PENGUI...

RIPL...

Patricia Highsmith was born in Fort Worth, Texas, in 1921. Her parents moved to New York when she was six, and she attended the Julia Richmond High School and Barnard College. In her senior year she edited the college magazine, having decided at the age of sixteen to become a writer. Her first novel, *Strangers on a Train*, was filmed by Alfred Hitchcock, and her fourth, *The Talented Mr Ripley*, was awarded the Edgar Allan Poe Scroll by the Mystery Writers of America. She has commented that she is 'interested in the effects of guilt' on her heroes. Miss Highsmith enjoys gardening and carpentering, drawing and sculpture; some of her works have been exhibited. She now lives in Switzerland.

Patricia Highsmith's many books include *The Blunderer*, *Deep Water*, *A Game for the Living*, *This Sweet Sickness*, *The Two Faces of January*, *The Glass Cell*, *Ripley Under Ground*, *Those Who Walk Away*, *The Tremor of Forgery*, *Ripley's Game*, *Edith's Diary*, *The Boy Who Followed Ripley*, *People Who Knock on the Door*, *Found in the Street*, *Ripley Under Water* and several collections of short stories, *Eleven*, *The Animal Lover's Book of Beastly Murder*, *Little Tales of Misogyny*, *Slowly, Slowly in the Wind*, *The Black House* and *Mermaids on the Golf Course* (all published by Penguin). Her novel *Carol*, originally published pseudonymously in 1952, is also published by Penguin.

PATRICIA HIGHSMITH

RIPLEY

THE TALENTED MR RIPLEY
RIPLEY UNDER GROUND
RIPLEY'S GAME
THE BOY WHO FOLLOWED RIPLEY

PENGUIN BOOKS

PENGUIN BOOKS

Published by the Penguin Group
Penguin Books Ltd, 27 Wrights Lane, London W8 5TZ, England
Penguin Books USA Inc., 375 Hudson Street, New York, New York 10014, USA
Penguin Books Australia Ltd, Ringwood, Victoria, Australia
Penguin Books Canada Ltd, 2801 John Street, Markham, Ontario, Canada L3R 1B4
Penguin Books (NZ) Ltd, 182–190 Wairau Road, Auckland 10, New Zealand

Penguin Books Ltd, Registered Offices: Harmondsworth, Middlesex, England

The Talented Mr Ripley first published in the USA by
Coward-McCann, Inc., 1955
Published in Great Britain by the Cresset Press 1956
Published in Great Britain by William Heinemann Ltd 1966
Published in Penguin Books 1976

Copyright © Patricia Highsmith, 1955
Copyright © renewed Patricia Highsmith, 1983

Ripley Under Ground first published in the USA by
Doubleday & Company 1970
Published in Great Britain by William Heinemann Ltd 1971
Published in Penguin Books 1973

Copyright © Patricia Highsmith, 1970

Ripley's Game first published in Great Britain by William Heinemann Ltd 1974
First published in the USA by Alfred A. Knopf, Inc., 1974
Published in Penguin Books 1976

Copyright © Patricia Highsmith, 1974

The Boy Who Followed Ripley first published in Great Britain by
William Heinemann Ltd 1980
First published in the USA by Lippincott and Crowell 1980
Published in Great Britain in Penguin Books 1981
Published in the USA in Penguin Books 1985

Copyright © Patricia Highsmith, 1980

The Talented Mr Ripley, *Ripley Under Ground* and *Ripley's Game*
published in one volume as *The Mysterious Mr Ripley* in Penguin Books 1985
Reprinted, together with *The Boy Who Followed Ripley*, as *Ripley* 1992
1 3 5 7 9 10 8 6 4 2

All rights reserved

Typeset by DatIX International Limited, Bungay, Suffolk
Filmset in Monophoto Photina
Printed in England by Clays Ltd, St Ives plc

CONTENTS

THE TALENTED
MR RIPLEY

ONE

Tom glanced behind him and saw the man coming out of the Green Cage, heading his way. Tom walked faster. There was no doubt that the man was after him. Tom had noticed him five minutes ago, eyeing him carefully from a table, as if he weren't *quite* sure, but almost. He had looked sure enough for Tom to down his drink in a hurry, pay and get out.

At the corner Tom leaned forward and trotted across Fifth Avenue. There was Raoul's. Should he take a chance and go in for another drink? Tempt fate and all that? Or should he beat it over to Park Avenue and try losing him in a few dark doorways? He went into Raoul's.

Automatically, as he strolled to an empty space at the bar, he looked around to see if there was anyone he knew. There was the big man with red hair, whose name he always forgot, sitting at a table with a blonde girl. The red-haired man waved a hand, and Tom's hand went up limply in response. He slid one leg over a stool and faced the door challengingly, yet with a flagrant casualness.

'Gin and tonic, please,' he said to the barman.

Was this the kind of man they would send after him? Was he, wasn't he, was he? He didn't look like a policeman or a detective at all. He looked like a businessman, somebody's father, well-dressed, well-fed, greying at the temples, an air of uncertainty about him. Was that the kind they sent on a job like this, maybe to start chatting with you in a bar, and then *bang!* – the hand on the shoulder, the other hand displaying a policeman's badge. *Tom Ripley, you're under arrest.* Tom watched the door.

Here he came. The man looked around, saw him and immediately looked away. He removed his straw hat, and took a place around the curve of the bar.

My God, what did he want? He certainly wasn't a *pervert*, Tom thought for the second time, though now his tortured brain groped and produced the actual word, as if the word could protect him, because he would rather the man be a pervert than a policeman. To a pervert, he could simply say, 'No, thank you,' and smile and walk away. Tom slid back on the stool, bracing himself.

Tom saw the man make a gesture of postponement to the barman, and come around the bar towards him. Here it was! Tom stared at him, paralysed. They couldn't give you more than ten years, Tom thought. Maybe fifteen, but with good conduct – In the instant the man's lips parted to speak, Tom had a pang of desperate, agonized regret.

'Pardon me, are you Tom Ripley?'

'Yes.'

'My name is Herbert Greenleaf. Richard Greenleaf's father.' The expression on his face was more confusing to Tom than if he had focused a gun on him. The face was friendly, smiling and hopeful. 'You're a friend of Richard's, aren't you?'

It made a faint connection in his brain. Dickie Greenleaf. A tall blond fellow. He had quite a bit of money, Tom remembered. 'Oh, Dickie Greenleaf. Yes.'

'At any rate, you know Charles and Marta Schriever. They're the ones who told me about you, that you might – uh – Do you think we could sit down at a table?'

'Yes,' Tom said agreeably, and picked up his drink. He followed the man towards an empty table at the back of the little room. Reprieved, he thought. Free! Nobody was going to arrest him. This was about something else. No matter what it was, it wasn't grand larceny or tampering with the mails or whatever they called it. Maybe Richard was in some kind of jam. Maybe Mr Greenleaf wanted help, or advice. Tom knew just what to say to a father like Mr Greenleaf.

'I wasn't quite sure you were Tom Ripley,' Mr Greenleaf said. 'I've seen you only once before, I think. Didn't you come up to the house once with Richard?'

'I think I did.'

'The Schrievers gave me a description of you, too. We've all been trying to reach you, because the Schrievers wanted us to meet at their house. Somebody told them you went to the Green Cage bar now and then. This is the first night I've tried to find you, so I suppose I should consider myself lucky.' He smiled. 'I wrote you a letter last week, but maybe you didn't get it.'

'No, I didn't.' Marc wasn't forwarding his mail, Tom thought. Damn him. Maybe there was a cheque there from Auntie Dottie. 'I moved a week or so ago,' Tom added.

'Oh, I see. I didn't say much in my letter. Only that I'd like to see you and have a chat with you. The Schrievers seemed to think you knew Richard quite well.'

'I remember him, yes.'

'But you're not writing to him now?' He looked disappointed.

'No. I don't think I've seen Dickie for a couple of years.'

'He's been in Europe for two years. The Schrievers spoke very highly of you, and thought you might have some influence on Richard if you were to write to him. I want him to come home. He has responsibilities here – but just now he ignores anything that I or his mother try to tell him.'

Tom was puzzled. 'Just what did the Schrievers say?'

'They said – apparently they exaggerate a little – that you and Richard were very good friends. I suppose they took it for granted you were writing him all along. You see, I know so few of Richard's friends any more –' He glanced at Tom's glass, as if he would have liked to offer him a drink, at least, but Tom's glass was nearly full.

Tom remembered going to a cocktail party at the Schrievers' with Dickie Greenleaf. Maybe the Greenleafs were more friendly with the Schrievers than he was, and that was how it had all come about, because he hadn't seen the Schrievers more than three or four times in his life. And the last time, Tom thought, was the night he had worked out Charley Schriever's income tax for him. Charley was a TV director, and he had been in a complete muddle with his free-lance accounts. Charley had thought he was a genius for having doped out his tax and made it lower than the one Charley had arrived at, and perfectly legitimately lower. Maybe that was what had prompted Charley's recommendation of him to Mr Greenleaf. Judging him from that night, Charley could have told Mr Greenleaf that he was intelligent, level-headed, scrupulously honest, and very willing to do a favour. It was a slight error.

'I don't suppose you know of anybody else close to Richard who might be able to wield a little influence?' Mr Greenleaf asked rather pitifully.

There was Buddy Lankenau, Tom thought, but he didn't want to wish a chore like this on Buddy. 'I'm afraid I don't,' Tom said, shaking his head. 'Why won't Richard come home?'

'He says he prefers living over there. But his mother's quite ill right now – Well, those are family problems. I'm sorry to annoy you like this.' He passed a hand in a distraught way over his thin, neatly combed grey hair. 'He says he's painting. There's no harm in that, but he hasn't the talent to be a painter. He's got great talent for boat designing, though, if he'd just put his mind to it.' He looked up as a waiter spoke to him. 'Scotch and soda, please. Dewar's. You're not ready?'

'No, thanks,' Tom said.

Mr Greenleaf looked at Tom apologetically. 'You're the first of Richard's friends who's even been willing to listen. They all take the attitude that I'm trying to interfere with his life.'

Tom could easily understand that. 'I certainly wish I could help,' he said politely. He remembered now that Dickie's money came from a ship-building company. Small sailing boats. No doubt his father wanted him to come home and take over the family firm. Tom smiled at Mr Greenleaf, meaninglessly, then finished his drink. Tom was on the edge of his chair, ready to leave, but the disappointment across the table was almost palpable. 'Where is he staying in Europe?' Tom asked, not caring a damn where he was staying.

'In a town called Mongibello, south of Naples. There's not even a library there, he tells me. Divides his time between sailing and painting. He's bought a house there. Richard has his own income – nothing huge, but enough to live on in Italy, apparently. Well, every man to his own taste, but I'm sure I can't see the attractions of the place.' Mr Greenleaf smiled bravely. 'Can't I offer you a drink, Mr Ripley?' he asked when the waiter came with his Scotch and soda.

Tom wanted to leave. But he hated to leave the man sitting alone with his fresh drink. 'Thanks, I think I will,' he said, and handed the waiter his glass.

'Charley Schriever told me you were in the insurance business,' Mr Greenleaf said pleasantly.

'That was a little while ago. I –' But he didn't want to say he was working for the Department of Internal Revenue, not now. 'I'm in the accounting department of an advertising agency at the moment.'

'Oh?'

Neither said anything for a minute. Mr Greenleaf's eyes were fixed on him with a pathetic, hungry expression. What on earth could he say? Tom was sorry he had accepted the drink. 'How old is Dickie now, by the way?' he asked.

'He's twenty-five.'

So am I, Tom thought. Dickie was probably having the time of his life over there. An income, a house, a boat. Why should he want to come home? Dickie's face was becoming clearer in his memory: he had a big smile, blondish hair with crisp waves in it, a happy-go-lucky face. Dickie was lucky. What was he himself doing at twenty-five? Living from week to week. No bank account. Dodging cops now for the first time in his life. He had a talent for mathematics. Why in hell didn't they pay him for it, somewhere? Tom realized that all his muscles had tensed, that the matchcover in his fingers was mashed sideways, nearly flat. He was bored, Goddamned bloody bored, bored, bored! He wanted to be back at the bar, by himself.

Tom took a gulp of his drink. 'I'd be very glad to write to Dickie, if you give me his address,' he said quickly. 'I suppose he'll remember me. We were at a weekend party once out on Long Island, I remember. Dickie and

I went out and gathered mussels, and everyone had them for breakfast.'
Tom smiled. 'A couple of us got sick, and it wasn't a very good party. But
I remember Dickie talking that weekend about going to Europe. He must
have left just –'

'I remember!' Mr Greenleaf said. 'That was the last weekend Richard
was here. I think he told me about the mussels.' He laughed rather loudly.

'I came up to your apartment a few times, too,' Tom went on, getting
into the spirit of it. 'Dickie showed me some ship models that were sitting
on a table in his room.'

'Those are only childhood efforts!' Mr Greenleaf was beaming. 'Did he
ever show you his frame models? Or his drawings?'

Dickie hadn't, but Tom said brightly, 'Yes! Of course he did. Pen-and-
ink drawings. Fascinating, some of them.' Tom had never seen them, but
he could see them now, precise draughtsman's drawings with every line
and bolt and screw labelled, could see Dickie smiling, holding them up for
him to look at, and he could have gone on for several minutes describing
details for Mr Greenleaf's delight, but he checked himself.

'Yes, Richard's got talent along those lines,' Mr Greenleaf said with a
satisfied air.

'I think he has,' Tom agreed. His boredom had slipped into another gear.
Tom knew the sensations. He had them sometimes at parties, but generally when he was having dinner with someone with whom he hadn't
wanted to have dinner in the first place, and the evening got longer and
longer. Now he could be maniacally polite for perhaps another whole
hour, if he had to be, before something in him exploded and sent him
running out of the door. 'I'm sorry I'm not quite free now or I'd be very
glad to go over and see if I could persuade Richard myself. Maybe I could
have some influence on him,' he said, just because Mr Greenleaf wanted
him to say that.

'If you seriously think so – that is, I don't know if you're planning a trip
to Europe or not.'

'No, I'm not.'

'Richard was always so influenced by his friends. If you or somebody
like you who knew him could get a leave of absence, I'd even send them
over to talk to him. I think it'd be worth more than my going over, anyway.
I don't suppose you could possibly get a leave of absence from your present
job, could you?'

Tom's heart took a sudden leap. He put on an expression of reflection.
It was a possibility. Something in him had smelt it out and leapt at it even
before his brain. Present job: nil. He might have to leave town soon,

anyway. He wanted to leave New York. 'I might,' he said carefully, with
the same pondering expression, as if he were even now going over the
thousands of little ties that could prevent him.

'If you did go, I'd be glad to take care of your expenses, that goes without
saying. Do you really think you might be able to arrange it? Say, this fall?'

It was already the middle of September. Tom stared at the gold signet
ring with the nearly worn-away crest on Mr Greenleaf's little finger. 'I
think I might. I'd be glad to see Richard again – especially if you think I
might be of some help.'

'I do! I think he'd listen to you. Then the mere fact that you don't know
him very well – If you put it to him strongly why you think he ought to
come home, he'd know you hadn't any axe to grind.' Mr Greenleaf leaned
back in his chair, looking at Tom with approval. 'Funny thing is, Jim Burke
and his wife – Jim's my partner – they went by Mongibello last year when
they were on a cruise. Richard promised he'd come home when the winter
began. Last winter. Jim's given him up. What boy of twenty-five listens
to an old man sixty or more? You'll probably succeed where the rest of
us have failed!'

'I hope so,' Tom said modestly.

'How about another drink? How about a nice brandy?'

TWO

It was after midnight when Tom started home, Mr Greenleaf had offered
to drop him off in a taxi, but Tom had not wanted him to see where he
lived – in a dingy brownstone between Third and Second with a ROOMS
TO LET sign hanging out. For the last two and half weeks Tom had been
living with Bob Delancey, a young man he hardly knew, but Bob had been
the only one of Tom's friends and acquaintances in New York who had
volunteered to put him up when he had been without a place to stay. Tom
had not asked any of his friends up to Bob's, and had not even told anybody
where he was living. The main advantage of Bob's place was that he could
get his George McAlpin mail there with the minimum chance of detection.
But the smelly john down the hall that didn't lock, that grimy single room

that looked as if it had been lived in by a thousand different people who had left behind their particular kind of filth and never lifted a hand to clean it, those slithering stacks of *Vogue* and *Harper's Bazaar* and those big chi-chi smoked-glass bowls all over the place, filled with tangles of string and pencils and cigarette butts and decaying fruit! Bob was a free-lance window decorator for shops and department stores, but now the only work he did was occasional jobs for Third Avenue antique shops, and some antique shop had given him the smoked-glass bowls as a payment for something. Tom had been shocked at the sordidness of the place, shocked that he even knew anybody who lived like that, but he had known that he wouldn't live there very long. And now Mr Greenleaf had turned up. Something always turned up. That was Tom's philosophy.

Just before he climbed the brownstone steps, Tom stopped and looked carefully in both directions. Nothing but an old woman airing her dog, and a weaving old man coming around the corner from Third Avenue. If there was any sensation he hated, it was that of being followed, by *anybody*. And lately he had it all the time. He ran up the steps.

A lot the sordidness mattered now, he thought as he went into the room. As soon as he could get a passport, he'd be sailing for Europe, probably in a first-class cabin. Waiters to bring him things when he pushed a button! Dressing for dinner, strolling into a big dining-room, talking with people at his table like a gentleman! He could congratulate himself on tonight, he thought. He had behaved just right. Mr Greenleaf couldn't possibly have had the impression that he had wangled the invitation to Europe. Just the opposite. He wouldn't let Mr Greenleaf down. He'd do his very best with Dickie. Mr Greenleaf was such a decent fellow himself, he took it for granted that everybody else in the world was decent, too. Tom had almost forgotten such people existed.

Slowly he took off his jacket and untied his tie, watching every move he made as if it were somebody else's movements he was watching. Astonishing how much straighter he was standing now, what a different look there was in his face. It was one of the few times in his life that he felt pleased with himself. He put a hand into Bob's glutted closet and thrust the hangers aggressively to right and left to make room for his suit. Then he went into the bathroom. The old rusty showerhead sent a jet against the shower curtain and another jet in an erratic spiral that he could hardly catch to wet himself, but it was better than sitting in the filthy tub.

When he woke up the next morning Bob was not there, and Tom saw from a glance at his bed that he hadn't come home. Tom jumped out of bed, went to the two-ring burner and put on coffee. Just as well Bob wasn't home this morning. He didn't want to tell Bob about the European trip. All that crummy bum would see in it was a free trip. And Ed Martin, too, probably, and Bert Visser, and all the other crumbs he knew. He wouldn't tell any of them, and he wouldn't have anybody seeing him off. Tom began to whistle. He was invited to dinner tonight at the Greenleafs' apartment on Park Avenue.

Fifteen minutes later, showered, shaved, and dressed in a suit and a striped tie that he thought would look well in his passport photo, Tom was strolling up and down the room with a cup of black coffee in his hand, waiting for the morning mail. After the mail, he would go over to Radio City to take care of the passport business. What should he do this afternoon? Go to some art exhibits, so he could chat about them tonight with the Greenleafs? Do some research on Burke–Greenleaf Watercraft, Inc., so Mr Greenleaf would know that he took an interest in his work?

The whack of the mailbox came faintly through the open window, and Tom went downstairs. He waited until the mailman was down the front steps and out of sight before he took the letter addressed to George McAlpin down from the edge of the mailbox frame where the mailman had stuck it. Tom ripped it open. Out came a cheque for one hundred and nineteen dollars and fifty-four cents, payable to the Collector of Internal Revenue. Good old Mrs Edith W. Superaugh! Paid without a whimper, without even a telephone call. It was a good omen. He went upstairs again, tore up Mrs Superaugh's envelope and dropped it into the garbage bag.

He put her cheque into a manila envelope in the inside pocket of one of his jackets in the closet. This raised his total in cheques to one thousand eight hundred and sixty-three dollars and fourteen cents, he calculated in his head. A pity that he couldn't cash them. Or that some idiot hadn't paid in cash yet, or made out a cheque to George McAlpin, but so far no one had. Tom had a bank messenger's identification card that he had found somewhere with an old date on it that he could try to alter, but he was afraid he couldn't get away with cashing the cheques, even with a forged letter of authorization for whatever the sum was. So it amounted to no more than a practical joke, really. Good clean sport. He wasn't stealing money from anybody. Before he went to Europe, he thought, he'd destroy the cheques.

There were seven more prospects on his list. Shouldn't he try just one more in these last ten days before he sailed? Walking home last evening, after seeing Mr Greenleaf, he had thought that if Mrs Superaugh and Carlos de Sevilla paid up, he'd call it quits. Mr de Sevilla hadn't paid up yet – he needed a good scare by telephone to put the fear of God into him,

Tom thought – but Mrs Superaugh had been so easy, he was tempted to try just *one* more.

Tom took a mauve-coloured stationery box from his suitcase in the closet. There were a few sheets of stationery in the box, and below them a stack of various forms he had taken from the Internal Revenue office when he had worked there as a stockroom clerk a few weeks ago. On the very bottom was his list of prospects – carefully chosen people who lived in the Bronx or in Brooklyn and would not be too inclined to pay the New York office a personal visit, artists and writers and free-lance people who had no withholding taxes, and who made from seven to twelve thousand a year. In that bracket, Tom figured that people seldom hired professional tax men to compute their taxes, while they earned enough money to be logically accused of having made a two- or three-hundred dollar error in their tax computations. There was William J. Slatterer, journalist; Philip Robillard, musician; Frieda Hoehn, illustrator; Joseph J. Gennari, photographer; Frederick Reddington, artist; Frances Karnegis – Tom had a hunch about Reddington. He was a comic-book artist. He probably didn't know whether he was coming or going.

He chose two forms headed NOTICE OF ERROR IN COMPUTATION, slipped a carbon between them, and began to copy rapidly the data below Reddington's name on his list. Income: $11,250 Exemptions: 1. Deductions: $600. Credits: nil. Remittance: nil. Interest: (he hesitated a moment) $2.16. Balance due: $233.76. Then he took a piece of typewriter paper stamped with the Department of Internal Revenue's Lexington Avenue address from his supply in his carbon folder, crossed out the address with one slanting line of his pen, and typed below it:

Dear Sir:

Due to an overflow at our regular Lexington Avenue office, your reply should be sent to:

> Adjustment Department
> Attention of George McAlpin
> 187 E. 51 Street
> New York 22, New York

Thank you.

> Ralph F. Fischer
> Gen. Dir. Adj. Dept.

Tom signed it with a scrolly, illegible signature. He put the other forms away in case Bob should come in suddenly, and picked up the telephone. He had decided to give Mr Reddington a preliminary prod. He got Mr

Reddington's number from information and called it. Mr Reddington was at home. Tom explained the situation briefly, and expressed surprise that Mr Reddington had not yet received the notice from the Adjusting Department.

'That should have gone out a few days ago,' Tom said. 'You'll undoubtedly get it tomorrow. We've been a little rushed around here.'

'But I've *paid* my tax,' said the alarmed voice at the other end. 'They were all –'

'These things can happen, you know, when the income's earned on a free-lance basis with no withholding tax. We've been over your return very carefully, Mr Reddington. There's no mistake. And we wouldn't like to slap a lien on the office you work for or your agent or whatever –' Here he chuckled. A friendly, personal chuckle generally worked wonders. '– but we'll have to do that unless you pay within forty-eight hours. I'm sorry the notice hasn't reached you before now. As I said, we've been pretty –'

'Is there anyone there I can talk to about it if I come in?' Mr Reddington asked anxiously. 'That's a hell of a lot of money!'

'Well, there is, of course.' Tom's voice always got folksy at this point. He sounded like a genial old codger of sixty-odd, who might be as patient as could be if Mr Reddington came in, but who wouldn't yield by so much as a red cent, for all the talking and explaining Mr Reddington might do. George McAlpin represented the Tax Department of the United States of America, suh. 'You can talk to *me*, of course,' Tom drawled, 'but there's absolutely no mistake about this, Mr Reddington. I'm just thinking of saving you your time. You can come in if you want to, but I've got all your records right here in my hand.'

Silence. Mr Reddington wasn't going to ask him anything about records, because he probably didn't know what to begin asking. But if Mr Reddington were to ask him to explain what it was all about, Tom had a lot of hash about net income versus accrued income, balance due versus computation, interest at six per cent per annum accruing from due date of the tax until paid on any balance which represents tax shown on original return, which he could deliver in a slow voice as incapable of interruption as a Sherman tank. So far, no one had insisted in coming in person to hear more of that. Mr Reddington was backing down, too. Tom could hear it in the silence.

'All right,' Mr Reddington said in a tone of collapse. 'I'll read the notice when I get it tomorrow.'

'All right, Mr Reddington,' he said, and hung up.

Tom sat there for a moment, giggling, the palms of his thin hands pressed together between his knees. Then he jumped up, put Bob's type-writer away again, combed his light-brown hair neatly in front of the mirror, and set off for Radio City.

THREE

'Hello-o, Tom, my boy!' Mr Greenleaf said in a voice that promised good martinis, a gourmet's dinner, and a bed for the night in case he got too tired to go home. 'Emily, this is Tom Ripley!'

'I'm so happy to meet you!' she said warmly.

'How do you do, Mrs Greenleaf?'

She was very much what he had expected – blonde, rather tall and slender, with enough formality to keep him on his good behaviour, yet with the same naïve good-will-towards-all that Mr Greenleaf had. Mr Greenleaf led them into the living-room. Yes, he had been here before with Dickie.

'Mr Ripley's in the insurance business,' Mr Greenleaf announced, and Tom thought he must have had a few already, or he was very nervous tonight, because Tom had given him quite a description last night of the advertising agency where he had said he was working.

'Not a very exciting job,' Tom said modestly to Mrs Greenleaf.

A maid came into the room with a tray of martinis and canapés.

'Mr Ripley's been here before,' Mr Greenleaf said. 'He's come here with Richard.'

'Oh, has he? I don't believe I met you, though.' She smiled. 'Are you from New York?'

'No, I'm from Boston,' Tom said. That was true.

About thirty minutes later – just the right time later, Tom thought, because the Greenleafs had kept insisting that he drink another and another martini – they went into a dining-room off the living-room, where a table was set for three with candles, huge dark-blue dinner napkins, and a whole cold chicken in aspic. But first there was céleri rémoulade. Tom was very fond of it. He said so.

'So is Richard!' Mrs Greenleaf said. 'He always liked it the way our cook makes it. A pity you can't take him some.'

'I'll put it with the socks,' Tom said, smiling, and Mrs Greenleaf laughed. She had told him she would like him to take Richard some black woollen socks from Brooks Brothers, the kind Richard always wore.

The conversation was dull, and the dinner superb. In answer to a question of Mrs Greenleaf's, Tom told her that he was working for an advertising firm called Rothenberg, Fleming and Barter. When he referred to it again, he deliberately called it Reddington, Fleming and Parker. Mr Greenleaf didn't seem to notice the difference. Tom mentioned the firm's name a second time when he and Mr Greenleaf were alone in the living room after dinner.

'Did you go to school in Boston?' Mr Greenleaf asked.

'No, sir. I went to Princeton for a while, then I visited another aunt in Denver and went to college there.' Tom waited, hoping Mr Greenleaf would ask him something about Princeton, but he didn't. Tom could have discussed the system of teaching history, the campus restrictions, the atmosphere at the week-end dances, the political tendencies of the student body, anything. Tom had been very friendly last summer with a Princeton junior who had talked of nothing but Princeton, so that Tom had finally pumped him for more and more, foreseeing a time when he might be able to use the information. Tom had told the Greenleafs that he had been raised by his Aunt Dottie in Boston. She had taken him to Denver when he was sixteen, and actually he had only finished high school there, but there had been a young man named Don Mizell rooming in his Aunt Bea's house in Denver who had been going to the University of Colorado. Tom felt as if he had gone there, too.

'Specialize in anything in particular?' Mr Greenleaf asked.

'Sort of divided myself between accounting and English composition,' Tom replied with a smile, knowing it was such a dull answer that nobody would possibly pursue it.

Mrs Greenleaf came in with a photograph album, and Tom sat beside her on the sofa while she turned through it. Richard taking his first step, Richard in a ghastly full-page colour photograph dressed and posed as the Blue Boy, with long blond curls. The album was not interesting to him until Richard got to be sixteen or so, long-legged, slim, with the wave tightening in his hair. So far as Tom could see, he had hardly changed between sixteen and twenty-three or -four, when the pictures of him stopped, and it was astonishing to Tom how little the bright, naïve smile changed. Tom could not help feeling that Richard was not very intelligent or else he loved to be photographed and thought he looked best with his mouth spread from ear to ear, which was not very intelligent of him, either.

'I haven't gotten round to pasting these in yet,' Mrs Greenleaf said, handing him a batch of loose pictures. 'These are all from Europe.'

They were more interesting: Dickie in what looked like a café in Paris, Dickie on a beach. In several of them he was frowning.

'This is Mongibello, by the way,' Mrs Greenleaf said, indicating a picture of Dickie pulling a rowboat up on the sand. The picture was backgrounded by dry, rocky mountains and a fringe of little white houses along the shore. 'And here's the girl there, the only other American who lives there.'

'Marge Sherwood,' Mr Greenleaf supplied. He sat across the room, but he was leaning forward, following the picture-showing intently.

The girl was in a bathing suit on the beach, her arms around her knees, healthy and unsophisticated-looking, with tousled, short blonde hair – the good-egg type. There was a good picture of Richard in shorts, sitting on the parapet of a terrace. He was smiling, but it was not the same smile, Tom saw. Richard looked more poised in the European pictures.

Tom noticed Mrs Greenleaf was staring down at the rug in front of her. He remembered the moment at the table when she had said, 'I wish I'd never heard of Europe!' and Mr Greenleaf had given her an anxious glance and then smiled at him, as if such outbursts had occurred before. Now he saw tears in her eyes. Mr Greenleaf was getting up to come to her.

'Mrs Greenleaf,' Tom said gently, 'I want you to know that I'll do everything I can to make Dickie come back.'

'Bless you, Tom, bless you.' She pressed Tom's hand that rested on his thigh.

'Emily, don't you think it's time you went to bed?' Mr Greenleaf asked, bending over her.

Tom stood up as Mrs Greenleaf did.

'I hope you'll come again to pay us a visit before you go, Tom,' she said. 'Since Richard's gone, we seldom have any young men to the house. I miss them.'

'I'd be delighted to come again,' Tom said.

Mr Greenleaf went out of the room with her. Tom remained standing, his hands at his sides, his head high. In a large mirror on the wall he could see himself: the upright, self-respecting young man again. He looked quickly away. He was doing the right thing, behaving the right way. Yet he had a feeling of guilt. When he had said to Mrs Greenleaf just now, *I'll do everything I can* ... Well, he meant it. He wasn't trying to fool anybody.

He felt himself beginning to sweat, and he tried to relax. What was he so worried about? He'd felt so well tonight! When he had said that about Aunt Dottie –

Tom straightened, glancing at the door, but the door had not opened. That had been the only time tonight when he had felt uncomfortable, unreal, the way he might have felt if he had been lying, yet it had been practically the only thing he had said that *was* true: *My parents died when I was very small. I was raised by my aunt in Boston.*

Mr Greenleaf came into the room. His figure seemed to pulsate and grow larger and larger. Tom blinked his eyes, feeling a sudden terror of him, an impulse to attack him before he was attacked.

'Suppose we sample some brandy?' Mr Greenleaf said, opening a panel beside the fireplace.

'It's like a movie, Tom thought. In a minute, Mr Greenleaf or somebody else's voice would say, 'Okay, *cut!*' and he would relax again and find himself back in Raoul's with the gin and tonic in front of him. No, back in the Green Cage.

'Had enough?' Mr Greenleaf asked. 'Don't drink this, if you don't want it.'

Tom gave a vague nod, and Mr Greenleaf looked puzzled for an instant, then poured the two brandies.

A cold fear was running over Tom's body. He was thinking of the incident in the drugstore last week, though that was all over and he wasn't *really* afraid, he reminded himself, not now. There was a drugstore on Second Avenue whose phone number he gave out to people who insisted on calling him again about their income tax. He gave it out as the phone number of the Adjustment Department where he could be reached only between three-thirty and four on Wednesday and Friday afternoons. At these times, Tom hung around the booth in the drugstore, waiting for the phone to ring. When the druggist had looked at him suspiciously the second time he had been there, Tom had said that he was waiting for a call from his girl friend. Last Friday when he had answered the telephone, a man's voice had said, 'You know what we're talking about, don't you? We know where you live, if you want us to come to your place ... We've got the stuff for you, if you've got it for us.' An insistent yet evasive voice, so that Tom had thought it was some kind of a trick and hadn't been able to answer anything. Then, 'Listen, we're coming right over. To your *house.*'

Tom's legs had felt like jelly when he got out of the phone booth, and then he had seen the druggist staring at him, wide-eyed, panicky-looking, and the conversation had suddenly explained itself: the druggist sold dope, and he was afraid that Tom was a police detective who had come to get the goods on *him*. Tom had started laughing, had walked out laughing uproariously, staggering as he went, because his legs were still weak from his own fear.

'Thinking about Europe?' Mr Greenleaf's voice said.

Tom accepted the glass Mr Greenleaf was holding out to him. 'Yes, I was,' Tom said.

'Well, I hope you enjoy your trip, Tom, as well as have some effect on Richard. By the way, Emily likes you a lot. She told me so. I didn't have to ask her.' Mr Greenleaf rolled his brandy glass between his hands. 'My wife has leukaemia, Tom.'

'Oh. That's very serious, isn't it?'

'Yes. She may not live a year.'

'I'm sorry to hear that,' Tom said.

Mr Greenleaf pulled a paper out of his pocket. 'I've got a list of boats. I think the usual Cherbourg way is quickest, and also the most interesting. You'd take the boat train to Paris, then a sleeper down over the Alps to Rome and Naples.'

'That'd be fine.' It began to sound exciting to him.

'You'll have to catch a bus from Naples to Richard's village. I'll write him about you – not telling him that you're an emissary from me,' he added, smiling, 'but I'll tell him we've met. Richard ought to put you up, but if he can't for some reason, there're hotels in the town. I expect you and Richard'll hit it off all right. Now as to money –' Mr Greenleaf smiled his fatherly smile. 'I propose to give you six hundred dollars in traveller's cheques apart from your round-trip ticket. Does that suit you? The six hundred should see you through nearly two months, and if you need more, all you have to do is wire me, my boy. You don't look like a young man who'd throw money down the drain.'

'That sounds ample, sir.'

Mr Greenleaf got increasingly mellow and jolly on the brandy, and Tom got increasingly close-mouthed and sour. Tom wanted to get out of the apartment. And yet he still wanted to go to Europe, and wanted Mr Greenleaf to approve of him. The moments on the sofa were more agonizing than the moments in the bar last night when he had been so bored, because now that break into another gear didn't come. Several times Tom got up with his drink and strolled to the fireplace and back, and when he looked into the mirror he saw that his mouth was turned down at the corners.

Mr Greenleaf was rollicking on about Richard and himself in Paris, when Richard had been ten years old. It was not in the least interesting. If anything happened with the police in the next ten days, Tom thought, Mr Greenleaf would take him in. He could tell Mr Greenleaf that he'd sublet his apartment in a hurry, or something like that, and simply hide out here. Tom felt awful, almost physically ill.

'Mr Greenleaf, I think I should be going.'

'Now? But I wanted to show you – Well, never mind. Another time.'

Tom knew he should have asked, 'Show me what?' and been patient while he was shown whatever it was, but he couldn't.

'I want you to visit the yards, of course!' Mr Greenleaf said cheerfully. 'When can you come out? Only during your lunch hour, I suppose. I think you should be able to tell Richard what the yards look like these days.'

'Yes – I could come in my lunch hour.'

'Give me a call any day, Tom. You've got my card with my private number. If you give me half an hour's notice, I'll have a man pick you up at your office and drive you out. We'll have a sandwich as we walk through, and he'll drive you back.'

'I'll call you,' Tom said. He felt he would faint if he stayed one minute longer in the dimly lighted foyer, but Mr Greenleaf was chuckling again, asking him if he had read a certain book by Henry James.

'I'm sorry to say I haven't, sir, not that one,' Tom said.

'Well, no matter,' Mr Greenleaf smiled.

Then they shook hands, a long suffocating squeeze from Mr Greenleaf, and it was over. but the pained, frightened expression was still on his face as he rode down in the elevator, Tom saw. He leaned in the corner of the elevator in an exhausted way, though he knew as soon as he hit the lobby he would fly out of the door and keep on running, running, all the way home.

FOUR

The atmosphere of the city became stranger as the days went on. It was as if something had gone out of New York – the realness or the importance of it – and the city was putting on a show just for him, a colossal show with its buses, taxis, and hurrying people on the sidewalks, its television shows in all the Third Avenue bars, its movie marquees lighted up in broad daylight, and its sound effects of thousands of honking horns and human voices, talking for no purpose whatsoever. As if when his boat left the pier on Saturday, the whole city of New York would collapse with a *poof* like a lot of cardboard on a stage.

Or maybe he was afraid. He hated water. He had never been anywhere before on water, except to New Orleans from New York and back to New York again, but then he had been working on a banana boat mostly below deck, and he had hardly realized he was on water. The few times he had been on deck the sight of water had at first frightened him, then made him feel sick, and he had always run below deck again, where, contrary to what people said, he had felt better. His parents had drowned in Boston Harbour, and Tom had always thought that probably had something to do with it, because as long as he could remember he had been afraid of water, and he had never learned how to swim. It gave Tom a sick, empty feeling at the pit of his stomach to think that in less than a week he would have water below him, miles deep, and that undoubtedly he would have to look at it most of the time; because people on ocean liners spent most of their time on deck. And it was particularly un-chic to be seasick, he felt. He had never been seasick, but he came very near it several times in those last days, simply thinking about the voyage to Cherbourg.

He had told Bob Delancey that he was moving in a week, but he hadn't said where. Bob did not seem interested, anyway. They saw very little of each other at the Fifty-first Street place. Tom had gone to Marc Priminger's house in East Forty-fifth Street – he still had the keys – to pick up a couple of things he had forgotten, and he had gone at an hour when he had thought Marc wouldn't be there, but Marc had come in with his new housemate, Joel, a thin drip of a young man who worked for a publishing house, and Marc had put on one of his suave 'Please-do-*just*-as-you-like' acts for Joel's benefit, though if Joel hadn't been there Marc would have cursed him out in language that even a Portuguese sailor wouldn't have used. Marc (his given name was, of all things, Marcellus) was an ugly mug of a man with a private income and a hobby of helping out young men in temporary financial difficulties by putting them up in his two-storey, three-bedroom house, and playing God by telling them what they could and couldn't do around the place and by giving them advice as to their lives and their jobs, generally rotten advice. Tom had stayed there three months, though for nearly half that time Marc had been in Florida and he had had the house all to himself, but when Marc had come back he had made a big stink about a few pieces of broken glassware – Marc playing God again, the Stern Father – and Tom had gotten angry enough, for once, to stand up for himself and talk to him back. Whereupon Marc had thrown him out, after collecting sixty-three dollars from him for broken glassware. The old tightwad! He should have been an old maid, Tom thought, at the head of a girls' school. Tom was bitterly sorry he had ever laid eyes on Marc Priminger, and the sooner he could forget Marc's stupid, pig-like eyes, his massive jaw, his ugly hands with the gaudy rings (waving through the air, ordering this and that from everybody), the happier he would be.

The only one of his friends he felt like telling about his European trip was Cleo, and he went to see her on the Thursday before he sailed. Cleo Dobelle was a slim dark-haired girl who could have been anything from twenty-three to thirty, Tom didn't know, who lived with her parents in Gracie Square and painted in a small way – a *very* small way, in fact, on little pieces of ivory no bigger than postage stamps that had to be viewed through a magnifying glass, and Cleo used a magnifying glass when she painted them. 'But think how convenient it is to be able to carry *all* my paintings in a cigar box! Other painters have rooms and rooms to hold their canvases!' Cleo said. Cleo lived in her own suite of rooms with a little bath and kitchen at the back of her parents' section of the apartment, and Cleo's apartment was always rather dark since it had no exposure except to a tiny backyard overgrown with ailanthus trees that blocked out the light. Cleo always had the lights on, dim ones, which gave a nocturnal atmosphere whatever the time of day. Except for the night when he had met her, Tom had seen Cleo only in close-fitting velvet slacks of various colours and gaily striped silk shirts. They had taken to each other from the very first night, when Cleo had asked him to dinner at her apartment on the following evening. Cleo always asked him up to her apartment, and there was somehow never any thought that he might ask her out to dinner or the theatre or do any of the ordinary things that a young man was expected to do with a girl. She didn't expect him to bring her flowers or books or candy when he came for dinner or cocktails, though Tom did bring her a little gift sometimes, because it pleased her so. Cleo was the one person he could tell that he was going to Europe and why. He did.

Cleo was enthralled, as he had known she would be. Her red lips parted in her long, pale face, and she brought her hands down on her velvet thighs and exclaimed, '*Tom*-mie! How too, too marvellous! It's just like out of Shakespeare or something!'

That was just what Tom thought, too. That was just what he had needed someone to say.

Cleo fussed around him all evening, asking him if he had this and that, Kleenexes and cold tablets and woollen socks because it started raining in Europe in the fall, and his vaccinations. Tom said he felt pretty well prepared.

'Just don't come to see me off, Cleo. I don't want to be seen off.'

'Of course not!' Cleo said, understanding perfectly. 'Oh, Tommie, I think that's such fun! Will you write me everything that happens with Dickie? You're the only person I know who ever went to Europe for a *reason*.'

He told her about visiting Mr Greenleaf's shipyards in Long Island, the miles and miles of tables with machines making shiny metal parts, varnishing and polishing wood, the dry-docks with boat skeletons of all sizes, and impressed her with the terms Mr Greenleaf had used – coamings, inwales, keelsons, and chines. He described the second dinner at Mr Greenleaf's house, when Mr Greenleaf had presented him with a wrist-watch. He showed the wrist-watch to Cleo, not a fabulously expensive wrist-watch, but still an excellent one and just the style Tom might have chosen for himself – a plain white face with fine black Roman numerals in a simple gold setting with an alligator strap.

'Just because I happened to say a few days before that I didn't own a watch,' Tom said. 'He's really adopted me like a son.' And Cleo, too, was the only person he knew to whom he could say that.

Cleo sighed. 'Men! You have all the luck. Nothing like that could ever happen to a girl. Men're so *free*!'

Tom smiled. It often seemed to him that it was the other way around. 'Is that the lamb chops burning?'

Cleo jumped up with a shriek.

After dinner, she showed him five or six of her latest paintings, a couple of romantic portraits of a young man they both knew, in an open-collared white shirt, three imaginary landscapes of a junglelike land, derived from the view of ailanthus trees out her window. The hair of the little monkeys in the paintings was really astoundingly well done, Tom thought. Cleo had a lot of brushes with just one hair in them, and even these varied from comparatively coarse to ultra fine. They drank nearly two bottles of Médoc from her parents' liquor shelf, and Tom got so sleepy he could have spent the night right where he was lying on the floor – they had often slept side by side on the two big bear rugs in front of the fireplace, and it was another of the wonderful things about Cleo that she never wanted or expected him to make a pass at her, and he never had – but Tom hauled himself up at a quarter to twelve and took his leave.

'I won't see you again, will I?' Cleo said dejectedly at the door.

'Oh, I should be back in about six weeks,' Tom said, though he didn't think so at all. Suddenly he leaned forward and planted a firm, brotherly kiss on her ivory cheek. 'I'll miss you, Cleo.'

She squeezed his shoulder, the only physical touch he could recall her ever having give him. 'I'll miss you,' she said.

The next day he took care of Mrs Greenleaf's commissions at Brooks Brothers, the dozen pairs of black woollen socks and the bathrobe. Mrs Greenleaf had not suggested a colour for the bathrobe. She would leave that up to him, she had said. Tom chose a dark maroon flannel with a navy-blue belt and lapels. It was not the best-looking robe of the lot, in Tom's opinion, but he felt it was exactly what Richard would have chosen, and that Richard would be delighted with it. He put the socks and robe on the Greenleafs' charge account. He saw a heavy linen sport shirt with wooden buttons that he liked very much, that would have been easy to put on the Greenleafs' charge account, too, but he didn't. He bought it with his own money.

FIVE

The morning of his sailing, the morning he had looked forward to with such buoyant excitement, got off to a hideous start. Tom followed the steward to his cabin congratulating himself that his firmness with Bob about not wanting to be seen off had taken effect, and had just entered the room when a bloodcurdling whoop went up.

'Where's all the champagne, Tom? We're waiting!'

'Boy, is this a stinking room! Why don't you ask them for something decent?'

'Tommie, take *me?*' from Ed Martin's girl friend, whom Tom couldn't bear to look at.

There they all were, mostly Bob's lousy friends, sprawled on his bed, on the floor, everywhere. Bob had found out he was sailing, but Tom had never thought he would do a thing like this. It took self-control for Tom not to say in an icy voice, 'There *isn't* any champagne.' He tried to greet them all, tried to smile, though he could have burst into tears like a child. He gave Bob a long, withering look, but Bob was already high, on something. There were very few things that got under his skin, Tom thought self-justifyingly, but this was one of them: noisy surprises like this, the riffraff, the vulgarians, the slobs he had thought he had left behind when he crossed the gangplank, littering the very stateroom where he was to spend the next five days!

Tom went over to Paul Hubbard, the only respectable person in the room, and sat down beside him on the short, built-in sofa. 'Hello, Paul,' he said quietly. 'I'm sorry about all this.'

'Oh!' Paul scoffed. 'How long'll you be gone? – What's the matter, Tom? Are you sick?'

It was awful. It went on, the noise and the laughter and the girls feeling the bed and looking in the john. Thank God the Greenleafs hadn't come to see him off! Mr Greenleaf had had to go to New Orleans on business, and Mrs Greenleaf, when Tom had called this morning to say good-bye, had said that she didn't feel quite up to coming down to the boat.

Finally, Bob or somebody produced a bottle of whisky, and they all began to drink out of the two glasses from the bathroom, and then a steward came in with a tray of glasses. Tom refused to have a drink. He was sweating so heavily, he took off his jacket so as not to soil it. Bob came over and rammed a glass in his hand, and Bob was not exactly joking, Tom saw, and he knew why – because he had accepted Bob's hospitality for a month, and he might at least put on a pleasant face, but Tom could not put on a pleasant face any more than if his face had been made of granite. So what if they all hated him after this, he thought, what had he lost?

'I can fit in here, Tommie,' said the girl who was determined to fit in somewhere and go with him. She had wedged herself sideways into a narrow closet about the size of a broom closet.

'I'd like to see Tom caught with a girl in his room!' Ed Martin said, laughing.

Tom glared at him. 'Let's get out of here and get some air,' he murmured to Paul.

The others were making so much noise, nobody noticed their leaving.

They stood at the rail near the stern. It was a sunless day, and the city on their right was already like some grey, distant land that he might be looking at from mid-ocean – except for those bastards inside his stateroom.

'Where've you been keeping yourself?' Paul asked. 'Ed called up to tell me you were leaving. I haven't seen you in weeks.'

Paul was one of the people who thought he worked for the Associated Press. Tom made a fine story about an assignment he had been sent on. Possibly the Middle East, Tom said. He made it sound rather secret. 'I've been doing quite a lot of night work lately, too,' Tom said, 'which is why I haven't been around much. It's awfully nice of you to come down and see me off.'

'I hadn't any classes this morning,' Paul took the pipe out of his mouth and smiled. 'Not that I wouldn't have come anyway, probably. Any old excuse!'

Tom smiled. Paul taught music at a girls' school in New York to earn his living, but he preferred to compose music on his own time. Tom could not remember how he had met Paul, but he remembered going to his Riverside Drive apartment for Sunday brunch with some other people, and Paul had played some of his own compositions on the piano, and Tom had enjoyed it immensely. 'Can't I offer you a drink? Let's see if we can find the bar,' Tom said.

But just then a steward came out, hitting a gong and shouting, 'Visitors ashore, please! All visitors ashore!'

'That's me,' Paul said.

They shook hands, patted shoulders, promised to write postcards to each other. Then Paul was gone.

Bob's gang would stay till the last minute, he thought, probably have to be blasted out. Tom turned suddenly and ran up a narrow, ladderlike flight of stairs. At the top of it he was confronted by a CABIN CLASS ONLY sign hanging from a chain, but he threw a leg over the chain and stepped on to the deck. They surely wouldn't object to a first-class passenger going into second-class, he thought. He couldn't bear to look at Bob's gang again. He had paid Bob half a month's rent and given him a good-bye present of a good shirt and tie. What more did Bob want?

The ship was moving before Tom dared to go down to his room again. He went into the room cautiously. Empty. The neat blue bedcover was smooth again. The ashtrays were clean. There was no sign they had ever been here. Tom relaxed and smiled. This was service! The fine old tradition of the Cunard Line, British seamanship and all that! He saw a big basket of fruit on the floor by his bed. He seized the little white envelope eagerly. The card inside said:

> Bon voyage and bless you, Tom. All our good wishes go with you.
> Emily and Herbert Greenleaf

The basket had a tall handle and it was entirely under yellow cellophane – apples and pears and grapes and a couple of candy bars and several little bottles of liqueurs. Tom had never received a bon voyage basket. To him, they had always been something you saw in florists' windows for fantastic prices and laughed at. Now he found himself with tears in his eyes, and he put his face down in his hands suddenly and began to sob.

SIX

His mood was tranquil and benevolent, but not at all sociable. He wanted his time for thinking, and he did not care to meet any of the people on the ship, not any of them, though when he encountered the people with whom he sat at his table, he greeted them pleasantly and smiled. He began to play a role on the ship, that of a serious young man with a serious job ahead of him. He was courteous, poised, civilized and preoccupied.

He had a sudden whim for a cap and bought one in the haberdashery, a conservative bluish-grey cap of soft English wool. He could pull it down over nearly his whole face when he wanted to nap in his deck-chair, or wanted to look as if he were napping. A cap was the most versatile of head-gears, he thought, and he wondered why he had never thought of wearing one before. He could look like a country gentleman, a thug, an Englishman, a Frenchman, or a plain American eccentric, depending on how he wore it. Tom amused himself with it in his room in front of the mirror. He had always thought he had the world's dullest face, a thoroughly forgettable face with a look of docility that he could not understand, and a look also of vague fright that he had never been able to erase. A real conformist's face, he thought. The cap changed all that. It gave him a country air, Greenwich, Connecticut, country. Now he was a young man with a private income, not long out of Princeton, perhaps. He bought a pipe to go with the cap.

He was starting a new life. Good-bye to all the second-rate people he had hung around and had let hang around him in the past three years in New York. He felt as he imagined immigrants felt when they left everything behind them in some foreign country, left their friends and relations and their past mistakes, and sailed for America. A clean slate! Whatever happened with Dickie, he would acquit himself well, and Mr Greenleaf would know that he had, and would respect him for it. When Mr Greenleaf's money was used up, he might not come back to America. He might get an interesting job in a hotel, for instance, where they needed somebody bright and personable who spoke English. Or he might become a representative for some European firm and travel everywhere in the world. Or somebody might come along who needed a young man exactly like himself, who could drive a car, who was quick at figures, who could entertain an old grandmother or squire somebody's daughter to a dance. He was versatile, and the world was wide! He swore to himself he would stick to a job once he got it. Patience and perseverance! Upward and onward!

'Have you Henry James's *The Ambassadors?*' Tom asked the officer in charge of the first-class library. The book was not on the shelf.

'I'm sorry, we haven't, sir,' said the officer.

Tom was disappointed. It was the book Mr Greenleaf had asked him if he had read. Tom felt he ought to read it. He went to the cabin-class library. He found the book on the shelf, but when he started to check it out and gave his cabin number, the attendant told him sorry, that first-class passengers were not allowed to take books from the cabin-class library. Tom had been afraid of that. He put the book back docilely, though it would have been easy, so easy, to make a pass at the shelf and slip the book under his jacket.

In the mornings he strolled several times round the deck, but very slowly, so that the people puffing around on their morning constitutionals always passed him two or three times before he had been around once, then settled down in his deck-chair for bouillon and more thought on his own destiny. After lunch, he pottered around in his cabin, basking in its privacy and comfort, doing absolutely nothing. Sometimes he sat in the writing-room, thoughtfully penning letters on the ship's stationery to Marc Priminger, to Cleo, to the Greenleafs. The letter to the Greenleafs began as a polite greeting and a thank-you for the bon voyage basket and the comfortable accommodations, but he amused himself by adding an imaginary postdated paragraph about finding Dickie and living with him in his Mongibello house, about the slow but steady progress he was making in persuading Dickie to come home, about the swimming, the fishing, the café life, and he got so carried away that it went on for eight or ten pages and he knew he would never mail any of it, so he wrote on about Dickie's not being romantically interested in Marge (he gave a complete character analysis of Marge) so it was not Marge who was holding Dickie, though Mrs Greenleaf had thought it might be, etc., etc., until the table was covered with sheets of paper and the first call came for dinner.

On another afternoon, he wrote a polite note to Aunt Dottie:

Dear Auntie [which he rarely called her in a letter and never to her face],

As you see by the stationery, I am on the high seas. An unexpected business offer which I cannot explain now. I had to leave rather suddenly, so I was not able to get up to Boston and I'm sorry, because it may be months or even years before I come back.

I just wanted you not to worry and not to send me any more cheques, thank you. Thank you very much for the last one of a month or so ago. I don't suppose you have sent any more since then. I am well and extremely happy.

Love,
Tom

No use sending any good wishes about her health. She was as strong as an ox. He added:

P.S. I have no idea what my address will be, so I cannot give you any.

That made him feel better, because it definitely cut him off from her. He needn't ever tell her where he was. No more of the snidely digging letters, the sly comparisons of him to his father, the piddling cheques for the strange sums of six dollars and forty-eight cents and twelve dollars and ninety-five, as if she had had a bit left over from her latest bill-paying, or taken something back to a store and had tossed the money to him, like a crumb. Considering what Aunt Dottie might have sent him, with her income, the cheques were an insult. Aunt Dottie insisted that his upbringing had cost her more than his father had left in insurance, and maybe it had, but did she have to keep rubbing it in his face? Did anybody human keep rubbing a thing like that in a child's face? Lots of aunts and even strangers raised a child for nothing and were delighted to do it.

After his letter to Aunt Dottie, he got up and strode around the deck, walking it off. Writing her always made him feel angry. He resented the courtesy to her. Yet until now he had always wanted her to know where he was, because he had always needed her piddling cheques. He had had to write a score of letters about his changes of address to Aunt Dottie. But he didn't need her money now. He would hold himself independent of it, forever.

He thought suddenly of one summer day when he had been about twelve, when he had been on a cross-country trip with Aunt Dottie and a woman friend of hers, and they had got stuck in a bumper-to-bumper traffic jam somewhere. It had been a hot summer day, and Aunt Dottie had sent him out with the Thermos to get some ice water at a filling station, and suddenly the traffic had started moving. He remembered running between huge, inching cars, always about to touch the door of Aunt Dottie's car and never being quite able to, because she had kept inching along as fast as she could go, not willing to wait for him a minute, and yelling, 'Come on, come on, slowpoke!' out the window all the time. When he had finally made it to the car and got in, with tears of frustration and anger running down his cheeks, she had said gaily to her friend, 'Sissy! He's a sissy from the ground up. Just like his father!' It was a wonder he had emerged from such treatment as well as he had. And just what, he wondered, made Aunt Dottie think his father had been a sissy? Could she, had she, ever cited a single thing? No.

Lying in his deck-chair, fortified morally by the luxurious surroundings and inwardly by the abundance of well-prepared food, he tried to take an objective look at his past life. The last four years had been for the most part a waste, there was no denying that. A series of haphazard jobs, long perilous intervals with no job at all and consequent demoralization because of having no money, and then taking up with stupid, silly people in order not to be lonely, or because they could offer him something for a while, as Marc Priminger had. It was not a record to be proud of, considering he had come to New York with such high aspirations. He had wanted to be an actor, though at twenty he had not had the faintest idea of the difficulties, the necessary training, or even the necessary talent. He had thought he had the necessary talent and that all he would have to do was show a producer a few of his original one-man skits – Mrs Roosevelt writing 'My Day' after a visit to a clinic for unmarried mothers for instance – but his first three rebuffs had killed all his courage and his hope. He had had no reserve of money, so he had taken the job on the banana boat, which at least had removed him from New York. He had been afraid that Aunt Dottie had called the police to look for him in New York, though he hadn't done anything wrong in Boston, just run off to make his own way in the world as millions of young men had done before him.

His main mistake had been that he had never stuck to anything, he thought, like the accounting job in the department store that might have worked into something, if he had not been so completely discouraged by the slowness of department-store promotions. Well, he blamed Aunt Dottie to some extent for his lack of perseverance, never giving him credit when he was younger for anything he had stuck to – like his paper route when he was thirteen. He had won a silver medal from the newspaper for 'Courtesy, Service, and Reliability'. It was like looking back at another person to remember himself then, a skinny, snivelling wretch with an eternal cold in the nose, who had still managed to win a medal for courtesy, service, and reliability. Aunt Dottie had hated him when he had a cold; she used to take her handkerchief and nearly wrench his nose off, wiping it.

Tom writhed in his deck-chair as he thought of it, but he writhed elegantly, adjusting the crease of his trousers.

He remembered the vows he had made, even at the age of eight, to run away from Aunt Dottie, the violent scenes he had imagined – Aunt Dottie trying to hold him in the house, and he hitting her with his fists, flinging her to the ground and throttling her, and finally tearing the big brooch off her dress and stabbing her a million times in the throat with it. He had run away at seventeen and had been brought back, and he had done it again at twenty and succeeded. And it was astounding and pitiful how naïve he had been, how little he had known about the way the world worked, as if he had spent so much of his time hating Aunt Dottie and scheming how to escape her, that he had not had enough time to learn and grow. He remembered the way he had felt when he had been fired from the warehouse job during his first month in New York. He had held the job less than two weeks, because he hadn't been strong enough to lift orange crates eight hours a day, but he had done his best and knocked himself out trying to hold the job, and when they had fired him, he remembered how horribly unjust he had thought it. He remembered deciding then that the world was full of Simon Legrees, and that you had to be an animal, as tough as the gorillas who worked with him at the warehouse, or starve. He remembered that right after that, he had stolen a loaf of bread from a delicatessen counter and had taken it home and devoured it, feeling that the world owed a loaf of bread to him, and more.

'Mr Ripley?' One of the Englishwomen who had sat on the sofa with him in the lounge the other day during tea was bending over him. 'We were wondering if you'd care to join us in a rubber of bridge in the game room? We're going to start in about fifteen minutes.'

Tom sat up politely in his chair. 'Thank you very much, but I think I prefer to stay outside. Besides, I'm not too good at bridge.'

'Oh, neither are we! All right, another time.' She smiled and went away.

Tom sank back in his chair again, pulled his cap down over his eyes and folded his hands over his waist. His aloofness, he knew, was causing a little comment among the passengers. He had not danced with either of the silly girls who kept looking at him hopefully and giggling during the after-dinner dancing every night. He imagined the speculations of the passengers: Is he an American! I *think* so, but he doesn't act like an American, does he? Most Americans are so *noisy*. He's terribly serious, isn't he, and he can't be more than twenty-three. He must have something very important on his mind.

Yes, he had. The present and the future of Tom Ripley.

SEVEN

Paris was no more than a glimpse out of a railroad station window of a lighted café front, complete with rain-streaked awning, sidewalk tables, and boxes of hedges, like a tourist poster illustration, and otherwise a series of long station platforms down which he followed dumpy little blue-clad porters with his luggage, and at last the sleeper that would take him all the way to Rome. He could come back to Paris at some other time, he thought. He was eager to get to Mongibello.

When he woke up the next morning, he was in Italy. Something very pleasant happened that morning. Tom was watching the landscape out of the window, when he heard some Italians in the corridor outside his compartment say something with the word 'Pisa' in it. A city was gliding by on the other side of the train. Tom went into the corridor to get a better look at it, looking automatically for the Leaning Tower, though he was not at all sure that the city was Pisa or that the tower would even be visible from here, but there it was! – a thick white column sticking up out of the low chalky houses that formed the rest of the town, and *leaning*, leaning at an angle that he wouldn't have thought possible! He had always taken it for granted that the leaning of the Leaning Tower of Pisa was exaggerated. It seemed to him a good omen, a sign that Italy was going to be everything that he expected, and that everything would go well with him and Dickie.

He arrived in Naples late that afternoon, and there was no bus to Mongibello until tomorrow morning at eleven. A boy of about sixteen in dirty shirt and trousers and G.I. shoes latched on to him at the railroad station when he was changing some money, offering him God knew what, maybe girls, maybe dope, and in spite of Tom's protestations actually got into the taxi with him and instructed the driver where to go, jabbering on and holding a finger up as if he was going to fix him up fine, wait and see. Tom gave up and sulked in a corner with his arms folded, and finally the taxi stopped in front of a big hotel that faced the bay. Tom would have been afraid of the imposing hotel if Mr Greenleaf had not been paying the bill.

'Santa Lucia!' the boy said triumphantly, pointing seaward.

Tom nodded. After all, the boy seemed to mean well. Tom paid the driver and gave the boy a hundred-lire bill, which he estimated to be sixteen and a fraction cents and appropriate as a tip in Italy, according to an article on Italy he had read on the ship, and when the boy looked outraged, gave him another hundred, and when he still looked outraged, waved a hand at him and went into the hotel behind the bellboys who had already gathered up his luggage.

Tom had dinner that evening at a restaurant down on the water called Zi' Teresa, which had been recommended to him by the English-speaking manager of the hotel. He had a difficult time ordering, and he found himself with a first course of miniature octopuses, as virulently purple as if they had been cooked in the ink in which the menu had been written. He tasted the tip of one tentacle, and it had a disgusting consistency like cartilage. The second course was also a mistake, a platter of fried fish of various kinds. The third course – which he had been sure was a kind of dessert – was a couple of small reddish fish. Ah, Naples! The food didn't matter. He was feeling mellow on the wine. Far over on the left, a three-quarter moon drifted above the jagged hump of Mount Vesuvius. Tom gazed at it calmly, as if he had seen it a thousand times before. Around the corner of land there, beyond Vesuvius, lay Richard's village.

He boarded the bus the next morning at eleven. The road followed the shore and went through little towns where they made brief stops – Torre del Greco, Torre Annunciata, Castellammare, Sorrento. Tom listened eagerly to the names of the towns that the driver called out. From Sorrento, the road was a narrow ridge cut into the side of the rock cliffs that Tom had seen in the photographs at the Greenleafs'. Now and then he caught glimpses of little villages down at the water's edge, houses like white crumbs of bread, specks that were the heads of people swimming near the shore. Tom saw a boulder-sized rock in the middle of the road that had evidently broken off a cliff. The driver dodged it with a nonchalant swerve.

'Mongibello!'

Tom sprang up and yanked his suitcase down from the rack. He had another suitcase on the roof, which the bus boy took down for him. Then the bus went on, and Tom was alone at the side of the road, his suitcases at his feet. There were houses above him, straggling up the mountain, and houses below, their tile roofs silhouetted against the blue sea. Keeping an eye on his suitcases, Tom went into a little house across the road marked POSTA, and inquired of the man behind the window where Richard Greenleaf's house was. Without thinking, he spoke in English, but the man seemed to understand, because he came out and pointed from the door up the road Tom had come on the bus, and gave in Italian what seemed to be explicit directions how to get there.

'Sempre seeneestra, seeneestra!'

Tom thanked him, and asked if he could leave his two suitcases in the post office for a while, and the man seemed to understand this, too, and helped Tom carry them into the post office.

He had to ask two more people where Richard Greenleaf's house was, but everybody seemed to know it, and the third person was able to point it out to him – a large two-storey house with an iron gate on the road, and a terrace that projected over the cliff's edge. Tom rang the bell beside the gate. An Italian woman came out of the house, wiping her hands on her apron.

'Mr Greenleaf?' Tom asked hopefully.

The woman gave him a long, smiling answer in Italian and pointed downward towards the sea. 'Jew,' she seemed to keep saying. 'Jew.'

Tom nodded. 'Grazie.'

Should he go down to the beach as he was, or be more casual about it and get into a bathing suit? Or should he wait until the tea or cocktail hour? Or should he try to telephone him first? He hadn't brought a bathing suit with him, and he'd certainly have to have one here. Tom went into one of the little shops near the post office that had shirts and bathing shorts in its tiny front window, and after trying on several pairs of shorts that did not fit him, or at least not adequately enough to serve as a bathing suit, he bought a black-and-yellow thing hardly bigger than a G-string.

He made a neat bundle of his clothing inside his raincoat, and started out of the door barefoot. He leapt back inside. The cobblestones were as hot as coals.

'Shoes? Sandals?' he asked the man in the shop.

The man didn't sell shoes.

Tom put on his own shoes again and walked across the road to the post office, intending to leave his clothes with his suitcases, but the post office was locked. He had heard of this in Europe, places closing from noon to four sometimes. He turned and walked down a cobbled lane which he supposed led towards the beach. He went down a dozen steep stone steps, down another cobbled slope past shops and houses, down more steps, and finally he came to a level length of broad sidewalk slightly raised from the beach, where there were a couple of cafés and a restaurant with outdoor tables. Some bronzed adolescent Italian boys sitting on wooden benches at the edge of the pavement inspected him thoroughly as he walked by. He felt mortified at the big brown shoes on his feet and at his ghost-white skin. He had not been to a beach all summer. He hated beaches. There was a wooden walk that led half across the beach, which Tom knew must be hot as hell to walk on, because everybody was lying on a towel or something else, but he took his shoes off anyway and stood for a moment on the hot wood, calmly surveying the groups of people near him. None of the people looked like Richard, and the shimmering heat waves kept him from making out the people very far away. Tom put one foot out on the sand and drew it back. Then he took a deep breath, raced down the rest of the walk, sprinted across the sand, and sank his feet into the blissfully cool inches of water at the sea's edge. He began to walk.

Tom saw him from a distance of about a block – unmistakably Dickie, though he was burnt a dark brown and his crinkly blond hair looked lighter than Tom remembered it. He was with Marge.

'Dickie Greenleaf?' Tom asked, smiling.

Dickie looked up. 'Yes?'

'I'm Tom Ripley. I met you in the States several years ago. Remember?' Dickie looked blank.

'I think your father said he was going to write you about me.'

'Oh, yes!' Dickie said, touching his forehead as if it was stupid of him to have forgotten. He stood up. 'Tom *what* is it?'

'Ripley.'

'This is Marge Sherwood,' he said. 'Marge, Tom Ripley.'

'How do you do?' Tom said.

'How do you do?'

'How long are you here for?' Dickie asked.

'I don't know yet,' Tom said. 'I just got here. I'll have to look the place over.'

Dickie was looking him over, not entirely with approval, Tom felt. Dickie's arms were folded, his lean brown feet planted in the hot sand that didn't seem to bother him at all. Tom had crushed his feet into his shoes again.

'Taking a house?' asked Dickie.

'I don't know,' Tom said undecidedly, as if he had been considering it.

'It's a good time to get a house, if you're looking for one for the winter,' the girl said. 'The summer tourists have practically all gone. We could use a few more Americans around here in winter.'

Dickie said nothing. He had reseated himself on the big towel beside the girl, and Tom felt that he was waiting for him to say good-bye and move on. Tom stood there, feeling pale and naked as the day he was born. He hated bathing suits. This one was very revealing. Tom managed to extract his pack of cigarettes from his jacket inside his raincoat, and offered it to Dickie and the girl. Dickie accepted one, and Tom lighted it with his lighter.

'You don't seem to remember me from New York,' Tom said.

'I can't really say I do,' Dickie said. 'Where did I meet you?'

'I think – Wasn't it at Buddy Lankenau's?' It wasn't, but he knew Dickie knew Buddy Lankenau, and Buddy was a very respectable fellow.

'Oh,' said Dickie, vaguely. 'I hope you'll excuse me. My memory's rotten for America these days.'

'It certainly is,' Marge said, coming to Tom's rescue. 'It's getting worse and worse. When did you get here, Tom?'

'Just about an hour ago. I've just parked my suitcases at the post office.' He laughed.

'Don't you want to sit down? Here's another towel.' She spread a smaller white towel beside her on the sand.

Tom accepted it gratefully.

'I'm going in for a dip to cool off,' Dickie said, getting up.

'Me too!' Marge said. 'Coming in, Tom?'

Tom followed them. Dickie and the girl went out quite far – both seemed to be excellent swimmers – and Tom stayed near the shore and came in much sooner. When Dickie and the girl came back to the towels, Dickie said, as if he had been prompted by the girl, 'We're leaving. Would you like to come up to the house and have lunch with us?'

'Why, yes. Thanks very much.' Tom helped them gather up the towels, the sunglasses, the Italian newspapers.

Tom thought they would never get there. Dickie and Marge went in front of him, taking the endless flights of stone steps slowly and steadily, two at a time. The sun had enervated Tom. The muscles of his legs trembled on the level stretches. His shoulders were already pink, and he had put on his shirt against the sun's rays, but he could feel the sun burning through his hair, making him dizzy and nauseous.

'Having a hard time?' Marge asked, not out of breath at all. 'You'll get used to it, if you stay here. You should have seen this place during the heat wave in July.'

Tom hadn't breath to reply anything.

Fifteen minutes later he was feeling better. He had had a cool shower, and he was sitting in a comfortable wicker chair on Dickie's terrace with a martini in his hand. At Marge's suggestion, he had put his swimming outfit on again, with his shirt over it. The table on the terrace had been set for three while he was in the shower, and Marge was in the kitchen now, talking in Italian to the maid. Tom wondered if Marge lived here. The house was certainly big enough. It was sparsely furnished, as far as Tom could see, in a pleasant mixture of Italian antique and American bohemian. He had seen two original Picasso drawings in the hall.

Marge came out on the terrace with her martini. 'That's my house over there.' She pointed. 'See it? The square-looking white one with the darker red roof than the houses just beside it.'

It was hopeless to pick it out from the other houses, but Tom pretended he saw it. 'Have you been here long?'

'A year. All last winter, and it was quite a winter. Rain every day except one for three whole months!'

'Really!'

'Um-hm.' Marge sipped her martini and gazed out contentedly at her little village. She was back in her bathing suit, too, a tomato-coloured bathing suit, and she wore a striped shirt over it. She wasn't bad-looking, Tom supposed, and she even had a good figure, if one liked the rather solid type. Tom didn't, himself.

'I understand Dickie has a boat,' Tom said.

'Yes, the *Pipi*. Short for *Pipistrello*. Want to see it?'

She pointed at another indiscernible something down at the little pier that they could see from the corner of the terrace. The boats looked very much alike, but Marge said Dickie's boat was larger than most of them and had two masts.

Dickie came out and poured himself a cocktail from the pitcher on the table. He wore badly ironed white duck trousers and a terra cotta linen shirt the colour of his skin. 'Sorry there's no ice. I haven't got a refrigerator.'

Tom smiled. 'I brought a bathrobe for you. Your mother said you'd asked for one. Also some socks.'

'Do you know my mother?'

'I happened to meet your father just before I left New York, and he asked me to dinner at his house.'

'Oh? How was my mother?'

'She was up and around that evening. I'd say she gets tired easily.'

Dickie nodded. 'I had a letter this week saying she was a little better. At least there's no particular crisis right now, is there?'

'I don't think so. I think your father was more worried a few weeks ago.' Tom hesitated. 'He's also a little worried because you won't come home.'

'Herbert's always worried about something,' Dickie said.

Marge and the maid came out of the kitchen carrying a steaming platter of spaghetti, a big bowl of salad, and a plate of bread. Dickie and Marge began to talk about the enlargement of some restaurant down on the beach. The proprietor was widening the terrace so there would be room for people to dance. They discussed it in detail, slowly, like people in a small town who take an interest in the most minute changes in the neighbour-hood. There was nothing Tom could contribute.

He spent the time examining Dickie's rings. He liked them both: a large rectangular green stone set in gold on the third finger of his right hand, and on the little finger of the other hand a signet ring, larger and more ornate than the signet Mr Greenleaf had worn. Dickie had long, bony hands, a little like his own hands, Tom thought.

'By the way, your father showed me around the Burke-Greenleaf yards before I left,' Tom said. 'He told me he'd made a lot of changes since you've seen it last. I was quite impressed.'

'I suppose he offered you a job, too. Always on the lookout for promising young men.' Dickie turned his fork round and round, and thrust a neat mass of spaghetti into his mouth.

'No, he didn't.' Tom felt the luncheon couldn't have been going worse. Had Mr Greenleaf told Dickie that he was coming to give him a lecture on why he should go home? Or was Dickie just in a foul mood? Dickie had certainly changed since Tom had seen him last.

Dickie brought out a shiny espresso machine about two feet high, and plugged it into an outlet on the terrace. In a few moments there were four little cups of coffee, one of which Marge took into the kitchen to the maid.

'What hotel are you staying at?' Marge asked Tom.

Tom smiled. 'I haven't found one yet. What do you recommend?'

'The Miramare's the best. It's just this side of Giorgio's. The only other hotel is Georgio's, but –'

'They say Georgio's got pulci in his beds,' Dickie interrupted.

'That's fleas. Giorgio's is cheap,' Marge said earnestly, 'but the service is –'

'Non-existent,' Dickie supplied.

'You're in a fine mood today, aren't you?' Marge said to Dickie, flicking a crumb of gorgonzola at him.

'In that case, I'll try the Miramare,' Tom said, standing up. 'I must be going.'

Neither of them urged him to stay. Dickie walked with him to the front gate. Marge was staying on. Tom wondered if Dickie and Marge were having an affair, one of those old, faute de mieux affairs that wouldn't necessarily be obvious from the outside, because neither was very enthusiastic. Marge was in love with Dickie, Tom thought, but Dickie couldn't have been more indifferent to her if she had been the fifty-year-old Italian maid sitting there.

'I'd like to see some of your paintings sometimes,' Tom said to Dickie.

'Fine. Well, I suppose we'll see you again if you're around,' and Tom thought he added it only because he remembered that he had brought the bathrobe and the socks.

'I enjoyed the lunch. Good-bye, Dickie,'

'Good-bye.'

The iron gate clanged.

EIGHT

Tom took a room at the Miramare. It was four o'clock by the time he got his suitcases up from the post office, and he had barely the energy to hang up his best suit before he fell down on the bed. The voices of some Italian boys who were talking under his window drifted up as distinctly as if they had been in the room with him, and the insolent, cackling laugh of one of them, bursting again and again through the pattering syllables, made

Tom twitch and writhe. He imagined them discussing his expedition to Signor Greenleaf, and making unflattering speculations as to what might happen next.

What was he doing here? He had no friends here and he didn't speak the language. Suppose he got sick? Who would take care of him?

Tom got up, knowing he was going to be sick, yet moving slowly because he knew just when he was going to be sick and that there would be time for him to get to the bathroom. In the bathroom he lost his lunch, and also the fish from Naples, he thought. He went back to his bed and fell instantly asleep.

When he awoke groggy and weak, the sun was still shining and it was five-thirty by his new watch. He went to a window and looked out, looking automatically for Dickie's big house and projecting terrace among the pink and white houses that dotted the climbing ground in front of him. He found the sturdy reddish balustrade of the terrace. Was Marge still there? Were they talking about him? He heard a laugh rising over the little din of street noises, tense and resonant, and as American as if it had been a sentence in American. For an instant he saw Dickie and Marge as they crossed a space between houses on the main road. They turned a corner, and Tom went to his side window for a better view. There was an alley by the side of the hotel just below his window, and Dickie and Marge came down it, Dickie in his white trousers and terra cotta shirt, Marge in a skirt and blouse. She must have gone home, Tom thought. Or else she had clothes at Dickie's house. Dickie talked with an Italian on the little wooden pier, gave him some money, and the Italian touched his cap, then untied the boat from the pier. Tom watched Dickie help Marge into the boat. The white sail began to climb. Behind them, to the left, the orange sun was sinking into the water. Tom could hear Marge's laugh, and a shout from Dickie in Italian towards the pier. Tom realized he was seeing them on a typical day – a siesta after the late lunch, probably, then the sail in Dickie's boat at sundown. Then aperitifs at one of the cafés on the beach. They were enjoying a perfectly ordinary day, as if he did not exist. Why should Dickie want to come back to subways and taxis and starched collars and a nine-to-five job? Or even a chauffeured car and vacations in Florida and Maine? It wasn't as much fun as sailing a boat in old clothes and being answerable to nobody for the way he spent his time, and having his own house with a good-natured maid who probably took care of everything for him. And money besides to take trips, if he wanted to. Tom envied him with a heartbreaking surge of envy and self-pity.

Dickie's father had probably said in his letter the very things that would set Dickie against him, Tom thought. How much better it would have been if he had just sat down in one of the cafés down at the beach and struck up an acquaintance with Dickie out of the blue! He probably could have persuaded Dickie to come home eventually, if he had begun like that, but this way it was useless. Tom cursed himself for having been so heavy-handed and so humourless today. Nothing he took desperately seriously ever worked out. He'd found that out years ago.

He'd let a few days go by, he thought. The first step, anyway, was to make Dickie like him. That he wanted more than anything else in the world.

NINE

Tom let three days go by. Then he went down to the beach on the fourth morning around noon, and found Dickie alone, in the same spot Tom had seen him first, in front of the grey rocks that extended across the beach from the land.

'Morning!' Tom called. 'Where's Marge?'

'Good morning. She's probably working a little later. She'll be down.'

'Working?'

'She's a writer.'

'Oh.'

Dickie puffed on the Italian cigarette in the corner of his mouth. 'Where've you been keeping yourself? I thought you'd gone.'

'Sick,' Tom said casually, tossing his rolled towel down on the sand, but not too near Dickie's towel.

'Oh, the usual upset stomach?'

'Hovering between life and the bathroom,' Tom said, smiling. 'But I'm all right now.' He actually had been too weak even to leave the hotel, but he had crawled around on the floor of his room, following the patches of sunlight that came through his windows, so that he wouldn't look so white the next time he came down to the beach. And he had spent the remainder of his feeble strength studying an Italian conversation book that he had bought in the hotel lobby.

Tom went down to the water, went confidently up to his waist and stopped there, splashing the water over his shoulders. He lowered himself until the water reached his chin, floated around a little, then came slowly in.

'Can I invite you for a drink at the hotel before you go up to your house?' Tom asked Dickie. 'And Marge, too, if she comes. I wanted to give you your bathrobe and socks, you know.'

'Oh yes. Thanks very much. I'd like to have a drink.' He went back to his Italian newspaper.

Tom stretched out on his towel. He heard the village clock strike one.

'Doesn't look as if Marge is coming down,' Dickie said. 'I think I'll be going along.'

Tom got up. They walked up to the Miramare, saying practically nothing to each other, except that Tom invited Dickie to lunch with him, and Dickie declined because the maid had his lunch ready at the house, he said. They went up to Tom's room, and Dickie tried the bathrobe on and held the socks up to his bare feet. Both the bathrobe and the socks were the right size, and, as Tom had anticipated, Dickie was extremely pleased with the bathrobe.

'And this,' Tom said, taking a square package wrapped in drugstore paper from a bureau drawer. 'Your mother sent you some nosedrops, too.'

Dickie smiled. 'I don't need them any more. That was sinus. But I'll take them off your hands.'

Now Dickie had everything, Tom thought, everything he had to offer. He was going to refuse the invitation for a drink, too, Tom knew. Tom followed him towards the door. 'You know, your father's very concerned about your coming home. He asked me to give you a good talking to, which of course I won't, but I'll still have to tell him something. I promised to write him.'

Dickie turned with his hand on the doorknob. 'I don't know what my father thinks I'm doing over here – drinking myself to death or what. I'll probably fly home this winter for a few days, but I don't intend to stay over there. I'm happier here. If I went back there to live, my father would be after me to work in Burke-Greenleaf. I couldn't possibly paint. I happen to like painting, and I think it's my business how I spend my life.'

'I understand. But he said he wouldn't try to make you work in his firm if you come back, unless you wanted to work in the designing department, and he said you liked that.'

'Well – my father and I have been over that. Thanks, anyway, Tom, for delivering the message and the clothes. It was very nice of you.' Dickie held out his hand.

Tom couldn't have made himself take the hand. This was the very edge of failure, failure as far as Mr Greenleaf was concerned, and failure with Dickie. 'I think I ought to tell you something else,' Tom said with a smile. 'Your father sent me over here especially to ask you to come home.'

'What do you mean?' Dickie frowned. 'Paid your way?'

'Yes.' It was his one last chance to amuse Dickie or to repel him, to make Dickie burst out laughing or go out and slam the door in disgust. But the smile was coming, the long corners of his mouth going up, the way Tom remembered Dickie's smile.

'Paid your way! What do you know! He's getting desperate, isn't he?' Dickie closed the door again.

'He approached me in a bar in New York,' Tom said. 'I told him I wasn't a close friend of yours, but he insisted I could help if I came over. I told him I'd try.'

'How did he ever meet you?'

'Through the Schrievers. I hardly know the Schrievers, but there it was! I was your friend and I could do you a lot of good.'

They laughed.

'I don't want you to think I'm someone who tried to take advantage of your father,' Tom said. 'I expect to find a job somewhere in Europe soon, and I'll be able to pay him back my passage money eventually. He bought me a round-trip ticket.'

'Oh, don't bother! It goes on the Burke-Greenleaf expense list. I can just see Dad approaching you in a bar! Which bar was it?'

'Raoul's. Matter of fact, he followed me from the Green Cage.' Tom watched Dickie's face for a sign of recognition of the Green Cage, a very popular bar, but there was no recognition.

They had a drink downstairs in the hotel bar. They drank to Herbert Richard Greenleaf.

'I just realized today's Sunday,' Dickie said. 'Marge went to church. You'd better come up and have lunch with us. We always have chicken on Sunday. You know it's an old American custom, chicken on Sunday.'

Dickie wanted to go by Marge's house to see if she was still there. They climbed some steps from the main road up the side of a stone wall, crossed part of somebody's garden, and climbed more steps. Marge's house was a rather sloppy-looking one-storey affair with a messy garden at one end, a couple of buckets and a garden hose cluttering the path to the door, and the feminine touch represented by her tomato-coloured bathing suit and a bra hanging over a window-sill. Through an open window, Tom had a glimpse of a disorderly table with a typewriter on it.

'Hi!' she said, opening the door. 'Hello, Tom! Where've you been all this time?'

She offered them a drink, but discovered there was only half an inch of gin in her bottle of Gilbey's.

'It doesn't matter, we're going to my house,' Dickie said. He strolled around Marge's bedroom–living-room with an air of familiarity, as if he lived half the time here himself. He bent over a flower pot in which a tiny plant of some sort was growing, and touched its leaf delicately with his forefinger. 'Tom has something funny to tell you,' he said. 'Tell her, Tom.'

Tom took a breath and began. He made it very funny and Marge laughed like someone who hadn't had anything funny to laugh at in years. 'When I saw him coming in Raoul's after me, I was ready to climb out of a back window!' His tongue rattled on almost independently of his brain. His brain was estimating how high his stock was shooting up with Dickie and Marge. He could see it in their faces.

The climb up the hill to Dickie's house didn't seem half so long as before. Delicious smells of roasting chicken drifted out on the terrace. Dickie made some martinis. Tom showered and then Dickie showered, and came out and poured himself a drink, just like the first time, but the atmosphere now was totally changed.

Dickie sat down in a wicker chair and swung his legs over one of the arms. 'Tell me more,' he said, smiling. 'What kind of work do you do? You said you might take a job.'

'Why? Do you have a job for me?'

'Can't say that I have.'

'Oh, I can do a number of things – valeting, baby-sitting, accounting – I've got an unfortunate talent for figures. No matter how drunk I get, I can always tell when a waiter's cheating me on a bill. I can forge a signature, fly a helicopter, handle dice, impersonate practically anybody, cook – and do a one-man show in a nightclub in case the regular entertainer's sick. Shall I go on?' Tom was leaning forward, counting them off on his fingers. He could have gone on.

'What kind of a one-man show?' Dickie asked.

'Well –' Tom sprang up. 'This for example.' He struck a pose with one hand on his hip, one foot extended. 'This is Lady Assburden sampling the American subway. She's never even been in the underground in London, but she wants to take back some American experiences.' Tom did it all in pantomime, searching for a coin, finding it didn't go into the slot, buying a token, puzzling over which stairs to go down, registering alarm at the noise and the long express ride, puzzling again as to how to get out of the place – here Marge came out, and Dickie told her it was an Englishwoman in the subway, but Marge didn't seem to get it and asked, 'What?' – walking through a door which could only be the door of the men's room from her twitching horror of this and that, which augmented until she fainted. Tom fainted gracefully on to the terrace glider.

'Wonderful!' Dickie yelled, clapping.

Marge wasn't laughing. She stood there looking a little blank. Neither of them bothered to explain it to her. She didn't look as if she had that kind of sense of humour, anyway, Tom thought.

Tom took a gulp of his martini, terribly pleased with himself. 'I'll do another for you sometime,' he said to Marge, but mostly to indicate to Dickie that he had another one to do.

'Dinner ready?' Dickie asked her. 'I'm starving.'

'I'm waiting for the darned artichokes to get done. You know that front hole. It'll barely make anything come to a boil.' She smiled at Tom. 'Dickie's very old-fashioned about some things, Tom, the things he doesn't have to fool with. There's still only a wood stove here, and he refuses to buy a refrigerator or even an icebox.'

'One of the reasons I fled America,' Dickie said. 'Those things are a waste of money in a country with so many servants. What'd Ermelinda do with herself, if she could cook a meal in half an hour?' He stood up. 'Come on in, Tom, I'll show you some of my paintings.'

Dickie led the way into the big room Tom had looked into a couple of times on his way to and from the shower, the room with a long couch under the two windows and the big easel in the middle of the floor. 'This is one of Marge I'm working on now.' He gestured to the picture on the easel.

'Oh,' Tom said with interest. It wasn't good in his opinion, probably in anybody's opinion. The wild enthusiasm of her smile was a bit off. Her skin was as red as an Indian's. If Marge hadn't been the only girl around with blonde hair, he wouldn't have noticed any resemblance at all.

'And these – a lot of landscapes,' Dickie said with a deprecatory laugh, though obviously he wanted Tom to say something complimentary about them, because obviously he was proud of them. They were all wild and hasty and monotonously similar. The combination of terra cotta and electric blue was in nearly every one, terra cotta roofs and mountains and bright electric-blue seas. It was the blue he had put in Marge's eyes, too.

'My surrealist effort,' Dickie said, bracing another canvas against his knee.

Tom winced with almost a personal shame. It was Marge again, undoubtedly, though with long snakelike hair, and worst of all two horizons in her eyes, with a miniature landscape of Mongibello's houses and mountains in one eye, and the beach in the other full of little red people. 'Yes, I like that,' Tom said. Mr Greenleaf had been right. Yet it gave Dickie something to do, kept him out of trouble, Tom supposed, just as it gave thousands of lousy amateur painters all over America something to do. He was only sorry that Dickie fell into this category as a painter, because he wanted Dickie to be much more.

'I won't ever set the world on fire as a painter,' Dickie said, 'but I get a great deal of pleasure out of it.'

'Yes,' Tom wanted to forget all about the paintings and forget that Dickie painted. 'Can I see the rest of the house?'

'Absolutely! You haven't seen the salon, have you?'

Dickie opened a door in the hall that led into a very large room with a fireplace, sofas, bookshelves, and three exposures – to the terrace, to the land on the other side of the house, and to the front garden. Dickie said that in summer he did not use the room, because he liked to save it as a change of scene for the winter. It was more of a bookish den than a living-room, Tom thought. It surprised him. He had Dickie figured out as a young man who was not particularly brainy, and who probably spent most of his time playing. Perhaps he was wrong. But he didn't think he was wrong in feeling that Dickie was bored at the moment and needed someone to show him how to have fun.

'What's upstairs?' Tom asked.

The upstairs was disappointing: Dickie's bedroom in the corner of the house above the terrace was stark and empty – a bed, a chest of drawers, and a rocking chair, looking lost and unrelated in all the space – a narrow bed, too, hardly wider than a single bed. The other three rooms of the second floor were not even furnished, or at least not completely. One of them held only firewood and a pile of canvas scraps. There was certainly no sign of Marge anywhere, least of all in Dickie's bedroom.

'How about going to Naples with me sometime?' Tom asked. 'I didn't have much of a chance to see it on my way down.'

'All right,' Dickie said. 'Marge and I are going Saturday afternoon. We have dinner there nearly every Saturday night and treat ourselves to a taxi or a carrozza ride back. Come along.'

'I mean in the daytime or some weekday so I could see a little more,'

Tom said, hoping to avoid Marge in the excursion. 'Or do you paint all day?'

'No. There's a twelve o'clock bus Mondays, Wednesdays, and Fridays. I suppose we could go tomorrow, if you feel like it.'

'Fine,' Tom said, though he still wasn't sure that Marge wouldn't be asked along. 'Marge is a Catholic?' he asked as they went down the stairs.

'With a vengeance! She was converted about six months ago by an Italian she had a mad crush on. Could that man talk! He was here for a few months, resting up after a ski accident. Marge consoles herself for the loss of Eduardo by embracing his religion.'

'I had the idea she was in love with you.'

'With me? Don't be silly!'

The dinner was ready when they went out on the terrace. There were even hot biscuits with butter, made by Marge.

'Do you know Vic Simmons in New York?' Tom asked Dickie.

Vic had quite a salon of artists, writers and dancers in New York, but Dickie didn't know of him. Tom asked him about two or three other people, also without success.

Tom hoped Marge would leave after the coffee, but she didn't. When she left the terrace for a moment Tom said, 'Can I invite you for dinner at my hotel tonight?'

'Thank you. At what time?'

'Seven-thirty? So we'll have a little time for cocktails? – After all, it's your father's money,' Tom added with a smile.

Dickie laughed. 'All right, cocktails and a good bottle of wine, Marge!' Marge was just coming back. 'We're dining tonight at the Miramare, compliments of Greenleaf père!'

So Marge was coming, too, and there was nothing Tom could do about it. After all, it was Dickie's father's money.

The dinner that evening was pleasant, but Marge's presence kept Tom from talking about anything he would have liked to talk about, and he did not feel even like being witty in Marge's presence. Marge knew some of the people in the dining-room, and after dinner she excused herself and took her coffee over to another table and sat down.

'How long are you going to be here?' Dickie asked.

'Oh, at least a week, I'd say,' Tom replied.

'Because –' Dickie's face had flushed a little over the cheekbones. The chianti had put him into a good mood. 'If you're going to be here a little longer, why don't you stay with me? There's no use staying in a hotel, unless you really prefer it.'

'Thank you very much,' Tom said.

'There's a bed in the maid's room, which you didn't see. Ermelinda doesn't sleep in. I'm sure we can make out with the furniture that's scattered around, if you think you'd like to.'

'I'm sure I'd like to. By the way, your father gave me six hundred dollars for expenses, and I've still got about five hundred of it. I think we both ought to have a little fun on it, don't you?'

'Five hundred!' Dickie said, as if he'd never seen that much money in one lump in his life. 'We could pick up a little car for that!'

Tom didn't contribute to the car idea. That wasn't his idea of having fun. He wanted to fly to Paris. Marge was coming back, he saw.

The next morning he moved in.

Dickie and Ermelinda had installed an armoire and a couple of chairs in one of the upstairs rooms, and Dickie had thumb-tacked a few reproductions of mosaic portraits from St Mark's Cathedral on the walls. Tom helped Dickie carry up the narrow iron bed from the maid's room. They were finished before twelve, a little lightheaded from the frascati they had been sipping as they worked.

'Are we still going to Naples?' Tom asked.

'Certainly.' Dickie looked at his watch. 'It's only a quarter to twelve. We can make the twelve o'clock bus.'

They took nothing with them but their jackets and Tom's book of traveller's cheques. The bus was just arriving as they reached the post office. Tom and Dickie stood by the door, waiting for people to get off; then Dickie pulled himself up, right into the face of a young man with red hair and a loud sports shirt, an American.

'Dickie!'

'Freddie!' Dickie yelled. 'What're you doing here?'

'Came to see you! And the Cecchis. They're putting me up for a few days.'

'Ch'elegante! I'm off to Naples with a friend. Tom?' Dickie beckoned Tom over and introduced them.

The American's name was Freddie Miles. Tom thought he was hideous. Tom hated red hair, especially this kind of carrot-red hair with white skin and freckles. Freddie had large red-brown eyes that seemed to wobble in his head as if he were cock-eyed, or perhaps he was only one of those people who never looked at anyone they were talking to. He was also overweight. Tom turned away from him, waiting for Dickie to finish his conversation. They were holding up the bus, Tom noticed. Dickie and Freddie were talking about skiing, making a date for some time in December in a town Tom had never heard of.

'There'll be about fifteen of us at Cortina by the second,' Freddie said. 'A real bang-up party like last year! Three weeks, if our money holds out!'

'If we hold out!' Dickie said. 'See you tonight, Fred!'

Tom boarded the bus after Dickie. There were no seats, and they were wedged between a skinny, sweating man who smelled, and a couple of old peasant women who smelled worse. Just as they were leaving the village Dickie remembered that Marge was coming for lunch as usual, because they had thought yesterday that Tom's moving would cancel the Naples trip. Dickie shouted for the driver to stop. The bus stopped with a squeal of brakes and a lurch that threw everybody who was standing off balance, and Dickie put his head through a window and called, 'Gino! Gino!'

A little boy on the road came running up to take the hundred-lire bill that Dickie was holding out to him. Dickie said something in Italian, and the boy said, 'Subito, signor!' and flew up the road, Dickie thanked the driver, and the bus started again. 'I told him to tell Marge we'd be back tonight, but probably late,' Dickie said.

'Good.'

The bus spilled them into a big, cluttered square in Naples, and they were suddenly surrounded by push-carts of grapes, figs, pastry, and watermelon, and screamed at by adolescent boys with fountain pens and mechanical toys. The people made way for Dickie.

'I know a good place for lunch,' Dickie said. 'A real Neapolitan pizzeria. Do you like pizza?'

'Yes.'

The pizzeria was up a street too narrow and steep for cars. Strings of beads hanging in the doorway, a decanter of wine on every table, and there were only six tables in the whole place, the kind of place you could sit in for hours and drink wine and not be disturbed. They sat there until five o'clock, when Dickie said it was time to move on to the Galleria. Dickie apologized for not taking him to the art museum, which had original da Vincis and El Grecos, he said, but they could see that at another time. Dickie had spent most of the afternoon talking about Freddie Miles, and Tom had found it as uninteresting as Freddie's face. Freddie was the son of an American hotel-chain owner, and a playwright – self-styled, Tom gathered, because he had written only two plays, and neither had seen Broadway. Freddie had a house in Cagnes-sur-Mer, and Dickie had stayed with him several weeks before he came to Italy.

'This is what I like,' Dickie said expansively in the Galleria, 'sitting at a table and watching the people go by. It does something to your outlook on life. The Anglo-Saxons make a great mistake not staring at people from a sidewalk table.'

Tom nodded. He had heard it before. He was waiting for something profound and original from Dickie. Dickie was handsome. He looked unusual with his long, finely cut face, his quick, intelligent eyes, the proud way he carried himself regardless of what he was wearing. He was wearing broken-down sandals and rather soiled white pants now, but he sat there as if he owned the Galleria, chatting in Italian with the waiter when he brought their espressos.

'Ciao!' he called to an Italian boy who was passing by.

'Ciao, Dickie?'

'He changes Marge's traveller's cheques on Saturdays,' Dickie explained to Tom.

A well-dressed Italian greeted Dickie with a warm handshake and sat down at the table with them. Tom listened to their conversation in Italian, making out a word here and there. Tom was beginning to feel tired.

'Want to go to Rome?' Dickie asked him suddenly.

'Sure,' Tom said. 'Now?' He stood up, reaching for the money to pay the little tabs that the waiter had stuck under their coffee cups.

The Italian had a long grey Cadillac equipped with venetian blinds, a four-toned horn, and a blaring radio that he and Dickie seemed content to shout over. They reached the outskirts of Rome in about two hours. Tom sat up as they drove along the Appian Way, especially for his benefit, the Italian told Tom, because Tom had not seen it before. The road was bumpy in spots. These were stretches of original Roman brick left bare to show people how Roman roads felt, the Italian said. The flat fields to left and right looked desolate in the twilight, like an ancient graveyard, Tom thought, with just a few tombs and remains of tombs still standing. The Italian dropped them in the middle of a street in Rome and said an abrupt good-bye.

'He's in a hurry,' Dickie said. 'Got to see his girl friend and get away before the husband comes home at eleven. There's the music hall I was looking for. Come on.'

They bought tickets for the music-hall show that evening. There was still an hour before the performance, and they went to the Via Veneto, took a sidewalk table at one of the cafés, and ordered americanos. Dickie didn't know anybody in Rome, Tom noticed, or at least none who passed by, and they watched hundreds of Italians and Americans pass by their table. Tom got very little out of the music-hall show, but he tried his very best. Dickie proposed leaving before the show was over. Then they caught a carrozza and drove around the city, past fountain after fountain, through the Forum and around the Colosseum. The moon had come out. Tom was still a little sleepy, but the sleepiness, underlaid with excitement at being in Rome for the first time, put him into a receptive, mellow mood. They sat slumped in the carrozza, each with a sandalled foot propped on a knee, and it seemed to Tom that he was looking in a mirror when he looked at Dickie's leg and his propped foot beside him. They were the same height, and very much the same weight, Dickie perhaps a bit heavier, and they wore the same size bathrobe, socks, and probably shirts.

Dickie even said, 'Thank you, Mr Greenleaf,' when Tom paid the carrozza driver. Tom felt a little weird.

They were in even finer mood by one in the morning, after a bottle and a half of wine between them at dinner. They walked with their arms around each other's shoulders, singing, and around a dark corner they somehow bumped into a girl and knocked her down. They lifted her up, apologizing, and offered to escort her home. She protested, they insisted, one on either side of her. She had to catch a certain trolley, she said. Dickie wouldn't hear of it. Dickie got a taxi. Dickie and Tom sat very properly on the jump seats with their arms folded like a couple of footmen, and Dickie talked to her and made her laugh. Tom could understand nearly everything Dickie said. They helped the girl out in a little street that looked like Naples again, and she said, 'Grazie tante!' and shook hands with both of them, then vanished into an absolutely black doorway.

'Did you hear that?' Dickie said. 'She said we were the nicest Americans she'd ever met!'

'You know what most crummy Americans would do in a case like that – rape her,' Tom said.

'Now where are we?' Dickie asked, turning completely around.

Neither had the slightest idea where they were. They walked for several blocks without finding a landmark or a familiar street name. They urinated against a dark wall, then drifted on.

'When the dawn comes up, we can see where we are,' Dickie said cheerfully. He looked at his watch. ''S only a couple of more hours.'

'Fine.'

'It's worth it to see a nice girl home, isn't it?' Dickie asked, staggering a little.

'Sure it is. I like girls,' Tom said protestingly. 'But it's just as well Marge isn't here tonight. We never could have seen that girl home with Marge with us.'

'Oh, I don't know,' Dickie said thoughtfully, looking down at his weaving feet. 'Marge isn't –'

'I only mean, if Marge was here, we'd be worrying about a hotel for the night. We'd be *in* the damned hotel, probably. We wouldn't be seeing half of Rome!'

'That's right!' Dickie swung an arm around his shoulder.

Dickie shook his shoulder, roughly. Tom tried to roll out from under it and grab his hand, 'Dickie-e!' Tom opened his eyes and looked into the face of a policeman.

Tom sat up. He was in a park. It was dawn. Dickie was sitting on the grass beside him, talking very calmly to the policeman in Italian. Tom felt for the rectangular lump of his traveller's cheques. They were still in his pocket.

'Passporti!' the policeman hurled at them again, and again Dickie launched into his calm explanation.

Tom knew exactly what Dickie was saying. He was saying that they were Americans, and they didn't have their passports because they had only gone out for a little walk to look at the stars. Tom had an impulse to laugh. He stood up and staggered, dusting his clothing. Dickie was up, too, and they began to walk away, though the policeman was still yelling at them. Dickie said something back to him in a courteous, explanatory tone. At least the policeman was not following them.

'We do look pretty cruddy,' Dickie said.

Tom nodded. There was a long rip in his trouser knee where he had probably fallen. Their clothes were crumpled and grass-stained and filthy with dust and sweat, but now they were shivering with cold. They went into the first café they came to, and had caffè latte and sweet rolls, then several Italian brandies that tasted awful but warmed them. Then they began to laugh. They were still drunk.

By eleven o'clock they were in Naples, just in time to catch the bus for Mongibello. It was wonderful to think of going back to Rome when they were more presentably dressed and seeing all the museums they had missed, and it was wonderful to think of lying on the beach at Mongibello this afternoon, baking in the sun. But they never got to the beach. They had showers at Dickie's house, then fell down on their respective beds and slept until Marge woke them up around four. Marge was annoyed because Dickie hadn't sent her a telegram saying he was spending the night in Rome.

'Not that I minded you spending the night, but I thought you were in Naples and anything can happen in Naples.'

'Oh-h,' Dickie drawled with a glance at Tom. He was making Bloody Marys for all of them.

Tom kept his mouth mysteriously shut. He wasn't going to tell Marge anything they had done. Let her imagine what she pleased. Dickie had made it evident that they had had a very good time. Tom noticed that she looked Dickie over with disapproval of his hangover, his unshaven face, and the drink he was taking now. There was something in Marge's eyes when she was very serious that made her look wise and old in spite of the naïve clothes she wore and her windblown hair and her general air of a Girl Scout. She had the look of a mother or an older sister now – the old feminine disapproval of the destructive play of little boys and men. La dee da! Or was it jealousy? She seemed to know that Dickie had formed a closer bond with him in twenty-four hours, just because he was another man, than she could ever have with Dickie, whether he loved her or not, and he didn't. After a few moments she loosened up, however, and the look went out of her eyes. Dickie left him with Marge on the terrace. Tom asked her about the book she was writing. It was a book about Mongibello, she said, with her own photographs. She told him she was from Ohio and showed him a picture, which she carried in her wallet, of her family's house. It was just a plain clapboard house, but it was home, Marge said with a smile. She pronounced the adjective 'clabbered', which amused Tom, because that was the word she used to describe people who were drunk, and just a few minutes before she had said to Dickie, 'You look absolutely clabbered!' her speech, Tom thought, was abominable, both her choice of words and her pronunciation. He tried to be especially pleasant to her. He felt he could afford to be. He walked with her to the gate, and they said a friendly good-bye to each other, but neither said anything about their all getting together later that day or tomorrow. There was no doubt about it, Marge was a little angry with Dickie.

TEN

For three or four days they saw very little of Marge except down at the beach, and she was noticeably cooler towards both of them on the beach. She smiled and talked just as much or maybe more, but there was an element of politeness now, which made for the coolness. Tom noticed that Dickie was concerned, though not concerned enough to talk to Marge alone, apparently, because he hadn't seen her alone since Tom had moved into the house. Tom had been with Dickie every moment since he had moved into Dickie's house.

Finally Tom, to show that he was not obtuse about Marge, mentioned to Dickie that he thought she was acting strangely.

'Oh, she has moods,' Dickie said. 'Maybe she's working well. She doesn't like to see people when she's in a streak of work.'

The Dickie–Marge relationship was evidently just what he had supposed it to be at first, Tom thought. Marge was much fonder of Dickie than Dickie was of her.

Tom, at any rate, kept Dickie amused. He had lots of funny stories to tell Dickie about people he knew in New York, some of them true, some of them made up. They went for a sail in Dickie's boat every day. There was no mention of any date when Tom might be leaving. Obviously Dickie was enjoying his company. Tom kept out of Dickie's way when Dickie wanted to paint, and he was always ready to drop whatever he was doing and go with Dickie for a walk or a sail or simply sit and talk. Dickie also seemed pleased that Tom was taking his study of Italian seriously. Tom spent a couple of hours a day with his grammar and conversation books.

Tom wrote to Mr Greenleaf that he was staying with Dickie now for a few days, and said that Dickie had mentioned flying home for a while in the winter, and that probably he could by that time persuade him to stay longer. This letter sounded much better now that he was staying at Dickie's house than his first letter in which he had said he was staying at a hotel in Mongibello. Tom also said that when his money gave out he intended to try to get himself a job, perhaps at one of the hotels in the village, a casual statement that served the double purpose of reminding Mr Greenleaf that six hundred dollars could run out, and also that he was a young man ready and willing to work for a living. Tom wanted to convey the same good impression to Dickie, so he gave Dickie the letter to read before he sealed it.

Another week went by, of ideally pleasant weather, ideally lazy days in which Tom's greatest physical exertion was climbing the stone steps from the beach every afternoon and his greatest mental effort trying to chat in Italian with Fausto, the twenty-three-year-old Italian boy whom Dickie had found in the village and had engaged to come three times a week to give Tom Italian lessons.

They went to Capri one day in Dickie's sailboat. Capri was just far enough away not to be visible from Mongibello. Tom was filled with anticipation, but Dickie was in one of his preoccupied moods and refused to be enthusiastic about anything. He argued with the keeper of the dock where they tied the *Pipistrello*. Dickie didn't even want to take a walk through the wonderful-looking little streets that went off in every direction from the plaza. They sat in a café on the plaza and drank a couple of Fernet-Brancas, and then Dickie wanted to start home before it became dark, though Tom would have willingly paid their hotel bill if Dickie had agreed to stay overnight. Tom supposed they would come again to Capri, so he wrote that day off and tried to forget it.

A letter came from Mr Greenleaf, which had crossed Tom's letter, in which Mr Greenleaf reiterated his arguments for Dickie's coming home, wished Tom success, and asked for a prompt reply as to his results. Once more Tom dutifully took up the pen and replied. Mr Greenleaf's letter had been in such a shockingly businesslike tone – really as if he had been checking on a shipment of boat parts, Tom thought – that he found it very easy to reply in the same style. Tom was a little high when he wrote the letter, because it was just after lunch and they were always slightly high on wine just after lunch, a delicious sensation that could be corrected at once with a couple of espressos and a short walk, or prolonged with another glass of wine, sipped as they went about their leisurely afternoon routine. Tom amused himself by injecting a faint hope in this letter. He wrote in Mr Greenleaf's own style:

... If I am not mistaken, Richard is wavering in his decision to spend another winter here. As I promised you, I shall do everything in my power to dissuade him from spending another winter here, and in time – though it may be as long as Christmas – I may be able to get him to stay in the States when he goes over.

Tom had to smile as he wrote it, because he and Dickie were talking of cruising around the Greek islands this winter, and Dickie had given up the idea of flying home even for a few days, unless his mother should be really seriously ill by then. They had talked also of spending January and February, Mongibello's worst months, in Majorca. And Marge would not be going with them, Tom was sure. Both he and Dickie excluded her from their travel plans whenever they discussed them, though Dickie had made the mistake of dropping to her that they might be taking a winter cruise somewhere. Dickie was so damned open about everything! And now, though Tom knew Dickie was still firm about their going alone, Dickie was being more than usually attentive to Marge, just because he realized that she would be lonely here by herself, and that it was essentially unkind of them not to ask her along. Dickie and Tom both tried to cover it up by impressing on her that they would be travelling in the cheapest and worst possible way around Greece, cattleboats, sleeping with peasants on the decks and all that, no way for a girl to travel. But Marge still looked dejected, and Dickie still tried to make it up by asking her often to the house now for lunch and dinner. Dickie took Marge's hand sometimes as they walked up from the beach, though Marge didn't always let him keep it. Sometimes she extricated her hand after a few seconds in a way that looked to Tom as if she were dying for her hand to be held.

And when they asked her to go along with them to Herculaneum, she refused.

'I think I'll stay home. You boys enjoy yourselves,' she said with an effort at a cheerful smile.

'Well, if she won't, she won't,' Tom said to Dickie, and drifted tactfully into the house so that she and Dickie could talk alone on the terrace if they wanted to.

Tom sat on the broad window-sill in Dickie's studio and looked out at the sea, his brown arms folded on his chest. He loved to look out at the blue Mediterranean and think of himself and Dickie sailing where they pleased. Tangier, Sofia, Cairo, Sevastopol ... By the time his money ran out, Tom thought, Dickie would probably be so fond of him and so used to him that he would take it for granted they would go on living together. He and Dickie could easily live on Dickie's five hundred a month income. From the terrace he could hear a pleading tone in Dickie's voice, and Marge's monosyllabic answers. Then he heard the gate clang. Marge had left. She had been going to stay for lunch. Tom shoved himself off the window-sill and went out to Dickie on the terrace.

'Was she angry about something?' Tom asked.

'No. She feels kind of left out, I suppose.'

'We certainly tried to include her.'

'It isn't just this.' Dickie was walking slowly up and down the terrace. 'Now she says she doesn't even want to go to Cortina with me.'

'Oh, she'll probably come around about Cortina before December.'

'I doubt it,' Dickie said.

Tom supposed it was because he was going to Cortina, too. Dickie had asked him last week. Freddie Miles had been gone when they got back from their Rome trip: he had had to go to London suddenly, Marge had told them. But Dickie had said he would write Freddie that he was bringing a friend along. 'Do you want me to leave, Dickie?' Tom asked, sure that Dickie didn't want him to leave. 'I feel I'm intruding on you and Marge.'

'Of course not! Intruding on what?'

'Well, from her point of view.'

'No. It's just that I owe her something. And I haven't been particularly nice to her lately. We haven't.'

Tom knew he meant that he and Marge had kept each other company over the long, dreary last winter, when they had been the only Americans in the village, and that he shouldn't neglect her now because somebody else was here. 'Suppose I talk to her about going to Cortina,' Tom suggested.

'Then she surely won't go,' Dickie said tersely, and went into the house.

Tom heard him telling Ermelinda to hold the lunch because he wasn't ready to eat yet. Even in Italian Tom could hear that Dickie said he wasn't ready for lunch, in the master-of-the-house tone. Dickie came out on the terrace, sheltering his lighter as he tried to light his cigarette. Dickie had a beautiful silver lighter, but it didn't work well in the slightest breeze. Tom finally produced his ugly, flaring lighter, as ugly and efficient as a piece of military equipment, and lighted it for him. Tom checked himself from proposing a drink: it wasn't his house, though as it happened he had bought the three bottles of Gilbey's that now stood in the kitchen.

'It's after two,' Tom said. 'Want to take a little walk and go by the post office?' Sometimes Luigi opened the post office at two-thirty, sometimes not until four, they could never tell.

They walked down the hill in silence. What had Marge said about him, Tom wondered. The sudden weight of guilt made sweat come out on Tom's forehead, an amorphous yet very strong sense of guilt, as if Marge had told Dickie specifically that he had stolen something or had done some other shameful thing. Dickie wouldn't be acting like this only because Marge had behaved coolly, Tom thought. Dickie walked in his slouching, down-hill gait that made his bony knees jut out in front of him, a gait that Tom had unconsciously adopted, too. But now Dickie's chin was sunk down on his chest and his hands were rammed into the pockets of his shorts. He came out of silence only to greet Luigi and thank him for his letter. Tom had no mail. Dickie's letter was from a Naples bank, a form slip on which Tom saw typewritten in a blank space: $500.00. Dickie pushed the slip carelessly into a pocket and dropped the envelope into a wastebucket. The monthly announcement that Dickie's money had arrived in Naples, Tom supposed. Dickie had said that his trust company sent his money to a Naples bank. They walked on down the hill, and Tom assumed that they would walk up the main road to where it curved around a cliff on the other side of the village, as they had done before, but Dickie stopped at the steps that led up to Marge's house.

'I think I'll go up to see Marge,' Dickie said. 'I won't be long, but there's no use in your waiting.'

'All right,' Tom said, feeling suddenly desolate. He watched Dickie climb a little way up the steep steps cut into the wall, then he turned abruptly and started back towards the house.

About half-way up the hill he stopped with an impulse to go down to Giorgio's for a drink (but Giorgio's martinis were terrible), and with another impulse to go up to Marge's house, and, on a pretence of apologizing to her, vent his anger by surprising them and annoying them. He suddenly felt that Dickie was embracing her, or at least touching her, at this minute, and partly he wanted to see it, and partly he loathed the idea of seeing it. He turned and walked back to Marge's gate. He closed the gate carefully behind him, though her house was so far above she could not possibly have heard it, then ran up the steps two at a time. He slowed as he climbed the last flight of steps. He would say, 'Look here, Marge, I'm sorry if *I've* been causing the strain around here. We asked you to go today, and we mean it. *I* mean it.'

Tom stopped as Marge's window came into view: Dickie's arm was around her waist. Dickie was kissing her, little pecks on her cheek, smiling at her. They were only about fifteen feet from him, but the room was shadowed compared to the bright sunlight he stood in, and he had to strain to see. Now Marge's face was tipped straight up to Dickie's, as if she were fairly lost in ecstasy, and what disgusted Tom was that he knew Dickie didn't mean it, that Dickie was only using this cheap, obvious, easy way to hold on to her friendship. What disgusted him was the big bulge of her behind in the peasant skirt below Dickie's arm that circled her waist. And Dickie –! Tom really wouldn't have believed it possible of Dickie!

Tom turned away and ran down the steps, wanting to scream. He banged the gate shut. He ran all the way up the road home, and arrived gasping, supporting himself on the parapet after he entered Dickie's gate. He sat on the couch in Dickie's studio for a few moments, his mind stunned and blank. That kiss – it hadn't looked like a first kiss. He walked to Dickie's easel, unconsciously avoiding looking at the bad painting that was on it, picked up the kneaded eraser that lay on the palatte and flung it violently out of the window, saw it arc down and disappear towards the sea. He picked up more erasers from Dickie's table, pen points, smudge sticks, charcoal and pastel fragments, and threw them one by one into corners or out of the windows. He had a curious feeling that his brain remained calm and logical and that his body was out of control. He ran out on the terrace with an idea of jumping on to the parapet and doing a dance or standing on his head, but the empty space on the other side of the parapet stopped him.

He went up to Dickie's room and paced around for a few moments, his hands in his pockets. He wondered when Dickie was coming back? Or was he going to stay and make an afternoon of it, really take her to bed with him? He jerked Dickie's closet door open and looked in. There was a freshly pressed, new-looking grey flannel suit that he had never seen Dickie wearing. Tom took it out. He took off his knee-length shorts and put on the grey flannel trousers. He put on a pair of Dickie's shoes. Then he opened the bottom drawer of the chest and took out a clean blue-and-white striped shirt.

He chose a dark-blue silk tie and knotted it carefully. The suit fitted him. He re-parted his hair and put the part a little more to one side, the way Dickie wore his.

'Marge, you must understand that I don't *love* you,' Tom said into the mirror in Dickie's voice, with Dickie's higher pitch on the emphasized words, with the little growl in his throat at the end of the phrase that could be pleasant or unpleasant, intimate or cool, according to Dickie's mood. 'Marge, stop it!' Tom turned suddenly and made a grab in the air as if he were seizing Marge's throat. He shook her, twisted her, while she sank lower and lower, until at last he left her, limp, on the floor. He was panting. He wiped his forehead the way Dickie did, reached for a handkerchief and, not finding any, got one from Dickie's top drawer, then resumed in front of the mirror. Even his parted lips looked like Dickie's lips when he was out of breath from swimming, drawn down a little from his lower teeth. 'You know why I had to do that,' he said, still breathlessly, addressing Marge, though he watched himself in the mirror. 'You were interfering between Tom and me – No, not that! But there *is* a bond between us!'

He turned, stepped over the imaginary body, and went stealthily to the window. He could see, beyond the bend of the road, the blurred slant of the steps that went up to Marge's house level. Dickie was not on the steps or on the parts of the road that he could see. Maybe they were sleeping together, Tom thought with a tighter twist of disgust in his throat. He imagined it, awkward, clumsy, unsatisfactory for Dickie, and Marge loving it. She'd love it even if he tortured her! Tom darted back to the closet again and took a hat from the top shelf. It was a little grey Tyrolean hat with a green-and-white feather in the brim. He put it on rakishly. It surprised him how much he looked like Dickie with the top part of his head covered. Really it was only his darker hair that was very different from Dickie. Otherwise, his nose – or at least its general form – his narrow jaw, his eyebrows if he held them right –

'What're you *doing?*'

Tom whirled around. Dickie was in the doorway. Tom realized that he must have been right below at the gate when he had looked out. 'Oh – just amusing myself,' Tom said in the deep voice he always used when he was embarrassed. 'Sorry, Dickie.'

Dickie's mouth opened a little, then closed, as if anger churned his words too much for them to be uttered. To Tom, it was just as bad as if he had spoken. Dickie advanced to the room.

'Dickie, I'm sorry if it –'

The violent slam of the door cut him off. Dickie began opening his shirt scowling, just as he would have if Tom had not been there, because this was his room, and what was Tom doing in it? Tom stood petrified with fear.

'I wish you'd get out of my clothes,' Dickie said.

Tom started undressing, his fingers clumsy with his mortification, his shock, because up until now Dickie had always said wear this and wear that that belonged to him. Dickie would never say it again.

Dickie looked at Tom's feet. 'Shoes, too? Are you crazy?'

'No.' Tom tried to pull himself together as he hung up the suit, then he asked, 'Did you make it up with Marge?'

'Marge and I are fine,' Dickie snapped in a way that shut Tom out from them. 'Another thing I want to say, but clearly,' he said, looking at Tom, 'I'm not queer. I don't know if you have the idea that I am or not.'

'Queer?' Tom smiled faintly. 'I never thought you were queer.'

Dickie started to say something else, and didn't. He straightened up, the ribs showing in his dark chest. 'Well, Marge thinks you are.'

'Why?' Tom felt the blood go out of his face. He kicked off Dickie's second shoe feebly, and set the pair in the closet. 'Why should she? What've I ever done?' He felt faint. Nobody had ever said it outright to him, not in this way.

'It's just the way you act,' Dickie said in a growling tone, and went out of the door.

Tom hurried back into his shorts. He had been half concealing himself from Dickie behind the closet door, though he had his underwear on. Just because Dickie liked him, Tom thought, Marge had launched her filthy accusations of him at Dickie. And Dickie hadn't had the guts to stand up and deny it to her!

He went downstairs and found Dickie fixing himself a drink at the bar shelf on the terrace. 'Dickie, I want to get this straight,' Tom began. 'I'm not queer either, and I don't want anybody thinking I am.'

'All right,' Dickie growled.

The tone reminded Tom of the answers Dickie had given him when he had asked Dickie if he knew this person and that in New York. Some of the people he had asked Dickie about were queer, it was true, and he had often suspected Dickie of deliberately denying knowing them when he did know them. All right! Who was making an issue of it, anyway? Dickie was. Tom hesitated while his mind tossed in a welter of things he might have said, bitter things, conciliatory things, grateful and hostile. His mind went back to certain groups of people he had known in New York, known and dropped finally, all of them, but he regretted now having ever known them. They had taken him up because he amused them, but *he* had never had anything to do with any of them! When a couple of them had made a pass at him, he had rejected them – though he remembered how he had tried to make it up to them later by getting ice for their drinks, dropping them off in taxis when it was out of his way, because he had been afraid they would start to dislike him. He'd been an ass! And he remembered, too, the humiliating moment when Vic Simmons had said, *Oh, for Christ sake, Tommie, shut up!* when he had said to a group of people, for perhaps the third or fourth time in Vic's presence, 'I can't make up my mind whether I like men or women, so I'm thinking of giving them *both* up.' Tom had used to pretend he was going to an analyst, because everybody else was going to an analyst, and he had used to spin wildly funny stories about his sessions with his analyst to amuse people at parties, and the line about giving up men and women both had always been good for a laugh, the way he delivered it, until Vic had told him for Christ sake to shut up, and after that Tom had never said it again and never mentioned his analyst again, either. As a matter of fact, there was a lot of truth in it, Tom thought. As people went, he was one of the most innocent and clean-minded he had ever known. That was the irony of this situation with Dickie.

'I feel as if I've –' Tom began, but Dickie was not even listening. Dickie turned away with a grim look around his mouth and carried his drink to the corner of the terrace. Tom advancd towards him, a little fearfully, not knowing whether Dickie would hurl him off the terrace, or simply turn around and tell him to get the hell out of the house. Tom asked quietly, 'Are you in love with Marge, Dickie?'

'No, but I feel sorry for her. I care about her. She's been very nice to me. We've had some good times together. You don't seem to be able to understand that.'

'I do understand. That was my original feeling about you and her – that it was a platonic thing as far as you were concerned, and that she was probably in love with you.'

'She is. You go out of your way not to hurt people who're in love with you, you know.'

'Of course.' He hesitated again, trying to choose his words. He was still in a state of trembling apprehension, though Dickie was not angry with him any more. Dickie was not going to throw him out. Tom said in a more self-possessed tone, 'I can imagine that if you both were in New York you wouldn't have seen her nearly so often – or at all – but this village being so lonely –'

'That's exactly right. I haven't been to bed with her and I don't intend to, but I do intend to keep her friendship.'

'Well, have I done anything to prevent you? I told you, Dickie, I'd rather leave than do anything to break up your friendship with Marge.'

Dickie gave a glance. 'No, you haven't done anything, specifically, but it's obvious you don't like her around. Whenever you make an effort to say anything nice to her, it's so obviously an effort.'

'I'm sorry,' Tom said contritely. He was sorry he hadn't made more of an effort, that he had done a bad job when he might have done a good one.

'Well, let's let it go. Marge and I are okay,' Dickie said defiantly. He turned away and stared off at the water.

Tom went into the kitchen to make himself a little boiled coffee. He didn't want to use the espresso machine, because Dickie was very particular about it and didn't like anyone using it but himself. He'd take the coffee up to his room, and study some Italian before Fausto came, Tom thought. This wasn't the time to make it up with Dickie. Dickie had his pride. He would be silent for most of the afternoon, then come around by about five o'clock after he had been painting for a while, and it would be as if the episode with the clothes had never happened. One thing Tom was sure of: Dickie was glad to have him here. Dickie was bored with living by himself, and bored with Marge, too. Tom still had three hundred dollars of the money Mr Greenleaf had given him, and he and Dickie were going to use it on a spree in Paris. Without Marge. Dickie had been amazed when Tom had told him he hadn't had more than a glimpse of Paris through a railroad station window.

While he waited for his coffee, Tom put away the food that was to have been their lunch. He set a couple of pots of food in bigger pots of water to keep the ants away from them. There was also the little paper of fresh butter, the pair of eggs, the paper of four rolls that Ermelinda had brought for their breakfast tomorrow. They had to buy small quantities of everything every day, because there was no refrigerator. Dickie wanted to buy a refrigerator with part of his father's money. He had mentioned it a couple of times. Tom hoped he changed his mind, because a refrigerator would cut down their travelling money, and Dickie had a very definite budget for his own five hundred dollars every month. Dickie was cautious about money, in a way, yet down at the wharf, and in the village bars, he gave enormous tips right and left, and gave five-hundred-lire bills to any beggar who approached him.

Dickie was back to normal by five o'clock. He had had a good afternoon of painting, Tom supposed, because he had been whistling for the last hour in his studio. Dickie came out on the terrace where Tom was scanning his Italian grammar, and gave him some pointers on his pronunciation.

'They don't always say "voglio" so clearly,' Dickie said. 'They say "io vo' presentare mia amica Marge, per esempio."' Dickie drew his long hand backwards through the air. He always made gestures when he spoke Italian, graceful gestures as if he were leading an orchestra in a legato. 'You'd better listen to Fausto more and read that grammar less. I picked my Italian up off the streets.' Dickie smiled and walked away down the garden path. Fausto was just coming in the gate.

Tom listened carefully to their laughing exchanges in Italian, straining to understand every word.

Fausto came out on the terrace smiling, sank into a chair, and put his bare feet up on the parapet. His face was either smiling or frowning, and it could change from instant to instant. He was one of the few people in the village, Dickie said, who didn't speak in a southern dialect. Fausto lived in Milan, and he was visiting an aunt in Mongibello for a few months. He came, dependably and punctually, three times a week between five and five-thirty, and they sat on the terrace and sipped wine or coffee and chatted for about an hour. Tom tried his utmost to memorize everything Fausto said about the rocks, the water, politics (Fausto was a Communist, a card-carrying Communist, and he showed his card to Americans at the drop of a hat, Dickie said, because he was amused by their astonishment at his having it), and about the frenzied, catlike sex-life of some of the village inhabitants. Fausto found it hard to think of things to talk about sometimes, and then he would stare at Tom and burst out laughing. But Tom was making great progress. Italian was the only thing he had ever studied that he enjoyed and felt he could stick to. Tom wanted his Italian to be as good as Dickie's, and he thought he could make it that good in another month, if he kept on working hard at it.

ELEVEN

Tom walked briskly across the terrace and into Dickie's studio. 'Want to go to Paris in a coffin?' he asked.

'What?' Dickie looked up from his watercolour.

'I've been talking to an Italian in Giorgio's. We'd start out from Trieste, ride in coffins in the baggage car escorted by some Frenchmen, and we'd get a hundred thousand lire apiece. I have the idea it concerns dope.'

'Dope in the coffins? Isn't that an old stunt?'

'We talked in Italian, so I didn't understand everything, but he said there'd be three coffins, and maybe the third has a real corpse in it and they've put the dope into the corpse. Anyway, we'd get the trip plus the experience.' He emptied his pockets of the packs of ship's store Lucky Strikes that he had just bought from a street pedlar for Dickie. 'What do you say?'

'I think it's a marvellous idea. To Paris in a coffin!'

There was a funny smile on Dickie's face, as if Dickie were pulling his leg by pretending to fall in with it, when he hadn't the least intention of falling in with it. 'I'm serious,' Tom said. 'He really is on the lookout for a couple of willing young men. The coffins are supposed to contain the bodies of French casualties from Indo-China. The French escort is sup- posed to be the relative of one of them, or maybe all of them.' It wasn't exactly what the man had said to him, but it was near enough. And two hundred thousand lire was over three hundred dollars, after all, plenty for a spree in Paris. Dickie was still hedging about Paris.

Dickie looked at him sharply, put out the bent wisp of the Nazionale he was smoking, and opened one of the packs of Luckies. 'Are you sure the guy you were talking to wasn't under the influence of dope himself?'

'You're so damned cautious these days!' Tom said with a laugh. 'Where's your spirit? You look as if you don't even believe me! Come with me and I'll show you the man. He's still down there waiting for me. His name's Carlo.'

Dickie showed no sign of moving. 'Anybody with an offer like that doesn't explain all the particulars to you. They get a couple of toughs to ride from Trieste to Paris, maybe, but even that doesn't make sense to me.'

'Will you come with me and talk to him? If you don't believe me, at least look at him.'

'Sure.' Dickie got up suddenly. 'I might even do it for a hundred thousand lire.' Dickie closed a book of poems that had been lying face down on his studio couch before he followed Tom out of the room. Marge had a lot of books of poetry. Lately Dickie had been borrowing them.

The man was still sitting at the corner table in Giorgio's when they came in. Tom smiled at him and nodded.

'Hello, Carlo,' Tom said. 'Posso sedermi?'

'Si, si,' the man said, gesturing to the chairs at his table.

'This is my friend,' Tom said carefully in Italian. 'He wants to know if the work with the railroad journey is correct.' Tom watched Carlo looking Dickie over, sizing him up, and it was wonderful to Tom how the man's dark, tough, callous-looking eyes betrayed nothing but polite interest, how in a split second he seemed to take in and evaluate Dickie's faintly smiling but suspicious expression, Dickie's tan that could not have been acquired except by months of lying in the sun, his worn, Italian-made clothes and his American rings.

A smile spread slowly across the man's pale, flat lips, and he glanced at Tom.

'Allora?' Tom prompted, impatient.

The man lifted his sweet martini and drank. 'The job is real, but I do not think your friend is the right man.'

Tom looked at Dickie. Dickie was watching the man alertly, with the same neutral smile that suddenly struck Tom as contemptuous. 'Well, at least it's true, you see!' Tom said to Dickie.

'Mm-m,' Dickie said, still gazing at the man as if he were some kind of animal which interested him, and which he could kill if he decided to.

Dickie could have talked Italian to the man. Dickie didn't say a word. Three weeks ago, Tom thought Dickie would have taken the man up on his offer. Did he have to sit there looking like a stool pigeon or a police detective waiting for reinforcements so he could arrest the man? 'Well,' Tom said finally, 'you believe me, don't you?'

Dickie glanced at him. 'About the job? How do I know?'

Tom looked at the Italian expectantly.

The Italian shrugged. 'There is no need to discuss it, is there?' he asked in Italian.

'No,' Tom said. A crazy, directionless fury boiled in his blood and made him tremble. He was furious at Dickie. Dickie was looking over the man's dirty nails, dirty shirt collar, his ugly dark face that had been recently shaven though not recently washed, so that where the beard had been was much lighter than the skin above and below it. But the Italian's dark eyes were cool and amiable, and stronger than Dickie's. Tom felt stifled. He was conscious that he could not express himself in Italian. He wanted to speak both to Dickie and to the man.

'Niente, grazie, Berto,' Dickie said calmly to the waiter who had come over to ask what they wanted. Dickie looked at Tom. 'Ready to go?'

Tom jumped up so suddenly his straight chair upset behind him. He set it up again, and bowed a good-bye to the Italian. He felt he owed the Italian an apology, yet he could not open his mouth to say even a conventional good-bye. The Italian nodded good-bye and smiled. Tom followed Dickie's long white-clad legs out of the bar.

Outside, Tom said, 'I just wanted you to see that it's true at least. I hope you see.'

'All right, it's true,' Dickie said, smiling. 'What's the matter with you?'

'What's the matter with *you*?' Tom demanded.

'The man's a crook. Is that what you want me to admit? Okay!'

'Do you have to be so damned superior about it? Did he do anything to you?'

'Am I supposed to get down on my knees to him? I've seen crooks before. This village gets lots of them.' Dickie's blond eyebrows frowned. 'What the hell *is* the matter with you? Do you want to take him up on his crazy proposition? Go ahead!'

'I couldn't now if I wanted to. Not after the way you acted.'

Dickie stopped in the road, looking at him. They were arguing so loudly, a few people around them were looking, watching.

'It could have been fun,' Tom said, 'but not the way you chose to take it. A month ago when we went to Rome, you'd have thought something like this was fun.'

'Oh, no,' Dickie said, shaking his head. 'I doubt it.'

The sense of frustration and inarticulateness was agony to Tom. And the fact that they were being looked at. He forced himself to walk on, in tense little steps at first, until he was sure that Dickie was coming with him. The puzzlement, the suspicion, was still in Dickie's face, and Tom knew Dickie was puzzled about his reaction. Tom wanted to explain it, wanted to break through to Dickie so he would understand and they would feel the same way. Dickie had felt the same way he had a month ago. 'It's the way you acted,' Tom said. 'You didn't have to act that way. The fellow wasn't doing you any harm.'

'He looked like a dirty crook!' Dickie retorted. 'For Christ sake, go back if you like him so much. You're under no obligation to do what I do!'

Now Tom stopped. He had an impulse to go back, not necessarily to go back to the Italian, but to leave Dickie. Then his tension snapped suddenly. His shoulders relaxed, aching, and his breath began to come fast, through his mouth. He wanted to say at least, 'All right Dickie,' to make it up, to make Dickie forget it. He felt tongue-tied. He stared at Dickie's blue eyes that were still frowning, the sun-bleached eyebrows white and the eyes themselves shining and empty, nothing but little pieces of blue jelly with a black dot in them, meaningless, without relation to him. You were supposed to see the soul through the eyes, to see love through the eyes, the one place you could look at another human being and see what really went on inside, and in Dickie's eyes Tom saw nothing more now than he would have seen if he had looked at the hard, bloodless surface of a mirror. Tom felt a painful wrench in his breast, and he covered his face with his hands. It was as if Dickie had been suddenly snatched away from him. They were not friends. They didn't know each other. It struck Tom like a horrible truth, true for all time, true for the people he had known in the past and for those he would know in the future: each had stood and would stand before him, and he would know time and time again that he would never know them, and the worst was that there would always be the illusion, for a time, that he did know them, and that he and they were completely in harmony and alike. For an instant the wordless shock of his realization seemed more than he could bear. He felt in the grip of a fit, as if he would fall to the ground. It was too much: the foreignness around him, the different language, his failure, and the fact that Dickie hated him. He felt surrounded by strangeness, by hostility. He felt Dickie yank his hand down from his eyes.

'What's the matter with you?' Dickie asked. 'Did that guy give you a shot of something?'

'No.'

'Are you sure? In your drink?'

'No.' The first drops of the evening rain fell on his head. There was a rumble of thunder. Hostility from above, too. 'I want to die,' Tom said in a small voice.

Dickie yanked him by the arm. Tom tripped over a doorstep. They were in the little bar opposite the post office. Tom heard Dickie ordering a brandy, specifying Italian brandy because he wasn't good enough for French, Tom supposed. Tom drank it off, slightly sweetish, medicinal-tasting, drank three of them, like a magic medicine to bring him back to what his mind knew was usually called reality: the smell of the Nazionale in Dickie's hand, the curlicued grain in the wood of the bar under his fingers, the fact that his stomach had a hard pressure in it as if someone were holding a fist against his navel, the vivid anticipation of the long steep walk from here up to the house, the faint ache that would come in his thighs from it.

'I'm okay,' Tom said in a quiet, deep voice. 'I don't know what was the matter. Must have been the heat that got me for a minute.' He laughed a little. That was reality, laughing it off, making it silly, something that was more important than anything that had happened to him in the five weeks since he had met Dickie, maybe that had ever happened to him.

Dickie said nothing, only put the cigarette in his mouth and took a couple of hundred-lire bills from his black alligator wallet and laid them on the bar. Tom was hurt that he said nothing, hurt like a child who has been sick and probably a nuisance, but who expects at least a friendly word when the sickness is over. But Dickie was indifferent. Dickie had bought him the brandies as coldly as he might have bought them for a stranger he had encountered who felt ill and had no money. Tom thought suddenly, *Dickie doesn't want me to go to Cortina*. It was not the first time Tom had thought that. Marge was going to Cortina now. She and Dickie had bought a new giant-sized Thermos to take to Cortina the last time they had been in Naples. They hadn't asked him if he had liked the Thermos, or anything else. They were just quietly and gradually leaving him out of their preparations. Tom felt that Dickie expected him to take off, in fact, just before the Cortina trip. A couple of weeks ago, Dickie had said he would show him some of the ski trails around Cortina that were marked on a map that he had. Dickie had looked at the map one evening, but he had not talked to him.

'Ready?' Dickie asked.

Tom followed him out of the bar like a dog.

'If you can get home all right by yourself, I thought I'd run up and see Marge for a while,' Dickie said on the road.

'I feel fine,' Tom said.

'Good.' Then he said over his shoulder as he walked away, 'Want to pick up the mail? I might forget.'

Tom nodded. He went into the post office. There were two letters, one to him from Dickie's father, one to Dickie from someone in New York whom Tom didn't know. He stood in the doorway and opened Mr Greenleaf's letter, unfolded the typewritten sheet respectfully. It had the impressive pale green letterhead of Burke-Greenleaf Watercraft, Inc., with the ship's wheel-trademark in the centre.

10 Nov. 19—

My dear Tom,

In view of the fact you have been with Dickie over a month and that he shows no more sign of coming home than before you went, I can only conclude that you haven't been successful. I realize that with the best intentions you reported that he is considering returning, but frankly, I don't see it anywhere in his letter of 26 October. As a matter of fact, he seems more determined than ever to stay where he is.

I want you to know that I and my wife appreciate whatever efforts you have made on our behalf, and his. You need no longer consider yourself obligated to me in any way. I trust you have not inconvenienced yourself greatly by your efforts of the past month, and I sincerely hope the trip has afforded you some pleasure despite the failure of its main objective.

Both my wife and I send you greetings and our thanks.

Sincerely,
H. R. Greenleaf

It was the final blow. With the cool tone – even cooler than his usual businesslike coolness, because this was a dismissal and he had injected a note of courteous thanks in it – Mr Greenleaf had simply cut him off. He had failed. 'I trust you have not inconvenienced yourself greatly ...' Wasn't that sarcastic? Mr Greenleaf didn't even say that he would like to see him again when he returned to America.

Tom walked mechanically up the hill. He imagined Dickie in Marge's house now, narrating to her the story of Carlo in the bar, and his peculiar behaviour on the road afterwards. Tom knew what Marge would say: 'Why don't you get *rid* of him, Dickie?' Should he go back and explain to them, he wondered, force them to listen? Tom turned around, looking at the inscrutable square front of Marge's house up on the hill, at its empty, dark-looking window. His denim jacket was getting wet from the rain. He turned its collar up. Then he walked on quickly up the hill towards Dickie's house. At least, he thought proudly, he hadn't tried to wheedle any more money out of Mr Greenleaf, and he might have. He might have, even with Dickie's cooperation, if he had ever approached Dickie about it when Dickie had been in a good mood. Anybody else would have, Tom thought, anybody, but he hadn't, and that counted for *something*.

He stood at the corner of the terrace, staring out at the vague empty line of the horizon and thinking of nothing, feeling nothing except a faint, dreamlike lostness and aloneness. Even Dickie and Marge seemed far away, and what they might be talking about seemed unimportant. He was alone. That was the only important thing. He began to feel a tingling fear at the end of his spine, tingling over his buttocks.

He turned as he heard the gate open. Dickie walked up the path, smiling, but it struck Tom as a forced, polite smile.

'What're you doing standing there in the rain?' Dickie asked, ducking into the hall door.

'It's very refreshing,' Tom said pleasantly. 'Here's a letter for you.' He handed Dickie his letter and stuffed the one from Mr Greenleaf into his pocket.

Tom hung his jacket in the hall closet. When Dickie had finished reading his letter – a letter that had made him laugh out loud as he read it – Tom said, 'Do you think Marge would like to go up to Paris with us when we go?'

Dickie looked surprised. 'I think she would.'

'Well, ask her,' Tom said cheerfully.

'I don't know if I should go up to Paris,' Dickie said. 'I wouldn't mind getting away somewhere for a few days, but Paris –' He lighted a cigarette. 'I'd just as soon go up to San Remo or even Genoa. That's quite a town.'

'But Paris – Genoa can't compare with Paris, can it?'

'No, of course not, but it's a lot closer.'

'But when *will* we get to Paris?'

'I don't know. Any old time. Paris'll still be there.'

Tom listened to the echo of the words in his ears, searching their tone. The day before yesterday, Dickie had received a letter from his father. He had read a few sentences aloud and they had laughed about something, but he had not read the whole letter as he had a couple of times before. Tom had no doubt that Mr Greenleaf had told Dickie that he was fed up with Tom Ripley, and probably that he suspected him of using his money for his own entertainment. A month ago Dickie would have laughed at something like that, too, but not now, Tom thought. 'I just thought while

I have a little money left, we ought to make our Paris trip,' Tom persisted.

'You go up. I'm not in the mood right now. Got to save my strength for Cortina.'

'Well – I suppose we'll make it San Remo then,' Tom said, trying to sound agreeable, though he could have wept.

'All right.'

Tom darted from the hall into the kitchen. The huge white form of the refrigerator sprang out of the corner at him. He had wanted a drink, with ice in it. Now he didn't want to touch the thing. He had spent a whole day in Naples with Dickie and Marge, looking at refrigerators, inspecting ice trays, counting the number of gadgets, until Tom hadn't been able to tell one refrigerator from another, but Dickie and Marge had kept at it with the enthusiasm of newlyweds. Then they had spent a few more hours in a café discussing the respective merits of all the refrigerators they had looked at before they decided on the one they wanted. And now Marge was popping in and out more often than ever, because she stored some of her own food in it, and she often wanted to borrow ice. Tom realized suddenly why he hated the refrigerator so much. It meant that Dickie was staying put. It finished not only their Greek trip this winter, but it meant Dickie probably never would move to Paris or Rome to live, as he and Tom had talked of doing in Tom's first weeks here. Not with a refrigerator that had the distinction of being one of only about four in the village, a refrigerator with six ice trays and so many shelves on the door that it looked like a supermarket swinging out at you every time you opened it.

Tom fixed himself an iceless drink. His hands were shaking. Only yesterday Dickie had said, 'Are you going home for Christmas?' very casually in the middle of some conversation, but Dickie knew damned well he wasn't going home for Christmas. He didn't have a home, and Dickie knew it. He had told Dickie all about Aunt Dottie in Boston. It had simply been a big hint, that was all. Marge was full of plans about Christmas. She had a can of English plum pudding she was saving, and she was going to get a turkey from some contadino. Tom could imagine how she would slop it up with her saccharine sentimentality. A Christmas tree, of course, probably cut out of cardboard. 'Silent Night.' Eggnog. Gooey presents for Dickie. Marge knitted. She took Dickie's socks home to darn all the time. And they'd both slightly, politely, leave him out. Every friendly thing they would say to him would be a painful effort. Tom couldn't bear to imagine it. All right, he'd leave. He'd do something rather than endure Christmas with them.

TWELVE

Marge said she didn't care to go with them to San Remo. She was in the middle of a 'streak' on her book. Marge worked in fits and starts, always cheerfully, though it seemed to Tom that she was bogged down, as she called it, about seventy-five per cent of the time, a condition that she always announced with a merry little laugh. The book must stink, Tom thought. He had known writers. You didn't write a book with your little finger, lolling on a beach half the day, wondering what to eat for dinner. But he was glad she was having a 'streak' at the time he and Dickie wanted to go to San Remo.

'I'd appreciate it if you'd try to find that cologne, Dickie,' she said. 'You know, the Stradivari I couldn't find in Naples. San Remo's bound to have it, they have so many shops with French stuff.'

Tom could see them spending a whole day looking for it in San Remo, just as they had spent hours looking for it in Naples one Saturday.

They took only one suitcase of Dickie's between them, because they planned to be away only three nights and four days. Dickie was in a slightly more cheerful mood, but the awful finality was still there, the feeling that this was the last trip they would make together anywhere. To Tom, Dickie's polite cheerfulness on the train was like the cheerfulness of a host who has loathed his guest and is afraid the guest realizes it, and who tries to make it up at the last minute. Tom had never before in his life felt like an unwelcome, boring guest. On the train, Dickie told Tom about San Remo and the week he had spent there with Freddie Miles when he first arrived in Italy. San Remo was tiny, but it had a famous name as an international shopping centre, Dickie said, and people came across the French border to buy things there. It occurred to Tom that Dickie was trying to sell him on the town and might try to persuade him to stay there alone instead of coming back to Mongibello. Tom began to feel an aversion to the place before they got there.

Then, almost as the train was sliding into the San Remo station, Dickie said, 'By the way, Tom – I hate to say this to you, if you're going to mind terribly, but I really would prefer to go to Cortina d'Ampezzo alone with Marge. I think she'd prefer it, and after all I owe something to her, a pleasant holiday at least. You don't seem to be too enthusiastic about skiing.'

Tom went rigid and cold, but he tried not to move a muscle. Blaming it on Marge! 'All right,' he said. 'Of course.' Nervously he looked at the map in his hands, looking desperately around San Remo for somewhere else to go, though Dickie was already swinging their suitcase down from the rack. 'We're not far from Nice, are we?' Tom asked.

'No.'

'And Cannes. I'd like to see Cannes as long as I'm this far. At least Cannes is France,' he added on a reproachful note.

'Well, I suppose we could. You brought your passport, didn't you?'

Tom had brought his passport. They boarded a train for Cannes, and arrived around eleven o'clock that night.

Tom thought it beautiful – the sweep of curving harbour extended by little lights to long thin crescent tips, the elegant yet tropical-looking main boulevard along the water with its rows of palm trees, its row of expensive hotels. France! It was more sedate than Italy, and more chic, he could feel that even in the dark. They went to a hotel on the first back street, the Gray d'Albion, which was chic enough but wouldn't cost them their shirts, Dickie said, though Tom would gladly have paid whatever it cost at the best hotel on the ocean front. They left their suitcase at the hotel, and went to the bar of the Hotel Carlton, which Dickie said was the most fashionable bar in Cannes. As he had predicted, there were not many people in the bar, because there were not many people in Cannes at this time of year. Tom proposed a second round of drinks but Dickie declined.

They breakfasted at a café the next morning, then strolled down to the beach. They had their swimming trunks on under their trousers. The day was cool, but not impossibly cool for swimming. They had been swimming in Mongibello on colder days. The beach was practically empty – a few isolated pairs of people, a group of men playing some kind of game up the embankment. The waves curved over and broke on the sand with a wintry violence. Now Tom saw that the group of men were doing acrobatics.

'They must be professionals,' Tom said. 'They're all in the same yellow G-strings.'

Tom watched with interest as a human pyramid began building, feet braced on bulging thighs, hands gripping forearms. He could hear their 'Allez!' and their 'Un – deux!'

'Look!' Tom said. 'There goes the top!' He stood still to watch the smallest one, a boy of about seventeen, as he was boosted to the shoulders of the centre man in the three top men. He stood poised, hs arms open, as if receiving applause. 'Bravo!' Tom shouted.

The boy smiled at Tom before he leapt down, lithe as a tiger. Tom looked at Dickie. Dickie was looking at a couple of men sitting near by on the beach.

'Ten thousand saw I at a glance, nodding their heads in sprightly dance,' Dickie said sourly to Tom.

It startled Tom, then he felt that sharp thrust of shame, the same shame he had felt in Mongibello when Dickie had said, *Marge thinks you are.* All right, Tom thought, the acrobats were fairies. Maybe Cannes was full of fairies. So what? Tom's fists were clenched tight in his trousers pockets. He remembered Aunt Dottie's taunt: *Sissy! He's a sissy from the ground up. Just like his father!* Dickie stood with his arms folded, looking out at the ocean. Tom deliberately kept himself from even glancing at the acrobats again, though they were certainly more amusing to watch than the ocean. 'Are you going in?' Tom asked, boldly unbuttoning his shirt, though the water suddenly looked cold as hell.

'I don't think so,' Dickie said. 'Why don't you stay here and watch the acrobats? I'm going back.' He turned and started back before Tom could answer.

Tom buttoned his clothes hastily, watching Dickie as he walked diagonally away, away from the acrobats, though the next stairs up to the sidewalk were twice as far as the stairs nearer the acrobats. Damn him anyway, Tom thought. Did he have to act so damned aloof and superior all the time? You'd think he'd never seen a pansy! Obvious what was the matter with Dickie, all right! Why didn't he break down, just for once? What did he have that was so important to lose? A half-dozen taunts sprang to his mind as he ran after Dickie. Then Dickie glanced around at him coldly, with distaste, and the first taunt died in his mouth.

They left for San Remo that afternoon, just before three o'clock, so there would not be another day to pay on the hotel bill. Dickie had proposed leaving by three, though it was Tom who paid the 3,430-franc bill, ten dollars and eight cents American, for one night. Tom also bought their railroad tickets to San Remo, though Dickie was loaded with francs. Dickie had brought his monthly remittance cheque from Italy and cashed it in francs, figuring that he would come out better converting the francs back into lire later, because of a sudden recent strengthening of the franc.

Dickie said absolutely nothing on the train. Under a pretence of being sleepy, he folded his arms and closed his eyes. Tom sat opposite him, staring at his bony, arrogant, handsome face, at his hands with the green ring and the gold signet ring. It crossed Tom's mind to steal the green ring when he left. It would be easy: Dickie took it off when he swam. Sometimes he took it off even when he showered at the house. He would do it the very last day, Tom thought. Tom stared at Dickie's closed eyelids. A crazy emotion of hate, of affection, of impatience and frustration was swelling in him, hampering his breathing. He wanted to kill Dickie. It was not the first time he had thought of it. Before, once or twice or three times, it had been an impulse caused by anger or disappointment, an impulse that vanished immediately and left him with a feeling of shame. Now he thought about it for an entire minute, two minutes, because he was leaving Dickie anyway, and what was there to be ashamed of any more? He had failed with Dickie, in every way. He hated Dickie, because, however he looked at what had happened, his failing had not been his own fault, not due to anything he had done, but due to Dickie's inhuman stubbornness. And his blatant rudeness! He had offered Dickie friendship, companionship, and respect, everything he had to offer, and Dickie had replied with ingratitude and now hostility. Dickie was just shoving him out in the cold. If he killed him on this trip, Tom thought, he could simply say that some accident had happened. He could – He had just thought of something brilliant: he could become Dickie Greenleaf himself. He could do everything that Dickie did. He could go back to Mongibello first and collect Dickie's things, tell Marge any damned story, set up an apartment in Rome or Paris, receive Dickie's cheque every month and forge Dickie's signature on it. He could step right into Dickie's shoes. He could have Mr Greenleaf, Sr, eating out of his hand. The danger of it, even the inevitable temporariness of it when he vaguely realized, only made him more enthusiastic. He began to think of *how*.

The water. But Dickie was such a good swimmer. The cliffs. It would be easy to push Dickie off some cliff when they took a walk, but he imagined Dickie grabbing at him and pulling *him* off with him, and he tensed in his seat until his thighs ached and his nails cut red scallops in his thumbs. He would have to get the other ring off, too. He would have to tint his hair a little lighter. But he wouldn't live in a place, of course, where anybody who knew Dickie lived. He had only to look enough like Dickie to be able to use his passport. Well, he did. If he –

Dickie opened his eyes, looking right at him, and Tom relaxed, slumped into the corner with his head back and his eyes shut, as quickly as if he had passed out.

'Tom, are you okay?' Dickie asked, shaking Tom's knee.

'Okay,' Tom said, smiling a little. He saw Dickie sit back with an air of irritation, and Tom knew why; because Dickie had hated giving him even that much attention. Tom smiled to himself, amused at his own quick reflex in pretending to collapse, because that had been the only way to keep Dickie from seeing what must have been a very strange expression on his face.

San Remo. Flowers. A main drag along the beach again, shops and stores and French and English and Italian tourists. Another hotel, with flowers in the balconies. Where? In one of these little streets tonight? The town would be dark and silent by one in the morning, if he could keep Dickie up that long. In the water? It was slightly cloudy, though not cold. Tom racked his brain. It would be easy in the hotel room, too, but how would he get rid of the body? The body had to *disappear*, absolutely. That left only the water, and the water was Dickie's element. There were boats, rowboats and little motor-boats, that people could rent down at the beach. In each motor-boat, Tom noticed, was a round weight of cement attached to a line, for anchoring the boat.

'What do you say we take a boat, Dickie?' Tom asked, trying not to sound eager, though he did, and Dickie looked at him, because he had not been eager about anything since they had arrived here.

They were little blue-and-white and green-and-white motor-boats, about ten of them, lined up at the wooden pier, and the Italian was anxious for customers because it was a chilly and rather gloomy morning. Dickie looked out at the Mediterranean, which was slightly hazy though not with a presage of rain. This was the kind of greyness that would not disappear all day, and there would be no sun. It was about ten-thirty – that lazy hour after breakfast, when the whole long Italian morning lay before them.

'Well, all right. For an hour around the port,' Dickie said, almost immediately jumping into a boat, and Tom could see from his little smile that he had done it before, that he was looking forward to remembering, sentimentally, other mornings or some other morning here, perhaps with Freddie, or Marge. Marge's cologne bottle bulged the pocket of Dickie's corduroy jacket. They had bought it a few minutes ago at a store very much like an American drugstore on the main drag.

The Italian boatkeeper started the motor with a yanked string, asking Dickie if he knew how to work it, and Dickie said yes. And there was an oar, a single oar in the bottom of the boat, Tom saw. Dickie took the tiller. They headed straight out from the town.

'Cool!' Dickie yelled, smiling. His hair was blowing.

Tom looked to right and left. A vertical cliff on one side, very much like Mongibello, and on the other a flattish length of land fuzzing out in the mist that hovered over the water. Off-hand he couldn't say in which direction it was better to go.

'Do you know the land around here?' Tom shouted over the roar of the motor.

'Nope!' Dickie said cheerfully. He was enjoying the ride.

'Is that thing hard to steer?'

'Not a bit! Want to try it?'

Tom hesitated. Dickie was still steering straight out to the open sea. 'No, thanks.' He looked,to right and left. There was a sailboat off to the left. 'Where're you going?' Tom shouted.

'Does it matter?' Dickie smiled.

No, it didn't.

Dickie swerved suddenly to the right, so suddenly that they both had to duck and lean to keep the boat righted. A wall of white spray rose on Tom's left, then gradually fell to show the empty horizon. They were streaking across the empty water again, towards nothing. Dickie was trying the speed, smiling, his blue eyes smiling at the emptiness.

'In a little boat it always feels so much faster than it is!' Dickie yelled.

Tom nodded, letting his understanding smile speak for him. Actually, he was terrified. God only knew how deep the water was here. If something happened to the boat suddenly, there wasn't a chance in the world that they could get back to shore, or at least that *he* could. But neither was there a chance that anybody could see anything that they did here. Dickie was swerving very slightly towards the right again, towards the long spit of fuzzy grey land, but he could have hit Dickie, sprung on him, or kissed him, or thrown him overboard, and nobody could have seen him at this distance. Tom was sweating, hot under his clothes, cold on his forehead. He felt afraid, but it was not of the water, it was of Dickie. He knew that he was going to do it, that he would not stop himself now, maybe *couldn't* stop himself, and that he might not succeed.

'You dare me to jump in?' Tom yelled, beginning to unbutton his jacket.

Dickie only laughed at this proposal from him, opening his mouth wide, keeping his eyes fixed on the distance in front of the boat. Tom kept on undressing. He had his shoes and socks off. Under his trousers he wore his swimming trunks, like Dickie. 'I'll go in if you will!' Tom shouted. 'Will you?' He wanted Dickie to slow down.

'Will I? Sure!' Dickie slowed the motor abruptly. He released the tiller and took off his jacket. The boat bobbled, losing its momentum. 'Come on,' Dickie said, nodding at Tom's trousers that were still on.

Tom glanced at the land. San Remo was a blur of chalky white and pink. He picked up the oar, as casually as if he were playing with it between his knees, and when Dickie was shoving his trousers down, Tom lifted the oar and came down with it on the top of Dickie's head.

'Hey!' Dickie yelled, scowling, sliding half off the wooden seat. His pale brows lifted in groggy surprise.

Tom stood up and brought the oar down again, sharply, all his strength released like the snap of a rubber band.

'For God's sake!' Dickie mumbled, glowering, fierce, though the blue eyes wobbled, losing consciousness.

Tom swung a left-handed blow with the oar against the side of Dickie's head. The edge of the oar cut a dull gash that filled with a line of blood as Tom watched. Dickie was on the bottom of the boat, twisted. Dickie gave a groaning roar of protest that frightened Tom with its loudness and its strength. Tom hit him in the side of the neck three times, chopping strokes with the edge of the oar, as if the oar were an axe and Dickie's neck a tree. The boat rocked, and water splashed over his foot that was braced on the gunwale. He sliced at Dickie's forehead, and a broad patch of blood came slowly where the oar had scraped. For an instant Tom was aware of tiring as he raised and swung, and still Dickie's hands slid towards him on the bottom of the boat. Dickie's long legs straightened to thrust him forward. Tom got a bayonet grip on the oar and plunged its handle into Dickie's side. Then the prostrate body relaxed, limp and still. Tom straightened, getting his breath back painfully. He looked around him. There were no boats, nothing, except far, far away a little white spot creeping from right to left, a speeding motor-boat heading for the shore.

He stopped and yanked at Dickie's green ring. He pocketed it. The other ring was tighter, but it came off, over the bleeding scuffed knuckle. He looked in the trousers pockets. French and Italian coins. He left them. He took a keychain with three keys. Then he picked up Dickie's jacket and took Marge's cologne package out of the pocket. Cigarettes and Dickie's silver lighter, a pencil stub, the alligator wallet and several little cards in the inside breast pocket. Tom stuffed it all into his own corduroy jacket. Then he reached for the rope that was tumbled over the white cement weight. The end of the rope was tied to the metal ring at the prow. Tom tried to untie it. It was a hellish, water-soaked, immovable knot that must have been there for years. He banged at it with his fist. He had to have a knife.

He looked at Dickie. Was he dead? Tom crouched in the narrowing prow of the boat, watching Dickie for a sign of life. He was afraid to touch him, afraid to touch his chest or his wrist to feel a pulse. Tom turned and yanked at the rope frenziedly, until he realized that he was only making it tighter.

His cigarette lighter. He fumbled for it in the pocket of his trousers on the bottom of the boat. He lighted it, then held a dry portion of the rope over its flame. The rope was about an inch and a half thick. It was slow, very slow, and Tom used the minutes to look all round him again. Would the Italian with the boats be able to see him at this distance? The hard grey rope refused to catch fire, only glowed and smoked a little, slowly parting, strand by strand. Tom yanked it, and his lighter went out. He lighted it again, and kept on pulling at the rope. When it parted, he looped it four times around Dickie's bare ankles before he had time to feel afraid, and tied a huge, clumsy knot, overdoing it to make sure it would not come undone, because he was not very good at tying knots. He estimated the rope to be about thirty-five or forty feet long. He began to feel cooler, and smooth and methodical. The cement weight should be just enough to hold a body down, he thought. The body might drift a little, but it would not come up to the surface.

Tom threw the weight over. It made a *ker-plung* and sank through the transparent water with a wake of bubbles, disappeared, and sank and sank until the rope drew taut on Dickie's ankles, and by that time Tom had lifted the ankles over the side and was pulling now at an arm to lift the heaviest part, the shoulders, over the gunwale. Dickie's limp hand was warm and clumsy. The shoulders stayed on the bottom of the boat, and when he pulled, the arm seemed to stretch like rubber, and the body not to rise at all. Tom got down on one knee and tried to heave him out over the side. It made the boat rock. He had forgotten the water. It was the only thing that scared him. He would have to get him out over the stern, he thought, because the stern was lower in the water. He pulled the limp body towards the stern, sliding the rope along the gunwale. He could tell from the buoyancy of the weight in the water that the weight had not touched bottom. Now he began with Dickie's head and shoulders, turned Dickie's body on its belly and pushed him out little by little. Dickie's head was in the water, the gunwale cutting aross his waist, and now the legs were in a dead weight, resisting Tom's strength with their amazing weight, as his shoulders had done, as if they were magnetized to the boat bottom. Tom took a deep breath and heaved. Dickie went over, but Tom lost his balance and fell against the tiller. The idling motor roared suddenly.

Tom made a lunge for the control lever, but the boat swerved at the same time in a crazy arc. For an instant he saw water underneath him and his own hand outstretched towards it, because he had been trying to grab the gunwale and the gunwale was no longer there.

He was in the water.

He gasped, contracting his body in an upward leap, grabbing at the boat. He missed. The boat had gone into a spin. Tom leapt again, then sank lower, so low the water closed over his head again with a deadly, fatal slowness, yet too fast for him to get a breath, and he inhaled a noseful of water just as his eyes sank below the surface. The boat was farther away. He had seen such spins before: they never stopped until somebody climbed in and stopped the motor, and now in the deadly emptiness of the water he suffered in advance the sensations of dying, sank threshing below the surface again, and the crazy motor faded as the water *thugged* into his ears, blotting out all sound except the frantic sounds that he made inside himself, breathing, struggling, the desperate pounding of his blood. He was up again and fighting automatically towards the boat, because it was the only thing that floated, though it was spinning and impossible to touch, and its sharp prow whipped past him twice, three times, four, while he caught one breath of air.

He shouted for help. He got nothing but a mouthful of water. His hand touched the boat beneath the water and was pushed aside by the animal-like thrust of the prow. He reached out wildly for the end of the boat, heedless of the propeller's blades. His fingers felt the rudder. He ducked, but not in time. The keel hit the top of his head, passing over him. Now the stern was close again, and he tried for it, fingers slipping down off the rudder. His other hand caught the stern gunwale. He kept an arm straight, holding his body away from the propeller. With an unpremeditated energy, he hurled himself towards a stern corner, and caught an arm over the side. Then he reached up and touched the lever.

The motor began to slow.

Tom clung to the gunwale with both hands, and his mind went blank with relief, with disbelief, until he became aware of the flaming ache in his throat, the stab in his chest with every breath. He rested for what could have been two or ten minutes, thinking of nothing at all but the gathering of strength enough to haul himself into the boat, and finally he made slow jumps up and down in the water and threw his weight over and lay face down in the boat, his feet dangling over the gunwale. He rested, faintly conscious of the slipperiness of Dickie's blood under his fingers, a wetness mingled with the water that ran out of his own nose and mouth. He began to think before he could move, about the boat that was all bloody and could not be returned, about the motor that he would have to get up and start in a moment. About the direction.

About Dickie's rings. He felt for them in his jacket pocket. They were still there, and after all what could have happened to them? He had a fit of coughing, and tears blurred his vision as he tried to look all around him to see if any boat was near, or coming towards him. He rubbed his eyes. There was no boat except the gay little motor-boat in the distance, still dashing around in wide arcs, oblivious of him. Tom looked at the boat bottom. *Could* he wash it all out? But blood was hell to get out, he had always heard. He had been going to return the boat, and say, if he were asked by the boatkeeper where his friend was, that he had set him ashore at some other point. Now that couldn't be.

Tom moved the lever cautiously. The idling motor picked up and he was afraid even of that, but the motor seemed more human and manageable than the sea, and therefore less frightening. He headed obliquely towards the shore, north of San Remo. Maybe he could find some place, some little deserted cove in the shore where he could beach the boat and get out. But if they found the boat? The problem seemed immense. He tried to reason himself back to coolness. His mind seemed blocked as to how to get rid of the boat.

Now he could see pine trees, a dry empty-looking stretch of tan beach and the green fuzz of a field of olive trees. Tom cruised slowly to right and left of the place, looking for people. There were none. He headed in for the shallow, short beach, handling the throttle respectfully, because he was not sure it wouldn't flare up again. Then he felt the scrape and jolt of earth under the prow. He turned the lever to FERMA, and moved another lever that cut the motor. He got out cautiously into about ten inches of water, pulled the boat up as far as he could, then transferred the two jackets, his sandals, and Marge's cologne box from the boat to the beach. The little cove where he was – not more than fifteen feet wide – gave him a feeling of safety and privacy. There was not a sign anywhere that a human foot had ever touched the place. Tom decided to try to scuttle the boat.

He began to gather stones, all about the size of a human head because that was all he had the strength to carry, and to drop them one by one into the boat, but finally he had to use smaller stones because there were no more big ones near enough by. He worked without a halt, afraid that he would drop in a faint of exhaustion if he allowed himself to relax even for an instant, and that he might lie there until he was found by somebody. When the stones were nearly level with the gunwale, he shoved the boat off and rocked it, more and more, until water slopped in at the sides. As the boat began to sink, he gave it a shove towards deeper water, shoved and walked with it until the water was up to his waist, and the boat sank below his reach. Then he ploughed his way back to the shore and lay down for a while, face down on the sand. He began to plan his return to the hotel, and his story, and his next moves: leaving San Remo before nightfall, getting back to Mongibello. And the story there.

THIRTEEN

At sundown, just the hour when the Italians and everybody else in the village had gathered at the sidewalk tables of the cafés, freshly showered and dressed, staring at everybody and everything that passed by, eager for whatever entertainment the town could offer, Tom walked into the village wearing only his swimming shorts and sandals and Dickie's corduroy jacket, and carrying his slightly bloodstained trousers and jacket under his arm. He walked with a languid casualness because he was exhausted, though he kept his head up for the benefit of the hundreds of people who stared at him as he walked past the cafés, the only route to his beachfront hotel. He had fortified himself with five espressos full of sugar and three brandies at a bar on the road just outside San Remo. Now he was playing the role of an athletic young man who had spent the afternoon in and out of the water because it was his peculiar taste, being a good swimmer and impervious to cold, to swim until late afternoon on a chilly day. He made it to the hotel, collected the key at the desk, went up to his room and collapsed on the bed. He would allow himself an hour to rest, he thought, but he must not fall asleep lest he sleep longer. He rested, and when he felt himself falling asleep, got up and went to the basin and wet his face, took a wet towel back to his bed to waggle in his hand to keep from falling asleep.

Finally he got up and went to work on the blood smear on one leg of his corduroy trousers. He scrubbed it over and over with soap and a nailbrush, got tired and stopped for a while to pack the suitcase. He packed Dickie's things just as Dickie had always packed them, toothpaste and toothbrush in the back left pocket. Then he went back to finish the trouser leg. His own jacket had too much blood on it ever to be worn again, and he would have to get rid of it, but he could wear Dickie's jacket, because it was the same beige colour and almost identical in size. Tom had had his suit copied from Dickie's, and it had been made by the same tailor in Mongibello. He put his own jacket into the suitcase. Then he went down with the suitcase and asked for his bill.

The man behind the desk asked where his friend was, and Tom said he was meeting him at the railroad station. The clerk was pleasant and smiling, and wished Tom 'Buon' viaggio'.

Tom stopped in a restaurant two streets away and forced himself to eat a bowl of minestrone for the strength it would give him. He kept an eye out for the Italian who owned the boats. The main thing, he thought, was to leave San Remo tonight, take a taxi to the next town, if there was no train or bus.

There was a train south at ten twenty-four, Tom learned at the railroad station. A sleeper. Wake up tomorrow in Rome, and change trains for Naples. It seemed absurdly simple and easy suddenly, and in a burst of self-assurance he thought of going to Paris for a few days.

''Spetta un momento,' he said to the clerk who was ready to hand him his ticket. Tom walked around his suitcase, thinking of Paris. Overnight. Just to see it, for two days, for instance. It wouldn't matter whether he told Marge or not. He decided abruptly against Paris. He wouldn't be able to relax. He was too eager to get to Mongibello and see about Dickie's belongings.

The white, taut sheets of his berth on the train seemed the most wonderful luxury he had ever known. He caressed them with his hands before he turned the light out. And the clean blue-grey blankets, the spanking efficiency of the little black net over his head – Tom had an esctatic moment when he thought of all the pleasures that lay before him now with Dickie's money, other beds, tables, seas, ships, suitcases, shirts, years of freedom, years of pleasure. Then he turned the light out and put his head down and almost at once fell asleep, happy, content, and utterly confident, as he had never been before in his life.

In Naples he stopped in the men's room of the railway station and removed Dickie's toothbrush and hairbrush from the suitcase, and rolled them up in Dickie's raincoat together with his own corduroy jacket and Dickie's blood-spotted trousers. He took the bundle across the street from the station and pressed it into a huge burlap of garbage that leaned against an alley wall. Then he breakfasted on caffe latte and a sweet roll at a café on the bus-stop square, and boarded the old eleven o'clock bus for Mongibello.

He stepped off the bus almost squarely in front of Marge, who was in her bathing suit and the loose white jacket she always wore to the beach.

'Where's Dickie?' she asked.

'He's in Rome.' Tom smiled easily, absolutely prepared. 'He's staying up there for a few days. I came down to get some of his stuff to take up to him.'

'Is he staying with somebody?'

'No, just in a hotel.' With another smile that was half a good-bye, Tom started up the hill with his suitcase. A moment later he heard Marge's cork-soled sandals trotting after him. Tom waited. 'How's everything been in our home sweet home?' he asked.

'Oh, dull. As usual.' Marge smiled. She was ill at ease with him. But she followed him into the house – the gate was unlocked, and Tom got the big iron key to the terrace door from its usual place, back of a rotting wooden tub that held earth and a half-dead shrub – and they went on to the terrace together. The table had been moved a little. There was a book on the glider. Marge had been here since they left, Tom thought. He had been gone only three days and nights. It seemed to him that he had been away for a month.

'How's Skippy?' Tom asked brightly, opening the refrigerator, getting out an ice tray. Skippy was a stray dog Marge had acquired a few days ago, an ugly black-and-white bastard that Marge pampered and fed like a doting old maid.

'He went off. I didn't expect him to stay.'

'Oh.'

'You look like you've had a good time,' Marge said, a little wistfully.

'We did.' Tom smiled. 'Can I fix you a drink?'

'No, thanks. How long do you think Dickie's going to be away?'

'Well –' Tom frowned thoughtfully. 'I don't really know. He says he wants to see a lot of art shows up there. I think he's just enjoying a change of scene.' Tom poured himself a generous gin and added soda and a lemon slice. 'I suppose he'll be back in a week. By the way!' Tom reached for the suitcase, and took out the box of cologne. He had removed the shop's wrapping paper, because it had had blood smears on it. 'Your Stradivari. We got it in San Remo.'

'Oh, thanks – very much.' Marge took it, smiling, and began to open it, carefully, dreamily.

Tom strolled tensely around the terrace with his drink, not saying a word to Marge, waiting for her to go.

'Well –' Marge said finally, coming out on the terrace. 'How long are you staying?'

'Where?'

'Here.'

'Just overnight. I'll be going up to Rome tomorrow. Probably in the afternoon,' he added, because he couldn't get the mail tomorrow until perhaps after two.

'I don't suppose I'll see you again, unless you're at the beach,' Marge said with an effort at friendliness. 'Have a good time in case I don't see you. And tell Dickie to write a postcard. What hotel is he staying at?'

'Oh – uh – what's the name of it? Near the Piazza di Spagna?'

'The Inghilterra?'

'That's it. But I think he said to use the American Express as a mailing address.' She wouldn't try to telephone Dickie, Tom thought. And he could be at the hotel tomorrow to pick up a letter if she wrote. 'I'll probably go down to the beach tomorrow morning,' Tom said.

'All right. Thanks for the cologne.'

'Don't mention it!'

She walked down the path to the iron gate, and out.

Tom picked up the suitcase and ran upstairs to Dickie's bedroom. He slid Dickie's top drawer out: letters, two address books, a couple of little notebooks, a watchchain, loose keys, and some kind of insurance policy. He slid the other drawers out, one by one, and left them open. Shirts, shorts, folded sweaters and disordered socks. In the corner of the room a sloppy mountain of portfolios and old drawing pads. There was a lot to be done. Tom took off all his clothes, ran downstairs naked and took a quick, cool shower, then put on Dickie's old white duck trousers that were hanging on a nail in the closet.

He started with the top drawer, for two reasons: the recent letters were important in case there were current situations that had to be taken care of immediately, and also because, in case Marge happened to come back this afternoon, it wouldn't look as if he were dismantling the entire house so soon. But at least he could begin, even this afternoon, packing Dickie's biggest suitcase with his best clothes, Tom thought.

Tom was still pottering about the house at midnight. Dickie's suitcases were packed, and now he was assessing how much the house furnishings were worth, what he would bequeath to Marge, and how he would dispose of the rest. Marge could have the damned refrigerator. That ought to please her. The heavy carved chest in the foyer, which Dickie used for his linens, ought to be worth several hundred dollars, Tom thought. Dickie had said it was four hundred years old, when Tom had asked him about it. Cinquecento. He intended to speak to Signor Pucci, the assistant manager of the Miramare, and ask him to act as an agent for the sale of the house and the furniture. And the boat, too. Dickie had told him that Signor Pucci did jobs like that for residents of the village.

He had wanted to take all Dickie's possessions straight away to Rome, but in view of what Marge might think about his taking so much for presumably such a short time, he decided it would be better to pretend that Dickie had later made a decision to move to Rome.

Accordingly, Tom went down to the post office around three the next afternoon, claimed one interesting letter for Dickie from a friend in America and nothing for himself, but as he walked slowly back to the house again he imagined that he was reading a letter from Dickie. He imagined the exact words, so that he could quote them to Marge, if he had to, and he even made himself feel the slight surprise he would have felt at Dickie's change of mind.

As soon as he got home he began packing Dickie's best drawings and best linens into the big cardboard box he had gotten from Aldo at the grocery store on the way up the hill. He worked calmly and methodically, expecting Marge to drop in at any minute, but it was after four before she came.

'Still here?' she asked as she came into Dickie's room.

'Yes. I had a letter from Dickie today. He's decided he's going to move to Rome.' Tom straightened up and smiled a little, as if it were a surprise to him, too. 'He wants me to pick up all his things, all I can handle.'

'*Move* to Rome? For how long?'

'I don't know. The rest of the winter apparently, anyway.' Tom went on tying canvases.

'He's not coming back all winter?' Marge's voice sounded lost already.

'No. He said he might even sell the house. He said he hadn't decided yet.'

'Gosh! – What happened?'

Tom shrugged. 'He apparently wants to spend the winter in Rome. He said he was going to write to you. I thought you might have got a letter this afternoon, too.'

'No.'

Silence. Tom kept on working. It occurred to him that he hadn't packed up his own things at all. He hadn't even been into his room.

'He's still going to Cortina, isn't he?' Marge asked.

'No, he's not. He said he was going to write to Freddie and cancel it. But that shouldn't prevent your going.' Tom watched her. 'By the way, Dickie said he wants you to take the refrigerator. You can probably get somebody to help you move it.'

The present of the refrigerator had no effect at all on Marge's stunned face. Tom knew she was wondering whether he was going to live with Dickie or not, and that she was probably concluding, because of his cheerful manner, that he was going to live with him. Tom felt the question creeping up to her lips – she was as transparent as a child to him – then she asked: 'Are you going to stay with him in Rome?'

'Maybe for a while. I'll help him get settled. I want to go to Paris this month, then I suppose around the middle of December I'll be going back to the States.'

Marge looked crestfallen. Tom knew she was imagining the lonely weeks ahead – even if Dickie did make periodic little visits to Mongibello to see her – the empty Sunday mornings, the lonely dinners. 'What's he going to do about Christmas? Do you think he wants to have it here or in Rome?'

Tom said with a trace of irritation, 'Well, I don't think here. I have the feeling he wants to be alone.'

Now she was shocked to silence, shocked and hurt. Wait till she got the letter he was going to write from Rome, Tom thought. He'd be gentle with her, of course, as gentle as Dickie, but there would be no mistaking that Dickie didn't want to see her again.

A few minutes later, Marge stood up and said good-bye in an absent-minded way. Tom suddenly felt that she might be going to telephone Dickie today. Or maybe even go up to Rome. But what if she did? Dickie could have changed his hotel. And there were enough hotels in Rome to keep her busy for days, even if she came to Rome to find him. When she didn't find him, by telephone or by coming to Rome, she would suppose that he had gone to Paris or to some other city with Tom Ripley.

Tom glanced over the newspapers from Naples for an item about a scuttled boat's having been found near San Remo. *Barca affondata vicino San Remo*, the caption would probably say. And they would make a great to-do over the bloodstains in the boat, if the bloodstains were still there. It was the kind of thing the Italian newspapers loved to write up in their melodramatic journalese: 'Giorgio di Stefani, a young fisherman of San Remo, yesterday at three o'clock in the afternoon made a most terrible discovery in two metres of water. A little motor-boat, its interior covered with horrible bloodstains ...' But Tom did not see anything in the paper. Nor had there been anything yesterday. It might take months for the boat to be found, he thought. It might never be found. And if they did find it, how could they know that Dickie Greenleaf and Tom Ripley had taken the boat out together? They had not told their names to the Italian boatkeeper at San Remo. The boatkeeper had given them only a little orange ticket which Tom had had in his pocket, and had later found and destroyed.

Tom left Mongibello by taxi around six o'clock, after an espresso at Giorgio's, where he said good-bye to Giorgio, Fausto, and several other village acquaintances of his and Dickie's. To all of them he told the same story, that Signor Greenleaf was staying in Rome for the winter, and that he sent his greetings until he saw them again. Tom said that undoubtedly Dickie would be down for a visit before long.

He had had Dickie's linens and paintings crated by the American Express that afternoon, and the boxes sent to Rome along with Dickie's trunk and two heavier suitcases, to be claimed in Rome by Dickie Green-leaf. Tom took his own two suitcases and one other of Dickie's in the taxi with him. He had spoken to Signor Pucci at the Miramare, and had said that there was a possibility that Signor Greenleaf would want to sell his house and furniture, and could Signor Pucci handle it? Signor Pucci had said he would be glad to. Tom had also spoken to Pietro, the dock-keeper, and asked him to be on the lookout for someone who might want to buy the *Pipistrello*, because there was a good chance that Signor Greenleaf would want to get rid of it this winter. Tom said that Signor Greenleaf would let it go for five hundred thousand lire, hardly eight hundred dollars, which was such a bargain for a boat that slept two people, Pietro thought he could sell it in a matter of weeks.

On the train to Rome Tom composed the letter to Marge so carefully that he memorized it in the process, and when he got to the Hotel Hassler he sat down at Dickie's Hermes Baby, which he had brought in one of Dickie's suitcases, and wrote the letter straight off.

Rome

28 November, 19—

Dear Marge,

I've decided to take an apartment in Rome for the winter, just to have a change of scene and get away from old Mongy for a while. I feel a terrific urge to be by myself. I'm sorry it was so sudden and that I didn't get a chance to say good-bye, but actually I'm not far away, and I hope I'll be seeing you now and then. I just didn't feel like going to pack my stuff, so I threw the burden on Tom.

As to us, it can't harm anything and possibly may improve everything if we don't see each other for a while. I had a terrible feeling I was boring you, though you weren't boring *me*, and please don't think I am running away from anything. On the contrary Rome should bring me closer to reality. Mongy certainly didn't. Part of my discontent was you. My going away doesn't solve anything, of course, but it will help me to discover how I really feel about you. For this reason, I prefer not to see you for a while, darling, and I hope you'll understand. If you don't – well, you don't, and that's the risk I run. I may go up to Paris for a couple of weeks with Tom, as he's dying to go. That is, unless I start painting right away. Met a painter named Di Massimo whose work I like very much, an old fellow without much money who seems to be very glad to have me as a student if I pay him a little bit. I am going to paint with him in his studio.

The city looks marvellous with its fountains going all night and everybody up all night, contrary to old Mongy. You were on the wrong track about Tom. He's going back to the States soon and I don't care when, though he's really not a bad guy and I don't dislike him. He has nothing to do with us, anyway, and I hope you realize that.

Write me c/o American Express, Rome until I know where I am. Shall let you know when I find an apartment. Meanwhile keep the home fires burning, the refrigerators working and your typewriter also. I'm terribly sorry about Xmas, darling, but I don't think I should see you that soon, and you can hate me or not for that.

All my love,
Dickie

Tom had kept his cap on since entering the hotel, and he had given Dickie's passport in at the desk instead of his own, though hotels, he had noticed, never looked at the passport photo, only copied the passport number which was on the front cover. He had signed the register with Dickie's hasty and rather flamboyant signature with the big looping capitals R and G. When he went out to mail the letter he walked to a drugstore several streets away and bought a few items of make-up that he thought he might need. He had fun with the Italian salesgirl, making her think that he was buying them for his wife who had lost her make-up kit, and who was indisposed in the hotel with the usual upset stomach.

He spent that evening practising Dickie's signature for the bank cheques. Dickie's monthly remittance was going to arrive from America in less than ten days.

FOURTEEN

He moved the next day to the Hotel Europa, a moderately priced hotel near the Via Veneto, because the Hassler was a trifle flashy, he thought, the kind of hotel that was patronized by visiting movie people, and where Freddie Miles, or people like him who knew Dickie, might choose to stay if they came to Rome.

Tom held imaginary conversations with Marge and Fausto and Freddie in his hotel room. Marge was the most likely to come to Rome, he thought. He spoke to her as Dickie, if he imagined it on the telephone, and as Tom, if he imagined her face to face with him. She might, for instance, pop up to Rome and find his hotel and insist on coming up to his room, in which case he would have to remove Dickie's rings and change his clothing.

'I don't know,' he would say to her in Tom's voice. 'You know how he is – likes to feel he's getting away from everything. He said I could use his hotel room for a few days, because mine happens to be so badly heated ... Oh, he'll be back in a couple of days, or there'll be a postcard from him saying he's all right. He went to some little town with Di Massimo to look at some paintings in a church.'

('But you don't know whether he went north or south?')

'I really don't. I guess south. But what good does that do us?'

('It's just my bad luck to miss him, isn't it? Why couldn't he at least have said where he was going?')

'I know. I asked him, too. Looked the room over for a map or anything else that might have shown where he was going. He just called me up three days ago and said I could use his room if I cared to.'

It was a good idea to practise jumping into his own character again, because the time might come when he would need to in a matter of seconds, and it was strangely easy to forget the exact timbre of Tom Ripley's voice. He conversed with Marge until the sound of his own voice in his ears was exactly the same as he remembered it.

But mostly he was Dickie, discoursing in a low tone with Freddie and Marge, and by long distance with Dickie's mother, and with Fausto, and with a stranger at a dinner party, conversing in English and Italian, with Dickie's portable radio turned on so that if a hotel employee passed by in the hall and happened to know that Signor Greenleaf was alone he would not think him an eccentric. Sometimes, if the song on the radio was one that Tom liked, he merely danced by himself, but he danced as Dickie would have with a girl – he had seen Dickie once on Giorgio's terrace, dancing with Marge, and also in the Giardino degli Orangi in Naples – in long strides yet rather stiffly, not what could be called exactly good dancing. Every moment to Tom was a pleasure, alone in his room or walking the streets of Rome, when he combined sightseeing with looking around for an apartment. It was impossible ever to be lonely or bored, he thought, so long as he was Dickie Greenleaf.

They greeted him as Signor Greenleaf at the American Express, where he called for his mail. Marge's first letter said:

Dickie,

Well, it was a bit of a surprise. I wonder what came over you so suddenly in Rome or San Remo or wherever it was? Tom was most mysterious except to say that he would be staying with you. I'll believe he's leaving for America when I see it. At the risk of sticking my neck out, old boy, may I say that *I* don't like that guy? From my point of view or anybody else's he is using you for what you are worth. If you want to make some changes for your own good, for gosh sakes get *him* away from you. All right, he may not be queer. He's just a nothing, which is worse. He isn't normal enough to have *any* kind of sex life, if you know what I mean. However, I'm not interested in Tom but in you. Yes, I can bear the few weeks without you, darling, and even Christmas, though I prefer not to think of Christmas. I prefer not to think about you and – as you said – let the feelings come or not. But it's impossible not to think of you here because every inch of the village is haunted with you as far as I'm concerned, and in this house, everywhere I look there is some sign of you, the hedge we planted, the fence we started repairing and never finished, the books I borrowed from you and never returned. And your chair at the table, that's the worst.

To continue with the neck-sticking, I don't say that Tom is going to do anything actively bad to you, but I know that he has a subtly bad influence on you. You act vaguely ashamed of being around him when you *are* around him, do you know that? Did you ever try to analyse it? I thought you were beginning to realize all this in the last few weeks, but now you're with him again and frankly, dear boy, I don't know what to make of it. If you really 'don't care when' he takes off, for God's sake send him packing! He'll never help you or anybody else to get straightened out about anything. In fact it's greatly to his interest to keep you muddled and string you along and your father too.

Thanks loads for the cologne, darling. I'll save it – or most of it – for when I see you next. I haven't got the refrigerator over to my house yet. You can have it, of course, any time you want it back.

Maybe Tom told you that Skippy skipped out. Should I capture a gecko and tie a string around its neck? I have to get to work on the house wall right away before it mildews completely and collapses on me. Wish you were here, darling – of course.

Lots of love and *write*,

XX
Marge

c/o American Express
Rome
12 Dec. 19—

Dear Mother and Dad,

I'm in Rome looking for an apartment, though I haven't found exactly what I want yet. Apartments here are either too big or too small, and if too big you have to shut off every room but one in winter in order to heat it properly anyway. I'm trying to get a medium-sized, medium-priced place that I can heat completely without spending a fortune for it.

Sorry I've been so bad about letters lately. I hope to do better with the quieter life I'm leading here. I felt I needed a change from Mongibello – as you've both been saying for a long time – so I've moved bag and baggage and may even sell the house and the boat. I've met a wonderful painter called Di Massimo who is willing to give me instruction in his studio. I'm going to work like blazes for a few months and see what happens. A kind of trial period. I realize this doesn't interest you, Dad, but since you're always asking how I spend my time, this is how. I'll be leading a very quiet, studious life until next summer.

Apropos of that, could you sent me the latest folders from Burke-Greenleaf? I like to keep up with what you're doing, too, and it's been a long time since I've seen anything.

Mother, I hope you haven't gone to great trouble for my Christmas. I don't really need anything I can think of. How are you feeling? Are you able to get out very much? To the theatre, etc.? How is Uncle Edward now? Send him my regards and keep me posted.

With love,
Dickie

Tom read it over, decided there were probably too many commas, and retyped it patiently and signed it. He had once seen a half-finished letter of Dickie's to his parents in Dickie's typewriter, and he knew Dickie's general style. He knew that Dickie had never taken more than ten minutes writing any letter. If this letter was different, Tom thought, it could be different only in being a little more personal and enthusiastic than usual. He felt rather pleased with the letter when he read it over for the second time. Uncle Edward was a brother of Mrs Greenleaf, who was ill in an Illinois hospital with some kind of cancer, Tom had learned from the latest letter to Dickie from his mother.

A few days later he was off to Paris by plane. He had called the Inghilterra before he left Rome: no letters or phone calls for Richard Greenleaf. He landed at Orly at five in the afternoon. The passport inspector stamped his passport after only a quick glance at him, though Tom had lightened his hair slightly with a peroxide wash and had forced some waves into it, aided by hair oil, and for the inspector's benefit he had put on the rather tense, rather frowning expression of Dickie's passport photograph. Tom checked in at the Hôtel du Quai-Voltaire, which had been recommended to him by some Americans with whom he had struck up an acquaintance at a Rome café, as being conveniently located and not too full of Americans. Then he went out for a stroll in the raw, foggy December evening. He walked with his head up and a smile on his face. It was the atmosphere of the city that he loved, the atmosphere that he had always heard about, crooked streets, grey-fronted houses with sky-lights, noisy car horns, and everywhere public urinals and columns with brightly coloured theatre notices on them. He wanted to let the atmosphere seep in slowly, perhaps for several days, before he visited the Louvre or went up in the Eiffel Tower or anything like that. He bought a *Figaro*, sat down at a table in the Flore, and ordered a fine à l'eau, because Dickie had once said that fine à l'eau was his usual drink in France. Tom's French was limited, but so was Dickie's, Tom knew. Some interesting people stared at him through the glass-enclosed front of the café, but no one came in to speak to him. Tom was prepared for someone to get up from one of the tables at any moment, and come over and say, 'Dickie Greenleaf! Is it really you?'

He had done so little artificially to change his appearance, but his very expression, Tom thought, was like Dickie's now. He wore a smile that was dangerously welcoming to a stranger, a smile more fit to greet an old friend or a lover. It was Dickie's best and most typical smile when he was in a good humour. Tom was in a good humour. It was Paris. *Wonderful* to sit in a famous café, and to think of tomorrow and tomorrow and tomorrow being Dickie Greenleaf! The cuff links, the white silk shirts, even the old clothes – the worn brown belt with the brass buckle, the old brown grain-leather shoes, the kind advertised in *Punch* as lasting a lifetime, the old mustard-coloured coat sweater with the sagging pockets, they were all his and he loved them all. And the black fountain pen with little gold initials. And the wallet, a well-worn alligator wallet from Gucci's. And there was plenty of money to go in it.

By the next afternoon he had been invited to a party in the Avenue Kléber by some people – a French girl and an American young man – with whom he had started a conversation in a large café-restaurant on the Boulevard Saint-Germain. The party consisted of thirty or forty people, most of them middle-aged, standing around rather frigidly in a huge, chilly, formal apartment. In Europe, Tom gathered, inadequate heating was a hallmark of chic in winter, like the iceless martini in summer. He had moved to a more expensive hotel in Rome, finally, in order to be warmer, and had found that the more expensive hotel was even colder. In a gloomy, old-fashioned way the house was chic, Tom supposed. There were a butler and a maid, a vast table of pâtés en croûte, sliced turkey, and petits fours, and quantities of champagne, although the upholstery of the sofa and the long drapes at the windows were threadbare and rotting with age, and he had seen mouseholes in the hall by the elevator. At least half a dozen of the guests he had been presented to were counts and countesses. An American informed Tom that the young man and the girl who had invited him were going to be married, and that her parents were not enthusiastic. There was an atmosphere of strain in the big room, and Tom made an effort to be as pleasant as possible to everyone, even the severe-looking French people to whom he could say little more than 'C'est très agréable, n'est-ce pas?' He did his very best, and won at least a smile from the French girl who had invited him. He considered himself lucky to be there. How many Americans alone in Paris could get themselves invited to a French home after only a week or so in the city? The French were especially slow in inviting strangers to their homes, Tom had always heard. Not a single one of the Americans seemed to know his name. Tom felt completely comfortable, as he had never felt before at any party that he could remember. He behaved as he had always wanted to behave at a party. This was the clean slate he had thought about on the boat coming over from America. This was the real annihilation of his past and of himself, Tom Ripley, who was made up of the past and his rebirth as a completely new person. One Frenchwoman and two of the Americans invited him to parties, but Tom declined with the same reply to all of them: 'Thank you very much, but I'm leaving Paris tomorrow.'

It wouldn't do to become too friendly with any of these, Tom thought. One of them might know somebody who knew Dickie very well, someone who might be at the next party.

At eleven-fifteen, when he said good-bye to his hostess and to her parents, they looked very sorry to see him go. But he wanted to be at Notre Dame by midnight. It was Christmas Eve.

The girl's mother asked his name again.

'Monsieur Granelafe,' the girl repeated for her. 'Deekie Granelafe. Correct?'

'Correct,' Tom said, smiling.

Just as he reached the downstairs hall he remembered Freddie Miles's party at Cortina. December second. Nearly a month ago! He had meant to write to Freddie to say that he wasn't coming. Had Marge gone, he wondered? Freddie would think it very strange that he hadn't written to say he wasn't coming, and Tom hoped Marge had told Freddie, at least. He must write Freddie at once. There was a Florence address for Freddie in Dickie's address book. It was a slip, but nothing serious, Tom thought. He just mustn't let such a thing happen again.

He walked out into the darkness and turned in the direction of the illuminated, bone-white Arc de Triomphe. It was strange to feel so alone, and yet so much a part of things, as he had felt at the party. He felt it again, standing on the outskirts of the crowd that filled the square in front of Notre Dame. There was such a crowd he couldn't possibly have gone into the cathedral, but the amplifiers carried the music clearly to all parts of the square. French Christmas carols whose names he didn't know. 'Silent Night'. A solemn carol, and then a lively, babbling one. The chanting of male voices. Frenchmen near him removed their hats. Tom removed his.

He stood tall, straight, sober-faced, yet ready to smile if anyone had addressed him. He felt as he had felt on the ship, only more intensely, full of good will, a gentleman, with nothing in his past to blemish his character. He was Dickie, good-natured, naïve Dickie, with a smile for everyone and a thousand francs for anyone who asked him. An old man did ask him for money as Tom was leaving the cathedral square, and he gave him a crisp blue thousand-franc bill. The old man's face exploded in a smile, and he tipped his hat.

Tom felt a little hungry, though he rather liked the idea of going to bed hungry tonight. He would spend an hour or so with his Italian conversation book, he thought, then go to bed. Then he remembered that he had decided to try to gain about five pounds, because Dickie's clothes were just a trifle loose on him and Dickie looked heavier than he in the face, so he stopped at a bar-tabac and ordered a ham sandwich on long crusty bread and a glass of hot milk, because a man next to him at the counter was drinking hot milk. The milk was almost tasteless, pure and chastening, as Tom imagined a wafer tasted in church.

He came down in a leisurely way from Paris, stopping overnight in Lyon and also in Arles to see the places that Van Gogh had painted there. He maintained his cheerful equanimity in the face of atrociously bad weather. In Arles, the rain borne on the violent mistral soaked him through as he tried to discover the exact spots where Van Gogh had stood to paint from. He had bought a beautiful book of Van Gogh reproductions in Paris, but he could not take the book out in the rain, and he had to make a dozen trips back to his hotel to verify the scenes. He looked over Marseilles, found it drab except for the Cannebière, and moved on eastward by train, stopping for a day in St Tropez, Cannes, Nice, Monte Carlo, all the places he had heard of and felt such affinity for when he saw them, though in the month of December they were overcast by grey winter clouds, and the gay crowds were not there, even on New Year's Eve in Menton. Tom put the people there in his imagination, men and women in evening clothes descending the broad steps of the gambling palace in Monte Carlo, people in bright bathing costumes, light and brilliant as a Dufy watercolour, walking under the palms of the Boulevard des Anglais at Nice. People – American, English, French, German, Swedish, Italian. Romance, disappointment, quarrels, reconciliations, murder. The Côte d'Azur excited him as no other place he had yet seen in the world excited him. And it was so tiny, really, this curve in the Mediterranean coastline with the wonderful names strung like beads – Toulon, Fréjus, St Raphael, Cannes, Nice, Menton, and then San Remo.

There were two letters from Marge when he got back to Rome on the fourth of January. She was giving up her house on the first of March, she said. She had not quite finished the first draft of her book, but she was sending three-quarters of it with all the photographs to the American publisher who had been interested in her idea when she wrote him about it last summer. She wrote:

When am I going to see you? I hate passing up a summer in Europe after I've weathered another awful winter, but I think I'll go home early in March. Yes, I'm *homesick*, finally, *really*. Darling, it would be so wonderful if we could go home on the same boat together. Is there a possibility? I don't suppose there *is*. You're not going back to the U.S. even for a short visit this winter?

I was thinking of sending all my stuff (eight pieces of luggage, two trunks, three boxes of books and miscellaneous!) by slow boat from Naples and coming up through Rome and if you were in the mood we could at least go up the coast again and see Forte dei Marmi and Viareggio and the other spots we like – a last look. I'm not in the mood to care about the weather, which I know will be *horrid*. I wouldn't ask you to accompany me to Marseilles, where I catch the boat, but from Genoa? ? ? What do you think? ...

The other letter was more reserved. Tom knew why: he had not sent her even a postcard for nearly a month. She said:

Have changed my mind about the Riviera. Maybe this damp weather has taken away my enterprise or my book has. Anyway, I'm leaving for Naples on an earlier boat – the *Constitution* on 28 Feb. Imagine – back to America as soon as I step aboard. American food, Americans, dollars for drinks and the horseraces – Darling, I'm sorry not to be seeing you, as I gather from your silence you still don't want to see me, so don't give it a thought. Consider me off your hands.

Of course I do hope I see you again, in the States or anywhere else. Should you possibly be inspired to make a trip down to Mongy before the 28th, you know damned well you are welcome.

As ever,

Marge

P.S. I don't even know if you're still in Rome.

Tom could see her in tears as she wrote it. He had an impulse to write her a very considerate letter, saying he had just come back from Greece, and had she gotten his two postcards? But it was safer, Tom thought, to let her leave without being sure where he was. He wrote her nothing.

The only thing that made him uneasy, and that was not very uneasy, was the possibility of Marge's coming up to see him in Rome before he could get settled in an apartment. If she combed the hotels she could find him, but she could never find him in an apartment. Well-to-do Americans didn't have to report their places of residence at the questura, though, according to the stipulation of the Permesso di Soggiorno, one was supposed to register every change of address with the police. Tom had talked with an American resident of Rome who had an apartment and who had said he never bothered with the questura, and it never bothered him. If Marge did come up to Rome suddenly, Tom had a lot of his own clothing hanging ready in the closet. The only thing he had changed about himself, physically, was his hair, but that could always be explained as being the effect of the sun. He wasn't really worried. Tom had at first amused himself with an eyebrow pencil – Dickie's eyebrows were longer and turned up a little at the outer edges – and with a touch of putty at the end of his nose to make it longer and more pointed, but he abandoned these as too likely to be noticed. The main thing about impersonation, Tom thought, was to maintain the mood and temperament of the person one was impersonating, and to assume the facial expressions that went with them. The rest fell into place.

On the tenth of January Tom wrote Marge that he was back in Rome after three weeks in Paris alone, that Tom had left Rome a month ago, saying he was going up to Paris, and from there to America though he hadn't run into Tom in Paris, and that he had not yet found an apartment in Rome but he was looking and would let her know his address as soon as he had one. He thanked her extravagantly for the Christmas package: she had sent the white sweater with the red V stripes that she had been knitting and trying on Dickie for size since October, as well as an art book of quattrocento painting and a leather shaving kit with his initials, H.R.G., on the lid. The package had arrived only on January sixth, which was the main reason for Tom's letter: he didn't want her to think he hadn't claimed it, imagine that he had vanished into thin air, and then start a search for him. He asked if she had received a package from him? He had mailed it from Paris, and he supposed it was late. He apologized. He wrote:

I'm painting again with Di Massimo and am reasonably pleased. I miss you, too, but if you can still bear with my experiment, I'd prefer not to see you for several more weeks (unless you do suddenly go home in February, which I still doubt!) by which time you may not care to see me again. Regards to Giorgio and wife and Fausto if he's still there and Pietro down at the dock …

It was a letter in the absent-minded and faintly lugubrious tone of all Dickie's letters, a letter that could not be called warm or unwarm, and that said essentially nothing.

Actually he had found an apartment in a large apartment house in the

Via Imperiale near the Pincian Gate, and had signed a year's lease for it, though he did not intend to spend most of his time in Rome, much less the winter. He only wanted a home, a base somewhere, after years of not having any. And Rome was chic. Rome was part of his new life. He wanted to be able to say in Majorca or Athens or Cairo or wherever he was: 'Yes, I live in Rome. I keep an apartment there.' 'Keep' was the word for apartments among the international set. You kept an apartment in Europe the way you kept a garage in America. He also wanted his apartment to be elegant, though he intended to have the minimum of people up to see him, and he hated the idea of having a telephone, even an unlisted telephone, but he decided it was more of a safety measure than a menace, so he had one installed. The apartment had a large living-room, a bed-room, a kind of sitting-room, kitchen, and bath. It was furnished some-what ornately, but it suited the respectable neighbourhood and the respectable life he intended to lead. The rent was the equivalent of a hundred and seventy-five dollars a month in winter including heat, and a hundred and twenty-five in summer.

Marge replied with an ecstatic letter saying she had just received the beautiful silk blouse from Paris which she hadn't expected *at all* and it fitted to perfection. She said she had had Fausto and the Cecchis for Christmas dinner at her house and the turkey had been divine, with marrons and giblet gravy and plum pudding and blah blah blah and everything but *him*. And what was he doing and thinking about? And was he happier? And that Fausto would look him up on his way to Milan if he sent an address in the next few days, otherwise leave a message for Fausto at the American Express, saying where Fausto could find him.

Tom supposed her good humour was due mostly to the fact that she now thought Tom had departed for America via Paris. Along with Marge's letter came one from Signor Pucci, saying that he had sold three pieces of his furniture for a hundred and fifty thousand lire in Naples, and that he had a prospective buyer for the boat, a certain Anastasio Martino of Mongibello, who had promised to pay the first down payment within a week, but that the house probably couldn't be sold until summer when the Americans began coming in again. Less fifteen per cent for Signor Pucci's commission, the furniture sale amounted to two hundred and ten dollars, and Tom celebrated that night by going to a Roman nightclub and ordering a superb dinner which he ate in elegant solitude at a candlelit table for two. He did not at all mind dining and going to the theatre alone. It gave him the opportunity to concentrate on being Dickie Greenleaf. He broke his bread as Dickie did, thrust his fork into his mouth with his left hand as Dickie did, gazed off at the other tables and at the dancers in such a profound and benevolent trance that the waiter had to speak to him a couple of times to get his attention. Some people waved to him from a table, and Tom recognized them as one of the American couples he had met at the Christmas Eve party in Paris. He made a sign of greeting in return. He even remembered their name, Souders. He did not look at them again during the evening, but they left before he did and stopped by his table to say hello.

'All by yourself?' the man asked. He looked a little tipsy.

'Yes. I have a yearly date with myself,' Tom replied. 'I celebrate a certain anniversary.'

The American nodded a little blankly, and Tom could see that he was stymied for anything intelligent to say, as uneasy as any small-town American in the presence of cosmopolitan poise and sobriety, money and good clothes, even if the clothes were on another American.

'You said you were living in Rome, didn't you?' his wife asked. 'You know, I think we've forgotten your name, but we remember you very well from Christmas Eve.'

'Greenleaf,' Tom replied. 'Richard Greenleaf.'

'Oh, yes!' she said, relieved. 'Do you have an apartment here?'

She was all ready to take down his address in her memory.

'I'm staying at a hotel at the moment, but I'm planning to move into an apartment any day, as soon as the decorating's finished. I'm at the Eliseo. Why don't you give me a ring?'

'We'd love to. We're on our way to Majorca in three more days, but that's plenty of time!'

'Love to see you,' Tom said. 'Buona sera!'

Alone again, Tom returned to his private reveries. He ought to open a bank account for Tom Ripley, he thought, and from time to time put a hundred dollars or so into it. Dickie Greenleaf had two banks, one in Naples and one in New York, with about five thousand dollars in each account. He might open the Ripley account with a couple of thousand, and put into it the hundred and fifty thousand lire from the Mongibello furniture. After all, he had two people to take care of.

FIFTEEN

He visited the Capitoline and the Villa Borghese, explored the Forum thoroughly, and took six Italian lessons from an old man in his neighbourhood who had a tutoring sign in his window, and to whom Tom gave a false name. After the sixth lesson, Tom thought that his Italian was on a par with Dickie's. He remembered verbatim several sentences that Dickie had said at one time or another which he now knew were incorrect. For example. 'Ho paura che non c'e arrivata, Giorgio,' one evening in Giorgio's, when they had been waiting for Marge and she had been late. It should have been 'sia arrivata' in the subjunctive after an expression of fearing. Dickie had never used the subjunctive as often as it should be used in Italian. Tom studiously kept himself from learning the proper uses of subjunctive.

Tom bought dark red velvet for the drapes in his living-room, because the drapes that had come with the apartment offended him. When he had asked Signora Buffi, the wife of the house superintendent, if she knew of a seamstress who could make them up, Signora Buffi had offered to make them herself. Her price was two thousand lire, hardly more than three dollars. Tom forced her to take five thousand. He bought several minor items to embellish his apartment, though he never asked anyone up – with the exception of one attractive but not very bright young man, an American, whom he had met in the Café Greco when the young man had asked him how to get to the Hotel Excelsior from there. The Excelsior was on the way to Tom's house, so Tom asked him to come up for a drink. Tom had only wanted to impress him for an hour and then say good-bye to him for ever, which he did, after serving him his best brandy and strolling about his apartment discoursing on the pleasure of life in Rome. The young man was leaving for Munich the following day.

Tom carefully avoided the American residents of Rome who might expect him to come to their parties and ask them to his in return, though he loved to chat with Americans and Italians in the Café Greco and in the students' restaurants in the Via Margutta. He told his name only to an Italian painter named Carlino, whom he met in a Via Margutta tavern, told him also that he painted and was studying with a painter called Di Massimo. If the police ever investigated Dickie's activities in Rome, perhaps long after Dickie had disappeared and become Tom Ripley again, this one Italian painter could be relied upon to say that he knew Dickie Greenleaf had been painting in Rome in January. Carlino had never heard of Di Massimo, but Tom described him so vividly that Carlino would probably never forget him.

He felt alone, yet not at all lonely. It was very much like the feeling on Christmas Eve in Paris, a feeling that everyone was watching him, as if he had an audience made up of the entire world, a feeling that kept him on his mettle, because to make a mistake would be catastrophic. Yet he felt absolutely confident he would not make a mistake. It gave his existence a peculiar, delicious atmosphere of purity, like that, Tom thought, which a fine actor probably feels when he plays an important role on a stage with the conviction that the rôle he is playing could not be played better by anyone else. He was himself and yet not himself. He felt blameless and free, despite the fact that he consciously controlled every move he made. But he no longer felt tired after several hours of it, as he had at first. He had no need to relax when he was alone. Now, from the moment when he got out of bed and went to brush his teeth, he was Dickie, brushing his teeth with his elbow jutted out, Dickie rotating the eggshell on his spoon for the last bite, Dickie invariably putting back the first tie he pulled off the rack and selecting a second. He had even produced a painting in Dickie's manner.

By the end of January Tom thought that Fausto must have come and gone through Rome, though Marge's last letters had not mentioned him. Marge wrote, care of the American Express, about once a week. She asked if he needed any socks or a muffler, because she had plenty of time to knit, besides working on her book. She always put a funny anecdote about somebody they knew in the village, just so Dickie wouldn't think she was eating her heart out for him, though obviously she was, and obviously she wasn't going to leave for the States in February without making another desperate try for him in person, Tom thought, hence the investments of the long letters and the knitted socks and muffler which Tom knew were coming, even though he hadn't replied to her letters. Her letters repelled him. He disliked even touching them, and after he glanced through them he tore them up and dropped them into the garbage.

He wrote finally:

I'm giving up the idea of an apartment in Rome for the time being. Di Massimo is going to Sicily for several months, and I may go with him and go on somewhere from there. My plans are vague, but they have the virtue of freedom and they suit my present mood.

Don't send me any socks, Marge. I really don't need a thing. Wish you much luck with 'Mongibello'.

He had a ticket for Majorca – by train to Naples, then the boat from Naples to Palma over the night of January thirty-first and February first. He had bought two new suitcases from Gucci's, the best leather goods store in Rome, one a large, soft suitcase of antelope hide, the other a neat tan canvas with brown leather straps. Both bore Dickie's initials. He had thrown the shabbier of his own two suitcases away, and the remaining one he kept in the closet of his apartment, full of his own clothes, in case of emergency. But Tom was not expecting any emergencies. The scuttled boat in San Remo had never been found. Tom looked through the papers every day for something about it.

While Tom was packing his suitcases one morning his doorbell rang. He supposed it was a solicitor of some kind, or a mistake. He had no name on his doorbell, and he had told the superintendent that he did not want his name on the doorbell because he didn't like people to drop in on him. It rang for the second time, and Tom still ignored it, and went on with his lackadaisical packing. He loved to pack, and he took a long time about it, a whole day or two days, laying Dickie's clothes affectionately into suitcases, now and then trying on a good-looking shirt or a jacket in front of the mirror. He was standing in front of the mirror, buttoning a blue-and-white seahorse-patterned sport shirt of Dickie's that he had never worn, when there came a knock at his door.

It crossed his mind that it might be Fausto, that it would be just like Fausto to hunt him down in Rome and try to surprise him. That was silly, he told himself. But his hands were cool with sweat as he went to the door. He felt faint, and the absurdity of his faintness, plus the danger of keeling over and being found prostrate on the floor, made him wrench the door open with both hands, though he opened it only a few inches.

'Hello!' the American voice said out of the semi-darkness of the hall. 'Dickie? It's Freddie!'

Tom took a step back, holding the door open. 'He's – Won't you come in? He's not here right now. He should be back in a little later.'

Freddie Miles came in, looking around. His ugly, freckled face gawked in every direction. How in hell had he found the place, Tom wondered. Tom slipped his rings off quickly and pocketed them. And what else? He glanced around the room.

'You're staying with him?' Freddie asked with the wall-eyed stare that made his face look idiotic and rather scared.

'Oh, no. I'm just staying here for a few hours,' Tom said, casually removing the seahorse shirt. He had another shirt on under it. 'Dickie's out for lunch. Otello's, I think he said. He should be back around three at the latest.' One of the Buffis must have let Freddie in, Tom thought, and told him which bell to press, and told him Signor Greenleaf was in, too. Freddie had probably said he was an old friend of Dickie's. Now he would have to get Freddie out of the house without running into Signora Buffi downstairs because she always sang out, 'Buon' giorno, Signor Greenleaf!'

'I met you in Mongibello, didn't I?' Freddie asked. 'Aren't you Tom? I thought you were coming to Cortina.'

'I couldn't make it, thanks. How was Cortina?'

'Oh, fine. What happened to Dickie?'

'Didn't he write to you? He decided to spend the winter in Rome. He told me he'd written to you.'

'Not a word – unless he wrote to Florence. But I was in Salzburg, and he had my address.' Freddie half sat on Tom's long table, rumpling the green silk runner. He smiled. 'Marge told me he'd moved to Rome, but she didn't have any address except the American Express. It was only by the damnedest luck I found his apartment. I ran into somebody at the Greco last night who just happened to know his address. What's this idea of –'

'Who?' Tom asked. 'An American?'

'No, an Italian fellow. Just a young kid.' Freddie was looking at Tom's shoes. 'You've got the same kind of shoes Dickie and I have. They wear like iron, don't they? I bought my pair in London eight years ago.'

They were Dickie's grain-leather shoes. 'These came from America,' Tom said. 'Can I offer you a drink or would you rather try to catch Dickie at Otello's? Do you know where it is? There's not much use in your waiting, because he generally takes till three with his lunches. I'm going out soon myself.'

Freddie had strolled towards the bedroom and stopped, looking at the suitcases on the bed. 'Is Dickie leaving for somewhere or did he just get here?' Freddie asked, turning.

'He's leaving. Didn't Marge tell you? He's going to Sicily for a while.'

'When?'

'Tomorrow. Or late tonight, I'm not quite sure.'

'Say, what's the matter with Dickie lately?' Freddie asked, frowning. 'What's the idea of all the seclusion?'

'He says he's been working pretty hard this winter,' Tom said in an offhand tone. 'He seems to want privacy, but as far as I know he's still on good terms with everybody, including Marge.'

Freddie smiled again, unbuttoning his big polo coat. 'He's not going to stay on good terms with me if he stands me up a few more times. Are you sure he's on good terms with Marge? I got the idea from her that they'd had a quarrel. I thought maybe that was why they didn't go to Cortina.' Freddie looked at him expectantly.

'Not that I know of.' Tom went to the closet to get his jacket, so that Freddie would know he wanted to leave, then realized just in time that the grey flannel jacket that matched his trousers might be recognizable as Dickie's, if Freddie knew Dickie's suit. Tom reached for a jacket of his own and for his own overcoat that were hanging at the extreme left of the closet. The shoulders of the overcoat looked as if the coat had been on a hanger for weeks, which it had. Tom turned around and saw Freddie staring at the silver identification bracelet on his left wrist. It was Dickie's bracelet, which Tom had never seen him wearing, but had found in Dickie's studbox. Freddie was looking at it as if he had seen it before. Tom put on his overcoat casually.

Freddie was looking at him now with a different expression, with a little surprise. Tom knew what Freddie was thinking. He stiffened, sensing danger. You're not out of the woods yet, he told himself. You're not out of the house yet.

'Ready to go?' Tom asked.

'You do live here, don't you?'

'No!' Tom protested, smiling. The ugly, freckle-blotched face stared at him from under the garish thatch of red hair. If they could only get out without running into Signora Buffi downstairs, Tom thought. 'Let's go.'

'Dickie's loaded you up with all his jewellery, I see.'

Tom couldn't think of a single thing to say, a single joke to make. 'Oh, it's a loan,' Tom said in his deepest voice. 'Dickie got tired of wearing it, so he told me to wear it for a while.' He meant the identification bracelet, but there was also the silver clip on his tie, he realized, with the G on it. Tom had bought the tieclip himself. He could feel the belligerence growing in Freddie Miles as surely as if his huge body were generating a heat that he could feel across the room. Freddie was the kind of ox who might beat up somebody he thought was a pansy, especially if the conditions were as propitious as these. Tom was afraid of his eyes.

'Yes, I'm ready to go,' Freddie said grimly, getting up. He walked to the door and turned with a swing of his broad shoulders. 'That's the Otello not far from the Inghilterra?'

'Yes,' Tom said. 'He's supposed to be there by one o'clock.'

Freddie nodded. 'Nice to see you again,' he said unpleasantly, and closed the door.

Tom whispered a curse. He opened the door slightly and listened to the quick *tap-tap – tap-tap* of Freddie's shoes descending the stairs. He wanted to make sure Freddie got out without speaking to one of the Buffis again. Then he heard Freddie's 'Buon' giorno, signora.' Tom leaned over the stairwell. Three storeys down, he could see part of Freddie's coatsleeve. He was talking in Italian with Signora Buffi. The woman's voice came more clearly.

'. . . only Signor Greenleaf,' she was saying. 'No, only one . . . Signor Chi? . . . No, signor . . . I do not think he has gone out today at all, but I could be wrong!' She laughed.

Tom twisted the stair rail in his hands as if it were Freddie's neck. Then Tom heard Freddie's footsteps running up the stairs. Tom stepped back into the apartment and closed the door. He could go on insisting that he didn't live here, that Dickie was at Otello's, or that he didn't know where Dickie was, but Freddie wouldn't stop now until he found Dickie. Or Freddie would drag him downstairs and ask Signora Buffi who he was.

Freddie knocked on the door. The knob turned. It was locked. Tom picked up a heavy glass ash-tray. He couldn't get his hand across it, and he had to hold it by the edge. He tried to think just for two seconds more: wasn't there another way out? What would he do with the body? He couldn't think. This was the only way out. He opened the door with his left hand. His right hand with the ash-tray was drawn back and down.

Freddie came into the room. 'Listen, would you mind telling –'

The curved edge of the ash-tray hit the middle of his forehead. Freddie looked dazed. Then his knees bent and he went down like a bull hit between the eyes with a hammer. Tom kicked the door shut. He slammed the edge of the ash-tray into the back of Freddie's neck. He hit the neck again and again, terrified that Freddie might be only pretending and that one of his huge arms might suddenly circle his legs and pull him down. Tom struck his head a glancing blow, and blood came. Tom cursed himself. He ran and got a towel from the bathroom and put it under Freddie's head. Then he felt Freddie's wrist for a pulse. There was one, faint, and it seemed to flutter away as he touched it as if the pressure of his own fingers stilled it. In the next second it was gone. Tom listened for any sound behind the door. He imagined Signora Buffi standing behind the door with the hesitant smile she always had when she felt she was interrupting. But there wasn't any sound. There hadn't been any loud sound, he thought, either from the ash-tray or when Freddie fell. Tom looked down at Freddie's mountainous form on the floor and he felt a sudden disgust and a sense of helplessness.

It was only twelve-forty, hours until dark. He wondered if Freddie had people waiting for him anywhere? Maybe in a car downstairs? He searched Freddie's pockets. A wallet. The American passport in the inside breast pocket of the overcoat. Mixed Italian and some other kind of coins. A keycase. There were two car keys on a ring that said FIAT. He searched the wallet for a licence. There it was, with all the particulars: FIAT 1400 nero – convertible – 1955. He could find it if it was in the neighbourhood. He searched every pocket, and the pockets in the buff-coloured vest, for a garage ticket, but he found none. He went to the front window, then nearly smiled because it was so simple: there stood the black convertible across the street almost directly in front of the house. He could not be sure, but he thought there was no one in it.

He suddenly knew what he was going to do. He set about arranging the room, bringing out the gin and vermouth bottles from his liquor cabinet and on second thought the pernod because it smelled so much stronger. He set the bottles on the long table and mixed a martini in a tall glass with a couple of ice cubes in it, drank a little of it so that the glass would be soiled, then poured some of it into another glass, took it over to Freddie and crushed his limp fingers around it and carried it back to the table. He looked at the wound, and found that it had stopped bleeding or was stopping and had not run through the towel on to the floor. He propped Freddie up against the wall, and poured some straight gin from the bottle down his throat. It didn't go down very well, most of it went on to his shirtfront, but Tom didn't think the Italian police would actually make a blood test to see how drunk Freddie had been. Tom let his eyes rest absently on Freddie's limp, messy face for a moment, and his stomach contracted sickeningly and he quickly looked away. He mustn't do that again. His head had begun ringing as if he were going to faint.

That'd be a fine thing, Tom thought as he wobbled across the room towards the window, to faint now! He frowned at the black car down below, and breathed the fresh air in deeply. He wasn't going to faint, he told himself. He knew exactly what he was going to do. At the last minute, the pernod, for both of them. Two other glasses with their fingerprints and pernod. And the ash-trays must be full. Freddie smoked Chesterfields. Then the Appian Way. One of those dark places behind the tombs. There weren't any street lights for long stretches on the Appian Way. Freddie's wallet would be missing. Objective: robbery.

He had hours of time, but he didn't stop until the room was ready, the dozen lighted Chesterfields and the dozen or so Lucky Strikes burnt down and stubbed out in the ash-trays, and a glass of pernod broken and only half cleaned up from the bathroom tiles, and the curious thing was that as he set his scene so carefully, he pictured having hours more time to clean it up – say between nine this evening when the body might be found, and midnight, when the police just might decide he was worth questioning, because somebody just might have known that Freddie Miles was going to call on Dickie Greenleaf today – and he knew that he *would* have it all cleared up by eight o'clock, probably, because according to the story he was going to tell, Freddie would have left his house by seven (as indeed Freddie was going to leave his house by seven), and Dickie Greenleaf was a fairly tidy young man, even with a few drinks in him. But the point of the messy house was that the messiness substantiated merely for his own benefit the story that he was going to tell, and that therefore he had to believe himself.

And he would still leave for Naples and Palma at ten-thirty tomorrow morning, unless for some reason the police detained him. If he saw in the newspaper tomorrow morning that the body had been found, and the police did not try to contact him, it was only decent that he should volunteer to tell them that Freddie Miles had been at his house until late afternoon, Tom thought. But it suddenly occurred to him that a doctor might be able to tell that Freddie had been dead since noon. And he couldn't get Freddie out now, not in broad daylight. No, his only hope was that the body wouldn't be found for so many hours that a doctor couldn't tell exactly how long he had been dead. And he must try to get out of the house without *anybody* seeing him – whether he could carry Freddie down with a fair amount of ease like a passed-out drunk or not – so that if he had to make any statement, he could say that Freddie left the house around four or five in the afternoon.

He dreaded the five- or six-hour wait until nightfall so much that for a few moments he thought he *couldn't* wait. That mountain on the floor! And he hadn't wanted to kill him at all. It had been so unnecessary, Freddie and his stinking, filthy suspicions. Tom was trembling, sitting on the edge of a chair cracking his knuckles. He wanted to go out and take a walk, but he was afraid to leave the body lying there. There had to be noise, of course, if he and Freddie were supposed to be talking and drinking all afternoon. Tom turned the radio on to a station that played dance music. He could have a drink, at least. That was part of the act. He made another couple of martinis with ice in the glass. He didn't even want it, but he drank it.

The gin only intensified the same thoughts he had had. He stood looking down at Freddie's long, heavy body in the polo coat that was crumpled under him, that he hadn't the energy or the heart to straighten out, though it annoyed him, and thinking how sad, stupid, clumsy, dangerous and unnecessary his death had been, and how brutally unfair to Freddie. Of course, one could loathe Freddie, too. A selfish, stupid bastard who had sneered at one of his best friends – Dickie certainly was one of his best friends – just because he suspected him of sexual deviation. Tom laughed at that phrase 'sexual deviation'. Where was the sex? Where was the deviation? He looked at Freddie and said low and bitterly: 'Freddie Miles, you're a victim of your own dirty mind.'

SIXTEEN

He waited after all until nearly eight, because around seven there were always more people coming in and out of the house than at other times. At ten to eight, he strolled downstairs, to make sure that Signora Buffi was not pottering around in the hall and that her door was not open, and to make sure there really was no one in Freddie's car, though he had gone down in the middle of the afternoon to look at the car and see if it was Freddie's. He tossed Freddie's polo coat into the back seat. He came back upstairs, knelt down and pulled Freddie's arm around his neck, set his teeth, and lifted. He staggered, jerking the flaccid weight higher on his shoulder. He had lifted Freddie earlier that afternoon, just to see if he could, and he had seemed barely able to walk two steps in the room with Freddie's pounds pressing his own feet against the floor, and Freddie was exactly as heavy now, but the difference was that he knew he had to get him out now. He let Freddie's feet drag to relieve some of his weight, managed to pull his door shut with his elbow, then began to descend the stairs. Halfway down the first flight, he stopped, hearing someone come out of an apartment on the second floor. He waited until the person had gone down the stairs and out the front door, then recommenced his slow, bumping descent. He had pulled a hat of Dickie's well down over Freddie's head so that the bloodstained hair would not show. On a mixture of gin and pernod, which he had been drinking for the last hour, Tom had gotten himself to a precisely calculated state of intoxication in which he thought he could move with a certain nonchalance and smoothness and at the same time be courageous and even foolhardy enough to take chances without flinching. The first chance, the worst thing that could happen, was that he might simply collapse under Freddie's weight before he got him to the car. He had sworn that he would not stop to rest going down the stairs. He didn't. And nobody else came out of any of the apartments, and nobody came to the front door. During the hours upstairs, Tom had imagined so tortuously everything that might happen – Signora Buffi or her husband coming out of their apartment just as he reached the bottom of the stairs, or himself fainting so that both he and Freddie would be discovered sprawled on the stairs together, or being unable to pick Freddie up again if he had to put him down to rest – imagined it all with such intensity, writhing upstairs in his apartment, that to have descended all the stairs without a single one of his imaginings happening made him feel he was gliding down under a magical protection of some kind, with ease in spite of the mass on his shoulder.

He looked out of the glass of the two front doors. The street looked normal: a man was walking on the opposite sidewalk, but there was always someone walking on one sidewalk or the other. He opened the first door with one hand, kicked it aside and dragged Freddie's body through. Between the doors, he shifted Freddie to the other shoulder, rolling his head under Freddie's body, and for a second a certain pride went through him at his own strength, until the ache in his relaxing arm staggered him with its pain. The arm was too tired even to circle Freddie's body. He set his teeth harder and staggered down the four front steps, banging his hip against the stone newel post.

A man approaching him on the sidewalk slowed his steps as if he were going to stop, but he went on.

If anyone came over, Tom thought, he would blow such a breath of pernod in his face there wouldn't be any reason to ask what was the matter. Damn them, damn them, damn them, he said to himself as he jolted down the kerb. Passers-by, innocent passers-by. Four of them now. But only two of them so much as glanced at him, he thought. He paused a moment for a car to pass. Then with a few quick steps and a heave he thrust Freddie's head and one shoulder through the open window of the car, far enough in that he could brace Freddie's body with his own body while he got his breath. He looked around, under the glow of light from the street lamp across the street, into the shadows in front of his own apartment house.

At that instant the Buffis' youngest son ran out of the door and down the sidewalk without looking in Tom's direction. Then a man crossing the street walked within a yard of the car with only a brief and faintly surprised look at Freddie's bent figure, which did look almost natural now, Tom thought, practically as if Freddie were only leaning into the car talking to someone, only he really *didn't* look quite natural, Tom knew. But that was the advantage of Europe, he thought. Nobody helped anybody, nobody meddled. If this had been America –

'Can I help you?' a voice asked in Italian.

'Ah, no, no, grazie,' Tom replied with drunken good cheer. 'I know where he lives,' he added in mumbled English.

The man nodded, smiling a little, too, and walked on. A tall thin man in a thin overcoat, hatless, with a moustache. Tom hoped he wouldn't remember. Or remember the car.

Tom swung Freddie out on the door, pulled him around the door and on to the car seat, came around the car and pulled Freddie into the seat beside the driver's seat. Then he put on the pair of brown leather gloves he had stuck into his overcoat pocket. He put Freddie's key into the dashboard. The car started obediently. They were off. Down the hill to the Via Veneto, past the American Library, over to the Piazza Venezia, past the balcony on which Mussolini used to stand to make his speeches, past the gargantuan Victor Emmanuel Monument and through the Forum, past the Colosseum, a grand tour of Rome that Freddie could not appreciate at all. It was just as if Freddie were sleeping beside him, as sometimes people did sleep when you wanted to show them scenery.

The Via Appia Antica stretched out before him, grey and ancient in the soft lights of its infrequent lamps. Black fragments of tombs rose up on either side of the road, silhouetted against the still not quite dark sky. There was more darkness than light. And only a single car ahead, coming this way. Not many people chose to take a ride on such a bumpy, gloomy road after dark in the month of January. Except perhaps lovers. The approaching car passed him. Tom began to look around for the right spot. Freddie ought to have a handsome tomb to lie behind, he thought. There was a spot ahead with three or four trees near the edge of the road and doubtless a tomb behind them or part of a tomb. Tom pulled off the road by the trees and shut off his lights. He waited a moment, looking at both ends of the straight, empty road.

Freddie was still as limp as a rubber doll. What was all this about rigor mortis? He dragged the limp body roughly now, scraping the face in the dirt, behind the last tree and behind the little remnant of tomb that was only a four-feet-high, jagged arc of wall, but which was probably a remnant of the tomb of a patrician, Tom thought, and quite enough for this pig. Tom cursed his ugly weight and kicked him suddenly in the chin. He was tired, tired to the point of crying, sick of the sight of Freddie Miles, and the moment when he could turn his back on him for the last time seemed never to come. There was still the Goddamned coat! Tom went back to the car to get it. The ground was hard and dry, he noticed as he walked back, and should not leave any traces of his steps. He flung the coat down beside the body and turned away quickly and walked back to the car on his numb, staggering legs, and turned the car around towards Rome again.

As he drove, he wiped the outside of the car door with his gloved hand to get the fingerprints off, the only place he had touched the car before he put his gloves on, he thought. On the street that curved up to the American Express, opposite the Florida nightclub, he parked the car and got out and left it with the keys in the dashboard. He still had Freddie's wallet in his pocket, though he had transferred the Italian money to his own billfold and had burnt a Swiss twenty-franc note and some Austrian schilling notes in his apartment. Now he took the wallet out of his pocket, and as he passed a sewer grate he leaned down and dropped it in.

There were only two things wrong, he thought as he walked towards his house: robbers would logically have taken the polo coat, because it was a good one, and also the passport, which was still in the overcoat pocket. But not every robber was logical, he thought, maybe especially an Italian robber. And not every murderer was logical, either. His mind drifted back to the conversation with Freddie. '... *an Italian fellow. Just a young kid* ...' Somebody had followed him home at some time, Tom thought, because he hadn't told *anybody* where he lived. It shamed him. Maybe two or three delivery boys might know where he lived, but a delivery boy wouldn't be sitting in a place like the Café Greco. It shamed him and made him shrink inside his overcoat. He imagined a dark, dark, panting young face following him home, staring up to see which window had lighted up after he had gone in. Tom hunched in his overcoat and walked faster as if he were fleeing a sick, passionate pursuer.

SEVENTEEN

Tom went out before eight in the morning to buy the papers. There was nothing. They might not find him for days, Tom thought. Nobody was likely to walk around an unimportant tomb like the one he had put Freddie behind. Tom felt quite confident of his safety, but physically he felt awful. He had a hangover, the terrible, jumpy kind that made him stop halfway in everything he began doing, even stop halfway in brushing his teeth to go and see if his train really left at ten-thirty or at ten forty-five. It left at ten-thirty.

He was completely ready by nine, dressed and with his overcoat and raincoat out on the bed. He had even spoken to Signora Buffi to tell her he would be gone for at least three weeks and possibly longer. Signora Buffi had behaved just as usual, Tom thought, and had not mentioned his American visitor yesterday. Tom tried to think of something to ask her, something quite normal in view of Freddie's questions yesterday, that would show him what Signora Buffi really thought about the questions, but he couldn't think of anything, and decided to let well enough alone. Everything was fine. Tom tried to reason himself out of the hangover, because he had had only the equivalent of three martinis and three pernods at most. He knew it was a matter of mental suggestion, and that he had a hangover because he had intended to pretend that he had been drinking a great deal with Freddie. And now when there was no need of it, he was still pretending, uncontrollably.

The telephone rang, and Tom picked it up and said 'Pronto,' sullenly.

'Signor Greenleaf?' asked the Italian voice.

'Si.'

'Qui parla la stazione polizia numero ottantatre. Lei e un amico di un' americano chi se chiama Fred-derick Meelays?'

'Frederick Miles? Si,' Tom said.

The quick, tense voice stated that the corpse of Fred-derick Mee-lays had been found that morning on the Via Appia Antica, and that Signor Mee-lays had visited him at some time yesterday, was that not so?

'Yes, that is so.'

'At what time exactly?'

'From about noon to – perhaps five or six in the afternoon, I am not quite sure.'

'Would you be kind enough to answer some questions? ... No, it is not necessary that you trouble yourself to come to the station. The interrogator will come to you. Will eleven o'clock this morning be convenient?'

'I'll be very glad to help if I can,' Tom said in a properly excited voice, 'but can't the interrogator come now? It is necessary for me to leave the house at ten o'clock.'

The voice made a little moan and said it was doubtful, but they would try it. If they could not come before ten o'clock, it was very important that he should not leave the house.

'Va bene,' Tom said, acquiescently, and hung up.

Damn them! He'd miss his train *and* his boat now. All he wanted to do was get out, leave Rome and leave his apartment. He started to go over what he would tell the police. It was all so simple, it bored him. It was the absolute truth. They had had drinks, Freddie had told him about Cortina, they had talked a lot, and then Freddie had left, maybe a little high but in a very good mood. No, he didn't know where Freddie had been going. He had supposed Freddie had a date for the evening.

Tom went into the bedroom and put a canvas, which he had begun a few days ago, on the easel. The paint on the palette was still moist because he had kept it under water in a pan in the kitchen. He mixed some more blue and white and began to add to the greyish-blue sky. The picture was still in Dickie's bright reddish-browns and clear whites – the roofs and walls of Rome out of his window. The sky was the only departure, because the winter sky of Rome was so gloomy, even Dickie would have painted it greyish-blue instead of blue, Tom thought. Tom frowned, just as Dickie frowned when he painted.

The telephone rang again. 'God damn it!' Tom muttered, and went to answer it. 'Pronto!'

'Pronto! Fausto!' the voice said. 'Come sta?' And the familiar bubbling, juvenile laugh.

'Oh-h! Fausto! Bene, grazie! Excuse me'; Tom continued in Italian in Dickie's laughing, absent voice. 'I've been trying to paint – trying.' It was calculated to be possibly the voice of Dickie after having lost a friend like Freddie, and also the voice of Dickie on an ordinary morning of absorbing work.

'Can you have lunch?' Fausto asked. 'My train leaves at four-fifteen for Milano.'

Tom groaned, like Dickie. 'I'm just taking off for Naples. Yes, immediately, in twenty minutes!' If he could escape Fausto now, he thought, he needn't let Fausto know that the police had called him at all. The news about Freddie wouldn't be in the papers until noon or later.

'But I'm here! In Roma! Where's your house? I'm at the railroad station!' Fausto said cheerfully, laughing.

'Where'd you get my telephone number?'

'Ah! allora, I called up information. They told me you didn't give the number out, but I told the girl a long story about a lottery you won in Mongibello. I don't know if she believed me, but I made it sound very important. A house and a cow and a well and even a refrigerator! I had to call her back three times, but finally she gave it to me. Allora, Deekie, where are you?'

'That's not the point. I'd have lunch with you if I didn't have this train, but –'

'Va bene, I'll help you carry your bags! Tell me where you are and I'll come over with a taxi for you!'

'The time's too short. Why don't I see you at the railroad station in about half an hour? It's the ten-thirty train for Naples.'

'Okay!'

'How is Marge?'

'Ah – inamorata di te,' Fausto said, laughing. 'Are you going to see her in Naples?'

'I don't think so. I'll see you in a few minutes, Fausto. Got to hurry. Arrividerch.'

''Rividerch, Deekie! Addio!' He hung up.

When Fausto saw the papers this afternoon, he would understand why he hadn't come to the railroad station, otherwise Fausto would just think they had missed each other somehow. But Fausto probably would see the papers by noon, Tom thought, because the Italian papers would play it up big – the murder of an American on the Appian Way. After the interview with the police, he would take another train to Naples – after four o'clock, so Fausto wouldn't be still around the station – and wait in Naples for the next boat to Majorca.

He only hoped that Fausto wouldn't worm the address out of information, too, and decide to come over before four o'clock. He hoped Fausto wouldn't land here just when the police were here.

Tom shoved a couple of suitcases under the bed, and carried the other to a closet and shut the door. He didn't want the police to think he was just about to leave town. But what was he so nervous about? They probably hadn't any clues. Maybe a friend of Freddie's had known that Freddie was going to try to see him yesterday, that was all. Tom picked up a brush and moistened it in the turpentine cup. For the benefit of the police, he wanted to look as if he was not too upset by the news of Freddie's death to do a little painting while he waited for them, though he was dressed to go out, because he had said he intended to go out. He was going to be a friend of Freddie's, but not too close a friend.

Signora Buffi let the police in at ten-thirty. Tom looked down the stairwell and saw them. They did not stop to ask her any questions. Tom went back into his apartment. The spicy smell of turpentine was in the room.

There were two: an older man in the uniform of an officer, and a younger man in an ordinary police uniform. The older man greeted him politely and asked to see his passport. Tom produced it, and the officer looked sharply from Tom to the picture of Dickie, more sharply than anyone had ever looked at it before, and Tom braced himself for a challenge, but there was none. The officer handed him the passport with a little bow and a smile. He was a short, middle-aged man who looked like thousands of other middle-aged Italians, with heavy grey-and-black eyebrows and a short, bushy grey-and-black moustache. He looked neither particularly bright nor stupid.

'How was he killed?' Tom asked.

'He was struck on the head and in the neck by some heavy instrument,' the officer replied, 'and robbed. We think he was drunk. Was he drunk when he left your apartment yesterday afternoon?'

'Well – somewhat. We had both been drinking. We were drinking martinis and pernod.'

The officer wrote it down in his tablet, and also the time that Tom said Freddie had been there, from about twelve until about six.

The younger policeman, handsome and blank of face, was strolling around the apartment with his hands behind him, bending close to the easel with a relaxed air as if he were alone in a museum.

'Do you know where he was going when he left?' the officer asked.

'No, I don't.'

'But you thought he was able to drive?'

'Oh, yes. He was not too drunk to drive or I would have gone with him.'

The officer asked another question that Tom pretended not to quite grasp. The officer asked it a second time, choosing different words, and exchanged a smile with the younger officer. Tom glanced from one to the other of them, a little resentfully. The officer wanted to know what his relationship to Freddie had been.

'A friend,' Tom said. 'Not a very close friend. I had not seen or heard from him in about two months. I was terribly upset to hear about the disaster this morning.' Tom let his anxious expression make up for his rather primitive vocabulary. He thought it did. He thought the questioning was very perfunctory, and that they were going to leave in another minute or so. 'At exactly what time was he killed?' Tom asked.

The officer was still writing. He raised his bushy eyebrows. 'Evidently just after the signor left your house, because the doctors believe that he had been dead at least twelve hours, perhaps longer.'

'At what time was he found?'

'At dawn this morning. By some workmen who were walking along the road.'

'Dio mio!' Tom murmured.

'He said nothing about making an excursion yesterday to the Via Appia when he left your apartment?'

'No,' Tom said.

'What did you do yesterday after Signor Mee-lays left?'

'I stayed here,' Tom said, gesturing with open hands as Dickie would have done, 'and then I had a little sleep, and later I went out for a walk around eight or eight-thirty.' A man who lived in the house, whose name Tom didn't know, had seen him come in last night at about a quarter to nine, and they had said good evening to each other.

'You took a walk alone?'

'Yes.'

'And Signor Mee-lays left here alone? He was not going to meet anybody that you know of?'

'No. He didn't say so.' Tom wondered if Freddie had had friends with him at his hotel, or wherever he had been staying? Tom hoped that the police wouldn't confront him with any of Freddie's friends who might know Dickie. Now his name – Richard Greenleaf – would be in the Italian newspapers, Tom thought, and also his address. He'd have to move. It was hell. He cursed to himself. The police officer saw him, but it looked like a muttered curse against the sad fate that had befallen Freddie, Tom thought.

'So –' the officer said, smiling, and closed his tablet.

'You think it was –' Tom tried to think of the word for hoodlum '– violent boys, don't you? Are there any clues?'

'We are searching the car for fingerprints now. The murderer may have been somebody he picked up to give a ride to. The car was found this morning in the vicinity of the Piazza di Spagna. We should have some clues before tonight. Thank you very much, Signor Greenleaf.'

'Di niente! If I can be of any further assistance –'

The officer turned at the door. 'Shall we be able to reach you here for the next few days, in case there are any more questions?'

Tom hesitated. 'I was planning to leave for Majorca tomorrow.'

'But the questions may be, who is such-and-such a person who is a suspect,' the officer explained. 'You may be able to tell us who the person is in relation to the deceased.' He gestured.

'All right. But I do not think I knew Signor Miles that well. He probably had closer friends in the city.'

'Who?' The officer closed the door and took out his tablet.

'I don't know,' Tom said. 'I only know he must have had several friends here, people who knew him better than I did.'

'I am sorry, but we still must expect you to be in reach for the next couple of days,' he repeated quietly, as if there were no question of Tom's arguing about it, even if he was an American. 'We shall inform you as soon as you may go. I am sorry if you have made travel plans. Perhaps there is still time to cancel them. Good day, Signor Greenleaf.'

'Good day.' Tom stood there after they had closed the door. He could move to a hotel, he thought, if he told the police what hotel it was. He didn't want Freddie's friends or any friends of Dickie's calling on him after they saw his address in the newspapers. He tried to assess his behaviour from the polizia's point of view. They hadn't challenged him on anything. He had not acted horrified at the news of Freddie's death, but that jibed with the fact that he was not an especially close friend of Freddie's either. No, it wasn't bad, except that he had to be on tap.

The telephone rang, and Tom didn't answer it, because he had a feeling that it was Fausto calling from the railroad station. It was eleven-five, and the train for Naples would have departed. When the phone stopped ringing, Tom picked it up and called the Inghilterra. He reserved a room, and said he would be there in about half an hour. Then he called the police station – he remembered that it was number eighty-three – and after nearly ten minutes of difficulties because he couldn't find anyone who knew or cared who Richard Greenleaf was, he succeeded in leaving a message that Signor Richard Greenleaf could be found at the Albergo Inghilterra, in case the police wanted to speak to him.

He was at the Inghilterra before an hour was up. His three suitcases, two of them Dickie's and one his own, depressed him: he had packed them for such a different purpose. And now this!

He went out at noon to buy the papers. Every one of the papers had it: AMERICANO MURDERED ON THE VIA APPIA ANTICA ... SHOCKING MURDER OF RICCISSIMO AMERICANO FREDERICK MILES LAST NIGHT ON THE VIA APPIA ... VIA APPIA MURDER OF AMERICANO WITHOUT CLUES ... Tom read every word. There really were no clues, at least not yet, no tracks, no fingerprints, no suspects. But every paper carried the name Herbert Richard Greenleaf and gave his address as the place where Freddie had last been seen by anybody. Not one of the papers implied that Herbert Richard Greenleaf was under suspicion, however. The papers said that Miles had apparently had a few drinks and the drinks, in typical Italian journalistic style, were all enumerated and ran from americanos through Scotch whisky, brandy, champagne, even grappa. Only gin and pernod were omitted.

Tom stayed in his hotel room over the lunch hour, walking the floor and feeling depressed and trapped. He telephoned the travel office in Rome that had sold him his ticket to Palma, and tried to cancel it. He could have twenty per cent of his money back, they said. There was not another boat to Palma for about five days.

Around two o'clock his telephone rang urgently.

'Hello,' Tom said in Dickie's nervous, irritable tone.

'Hello, Dick. This is Van Houston.'

'Oh-h,' Tom said, as if he knew him, yet the single word conveyed no excess of surprise or warmth.

'How've you been? It's been a long time, hasn't it?' the hoarse, strained voice asked.

'Certainly has. Where are you?'

'At the Hassler. I've been going over Freddie's suitcases with the police. Listen, I want to see you. What was the matter with Freddie yesterday? I tried to find you all last evening, you know, because Freddie was supposed to be back at the hotel by six. I didn't have your address. What happened yesterday?'

'I wish I knew! Freddie left the house around six. We both had taken on quite a lot of martinis, but he looked capable of driving or naturally I wouldn't have let him go off. He said he had his car downstairs. I can't imagine what happened, except that he picked up somebody to give them a lift, and they pulled a gun on him or something.'

'But he wasn't killed by a gun. I agree with you somebody must have forced him to drive out there, or he blotted out, because he'd have to get clear across town to get to the Appian Way. The Hassler's only a few blocks from where you live.'

'Did he ever black out before? At the wheel of a car?'

'Listen, Dickie, can I see you? I'm free now, except that I'm not supposed to leave the hotel today.'

'Neither am I.'

'Oh, come on. Leave a message where you are and come over.'

'I can't, Van. The police are coming over in about an hour and I'm supposed to be here. Why don't you call me later? Maybe I can see you tonight.'

'All right. What time?'

'Call me around six.'

'Right. Keep your chin up, Dickie.'

'You too.'

Tom hung up. Van had sounded as if he were about to cry at the last. 'Pronto?' Tom said, clicking the telephone to get the hotel operator. He left a message that he was not in to anybody except the police, and that they were to let nobody up to see him. Positively no one.

After that the telephone did not ring all afternoon. At about eight, when it was dark, Tom went downstairs to buy the evening papers. He looked around the little lobby and into the hotel bar whose door was off the main hall, looking for anybody who might be Van. He was ready for anything, ready even to see Marge sitting there waiting for him, but he saw no one who looked even like a police agent. He bought the evening papers and sat in a little restaurant a few streets away, reading them. Still no clues. He learned that Van Houston was a close friend of Freddie's, aged twenty-eight, travelling with him from Austria to Rome on a holiday that was to have ended in Florence, where both Miles and Houston had residences, the papers said. They had questioned three Italian youths, two of them eighteen and one sixteen, on suspicion of having done the 'horrible deed', but the youths had been later released. Tom was relieved to read that no fingerprints that could be considered fresh or usable had been found on Miles's 'bellissimo Fiat 1400 convertible'.

Tom ate his costoletta di vitello slowly, sipped his wine, and glanced through every column of the papers for the last-minute items that were sometimes put into Italian papers just before they went to press. He found nothing more on the Miles case. But on the last page of the last newspaper he read:

BARCA AFFONDATA CON MACCHIE DI SANGUE TROVATA
NELL' ACQUA POCO FONDO VICINO SAN REMO

He read it rapidly, with more terror in his heart than he had felt when he had carried Freddie's body down the stairs, or when the police had come to question him. This was like a nemesis, like a nightmare come true, even the wording of the headline. The boat was described in detail and it brought the scene back to him, Dickie sitting in the stern at the throttle, Dickie smiling at him, Dickie's body sinking through the water with its

wake of bubbles. The text said that the stains were believed to be bloodstains, not that they were. It did not say what the police or anybody else
intended to do about them. But the police would do something, Tom
thought. The boatkeeper could probably tell the police the very day the
boat was lost. The police could then check the hotels for that day. The
Italian boatkeeper might even remember that it was two Americans who
had not come back with the boat. If the police bothered to check the hotel
registers around that time, the name Richard Greenleaf would stand out
like a red flag. In which case, of course, it would be Tom Ripley who would
be missing, who might have been murdered that day. Tom's imagination
went in several directions: suppose they searched for Dickie's body and
found it? It would be assumed to be Tom Ripley's now. Dickie would be
suspected of murder. Ergo, Dickie would be suspected of Freddie's murder,
too. Dickie would become overnight 'a murderous type'. On the other
hand, the Italian boatkeeper might not remember the day that one of his
boats had not been brought back. Even if he did remember, the hotels
might not be checked. The Italian police just might not be that interested.
Might, might, *might* not.

Tom folded up his papers, paid his check, and went out.

He asked at the hotel desk if there were any messages for him.

'Si, signor. Questo e questo e questo –' The clerk laid them out on the
desk before him like a card player laying down a winning straight.

Two from Van. One from Robert Gilbertson. (Wasn't there a Robert
Gilbertson in Dickie's address book? Check on that.) One from Marge. Tom
picked it up and read its Italian carefully: Signorina Sherwood had called
at three thirty-five P.M. and would call again. The call was long distance
from Mongibello.

Tom nodded, and picked them up. 'Thanks very much.' He didn't like
the looks of the clerk behind the desk. Italians were so damned curious!

Upstairs he sat hunched forward in an armchair, smoking and thinking.
He was trying to figure out what would logically happen if he did nothing,
and what he could make happen by his own actions. Marge would very
likely come up to Rome. She had evidently called the Rome police to get
his address. If she came up, he would have to see her as Tom, and try to
convince her that Dickie was out for a while, as he had with Freddie. And
if he failed – Tom rubbed his palms together nervously. He mustn't see
Marge, that was all. Not now with the boat affair brewing. Everything
would go haywire if he saw her. It'd be the end of everything! But if he
could only sit tight, nothing at all would happen. It was just this moment,
he thought, just this little crisis with the boat story and the unsolved

Freddie Miles murder, that made things so difficult. But absolutely nothing would happen to him, if he could keep on doing and saying the right things to everybody. Afterwards it could be smooth sailing again. Greece, or India. Ceylon. Some place far, far away, where no old friend could possibly come knocking on his door. What a fool he had been to think he could stay in Rome! Might as well have picked Grand Central Station, or put himself on exhibition in the Louvre!

He called the Stazione Termini, and asked about the trains for Naples tomorrow. There were four or five. He wrote down the times for all of them. It would be five days before a boat left from Naples for Majorca, and he would sit the time out in Naples, he thought. All he needed was a release from the police, and if nothing happened tomorrow he should get it. They couldn't hold a man forever, without even any grounds for suspicion, just in order to throw an occasional question at him! He began to feel he would be released tomorrow, that it was absolutely logical that he should be released.

He picked up the telephone again, and told the clerk that if Miss Marjorie Sherwood called again, he would accept the call. If she called again, he thought, he could convince her in two minutes that everything was all right, that Freddie's murder didn't concern him at all, that he had moved to a hotel just to avoid annoying telephone calls from total strangers and yet still be within reach of the police in case they wanted him to identify any suspects they picked up. He would tell her that he was flying to Greece tomorrow or the next day, so there was no use in her coming to Rome. As a matter of fact, he thought, he could fly to Palma from Rome. He hadn't even thought of that before.

He lay down on the bed, tired, but not ready to undress, because he felt that something else was going to happen tonight. He tried to concentrate on Marge. He imagined her at this moment sitting in Giorgio's, or treating herself to a long, slow Tom Collins in the Miramare bar, and debating whether to call him up again. He could see her troubled eyebrows, her tousled hair as she sat brooding about what might be happening in Rome. She would be alone at the table, not talking to anyone. He saw her getting up and going home, taking a suitcase and catching the noon bus tomorrow. He was there on the road in front of the post office, shouting to her not to go, trying to stop the bus, but it pulled away ...

The scene dissolved in swirling yellow-greyness, the colour of the sand in Mongibello. Tom saw Dickie smiling at him, dressed in the corduroy suit that he had worn in San Remo. The suit was soaking wet, the tie a dripping string. Dickie bent over him, shaking him. 'I swam!' he said. 'Tom, wake up! I'm all right! I swam! I'm alive!' Tom squirmed away from his touch. He heard Dickie laugh at him, Dickie's happy, deep laugh. 'Tom!' The timbre of the voice was deeper, richer, *better* than Tom had even been able to make it in his imitations. Tom pushed himself up. His body felt leaden and slow, as if he were trying to raise himself out of deep water.

'I swam!' Dickie's voice shouted, ringing and ringing in Tom's ears as if he heard it through a long tunnel.

Tom looked around the room, looking for Dickie in the yellow light under the bridge lamp, in the dark corner by the tall wardrobe. Tom felt his own eyes stretched wide, terrified, and though he knew his fear was senseless, he kept looking everywhere for Dickie, below the half-drawn shades at the window, and on the floor on the other side of the bed. He hauled himself up from the bed, staggered across the room, and opened a window. Then the other window. He felt drugged. *Somebody put something in my wine*, he thought suddenly. He knelt below the window, breathing the cold air in, fighting the grogginess as if it were something that was going to overcome him if he didn't exert himself to the utmost. Finally he went into the bathroom and wet his face at the basin. The grogginess was going away. He knew he hadn't been drugged. He had let his imagination run away with him. He had been out of control.

He drew himself up and calmly took off his tie. He moved as Dickie would have done, undressed himself, bathed, put his pyjamas on and lay down in bed. He tried to think about what Dickie would be thinking about. His mother. Her last letter had enclosed a couple of snapshots of herself and Mr Greenleaf sitting in the living-room over coffee, the scene he remembered from the evening he had had coffee with them after dinner. Mrs Greenleaf had said that Herbert had taken the pictures himself by squeezing a bulb. Tom began to compose his next letter to them. They were pleased that he was writing more often. He must set their minds at rest about the Freddie affair, because they knew of Freddie. Mrs Greenleaf had asked about Freddie Miles in one of his letters. But Tom was listening for the telephone while he tried to compose the letter, and he couldn't really concentrate.

EIGHTEEN

The first thing he thought of when he woke up was Marge. He reached for the telephone and asked if she had called during the night. She had not. He had a horrible premonition that she was coming up to Rome. It shot him out of bed, and then as he moved in his routine of shaving and bathing, his feeling changed. Why should he worry so much about Marge? He had always been able to handle her. She couldn't be here before five or six, anyway, because the first bus left Mongibello at noon, and she wasn't likely to take a taxi to Naples.

Maybe he would be able to leave Rome this morning. At ten o'clock he would call the police and find out.

He ordered caffè latte and rolls sent up to his room, and also the morning papers. Very strangely, there was not a thing in any of the papers about either the Miles case or the San Remo boat. It made him feel odd and frightened, with the same fear he had had last night when he had imagined Dickie standing in the room. He threw the newspapers away from him into a chair.

The telephone rang and he jumped for it obediently. It was either Marge or the police. 'Pronto?'

'Pronto. There are two signori of the police downstairs to see you, signor.'

'Very well. Will you tell them to come up?'

A minute later he heard their footsteps in the carpeted hall. It was the same older officer as yesterday, with a different younger policeman.

'Buon' giorno,' said the officer politely, with his little bow.

'Buon' giorno,' Tom said. 'Have you found anything new?'

'No,' said the officer on a questioning note. He took the chair that Tom offered him, and opened his brown leather briefcase. 'Another matter has come up. You are also a friend of the American Thomas Reepley?'

'Yes,' Tom said.

'Do you know where he is?'

'I think he went back to America about a month ago.'

The officer consulted his paper. 'I see. That will have to be confirmed by the United States Immigration Department. You see, we are trying to find Thomas Reepley. We think he may be dead.'

'Dead? Why?'

The officer's lips under his bushy iron-grey moustache compressed softly between each statement so that they seemed to be smiling. The smile had thrown Tom off a little yesterday, too. 'You were with him on a trip to San Remo in November, were you not?'

They had checked the hotels. 'Yes.'

'Where did you last see him? In San Remo?'

'No. I saw him again in Rome.' Tom remembered that Marge knew he had gone back to Rome after Mongibello, because he had said he was going to help Dickie get settled in Rome.

'When did you last see him?'

'I don't know if I can give you the exact date. Something like two months ago, I think. I think I had a postcard from – from Genoa from him, saying that he was going to go back to America.'

'You think?'

'I know I had,' Tom said. 'Why do you think he is dead?'

The officer looked at his form paper dubiously. Tom glanced at the younger policeman, who was leaning against the bureau with his arms folded, staring impersonally at him.

'Did you take a boat ride with Thomas Reepley in San Remo?'

'A boat ride? Where?'

'In a little boat? Around the port?' the officer asked quietly, looking at Tom.

'I think we did. Yes, I remember. Why?'

'Because a little boat has been found sunken with some kind of stains on it that may be blood. It was lost on November twenty-fifth. That is, it was not returned to the dock from which it was rented. November twenty-fifth was the day you were in San Remo with Signor Reepley.' The officer's eyes rested on him without moving.

The very mildness of the look offended Tom. It was dishonest, he felt. But Tom made a tremendous effort to behave in the proper way. He saw himself as if he were standing apart from himself and watching the scene. He corrected even his stance, and made it more relaxed by resting a hand on the end post of the bed. 'But nothing happened to us on that boat ride. There was no accident.'

'Did you bring the boat back?'

'Of course.'

The officer continued to eye him. 'We cannot find Signor Reepley registered in any hotel after November twenty-fifth.'

'Really? – How long have you been looking?'

'Not long enough to search every little village in Italy, but we have checked the hotels in the major cities. We find you registered at the Hassler on November twenty-eighth to thirtieth, and then –'

'Tom didn't stay with me in Rome – Signor Ripley. He went to Mongi-bello around that time and stayed for a couple of days.'

'Where did he stay when he came up to Rome?'

'At some small hotel. I don't remember which it was. I didn't visit him.'

'And where were you?'

'When?'

'On November twenty-sixth and twenty-seventh. That is, just after San Remo.'

'In Forte dei Marmi,' Tom replied. 'I stopped off there on the way down. I stayed at a pension.'

'Which one?'

Tom shook his head. 'I don't recall the name. A very small place.' After all, he thought, through Marge he could prove that Tom was in Mongi-bello, alive, after San Remo, so why should the police investigate what pension Dickie Greenleaf had stayed at on the twenty-sixth and twenty-seventh? Tom sat down on the side of his bed. 'I do not understand yet why you think Tom Ripley is dead.'

'We think *somebody* is dead,' the officer replied, 'in San Remo. Somebody was killed in that boat. That was why the boat was sunk – to hide the bloodstains.'

Tom frowned. 'They are sure they are bloodstains?'

The officer shrugged.

Tom shrugged, too. 'There must have been a couple of hundred people renting boats that day in San Remo.'

'Not so many. About thirty. It's quite true, it could have been any one of the thirty – or any pair of the fifteen,' he added with a smile. 'We don't even know all their names. But we are beginning to think Thomas Reepley is missing.' Now he looked off at a corner of the room, and he might have been thinking of something else, Tom thought, judging from his expression. Or was he enjoying the warmth of the radiator beside his chair?

Tom recrossed his legs impatiently. What was going on in the Italian's head was obvious: Dickie Greenleaf had twice been on the scene of a murder, or near enough. The missing Thomas Ripley had taken a boat ride November twenty-fifth with Dickie Greenleaf. Ergo – Tom straightened up, frowning. 'Are you saying that you do not believe me when I tell you that I saw Tom Ripley in Rome around the first of December?'

'Oh, no, I didn't say that, no indeed!' The officer gestured placatingly. 'I wanted to hear what you would say about your – your travelling with Signor Reepley after San Remo, because we cannot find him.' He smiled again, a broad, conciliatory smile that showed yellowish teeth.

Tom relaxed with an exasperated shrug. Obvious that the Italian police didn't want to accuse an American citizen outright of murder. 'I'm sorry that I can't tell you exactly where he is right now. Why don't you try Paris? Or Genoa? He'd always stay in a small hotel, because he prefers them.'

'Have you got the postcard that he sent you from Genoa?'

'No, I haven't,' Tom said. He ran his fingers through his hair, as Dickie sometimes did when he was irritated. He felt better, concentrating on being Dickie Greenleaf for a few seconds, pacing the floor once or twice.

'Do you know any friends of Thomas Reepley?'

Tom shook his head. 'No, I don't even know him very well, at least not for a very long time. I don't know if he has many friends in Europe. I think he said he knew someone in Faenza. Also in Florence. But I don't remember their names.' If the Italian thought he was protecting Tom's friends from a lot of police questioning by not giving their names, then let him, Tom thought.

'Va bene, we shall inquire,' the officer said. He put his papers away. He had made at least a dozen notations on them.

'Before you go,' Tom said in the same nervous, frank tone, 'I want to ask when I can leave the city. I was planning to go to Sicily. I should like very much to leave today if it is possible. I intend to stay at the Hotel Palma in Palermo. It will be very simple for you to reach me if I am needed.'

'Palermo,' the officer repeated. 'Ebbene, that may be possible. May I use the telephone?'

Tom lighted an Italian cigarette and listened to the officer asking for Capitano Aulicino, and then stating quite impassively that Signor Greenleaf did not know where Signor Reepley was, and that he might have gone back to America, or he might be in Florence or Faenza in the opinion of Signor Greenleaf. 'Faenza,' he repeated carefully, 'vicino Bologna.' When the man had got that, the officer said Signor Greenleaf wished to go to Palermo today. 'Va bene. Benone.' The officer turned to Tom, smiling. 'Yes, you may go to Palermo today.'

'Benone. Grazie.' He walked with the two to the door. 'If you find where Tom Ripley is, I wish you would let me know, too,' he said ingenuously.

'Of course! We shall keep you informed, signor. Buon' giorno!'

Alone, Tom began to whistle as he repacked the few things he had taken from his suitcase. He felt proud of himself for having proposed Sicily instead of Majorca, because Sicily was still Italy and Majorca wasn't, and naturally the Italian police would be more willing to let him leave if he stayed in their territory. He had thought of that when it had occurred to him that Tom Ripley's passport did not show that he had been to France again after the San Remo–Cannes trip. He remembered he had told Marge that Tom Ripley had said he was going up to Paris and from there back to America. If they ever questioned Marge as to whether Tom Ripley was in Mongibello after San Remo, she might also add that he later went to Paris. And if he ever had to become Tom Ripley again, and show his passport to the police, they would see that he hadn't been to France again after the Cannes trip. He would just have to say that he had changed his mind after he told Dickie that, and had decided to stay in Italy. That wasn't important.

Tom straightened up suddenly from a suitcase. Could it all be a trick, really? Were they just letting him have a little more rope in letting him go to Sicily, apparently unsuspected? A sly little bastard, that officer. He'd said his name once. What was it? Ravini? Roverini? Well, what could be the advantage of letting him have a little more rope? He'd told them exactly where he was going. He had no intention of trying to run away from anything. All he wanted was to get out of Rome. He was frantic to get out! He threw the last items into his suitcase and slammed the lid down and locked it.

The phone again! Tom snatched it up. 'Pronto?'

'Oh, Dickie –!' breathlessly.

It was Marge and she was downstairs, he could tell from the sound. Flustered, he said in Tom's voice, 'Who's this?'

'Is this Tom?'

'Marge! Well, hello! Where are you?'

'I'm downstairs. Is Dickie there? Can I come up?'

'You can come up in about five minutes,' Tom said with a laugh. 'I'm not quite dressed yet.' The clerks always sent people to a booth downstairs, he thought. The clerks wouldn't be able to overhear them.

'Is Dickie there?'

'Not at the moment. He went out about half an hour ago, but he'll be back any minute. I know where he is, if you want to find him.'

'Where?'

'At the eighty-third police station. No, excuse me, it's the eighty-seventh.'

'Is he in any trouble?'

'No, just answering questions. He was supposed to be there at ten. Want me to give you the address?' He wished he hadn't started talking in Tom's voice: he could so easily have pretended to be a servant, some friend of Dickie's, anybody, and told her that Dickie was out for hours.

Marge was groaning. 'No-o. I'll wait for him.'

'Here it is!' Tom said as if he had found it. 'Twenty-one Via Perugia. Do you know where that is?' Tom didn't, but he was going to send her in the opposite direction from the American Express, where he wanted to go for his mail before he left town.

'I don't want to go,' Marge said. 'I'll come up and wait with you, if it's all right.'

'Well, it's –' He laughed, his own unmistakable laugh that Marge knew well. 'The thing is, I'm expecting somebody any minute. It's a business interview. About a job. Believe it or not, old believe-it-or-not Ripley's trying to put himself to work.'

'Oh,' said Marge, not in the least interested. 'Well, how is Dickie? Why does he have to talk to the police?'

'Oh, just because he had some drinks with Freddie that day. You saw the papers, didn't you? The papers make it ten times more important than it was for the simple reason that the dopes haven't got any clues at all about anything.'

'How long has Dickie been living here?'

'Here? Oh, just overnight. I've been up north. When I heard about Freddie, I came down to Rome to see him. If it hadn't been for the police, I'd never have found him!'

'You're telling me! I went to the police in desperation! I've been so worried, Tom. He might at least have phoned me – at Giorgio's or some-where –'

'I'm awfully glad you're in town, Marge. Dickie'll be tickled pink to see you. He's been worried about what you might think of all this in the papers.'

'Oh, has he?' Marge said disbelievingly, but she sounded pleased.

'Why don't you wait for me in Angelo's? It's that bar right down the street in front of the hotel going towards the Piazza di Spagna steps. I'll see if I can sneak out and have a drink or a coffee with you in about five minutes, okay?'

'Okay. But there's a bar right here in the hotel.'

'I don't want to be seen by my future boss in a bar.'

'Oh, all right. Angelo's?'

'You can't miss it. On the street straight in front of the hotel. Bye-bye.'

He whirled around to finish his packing. He really was finished except for the coats in the closet. He picked up the telephone and asked for his bill to be prepared, and for somebody to carry his luggage. Then he put his luggage in a neat heap for the bellboys and went down via the stairs.

He wanted to see if Marge was still in the lobby, waiting there for him, or possibly still there making another telephone call. She couldn't have been downstairs waiting when the police were here, Tom thought. About five minutes had passed between the time the police left and Marge called up. He had put on a hat to conceal his blonder hair, a raincoat which was new, and he wore Tom Ripley's shy, slightly frightened expression.

She wasn't in the lobby. Tom paid his bill. The clerk handed him another message: Van Houston had been here. The message was in his own writing, dated ten minutes ago.

Waited for you half an hour. Don't you ever go for a walk? They won't let me up. Call me at the Hassler.

Van

Maybe Van and Marge had run into each other, if they knew each other, and were sitting together in Angelo's now.

'If anybody else asks for me, would you say that I've left the city?' Tom said to the clerk.

'Va bene, signor.'

Tom went out to his waiting taxi. 'Would you stop at the American Express, please?' he asked the driver.

The driver did not take the street that Angelo's was on. Tom relaxed and congratulated himself. He congratulated himself above all on the fact that he had been too nervous to stay in his apartment yesterday and had taken a hotel room. He never could have evaded Marge in his apartment. She had the address from the newspapers. If he had tried the same trick, she would have insisted on coming up and waiting for Dickie in the apartment. Luck was with him!

He had mail at the American Express – three letters, one from Mr Greenleaf.

'How are you today?' asked the young Italian girl who had handed him his mail.

She'd read the papers, too, Tom thought. He smiled back at her naïvely curious face. Her name was Maria. 'Very well, thanks, and you?'

As he turned away, it crossed his mind that he could never use the Rome American Express as an address for Tom Ripley. Two or three of the clerks knew him by sight. He was using the Naples American Express for Tom Ripley's mail now, though he hadn't claimed anything there or written them to forward anything, because he wasn't expecting anything important for Tom Ripley, not even another blast from Mr Greenleaf. When things cooled off a little, he would just walk into the Naples American

Express some day and claim it with Tom Ripley's passport, he thought.

He couldn't use the Rome American Express as Tom Ripley, but he had to keep Tom Ripley with him, his passport and his clothes in order for emergencies like Marge's telephone call this morning. Marge had come damned close to being right in the room with him. As long as the innocence of Dickie Greenleaf was debatable in the opinion of the police, it was suicidal to think of leaving the country as Dickie, because if he had to switch suddenly to Tom Ripley, Ripley's passport would not show that he had left Italy. If he wanted to leave Italy – to take Dickie Greenleaf entirely away from the police – he would have to leave as Tom Ripley, and re-enter later as Tom Ripley and become Dickie again once the police investigations were over. That was a possibility.

It seemed simple and safe. All he had to do was weather the next few days.

NINETEEN

The boat approached Palermo harbour slowly and tentatively, nosing its white prow gently through the floating orange peels, the straw and the pieces of broken fruit crates. It was the way Tom felt, too, approaching Palermo. He had spent two days in Naples, and there had been nothing of any interest in the papers about the Miles case and nothing at all about the San Remo boat, and the police had made no attempt to reach him that he knew of. But maybe they had just not bothered to look for him in Naples, he thought, and were waiting for him in Palermo at the hotel.

There were no police waiting for him on the dock, anyway. Tom looked for them. He bought a couple of newspapers, then took a taxi with his luggage to the Hotel Palma. There were no police in the hotel lobby, either. It was an ornate old lobby with great marble supporting columns and big pots of palms standing around. A clerk told him the number of his reserved room, and handed a bellboy the key. Tom felt so much relieved that he went over to the mail counter and asked boldly if there was any message for Signor Richard Greenleaf. The clerk told him there was not.

Then he began to relax. That meant there was not even a message from

Marge. Marge would undoubtedly have gone to the police by now to find out where Dickie was. Tom had imagined horrible things during the boat trip: Marge beating him to Palermo by plane, Marge leaving a message for him at the Hotel Palma that she would arrive on the next boat. He had even looked for Marge on the boat when he got aboard in Naples.

Now he began to think that perhaps Marge had given Dickie up after this episode. Maybe she'd caught on to the idea that Dickie was running away from her and that he wanted to be with Tom, alone. Maybe that had even penetrated *her* thick skull. Tom debated sending her a letter to that effect as he sat in his deep warm bath that evening, spreading soapsuds luxuriously up and down his arms. Tom Ripley ought to write the letter, he thought. It was about time. He would say that he'd wanted to be tactful all this while, that he hadn't wanted to come right out with it on the telephone in Rome, but that by now he had the feeling she understood, anyway. He and Dickie were very happy together, and that was that. Tom began to giggle merrily, uncontrollably, and squelched himself by slipping all the way under the water, holding his nose.

Dear Marge, he would say, I'm writing this because I don't think Dickie ever will, though I've asked him to many times. You're much too fine a person to be strung along like this for so long ...

He giggled again, then sobered himself by deliberately concentrating on the little problem that he hadn't solved yet: Marge had also probably told the Italian police that she had talked to Tom Ripley at the Inghilterra. The police were going to wonder where the hell he went to. The police might be looking for him in Rome now. The police would certainly look for Tom Ripley around Dickie Greenleaf. It was an added danger – if they were, for instance, to think that he was Tom Ripley now, just from Marge's description of him, and strip him and search him and find both his and Dickie's passports. But what had he said about risks? Risks were what made the whole thing fun. He burst out singing:

> *Papa non vuole, Mama ne meno,*
> *Come faremo far' l'amor'?*

He boomed it out in the bathroom as he dried himself. He sang in Dickie's loud baritone that he had never heard, but he felt sure Dickie would have been pleased with his ringing tone.

He dressed, put on one of his non-wrinkling travelling suits, and strolled out into the Palermo dusk. There across the plaza was the great Norman-influenced cathedral he had read about, built by the English archbishop Walter-of-the-Mill, he remembered from a guidebook. Then there was

Siracusa to the south, scene of a mighty naval battle between the Latins and the Greeks. And Dionysius' Ear. And Taormina. And Etna! It was a big island and brand-new to him. Sicilia! Stronghold of Giuliano! Colonized by the ancient Greeks, invaded by Norman and Saracen! Tomorrow he would commence his tourism properly, but this moment was glorious, he thought as he stopped to stare at the tall, towered cathedral in front of him. Wonderful to look at the dusty arches of its façade and to think of going inside tomorrow, to imagine its musty, sweetish smell, composed of the uncounted candles and incense-burnings of hundreds and hundreds of years. Anticipation! It occurred to him that his anticipation was more pleasant to him than his experiencing. Was it always going to be like that? When he spent evenings alone, handling Dickie's possessions, simply looking at his rings on his own fingers, or his woollen ties, or his black alligator wallet, was that experiencing or anticipation?

Beyond Sicily came Greece. He definitely wanted to see Greece as Dickie Greenleaf with Dickie's money. Dickie's clothes, Dickie's way of behaving with strangers. But would it happen that he couldn't see Greece as Dickie Greenleaf? Would one thing after another come up to thwart him – murder, suspicion, *people*? He hadn't wanted to murder, it had been a necessity. The idea of going to Greece, trudging over the Acropolis as Tom Ripley, American tourist, held no charm for him at all. He would as soon not go. Tears came in his eyes as he stared up at the campanile of the cathedral, and then he turned away and began to walk down a new street.

There was a letter for him the next morning, a fat letter from Marge. Tom squeezed it between his fingers and smiled. It was what he had expected, he felt sure, otherwise it wouldn't have been so fat. He read it at breakfast. He savoured every line of it along with his fresh warm rolls and his cinnamon-flavoured coffee. It was all he could have expected, and more.

... If you really *didn't* know that I had been by your hotel, that only means that Tom didn't tell you, which leaves the same conclusion to be drawn. It's pretty obvious now that you're running out and can't face me. Why don't you admit that you can't live without your little chum! I'm only sorry, old boy, that you didn't have the courage to tell me this before and *outright*. What do you think I am, a small-town hick who doesn't know about such things? *You're* the only one who's acting small-town! At any rate, I hope my telling you what you hadn't the courage to tell me relieves your conscience a little bit and lets you hold your head up. There's nothing like being proud of the person you love, is there! Didn't we once talk about this?

Accomplishment Number Two of my Roman holiday is informing the police that

Tom Ripley is with you. They seemed in a perfect tizzy to find him. (I wonder why? What's he done now?) I also informed the police in my best Italian that you and Tom are inseparable and how they could have found you and still missed *Tom*, I could not imagine.

Changed my boat and I'll be leaving for the States around the end of March, after a short visit to Kate in Munich, after which I presume our paths will never cross again. No hard feelings, Dickie boy. I'd just given you credit for a lot more guts.

Thanks for all the wonderful memories. They're like something in a museum already or something preserved in amber, a little unreal, as you must have felt yourself always to me. Best wishes for the future,

Marge

Ugh! That corn at the end! Ah, Clabber Girl! Tom folded the letter and stuck it into his jacket pocket. He glanced at the two doors of the hotel restaurant, automatically looking for police. If the police thought that Dickie Greenleaf and Tom Ripley were travelling together, they must have checked the Palermo hotels already for Tom Ripley, he thought. But he hadn't noticed any police watching him, or following him. Or maybe they'd given the whole boat scare up, since they were sure Tom Ripley was alive. Why on earth should they go on with it? Maybe the suspicion against Dickie in San Remo and in the Miles murder, too, had already blown over. Maybe.

He went up to his room and began a letter to Mr Greenleaf on Dickie's portable Hermes. He began by explaining the Miles affair very soberly and logically, because Mr Greenleaf would probably be pretty alarmed by now. He said that the police had finished their questioning and that all they conceivably might want now was for him to try to identify any suspects they might find, because the suspect might be a mutual acquaintance of his and Freddie's.

The telephone rang while he was typing. A man's voice said that he was a Tenente Somebody of the Palermo police force.

'We are looking for Thomas Phelps Ripley. Is he with you in your hotel?' he asked courteously.

'No, he is not,' Tom replied.

'Do you know where he is?'

'I think he is in Rome. I saw him just three or four days ago in Rome.'

'He has not been found in Rome. You do not know where he might have been going from Rome?'

'I'm sorry, I haven't the slightest idea,' Tom said.

'Peccato,' sighed the voice, with disappointment. 'Grazie tante, signor.'

'Di niente.' Tom hung up and went back to his letter.

The dull yards of Dickie's prose came out more fluently now than Tom's own letters ever had. He addressed most of the letter to Dickie's mother, told her the state of his wardrobe, which was good, and his health, which was also good, and asked if she had received the enamel triptych he had sent her from an antique store in Rome a couple of weeks ago. While he wrote, he was thinking of what he had to do about Thomas Ripley. The quest was apparently very courteous and lukewarm, but it wouldn't do to take wild chances. He shouldn't have Tom's passport lying right in a pocket of his suitcase, even if it was wrapped up in a lot of old income tax papers of Dickie's so that it wasn't visible to a custom inspector's eyes. He should hide it in the lining of the new antelope suitcase, for instance, where it couldn't be seen even if the suitcase were emptied, yet where he could get at it on a few minutes' notice if he had to. Because some day he might have to. There might come a time when it would be more dangerous to be Dickie Greenleaf than to be Tom Ripley.

Tom spent half the morning on the letter to the Greenleafs. He had a feeling that Mr Greenleaf was getting restless and impatient with Dickie, not in the same way that he had been impatient when Tom had seen him in New York, but in a much more serious way. Mr Greenleaf thought his removal from Mongibello to Rome had been merely an erratic whim, Tom knew. Tom's attempt to make his painting and studying in Rome sound constructive had really been a failure. Mr Greenleaf had dismissed it with a withering remark: something about his being sorry that he was still torturing himself with painting at all, because he should have learned by now that it took more than beautiful scenery or a change of scene to make a painter. Mr Greenleaf had also not been much impressed by the interest Tom had shown in the Burke-Greenleaf folders that Mr Greenleaf had sent him. It was a far cry from what Tom had expected by this time: that he would have Mr Greenleaf eating out of his hand, that he would have made up for all Dickie's negligence and unconcern for his parents in the past, and that he could ask Mr Greenleaf for some extra money and get it. He couldn't possibly ask Mr Greenleaf for money now.

Take care of yourself, moms [he wrote]. Watch out for those colds. [She had said she'd had four colds this winter, and had spent Christmas propped up in bed, wearing the pink woollen shawl he had sent her as one of his Christmas presents.] If you'd been wearing a pair of those wonderful woollen socks you sent me, you never would have caught the colds. I haven't had a cold this winter, which is something to boast about in a European winter . . . Moms, can I send you something from here? I enjoy buying things for you . . .

TWENTY

Five days passed, calm, solitary but very agreeable days in which he rambled about Palermo, stopping here and there to sit for an hour or so in a café or a restaurant and read his guidebooks and the newspapers. He took a carrozza one gloomy day and rode all the way to Monte Pelligrino to visit the fantastic tomb of Santa Rosalia, the patron saint of Palermo, depicted in a famous statue, which Tom had seen pictures of in Rome, in one of those states of frozen ecstasy that are given other names by psychiatrists. Tom found the tomb vastly amusing. He could hardly keep from giggling when he saw the statue: the lush, reclining female body, the groping hands, the dazed eyes, the parted lips. It was all there but the actual sound of the panting. He thought of Marge. He visited a Byzantine palace, the Palermo library with its paintings and old cracked manuscripts in glass cases, and studied the formation of the harbour, which was carefully diagrammed in his guidebook. He made a sketch of a painting by Guido Reni, for no particular purpose, and memorized a long inscription by Tasso on one of the public buildings. He wrote letters to Bob Delancey and to Cleo in New York, a long letter to Cleo describing his travels, his pleasures, and his multifarious acquaintances with the convincing ardour of Marco Polo describing China.

But he was lonely. It was not like the sensation in Paris of being alone yet not alone. He had imagined himself acquiring a bright new circle of friends with whom he would start a new life with new attitudes, standards, and habits that would be far better and clearer than those he had had all his life. Now he realized that it couldn't be. He would have to keep a distance from people, always. He might acquire the different standards and habits, but he could never acquire the circle of friends – not unless he went to Istanbul or Ceylon, and what was the use of acquiring the kind of people he would meet in those places? He was alone, and it was a lonely game he was playing. The friends he might make were most of the danger, of course. If he had to drift about the world entirely alone, so much the better: there was that much less chance that he would be found out. That was one cheerful aspect of it, anyway, and he felt better having thought of it.

He altered his behaviour slightly, to accord with the role of a more detached observer of life. He was still courteous and smiling to everyone, to people who wanted to borrow his newspaper in restaurants and to clerks he spoke to in the hotel, but he carried his head even higher and he spoke a little less when he spoke. There was a faint air of sadness about him now. He enjoyed the change. He imagined that he looked like a young man who had had an unhappy love affair or some kind of emotional disaster, and was trying to recuperate in a civilized way, by visiting some of the more beautiful places on the earth.

That reminded him of Capri. The weather was still bad, but Capri was Italy. That glimpse he had had of Capri with Dickie had only whetted his appetite. Christ, had Dickie been a bore *that* day! Maybe he should hold out until summer, he thought, hold the police off until then. But even more than Greece and the Acropolis, he wanted one happy holiday in Capri, and to hell with culture for a while. He had read about Capri in winter – wind, rain, and solitude. But still Capri! There was Tiberius' Leap and the Blue Grotto, the plaza without people but still the plaza, and not a cobblestone changed. He might even go today. He quickened his steps towards his hotel. The lack of tourists hadn't detracted from the Côte d'Azur. Maybe he could fly to Capri. He had heard of a seaplane service from Naples to Capri. If the seaplane wasn't running in February, he could charter it. What was money for?

'Buon' Giorno! Come sta?' He greeted the clerk behind the desk with a smile.

'A letter for you, signor. Urgentissimo,' the clerk said, smiling, too.

It was from Dickie's bank in Naples. Inside the envelope was another envelope from Dickie's trust company in New York. Tom read the letter from the Naples bank first.

10 Feb. 19—

Most esteemed signor:

It has been called to our attention by the Wendell Trust Company of New York, that there exists a doubt whether your signature of receipt of your remittance of five hundred dollars of January last is actually your own. We hasten to inform you so that we may take the necessary action.

We have already deemed it proper to inform the police, but we await your confirmation of the opinion of our Inspector of Signatures and the Inspector of Signatures of the Wendell Trust Company of New York. Any information you may be able to give us will be most appreciated, and we urge you to communicate with us at your earliest possible convenience.

> Most respectfully and obediently yours,
> Emilio di Braganzi
> Segretario Generale della Banca di Napoli

P.S. In the case that your signature is in fact valid, we urge you despite this to visit our offices in Naples as soon as possible in order to sign your name again for our permanent records. We enclose a letter to you sent in our care from the Wendell Trust Company.

Tom ripped open the trust company's letter.

5 Feb. 19—

Dear Mr Greenleaf:

Our Department of Signatures has reported to us that in its opinion your signature of January on your regular monthly remittance, No. 8747, is invalid.
Believing this may for some reason have escaped your notice, we are hastening to
inform you, so that you may confirm the signing of the said cheque or confirm our
opinion that the said cheque has been forged. We have called this to the attention
of the Bank of Naples also.

Enclosed is a card for our permanent signature file which we request you to sign
and return to us.

Please let us hear from you as soon as possible.

Sincerely,
Edward T. Cavanach
Secretary

Tom wet his lips. He'd write to both banks that he was not missing any
money at all. But would that hold them off for long? He had signed three
remittances, beginning in December. Were they going to go back and
check on all his signatures now? Would an expert be able to tell that all
three signatures were forged?

Tom went upstairs and immediately sat down at the typewriter. He put
a sheet of hotel stationery into the roller and sat there for a moment,
staring at it. They wouldn't rest with this, he thought. If they had a board
of experts looking at the signatures with magnifying glasses and all that,
they probably would be able to tell that the three signatures were forgeries.
But they were such damned good forgeries, Tom knew. He'd signed the
January remittance a little fast, he remembered, but it wasn't a bad job
or he never would have sent it off. He would have told the bank he lost
the remittance and would have had them send him another. Most forgeries took months to be discovered, he thought. Why had they spotted
this one in four weeks? Wasn't it because they were checking on him in
every department of his life, since the Freddie Miles murder and the San
Remo boat story? They wanted to see him personally in the Naples bank.
Maybe some of the men there knew Dickie by sight. A terrible, tingling
panic went over his shoulders and down his legs. For a moment he felt
weak and helpless, too weak to move. He saw himself confronted by a
dozen policemen, Italian and American, asking him where Dickie Greenleaf was, and being unable to produce Dickie Greenleaf or tell them where
he was or prove that he existed. He imagined himself trying to sign H.
Richard Greenleaf under the eyes of a dozen handwriting experts, and

going to pieces suddenly and not being able to write at all. He brought his hands up to the typewriter keys and forced himself to begin. He addressed the letter to the Wendell Trust Company of New York.

12 Feb. 19—

Dear Sirs:

In regard to your letter concerning my January remittance:

I signed the cheque in question myself and received the money in full. If I had missed the cheque, I should of course have informed you at once.

I am enclosing the card with my signature for your permanent record as you requested.

Sincerely,
H. Richard Greenleaf

He signed Dickie's signature several times on the back of the trust company's envelope before he signed his letter and then the card. Then he wrote a similar letter to the Naples bank, and promised to call at the bank within the next few days and sign his name again for their permanent record. He marked both envelopes 'Urgentissimo', went downstairs and bought stamps from the porter and posted them.

Then he went out for a walk. His desire to go to Capri had vanished. It was four-fifteen in the afternoon. He kept walking, aimlessly. Finally, he stopped in front of an antique shop window and stared for several minutes at a gloomy oil painting of two bearded saints descending a dark hill in moonlight. He went into the shop and bought it for the first price the man quoted to him. It was not even framed, and he carried it rolled up under his arm back to his hotel.

TWENTY-ONE

Stazione Polizia
Roma
14 Feb. 19—

Most esteemed Signor Greenleaf:

You are urgently requested to come to Rome to answer some important questions concerning Thomas Ripley. Your presence would be most appreciated and would greatly expedite our investigations.

Failure to present yourself within a week will cause us to take certain measures which will be inconvenient both to us and to you.

Most respectfully yours,
Cap. Enrico Farrara

So they were still looking for Tom. But maybe it meant that something had happened on the Miles case, too, Tom thought. The Italians didn't summon an American in words like these. That last paragraph was a plain threat. And of course they knew about the forged cheque by now.

He stood with the letter in his hand, looking blankly around the room. He caught sight of himself in the mirror, the corners of his mouth turned down, his eyes anxious and scared. He looked as if he were trying to convey the emotions of fear and shock by his posture and his expression, and because the way he looked was involuntary and real, he became suddenly twice as frightened. He folded the letter and pocketed it, then took it out of his pocket and tore it to bits.

He began to pack rapidly, snatching his robe and pyjamas from the bathroom door, throwing his toilet articles into the leather kit with Dickie's initials that Marge had given him for Christmas. He stopped suddenly. He had to get rid of Dickie's belongings, all of them. Here? Now? Should he throw them overboard on the way back to Naples?'

The question didn't answer itself, but he suddenly knew what he had to do, what he was going to do when he got back to Italy. He would not go anywhere near Rome. He could go straight up to Milan or Turin, or maybe somewhere near Venice, and buy a car, secondhand, with a lot of mileage on it. He'd say he'd been roaming around Italy for the last two or three months. He hadn't heard anything about the search for Thomas Ripley. Thomas Reepley.

He went on packing. This was the end of Dickie Greenleaf, he knew. He hated becoming Thomas Ripley again, hated being nobody, hated putting on his old set of habits again, and feeling that people looked down on him and were bored with him unless he put on an act for them like a clown, feeling incompetent and incapable of doing anything with himself except entertaining people for minutes at a time. He hated going back to himself as he would have hated putting on a shabby suit of clothes, a grease-spotted, unpressed suit of clothes that had not been very good even when it was new. His tears fell on Dickie's blue-and-white-striped shirt that lay uppermost in the suitcase, starched and clean and still as new-looking as when he had first taken it out of Dickie's drawer in Mongibello. But it had

Dickie's initials on the pocket in little red letters. As he packed he began to reckon up defiantly the things of Dickie's that he could still keep because they had no initials, or because no one would remember that they were Dickie's and not his own. Except maybe Marge would remember a few, like the new blue leather address book that Dickie had written only a couple of addresses in, and that Marge had very likely given to him. But he wasn't planning to see Marge again.

Tom paid his bill at the Palma, but he had to wait until the next day for a boat to the mainland. He reserved the boat ticket in the name of Greenleaf, thinking that this was the last time he would ever reserve a ticket in the name of Greenleaf, but that maybe it wouldn't be, either. He couldn't give up the idea that it might all blow over. Just might. And for that reason it was senseless to be despondent. It was senseless to be despondent, anyway, even as Tom Ripley. Tom Ripley had never really been despondent, though he had often looked it. Hadn't he learned something from these last months? If you wanted to be cheerful, or melancholic, or wistful, or thoughtful, or courteous, you simply had to *act* those things with every gesture.

A very cheerful thought came to him when he awoke on the last morning in Palermo: he could check all Dickie's clothes at the American Express in Venice under a different name and reclaim them at some future time, if he wanted to or had to, or else never claim them at all. It made him feel much better to know that Dickie's good shirts, his studbox with all the cuff-links and the identification bracelet and his wrist-watch would be safely in storage somewhere, instead of at the bottom of the Tyrrhenian Sea or in some ashcan in Sicily.

So, after scraping the initials off Dickie's two suitcases, he sent them, locked, from Naples to the American Express Company, Venice, together with two canvases he had begun painting in Palermo, in the name of Robert S. Fanshaw, to be stored until called for. The only things, the only revealing things, he kept with him were Dickie's rings, which he put into the bottom of an ugly little brown leather box belonging to Thomas Ripley, that he had somehow kept with him for years everywhere he travelled or moved to, and which was otherwise filled with his own interesting collection of cuff-links, collar pins, odd buttons, a couple of fountain-pen points, and a spool of white thread with a needle stuck in it.

Tom took a train from Naples up through Rome, Florence, Bologna, and Verona, where he got out and went by bus to the town of Trento about forty miles away. He did not want to buy a car in a town as big as Verona, because the police might notice his name when he applied for his licence plates, he thought. In Trento he bought a secondhand cream-coloured Lancia for the equivalent of about eight hundred dollars. He bought it in the name of Thomas Ripley, as his passport read, and took a hotel room in that name to wait for twenty-four hours until his licence plates should be ready. Six hours later nothing had happened. Tom had been afraid that even this small hotel might recognize his name, that the office that took care of the applications for plates might also notice his name, but by noon the next day he had his plates on his car and nothing had happened. Neither was there anything in the papers about the quest for Thomas Ripley, or the Miles case or the San Remo boat affair. It made him feel rather strange, rather safe and happy, and as if perhaps all of it were unreal. He began to feel happy even in his dreary role as Thomas Ripley. He took a pleasure in it, overdoing almost the old Tom Ripley reticence with strangers, the inferiority in every duck of his head and wistful, sidelong glance. After all, would anyone, *anyone*, believe that such a character had ever done a murder? And the only murder he could possibly be suspected of was Dickie's in San Remo, and they didn't seem to be getting very far on that. Being Tom Ripley had one compensation, at least: it relieved his mind of guilt for the stupid, unnecessary murder of Freddie Miles.

He wanted to go straight to Venice, but he thought he should spend one night doing what he intended to tell the police he had been doing for several months: sleeping in his car on a country road. He spent one night in the back seat of the Lancia, cramped and miserable, somewhere in the neighbourhood of Brescia. He crawled into the front seat at dawn with such a painful crick in his neck he could hardly turn his head sufficiently to drive, but that made it authentic, he thought, that would make him tell the story better. He bought a guidebook of Northern Italy, marked it up appropriately with dates, turned down corners of its pages, stepped on its covers and broke its binding so that it fell open at Pisa.

The next night he spent in Venice. In a childish way Tom had avoided Venice simply because he expected to be disappointed in it. He had thought only sentimentalists and American tourists raved over Venice, and that at best it was only a town for honeymooners who enjoyed the inconvenience of not being able to go anywhere except by a gondola moving at two miles an hour. He found Venice much bigger than he had supposed, full of Italians who looked like Italians anywhere else. He found he could walk across the entire city via the narrow streets and bridges without setting foot in a gondola, and that the major canals had a transportation system of motor launches just as fast and efficient as the subway system, and that the canals did not smell bad, either. There was a tremendous choice of hotels, from the Gritti and the Danieli, which he had heard of, down to crummy little hotels and pensions in back alleys so off the beaten track, so removed from the world of police and American tourists, that Tom could imagine living in one of them for months without being noticed by anyone. He chose a hotel called the Costanza, very near the Rialto bridge, which struck the middle between the famous luxury hotels and the obscure little hostelries on the back streets. It was clean, inexpensive, and convenient to points of interest. It was just the hotel for Tom Ripley.

Tom spent a couple of hours pottering around in his room, slowly unpacking his old familiar clothes, and dreaming out of the window at the dusk falling over the Canale Grande. He imagined the conversation he was going to have with the police before long ... Why, I haven't any idea. I saw him in Rome. If you've any doubt of that, you can verify it with Miss Marjorie Sherwood ... Of course I'm Tom Ripley! (He would give a laugh.) I can't understand what all the fuss is about! ... San Remo? Yes, I remember. We brought the boat back after an hour ... Yes, I came back to Rome after Mongibello, but I didn't stay more than a couple of nights. I've been roaming around the north of Italy ... I'm afraid I haven't any idea where he is, but I saw him about three weeks ago ... Tom got up from the windowsill smiling, changed his shirt and tie for the evening, and went out to find a pleasant restaurant for dinner. A good restaurant, he thought. Tom Ripley could treat himself to something expensive for once. His billfold was so full of long ten- and twenty-thousand-lire notes it wouldn't bend. He had cashed a thousand dollars' worth of travellers' cheques in Dickie's name before he left Palermo.

He bought two evening newspapers, tucked them under his arm and walked on, over a little arched bridge, through a long street hardly six feet wide full of leather shops and men's shirt shops, past windows glittering with jewelled boxes that spilled out necklaces and rings like the boxes Tom had always imagined that treasures spilled out of in fairy tales. He liked the fact that Venice had no cars. It made the city human. The streets were like veins, he thought, and the people were the blood, circulating everywhere. He took another street back and crossed the great quadrangle of San Marco's for the second time. Pigeons everywhere, in the air, in the light of shops – even at night, pigeons walking along under people's feet like sightseers themselves in their own home town! The chairs and tables of the cafés spread across the arcade in the plaza itself, so that people and pigeons had to look for little aisles through them to get by. From either end of the plaza blaring phonographs played in disharmony. Tom tried to imagine the place in summer, in sunlight, full of people tossing handfuls of grain up into the air for the pigeons that fluttered down for it. He entered another little lighted tunnel of a street. It was full of restaurants, and he chose a very substantial and respectable-looking place with white table-cloths and brown wooden walls, the kind of restaurant which experience had taught him by now concentrated on food and not the passing tourist. He took a table and opened one of his newspapers.

And there it was, a little item on the second page:

POLICE SEARCH FOR MISSING AMERICAN
Dickie Greenleaf, Friend of the Murdered Freddie Miles,
Missing After Sicilian Holiday

Tom bent close over the paper, giving it his full attention, yet he was conscious of a certain sense of annoyance as he read it, because in a strange way it seemed silly, silly of the police to be so stupid and ineffectual, and silly of the newspaper to waste space printing it. The text stated that H. Richard ('Dickie') Greenleaf, a close friend of the late Frederick Miles, the American murdered three weeks ago in Rome, had disappeared after presumably taking a boat from Palermo to Naples. Both the Sicilian and Roman police had been alerted and were keeping a vigilantissimo watch for him. A final paragraph said that Greenleaf had just been requested by the Rome police to answer questions concerning the disappearance of Thomas Ripley, also a close friend of Greenleaf. Ripley had been missing for about three months, the paper said.

Tom put the paper down, unconsciously feigning so well the astonishment that anybody might feel on reading in a newspaper that he was 'missing', that he didn't notice the waiter trying to hand him the menu until the menu touched his hand. This was the time, he thought, when he ought to go straight to the police and present himself. If they had nothing against him – and what could they have against Tom Ripley? – they wouldn't likely check as to when he had bought the car. The newspaper item was quite a relief to him, because it meant that the police really had not picked up his name at the bureau of automobile registration in Trento.

He ate his meal slowly and with pleasure, ordered an espresso after-wards, and smoked a couple of cigarettes as he thumbed through his guidebook on Northern Italy. By then he had had some different thoughts. For example, why should he have seen an item this small in the news-paper? And it was in only one newspaper. No, he oughtn't to present himself until he had seen two or three such items, or one big one that would logically catch his attention. They probably would come out with a big item before long: when a few days passed and Dickie Greenleaf still had not appeared, they would begin to suspect that he was hiding away because he had killed Freddie Miles and possibly Tom Ripley, too. Marge might have told the police she spoke with Tom Ripley two weeks ago in Rome, but the police hadn't seen him yet. He leafed through the guidebook, letting his eyes run over the colourless prose and statistics while he did some more thinking.

He thought of Marge, who was probably winding up her house in Mongibello now, packing for America. She'd see in the papers about Dickie's being missing, and Marge would blame him, Tom knew. She'd write to Dickie's father and say that Tom Ripley was a vile influence, at very least. Mr Greenleaf might decide to come over.

What a pity he couldn't present himself as Tom Ripley and quiet them down about that, then present himself as Dickie Greenleaf, hale and hearty, and clear up that little mystery, too!

He might play up Tom a little more, he thought. He could stoop a little more, he could be shyer than ever, he could even wear horn-rimmed glasses and hold his mouth in an even sadder, droopier manner to contrast with Dickie's tenseness. Because some of the police he might talk to might be the ones who had seen him as Dickie Greenleaf. What was the name of that one in Rome? Rovassini? Tom decided to rinse his hair again in a stronger solution of henna, so that it would be even darker than his normal hair.

He looked through all the papers a third time for anything about the Miles case. Nothing.

TWENTY-TWO

The next morning there was a long account in the most important newspaper, saying in only a small paragraph that Thomas Ripley was missing, but saying very boldly that Richard Greenleaf was 'exposing himself to suspicion of participation' in the murder of Miles, and that he must be considered as evading the 'problem', unless he represented himself to be cleared of suspicion. The paper also mentioned the forged cheques. It said that the last communication from Richard Greenleaf had been his letter to the Bank of Naples, attesting that no forgeries had been committed against him. But two experts out of three in Naples said that they believed Signor Greenleaf's January and February cheques were forgeries, concurring with the opinion of Signor Greenleaf's American bank, which had sent photostats of his signatures back to Naples. The newspaper ended on a slightly facetious note: 'Can anybody commit a forgery against himself? Or is the wealthy American shielding one of his friends?'

To hell with them, Tom thought. Dickie's own handwriting changed often enough: he had seen it on an insurance policy among Dickie's papers, and he had seen it in Mongibello, right in front of his eyes. Let them drag out everything he had signed in the last three months, and see where it got them! They apparently hadn't noticed that the signature on his letter from Palermo was a forgery, too.

The only thing that really interested him was whether the police had found anything that actually incriminated Dickie in the murder of Freddie Miles. And he could hardly say that that really interested him, personally. He bought *Oggi* and *Epoca* at a news-stand in the corner of San Marco's. They were tabloid-sized weeklies full of photographs, full of anything from murder to flagpole-sitting, anything spectacular that was happening anywhere. There was nothing in them yet about the missing Dickie Greenleaf. Maybe next week, he thought. But they wouldn't have any photographs of him in them, anyway. Marge had taken pictures of Dickie in Mongibello, but she had never taken one of him.

On his ramble around the city that morning he bought some rimmed glasses at a shop that sold toys and gadgets for practical jokers. The lenses were of plain glass. He visited San Marco's cathedral and looked all around inside it without seeing anything, but it was not the fault of the glasses. He was thinking that he had to identify himself, immediately. It would look worse for him, whatever happened, the longer he put it off. When he left the cathedral he inquired of a policeman where the nearest police station was. He asked it sadly. He felt sad. He was not afraid, but he felt that identifying himself as Thomas Phelps Ripley was going to be one of the saddest things he had ever done in his life.

'*You* are Thomas Reepley?' the captain of police asked, with no more interest than if Tom had been a dog that had been lost and was now found. 'May I see your passport?'

Tom handed it to him. 'I don't know what the trouble is, but when I saw in the papers that I am believed missing –' It was all dreary, dreary, just as he had anticipated. Policemen standing around blank-faced, staring at him. 'What happens now?' Tom asked the officer.

'I shall telephone to Rome,' the officer answered calmly, and picked up the telephone on his desk.

There was a few minutes' wait for the Rome line, and then, in an impersonal voice, the officer announced to someone in Rome that the American, Thomas Reepley, was in Venice. More inconsequential exchanges, then the officer said to Tom, 'They would like to see you in Rome. Can you go to Rome today?'

Tom frowned. 'I wasn't planning to go to Rome.'

'I shall tell them,' the officer said mildly, and spoke into the telephone again.

Now he was arranging for the Rome police to come to him. Being an American citizen still commanded certain privileges, Tom supposed.

'At what hotel are you staying?' the officer asked.

'At the Costanza.'

The officer gave this piece of information to Rome. Then he hung up and informed Tom politely that a representative of the Rome police would be in Venice that evening after eight o'clock to speak to him.

'Thank you,' Tom said, and turned his back on the dismal figure of the officer writing on his form sheet. It had been a very boring little scene.

Tom spent the rest of the day in his room, quietly thinking, reading, and making further small alterations in his appearance. He thought it quite possible that they would send the same man who had spoken to him in Rome, Tenente Rovassini or whatever his name was. He made his eyebrows a trifle darker with a lead pencil. He lay around all afternoon in his brown tweed suit, and even pulled a button off the jacket. Dickie had been rather on the neat side, so Tom Ripley was going to be notably sloppy by contrast. He ate no lunch, not that he wanted any, anyway, but he wanted to continue losing the few pounds he had added for the role of Dickie Greenleaf. He would make himself thinner than he had ever been before as Tom Ripley. His weight on his own passport was one hundred and fifty-five. Dickie's was a hundred and sixty-eight, though they were the same height, six feet one and one-half.

At eight-thirty that evening his telephone rang, and the switchboard operator announced that Tenente Roverini was downstairs.

'Would you have him come up, please?' Tom said.

Tom went to the chair that he intended to sit in, and drew it still farther back from the circle of light cast by the standing lamp. The room was arranged to look as if he had been reading and killing time for the last few hours – the standing lamp and a tiny reading lamp were on, the counterpane was not smooth, a couple of books lay open face down, and he had even begun a letter on the writing table, a letter to Aunt Dottie.

The tenente knocked.

Tom opened the door in a languid way. 'Buona sera.'

'Buona sera. Tenente Roverini della Polizia Romana.' The tenente's homely, smiling face did not look the least surprised or suspicious. Behind him came another tall, silent young police officer – not another, Tom realized suddenly, but the one who had been with the tenente when Tom had first met Roverini in the apartment in Rome. The officer sat down in the chair Tom offered him, under the light. 'You are a friend of Signor Richard Greenleaf?' he asked.

'Yes.' Tom sat down in the other chair, an armchair that he could slouch in.

'When did you last see him and where?'

'I saw him briefly in Rome, just before he went to Sicily.'

'And did you hear from him when he was in Sicily?' The tenente was writing it all down in the notebook that he had taken from his brown briefcase.

'No, I didn't hear from him.'

'Ah-hah,' the tenente said. He was spending more time looking at his papers than at Tom. Finally, he looked up with a friendly, interested expression. 'You did not know when you were in Rome that the police wanted to see you?'

'No. I did not know that. I cannot understand why I am said to be missing.' He adjusted his glases, and peered at the man.

'I shall explain later. Signor Greenleaf did not tell you in Rome that the police wanted to speak to you?'

'No.'

'Strange,' he remarked quietly, making another notation. 'Signor Greenleaf knew that we wanted to speak to you. Signor Greenleaf is not very cooperative.' He smiled at Tom.

Tom kept his face serious and attentive.

'Signor Reepley, where have you been since the end of November?'

'I have been travelling. I have been mostly in the north of Italy.' Tom made his Italian clumsy, with a mistake here and there, and with quite a different rhythm from Dickie's Italian.

'Where?' The tenente gripped his pen again.

'Milano, Torino, Faenza – Pisa –'

'We have inquired at the hotels in Milano and Faenza, for example. Did you stay all the time with friends?'

'No, I – slept quite often in my car.' It was obvious that he hadn't a great deal of money, Tom thought, and also that he was the kind of young man who would prefer to rough it with a guidebook and a volume of Silone or

Dante, than to stay in a fancy hotel. 'I am sorry that I did not renew my permisso di soggiorno,' Tom said contritely. 'I did not know that it was such a serious matter.' But he knew that tourists in Italy almost never took the trouble to renew their soggiorno, and stayed for months after stating on entering the country that they intended to be there for only a few weeks.

'*Permesso* di soggiorno,' the tenete said in a tone of gentle, almost paternal correction.

'Grazie.'

'May I see your passport?'

Tom produced it from his inside jacket pocket. The tenente studied the picture closely, while Tom assumed the faintly anxious expression, the firmly parted lips, of the passport photograph. The glasses were missing from the photograph, but his hair was parted in the same manner, and his tie was tied in the same loose, triangular knot. The tenente glanced at the few stamped entries that only partially filled the first two pages of the passport.

You have been in Italy since October second, except for the short trip to France with Signor Greenleaf?'

'Yes.'

The tenente smiled, a pleasant Italian smile now, and leaned forward on his knees. 'Ebbene, this settles one important matter – the mystery of San Remo boat.'

Tom frowned. 'What is that?'

'A boat was found sunken there with some stains that were believed to be bloodstains. Naturally, when you were missing so far as we knew, immediately after San Remo –' He threw his hands out and laughed. 'We thought it might have been advisable to ask Signor Greenleaf what had happened to you. Which we did. The boat was missed the same day that you two were in San Remo!' He laughed again.

Tom pretended not to see the joke. 'But did not Signor Greenleaf tell you that I went to Mongibello after San Remo? I did some –' he groped for a word '– little labours for him.'

'Benone!' Tenente Roverini said, smiling. He loosened his brass-buttoned overcoat comfortably, and rubbed a finger back and forth across the crisp, bushy moustache. 'Did you also know Fred-erick Mee-lays?' he asked.

Tom gave an involuntary sigh, because the boat incident was apparently closed. 'No. I only met him once when he was getting off the bus in Mongibello. I never saw him again.'

'Ah-hah,' said the tenente, taking this in. He was silent a minute, as if he had run out of questions, then he smiled. 'Ah Mongibello! A beautiful village, is it not? My wife comes from Mongibello.'

'Ah, indeed!' Tom said pleasantly.

'Si. My wife and I went there on our honeymoon.'

'A most beautiful village,' Tom said. 'Grazie.' He accepted the Nazionale that the tenente offered him. Tom felt that this was perhaps a polite Italian interlude, a rest between rounds. They were surely going to get into Dickie's private life, the forged cheques and all the rest. Tom said seriously in his plodding Italian, 'I have read in a newspaper that the police think that Signor Greenleaf may be guilty of the murder of Freddie Miles, if he does not present himself. It is true that they think he is guilty?'

'Ah, no, no, no!' the tenente protested. 'But it is imperative that he present himself! Why is he hiding from us?'

'I don't know. As you say – he is not very cooperative,' Tom commented solemnly. 'He was not enough cooperative to tell me in Rome that the police wanted to speak with me. But at the same time – I cannot believe it is possible that he killed Freddie Miles.'

'*But* – you see, a man has said in Rome that he saw two men standing beside the car of Signor Mee-lays across the street from the house of Signor Greenleaf, and that they were both drunk or' – he paused for effect, looking at Tom '– perhaps one man was dead, because the other was holding him up beside the car! Of course, we cannot say that the man who was being supported was Signor Mee-lays or Signor Greenleaf,' he added, 'but if we could find Signor Greenleaf, we could at least ask him if he was so drunk that Signor Mee-lays had to hold him up.' He laughed. 'It is a very serious matter.'

'Yes, I can see that.'

'You have absolutely no idea where Signor Greenleaf might be at this moment?'

'No. Absolutely no.'

The tenente mused. 'Signor Greenleaf and Signor Mee-lays had no quarrel that you know of?'

'No, but –'

'But?'

Tom continued slowly, doing it just right. 'I know that Dickie did not go to a ski party that Freddie Miles had invited him to. I remember that I was surprised that he had not gone. He did not tell me why.'

'I know about the ski party. In Cortina d'Ampezzo. Are you sure there was no woman involved?'

Tom's sense of humour tugged at him, but he pretended to think this one over carefully. 'I do not think so.'

'What about the girl, Marjorie Sherwood?'

'I suppose it is *possible*,' Tom said, 'but I do not think so. I am perhaps not the person to answer questions about Signor Greenleaf's personal life.'

'Signor Greenleaf never talked to you about his affairs of the heart?' the tenente asked with a Latin astonishment.

He could lead them on indefinitely, Tom thought. Marge would back it up, just by the emotional way she would react to questions about Dickie, and the Italian police could never get to the bottom of Signor Greenleaf's emotional involvements. He hadn't been able to himself! 'No,' Tom said. 'I cannot say that Dickie ever talked to me about his most personal life. I know he is very fond of Marjorie.' He added, 'She also knew Freddie Miles.'

'How well did she know him?'

'Well –' Tom acted as if he might say more if he chose.

The tenente leaned forward. 'Since you lived for a time with Signor Greenleaf in Mongibello, you are perhaps in a position to tell us about Signor Greenleaf's attachments in general. They are most important.'

'Why don't you speak to Signorina Sherwood?' Tom suggested.

'We have spoken to her in Rome – before Signor Greenleaf disappeared. I have arranged to speak to her again when she comes to Genoa to embark for America. She is now in Munich.'

Tom waited, silent. The tenente was waiting for him to contribute something more. Tom felt quite comfortable now. It was going just as he had hoped in his most optimistic moments: the police held nothing against him at all, and they suspected him of nothing. Tom felt suddenly innocent and strong, as free of guilt as his old suitcase from which he had carefully scrubbed the *Deponimento* sticker from the Palermo baggage-room. He said in his earnest, careful, Ripley-like way, 'I remember that Marjorie said for a while in Mongibello that she would *not* go to Cortina, and later she changed her mind. But I do not know why. If that could mean anything –'

'But she never went to Cortina.'

'No, but only because Signor Greenleaf did not go, I think. At least, Signorina Sherwood likes him so much that she would not go alone on a holiday after she expected to go on the holiday with him.'

'Do you think they had a quarrel, Signors Mee-lays and Greenleaf, about Signorina Sherwood?'

'I cannot say. It is possible. I know that Signor Miles was very fond of her, too.'

'Ah-hah.' The tenente frowned, trying to figure all that out. He glanced up at the younger policeman, who was evidently listening, though, from his immobile face, he had nothing to contribute.

What he had said gave a picture of Dickie as a sulking lover, Tom thought, unwilling to let Marge go to Cortina to have some fun, because she liked Freddie Miles too much. The idea of anybody, Marge especially, liking that wall-eyed ox in preference to Dickie made Tom smile. He turned the smile into an expression of non-comprehension. 'Do you actually think Dickie is running away from something, or do you think it is an accident that you cannot find him?'

'Oh, no. This is too much. First, the matter of the cheques. You perhaps know about that from the newspapers.'

'I do not completely understand about the cheques.'

The officer explained. He knew the dates of the cheques and the number of people who believed they were forged. He explained that Signor Greenleaf had denied the forgeries. 'But when the bank wishes to see him again about a forgery against himself, and also the police in Rome wish to see him again about the murder of his friend, and he suddenly vanishes –' The tenente threw out his hands. 'That can only mean that he is running away from us.'

'You don't think someone may have murdered *him*?' Tom said softly.

The officer shrugged, holding his shoulders up under his ears for at least a quarter of a minute. 'I do not think so. The facts are not like that. Not quite. Ebbene – we have checked by radio every boat of any size with passengers which has left from Italy. He has either taken a small boat, and it must have been as small as a fishing boat, or else he is hiding in Italy. Or of course, anywhere else in Europe, because we do not ordinarily take the names of people leaving our country, and Signor Greenleaf had several days in which to leave. In any case, he is hiding. In any case, he acts guilty. *Something* is the matter.'

Tom stared gravely at the man.

'Did you ever *see* Signor Greenleaf sign any of those remittances? In particular, the remittances of January and February?'

'I saw him sign one of them,' Tom said. 'But I am afraid it was in December. I was not with him in January and February. – Do you seriously suspect that he might have killed Signor Miles?' Tom asked again, in-credulously.

'He has no actual alibi,' the officer replied. 'He says he was taking a walk after Signor Mee-lays departed, but nobody saw him taking the walk.' He pointed a finger at Tom suddenly. '*And* – we have learned from the friend

of Signor Mee-lays, Signor Van Houston, that Signor Mee-lays had a
difficult time finding Signor Greenleaf in Rome – as if Signor Greenleaf
were trying to hide from him. Signor Greenleaf might have been angry
with Signor Mee-lays, though, according to Signor Van Houston, Signor
Mee-lays was not at all angry with Signor Greenleaf!'

'I see,' Tom said.

'Ecco,' the tenente said conclusively. He was staring at Tom's hands.

Or at least Tom imagined that he was staring at his hands. Tom had
his own ring on again, but did the tenente possibly notice some resemblance? Tom boldly thrust this hand forward to the ashtray and put out
his cigarette.

'Ebbene,' the tenente said, standing up. 'Thank you so much for your
help, Signor Reepley. You are one of the very few people from whom we
can find out about Signor Greenleaf's personal life. In Mongibello, the
people he knew are extremely quiet. An Italian trait, alas! You know,
afraid of the police.' He chuckled. 'I hope we can reach you more easily
the next time we have questions to ask you. Stay in the cities a little more
and in the country a little less. Unless, of course, you are addicted to our
countryside.'

'I am!' Tom said heartily. 'In my opinion, Italy is the most beautiful
country of Europe. But if you like, I shall keep in touch with you in Rome
so you will always know where I am. I am as much interested as you in
finding my friend.' He said it as if his innocent mind had already forgotten
the possibility that Dickie could be a murderer.

The tenente handed him a card with his name and the address of his
headquarters in Rome. He bowed. 'Grazie tante, Signor Reepley. Buona
sera!'

'Buona sera,' Tom said.

The younger policeman saluted him as he went out, and Tom gave him
a nod and closed the door.

He could have flown – like a bird, out of the window, with spread arms!
The idiots! All around the thing and never guessing it! Never guessing that
Dickie was running from the forgery questions because he wasn't Dickie
Greenleaf in the first place! The one thing they were bright about was that
Dickie Greenleaf might have killed Freddie Miles. But Dickie Greenleaf was
dead, dead, deader than a doornail and he, Tom Ripley, was safe! He picked
up the telephone.

'Would you give me the Grand Hotel, please,' he said in Tom Ripley's
Italian. 'Il ristorante, per piacere. – Would you reserve a table for one for
nine-thirty? Thank you. The name is Ripley. R-i-p-l-e-y.'

Tonight he was going to have a dinner. And look out at the moonlight on the Grand Canal. And watch the gondolas drifting as lazily as they ever drifted for any honeymooner, with the gondoliers and their oars silhouetted against the moonlit water. He was suddenly ravenous. He was going to have something luscious and expensive to eat – whatever the Grand Hotel's speciality was, breast of pheasant or petto di pollo, and perhaps cannelloni to begin with, creamy sauce over delicate pasta, and a good valpolicella to sip while he dreamed about his future and planned where he went from here.

He had a bright idea while he was changing his clothes: he ought to have an envelope in his possession, on which should be written that it was not to be opened for several months to come. Inside it should be a will signed by Dickie, bequeathing him his money and his income. Now that was an idea.

TWENTY-THREE

Venice
28 Feb. 19—

Dear Mr Greenleaf:

I thought under the circumstances you would not take it amiss if I wrote you whatever personal information I have in regard to Richard – I being one of the last people, it seems, who saw him.

I saw him in Rome around 2 February at the Inghilterra Hotel. As you know, this was only two or three days after the death of Freddie Miles. I found Dickie upset and nervous. He said he was going to Palermo as soon as the police finished their questioning him in regard to Freddie's death, and he seemed eager to get away, which was understandable, but I wanted to tell you that there was a certain depression underlying all this that troubled me much more than his obvious nervousness. I had the feeling he would try to do something violent – perhaps to himself. I knew also that he didn't want to see his friend Marjorie Sherwood again, and he said he would try to avoid her if she came up from Mongibello to see him because of the Miles affair. I tried to persuade him to see her. I don't know if he did. Marge has a soothing effect on people, as perhaps you know.

What I am trying to say is that I feel Richard may have killed himself. At the time of writing he has not been found. I certainly hope he will be before this reaches you. It goes without saying that I am sure Richard had nothing to do, directly or indirectly, with Freddie's death, but I think the shock of it and the questioning that followed did do something to upset his equilibrium. This is a depressing message to send to you and I regret it. It may be all completely unnecessary and Dickie may be (again understandably, according to his temperament) simply in hiding until these unpleasantnesses blow over. But as the time goes on, I begin to feel more uneasy myself. I thought it my duty to write you this, simply by way of letting you know ...

Munich
3 March, 19—

Dear Tom:

Thanks for your letter. It was very kind of you. I've answered the police in writing, and one came up to see me. I won't be coming by Venice, but thanks for your invitation. I am going to Rome day after tomorrow to meet Dickie's father, who is flying over. Yes, I agree with you that it was a good idea for you to write to him.

I am so bowled over by all this, I have come down with something resembling undulant fever, or maybe what the Germans call Foehn, but with some kind of virus thrown in. Literally unable to get out of bed for four days, otherwise I'd have gone to Rome before now. So please excuse this disjointed and probably feeble-minded letter which is such a bad answer to your very nice one. But I did want to say I don't agree with you at all that Dickie might have committed suicide. He just isn't the type, though I know all you're going to say about people never acting like they're going to do it, etc. No, anything else but this for Dickie. He might have been murdered in some back alley of Naples – or even Rome, because who knows whether he got up to Rome or not after he left Sicily? I can also imagine him running out on obligations to such an extent that he'd be *hiding* now. I think that's what he's doing.

I'm glad you think the forgeries are a mistake. Of the bank, I mean. So do I. Dickie has changed so much since November, it could easily have changed his hand-writing, too. Let's hope something's happened by the time you get this. Had a wire from Mr Greenleaf about Rome – so must save all my energy for that.

Nice to know your address finally. Thanks again for your letter, your advice, and invitations.

Best,
Marge

P.S. I didn't tell you my *good* news. I've got a publisher interested in 'Mongibello'! Says he wants to see the whole thing before he can give a contract, but it really sounds hopeful! Now if I can only finish the damn thing!

M.

She had decided to be on good terms with him, Tom supposed. She'd probably changed her tune about him to the police, too.

Dickie's disappearance was stirring up a great deal of excitement in the Italian press. Marge, or somebody, had provided the reporters with photographs. There were pictures in *Epoca* of Dickie sailing his boat in Mongibello, pictures of Dickie in *Oggi* sitting on the beach in Mongibello and also on Giorgio's terrace, and a picture of Dickie and Marge – 'girl friend of both il sparito Dickie and il assassinato Freddie' – smiling, with their arms around each other's shoulders, and there was even a businesslike portrait of Herbert Greenleaf, Sr. Tom had gotten Marge's Munich address right out of a newspaper. *Oggi* had been running a life story of Dickie for the past two weeks, describing his school years as 'rebellious' and embroidering his social life in America and his flight to Europe for the sake of his art to such an extent that he emerged as a combination of Errol Flynn and Paul Gauguin. The illustrated weeklies always gave the latest police reports, which were practically nil, padded with whatever theorizing the writers happened to feel like concocting that week. A favourite theory was that he had run off with another girl – a girl who might have been signing his remittances – and was having a good time, incognito, in Tahiti or South America or Mexico. The police were still combing Rome and Naples and Paris, that was all. No clues as to Freddie Miles's killer, and nothing about Dickie Greenleaf's having been seen carrying Freddie Miles, or vice versa, in front of Dickie's house. Tom wondered why they were holding that back from the newspapers. Probably because they couldn't write it up without subjecting themselves to charges of libel by Dickie. Tom was gratified to find himself described as 'a loyal friend' of the missing Dickie Greenleaf, who had volunteered everything he knew as to Dickie's character and habits, and who was as bewildered by his disappearance as anybody else. 'Signor Ripley, one of the young well-to-do American visitors in Italy,' said *Oggi*, 'now lives in a palazzo overlooking San Marco in Venice.' That pleased Tom most of all. He cut out the write-up.

Tom had not thought of it as a 'palace' before, but of course it was what the Italians called a palazzo – a two-storey house of formal design more than two hundred years old, with a main entrance on the Grand Canal approachable only by gondola, with broad stone steps descending into the water, and iron doors that had to be opened by an eight-inch-long key, besides the regular doors behind the iron doors which also took an enormous key. Tom used the less formal 'back door' usually, which was on the Viale San Spiridione, except when he wanted to impress his guests by bringing them to his home in a gondola. The back door – itself fourteen feet high like the stone wall that enclosed the house from the street – led into a garden that was somewhat neglected but still green, and which boasted two gnarled olive trees and a birdbath made of an ancient-looking statue of a naked boy holding a wide shallow bowl. It was just the garden for a Venetian palace, slightly run down, in need of some restoration which it was not going to get, but indelibly beautiful because it had sprung into the world so beautiful more than two hundred years ago. The inside of the house was Tom's ideal of what a civilized bachelor's home should look like, in Venice, at least: a checkerboard black-and-white marble floor downstairs extending from the formal foyer into each room, pink-and-white marble floor upstairs, furniture that did not resemble furniture at all but an embodiment of cinquecento music played on hautboys, recorders, and violas da gamba. He had his servants – Anna and Ugo, a young Italian couple who had worked for an American in Venice before, so that they knew the difference between a Bloody Mary and a crème de menthe frappé – polish the carved fronts of the armoires and chests and chairs until they seemed alive with dim lustrous lights that moved as one moved around them. The only thing faintly modern was the bathroom. In Tom's bedroom stood a gargantuan bed, broader than it was long. Tom decorated his bedroom with a series of panoramic pictures of Naples from 1540 to about 1880, which he found at an antique store. He had given his undivided attention to decorating his house for more than a week. There was a sureness in his taste now that he had not felt in Rome, and that his Rome apartment had not hinted at. He felt surer of himself now in every way.

His self-confidence had even inspired him to write to Aunt Dottie in a calm, affectionate and forbearing tone that he had never wanted to use before, or had never before been able to use. He had inquired about her flamboyant health, about her little circle of vicious friends in Boston, and had explained to her why he liked Europe and intended to live here for a while, explained so eloquently that he had copied that section of his letter and put it into his desk. He had written this inspired letter one morning after breakfast, sitting in his bedroom in a new silk dressing-gown made to order for him in Venice, gazing out of the window now and then at the Grand Canal and the Clock Tower of the Piazza San Marco across the water. After he had finished the letter he had made some more coffee and on Dickie's own Hermes he had written Dickie's will, bequeathing him his income and the money he had in various banks, and had signed it Herbert Richard Greenleaf, Jr. Tom thought it better not to add a witness, lest the banks or Mr Greenleaf challenge him to the extent of demanding to know who the witness was, though Tom had thought of making up an Italian name, presumably someone Dickie might have called into his apartment in Rome for the purpose of witnessing the will. He would just have to take his chances on an unwitnessed will, he thought, but Dickie's typewriter was so in need of repair that its quirks were as recognizable as a particular handwriting, and he had heard that holograph wills required no witness. But the signature was perfect, exactly like the slim, tangled signature on Dickie's passport. Tom practised for half an hour before he signed the will, relaxed his hands, then signed a piece of scrap paper, then the will, in rapid succession. And he would defy anybody to prove that the signature on the will wasn't Dickie's. Tom put an envelope into the typewriter and addressed it To Whom It May Concern, with a notation that it was not to be opened until June of this year. He tucked it into a side pocket of his suitcase, as if he had been carrying it there for some time and hadn't bothered unpacking it when he moved into the house. Then he took the Hermes Baby in its case downstairs and dropped it into the little inlet of the canal, too narrow for a boat, which ran from the front corner of his house to the garden wall. He was glad to be rid of the typewriter, though he had been unwilling to part with it until now. He must have known, subconsciously, he thought, that he was going to write the will or something else of great importance on it, and that was the reason why he had kept it.

Tom followed the Italian newspapers and the Paris edition of the *Herald-Tribune* on the Greenleaf and Miles cases with the anxious concern befitting a friend of both Dickie and Freddie. The papers were suggesting by the end of March that Dickie might be dead, murdered by the same man or men who had been profiting by forging his signature. A Rome paper said that one man in Naples now held that the signature on the letter from Palermo, stating that no forgeries had been committed against him, was also a forgery. Others, however, did not concur. Some man on the police force, not Roverini, thought that the culprit or culprits had been 'intimo' with Greenleaf, that they had had access to the bank's letter and had had the audacity to reply to it themselves. 'The mystery is,' the officer was quoted, 'not only who the forger was but how he gained access to the letter, because the porter of the hotel remembers putting the registered bank letter into Greenleaf's hands. The hotel porter also recalls that Greenleaf was always alone in Palermo . . .'

More hitting around the answer without ever hitting it. But Tom was shaken for several minutes after he read it. There remained only one more step for them to take, and wasn't somebody going to take it today or tomorrow or the next day? Or did they really already know the answer, and were they just trying to put him off guard – Tenente Roverini sending him personal messages every few days to keep him abreast of what was happening in the search for Dickie – and were they going to pounce on him one day soon with every bit of evidence they needed?

It gave Tom the feeling that he was being followed, especially when he walked through the long, narrow street to his house door. The Viale San Spiridione was nothing but a functional slit between vertical walls of houses, without a shop in it and with hardly enough light for him to see where he was going, nothing but unbroken housefronts and the tall, firmly locked doors of the Italian house gates that were flush with the walls. Nowhere to run to if he were attacked, no house door to duck into. Tom did not know who would attack him, if he were attacked. He did not imagine police, necessarily. He was afraid of nameless, formless things that haunted his brain like the Furies. He could go through San Spiridione comfortably only when a few cocktails had knocked out his fear. Then he walked through swaggering and whistling.

He had his pick of cocktail parties, though in his first two weeks in his house he went to only two. He had his choice of people because of a little incident that had happened the first day he had started looking for a house. A rental agent, armed with three huge keys, had taken him to see a certain house in San Stefano parish, thinking it would be vacant. It had not only been occupied but a cocktail party had been in progress, and the hostess had insisted on Tom and the rental agent, too, having a cocktail by way of making amends for their inconvenience and her remissness. She had put the house up for rent a month ago, had changed her mind about leaving, and had neglected to inform the rental agency. Tom stayed for a drink, acted his reserved, courteous self, and met all her guests, who he supposed were most of the winter colony of Venice and rather hungry for new blood, judging from the way they welcomed him and offered their assistance in finding a house. They recognized his name, of course, and the fact that he knew Dickie Greenleaf raised his social value to a degree that surprised even Tom. Obviously they were going to invite him everywhere and quiz him and drain him of every last little detail to add some spice to their dull lives. Tom behaved in a reserved but friendly manner appropriate for a young man in his position – a sensitive young man, unused to garish publicity, whose primary emotion in regard to Dickie was anxiety as to what had happened to him.

He left that first party with the addresses of three other houses he might look at (one being the one he took) and invitations to two other parties. He went to the party whose hostess had a title, the Condessa Roberta (Titi) della Latta-Cacciaguerra. He was not at all in the mood for parties. He seemed to see people through a mist, and communication was slow and difficult. He often asked people to repeat what they had said. He was terribly bored. But he could use them, he thought, to practise on. The naïve questions they asked him ('Did Dickie drink a lot?' and 'But he *was* in love with Marge, wasn't he?' and 'Where do you *really* think he went?') were good practice for the more specific questions Mr Greenleaf was going to ask him when he saw him, if he ever saw him. Tom began to be uneasy about ten days after Marge's letter, because Mr Greenleaf had not written or telephoned him from Rome. In certain frightened moments, Tom imagined that the police had told Mr Greenleaf that they were playing a game with Tom Ripley, and had asked Mr Greenleaf not to talk to him.

Each day he looked eagerly in his mailbox for a letter from Marge or Mr Greenleaf. His house was ready for their arrival. His answers to their questions were ready in his head. It was like waiting interminably for a show to begin, for a curtain to rise. Or maybe Mr Greenleaf was so resentful of him (not to mention possibly being actually suspicious) that he was going to ignore him entirely. Maybe Marge was abetting him in that. At any rate, he couldn't take a trip until *something* happened. Tom wanted to take a trip, the famous trip to Greece. He had bought a guidebook of Greece, and he had already planned his itinerary over the islands.

Then, on the morning of April fourth, he got a telephone call from Marge. She was in Venice, at the railroad station.

'I'll come and pick you up!' Tom said cheerfully. 'Is Mr Greenleaf with you?'

'No, he's in Rome. I'm alone. You don't have to pick me up. I've only got an overnight bag.'

'Nonsense!' Tom said, dying to do something. 'You'll never find the house by yourself.'

'Yes, I will. It's next to della Salute, isn't it? I take the motoscafo to San Marco's, then take a gondola across.'

She knew, all right. 'Well, if you insist.' He had just thought that he had better take one more good look around the house before she got there. 'Have you had lunch?'

'No.'

'Good! We'll lunch together somewhere. Watch your step on the motoscafo!'

They hung up. He walked soberly and slowly through the house, into both large rooms upstairs, down the stairs and through his living-room. Nothing, anywhere, that belonged to Dickie. He hoped the house didn't look too plush. He took a silver cigarette box, which he had bought only two days ago and had had initialled, from the living-room table and put it in the bottom drawer of a chest in the dining-room.

Anna was in the kitchen, preparing lunch.

'Anna, there'll be one more for lunch,' Tom said. 'A young lady.'

Anna's face broke into a smile at the prospect of a guest. 'A young American lady?'

'Yes. An old friend. When the lunch is ready, you and Ugo can have the rest of the afternoon off. We can serve ourselves.'

'Va bene,' Anna said.

Anna and Ugo came at ten and stayed until two, ordinarily. Tom didn't want them here when he talked with Marge. They understood a little English, not enough to follow a conversation perfectly, but he knew both of them would have their ears out if he and Marge talked about Dickie, and it irritated him.

Tom made a batch of martinis, and arranged the glasses and a plate of canapés on a tray in the living-room. When he heard the door knocker, he went to the door and swung it open.

'Marge! Good to see you! Come in!' He took the suitcase from her hand.

'How are you, Tom? My! – Is all this yours?' She looked around her, and up at the high coffered ceiling.

'I rented it. For a song,' Tom said modestly. 'Come and have a drink. Tell me what's new. You've been talking to the police in Rome?' He carried her topcoat and her transparent raincoat to a chair.

'Yes, and to Mr Greenleaf. He's very upset – naturally.' She sat down on the sofa.

Tom settled himself in a chair opposite her. 'Have they found anything new? One of the police officers there has been keeping me posted, but he hasn't told me anything that really matters.'

'Well, they found out that Dickie cashed over a thousand dollars' worth of traveller's cheques before he left Palermo. *Just* before. So he must have gone off somewhere with it, like Greece or Africa. He couldn't have gone off to kill himself after just cashing a thousand dollars, anyway.'

'No,' Tom agreed. 'Well, that sounds hopeful. I didn't see that in the papers.'

'I don't think they put it in.'

'No. Just a lot of nonsense about what Dickie used to eat for breakfast in Mongibello,' Tom said as he poured the martinis.

'Isn't it awful! It's getting a little better now, but when Mr Greenleaf arrived, the papers were at their worst. Oh, thanks!' She accepted the martini gratefully.

'How is he?'

Marge shook her head. 'I feel so sorry for him. He keeps saying the

American police could do a better job and all that, and he doesn't know any Italian, so that makes it twice as bad.'

'What's he doing in Rome?'

'Waiting. What can any of us do? I've postponed my boat again. Mr Greenleaf and I went to Mongibello and I questioned everyone there, mostly for Mr Greenleaf's benefit, of course, but they can't tell us anything. Dickie hasn't been back there since November.'

'No.' Tom sipped his martini thoughtfully. Marge was optimistic, he could see that. Even now she had that energetic buoyancy that made Tom think of the typical Girl Scout, that look of taking up a lot of space, of possibly knocking something over with a wild movement, of rugged health and vague untidiness. She irritated him intensely suddenly, but he put on a big act, got up and patted her on the shoulder, and gave her an affectionate peck on the cheek. 'Maybe he's sitting in Tangier or somewhere living the life of Riley and waiting for all this to blow over.'

'Well, it's damned inconsiderate of him if he is!' Marge said, laughing. 'I certainly didn't mean to alarm anybody when I said what I did about his depression. I felt it was a kind of duty to tell you and Mr Greenleaf.'

'I understand. No, I think you were right to tell us. I just don't think it's true.' She smiled her broad smile, her eyes glowing with an optimism that struck Tom as completely insane.

He began asking her sensible, practical questions about the opinions of the Rome police, about the leads that they had (they had none worth mentioning), and what she had heard on the Miles case. There was nothing new on the Miles case, either, but Marge did know about Freddie and Dickie's having been seen in front of Dickie's house around eight o'clock that night. She thought the story was exaggerated.

Maybe Freddie was drunk, or maybe Dickie just had an arm around him. How could anybody tell in the dark? Don't tell me Dickie murdered him!'

'Have they any concrete clues at all that would make them think Dickie killed him?'

'Of course not!'

'Then why don't the so-and-so's get down to the business of finding out who really did kill him? And also where Dickie is?'

'Ecco!' Marge said emphatically. 'Anyway, the police are sure now that Dickie at least got from Palermo to Naples. A steward remembers carrying his bags from his cabin to the Naples dock.'

'Really,' Tom said. He remembered the steward, too, a clumsy little oaf who had dropped his canvas suitcase, trying to carry it under one arm.

'Wasn't Freddie killed hours after he left Dickie's house?' Tom asked suddenly.

'No. The doctors can't say exactly. And it seems Dickie didn't have an alibi, of course, because he was undoubtedly alone. Just more of Dickie's bad luck.'

'They don't actually *believe* Dickie killed him, do they?'

'They don't say it, no. It's just in the air. Naturally, they can't make rash statements right and left about an American citizen, but as long as they haven't any suspects and Dickie's disappeared – Then also his landlady in Rome said that Freddie came down to ask her who was living in Dickie's apartment or something like that. She said Freddie looked angry, as if they'd been quarrelling. She said he asked if Dickie was living alone.'

Tom frowned. 'I wonder why?'

'I can't imagine. Freddie's Italian wasn't the best in the world, and maybe the landlady got it wrong. Anyway, the mere fact that Freddie was angry about something looks bad for Dickie.'

Tom raised his eyebrows. 'I'd say it looked bad for Freddie. Maybe Dickie wasn't angry at all.' He felt perfectly calm, because he could see that Marge hadn't smelled out anything about it. 'I wouldn't worry about that unless something concrete comes out of it. Sounds like nothing at all to me.' He refilled her glass. 'Speaking of Africa, have they inquired around Tangier yet? Dickie used to talk about going to Tangier.'

'I think they've alerted the police everywhere. I think they ought to get the French police down here. The French are terribly good at things like this. But of course they can't. This is Italy,' she said with the first nervous tremor in her voice.

'Shall we have lunch here?' Tom asked. 'The maid is functioning over the lunch hour and we might as well take advantage of it.' He said it just as Anna was coming in to announce that the lunch was ready.

'Wonderful!' Marge said. 'It's raining a little, anyway.'

'Pronto la collazione, signor,' Anna said with a smile, staring at Marge.

Anna recognized her from the newspaper pictures, Tom saw. 'You and Ugo can go now if you like, Anna. Thanks.'

Anna went back into the kitchen – there was a door from the kitchen to a little alley at the side of the house, which the servants used – but Tom heard her pottering around with the coffee maker, stalling for another glimpse, no doubt.

'And Ugo?' Marge said. 'Two servants, no less?'

'Oh, they come in couples around here. You may not believe it, but I got this place for fifty dollars a month, not counting heat.'

'I don't believe it! That's practically like Mongibello rates!'

'It's true. The heating's fantastic, of course, but I'm not going to heat any room except my bedroom.'

'It's certainly comfortable here.'

'Oh, I opened the whole furnace for your benefit,' Tom said, smiling.

'What happened? Did one of your aunts die and leave you a fortune?' Marge asked, still pretending to be dazzled.

'No, just a decision of my own. I'm going to enjoy what I've got as long as it lasts. I told you that job I was after in Rome didn't pan out, and here I was in Europe with only about two thousand dollars to my name, so I decided to live it up and go home – broke – and start over again.' Tom had explained to her in his letter that the job he had applied for had been selling hearing aids in Europe for an American company, and he hadn't been able to face it, and the man who had interviewed him, he said, hadn't thought him the right type, either. Tom had also told her the man had appeared one minute after he spoke to her, which was why he had been unable to keep his appointment with her in Angelo's that day in Rome.

'Two thousand dollars won't last you long at this rate.'

She was probing to see if Dickie had given him anything, Tom knew. 'It will last till summer,' Tom said matter-of-factly. 'Anyway, I feel I deserve it. I spent most of the winter going around Italy like a gypsy on practically no money, and I've had about enough of that.'

'Where *were* you this winter?'

'Well, not with Tom, I mean, not with Dickie,' he said laughing, flustered at his slip of the tongue. 'I know you probably thought so. I saw about as much of Dickie as you did.'

'Oh, come on now,' Marge drawled. She sounded as if she were feeling her drinks.

Tom made two or three more martinis in the pitcher. 'Except for the trip to Cannes and the two days in Rome in February, I haven't seen Dickie at all.' It wasn't quite true, because he had written her that 'Tom was staying' with Dickie in Rome for several days after the Cannes trip, but now that he was face to face with Marge he found he was ashamed of her knowing, or thinking, that he had spent so much time with Dickie, and that he and Dickie might be guilty of what she had accused Dickie of in her letter. He bit his tongue as he poured their drinks, hating himself for his cowardice.

During lunch – Tom regretted very much that the main dish was cold roast beef, a fabulously expensive item on the Italian market – Marge quizzed him more acutely than any police officer on Dickie's state of mind while he was in Rome. Tom was pinned down to ten days spent in Rome with Dickie after the Cannes trip, and was questioned about everything from Di Massimo, the painter Dickie had worked with, to Dickie's appetite and the hour he got up in the morning.

'How do you think he felt about *me*? Tell me honestly. I can take it.'

'I think he was worried about you,' Tom said earnestly. 'I think – well, it was one of those situations that turn up quite often, a man who's terrified of marriage to begin with –'

'But I never asked him to marry me!' Marge protested.

'I know, but –' Tom forced himself to go on, though the subject was like vinegar in his mouth. 'Let's say he couldn't face the responsibility of your caring so much about him. I think he wanted a more casual relationship with you.' That told her everything and nothing.

Marge stared at him in that old, lost way for a moment, then rallied bravely and said, 'Well, all that's water under the bridge by now. I'm only interested in what Dickie might have done with himself.'

Her fury at his apparently having been with Dickie all winter was water under the bridge, too, Tom thought, because she hadn't wanted to believe it in the first place, and now she didn't have to. Tom asked carefully, 'He didn't happen to write to you when he was in Palermo?'

Marge shook her head. 'No. Why?'

'I wanted to know what kind of state you thought he was in then. Did you write to him?'

She hesitated. 'Yes – matter of fact, I did.'

'What kind of a letter? I only ask because an unfriendly letter might have had a bad effect on him just then.'

'Oh – it's hard to say what kind. A fairly friendly letter. I told him I was going back to the States.' She looked at him with wide eyes.

Tom enjoyed watching her face, watching somebody else squirm as they lied. That had been the filthy letter in which she said she had told the police that he and Dickie were always together. 'I don't suppose it matters then,' Tom said, with sweet gentleness, sitting back.

They were silent a few moments, then Tom asked her about her book, who the publisher was, and how much more work she had to do. Marge answered everything enthusiastically. Tom had the feeling that if she had Dickie back and her book published by next winter, she would probably just explode with happiness, make a loud, attractive *ploop!* and that would be the end of her.

'Do you think I should offer to talk to Mr Greenleaf, too?' Tom asked. 'I'd be glad to go to Rome –' Only he wouldn't be so glad, he remembered, because Rome had simply too many people in it who had seen him as Dickie Greenleaf. 'Or do you think he would like to come here? I could put him up. Where's he staying in Rome?'

'He's staying with some American friends who have a big apartment. Somebody called Northup in Via Quattro Novembre. I think it'd be nice if you called him. I'll write the address down for you.'

'That's a good idea. He doesn't like me, does he?'

Marge smiled a little. 'Well, frankly, no. I think he's a little hard on you, considering. He probably thinks you sponged off Dickie.'

'Well, I didn't. I'm sorry the idea didn't work out about my getting Dickie back home, but I explained all that. I wrote him the nicest letter I could about Dickie when I heard he was missing. Didn't that help any?'

'I think it did, but – Oh, I'm terribly sorry, Tom! All over this wonderful tablecloth!' Marge had turned her martini over. She daubed at the crocheted tablecloth awkwardly with her napkin.

Tom came running back from the kitchen with a wet cloth. 'Perfectly all right,' he said, watching the wood of the table turn white in spite of his wiping. It wasn't the tablecloth he cared about, it was the beautiful table.

'I'm so sorry,' Marge went on protesting.

Tom hated her. He suddenly remembered her bra hanging over the windowsill in Mongibello. Her underwear would be draped over his chairs tonight, if he invited her to stay here. The idea repelled him. He deliberately hurled a smile across the table at her. 'I hope you'll honour me by accepting a bed for the night. Not mine,' he added, laughing, 'but I've got two rooms upstairs and you're welcome to one of them.'

'Thanks a lot. All right, I will.' She beamed at him.

Tom installed her in his own room – the bed in the other room being only an outsized couch and not so comfortable as his double bed – and Marge closed her door to take a nap after lunch. Tom wandered restlessly through the rest of the house, wondering whether there was anything in his room that he ought to remove. Dickie's passport was in the lining of a suitcase in his closet. He couldn't think of anything else. But women had sharp eyes, Tom thought, even Marge. She might snoop around. Finally he went into the room while she was still asleep and took the suitcase from the closet. The floor squeaked, and Marge's eyes fluttered open.

'Just want to get something out of here,' Tom whispered. 'Sorry.' He continued tiptoeing out of the room. Marge probably wouldn't even remember, he thought, because she hadn't completely woken up.

Later he showed Marge all around the house, showed her the shelf of

leather-bound books in the room next to his bedroom, books that he said
had come with the house, though they were his own, bought in Rome and
Palermo and Venice. He realized that he had had about ten of them in
Rome, and that one of the young police officers with Roverini had bent
close to them, apparently studying their titles. But it was nothing really
to worry about, he thought, even if the same police officer were to come
back. He showed Marge the front entrance of the house, with its broad
stone steps. The tide was low and four steps were bared now, the lower
two covered with thick wet moss. The moss was a slippery, long-filament
variety, and hung over the edges of the steps like messy dark-green hair.
The steps were repellent to Tom, but Marge thought them very romantic.
She bent over them, staring at the deep water of the canal. Tom had an
impulse to push her in.

'Can we take a gondola and come in this way tonight?' she asked.

'Oh sure.' They were going out to dinner tonight, of course. Tom
dreaded the long Italian evening ahead of them, because they wouldn't
eat until ten, and then she'd probably want to sit in San Marco's over
espressos until two in the morning.

Tom looked up at the hazy, sunless Venetian sky, and watched a gull
glide down and settle on somebody else's front steps across the canal. He
was trying to decide which of his new Venetian friends he would telephone
and ask if he could bring Marge over for a drink around five o'clock. They
would all be delighted to meet her, of course. He decided on the Englishman Peter Smith-Kingsley. Peter had an Afghan, a piano, and a well-
equipped bar. Tom thought Peter would be best because Peter never
wanted anybody to leave. They could stay there until it was time for them
to go to dinner.

TWENTY-FOUR

Tom called Mr Greenleaf from Peter Smith-Kingsley's house at about seven
o'clock. Mr Greenleaf sounded friendlier than Tom had expected, and
sounded pitifully hungry for the little crumbs Tom gave him about Dickie.
Peter and Marge and the Franchettis – an attractive pair of brothers from

Trieste whom Tom had recently met – were in the next room and able to hear almost every word he said, so Tom did it better than he would have done it completely alone, he felt.

'I've told Marge all I know,' he said, 'so she'll be able to tell you anything I've forgotten. I'm only sorry that I can't contribute anything of real importance for the police to work on.'

'These police!' Mr Greenleaf said gruffly. 'I'm beginning to think Richard is dead. For some reason the Italians are reluctant to admit he might be. They act like amateurs – or old ladies playing at being detectives.'

Tom was shocked at Mr Greenleaf's bluntness about Dickie's possibly being dead. 'Do *you* think Dickie might have killed himself, Mr Greenleaf?' Tom asked quietly.

Mr Greenleaf sighed. 'I don't know. I think it's possible, yes. I never thought much of my son's stability, Tom.'

'I'm afraid I agree with you,' Tom said. 'Would you like to talk to Marge? She's in the next room.'

'No, no, thanks. When's she coming back?'

'I think she said she'd be going back to Rome tomorrow. If you'd possibly like to come to Venice, just for a slight rest, Mr Greenleaf, you're very welcome to stay at my house.'

But Mr Greenleaf declined the invitation. It wasn't necessary to bend over backwards, Tom realized. It was as if he were really inviting trouble, and couldn't stop himself. Mr Greenleaf thanked him for his telephone call and said a very courteous good night.

Tom went back into the other room. 'There's no more news from Rome,' he said dejectedly to the group.

'Oh,' Peter looked disappointed.

'Here's for the phone call, Peter,' Tom said, laying twelve hundred lire on top of Peter's piano. 'Thanks very much.'

'I have an idea,' Pietro Franchetti began in his English-accented English. 'Dickie Greenleaf has traded passports with a Neapolitan fisherman or maybe a Roman cigarette pedlar, so that he can lead the quiet life he always wanted to. It so happens that the bearer of the Dickie Greenleaf passport is not so good a forger as he thought he was, and he had to disappear suddenly. The police should find a man who can't produce his proper carta d'identità, find out who he is, then look for a man with his name, who will turn out to be Dickie Greenleaf!'

Everybody laughed, and Tom loudest of all.

'The trouble with that idea,' Tom said, 'is that lots of people who knew Dickie saw him in January and February –'

'*Who?*' Pietro interrupted with that irritating Italian belligerence in conversation that was doubly irritating in English.

'Well, I did, for one. Anyway, as I was going to say, the forgeries now date from December, according to the bank.'

'Still, it's an idea,' Marge chirruped, feeling very good on her third drink, lolling back on Peter's big chaise-longue. 'A very Dickie-like idea. He probably would have done it right after Palermo, when he had the bank forgery business on top of everything else. I don't believe those forgeries for one minute. I think Dickie'd changed so much that his handwriting changed.'

'I think so, too,' Tom said. 'The bank isn't unanimous, anyway, in saying they're all forged. America's divided about it, and Naples fell right in with America. Naples never would have noticed a forgery if the U.S. hadn't told them about it.'

'I wonder what's in the papers tonight?' Peter asked brightly, pulling on a slipper-like shoe that he had half taken off because it probably hurt. 'Shall I go out and get them?'

But one of the Franchettis volunteered to go, and dashed out of the room. Lorenzo Franchetti was wearing a pink embroidered waistcoat, all' inglese, and an English-made suit and heavy-soled English shoes, and his brother was dressed in much the same way. Peter, on the other hand, was dressed in Italian clothes from head to foot. Tom had noticed, at parties and at the theatre, that if a man was dressed in English clothes he was bound to be Italian, and vice versa.

Some more people arrived just as Lorenzo came back with the papers – two Italians and two Americans. The papers were passed around. More discussion, more exchanges of stupid speculation, more excitement over today's news: Dickie's house in Mongibello had been sold to an American for twice the price he originally asked for it. The money was going to be held by a Naples bank until Greenleaf claimed it.

The same paper had a cartoon of a man on his knees, looking under his bureau. His wife asked, 'Collar button?' And his answer was, 'No, I'm looking for Dickie Greenleaf.'

Tom had heard that the Rome music halls were taking off the search in skits, too.

One of the Americans who had just come in, whose name was Rudy something, invited Tom and Marge to a cocktail party at his hotel the following day. Tom started to decline, but Marge said she would be delighted to come. Tom hadn't thought she would be here tomorrow, because she had said something at lunch about leaving. The party would be deadly, Tom thought. Rudy was a loud-mouthed, crude man in flashy clothes who said he was an antique dealer. Tom manoeuvred himself and Marge out of the house before she accepted any more invitations that might be further into the future.

Marge was in a giddy mood that irritated Tom throughout their long five-course dinner, but he made the supreme effort and responded in kind – like a helpless frog twitching from an electric needle, he thought – and when she dropped the ball, he picked it up and dribbled it a while. He said things like, 'Maybe Dickie's suddenly found himself in his painting, and he's gone away like Gauguin to one of the South Sea Islands.' It made him ill. Then Marge would spin a fantasy about Dickie and the South Sea Islands, making lazy gestures with her hands. The worst was yet to come, Tom thought: the gondola ride. If she dangled those hands in the water, he hoped a shark bit them off. He ordered a dessert that he hadn't room for, but Marge ate it.

Marge wanted a private gondola, of course, not the regular ferry-service gondola that took people over ten at a time from San Marco's to the steps of Santa Maria della Salute, so they engaged a private gondola. It was one-thirty in the morning. Tom had a dark-brown taste in his mouth from too many espressos, his heart was fluttering like bird wings, and he did not expect to be able to sleep until dawn. He felt exhausted, and lay back in the gondola's seat about as languidly as Marge, careful to keep his thigh from touching hers. Marge was still in ebullient spirits, entertaining herself now with a monologue about the sunrise in Venice, which she had apparently seen on some other visit. The gentle rocking of the boat and the rhythmic thrusts of the gondolier's oar made Tom feel slightly sickish. The expanse of water between the San Marco boat stop and his steps seemed interminable.

The steps were covered now except for the upper two, and the water swept just over the surface of the third step, stirring its moss in a disgusting way. Tom paid the gondolier mechanically, and was standing in front of the big doors when he realized he hadn't brought the keys. He glanced around to see if he could climb in anywhere, but he couldn't even reach a window ledge from the steps. Before he even said anything, Marge burst out laughing.

'You didn't bring the key! Of all things, stuck on the door step with the raging waters around us, and no key!'

Tom tried to smile. Why the hell should he have thought to bring two keys nearly a foot long that weighed as much as a couple of revolvers? He turned and yelled to the gondolier to come back.

'Ah!' the gondolier chuckled across the water. 'Mi dispiace, signor! Deb' ritornare a San Marco! Ho un appuntamento!' He kept on rowing.

'We have no keys!' Tom yelled in Italian.

'Mi dispiace, signor!' replied the gondolier. 'Mandarò un altro gondoliere!' Marge laughed again. 'Oh, some other gondolier'll pick us up. Isn't it beautiful?' She stood on tiptoe.

It was not at all a beautiful night. It was chilly, and a slimy little rain had started falling. He might get the ferry gondola to come over, Tom thought, but he didn't see it. The only boat he saw was the motoscafo approaching the San Marco pier. There was hardly a chance that the motoscafo would trouble to pick them up, but Tom yelled to it, anyway. The motoscafo, full of lights and people, went blindly on and nosed in at the wooden pier across the canal. Marge was sitting on the top step with her arms around her knees, doing nothing. Finally, a lowslung motor-boat that looked like a fishing boat of some sort slowed down, and someone yelled in Italian: 'Locked out?'

'We forgot the keys!' Marge explained cheerfully.

But she didn't want to get into the boat. She said she would wait on the steps while Tom went around and opened the street door. Tom said it might take fifteen minutes or more, and she would probably catch a cold there, so she finally got in. The Italian took them to the nearest landing at the steps of the Santa Maria della Salute church. He refused to take any money for his trouble, but he accepted the rest of Tom's packet of American cigarettes. Tom did not know why, but he felt more frightened that night, walking through San Spiridione with Marge, than if he had been alone. Marge, of course, was not affected at all by the street, and talked the whole way.

TWENTY-FIVE

Tom was awakened very early the next morning by the banging of his door knocker. He grabbed his robe and went down. It was a telegram, and he had to run back upstairs to get a tip for the man. He stood in the cold living-room and read it.

CHANGED MY MIND. WOULD LIKE TO SEE YE.
ARRIVING 11.45 A.M.

                                                    H. GREENLEAF

Tom shivered. Well, he had expected it, he thought. But he hadn't,
really. He dreaded it. Or was it just the hour? It was barely dawn. The
living-room looked grey and horrible. That 'YE' gave the telegram such
a creepy, archaic touch. Generally Italian telegrams had much funnier
typographical errors. And what if they'd put 'R.' or 'D.' instead of the 'H.'?
How would he be feeling then?

He ran upstairs and got back into his warm bed to try to catch some
more sleep. He kept wondering if Marge would come in or knock on his
door because she had heard that loud knocker, but he finally decided she
had slept through it. He imagined greeting Mr Greenleaf at the door,
shaking his hand firmly, and he tried to imagine his questions, but his
mind blurred tiredly and it made him feel frightened and uncomfortable.
He was too sleepy to form specific questions and answers, and too tense
to get to sleep. He wanted to make coffee and wake Marge up, so he would
have someone to talk to, but he couldn't face going into that room and
seeing the underwear and garter belts strewn all over the place, he
absolutely *couldn't*.

It was Marge who woke him up, and she had already made coffee
downstairs, she said.

'What do you think?' Tom said with a big smile. 'I got a telegram from
Mr Greenleaf this morning and he's coming at noon.'

'He *is*? When did you get the telegram?'

'This morning early. If I wasn't dreaming.' Tom looked for it. 'Here it
is.'

Marge read it. '"Would like to see ye,"' she said, laughing a little. 'Well,
that's nice. It'll do him good, I hope. Are you coming down or shall I bring
the coffee up?'

'I'll come down,' Tom said, putting on his robe.

Marge was already dressed in slacks and a sweater, black corduroy
slacks, well-cut and made to order, Tom supposed, because they fitted her
gourdlike figure as well as pants possibly could. They prolonged their
coffee drinking until Anna and Ugo arrived at ten with milk and rolls and
the morning papers. Then they made more coffee and hot milk and sat in
the living-room. It was one of the mornings when there was nothing in
the papers about Dickie or the Miles case. Some mornings were like that,
and then the evening papers would have something about them again,

even if there was no real news to report, just by way of reminding people that Dickie was still missing and the Miles murder was still unsolved.

Marge and Tom went to the railroad station to meet Mr Greenleaf at eleven forty-five. It was raining again, and so windy and cold that the rain felt like sleet on their faces. They stood in the shelter of the railroad station, watching the people come through the gate, and finally there was Mr Greenleaf, solemn and ashen. Marge rushed forward to kiss him on the cheek, and he smiled at her.

'Hello, Tom!' he said heartily, extending his hand. 'How're you?'

'Very well, sir. And you?'

Mr Greenleaf had only a small suitcase, but a porter was carrying it and the porter rode with them on the motoscafo, though Tom said he could easily carry the suitcase himself. Tom suggested they go straight to his house, but Mr Greenleaf wanted to install himself in a hotel first. He insisted.

'I'll come over as soon as I register. I thought I'd try the Gritti. Is that anywhere near your place?' Mr Greenleaf asked.

'Not too close, but you can walk to San Marco's and take a gondola over,' Tom said. 'We'll come with you, if you just want to check in. I thought we might all have lunch together – unless you'd rather see Marge by yourself for a while.' He was the old self-effacing Ripley again.

'Came here primarily to talk to you!' Mr Greenleaf said.

'Is there any news?' Marge asked.

Mr Greenleaf shook his head. He was casting nervous, absent-minded glances out the windows of the motoscafo, as if the strangeness of the city compelled him to look at it, though nothing of it was registering. He had not answered Tom's question about lunch. Tom folded his arms, put a pleasant expression on his face, and did not try to talk any more. The boat's motor made quite a roar, anyway. Mr Greenleaf and Marge were talking very casually about some people they knew in Rome. Tom gathered that Marge and Mr Greenleaf got along very well, though Marge had said she had not known him before she met him in Rome.

They went to lunch at a modest restaurant between the Gritti and the Rialto, which specialized in seafoods that were always displayed raw on a long counter inside. One of the plates held varieties of the little purple octopuses that Dickie had liked so much, and Tom said to Marge, nodding towards the plates as they passed, 'Too bad Dickie isn't here to enjoy some of those.'

Marge smiled gaily. She was always in a good mood when they were about to eat.

Mr Greenleaf talked a little more at lunch, but his face kept its stony expression, and he still glanced around as he spoke, as if he hoped that Dickie would come walking in at any moment. No, the police hadn't found a blessed thing that could be called a clue, he said, and he had just arranged for an American private detective to come over and try to clear the mystery up.

It made Tom swallow thoughtfully – he, too, must have a lurking suspicion, or illusion, perhaps, that American detectives were better than the Italian – but then the evident futility of it struck him as it was apparently striking Marge, because her face had gone long and blank suddenly.

'That may be a very good idea,' Tom said.

'Do you think much of the Italian police?' Mr Greenleaf asked him.

'Well – actually, I do,' Tom replied. 'There's also the advantage that they speak Italian and they can get around everywhere and investigate all kinds of suspects. I suppose the man you sent for speaks Italian?'

'I really don't know. I don't know,' Mr Greenleaf said in a flustered way, as if he realized he should have demanded that, and hadn't. 'The man's name is McCarron. He's said to be very good.'

He probably didn't speak Italian, Tom thought. 'When is he arriving?'

'Tomorrow or the next day. I'll be in Rome tomorrow to meet him if he's there.' Mr Greenleaf had finished his vitello alla parmigiana. He had not eaten much.

'Tom has the most beautiful house!' Marge said, starting in on her seven-layer rum cake.

Tom turned his glare at her into a faint smile.

The quizzing, Tom thought, would come at the house, probably when he and Mr Greenleaf were alone. He knew Mr Greenleaf wanted to talk to him alone, and therefore he proposed coffee at the restaurant where they were before Marge could suggest having it at home. Marge liked the coffee that his filter pot made. Even so, Marge sat around with them in the living-room for half an hour after they got home. Marge was incapable of sensing anything, Tom thought. Finally Tom frowned at her facetiously and glanced at the stairs, and she got the hint, clapped her hand over her mouth and announced that she was going up to have a wee nap. She was in her usual invincibly merry mood, and she had been talking to Mr Greenleaf all during lunch as if of *course* Dickie wasn't dead, and he mustn't, mustn't worry so much because it wasn't good for his digestion. As if she still had hopes of being his daughter-in-law one day, Tom thought.

Mr Greenleaf stood up and paced the floor with his hands in his jacket pockets, like an executive about to dictate a letter to his stenographer. He hadn't commented on the plushness of the house, or even much looked at it, Tom noticed.

'Well, Tom,' he began with a sigh, 'this is a strange end, isn't it?'

'End?'

'Well, you living in Europe now, and Richard –'

'None of us has suggested yet that he might have gone back to America,' Tom said pleasantly.

'No. That couldn't be. The immigration authorities in America are much too well alerted for that.' Mr Greenleaf continued to pace, not looking at him. 'What's your real opinion as to where he may be?'

'Well, sir, he could be hiding out in Italy – very easily if he doesn't use a hotel where he has to register.'

'Are there any hotels in Italy where one doesn't have to register?'

'No, not officially. But anyone who knows Italian as well as Dickie might get away with it. Matter of fact, if he bribed some little innkeeper in the south of Italy not to say anything, he could stay there even if the man knew his name was Richard Greenleaf.'

'And is that your idea of what he may be doing?' Mr Greenleaf looked at him suddenly, and Tom saw that pitiful expression he had noticed the first evening he had met him.

'No, I – It's possible. That's all I can say about it.' He paused. 'I'm sorry to say it, Mr Greenleaf, but I think there's a possibility that Dickie is dead.'

Mr Greenleaf's expression did not change. 'Because of that depression you mentioned in Rome? What exactly did he say to you?'

'It was his general mood.' Tom frowned. 'The Miles thing had obviously shaken him. He's the sort of man – He really does hate publicity of any kind, violence of any kind.' Tom licked his lips. His agony in trying to express himself was genuine. 'He did say if one more thing happened, he would blow his top – or he didn't know what he would do. Also for the first time, I felt he wasn't interested in his painting. Maybe it was only temporary, but up until then I'd always thought Dickie had his painting to go to, whatever happened to him.'

'Does he really take his painting so seriously?'

'Yes, he does,' Tom said firmly.

Mr Greenleaf looked up at the ceiling again, his hands behind him. 'A pity we can't find this Di Massimo. He might know something. I understand Richard and he were going to go together to Sicily.'

'I didn't know that,' Tom said. Mr Greenleaf had got that from Marge, he knew.

'Di Massimo's disappeared, too, if he ever existed. I'm inclined to think Richard made him up to try to convince me he was painting. The police can't find a painter called Di Massimo on their – their identity lists or whatever it is.'

'I never met him,' Tom said. 'Dickie mentioned him a couple of times. I never doubted his identity – or his actuality.' He laughed a little.

'What did you say before about "if one more thing happened to him"? What else had happened to him?'

'Well, I didn't know then, in Rome, but I think I know what he meant now. They'd questioned him about the sunken boat in San Remo. Did they tell you about that?'

'No.'

'They found a boat in San Remo, scuttled. It seems the boat was missed on the day or around the day Dickie and I were there, and we'd taken a ride in the same kind of boat. They were the little motor-boats people rented there. At any rate, the boat was scuttled, and there were stains on it that they thought were bloodstains. They happened to find the boat just after the Miles murder, and they couldn't find *me* at that time, because I was travelling around the country, so they asked Dickie where I was. I think for a while, Dickie must have thought they suspected him of having murdered me!' Tom laughed.

'Good lord!'

'I only know this, because a police inspector questioned me about it in Venice just a few weeks ago. He said he'd questioned Dickie about it before. The strange thing is that I didn't know I was being looked for – not very seriously, but still being looked for – until I saw it in the newspaper in Venice. I went to the police station here and presented myself.' Tom was still smiling. He had decided days ago that he had better narrate all this to Mr Greenleaf, if he ever saw him, whether Mr Greenleaf had heard about the San Remo boat incident or not. It was better than having Mr Greenleaf learn about it from the police, and be told that he had been in Rome with Dickie at a time when he should have known the police were looking for him. Besides, it fitted in with what he was saying about Dickie's depressed mood at that time.

'I don't quite understand all this,' Mr Greenleaf said. He was sitting on the sofa, listening attentively.

'It's blown over now, since Dickie and I are both alive. The reason I mention it at all is that Dickie knew I was being looked for by the police, because they had asked him where I was. He may not have known exactly where I was at the first interview with the police, but he did know at least that I was still in the country. But even when I came to Rome and saw him, he didn't tell the police he'd seen me. He wasn't going to be that cooperative, he wasn't in the mood. I know this because at the very time Marge talked to me in Rome at the hotel, Dickie was out talking to the police. His attitude was, let the police find me themselves, he wasn't going to tell them where I was.'

Mr Greenleaf shook his head, a kind of fatherly, mildly impatient shake of the head, as if he could easily believe it of Dickie.

'I think that was the night he said, if one more thing happened to him – It caused me a little embarrassment when I was in Venice. The police probably thought I was a moron for not knowing before that I was being looked for, but the fact remains I didn't.'

'Hm-m,' Mr Greenleaf said uninterestedly.

Tom got up to get some brandy.

'I'm afraid I don't agree with you that Richard committed suicide,' Mr Greenleaf said.

'Well, neither does Marge. I just said it's a possibility. I don't even think it's the most likely thing that's happened.'

'You don't? What do you think is?'

'That he's hiding,' Tom said. 'May I offer you some brandy, sir? I imagine this house feels pretty chilly after America.'

'It does, frankly.' Mr Greenleaf accepted his glass.

'You know, he could be in several other countries besides Italy, too,' Tom said. 'He could have gone to Greece or France or anywhere else after he got back to Naples, because no one was looking for him until days later.'

'I know, I know,' Mr Greenleaf said tiredly.

TWENTY-SIX

Tom had hoped Marge would forget about the cocktail party invitation of the antique dealer at the Danieli, but she didn't. Mr Greenleaf had gone back to his hotel to rest around four o'clock, and as soon as he had gone Marge reminded Tom of the party at five o'clock.

'Do you really want to go?' Tom asked. 'I can't even remember the man's name.'

'Maloof. M-a-l-o-o-f,' Marge said. 'I'd like to go. We don't have to stay long.'

So that was that. What Tom hated about it was the spectacle they made of themselves, not one but two of the principals in the Greenleaf case, conspicuous as a couple of spotlighted acrobats at a circus. He felt – he knew – they were nothing but a pair of names that Mr Maloof had bagged, guests of honour that had actually turned up, because certainly Mr Maloof would have told everybody today that Marge Sherwood and Tom Ripley were attending his party. It was unbecoming, Tom felt. And Marge couldn't excuse her giddiness simply by saying that she wasn't worried a bit about Dickie's being missing. It even seemed to Tom that Marge guzzled the martinis because they were free, as if she couldn't get all she wanted at his house, or as if he wasn't going to buy her several more when they met Mr Greenleaf for dinner.

Tom sipped one drink slowly and managed to stay on the other side of the room from Marge. He was the friend of Dickie Greenleaf, when anybody began a conversation by asking him if he was, but he knew Marge only slightly.

'Miss Sherwood is my house guest,' he said with a troubled smile.

'Where's Mr Greenleaf? Too bad you didn't bring him,' Mr Maloof said, sidling up like an elephant with a huge Manhattan in a champagne glass. He wore a checked suit of loud English tweed, the kind of pattern, Tom supposed, the English made, reluctantly, especially for such Americans as Rudy Maloof.

'I think Mr Greenleaf is resting,' Tom said. 'We're going to see him later for dinner.'

'Oh,' said Mr Maloof. 'Did you see the papers tonight?' This last politely, with a respectfully solemn face.

'Yes, I did,' Tom replied.

Mr Maloof nodded, without saying anything more. Tom wondered what inconsequential item he could have been going to report if he had said he hadn't read the papers. The papers tonight said that Mr Greenleaf had arrived in Venice and was staying at the Gritti Palace. There was no mention of a private detective from America arriving in Rome today, or that one was coming at all, which made Tom question Mr Greenleaf's story about the private detective. It was like one of those stories told by someone else, or one of his own imaginary fears, which were never based on the least fragment of fact and which, a couple of weeks later, he was ashamed that he *could* have believed. Such as that Marge and Dickie were having an affair in Mongibello, or were even on the brink of having an affair. Or that the forgery scare in February was going to ruin him and expose him if he continued in the role of Dickie Greenleaf. The forgery scare had blown over, actually. The latest was that seven out of ten experts in America had said that they did not believe the cheques were forged. He could have signed another remittance from the American bank, and gone on forever as Dickie Greenleaf, if he hadn't let his imaginary fears get the better of him. Tom set his jaw. He was still listening with a fraction of his brain to Mr Maloof, who was trying to sound intelligent and serious by describing his expedition to the islands of Murano and Burano that morning. Tom set his jaw, frowning, listening, and concentrating doggedly on his own life. Perhaps he should believe Mr Greenleaf's story about the private detective coming over, until it was disproven, but he would not let it rattle him or cause him to betray fear by so much as the blink of an eye.

Tom made an absent-minded reply to something Mr Maloof had said, and Mr Maloof laughed with inane good cheer and drifted off. Tom followed his broad back scornfully with his eyes, realizing that he had been rude, was being rude, and that he ought to pull himself together, because behaving courteously even to this handful of second-rate antique dealers and bric-à-brac and ash-tray buyers – Tom had seen the samples of their wares spread out on the bed in the room where they had put their coats – was part of the business of being a gentleman. But they reminded him too much of the people he had said good-bye to in New York, he thought, that was why they got under his skin like an itch and made him want to run.

Marge was the reason he was here, after all, the only reason. He blamed *her*. Tom took a sip of his martini, looked up at the ceiling, and thought that in another few months his nerves, his patience, would be able to bear even people like this, if he ever found himself with people like this again. He had improved, at least, since he left New York, and he would improve still more. He stared up at the ceiling and thought of sailing to Greece, down the Adriatic from Venice, into the Ionian Sea to Crete. That was what he would do this summer. June. *June.* How sweet and soft the word was, clear and lazy and full of sunshine! His reverie lasted only a few seconds, however. The loud grating American voices forced their way into his ears again, and sank like claws into the nerves of his shoulders and his back. He moved involuntarily from where he stood, moved towards Marge. There were only two other women in the room, the horrible wives of a couple of the horrible businessmen, and Marge, he had to admit, was better-looking than either of them, but her voice, he thought, was worse, like theirs only worse.

He had something on the tip of his tongue to say about their leaving, but, since it was unthinkable for a man to propose leaving, he said nothing at all, only joined Marge's group and smiled. Somebody refilled his glass. Marge was talking about Mongibello, telling them about her book, and the three grey-templed, seamy-faced, bald-headed men seemed to be entranced with her.

When Marge herself proposed leaving a few minutes later, they had a ghastly time getting clear of Maloof and his cohorts, who were a little drunker now and insistent that they *all* get together for dinner, and Mr Greenleaf, too.

'That's what Venice is for – a good time!' Mr Maloof kept saying idiotically, taking the opportunity to put his arm around Marge and maul her a little as he tried to make her stay, and Tom thought it was a good thing he hadn't eaten yet because he would have lost it right then. 'What's Mr Greenleaf's number? Let's call him up!' Mr Maloof weaved his way to the telephone.

'I think we'd better get out of here!' Tom said grimly into Marge's ear. He took a hard, functional grip on her elbow and steered her towards the door, both of them nodding and smiling good-bye as they went.

'What's the *matter?*' Marge asked when they were in the corridor.

'Nothing. I just thought the party was getting out of hand,' Tom said, trying to make light of it with a smile. Marge was a little higher, but not too high to see that something was the matter with him. He was perspiring. It showed on his forehead, and he wiped it. 'People like that get me down,' he said, 'talking about Dickie all the time, and we don't even know them and I don't want to. They make me ill.'

'Funny. Not a soul talked to me about Dickie or even mentioned his name. I thought it was much better than yesterday at Peter's house.'

Tom lifted his head as he walked and said nothing. It was the class of people he despised, and why say that to Marge, who was of the same class?

They called for Mr Greenleaf at his hotel. It was still early for dinner, so they had aperitifs at a café in a street near the Gritti. Tom tried to make up for his explosion at the party by being pleasant and talkative during dinner. Mr Greenleaf was in a good mood, because he had just telephoned his wife and found her in very good spirits and feeling much better. Her doctor had been trying a new system of injections for the past ten days,

Mr Greenleaf said, and she seemed to be responding better than to anything he had tried before.

It was a quiet dinner. Tom told a clean, mildly funny joke, and Marge laughed hilariously. Mr Greenleaf insisted on paying for the dinner, and then said he was going back to his hotel because he didn't feel quite up to par. From the fact that he carefully chose a pasta dish and ate no salad, Tom thought that he might be suffering from the tourist's complaint, and he wanted to suggest an excellent remedy, obtainable in every drugstore, but Mr Greenleaf was not quite the person one could say a thing like that to, even if they had been alone.

Mr Greenleaf said he was going back to Rome tomorrow, and Tom promised to give him a ring around nine o'clock the next morning to find out which train he had decided on. Marge was going back to Rome with Mr Greenleaf, and she was agreeable to either train. They walked back to the Gritti – Mr Greenleaf with his taut face-of-an-industrialist under his grey homburg looking like a piece of Madison Avenue walking through the narrow, zigzagging streets – and they said good night.

'I'm terribly sorry I didn't get to spend more time with you,' Tom said.

'So am I, my boy. Maybe some other time,' Mr Greenleaf patted his shoulder.

Tom walked back home with Marge in a kind of glow. It had all gone awfully well, Tom thought. Marge chattered to him as they walked, giggling because she had broken a strap of her bra and had to hold it up with one hand, she said. Tom was thinking of the letter he had received from Bob Delancey this afternoon, the first word he'd gotten from Bob except one postcard ages ago, in which Bob had said that the police had questioned everybody in his house about an income tax fraud of a few months ago. The defrauder, it seemed, had used the address of Bob's house to receive his cheques, and had gotten the cheques by the simple means of taking the letters down from the letterbox edge where the postman had stuck them. The postman had been questioned, too, Bob had said, and remembered the name George McAlpin on the letters. Bob seemed to think it was rather funny. He described the reactions of some of the people in the house when they were questioned by the police. The mystery was, who took the letters addressed to George McAlpin? It was very reassuring. That income tax episode had been hanging over his head in a vague way, because he had known there would be an investigation at some time. He was glad it had gone this far and no further. He couldn't imagine how the police would ever, could ever, connect Tom Ripley with George McAlpin. Besides, as Bob had remarked, the defrauder had not even tried to cash the cheques.

He sat down in the living-room to read Bob's letter again when he got home. Marge had gone upstairs to pack her things and to go to bed. Tom was tired too, but the anticipation of freedom tomorrow, when Marge and Mr Greenleaf would be gone, was so pleasant to relish he would not have minded staying up all night. He took his shoes off so he could put his feet up on the sofa, lay back on a pillow, and continued reading Bob's letter. 'The police think it's some outsider who dropped by occasionally to pick up his mail, because none of the dopes in this house look like criminal types ...' It was strange to read about the people he knew in New York, Ed and Lorraine, the newt-brained girl who had tried to stow herself away in his cabin the day he sailed from New York. It was strange and not at all attractive. What a dismal life they led, creeping around New York, in and out of subways, standing in some dingy bar on Third Avenue for their entertainment, watching television, or even if they had enough money for a Madison Avenue bar or a good restaurant now and then, how dull it all was compared to the worst little trattoria in Venice with its tables of green salads, trays of wonderful cheeses, and its friendly waiters bringing you the best wine in the world! 'I certainly do envy you sitting there in Venice in an old palazzo!' Bob wrote. 'Do you take a lot of gondola rides? How are the girls? Are you getting so cultured you won't speak to any of us when you come back? How long are you staying, anyway?'

Forever, Tom thought. Maybe he'd never go back to the States. It was not so much Europe itself as the evenings he had spent alone, here and in Rome, that made him feel that way. Evenings by himself simply looking at maps, or lying around on sofas thumbing through guidebooks. Evenings looking at his clothes – his clothes and Dickie's – and feeling Dickie's rings between his palms, and running his fingers over the antelope suitcase he had bought at Gucci's. He had polished the suitcase with a special English leather dressing, not that it needed polishing because he took such good care of it, but for its protection. He loved possessions, not masses of them, but a select few that he did not part with. They gave a man self-respect. Not ostentation but quality, and the love that cherished the quality. Possessions reminded him that he existed, and made him enjoy his existence. It was as simple as that. And wasn't that worth something? He existed. Not many people in the world knew how to, even if they had the money. It really didn't take money, masses of money, it took a certain security. He had been on the road to it, even with Marc Priminger. He had appreciated Marc's possessions, and they were what had attracted him to the house, but they were not his own, and it had been impossible to make a beginning at acquiring anything of his own on forty dollars a week. It would have taken him the best years of his life, even if he had economized stringently, to buy the things he wanted. Dickie's money had given him only an added momentum on the road he had been travelling. The money gave him the leisure to see Greece, to collect Etruscan pottery if he wanted (he had recently read an interesting book on that subject by an American living in Rome), to join art societies if he cared to and to donate to their work. It gave him the leisure, for instance, to read his Malraux tonight as late as he pleased, because he did not have to go to a job in the morning. He had just bought a two-volume edition of Malraux's *Psychologie de l'art* which he was now reading, with great pleasure, in French with the aid of a dictionary. He thought he might nap for a while, then read some of it, whatever the hour. He felt cosy and drowsy, in spite of the espresso. The curve of the sofa fitted his shoulders like somebody's arm, or rather fitted it better than somebody's arm. He decided he would spend the night here. It was more comfortable than the sofa upstairs. In a few minutes he might go up and get a blanket.

'Tom?'

He opened his eyes. Marge was coming down the stairs, barefoot. Tom sat up. She had his brown leather box in her hand.

'I just found Dickie's rings in here,' she said rather breathlessly.

'Oh. He gave them to me. To take care of.' Tom stood up.

'When?'

'In Rome, I think.' He took a step back, struck one of his shoes and picked it up, mostly in an effort to seem calm.

'What was he going to do? Why'd he give them to you?'

She'd been looking for a thread to sew her bra, Tom thought. Why in hell hadn't he put the rings somewhere else, like in the lining of that suitcase? 'I don't really know,' Tom said. 'A whim or something. You know how he is. He said if anything ever happened to him, he wanted me to have his rings.'

Marge looked puzzled. 'Where was he going?'

'To Palermo. Sicily.' He was holding the shoe in both hands in a position to use the wooden heel of it as a weapon. And how he would do it went quickly through his head: hit her with the shoe, then haul her out by the front door and drop her into the canal. He'd say she'd fallen, slipped on the moss. And she was such a good swimmer, he'd thought she could keep afloat.

Marge stared down at the box. 'Then he *was* going to kill himself.'

'Yes – if you want to look at it that way, the rings – They make it look more likely that he did.'

'Why didn't you say anything about it before?'

'I think I absolutely forgot them. I put them away so they wouldn't get lost and I never thought of looking at them since the day he gave them to me.'

'He either killed himself or changed his identity – didn't he?'

'Yes.' Tom said it sadly and firmly.

'You'd better tell Mr Greenleaf.'

'Yes, I will. Mr Greenleaf and the police.'

'This practically *settles* it,' Marge said.

Tom was wringing the shoe in his hands like a pair of gloves now, yet still keeping the shoe in position, because Marge was staring at him in a funny way. She was still thinking. Was she kidding him? Did she know now?

Marge said earnestly, 'I just can't imagine Dickie ever being without his rings,' and Tom knew then that she hadn't guessed the answer, that her mind was miles up some other road.

He relaxed then, limply, sank down on the sofa and pretended to busy himself with putting on his shoes. 'No,' he agreed, automatically.

'If it weren't so late, I'd call Mr Greenleaf now. He's probably in bed, and he wouldn't sleep all night if I told him, I know.'

Tom tried to push a foot into the second shoe. Even his fingers were limp, without strength. He racked his brain for something sensible to say. 'I'm sorry I didn't mention it sooner,' he brought out in a deep voice. 'It was just one of those –'

'Yes, it makes it kind of silly at this point for Mr Greenleaf to bring a private detective over, doesn't it?' Her voice shook.

Tom looked at her. She was about to cry. This was the very first moment, Tom realized, that she was admitting to herself that Dickie could be dead, that he probably was dead. Tom went towards her slowly. 'I'm sorry, Marge. I'm sorry above all that I didn't tell you sooner about the rings.' He put his arm around her. He fairly had to, because she was leaning against him. He smelled her perfume. The Stradivari, probably. 'That's one of the reasons I felt sure he'd killed himself – at least that he might have.'

'Yes,' she said in a miserable, wailing tone.

She was not crying, actually, only leaning against him with her head rigidly bent down. Like someone who just heard the news of a death, Tom thought. Which she had.

'How about a brandy?' he said tenderly.

'No.'

'Come over and sit on the sofa.' He led her towards it.

She sat down, and he crossed the room to get the brandy, poured brandy into two inhalers. When he turned around, she was gone. He had just time to see the edge of her robe and her bare feet disappear at the top of the stairs.

She preferred to be by herself, he thought. He started to take a brandy up to her, then decided against it. She was probably beyond the help of brandy. He knew how she felt. He had meant to pour only one back, but he poured them both back, and then let it go and replaced the bottle among the other bottles.

He sank down on the sofa again, stretched a leg out with his foot dangling, too exhausted now even to remove his shoes. As tired as after he had killed Freddie Miles, he thought suddenly, or as after Dickie in San Remo. He had come so close! He remembered his cool thoughts of beating her senseless with his shoe heel, yet not roughly enough to break the skin anywhere, of dragging her through the front hall and out of the doors with the lights turned off so that no one would see them, and his quickly invented story, that she had evidently slipped, and thinking she could surely swim back to the steps, he hadn't jumped in or shouted for help until – In a way, he had even imagined the exact words that he and Mr Greenleaf would say to each other afterwards, Mr Greenleaf shocked and astounded, and he himself just as apparently shaken, but only apparently. Underneath he would be as calm and sure of himself as he had been after Freddie's murder, because his story would be unassailable. Like the San Remo story. His stories were good because he imagined them intensely, so intensely that he came to believe them.

For a moment he heard his own voice saying: '... I stood there on the steps calling to her, thinking she'd come up any second, or even that she might be playing a trick on me ... But I wasn't *sure* she'd hurt herself, and she'd been in such good humour standing there a moment before ...' He tensed himself. It was like a phonograph playing in his head, a little drama taking place right in the living-room that he was unable to stop. He could see himself with the Italian police and Mr Greenleaf by the big doors that opened to the front hall. He could see and hear himself talking earnestly. And being believed.

But what seemed to terrify him was not the dialogue or his halluci-natory belief that he had done it (he knew he hadn't), but the memory of himself standing in front of Marge with the shoe in his hand, imagining all this in a cool, methodical way. And the fact that he had done it twice before. Those two other times were *facts*, not imagination. He could say he hadn't wanted to do them, but he had done them. He didn't want to be a murderer. Sometimes he could absolutely forget that he had murdered, he realized. But sometimes – like now – he couldn't. He had surely forgotten for a while tonight, when he had been thinking about the meaning of possessions, and why he liked to live in Europe.

He twisted on to his side, his feet drawn up on the sofa. He was sweating and shaking. What was happening to him? What had happened? Was he going to blurt out a lot of nonsense tomorrow when he saw Mr Greenleaf, about Marge falling into the canal, and his screaming for help and jumping in and not finding her? Even with Marge standing there with them, would he go berserk and spill the story out and betray himself as a maniac?

He had to face Mr Greenleaf with the rings tomorrow. He would have to repeat the story he had told to Marge. He would have to give it details to make it better. He began to invent. His mind steadied. He was imagining a Roman hotel room, Dickie and he standing there talking, and Dickie taking off both his rings and handing them to him. Dickie said: 'It's just as well you don't tell anybody about this ...'

TWENTY-SEVEN

Marge called Mr Greenleaf at eight-thirty the next morning to ask how soon they could come over to his hotel, she had told Tom. But Mr Greenleaf must have noticed that she was upset. Tom heard her starting to tell him the story of the rings. Marge used the same words that Tom had used to her about the rings – evidently Marge had believed him – but Tom could not tell what Mr Greenleaf's reaction was. He was afraid this piece of news might be just the one that would bring the whole picture into focus, and that when they saw Mr Greenleaf this morning he might be in the company of a policeman ready to arrest Tom Ripley. This possibility rather offset the advantage of his not being on the scene when Mr Greenleaf heard about the rings.

'What did he say?' Tom asked when Marge had hung up.

Marge sat down tiredly on a chair across the room. 'He seems to feel the way I do. He said it himself. It looks as if Dickie meant to kill himself.'

But Mr Greenleaf would have a little time to think about it before they got there, Tom thought. 'What time are we due?' Tom asked.

'I told him about nine-thirty or before. As soon as we've had some coffee. The coffee's on now.' Marge got up and went into the kitchen. She was already dressed. She had on the travelling suit that she had worn when she arrived.

Tom sat up indecisively on the edge of the sofa and loosened his tie. He had slept in his clothes on the sofa, and Marge had awakened him when she had come down a few minutes ago. How he had possibly slept all night in the chilly room he didn't know. It embarrassed him. Marge had been amazed to find him there. There was a crick in his neck, his back, and his right shoulder. He felt wretched. He stood up suddenly. 'I'm going upstairs to wash,' he called to Marge.

He glanced into his room upstairs and saw that Marge had packed her suitcase. It was lying in the middle of the floor, closed. Tom hoped that she and Mr Greenleaf were still leaving on one of the morning trains. Probably they would, because Mr Greenleaf was supposed to meet the American detective in Rome today.

Tom undressed in the room next to Marge's, then went into the bathroom and turned on the shower. After a look at himself in the mirror he decided to shave first, and he went back to the room to get his electric razor which he had removed from the bathroom, for no particular reason, when Marge arrived. On the way back he heard the telephone ring. And Marge answered it. Tom leaned over the stairwell, listening.

'Oh, that's fine,' she said. 'Oh, that doesn't matter if we don't . . . Yes, I'll tell him . . . All right, we'll hurry. Tom's just washing up . . . Oh, less than an hour. Bye-bye.'

He heard her walking towards the stairs, and he stepped back because he was naked.

'Tom?' she yelled up. 'The detective from America just got here! He just called Mr Greenleaf and he's coming from the airport!'

'Fine!' Tom called back, and angrily went into the bedroom. He turned the shower off, and plugged his razor into the wall outlet. Suppose he'd been under the shower? Marge would have yelled up, anyway, simply assuming that he would be able to hear her. He would be glad when she was gone, and he hoped she left this morning. Unless she and Mr Greenleaf decided to stay to see what the detective was going to do with him. Tom knew that the detective had come to Venice especially to see him, otherwise he would have waited to see Mr Greenleaf in Rome. Tom wondered if Marge realized that too. Probably she didn't. That took a minimum of deduction.

Tom put on a quiet suit and tie, and went down to have coffee with Marge. He had taken his shower as hot as he could bear it, and he felt much better. Marge said nothing during the coffee except that the rings should make a great difference both to Mr Greenleaf and the detective, and she meant that it should look to the detective, too, as if Dickie had killed himself. Tom hoped she was right. Everything depended on what kind of man the detective would be. Everything depended on the first impression he made on the detective.

It was another grey, clammy day, not quite raining at nine o'clock, but it had rained, and it would rain again, probably towards noon. Tom and Marge caught the gondola from the church steps to San Marco, and walked from there to the Gritti. They telephoned up to Mr Greenleaf's room. Mr Greenleaf said that Mr McCarron was there, and asked them to come up.

Mr Greenleaf opened his door for them. 'Good morning,' he said. He pressed Marge's arm in a fatherly way. 'Tom –'

Tom came in behind Marge. The detective was standing by the window, a short chunky man of about thirty-five. His face looked friendly and alert. Moderately bright, but only moderately, was Tom's first impression.

'This is Alvin McCarron,' Mr Greenleaf said. 'Miss Sherwood and Mr Ripley.'

They all said, 'How do you do?'

Tom noticed a brand-new briefcase on the bed with some papers and photographs lying around it. McCarron was looking him over.

'I understand you're a friend of Richard's?' he asked.

'We both are,' Tom said.

They were interrupted for a minute while Mr Greenleaf saw that they were all seated. It was a good-sized, heavily furnished room with windows on the canal. Tom sat down in an armless chair upholstered in red. McCarron had installed himself on the bed, and was looking through his sheaf of papers. There were a few photostated papers, Tom saw, that looked like pictures of Dickie's cheques. There were also several loose photographs of Dickie.

'Do you have the rings?' McCarron asked, looking from Tom to Marge.

'Yes,' Marge said solemnly, getting up. She took the rings from her handbag and gave them to McCarron.

McCarron held them out in his palm to Mr Greenleaf. 'These are his rings?' he asked, and Mr Greenleaf nodded after only a glance at them, while Marge's face took on a slightly affronted expression as if she were about to say, 'I know his rings just as well as Mr Greenleaf and probably better.' McCarron turned to Tom. 'When did he give them to you?' he asked.

'In Rome. As nearly as I can remember, around February third, just a few days after the murder of Freddie Miles,' Tom answered.

The detective was studying him with his inquisitive, mild brown eyes. His lifted eyebrows put a couple of wrinkles in the thick-looking skin of his forehead. He had wavy brown hair, cut very short on the sides, with a high curl above his forehead, in a rather cute college-boy style. One couldn't tell a thing from that face, Tom thought: it was trained. 'What did he say when he gave them to you?'

'He said that if anything happened to him he wanted me to have them. I asked him what he thought was going to happen to him. He said he didn't know, but something might.' Tom paused deliberately. 'He didn't seem more depressed at that particular moment than a lot of other times. I'd talked to him, so it didn't cross my mind that he was going to kill himself. I knew he intended to go away, that was all.'

'Where?' asked the detective.

'To Palermo,' he said. Tom looked at Marge. 'He must have given them to me the day you spoke to me in Rome – at the Inghilterra. That day or the day before. Do you remember the date?'

'February second,' Marge said in a subdued voice.

McCarron was making notes. 'What else?' he asked Tom. 'What time of day was it? Had he been drinking?'

'No. He drinks very little. I think it was early afternoon. He said it would be just as well if I didn't mention the rings to anybody, and of course I agreed. I put the rings away and completely forgot about them, as I told Miss Sherwood – I supposed because I'd so impressed on myself that he didn't want me to say anything about them.' Tom spoke straightforwardly, stammering a little, inadvertently, just as anybody might stammer under the circumstances, Tom thought.

'What did you do with the rings?'

'I put them in an old box that I have – just a little box I keep odd buttons in.'

McCarron regarded him for a moment in silence, and Tom took the moment to brace himself. Out of that placid yet alert Irish face could come anything, a challenging question, a flat statement that he was lying. Tom clung harder in his mind to his own facts, determined to defend them unto death. In the silence, Tom could almost hear Marge's breathing, and a cough from Mr Greenleaf made him start. Mr Greenleaf looked remarkably calm, almost bored. Tom wondered if he had fixed up some scheme with McCarron against him, based on the rings story?

'Is he the kind of man to lend you the rings for luck for a short time? Had he ever done anything else like that?' McCarron asked.

'No,' Marge said before Tom could answer.

Tom began to breathe more easily. He could see that McCarron didn't know yet what he should make out of it. McCarron was waiting for him to answer. 'He had lent me certain things before,' Tom said. 'He'd told me to help myself to his ties and jackets now and then. But that's quite a different matter from the rings, of course.' He had felt a compulsion to say that, because Marge undoubtedly knew about the time Dickie had found him in his clothes.

'I can't imagine Dickie without his rings,' Marge said to McCarron. 'He took the green one off when he went swimming, but he always put it right on again. They were just like part of his dressing. That's why I think he was either intending to kill himself or he meant to change his identity.'

McCarron nodded. 'Had he any enemies that you know of?'

'Absolutely none,' Tom said. 'I've thought of that.'

'Any reason you can think of why he might have wanted to disguise himself, or assume another identity?'

Tom said carefully, twisting his aching neck, 'Possibly – but it's next to impossible in Europe. He'd have had to have a different passport. Any country he'd have entered, he would have had to have a passport. He'd have had to have a passport even to get into a hotel.'

'You told me he might not have had to have a passport,' Mr Greenleaf said.

'Yes, I said that about small hotels in Italy. It's a remote possibility, of course. But after all this publicity about his disappearance, I don't see how he could still be keeping it up,' Tom said. 'Somebody would surely have betrayed him by this time.'

'Well, he left with his passport, obviously,' McCarron said, 'because he got into Sicily with it and registered at a big hotel.'

'Yes,' Tom said.

McCarron made notes for a moment, then looked up at Tom. 'Well, how do you see it, Mr Ripley?'

McCarron wasn't nearly finished, Tom thought. McCarron was going to see him alone later. 'I'm afraid I agree with Miss Sherwood that it looks as if he's killed himself, and it looks as if he intended to all along. I've said that before to Mr Greenleaf.'

McCarron looked at Mr Greenleaf, but Mr Greenleaf said nothing, only looked expectantly at McCarron. Tom had the feeling that McCarron was now inclined to think that Dickie was dead, too, and that it was a waste of time and money for him to have come over.

'I just want to check these facts again,' McCarron said, still plodding on, going back to his papers. 'The last time Richard was seen by anybody is February fifteenth, when he got off the boat in Naples, coming from Palermo.'

'That's correct,' Mr Greenleaf said. 'A steward remembers seeing him.'

'But no sign of him at any hotel after that, and no communications from him since.' McCarron looked from Mr Greenleaf to Tom.

'No,' Tom said.

McCarron looked at Marge.

'No,' Marge said.

'And when was the last time you saw him, Miss Sherwood?'

'On November twenty-third, when he left for San Remo,' Marge said promptly.

'You were then in Mongibello?' McCarron asked, pronouncing the town's name with a hard 'g', as if he had no knowledge of Italian.

'Yes,' Marge said. 'I just missed seeing him in Rome in February, but the last time I saw him was in Mongibello.'

Good old Marge! Tom felt almost affectionate towards her – underneath everything. He had begun to feel affectionate this morning, even though she had irritated him. 'He was trying to avoid everyone in Rome,' Tom put in. 'That's why, when he first gave me the rings, I thought he was on some tack of getting away from everyone he had known, living in another city, and just vanishing for a while.'

'Why, do you think?'

Tom elaborated, mentioning the murder of his friend Freddie Miles, and its effect on Dickie.

'Do you think Richard knew who killed Freddie Miles?'

'No. I certainly don't.'

McCarron waited for Marge's opinion.

'No,' Marge said, shaking her head.

'Think a minute,' McCarron said to Tom. 'Do you think that might have explained his behaviour? Do you think he's avoiding answering the police by hiding out now?'

Tom thought for a minute. 'He didn't give me a single clue in that direction.'

'Do you think Dickie was afraid of something?'

'I can't imagine of what,' Tom said.

McCarron asked Tom how close a friend Dickie had been of Freddie Miles, whom else he knew who was a friend of both Dickie and Freddie, if he knew of any debts between them, any girl friends – 'Only Marge that

I know of,' Tom replied, and Marge protested that she wasn't a *girl* friend of Freddie's, so there couldn't possibly have been any *rivalry* over her – and could Tom say that he was Dickie's best friend in Europe?

'I wouldn't say that,' Tom answered. 'I think Marge Sherwood is. I hardly know any of Dickie's friends in Europe.'

McCarron studied Tom's face again. 'What's your opinion about these forgeries?'

'Are they forgeries? I didn't think anybody was sure.'

'I don't think they are,' Marge said.

'Opinion seems to be divided,' McCarron said. 'The experts don't think the letter he wrote to the bank in Naples is a forgery, which can only mean that if there is a forgery somewhere, he's covering up for someone. Assuming there is a forgery, do you have any idea who he might be trying to cover up for?'

Tom hesitated a moment, and Marge said, 'Knowing him, I can't imagine him covering up for anyone. Why should he?'

McCarron was staring at Tom, but whether he was debating his honesty or mulling over all they had said to him, Tom couldn't tell. McCarron looked like a typical American automobile salesman, or any other kind of salesman, Tom thought – cheerful, presentable, average in intellect, able to talk baseball with a man or pay a stupid compliment to a woman. Tom didn't think too much of him, but, on the other hand, it was not wise to underestimate one's opponent. McCarron's small, soft mouth opened as Tom watched him, and he said, 'Would you mind coming downstairs with me for a few minutes, Mr Ripley, if you've still got a few minutes?'

'Certainly,' Tom said, standing up.

'We won't be long,' McCarron said to Mr Greenleaf and Marge.

Tom looked back from the door, because Mr Greenleaf had gotten up and was starting to say something, though Tom didn't listen. Tom was suddenly aware that it was raining, that thin, grey sheets of rain were slapping against the window-panes. It was like a last glimpse, blurred and hasty – Marge's figure looking small and huddled across the big room, Mr Greenleaf doddering forward like an old man, protesting. But the comfortable room was the thing, and the view across the canal to where his house stood – invisible now because of the rain – which he might never see again.

Mr Greenleaf was asking, 'Are you – you are coming back in a few minutes?'

'Oh, yes,' McCarron answered with the impersonal firmness of an executioner.

They walked towards the elevator. Was this the way they did it? Tom

wondered. A quiet word in the lobby. He would be handed over to the
Italian police, and then McCarron would return to the room just as he had
promised. McCarron had brought a couple of the papers from his briefcase
with him. Tom stared at an ornamental vertical moulding beside the floor
number panel in the elevator: an egg-shaped design framed by four raised
dots, egg-shape, dots, all the way down. *Think of some sensible, ordinary
remark to make about Mr Greenleaf, for instance*, Tom said to himself. He
ground his teeth. If he only wouldn't start sweating now. He hadn't started
yet, but maybe it would break out all over his face when they reached the
lobby. McCarron was hardly as tall as his shoulder. Tom turned to him
just as the elevator stopped, and said grimly, baring his teeth in a smile,
'Is this your first trip to Venice?'

'Yes,' said McCarron. He was crossing the lobby. 'Shall we go in here?'
He indicated the coffee bar. His tone was polite.

'All right,' Tom said agreeably. The bar was not crowded, but there was
not a single table that would be out of earshot of some other table. Would
McCarron accuse him in a place like this, quietly laying down fact after
fact on the table? He took the chair that McCarron pulled out for him.
McCarron sat with his back to the wall.

A waiter came up. 'Signori?'

'Coffee,' McCarron said.

'Cappuccino,' Tom said. 'Would you like cappuccino or an espresso?'

'Which is the one with milk? Cappuccino?'

'Yes.'

'I'll have that.'

Tom gave the order.

McCarron looked at him. His small mouth smiled on one side. Tom
imagined three or four different beginnings: 'You killed Richard, didn't
you? The rings are just too much, aren't they?' Or 'Tell me about the San
Remo boat, Mr Ripley, in detail.' Or simply, leading up quietly, 'Where
were you on February fifteenth, when Richard landed in ... Naples? All
right, but where were you living then? Where were you in January, for
instance? ... Can you prove it?'

McCarron was saying nothing at all, only looking down at his plump
hands now, and smiling faintly. As if it had been so absurdly simple for
him to unravel, Tom thought, that he could hardly force himself to put
it into words.

At a table next to them four Italian men were babbling away like a
madhouse, screeching with wild laughter. Tom wanted to edge away from
them. He sat motionless.

Tom braced himself until his body felt like iron, until sheer tension created defiance. He heard himself asking, in an incredibly calm voice, 'Did you have time to speak to Tenente Roverini when you came to Rome?' and at the same time he asked it, he realized that he had even an objective in the question: to find out if McCarron had heard about the San Remo boat.

'No, I didn't,' McCarron said. 'There was a message for me that Mr Greenleaf would be in Rome today, but I'd landed in Rome so early, I thought I'd fly over and catch him – and also talk to you.' McCarron looked down at his papers. 'What kind of a man is Richard? How would you describe him as far as his personality goes?'

Was McCarron going to lead up to it like this? Pick out more little clues from the words he chose to describe him? Or did he only want the objective opinion that he couldn't get from Dickie's parents? 'He wanted to be a painter,' Tom began, 'but he knew he'd never be a very good painter. He tried to act as if he didn't care, and as if he were perfectly happy and leading exactly the kind of life he wanted to lead over here in Europe.' Tom moistened his lips. 'But I think the life was beginning to get him down. His father disapproved, as you probably know. And Dickie had got himself into an awkward spot with Marge.'

'How do you mean?'

'Marge was in love with him, and he wasn't with her, and at the same time he was seeing her so much in Mongibello, she kept on hoping –' Tom began to feel on safer ground, but he pretended to have difficulty in expressing himself. 'He never actually discussed it with me. He always spoke very highly of Marge. He was very fond of her, but it was obvious to everybody – Marge too – that he never would marry her. But Marge never quite gave up. I think that's the main reason Dickie left Mongibello.'

McCarron listened patiently and sympathetically, Tom thought. 'What do you mean never gave up? What did she do?'

Tom waited until the waiter had set down the two frothy cups of cappuccino and stuck the tab between them under the sugar bowl. 'She kept writing to him, wanting to see him, and at the same time being very tactful, I'm sure, about not intruding on him when he wanted to be by himself. He told me all this in Rome when I saw him. He said, after the Miles murder, that he certainly wasn't in the mood to see Marge, and he was afraid that she'd come up to Rome from Mongibello when she heard of all the trouble he was in.'

'Why do you think he was nervous after the Miles murder?' McCarron took a sip of the coffee, winced from the heat or the bitterness, and stirred it with the spoon.

Tom explained. They'd been quite good friends, and Freddie had been killed just a few minutes after leaving his house.

'Do you think Richard might have killed Freddie?' McCarron asked quietly.

'No, I don't.'

'Why?'

'Because there was no reason for him to kill him – at least no reason that I happen to know of.'

'People usually say, because so-and-so wasn't the type to kill anybody,' McCarron said. 'Do you think Richard was the type who could have killed anyone?'

Tom hesitated, seeking earnestly for the truth. 'I never thought of it. I don't know what kind of people are apt to kill somebody. I've seen him angry –'

'When?'

Tom described the two days in Rome, when Dickie, he said, had been angry and frustrated because of the police questioning, and had actually moved out of his apartment to avoid phone calls from friends and strangers. Tom tied this in with a growing frustration in Dickie, because he had not been progressing as he had wanted to in his painting. He depicted Dickie as a stubborn, proud young man, in awe of his father and therefore determined to defy his father's wishes, a rather erratic fellow who was generous to strangers as well as to his friends, but who was subject to changes of mood – from sociability to sullen withdrawal. He summed it up by saying that Dickie was a very ordinary young man who liked to think he was extraordinary. 'If he killed himself,' Tom concluded, 'I think it was because he realized certain failures in himself – inadequacies. It's much easier for me to imagine him a suicide than a murderer.'

'But I'm not so sure that he didn't kill Freddie Miles. Are you?'

McCarron was perfectly sincere. Tom was sure of that. McCarron was even expecting him to defend Dickie now, because they had been friends. Tom felt some of his terror leaving him, but only some of it, like something melting very slowly inside him. 'I'm not sure,' Tom said, 'but I just don't believe that he did.'

'I'm not sure either. But it would explain a lot, wouldn't it?'

'Yes,' Tom said. 'Everything.'

'Well, this is only the first day of work,' McCarron said with an optimistic smile. 'I haven't even looked over the report in Rome. I'll probably want to talk to you again after I've been to Rome.'

Tom stared at him. It seemed to be over. 'Do you speak Italian?'

'No, not very well, but I can read it. I do better in French, but I'll get along,' McCarron said, as if it were not a matter of much importance.

It was very important, Tom thought. He couldn't imagine McCarron extracting everything that Roverini knew about the Greenleaf case solely through an interpreter. Neither would McCarron be able to get around and chat with people like Dickie Greenleaf's landlady in Rome. It was most important. 'I talked with Roverini here in Venice a few weeks ago,' Tom said. 'Give him my regards.'

'I'll do that.' McCarron finished his coffee. 'Knowing Dickie, what places do you think he would be likely to go if he wanted to hide out?'

Tom squirmed back a little on his chair. This was getting down to the bottom of the barrel, he thought. 'Well, I know he likes Italy best. I wouldn't bet on France. He also likes Greece. He talked about going to Majorca at some time. All of Spain is a possibility, I suppose.'

'I see,' McCarron said, sighing.

'Are you going back to Rome today?'

McCarron raised his eyebrows. 'I imagine so, if I can catch a few hours' sleep here. I haven't been to bed in two days.'

He held up very well, Tom thought. 'I think Mr Greenleaf was wondering about the trains. There are two this morning and probably some more in the afternoon. He was planning to leave today.'

'We can leave today.' McCarron reached for the check. 'Thanks very much for your help, Mr Ripley. I have your address and phone number, in case I have to see you again.'

They stood up.

'Mind if I go up and say good-bye to Marge and Mr Greenleaf?'

McCarron didn't mind. They rode up in the elevator again. Tom had to check himself from whistling. *Papa non vuole* was going around in his head.

Tom looked closely at Marge as they went in, looking for signs of enmity. Marge only looked a little tragic, he thought. As if she had recently been made a widow.

'I'd like to ask you a few questions alone, too, Miss Sherwood,' McCarron said. 'If you don't mind,' he said to Mr Greenleaf.

'Certainly not. I was just going down to the lobby to buy some newspapers,' Mr Greenleaf said.

McCarron was carrying on. Tom said good-bye to Marge and to Mr Greenleaf, in case they were going to Rome today and he did not see them again. He said to McCarron, 'I'd be very glad to come to Rome at any time, if I can be of any help. I expect to be here until the end of May, anyway.'

'We'll have something before then,' McCarron said with his confident Irish smile.

Tom went down to the lobby with Mr Greenleaf.

'He asked me the same questions all over again,' Tom told Mr Greenleaf, 'and also my opinion of Richard's character.'

'Well, what is your opinion?' Mr Greenleaf asked in a hopeless tone.

Whether he was a suicide or had run away to hide himself would be conduct equally reprehensible in Mr Greenleaf's eyes, Tom knew. 'I told him what I think is the truth,' Tom said, 'that he's capable of running away and also capable of committing suicide.'·

Mr Greenleaf made no comment, and only patted Tom's arm. 'Good-bye, Tom.'

'Good-bye,' Tom said. 'Let me hear from you.'

Everything was all right between him and Mr Greenleaf, Tom thought. And everything would be all right with Marge, too. She had swallowed the suicide explanation, and that was the direction her mind would run in from now on, he knew.

Tom spent the afternoon at home, expecting a telephone call, one telephone call at least from McCarron, even if it was not about anything important, but none came. There was only a call from Titi, the resident countess, inviting him for cocktails that afternoon. Tom accepted.

Why should he expect any trouble from Marge, he thought. She never had given him any. The suicide was an idée fixe, and she would arrange everything in her dull imagination to fit it.

TWENTY-EIGHT

McCarron called Tom the next day from Rome, wanting the names of everyone Dickie had known in Mongibello. That was apparently all that McCarron wanted to know, because he took a leisurely time getting them all, and checking them off against the list that Marge had given him. Most of the names Marge had already given him, but Tom went through them all, with their difficult addresses – Giorgio, of course, Pietro the boatkeeper, Fausto's Aunt Maria whose last name he didn't know though he told

McCarron in a complicated way how to get to her house, Aldo the grocer, the Cecchis, and even old Stevenson, the recluse painter who lived just outside the village and whom Tom had never even met. It took Tom several minutes to list them all, and it would take McCarron several days to check on them, probably. He mentioned everybody but Signor Pucci, who had handled the sale of Dickie's house and boat, and who would undoubtedly tell McCarron, if he hadn't learned it through Marge, that Tom Ripley had come to Mongibello to arrange Dickie's affairs. Tom did not think it very serious, one way or the other, if McCarron did know that he had taken care of Dickie's affairs. And as to people like Aldo and Stevenson, McCarron was welcome to all he could get out of them.

'Anyone in Naples?' McCarron asked.

'Not that I know of.'

'Rome?'

'I'm sorry, I never saw him with any friends in Rome.'

'Never met this painter – uh – Di Massimo?'

'No. I saw him once,' Tom said, 'but I never met him.'

'What does he look like?'

'Well, it was just on a street corner. I left Dickie as he was going to meet him, so I wasn't very close to him. He looked about five feet nine, about fifty, greyish-black hair – that's about all I remember. He looked rather solidly built. He was wearing a light-grey suit, I remember.'

'Hm-m – okay,' McCarron said absently, as if he were writing all that down. 'Well, I guess that's about all. Thanks very much, Mr Ripley.'

'You're very welcome. Good luck.'

Then Tom waited quietly in his house for several days, just as anybody would do, if the search for a missing friend had reached its intensest point. He declined three or four invitations to parties. The newspapers had renewed their interest in Dickie's disappearance, inspired by the presence in Italy of an American private detective who had been hired by Dickie's father. When some photographers from *Europeo* and *Oggi* came to take pictures of him and his house, he told them firmly to leave, and actually took one insistent young man by the elbow and propelled him across the living-room towards the door. But nothing of any importance happened for five days – no telephone calls, no letters, even from Tenente Roverini. Tom imagined the worst sometimes, especially at dusk when he felt more depressed than at any other time of day. He imagined Roverini and McCarron getting together and developing the theory that Dickie could have disappeared in November, imagined McCarron checking on the time he had bought his car, imagined him picking up a scent when he found

out that Dickie had not come back after the San Remo trip and that Tom
Ripley had come down to arrange for the disposal of Dickie's things. He
measured and remeasured Mr Greenleaf's tired, indifferent good-bye that
last morning in Venice, interpreted it as unfriendly, and imagined Mr
Greenleaf flying into a rage in Rome when no results came of all the efforts
to find Dickie, and suddenly demanding a thorough investigation of Tom
Ripley, that scoundrel he had sent over with his own money to try to get
his son home.

But each morning Tom was optimistic again. On the good side was the
fact that Marge unquestioningly believed that Dickie had spent those
months sulking in Rome, and she would have kept all his letters and she
would probably bring them all out to show to McCarron. Excellent letters
they were, too. Tom was glad he had spent so much thought on them.
Marge was an asset rather than a liability. It was really a very good thing
that he had put down his shoe that night that she had found the rings.

Every morning he watched the sun, from his bedroom window, rising
through the winter mists, struggling upwards over the peaceful-looking
city, breaking through finally to give a couple of hours of actual sunshine
before noon, and the quiet beginning of each day was like a promise of
peace in the future. The days were growing warmer. There was more light,
and less rain. Spring was almost here, and one of these mornings, one
morning finer than these, he would leave the house and board a ship for
Greece.

On the evening of the sixth day after Mr Greenleaf and McCarron had
left, Tom called him in Rome. Mr Greenleaf had nothing new to report,
but Tom had not expected anything. Marge had gone home. As long as
Mr Greenleaf was in Italy, Tom thought, the papers would carry something about the case every day. But the newspapers were running out of
sensational things to say about the Greenleaf case.

'And how is your wife?' Tom asked.

'Fair. I think the strain is telling on her, however. I spoke to her again
last night.'

'I'm sorry,' Tom said. He ought to write her a nice letter, he thought,
just a friendly word while Mr Greenleaf was away and she was by herself.
He wished he had thought of it before.

Mr Greenleaf said he would be leaving at the end of the week, via Paris,
where the French police were also carrying on the search. McCarron was
going with him, and if nothing happened in Paris they were both going
home. 'It's obvious to me or to anybody,' Mr Greenleaf said, 'that he's
either dead or deliberately hiding. There's not a corner of the world where

the search for him hasn't been publicized. Short of Russia, maybe. My God, he never showed any liking for that place, did he?'

'Russia? No, not that I know of.'

Apparently Mr Greenleaf's attitude was that Dickie was either dead or to hell with him. During that telephone call, the to-hell-with-him attitude seemed to be uppermost.

Tom went over to Peter Smith-Kingsley's house that same evening. Peter had a couple of English newspapers that his friends had sent him, one with a picture of Tom ejecting the *Oggi* photographer from his house. Tom had seen it in the Italian newspapers too. Pictures of him on the streets of Venice and pictures of his house had also reached America. Bob and Cleo both had airmailed him photographs and write-ups from New York tabloids. They thought it was all terribly exciting.

'I'm good and sick of it,' Tom said. 'I'm only hanging around here to be polite and to help if I can. If any more reporters try to crash my house, they're going to get it with a shotgun as soon as they walk in the door.' He really was irritated and disgusted, and it sounded in his voice.

'I quite understand,' Peter said. 'I'm going home at the end of May, you know. If you'd like to come along and stay at my place in Ireland, you're more than welcome. It's deadly quiet there, I can assure you.'

Tom glanced at him. Peter had told him about his old Irish castle and had shown him pictures of it. Some quality of his relationship with Dickie flashed across his mind like the memory of a nightmare, like a pale and evil ghost. It was because the same thing could happen with Peter, he thought, Peter the upright, unsuspecting, naïve, generous good fellow – except that he didn't look enough like Peter. But one evening, for Peter's amusement, he had put on an English accent and had imitated Peter's mannerisms and his ways of jerking his head to one side as he talked, and Peter had thought it hilariously funny. He shouldn't have done that, Tom thought now. It made Tom bitterly ashamed, that evening and the fact that he had thought even for an instant that the same thing that had happened with Dickie could happen with Peter.

'Thanks,' Tom said. 'I'd better stay by myself for a while longer. I miss my friend Dickie, you know. I miss him terribly.' He was suddenly near tears. He could remember Dickie's smiles that first day they began to get along, when he had confessed to Dickie that his father had sent him. He remembered their crazy first trip to Rome. He remembered with affection even that half-hour in the Carlton Bar in Cannes, when Dickie had been so bored and silent, but there had been a reason why Dickie had been bored, after all: he had dragged Dickie there, and Dickie didn't care for the

Côte d'Azur. If he'd only gotten his sightseeing done all by himself, Tom thought, if he only hadn't been in such a hurry and so greedy, if he only hadn't misjudged the relationship between Dickie and Marge so stupidly, or had simply waited for them to separate of their own volition, then none of this would have happened, and he *could* have lived with Dickie for the rest of his life, travelled and lived and enjoyed living for the rest of his life. If he only hadn't put on Dickie's clothes that day –

'I understand, Tommie boy, I really do,' Peter said, patting his shoulder.

Tom looked up at him through distorting tears. He was imagining travelling with Dickie on some liner back to America for Christmas holidays, imagining being on as good terms with Dickie's parents as if he and Dickie had been brothers. 'Thanks,' Tom said. It came out a childlike 'blub'.

'I'd really think something was the matter with you if you didn't break down like this,' Peter said sympathetically.

TWENTY-NINE

Venice
3 June, 19—

Dear Mr Greenleaf:

While packing a suitcase today, I came across an envelope that Richard gave me in Rome, and which for some unaccountable reason I had forgotten until now. On the envelope was written 'Not to be opened until June' and, as it happens, it is June. The envelope contained Richard's will, and he leaves his income and possessions to me. I am as astounded by this as you probably are, yet from the wording of the will (it is typewritten) he seems to have been in possession of his senses.

I am only bitterly sorry I did not remember having the envelope, because it would have proven much earlier that Dickie intended to take his own life. I put it into a suitcase pocket, and then I forgot it. He gave it to me on the last occasion I saw him, in Rome, when he was so depressed.

On second thought, I am enclosing a photostat copy of the will so that you may see it for yourself. This is the first will I have ever seen in my life, and I am absolutely unfamiliar with the usual procedure. What should I do?

Please give my kindest regards to Mrs Greenleaf and realize that I sympathize deeply with you both, and regret the necessity of writing this letter. Please let me hear from you as soon as possible. My next address will be:

c/o American Express
Athens, Greece
Most sincerely yours,
Tom Ripley

In a way it was asking for trouble, Tom thought. It might start a new investigation of the signatures, on the will and also the remittances, one of the relentless investigations that insurance companies and probably trust companies also launched when it was a matter of money out of their own pockets. But that was the mood he was in. He had bought his ticket for Greece in the middle of May, and the days had grown finer and finer, making him more and more restless. He had taken his car out of the Fiat garage in Venice and had driven over the Brenner to Salzburg and Munich, down to Trieste and over to Bolzano, and the weather had held everywhere, except for the mildest, most springlike shower in Munich when he had been walking in the Englischer Garten, and he had not even tried to get under cover from it but had simply kept on walking, thrilled as a child at the thought that this was the first German rain that had ever fallen on him. He had only two thousand dollars in his own name, transferred from Dickie's bank account and saved out of Dickie's income, because he hadn't dared to withdraw any more in so short a time as three months. The very chanciness of trying for all of Dickie's money, the peril of it, was irresistible to him. He was so bored after the dreary, eventless weeks in Venice, when each day that went by had seemed to confirm his personal safety and to emphasize the dullness of his existence. Roverini had stopped writing to him. Alvin McCarron had gone back to America (after nothing more than another inconsequential telephone call to him from Rome), and Tom supposed that he and Mr Greenleaf had concluded Dickie was either dead or hiding of his own will, and that further search was useless. The newspapers had stopped printing anything about Dickie for want of anything to print. Tom had a feeling of emptiness and abeyance that had driven him nearly mad until he made the trip to Munich in his car. When he came back to Venice to pack for Greece and to close his house, the sensation had been worse: he was about to go to Greece, to those ancient heroic islands, as little Tom Ripley, shy and meek, with a dwindling two-thousand-odd in his bank, so that he would practically have to think twice before he bought himself even a book on Greek art. It was intolerable.

He had decided in Venice to make his voyage to Greece an heroic one.

He would see the islands, swimming for the first time into his view, as a living, breathing, courageous individual – not as a cringing little nobody from Boston. If he sailed right into the arms of the police in Piraeus, he would at least have known the days just before, standing in the wind at the prow of a ship, crossing the wine-dark sea like Jason or Ulysses returning. So he had written the letter to Mr Greenleaf and mailed it three days before he was to sail from Venice. Mr Greenleaf would probably not get the letter for four or five days, so there would be no time for Mr Greenleaf to hold him in Venice with a telegram and make him miss his ship. Besides, it looked better from every point of view to be casual about the thing, not to be reachable for another week or so until he got to Greece, as if he were so unconcerned as to whether he got the money or not, he had not let the fact of the will postpone even a little trip he had planned to make.

Two days before his sailing, he went to tea at the house of Titi della Latta-Cacciaguerra, the countess he had met the day he had started looking for a house in Venice. The maid showed him into the living room, and Titi greeted him with the phrase he had not heard for many weeks: 'Ah, ciao, Tomaso! Have you seen the afternoon paper? They have found Dickie's suitcases! And his paintings! Right here in the American Express in Venice!' Her gold earrings trembled with her excitement.

'What?' Tom hadn't seen the papers. He had been too busy packing that afternoon.

'Read it! Here! All his clothes deposited only in February! They were sent from Naples. Perhaps he is here in Venice!'

Tom was reading it. The cord around the canvases had come undone, the paper said, and in wrapping them again a clerk had discovered the signature of R. Greenleaf on the paintings. Tom's hands began to shake so that he had to grip the sides of the paper to hold it steady. The paper said that the police were now examining everything carefully for finger-prints.

'Perhaps he is alive!' Titi shouted.

'I don't think – I don't see why this proves he is alive. He could have been murdered or killed himself after he sent the suitcases. The fact that it's under another name – Fanshaw –' He had the feeling the countess, who was sitting rigidly on the sofa staring at him, was startled by his nervousness, so he pulled himself together abruptly, summoned all his courage and said, 'You see? They're looking through everything for finger-prints. They wouldn't be doing that if they were sure Dickie had sent the suitcases himself. Why should he deposit them under Fanshaw, if he expected to claim them against himself? His passport's even here. He packed his passport.'

'Perhaps he is hiding himself under the name of Fanshaw! Oh, caro mio, you need some tea!' Titi stood up. 'Giustina! Il te, per piacere, subitissimo!'

Tom sank down weakly on the sofa, still holding the newspaper in front of him. What about the knot on Dickie's body? Wouldn't it be just his luck to have that come undone now?

'Ah, carissimo, you are so pessimistic,' Titi said, patting his knee. 'This is good news! Suppose all the fingerprints are his? Wouldn't you be happy then? Suppose tomorrow, when you are walking in some little street of Venice, you will come face to face with Dickie Greenleaf, alias Signor Fanshaw!' She let out her shrill, pleasant laugh that was as natural to her as breathing.

'It says here that the suitcases contained everything – shaving kit, toothbrush, shoes, overcoat, complete equipment,' Tom said, hiding his terror in gloom. 'He couldn't be alive and leave all that. The murderer must have stripped his body and deposited his clothes there because it was the easiest way of getting rid of them.'

This gave even Titi pause. Then she said, 'Will you not be so down-hearted until you know what the fingerprints are? You are supposed to be off on a pleasure trip tomorrow. Ecco il te!'

The day after tomorrow, Tom thought. Plenty of time for Roverini to get his fingerprints and compare them with those on the canvases and in the suitcases. He tried to remember any flat surfaces on the canvas frames and on things in the suitcases from which fingerprints could be taken. There was not much, except the articles in the shaving kit, but they could find enough, in fragments and smears, to assemble ten perfect prints if they tried. His only reason for optimism was that they didn't have his fingerprints yet, and they might not ask for them because he was not yet under suspicion. But if they already had Dickie's fingerprints from somewhere? Wouldn't Mr Greenleaf send Dickie's fingerprints from America the very first thing, by way of checking? There could be any number of places they could find Dickie's fingerprints: on certain possessions of his in America, in the house in Mongibello –

'Tomaso! Take your tea!' Titi said, with another gentle press of his knee. 'Thank you.'

'You will see. At least this is a step towards the truth, what *really* happened. Now let us talk about something else, if it makes you so unhappy! Where do you go from Athens?'

He tried to turn his thoughts to Greece. For him, Greece was gilded, with the gold of warriors' armour and with its own famous sunlight. He saw stone statues with calm, strong faces, like the women on the porch of the Erechtheum. He didn't want to go to Greece with the threat of the fingerprints in Venice hanging over him. It would debase him. He would feel as low as the lowest rat that scurried in the gutters of Athens, lower than the dirtiest beggar who would accost him in the streets of Salonika. Tom put his face in his hands and wept. Greece was finished, exploded like a golden balloon.

Titi put her firm, plump arm around him. 'Tomaso, cheer up! Wait until you have reason to feel so downcast!'

'I can't see why you don't see that this is a bad sign!' Tom said desperately. 'I really don't!'

THIRTY

The worst sign of all was that Roverini, whose messages had been so friendly and explicit up to now, sent him nothing at all in regard to the suitcases and canvases having been found in Venice. Tom spent a sleepless night and then a day, of pacing his house while he tried to finish the endless little chores pertaining to his departure, paying Anna and Ugo, paying various tradesmen. Tom expected the police to come knocking on his door at any hour of the day or night. The contrast between his tranquil self-confidence of five days ago and his present apprehension almost tore him apart. He could neither sleep nor eat nor sit still. The irony of Anna's and Ugo's commiseration with him, and also of the telephone calls from his friends, asking him if he had any ideas as to what might have happened in view of the finding of the suitcases, seemed more than he could bear. Ironic, too, that he could let them know that he was upset, pessimistic, desperate even, and they thought nothing of it. They thought it was perfectly normal, because Dickie after all might have been murdered: everybody considered it very significant that all Dickie's possessions had been in the suitcases in Venice, down to his shaving kit and comb.

Then there was the matter of the will. Mr Greenleaf would get it the day after tomorrow. By that time they might know that the fingerprints were not Dickie's. By that time they might have intercepted the *Hellenes*, and taken his own fingerprints. If they discovered that the will was a forgery, too, they would have no mercy on him. Both murders would come out, as naturally as ABC.

By the time he boarded the *Hellenes* Tom felt like a walking ghost. He was sleepless, foodless, full of espressos, carried along only by his twitching nerves. He wanted to ask if there was a radio, but he was positive there was a radio. It was a good-sized triple-deck ship with forty-eight passengers. He collapsed about five minutes after the stewards had brought his luggage into his cabin. He remembered lying face down on his bunk with one arm twisted under him, and being too tired to change his position, and when he awakened the ship was moving, not only moving but rolling gently with a pleasant rhythm that suggested a tremendous reserve of power and a promise of unending, unobstructable forward movement that would sweep aside anything in its way. He felt better except that the arm he had been lying on hung limply at his side like a dead member, and flopped against him when he walked through the corridor so that he had to grip it with the other hand to hold it in place. It was a quarter of ten by his watch, and utterly dark outside.

There was some kind of land on his extreme left, probably part of Yugoslavia, five or six little dim white lights, and otherwise nothing but black sea and black sky, so black that there was no trace of an horizon and they might have been sailing against a black screen, except that he felt no resistance to the steadily ploughing ship, and the wind blew freely on his forehead as if out of infinite space. There was no one around him on the deck. They were all below, eating their late dinner, he supposed. He was glad to be alone. His arm was coming back to life. He gripped the prow where it separated in a narrow V and took a deep breath. A defiant courage rose in him. What if the radio-man were receiving at this very minute a message to arrest Tom Ripley? He would stand up just as bravely as he was standing now. Or he might hurl himself over the ship's gunwale – which for him would be the supreme act of courage as well as escape. Well, what if? Even from where he stood, he could hear the faint *beep-beep-beep* from the radio room at the top of the superstructure. He was not afraid. This was it. This was the way he had hoped he would feel, sailing to Greece. To look out at the black water all around him and not be afraid was almost as good as seeing the islands of Greece coming into view. In the soft June darkness ahead of him he could construct in imagination the little islands, the hills of Athens dotted with buildings, and the Acropolis.

There was an elderly Englishwoman on board the ship, travelling with her daughter who herself was forty, unmarried and so wildly nervous she could not even enjoy the sun for fifteen minutes in her deck-chair without leaping up and announcing in a loud voice that she was 'off for a walk'. Her mother, by contrast, was extremely calm and slow, she had some kind of paralysis in her right leg, which was shorter than the other so that she had to wear a thick heel on her right shoe and could not walk except with a cane – the kind of person who would have driven Tom insane in New York with her slowness and her unvarying graciousness of manner, but now Tom was inspired to spend time with her in the deck-chair, talking to her and listening to her talk about her life in England and about Greece, when she had last seen Greece in 1926. He took her for a slow walk around the deck, she leaning on his arm and apologizing constantly for the trouble she was giving him, but obviously she loved the attention. And the daughter was obviously delighted that someone was taking her mother off her hands.

Maybe Mrs Cartwright had been a hellcat in her youth, Tom thought, maybe she was responsible for every one of her daughter's neuroses, maybe she had clutched her daughter so closely to her that it had been impossible for the daughter to lead a normal life and marry, and maybe she deserved to be kicked overboard instead of walking around the deck and listened to for hours while she talked, but what did it matter? Did the world always mete out just deserts? Had the world meted his out to him? He considered that he had been lucky beyond reason in escaping detection for two murders, lucky from the time he had assumed Dickie's identity until now. In the first part of his life fate had been grossly unfair, he thought, but the period with Dickie and afterwards had more than compensated for it. But something was going to happen now in Greece, he felt, and it couldn't be good. His luck had held just too long. But supposing they got him on the fingerprints, and on the will, and they gave him the electric chair – could that death in the electric chair equal in pain, or could death itself, at twenty-five, be so tragic, that he could not say that the months from November until now had not been worth it? Certainly not.

The only thing he regretted was that he had not seen all the world yet. He wanted to see Australia. And India. He wanted to see Japan. Then there was South America. Merely to look at the art of those countries would be a pleasant, rewarding life's work, he thought. He had learned a lot about painting, even in trying to copy Dickie's mediocre paintings. At the art galleries in Paris and Rome he had discovered an interest in paintings that he had never realized before, or perhaps that had not been in him before. He did not want to be a painter himself, but if he had the money, he-thought, his greatest pleasure would be to collect paintings that he liked, and to help young painters with talent who needed money.

His mind went off on such tangents as he walked with Mrs Cartwright around the deck, or listened to her monologues that were not always interesting. Mrs Cartwright thought him charming. She told him several times, speaking with fervour, how much he had contributed to her enjoyment of the voyage, and they made plans about meeting at a certain hotel in Crete on the second of July, Crete being the only place their itineraries crossed. Mrs Cartwright was travelling by bus on a special tour. Tom acquiesced to all her suggestions, though he never expected to see her again once they got off the ship. He imagined himself seized at once and taken on board another ship, or perhaps a plane, back to Italy. No radio messages had come about him – that he knew of – but would they necessarily inform him if any had come? The ship's paper, a little one-page mimeographed sheet that appeared every evening at each place on the dinner tables, was entirely concerned with international political news, and would not have contained anything about the Greenleaf case even if something important had happened. During the brief voyage Tom lived in a peculiar atmosphere of doom and of heroic, unselfish courage. He imagined strange things: Mrs Cartwright's daughter falling overboard and he jumping after her and saving her. Or fighting through the waters of a ruptured bulkhead to close the breach with his own body. He felt possessed of a preternatural strength and fearlessness.

When the boat approached the mainland of Greece Tom was standing at the rail with Mrs Cartwright. She was telling him how the port of Piraeus had changed in appearance since she had seen it last, and Tom was not interested at all in the changes. It existed, that was all that mattered to him. It wasn't a mirage ahead of him, it was a solid hill that he could walk on, with buildings that he could touch – if he got that far.

The police were waiting on the dock. He saw four of them, standing with folded arms, looking up at the ship. Tom helped Mrs Cartwright to the very last, boosted her gently over the kerb at the end of the gangplank, and said a smiling good-bye to her and her daughter. He had to wait under the R's and they under the C's to receive their luggage, and the two Cartwrights were leaving right away for Athens on their special bus.

With Mrs Cartwright's kiss still warm and slightly moist on his cheek, Tom turned and walked slowly towards the policemen. No fuss, he thought, he'd just tell them himself who he was. There was a big newsstand behind the policemen, and he thought of buying a paper. Perhaps they would let him. The policemen stared back at him from over their folded arms as he approached them. They wore black uniforms with visored caps. Tom smiled at them faintly. One of them touched his cap and stepped aside. But the others did not close in. Now Tom was practically between two of them, right in front of the news-stand, and the policemen were staring forward again, paying no attention to him at all.

Tom looked over the array of papers in front of him, feeling dazed and faint. His hand moved automatically to take a familiar paper of Rome. It was only three days old. He pulled some lire out of his pocket, realized suddenly that he had no Greek money, but the newsdealer accepted the lire as readily as if he were in Italy, and even gave him back change in lire.

'I'll take these, too,' Tom said in Italian, choosing three more Italian papers and the Paris *Herald-Tribune*. He glanced at the police officers. They were not looking at him.

Then he walked back to the shed on the dock where the ship's passengers were awaiting their luggage. He heard Mrs Cartwright's cheerful halloo to him as he went by, but he pretended not to have heard. Under the R's he stopped and opened the oldest Italian paper, which was four days old.

NO ONE NAMED ROBERT S. FANSHAW FOUND, DEPOSITOR OF GREENLEAF BAGGAGE

said the awkward caption on the second page. Tom read the long column below it, but only the fifth paragraph interested him:

The police ascertained a few days ago that the fingerprints on the suitcases and paintings are the same as the fingerprints found in Greenleaf's abandoned apartment in Rome. Therefore, it has been assumed that Greenleaf deposited the suitcases and the paintings himself ...

Tom fumbled open another page. Here it was again:

... In view of the fact that the fingerprints on the articles in the suitcases are identical with those in Signor Greenleaf's apartment in Rome, the police have concluded that Signor Greenleaf packed and dispatched the suitcases to Venice, and there is speculation that he may have committed suicide, perhaps in the water in a state of total nudity. An alternative speculation is that he exists at present under the alias of Robert S. Fanshaw or another alias. Still another possibility is that he was murdered, after packing or being made to pack his own baggage – perhaps for the express purpose of confusing the police inquiries through fingerprints ...

In any case, it is futile to search for 'Richard Greenleaf' any longer, because, even if he is alive, he has not his 'Richard Greenleaf' passport ...

Tom felt shaky and lightheaded. The glare of sunlight under the edge of the roof hurt his eyes. Automatically he followed the porter with his luggage towards the customs counter, and tried to realize, as he stared down at his open suitcase that the inspector was hastily examining, exactly what the news meant. It meant he was not suspected at all. It meant that the fingerprints really had guaranteed his innocence. It meant not only that he was not going to jail, and not going to die, but that he was not suspected at all. He was free. Except for the will.

Tom boarded the bus for Athens. One of his table companions was sitting next to him, but he gave no sign of greeting, and couldn't have answered anything if the man had spoken to him. There would be a letter concerning the will at the American Express in Athens, Tom was sure. Mr Greenleaf had had just time to reply. Perhaps he had put his lawyers on to it right away, and there would be only a polite negative reply in Athens from a lawyer, and maybe the next message would come from the American police, saying that he was answerable for forgery. Maybe both messages were awaiting him at the American Express. The will could undo it all. Tom looked out of the window at the primitive, dry landscape. Nothing was registering on him. Maybe the Greek police were waiting for him at the American Express. Maybe the four men he had seen had not been police but some kind of soldiers.

The bus stopped. Tom got out, corralled his luggage, and found a taxi.

'Would you stop at the American Express, please?' he asked the driver in Italian, but the driver apparently understood 'American Express' at least, and drove off. Tom remembered when he had said the same words to the taxi driver in Rome, the day he had been on his way to Palermo. How sure of himself he'd been that day, just after he had given Marge the slip at the Inghilterra!

He sat up when he saw the American Express sign, and looked around the building for policemen. Perhaps the police were inside. In Italian, he asked the driver to wait, and the driver seemed to understand this too, and touched his cap. There was a specious ease about everything, like the moment just before something was going to explode. Tom looked around inside the American Express lobby. Nothing unusual. Maybe the minute he mentioned his name –

'Have you any letters for Thomas Ripley?' he asked in a low voice in English.

'Reepley? Spell it, if you please.'

He spelt it.

She turned and got some letters from a cubbyhole.

Nothing was happening.

'Three letters,' she said in English, smiling.

One from Mr Greenleaf. One from Titi in Venice. One from Cleo, forwarded. He opened the letter from Mr Greenleaf.

9 June, 19—

Dear Tom,

Your letter of 3 June received yesterday.

It was not so much of a surprise to my wife and me as you may have imagined. We were both aware that Richard was very fond of you, in spite of the fact he never went out of his way to tell us this in any of his letters. As you pointed out, this will does, unhappily, seem to indicate that Richard has taken his own life. It is a conclusion that we here have at last accepted – the only other chance being that Richard has assumed another name and for reasons of his own has chosen to turn his back on his family.

My wife concurs with me in the opinion that we should carry out Richard's preferences and the spirit of them, whatever he may have done with himself. So you have, insofar as the will is concerned, my personal support. I have put your photostat copy into the hands of my lawyers, who will keep you informed as to their progress in making over Richard's trust fund and other properties to you.

Once more, thank you for your assistance when I was overseas. Let us hear from you.

With best wishes
Herbert Greenleaf

Was it a joke? But the Burke-Greenleaf letterpaper in his hand felt authentic – thick and slightly pebbled and the letterhead engraved – and besides, Mr Greenleaf wouldn't joke like this, not in a million years. Tom walked on to the waiting taxi. It was no joke. It was his! Dickie's money and his freedom. And the freedom, like everything else, seemed combined, his and Dickie's combined. He could have a house in Europe, and a house in America too, if he chose. The money for the house in Mongibello was still waiting to be claimed, he thought suddenly, and he supposed he should send that to the Greenleafs, since Dickie put it up for sale before he wrote the will. He smiled, thinking of Mrs Cartwright. He must take her a big box of orchids when he met her in Crete, if they had any orchids in Crete.

He tried to imagine landing in Crete – the long island, peaked with the dry, jagged lips of craters, the little bustle of excitement on the pier as his boat moved into the harbour, the small-boy porters, avid for his luggage and his tips, and he would have plenty to tip them with, plenty for everything and everybody. He saw four motionless figures standing on the imaginary pier, the figures of Cretan policemen waiting for him, patiently waiting with folded arms. He grew suddenly tense, and his vision vanished. Was he going to see policemen waiting for him on every pier that he ever approached? In Alexandria? Istanbul? Bombay? Rio? No use thinking about that. He pulled his shoulders back. No use spoiling his trip worrying about imaginary policemen. Even if there *were* policemen on the pier, it wouldn't necessarily mean –

'A donda, a donda?' the taxi driver was saying, trying to speak Italian for him.

'To a hotel, please,' Tom said. 'Il meglio albergo. Il meglio, il meglio!'

RIPLEY
UNDER GROUND

To my Polish neighbours,
Agnès and Georges Barylski,
my friends of France, 77.

I think I would more readily die for what I do not
believe in than for what I hold to be true...
Sometimes I think that the artistic life is a long and
lovely suicide, and I am not sorry that it is so.

Oscar Wilde in his Personal Letters

ONE

Tom was in the garden when the telephone rang. He let Mme Annette, his housekeeper, answer it, and went on scraping at the soppy moss that clung to the sides of the stone steps. It was a wet October.

'M. *Tome*!' came Mme Annette's soprano voice. 'It's London!'

'Coming,' Tom called. He tossed down the trowel and went up the steps.

The downstairs telephone was in the living-room. Tom did not sit down on the yellow satin sofa, because he was in levis.

'Hello, Tom. Jeff Constant. Did you ...' *Burp.*

'Can you talk louder? It's a bad connection.'

'Is this better? I can hear you fine.'

People in London always could. 'A little.'

'Did you get my letter?'

'No,' Tom said.

'Oh. We're in trouble. I wanted to warn you. There's a ...'

Crackling, a buzz, a dull click, and they were cut off.

'Damn,' Tom said mildly. Warn him? Was something wrong at the gallery? With Derwatt Ltd? Warn *him*? Tom was hardly involved. He had dreamed up the idea of Derwatt Ltd, true, and he derived a little income from it, but – Tom glanced at the telephone, expecting it to ring again at any moment. Or should he ring Jeff? No, he didn't know if Jeff was at his studio or at the gallery. Jeff Constant was a photographer.

Tom walked towards the french windows that gave onto the back garden. He'd scrape a bit more at the moss, he thought. Tom gardened casually, and he liked spending an hour at it every day, mowing with a push-powered lawnmower, raking and burning twigs, weeding. It was exercise, and he could also daydream. He had hardly resumed with the trowel, when the telephone rang.

Mme Annette was coming into the living-room, carrying a duster. She was short and sturdy, about sixty, and rather jolly. She knew not a word of English and seemed incapable of learning any, even 'Good morning', which suited Tom perfectly.

'I'll get it, madame,' said Tom, and took the telephone.

'*Hello*,' Jeff's voice said. 'Look, Tom, I'm wondering if you could come over. To London, I ...'

'You what?' It was again a poor connection, but not as bad.

'I said – I've explained it in a letter. I can't explain here. But it's important, Tom.'

'Has somebody made a mistake? – Bernard?'

'In a way. There's a man coming from New York, probably tomorrow.'

'Who?'

'I explained it in my letter. You know Derwatt's show opens on Tuesday. I'll hold him off till then. Ed and I just won't be available.' Jeff sounded quite anxious. 'Are you free, Tom?'

'Well – yes.' But Tom didn't want to go to London.

'Try to keep it from Heloise. That you're coming to London.'

'Heloise is in Greece.'

'Oh, that's good.' The first hint of relief in Jeff's voice.

Jeff's letter came that afternoon at five, express and registered.

> 104 Charles Place
> N.W.8

Dear Tom,

 The new Derwatt show opens on Tuesday, the 15th, his first in two years. Bernard has nineteen new canvases and other pictures will be lent. Now for the bad news.

 There is an American named Thomas Murchison, not a dealer but a collector – retired with plenty of lolly. He bought a Derwatt from us three years ago. He compared it with an earlier Derwatt he has just seen in the States, and now he says his is phoney. It is, of course, as it is one of Bernard's. He wrote to the Buckmaster Gallery (to me) saying he thinks the painting he has is not genuine, because the technique and colours belong to a period of five or six years ago in Derwatt's work. I have the distinct feeling Murchison intends to make a stink here. And what to do about it? You're always good on ideas, Tom.

 Can you come over and talk to us? All expenses paid by the Buckmaster Gallery? We need an injection of confidence more than anything. I don't think Bernard has messed up any of the new canvases. But Bernard is in a flap, and we don't want him around even at the opening, especially at the opening.

> Please come at once if you can!
> Best,
> Jeff.

P.S. Murchison's letter was courteous, but supposing he's the kind who will insist on looking up Derwatt in Mexico to verify, etc?

 The last was a point, Tom thought, because Derwatt didn't exist. The story (invented by Tom) which the Buckmaster Gallery and Derwatt's loyal little band of friends put out, was that Derwatt had gone to a tiny village in Mexico to live, and he saw no one, had no telephone, and forbade the gallery to give his address to anyone. Well, if Murchison went to Mexico, he would have an exhausting search, enough to keep any man busy for a lifetime.

What Tom could see happening was Murchison – who would probably bring his Derwatt painting over – talking to other art dealers and then the press. It could arouse suspicion, and Derwatt might go up in smoke. Would the gang drag him into it? (Tom always thought of the gallery batch, Derwatt's old friends, as 'the gang', though he hated the term every time it came into his head.) And Bernard might mention Tom Ripley, Tom thought, not out of malice but out of his own insane – almost Christlike – honesty.

Tom had kept his name and his reputation clean, amazingly clean, considering all he did. It would be most embarrassing if it were in the French papers that Thomas Ripley of Villeperce-sur-Seine, husband of Heloise Plisson, daughter of Jacques Plisson, millionaire owner of Pharmaceutiques Plisson, had dreamed up the money-making fraud of Derwatt Ltd, and had for years been deriving a percentage from it, even if it was only ten per cent. It would look exceedingly shabby. Even Heloise, whose morals Tom considered next to non-existent, might react to this, and certainly her father would put the pressure on her (by stopping her allowance) to get a divorce.

Derwatt Ltd was now big, and a collapse would have ramifications. Down would go the lucrative art supply line of materials labelled 'Derwatt', from which the gang, and Tom, got royalties also. Then there was the Derwatt School of Art in Perugia, mainly for nice old ladies and American girls on holiday, but still a source of income, too. The art school got its money not so much from teaching art and selling 'Derwatt' supplies as from acting as a rental agent, finding houses and furnished apartments, of the most expensive order, for well-heeled tourist-students, and taking a cut from it all. The school was run by a pair of English queens, who were not in on the Derwatt hoax.

Tom couldn't make up his mind whether to go to London or not. What could he say to them? And Tom didn't understand the problem: couldn't a painter conceivably return to an earlier technique, for one painting?

'Would m'sieur prefer lamb chops or cold ham this evening?' Mme Annette asked Tom.

'Lamb chops, I think. Thank you. And how is your tooth?' That morning, Mme Annette had been to the village dentist, in whom she had the greatest confidence, for a tooth that had kept her awake all night.

'No pain now. He is so nice, Dr Grenier! He said it was an abscess but he opened the tooth and he said the nerve would fall out.'

Tom nodded, but wondered how a nerve could fall out; gravity, presumably. They'd had to dig hard for one of his nerves once, and in an upper tooth, too.

'You had good news from London?'

'No, well – just a ring from a friend.'

'Any news from Mme Heloise?'

'Not today.'

'Ah, imagine sunlight! Greece!' Mme Annette was wiping the already shining surface of a large oak chest beside the fireplace. 'Look! Villeperce has no sun. The winter has arrived.'

'Yes.' Mme Annette said the same thing every day lately.

Tom didn't expect to see Heloise until close to Christmas. On the other hand, she could turn up unexpectedly – having had a slight but reparable tiff with her friends, or simply having changed her mind about staying on a boat so long. Heloise was impulsive.

Tom put on a Beatles record to lift his spirits, then walked about the large living-room, hands in his pockets. He loved the house. It was a two-storey squarish grey stone house with four turrets over four round rooms in the upstairs corners, making the house look like a little castle. The garden was vast, and even by American standards the place had cost a fortune. Heloise's father had given the house to them three years ago as a wedding present. In the days before he married, Tom had needed some extra money, the Greenleaf money not being enough for him to enjoy the kind of life he had come to prefer, and Tom had been interested in his cut of the Derwatt affair. Now he regretted that. He had accepted ten per cent, when ten per cent had been very little. Even he had not realized that Derwatt would flourish the way it had.

Tom spent that evening as he did most of his evenings, quietly and alone, but his thoughts were troubled. He played the stereo softly while he ate, and he read Servan-Schreiber in French. There were two words Tom didn't know. He would look them up tonight in his Harrap's beside his bed. He was good at holding words in his memory to look up.

After dinner he put on a raincoat, though it wasn't raining, and walked to a little bar-café a quarter of a mile distant. Here he took coffee some evenings, standing at the bar. Invariably the proprietor Georges inquired about Mme Heloise, and expressed regret that Tom had to spend so much time alone. Tonight Tom said cheerfully:

'Oh, I am not sure she will stay on that yacht another two months. She will get bored.'

'*Quel luxe,*' murmured Georges dreamily. He was a paunchy man with a round face.

Tom mistrusted his mild and unfailing good-humour. His wife Marie, a big energetic brunette who wore bright red lipstick, was frankly tough, but she had a wild happy way of laughing that redeemed her. This was a workman's bar, and Tom did not object to that fact, but it was not his favourite bar. It just happened to be the closest. At least Georges and Marie had never referred to Dickie Greenleaf. A few people in Paris, acquaintances of his or Heloise's, had, and so had the owner of the Hotel St Pierre, Villeperce's only hostelry. The owner had asked, 'You are perhaps the M. Ripley who was a friend of the American Granelafe?' Tom had acknowledged that he was. But that had been three years ago, and such a question – if it never went any further – did not make Tom nervous, but he preferred to avoid the subject. The newspapers had said that he had received quite a sum of money, some said a regular income, which was true, from Dickie's will. At least no newspaper had ever implied that Tom had written the will himself, which he had. The French always remembered financial details.

After his coffee, Tom walked home, saying '*Bonsoir*' to a villager or two on the road, slipping now and then in the sodden leaves that cluttered the edge of the road. There was no sidewalk to mention. He had brought a flashlight, because the streetlights were too infrequent. He caught glimpses of cosy families in kitchens, watching television, sitting around oilcloth-covered tables. Chained dogs barked in a few courtyards. Then he opened the iron gates – ten feet high – of his own house, and his shoes crunched on gravel. Mme Annette's light was on in her side room, Tom saw from the glow. She had her own television set. Often Tom painted at night, for his amusement only. He knew he was a bad painter, worse than Dickie. But tonight he was not in the mood. Instead, he wrote to a friend in Hamburg, Reeves Minot, an American, asking when did he expect to need him? Reeves was to plant a microfilm – or something – on a certain Italian Count Bertolozzi. The Count would then visit Tom for a day or so in Villeperce, and Tom would remove the object from the place in the suitcase or wherever, which Reeves would tell him, and post it to a man Tom didn't know at all in Paris. Tom frequently performed these fence-like services, sometimes for jewellery thefts. It was easier if Tom removed the objects from his guests than if someone tried to do the same thing in a Paris hotel room, when the carrier was not in. Tom knew Count Bertolozzi slightly from a recent trip to Milan, when Reeves, who lived in Hamburg, had been in Milan also. Tom had discussed paintings with the Count. It was usually easy for Tom to persuade people with a bit of leisure to stay with him a day or so in Villeperce and look at his paintings – he had, besides Derwatts, a Soutine, of whose work Tom was especially fond, a Van Gogh, two Magrittes, and drawings by Cocteau and Picasso, and many drawings of less famous painters which he thought equally good or better. Villeperce was near Paris, and it was nice for his guests to enjoy a bit of country before going up. In fact, Tom often fetched them from Orly in his car, Villeperce being some forty miles south of Orly. Only once had Tom failed, when an American guest had become immediately ill in Tom's house from something he must have eaten before arriving, and Tom had not been able to get to his suitcase because the guest was constantly in bed and awake in his room. That object – another microfilm of some sort – had been recovered with difficulty by a Reeves man in Paris. Tom could not understand the value of some of these things, but neither could he always when he read spy novels, and Reeves was only a fence himself and took a percentage. Tom always drove to another town to post these things, and he always sent them with a false return name and address.

That night, Tom could not fall asleep, so he got out of bed, put on his purple woollen dressing-gown – new and thick, full of military frogs and tassels, a birthday present from Heloise – and went down to the kitchen. He had thought of taking up a bottle of Super Valstar beer, but decided to make some tea. He almost never drank tea, so in a way it was appropriate, as he felt it was a strange night. He tiptoed around the kitchen, so as not to awake Mme Annette. The tea Tom made was dark red. He had put too much in the pot. He carried a tray into the living-room, poured a cup, and walked about, noiseless in felt house-shoes. Why not impersonate Derwatt, he thought. My God, yes! That was the solution, the perfect solution, and the only solution.

Derwatt was about his age, close enough – Tom was thirty-one and Derwatt would be about thirty-five. Blue-grey eyes, Tom remembered Cynthia (Bernard's girl friend) or maybe Bernard saying in one of their gushing descriptions of Derwatt the Untarnishable. Derwatt had had a short beard, which was a tremendous help, would be, for Tom.

Jeff Constant would surely be pleased with the idea. A press interview. Tom must brush up on the questions he might have to answer, and the stories he would have to tell. Was Derwatt as tall as he? Well, who among the press would know? Derwatt's hair had been darker, Tom thought. But that could be fixed. Tom drank more tea. He continued walking about the room. His should be a surprise appearance, a surprise presumably even to Jeff and Ed – and Bernard, of course. Or so they would tell the press.

Tom tried to imagine confronting Mr Thomas Murchison. Be calm, self-assured, that was the essence. If Derwatt said a picture was his own, that he had painted it, who was Murchison to say him nay?

On a crest of enthusiasm, Tom went to his telephone. Often the operators were asleep at this hour – 2 A.M. and a bit after – and took ten minutes to answer. Tom sat patiently on the edge of the yellow sofa. He was thinking that Jeff or somebody would have to get some very good make-up in readiness. Tom wished he could count on a girl, Cynthia for instance, to supervise it, but Cynthia and Bernard had broken up two or three years ago. Cynthia knew the score about Derwatt and Bernard's forgeries, and would have none of it, not a penny of the profits, Tom remembered.

'Allo, j'écoute,' said the female operator in an annoyed tone, as if Tom had got her out of bed to do him a favour. Tom gave the number of Jeff's studio, which he had in an address book by the telephone. Tom was rather lucky, and the call came through in five minutes. He pulled his third cup of filthy tea nearer the telephone.

'Hello, Jeff. Tom. How are things?'

'Not any better. Ed's here. We were just thinking of ringing you. Are you coming over?'

'Yes, and I have a better idea. How about my playing – our missing friend – for a few hours, anyway?'

Jeff took an instant to comprehend. 'Oh, Tom, great! Can you be here for Tuesday?'

'Yes, sure.'

'Can you make it Monday. The day after tomorrow?'

'I don't think I can. But Tuesday, yes. Now listen, Jeff, the make-up – it's got to be good.'

'Don't worry! Just a sec!' He left off to speak with Ed, then returned. 'Ed says he has a source – of supply.'

'Don't announce it to the public,' Tom continued in his calm voice, because Jeff sounded as if he were leaping off his feet with joy. 'And another thing, if it doesn't work, if I fail – we must say it's a joke a friend of yours dreamed up – me. That it has nothing to do with – you know.' Tom meant with validating Murchison's forgery, but Jeff grasped this at once.

'Ed wants to say a word.'

'Hello, Tom,' Ed's deeper voice said. 'We're delighted you're coming over. It's a marvellous idea. And you know – Bernard's got some of his clothes and things.'

'I'll leave that to you.' Tom felt suddenly alarmed. 'The clothes are the least. It's the face. Get cracking, will you?'

'Right you are. Bless you.'

They hung up. Then Tom slumped back on the sofa and relaxed, almost horizontal. No, he wouldn't go to London too soon. Go on stage at the last moment, with dash and momentum. Too much briefing and rehearsal could be a bad thing.

Tom got up with the cold cup of tea. It would be amusing and funny if he could bring it off, he thought, as he stared at the Derwatt over his fireplace. This was a pinkish picture of a man in a chair, a man with several outlines, so it seemed one was looking at the picture through someone else's distorting eyeglasses. Some people said Derwatts hurt their eyes. But from a distance of three or four yards, they didn't. This was not a genuine Derwatt, but an early Bernard Tufts forgery. Across the room hung a genuine Derwatt, 'The Red Chairs'. Two little girls sat side by side, looking terrified, as if it were their first day in school, or as if they were listening to something frightening in church. 'The Red Chairs' was eight or nine years old. Behind the little girls, wherever they were sitting, the whole place was on fire. Yellow and red flames leapt about, hazed by touches of white, so that the fire didn't immediately catch the attention of the beholder. But when it did, the emotional effect was shattering. Tom loved both pictures. By now he had almost forgotten to remember, when he looked at them, that one was a forgery and the other genuine.

Tom recalled the early amorphous days of what was now Derwatt Ltd. Tom had met Jeffrey Constant and Bernard Tufts in London just after Derwatt had drowned – presumably intentionally – in Greece. Tom had just returned from Greece himself; it was not long after Dickie Green-leaf's death. Derwatt's body had never been found, but some fishermen of the village said they had seen him go swimming one morning, and had not seen him return. Derwatt's friends – and Tom had met Cynthia Gradnor on the same visit – had been profoundly disturbed, affected in a way that Tom had never seen after a death, not even in a family. Jeff, Ed, Cynthia, Bernard had been dazed. They had spoken dreamily, passionately, of Derwatt not only as an artist but as a friend, and as a human being. He had lived simply, in Islington, eating badly at times,

but he had always been generous to others. Children in his neighbourhood had adored him, and had sat for him without expecting any payment, but Derwatt had always reached in his pockets for what were
perhaps his last pennies to give them. Then just before he had gone to
Greece, Derwatt had had a disappointment. He had painted a mural on
a government assignment for a post office in a town in the north of
England. It had been approved in sketch form, but rejected when finished:
somebody was nude in it, or too nude, and Derwatt had refused to change
it. ('And he was right, of course!' Derwatt's loyal friends had assured
Tom.) But this had deprived Derwatt of a thousand pounds that he had
counted on. It seemed to have been a last straw in a series of disappointments – the depth of which Derwatt's friends had not realized,
and for this they reproached themselves. There had been a woman in
the picture too, Tom recalled vaguely, the cause of another disappointment
to Derwatt, but it seemed that the woman was not so important to him
as his work disappointments. All Derwatt's friends were professionals also,
mostly freelance, and were quite busy, and in the last days when Derwatt
had called on them – not for money but for company on several evenings
– they had said they hadn't time to see him. Unbeknownst to his friends,
Derwatt had sold what furniture he had in his studio and got himself to
Greece where he had written a long and depressed letter to Bernard. (Tom
had never seen the letter.) Then had come the news of his disappearance
or death.

The first thing Derwatt's friends, including Cynthia, had done was
gather all his paintings and drawings and try to sell them. They had
wanted to keep his name alive, had wanted the world to know and
appreciate what he had done. Derwatt had had no relatives, and as Tom
recalled, he had been a foundling without even known parents. The legend
of his tragic death had helped instead of hindered; usually galleries were
uninterested in paintings by a young and unknown artist who was already
dead – but Edmund Banbury, a freelance journalist, had used his
entrées and his talent for articles on Derwatt in newspapers, colour
supplements and art magazines, and Jeffrey Constant had made photographs of Derwatt's paintings to illustrate them. Within a few months
of Derwatt's death they found a gallery, the Buckmaster Gallery and moreover in Bond Street, which was willing to handle his work, and soon
Derwatt's canvases were selling for six and eight hundred pounds.

Then had come the inevitable. The paintings were all sold, or nearly,
and this was when Tom had been living in London (he had lived for
two years in a flat in S.W.1, near Eaton Square) and had run into Jeff

and Ed and Bernard one night in the Salisbury pub. They had again been sad, because Derwatt's paintings were coming to an end, and it had been Tom who had said, 'You're doing so well, it's a shame to end like this. Can't Bernard knock off a few paintings in Derwatt's style?' Tom had meant it as a joke, or a half-joke. He hardly knew the trio, only knew that Bernard was a painter. But Jeff, a practical type like Ed Banbury (and not a bit like Bernard), had turned to Bernard and said, 'I've thought of that, too. What do you think, Bernard?' Tom had forgot Bernard's exact reply, but he remembered that Bernard had lowered his head as if in shame or plain terror at the idea of falsifying his idol, Derwatt. Months later, Tom had encountered Ed Banbury in a street in London, and Ed had said cheerfully that Bernard had brought off two excellent 'Derwatts' and they had sold one at the Buckmaster as genuine.

Then still later, just after Tom had married Heloise, and was no longer living in London, Tom, Heloise, and Jeff were at the same party, a large cocktail party of the kind where you never meet or even see the host, and Jeff had beckoned Tom into a corner.

Jeff had said, 'Can we meet somewhere later? This is my address,' handing Tom a card. 'Can you come round about eleven tonight?

So Tom had gone to Jeff's alone, which had been simple, because Heloise – who at that time did not speak much English – had had enough after the cocktail party, and wanted to go back to their hotel. Heloise loved London – English sweaters and Carnaby Street, and the shops that sold Union Jack wastebaskets and signs that said things like 'Piss off', things that Tom often had to translate for her, but she said her head ached after trying to speak English for an hour.

'Our problem is,' Jeff had said that night, 'we can't go on pretending we've found another Derwatt somewhere. Bernard is doing fine but – Do you think we could dare dig up a big trove of Derwatts somewhere, like Ireland where he painted for a bit, and sell them and then call it quits? Bernard isn't keen about going on. He feels he's betraying Derwatt – in a way.'

Tom had reflected a moment, then said, 'What's the matter with Derwatt being still alive somewhere? A recluse somewhere, sending his paintings to London? That is, if Bernard can keep going.'

'Um-m. Well – yes. Greece, maybe. What a super idea, Tom! It can go on for ever!'

'How about Mexico? I think it's safer than Greece. Let's say Derwatt's living in some little village. He won't tell anyone the name of the village – except maybe you and Ed and Cynthia –'

'Not Cynthia, she's – Well, Bernard doesn't see much of her any more. Consequently neither do we. Just as well she doesn't know too much about this.'

Jeff had rung up Ed that night to tell him the idea, Tom recalled.

'It's just an idea,' Tom had said. 'I don't know if it'll work.'

But it had worked. Derwatt's paintings had begun coming from Mexico, it was said, and the dramatic story of Derwatt's 'resurrection' had been exploited to advantage by Ed Banbury and Jeff Constant in more magazine articles, with photographs of Derwatt and his (Bernard's) latest paintings, though not of Derwatt himself *in* Mexico, because Derwatt permitted no interviewers or photographers. The paintings were sent from Vera Cruz and not even Jeff or Ed knew the name of his village. Derwatt was perhaps mentally sick to be such a recluse. His paintings were sick and depressed, according to some critics. But were now among the highest priced paintings of any living artist in England or on the Continent or in America. Ed Banbury wrote to Tom in France, offering him ten per cent of the profits, the loyal little group (now numbering only three, Bernard, Jeff and Ed) being the sole beneficiaries of Derwatt's sales. Tom had accepted, mainly because he considered it, his acceptance, rather a guarantee of his silence about the duplicity. But Bernard Tufts was painting like a demon.

Jeff and Ed bought the Buckmaster Gallery. Tom was not sure if Bernard owned any part of it. Several Derwatts were in a permanent collection of the gallery, and the gallery showed the paintings of other artists as well, of course. This was more Jeff's job than Ed's, and Jeff had hired an assistant, a sort of manager for the gallery. But this step up, the purchase of the Buckmaster Gallery, had come after Jeff and Ed had been approached by an art materials manufacturer called George Janopolos or some such, who wanted to start a line of goods to be labelled 'Derwatt', which would include everything from erasers to oil paint sets, and for which he offered Derwatt a royalty of one per cent. Ed and Jeff had decided to accept for Derwatt (presumably with Derwatt's consent). A company had then been formed called Derwatt Ltd.

All this Tom recollected at four in the morning, shivering a little despite his princely dressing-gown. Mme Annette always thriftily turned the central heating down at night. He held the cup of cold sweet tea between his hands and stared unseeing at a photograph of Heloise – long blonde hair on either side of a slender face, a pleasant and meaningless design to Tom just now rather than a face – and he thought of Bernard working in secret on his Derwatt forgeries in a closed, even locked room

in his studio apartment. Bernard's place was pretty crummy, as it always
had been. Tom had never seen the sanctum sanctorum where he painted
his masterpieces, the Derwatts that brought in thousands of quid. If one
painted more forgeries than one's own paintings, wouldn't the forgeries
become more natural, more real, more genuine to oneself, even, than
one's own painting? Wouldn't the effort finally go out of it and the work
become second nature?

At last Tom curled up on the yellow sofa, slippers off and feet drawn
under his robe, and slept. He did not sleep long before Mme Annette
arrived and awaked him with a shriek, or a shrill gasp, of surprise.

'I must have fallen asleep reading,' Tom said, smiling, sitting up.

Mme Annette hurried off to make his coffee.

TWO

Tom booked a flight to London at noon on Tuesday. It would give him
only a couple of hours to get made-up and to be briefed. Not enough
time to grow nervous. Tom drove to Melun to pick up some cash – francs
– at his bank.

It was eleven-forty, and the bank closed at twelve. Tom was third in
the queue at the window where people received cash, but unfortunately
a woman was delivering payroll money or some such at this window,
heaving up bags of coins, while keeping her feet braced against the
bags that remained on the floor. Behind the grille, a clerk with wetted
thumb was counting stacks of banknotes as quickly as possible and making
notations of their sums on two separate papers. How long would this
go on, Tom wondered, as the clock crept towards twelve. Tom watched
with amusement as the queue broke up. Three men now and two women
pressed near the grille, staring glassy-eyed, like fascinated snakes, at all
the dough, as if it were a heritage left them by a relative who had worked
a lifetime for it. Tom gave it up and left the bank. He could manage
without the cash, he thought, and in fact he had only been thinking
of giving it or selling it to English friends who might be coming to France.

On Tuesday morning, when Tom was packing his bag, Mme Annette knocked on his bedroom door. 'I'm off for Munich,' Tom said cheerily. 'There's a concert.'

'Ah, Munich! Bavière! You must take warm clothing.' Mme Annette was used to his impromptu trips. 'For how long, M. Tome?'

'Two days, maybe three. Don't worry about messages. I may ring to see if any have come.'

Then Tom thought of something possibly useful, a Mexican ring that he had – he thought – in his studbox. Yes, there it was, among cufflinks and buttons, a heavy ring of silver whose design was two coiled snakes. Tom disliked it and had forgot how he acquired it, but at least it was Mexican. Tom blew on it, rubbed it against a trouser leg, and pocketed it.

The post at 10.30 A.M. brought three items, a telephone bill, lumpy in its envelope because of separate tabs for each non-Villeperce call; a letter from Heloise; and an American airmail letter addressed in a hand Tom didn't know. He turned the envelope over and was surprised to see the name Christopher Greenleaf on the back with a San Francisco return address. Who was Christopher? He opened Heloise's letter first.

11 octobre 19—

Chéri,

I am happy and very quite now. Very good repastes. We catch fishs off the boat. Zeppo sends love. [Zeppo was her swarthy Greek host and Tom could tell him what to do with his love.]

I learn better to mount a bicycle. We have made many voyages into the land which is dry. Zeppo makes photos. How goes it at Belle Ombre? I miss you. Are you happy? Many invites? [Did that mean guests or invitations?] Are you painting? I have received no word from Papa.

Kiss Mme A. I embrace you.

The rest was in French. She wanted him to send a red bathing-suit which he would find in a small *commode* in her bathroom. He should send it airmail. The yacht had a heated swimming-pool. Tom at once went upstairs where Mme Annette was still working in his room, and entrusted this task to her, giving her a hundred-franc note for it, because he thought she might be scandalized at the price of the airmail package and be tempted to send it slow post.

Then he went down and opened the Greenleaf letter hastily, because he had to leave for Orly in a few minutes.

Oct. 12 19—

Dear Mr Ripley,

I am a cousin of Dickie's and am coming to Europe next week, probably going to London first, though I cannot make up my mind whether to go to Paris first.

Anyway, I thought it would be nice if we could meet. My uncle Herbert gave me your address, and he says you are not far from Paris. Haven't got your telephone number, but I can look it up.

To tell you a bit about myself, I am twenty and I go to Stanford University. I spent one year in military service, during which my college was interrupted. I'll return to Stanford for a degree in engineering but meanwhile I am taking a year off to see Europe and relax. Lots of fellows do this now. The pressure everywhere is quite something. I mean in America, but maybe you have been in Europe so long you don't know what I mean.

My uncle has told me a lot about you. He says you were a good friend of Dickie's. I met Dickie when I was 11 and he was 21. I remember a tall blond fellow. He visited my family in California.

Please tell me if you will be in Villeperce in late October, early November. Meanwhile here's hoping to meet you.

Sincerely

Chris Greenleaf

He would get out of that one politely, Tom thought. No use making closer contact with the Greenleaf family. Once in a blue moon Herbert Greenleaf wrote him, and Tom always replied, nice polite letters.

'Mme Annette, keep the home fires burning,' Tom said as he took off.

'What did you say?'

He translated it into French as best he could.

'Au revoir, M. Tome! Bon voyage!' Mme Annette waved to him from the front door.

Tom took the red Alfa-Romeo, one of the two cars in the garage. At Orly, he put the car in the indoor garage, saying it was for two or three days. He bought a bottle of whisky in the terminus to take to the gang. He had already a big bottle of Pernod in his suitcase (since he was permitted to enter London with only one bottle), because Tom had found that if he went through the green aisle and showed the visible bottle, the inspector never asked him to open his suitcase. On the plane he bought untipped Gauloises, always popular in London.

It was raining lightly in England. The bus crept along on the left side of the road, past the family houses whose names always amused Tom, though now he could hardly read them through the murk. Bide-a-wee. Unbelievable. Milford Haven. Dun Wandering. They hung on little signboards. Inglenook. Sit-Ye-Doon. Good God. Then came the stretch of jammed-together Victorian houses that had been converted into small hotels with grandiose names in neon lights between Doric doorway pillars: Manchester Arms, King Alfred, Cheshire House. Tom knew that behind the genteel respectability of those narrow lobbies some of the best murderers of the present day took refuge for a night or so, looking equally respectable themselves. England was England, God bless it!

The next thing that caught Tom's attention was a poster on a lamppost on the left side of the road. DERWATT was written in bold black script slanting downward – Derwatt's signature – and the picture reproduced in colour looked in the dim light dark purple or black and somewhat resembled the raised top of a grand piano. A new Bernard Tufts forgery, doubtless. There was another such poster a few yards on. It was odd to feel so 'announced' all over London, and to arrive so quietly, Tom thought as he stepped down from the bus at the West Kensington Terminal unnoticed by anyone.

From the terminal, Tom rang Jeff Constant at this studio. Ed Banbury answered.

'Hop in a taxi and come straight here!' Ed said, sounding wildly happy.

Jeff's studio was in St John's Wood. Second floor – first to the English – on the left. It was a proper neat little building, neither swank nor shabby.

Ed whipped the door open. 'My God, Tom, it's great to see you!'

They shook hands firmly. Ed was taller than Tom with lank blond hair that was apt to fall over his ears, so he was constantly shoving it aside. He was about thirty-five.

'And where's Jeff?' Tom fished out Gauloises and whisky from the red net bag, then the smuggled Pernod from his suitcase. 'For the house.'

'Oh, super! Jeff's at the gallery. Listen, Tom, you'll *do* it? – Because I've got the stuff here and there isn't too much time.'

'I'll try it,' Tom said.

'Bernard's due. He'll help us. Briefing.' Ed looked hectically at his wristwatch.

Tom had removed his topcoat and jacket. 'Can't Derwatt be a little late? Isn't the opening at five?'

'Oh, of course. No need to get there till six, anyway, but I do want to try the make-up. Jeff said to remind you you're not much shorter than Derwatt was – and who remembers those statistics? Assuming I ever wrote them anywhere? And Derwatt had bluish-grey eyes. But yours'll do.' Ed laughed. 'Want some tea?'

'No thanks.' Tom was looking at the dark-blue suit on Jeff's couch. It looked too wide and it was unpressed. A pair of awful black shoes were on the floor by the couch. 'Why don't you have a drink?' Tom suggested to Ed, because Ed looked as jumpy as a cat. As usual, another person's nervousness was making Tom feel calm.

The doorbell rang.

Ed let Bernard Tufts in.

Tom extended a hand. 'Bernard, how are you?'

'All right, thank you,' Bernard said, sounding miserable. Bernard was thin and olive-skinned, with straight black hair and gentle dark eyes.

Tom thought it best not to try to talk to Bernard just now, but to be simply efficient.

Ed drew a basin of water in Jeff's tiny but modern bathroom, and Tom submitted to a hair rinse to make his hair darker. Bernard began to talk, but only after deliberate, then more importunate prodding from Ed.

'He walked with a slight stoop,' Bernard said. 'His voice – He was a little shy in public. It was a sort of monotone, I suppose. Like this, if I can illustrate,' Bernard said in a monotone. 'Now and then he laughed.'

'Don't we all!' Tom said, laughing nervously himself. Now Tom was sitting in a straight chair, being combed by Ed. On Tom's right was a platter of what looked like barbershop floor sweepings, but Ed shook this out, and it was a beard fastened to fine flesh-coloured gauze. 'Good God, I hope the lights are dim,' Tom murmured.

'We'll see to that,' said Ed.

While Ed worked with a moustache, Tom pulled off his two rings, one a wedding ring, one Dickie Greenleaf's ring, and pocketed them. He asked Bernard to bring him the ring from his left trouser pocket, and Bernard did. Bernard's thin fingers were cold and shaking. Tom wanted to ask him how Cynthia was, and remembered that Bernard was not seeing her any more. They had been going to marry, Tom remembered. Ed was snipping at Tom's hair with scissors, creating a bush in front.

'And Derwatt –' Bernard stopped, because his voice had cracked.

'Oh, shut up, Bernard!' Ed said, laughing hysterically.

Bernard laughed also. 'Sorry. Really, I'm sorry.' He sounded contrite, as if he meant it.

The beard was going on, with glue.

Ed said, 'I want you to walk around a bit here, Tom. Get used to it. At the gallery – You won't have to go in with the crowd, we decided against that. There's a back door, and Jeff will let us in. We'll invite some of the press to come into the office, you see, and we'll have just one standing lamp on across the room. We've removed a little lamp and the ceiling bulb, so that *can't* go on.'

The gluey beard felt cool on Tom's face. In the mirror in Jeff's loo, he looked a little like D. H. Lawrence, he thought. His mouth was surrounded by hair. It was a sensation Tom did not like. Below the mirror on a little shelf three snapshots of Derwatt were propped up – Derwatt reading a book in shirtsleeves in a deckchair, Derwatt standing with a man Tom did not know, facing the camera. Derwatt had glasses in all the pictures.

'The specs,' Ed said, as if he read Tom's thoughts.

Tom took the round-rimmed glasses Ed handed him, and put them on. That was better. Tom smiled, gently so as not to spoil the drying beard. The specs were plain glass, apparently. Tom walked with a stoop back into the studio, and said in what he hoped was Derwatt's voice, 'Now tell me about this man Murchison –'

'Deeper!' Bernard said, his skinny hands flailing wildly.

'This man Murchison,' Tom said.

Bernard said, 'M-Murchison, according to Jeff, thinks – Derwatt has returned to an old technique. In his painting "The Clock", you see. I don't know what he means – specifically – to tell you the truth.' Bernard shook his head quickly, pulled a handkerchief from somewhere and blew his nose. 'I was just looking at one of Jeff's shots of "The Clock". I haven't seen it in three years, you see. Not the picture itself.' Bernard was talking softly, as if the walls might be listening.

'Is Murchison an expert?' Tom asked, thinking, what was an expert?

'No, he's just an American businessman,' Ed said. 'He collects. He's got a bee in his bonnet.'

It was more than that, Tom thought, or they wouldn't all be so upset. 'Am I supposed to be prepared for anything specific?'

'No,' Ed said. 'Is he, Bernard?'

Bernard almost gasped, then tried to laugh, and for an instant he looked as he had looked years ago, younger, naïve. Tom realized that Bernard was thinner than when he had last seen him three or four years ago.

'I wish I knew,' Bernard said. 'You must only – stand by the fact that the picture, "The Clock", is Derwatt's.'

'Trust me,' Tom said. He was walking about, practising the stoop, assuming a slowish rhythm which he hoped was correct.

'But,' Bernard went on, 'if Murchison wants to continue whatever he's talking about, whatever it is – "Man in Chair" you've got, Tom –'

A forgery. 'He need never see that,' said Tom. 'I love it, myself.'

' "The Tub",' Bernard added. 'It's in the show.'

'You're worried about that?' Tom asked.

'It's in the same technique,' Bernard said. 'Maybe.'

'Then you know what technique Murchison is talking about? Why don't you take "The Tub" out of the show if you're worried about it?'

Ed said, 'It was announced on the programme. We were afraid if we removed it, Murchison might want to see it, want to know who bought it and all that.'

The conversation got nowhere, because Tom could not get a clear statement of what they, or Murchison, meant by the technique in these particular pictures.

'You'll never meet Murchison, so stop worrying,' Ed said to Bernard.

'Have you met him?' Tom asked Ed.

'No, only Jeff has. This morning.'

'And what's he like?'

'Jeff said about fifty or so, a big American type. Polite enough but stubborn. Wasn't there a belt in those trousers?'

Tom tightened the belt in his trousers. He sniffed at the sleeve of his jacket. There was a faint smell of mothballs, which probably wouldn't be noticed in all the cigarette smoke. And anyway, Derwatt could have been wearing Mexican clothes for the past few years, and his European clothes might have been put away. Tom looked at himself in a long mirror, under one of Jeff's very bright spotlights that Ed had put on, and suddenly doubled over with laughter. Tom turned around and said, 'Sorry, I was just thinking that considering Derwatt's fantastic earnings, he certainly hangs on to his old gear!'

'That's okay, he's a recluse,' Ed said.

The telephone rang. Ed answered, and Tom heard him assuring someone, no doubt Jeff, that Tom had arrived and was ready to go.

Tom did not feel quite ready to go. He felt sweaty from nerves. He said to Bernard, trying to sound cheerful, 'How's Cynthia? Do you ever see her?'

'I don't see her any more. Not very often, anyway,' Bernard glanced at Tom, then looked back at the floor.

'What's she going to say when she finds out Derwatt's come back to London for a few days?' Tom asked.

'I don't think she'll say anything,' Bernard replied dully. 'She's not – going to spoil things, I'm sure.'

Ed finished his telephone conversation. 'Cynthia won't say anything, Tom. She's like that. You remember her, don't you, Tom?'

'Yes. Slightly,' Tom said.

'If she hasn't said anything by now, she's not going to,' Ed said. The way he said it made it sound like, 'She's not a bad sport or a babble-mouth.'

'She *is* quite wonderful,' Bernard said dreamily, to nobody. He suddenly got up and darted for the bathroom, perhaps because he had to go there, but it might have been to throw up.

'Don't worry about Cynthia, Tom,' Ed said softly. 'We live with her, you see. I mean, here in London. She's been quiet for three years or so. Well, you know – since she broke up with Bernard. Or he broke up with her.'

'Is she happy? Found somebody else?'

'Oh, she has a boy-friend, I think.'

Bernard was coming back.

Tom had a Scotch. Bernard took a Pernod, and Ed drank nothing. He was afraid to, he said, because he'd had a sedative. By five o'clock, Tom had been briefed or refreshed on several things: the town in Greece where Derwatt had officially last been seen nearly six years ago. Tom, in case he was queried, was to say he had left Greece under another name on a Greek tanker bound for Vera Cruz, working as oiler and ship's painter.

They borrowed Bernard's topcoat, which was older looking than Tom's or any of Jeff's in his closet. Then Tom and Ed set off, leaving Bernard in Jeff's studio, where they all were to meet later.

'My God, he's down in the mouth,' Tom said on the pavement. He was walking with a slump. 'How long can he go on like this?'

'Don't judge by today. He'll go on. He's always like this when there's a show.'

Bernard was the old workhorse, Tom supposed. Ed and Jeff were burgeoning on extra money, good food, good living. Bernard merely produced the pictures that made it possible.

Tom drew back sharply from a taxi, not having expected it to be bowling along on the left side of the road.

Ed smiled. 'That's great. Keep it up.'

They came to a taxi rank and got into a cab.

'And this – caretaker or manager at the gallery,' Tom said. 'What's his name?'

'Leonard Hayward,' Ed said. 'He's about twenty-six. Queer as Dick's hatband, belongs in a King's Road boutique, but he's okay. Jeff and I let him into the circle. Had to. It's really safer, because he can't spring any blackmail, if he signed a written agreement with us to caretake the place, which he did. We pay him well enough and he's amused. He also sends us some good buyers.' Ed looked at Tom and smiled. 'Don't forget a bit of woikin' class accent. You can do it quite well as I remember.'

THREE

Ed Banbury rang a bell at a dark-red door flush with the back of a building. Tom heard a key being turned, then the door opened and Jeff stood there, beaming at them.

'Tom! It's *super*!' Jeff whispered.

They went down a short corridor, then into a cosy office with a desk and typewriter, books, cream-coloured wall-to-wall carpeting. Canvases and portfolios of drawings leaned against the wall.

'I can't tell you how right you look – Derwatt!' Jeff slapped Tom's shoulder. 'I hope that won't make your beard fall off.'

'Even a high wind wouldn't,' Ed put in.

Jeff Constant had gained weight, and his face was flushed – or perhaps he had been using a sun-tan lamp. His shirt cuffs were adorned with square gold links, and his blue and black striped suit looked brand-new. Tom noticed that a toupee – what they called a hair-piece – covered the bald spot on the top of Jeff's head, which Tom knew must be quite barren by now. Through the closed door that led to the gallery came a hubbub of voices, lots of voices out of which a woman's laugh leapt like a porpoise over the surface of a troubled sea, Tom thought, though he was not in the mood for poetry now.

'Six o'clock,' Jeff announced, flashing more cuff to see his watch. 'I shall now quietly tell a few of the press that Derwatt is here. This being England, there will not be a –'

'Ha-ha! Not be a what?' Ed interrupted.

'– not be a *stampede*,' Jeff said firmly. 'I'll see to that.'

'You'll sit back here. Or stand, as you like,' Ed said, indicating the desk which was set at an angle and had a chair behind it.

'This Murchison chap is here?' Tom asked in Derwatt tones.

Jeff's fixed smile widened, but a little uneasily. 'Oh, yes. You ought to see him, of course. But after the press.' Jeff was jumpy, eager to be off, though he looked as if he might have said more, and he went out. The key turned in the lock.

'Any water anywhere?' Tom asked.

Ed showed him a small bathroom, which had been concealed by a section of bookshelf that swung out. Tom took a hasty gulp, and as he stepped out of the bathroom, two gentlemen of the press were coming in with Jeff, their faces blank with surprise and curiosity. One was fifty-odd, the other in his twenties, but their expressions were much alike.

'May I present Mr Gardiner of the *Telegraph*,' Jeff said. 'Derwatt. And Mr –'

'Perkins,' said the younger man. '*Sunday* . . .'

Another knock on the door before they could exchange greetings. Tom walked with a stoop, almost rheumatically, towards the desk. The single lamp in the room was near the door to the gallery, a good ten feet away from him. But Tom had noticed that Mr Perkins carried a flash camera.

Four more men and one woman were admitted. Tom feared a woman's eyes, under the circumstances, more than anything. She was introduced to him as a Miss Eleanor Somebody of the *Manchester* Something or other.

Then the questions began to fly, although Jeff suggested that each reporter should ask his questions in turn. This was a useless proposal, as each reporter was too eager to get his own questions answered.

'Do you intend to live in Mexico indefinitely, Mr Derwatt?'

'Mr Derwatt, we're so surprised to see you here. What made you decide to come to London?'

'Don't call me *Mister* Derwatt,' Tom said grumpily. 'Just Derwatt.'

'Do you like the latest – group of canvases you've done? Do you think they're your best?'

'Derwatt – are you living alone in Mexico?' asked Eleanor Somebody.

'Yes.'

'Could you tell us the name of your village?'

Three more men came in, and Tom was aware of Jeff urging one of them to wait outside.

'One thing I will not tell you is the name of my village,' Tom said slowly. 'It wouldn't be fair to the inhabitants.'

'Derwatt, uh –'

'Derwatt, certain critics have said –'

Someone was banging with fists on the door.

Jeff banged back and yelled, 'No more just now, please!'

'Certain critics have said –'

Now the door gave a sound of splitting, and Jeff set his shoulder against it. The door was not giving, Tom saw, and turned his calm eyes from it to regard his questioner.

'– have said that your work resembles a period of Picasso's related to his cubist period, when he began to split faces and forms.'

'I have no periods,' Tom said. 'Picasso has periods. That's why you can't put your finger on Picasso – if anybody wants to. It's impossible to say "I like Picasso", because no one period comes to mind. Picasso plays. That's all right. But by doing this he destroys what might be a genuine – a genuine and integrated personality. What *is* Picasso's personality?'

The reporters scribbled diligently.

'What is your favourite painting in this show? Which do you think you like best?'

'I have no – No, I can't say that I have a favourite painting in this show. Thank you.' Did Derwatt smoke? What the hell. Tom reached for Jeff's Craven A's and lit one with a table lighter before two reporters could spring to his cigarette. Tom drew back to protect his beard from their fire. 'My favourites perhaps are the old ones – "The Red Chairs", "Falling Woman", maybe. Sold alas.' Out of nowhere, Tom had recalled the last title. It did exist.

'Where is that? I don't know that, but I know the name,' someone said.

Shyly, recluse-like, Tom kept his eyes on the leather-bound blotter on Jeff's desk. 'I've forgot. "Falling Woman". Sold to an American, I think.'

The reporters plunged in again: 'Are you pleased with your sales, Derwatt?'

(Who wouldn't be?)

'Does Mexico inspire you? I notice there are no canvases in the show with a Mexican setting.'

(A slight hurdle, but Tom got over it. He had always painted from imagination.)

'Can you at least describe the house where you live in Mexico, Derwatt?' asked Eleanor.

(This Tom could do. A one-storey house with four rooms. A banana tree out front. A girl came to clean every morning at ten, and did a little shopping for him at noon, bringing back freshly baked tortillas, which he ate with red beans – frijoles – for lunch. Yes, meat was scarce, but there was some goat. The girl's name? Juana.)

'Do they call you Derwatt in the village?'

'They used to, and they had a very different way of pronouncing it, I can tell you. Now it's Filipo. There's no need of another name but Don Filipo.'

'They have no idea that you're *Derwatt*?'

Tom laughed a little again. 'I don't think they're much interested in *The Times* or *Arts Review* or whatever.'

'Have you missed London? How does it look to you?'

'Was it just a whim that made you come back now?' young Perkins asked.

'Yes. Just a whim.' Tom smiled the worn, philosophic smile of a man who had gazed upon Mexican mountains, alone, for years.

'Do you ever go to Europe – incognito? We know you like seclusion –'

'Derwatt, I'd be most grateful if you could find ten minutes tomorrow. May I ask where you're –'

'I'm sorry, I haven't yet decided where I'm staying,' Tom said.

Jeff gently urged the reporters to take leave, and the cameras began to flash. Tom looked downward, then upward for one or two photographs on request. Jeff admitted a waiter in a white jacket with a tray of drinks. The tray was emptied in a trice.

Tom lifted a hand in a gesture of shy, gracious farewell. 'Thank you all.'

'No more please,' Jeff said at the door.

'But I –'

'Ah, Mr Murchison. Come in, please,' Jeff said. He turned to Tom. 'Derwatt, this is Mr Murchison. From America.'

Mr Murchison was large, with a pleasant face. 'How do you do, Mr Derwatt?' he said, smiling. 'What an unexpected treat to meet you here in London!'

They shook hands.

'How do you do?' Tom said.

'And this is Edmund Banbury,' Jeff said. 'Mr Murchison.'

Ed and Mr Murchison exchanged greetings.

'I've got one of your paintings – "The Clock". In fact, I brought it with me.' Mr Murchison was smiling widely now, staring with fascination and respect at Tom, and Tom hoped his gaze was dazzled by the surprise of actually seeing him.

'Oh, yes,' Tom said.

Jeff again quietly locked the door. 'Won't you sit down, Mr Murchison?'

'Yes, thank you.' Murchison sat, on a straight chair.

Jeff quietly began gathering empty glasses from the edges of bookshelves and the desk.

'Well, to come to the point, Mr Derwatt, I – I'm interested in a certain change of technique that you show in "The Clock". You know, of course, the picture I mean?' Murchison asked.

Was that a casual or a pointed question, Tom wondered? 'Of course,' Tom said.

'Can you describe it?'

Tom was still standing up. A slight chill went over him. Tom smiled.

'I can never describe my pictures. It wouldn't surprise me if there were
no clock in it. Did you know, Mr Murchison, I don't always make up
my own titles? And how anyone got "Sunday Noon" out of the particular
canvas is beyond me.' (Tom had glanced at the gallery programme of
twenty-eight Derwatts now on exhibit, a programme which Jeff or someone had thoughtfully opened and placed on the blotter of the desk.) 'Is
that your effort, Jeff?'

Jeff laughed. 'No, I think it's Ed's. Would you like a drink, Mr Murchison?
I'll get you one from the bar.'

'No, thank you, I'm fine.' Then Mr Murchison addressed Tom. 'It's
a bluish-black clock held by – Do you remember?' He smiled as if he
were asking an innocent riddle.

'I think a little girl – who's facing the beholder, shall we say?'

'Hm-m. Right,' said Murchison. 'But then you don't do little boys, do
you?'

Tom chuckled, relieved that he'd guessed right. 'I suppose I prefer little
girls.'

Murchison lit a Chesterfield. He had brown eyes, light-brown wavy
hair, and a strong jaw covered with just a little too much flesh, like
the rest of him. 'I'd like you to see my picture. I have a reason. Excuse
me a minute. I left it with the coats.'

Jeff let him out the door, then locked the door again.

Jeff and Tom looked at each other. Ed was standing against a wall
of books, silent. Tom said in a whisper:

'Really, boys, if the damned canvas has been in the coat-room all this
time, couldn't one of you've whisked it out and burnt it?'

'Ha-ha!' Ed laughed, nervously.

Jeff's plump smile was a twitch, though he kept his poise, as if Murchison
were still in the room.

'Well, let us hear him out,' Tom said in a slow and confident Derwatt
tone. He tried to shoot his cuffs, but they didn't shoot.

Murchison came back carrying a brown-paper-wrapped picture under
one arm. It was a medium-sized Derwatt, perhaps two feet by three. 'I
paid ten thousand dollars for this,' he said, smiling. 'You may think it
careless of me to leave it in the cloakroom, but I'm inclined to trust
people.' He was undoing the wrapping with the aid of a penknife. 'Do
you know this picture?' he asked Tom.

Tom smiled at the picture. 'Of course I do.'

'You remember painting it?'

'It's my picture,' Tom said.

'It's the purples in this that interest me. The purple. This is straight cobalt violet – as you can probably see better than I.' Mr Murchison smiled almost apologetically for a moment. 'The picture is at least three years old, because I bought it three years ago. But if I'm not mistaken, you abandoned cobalt violet for a mixture of cad red and ultramarine five or six years ago. I can't exactly fix the date.'

Tom was silent. In the picture Murchison had, the clock was black and purple. The brushstrokes and the colour resembled those of 'Man in Chair' (painted by Bernard) at home. Tom didn't know quite what, in the purple department, Murchison was hammering at. A little girl in a pink-and-apple-green dress was holding the clock, or rather resting her hand on it, as the clock was large and stood on a table. 'To tell you the truth, I've forgot,' Tom said. 'Perhaps I did use straight cobalt violet there.'

'And also in the painting called "The Tub" outside,' Murchison said, with a nod towards the gallery. 'But in none of the others. I find it curious. A painter doesn't usually go back to a colour he's discarded. The cad red and ultramarine combination is far more interesting – in my opinion. Your newer choice.'

Tom was unworried. Ought he to be more worried? He shrugged slightly.

Jeff had gone into the little bathroom and was fussing about with glasses and ashtrays.

'How many years ago did you paint "The Clock"?' Murchison asked.

'That I'm afraid I can't tell you,' Tom said in a frank manner. He had grasped Murchison's point, at least in regard to time, and he added, 'It could have been four or five years ago. It's an old picture.'

'It wasn't sold to me as an old one. And "The Tub". That's dated only last year, and it has the same straight cobalt violet in it.'

The cobalt for the purpose of shadow, one might say, was not dominant in 'The Clock'. Murchison had an eagle eye. Tom thought 'The Red Chairs' – the earlier and genuine Derwatt – had the same straight cobalt, and he wondered if it had a fixed date? If he could say 'The Red Chairs' was only three years old, prove it somehow, Murchison could simply go to hell. Check with Jeff and Ed later on that, Tom thought.

'You definitely remember painting "The Clock"?' Murchison asked.

'I know it's my picture,' Tom said. 'I might have been in Greece or even Ireland when I painted it, because I don't remember dates, and the dates the gallery might have are not always the dates when I painted something.'

'I don't think "The Clock" is your work,' Murchison said with good-natured American conviction.

'Good heavens, why not?' Tom's good-nature matched Murchison's.

'I have a nerve sticking my neck out like this, I know. But I've seen some of your earlier work in a museum in Philadelphia. If I may say so Mr Derwatt, you're –'

'Just call me Derwatt. I like it better.'

'Derwatt. You're so prolific, I think you might forget – I should say not remember a painting. Granted "The Clock" is in your style and the theme is typical of your –'

Jeff, like Ed, was listening attentively, and in this pause Jeff said, 'But after all this picture came from Mexico along with a few others of Derwatt's. He always sends two or three at a time.'

'Yes. "The Clock" has a date on the back. It's three years old, written in the same black paint as Derwatt's signature,' Murchison said, swinging his painting round so all could see it. 'I had the signature and the date analysed in the States. That's how carefully I've gone into this,' Murchison said, smiling.

'I don't quite know what the trouble is,' Tom said. 'I painted it in Mexico if the date's three years old in my own writing.'

Murchison looked at Jeff. 'Mr Constant, you say you received "The Clock" along with two others, perhaps, in a certain shipment?'

'Yes. Now that I recall – I think the other two are here now lent by London owners – "The Orange Barn" and – Do you recall the other, Ed?'

'I think it's "Bird Spectre" probably. Isn't it?'

From Jeff's nod, Tom could see it was true, or else Jeff was doing well at pretending.

'That's it,' said Jeff.

'They're not in this technique. There's purple in them, but made by mixed colours. The two you're talking about are genuine – genuinely later pictures at any rate.'

Murchison was slightly wrong, they were phoneys as well. Tom scratched his beard, but very gently. He kept a quiet, somewhat amused air.

Murchison looked from Jeff to Tom. 'You may think I'm being bumptious, but if you'll excuse me, Derwatt, I think you've been forged. I'll stick my neck our farther, I'll bet my life that "The Clock" isn't yours.'

'But Mr Murchison,' Jeff said, 'that's a matter of simply –'

'Of showing me a receipt for a certain number of paintings in a certain year? Paintings received from Mexico which might not be even titled? What if Derwatt doesn't give them a title?'

'The Buckmaster Gallery is the only authorized dealer for Derwatt's work. You bought that picture from us.'

'I'm aware of that,' said Murchison. 'And I'm not accusing you – or Derwatt. I'm just saying, I don't think this is a *Derwatt*. I can't tell you what *happened*.' Murchison looked at all of them in turn, a bit embarrassed by his own outburst, but still carried along by this conviction. 'My theory is that a painter never reverts to a single colour which he once used or any combination of colours once he has made a change to another colour as subtle and yet as important as lavender is in Derwatt's paintings. Do you agree, Derwatt?'

Tom sighed and touched his moustache with a forefinger. 'I can't say. I'm not so much of a theoretician as you, it seems.'

A pause.

'Well, Mr Murchison, what would you like us to do about "The Clock"? Refund your money?' Jeff asked. 'We'll be happy to do that, because – Derwatt has just verified it, and frankly it's worth more than ten thousand dollars now.'

Tom hoped Mr Murchison would accept, but he was not that kind of man.

Murchison took his time, pushed his hands into his trousers pockets and looked at Jeff. 'Thank you, but I'm more interested in my theory – my opinion, than in the money. And since I'm in London, where there're as good judges of painting as anywhere in the world, maybe the best, I intend to have "The Clock" looked at by an expert and compared with – certain indisputable Derwatts.'

'Very well,' said Tom amiably.

'Thank you very much for seeing me, Derwatt. A pleasure to meet you.' Murchison held out his hand.

Tom shook it firmly. 'A pleasure, Mr Murchison.'

Ed helped Murchison wrap up his painting, and provided more string, as Murchison's string would no longer tie.

'Can I reach you through the gallery here?' Murchison said to Tom. 'Say tomorrow?'

'Oh, yes,' Tom said. 'They'll know where I am.'

When Murchison had left the room, Jeff and Ed gave huge sighs.

'Well – how serious is it?' Tom asked.

Jeff knew more about pictures. He spoke first, with difficulty. 'It's serious if he drags in an expert, I suppose. And he will. He may have a point about the purples. One might call it a clue that could lead to worse.'

Tom said, 'Why don't we go back to your studio, Jeff? Can you whisk me out the back door again – like Cinderella?'

'Yep, but I want to speak to Leonard.' Jeff grinned. 'I'll drag him in to meet you.' He went out.

The hum from the gallery was less now. Tom looked at Ed, whose face was a bit pale. *I can disappear, but you can't,* Tom thought. Tom squared his shoulders, and lifted his fingers in a V. 'Chin up, Banbury. We'll see this one through.'

'Or that's what they'll do to *us,*' Ed replied, with a more vulgar gesture.

Jeff came back with Leonard, a smallish, neat young man in an Edwardian suit with many buttons and velvet facings. Leonard burst into laughter at the sight of Derwatt, and Jeff shushed him.

'It is marvellous, marvellous!' Leonard said, looking Tom over with a genuine admiration. 'I've seen so many pictures, you know! I haven't seen anything so good since I did Toulouse-Lautrec with my feet tied up behind me! That was last year.' Leonard stared at Tom. 'Who *are* you?'

'That,' Jeff said, 'you are not to know. Suffice it to say –'

'Suffice it to say,' Ed said, 'Derwatt has just given a brilliant interview to the press.'

'And tomorrow Derwatt is no more. He will return to Mexico,' Jeff said in a whisper. 'Now back to your duties, Leonard.'

'*Ciao,*' said Tom, raising a hand.

'*Hommage,*' said Leonard, bowing. He backed towards the door, and added, 'The crowd's nearly all gone. So's the booze.' He slipped out.

Tom was not quite so cheerful. He very much wanted out of his disguise. The situation was a problem, not yet solved.

Back at Jeff's studio, they found that Bernard Tufts had gone. Ed and Jeff seemed surprised. And Tom was a little uneasy, because Bernard ought to know what was going on.

'You can reach Bernard of course,' Tom said.

'Oh, sure,' said Ed. He was making some tea for himself in Jeff's kitchen. 'Bernard's always *chez lui.* He's got a telephone.'

It crossed Tom's mind that even the telephone might not be safe to use for long.

'Mr Murchison is going to want to see you again probably,' Jeff said. 'With the expert. So you've got to disappear. You'll leave for Mexico tomorrow – officially. Maybe even tonight.' Jeff was sipping a Pernod. He looked more confident, perhaps because the press interview and even the Murchison interview had gone reasonably well, Tom thought.

'Mexico my foot,' Ed said, coming in with his cup of tea. 'Derwatt will be somewhere in England staying with friends, and even we won't know where. Let some days pass. *Then* he'll go to Mexico. By what means? Who knows?'

Tom removed his baggy jacket. 'Is there a date for "The Red Chairs"?'

'Yes,' Jeff said. 'It's six years old.'

'Printed here and there, I suppose?' Tom asked. 'I was thinking of updating it – to get over this purple business.'

Ed and Jeff glanced at each other, and Ed said quickly, 'No, it's in too many catalogues.'

'There's one way out, have Bernard do several canvases – two anyway – with the plain cobalt violet. Sort of prove that he uses both kinds of purple.' But Tom felt discouraged as he said it, and he knew why. Tom felt that it might be Bernard that they couldn't count on any longer. Tom looked away from Jeff and Ed. They were dubious. He tried standing up, straight, feeling confident of his Derwatt disguise. 'Did I ever tell you about my honeymoon?' Tom asked in Derwatt's monotone.

'No, tell us about your honeymoon!' Jeff said, ready for a laugh and grinning already.

Tom assumed Derwatt's stoop. 'It was – most inhibiting – the atmosphere. In Spain. We'd taken a hotel suite, you see, and there I was with Heloise, and downstairs in the patio a parrot sang *Carmen* – badly. And every time we – Well, there it came: "Ah-ha-ha-ha-ha-ha-ha-haaaaaa! Ah-*ha*-ha-ha-ha-ha-ha-ha-ha-ha-ha-*haaaa*!" People leaned out windows yelling in Spanish, "Shut your filthy beak! Who taught that – unmentionable object to sing *Carmen*? Kill it! Boil it in soup!" It is impossible to make love while laughing. Have you ever tried it? Well – they say laughter distinguishes the human from the animal. And – the other thing certainly doesn't. Ed, can you get me out of this foliage?'

Ed was laughing, and Jeff rolling on the sofa in relief – which Tom knew would be temporary – from the recent strain.

'Come in the loo.' Ed turned on the hot water in the basin.

Tom changed into his own trousers and shirt. If he could lure Murchison to his house somehow, before Murchison spoke to the expert he was talking about, perhaps something – Tom didn't know what – could be done about the situation. 'Where's Murchison staying in London?'

'Some hotel,' Jeff said. 'He didn't say which.'

'Can you ring a few hotels and see if you can find him?'

Before Jeff got to the telephone, it rang. Tom heard Jeff telling someone that Derwatt had taken a train north, and Jeff did not know where he was going. 'He's very much a loner,' Jeff said. 'Another gentleman of the press,' Jeff said when he had hung up, 'trying to get a personal interview.' He opened a telephone book. 'I'll try the Dorchester first. He looks like a Dorchester type.'

'Or a Westbury type,' Ed said.

It took a lot of delicately applied water to remove the gauze of the beard. Afterwards came a shampoo to get the rinse out of his hair. Tom finally heard Jeff say in a cheerful tone, 'No, thank you, I'll ring back later.'

Then Jeff said, 'It's the Mandeville. That's off Wigmore Street.'

Tom put on his own pink shirt from Venice. Then he went to the telephone and booked a room at the Mandeville under the name Thomas Ripley. He would arrive by 8 p.m. or so, he said.

'What're you going to do?' Ed asked.

Tom smiled a little. 'I don't know just yet,' he said, which was true.

FOUR

The Hotel Mandeville was rather plush, but by no means as expensive as the Dorchester. Tom arrived at 8.15 p.m. and registered, giving his address as Villeperce-sur-Seine. It had crossed his mind to give a false name and some English country address, because he might get into considerable difficulties with Mr Murchison and have to disappear quickly, but there was also the possibility of inviting Murchison to France, in which case Tom might need his real name. Tom asked a bellhop to take his suitcase to his room, and then he looked into the bar, hoping Mr Murchison might be there. Mr Murchison was not there, but Tom decided to have a lager and wait a few moments.

A ten-minute wait with a lager and an *Evening Standard* brought no Mr Murchison. The neighbourhood was full of restaurants, Tom knew, but he could hardly approach Murchison's table and strike up an acquaintance on the strength of saying he had seen Murchison at the Derwatt show that day. Or could he – saying he had also seen Murchison going into the back room to meet Derwatt? Yes. Tom was just about to venture out to explore the local restaurants, when he saw Mr Murchison coming into the bar, gesturing to someone to follow him.

And to Tom's surprise, horror even, he saw that the other person was Bernard Tufts. Tom slipped quickly out of the door on the other side of the bar, which opened onto the pavement. Bernard hadn't seen him. Tom was fairly sure. He looked around for a telephone booth, for another hotel from which to telephone, and, finding none, he went back into the Mandeville by the main entrance and took his key for his room, number four eleven.

In his room, Tom rang Jeff's studio. Three rings, four, five, then to Tom's relief, Jeff answered.

'Hello, Tom! I was just going down the stairs with Ed when I heard the phone. What's up?'

'Do you happen to know where Bernard is now?'

'Oh, we're leaving him alone tonight. He's upset.'

'He's having a drink with Murchison in the bar of the Mandeville.'

'What?'

'I'm ringing from my room. Now whatever you do, Jeff – Are you listening?'

'Yes-yes.'

'Don't tell Bernard I saw him. Don't tell Bernard I'm at the Mandeville. And don't get in a flap about anything. That's providing Bernard isn't spilling the beans now, I don't know.'

'Oh, my God,' Jeff groaned. 'No-no. Bernard wouldn't spill the *beans*. I don't *think* he would.'

'Are you in later tonight?'

'Yes, by – Oh, home before midnight, anyway.'

'I'll try to ring you. But don't be worried if I don't. Don't try to ring me because – I just might have somebody in my room,' Tom said with a sudden laugh.

Jeff laughed, but a bit sickly. 'Okay, Tom.'

Tom hung up.

He definitely wanted to see Murchison tonight. Would Murchison and Bernard have dinner? That would be a bore to wait out. Tom hung up a suit and stuck a couple of shirts in a drawer. He splashed some more water on his face and looked in the mirror to make sure every bit of glue was gone.

Out of restlessness, he left his room, his topcoat over his arm. He would take a walk, to Soho perhaps, and find a place for dinner. In the lobby, he looked through the glass doors of the Mandeville bar.

He was in luck. Murchison sat alone, signing the bill, and the street door of the bar was just closing, perhaps even with Bernard's departure. Still, Tom glanced around in the lobby, in case Bernard had slipped out to the men's room and might be coming back. Tom did not see Bernard, and he waited until Murchison was actually standing up to leave before he went into the bar. Tom looked depressed and thoughtful, and in fact he felt that way. He looked twice at Murchison, whose eyes met his once, as if he were recalling Murchison from somewhere.

Then Tom approached him. 'Excuse me. I think I saw you at the Derwatt show today.' Tom had put on an American accent, mid-western with a hard r in Derwatt.

'Why, yes, I was there,' Murchison said.

'I thought you looked like an American. So am I. Do you like Derwatt?' Tom was being as naïve and straightforward as possible without seeming dim-witted.

'Yes, I certainly do.'

'I own two of his canvases,' Tom said with pride. 'I may buy one of the ones in the show today – if it's left. I haven't decided yet. "The Tub".'

'Oh? So do I own one,' Murchison said with equal candour.

'Y'do? What's it called?'

'Why don't you sit down?' Murchison was standing, but indicated the chair opposite him. 'Would you care for a drink?'

'Thanks, I don't mind if I do.'

Murchison sat down. 'My picture is called "The Clock". How nice to run into someone who owns a Derwatt, too – or a couple of them!'

A waiter came.

'Scotch for me, please. And you?' he asked Tom.

'A gin and tonic,' Tom said. He added, 'I'm staying here at the Mandeville, so these drinks are on me.'

'We'll argue about that later. Tell me what pictures you have.'

' "The Red Chairs",' Tom said, 'and –'

'Really? That's a gem! "The Red Chairs". Do you live in London?'

'No, in France.'

'Oh,' with disappointment. 'And what's the other picture?'

' "Man in Chair".'

'I don't know that,' Murchison said.

For a few minutes, they discussed Derwatt's odd personality, and Tom said he had seen Murchison go into a back room of the gallery where he had heard Derwatt was.

'Only the press was let in, but I crashed the gate,' Murchison told

Tom. 'You see, I've got a rather special reason for being here just now,
and when I heard Derwatt was *here* this afternoon at the gallery, I wasn't
going to let the opportunity slip.'

'Yes? What's your reason?' Tom asked.

Murchison explained. He explained his reasons for thinking Derwatt
might be being forged, and Tom listened with rapt attention. It was a
matter of Derwatt using a mixture of ultramarine and cadmium red now,
for the past five years or so (since before his death, Tom realized, so
Derwatt had begun this, not Bernard), and of having in 'The Clock' and
in 'The Tub' gone back to his early simple cobalt violet. Murchison himself painted, he told Tom, as a hobby.

'I'm no expert, believe me, but I've read almost every book about painters and painting that exists. It wouldn't take an expert or a microscope
to tell the difference between a single colour and a mixture, but what
I mean is, you'll never find a painter going back to a colour that he
has consciously or unconsciously discarded. I say unconsciously, because
when a painter chooses a new colour or colours it is usually a decision
made by his unconscious. Not that Derwatt uses lavender in every picture, no indeed. But my conclusion is that my "Clock" and possibly some
other pictures including "The Tub" that you're interested in, by the way,
are not Derwatts.'

'That's interesting. Very. Because as it happens my "Man in Chair"
sort of corresponds to what you're saying. I think. And "Man in Chair"
is about four years old now. I'd love you to see it. Well, what're you
going to do about your "Clock"?'

Murchison lit one of his Chesterfields. 'I haven't finished my story yet.
I just had a drink with an Englishman whose name is Bernard Tufts,
a painter also, and he seems to suspect the same thing about Derwatt.'

Tom frowned hard. 'Really? It's pretty important if someone's forging
Derwatts. What did the man say?'

'I have the feeling he knows more than he's saying. I doubt if he's
in on any of it. He's not a crooked type, and he doesn't look as if he
has much money, either. But he seems to know the London art scene.
He simply warned me, "Don't buy any more Derwatts, Mr Murchison."
Now what do you think of *that*?'

'Hm-m. But what's he got to go on?'

'As I say, I don't know. I couldn't get anything out of him. But he
took the trouble to look me up here, and he said he called eight London
hotels before he found me. I asked him how he knew my name, and
he said, "Oh, word gets around." Very strange, since the Buckmaster

Gallery people are the only people I've spoken to. Don't you think? I have an appointment with a man from the Tate Gallery tomorrow, but even he doesn't know it's in regard to a Derwatt.' Murchison drank some of his Scotch and said, 'When paintings start coming from Mexico – Do you know what I'm going to do tomorrow besides showing "The Clock" to Mr Reimer at the Tate Gallery, I'm going to ask if I or he has the right to see the receipts or books of the Buckmaster Gallery people in regard to Derwatt paintings sent from Mexico. It's not the titles I'm so interested in, and Derwatt told me he doesn't always title them, it's the number of paintings. Surely they're let in by the customs or something, and if some paintings aren't recorded, there's a reason. Wouldn't it be amazing if Derwatt himself were being hood-winked and a few Derwatts – well, some said to be four or five years old, for instance – were being painted right here in London?'

Yes, Tom thought. Amazing. 'But you said you spoke with Derwatt. Did you talk to him about your painting?'

'I showed it to him! He said it was his, but he wasn't dead sure of it in my opinion. He didn't say, "By God, that's mine!" He looked at it for a couple of minutes and said, "Of course, it's mine." It was maybe presumptuous of me, but I said to Derwatt I thought it was possible he could forget a canvas or two, an untitled canvas that he'd done years ago.'

Tom frowned as if he doubted this, which he did. Even a painter who did not give titles to his paintings would remember a painting, Tom thought, less a drawing, perhaps. But he let Murchison continue.

'And for another thing, I don't quite like the men at the Buckmaster Gallery. Jeffrey Constant. And the journalist Edmund Banbury, who's obviously a close friend of Constant's. They're old friends of Derwatt's, I realize that. I get *The Listener* and *Arts Review* and also the *Sunday Times* in Long Island where I live. I see articles by Banbury quite often, usually with a plug for Derwatt, if the article isn't on Derwatt. And do you know what occurred to me?'

'What?' Tom asked.

'That – just maybe Constant and Banbury are putting up with a few forgeries in order to sell more Derwatts than Derwatt can produce. I don't go so far as to say Derwatt's in on it. But wouldn't that be a funny story, if Derwatt's so absent-minded he can't even remember how many pictures he's painted?' Murchison laughed.

It was funny, Tom supposed, but not hilarious. Not as funny as the truth, Mr Murchison. Tom smiled. 'So you're going to show your picture to the expert tomorrow?'

'Come up and see it now!'

Tom tried to take the bill, but Murchison insisted upon signing.

Tom went with him in the lift. Murchison had his painting in a corner of his closet, wrapped as Ed had wrapped it that afternoon. Tom looked at it with interest.

'It's a handsome picture,' Tom said.

'Ah, no one can deny that!'

'You know?' Tom propped it on the writing-desk and was now looking at it from across the room with all the lights turned on. 'It does have a similarity to my "Man in Chair". Why don't you come over and look at my picture? I'm very near Paris. If you think my picture might be forged, too, I'll let you take it back with you to show in London.'

'Hum,' said Murchison, thinking. 'I could.'

'If you've been taken in, so have I, I think.' It would only be insulting to offer to pay for Murchison's flight, Tom thought, so he did not. 'I've a pretty big house and I'm alone at the moment, except for my housekeeper.'

'All right, I will,' said Murchison, who hadn't sat down.

'I intend to leave tomorrow afternoon.'

'All right, I'll postpone that Tate Gallery appointment.'

'I've lots of other paintings. Not that I'm a collector.' Tom sat down in the largest chair. 'I'd like you to have a look at them. A Soutine. Two Magrittes.'

'Really?' Murchison's eyes began to look a little dreamy. 'How far are you from Paris?'

Ten minutes later, Tom was in his own room one floor below. Murchison had proposed that they have dinner together, but Tom had thought it best to say he had an appointment at 10 p.m. in Belgravia, so there was hardly time. Murchison had entrusted Tom with booking their plane tickets for tomorrow afternoon to Paris, a round-trip for Murchison. Tom picked up the telephone and booked two seats on a flight that left tomorrow afternoon, Wednesday, at 2 p.m. for Orly. Tom had his own return ticket. He left a message downstairs for Murchison in regard to the flight. Then Tom ordered a sandwich and a half bottle of Médoc. After this, he napped until eleven, and put in a telephone call to Reeves Minot in Hamburg. This took nearly half an hour.

Reeves was not in, a man's German-accented voice said.

Tom decided to chance it, because he was fed up with Reeves, and said, 'This is Tom Ripley. Has Reeves any message for me?'

'Yes. The message is Wednesday. The Count arrives in Milan tomorrow. Can you come to Milan tomorrow?'

'No, I cannot come to Milan tomorrow. *Es tut mir leid.*' Tom didn't, as yet, want to say to this man, no matter who he was, that the Count already had an invitation to visit him when he next came to France. Reeves couldn't expect him to drop everything all the time – Tom had done so on two other occasions – to fly to Hamburg or Rome (much as Tom enjoyed little excursions), pretend to be in those cities by accident, and invite the 'host', as Tom always thought of the carrier, to his Ville-perce house. 'I think there's no great complication,' Tom said. 'Can you tell me the Count's address in Milan?'

'Grand Hotel,' said the voice brusquely.

'Would you tell Reeves I'll be in touch, tomorrow probably. Where can I reach him?'

'Tomorrow morning at the Grand Hotel in Milan. He is taking a train to Milan tonight. He does not like aeroplanes, you know.'

Tom hadn't known. It was odd, a man like Reeves not liking aeroplanes. 'I'll ring him. And I'm not in Munich now. I'm in Paris.'

'Paris?' with surprise. 'I know Reeves tried to ring you in Munich at the Vierjahreszeiten.'

That was too bad. Tom hung up politely.

The hands of his wristwatch moved towards midnight. Tom puzzled about what to tell Jeff Constant tonight. And what to do about Bernard. A speech of reassurance sprang full-blown to Tom's mind, and there was time to see Bernard before he left tomorrow afternoon, but Tom was afraid Bernard might be more upset and negative, if anybody made an obvious effort to reassure him. If Bernard had said to Murchison, 'Don't buy any more Derwatts,' it sounded as if Bernard wasn't going to paint any more Derwatts, and that, of course, was going to be very bad for business. A still worse possibility, which Bernard might be on the brink of, was a confession to the police or to one or several purchasers of phoney Derwatts.

What state of mind was Bernard really in, and what was he up to?

Tom decided he should not say anything to Bernard. Bernard knew that he, Tom, had proposed his forging. Tom took a shower and began to sing:

> Babbo non vuole
> Mamma nemmeno
> Come faremo
> A far all' amor . . .

The Mandeville's walls gave a feeling – maybe an illusion – of being soundproof. Tom had not sung the song in a long time. He was pleased that it had come to him out of the blue, because it was a happy song, and Tom associated it with good luck.

He got into pyjamas and rang Jeff's studio.

Jeff answered at once. 'Hello. What's up?'

'I spoke with Mr M. tonight, and we got along fine. He's coming to France with me tomorrow. So that will delay things, you see.'

'And – you'll try to persuade him or something, you mean.'

'Yes. Something like that.'

'Want me to come to your hotel, Tom? You're probably too tired to pop over here. Or are you?'

'No, but there's no need. And you might just run into Mr M. if you came here, and we don't want that.'

'No.'

'Did you hear from Bernard?' Tom asked.

'No.'

'Please tell him –' Tom tried to find the right words. 'Tell him that you – not me – happen to know Mr M. is going to wait a few days before he does anything about his painting. I'm mainly concerned that Bernard doesn't blow up. Will you try to take care of that?'

'Why don't *you* speak to Bernard?'

'Because it would be wrong,' Tom said somewhat crossly. Some people had no inkling of psychology!

'Tom, you were marvellous today,' Jeff said. 'Thank you.'

Tom smiled, gratified by Jeff's ecstatic tone. 'Take care of Bernard. I'll ring you before I take off.'

'I expect to be in my studio all morning tomorrow.'

They said good night.

If he had told Jeff about Murchison's intention to ask for receipts, the records of paintings sent from Mexico, Jeff would have been in a tizzy, Tom thought. He must warn Jeff about that tomorrow morning, ring him from a pavement telephone booth, or from a post office. Tom was wary of hotel switchboard listeners. Of course, he hoped to dissuade Murchison from his theory, but if he couldn't, it would be just as well if Buckmaster Gallery made some records that looked authentic.

FIVE

The next morning, breakfasting in bed – a privilege for which one paid a few puritan shillings extra in England – Tom rang Mme Annette. It was only eight o'clock, but Tom knew she would have been up for nearly an hour, singing as she went about her chores of turning up the heat (a little gauge in the kitchen), making her delicate *infusion* (tea), because coffee in the morning made her heart beat fast, and adjusting her plants on various windowsills so they would catch the most sun. And she would be mightily pleased by a *coup de fil* from him in Londres.

'Allo! – Allo-*allo*!' Operator furious.

'Allo?' Quizzical.

'*Allo!*'

Three French operators were on the telephone at once, plus the woman at the Mandeville switchboard.

At last, Mme Annette came on. 'It is very beautiful here this morning. Sunlight!' Mme Annette said.

Tom smiled. He badly needed a voice of cheer. 'Mme Annette ... Yes, I am very well, thank you. How is the tooth? ... Good! I am telephoning to say I will be home this afternoon around four with an American gentleman.'

'Ah-h!' said Mme Annette, pleased.

'Our guest for tonight, perhaps for two nights, who knows? Will you prepare the guest-room nicely? With some flowers? And for dinner perhaps *tournedos* with your own delicious *béarnaise?*'

Mme Annette sounded delirious with joy that Tom would have a guest and she would have something definite to do.

Then Tom rang Mr Murchison, and they agreed to meet in the hotel lobby around noon and to take a taxi together to Heathrow.

Tom went out, intending to walk to Berkeley Square, off which was a haberdashery where he bought a pair of silk pyjamas as a small ritual nearly every time he came to London. It might also be his last chance this trip for a ride on the Underground. The Underground was a part of the atmosphere of London life, and Tom also was an admirer of Underground graffiti. The sun was struggling rather hopelessly through a wet haze, though it was not actually raining. Tom ducked into Bond Street station along with some last stragglers, perhaps, of the morning rush hour. What Tom admired about London graffiti-writers was their ability to scrawl things from moving escalators. Underwear posters abounded on the escalator routes, nothing but girls in girdles and panties, and they were adorned by anatomical additions male and female, sometimes whole phrases: I LOVE BEING HERMAPHRODITE! How did they do it? By running in an opposite direction from the escalator's while writing? WOGS OUT NOW! Down on the train platform, Tom spotted a poster for the Zeffirelli *Romeo and Juliet* with Romeo naked on his back and Juliet crawling over him with a shocking proposal coming out of her breath. Romeo's reply in a balloon was 'Okay, why don't you?'

Tom had his pyjamas by 10.30. He bought a yellow pair. He had wanted purple, as he had none now, but he had heard enough about purple lately. Tom took a taxi to Carnaby Street. For himself, he bought a pair of narrow satin-like trousers, as he did not care for flared cuffs. And for Heloise flared hipsters of black wool, waist twenty-six. The booth where Tom tried on his own trousers was so tiny, he could not step back from the mirror to see if the length was right, but Mme Annette loved to adjust little things like that for him and Heloise. Besides, two Italians who kept saying *'Bellissimo!'* were pulling back the curtains every few seconds, wanting to come in and try on their own gear. When Tom was paying, two Greeks arrived and began discussing prices loudly in drachmas. The shop was about six feet by twelve, and no wonder there was only one assistant, because there would have been no room for two.

With his purchases in big crisp paper bags, Tom went to a pavement telephone booth and rang Jeff Constant.

'I spoke to Bernard,' Jeff said, 'and he's absolutely terrified of Murchison. I asked him what he said to Murchison, because Bernard told me he'd spoken with Murchison, you see. Bernard said he'd told Murchison not to buy any more – paintings. That's bad enough, isn't it?'

'Yes,' said Tom. 'And what else?'

'Well – I tried to tell Bernard he'd already said all he could or should. It's difficult to explain because you don't know Bernard, but he's got such a guilt thing about Derwatt's genius and all that. I tried to convince Bernard that he'd eased his own conscience by *saying* that to Murchison, and why not let well enough alone?'

'What did Bernard say to that?'

'He's so down in the mouth, it's hard to tell what he said. The show was a sell-out, you see, except for one picture. Imagine! And Bernard feels guilty about that!' Jeff laughed. ' "The Tub." It's one of the ones Murchison is picking on.'

'If he doesn't want to paint more just now, don't force him.'

'That's exactly my attitude. You're so right, Tom. But I think in about a fortnight, he'll be on his feet again. Painting. It's the strain of the show, and seeing you as Derwatt. He thinks more of Derwatt than most people do of Jesus Christ.'

Tom didn't have to be told that. 'One small thing, Jeff. Murchison may want to see the gallery's books for Derwatt's paintings. From Mexico. Do you keep some kind of record?'

'N-not from Mexico.'

'Can you fake something? Just in case I can't persuade him to drop the whole thing?'

'I'll try, Tom.' Jeff sounded a bit off balance.

Tom was impatient. 'Fake something. Age it. Regardless of Mr M., isn't it a good idea to have a few books to substantiate –?' Tom broke off. Some people didn't know how to run a business, even a successful business like Derwatt Ltd.

'All right, Tom.'

Tom detoured to the Burlington Arcade, where he stopped in a jewellery shop and bought a gold pin – a little crouched monkey – for Heloise, which he paid for with American travellers' cheques. Heloise's birthday was next month. Then he walked on towards his hotel, via Oxford Street, which was crowded as usual with shoppers, women with bulging bags and boxes, children in tow. A sandwich man advertised a passport photo studio, service fast and cheap. The old fellow wore an ancient overcoat, a limp hat, and a sordid unlit cigarette hung from between his lips. Get a passport for your cruise to the Greek islands, Tom thought, but this old guy was never going anywhere. Tom removed the cigarette butt and stuck a Gauloise between the man's lips.

'Have a cigarette,' Tom said. 'Here's a light.' Tom lit it quickly with his matches.

'Ta,' said the man, through his beard.

Tom pushed the rest of the Gauloise pack, then his matches, into the torn pocket of the overcoat, and dashed away, his head ducked, hoping no one had seen him.

Tom rang Murchison from his room, and they met downstairs with their luggage.

'Been doing a little shopping for my wife this morning,' Murchison said in the taxi. He seemed in a good mood.

'Yes? So have I. A pair of Carnaby Street trousers.'

'For Harriet, it's Marks and Spencer sweaters. And Liberty scarves.

Sometimes balls of wool. She knits, and she likes to think the wool came from old England, y'know?'

'You cancelled your appointment for this morning?'

'Yep. Made it for Friday morning. At the man's house.'

At the airport, they had a rather good lunch with a bottle of claret. Murchison insisted on paying. During lunch Murchison told Tom about his son who was an inventor working in a California laboratory. His son and daughter-in-law had just had their first baby. Murchison showed Tom a photograph of her, and laughed at himself for being a doting grandfather, but it was his first grandchild, named Karin after her grandmother on her maternal side. In answer to Murchison's questions, Tom said he had chosen to live in France because he had married a French girl three years ago. Murchison was not blunt enough to ask how Tom earned his living, but he did ask how he spent his time.

'I read history,' Tom said casually. 'I study German. Not to mention that my French still needs work. And gardening. I've got a pretty big garden in Villeperce. Also I paint,' he added, 'just for my amusement.'

They were at Orly by 3 p.m., and Tom went off in the little GASO bus to fetch his car from the garage, and then he picked up Murchison near the taxi rank with their suitcases. The sun was shining, and it was not so cold as in England. Tom drove to Fontainebleau and went past the château so that Murchison could see it. Murchison said he hadn't seen it in fifteen years. They reached Villeperce around 4.30 p.m.

'Where we buy most of our groceries,' Tom said, indicating a store on his left on the main village street.

'Very pretty. Unspoilt,' Murchison said. And when they came to Tom's house: 'Why this is terrific! Really beautiful!'

'You should see it in the summer,' Tom said, modestly.

Mme Annette, hearing the car, came out to greet them and to help with the luggage, but Murchison could not bear to see a woman carrying the heavy things, only the little bags of cigarettes and spirits.

'Everything goes well, Mme Annette?' Tom asked.

'Everything. Even the plumber came to repair the W.C.'

One of the W.C.s had been dripping, Tom remembered.

Tom and Annette showed Murchison up to his room which had an adjoining bath. It was actually Heloise's bath, and her room was on the other side of the bath. Tom explained that his wife was in Greece now, with friends. He left Murchison to wash and to open his suitcase, and said he would be downstairs in the living-room. Murchison was already gazing with interest at some drawings on the walls.

Tom went down and asked Mme Annette to make some tea. He presented her with a bottle of toilet water from England, 'Lake Mist' – which he had bought at Heathrow.

'Oh, M. Tome, *comme vous êtes gentil*!'

Tom smiled. Mme Annette always made him feel grateful for her gratitude. 'Good *tournedos* for tonight?'

'Ah, *oui*! And for dessert *mousse au chocolat*.'

Tom went into the living-room. Here were flowers, and Mme Annette had turned up the heat. There was a fireplace, and Tom loved fires, but he felt he had to watch them constantly, or he loved watching them so much he could not tear himself away, so he decided not to light one now. He stared at 'Man in Chair' over the fireplace, and bounced on his heels with satisfaction – satisfaction with its familiarity, its excellence. Bernard was good. He'd just made a couple of mistakes in his periods. Damn periods anyway. Logically, 'The Red Chairs', a genuine Derwatt, should have the place of honour in the room over the fireplace. Typical of him that he had put the phoney in the choice spot, he supposed. Heloise didn't know that 'Man in Chair' was bogus, and knew nothing of the Derwatt forgeries, in fact. Her interest in painting was casual. If she had any passions, they were for travelling, sampling exotic food, and buying clothes. The contents of her two closets in her room looked like an international costume museum without the dummies. She had waistcoats from Tunisia, fringed sleeveless jackets from Mexico, Greek soldiers' baggy pants in which she looked quite charming, and embroidered coats from China that she had bought somehow in London.

Then Tom suddenly remembered Count Bertolozzi, and went to his telephone. He didn't particularly want Murchison to hear the Count's name, but on the other hand Tom was not going to do any harm to the Count, and perhaps maintaining his open manner was all to the good. Tom asked for inquiries for Milan, got the number, and gave it to the French operator. She told Tom the call might take half an hour.

Mr Murchison came down. He had changed his clothes, and wore grey flannel trousers and a green and black tweed jacket. 'The country life!' he said, beaming. 'Ah!' He had caught sight of 'The Red Chairs' facing him across the room, and went over for closer inspection. 'That's a masterpiece. That's the real McCoy!'

No doubt of that, Tom thought, and a thrill of pride went over him which made him feel slightly foolish. 'Yes, I like it.'

'I think I've heard about it. I remember the title from somewhere. I congratulate you, Tom.'

'And there's my "Man in Chair",' Tom said, nodding towards the fire-place.

'Ah,' Murchison said on a different note. He went nearer, and Tom saw his tall, sturdy figure grow tense with concentration. 'And how old is this?'

'About four years old,' Tom said truthfully.

'What did you pay, to ask a rude question?'

'Four thousand quid. Before devaluation. About eleven thousand and two hundred dollars,' Tom said, calculating the pound at two eighty.

'I'm delighted to see this,' Murchison said, nodding. 'You see, the same purple turns up again. Very little of it here, but look.' He pointed to the bottom of the chair. Due to the height of the picture and the width of the fireplace, Murchison's finger was inches away from the canvas, but Tom knew the streak of purple that he meant. 'Plain cobalt violet.' Murchison crossed the room and looked again at 'The Red Chairs', peering at it at a distance of ten inches. 'And this is one of the old ones. Plain cobalt violet too.'

'You really think "Man in Chair" is a forgery?'

'Yes, I do. Like my "Clock". The quality is different. Inferior to "The Red Chairs". Quality is something one can't measure with the aid of a microscope. But I can see it here. *And* – I'm also sure about the plain cobalt violet here.'

'Then,' Tom said in an unperturbed way, 'maybe it means Derwatt is using plain cobalt violet and the mixture you mentioned – alternately.'

Murchison, frowning, shook his head. 'I don't see it that way.'

Mme Annette was pushing the tea in on a cart. One wheel of the cart squeaked slightly. '*Voilà le thé*, M. Tome.'

Mme Annette had made flat brown-edged cookies, and they gave off a rosy smell of warm vanilla. Tom poured the tea.

Murchison sat on the sofa. He might not have seen Mme Annette come and go. He stared at 'Man in Chair' as if dazed or fascinated. Then he blinked at Tom, smiled, and his faced was genial again. 'You don't believe me, I think. That's your privilege.'

'I don't know what to say. I don't see the difference in quality, no. Maybe I'm obtuse. If, as you say, you'll get an expert to look at yours, I'll abide by what an expert says. And by the way, "Man in Chair" is the picture you can take back to London with you, if you like.'

'I'd most certainly like. I'll write write you a receipt for it and even insure it for you.' Murchison chuckled.

'It's insured. Don't worry.'

Over two cups of tea, Murchison asked Tom about Heloise, and what she was doing. Had they any children? No. Heloise was twenty-five. No, Tom didn't think Frenchwomen were more difficult than other women, but they had their own idea of the respect with which they should be treated. This subject did not make much progress, because every woman wanted to be treated with a certain respect, and though Tom knew Heloise's kind, he absolutely could not put it into words.

The telephone rang, and Tom said, 'Excuse me, I think I'll take that up in my room.' He dashed up the stairs. After all, Murchison might suppose it was Heloise, and that he wanted to speak with her alone.

'Hello?' Tom said. 'Eduardo! How are you? I'm in luck to get you ... Via the grapevine. A mutual friend in Paris rang today and told me you were in Milan ... Now you can pay me a visit? After all, you promised.'

The Count, a bon-vivant ever willing to be distracted from the swift pursuit of his business (export-import) showed a slight hesitation about changing his Paris plans, then agreed with enthusiasm to come to Tom. 'But not tonight. Tomorrow. Is that all right?'

That was quite soon enough for Tom, who wasn't quite sure what problems Murchison would present. 'Yes, even Friday would be –'

'Thursday,' said the Count, firmly, not getting the point.

'All right. I'll pick you up at Orly. At what time?'

'My plane is at – just a minute.' The Count took quite a time looking it up, came back to the telephone and said. 'Arriving at five fifteen. Flight three zero six Alitalia.'

Tom wrote this down. 'I'll be there. Delighted you can come, Eduardo!'

Then Tom went back downstairs to Thomas Murchison. By now they called each other Tom, though Murchison said his wife called him Tommy. Murchison said he was an hydraulic engineer with a pipe-laying company whose main office was in New York. Murchison was one of the directors.

They took a walk around Tom's back garden, which blended into virgin woods. Tom rather liked Murchison. Surely he could persuade him, convert him, Tom thought. What *should* he do?

During dinner, while Murchison talked about something brand-new in his plant, packaged transport by pipe of anything and everything in soup-tin-sized containers – Tom wondered if he should bother to ask Jeff and Ed to get Mexican letterheads from some shipping company on which to list Derwatt's paintings? And how quickly could this be done? Ed was the journalist, and couldn't he handle a clerical job like this, and have Leonard, the gallery manager, and Jeff walk all over them on the floor to make them look five or six years old? The dinner was excellent, and

Murchison had praise for Mme Annette, which he delivered in quite passable French, for her *mousse* and even the Brie.

'We'll have coffee in the living-room,' Tom said to her. 'And can you bring the brandy?'

Mme Annette had lit the fire. Tom and Murchison settled themselves on the big yellow sofa.

'It's a funny thing,' Tom began, 'I like "Man in Chair" just as much as "The Red Chairs". If it's phoney. Funny, isn't it?' Tom was still talking in a mid-western accent. 'You can see it's got the place of honour in the house.'

'Well, you didn't know it was a forgery!' Murchison laughed a little. 'It'd be very interesting – very – to know who's forging.'

Tom stretched his legs out in front of him and puffed on a cigar. 'What a funny thing it would be,' he began, playing his last and best card, 'if a forger was doing all the Buckmaster Gallery Derwatts now, all the ones we saw yesterday. Someone as good as Derwatt, in other words.'

Murchison smiled. 'Then what's Derwatt doing? Sitting back and taking it! Don't be ridiculous. Derwatt was much as I'd thought he would be. Withdrawn and sort of old-fashioned.'

'Have you ever thought of collecting forgeries? I know a man in Italy who collects them. First as a hobby, and now he sells them to other collectors at quite high prices.'

'Oh, I've heard of that. Yes. But I like to know I'm buying a forgery when I buy one.'

Tom sensed that he was reaching a narrow and unpleasant spot. He tried again. 'I like to daydream – about absurd things like that. In a sense, why disturb a forger who's doing such good work? I intend to hang onto "Man in Chair".'

Murchison might not have heard Tom's remarks. 'And you know,' Murchison said, still gazing at the picture Tom was talking about, 'it's not merely the lavender, it's the soul of the painting. I wouldn't put it that way, if I weren't mellow on your good food and drink.'

They had finished a delicious bottle of Margaux, the best from Tom's cellar.

'Do you think the Buckmaster Gallery people might be crooks?' Murchison asked. 'They *must* be. Why would they be putting up with a forger? Shoving forgeries among the real ones?'

Murchison thought the other new Derwatts, all of them in the current show, except 'The Tub', were genuine, Tom realized. 'That's if these are really forgeries – your "Clock" and so forth. I suppose I'm not yet convinced.'

Murchison smiled with good humour. 'Just because you like your "Man in Chair". If your picture is four years old and mine's at least three, these forgeries have been going on quite a while. Maybe there's more in London that weren't lent for the show. Frankly, it's Derwatt I suspect. I suspect him of being in cahoots with the Buckmaster people to earn more money. Another thing – there've been no drawings by Derwatt for years now. That's odd.'

'Really?' Tom asked with a feigned surprise. He knew this, and he knew what Murchison was driving at.

'Drawings reveal an artist's personality,' Murchison said. 'I realized that myself, and then I read it somewhere – just to corroborate myself.' He laughed. 'Just because I manufacture pipe, people never give me credit for sensitivity! But a drawing is like a signature for a painter, a very complicated signature at that. You might say, you can forge a signature or a painting more easily than you can forge a drawing.'

'Never thought of that,' said Tom, and rolled his cigar end in the ashtray. 'You say Saturday you're going to speak to the Tate Gallery man?'

'Yes. There's a couple of old Derwatts at the Tate as you probably know. Then I'll speak to the Buckmaster people without giving them any warning – if Riemer corroborates me.'

Tom's mind began to make painful leaps. Saturday was the day after tomorrow. Riemer might want to compare 'The Clock' and 'Man in Chair' with the Tate Gallery Derwatts and those in the current show. Could Bernard Tufts's paintings stand up to it? And if they couldn't? He poured more brandy for Murchison and a bit for himself which he did not want. He folded his hands on his chest. 'You know, I don't think I'll sue – or whatever one does – if there's forging going on.'

'Hah! I'm a little more orthodox. Old-fashioned, maybe. My attitude. Suppose Derwatt's really in on it?'

'Derwatt's rather a saint, I hear.'

'That's the legend. He might've been more of a saint when he was younger and poorer. He's been in seclusion. His friends in London put him on the map, that's plain. A lot can happen to a poor man, if he suddenly becomes rich.'

Tom got no further during the evening. Murchison wanted to turn in early, because he was tired.

'I'll see about a plane in the morning. I should've booked one in London. That was stupid of me.'

'Oh, not in the morning, I hope,' Tom said.

'I'll book it in the morning. I'll take off in the afternoon, if that's all right with you.'

Tom saw his guest up to his room, made sure he had everything he needed.

It crossed his mind to ring Jeff or Ed. But what news had he, except that he wasn't getting anywhere in trying to persuade Murchison not to see the Tate Gallery man? And also Tom did not want Jeff's telephone number appearing too often on his bill.

SIX

Tom began the morning with a determined optimism. He put on old comfortable clothes – after having in bed Mme Annette's delicious coffee, one black cup to wake him up – and went down to see if Murchison was stirring as yet. It was a quarter to nine.

'Le m'sieur takes his breakfast in his room,' Mme Annette said.

While Mme Annette tidied his room, Tom shaved in his bathroom. 'M. Murchison is leaving this afternoon, I think,' Tom said in answer to Mme Annette's question about the dinner menu for that evening. 'But today is Thursday. Do you think you could catch a nice pair of soles –' Tom gulped and thought of 'shoes, skates' in English '– from the fish merchant for lunch?' A fish van came to the village twice a week. There was no fish shop in the town, because Villeperce was too small.

Mme Annette was inspired by this suggestion. 'The grapes are lovely at the fruit merchant's,' she said. 'You wouldn't believe it ...'

'Buy some.' Tom scarcely listened to her.

At 11 a.m. Tom and Murchison were walking in the woods behind Tom's property. Tom was in an odd mood, or state of mind. In a burst of bare-faced friendliness, honesty, or whatever one might call it, Tom had shown Murchison his own artistic efforts in the upstairs room where he painted. Tom painted landscapes and portraits mainly. He was ever trying to simplify, to keep the example of Matisse before him, but with little success, he thought. One portrait of Heloise, possibly Tom's twelfth, was not bad, and Murchison had praised it. *My God*, Tom thought, *I'll lay my soul bare, show him the poems I've written to Heloise, take my*

clothes off and do a sword dance, if he'll only – see things my way! It was
no use.

Murchison's plane was at 4 p.m. for London. Time for a decent lunch
here, as Orly was about an hour away by car under good conditions.
While Murchison had been changing his shoes for their little walk, Tom
had wrapped 'Man in Chair' in three thicknesses of corrugated paper,
string, brown paper and more string. Murchison was going to keep the
painting with him on the plane, he had told Tom. Murchison said he
had reserved a room at the Mandeville for this evening.

'But remember, no charges pressed on my part,' Tom said, 'about "Man
in Chair".'

'That doesn't mean you'll deny it's a fake,' Murchison said with a smile.
'You're not going to insist it's genuine?'

'No,' Tom said. *'Touché.* I'll bow to the experts.'

The open woods was not the place for a conversation which had to
get down to a pinpoint, Tom felt. Or did it have to expand into a huge
grey cloud? Tom was not happy at any rate, talking to Murchison in
the woods.

Tom asked Mme Annette to prepare the lunch rather early, because
of M. Murchison's departure, and they began at a quarter to one.

Tom was determined to keep the conversation on the subject, because
he did not want to abandon all hope. He brought up Van Meegeren,
with whose career Murchison was acquainted. Van Meegeren's forgeries
of Vermeer had finally achieved some value of their own. Van Meegeren
may have started it first in self-defence, in bravado, but aesthetically there
was no doubt that Van Meegeren's inventions of 'new' Vermeers had
given pleasure to the people who had bought them.

'I cannot understand your total disconnection with the *truth* of things,'
Murchison said. 'An artist's style is his truth, his honesty. Has another
man the right to copy it, in the same way that a man copies another
man's signature? And for the same purpose, to draw on his reputation,
his bank account? A reputation already built by a man's talent?'

They were chasing the last morsels of sole and butter around their
plates, with the last morsels of potato. The sole had been superb, the
white wine still was. It was the kind of lunch that under any other
circumstances would have given contentment, even happiness, would
have inspired lovers to go to bed – perhaps after coffee – and make love
and then sleep. The beauty of the lunch was today wasted on Tom.

'I speak for myself,' Tom said. 'I usually do. I don't mean to influence
you. I'm sure I couldn't. But you have my permission to say to – who

is it, Mr Constant, yes, that I'm rather happy with my forgery and I want to keep it.'

'I'll tell him that. But don't you think of the future? If there's somebody continuing to do this –'

There was a lemon soufflé. Tom struggled. He was convinced. Why couldn't he put it into words, put it well enough to convince Murchison? *Murchison was not artistic.* Or he wouldn't be talking like this. Murchison didn't appreciate Bernard. What the hell was Murchison doing dragging in truth and signatures and possibly even the police, compared to what Bernard was doing in his studio, which was undeniably the work of a fine painter? How had Van Meegeren put it (or had Tom himself put it that way, in one of his notebooks)? 'An artist does things naturally, without effort. Some power guides his hand. A forger struggles, and if he succeeds, it is a genuine achievement.' Tom realized it was his own paraphrase. But goddam it, that smug Murchison, holier-than-thou! At least Bernard was a man of talent, of more talent than Murchison with his plumbing, his pipe-laying, his packaging of transportable items, an idea which anyway had come from a young engineer in Canada, Murchison had said.

Coffee. Neither took brandy, though the bottle was at hand.

Thomas Murchison's face, full of flesh, somewhat ruddy – his face might have been stone to Tom. Murchison's eyes were bright, quite intelligent, and against him.

It was 1.30. They were to leave for Orly in half an hour or so. Should he go back to London as soon as possible after the Count left, Tom wondered? But what could be accomplished in London? Damn the Count, Tom thought. Derwatt Ltd was more important than the crap or the trinket that the Count was carrying. Tom realized that Reeves had not told him where to look in the Count's suitcase or briefcase or whatever. Tom supposed Reeves would telephone this evening. Tom felt wretched, and he simply had to move, now, from the chair where he had been squirming for the past ten minutes.

'I wanted you to take a bottle of wine from my cellar,' Tom said. 'Shall we go down and have a look?'

Murchison's smile became broader. 'What a marvellous idea! Thank you, Tom.'

The cellar was approachable from outdoors, down a few stone steps to a green door, or via a door in a downstairs spare loo, next to a little hall where guests hung their coats. Tom and Heloise had had the indoor stairs put in to avoid going outdoors in bad weather.

'I'll take the wine back to the States with me. It'd be a pity to crack it by myself in London,' Murchison said.

Tom put on the light in the cellar. The cellar was big, grey and as cool as a refrigerator, or so it seemed in contrast to the centrally heated house. There were five or six big barrels on stands, not all of them full, and many racks of wine bottles against all the walls. In one corner was the big fuel storage tank for the heating, and another tank that held hot water.

'Here are the clarets,' Tom said, indicating a wall of wine racks which were more than half full of dusty dark bottles.

Murchison whistled appreciatively.

It's got be done down here, Tom thought, if anything has to be done. Yet he had not planned nearly enough, he had not planned anything. Keep moving, he told himself, but all he did was stroll about slowly, looking over his bottles, touching one or two of the red tinfoil-wrapped necks. He pulled one out. 'Margaux. You liked that.'

'Superb,' Murchison said. 'Thank you very much, Tom. I'll tell the folks about the cellar it came from.' Murchison took the bottle reverently.

Tom said, 'You won't possibly change your mind – just for the sake of sportsmanship – about speaking to the expert in London. About the forgeries.'

Murchison laughed a little. 'Tom, I can't. Sportsmanship! I can't for the life of me see why you want to protect them, unless –'

Murchison had had a thought, and Tom knew what that thought was, that Tom Ripley was in on it, deriving some kind of benefit or profit from it. 'Yes, I have an interest in it,' Tom said quickly. 'You see, I know the young man who spoke to you in your hotel the other day. I know all about him. He's the forger.

'*What?* That – that –'

'Yes, that nervous fellow. Bernard. He knew Derwatt. It started out quite idealistically, you see –'

'You mean, Derwatt *knows* about it?'

'Derwatt is dead. They got someone to impersonate him.' Tom blurted it out, feeling he had nothing any longer to lose, and maybe something to gain. Murchison had his life to gain, but Tom could not quite put that into words, not plain words, as yet.

'So Derwatt's dead – since how long?'

'Five or six years. He really died in Greece.'

'So all the pictures –'

'Bernard Tufts – You saw what kind of fellow he is. He'd commit suicide if it came out he was forging his dead friend's paintings. He told you not to buy any more. Isn't that enough? The gallery asked Bernard to paint a couple of pictures in Derwatt's style, you see –' Tom realized *he* had suggested that, but no matter. Tom also realized that he was arguing hopelessly, not only because Murchison was adamant, but because there was a split in Tom's own reasoning, a split he was well acquainted with. He saw the right and the wrong. Yet both sides of himself were equally sincere: save Bernard, save the forgeries, save even Derwatt, was what Tom was arguing. Murchison would never understand. 'Bernard wants out of it, I know. I don't think you'd like to risk a man's killing himself out of shame just to prove a point, would you?'

'He might've thought of shame when he began!' Murchison looked at Tom's hands, his face, back to his hands again. 'Was it *you* impersonating Derwatt? Yes. I noticed Derwatt's hands.' Murchison smiled bitterly. 'And people think I don't notice little things!'

'You're very observant,' Tom said quickly. He suddenly felt angry.

'My God, I might've mentioned it yesterday. I thought of it yesterday. Your hands. You can't put a beard on those, can you?'

Tom said, 'Let them alone, would you? Are they doing much harm? Bernard's pictures are good, you can't deny that.'

'I'm damned if I'll keep my mouth shut about it! No! Not even if you or anybody else offers me a whacking lot of money to keep my mouth shut!' Murchison's face was redder, and his jowls trembled. He set the wine down rather hard on the floor, but it didn't break.

The rejection of his wine was a slight insult, or so Tom felt now, a minuscule but further insult and annoyance. Tom picked up the bottle almost at once and swung it at Murchison, hitting him on the side of the head. This time the bottle broke, wine splashed, and the base of the bottle fell to the floor. Murchison reeled against the wine racks, jiggling it all, but nothing else fell, except Murchison, who slumped down, bumping wine-bottle tops but not disturbing any. Tom seized the first thing to hand – which happened to be an empty coal scuttle – and swung it at Murchison's head. Tom struck a second blow. The base of the scuttle was heavy. Murchison was bleeding, lying sideways, his body somewhat twisted, on the stone floor. He wasn't moving.

What to do about the blood? Tom turned around in circles, looking for an old rag anywhere, even newspaper. He went over to the fuel tank. Under the tank was a large rag, stiff with age and dirt. He went back with it and mopped, but gave up the useless task after a moment, and looked around again. Put him under a barrel, he thought. He grabbed

Murchison by the ankles, then at once dropped the ankles and felt Murchison's neck. There seemed to be no pulse. Tom took a huge breath, and got his hands under Murchison's arms. He pulled and jerked, dragging the heavy body towards the barrel. The corner behind the barrel was dark. Murchison's feet stuck out a little. Tom bent Murchison's knees so that the feet did not show. But since the barrel stood some sixteen inches above the floor on its stand, Murchison was more or less visible, if someone stood in the middle of the cellar and looked into that particular corner. By stooping, one had a view of Murchison's whole body. Of all times, Tom thought, not to find an old sheet, a piece of tarpaulin, newspaper, anything to cover something up with! That was Mme Annette's tidiness!

Tom kicked the bloodstained rag, and it landed on Murchison's feet. He kicked at a couple of pieces of broken bottle on the floor – the wine had mingled with the blood now – then quickly picked up the neck of the bottle, and hit the light bulb which hung on a cord from the ceiling. The bulb broke and tinkled to the floor.

Then, gasping a little, trying to get his breathing back to normal, Tom moved in the darkness towards the stairs and climbed them. He closed the door. The spare john had a basin, and here he washed his hands quickly. Some blood showed pink in the running water, and Tom thought it was Murchison's, until he saw that it kept coming, and that he had a cut at the base of his thumb. But it wasn't a bad cut, it could have been worse, so he considered himself lucky. He pulled toilet paper from the roll on the wall and wrapped it around his thumb.

Mme Annette was busy in the kitchen now, which was another piece of luck. If she came out, Tom thought, he would say that M. Murchison was already in the car – in case Mme Annette asked where he was. It was time to go.

Tom ran up to Murchison's room. The only things Murchison had not packed were his topcoat and toilet articles in the loo. Tom put the toilet articles into a pocket of Murchison's suitcase and closed it. Then he carried the suitcase and the topcoat down the stairs and out of the front door. He put these things into the Alfa-Romeo, then ran back upstairs for Murchison's 'Clock', which was still wrapped. Murchison had been so sure of himself, he hadn't bothered unwrapping 'The Clock' to compare it with 'Man in Chair'. Pride goeth before a fall, Tom thought. He took his wrapped 'Man in Chair' from Murchison's room into his own room, and stuck it in a back corner of his closet, then carried 'The Clock' downstairs. He grabbed his raincoat from a hook outside the spare loo, and went out to the car. He drove off for Orly.

Murchison's passport and airline ticket might be in the pocket of his jacket, Tom thought. He would take care of that later, burn them preferably, when Mme Annette was out of the house in the morning on her usual leisurely shopping tour. It also occurred to Tom that he had not told Mme Annette about the Count's arrival. Tom would ring her from somewhere, but not from Orly Airport, he thought, because he did not want to linger there.

The time was right, as if Murchison were actually going to make his plane.

Tom made for the departures doorway. Here taxis and private cars, as long as they did not pause too long, could deposit luggage and people or pick them up. Tom stopped, got Murchison's suitcase out, and set it on the pavement, then set 'The Clock' against the suitcase, and laid Murchison's coat on top. Tom drove off. There were a few other little assemblies of luggage on the pavement, he noticed. He drove out in the Fontainebleau direction, and stopped at a roadside bar-café, one of many medium-sized bar-cafés along the route between Orly and the beginning of the Autoroute du Sud.

He ordered a beer, and asked for a jeton to make a telephone call. No jeton was necessary, so Tom took the telephone on the bar near the cash register, and dialled the number of his house.

'Hello, it's me,' said Tom. 'M. Murchison had to hurry at the last moment, so he asked me to tell you good-bye and to thank you.'

'Oh, I understand.'

'*Alors* – there is another guest coming this evening, a Count Bertolozzi, an Italian. I shall find him at Orly, and we'll be home before six. Now can you buy perhaps some – calves' liver?'

'The butcher at the moment has beautiful *gigot*!'

Tom was not in the mood for anything with a bone in it, somehow. 'If it is not too much trouble, I think I prefer calves' liver.'

'And a Margaux? A Meursault?'

'Leave the wine to me.'

Tom paid – he said he had telephoned Sens, which was farther than his village – and went out to his car. He drove at a leisurely speed back to Orly, past the arrivals and departures section, and noticed that Murchison's things were still where he had left them. The coat would be the first to go, Tom thought, nicked by some enterprising young man. And if Murchison's passport were in the topcoat, the nicker might turn it to some advantage. Tom smiled a little as he drove into P-4, one of the one-hour parking lots.

Tom walked slowly through the glass doors which opened before him, bought a *Neue Zürcher Zeitung* at the news-stand, then checked on the arrival time of Eduardo's plane. The flight was on time, and he had a few minutes to spare. Tom went to the crowded bar – it was always crowded – and at last got an elbow in and managed to order coffee. After the coffee, he bought a ticket and went up to where people met the arrivals.

The Count was wearing a grey homburg. He had a long thin black moustache and a bulging abdomen, which was visible even under his unbuttoned topcoat. The Count broke into a smile, a real spontaneous Italian smile, and he waved a greeting. The Count was presenting his passport.

Then they were shaking hands, giving each other a quick embrace, and Tom helped him with packages and carry-alls. The Count had also an attaché case. What was the Count carrying, and where? His suitcase was not even opened, only motioned through by the French official.

'If you'll wait here a minute, I'll fetch my car,' Tom said when they were on the pavement. 'It's just a few yards away.' Tom went off at a trot, and was back in five minutes.

He had to drive past the departures gate, and he noticed that Murchison's suitcase and painting were still there, but the coat was gone. One down and two to go.

On the drive homeward, they discussed, not very profoundly, Italian politics, French politics of the moment, and the Count inquired about Heloise. Tom scarcely knew the Count, and thought this was the second time they had seen each other, but in Milan they had talked about painting, which was a passionate interest of the Count's.

'At the moment, there is an *esposizione* of Derwatt in London. I look forward to that next week. And what do you think of Derwatt coming to London? I was *astound*! The first photographs of him in years!'

Tom had not bothered to buy a London newspaper. 'A big surprise. He hasn't changed much, they say.' Tom was not going to mention that he had been recently in London and had seen the show.

'I look forward to seeing your picture at home. What is it? The one with the little girls?'

'"The Red Chairs",' Tom said, surprised that the Count remembered. He smiled and gripped the wheel tighter. Despite the corpse in the cellar, despite the ghastly day, the nerve-racking afternoon, Tom was going to be very happy to get back home – to the scene of the crime, as they said. Tom didn't feel that it was a crime. Or was he due for a delayed reaction tomorrow, even tonight? He hoped not.

'Italy is producing worse expresso. In the cafés,' the Count announced in a solemn baritone. 'I am *convince*. Probably some Mafia business at the bottom of it.' He mused sourly out the window for a few moments, then continued, 'And the hairdressers in Italy, my goodness! I begin to wonder if I know my own country! Now in my old favourite barbershop off the Via Veneto, they have new young men who ask me what kind of shampoo I want. I say, "Just wash my hair, please – what's left of it!" "But is it oily or dry, signor? We have three kinds of shampoo. Have you dandruff?" "No!" I say. "Can't somebody have *normal* hair these days, or doesn't ordinary shampoo exist any more?"'

Like Murchison, the Count praised the sturdy symmetry of Belle Ombre. The garden, though there was hardly a rose left from summer, showed its handsome rectangular lawn surrounded by thick and formidable pines. It was home, and not exactly humble. Again Mme Annette met them on the doorstep, and was as helpful and welcoming as yesterday when Thomas Murchison had arrived. Again Tom showed his guest to his room, which Mme Annette had made ready. It was late for tea, so Tom said he would be downstairs when the Count wished to join him. Dinner was at eight.

Then Tom unwrapped 'Man in Chair' in his room, and took it downstairs and hung it in its usual place. Mme Annette might well have noticed its absence for a few hours, but if she asked him anything about it, Tom intended to say that Mr Murchison had taken it to his room, Tom's, to look at under a different light.

Tom parted the heavy red curtains of the french windows, and looked at his back garden. The dark green shadows were becoming black with the fall of night. Tom realized he was standing directly over Murchison in the cellar, and he edged away. He must, even if it had to be late tonight, go down and do what he could about cleaning up the wine and bloodstains. Mme Annette might have a reason to go to the cellar; she kept a good eye on the fuel supply. And then, how to get the body out of the house? There was a wheelbarrow in the toolshed. Could he wheel Murchison – covered by a tarpaulin which was in the toolshed also – into the woods behind the house and bury him? Primitive, unpleasantly close to the house, but it might be the best solution.

The Count came down, spry and bouncing in spite of his bulk. He was a rather tall man.

'A-hah! A-*hah*!' Like Murchison he was struck by 'The Red Chairs' which hung on the other side of the room. But the Count turned at once, and looked towards the fireplace, and seemed even more impressed by

'Man in Chair'. 'Lovely! Delicious!' He peered at both pictures. 'You did
not disappoint me. They are a pleasure. So is your entire house. I mean
the drawings in my room.'

Mme Annette came in with the ice bucket and some glasses on the
bar cart.

The Count, seeing Punt e Mes, said he would have that.

'Did the gallery in London ask you to lend your pictures for the
esposizione?'

Murchison had asked that question twenty-four hours ago, but about
'Man in Chair' only, and had asked it because he was curious about the
gallery's attitude to paintings they must know to be forgeries. Tom felt
a little dizzy in the head, as if he were going to faint. He had been bending
over the bar cart, and now he straightened up. 'They did. But it's such
trouble, you know, shipping and insuring. I lent "The Red Chairs" for
a show two years ago.'

'I may buy a Derwatt,' said the Count thoughtfully. 'That is if I can
afford one. It will be to a small one, at his prices.'

Tom poured a straight Scotch on ice for himself.

The telephone rang.

'Excuse me,' Tom said, and answered it.

Eduardo was walking about, looking at other things on the walls.

It was Reeves Minot. He asked if the Count had arrived, then if Tom
were alone.

'No, I'm not.'

'It's in the –'

'I can't quite hear.'

'*Toothpaste,*' Reeves said.

'O-oh.' It was almost a groan from Tom, of fatigue, contempt, boredom
even. Was this a child's game? Or something in a lousy film? 'Very good.
And the address? Same as last time?' Tom had an address in Paris, three
or four actually, where he had sent Reeves's items on other occasions.

'That'll do. The last one. Is everything all right?'

'Yes, I think so, thank you,' Tom said pleasantly. He might have
suggested Reeves have a word with the Count, just to be friendly, but
it was probably better the Count didn't know that Reeves had rung. Tom
felt quite off his form, off on the wrong foot. 'Thanks for ringing.'

'No need to ring me if everything's okay,' said Reeves and hung up.

'Would you excuse me a second, Eduardo,' Tom said, and ran upstairs.

He went into the Count's room. One of his suitcases was open on the
antique wood-box where guests and Mme Annette usually put suitcases,

but Tom looked first in the bathroom. The Count had not put out his toilet articles. Tom went to the suitcase and found an opaque plastic bag with a zipper. He tried this and ran into tobacco. There was another plastic bag in which were shaving gear, toothbrush and toothpaste, and he took the toothpaste. The end of the tube was a little rough, but sealed. Reeves's man probably had some kind of clamp with which to seal the metal again. Tom squeezed the tube cautiously and felt a hard lump near the end of it. He shook his head in disgust, pocketed the toothpaste, replaced the plastic kit. He went to his own room and put the toothpaste at the back of his top left drawer which contained a stud box and a lot of starched collars.

Tom rejoined the Count downstairs.

During dinner they talked about Derwatt's surprising return, and his interview which the Count had read in the press.

'He's living in Mexico, isn't he?' Tom asked.

'Yes. And he won't say where. Like B. Traven, you know. Ha! Ha!'

The Count praised the dinner and ate heartily. He had the European faculty of being able to talk with his mouth full, which no American could manage without looking or feeling extremely messy.

After dinner, the Count, seeing Tom's gramophone, expressed a desire for some music, and chose *Pelléas et Mélisande*. The Count wanted the third act – the duet, somewhat hectic, between soprano and deep male voice. While listening, even singing along, the Count managed to talk.

Tom tried to pay attention to the Count and to exclude the music, but Tom always found it hard to exclude music. He was in no mood for *Pelléas et Mélisande*. What he needed was the music from *A Midsummer Night's Dream*, the fabulous overture, and now as the other thing played on with its heavy drama, Mendelssohn's overture danced in Tom's inner ear – nervous, comic, full of invention. He desperately needed to be full of invention.

They were dipping into the brandy. Tom suggested that tomorrow morning they might take a drive and lunch at Moret-sur-Loing. Eduardo had said he wanted to take an afternoon train to Paris. But first he wanted to make sure he had seen all Tom's art treasures, so Tom took him on a tour of the house. Even in Heloise's room, there was a Marie Laurencin.

Then they said good night, and Eduardo retired with a couple of Tom's art books.

In his room, Tom got the tube of Vademecum toothpaste from his drawer, tried to open the bottom with a thumbnail, and failed. He went into the room where he painted, and got some pliers from his worktable. Back in his room, he cut the tube open, and out came a black cylinder. A microfilm, of course. Tom wondered if it could survive rinsing, decided against it, and merely wiped the thing with a Kleenex. It smelled of peppermint. He addressed an envelope to:

M. Jean-Marc Cahannier
16 Rue de Tison
Paris IX

then put the cylinder into a couple of sheets of writing-paper and stuck it all into the envelope. Tom swore to himself to pull out of this silly business, because it was degrading. He could tell Reeves without offending him. Reeves had a strange idea that the more an item changed hands, the safer it was. Reeves was fence-minded. But surely he lost money paying everybody, even paying them a little bit. Or did some people take it out in favours asked from Reeves?

Tom got into pyjamas and dressing-gown, looked into the hall, and was gratified to see that there was no light showing under Eduardo's door. He went quietly down to the kitchen. There were two doors between the kitchen and Mme Annette's bedroom, because there was a little hall with servants' entrance beyond the kitchen, so she was not likely to hear him or see the kitchen light. Tom got a sturdy grey cleaning rag and a container of Ajax, took a light bulb from a cabinet and put it in a pocket. He went down to the cellar. He shivered. Now he realized he had to have a torch and a chair to stand on, so he went back to the kitchen and took one of the wooden stools that belonged to the kitchen table, and picked up a torch from the hall table drawer.

He held the torch under his arm, and removed the shattered bulb and put in the new one. The cellar lit up. Murchison's shoes still showed. Then Tom realized to his horror that the legs had straightened with rigor mortis. Or he wasn't possibly still alive? Tom forced himself to make sure, or he knew he wouldn't be able to sleep that night. Tom put the back of his fingers against Murchison's hand. That was enough. Murchison's hand was cold and also stiff. Tom pulled the grey rag over Murchison's shoes.

There was a sink with cold water in a corner. Tom wet his cleaning rag and got to work. Some colour came off on the rag, which he washed out, but he could not see much improvement in the colour of the floor, though the dark of it might be due to its wetness now. Well, he could say to Mme Annette that he dropped a bottle of wine, in case she asked anything. Tom got up the last fragments of broken light bulb and wine bottle, rinsed the rag out in the sink cautiously, recovered the pieces of glass from the sink's drain, and put them into his dressing-gown pocket. He again worked on the floor with the rag. Then he went back upstairs, and in the better light of the kitchen made sure that the reddish tint in the rag was gone or almost gone. He laid the rag over the drainpipe under the sink.

But the blasted body. Tom sighed, and thought of locking the cellar until he returned tomorrow after seeing Eduardo off, but wouldn't this look pretty strange if Mme Annette wanted to go in? And she had her own key, and one to the outside door as well, which had a different lock. Tom took the precaution of bringing up a bottle of *rosé* and two of Margaux, and put them on the kitchen table. There were times when having a servant was annoying.

When Tom went to bed, more tired than the night before, he thought of putting Murchison into a barrel. But it would take a cooper to get the damned hoops back on it properly, he supposed. And Murchison would have to be in liquid of some sort or he would bump around in an empty barrel. And how could he manage Murchison's weight in a barrel by himself? Impossible.

Tom thought of Murchison's suitcase and 'The Clock' at Orly. Surely someone had removed them by now. Murchison would perhaps have an address book, some old envelope in his suitcase. By tomorrow, Murchison might be declared 'missing'. Or the day after tomorrow. The Tate Gallery man was expecting Murchison tomorrow morning. Tom wondered if Murchison had told anyone that he was going to stay with Tom Ripley. Tom hoped not.

SEVEN

Friday was sunny and cool, though not cool enough to be called crisp. Tom and Eduardo breakfasted in the living-room near the french windows through which the sun came. The Count was in pyjamas and dressing-gown, which he would not be wearing, he said, if there were a lady in the house, but he hoped Tom did not mind.

A little after 10 a.m., the Count went up to dress, and came downstairs with his suitcases, ready to take off for a drive before lunch. 'I wonder if I can borrow some toothpaste,' said Eduardo. 'I think I forgot mine in my hotel in Milano. Very stupid of me.'

Tom had been expecting the Count to ask this, and was rather glad that he had, at last. Tom went to speak with Mme Annette who was in the kitchen. Since the Count's toilet kit was in his suitcase downstairs, Tom supposed, Tom thought it best to show him the spare loo with the basin. Mme Annette brought some toothpaste to him.

The post arrived, and Tom excused himself to glance at it. A postcard from Heloise, saying nothing really. And another letter from Christopher Greenleaf. Tom tore this open. It said:

Oct. 15 19—

Dear Mr Ripley,

I just found out I can get a charter flight to Paris so I am coming earlier than I thought. I hope you are home just now. I am flying with a friend, Gerald Hayman, also my age, but I assure you I will not bring him to meet you because that might be a drag although he's a nice fellow. I am arriving in Paris Sat. 19th Oct. and will try to call you. Of course I will spend Saturday night in a Paris hotel somewhere, as the plane gets in 7 p.m. French time.

Meanwhile, greetings and yours sincerely,

Chris Greenleaf.

Saturday was tomorrow. At least Chris wasn't going to arrive here tomorrow. Good God, Tom thought, all he needed now was for Bernard to turn up. Tom thought of asking Mme Annette not to answer the telephone for the next two days, but that would seem strange, and would furthermore annoy Mme Annette, who received at least one telephone call a day from one of her friends, usually Mme Yvonne, another housekeeper in the village.

'Bad news?' asked Eduardo.

'Oh, no, not in the least,' Tom replied. He had to get Murchison's body out. Preferably tonight. And of course he could put Chris off, tell him he was busy at least until Tuesday. Tom had a vision of French police walking in tomorrow, looking for Murchison, and finding him within seconds in the most logical place, the cellar.

Tom went into the kitchen to say good-bye to Mme Annette. She was polishing a big silver tureen and a lot of soup spoons, all adorned with Heloise's family's initials P.F.P. 'I'm off for a little tour. M. the Count is leaving. Shall I bring anything back for the house?'

'If you find some really fresh parsley, M. Tome –'

'I'll remember it. *Persil*. I shall return before five o'clock, I think. Dinner tonight by myself. Something simple.'

'Shall I help with the valises?' Mme Annette stood up. 'I don't know where my mind is today.'

Tom assured her it was not necessary, but she came out to say good-bye to the Count – who bowed to her and paid compliments in French on her cooking.

They drove to Nemours, looked at the market-place with its fountain, then went northward along the Loing to Moret, whose one-way streets Tom negotiated very knowledgeably now. The town had splendid grey stone towers, formerly the town gates, on both sides of the bridge over the river. The Count was enchanted.

'It is not so *dusty* as Italy,' he remarked.

Tom did his best not to appear nervous during their slow lunch, and he gazed frequently out the window at the weeping willows on the river bank, wishing he could achieve within himself the easy rhythm of their branches that the breeze swung this way and that. The Count told a very long story of his daughter's second marriage to a young man of a titled family who had for a while been disowned by his Bologna family for marrying a girl who had been once married. Tom barely hung onto this story, because he was thinking about disposing of Murchison. Should he risk trying to dump him in some river? Could he manage Murchison's weight over a bridge parapet, plus the weight of stones? And not be seen? If he simply dragged him down the bank of a river, could he be sure Murchison would sink deep enough, even weighted? It had begun to rain slightly. That would make the earth easier to dig, Tom thought. The woods behind the house might be the best idea after all.

At the Melun station, Eduardo had only a ten-minute wait for his train to Paris. When he and Tom had said an affectionate good-bye, Tom drove to the nearest *tabac* and bought an excess of stamps to put on his envelope to Reeves's man, so that it would not be stopped by some petty post office clerk for want of five centimes.

Tom bought parsley for Mme Annette. *Persil*, French. *Petersilie*, German. *Prezzemolo*, Italian. Tom then drove homeward. The sun was setting. Tom wondered if a torch or any kind of light in the woods would attract Mme Annette's attention if she looked out the window of her bath-room, which gave onto the back garden. If she would come up to his room (and find him gone) to tell him she had seen a light in the woods. The woods were never visited by anybody that Tom knew of, neither picnickers nor mushroom gatherers. Tom intended to go some distance into the woods, however, and perhaps Mme Annette would not notice a light.

When he got home, Tom had a compulsion to put on levis at once and get the wheelbarrow out of the toolshed. He rolled the wheelbarrow near the stone steps that led down from the back terrace. Then, since there was still enough light, he trotted across the lawn to the shed again. If Mme Annette noticed anything, he would say that he was considering making a compost heap in the woods.

Mme Annette's light was on in her bathroom, which had a clouded glass window, and he supposed she was taking her bath, as she did at this hour if there was not too much to do in the kitchen. Tom got a four-pronged fork from the shed and took it to the woods. He was in search of a likely spot, and he hoped to start a hole which would give him a bit of cheer when he really had to finish the job tomorrow, very early tomorrow morning. He found a place among a few slender trees, where hopefully there would not be too many big roots to get through. In the dimness, Tom believed it was the best spot, even though it was only some eighty yards from the edge of the woods, where his lawn began. Tom dug vigorously, releasing some of the nervous energy that had bothered him all day.

Next the garbage, he thought, and he stopped, panting, laughing out loud as he turned his face up to gulp air. Collect the potato peelings in the garbage bin now, and apple cores, and stick them all in with Murchison? And a big sprinkling of the powder that started the decomposition? There was a sack of it in the kitchen.

Now it was rather dark.

Tom went back with his fork, replaced it in the toolshed, and seeing that Mme Annette's bathroom light was still on – it was only seven – Tom went down to the cellar. Now he had more courage to touch Murchison, or *the thing* as they called it, and he reached at once into the inside pocket of Murchison's jacket. Tom was curious about the plane ticket and the passport. He found only a wallet, and two business cards fell out of it onto the floor. Tom hesitated, then shoved the wallet, with the cards replaced in it, back into the pocket. A side pocket of the jacket held a key on a ring, which Tom left. The other pocket, on which Murchison was lying, was more difficult, as Murchison was stiff as a piece of sculpture and seemed to weigh nearly as much. The left pocket yielded nothing. The trouser pockets had only some French coins mixed with English, which Tom let remain. Tom also left Murchison's two rings on his fingers. If Murchison was going to be found on his grounds, there would be no doubt who he was: Mme Annette had met him. Tom left the cellar and turned out the light at the top of the stairs.

Then Tom took a bath, and had just finished when the telephone rang. Tom lunged for it, hoping, expecting it was Jeff, perhaps with good news – but what *could* be good news?

'Ello, Tom! Jacqueline here. How are you?'

It was one of their neighbours, Jacqueline Berthelin, who with her husband Vincent lived in a town a few kilometres away. She wanted him to come for dinner Thursday. She was having les Clegg, a middle-aged English couple whom Tom knew, who lived near Melun.

'You know, my dear, it's bad luck for me. I have a guest coming. A young man from America.'

'Bring him. He is welcome.'

Tom tried to get out of it and couldn't completely. He said he would ring back in a couple of days and let her know, because he was not sure how long his American friend would be staying.

Tom was leaving his room when the telephone rang again.

This time it was Jeff, ringing from the Strand Palace Hotel, he said. 'How are things there?' Jeff asked.

'Oh all right, thanks,' Tom said with a smile, and pushed his fingers through his hair, as if he couldn't care less that there was a corpse in his cellar, a man Tom had killed for the protection of Derwatt Ltd. 'And how are things with you?'

'Where is Murchison? Is he still with you?'

'He left yesterday afternoon for London. But – I don't think he's going to talk to – you know, the Tate Gallery man. I'm sure of it.'

'You persuaded him?'

'Yes,' Tom said.

Jeff's sigh, or gasp of relief, was audible across the Channel. 'Super, Tom. You're a genius.'

'Tell them to calm down there. Especially Bernard.'

'Well – that's our problem. Sure, I'll tell him, with pleasure. He's – he's depressed. We're trying to get him to go somewhere, Malta, any damned place until the show's over. He's always like this with a show, but now it's worse because of – you know.'

'What's he doing?'

'Moping, frankly. We even rang up Cynthia – who still sort of likes him, I thought. Not that we told her about – about this scare,' Jeff hastened to add. 'We just asked her if she could spend some time with Bernard.'

'I gather she said no.'

'Right.'

'Does Bernard know you spoke with her?'

'Ed told him. I know, Tom, maybe it was a mistake.'

Tom was impatient. 'Will you just keep Bernard quiet for a few days?'

'We're giving him sedatives, mild ones. I slipped one in his tea this afternoon.'

'Would you tell him Murchison is – sedated?'

Jeff laughed. 'Yes, Tom. What's he going to do in London?'

'He said he had some things to do there. Then he's going back to the States. Listen, Jeff, no more rings for a few days, eh? I'm not sure I'm going to be home, anyway.'

Tom thought he could explain the few telephone calls he had made to Jeff, or received from Jeff, if the police bothered to look for them: he had considered buying 'The Tub', and had spoken to the Buckmaster Gallery about it.

That evening Tom went out to the toolshed and brought back a tarpaulin and a rope. While Mme Annette tidied in the kitchen, Tom wrapped Murchison's body and tied the rope so he could get a grip on it. The corpse was unwieldy, resembling a tree trunk and weighing more, Tom thought. He dragged it to the cellar steps. The fact that the body was covered made him feel slightly better, but now its nearness to the door, the steps, the front door, exacerbated his nerves all over again. What could he say if Mme Annette saw him, if one of the eternal doorbell-ringers – a gypsy selling baskets, Michel the town handyman asking if there was a job for him, a boy selling Catholic pamphlets – what would he say about the monstrous object that he was about to load on the wheelbarrow? People might not ask about it, but they would stare, and make a typical French comment in the negative:

'Not a very light weight, is it?' And they would remember.

Tom slept badly, and was curiously aware of his own snoring. He never quite fell asleep, so it was easy for him to get up at 5 a.m.

Downstairs, he pushed aside the mat before the front door, then went down to the cellar. Murchison went up half the steps very nicely, but Tom had spent a lot of energy on it, and had to pause. The rope was cutting his hands a bit, and he was too impatient to run to the toolshed for his gardening gloves. He took another grip and made it to the top. It was easier going across the marble floor. He varied his task by rolling the wheelbarrow round to the front and tipping it on its side. He would have preferred to get Murchison out via the french windows, but he couldn't cross the living-room with him without taking up the rug. Now Tom pulled the elongated lump down the four or five outside steps. He tried to put the thing sufficiently into the wheelbarrow, so that if he lifted one side of the wheelbarrow, he could right it. He did this, but the wheelbarrow tipped all the way over and spilled Murchison out the other side onto the ground again. It was almost funny.

The thought of having to drag the corpse back into the cellar was awful. Unthinkable. Tom spent a moment, thirty seconds, trying to recover his energies, staring at the damned thing on the ground. Then he flung himself at it as if it were a live, screaming dragon, or something supernatural that he had to kill before it killed him, and hoisted it into the upright barrow.

The front wheel of the barrow sank into the gravel. Tom knew at once it would be hopeless to take it across the lawn, already a bit soft from yesterday's showers. Tom ran and opened the big gates of his home. There were irregular flagstones between front steps and gate, and this went quite well, and then the wheelbarrow was on the hard sandy ground of the road. A lane to Tom's right led to the woods behind his house, a narrow lane that was more of a footpath or a way for carts than cars, though it was just wide enough for a car. Tom steered the barrow round little holes and puddles in the lanes, and eventually he reached his woods – not his, certainly, but he rather felt they were his now, he was so glad to reach the concealment they offered.

Tom pushed the barrow some distance, then stopped and looked for the place where he had started to dig. He soon found it. There was a slope from the lane up to the woods, which Tom had not reckoned on, so he had to dump the corpse in the lane and drag it up. Then Tom pulled the wheelbarrow into the woods, so in case anyone passed along the lane, the wheelbarrow wouldn't be seen. By now there was a bit more light. Tom went off at a trot towards the toolshed for the fork. He also took a shovel – rusted, left behind by somebody when he and Heloise had bought the house. The shovel had a hole in it, but would still be of help. Tom went back and continued his digging. He struck roots. After fifteen minutes, it became obvious that he could not finish the hole that morning. By 8.30, Mme Annette would come upstairs to his bedroom with his coffee, for one thing.

Tom ducked as a man in faded blue came walking along the lane, pushing a wooden home-made wheelbarrow full of firewood. The man did not glance Tom's way. He was walking towards the road that ran in front of Tom's house. Where had he come from? Maybe he was pinching state wood, and was as glad to avoid Tom as Tom was to avoid him.

Tom dug until the trench was nearly four feet deep, traversed by roots that would take a saw to cut. Then he climbed out and looked around for a slope, any depression in which to hide Murchison temporarily. Tom found one fifteen feet away, and dragged the corpse by the ropes once more. He covered the grey tarpaulin with fallen branches and leaves. At least it would not catch the eye of someone in the lane, he thought.

Then he pushed the now feather-light barrow onto the lane, and for good measure returned the barrow to the shed, so that Mme Annette would not ask him a question about it if she saw it out.

He had to enter by the front door, because the french windows were locked. His forehead was wet with sweat.

Upstairs, he wiped himself with a hot wet towel, got back into pyjamas and went to bed. It was twenty to eight. He had done too much for Derwatt Ltd, he thought. Were they worth it? Curiously, Bernard was. If they could get Bernard past this *crise*.

But that wasn't the way to look at it. He wouldn't have killed someone just to save Derwatt Ltd or even Bernard, Tom supposed. Tom killed Murchison because Murchison had realized, in the cellar, that he had impersonated Derwatt. Tom had killed Murchison to save himself. And yet, Tom tried to ask himself, had he intended to kill Murchison anyway when they went down to the cellar together? Had he not intended to kill him? Tom simply could not answer that. And did it matter, much?

Bernard was the only one of the trio whom he could not understand perfectly, and yet Tom liked Bernard best. The motive of Ed and Jeff was so simple, to make money. Tom doubted that Cynthia had done the breaking off with Bernard. It would not have surprised Tom if Bernard (who certainly at one point had been in love with Cynthia) had broken it off, because he was ashamed of his forging. It would be interesting to sound Bernard out about this some time. Yes, in Bernard there was a mystery, and it was mystery that made people attractive, Tom thought, that caused people to fall in love, too. Despite the ugly, tarpaulin-bound lump in the woods behind his house, Tom felt his own thoughts bearing him away as if he were on a cloud. It was strange, and exceedingly pleasant, to daydream about Bernard's drives, fears, shames and possible loves. Bernard, like the real Derwatt, was a bit of a saint.

A pair of flies, insane as usual, were annoying Tom. He pulled one out of his hair. They were zooming around his night table. Late for flies, and he'd had quite enough of them this summer. The French countryside was famous for its variety of flies, which outnumbered the variety of cheeses, Tom had read somewhere. One fly jumped on the other's back. In plain view! Quickly Tom struck a match and held it to the bastards. Wings sizzled. *Buzz-buzz.* Legs struck in the air and flailed their last. Ah, Liebestod, united even in death!

If it could happen in Pompeii, why not at Belle Ombre, Tom thought.

EIGHT

Tom spent Saturday morning lazily, writing a letter to Heloise c.o. American Express, Athens, and at 2.30 p.m. he listened to a comic programme on the radio, as he often did. Mme Annette, on Saturday afternoons, sometimes found Tom convulsed on the yellow sofa, and Heloise now and then asked him to translate, but much of it didn't translate, not the puns. At four, responding to an invitation that had come that noon by telephone, Tom went to take tea with Antoine and Agnès Grais, who lived on the other side of Villeperce, walking distance. Antoine was an architect who worked in Paris and spent weekdays there in his atelier. Agnès, a quiet blonde of about twenty-eight, stayed in Villeperce and took care of their two small children. There were four other guests at the Grais's, all Parisians.

'What have you been doing, Tome?' Agnès asked, bringing out her husband's speciality at the end of the tea, a bottle of strong old Holland gin, which the Grais recommended to be drunk neat.

'Painting a little. Wandering around the garden cleaning the wrong things, probably.' The French said cleaning for weeding.

'Not lonely? When is Heloise coming back?'

'Maybe in a month.'

The hour and a half at the Grais' was soothing to Tom. The Grais made no comment on his two guests, Murchison and Count Bertolozzi, and perhaps had not noticed them or heard of them via Mme Annette, who chatted freely in the food shops. Nor did the Grais notice his pink and almost bleeding palms sore from the ropes around Murchison.

That evening, Tom lay with his shoes off on the yellow sofa, browsing in *Harrap's Dictionary*, which was so heavy he had to hold it against his thighs or rest it upon a table. He anticipated a telephone call, without being quite sure who would ring, and at a quarter past one, one came. Chris Greenleaf in Paris.

'Is this – Tom Ripley?'

'Yes. Hello, Chris. How are you?'

'Fine, thanks. I just got here with my friend. I'm awfully glad you're in. I didn't have time to get a letter from you, in case you wrote. Well – look –'

'Where're you staying?'

'At the Hotel Louisiane. Highly recommended by the fellows back home! It's my first night in Paris. I haven't even opened my suitcase. But I thought I'd call you.'

'What're your plans? When would you like to visit?'

'Oh, any time. Of course I want to do some tourism. The Louvre first, maybe.'

'How about Tuesday?'

'Well – all right, but I was thinking of tomorrow, because my friend is busy all day tomorrow. He has a cousin living here, an older man, an American. So I was hoping ...'

Somehow Tom couldn't turn him down, or think of a good excuse. 'Tomorrow. All right. In the afternoon? I'm a little busy in the morning.' Tom explained that he would have to take a train at Gare de Lyon for Moret-les-Sablons, and that he should ring again when he had chosen his train, so that Tom would know when to meet him.

Obviously Chris would stay overnight tomorrow. Tom realized that he would have to finish Murchison's grave and get him into it tomorrow morning. That was, in fact, probably why he had allowed Chris to come tomorrow. It was an added prod for himself.

Chris sounded naïve, but perhaps he had some of the Greenleaf good manners and would not outstay a welcome. Tom winced as this crossed his mind, because he had certainly outstayed his welcome at Dickie's in Mongibello in his callow youth, when he'd been twenty-five, not twenty. Tom had come from America, or rather had been sent by Dickie's father, Herbert Greenleaf, to bring Dickie back home. It had been a classic situation. Dickie hadn't wanted to go back to the United States. And Tom's *naïveté* at the time, was something that now made him cringe. The things he had had to learn! And then – well, Tom Ripley had stayed in Europe. He had learned a bit. After all he had some money – Dickie's – the girls had liked him well enough, and in fact Tom had felt a bit pursued.

Heloise Plisson had been one of the ones who had liked him. And from Tom's point of view, she wasn't a piece of cement, orthodox, or far out, or another bore. Tom had not proposed marriage, nor had Heloise. It was a dark chapter in his life, a brief one. Heloise had said, in their rented bungalow in Cannes, 'Since we're living together, why not get married? ... *Apropos*, I am not sure Papa will countenance' (how had she said countenance in French? look that up) 'our living together much longer, whereas if we were really married – *ça serait un fait accompli*.' Tom had turned green at the wedding, even though it had been a civil wedding with no audience in a courtroom of some kind. Heloise had said later, laughing, 'You were green.' True. But Tom had at least gone through with it. He had hoped for a word of praise from Heloise, though he knew this was absurd on his part. It was for the bridegroom to say, 'Darling, you were gorgeous!' or 'Your cheeks were glowing with beauty and happiness!' or some such rot. Well, Tom's had been pale green. At least he hadn't collapsed going up the aisle – which had been a dingy passage between a few straight empty chairs in a magistrate's office in the South of France. Marriages ought to be secret, Tom thought, as private as the wedding night – which wasn't saying much. Since everybody's mind was frankly on the wedding night anyway at weddings, why was the affair itself so blatantly public? There was something rather vulgar about it. Why couldn't people surprise their friends by saying, 'Oh, but we've been married for three months now!' It was easy to see the reason for public weddings in the past – she's off our hands and you can't wriggle out of this one, old cock, or fifty relatives of the bride will boil you in oil – but why these days?

Tom went to bed.

On Sunday morning, again around 5 a.m., Tom donned his levis and went quietly down the stairs.

This time, he ran into Mme Annette, who opened the door from the kitchen into the hall, just as Tom was about to open the front door to go out. Mme Annette had a white cloth pressed to her cheek – no doubt the cloth contained hot salt of the coarse cooking type – and there was a dolorous expression on her face.

'Mme Annette – it's the tooth,' Tom said sympathetically.

'I could not sleep all night,' said Mme Annette. 'You are up early, M. Tome.'

'Damn that dentist,' Tom said in English. He continued in French, 'The idea of a nerve *falling* out! He doesn't know what he's doing. Now listen, Mme Annette, I have some yellow pills upstairs, I just remembered them.

From Paris. Especially for toothache. Wait a second.' Tom ran back up the stairs.

She took one of the capsules. Mme Annette blinked as she swallowed. She had pale blue eyes. Her thin upper lids, drawn downward at the outer corners, looked Nordic. She was a Breton on her father's side.

'If you like, I can drive you to Fontainebleau today,' Tom said. Tom and Heloise had a dentist in Fontainebleau, and Tom thought he would see Mme Annette on a Sunday.

'Why are you up so early?' Mme Annette's curiosity was greater than her pain, it seemed.

'I'm going to work a little in the garden and go back to sleep for an hour or so. I also had a difficult time sleeping.'

Tom persuaded her gently back to her room, and left the bottle of capsules with her. Four in twenty-four hours were all right to take, he told her. 'Don't bother with breakfast or lunch for me, dear Madame. Repose yourself today.'

Then Tom went out to his task. He took it at a reasonable rate, or what he thought was reasonable. The trench ought to be five feet deep, and no nonsense about it. He had taken a rather rusty but still effective buck-saw from the tool shed, and with this he attacked the criss-crossing roots, heedless of the damp soil that stuck in the saw's teeth. He made progress. It was fairly light, though the sun was by no means up, when he finished the trench and hauled himself out, muddying the whole front of his sweater, unfortunately a beige cashmere. He looked around, but saw no one on the little lane that ran through the woods. A good thing, he thought, that the French tied up their dogs in the country, because a dog during last night might have snuffed up the branches that covered Murchison's corpse and barked an announcement that would have carried a kilometre. Again Tom tugged on the ropes that bound Murchison's tarpaulin. The body fell in with a thud positively delicious to Tom's ears. The shovelling in of earth was also a pleasure. There was soil to spare, and after stamping down the grave, Tom scattered the rest of the soil about in all directions. Then he walked slowly, but with a sense of achievement, back across his lawn and around to the front door.

He washed his sweater in some kind of delicate suds from Heloise's bathroom. Then he slept excellently till after 10 a.m.

Tom made some coffee in the kitchen, then went out to pick up his *Observer* and *Sunday Times* at the newspaper shop. Usually he stopped for a coffee somewhere while he glanced at the two newspapers – always a treasure to him – but today he wanted to be alone when he looked at the Derwatt write-ups. Tom almost forgot to buy Mme Annette's daily, the local edition of *Le Parisien*, whose headline was always in red. Today, something about a strangled twelve-year-old. The placards outside the shop touting various newspapers were equally bizarre but in a different way:

JEANNE AND PIERRE KISS AGAIN!

Who were they?

MARIE FURIOUS WITH CLAUDE!

The French were never merely annoyed, they were *furieux*.

ONASSIS FEARS THEY WILL STEAL JACKY
FROM HIM!

Were the French lying awake worrying about that?

A BABY FOR NICOLE!

Nicole *who*, for Christ's sake? Tom never knew who most of these people were – film stars, pop singers, perhaps – but they evidently sold newspapers. The activities of the English Royal Family were unbelievable, Elizabeth and Philip on the brink of divorce three times a year, and Margaret and Tony spitting in each other's faces.

Tom put Mme Annette's paper on the kitchen table, then went up to his room. Both the *Observer* and the *Sunday Times* had a picture of him as Philip Derwatt on their arts review pages. In one, his mouth was open in the act of replying to questions, open in the disgusting beard. Tom looked quickly at the write-ups, not really wanting to read every word.

The *Observer* said: '... breaking his long retreat with a surprise appearance Wednesday afternoon at the Buckmaster Gallery, Philip Derwatt, who prefers to be called simply Derwatt, was reticent about his Mexican whereabouts but voluble enough when questioned about his work and that of his contemporaries. On Picasso: "Picasso has periods. I have no periods."' In the *Sunday Times* photograph, he stood behind Jeff's desk gesticulating with his left fist raised, an action Tom did not remember having made, but here it was. '... wearing clothes that had obviously been in a cupboard for years ... held his own against a battery of twelve reporters, which must have been a trial after six years of seclusion, we assume.' Was that 'we assume' a dig? Tom thought not, really, because the rest of the comment was favourable. 'Derwatt's current canvases maintain his high standards – idiosyncratic, bizarre,

even sick, perhaps? ... None of Derwatt's paintings is dashed off or un-
resolved. They are labours of love, though his technique appears quick,
fresh and easy to him. This is not to be confused with facility or the
look of it. Derwatt says he has never painted a picture in less than two
weeks ...' Had he said that? '... and he works daily, often for more than
seven hours per day ... Men, little girls, chairs, tables, strange things
on fire, these still predominate ... The show is going to be another sell-
out.' No mention was made of Derwatt's disappearance after the interview.

A pity, Tom thought, that some of these compliments couldn't be
engraved upon Bernard Tufts's own tomb, wherever that might be finally.
Tom was reminded of 'Here lies one whose name was writ in water',
a line that had made Tom's eyes fill with tears on the three occasions
he had seen it in the English Protestant Cemetery in Rome, and could
sometimes make his eyes water when he merely thought of it. Perhaps
Bernard, the plodder, the artist, would compose his own lines before he
died. Or would he be anonymously famous because of one 'Derwatt', one
splendid picture which he had yet to paint?

Or would Bernard ever paint another Derwatt? Good God, he didn't
even know, Tom realized. And was Bernard painting any more of his
own paintings, that might be called Tufts?

Mme Annette was feeling better before noon. And as Tom had foreseen,
because of the anodynal pills, she did not want to be taken to the
better dentist at Fontainebleau.

'Madame – I am inundated with *invités* just now, it seems. A pity Mme
Heloise is not here. But tonight there is another for dinner, a young man
called M. Christophe, an American. I can do all the shopping necessary
in the village ... *Non-non*, you repose yourself.'

And Tom did the shopping straight away and was back home before
two. Mme Annette said an American had rung, but they could not understand each other, and the American would ring back.

Chris did, and Tom was to pick him up at 6.30 at Moret.

Tom put on old flannels, a turtleneck sweater, and desert boots, and
left in the Alfa-Romeo. The menu tonight was *viande hâchée* – the French
hamburger which was so red and delicious one could eat it raw. Tom
had seen Americans swoon over hamburgers with onion and ketchup
in the Paris Drugstores, when they had been away from America only
twenty-four hours.

Tom recognized Chris Greenleaf at his first glimpse, as he had thought
he might. Though Tom's view was obscured by several people,

Christopher's blond head stuck a bit above them. His eyes and his brows had the same slight frown that Dickie's had had. Tom raised an arm in greeting, but Christopher was hesitant until their eyes actually met, and Tom smiled. The boy's smile was like Dickie's, but if there was a difference, it was in the lips, Tom thought. Christopher's lips were fuller, with a fullness unrelated to Dickie and no doubt from Christopher's mother's side.

They gripped hands.

'It's really like the country out here.'

'How do you like Paris?'

'Oh, I like it. It's bigger than I thought.'

Christopher took in everything, craning his neck at the most ordinary bar-cafés, plane trees, private houses along the way. His friend Gerald might go for two or three days to Strasbourg, Christopher told Tom. 'This is the first French village I've seen. It's real, isn't it?' he asked, as if it might be a stage-set.

Tom found it amusing, strangely nervous-making, Chris's enthusiasm. Tom remembered his own mad joy – though there'd been no one for him to speak to – at his first glimpse of the Leaning Tower of Pisa from a moving train, his first view of the curving lights of Cannes's shore.

Belle Ombre was not fully visible in the dark now, but Mme Annette had put the light on at the front door, and its proportions could be guessed from a light in the front left corner, where the kitchen was. Tom smiled to himself at Chris's ecstatic comments, but they pleased Tom nevertheless. Sometimes Tom felt like kicking Belle Ombre and the Plisson family, too, to pieces, as if they were a conglomerate sand castle that he could destroy with a foot. These times came when he was maddened by some incident of French bloodymindedness, greed, a lie that was not exactly a lie but a deliberate concealment of fact. When other people praised Belle Ombre, Tom liked it, too. Tom drove into the garage, and carried one of Chris's two suitcases. Chris said he had everything with him.

Mme Annette opened the front door.

'My housekeeper, faithful retainer, without whom I couldn't live,' Tom said, 'Mme Annette. M. Christophe.'

'How do you do? *Bonsoir*,' Chris said.

'Bonsoir, m'sieur. The room of m'sieur is ready.'

Tom took Chris upstairs.

'This is marvellous,' Chris said. 'It's like a museum!'

There was, Tom supposed, a considerable amount of satin and ormolu. 'It's my wife, I think – the decorating. She's not here just now.'

'I saw a picture of her with you. Uncle Herbert showed it to me in New York just the other day. She's blonde. Her name's Heloise.'

Tom left Christopher to wash up, and said he would be downstairs.

Tom's thoughts drifted to Murchison again: Murchison would be missing from his plane's passenger list. The police would check Paris hotels and find that Murchison had not been at any. An immigration check would show that Murchison had been at the Hotel Mandeville October 14th and 15th, and had said he would be back on the 17th. Tom's own name and address was on the Hotel Mandeville register for the night of 15 October. But he would not be the only resident of France in the Mandeville that night, surely. Would the police come to question him or would they not?

Christopher came downstairs. He had combed his wavy brown hair, and still wore his corduroy trousers and army boots. 'Hope you're not having guests for dinner. If you are, I'll change.'

'We're alone. It's the country, so wear what you like.'

Christopher looked at Tom's paintings, and paid more attention to a pinkish Pascin nude, a drawing, than to the paintings. 'You live here all year round? It must be a pleasure.'

He accepted a Scotch. Tom had to account for his time again, and mentioned his gardening and his informal study of languages, though in fact Tom's routine of study was stricter than he admitted. Tom loved his leisure, however, as only an American could, he thought – once an American got the hang of it, and so few did. It was not a thing he cared to put into words to anyone. He had longed for leisure and a bit of luxury when he had met Dickie Greenleaf, and now that he had attained it, the charm had not palled.

At the table, Christopher began to talk of Dickie. He said he had photographs of Dickie that someone had taken in Mongibello, and that Tom was in one of the photographs. Christopher spoke with a little difficulty of Dickie's death – his suicide, as everyone thought. Chris had something better than manners, Tom saw, which was sensitivity. Tom was fascinated by the candlelight through the irises of his blue eyes, because so often Dickie's eyes had looked the same late at night in Mongibello, or in some candlelit restaurant in Naples.

Christopher said, standing tall and looking at the french windows, and up at the cream-coloured coffered ceiling, 'It's fabulous to live in a house like this. And you have music besides – and paintings!'

Tom was reminded painfully of himself at twenty. Chris's family wasn't poor, Tom was sure, but their house wouldn't be quite like this one.

While they drank coffee, Tom played *A Midsummer Night's Dream* music.

Then the telephone rang. It was about 10 p.m.

The French telephone operator asked him if his number was so-and-so, then told him not to quit for a call from London.

'Hello. This is Bernard Tufts,' said the tense voice, and there followed crackles.

'Hello? Yes. Tom here. Can you hear me?'

'Can you speak louder? I'm ringing to say ...' Bernard's voice faded out as if drowned in a deep sea.

Tom glanced at Chris, who was reading the sleeve of a record. 'Is this *better?*' Tom roared into the telephone, and as if to spite him, the telephone gave a fart, then a crack like a mountain splitting beneath a stroke of lightning. Tom's left ear rang from the impact, and he switched to the right ear. He could hear Bernard struggling on slowly, loudly, but alas the words were quite unintelligible. Tom heard only 'Murchison'. *'He's in London!'* Tom shouted, glad to have something definite to convey. Now it was something about the Mandeville. Had the man from the Tate Gallery tried to reach Murchison at the Mandeville, then spoken to the Buckmaster Gallery, Tom wondered? 'Bernard, it is *hopeless!*' Tom yelled desperately. 'Can you write me?' Tom didn't know whether Bernard hung up or not, but a buzzing silence followed, and Tom assumed Bernard had given up, so he put the telephone down. 'To think one pays a hundred and twenty bucks just to *get* a telephone in this country,' Tom said. 'I'm sorry for all the shouting.'

'Oh, I've always heard French telephones are lousy,' Chris said. 'Was it important? Heloise?'

'No, no.'

Chris stood up. 'I'd like to show you my guide books. Can I?' He ran upstairs.

A matter of time, Tom thought, till the French police or the English – maybe even the American – questioned him about Murchison. Tom hoped Chris would not be here when it happened.

Chris came down with three books. He had the *Guide Bleu* for France, an art book on French châteaux, and a big book on the Rhineland, where he intended to go with Gerald Hayman when Gerald came back from Strasbourg.

Christopher sipped with pleasure at a single brandy, prolonging it. 'I have serious doubts about the value of democracy. That's a terrible thing for an American to say, isn't it? Democracy depends on a certain minimal level of education for everybody, and America tries to give it to everybody – but we really haven't got it. And it isn't even true that everybody wants it . . .'

Tom half listened. But his occasional comments seemed to satisfy Chris, at least this evening.

The telephone rang again. Tom noticed that it was five to eleven by the little silver clock on the telephone table.

A man's voice said in French that he was an agent of police, and apologized for ringing at this hour, but was M. Ripley there? 'Good evening, m'sieur. Do you by any chance know an American named Thomas Murchison?'

'Yes,' Tom said.

'Did he by chance visit you recently? Wednesday? Or Thursday?'

'Yes, he did.'

'Ah *bon!* Is he with you now?'

'No, he went back to London on Thursday.'

'No, he did not. But his suitcase was found at Orly. He did not take the sixteen hours plane he was supposed to.'

'Oh?'

'You are a friend of M. Murchison, M. Reeply?'

'No, not a friend. I have known him for only a short time.'

'How did he depart from your house to Orly?'

'I drove him to Orly – around three-thirty Thursday afternoon.'

'Do you know any friends of his in Paris – where he might be staying? Because he is not in any hotel in Paris.'

Tom paused, thinking. 'No. He did not mention anyone.'

This was evidently disappointing to the agent. 'You are at home in the next days, M. Reeply? . . . We may wish to speak with you . . .'

This time Christopher was curious. 'What's that all about?'

Tom smiled. 'Oh – someone asking me where a friend is. I don't know.'

Who was making the fuss about Murchison, Tom wondered? The man at the Tate Gallery? The French police at Orly, had they started it? Or even Murchison's wife in America?

'What's Heloise like?' Christopher asked.

NINE

When Tom came downstairs the next morning, Mme Annette told him that M. Christophe had gone out for a walk. Tom hopéd not into the woods behind the house, but it was more likely Chris would look around the village. Tom picked up the London Sundays, which he had barely glanced at yesterday, and looked through the news sections for any item, however small, about Murchison, or a disappearance at Orly. There was nothing.

Chris came in, pink-cheeked and smiling. He had bought a wire whisk, the kind the French beat eggs with, at the local *droguerie*. 'Little present for my sister,' Chris said. 'It doesn't weigh much in a suitcase. I'll tell her it came from your village.'

Tom asked if Chris would like to take a drive and have lunch in another town. 'Bring your *Guide Bleu* along. We'll drive along the Seine.' Tom wanted to wait a few minutes for the post.

The post brought only one letter addressed in a tall angular hand in black ink. Tom felt at once it was from Bernard, though he didn't know Bernard's writing. He opened the letter and saw from the signature at the bottom that he was correct.

> 127 Copperfield St
> S.E.I.
>
> Dear Tom,
>
> Forgive this unexpected letter. I would like very much to see you. Can I come over? You do not need to put me up. It would be good for me to speak with you for a bit, providing you are willing.
>
> Yours,
> Bernard T.
>
> P.S. I may try to ring you before you receive this.

He would have to cable Bernard at once. Cable him what? A refusal would depress Bernard further, Tom supposed, although Tom certainly did not want to see him – not just now. Perhaps he could cable Bernard from a small town post office this morning, and give a false last name and address for himself, since the sender's name and address were demanded at the bottom of French telegram forms. He must send Chris on his way as soon as possible, which he disliked doing. 'Shall we shove off?'

Chris got up from the sofa, where he had been writing a postcard. 'Fine.'

Tom opened the front door in the faces of two French police officers who had been about to knock. In fact, Tom stepped back from the upraised fist in the white glove.

'Bonjour. M. Reeply?'

'Yes. Come in, please.' They must be from Melun, Tom thought, because the two police in Villeperce knew him, and Tom knew their faces, too, but not these faces.

The agents came in but declined to sit down. They removed their caps, stuck them under their arms, and the younger officer pulled a tablet and pencil from a pocket.

'I telephoned you last evening in regard to a M. Murchison,' said the older officer, who was a *commissaire*. 'We have spoken with London and after some telephone calls we ascertained that you and M. Murchison arrived at Orly on the same plane Wednesday and were also at the same hotel in London, the Mande*veel*. So —' The *commissaire* smiled with satisfaction. 'You say you brought M. Murchison to Orly at three-thirty on Thursday afternoon?'

'Yes.'

'And you accompanied M. Murchison into the terminal?'

'No, because I couldn't park my car at the pavement, you see, so I let him out.'

'Did you see him go through the doors of the terminal?'

Tom thought. 'I did not look back as I drove away.'

'Because he left his suitcase on the pavement and he has simply disappeared. Was he expecting to meet someone at Orly?'

'He did not say anything about that.'

Christopher Greenleaf was standing some distance away, listening to all this, but Tom was sure he could not understand much.

'He mentioned friends in London he was going to see?'

'No. Not that I recall.'

'This morning we telephoned again to the Mande*veel*, where he was supposed to go, to ask if they had news. They informed us no, but a M. —' He turned to his colleague.

'M. Riemer,' the younger officer supplied.

'M. Riemer had telephoned to the hotel, because he had an appointment with M. Murchison on Friday. We also learned from the London police that M. Murchison is interested in verifying a painting in his possession. One by Derwatt. Do you know anything about this?'

'Oh, yes,' Tom said. 'M. Murchison had his painting with him. He wanted to see my Derwatts here.' Tom indicated them on his walls. 'That is why he came over from London with me.'

'Ah, I understand. How long have you known M. Murchison?'

'Since Tuesday last. I saw him at the art gallery, where the Derwatt exhibition is on, and then I saw him in my hotel that evening, and we began talking.' Tom turned and said, 'Excuse me, Chris, but this is important.'

'Oh, go ahead, I don't mind,' Chris said.

'Where is the painting of M. Murchison?'

'He took it with him,' Tom said.

'It was in his suitcase? It is not in his suitcase.' The *commissaire* looked at his colleague, and both men's faces showed some surprise.

It had been stolen at Orly, and thank God, Tom thought. 'It was wrapped in brown paper. M. Murchison was carrying it. I hope it wasn't stolen.'

'Ah, well – apparently it is. What was the picture called? And how big was it? Can you describe it?'

Tom replied to all this accurately.

'This is complicated for us, and perhaps is a matter for the London police, but we must tell them all we can. This is the picture – "L'Horloge" – of whose authenticity Murchison doubts?'

'Yes, he did doubt it at first. He is more of an expert than I am,' Tom said. 'I was interested in what he said, because of my own two Derwatts, so I invited him to come to see them.'

'And –' the *commissaire* frowned in a puzzled way, '– what did he say about yours?' It might have been a question inspired by simple curiosity.

'Certainly he thinks mine are genuine and so do I,' Tom replied. 'I think he began to think his own was genuine, too. He said he might cancel his appointment with M. Riemer.'

'Ah-hah.' The *commissaire* looked at the telephone, perhaps debating ringing Melun, but he did not ask to use the telephone.

'May I offer you a glass of wine?' Tom asked, including the two officers in his question.

They declined the wine, but they did wish to look at his paintings. Tom was pleased to show them. The two agents walked about, murmuring comments which might have been quite knowledgeable, judging from their fascinated faces and their gestures as they looked at canvases and drawings. They might have been visiting a gallery in their spare time.

'A famous painter in England, Derwatt,' said the younger officer.

'Yes,' Tom said.

The interview was over. They thanked Tom and took their leave.

Tom was glad Mme Annette had been out on her morning shopping round.

Christopher laughed a little when Tom had closed the door. 'Well, what was that all about? All I could understand was "Orly" and "Murchison".'

'It seems that Thomas Murchison, an American who visited me last week, didn't take his plane back to London from Orly. He seems to have disappeared. And they found his suitcase on the pavement at Orly – where I left him Thursday.'

'Disappeared? Gosh! – That's four days ago.'

'I didn't know anything about it till last night. That was the telephone call I had last night. From the police.'

'Gosh. How strange.' Chris asked a few questions, and Tom answered them, as he had answered the police. 'Sounds like he had a black-out, leaving his luggage like that. Was he sober?'

Tom laughed. 'Absolutely. I can't understand it.'

They rambled along the Seine in the Alfa-Romeo, and near Samois, Tom showed Chris the bridge where General Patton had crossed the Seine with his army, on the way to Paris in 1944. Chris got out and read the inscription on the grey little column, and came back as wet-eyed as Tom after the grave of Keats. Lunch in Fontainebleau, because Tom disliked the main restaurant in Bas Samois – Chez Bertrand or some such – where he and Heloise had never yet received an honest *addition*, and where the family who ran it had the habit of starting to mop the floors before people were finished eating, dragging metal-legged chairs across tiles with merciless unconcern for the human ear. Later, Tom did not forget his little chores for Mme Annette – *champignons à la grecque*, *céleri rémoulade*, and some sausages whose name Tom could not remember, because he did not care for them – things one could not buy in Villeperce. He got them in Fontainebleau, and also some batteries for his transistor.

On the way home, Chris burst out laughing and said, 'This morning in the woods I came across what looked like a fresh grave. Really fresh. I thought it was funny because of the police this morning. They're looking for a missing man who was at your house, and if they saw that *grave* shape in the woods –' He went off in guffaws.

Yes, it was funny, damned funny. Tom laughed at the crazy danger of it. But he made no comment.

TEN

The next day was overcast, and it began to rain around nine o'clock. Mme Annette went out to fasten a shutter that was banging somewhere. She had listened to her radio, and there were dire pronouncements of an *orage*, she warned Tom.

Wind made Tom jumpy. Tourism, that morning, was out for him and Chris. By midday, the storm was worse, and the wind bent the tops of the tall poplars like whips or sword-tips. Now and then a branch – small and dead, probably – was blown from a tree near the house and rattled as it hit the roof and rolled down.

'I really never saw anything like it – here,' Tom said at lunch.

But Chris, with the coolness of Dickie, or maybe of his whole family, smiled and enjoyed the disturbance.

The lights went out for half an hour, which Tom said happened all the time in the French countryside, even if the storm was a mild one.

After lunch, Tom went up the room where he painted. Sometimes painting helped when he was nervous. He painted standing up at his worktable, with the canvas propped against a heavy vice and a few thick art books and books on horticulture.

The bottom of the canvas rested on some newspapers plus a large paint rag which had been part of an old bed sheet. Tom bent zealously over his work, stepping back frequently to look at it. This was a portrait of Mme Annette done in – perhaps – rather a de Kooning style, which meant Mme Annette would never possibly recognize it as an attempted likeness. Tom was not consciously imitating de Kooning, and had not consciously thought of him when he began this opus, but there was no doubt the picture looked like a portrait in de Kooning's style. Mme Annette's pale lips were parted in a smile of slashing pink, her teeth decidedly off-white and irregular. She was in a pale purple dress with a white ruffle round the neck. All this was done with rather wide brushes and in long strokes. Tom's preliminary work for this had been several hasty cartoons of Mme Annette done on a pad on his knee in the living-room, when Mme Annette was unaware.

Now there was lightning. Tom straightened up and breathed, his chest aching from tension. On his transistor, *France Culture* was interviewing another uncomfortable-sounding author: 'Your book, M. Hubolt (Heublein?) seems to be (crackle) ... which is a departure from – as several critics have said – your up-to-now *challenge* to the concepts of anti-

Sartrisme. But rather now it seems to be reversing ...' Tom cut it off abruptly.

There was an ominous *crack* close by in the woods direction, and Tom looked out his window. The tops of pines and poplars still flexed, but if any tree had fallen in the woods, he could not see it from here in the grey-green murk of the forest. A tree might just fall, even a smallish tree, and cover the damned grave, Tom thought. He hoped so. Tom was mixing a reddish brown for Mme Annette's hair – he wanted to finish the painting today – when he heard voices, or thought he did, from downstairs. Men's voices.

Tom went into the hall.

The voices were speaking English, but he could not hear what they were saying, Chris and someone else. *Bernard*, Tom thought. An English accent. Yes, my God!

Tom laid his palette knife carefully across the turpentine cup. He closed the door behind him and trotted downstairs.

It was Bernard, standing bedraggled and wet on the mat just inside the front door. Tom was struck by his dark eyes which seemed deeper sunken under the straight black brows. Bernard looked terrified, Tom thought. Then in the next instant, Tom thought Bernard looked like death itself.

'Bernard!' Tom said. 'Welcome!'

'Hello,' Bernard said. He had a duffelbag at his feet.

'This is Christopher Greenleaf,' Tom said. 'Bernard Tufts. Maybe you've introduced yourselves.'

'Yes, we have,' said Chris, smiling, pleased to have company it seemed.

'I hope it's all right if I just arrived – like this,' Bernard said.

Tom assured him it was. Now Mme Annette came in, and Tom introduced them.

Mme Annette asked to take Bernard's coat.

Tom said to her in French, 'You might prepare the little room for M. Bernard.' This was a second guest-room, seldom used, with a single bed, which he and Heloise called 'the little bedroom'. 'And M. Bernard will dine with us tonight.' Then Tom said to Bernard, 'What did you do? Take a taxi from Melun? Or Moret?'

'Yes. Melun. I looked up the town on a map in London.' Thin and angular, like his writing, Bernard stood chafing his hands. Even his jacket looked wet.

'Want a sweater, Bernard? How about a brandy to warm you up?'

'Oh, no, no thank you.'

'Come in the living-room! Some tea? I'll ask Madame to make some when she comes down. Sit down, Bernard.'

Bernard looked anxiously at Chris, as if expecting him to sit down first or something. But in the next minutes, Tom realized that Bernard looked anxiously at everything, even at an ashtray on the coffee-table. The exchange of words, such as it was, was extremely sticky, and Bernard plainly wished that Christopher were not here. But Chris did not seem to grasp this, Tom could see, and on the contrary thought his presence might be useful, because Bernard, obviously, was in a state. Bernard stuttered, and his hands shook.

'I really won't disturb you for long,' Bernard said.

Tom laughed. 'But you're not going back today! We're being treated to the worst weather I've seen in the three years I've been here. Did the plane have a hard time landing?'

Bernard didn't remember. His eyes drifted to the – his own – 'Man in Chair' over the fireplace, and away again.

Tom thought of the cobalt violet in the picture. Now it was like a chemical poison to Tom. To Bernard, too, Tom supposed. 'You haven't seen "The Red Chairs" in a long time,' Tom said, getting up. The picture was behind Bernard.

Bernard got to his feet and twisted around, his legs still pressed against the sofa.

Tom's effort was rewarded by a faint but genuine smile on Bernard's face. 'Yes. It's beautiful,' Bernard said in his quiet voice.

'Are you a painter?' asked Chris.

'Yes.' Bernard sat down again. 'But not as good as – as Derwatt.'

'Mme Annette, could you put on some water for tea?' Tom asked.

Mme Annette had come down from upstairs, carrying towels or something. 'At once, M. Tome.'

'Can you tell me,' Christopher began to Bernard, 'what makes a painter good – or not? For instance, it seems to me several painters are painting like Derwatt now. I can't remember their names off hand, because they're not as famous. Oh, yes, Parker Nunnally, for one. Do you know his work? What is it that makes Derwatt so good?'

Tom also tried for a correct answer, perhaps 'originality'. But the word 'publicity' flashed into his mind, too. He was waiting for Bernard to speak.

'It is personality,' Bernard said carefully. 'It is Derwatt.'

'You know him?' Chris asked.

A slight pang went through Tom, a twinge of sympathy for Bernard.

Bernard nodded. Oh, yes.' Now his bony hands were clasped around one knee.

'Do you feel this personality when you meet him? See him, I mean?'

'Yes,' Bernard said more firmly. But he writhed, perhaps in agony, at the conversation. At the same time his dark eyes seemed to be searching for something else he might say on the subject.

'That probably wasn't a fair question,' Chris said. 'Most good artists don't show their personalities or waste their fire in their personal life, I think. They seem perfectly ordinary on the surface.'

Tea was served.

'You have no suitcase, Bernard?' Tom asked. Tom knew he had no suitcase, and was worried about Bernard's general comfort.

'No, I just came over on a hop,' Bernard said.

'Don't worry. I've got everything you might want.' Tom felt Chris's eyes on him and Bernard, speculating probably as to how and how well they knew each other. 'Hungry?' Tom asked Bernard. 'My housekeeper loves to make sandwiches.' There were only petits fours with the tea. 'Her name's Mme Annette. Ask for anything you want.'

'No, thank you.' Bernard's cup made three distinct clicks against the saucer as he set it down.

Tom wondered if Jeff and Ed had so sedated Bernard that he was in need of something now. Bernard had finished his tea, and Tom took him upstairs to show him his room.

'You'll have to share the bath with Chris,' Tom said. 'You go across the hall here and through my wife's room.' Tom left the doors open. 'Heloise isn't here, she's in Greece. I hope you can rest a bit here, Bernard. What's the matter, really? What's worrying you?'

They were back in Bernard's 'little bedroom', and the door was shut.

Bernard shook his head. 'I feel as if I'm at the end. That's all. The show was the end. It's the last show I can paint. The last picture. "The Tub". And now they're trying to bring – you know – bring him back to life.'

And I succeeded, Tom might have said, but his face remained as serious as Bernard's. 'Well – he's presumably *been* alive for the past five years. I'm sure they're not going to force you to go on painting if you don't want to, Bernard.'

'Oh, they're going to try, Jeff and Ed. But I've had enough, you see. Quite enough.'

'I think they know that. Don't worry about that. We can – Look, Derwatt can go into seclusion *again*. In Mexico. Let's say he's painting for the next many years, and refuses to show anything.' Tom walked up and down as he spoke. 'Years can pass. When Derwatt dies – we'll have him burn all his last paintings, something like that, so no one will ever see them!' Tom smiled.

Bernard's sombre eyes, staring at the floor, made Tom feel as if he had told a joke that his audience didn't get. Or worse, committed a sacrilege, cracked a bad joke in a cathedral.

'You need a rest, Bernard. Would you like a phenobarb? I have some mild ones, quarter grains.'

'No, thanks.'

'Want to wash up? Don't worry about Chris and me. We'll leave you in peace. Dinner at eight if you want to join us. Come down earlier if you want a drink.'

The wind just then made a '*Whoo-oo-oo*' and a huge tree bent – they both glanced at the window and saw it, it was in Tom's back garden – and it seemed to Tom as if the house bent, too, and he instinctively braced his feet. How could anyone be calm in this weather?

'Want me to close these curtains?' Tom asked.

'It doesn't matter.' Bernard looked at Tom. 'What did Murchison say when he saw "Man in Chair"?'

'He said he thought it was a forgery – at first. But I persuaded him it wasn't.'

'How could you? Murchison told me what he thought about – the lavenders. He's right. I made three mistakes, "Man in Chair", "The Clock" and now "The Tub". I don't know how it happened. I don't know why. I wasn't thinking. Murchison is right.'

Tom was silent. Then he said, 'Naturally it was a scare for all of us. Derwatt alive might have lived it down. It was the danger – the danger of his non-existence being exposed. But we're over that hump, Bernard.'

Bernard might not have followed this at all. He said, 'Did you offer to buy "The Clock" or something like that?'

'No. I persuaded him that Derwatt must've gone back – for a painting or two or maybe three – to a lavender he'd used before.'

'Murchison was even talking to me about the quality of the painting. Oh, Christ!' Bernard sat down on the bed and slumped back. 'What's Murchison doing now in London?'

'I don't know. But I know he's not going to see an expert, not going to do anything, Bernard – because I persuaded him our way,' Tom said soothingly.

'I can think of only one way you persuaded him, one wild way.'

'What do you mean?' Tom asked, smiling, a little frightened.

'You persuaded him to let me alone. As a thing of pity, a thing to be pitied. I don't wish to be pitied.'

'There was no mention of you – naturally.' *You're mad*, Tom felt like saying. Bernard was mad, or at least temporarily deranged. Yet what Bernard had said was exactly what Tom had tried to do in the cellar before he killed Murchison: persuade him to let Bernard alone, because Bernard would never paint any more 'Derwatts'. Tom had even tried to make Murchison understand Bernard's worship of Derwatt, his dead idol.

'I don't think Murchison could be persuaded,' Bernard said. 'You're not trying to make me feel better by lying to me, are you, Tom? Because I've had just about enough of *lies*.'

'No.' But Tom felt uncomfortable because he was lying to Bernard. It was seldom Tom felt uncomfortable, lying. Tom foresaw that he would have to tell Bernard at some time that Murchison was dead. It was the only way to reassure Bernard – reassure him partially, on the forgery score at least. But Tom couldn't tell him now, not in this nerve-racking storm, not in the state Bernard was in now, or Bernard would really go berserk. 'I'll be back in a minute,' Tom said.

Bernard got up from the bed at once and walked towards the window, just as the wind threw a hard spray of rain against the panes.

Tom winced at it, but Bernard did not. Tom went into his room, got some pyjamas and a Madras dressing-gown for Bernard, also house-slippers, and a new toothbrush still in its plastic box. He put the toothbrush in the bathroom in case Bernard had none, and brought the other things into Bernard's room. He told Bernard he would be downstairs if he wanted anything, and that he would leave him to rest for a while.

Chris had gone into his room, Tom saw from his light. The storm had made the house unnaturally dark. Tom went into his own room and got the Count's toothpaste from his top drawer. By rolling the bottom up, the tube was usable, and it was better that he use it than throw it away and run the risk of Mme Annette's seeing it in the garbage: inexplicable and wanton waste. Tom took his own toothpaste from the basin and put it in the bathroom used by Chris and Bernard.

What the hell would he do with Bernard, Tom wondered? And what if the police came back and Bernard was present, as Chris had been present? Bernard understood French pretty well, Tom thought.

Tom sat down and wrote a letter to Heloise. Writing to her always had a calming effect on him. When he was dubious about his French, he usually didn't bother running to the dictionary, because his errors amused Heloise.

Oct. 22 19—

Heloise chérie,

A cousin of Dickie Greenleaf, a nice boy named Christophe, is visiting for a couple of days. He is making his first visit to Paris. Imagine seeing Paris for the first time at the age of twenty? He is very astonished by its size. He is from California.

Today there is a terrible storm. Everyone is nervous. Wind and rain.

I miss you. Did you get the red bathing-suit? I told Mme Annette to airmail it and gave her lots of money, so if she did not send it airmail, I will hit her. Everyone asks when you are coming home. I had tea with the Grais. I feel myself very alone without you. Come back and we shall sleep in each other's arms.

Your solitary husband,
Tom

Tom stamped the letter and took it downstairs to put on the hall table.

Now Christopher was in the living-room, reading on the sofa. He jumped up. 'Listen –' He spoke quietly. 'What's the matter with your friend?'

'He's had a crisis. In London. He's depressed about his work. And I think he's had a – He's broken off with his girl-friend or she has with him. I don't know.'

'You know him well?'

'Not too. No.'

'I was wondering – since he's in such a funny state – if you'd like me to take off. Tomorrow morning. Even tonight.'

'Oh, certainly not tonight, Chris. In this weather? No, it doesn't bother me, your being here.'

'But I had the feeling it bothered him. Bernard.' Chris jerked his head towards the stairs.

'Well – there's plenty of room in this house for us to talk, Bernard and I, if he wants to. Don't worry.'

'All right. If you mean it. Till tomorrow then.' He shoved his hands in his back pockets and walked towards the french windows.

At any moment now, Mme Annette would come in and draw the curtains, Tom thought, which would at least be something calm in all this chaos.

'Look!' Chris pointed out towards the lawn.

'What is it?' A tree had fallen, Tom supposed, a minor matter. It took him a moment to see what Chris had seen, because it was so dark. Tom made out a figure walking slowly across the lawn, and his first thought was *Murchison's ghost*, and he jumped. But Tom didn't believe in ghosts.

'It's Bernard!' Chris said.

It was Bernard, of course. Tom opened the french windows and stepped out into the rain, which was now a cold spray blown in all directions. 'Hey, Bernard! What're you doing?' Tom saw that Bernard wasn't reacting, was still walking slowly, his head lifted, and Tom dashed off towards him. Tom tripped on the top step of his stone stairs, nearly fell down the rest of them, and caught himself only at the bottom, turning an ankle at the same time. 'Hey, Bernard, come in!' Tom yelled, limping towards him now.

Chris ran down and joined Tom. 'You'll get soaking wet!' Chris said with a laugh, and started to grab Bernard's arm, but evidently didn't dare.

Tom took Bernard's wrist firmly. 'Bernard, are you trying to catch a sensational cold?'

Bernard turned to them and smiled, and the rain dripped down his black hair that was plastered to his forehead. 'I like it. I really do. I *feel* like this!' He lifted his arms high, breaking Tom's hold.

'But you're coming in now? Please, Bernard.'

Bernard smiled at Tom. 'Oh, all right,' he said, as if he were humouring Tom.

The three walked back to the house together, but slowly, because Bernard seemed to want to absorb every drop. Bernard was in good humour, and made some cheerful comment as he removed his shoes at the french windows, so as not to soil the rug. He also removed his jacket.

'You've really got to change,' Tom said. 'I'll get something for you.' Tom was taking off his own shoes.

'Very well, I'll change,' Bernard said, in the same tone of condescension, and slowly climbed the stairs, shoes in hand.

Chris looked at Tom and frowned intently, like Dickie. 'That guy's nuts!' he whispered. 'Really nuts!'

Tom nodded, strangely shaken – shaken as he always was when in the presence of someone genuinely a bit off in the head. It was a feeling of being shattered. The sensation was setting in early: usually it took twenty-four hours. Tom stepped cautiously on his ankle and worked it round. It was not going to be serious, his ankle, he thought. 'You may be right,' he said to Chris. 'I'll go up and find some dry clothes for him.'

ELEVEN

Around ten o'clock that evening, Tom knocked on Bernard's door. 'It's me. Tom.'

'Oh, come in, Tom,' Bernard's voice said calmly. He was sitting at the writing-table, pen in hand. 'Please don't be alarmed by my walking in the rain tonight. I was myself in the rain. And that's become a rare thing.'

Tom understood, only too well.

'Sit down, Tom! Shut the door. Make yourself at home.'

Tom sat down on Bernard's bed. He had come to see Bernard as he had promised during dinner, in the presence of Chris, in fact. Bernard had been more cheerful during dinner. Bernard was wearing the Madras dressing-gown. There were a couple of sheets of paper covered with Bernard's black ink handwriting on the table, but Tom had the feeling Bernard was not writing a letter. 'I suppose a lot of the time you feel you're Derwatt,' Tom said.

'Sometimes. But who could be really him? And when I walk down a London street, no. Just sometimes when I paint, for seconds at a time, I've felt I'm him. And you know, I can talk easily now about it, and it's a pleasure, because I'm going to give it up, I hope.'

And that was perhaps a confession on the writing-table, Tom thought. A confession to whom?

Bernard put his arm over the back of his chair. 'And you know, my faking, my forgeries, have evolved in four or five years the way Derwatt's painting might have evolved. it's funny, isn't it?'

Tom didn't know what to say that would be correct, even respectful enough. 'Maybe it's not funny. You understood Derwatt. And critics have said the same thing, that the painting has developed.'

'You can't imagine how strange it is to paint like – Bernard Tufts. His painting hasn't developed as much. It's as if I'm faking Tufts now, because I'm painting the same Tufts as I did five years ago!' Bernard gave a real laugh. 'In a way, I have to make more of an effort to be myself than I do to be Derwatt. I *did*. And it was making me mad, you see. You can see that. I'd like to give myself a chance, if there's anything of me left.'

He meant give Bernard Tufts a chance, Tom knew. 'I'm positive that can be done. You should be the one that calls the tune.' Tom took his Gauloises from a pocket and offered Bernard one.

'I want to start with a clean slate. I intend to admit what I've done and start from there – or try to.'

'Oh, Bernard! You've got to get rid of *that* idea. You're not the only one involved. Think what it'd do to Jeff and Ed. All the pictures you've painted would – Really, Bernard, confess it to a priest, if you want to, but not the press. Or the English police.'

'You think I'm mad, I know. Well, I am sometimes. But I have only one life to lead. I've nearly ruined it. I don't intend to ruin the rest. And that's my affair, isn't it?'

Bernard's voice shook. Was he strong or weak, Tom wondered? 'I do understand,' Tom said gently.

'I don't mean to sound dramatic, but I have to see if people will accept me – see if they'll forgive me, if you like.'

They won't, Tom thought. The world absolutely wouldn't. Would it smash Bernard if he said this? Probably. Bernard might commit suicide instead of making a confession. Tom cleared his throat and tried to think, but nothing, nothing came to him.

'For another thing, I think Cynthia would like it if I made a clean breast of things. She loves me. I love her. I know she didn't want to see me just now. In London Ed told me. I don't blame her. Jeff and Ed presenting me like an invalid case: "Come to see Bernard, he needs you!"' Bernard said in a mincing voice. 'What woman would?' Bernard looked at Tom and opened his arms, smiling. 'You see how much good the rain did me, Tom? It did everything but wash away my sins.'

His laugh came again, and Tom envied him the carefreeness of it.

'Cynthia's the only woman I've ever loved. I don't mean – Well, she's had an affair or two since me, I'm sure. I was the one who more or less ended it. I got so – nervous, even scared in a way, when I began imitating Derwatt.' Bernard gulped. 'But I know she still loves me – if I'm *me*. Can you understand that?'

'I certainly can. Of course. Are you writing to Cynthia now?'

Bernard waved an arm at the sheets of paper and smiled. 'No, I'm writing – to anyone. It's just a statement. It's for the press or anyone.'

And that had to be stopped. Tom said calmly, 'I wish you'd think things over for a few days, Bernard.'

'Haven't I had enough time to think?'

Tom tried to think of something stronger, clearer to say to Bernard that would stop him, but half his mind was on Murchison, on the possibility of the police returning. How hard would they search here for clues? Would they look in the woods? Tom Ripley's reputation was already a bit – stained, perhaps, by the Dickie Greenleaf story. Though he'd been cleared of suspicion, he had for a time been under suspicion, there had been a story there, despite its happy ending. Why hadn't he put Murchison in the station wagon and driven him miles away to bury him, somewhere in the forest of Fontainebleau, camped out in the woods to get the job done, if he'd had to? 'Can we talk about it tomorrow?' Tom said. 'You might see things differently, Bernard.'

'Of course, we can talk about it any time. But I'm not going to feel any different tomorrow. I wanted to talk to you first, because you thought of the whole idea – of resurrecting Derwatt. I want to start with first things first, you see. I'm quite logical.' There was a touch of the insane in his dogmatic delivery of this, and Tom felt again a profound unease.

The telephone rang. There was a telephone in Tom's room, and the sound came clearly across the hall of the house.

Tom jumped up. 'You mustn't forget the others involved –'

'I won't drag you into it, Tom.'

'The telephone. Good night, Bernard,' Tom said quickly, and dashed across the hall to his room. He didn't want Chris to pick up the phone downstairs.

It was the police again. They apologized for ringing this late, but –

Tom said, 'I'm sorry, m'sieur, but could you ring back in perhaps five minutes? I am just now –'

The courteous voice said of course he could ring back.

Tom hung up and sank his face in his hands. He was sitting on the edge of the bed. He got up and shut his door. Events were getting a bit ahead of him. He'd been in a hurry about burying Murchison because of the damned Count. What a mistake! The Seine, the Loing were snaking around everywhere in the district, there were quiet bridges, quiet especially after one o'clock in the morning. The telephone call from the police could mean only bad news. Mrs Murchison – Harriet, had Murchison said her name was? – might have engaged an American or English detective to find her husband. She knew what Murchison's mission had been, to find out if a painting by an important artist was a forgery or not. Wouldn't she suspect foul play? If Mme Annette was questioned, wouldn't she say that she hadn't actually *seen* M. Murchison leave the house Thursday afternoon?

If the police wanted to see him tonight, Chris might volunteer the information about the grave-like patch in the woods. Tom envisaged Chris saying in English, 'Why don't you tell them about ...' and Tom wouldn't be able to say something else to the police in French, because Chris would probably want to watch them digging.

The telephone rang again, and Tom answered it calmly.

'Hello, M. Reeply. The prefecture of Melun here. We have had a telephone call from London. In the matter of M. Murchison, Mme Murchison has contacted the London Metropolitan Police, which wants us to provide all the information we can by tonight. The English Inspector will arrive tomorrow morning. Now, if you please, did M. Murchison make any telephone calls from your house? We should like to trace the numbers.'

'I can't remember,' Tom said, 'that he made a single telephone call. But I was not in the house all the time.' They could look at his telephone account, Tom thought, but let them think of that.

A moment later, they had hung up.

It was unfriendly, a little off-putting that the London police hadn't rung Tom direct to ask questions, Tom thought. He felt the London police were already treating him as suspect, and preferred to get information through official channels. Somehow Tom feared an English detective more than a French detective, although for overall minutiae and sticklership, he had to give the French high marks.

He had to do two things, get the body out of the woods and Chris out of the house. And Bernard? Tom's brain almost boggled at the task.

He went downstairs.

Chris was reading, but he yawned and stood up. 'I was just going to turn in. How's Bernard? I thought he was better at dinner.'

'Yes, I think so, too.' Tom hated what he had to say, or hinting at it, which was worse.

'I found a time-table by the telephone. There's a train in the morning at nine fifty-two and one at eleven thirty-two. I can get a taxi from here to the station.'

Tom was relieved. There were earlier trains, but it was impossible for him to propose them. 'Whichever one you want. I'll take you to the station. I don't know what to make of Bernard, but I think he wants to be alone with me for a couple of days.'

'I only hope it's safe,' Chris said earnestly. 'You know, I thought of staying on a day or so just to give you a hand with him, in case you needed it.' Chris was speaking softly. 'There was a fellow in Alaska – I did my service there – who cracked up, and he acted a lot like Bernard. Just all of a sudden he turned violent, socking everybody.'

'Well, I doubt that Bernard will. Maybe you and your friend Gerald can visit after Bernard leaves. Or after you get back from the Rhineland.'

Chris brightened at this prospect.

When Chris had gone upstairs (he wanted the 9.52 a.m. train tomorrow), Tom walked up and down the living-room. It was five minutes to midnight. Something had to be done about Murchison's corpse tonight. Quite a task for one person to dig it up in the dark, load it in the station wagon and dump it – where? Off some little bridge, maybe. Tom pondered the idea of asking Bernard to help him. Would Bernard blow up or be co-operative – confronted by reality? Tom sensed that he wasn't going to be able to persuade Bernard not to confess, as things were. Mightn't the corpse shock him into a sense of the seriousness of the situation?

It was a hell of a question.

Would Bernard take the leap into faith as Kierkegaard put it? Tom smiled as the phrase crossed his mind. But he had taken the leap when he had dashed to London to impersonate Derwatt. That leap had succeeded. He had taken another leap in killing Murchison. To hell with it. Nothing ventured, nothing gained.

Tom went to the stairway, but had to slow his pace because of the pain in his ankle. In fact, he paused with his bad foot on the first step, his hand on the gilt angel that formed the newel post. It had occurred to him that if Bernard balked tonight, Bernard would have to be disposed of, too. Killed. It was a sickening thought. Tom did not want to kill Bernard. Perhaps he would not even be able to. So if Bernard refused to help him, and added *Murchison* to his confession –

Tom climbed the stairs.

The hall was dark, except for the little light that came from Tom's own room. Bernard's light was off, and Chris's seemed to be too, but that didn't mean Chris was asleep. It was difficult for Tom to lift his hand and knock on Bernard's door. He knocked gently, because Chris's room was only eight feet away, and he did not want Chris to eavesdrop by way of protecting him from a possible assault by Bernard.

TWELVE

Bernard did not answer, and Tom opened the door and went in and closed it behind him.

'Bernard?'

'Hm-m? – Tom?'

'Yes. Excuse me. Can I put on the light?'

'Of course.' Bernard sounded quite calm, and found the bedside light himself. 'What's the matter?'

'Oh, nothing. I mean, it's just that I've got to talk to you and quietly, because I don't want Chris to hear.' Tom pulled the straight chair rather close to Bernard's bed, and sat down. 'Bernard – I'm in trouble, and I'd like you to give me a hand, if you will.'

Bernard frowned with attention. He reached for his pack of Capstan Full-strength and lit one. 'What's the trouble?'

'Murchison is dead,' Tom said softly. 'That's why you don't have to worry about him.'

'Dead?' Bernard frowned. 'Why didn't you tell me?'

'Because – I killed him. Here in the cellar.'

Bernard gasped. '*You* did? You don't mean that, Tom!'

'Sh-h.' Oddly, Tom had the feeling that Bernard was more sane than he at the moment. It made things more difficult for Tom, because he had anticipated a more bizarre reaction on Bernard's part. 'I had to kill him – here – and he's buried now in the woods behind the house. My problem is, I've got to get him away from here tonight. The police are already telephoning, you see. Tomorrow they may come and look around.'

'Killed him?' Bernard said, still incredulous. 'But why?'

Tom sighed, shuddering. 'First, need I point out, he was going to explode Derwatt? Derwatt Ltd. Second and worse, he recognized me down in the cellar. He recognized my hands. He said, "You pretended to be Derwatt in London." It was suddenly all up. I had no intention of killing him when I brought him here.'

'Dead,' Bernard repeated, stunned.

Tom was impatient as the minutes slipped by. 'Believe me. I did my best to make him let things alone. I even told him you were the forger, you the fellow he'd talked to in the bar of the Mandeville. Yes, I saw you there,' Tom said before Bernard could speak. 'I told him you weren't going to paint any more Derwatts. I asked him to let you alone. Murchison refused. So – will you help me get the corpse off my grounds?' Tom glanced at the door. It was still closed, and there had been no sound from the hall.

Bernard got slowly out of bed. 'And what do you want me to do?'

Tom stood up. 'In about twenty minutes, I'd be grateful if you gave me a hand. I'd like to take it away in the station wagon. It'll be much easier if there're two of us. I really can't do the whole thing alone. He's heavy.' Tom felt better, because he was talking the same way he often thought. 'If you don't want to help me, all right. I can try it alone, but –'

'All right, I'll help you.'

Bernard spoke in a resigned way, as if he meant it, yet Tom mistrusted it. Was Bernard going to have some unpredictable reaction later, in half an hour? Bernard's tone had been that of a saint saying to – well, someone superior to a saint, 'I will follow, wherever you lead.'

'Could you put some clothes on? Those trousers I gave you today. Try to be quiet. Chris mustn't hear us.'

'Right.'

'Can you be downstairs – outside the front steps in fifteen minutes?' Tom looked at his watch. 'Twelve twenty-seven now.'

'Yes.'

Tom went downstairs and unlocked the front door, which Mme Annette had locked for the night. Then he hobbled upstairs to his room where he took off his house-slippers and put on shoes and a jacket. He went back downstairs and picked up his car keys from the hall table. He turned off the living-room lights, except one: he often left one lamp burning all night. Then he took a raincoat and pulled on some rubber boots, which were on the floor in the spare loo, over the shoes. He took a torch from the hall-table drawer, and also a lantern which was in the spare loo. This light could stand upright on the ground.

He drove the Renault station wagon out, and into the lane that led to the woods. He used only his parking lights and having reached what he thought was the right spot, he cut them. He went into the woods with his torch, found the grave, then holding the torch so its beam was concealed as much as possible, he made his way to the toolshed, and got the shovel and the fork. These he took back to the muddy splotch which was Murchison's grave. Then he walked calmly, thinking of conserving his strength, back along the lane to the house. Tom expected Bernard to be late, and was fully braced for him not to appear at all.

Bernard was there, standing like a statue in the dark hall, in his own suit that had been wet a few hours ago, but which Bernard had draped over the long radiator in his room, Tom had noticed.

Tom gestured, and Bernard followed him.

In the lane, Tom saw that Chris's window was still dark. Only Bernard's light was on. 'It's not far. That's the trouble!' Tom said, crazily amused suddenly. He handed Bernard the fork and kept the shovel, because he thought the shovel work was harder. 'I regret to say it's pretty deep.'

Bernard went at the task with his odd resignation, but his plunges with the fork were strong and effective. Bernard tossed the earth out, but soon he was merely loosening it, and Tom was standing in the trench shovelling out the soil as fast as he could.

'I'll take a break,' Tom said at last, but his break was carrying two big stones, each of which weighed over thirty pounds, to the back of the car. He had opened the drop-door, and Tom pushed the stones in.

Bernard had reached the body. Tom got down and tried to use his shovel to prise it up, but the trench was too narrow. They both, feet apart on either side of the body, hauled at the ropes. Tom's broke or came undone, and he cursed and tied it again, while Bernard held the torch. Something might have been sucking Murchison's body into the earth: it was like some force working against them. Tom's hands were muddy and sore, maybe bleeding.

'It's very heavy,' said Bernard.

'Yes. We'd better say "one, two, three", and really give it a heave.'

'Yes.'

'One – two –' They were braced. '– three! *Oop!*'

Murchison went up onto ground level. Bernard had had the heavier end, the shoulders.

'The rest ought to be easier,' Tom said, just to be saying something.

They got the body into the car. The tarpaulin was still dripping clods, and the front of Tom's raincoat was a mess.

'Got to put the dirt back.' Tom's voice was hoarse with exhaustion.

Again this was the easiest part, and Tom for good measure pulled a couple of blown-down branches over it. Bernard casually dropped his fork to the ground, and Tom said, 'Let's put the tools back in the car.'

So they did. Then Tom and Bernard got into the car, and Tom drove in reverse, regretting the whine of the motor, towards the road. There was nowhere to turn in the lane. Then to Tom's horror, he saw Chris's light come on, just as he was backing into the road to start forward. Tom had glanced up at the dark window – Chris had a side window as well – and the light had blinked on then, as if in greeting. Tom said nothing to Bernard. There was no streetlight here, and Tom hoped that Chris could not make out the colour (dark green) of the car, though Tom's parking lights were on now, out of necessity.

'Where're we going?' Bernard asked.

'I know a spot eight kilometres from here. A bridge –'

There was not another car on the road just now, which was not unusual at the hour of 1.50 a.m. Tom had driven back from enough late dinner-parties to know that.

'Thanks, Bernard. Everything is fine,' Tom said.

Bernard was silent.

They came to the place Tom had thought of. It was beside a village called Voisy, a name Tom had never paid much attention to until tonight, when he had to pass the village marker and go through the village in order to get to the bridge he had recalled. The river was the Loing, Tom thought, which flowed into the Seine. Not that Murchison was going to flow very far with those stones on him. There was a dim and economical streetlight at this end of the bridge, but none at the other end which was black. Tom drove the car to the other end, and a few yards past the bridge. In the dark, with some aid from Tom's torch, they shoved the stones into the tarpaulin and re-tied the ropes.

'Now we drop it,' Tom said softly.

Bernard was moving with a calm efficiency, and seemed to know exactly what to do. The two of them carried the body, even with the stones, with fair ease. The wooden parapet of the bridge was four feet high. Tom, walking backwards, looked all around, at the dark village behind him where only two street-lights showed, ahead where the bridge disappeared into blackness.

'I think we can risk the middle,' Tom said.

So they went to the middle of the bridge, and set the corpse down for a few moments until they gathered strength. Then they bent and lifted, and with a mutual heave they raised it high and over it went.

The splash was shattering – giving the effect of a *boom* in the silence, like a cannon that might awaken the village – and then came a hail of splatters. They walked back towards the car.

'Don't run,' Tom said, perhaps unnecessarily. Had they any energy left?

They got into the car and started off straight ahead. Tom neither knowing nor caring where they were going.

'It's finished!' Tom said. 'The damned thing's off our hands!' He felt wonderfully happy, light and free. 'I didn't tell you, I think, Bernard,' Tom said in a gay tone, his throat now not even dry, 'I've told the police I dropped Murchison at Orly on Thursday. I did drop his luggage there. So if Murchison didn't take his plane, it's not my fault is it? Ha!' Tom laughed, as he had often laughed alone, with similar relief after ghastly moments. 'By the way, "The Clock" was stolen at Orly. Murchison had it with his suitcase. I'd imagine anyone seeing Derwatt's signature would hang onto the picture and say nothing about it!'

But was Bernard exactly with him? Bernard said nothing.

It was starting to rain again! Tom felt like cheering. The rain might, probably *would* erase his car tracks on the lane near his house, and would certainly aid the appearance of the now empty grave.

'I have to get out,' Bernard said, reaching for the door handle.

'What?'

'I feel sick.'

As soon as he could, Tom pulled closer to the edge of the road and stopped. Bernard got out.

'Want me to go with you?' Tom asked quickly.

'No, thanks.' Bernard went a couple of yards to the right, where a dark bank rose abruptly a few feet high. He bent over.

Tom felt sorry for him. Himself so merry and well, and Bernard sick at his stomach. Bernard stayed two minutes, three, four, Tom thought.

A car was approaching from behind, moving at an easy speed. Tom had an impulse to douse his lights, but left them as they were, normal headlights on, but not the brightest. Due to a curve in the road, the car's headlights swept over Bernard's figure for a second. A police car, for God's sake! The roof had a blue light on it. The police car veered around Tom's car and went on, at the same easy speed. Tom relaxed. Thank goodness. They had no doubt thought Bernard was stopping to pee, and in France that was certainly not against the law at the edge of a country road, even in plain view in broad daylight. Bernard said nothing about the car when he got back in, and neither did Tom.

Back at the house, Tom drove quietly into the garage. He took out the shovel and fork and leaned them against a wall, then wiped out the back of the car with a rag. He closed the drop-door till it half-latched, not wanting to make a bang by closing it. Bernard was waiting. Tom gestured, and they went out of the garage. Tom closed the doors and gently snapped the padlock.

At the front door, they took off their shoes and carried them. Tom noticed that Chris's light had not been on when the car approached the house. Now Tom used his torch and they climbed the stairs. Tom motioned for Bernard to go to his own room, and signalled that he would be back in a moment.

Tom emptied his raincoat pockets and dropped the raincoat in the tub. He rinsed his boots under the tub tap, and stuck the boots in a closet. He could later wash his raincoat and hang it in the closet, too, so Mme Annette would not see it in the morning.

Then he went silently, in pyjamas and house-slippers now, to see Bernard.

Bernard was standing in stocking feet, smoking a cigarette. His soiled jacket was over a straight chair.

'Not much more can happen to that suit,' Tom said. 'Let me take care of it.'

Bernard moved slowly, but he moved. He took off his trousers and handed them to Tom. Tom took the trousers and jacket into his room. He could wipe off the mud later, and get it to a fast cleaners. It was not a good suit, which was typical of Bernard. Jeff or Ed had told Tom that Bernard did not accept all the money they wanted to give him from Derwatt Ltd. Tom went back to Bernard's room. It was the first time Tom appreciated the solidity of his parquet floors: they didn't creak.

'Can I bring you a drink, Bernard? I think you could use one.' Now he could afford to be seen downstairs, Tom thought, by Mme Annette or even Chris. He could even say he and Bernard had had a whim to take a little drive, and they'd just come back.

'No, thanks,' Bernard said.

Tom wondered if Bernard could get to sleep, but he was afraid to propose anything else, like a sedative or even hot chocolate, because he thought Bernard would say again, 'No, thanks.' Tom said, whispering, 'I'm sorry I let you in for this. Will you sleep all morning if you feel like it? Chris is leaving in the morning.'

'All right.' Bernard's face was a pale olive colour. He did not look at Tom. His lips had a firm line, like lips that seldom smiled or spoke – and now his mouth looked disappointed.

He looked betrayed, Tom thought. 'I'll take care of your shoes, too.' Tom picked them up.

In his bathroom – his room door and bathroom door closed now, against Chris, possibly – Tom washed his own raincoat, and sponged Bernard's suit. He rinsed Bernard's desert boots and put them on a newspaper near the radiator in the loo. Mme Annette, though she brought his coffee and did his bed, did not go into his bathroom except perhaps once a week to give it a tidying, and the serious cleaning woman, a Mme Clusot, came once a week and was due today, in the afternoon.

At last, Tom took care of his own hands, which were not as bad as they felt. He put Nivea on them. In a curious way, he felt that he had dreamed the last hour or so – gone through the motions of it somewhere, which had made his hands sore – and that what had happened was not real.

The telephone gave an annunciatory *ping*. Tom leapt for it, catching it midway in its peal, which seemed shockingly loud.

It was nearly 3 a.m.

Beep-beep . . . burr-r-r-r . . . dup-dup-dup . . . beep?

Submarine sounds. Where was this call coming from?

'Vous êtes . . . ne quittez pas . . . Athènes vous appelle . . .'

Heloise.

'Ello, *Tome!* . . . *Tome!*'

That was all Tom could understand for a maddening several seconds. 'Can you talk louder?' he said in French.

Heloise was telling him, he barely gathered, that she was unhappy and bored, *terriblement ennuyée*. Something else, maybe someone, was absolutely *disgusting* also.

'... this woman who is called Norita ...' Lolita?

'Come home, darling! I miss you!' Tom yelled in English. 'To hell with those stinks!'

'I know what I should do.' This came clearly. 'I was trying since two hours to reach you. Even the telephone does not work here.'

'It's not supposed to work anywhere. It's just a device to extort money.' Tom was pleased to hear her laugh a little – like a siren laughing beneath the sea.

'Do you love me?'

'Of course I love you!'

Just as audibility was improving, they were cut off. Tom was sure Heloise had not hung up.

The telephone did not ring again. It was 5 a.m. in Greece, Tom supposed. Had Heloise rung from an Athens hotel? From that crazy yacht? He wanted very much to see her. He had grown used to her, and he missed her. Was that loving someone? Or marriage? But he wanted to clear away the present debris first. Heloise was rather amoral, but she would not be able to take all this. And of course she knew nothing about the Derwatt forgeries.

THIRTEEN

Tom awakened groggily at Mme Annette's tap at his door. She brought his cup of black coffee.

'Good morning, M. Tome! It's a beautiful day today!'

The sun was indeed shining, a fantastic change from yesterday. Tom sipped his coffee, letting its black magic creep through him, then he got up and dressed.

Tom knocked on Chris's door. There was still time to catch the 9.52 train.

Chris was in bed with a large map spread against his knees. 'I decided to take the eleven thirty-two – if it's all right. I so enjoy loafing in bed like this for a few minutes.'

'Sure it's all right,' Tom said. 'You should've asked Mme Annette to bring you some coffee.'

'Oh, that's *too* much.' Chris sprang out of bed. 'I thought I'd take a quick walk.'

'Okay. See you later, then.'

Tom went downstairs. He reheated the coffee and poured another cup in the kitchen and stood looking out the window, sipping it. He saw Chris walking from the house, opening the big gates. He turned left in the direction of the town. He was probably going to pick up a café au lait and a croissant in a bar-café, French style.

Evidently Bernard was still sleeping, which was all to the good.

At ten past nine, the telephone rang. An English voice spoke carefully: 'This is Detective-Inspector Webster, London Metropolitan Police. Is Mr Ripley there?'

Was this the theme song of his existence? 'Yes, speaking.'

'I'm ringing from Orly. I'd like very much to see you this morning, if possible.'

Tom wanted to say that this afternoon would be more convenient, but his usual boldness was not with him just then, and he felt, too, that the Inspector might suspect he would spend the morning trying to hide something. 'This morning would be quite all right. Are you coming by train?'

'I thought I'd take a taxi,' the voice said casually. 'It doesn't seem all that far. How long should it take by taxi?'

'About an hour.'

'I'll see you in about an hour then.'

Chris would still be here. Tom poured another cup of coffee and took it up for Bernard. He would have preferred to keep Bernard's presence a secret from Inspector Webster, but under the circumstances, and also not knowing what Chris might blurt out, Tom thought it wisest not to try to conceal Bernard.

Bernard was awake, lying on his back, with his head propped on two pillows and his fingers interlaced under his chin. He might have been in the middle of some matutinal meditation.

'Morning, Bernard. Like some coffee?'

'Yes, thank you.'

'There's a man from the London police arriving in an hour. He may want to talk with you. It's about Murchison, of course.'

'Yes,' Bernard said.

Tom waited until Bernard had had a sip or two of coffee. 'I didn't put any sugar in it. I didn't know if you liked it.'

'Doesn't matter. That's excellent coffee.'

'Now, Bernard, it's obviously best if you say you never met Murchison, never saw him. You never had that talk with him in the Mandeville bar. Do you understand?' Tom hoped it was penetrating.

'Yes.'

'And also, you never even *heard* of Murchison, even through Jeff and Ed. As you know, you're not supposed to be a very close friend of Jeff or Ed now. You all know one another, but Jeff and Ed wouldn't have troubled to tell *you* there was an American who – suspected "The Clock" wasn't genuine.'

'Yes,' Bernard said. 'Yes, of course.'

'And – the easiest thing to remember, because it's true,' Tom continued, as if he were talking to a class of schoolchildren who were not listening very carefully, 'is that you arrived here yesterday afternoon, a good twenty-four hours after Murchison left to go to London. Naturally, you never saw him or heard of him. All right, Bernard?'

'All right,' Bernard said. He was propped on one elbow.

'Want something to eat? Eggs? I can bring you a croissant. Mme Annette's been out and bought some.'

'No, thanks.'

Mme Annette was coming in from the kitchen. 'M. Tome, look.' She showed him the front page of her newspaper. 'Is this not the gentleman, the M. Murchison who visited Thursday? It says they are looking for M. Murchison!'

A la recherche de M. Murcheeson . . . Tom looked at the two-column-wide photograph of Murchison, full face, faintly smiling, in the lower left corner of *Le Parisien – Edition Seine et Marne.* 'Yes, it is,' Tom said. It read:

Thomas F. Murchison, 52 American, has been declared missing since Thursday afternoon, October 17th. His suitcase was found at the departure door at Orly Airport, but he did not board his airplane for London. M. Murchison is a business executive of New York, and had been visiting a friend in the region of Melun. His wife Harriet in America has begun inquiries with the aid of French and English police.

Tom was thankful that they had not mentioned his name.

Chris came in the front door, with a couple of magazines in his hand, but not a newspaper. 'Hello, Tom! Madame! It's a beautiful day!'

Tom greeted him, then said to Mme, Annette, 'I had thought by now he would have been found. But in fact – an Englishman is coming this morning to ask me some questions.'

'Oh, yes? This morning?'

'In half an hour or so.'

'What a mystery!' she said.

'What's a mystery?' Chris asked Tom.

'Murchison. A picture of him in today's paper.'

Chris looked at the photograph with interest, and slowly read aloud some of the phrases underneath it, translating. 'Gosh! Still missing!'

'Madame Annette,' Tom said, 'I am not sure if the Englishman will stay for lunch. Could you manage four?'

'But yes, M'sieur Tome.' She went off to the kitchen.

'What Englishman?' Chris asked. 'Another one?'

Chris's French was improving rapidly, Tom thought. 'Yes, he's coming to ask about Murchison. You know — if you want the eleven-thirty train —'

'Well — could I stay? There's a train just after twelve, and of course some trains this afternoon. I'm curious about Murchison, what they've found out. Naturally — I wouldn't stay in the living-room when you spoke with him, if you want to be alone.'

Tom was irked, but he said, 'Why not? No secrets.'

The Detective-Inspector arrived by taxi around 10.30. Tom had forgot to tell him how to find the house, but he said he had asked at the post office for the house of M. Ripley.

'What a lovely place you have!' said the Inspector cheerfully. He was about forty-five, in plain clothes. He had black, thinning hair and a slight paunch, and wore black-rimmed glasses through which he peered alertly and courteously. In fact his pleasant smile appeared to be fixed. 'Been living here long?'

'Three years,' Tom said. 'Won't you sit down?' Tom had opened the door, since Mme Annette had not seen the taxi come up, and Tom now took the Inspector's coat.

The Inspector carried a neat slender black case of the kind that could hold a suit, and this he took with him to the sofa, as if he were not in the habit of parting with it. 'Well — first things first. When did you last see Mr Murchison?'

Tom sat down on a straight chair. 'Last Thursday. About three-thirty in the afternoon. I took him to Orly. He was going to London.'

'I know.' Webster opened his black case a little and took a notebook from it, then pulled a pen from his pocket. He wrote notes for a few seconds. 'He was in good spirits?' he asked, smiling. He reached for a cigarette from his jacket pocket, and lit it quickly.

'Yes.' Tom started to say he had just made him a present of a nice Margaux, but he didn't want to refer to his cellar.

'And he had his picture with him. Called "The Clock", I think.'

'Yes. Wrapped in brown paper.'

'Apparently stolen at Orly, yes. This was the picture Mr Murchison thinks is a forgery?'

'He said he suspected it – at first.'

'How well do you know Mr Murchison? For how long?'

Tom explained. 'I remembered seeing him go into the back office at the gallery, where Derwatt was, I'd heard. So – when I saw Mr Murchison in the bar of my hotel that evening, I spoke to him. I wanted to ask him what Derwatt was like.'

'I see. And then?'

'We had a drink together, and Murchison told me his idea that a few of Derwatt's paintings were being forged – lately. I said I had a couple of Derwatts in my house in France, and I asked if he wanted to come over and see them. So we came over together Wednesday afternoon and he spent the night here.'

The Detective-Inspector was making a note or two. 'You went over to London especially for the Derwatt show?'

'Oh, no.' Tom smiled a little. 'For two things. Half for the Derwatt show, I admit, and the other half because my wife's birthday is in November, and she likes things from England. Sweaters and trousers. Carnaby Street. I bought something in the Burlington Arcade –' Tom glanced at the stairway and thought of going up to fetch it, the gold monkey pin, but checked himself. 'I didn't buy a Derwatt this time, but I was thinking of buying "The Tub". Just about the only one not sold then.'

'Did you – uh – ask Mr Murchison over with an idea that your paintings could be forgeries also?'

Tom hesitated. 'I admit I was curious. But I never doubted mine. And after seeing my two, Mr Murchison thought they were genuine.' Tom certainly wasn't going to go into Murchison's lavender theory. And Inspector Webster did not seem much interested in Tom's Derwatts, not enough to do more than turn his head to look for a few seconds at 'The Red Chairs' behind him, and then at 'Man in Chair' in front of him.

'Not my forte, I'm afraid. Modern painting. You live by yourself, Mr Ripley? You and your wife?'

'Yes, except for my housekeeper Mme Annette. My wife's in Greece just now.'

'I'd like to meet your housekeeper,' said the Inspector, still smiling.

Tom made a start towards the kitchen to fetch Mme Annette, but just then Chris came down the stairs. 'Ah, Chris. This is Detective-Inspector Webster. From London. My guest Christopher Greenleaf.'

'How do you do?' Chris said, extending a hand and looking awed at meeting a member of the London Police.

'How do you do?' Webster said pleasantly, leaning forward to shake Chris's hand. 'Greenleaf. Richard Greenleaf. He was a friend of yours, was he not, Mr Ripley?'

'Yes. And Chris is his cousin.' Webster must have looked that up recently, Tom thought, must have delved into files to see if Tom Ripley had any record, because Tom couldn't imagine anyone remembering Dickie's name over a period of six years. 'If you'll excuse me, I'll call Mme Annette.'

Mme Annette was peeling something at the sink. Tom asked if she could come in and meet the gentleman from London. 'He probably speaks French.'

Then, as Tom went back into the living-room, Bernard was coming downstairs. He wore Tom's trousers, and a sweater without a shirt. Tom introduced him to Webster. 'Mr Tufts is a painter. From London.'

'Oh,' said Webster. 'Did you meet Mr Murchison while you were here?'

'No,' Bernard said, sitting on one of the straight yellow-upholstered chairs. 'I only arrived yesterday.'

Mme Annette came in.

Detective-Inspector Webster stood up, smiled, and said, 'Enchanté, madame.' He continued in perfect French though with a determined British accent, 'I am here to inquire about Mr Thomas Murchison who has disappeared.'

'Ah, yes! I read about it only this morning in the newspaper,' Mme Annette said. 'He has not been found?'

'No, madame.' Another smile, as if he were talking about something much more amusing. 'It seems that you and M. Ripley were the last people to see him. Or were you here, Mr Greenleaf?' he asked Chris in English.

Chris stammered, but was indisputably sincere. 'I never met Mr Murchison, no.'

'What time did M. Murchison leave the house on Thursday, Mme Annette? Do you remember?'

'Ooh, perhaps – It was just after lunch. I prepared lunch a little early. Let us say two-thirty he left.'

Tom remained silent. Mme Annette was correct.

The Inspector said to Tom, 'Did he mention any friends at all in Paris? Excuse me, madame, I can just as well speak in French.'

But the conversation went on in both languages, sometimes Tom, sometimes Webster translating for Mme Annette, because Webster wanted her contributions, if she had any.

Murchison had not mentioned anyone in Paris, and Tom said he did not think Murchison had intended to meet anyone at Orly.

'You see, the disappearance of Mr Murchison *and* his painting – this might be connected,' Inspector Webster said. (Tom explained to Mme

Annette that a painting Murchison had had with him had been stolen at Orly, and Mme Annette happily remembered seeing it standing against the gentleman's suitcase in the hall before he left. She must have had a very brief glimpse, Tom thought, but it was piece of luck. Webster might have suspected that Tom had destroyed it.) 'The Derwatt corporation, as I think I have every reason to call it, is a large one. There's more to it than Derwatt himself, as a painter. Derwatt's friends, Constant and Banbury, own the Buckmaster Gallery as a sort of sideline to their own work, journalism and photography respectively. There's the Derwatt art supplies company. There's the Derwatt Art School in Perugia. If we throw forgery into all this, then we've really got something!' He turned to Bernard. 'I think you know Mr Constant and Mr Banbury, don't you, Mr Tufts?'

And Tom felt another sink of alarm, because Webster really must have dug for that one: for years Ed Banbury hadn't mentioned Bernard's name in his articles as being one of the original group of Derwatt's friends.

'Yes, I know them,' Bernard said in a somewhat dazed manner, but at least he was unruffled.

'Did you speak to Derwatt in London?' Tom asked the Inspector.

'He can't be found!' Inspector Webster said, positively beaming now. 'Not that I was particularly trying to find him, but one of my colleagues was – after Mr Murchison's disappearance. What is even more curious –' here he switched to French to include Mme Annette – 'there's no record that Derwatt entered England lately from Mexico or anywhere else. Not just in the last days, when presumably he arrived in England, but for years back. In fact the last record of the Emigration Bureau says that Philip Derwatt left the country six years ago bound for Greece. We have no record that he ever returned. As you perhaps know, Derwatt was believed to have drowned or committed suicide somewhere in Greece.'

Bernard sat forward, forearms on his kees. Was he rallying to the challenge, or about to blurt out all?

'Yes. I've heard that.' Tom said to Mme Annette, 'We speak about Derwatt the painter – his presumed suicide.'

'Yes, madame,' Webster said courteously, 'excuse us for a moment. Anything important, I shall say in French.' Then to Tom, 'So it means Derwatt entered and maybe even left England like the Scarlet Pimpernel or a ghost.' He chuckled. 'But you, Mr Tufts, you knew Derwatt in the old days, I understand. Did you see him in London?'

'No, I didn't.'

'But you went to his show, I suppose?' Webster's smile was in maniacal contrast to Bernard's gloom.

'No. I may go later,' Bernard said solemnly. 'I become – upset about anything to do with Derwatt.'

Webster seemed to look Bernard over with a new eye. 'Why?'

'I'm very fond of him. I know he doesn't like publicity. I thought – when all the fuss is over, I'll go to see him before he goes back to Mexico.'

Webster laughed and slapped his thigh. 'Well, if you can find him tell us where he is. We'd like to speak to him on this matter of possible forgery. I've spoken to Mr Banbury and Mr Constant. They saw "The Clock" and said it was genuine, but of course they might say that, if I may say so,' he added with a smiling glance at Tom, 'because they sold it. They also said Derwatt identified it positively as his own. But after all I've only – now – Mr Banbury's and Mr Constant's word for that, since I can't find Derwatt or Mr Murchison. It would be interesting if Derwatt had disowned it, or maybe was doubtful about it, and – Oh, well, I'm not writing mystery stories, even in my imagination!' Webster gave a hearty laugh, the corners of his mouth went up merrily, and he rolled a little on the sofa. His laugh was infectious and attractive, despite Webster's oversized and somewhat stained teeth.

Tom knew that Webster had been going to say: the Buckmaster Gallery people might have seen fit to shut Derwatt up somehow, or spirit him away. Shut Murchison up, too. Tom said, 'But Mr Murchison told me about his conversation with Derwatt. He said Derwatt acknowledged the painting. What worried Mr Murchison is that he thought Derwatt might've forgotten painting it. Or should I say *not* painting it. But Derwatt seems to have remembered it.' Now Tom laughed.

Detective-Inspector Webster looked at Tom and blinked, and kept what Tom felt was a polite silence. It was the same as saying, 'And now I have *your* word, which might not be worth much.' Webster finally said, 'I'm fairly sure someone for some reason thought it worth while to get rid of Thomas Murchison. What else can I think?' He translated this politely to Mme Annette.

Mme Annette said, *'Tiens!'* and Tom sensed her *frisson* of horror, though he did not glance at her.

Tom was glad that Webster didn't know that he knew Jeff and Ed, even slightly. It was funny Webster hadn't asked directly if he knew them, Tom thought. Or had Jeff and Ed already told him they knew Tom Ripley *slightly*, because he'd bought two pictures from them? 'Mme Annette, perhaps we might have some coffee. Can I offer you some coffee, Inspector, or a drink?'

'I saw some Dubonnet on your cart. I'd love some with a little ice and lemon peel, if it's not too much trouble.'

Tom conveyed this to Mme Annette.

Nobody wanted coffee. Chris, leaning on the back of a chair near the french windows, did not want anything. He seemed rapt by the goings on.

'Exactly why,' Webster said, 'did Mr Murchison think his painting was a forgery?'

Tom sighed thoughtfully. The question had been addressed to him. 'He spoke about the spirit of it. Something also about the brushstrokes.' All vague.

'I'm quite sure,' Bernard said, 'that Derwatt would not countenance any forgery of his work. It's out of the question. If he thought "The Clock" was a forgery, he would've been the first to say so. He would've gone straight to the – I don't know – the police, I suppose.'

'Or the Buckmaster Gallery people,' said the Inspector.

'Yes,' said Bernard firmly. He stood up suddenly. 'Would you excuse me a minute?' He went off towards the stairs.

Mme Annette served Webster's drink.

Bernard came down with a thick brown notebook, quite worn, in which he was trying to find something as he walked across the room. 'If you want to know a little about Derwatt – I copied several things from his journals here. They were left in a suitcase in London when he went to Greece. I borrowed them for a while. His journals are chiefly about painting, the difficulties he had from day to day, but there's one entry – Yes, here it is. It's seven years old. This is really Derwatt. May I read it?'

'Yes, please do,' said Webster.

Bernard read, '"There is no depression for the artist except that caused by a return to the Self." He spells Self with a capital. "The Self is that shy, vainglorious, egocentric, conscious magnifying glass which should never be looked at or through. A glimpse of it occurs in midstream sometimes, when it is a real horror, and between paintings, and on vacations – which should never be taken."' Bernard laughed a little. '"Such a depression consists in, besides wretchedness, vain questions such as what is it all about? And the exclamation, how badly I've fallen short! And the even worse discovery which I should have noticed long ago, I can't even depend on the people who are supposed to love me at a time when I need them. One doesn't need them when working well. I mustn't show myself in this moment of weakness. It will be, might be, thrown at me at some later date, like a crutch that should have been burnt – tonight. Let the memory of the black nights live only in me." Next paragraph,' said Bernard with reverence. '"Do people who can really talk to each other without fear of reprisals have the best marriages? Where has kindness, forgiveness gone in the world? I find more in the faces of children who sit for me, gazing at me, watching me with innocent wide eyes that make no judgement. And friends? In the moment of grappling with the enemy Death, the potential suicide calls upon them. One by one, they are not at home, the telephone doesn't answer, or if it does, they are busy tonight – something quite important that they can't get away from – one is too proud to break down and say, 'I've got to see you tonight or else!' This is the last effort to make contact. How pitiable, how human, how noble – for what is more godlike than communication? The suicide knows that it has magical powers."' Bernard closed the notebook. 'Of course he was rather young when he wrote that. Still not thirty.'

'Very moving,' said the Inspector. 'When did you say he wrote that?'

'Seven years ago. In November,' Bernard replied. 'He tried a suicide in London in October. He wrote this when he recovered. It wasn't a – bad bout. Sleeping pills.'

Tom listened uneasily. He hadn't heard of Derwatt's attempted suicide.

'Perhaps you think it melodramatic,' Bernard said to the Inspector. 'His journals weren't meant for anyone to read. The Buckmaster Gallery has the others. Unless Derwatt asked for them.' Bernard had begun to stammer, to look uncomfortable, probably because he was carefully trying to lie.

'He's the suicide type, then?' asked Webster.

'Oh, no! He has ups and downs. Perfectly normal. I mean, normal for a painter. At the time he wrote this, he was broke. A mural assignment had fallen through, and Derwatt had even finished the mural. The judges turned it down because there were a couple of nudes in it. It was for a post office somewhere.' Bernard laughed as if it were of no importance now.

And oddly, Webster's face was serious and thoughtful.

'I read this to show you that Derwatt is an honest man,' Bernard continued, undaunted. 'No dishonest man could have written this – or anything else that's in this book on the subject of painting – or simply life.' Bernard thumped the book with the back of his fingers. 'I was one of the ones who was too busy to see him when he needed me. I had no idea he was in such a bad state, you see. None of us did. He even needed money, and he was too proud to ask for any. Such a man doesn't steal, doesn't commit – I mean permit forgery.'

Tom thought Inspector Webster was going to say, with the solemnity proper to the occasion, 'I understand,' but he only sat with splayed knees, still thoughtful, with one hand turned inward on his thigh.

'I think that's great – what you read,' Chris said in the long silence.

When no one said anything, Chris ducked his head, then lifted it again, as if ready to defend his opinion.

'Any more later entries?' Webster asked. 'I'm quite interested in what you read, but –'

'One or two,' Bernard said, leafing through the notebook. 'But again six years ago. For instance, "The eternal falling short is the only thing that takes the terror out of the act of creation." Derwatt has always been – respectful of his talent. It's very hard for me to put into words.'

'I think I understand,' said Webster.

Tom sensed at once Bernard's severe, almost personal disappointment. He glanced at Mme Annette, standing discreetly mid-distance from the arched doorway and the sofa.

'Did you speak with Derwatt at all in London, even by telephone?' Webster asked Bernard.

'No,' Bernard said.

'Or with Banbury or Constant either – while Derwatt was there?'

'No. I don't often see them.'

No one, Tom thought, could suspect Bernard of lying. He looked the essence of probity.

'But you're on good terms with them?' Webster asked, cocking his head, looking a little apologetic for the question. 'I understand you knew them years ago when Derwatt lived in London?'

'Oh, yes. Why not? But I don't go out much in London.'

'Do you know if Derwatt has any friends,' Webster continued to Bernard in his rather gentle voice, 'with a helicopter or a boat or a couple of boats who could've whisked him into England and out again – like a Siamese cat or a Pakistani?'

'I don't know. I certainly don't know of any.'

'Another question, surely you wrote to Derwatt in Mexico when you learned he was alive, didn't you?'

'No, I didn't.' Bernard gulped, and his rather large Adam's apple seemed in distress. 'As I said, I have little contact with – Jeff and Ed at the Buckmaster. And they don't know Derwatt's village, I know that, because the paintings are sent from Vera Cruz by boat. I thought Derwatt could've written to me, if he wanted to. Since he didn't, I didn't try to write to him. I felt –'

'Yes? You felt?'

'I felt Derwatt had been through enough. In his spirit. Maybe in Greece or before Greece. I thought it might have changed him and even soured him on his past friends, and if he didn't want to communicate with me – that was his way of doing things, seeing things.'

Tom could have wept for Bernard. He was doing his painful best. Bernard was as miserable as someone, who was not an actor, trying to act on a stage and hating every minute of it.

Inspector Webster glanced at Tom, then looked at Bernard. 'Strange – You mean Derwatt was in such –'

'I think Derwatt was really fed up to the back teeth,' Bernard interrupted, 'fed up with people when he went to Mexico. If he wanted seclusion, I didn't make any effort to break it. I could have gone to Mexico and looked for him for ever – until I found him, I suppose.'

Tom almost believed the words he had just heard. He must believe them, he told himself. So he began to believe them. Tom went to the bar to freshen Webster's glass of Dubonnet.

'I see. And now – when Derwatt leaves again for Mexico, and perhaps he's already left, you won't know where to write to him?' asked Webster.

'Certainly not. I'll only know that he's painting and – I suppose, happy.'

'And the Buckmaster Gallery? They won't know where to find him either?' Bernard shook his head again. 'As far as I know, they won't.'

'Where do they send the money that he earns?'

'I think – to a bank in Mexico City which forwards it to Derwatt.'

For this smooth reply, much thanks, thought Tom, as he bent to pour the Dubonnet. He left room in the glass for ice, and brought the bucket from the cart. 'Inspector, will you stay for lunch with us? I've told my housekeeper I expected you would stay.'

Mme Annette had slipped away to the kitchen.

'No, no, thank you very much,' Inspector Webster said with a smile. 'I've a lunch appointment with the police of Melun. The only time I could speak with them at leisure, I think. That's very French, isn't it? I'm due in Melun at a quarter to one, so the next thing I should do is ring for a taxi.'

Tom rang a Melun taxi service for a cab.

'I would like to look around your grounds,' said the Inspector. 'They look lovely!'

This might have been a change of mood, Tom thought, like someone asking to have a look at the roses by way of escaping a deadly tea conversation, but Tom didn't think it was that.

Chris would have followed them, so fascinated was he by the British police, but Tom gave him a negative glance, and went out with the Inspector alone. Down the stone steps where Tom had nearly fallen yesterday, only yesterday, in pursuit of the rain-soaked Bernard. The sun was half-hearted, the grass almost dry. The Inspector shoved his hands into his baggy trousers. Webster might not definitely suspect him of wrongdoing, Tom thought, but he sensed that he was not entirely in the clear.

I have done that State some disservice and they know't. It was an odd morning for Shakespeare to be in his head.

'Apple trees. Peach. You must have a wonderful life here. Have you a profession, Mr Ripley?'

The question was sharp as that of an Immigration Inspector, but Tom was used to it by now. 'I garden, paint and study what I please. I have no occupation in the sense of having to go to Paris daily or even weekly. I seldom go to Paris.' Tom picked up a stone that was marring his lawn, and aimed it at a tree trunk. The stone hit the tree with a *tock*, and Tom suffered a twinge in his turned ankle.

'And woods. Are these yours?'

'No. As far as I know, they're communal. Or State. I sometimes get a bit of firewood from them, kindling, from trees that've already fallen. Do you want to take a little walk?' Tom indicated the lane.

Inspector Webster did go five or six steps farther towards the lane, into it, but having glanced down the lane, he turned. 'Not just now, thank you. I'd better be looking out for my taxi, I think.'

The taxi was at the door when they got back.

Tom said good-bye to the Inspector, and so did Chris. Tom wished him *'Bon appétit'*.

'Fascinating!' Chris said. 'Really! Did you show him the grave in the woods? I wasn't looking out the windows, because I thought it would be rude.'

Tom smiled. 'No.'

'I started to mention it, then I thought I'd be an idiot if I did. Bringing in false clues.' Chris laughed. Even his teeth were like Dickie's, sharp eye-teeth and the rest set rather narrowly in his mouth. 'Imagine the Inspector digging it up looking for Murchison!' Chris went off again.

Tom laughed, too. 'Yes, if I dropped him at Orly, how'd he get back here?'

'Who killed him?' Chris asked.

'I don't think he's *dead*,' said Tom.

'Kidnapped?'

'I dunno. Maybe. Along with his painting. I dunno what to think. Where's Bernard?'

'He went upstairs.'

Tom went upstairs to see him. Bernard's door was closed. Tom knocked and heard a mumble in response.

Bernard was sitting on the edge of the bed with his hands clasped. He looked defeated and exhausted.

Tom said as cheerfully as he could, or as he dared, 'That went well, Bernard. *Tout va bien.*'

' I failed,' Bernard said, with miserable eyes.

'What're you talking about? You were marvellous.'

'I failed. That's why he asked all those questions about Derwatt. About how to find him in Mexico. Derwatt failed and so did I.'

FOURTEEN

It was one of the worst lunches Tom had ever sat through, matching almost the lunch with Heloise and her parents after Heloise had told them they were already married. But at least this lunch did not last so long. Bernard was in the hopeless depression of an actor, Tom supposed, who had just given a performance that he believed was rotten, so no words of comfort helped. Bernard was suffering the exhaustion – Tom had known it – of the player who has given his all.

'You know, last night,' Chris said, finishing the last of a glass of milk which he drank along with wine, 'I saw a car backing out of that lane in the woods. Must've been about one. I don't suppose it's important. The car was backing with the minimum of lights on, like someone who didn't want to be seen.'

Tom said, 'Probably – lovers.' He was afraid Bernard would react some-how – how? – to this, but Bernard might not have heard it.

Bernard excused himself and got up.

'Gosh, it's a shame he's so upset,' Chris said when Bernard was out of earshot. 'I'll take off right away. I hope I haven't stayed too long.'

Tom wanted to check on the afternoon trains, but Chris had a different idea. He preferred to hitch-hike to Paris. There was no dissuading him. Chris was convinced it would be an adventure. The alternative was a train close to five, Tom knew. Chris came downstairs with his suitcases, and went into the kitchen to say good-bye to Mme Annette.

Then they went out to the garage.

'Please,' Chris said, 'say good-bye for me to Bernard, would you? His door was shut. I had the feeling he doesn't want to be disturbed, but I don't want him to think I'm rude.'

Tom assured him he would make things all right with Bernard. Tom took the Alfa-Romeo.

'You can drop me anywhere, really,' Chris said.

Tom thought Fontainebleau was the best bet, the highway to Paris by the Monument. Chris looked like what he was, a tall American boy on vacation, neither rich nor poor, and Tom thought he would have no trouble getting a lift into Paris.

'Shall I call you in a couple of days?' Chris asked. 'I'll be interested in what's happening. I'll look at the papers, too, of course.'

'Yes,' Tom said. 'Let me ring you. Hotel Louisiane, rue de Seine, isn't it?'

'Yes. I can't tell you how wonderful it's been for me – just seeing the inside of a French house.'

Yes, he could. Or rather, he didn't have to tell him, Tom thought. On the way home, Tom drove faster than usual. He felt very worried, but he did not know exactly what he ought to be worried about. He felt out of touch with Jeff and Ed, and for him or them to try to communicate would be unwise. He thought it best to try to persuade Bernard to stay on. It might be difficult. But going back to London would mean the Derwatt show in Bernard's face again, posters on the streets, perhaps seeing Jeff and Ed who were frightened and off-balance now themselves. Tom put the car in the garage and went directly up to Bernard's room and knocked.

No answer.

Tom opened the door. The bed was made as it had been made that morning when Bernard sat on it, and now Tom saw the faint depression in the bedspread where Bernard had sat. But everything of Bernard's was gone, his duffelbag, his unpressed suit which Tom had put in the closet. Tom took a quick look in his own room. Bernard was not there. And there was no note anywhere. Mme Clusot was vacuuming in his room, and Tom said, 'Bonjour, madame,' to her.

Tom went downstairs. 'Mme Annette!'

Mme Annette was not in the kitchen, she was in her bedroom. Tom knocked and, hearing a word from her, opened the door. Mme Annette was reclining on her bed under a mauve knitted coverlet, reading *Marie-Claire*.

'Don't disturb yourself, madame!' Tom said. 'I only wanted to ask where is M. Bernard?'

'Is he not in his room? Perhaps he has gone out for a walk.'

Tom did not want to tell her that he appeared to have taken his things and left. 'He didn't say anything to you?'

'No, m'sieur.'

'Well –' Tom managed to smile. 'Let's not worry about it. Were there any telephone calls?'

'No, m'sieur. And how many will there be for dinner this evening?'

'Two, I think, thank you, Mme Annette,' Tom said, thinking that Bernard might be back. He went out and closed the door.

My God, Tom thought, plunge into a couple of soothing Goethe poems. *Der Abschied* or some such. A little German solidity. Goethian conviction of superiority and – maybe genius. That was what he needed. Tom pulled the book down – *Goethes Gedichte* – from a shelf, and as fate or the unconscious would have it, he opened the book at *Der Abschied*. Tom knew it by heart almost, though he would never have dared recite it to anyone, being afraid his accent was not perfect. Now the first lines upset him:

> *Lass mein Aug' den Abschied sagen,*
> *Den mein Mund nicht nehmen kann!*
> > Let my eyes say the adieu that my mouth cannot.
> *Schwer, wie, schwer ist er zu tragen!*
> *Und ich bin –'*

Tom was startled by the closing of a car door. Someone was arriving. Bernard had taken a taxi back, Tom thought.

But no, it was Heloise.

She stood bareheaded, her long blonde hair blowing in the breeze, fumbling with her purse.

Tom bolted for the door and flung it open. 'Heloise!'

'Ah, *Tome!*'

They embraced. Ah, Tome, ah, Tome! Tom had grown used to his bookish name, and from Heloise, he liked it.

'You're all sunburnt!' Tom said in English, but he meant suntanned. 'Let me get rid of this guy. How much is it?'

'One hundred forty francs.'

'Bastard. From Orly he's –' Tom repressed, even in English, the words he had been going to use. Tom paid the bill. The driver did not assist with the luggage.

Tom took everything into the house.

'Ah, how good to be home!' Heloise said, stretching her arms. She flung a big tapestry-like bag – a Greek product – onto the yellow sofa. She was wearing brown leather sandals, pink, bell-bottomed trousers, an American Navy pea-jacket. Tom wondered where and how she had acquired the pea-jacket?

'All is well. Mme Annette is at ease in her bedroom,' Tom said, switching to French.

'What a terrible vacation I had!' Heloise plopped on the sofa and lit a cigarette. She would take several minutes to calm down, so he started to carry her suitcases upstairs. She screamed at one of them, because there was something in it which belonged downstairs, so Tom left that and took something else. 'Must you be so American and so efficient?'

What was the alternative? Standing and waiting for her to unwind? 'Yes.' He took the other things to her room.

When he came down, Mme Annette was in the living-room, and she and Heloise were talking about Greece, the yacht, the house there (evidently in a small fishing village), but not, Tom noticed, about Murchison as yet. Mme Annette was fond of Heloise, because Mme Annette liked to be of service to people, and Heloise liked to be served. Heloise did not want anything now, though at Mme Annette's insistence, she agreed to a cup of tea.

Then Heloise told him about her vacation on the *Princesse de Grèce*, the yacht of the oaf called Zeppo, a name which recalled the Marx Brothers to Tom. Tom had seen pictures of this hairy beast, whose self-esteem matched that of any of the Greek shipping tycoons, from what Tom could gather, and Zeppo was only the son of a minor real estate shark, small potatoes. A businessman screwing his own people, himself already screwed by the Fascist colonels there, according to Zeppo and Heloise, yet still making so much money that his son could cruise around on a yacht throwing caviare to the fish and filling the yacht's swimming-pool with champagne, which they later heated so they could swim in it. 'Zeppo had to hide the champagne, so he put it in the pool,' Heloise explained.

'And who was in bed with Zeppo? Not the wife of the President of the United States, I trust?'

'Any-body,' Heloise said in English, with disgust, and blew her smoke out.

Not Heloise, Tom was sure. Heloise was sometimes – not even too often – a tease, but Tom was sure she had not jumped into bed with anyone but him since they were married. Thank God, not Zeppo, who was a gorilla. Heloise would never go for that. Zeppo's treatment of women sounded repellent, but Tom's attitude to that – which he had never dared express to a woman – was that if women put up with it from the start, in order to get a diamond bracelet or a villa in the south of France, why should they complain about it later? Heloise's main irritation seemed to be due to the jealousy of one woman named Norita, because a certain man on the yacht had been paying attention to Heloise. Tom scarcely listened to this gossip-column drivel, because he was wondering how to tell Heloise some of his news in a manner that wouldn't upset her.

Tom was also half-expecting Bernard's gaunt figure to appear at the front door at any moment. He walked up and down the floor slowly, glancing at the front door at each turn. 'I went to London.'

'Yes? How was it?'

'I brought you something.' Tom ran up the stairs – his ankle was much better – and returned with the Carnaby Street trousers. Heloise put them on in the dining-room. They fitted well.

'I love them!' Heloise said, and gave Tom a hug and a kiss on his cheek.

'I came back with a man called Thomas Murchison,' Tom said, and proceeded to tell her what had happened.

Heloise had not heard of his disappearance. Tom explained Murchison's suspicion of his 'Clock' as a forgery, and Tom said he was convinced there was no forgery being done of Derwatt's paintings, and so, like the police, he could not account for Murchison's disappearance. Just as Heloise did not know about the forging, she did not know how much of an income Tom derived from Derwatt Ltd, about $12,000 per year, about the same as the income from the stocks he had acquired from Dickie Greenleaf. Heloise was interested in money, but not particularly in where it came from. She knew her family's money contributed as much to their household as Tom's, but she had never thrown this up to Tom, and Tom knew she couldn't have cared less, which was another thing he appreciated in Heloise. Tom had told her that Derwatt Ltd insisted on giving him a small percentage of their profits because he had helped them organize their business years ago, before he and Heloise met. Tom's Derwatt Ltd income was sent to him, or handled by the New York company which was a distributor of the Derwatt-labelled art supplies. Some of this Tom invested in New York, and some he had sent to France to be turned into francs. The head of the Derwatt art supply company (who also happened to be a Greek) was aware that Derwatt did not exist and was being falsified.

Tom continued: 'Another matter. Bernard Tufts – I don't think you ever met him – was visiting for a couple of days, and just this afternoon he appears to have taken a walk – with his things. I don't know if he's coming back or not.'

'Bernard Toofts? Un Anglais?'

'Yes. I don't know him well. He's a friend of friends. He's a painter, a little upset now because of his girl-friend. He's probably gone off to Paris. I thought I should tell you about him in case he comes back.' Tom laughed. He felt more and more convinced that Bernard would not come back. Had he taken a taxi perhaps, to Orly to hop on the first plane he could back to London? 'And – my other news is we're invited tomorrow night to the Berthelins for dinner. They'll be *enchanted* that you're back! Oh,

I almost forgot. I had still another guest – Christopher Greenleaf, a cousin of Dickie's. He was here two nights. Didn't you get my letter about him?' But she hadn't, because he had sent it only Tuesday.

'Mon dieu, you have been busy!' Heloise said in English, with a funny edge of jealousy in it. 'Did you miss me, Tom?'

He put his arms around her. 'I missed you – really I did.'

The item Heloise had for the downstairs was a vase, short and sturdy with two handles, and two black bulls on it lowering their heads at each other. It was attractive, and Tom did not ask if it was valuable, very old, or anything else, because at that moment he did not care. He put on Vivaldi's *Four Seasons*. Heloise was upstairs unpacking, and she said she wanted to take a bath.

By 6.30 p.m. Bernard had not arrived. Tom had a feeling Bernard was in Paris, not London, but it was only a feeling, something he shouldn't count on. During dinner, which he and Heloise took at home, Mme Annette chatted with Heloise about the English gentleman who had come that morning to ask about M. Murchison. Heloise was interested but only slightly, and certainly she wasn't worried, Tom saw. She was more interested in Bernard.

'You expect him back? Tonight?'

'In fact – now I don't,' Tom said.

Thursday morning came and went tranquilly, without even a telephone call, though Heloise rang up three or four people in Paris, including her father at his Paris office. Now Heloise wore faded levis and she went barefoot in the house. There was nothing in Mme Annette's *Parisien* today about Murchison. When Mme Annette went out in the afternoon – ostensibly to shop, but probably to call on her friend Mme Yvonne and inform her of Heloise's arrival and of the visit of an *agent* of the London police – Tom lay with Heloise on the yellow sofa, drowsily, his head against her breast. They had made love that morning. Amazing. It was supposed to be a dramatic fact. It was not so important to Tom as having fallen asleep with Heloise the night before, with Heloise in his arms. Heloise often said, 'You are nice to sleep with, because when you turn over it is not like an earthquake shaking the bed. Really I don't know when you turn over.' That pleased Tom. He had never even asked who the earthquakes had been. Heloise existed. It was odd for Tom. He could not make out her objectives in life. She was like a picture on the wall. She might want children, some time, she said. Meanwhile, she existed. Not that Tom could boast of having any objectives himself, now that he had attained the life he had now, but Tom had a certain zest in seizing the pleasures he was now able to seize, and this zest seemed lacking in Heloise, maybe because she had had everything she wished since birth. Tom felt odd sometimes making love with her, because he felt detached half the time, and as if he derived pleasure from something inanimate, unreal, from a body without an identity. Or was this some shyness or puritanism on his part? Or some fear of (mentally) giving himself completely, which would be to say to himself, 'If I should not have, if I should lose Heloise, I couldn't exist any longer.' Tom knew he was capable of believing that, even in regard to Heloise, but he did not like to admit it to himself, did not permit it, and had certainly never said it to Heloise, because it would (as things were now) be a lie. The condition of utter dependence on her he sensed merely as a possibility. It had little to do with sex, Tom thought, with any dependence on that. Usually Heloise was disrespectful of the same things he was. She was a partner, in a way, though a passive one. With a boy or a man, Tom would have laughed more – maybe that was the main difference. Yet Tom remembered one occasion with her parents, when he'd said, 'I'm sure every member of the Mafia is baptized, and what good does it do *them*?' and Heloise had laughed. Her parents hadn't. They (the parents) somehow ferreted out of Tom the fact that he hadn't been baptized in the United States – a point Tom actually was vague about, but certainly his Aunt Dottie had never mentioned it. Tom's parents had been drowned when he was very small, so he'd never heard anything on the subject from them. Impossible to explain to the Plissons, who were Catholics, that in the United States baptism and mass and confession and pierced ears and Hell and the Mafia were sort of, somehow, Catholic and not Protestant, not that Tom was anything, but if he was sure of anything, he was sure he wasn't Catholic.

The times that Heloise came most alive to Tom were when she flew into a temper. She had tempers and tempers. Tom did not count the tempers over a delayed delivery of something from Paris, when Heloise swore (untruthfully) that she would never patronize such-and-such a shop again. The more serious tempers were caused by boredom or a minor assault upon her ego, and could occur if a guest had bested or contradicted her in a discussion at the table. Heloise would control herself until the guest or guests had departed – which was something – but once the people had gone, she would walk up and down the floor ranting, throwing pillows at the walls, shouting, *Fous-moi la paix! – Salauds!'* ('Get the hell out of here! – Slobs!') with Tom as her only audience. Tom would say something soothing and irrelevant, Heloise would go limp, a tear would roll out of each eye, and she could be laughing a moment later. Tom supposed that was Latin. It certainly wasn't English.

Tom worked for an hour or so in the garden, then read a bit in *Les*

Armes Secrètes by Julio Cortazar. Then he went up and did the last work on his portrait of Mme Annette – this was her day off, Thursday. At 6 p.m. Tom asked Heloise to come in and look at it.

'It's not bad, you know? You have not worked too much on it. I like that.'

Tom was pleased by this. 'Don't mention it to Madame.' He put it in a corner to dry, face to the wall.

Then they got ready to go to the Berthelins. Dress was informal. Levis would do. Vincent was another husband who worked in Paris and came to his country house at weekends.

'What has Papa to say?' Tom asked.

'He is glad I am back in France.'

Papa didn't like him much, Tom knew, but Papa had a vague feeling that Heloise neglected him. Bourgeois virtue was at war with a nose for character, Tom supposed. 'And Noëlle?' Noëlle was a favourite friend of Heloise who lived in Paris.

'Oh, the same. Bored, she says. She never likes the autumn.'

The Berthelins, though quite well off, deliberately roughed it in the country, with an outside john, and no hot water in the kitchen sink. Hot water was made in a kettle on the stove which burnt wood. Their guests, the Cleggs, the English couple, were about fifty, the same age as the Berthelins. Vincent Berthelin's son, whom Tom had not met before, was a dark-haired young man of twenty-two (Vincent told Tom his age in the kitchen, when he and Tom were drinking Ricards, and Vincent was doing the cooking), living with a girl-friend now in Paris, and on the brink of abandoning his architectural studies at the Beaux Arts, which had Vincent in a tizzy. *'The girl is not worth it!'* Vincent stormed at Tom. 'It is the English influence, you know?' Vincent was a Gaullist.

The dinner was excellent, chicken, rice, salad, cheese, and apple tart made by Jacqueline. Tom's mind was on other things. But he was pleased, pleased to the point of smiling, because Heloise was in good spirits, talking about her Greek adventures, and at the last they all sampled the ouzo Heloise had brought.

'Disgusting taste, that ouzo! Worse than Pernod!' said Heloise at home, brushing her teeth at the basin in her bathroom. She was already in her nightdress, a short blue thing.

In his bedroom, Tom was putting on his new pyjamas from London.

'I'm going down to get some champagne!' Heloise called.

'I'll get it,' Tom hurried into his slippers.

'I have to get this taste out. Besides I want some champagne. You would think the Berthelins were paupers, the things they serve to drink. *Vin ordinaire!*' She was going down the stairs.

Tom intercepted her.

'I shall get it,' Heloise said. 'Get some ice.'

Tom somehow didn't want her to go into the cellar. He went on to the kitchen. He had just pulled an ice tray out, when he heard a scream – a muffled scream because of the distance, but Heloise's scream, and a terrible one. Tom dashed across the front hall.

There was a second scream, and he collided with her in the spare loo.

'Mon dieu! Someone has hanged himself down there!'

'Oh, Christ!' Tom half supported Heloise and guided her up the stairs.

'Don't go down, Tome! It is horrible!'

It was Bernard, of course. Tom was trembling as he walked up the stairs with her, she talking in French and he in English.

'Promise me you won't go down! Call the police, Tome!'

'All right, I'll call the police.'

'Who is it?'

'I don't know.'

They went into Heloise's bedroom.

'Stay here!' Tom said.

'No, don't leave me!'

'I insist!' Tom said in French, and ran out, and down the stairs. A straight Scotch was the best thing, he thought. Heloise hardly drank spirits, so it ought to help her at once. Then a sedative. Tom ran back upstairs with the bottle and a glass from the bar cart. He poured half a glassful, and when Heloise hesitated, drank some himself, then put the glass between her lips. Her teeth were chattering.

'You will call the police?'

'Yes!' At least this was suicide, Tom thought. That ought to be provable. It wasn't murder. Tom sighed, shuddering, almost as shaky as Heloise. She was sitting on the edge of the bed. 'How about the champagne? A lot of it.'

'Yes. Non! You must not go down there! Telephone the police!'

'Yes.' Tom went down the stairs.

He went into the spare loo, hesitated just an instant at the open doorway – the cellar light was still on – then started down the steps. A shock went through him at the sight of the dark, hanging figure, head askew. The rope was short. Tom blinked. There seemed to be no feet. He went closer.

It was a dummy.

Tom smiled, then he laughed. He slapped the limp legs – which were nothing but empty trousers, the trousers of Bernard Tufts. 'Heloise!' he yelled, running back up the stairs, not caring if he might waken Mme

Annette. 'Heloise, it's a *dummy*!' he said in English. 'It's not real! *C'est un mannequin*! You mustn't be afraid!'

It took a few seconds to convince her. It was a joke that perhaps Bernard had played – perhaps even Christopher, Tom added. At any rate, he had felt the legs, and he was sure.

Gradually, Heloise became angry, which was a sign of recovery. 'What stupid jokes these English play! Stupid! Imbecilic!'

Tom laughed with relief. 'I'm going down to get the champagne! And the ice!'

Tom went down again. The dummy hung from a belt which Tom recognized as one of his own. A hanger supported the dark grey jacket, the trousers were buttoned onto a button on the jacket, and the head was a grey rag, tied at the neck with a string. Tom got a chair quickly from the kitchen – happily Mme Annette had not awakened in all this – and returned to the cellar and took the thing down. The belt had hung from a nail in a rafter. Tom dropped the empty clothes on the floor. Then he chose a champagne quickly. He removed the hanger from the jacket, and also took the belt with him. He managed to take the ice bucket from the kitchen also, and to turn out the lights, and then he went upstairs.

FIFTEEN

Tom awakened just before seven. Heloise was sleeping soundly. Tom got gently out of bed, and took his dressing-gown which was hanging in Heloise's bedroom.

Mme Annette might be up. Tom went quietly down the stairs. He wanted to remove Bernard's suit from the cellar before Mme Annette found it. The stain of the spilt wine and Murchison's blood, Tom saw now, was not serious. If a technician examined it for blood, he would no doubt find traces, but Tom was optimistic enough to think this would not happen.

He unbuttoned the jacket from the trousers. A piece of white paper fluttered down, a note from Bernard, written in his tall pointed hand:

I hang myself in effigy in your house. It is Bernard Tufts that I hang, not Derwatt. For D. I do penance in the only way I can, which is to kill the self I have been for the last five years. Now to continue and try to do my work honestly in what is left of my life.

B.T.

Tom had an impulse to crumple the note and destroy it. Then he folded it, and stuck it in a pocket of his dressing-gown. He might need it. Who knew? Who knew where Bernard was and what he was doing? He shook out Bernard's crumpled suit, and tossed the rag in a corner. He'd send the suit to the cleaners. No harm in that. Tom started to take it up to his room, then decided to leave it on the hall table where he put clothes for Mme Annette to take to the cleaners.

'Bonjour, M. Tome!' Mme Annette said from the kitchen. 'Again you are up early! Mme Heloise also? Would she like her tea?'

Tom went to the kitchen. 'I think she wants to sleep this morning. She should sleep as late as she wishes. But I'd like some coffee now, please.'

Mme Annette said she would bring it up to him. Tom went upstairs and dressed. He wanted to take a look at the grave in the woods. Bernard might have done something odd – opened it partly, God knew what – maybe even buried himself in it.

After his coffee, he went downstairs. The sun was hazy and hardly up, the grass wet with dew. Tom idled by his shrubs, not wanting to make a bee-line for the grave, in case Heloise or Mme Annette was looking out a window. Tom did not look back at the house, because he believed one person's eye attracted the eye of another.

The grave was just as he and Bernard had left it.

Heloise did not awaken until after ten, and Mme Annette told Tom, who was in his workroom then, that Mme Heloise wanted to see him. Tom went into her bedroom. She was having her tea in bed.

She said, chewing grapefruit, 'I do not like the jokes of your friends.'

'There won't be any more. I removed the clothes – from the cellar. Don't think any more about that. Would you like to go to a nice place for lunch? Somewhere along the Seine? A late lunch?'

She liked this idea.

They found a restaurant new to them in a small town to the south, not on the Seine as it happened.

'Shall we go away somewhere? To Ibiza?' Heloise asked.

Tom hesitated. He would love to go somewhere by boat, take all the luggage he wanted, books, a record player, paints and drawing-pads. But it would look like an evasion, he felt, to Bernard, to Jeff and Ed, and to the police – even if they knew where he was going. 'I will think about it. Maybe.'

'Greece left an unpleasant taste. Like the ouzo,' Heloise said.

Tom was in the mood for a lovely snooze after lunch. So was Heloise. They would sleep in her bed, she said, until they woke up, or until time for dinner. Unplug the telephone in Tom's room, so it would only ring downstairs, and Mme Annette would answer it. It was at moments like these, Tom thought, as he drove lazily back through the woods towards Villeperce, that he enjoyed being jobless, rather well-off, and married.

Tom was certainly not prepared for what he saw as soon as he opened the front door with his key. Bernard was sitting in one of the yellow straight chairs, facing the door.

Heloise did not see Bernard at once, and said, 'Tome, chéri, can you bring me some Perrier and ice? Oh, I am so sle-epy!' Heloise fell into Tom's arms, and was surprised to find him tense.

'Bernard's here. You know, the Englishman I mentioned.' Tom walked into the living-room. 'Hello, Bernard. How are you?' Tom could not quite extend a hand, but he tried to smile.

Mme Annette came in from the kitchen. 'Ah, M. Tome! Mme Heloise! I did not hear the car. I must be growing deaf. M. Bernard has returned.' Mme Annette seemed flustered.

Tom said as calmly as he could, 'Yes. Good. I was expecting him,' though he had told Mme Annette he wasn't sure Bernard would come back, he remembered.

Bernard stood up. He needed a shave. 'Pardon me for returning unannounced.'

'Heloise, this is Bernard Tufts – a painter who lives in London. My wife, Heloise.'

'How do you do?' Bernard said.

Heloise stood where she was. 'How do you do?' she replied in English.

'My wife's a little tired.' Tom walked towards her. 'Want to go upstairs – or stay with us?'

With a motion of her head, Heloise asked Tom to come with her.

'Back in a moment, Bernard,' Tom said, and followed her.

'Is that the one who played the trick?' Heloise asked when they were in her bedroom.

'I'm afraid so. He's rather eccentric.'

'What is he doing here? I don't like him. Who is he? You never mentioned him before. And he's wearing your clothes?'

Tom shrugged. 'He's a friend of some friends of mine in London. I'm sure I can persuade him to take off this afternoon. He probably needs some extra money. Or clothes. I'll ask him.' Tom kissed her cheek. 'Get into bed, darling. I'll see you soon.'

Tom went to the kitchen and asked Mme Annette to take up Heloise's Perrier.

'M. Bernard will be here for dinner?' asked Mme Annette.

'I don't think so. But we shall be in. Something simple. We had a big lunch.' Tom went back to Bernard. 'Were you in Paris?'

'Yes, Paris.' Bernard was still standing.

Tom didn't know what tack to take. 'I found your effigy downstairs. It gave my wife quite a shock. You shouldn't play tricks like that – with women in the house.' Tom smiled. 'By the way, my housekeeper took your suit to be cleaned and I'll see that you get it in London – or wherever you are. Sit down.' Tom sat down on the sofa. 'What're your plans?' It was like asking an insane man how he felt, Tom thought. Tom was uneasy, and he felt worse when he realized that his heart was beating rather fast.

Bernard sat down. 'Oh –' Long pause.

'Not going back to London?' In desperation, Tom took a cigar from the box on the coffee-table. It was enough to gag him just now, but did it matter?

'I came to talk to you.'

'All right. What about?'

Another silence, and Tom was afraid to break it. Bernard might have been groping in clouds, infinite clouds of his own thoughts in the last days. It was as if he were trying to hunt down one fleecy little sheep amid a gigantic flock, Tom felt. 'I have all the time you want. You're among friends, Bernard.'

'It's quite simple. I must start my life over again. Cleanly.'

'Yes, I know. Well, you can.'

'Does your wife know – about my forging?'

Tom welcomed this logical question. 'No, of course not. No one knows. No one in France.'

'Or about Murchison?'

'I told her Murchison was missing. And that I dropped him at Orly.' Tom spoke softly, in case Heloise might be in the hall upstairs, listening. But he knew voices did not carry well from the living-room, up the faraway curve of the stairs.

Bernard said somewhat irritably, 'I really can't talk with other people in the house. Like your wife. Or the housekeeper.'

'All right, we can go somewhere.'

'No.'

'Well, I can hardly ask Mme Annette to leave. She runs this place. Want to take a walk? There's a quiet café –'

'No, thanks.'

Tom leaned back on the sofa with his cigar, which now smelled like a house burning down. Usually he liked the smell. 'By the way, I've heard nothing from the English Inspector since I saw you. Or the French.'

Bernard showed no reaction. Then he said, 'All right, let's take a walk.' He stood up and looked at the french windows. 'Out the back way, perhaps.'

They walked out, onto the lawn. Neither had put on a topcoat and it was chilly. Tom let Bernard go where he wished, and Bernard drifted towards the woods, towards the lane. Bernard walked slowly, a bit unsteadily. Was he weak from not having eaten, Tom wondered? Soon they were passing the spot where Murchison's corpse had been. Tom felt fear, a fear that made the hair on his neck and behind his ears prickle. It was not a fear of that spot, Tom realized, but a fear of Bernard. Tom kept his hands free, and walked a little to one side of Bernard.

Then Bernard slowed and turned around, and they began walking back towards the house.

'What's on your mind?' Tom asked.

'Oh, I – I don't know where this thing's going to end. It's already caused a man's death.'

'Well – regrettable, yes. I agree. But really nothing to do with you, is it? Since you're not painting any more Derwatts, the new Bernard Tufts can start over – cleanly.'

No reply from Bernard.

'Did you ring Jeff or Ed when you were in Paris?'

'No.'

Tom hadn't troubled to buy any English newspapers, and Bernard perhaps hadn't troubled, either. Bernard's anxieties were within himself. 'If you'd like to, you can ring Cynthia from the house. You can do it from my room.'

'I spoke to her from Paris. She doesn't want to see me.'

'Oh.' That was the trouble. That was the last straw, Tom supposed. 'Well, you can always write her. That may be better. Or see her when you go back to London. Storm her door!' Tom laughed.

'She said no.'

Silence.

Cynthia wanted to keep clear of it, Tom supposed. Not that she mistrusted Bernard's intention of stopping the forgeries – no one could doubt Bernard when he stated something – but she'd had enough. Bernard's hurt was beyond Tom's grasp, for the moment. They were standing on the stone terrace outside the french windows. 'I've got to go in, Bernard. I'm freezing. Come in.' Tom opened the doors.

Bernard came in, too.

Tom ran up to see Heloise. He was still rigid with cold, or fear. Heloise was in her bedroom, sitting on her bed, sorting snapshots and postcards.

'When is he leaving?'

'Darling – it's his girl-friend in London. He rang her from Paris. She doesn't want to see him. He's unhappy and I can't just ask him to leave. I don't know what he's going to do. Darling, would you like to visit your parents for a few days?'

'Non!'

'He wants to talk to me. I'm only hoping he'll get at it soon.'

'Why can't you put him out? He is not your friend. Also he is mad!'

Bernard stayed.

*

They had not finished dinner when the front doorbell sounded. Mme Annette answered it, and returned and said to Tom:

'It is two *agents* of police, M. Tome. They would like to speak with you.'

Heloise gave a sigh of impatience, and threw her napkin down. She had detested sitting at the table, and now she stood up. 'Again some intrusions!' she said in French.

Tom had stood up, too.

Only Bernard seemed unperturbed.

Tom went into the living-room. It was the same pair of agents who had visited him Monday.

'We are sorry to disturb you, m'sieur,' said the older man, 'but your telephone is not working. We have reported it.'

'Really?' The telephone's non-functioning happened, in fact, every six weeks or so, inexplicably, but now Tom wondered if Bernard had done something odd, like cut the line. 'I was not aware of it. Thank you.'

'We have been in touch with the English investigator. Rather he has been in touch with us.'

Heloise came in, out of both curiosity and anger, Tom supposed. Tom introduced her, and the officers gave their names again, Commissaire Delaunay, and the other name Tom missed.

Delaunay said, 'Now it is not merely M. Murchison but the painter Derwatt who is missing. The English investigator Webster, who also tried to ring you this afternoon, would like to know if you have heard from either of them?'

Tom smiled, actually a little amused. 'I have never met Derwatt, and he certainly doesn't know me,' Tom said, just as Bernard came into the room. 'And I have had no word from M. Murchison, I regret to say. May I present Bernard Tufts, an English friend. Bernard, two gentlemen of the police force.'

Bernard mumbled a greeting.

Bernard's name did not mean anything to the French police, Tom noticed.

'Even the people who own the gallery where Derwatt now has an exhibition do not know where Derwatt is,' said Delaunay. 'It is astounding, this.'

It was indeed odd, but Tom could not help them at all.

'Do you by an chance know the American, M. Murchison?' Delaunay asked Bernard.

'No,' Bernard said.

'Or you, madame?'

'No,' Heloise said.

Tom explained that his wife had just returned from Greece, but he had told her about M. Murchison's visit and his disappearance.

The officers looked as if they did not know what move to make next. Delaunay said, 'Because of the circumstances, M. Reeply, we have been asked by Inspector Webstair to make a search of your house. A formality, you understand, but necessary. We might come across a clue. I speak of M. Murchison, of course. We must aid our English *confrères* all we can!'

'But certainly! Would you like to begin now?'

It was rather dark, as far as the outdoors was concerned, but the police said they would begin now, and continue tomorrow morning. Both officers stood on the stone terrace, looking longingly, Tom felt, at the dark garden and the woods beyond.

They went over the house, under Tom's guidance. They were first interested in Murchison's bedroom, the one Chris had used afterwards. Mme Annette had emptied the waste-basket. The officers looked into drawers, all of which were empty except for two bottom drawers of a chest, or *commode* as the French called it, which contained bedspreads and a couple of blankets. There was no sign of Murchison or Chris. They looked into Heloise's bedroom. (Heloise was downstairs in a repressed fury, Tom knew.) They looked into Tom's atelier, even picked up one of his saws. There was an attic. The light had burnt out, and Tom had to get a lightbulb and a torch from downstairs. The attic was dusty. There were chairs under cloth covers, and an old sofa that Tom and Heloise had not removed from previous tenants. The policemen also looked behind things with the aid of their own torches. They were looking for something larger than a clue. Tom supposed, absurd as the idea might be that he would leave a corpse behind a sofa.

Then it was the cellar. Tom showed it with the same ease, standing right on the stain, and shining his torch into the corners, though the light was good. Tom was a bit afraid Murchison might have bled onto the cement floor behind the wine cask. Tom had not looked at that spot carefully enough. But if there was any blood, the officers did not see it, and gave the floor only a glance. This did not mean they would not make a more thorough search tomorrow, Tom thought.

They said they would be back at eight in the morning, if that was not too early for Tom. Tom told them that eight would be quite all right.

'Sorry,' Tom said to Heloise and Bernard, when he had closed the front door. Tom had the feeling Heloise and Bernard had been sitting in silence with their coffee the whole time.

'Why do they want to search the house?' Heloise demanded.

'Because this so-and-so American is still missing,' Tom said. 'M. Murchison.'

Heloise stood up. 'Can I speak to you upstairs, Tome?'

Tom excused himself to Bernard and went with her.

Heloise went into her bedroom. 'If you don't put this *fou* out, I am leaving the house tonight!'

That was a dilemma. He wanted Heloise to stay, and yet if she did, Tom knew he would get nowhere with Bernard. And like Bernard, he couldn't think with Heloise's indignant eyes glaring at him. 'I'll try again to get him out,' Tom said. He kissed Heloise on the neck. At least she permitted this.

Tom went downstairs. 'Bernard – Heloise is upset. Would you mind going back to Paris tonight? I could drive you to – Why not Fontaine-bleau? A couple of good hotels there. If you want to talk to me, I could come tomorrow to Fontainebleau –'

'No.'

Tom sighed. 'Then she'll take off tonight. I'll go and tell her.' Tom went back up the stairs and told Heloise.

'What is this, another Dickie Granelafe? You can't tell him to get out of your house?'

'I never – Dickie wasn't in *my* house.' Tom stopped, wordless. Heloise looked angry enough to oust Bernard herself, but she wouldn't be able to, Tom thought, because Bernard's adamance was beyond convention or etiquette.

She dragged a small leather suitcase down from the top of a closet and began to pack. Useless to say he felt responsible for Bernard, Tom supposed. Heloise would wonder why.

'Heloise, darling, I am sorry. Are you taking the car or do you want me to drive you to the station?'

'I take the Alfa to Chantilly. By the way, there is nothing wrong with the telephone. I just tried it in your room.'

'Maybe the word from the *flics* got it fixed.'

'I think maybe they lied. They wanted to surprise us.' She paused in the act of putting a shirt into her suitcase. 'What have you done, Tome? Did you do something to this Murchison?'

'No!' Tom said, startled.

'You know, my father is not going to support any more nonsense, any more scandal.'

She referred to the Greenleaf business. Tom had cleared his name there, to be sure, but there were always suspicions. The Latins made wild jokes, and the jokes in a curious way became Latin truths. Tom might have killed Dickie. And everyone knew that he derived some money from Dickie's death, much as Tom had tried to hide this. Heloise knew he had an income from Dickie, and so did Heloise's father, whose own hands were not immaculate in his business activities, but Tom's had, perhaps, blood on them. *Non olet pecunia, sed sanguis* . . .

'There won't be any more scandal,' Tom said. 'If you only knew, I'm trying my best to avoid scandal. That's my objective.'

She closed her suitcase. 'I never know what you are doing.'

Tom took the suitcase. Then he set it down and they embraced. 'I would like to be with you tonight.'

Heloise would have liked to be with him, too, and she did not have to say it in words. This was the other side of her *fous-moi-le-camp*! Now she was leaving. Frenchwomen had to leave a room, a house, or ask someone else to change his room, or go somewhere, and the more inconvenient it was for the other person, the better they liked it, but it was still less inconvenient than their screaming. Tom called it 'The Law of French Displacement.'

'Did you telephone your family?' Tom asked.

'If they are not there, the servants are there.'

It would take her nearly two hours to drive. 'Will you ring me when you get there?'

'Au revoir, Bernard!' Heloise shouted from the front door. Then to Tom, who walked out with her, *'Non!'*

Tom watched bitterly as the red lights of the Alfa-Romeo turned left at the gates and disappeared.

Bernard sat smoking a cigarette. From the kitchen came the faint clatter of the garbage pail's lid. Tom took his torch from the hall table, and went into the spare loo. He went down to the cellar and looked behind the wine cask where Murchison had been. Very luckily there was no bloodstain there. Tom went back upstairs.

'You know, Bernard, you're welcome here tonight, but tomorrow morning the police arrive to look the house over more thoroughly.' He suddenly thought, the woods, too. 'They might ask you questions. It'll be annoying to you. Do you want to leave before they arrive – at eight?'

'Possibly, possibly.'

It was nearly 10 p.m. Mme Annette came in to ask if they would like more coffee. Tom and Bernard declined.

'Mme Heloise has gone out?' Mme Annette asked.

'She decided to go and see her parents,' said Tom.

'At this hour! Ah, Mme Heloise!' She collected the coffee things.

Tom sensed that she disliked Bernard, or mistrusted him, in the same way Heloise did. It was regrettable, Tom thought, that Bernard's character did not come through, that it had such an off-putting surface for most people. Tom realized that neither Heloise nor Mme Annette could like him, because they knew nothing about him really, nothing about his devotion to Derwatt – which they would probably consider 'putting Derwatt to use'. Above all, neither Heloise nor Mme Annette, with their quite different backgrounds, would ever understand Bernard Tufts's progress from rather working-class origin (according to Jeff and Ed) to what might be called the edge of greatness by virtue of his talent – though he signed his work with another name. Bernard did not even care about the money side of it – which would again be incomprehensible to Mme Annette and Heloise. Mme Annette left the room rather quickly, and in what Tom felt was as much of a huff as she dared.

'There's something I'd like to tell you,' Bernard said. 'The night after

Derwatt died – We all heard about his death twenty-four hours after it happened in Greece – I-I had a vision of Derwatt standing in my bedroom. There was moonlight coming through the window. I'd broken a date with Cynthia, I remember, because I wanted to be alone. I could *see* Derwatt there and feel his presence. He was even smiling. He said, "Don't be alarmed, Bernard, I'm not badly off. I'm feeling no pain." Can you imagine Derwatt saying something as predictable as that? Yet I heard him.'

Bernard had heard his inner ear. Tom listened respectfully.

'I sat up in bed watching him for maybe a minute. Derwatt sort of drifted around my room, the room where I paint sometimes – and sleep.'

Bernard meant painted Tufts, not Derwatts.

Bernard continued, 'He said, "Carry on Bernard, I'm not sorry." I gathered he meant he wasn't sorry he'd killed himself. He meant, just go on living. That is –' Bernard looked at Tom for the first time since he had begun speaking '– for as long as it's supposed to last. It's hardly something one has control over, is it? Destiny does it for you.'

Tom hesitated. 'Derwatt had a sense of humour. Jeff says he might've appreciated your forging his work with such success.' Thank God, this went down not badly.

'To a point. Yes, the forging might have been a professional joke. Derwatt wouldn't have liked the business side of it. Money might have made him commit suicide as easily as being broke.'

Tom felt Bernard's thoughts starting to turn again, in a disorganized and hostile way, hostile to him. Should he make a move to call it a night? Or would Bernard take that as an insult? 'The blasted *flics* are arriving so early, I think I'll turn in.'

Bernard leaned forward. 'You didn't understand what I meant the other day when I said I'd failed. With that detective from London, when I was trying to explain Derwatt to him.'

'Because you didn't fail. Look, Chris knew what you meant. Webster said it was very moving, I remember.'

'Webster was still considering the possibility of forgery, of Derwatt's permitting it. I couldn't even convey Derwatt's character. I did my best and I failed.'

Tom said, trying desperately to get Bernard on the rails again, 'Webster is looking for Murchison. That's his assignment. Not Derwatt at all. I'm going upstairs.'

Tom went to his room and put on pyjamas. He opened the window a crack at the top, and got into bed – which Mme Annette had not turned down this evening – but he felt shaky and had an impulse to lock his door. Was that silly? Was it sensible? It seemed cowardly. He did not lock the door. He was midway in a volume of Trevelyan's *English Social History*, and started to pick it up, then took his *Harrap's Dictionary* instead. *To forge*. Old French *forge*, a workshop. *Faber*, a workman. *Forge* in French had only to do with a workshop for metal. The French for forgery was *falsification* or *contrefaire*. Tom already knew this. He closed the book.

He lay for an hour without falling asleep. Every few moments, the blood sang in his ears in a crescendo, loud enough to startle him, and he kept having sensations of falling from a height.

By the radium hands of his wristwatch, Tom saw that it was 12.30 a.m. Should he ring Heloise? He wanted to ring her, but he did not want to incur further disapproval of Papa by ringing at a late hour. Damn other people.

Then Tom was aware of being flung over by the shoulders, and of hands around his throat. Tom threshed his legs free of the covers. He was pulling ineffectively at Bernard's arms to get his hands from his throat, and at last Tom got his foot against Bernard's body and pushed. The hands left his throat. Bernard dropped with a thud to the floor, gasping. Tom turned on his lamp, nearly knocked it over, and did knock over a glass of water which spilt on the blue oriental rug.

Bernard was getting his breath back painfully.

So was Tom, in a sense.

'My God, Bernard,' Tom said.

Bernard didn't reply, or couldn't. He sat on the floor, propped on one arm, in the position of The Dying Gaul. Was he going to attack again as soon as he recovered his strength, Tom wondered? Tom stood up from his bed, and lit a Gauloise.

'Really, Bernard, what a stupid thing to do!' Tom burst out laughing, and coughed on his smoke. 'You wouldn't have had a chance! Even trying to escape! Mme Annette knows you're here, so do the police.' Tom watched as Bernard got to his feet. It was not often, Tom thought, that a near-victim could smoke a cigarette and walk around bare-foot, smiling at someone who had just tried to kill him. 'You shouldn't do that again.' Tom knew his words were absurd. Bernard didn't care what happened to himself. 'Aren't you going to say anything?'

'Yes,' Bernard said. 'I detest you – because all this is entirely your fault. I should never have agreed to it – true. But you're the origin.'

Tom knew. He was a mystic origin, a font of evil. 'We're all trying to wind the thing up, not continue it.'

And I am finished. Cynthia –'

Tom puffed on his cigarette. 'You said you felt like Derwatt sometimes when you painted. Think what you've done for his name! Because he wasn't famous at all when he died.'

'It has been corrupted,' Bernard said like the voice of doom or judgement or hell itself. He went to the door and went out, with more of a look of purpose than usual.

Where was he going, Tom wondered? Bernard was still dressed, though it was after 3 a.m. Was he going to wander out in the night? Or go downstairs and set the house on fire?

Tom turned the key in his door. If Bernard came back, he'd have to bang to get in, and of course Tom would let him in, but it was only fair to have a bit of warning.

Bernard would be no asset tomorrow morning with the police.

SIXTEEN

At 9.15 a.m., Saturday October 26th. Tom stood at his french windows looking out towards the woods, where the police had begun to dig up Murchison's old grave. Behind Tom, Bernard paced the living-room floor quietly and restlessly. And in his hand, Tom held a formal letter from Jeffrey Constant asking on behalf of the Buckmaster Gallery if he knew the whereabouts of Thomas Murchison, because they didn't.

Three police agents had arrived that morning, two new to Tom, and the other the Commissaire Delaunay, who Tom thought was not going to do any digging. 'Do you know what is the recently dug place in the woods?' they had asked. Tom said he knew nothing about it. The woods did not belong to him. The gendarme had gone across the lawn to speak to his confrères. They had been over the house again.

Tom also had a letter from Chris Greenleaf which he had not opened.

The police had now been digging for perhaps ten minutes.

Tom read Jeff's letter more carefully. Jeff had written it either with an idea that Tom's post was being looked at, or Jeff was in a mood to be droll, but Tom believed the first idea.

> The Buckmaster Gallery
> Bond Street W1
> Oct, 24 19—

Thomas P. Ripley, Esq.
Belle Ombre
Villeperce 77

Dear Mr Ripley,

We have been informed that Detective-Inspector Webster visited you recently with regard to Mr Thomas Murchison, who accompanied you last Wednesday to France. This is to inform you that we have heard nothing from Mr Murchison since Thursday 15th inst. when he came to our gallery.

We know that Mr Murchison wished to see Derwatt before he (Mr Murchison) returned to the United States. At the moment we do not know where Derwatt is in England, but we expect he will get in touch with us before returning to Mexico. It may be that Derwatt has arranged a meeting with Mr Murchison of which we know nothing. [A ghostly tea, perhaps, Tom thought.]

We as well as the police are concerned about the disappearance of the painting by Derwatt called 'The Clock'.

Please ring us and reverse the charges if you have information.

> Yours sincerely,
> Jeffrey Constant.

Tom turned around, in arrogant good spirits now – at least for the moment, and at any rate Bernard's sullenness bored him. Tom wanted to say, 'Listen, old crud, clot or cock, what the hell are you doing hanging around here anyway?' But Tom knew what Bernard was doing, waiting to have another go at him. So Tom only held his breath for a moment, smiling at Bernard who wasn't even looking at him, and Tom listened to blue tits twittering over some suet that Mme Annette had hung from a tree, heard Mme Annette's transistor faintly from the kitchen, and he heard also the *clink* of a police agent's spade, distant in the woods.

Tom said with the dead-pan coolness of Jeff's letter: 'Well, they're not going to find any signs of Murchison out there.'

'Let them drag the river,' Bernard said.

'Are you going to *tell* them to do that?'

'No.'

'Anyway, what river? I can't even remember which it was.' Tom was sure Bernard couldn't.

Tom was waiting for the police to return from the woods, and to say they hadn't found anything. Or maybe they would not bother saying that, maybe they would say nothing. Or they might go farther into the woods, searching. It might be an all-day affair. It was not a bad way, on a nice day, for the police to kill time. Lunch in the village or some village near by, or more likely their own homes in the district, then a return to the woods.

Tom opened Chris's letter.

Oct. 24, 19—

Dear Tom,

Thank you once more for the elegant days I spent with you. They are quite a contrast to my squalid abode here, but I sort of like it here. Last evening I had an adventure. I met a girl called Valerie in a St-Germain-des-Prés café. I asked her if she would like to come to my hotel for a glass of wine. (Ahem!) She accepted. I was with Gerald, but he tactfully disappeared like the gentleman he sometimes is. Valerie came upstairs a few minutes after me, her idea, though I don't think it would have mattered with the desk downstairs. She asked if she could wash up. I told her I had no bathroom, only a basin, so I offered to go out of the room while she washed up. When I knocked on the door again, she asked was there a bathroom with a tub. I said of course but I would have to get the key. This I did. Well, she disappeared in the bathroom for at least fifteen minutes. Then she came back and again wanted me to leave the room while she washed. Okay, so I did, but by this time I was wondering what on earth she could still be washing. I waited downstairs on the sidewalk. When I went up again, she was gone, the room was empty. I looked in the halls, everywhere. Gone! I thought, there's a girl who has washed herself right out of my life. Maybe I didn't do the right thing. Better luck next time, Chris!

I may go to Rome next with Gerald ...

Tom looked out of the window. 'I wonder when they'll be finished? Ah, here they come! Look! Swinging their empty shovels.'

Bernard did not look.

Tom sat down comfortably on the yellow sofa.

The French knocked at the back windows, and Tom gestured for them to come in, then jumped up to open the windows for them.

'Nothing in the trench except this,' said the Commissaire Delaunay, holding up a small coin. It was a 20-centime piece, gold-coloured. 'The date is nineteen hundred sixty-five.' He smiled.

Tom smiled, too, 'Funny you found that.'

'Our treasure for today,' said Delaunay, pocketing the coin. 'Yes, the hole was recently dug. Very strange. Just the size for a corpse, but no corpse. You saw no one digging there recently?'

'I certainly did not. But – one can't see the place from the house. It is concealed by trees.'

Tom went to speak with Mme Annette in the kitchen, but she was not there. Probably she was out shopping, a tour that would be longer than usual, because she would tell three or four acquaintances about the arrival of the police who searched the house for M. Murchison, whose picture was in the newspaper. Tom prepared a tray of cold beer and a bottle of wine, and brought it into the living-room. The French officer was chatting with Bernard. It was about painting.

'Who makes use of the woods there?' asked Delaunay.

'Oh, now and then some farmers, I think,' Tom replied, 'who get wood. I seldom see anybody in that lane.'

'And recently?'

Tom thought. 'I can't remember anybody.'

The three agents departed. They had ascertained a few matters: his telephone was working; his *femme de ménage* was out shopping just now (Tom said he thought they might find her in the village, if they wished to speak with her); Heloise had gone to visit her parents in Chantilly. Delaunay had not bothered to take her address.

'I want to open the windows,' Tom said when they had gone. He did, the front door and the french windows.

The chill did not bother Bernard.

'I'm going to see what they did out there,' Tom said, and walked across the lawn towards the woods. What a relief to have the men of the law out of the house!

They had filled in the hole. It stood a bit high, reddish-brown earth, but they had been quite tidy about it. Tom walked back to the house. Good God, he thought, how many more discussions, repetitions, could he bear? One thing, perhaps, he should be grateful for, Bernard was not self-pitying. Bernard accused him. That was at least active and positive and definite.

'Well,' Tom said, entering the living-room, 'a tidy job they did. And twenty centimes for their trouble. Why don't we leave before –'

Just then, Mme Annette opened the door from the kitchen – Tom heard it without seeing it – and Tom advanced to speak with her.

'Well, Mme Annette, the agents have departed. No clues for them, I'm afraid.' He was not going to mention the grave in the woods.

'It is very strange, is it not?' she said quickly, often a protocol in French for something else more important. 'It is a mystery here, is it not?'

'It is a mystery at Orly or Paris,' Tom replied. 'Not here.'

'Will you and M. Bernard be here for lunch?'

'Not today,' Tom said. 'We shall go out somewhere. And as for this evening, don't trouble yourself. If Mme Heloise telephones, would you tell her I shall ring back tonight? In fact –' Tom hesitated, 'I'll definitely ring back by five this afternoon. In any case, why don't you take the rest of the day off?'

'I bought some cutlets just in case. Yes, I have a rendezvous with Mme Yvonne at –'

'That's the spirit!' Tom interrupted. He turned to Bernard. 'Shall we take off somewhere?'

But they could not leave at once. Bernard wanted to do something in his room, he said. Mme Annette (Tom thought) left the house, possibly to have lunch with a friend in Villeperce. Tom at last knocked on Bernard's closed door.

Bernard was writing at the table in his room.

'If you want to be left alone –'

'In fact, I don't,' Bernard said, getting up readily enough.

Tom was mystified. What do you want to talk about? Tom wanted to ask. Why are you here? Tom could not bring himself to ask these questions. 'Let's go downstairs.'

Bernard came with him.

Tom wanted to ring Heloise. It was now 12.30 p.m. Tom could catch her before lunch. At home, the family ate on the hour, at 1 p.m. The telephone rang as Tom and Bernard entered the living-room. 'Maybe Heloise,' Tom said, and picked the telephone up.

'*Vous êtes ... blur-r-p ... Ne quittez pas. Londres vous appelle ...*'

Then Jeff came on. 'Hello, Tom. I'm ringing from a post office. Can you come over again – possibly?'

Tom knew he meant come over as Derwatt. 'Bernard is here.'

'We thought so. How is he?'

'He's – taking it easy,' Tom said. Tom did not think Bernard – gazing out the french windows – even cared to listen, but Tom was not sure. 'I *can't* just now,' Tom said. Didn't they realize, after all, that he had killed Murchison?

'Can't you think it over – please?'

'But I have a few obligations here, too, you know. What's happening?'

'That Inspector was here. He wanted to know where Derwatt was. He wanted to look at our books.' Jeff gulped, his voice had become perhaps unconsciously lower for reasons of secrecy, but at the same time he sounded so desperate that he might not have cared who heard or understood him. 'Ed and I – we made a few lists, recent ones. We said we'd always had an informal arrangement, that no pictures had ever been lost. I think that went down all right. But they are curious about Derwatt himself, and if you could carry it off again –'

'I don't think it's wise,' Tom said, interrupting.

'If you could confirm our books –'

Damn their books, Tom thought. Damn their income. What about Murchison's murder, was that his responsibility only? And what about Bernard and Bernard's life? In one strange instant, while he was not even thinking, Tom realized that Bernard was going to kill himself, was going to be a suicide somewhere. And Jeff and Ed were worried about *their* income, *their* reputation, and about going to prison! 'I have certain responsibilities here. It's impossible for me to go to London.' In Jeff's disappointed silence, Tom asked, 'Is Mrs Murchison coming over, do you know?'

'We haven't heard anything about that.'

'Let Derwatt stay where he is, wherever that is. Maybe he's got a friend with a private plane, who knows?' Tom laughed.

'By the way,' Jeff said, slightly more cheerful, 'what happened to "The Clock"? Was it really stolen?'

'Yes. Amazing, isn't it? I wonder who's enjoying that treasure?'

The note on which Jeff hung up was still a disappointed one: Tom was not coming over.

'Let's take a walk,' Bernard said.

So much for ringing Heloise, Tom thought. Tom started to ask if he might take ten minutes up in his room to ring her, then thought it better to humour Bernard. 'I'll get a jacket.'

They walked around the village. Bernard did not want a coffee, or a glass of wine, or lunch. They walked nearly a kilometre on two of the roads that led out of Villeperce, then turned back, stepping aside sometimes for wide farm trucks, for wagons pulled by Percheron horses. Bernard talked of Van Gogh and Arles, where Bernard had been twice.

'... Vincent like all the others had a certain span of life and no more. Can anybody imagine Mozart living to be eighty? I'd like to see Salzburg again. There's a café there, the Tomaselli. Marvellous coffee ... Can you imagine Bach dying at twenty-six, for example? Which proves a man is his work, nothing more or less. It's never a man we're talking about, but his work ...'

It was threatening to rain. Tom had long ago turned his jacket collar up.

'... Derwatt had a certain decent span, you see. It was absurd that I prolonged it. But of course I didn't. All that can be rectified,' Bernard said like a judge pronouncing sentence, a wise sentence – in the opinion of the judge.

Tom took his hands from his pockets and blew on them, and stuffed them back in his pockets.

Back at the house, Tom made tea and brought out the whisky and brandy. The drink would either calm Bernard or bring matters to a crisis by making Bernard angry, and something would happen.

'I must ring my wife,' Tom said. 'Help yourself to anything.' Tom fled up the stairs. Heloise, even if angry still, would be a voice of sanity.

Tom said the Chantilly number to the operator. The rain began to fall. It was gentle against the windowpanes. There was no wind just now. Tom sighed.

'Hello, Heloise!' She had answered. 'Yes, I am all right. I wanted to ring you last evening, but it became too late ... I was just out walking. (She had tried to ring him.) With Bernard ... Yes, he is still here but I think he's leaving this afternoon, maybe tonight. When will you come home?'

'When you get rid of that *foul*'

'Heloise, *je t'aime*. I may come to Paris. With Bernard, because I think it will help him to leave.'

'Why are you so nervous? What is happening?'

'Nothing!'

'Will you tell me when you are in Paris?'

Tom went back downstairs, and put on some music. He chose jazz. It was not good, not bad jazz, and as he had noticed in other crucial moments in his life, the jazz did nothing for him. Only classical music did something – it soothed or it bored, gave confidence or took confidence quite away, because it had order, and one either accepted that order or rejected it. Tom dumped a lot of sugar into his tea, now cold, and drank it off. Bernard had not shaved in two days, it seemed. Was he going to affect a Derwatt beard?

A few minutes later, they were strolling over the back lawn. One of Bernard's shoelaces was untied. Bernard wore desert boots, rather flattened with wear, their soles against the uppers like the beaks of new-born birds, which had a curious way of looking ancient. Was Bernard going to tie his shoelace or not?

'The other night,' Tom said, 'I tried to compose a limerick.

> There once was a match by computer.
> A nought was wed to a neuter.

Said the neuter to nought,
"I'm not what I ought,
But our offspring will be even mooter."

The trouble is, it's clean. But maybe you can think of a better last line.' Tom had two versions of middle part and last line, but was Bernard even listening?

They were going into the lane now, into the woods. The rain had stopped, and now it was merely drippy.

'Look at the little frog!' Tom said, bending to scoop it up, because he had almost trod on it, a little thing no bigger than a thumbnail.

The blow hit Tom on the back of the head, and might have been Bernard's fist. Tom heard Bernard's voice saying something, was aware of wet grass, a stone against his face, then he passed out – for all practical purposes, though he felt a second blow on the side of his head. *This is too much*, Tom thought. He imagined his empty hands groping stupidly over the ground, but he knew he was not moving.

Then he was being rolled over and over. Everything was silent, except for a ringing in his ears. Tom tried to move and could not. Was he face down or face up? He was thinking, in a way, without being able to see. He blinked his eyes, and they were gritty. He began to realize, to believe, that weights or a weight was descending on his spine, his legs. Through the ringing in his ears came the whispering sound of a shovel driving into soil. Bernard was burying him. Tom was sure now that his eyes were open. How deep was the hole? It was Murchison's grave, Tom was sure. How much time had passed?

Good God, Tom thought, he couldn't allow Bernard to bury him several feet under, or he'd never get out. Dimly, even with dim humour, Tom thought that there could be a limit to placating Bernard, and the limit was his own life. *Listen! Okay!* Tom imagined, believed that he had yelled this, but he hadn't.

'... not the first,' Bernard's voice said, thick and muffled by the earth that surrounded Tom.

What did that mean? Had he even heard it? Tom was able to turn his head a little, and he realized he was face down. He could turn his head to a very small degree.

And the weight had stopped falling. Tom concentrated on breathing, partly through his mouth. His mouth was dry, and he spat out gritty soil. If he didn't move, Bernard would leave. Now Tom was awake enough to realize that Bernard must have got the shovel from the toolshed, while he was knocked out. Tom felt a warm trickle on the back of his neck. That was blood, probably.

Maybe two, maybe five minutes passed, and Tom wanted to bestir himself, or at least try to, but was Bernard standing there watching him?

Impossible to hear anything, such as footfalls. Maybe Bernard had departed minutes ago. And anyway, would Bernard attack again if he saw him struggling out of the grave? It was a bit amusing. Later, if there was any later, Tom would laugh, he thought.

Tom risked it. He worked his knees. He got his hands in a position to push himself upwards, and then found he had no strength. So he began to dig upwards with his fingers like a mole. He cleared a space for his face, and tunnelled upwards for air, without reaching any air. The earth was wet and loose but very clinging. The weight on his spine was formidable. He began to push with his feet and to work upwards with his hands and arms, like someone trying to swim in unhardened cement. It couldn't be more than three feet of earth on top of him, Tom thought optimistically, maybe not even that. It took a long time to excavate three feet, even soft earth like this, and Bernard surely hadn't been at work very long. Tom felt sure he was now stirring the top of his prison, and if Bernard were standing there not reacting, not tossing more earth on or digging him up to hit him on the head again, he could afford to give a big heave and relax for a few seconds. Tom gave a big heave. It gained him more breathing space. He took some twenty inhalations of tomb-like wet air, then went at it again.

Two minutes later, he was standing reeling like a drunk, beside Murchison's – now his own – grave, covered from head to foot with mud and clods.

It was growing dark. There was no light on in the house, Tom saw when he staggered into the lane. Automatically, Tom thought of the appearance of the grave, thought of covering it back, wondered where the shovel was that Bernard had used, and then thought the hell with it all. He was still wiping dirt out of his eyes and ears.

Maybe he would find Bernard sitting in the more or less dark of the living-room, in which case Tom would say, 'Boo!' Bernard's had been a rather ponderous practical joke. Tom took his shoes off on the terrace and left them. The french windows were ajar. 'Bernard!' Tom called. He was really in no state to withstand another attack.

No answer.

Tom walked into his living-room, then turned and walked dazedly out again and dropped his muddy jacket on the terrace, also his trousers. In his shorts now, he put on lights and went upstairs to his bathroom. A bath refreshed him. He put a towel around his neck. The cut on his head was bleeding. Tom had touched it only once with his washcloth to get the mud out, and then tried to forget it, because there was nothing he could do about it alone. He put on his dressing-gown and went down to the kitchen, made a sandwich of sliced ham and poured a big glass of milk, and had this snack at the kitchen table. Then he hung his jacket and trousers in his bathroom. Brush them and send them to the cleaners, the redoubtable Mme Annette would say, and what a blessing she was not here now, but she'd be back by 10 p.m., Tom thought, maybe 11.30 p.m. if she'd gone to the cinema in Fontainebleau or Melun, but he shouldn't count on that. It was now ten minutes to eight.

What would Bernard do now, Tom wondered? Drift to Paris? Somehow Tom could not see Bernard going back to London, so he ruled that idea out. But Bernard was so deranged at the moment as to be really unpredictable by any standards. Would Bernard, for instance, inform Jeff and Ed that he had killed Tom Ripley? Bernard might as well shout anything from the house-tops now. In fact, Bernard was going to kill himself, and Tom sensed this the way he might have sensed a murder, because suicide was after all a form of murder. And in order for Bernard to go through, or carry out, whatever it was he intended, Tom knew that he himself had to continue to be dead.

And what a bore that was, in view of Mme Annette, Heloise, his neighbours, the police. How could he make all of them believe he was dead?

Tom put on levis and went back to the lane with the lantern from the spare loo. Sure enough, the shovel lay on the ground between the much used grave and the lane. Tom used it to fill in the grave. A beautiful tree ought to grow there at some time, Tom thought, because the ground was so well loosened. Tom even dragged back some of the old branches and leaves with which he had originally covered Murchison.

R.I.P. Tom Ripley, he thought.

Another passport might be useful, and who but Reeves Minot should he call on for it? It was high time he asked Reeves for a small favour.

Tom wrote a note to Reeves on his typewriter, and enclosed two, for safety, of his current passport photographs. He should ring Reeves tonight from Paris. Tom had decided to go to Paris, where he could hide out for a few hours and think. So Tom now took his muddy shoes and clothes up to the attic, where Mme Annette would probably not go. Tom changed clothes again, and took the estate wagon to the Melun railway station.

He was in Paris by 10.45 p.m., and he dropped the note to Reeves in a Gare de Lyon post box. Then he went to the Hotel Ritz, where he took a room under the name Daniel Stevens, wrote a made-up American passport number, saying he did not have his passport with him. Address: 14 rue du Docteur Cavet, Rouen, a street which as far as Tom knew did not exist.

SEVENTEEN

Tom telephoned Heloise from his room. She was not in. The maid said she had gone out to dinner with her parents. Tom put in a call to Reeves in Hamburg. This came through in twenty minutes, and Reeves was in.

'Greetings, Reeves. Tom here. I'm in Paris. How goes everything? ... Can you pop me a passport *tout de suite*? I've already sent you photographs.'

Reeves sounded flustered. Good heavens, was this a real request at last? A passport? Yes, those essential little things that were pinched all the time, everywhere. How much would Reeves want for it, Tom was polite enough to ask.

Reeves couldn't say just now.

'Put it on the bill,' Tom said with confidence. 'The point is to get it to me at once. If you get my pictures Monday morning, can you finish by Monday night? ... Yes, it is urgent. Have you got a friend flying to Paris late Monday night, for example?' If not, find one, Tom thought.

Yes, Reeves said, a friend could fly to Paris. Not another carrier (or host), Tom insisted, because he would not be in any position to pick someone's pockets or suitcase.

'Any American name,' Tom said. 'American passport preferred, English will do. Meanwhile I'm at the Ritz, Place Vendôme ... Daniel Stevens.' Tom gave the Ritz's telephone number for Reeves's convenience, and said he would meet Reeves's messenger personally, once he knew the time the man could get to Orly.

By this time, Heloise was back in Chantilly, and Tom spoke with her. '*Yes*, I am in Paris. Do you want to come in tonight?'

Heloise did. Tom was delighted. He had a vision of sitting across a table from Heloise, drinking champagne, in another hour or so, if Heloise wanted champagne, and she usually did.

Tom stood on the grey pavement, looking out at the round Place

Vendôme. Circles annoyed him. What direction should he take? Left towards l'Opéra, or right towards the rue de Rivoli? Tom preferred to think in squares or rectangles. Where was Bernard? Why do you want a passport, he asked himself? As an ace in the hole? An added measure of potential freedom? *I can't draw like Derwatt*, Bernard had said this afternoon. *I simply don't draw any more – seldom for myself even.* Was Bernard at this moment in some Paris hotel, cutting his wrists in a basin? Leaning over the Seine on one of the bridges about to jump over – gently – when no one was looking?

Tom walked in a straight line towards the rue de Rivoli. It was dull and dark at this time of night, and shop windows were barred with steel bands and chains against the theft of the tourist-aimed crap they displayed – silk handkerchiefs with 'Paris' printed on them, overpriced silk ties and shirts. He thought of taking a taxi to the sixth *arrondissement*, strolling about in that more cheerful atmosphere and having a beer at Lippe's. But he did not want possibly to run into Chris. He went back to his hotel, and put in a call to Jeff's studio.

This call (the operator said) would take forty-five minutes, the lines were crowded, but it came through in half an hour.

'Hello? – Paris?' Jeff's voice came like that of a drowning dolphin.

'*It's Tom in Paris!* Can you hear me?'

'*Badly!*'

It was not bad enough for Tom to attempt a second call. He pursued: 'I don't know where Bernard *is*. Have you heard from him?'

'Why are you in Paris?'

Rather useless, under the circumstances of near inaudibility, to explain that. Tom managed to learn that Jeff and Ed had not heard anything from Bernard.

Then Jeff said, 'They're trying to find *Derwatt* ...' (Muttered English curses.) 'My God, if I can't hear *you*, I doubt if anybody in between can hear a bloody ...'

'*D'accord!*' Tom responded. 'Tell me all your troubles.'

'Murchison's wife may ...'

'What?' Good God, the telephone was a maddening device. People should revert to pen and paper and the packet-boat. 'Can't hear a damned word!'

'We sold "The Tub" ... They are asking ... Derwatt! Tom, if you'd only ...'

They were suddenly cut off.

Tom banged the telephone down in anger, gripped it and lifted it again, ready to blast at the operator downstairs. But he put the telephone down. It wasn't her fault. It was nobody's fault, nobody who could be found.

Well, Mrs Murchison was coming over, as Tom had foreseen. And maybe she knew about the lavender theory. And 'The Tub' was sold, to whom? And Bernard was – where? Athens? Would he repeat Derwatt's act and drown himself off a Greek island? Tom saw himself going to Athens. What was that island of Derwatt's? Icaria? Where was it? Find out tomorrow in a tourist agency.

Tom sat down at the writing-table and dashed off a note:

Dear Jeff,

In case you see Bernard, I am supposed to be dead. Bernard thinks he has killed me. I will explain later. Don't pass this on to anyone, it is *only* in case you see Bernard and he says he has killed me – pretend to believe him and don't do anything. Stall Bernard, please.

All the best,
Tom

Tom went downstairs and posted the letter with a seventy-centime stamp bought at the desk. Jeff probably wouldn't get it till Tuesday. But it was not the kind of message he dared send by cable. Or did he? *I must lie low even under ground re Bernard.* No, that wasn't clear enough. He was still pondering when Heloise came in the door. Tom was glad to see that she had her small Gucci valise with her.

'Good evening, Mme Stevens,' Tom said in French. 'You are Mme Stevens this evening.' Tom thought of steering her to the desk to register, then decided not to bother, and led Heloise to the lift.

Three pairs of eyes followed them. Was she really his wife?

'Tome, you are pale!'

'I've had a busy day.'

'Ah, what is that –'

'Sh-h.' She meant the back of his head. Heloise noticed everything. Tom thought he could tell her a few things, but not everything. The grave – that would be too horrible. Besides, it would make Bernard out a killer, which he wasn't. Tom tipped the lift man, who insisted on carrying Heloise's valise.

'What happened to your head?'

Tom took off the dark green and blue muffler that he had been wearing high around his neck to catch the blood. 'Bernard hit me. Now don't be worried, darling. Take off your shoes. Your clothes. Make yourself comfortable. Would you like some champagne?'

'Yes. Why not?'

Tom ordered it by telephone. Tom felt light-headed, as if he had a fever, but he knew it was only fatigue and loss of blood. Had he checked over the house for blood drops? Yes, he remembered going upstairs at the last minute especially to look for blood anywhere.

'Where is Bernard?' Heloise had slipped off her shoes and was barefoot.

'I really don't know. Maybe Paris.'

'You had a fight? He wouldn't leave?'

'Oh – a slight fight. He is very nervous just now. It is nothing serious, nothing.'

'But why did you come to Paris? Is he still at the house?'

That was a possibility, Tom realized, though Bernard's things had been gone from the house. Tom had looked. And Bernard couldn't get back into the house without breaking a french window. 'He's not at the house, no.'

'I want to see your head. Come into the bathroom where there is more light.'

A knock came at the door. They were quick with the champagne. The portly, grey-haired waiter grinned as the cork popped. The bottle crunched pleasantly into a bucket of ice.

'Merci, m'sieur,' said the waiter, taking Tom's banknote.

Tom and Heloise lifted their glasses, Heloise a little uncertainly, and drank. She had to see his head. Tom submitted. He took off his shirt, and bent over and closed his eyes, as Heloise washed the back of his head in the basin with a face towel. He closed his ears, or tried to, to her exclamations which he had anticipated.

'It isn't a big cut, or it would've kept on bleeding!' Tom said. The washing was making it bleed again, of course. 'Get another towel – get something,' Tom said, and returned to the bedroom, where he sank gently to the floor. He was out, so he crawled to the bathroom where the floor was of tile.

Heloise was talking about adhesive tape.

Tom fainted for a minute, though he didn't mention it. He crawled to the toilet and threw up briefly. He used some of Heloise's wet towels for his face and forehead. Then a couple of minutes later, he was standing at the basin, sipping champagne, while Heloise made a bandage out of a small white handkerchief. 'Why do you carry adhesive tape?' Tom asked.

'I use it for my nails.'

How, Tom wondered? He held the tape while she cut it. 'Pink adhesive tape,' Tom said, 'it is a sign of racial discrimination. Black Power in the States ought to get onto that – and stop it.'

Heloise didn't understand. Tom had spoken in English.

'I will explain it tomorrow – maybe.'

Then they were in bed, in the luxurious wide bed with four thick pillows, and Heloise had donated her pyjamas to put under Tom's head, in case he bled any more, but he thought it had almost stopped. Heloise was naked, and she felt unbelievably smooth, like something of polished marble, only of course she was soft, and even warm. It was not an evening for making love, but Tom felt very happy, and not at all worried about tomorrow – which was perhaps unwise of him, but that night, or rather early morning, he indulged himself. In the darkness, he heard the hiss of champagne bubbles as Heloise sipped her glass, and the click as she set it down on the night-table. Then his cheek was against her breast. Heloise, you're the only woman in the world who has ever made me think of *now*, Tom wanted to say, but he was too tired, and the remark was probably not important.

In the morning, Tom had some explaining to do to Heloise, and he had to do it subtly. He said that Bernard Tufts was upset because of his English girl-friend, that he might kill himself, and Tom wanted to find him. He might be in Athens. And since the police wanted to keep Tom in their sight because of Murchison's disappearance, it was best that the police thought he was in Paris, staying with friends, perhaps. Tom explained that he was awaiting a passport which could come only by Monday evening at best. Tom and Heloise were breakfasting in bed.

'I don't understand why you bother about this *fou* who even hit you.'

'Friendship,' Tom said. 'Now, darling, why don't you go back to Belle Ombre and keep Mme Annette company? Or – we can ring her and you can spend today and tonight with me,' Tom said more cheerfully. 'But we'd better change hotels today, just for safety.'

'Oh, Tome –' But Heloise didn't mean her disappointed tone, Tom knew. She liked doing things that were a little sly, keeping secrets when secrets were unnecessary. The stories she'd told Tom about her adolescent intrigues with girl schoolmates, and boys, too, to evade her parents' surveillance, matched the inventions of Cocteau.

'We'll have another name today. What name would you like? Got to be something American or English, because of me. You're just my French wife, you see?' Tom was speaking in English.

'Hm-m. Gladstone?'

Tom laughed.

'Is there something funny about Gladstone?'

How Heloise hated the English language, because she thought it was full of dirty double meanings that she could never master. 'No, it's just that he invented a suitcase.'

'He invented the *suitcase!* I don't believe you! Who could invent a suitcase? It is too *simple!* Really, Tom!'

They moved to the Hotel Ambassadeur, in the boulevard Haussmann, in the ninth *arrondissement.* Conservative and respectable. Here, Tom registered as William Tenyck, with wife Mireille. Tom made a second call to Reeves, and left his new name, address and telephone number, PRO 72–21, with the man with the German accent who frequently answered Reeves's telephone.

Tom and Heloise went to a film in the afternoon, and returned to the hotel at 6 p.m. No message as yet from Reeves. Heloise rang Mme Annette, at Tom's suggestion, and Tom spoke with Madame also.

'Yes, we are in Paris,' Tom said. 'I am sorry I didn't leave you a note ... Perhaps Mme Heloise will return late tomorrow night, I am not sure.' He handed the phone back to Heloise.

Bernard had certainly not been in evidence at Belle Ombre, or Mme Annette would have mentioned him.

They went to bed early. Tom had unsuccessfully tried to persuade Heloise to cut away the silly strips of adhesive on the back of his head, and she had even bought some lavender-coloured French antiseptic with which she soaked the patch of bandage. She had rinsed his muffler out at the Ritz, and it had been dry by morning. Just before midnight, their telephone rang. Reeves said that a friend would bring him what he needed tomorrow night Monday on Lufthansa flight 311 due at Orly at 12.15 a.m.

'And his name?' Tom asked.

'It's a woman, Gerda Schneider. She knows what you look like.'

'Okay,' Tom said, quite pleased with the service in view of the fact Reeves hadn't yet received his photographs. 'Want to come with me tomorrow night to Orly?' Tom asked Heloise when he had hung up.

'I will drive you. I want to know if you are safe.'

Tom told her that the station wagon was at the Melun station. She perhaps could get André, a gardener they sometimes used, to go with her to fetch it.

They decided to stay another night at the Ambassadeur, in case there was any hitch about the passport on Monday night. Tom thought of catching a night-flight to Greece in the small hours of Tuesday, but this couldn't be determined until he had the passport in hand. There was also the matter of acquainting himself with the signature on the passport. All this, he realized, to save Bernard's life. Tom wished he could share his thoughts, his feelings, with Heloise, but he was afraid he could not make her understand. Would she understand if she knew about the forgeries? Yes, she might, intellectually, if he could use such a word. But Heloise would say, 'Why is it all on your shoulders? Can't Jeff and Ed look for their friend – their breadwinner?' Tom did not begin the story to her. It was best to be alone, stripped for action, in a sense. Stripped of sympathy, even of tender thoughts from home.

And all went well. Tom and Heloise arrived at Orly at midnight Monday, and the flight came in on time, and Gerda Schneider – or a woman who used that name – accosted Tom at the upstairs gate where he waited.

'Tom Ripley?' she said, smiling.

'Yes. Frau Schneider?'

She was a woman of about thirty, blonde, quite handsome and intelligent looking, and quite unmade up, as if she had just washed her face in cold water and put on some clothes. 'Mr Ripley, I am indeed honoured to meet you,' she said in English. 'I have heard so much about you.'

Tom laughed out loud at her polite and amused tone. It was a surprise to him that Reeves could muster such interesting people to work for him. 'I'm with my wife. She's downstairs. You're staying the night in Paris?'

She was. She even had a hotel room booked, at the Pont-Royal in the rue Montalembert. Tom introduced her to Heloise. Tom fetched the car, while Heloise and Frau Schneider waited for him not far from where Tom had deposited Murchison's suitcase. They drove all the way to Paris, to the Pont-Royal, before Frau Schneider said:

'I shall give you the package here.'

They were still in the car. Gerda Schneider opened her large handbag and removed a white envelope which was rather thick.

Tom was parked, and it was somewhat dark. He took out the green American passport and stuck it in his jacket pocket. The passport had been wrapped in apparently blank sheets of paper. 'Thank you,' Tom said. 'I'll be in touch with Reeves. How is he? . . .'

A few minutes later, Tom and Heloise were driving towards the Hotel Ambassadeur.

'She is quite pretty, for a German,' Heloise said.

In their room, Tom took a look at the passport. It was a well-worn thing, and Reeves had abrased his photograph to match it. *Robert Fiedler*

Mackay was his name, age 31, born in Salt Lake City, Utah, occupation engineer, dependants none. The signature was slender and high, all the letters connected, a handwriting Tom associated with a couple of boring characters, American men, he had known.

'Darling – Heloise – I am now *Robert*,' Tom said in French. 'If you'll excuse me, I have to practise my signature for a while.'

Heloise was leaning against the *commode*, watching him.

'Oh, darling! Don't worry!' Tom put his arms around her. 'Let's have champagne! All goes well!'

*

By 2 p.m. on Tuesday, Tom was in Athens – more chromed, cleaner than the Athens he had seen last, five or six years ago. Tom registered at the Hotel Grande Bretagne, tidied up a little in his room which gave onto Constitution Square, then went out to look around and to inquire at a few other hotels for Bernard Tufts. Impossible to believe Bernard had registered at the Grande Bretagne, Tom thought, the most expensive hotel in Athens. Tom was even sixty per cent sure Bernard was *not* in Athens, but he had made his way to Derwatt's island, or to some island; even so Tom felt it would be stupid not to ask at a few Athens hotels.

Tom's story was that he had been separated from a friend whom he was supposed to meet – Bernard Tufts. No, his own name didn't matter, but when asked it, Tom gave it – Robert Mackay.

'What is the situation now with the islands?' Tom asked at one reasonably decent hotel where he thought they might know something about tourism. Tom spoke in French here, though in other hotels, English had been spoken, a little. 'Icaria in particular.'

'Icaria?' with surprise.

It was considerably east, one of the northernmost of the Dodecanese. No airport. There were boats, but the man was not sure how frequently they went.

Tom got there on Wednesday. He had to hire a speedboat with a skipper from Mykonos. Icaria – after Tom's brief and instantaneous optimism about it – was a crashing disappointment. The town of Armemisti (or something like that) was sleepy-looking, and Tom saw no Westerners at all, only sailors mending nets, and locals sitting in tiny cafés. From here, after inquiring if there had been an Englishman named Bernard Tufts, dark-haired, slender, etc. Tom made a telephone call to another town on the island called Agios Kirycos. A hotel-keeper there checked for him, and said he would check at another hostelry and ring back. He did not ring back. Tom gave it up. A needle in a haystack, Tom thought. Maybe Bernard had chosen another island.

Still, *this* island, because it had been the scene of Derwatt's suicide, had a faint and filtered mystery for Tom. On these yellow-white beaches, somewhere, Philip Derwatt had taken a walk out to sea and had never returned. Tom doubted that any inhabitant of Icaria would react to the name Derwatt, but Tom tried it with the café proprietor, without success. Derwatt had been here scarcely a month, Tom thought, and that six long years ago. Tom refreshed himself at a little restaurant with a plate of stewed tomato and rice and lamb, then extricated the skipper from another bar-restaurant where the skipper had said he would be until 4 p.m., in case Tom wanted him.

They sped back to Mykonos, where the skipper was based. Tom had his suitcase with him. Tom felt restless, exhausted and frustrated. He decided to go back to Athens tonight. He sat in a café, dejectedly drinking a cup of sweet coffee. Then he went back to the dock where he had met the Greek skipper, and found him after going to his house, where he was having supper.

'How much to take me to Piraeus tonight?' Tom asked. Tom still had some American travellers' cheques.

Much to-do, a recitation of difficulties, but money solved everything. Tom slept part of the way, tied onto a wooden bench in the small cabin of the boat. It was 5 a.m., or so when they got to the Piraeus. The skipper Antinou was giddy with joy or money or fatigue, or maybe ouzo, Tom didn't know. Antinou said he had friends in Piraeus who were going to be happy to see him.

The dawn cold was cutting. Tom bludgeoned a taxi-driver, verbally, by promising handfuls of money, to take him to Constitution Square in Athens, and to the door of the Grande Bretagne.

Tom was given a room, not the same one he had had. They had not finished cleaning that, the night porter told him quite honestly. Tom wrote Jeff's studio number on a piece of paper and asked the porter to put the call through to London.

Then he went upstairs to his room and had a bath, listening all the while for the telephone ringing. It was a quarter to 8 a.m. before the call came through.

'This is Tom in Athens,' Tom said. He had been almost asleep in his bed.

'Athens?'

'Any news of Bernard?'

'No, nothing. What're you –'

'I'm coming over to London. By tonight, I mean. Get the make-up ready. All right?'

EIGHTEEN

On impulse on Thursday afternoon, Tom bought a green raincoat in Athens, a raincoat of a style he would never have chosen himself – that was to say, Tom Ripley would never have touched it. It had a lot of flaps and straps, some of which fastened with double rings, some of which had little buckles, as if the raincoat had been meant to be weighted down with dispatches, military water-bottles, cartridges, a mess kit, bayonet and a baton or two. It was in bad taste, and Tom thought it would help him on entering London – just in case one of the immigration inspectors actually remembered what Thomas Ripley looked like. Tom also changed the parting in his hair from left to right, though the parting did not show in the straight-on photographs. Luckily, his suitcase bore no initials. Money was now the problem, as Tom had only travellers' cheques in the name Ripley, which he couldn't hand out in London the way he had to the Greek skipper, but Tom had enough drachmas (obtained with French francs from Heloise) for a one-way ticket to London, and in London Jeff and Ed could finance him. Tom removed cards and anything identifying from his billfold, and stuck these things into the buttoned back pocket of his trousers. But he really was not expecting a search.

He survived the Heathrow Immigration Control desk. 'How long are you here for?' 'Not more than four days, I think.' 'A business trip?' 'Yes.' 'Where will you be staying?' 'The Londoner Hotel – Welbeck Street.'

Once more, the bus ride to the London Terminus, and Tom went to a booth and rang Jeff's studio. It was 10.15 p.m.

A woman answered.

'Is Mr Constant there?' Tom asked. 'Or Mr Banbury?'

'They're both out just now. Who is that, please?'

'Robert – Robert Mackay.' No reaction, because Tom had not given his new name to Jeff. Tom knew that Jeff and Ed must have left someone, someone who was an ally, in the studio to await Tom Ripley. 'Is this Cynthia?'

'Y-yes,' said the rather high voice.

Tom decided to risk it. 'This is Tom,' he said. 'When is Jeff coming back?'

'Oh, Tom! I wasn't sure it was you. They're due back in half an hour. Can you come here?'

Tom caught a taxi to the St John's Wood studio.

Cynthia Gradnor opened the door. 'Tom – hello.'

Tom had almost forgotten how she looked: medium height, brown hair that hung straight to her shoulders, rather large grey eyes. Now she looked thinner than he recalled. And she was nearly thirty. She seemed a trifle jumpy.

'You saw Bernard?'

'Yes, but I don't know where he went to.' Tom smiled. He assumed Jeff (and Ed) had obeyed him and not told anyone of Bernard's attempt on his life. 'He's probably in Paris.'

'Do sit down, Tom! Can I get you a drink?'

Tom smiled, and offered the parcel he had acquired at the Athens airport, White Horse Scotch. Cynthia was quite friendly – on the surface. Tom was glad.

'Bernard's always upset during a show,' said Cynthia, fixing the drinks. 'So I'm told. I haven't seen him much lately. As you may know.'

Tom emphatically wasn't going to mention that Bernard had told him Cynthia had rejected him – didn't want to see him. Maybe Cynthia didn't really mean that. Tom couldn't guess. 'Well,' Tom said cheerfully, 'he says he's not going to paint any more – Derwatts. That's one good thing for him, I'm sure. He's hated it, he says.'

Cynthia handed Tom his drink. 'It's a ghastly business. *Ghastly*!'

It was, Tom knew. Ghastly. Cynthia's visible shudder brought it home to Tom. A murder, lies, fraud – yes it was a ghastly business. 'Well – unfortunately it's gone this far,' Tom said, 'but it won't go further. This is Derwatt's final appearance, you might say. Unless Jeff and Ed have decided they – they don't want to me to play him any more. Even now, I mean.'

Cynthia seemed to pay no attention to this. It was odd. Tom had sat down, but Cynthia walked slowly up and down the floor, and seemed to be listening for the footsteps of Jeff and Ed on the stairs. 'What happened to the man called Murchison? His wife is arriving tomorrow, I think. Jeff and Ed think.'

'I don't know. I can't help you,' Tom said quite calmly. He could not afford to let Cynthia's questions upset him. He had work to do. Good God, the wife arriving tomorrow.

'Murchison knows the paintings are being forged. What did he base that on, exactly?'

'*His* opinion,' Tom said, and shrugged. 'Oh, he talked about the spirit of a painting, the personality – I doubt if he could have convinced a London expert. Who knows where the line divides between Derwatt and Bernard now frankly? Tedious bastards, these self-appointed art critics. Just about as amusing to listen to as art reviews are to read – spatial concepts, plastic values and all that jazz.' Tom laughed, shot his cuffs, and this time they shot. 'Murchison saw mine at home, one genuine and one of Bernard's. Naturally, I tried to discourage him, and if I may say so, I think I did. I don't think he was going to keep his appointment with – with the man at the Tate Gallery.'

'But where did he disappear to?'

Tom hesitated. 'It's a mystery. Where did Bernard disappear to? I don't know. Murchison may have had ideas of his own. Personal reasons for disappearing. Or else it's a mysterious shanghaiing at Orly!' Tom was nervous, and hated the subject.

'It doesn't simplify things here. It looks as if Murchison was eliminated or something, because he knew about the forging.'

'That is what I'm trying to correct. And then bow out. The forging has not been proven. Ah, yes, Cynthia, it's a nasty game, but having gone this far, we have to see it through – to a certain extent.'

'Bernard said he wanted to admit it all – to the police. Maybe he's doing that.'

That *was* a horrible possibility, and Tom shuddered a little at the thought, as Cynthia had shuddered. He tossed off his drink. Yes, if the British police crashed in tomorrow with amused smiles, while he was in the middle of his second Derwatt performance, that would be rather a catastrophe. 'I don't think Bernard's doing that,' Tom said, but he wasn't sure of what he said.

Cynthia looked at him. 'Did you try to persuade Bernard, too?'

Tom was suddenly stung by her hostility, a hostility of years' standing, Tom knew. *He* had dreamed up this whole mess. 'I did,' Tom said, 'for two reasons. One – it would finish Bernard's own career, and second –'

'I think Bernard's career is finished, if you mean Bernard Tufts as a painter.'

'Second,' Tom said as gently as he could, 'Bernard is not the only person involved, unfortunately. It would ruin also Jeff and Ed, the – whoever they are making the art supplies, unless they deny knowing about the fraud, which I doubt they could do successfully. The art school in Italy –'

Cynthia gave a tense sigh. She seemed unable to speak. Perhaps she did not want to say any more. She walked around the square studio again, and looked at a blown-up photograph of a kangaroo that Jeff had leaned against a wall. 'It's been two years since I was in this room. Jeff gets more posh all the time.'

Tom was silent. To his relief, he heard faint footsteps, a blur of male voices.

Someone knocked. 'Cynthia? It's us!' Ed called.

Cynthia opened the door.

'Well, *Tom!*' Ed yelled, and rushed to grip his hand.

'Tom! Greetings!' Jeff said, as merry as Ed.

Jeff carried a small black suitcase which contained the make-up, Tom knew.

'Had to call on our Soho friend for the make-up again,' Jeff said. 'How are you, Tom? How was Athens?'

'Gloomy,' Tom said. 'Have a drink, boys. The colonels, you know. Didn't hear any bouzoukis. Look, I hope there's no show tonight.' Jeff was opening the suitcase.

'No. Just checking to see if everything is here. Did you hear anything from Bernard?'

'What a question,' Tom said. 'No.' He glanced uneasily at Cynthia, who was leaning with folded arms against a cabinet across the room. Did she know he had gone to Greece especially to look for Bernard? Was it of any importance to tell her? No.

'Or Murchison?' Ed asked over his shoulder. He was helping himself to a drink.

'No,' Tom said. 'I understand Mrs Murchison is coming tomorrow?'

'She *may*,' Jeff replied. 'Webster rang us up today and said that. You know, Webster the Inspector.'

Tom simply could not speak with Cynthia in the room. He didn't speak. He wanted to say something casual, such as, 'Who bought "The Tub"?' but he couldn't even do this. Cynthia was hostile. She might not betray them, but she was anti.

'By the way, Tom,' Ed said, bringing Jeff a drink (Cynthia still had her drink), 'you can stay here tonight. We're hoping you will.'

'With pleasure,' Tom said.

'And tomorrow – morning, Jeff and I thought we'd ring Webster around ten-thirty, and if we can't get him we'll leave a message, that you arrived by train in London this morning – tomorrow, and rang us up. You've been staying with friends near Bury St Edmunds, something like that and you hadn't – uh –'

'You didn't consider the search for you serious enough for you to inform the police of your whereabouts,' Jeff put in, as if he were reciting a Mother Goose rhyme. 'Matter of fact they weren't combing the streets for you. They just asked us a couple of times where Derwatt was, and we said you were probably with friends in the country.'

'*D'accord,*' Tom said.

'I think I'll push off,' Cynthia said.

'Oh, Cynthia – not the other half of your drink?' Jeff asked.

'No.' She was putting on her coat, and Ed helped her. 'I really only wanted to know if there was news of Bernard, you know.'

'Thanks, Cynthia, for holding the fort for us here,' Jeff said.

An unfortunate metaphor, Tom thought. Tom stood up. 'I'll be sure to let you know if I hear anything, Cynthia. I'll be going back to Paris soon – maybe even tomorrow.'

Mumbled good-byes at the door among Cynthia, Jeff and Ed. Jeff and Ed came back.

'Is she really still in love with him?' Tom asked. 'I didn't think so. Bernard said –'

Both Jeff and Ed had vaguely pained expressions.

'Bernard said what?' Jeff asked.

'Bernard said he rang her from Paris last week and she said she didn't want to see him. Or maybe Bernard was exaggerating, I don't know.'

'Neither do we,' Ed said, and shoved his lank blond hair back. He went for another drink.

'I thought Cynthia had a boy-friend,' Tom said.

'Oh, it's the same one,' Ed said in a bored tone from the kitchen.

'Stephen something,' Jeff said. 'He hasn't set her on fire.'

'He's not the fireball type!' Ed said, laughing.

'She still has the same job,' Jeff went on. 'It pays well and she's Number One girl for some sort of a big shot.'

'She is *settled*,' Ed put in, with finality. 'Now where *is* Bernard, and what did you mean by he's supposed to think you're dead?'

Tom explained, briefly. Also about the burial, which he managed to make funny so that Jeff and Ed were enthralled, maybe morbidly fascinated, and laughing at the same time. 'Just a small tap on the head,'

Tom said. He had stolen Heloise's scissors and cut off the adhesive tape in the loo of the plane going to Athens.

'Let me touch you!' Ed said, seizing Tom's shoulder. 'Here's a man who's climbed out of the grave, Jeff!'

'More than we'll do. More than I'll do,' said Jeff.

Tom removed his jacket and seated himself more comfortably on Jeff's rust-coloured couch. 'I suppose you have guessed,' Tom said, 'that Murchison is dead?'

'We did *think* that,' Jeff said solemnly. 'What happened?'

'I killed him. In my cellar – with a wine bottle.' At this odd moment, it occurred to Tom that he might, that he ought to send Cynthia some flowers. She could toss them in the waste-basket or the fireplace, if she wished. Tom reproached himself for having been ungallant with Cynthia.

Jeff and Ed were still speechlessly recovering from what he had said.

'Where's the body?' asked Jeff.

'At the bottom of some river. Near me. I think the Loing,' Tom said. Should he tell them that Bernard assisted him? No. Why bother? Tom rubbed his forehead. He was tired, and he slumped on one elbow.

'My God,' Ed said. 'Then you took his stuff to Orly?'

'His stuff, yes.'

'Haven't you got a housekeeper?' Jeff asked.

'Yes. I had to do all this secretly. Around her,' Tom said. 'Early in the morning and all that.'

'But you spoke about the burial place in the woods – that Bernard used.' This from Ed.

'Yes, I – had Murchison buried in the woods first, then the police came investigating, so before they got to the woods, I thought I should get him – out of the woods, so I –' Tom gestured, a vague dumping motion. No, best not to mention that Bernard had helped him. If Bernard wanted to – what did he want to do, redeem himself? – the less complicity Bernard had, the better.

'Gosh,' Ed said. 'My God. Can you face his wife?'

'Sh-h,' said Jeff quickly, with a nervous smile.

'Of course,' Tom said. 'I had to do it, because Murchison got onto me – down in the cellar, matter of fact. He realized that I'd been playing Derwatt in London. So it was all up if I didn't get rid of him. You see?' Tom walked about trying to feel less sleepy.

They did see, and they were impressed. At the same time, Tom could sense their brains grinding: Tom Ripley had killed before. Dickie Greenleaf, no? And maybe the other fellow named Freddie something. That was a suspicion merely, but wasn't it true? How seriously was Tom taking this killing, and in fact how much gratitude was he going to expect from Derwatt Ltd? Gratitude, loyalty, money? Did it all come down to the same thing? Tom was idealistic enough to think not, to hope not. Tom hoped for a higher calibre in Jeff Constant and Ed Banbury. After all, they had been friends of the great Derwatt, even his best friends. How great was Derwatt? Tom dodged this question. How great was Bernard? Well, pretty great as a painter, if the truth be told. Tom stood up straighter, because of Bernard (who had avoided Jeff and Ed for years from the point of view of friendship), and said, 'Well, my friends – how about briefing me on tomorrow? Who else is turning up? I admit I'm tired and I wouldn't mind going to bed soon.'

Ed was standing facing him. 'Any clues against you about Murchison, Tom?'

'Not that I know of.' Tom smiled. 'Nothing except the facts.'

'Was "The Clock" really stolen?'

'The picture was with Murchison's suitcase – wrapped separately – at Orly. Somebody swiped it, that's plain,' Tom said. 'I wonder who's hanging it now? I wonder if they know what they've got? In which case it might not be hanging. Let's get on with the briefing, shall we? Can we have some music?'

To souped-up Radio Luxembourg, Tom submitted to a semi-dress rehearsal. The beard, on gauze, was still in one piece, and they tested it but did not glue it. Bernard had not taken back Derwatt's old dark-blue suit, and Tom put on the jacket.

'Do you know anything about Mrs Murchison?' Tom asked.

They didn't really, though they volunteered fragments of information which showed her, as far as Tom could see, neither aggressive nor timid, intelligent nor stupid. One datum cancelled out the other. Jeff had spoken with her by telephone at the Buckmaster Gallery, where she had rung by a cabled pre-arrangement.

'A miracle she didn't ring me,' Tom said.

'Oh, we said we didn't know your telephone number,' said Ed, 'and considering it was France, I suppose it gave her pause.'

'Mind if I ring my house tonight?' Tom asked, putting on Derwatt's voice. 'By the way, I'm broke here.'

Jeff and Ed could not have been more obliging. They had plenty of cash on hand. Jeff put in the call at once to Belle Ombre. Ed made Tom a small strong coffee, which Tom asked for. Tom showered and got into pyjamas. That was better – in a pair of Jeff's house-slippers as well. Tom was to sleep on the studio couch.

'I hope I've made it clear,' Tom said, 'Bernard wants to call it quits. Derwatt will go into permanent retirement and – maybe get eaten by ants in Mexico or devoured by fire, and presumably any future paintings along with him.'

Jeff nodded, started to nibble a fingernail, and whipped it out of his mouth. 'What have you told your wife?'

'Nothing,' Tom said. 'Nothing important, really.'

The telephone rang.

Jeff beckoned Ed to come into his bedroom with him.

'Hello, darling, it's *me*!' Tom said. 'No, I'm in London . . . Well, I changed my mind . . .'

When was he coming home? . . . And Mme Annette's tooth was hurting again.

'Give her the dentist's name in *Fontainebleau*!' Tom said.

It was surprising how comforting a telephone call could be in the circumstances in which he was now. It almost made Tom love the telephone.

NINETEEN

'Is Detective Inspector Webster there, please?' Jeff asked. 'Jeffrey Constant of the Buckmaster Gallery . . . Would you tell the Inspector that I had a ring from Derwatt this morning, and we expect to see him this morning at the gallery . . . I'm not sure of the exact time. Before twelve.'

It was a quarter to ten.

Tom stood in front of the long mirror again, examining his beard and the reinforcement of his eyebrows. Ed was looking at his face under one of Jeff's strongest lamps, which was glaring in Tom's eyes. His hair was lighter than the beard, but darker than his own, as before. Ed had been careful with the cut on the back of his head, and happily it was not bleeding. 'Jeff, old man,' Tom said in Derwatt's taut voice. 'Can you cut that music and get something else?'

'What would you like?'

'*A Midsummer Night's Dream*. Have you got a record?'

'No-o,' Jeff said.

'Can you get it? That's what I'm in the mood for. It inspires me, and I need inspiration.' Imagining the music this morning was not quite enough.

Jeff didn't know anyone, even, who he was sure had it.

'Can't you go out and get it, Jeff? Isn't there a music shop between here and St John's Wood Road?'

Jeff ran out.

'You didn't speak with Mrs Murchison, I suppose,' Tom said, relaxing for a moment with a Gauloise. 'I must buy some English cigarettes. I don't want to push my luck too much with these Gauloises.'

'Take these. If you run out, people'll offer you fags,' Ed said quickly, shoving a packet of something into Tom's pocket. 'No, I didn't speak with her. At least she hadn't sent over an American detective. That might be pretty rough if she did.'

She might be flying over with one, Tom thought. He removed his two rings. He had not, of course, the Mexican ring now. Tom picked up a ball-point pen and tried duplicating the bold DERWATT signature stamped on a blue pencil eraser on Jeff's table. Tom did the signature three times, then crumpled the paper on which he had written it, and dropped it into a basket.

Jeff arrived back, panting as if he had run.

'Turn it up loud – if you can,' Tom said.

The music began – rather loud. Tom smiled. It was *his* music. An audacious thought, but this was the time for audacity. Tom felt aglow now, stood up taller, then remembered Derwatt didn't stand tall. 'Jeff, can I ask another favour? Ring up a florist and have some flowers sent to Cynthia. Put it on my bill.'

'Are you talking about bills? Flowers – to Cynthia. Okay. What kind?'

'Oh, gladioli, if they have them. If not, two dozen roses.'

'Flowers, flowers, florists –' Jeff was looking in his telephone directory. 'From whom? Just signed "Tom"?'

'With love from Tom,' Tom said, and held still while Ed went over his upper lip again with pale lipstick. Derwatt's upper lip was fuller.

They left Jeff's studio while the first half of the record was still playing. It would turn off automatically, Jeff said. Jeff took the first taxi by himself. Tom felt sure enough to have gone on his own, but he sensed that Ed did not want to risk that, or didn't want to leave him. They went in a taxi together, and got out a street away from Bond Street.

'If somebody speaks to us, I happened to meet you walking to the Buckmaster,' Ed said.

'Relax. We shall carry the day.'

Again, Tom went in by the red-painted back door of the gallery. The office was empty, except for Jeff who was on the telephone. He motioned for them to sit down.

'Would you put that through as quickly as possible?' Jeff said. He hung up. 'I'm making a courtesy call to France. The police in Melun. To tell them Derwatt has turned up again. They did ring us, you know – Derwatt, and I promised to let them know if you got in touch with us.'

'I see,' Tom said. 'I suppose you haven't told any newspapers?'

'No, and I don't see why I should, do you?'

'No, let it go.'

Leonard, the blithe spirit who was the front manager, poked his head in the door. 'Hello! May I come in?'

'No-o!' Jeff whispered, not meaning it.

Leonard came in and closed the door, beaming at the second resurrection of Derwatt. 'I couldn't believe my eyes, if I weren't looking at it! Who're we expecting this morning?'

'Inspector Webster of the Metropolitan Police for a start,' said Ed.

'Am I to let anyone –'

'No, not just anyone,' Jeff said. 'Knock first, and I'll open the door, but I won't lock the door today. Now shoo!'

Leonard went out.

Tom was sunk in the armchair when Inspector Webster arrived.

Webster smiled like a happy rabbit with his big stained front teeth. 'How do you do, Mr Derwatt? Well! I never expected I'd have the pleasure of meeting you!'

'How do you do, Inspector?' Tom did not quite get up. Remember, he told himself, you are a little older, heavier, slower, more stooped than Tom Ripley. 'I am sorry,' Tom said easily, as if he were not very sorry and certainly not disturbed, 'that you were wondering where I was. I was with some friends down in Suffolk.'

'So I was told,' said the Inspector, taking a straight chair which was some two yards from Tom.

The venetian blind of the window was three-quarters down, partly closed, Tom had noticed. The light was adequate, even for writing a letter, but not bright.

'Well, your whereabouts were incidental, I think, to those of Thomas Murchison,' Webster said, smiling. 'It's my job to find him.'

'I read something or – Jeff said something about his disappearing in France.'

'Yes, and one of your pictures disappeared with him. "The Clock".'

'Yes. Probably not the first – theft,' Tom said philosophically. 'I understand his wife may come to London?'

'Indeed she has come.' Webster looked at his watch. 'She's due at 11 a.m. After a night flight, I dare say she'll want to rest for a couple of hours. Will you be here this afternoon, Mr Derwatt? Can you be here?'

Tom knew he had to say yes to be courteous. He said, with only a hint of reluctance, that he could be, of course. 'About what time? I have a few errands to do this afternoon.'

Webster stood up, like a busy man. 'Shall we say three-thirty? And in case of a change, I'll let you know through the gallery.' He turned to Jeff and Ed. 'Thank you so much for informing me about Mr Derwatt. Bye-bye, gentlemen.'

'Bye-bye, Inspector.' Jeff opened the door for him.

Ed looked at Tom and smiled a satisfied smile, with his lips closed. 'A little more lively for this afternoon. Derwatt was a little more – energetic. Nervous energy.'

'I have my reasons,' Tom said. He put his finger-tips together and stared into space, in the manner of Sherlock Holmes reflecting, an unconscious gesture perhaps, because he had been thinking of a certain Sherlock Holmes story which resembled this situation. Tom hoped his disguise would not be seen through so easily. At any rate, it was better than some of those exploded by Sir Arthur – when a nobleman forgot to remove his diamond ring or some such.

'What's your reason?' Jeff asked.

Tom jumped up. 'Tell you later. Now I could use a Scotch.'

They lunched at Norughe's, an Italian restaurant in the Edgware Road. Tom was hungry, and the restaurant was just to his taste – quiet, pleasant to look at, and the pasta was excellent. Tom had gnocchi with a delicious cheese sauce, and they drank two bottles of Verdicchio. A near-by table was occupied by some notables of the Royal Ballet, who plainly recognized Derwatt, as Tom recognized them, but in the English style, the exchanged glances soon stopped.

'I'd rather arrive at the gallery alone and through the front door this afternoon,' Tom said.

They all had cigars and brandy. Tom felt fit for anything, even Mrs Murchison.

'Let me out here,' Tom said in the taxi. 'I feel like walking.' He spoke in Derwatt's voice, which he had used throughout lunch, too. 'I know it's a bit of a walk, but at least there're not so many hills as in Mexico. Ah-hum.'

Oxford Street looked busy and inviting. Tom realized he had not asked Jeff or Ed if they had concocted any more receipts for paintings. Maybe Webster would not ask for them again. Maybe Mrs Murchison would. Who knew? Some of the crowd on Oxford Street glanced at him twice, perhaps recognizing hom – though Tom really doubted that – or perhaps their eyes were caught by his beard and his intense eyes. Tom supposed his eyes looked intense because of his brows, and because Derwatt frowned a little, though this had not meant ill-temper, Ed had assured him.

This afternoon is either success or failure, Tom thought. It would be, it had to be a success. Tom began to imagine what would happen if the afternoon were a failure, and his mind stopped when he came to Heloise – and her family. It would be the end of all that, the end of Belle Ombre. Of Mme Annette's kind services. In plain words, he would go to prison, because it would be more than obvious that he had eliminated Murchison. Perish the thought of going to prison.

Tom came head-on with the old bloke with the sandwich boards advertising quick passport photos. As if he were blind, the old man didn't step aside. Tom did. Tom ran in front of him again. 'Remember me? Greetings!'

'Eh? Um-m?' An unlighted half-cigarette again hung from between his lips.

'Here's for luck!' Tom said, and stuck what was left of his packet of cigarettes into the old tweed overcoat pocket. Tom hurried on, remembering to stoop.

Tom walked quietly into the Buckmaster Gallery, where all Derwatt's pictures, except those on loan, were graced with a little red star. Leonard gave him a smile and a nod that was almost a bow. There were five other people in the room, a young couple (the girl barefoot on the beige carpet), one elderly gentleman, two men. As Tom made his way towards the red door at the rear of the gallery, he could feel all eyes turn and follow him – until he was out of sight.

Jeff opened the door. 'Derwatt, hello. Come in. This is Mrs Murchison – Philip Derwatt.'

Tom bowed slightly to the woman seated in the armchair. 'How do you do, Mrs Murchison?' Tom nodded also to Inspector Webster, who was sitting on a straight chair.

Mrs Murchison looked about fifty, with short razor-cut hair that was red-blonde, bright blue eyes, a rather wide mouth – a face, Tom thought, that might have been cheerful if the circumstances had been different. She wore a good tweed suit of graceful cut, a necklace of jade, a pale green sweater.

Jeff had gone behind his desk, but was not seated.

'You saw my husband in London. Here,' Mrs Murchison said to Tom.

'Yes, for a few minutes. Yes. Perhaps ten minutes.' Tom moved towards the straight chair that Ed was offering. He felt Mrs Murchison's eyes on his shoes, the nearly cracked shoes that had actually belonged to Derwatt. Tom sat down gingerly, as if he had rheumatism, or worse. Now he was five feet away from Mrs Murchison, who had to turn her head a little to her right to see him.

'He was going to visit a Mr Ripley in France. He wrote me that,' said Mrs Murchison. 'He didn't make an appointment to see you later?'

'No,' Tom said.

'Do you happen to know Mr Ripley? I understand he has some of your pictures.'

'I've heard his name, never met him,' Tom said.

'I'm going to try to see him. After all – my husband may still be in France. What I would like to know, Mr Derwatt, is if you think there is any *ring* of your paintings – It's hard for me to put in words. Any people who would think it worth their while to do away with my husband to keep him from exposing a forgery? Or maybe several forgeries?'

Tom shook his head slowly. 'Not to my knowledge.'

'But you've been in Mexico.'

'I've talked with –' Tom looked up at Jeff, then at Ed who was leaning against the desk. 'This gallery knows of no group or ring and what is more, doesn't know of any forgeries. I saw the picture your husband brought, you know. "The Clock".'

'And that's been stolen.'

'Yes, so I'm told. But the point is, it's my picture.'

'My husband was going to show it to Mr Ripley.'

'He did,' Webster put in. 'Mr Ripley told me about their conversation –'

'I know, I know. My husband had his theory,' Mrs Murchison said with an air of pride or courage. 'He might be wrong. I admit I'm not such a connoisseur of paintings as my husband. But supposing he *is* right.' She waited for an answer, from anybody.

Tom hoped she didn't know about her husband's theory, or didn't understand it.

'What was his theory, Mrs Murchison?' Webster asked with an eager expression.

'Something about the purples in Mr Derwatt's later paintings – some of them. Surely he discussed it with you, Mr Derwatt?'

'Yes,' Tom said. 'He said the purples of my earlier paintings were darker. That may be so.' Tom smiled slightly. 'I hadn't noticed. If they're lighter now, I think there're more of 'em. Witness "The Tub" out there.' Tom had mentioned, without thinking, a painting Murchison had considered quite as obvious a forgery as 'The Clock' – the purples in both paintings being pure cobalt violet, in the old style.

No reaction from this.

'By the way,' Tom said to Jeff, 'you were trying to ring the French police this morning to say I was back in London. Did the call go through?'

Jeff started. 'No. No, by George, it didn't.'

Mrs Murchison said, 'Did my husband mention anyone besides Mr Ripley he was going to see in France, Mr Derwatt?'

Tom pondered. Start a small wild-goose chase? Or be honest. Tom said very honestly, 'Not that I recall. He didn't mention Mr Ripley to me, for that matter.'

'May I offer you some tea, Mrs Murchison?' Ed asked amiably.

'Oh, no thank you.'

'Anyone for tea? Or a spot of sherry?' Ed asked.

No one wanted or dared to accept anything.

It seemed to be a signal, in fact, for Mrs Murchison to take her leave. She wanted to ring Mr Ripley – she had his telephone number from the Inspector – and make an appointment to see him.

Jeff, with a coolness that was right up Tom's alley, said, 'Would you like to ring him from here, Mrs Murchison?' indicating the telephone on his desk.

'No, thanks very much, but I'll do it from my hotel.'

Tom stood up as Mrs Murchison left.

'Where're you staying in London, Mr Derwatt?' Inspector Webster asked.

'I'm staying at Mr Constant's studio.'

'May I ask how you arrived in England?' A big smile. 'The Immigration Control has no record of your entering.'

Tom looked deliberately vague and thoughtful. 'I have a Mexican passport now.' Tom had expected the question. 'And I have another name in Mexico.'

'You flew?'

'By boat,' Tom said. 'I don't much like aeroplanes.' Tom expected Webster to ask if he had landed at Southampton or where, but Webster said only:

'Thanks, Mr Derwatt. Good-bye.'

If he looked that up, Tom thought, what would he find? How many people from Mexico had entered London a fortnight ago? Probably not many.

Jeff closed the door once more. There were a few seconds of silence while their visitors moved out of hearing distance. Jeff and Ed had heard his last words.

'If he wants to look that up,' Tom said, 'I'll manufacture something else.'

'What?' asked Ed.

'Oh – a Mexican passport, for instance,' Tom replied. 'I did know – that I'd have to hop it back to France at once.' He spoke like Derwatt, but in almost a whisper.

'Not tonight, do you think?' Ed said. '*Surely* not.'

'No. Because I said I'd be at Jeff's. Don't yer know?'

'Good God,' said Jeff with relief, but he wiped the back of his neck with a handkerchief.

'We have succeeded,' Ed said, mock solemn, pulling a hand down the front of his face.

'Christ, I wish we could celebrate!' Tom said suddenly. 'How can I celebrate in this bloody beard? Out of which I had to keep the cheese sauce this *noon*? I've got to wear this beard all evening!'

'And sleep with it!' Ed yelped, falling all over the room with laughter.

'Gentlemen –' Tom drew himself up, and promptly slumped again. 'I must risk, because of need, a ring to Heloise. May I, Jeff? Subscriber Trunk Dialling, so I hope it isn't conspicuous on your bill. Too bad if it is, because I feel this is necessary.' Tom took the telephone.

Jeff made tea, and reinforced the tray with a whisky bottle.

Mme Annette answered, as Tom had hoped she wouldn't. He put on a woman's voice and asked in worse French than his own if Mme Ripley was there. 'Hush!' Tom said to Jeff and Ed who were laughing. 'Hello, Heloise.' Tom spoke in French. 'I must be brief, my darling. If anyone telephones to speak to me, I am staying in Paris with friends ... I expect a woman may ring you, a woman who speaks only English, I don't know. You must give a false number for me in Paris ... Invent one ... Thank you, darling ... I think tomorrow afternoon, but you must not say this to the American lady ... And don't tell Mme Annette I am in London ...'

When Tom hung up, he asked Jeff if he could have a look at the books Jeff said they had made, and Jeff got them out. They were two ledgers, one a bit worn, the other newer. Tom bent over them for a few minutes, reading titles of canvases and dates. Jeff was generous with space, and the Derwatts did not predominate, as the Buckmaster Gallery dealt with other painters. Jeff had entered some titles in different inks after some dates, because Derwatt did not always give his pictures titles.

'I like this page with the tea stain,' Tom said.

Jeff beamed. 'Ed's contribution. Two days old.'

'Speaking of celebrating,' Ed said, bringing his hands together with a subdued clap, 'what about Michael's party tonight? Ten-thirty, he said. Holland Park Road.'

'We'll think about that,' Jeff said.

'Look in for twenty minutes?' Ed said hopefully.

'The Tub' was correctly listed as one of the later pictures, Tom saw, there probably had been no avoiding that. The ledgers were mainly filled with purchasers' names and addresses, the prices they had paid, the purchases genuine, the arrival times sometimes faked, Tom supposed, but all in all, the thought Jeff and Ed had done quite a good job. 'And the Inspector looked at these?'

'Oh, yes,' Jeff said.

'He didn't raise any questions, did he, Jeff?' Ed said.

'No.'

Vera Cruz ... Vera Cruz ... Southampton ... Vera Cruz ...

If it had passed muster, it had passed, Tom supposed.

They said good-bye to Leonard – it was near closing time anyway – and took a taxi to Jeff's studio. Tom felt they both looked at him as if he were some sort of magical personage: it amused Tom, yet in a way he did not like it. They might have imagined him a saint, able to cure a dying plant by touching it, able to erase a headache by waving a hand, able to walk on water. But Derwatt hadn't been able to walk on water, or maybe hadn't wanted to. Yet Tom was Derwatt now.

'I want to ring Cynthia,' Tom said.

'She works till seven. It's a funny office,' Jeff said.

Tom rang Air France first and booked a 1 p.m. flight for tomorrow. He could pick up his ticket at the terminus. Tom had decided to be in London tomorrow morning, in case any difficulties arose. It mustn't look again as if Derwatt were fleeing the scene posthaste.

Tom drank sugared tea and reclined on Jeff's couch, without jacket and tie now, but still with the bothersome beard. 'I wish I could make Cynthia take Bernard back,' Tom said musingly, as if he were God having a weak moment.

'Why?' asked Ed.

'I'm afraid Bernard may destroy himself. I wish I knew where he was.'

'You mean really? Kill himself?' Jeff asked.

'Yes,' Tom said. 'I told you that – I thought. I didn't tell Cynthia. I thought it wasn't fair. It'd be like blackmail – to make her take him back. And I'm sure Bernard wouldn't like that.'

'You mean commit suicide somewhere?' Jeff said.

'Yes, I do mean that.' Tom hadn't been going to mention the effigy in his house, but he thought, why not? Sometimes the truth, dangerous as it was, could be turned to advantage to reveal something new, something more. 'He hanged himself in my cellar – in effigy. I should say he hung himself, since he was a batch of clothes. He labelled it "Bernard Tufts". The old Bernard, you see, the forger. Or maybe the real one. It's all muddled in Bernard's mind.'

'Wow! He's off his rocker, eh?' Ed said, looking at Jeff.

Both Jeff and Ed were wide-eyed, Jeff in his somewhat more calculating fashion. Were they only now realizing that Bernard Tufts was not going to paint any more Derwatts?

Tom said, 'I am speculating. No use getting upset before it's happened. But you see –' Tom got up. He started to say, *the important thing is that Bernard thinks he has killed me.* But Tom wondered, *was* it important? If so, how? Tom realized he had been glad no journalists had been on hand to write, tomorrow, 'Derwatt is back,' because if Bernard saw it in any newspaper, he would know that Tom was out of the grave, somehow, alive. That, in a sense, might be good for Bernard, because Bernard might be less inclined to kill himself, if he thought he had not killed Tom Ripley. Or would this really count, in Bernard's confused thinking just now? What was right and what was wrong?

After seven, Tom rang Cynthia at a Bayswater number. 'Cynthia – before I leave, I wanted to say – in case I see Bernard again, anywhere, can I tell him one small thing, that –'

'That what?' Cynthia asked, brisk, so much more on the defensive, or at least on the protective, than Tom.

'That you'll agree to see him again. In London. It'd be wonderful, you see, if I could just say something positive like that to him. He's very depressed.'

'But I see no use in seeing him again,' Cynthia said.

In her voice, Tom heard the bulwarks of castles, churches, the middle class. Grey and beige stones, impregnable. Decent behaviour. 'Under any circumstances, you just don't want to see him again?'

'I'm afraid I don't. It's much easier if I don't prolong things. Easier on Bernard, too.'

That was final. Stiff upper-lip stuff. But it was also petty, bloody petty. Tom at least understood where he was now. A girl had been neglected, jilted, ousted, abandoned – three years ago. It was Bernard who had broken it off. Let Bernard, under the best of circumstances, try to remedy that. 'All right, Cynthia.'

Would it do her pride any good, Tom wondered, to know Bernard would hang himself again because of her?

Jeff and Ed had been in Jeff's bedroom talking, and had not heard any of the conversation, but they asked Tom what Cynthia had said.

'She doesn't want to see Bernard again,' Tom said.

Neither Jeff nor Ed seemed to see the consequences of this.

Tom said, to bring the matter to a conclusion, 'Of course, I may never see Bernard again myself.'

TWENTY

They went to Michael's party. Michael who? They arrived around midnight. Half the guests were tiddly, and Tom could not see anyone who looked of any importance, as far as he was concerned. Tom sat in a deep chair, actually rather under a lamp, with a long Scotch and water, and chatted with a few people who seemed a little in awe of him, or at least respectful. Jeff was keeping an eye on him from across the room.

The decor was pink and full of huge tassels. Chairs resembled white meringues. Girls wore skirts so short that Tom's eye – unused to such gear – was drawn to intricate seaming of tights of various colours – then repelled. Goony, Tom thought. Absolutely nuts. Or was he seeing them as Derwatt would? Was it possible for anybody to imagine approachable

flesh under those tights that showed nothing but fortified seams and sometimes more panties under them? Breasts were visible when the girls bent
for cigarettes. Which half of the girl was one supposed to look at? Looking
higher, Tom was startled by brown-rimmed eyes. A colourless mouth
below the eyes said:

'Derwatt – can you tell me where you live in Mexico? I don't expect
a real answer, but a half-real answer will do.'

Through his undistorting glasses, Tom regarded her with contempla-
tive puzzlement, as if he were devoting half his great brain to the question
she had asked, but in fact he was bored. How he preferred, Tom thought,
Heloise's skirts to just above the knee, no make-up at all, and eyelashes
that didn't look like a handful of spears pointed at him. 'Ah, well,' Tom
said, ruminating on nothing. 'South of Durango.'

'Durango, where is that?'

'North of Mexico City. No, of course I can't tell you the name of my
village. It's a long Aztec name. Ah-hah-hah.'

'We're looking for something unspoilt. We meaning my husband Zach,
and we have two kids.'

'You might try Puerto Vallarta,' Tom said, and was rescued, or at least
beckoned by Ed Banbury from a distance. 'Excuse me,' said Tom, and
hauled himself up from the white meringue.

Ed thought it was time they slipped out. So did Tom think so. Jeff was
circulating smoothly, maintaining his easy smile, chatting. Commendable, Tom thought. Young men, older men regarded Tom, perhaps not
daring to approach, perhaps not wanting to.

'Shall we blow?' Tom said as Jeff joined them.

Tom insisted on finding his host, whom he had not met or seen for
the hour he had been there. Michael the host was the one in a black
bear parka with the hood not pulled over his head. He was not very
tall and had crew-cut black hair. 'Derwatt, you've been the jewel in my
carcanet tonight! I can't tell you how pleased I am and how grateful
I am to these old ...'

The rest was lost in noise.

Handshakes, and at last the door closed.

'Well,' Jeff said over his shoulder when they were safely down a flight
of stairs. He whispered the rest. 'The only reason we went to the party
is because the people are of no importance.'

'And yet they are, somehow,' Ed said. 'They're still people. Another
success tonight!'

Tom let it go. It was true, nobody had ripped off his beard.

They dropped Ed off somewhere in their taxi.

In the morning, Tom breakfasted in bed, Jeff's idea of a small consolation for having to eat through the beard. Then Jeff went out to pick up something from a photographer's supply shop, and said he would be back at 10.30 – though of course he couldn't accompany Tom to the West Kensington Terminal. It became 11. Tom went into the bathroom and started carefully removing the gauze of his beard.

The telephone rang.

Tom's first thought was not to answer it. But wouldn't that look just a little odd? Maybe evasive?

Tom braced himself for Webster and answered it, in Derwatt's voice. 'Yes? Hello?'

'Is Mr Constant there? . . . Or is that Derwatt? . . . Oh, good. Inspector Webster. What are your plans, Mr Derwatt?' Webster asked in his usual pleasant voice.

Tom had no plans, for Inspector Webster. 'Oh – I expect to leave this week. Back to the salt mines.' Tom chuckled. 'And quietude.'

'Could you – perhaps give me a ring before you go, Mr Derwatt?' Webster gave his number, plus an extension, and Tom wrote it down.

Jeff came back. Tom had almost his suitcase in his hand, so eager was he to be off. Their good-byes were brief, even perfunctory on Tom's part, though they knew, each knew, that their welfare depended on each other.

'Good-bye. God bless.'

'Good-bye.'

To hell with Webster.

Soon, Tom was in the cocoon of the aeroplane, the synthetic, strapped-in atmosphere of smiling hostesses, stupid yellow and white cards to fill out, the unpleasant nearness of elbows in business suits, which made Tom twitch away. He wished he had travelled first class.

Would he have to say to anyone where, as Tom Ripley, he had been in Paris? At least last night, for instance? Tom had a friend who would vouch, but he didn't want to involve another person, because there were enough people already involved.

The plane took off, standing on its tail. How boring, Tom thought, to be jetting at a few hundred miles an hour, hearing very little, letting the unfortunate people who lived below suffer the noise. Only trains excited Tom. The non-stop trains from Paris rocketing by on smooth rails past the platform in Melun – trains going so fast, one couldn't read the French and Italian names on their sides. Once Tom had almost crossed a track where it was forbidden to cross. The tracks had been empty, the station silent. Tom had decided not to risk it, and fifteen seconds later, two chromium express trains had passed each other going like hell, and Tom had imagined being chewed up between them, his body and his suitcase strewn for yards in either direction, unidentifiable. Tom thought of it now and winced in the jet aeroplane. He was glad, at least, that Mrs Murchison was not on the plane. He had even glanced round for her when he boarded.

TWENTY-ONE

France now, and as the plane descended, the tops of trees began to look like dark green and brown knots embroidered in a tapestry, or like the ornate frogs on Tom's dressing-gown at home. Tom sat in his ugly new raincoat. At Orly, the passport control glanced at him and at the picture in his Mackay passport, but did not stamp anything – nor had they when he had left Orly for London before. Only London inspectors stamped, it seemed. Tom went through the 'nothing to declare' aisle, and hopped into a taxi for home.

He was at Belle Ombre just before 3 p.m. In the taxi, he had put the parting in his hair back in its usual place, and he carried the raincoat over his arm.

Heloise was home. The heat was working. The furniture and floors gleamed with wax. Mme Annette took his bag upstairs. Then Tom and Heloise kissed.

'What did you do in Greece?' she asked a bit anxiously. 'And then in London?'

'I looked around,' Tom said, smiling.

'For that *fou*. Did you see him? How is your head?' She turned him around by the shoulders.

It was barely hurting. Tom was much relieved that Bernard hadn't turned up to alarm Heloise. 'Did the American woman telephone?'

'Ah, yes. Mme Murchison. She speaks some French, but very fon-ny. She telephoned this morning from London. She arrives at Orly this afternoon at three, and she wants to see you. Ah, *merde*, who *are* these people?'

Tom looked at his wristwatch. Mrs Murchison's plane should be touching down in ten minutes.

'Darling, do you want a cup of tea?' Heloise led him towards the yellow sofa. 'Did you see this Bernard anywhere?'

'No. I want to wash my hands. Just a minute.' Tom went into the downstairs loo and washed his hands and face. He hoped Mrs Murchison would not want to come to Belle Ombre, that she would be satisfied with seeing him in Paris, although Tom hated the idea of going to Paris today.

Mme Annette was coming downstairs as Tom went into the living-room. 'Madame, how goes the famous tooth? Better, I hope?'

'Yes, M. Tome. I went to the dentist in Fontainebleau this morning and he took out the nerve. He *really* took it out. I must go again on Monday.'

'Would we could all have our nerves taken out! All of them! No more pain now, you can count on that!' Tom was hardly aware of what he was saying. Should he have rung Webster? It had seemed to Tom a better idea *not* to ring him before leaving, because ringing might have looked too much as if he were trying to obey police orders. An innocent man wouldn't have rung, had been Tom's reasoning.

Tom and Heloise had tea.

'Noëlle wants to know if we can come to a party Tuesday night,' Heloise said. 'Tuesday is her birthday.'

Noëlle Hassler, Heloise's best friend in Paris, gave delightful parties. But Tom had been thinking about Salzburg, about going there at once, because he had decided that Bernard might have chosen Salzburg to go to. The home of Mozart, another artist who had died young. 'Darling, you must go. I am not sure I'll be here.'

'Why?'

'Because – now I may have to go to Salzburg.'

'In *Austria*? Not to look for this *fou* again! Soon it will be China!'

Tom glanced nervously at the telephone. Mrs Murchison was going to ring. When? 'You gave Mrs Murchison a telephone number in Paris where she could ring me?'

'Yes,' Heloise said. 'An invented number.' She was still speaking French, and becoming a bit annoyed with him.

Tom wondered how much he could dare explain to Heloise? 'And you told her I would be home – when?'

'I said I did not know.'

The telephone rang. If it was Mrs Murchison, she was ringing from Orly.

Tom stood up. 'The important thing,' he said quickly in English, because Mme Annette was coming in, 'is that I was not in London. Very important, darling. I was only in Paris. Don't mention London, if we have to see Mrs Murchison.'

'Is she coming *here?*'

'I hope not.' Tom picked the telephone up. 'Hello ... Yes ... How do you do, Mrs Murchison?' She wanted to come to see him. 'That would be quite all right, of course, but wouldn't it be easier for you if I came to Paris? ... Yes, it is *some* distance, farther than from Orly to Paris ...' He was having no luck. He might have discouraged her with difficult directions, but he didn't want to inconvenience the unfortunate woman any further. 'Then the easiest is to take a taxi.' Tom gave her the directions to the house.

Tom tried to explain to Heloise. Mrs Murchison would arrive in an hour, and would want to talk to him about her husband. Mme Annette had left the room, so Tom was able to speak in French to Heloise, though Mme Annette could have listened for all he cared. It had crossed Tom's mind, before Mrs Murchison rang, to tell Heloise why he had gone to London, to explain to her that he had twice impersonated Derwatt the painter, who was now dead. But this moment was not the time to spring all that on her. If they got through Mrs Murchison's visit successfully, that was all Tom could demand of Heloise.

'But what happened to her husband?' Heloise asked.

'I don't know, darling. But she has come to France and naturally she wants to speak to –' Tom didn't want to say to the last person who had seen her husband. 'She wants to see the house, because her husband was last here. I took him to Orly from here.'

Heloise stood up with a twist of impatience in her body. But she was not stupid enough to make a scene. She was not going to be uncontrollable, unreasonable. That might come later.

'I know what you're going to say. You don't want her here for the evening. All right. She will not be invited for dinner. We can say we have an engagement. But I must offer her tea or a drink or both. I would estimate – she will be here not more than an hour, and I'll handle everything politely. And correctly.'

Heloise subsided.

Tom went upstairs to his room. Mme Annette had emptied his suitcase and put it away, but there were some things not quite in their usual place, so Tom put them back as they were when he stayed at Belle Ombre for weeks on end. Tom had a shower, then put on grey flannels, a shirt and sweater, and he took a tweed jacket from his closet, in case Mrs Murchison might want to take a stroll on the lawn.

Mrs Murchison arrived.

Tom went to the front door to meet her, and to make sure the taxi was settled correctly. Mrs Murchison had French currency and over-tipped the driver, but Tom let it go.

'My wife, Heloise,' Tom said. 'Mrs Murchison – from America.'

'How do you do?'

'How do you do?' said Heloise.

Mrs Murchison agreed to a cup of tea. 'I hope you'll excuse me for inviting myself so abruptly,' she said to Tom and Heloise, 'but it's a matter of importance – and I wanted to see you as soon as possible.'

They were all seated now, Mrs Murchison on the yellow sofa, Tom on a straight chair, like Heloise. Heloise had a marvellous air of not being much interested in the situation, but of being polite enough to be present. But she was quite interested, Tom knew.

'My husband –'

'Tom, he told me to call him,' Tom said, smiling. He stood up. 'He looked at these pictures. Here on my right "Man in Chair". Behind you "The Red Chairs". It's an earlier one.' Tom spoke boldly. Carry it off or not, and to hell with propriety, ethics, kindness, truth, the law, or even fate – meaning the future. Either he brought it off now, or he did not. If Mrs Murchison wanted a tour of the house, it could even include the cellar as far as Tom was concerned. Tom waited for Mrs Murchison to ask a question, perhaps, about what her husband had thought about the validity of the paintings.

'You bought these from the Buckmaster?' Mrs Murchison.

'Yes, both of them.' Tom glanced at Heloise, who was smoking an un-accustomed Gitane maïs. 'My wife understands English,' Tom said.

'Were you here when my husband visited?'

'No, I was in Greece,' Heloise replied. 'I did not meet your husband.'

Mrs Murchison stood up and looked at the paintings, and Tom turned on two lamps in addition to the other light, so she could see them better.

'I'm fondest of "Man in Chair",' Tom said. 'That's why it's over the fireplace.'

Mrs Murchison seemed to like it, too.

Tom was expecting her to say something with regard to her husband's theory about Derwatt being forged. She did not. She did not make a comment on the lavenders or the purples in either of the paintings. Mrs Murchison asked the same questions that Inspector Webster had, whether

her husband had been feeling well when he left, whether he had an appointment with anyone.

'He seemed in very good spirits,' Tom said, 'and he didn't mention any appointments, as I said to Inspector Webster. What is strange is that your husband's painting was stolen. He had it with him at Orly, very well wrapped.'

'Yes, I know.' Mrs Murchison was smoking one of her Chesterfields. 'The painting hasn't been found. But neither has my husband or his passport.' She smiled. She had a comfortable, kindly face, a little plump, which precluded any creases of age as yet.

Tom poured another cup of tea for her. Mrs Murchison was looking at Heloise. An assessing glance? Wondering what Heloise thought of all this? Wondering how much Heloise knew? Wondering if there was anything to know in the first place? Or which side Heloise would be on if her husband were guilty of anything?

'Inspector Webster told me that you were a friend of Dickie Greenleaf who was killed in Italy,' Mrs Murchison said.

'Yes,' Tom said. 'He wasn't killed, he was a suicide. I'd known him about five months – maybe six.'

'If he was not a suicide – I think Inspector Webster seems doubtful about it – then who might have killed him? And why?' asked Mrs Murchison. 'Or have you any ideas on the subject?'

Tom was standing up, and he planted his feet firmly on the floor, and sipped the tea. 'I have no ideas on the subject. Dickie killed himself. I don't think he could find his way – as a painter, and certainly not in his father's business. Shipbuilding or boat-building. Dickie had lots of friends, but not sinister friends.' Tom paused, and so did everyone else. 'Dickie had no reason to have enemies,' Tom added.

'Nor did my husband – except possibly if there is some forging of Derwatts going on.'

'Well – that I wouldn't know about, living here.'

'There may be a ring of some kind.' She looked at Heloise. 'I hope you understand what we're saying, Mme Ripley.'

Tom said to Heloise in French, 'Mme Murchison wonders if there might be a gang of dishonest people – in regard to Derwatt's paintings.'

'I understand,' Heloise said.

Heloise was dubious about the Dickie affair, Tom knew. But Tom knew he could count on her. Heloise was that curious bit of a crook herself. At any rate, before a stranger, Heloise would not appear doubtful of what Tom said.

'Would you like to see the upstairs of the house?' Tom asked Mrs Murchison. 'Or the grounds before it gets dark?'

Mrs Murchison said she would.

She and Tom went upstairs. Mrs Murchison wore a light grey woollen dress. She was well-built – perhaps she rode horseback or golfed – though no one could have called her fat. People never did call these sturdy sports-women fat, though what else were they? Heloise had declined to come with them. Tom showed Mrs Murchison his guest-room, opening the door widely and putting on the light. Then in a free and easy manner, he showed her the rest of his upstairs rooms, including Heloise's, whose door he opened, without turning the light on, because Mrs Murchison did not seem much interested in seeing it.

'I thank you,' said Mrs Murchison, and they went downstairs.

Tom felt sorry for her. He felt sorry that he had killed her husband. But, he reminded himself, he could not afford to reproach himself for that now: if he did, he would be exactly like Bernard, who wanted to tell all at the expense of several other people. 'Did you see Derwatt in London?'

'I saw him, yes,' said Mrs Murchison seating herself on the sofa again, but rather on the edge of it.

'What's he like? I came within an inch of meeting him the day of the opening.'

'Oh, he has a beard – Pleasant enough but not talkative,' she finished, not interested in Derwatt. 'He did say he didn't think there was any forgery of his work going on – and that he'd said that to Tommy.'

'Yes, I think your husband told me that, too. And you believe Derwatt?'

'I think so. Derwatt seems sincere. What else can one say?' She leaned back on the sofa.

Tom stepped forward. 'Some tea? How about a Scotch?'

'I think I'd like a Scotch, thank you.'

Tom went to the kitchen for ice. Heloise joined him and helped him.

'What is this about Dickie?' Heloise asked.

'Nothing,' Tom said. 'I would tell you if it were something. She knows I was a friend of Dickie's. Would you like some white wine?'

'Yes.'

They carried the ice and glasses in. Mrs Murchison wanted a taxi. To Melun. She excused herself for asking for it just then, but she did not know how long it would take.

'I can drive you to Melun,' Tom said, 'if you want a train to Paris.'

'No, I wanted to go to Melun to speak with the police there. I called them from Orly.'

'Then I'll take you,' Tom said. 'How's your French? Mine's not perfect, but –'

'Oh, I think I can get along. Thank you very much.' She smiled a little. She wanted to speak with the police without him, Tom supposed.

'Was there anyone else at the house when my husband was here?' Mrs Murchison asked.

'Only our housekeeper, Mme Annette. Where is Mme Annette, Heloise?'

She was perhaps in her room, perhaps out for some last-minute shopping, Heloise thought, and Tom went to Mme Annette's room and knocked. Mme Annette was sewing something. Tom asked if she could come in for a moment and meet Mme Murchison.

In a moment or two, Mme Annette came in, and her face showed interest because Mme Murchison was the wife of the man who was missing. 'The last time I saw him,' said Mme Annette, 'm'sieur had lunch and then he left with M. Tome.'

Mme Annette had evidently forgot, Tom thought, that she had not actually seen M. Murchison walking out of the house.

'Is there something you wish, M. Tome?' Mme Annette asked.

But they didn't need anything, and Mrs Murchison apparently had no more questions. Mme Annette a bit reluctantly left the room.

'What do you think happened to my husband?' Mrs Murchison asked, looking at Heloise, then back at Tom.

'If I were to guess anything,' Tom said, 'it would be that someone knew he was carrying a valuable painting. Not a very valuable painting, to be sure, but a Derwatt. I gather that he spoke to a few people about it in London. If someone tried to kidnap him and the painting, they might have gone too far and killed him. Then they would have to hide his body somewhere. Or else – he's being held alive somewhere.'

'But that sounds as if my husband is right in thinking "The Clock" is a forgery. As you say, the picture wasn't very valuable, maybe because it isn't very big. But maybe they're trying to hush up the whole idea of Derwatt's being forged.'

'But I don't believe your husband's picture was a forgery. And *he* was dubious when he left. As I said to Webster, I don't think Tommy was going to bother showing "The Clock" to the expert in London. I didn't ask him, as I recall. But I had the idea he had second thoughts after seeing my two. I may be wrong.'

A silence. Mrs Murchison was wondering what to say or ask next. The only important thing was the people around the Buckmaster Gallery, Tom supposed. And how could she ask him about them?

The taxi arrived.

'Thank you, Mr Ripley,' Mrs Murchison said. 'And Madame. I may see you again if –'

'Any time,' Tom said. He saw her out to the taxi.

When he came back into the living-room, Tom walked slowly to the sofa and sank down in it. The Melun police couldn't tell Mrs Murchison anything new, or they would certainly have told him something by now, Tom thought. Heloise had said they had not rung while he had been gone. If the police had found Murchison's body in the Loing or wherever it was –

'Chéri, you are so nervous,' Heloise said. 'Take a drink.'

'I might,' Tom said, pouring it. There had been no item in the London papers that Tom had seen on the plane about Derwatt turning up again in London. The English didn't think it important apparently. Tom was glad, because he did not want Bernard, wherever he was, to know that he had somehow climbed out of the grave. Just why Tom didn't want Bernard to know this was hazy in Tom's mind. But it had something to do with what Tom felt was Bernard's destiny.

'You know, Tome, the Berthelins want us to come for an aperitif tonight at seven. It would do you good. I said you might be here tonight.'

The Berthelins lived in a town seven kilometres away. 'Can I –' The telephone interrupted Tom. He motioned for Heloise to answer it.

'Shall I say to anyone that you are here?'

He smiled, pleased at her concern. 'Yes. And maybe it's Noëlle asking your advice about what to wear Tuesday.'

'Oui. Yes. Bonjour.' She smiled at Tom. 'One moment.' She handed him the telephone. 'An English trying to speak French.'

'Hello, Tom, this is Jeff. Are you all right?'

'Oh, perfectly.'

Jeff wasn't, quite. His stutter had come back, and he was talking quickly and softly. Tom had to ask him to speak up.

'I said Webster is asking about Derwatt again, where he is. If he's left.'

'What did you tell him?'

'I said we didn't know if he'd left or not.'

'You might say to Webster that – he seemed depressed and might want to be by himself for a while.'

'I think Webster might want to see you again. He's coming over to join Mrs Murchison. That's the reason I'm ringing.'

Tom sighed. 'When?'

'It could be today. I can't tell what he's up to ...'

When they had hung up, Tom felt stunned, and also angry, or irritated. Face Webster again for what? Tom preferred to leave the house.

'Chéri, what is it?'

'I can't go to the Berthelins,' Tom said, and laughed. The Berthelins were the least of his problems. 'Darling, I must go to Paris tonight, to Salzburg tomorrow. Maybe Salzburg tonight, if there is a plane. The English Inspector Webster may telephone this evening. You must say I went to Paris on business, to talk to my accountant, anything. You don't know where I'm staying. At some hotel, you don't know which hotel.'

'But what are you running from, Tome?'

Tom gasped. Running? Running from? Running to? 'I don't know.' He had begun to sweat. He wanted another shower, but was afraid to take the time. 'Tell Mme Annette also that I had to dash up to Paris.'

Tom went upstairs and took his suitcase out of the closet. He would wear the ugly new raincoat again, re-part his hair and become Robert Mackay again. Heloise came in to help him.

'I'd love a shower,' Tom said, and at that instant heard Heloise turn on the shower in his bathroom. Tom jumped out of his clothes and stepped under the shower, which was lukewarm, just right.

'Can I come with you?'

How he wished she could! 'Darling, it's the passport thing. I can't have Mme Ripley crossing the French–German or Austrian border with Robert Mackay. Mackay, *that* swine!' Tom got out of the shower.

'The English Inspector is coming because of Murchison? Did you kill him, Tome?' Heloise looked at him, frowning, anxious, but far from hysteria, Tom saw.

She knew about Dickie, Tom realized. Heloise had never said it in so many words, but she knew. He might as well tell her, Tom thought, because she might be of help, and in any case the state of affairs was so desperate that if he lost, or tripped anywhere, everything was up, including his marriage. It occurred to him, couldn't he go as Tom Ripley to Salzburg? Take Heloise with him? But much as he would have liked to, he didn't know what he would have to do in Salzburg, or where the trail would lead from there. He should take both passports, however, his own and Mackay's.

'You killed him, Tome? Here?'

'I had to kill him to save a lot of other people.'

'The Derwatt people? Why?' She began to speak in French. 'Why are those people so important?'

'It's Derwatt who is dead – for years,' Tom said. 'Murchison was going to – to expose that fact.'

'He is *dead*?'

'Yes, and I impersonated him twice in London,' Tom said. The word in French sounded so innocent and gay: he had 'représenté' Derwatt twice in London. 'Now they are looking for Derwatt – maybe not desperately just now. But nothing falls into place just yet.'

'You have not been forging his paintings, too?'

Tom laughed. 'Heloise, you do me credit. It is Bernard the *fou* who has been forging. He wants to stop it. Oh, it is very complicated to explain.'

'Why must you look for the *fou* Bernard? Oh, Tome, stay away from it . . .'

Tom did not listen to the rest of what she said. He suddenly knew he must find Bernard. He had suddenly a vision. Tom picked up his suitcase. 'Good-bye, my angel. Can you drive me to Melun? And avoid the police station, please?'

Downstairs, Mme Annette was in the kitchen, and Tom said a hasty good-bye from the front hall, averting his head so she might not notice the different parting in his hair. The ugly, but perhaps lucky, raincoat was over his arm.

Tom promised to keep in touch with Heloise, though he said he would sign a different name to any telegram that he sent. They kissed good-bye in the Alfa-Romeo, and Tom left the comfort of her arms and boarded a first-class carriage for Paris.

In Paris, he discovered that there was no direct plane for Salzburg, and only one daily flight of use, on which one had to change planes at Frankfurt to get to Salzburg. The plane to Frankfurt left at 2.40 p.m. every day. Tom stayed in a hotel not far from the Gare de Lyon. Just before midnight, he risked a telephone call to Heloise. He could not bear to think of her there at the house alone, possibly facing Webster, not knowing where he was. She had said she was not going to to the Berthelins.

'Darling, hello. If Webster is there, say I have got the wrong number, and hang up,' Tom said.

'M'sieur, I think you have made a mistake,' Heloise's voice said, and the telephone was hung up.

Tom's spirit sank, his knees sank, and he sat down on his hotel room bed. He reproached himself for having rung her. It was better to work alone, always. Surely Webster would realize, or very much suspect, that it was he who had rung.

What was Heloise going through now? Was it better that he had told her the truth or not?

TWENTY-TWO

In the morning, Tom bought his airline ticket, and by 2.20 p.m. was at Orly. If Bernard were not in Salzburg, where then? Rome? Tom hoped not. It would be difficult to find anyone in Rome. Tom kept his head down and did not look around at Orly, because it was possible that Webster had called someone over from London to look out for him. That depended on how hot things were, and Tom didn't know. Why was Webster calling on *him* again? Did Webster suspect he had impersonated Derwatt? If so, his second impersonation with a different passport to enter and leave England was a slight point in his favour: at least Tom Ripley hadn't been in London during the second impersonation.

There was a wait of an hour in the Frankfurt terminus, then Tom boarded a four-engined plane of the Austrian Airlines with the charming name of *Johann Strauss* on its fuselage. At the Salzburg terminus, he began to feel safer. Tom rode in on the bus to Mirabeleplatz, and since he wanted to stay at the Goldener Hirsch, he thought it best to ring first, because it was the best hotel and often full. They had a room with bath to offer. Tom gave his name as Thomas Ripley. Tom decided to walk to the hotel, because the distance was short. He had been to Salzburg twice before, once with Heloise. On the pavements, there were a few men in Lederhosen and Tyrolean hats, their costume complete down to the hunting knives in their knee-high stockings. Rather large old hotels, which Tom recalled vaguely from his other trips, displayed their menus on big placards propped beside their front doors: full meals featuring Wienerschnitzel at twenty-five and thirty Schillings.

Then there was the River Salzach and the main bridge – the Staatsbrücke was it called? – and a couple of smaller bridges in view. Tom took the main bridge. He was watching everywhere for the gaunt and probably stooping figure of Bernard. The grey river flowed quickly, and there were sizeable rocks along either green bank over which the water frothed. It was dusk, just after 6 p.m. Lights began to come on irregularly in the older half of the city that he was approaching, lights that jumped higher like constellations onto the great hill of the Feste Hohensalzburg and onto the Mönchsberg. Tom entered a narrow short street that led to the Getreidegasse.

Tom's room had a view on the Sigmundsplatz at the rear of the hotel: to the right was the 'horse bath' fountain backed by a small rocky cliff, and in front was an ornate well. In the morning, they sold fruit and vegetables from push-carts here, Tom remembered. Tom took a few minutes to breathe, to open his suitcase, and walk in socked feet on the immaculately polished pinewood floors of his room. The furnishings were predominantly Austrian green, the walls white, the windows double-glazed with deep embrasures. Ah, Austria! Now to go down and have a Doppelespresso at the Café Tomaselli just a few steps away. And this might not be a bad idea, as it was a big coffee house and Bernard might be there.

But Tom had a slivowitz instead at Tomaselli's, because it wasn't the house for coffee. Bernard was not there. Newspapers in several languages hung on rotating racks, and Tom browsed in the London *Times* and the Paris *Herald-Tribune*, without finding anything about Bernard (not that he expected to in the *Herald-Tribune*) or about Thomas Murchison or his wife's visit to London or France. Good.

Tom wandered out, crossed the Staatsbrücke again, and went up the Linzergrasse, the main street that led from it. It was now after 9 p.m. Bernard, if he were here, would be at a medium-priced hotel, Tom thought, and as likely this side of the Salzach as the other. And he would have been here two or three days. Who knew? Tom stared into windows that displayed hunting knives, garlic presses, electric razors, and windows full of Tyrolian clothes – white blouses with ruffles, dirndl skirts. All the shops were closed. Tom tried the back streets. Some were not streets, but unlighted narrow alleys with closed doorways on either side. Towards ten, Tom was hungry, and went into a restaurant up and to the right of the Linzergrasse. Afterwards, he walked back by a different route to the Café Tomaselli, where he intended to spend an hour. In the street of his hotel, the Getreidegasse, was also the house where Mozart had been born. Perhaps Bernard, if he was lingering in Salzburg, frequented this area. Give the search twenty-four hours, Tom told himself.

No luck at Tomaselli's. The clientèle now seemed to be the regulars, the Salzburgers, families enjoying huge pieces of cake with espressos-with-cream, or glasses of pink Himbeersaft. Tom was impatient, bored by the newspapers, frustrated because he did not see Bernard, angry – because he was tired. He went back to his hotel.

Tom was out on the streets again by 9.30 a.m., and on the 'right bank' of Salzburg, the newer half, he rambled in a zigzag, watching out for Bernard, pausing sometimes to look into shop windows. Tom started back towards the river, with the idea of visiting the Mozart Museum in the street of his hotel. Tom walked through the Dreifaltigkeitsgasse into the Linzergasse, and as he approached the Staatsbrücke, Tom saw Bernard stepping off the bridge on the other side of the street.

Bernard's head was down, and he was almost hit by a car. Tom, who wanted to follow him, was held up by a long traffic light, but that didn't matter, because Bernard was in plain view. Bernard's raincoat was dirtier, and its belt hung out of one strap nearly to the ground. He looked almost like a tramp. Tom crossed the street and kept some thirty feet behind, ready to dash forward if Bernard turned a corner, because he did not want Bernard to vanish into a small hotel in a little street where there were perhaps a couple of hotels.

'Are you busy this morning?' asked a female voice in English.

Startled, Tom glanced into the face of a blond floozy who was standing in a doorway. Tom walked on quickly. My God, did he look that desperate, or that kooky in his green raincoat? At ten in the morning!

Bernard kept walking up the Linzergasse. Then Bernard crossed the street and half a block farther went into a doorway over which there was a sign: *Zimmer und Pension*. A drab doorway. Tom paused on the opposite pavement. Der Blaue something, the place was called. The sign was torn off. At least Tom knew where Bernard was staying. And he'd been right! Bernard was in Salzburg! Tom congratulated himself on his intuition. Or was Bernard only now engaging a room?

No, evidently he was staying at the Blaue Something, because he did not appear in the next minutes, and he had not been carrying his duffel-bag. Tom waited it out, and a dreary wait it was, because there was no café near by from which he might watch the doorway. And at the same time, Tom had to keep himself hidden, in case Bernard might look out a front window of the establishment and see him. But somehow people who looked like Bernard never got a room with a view. Still, Tom hid himself, and he had to wait until nearly eleven.

Then out came Bernard, shaven now, and Bernard turned right as if he had a destination.

Tom followed discreetly, and lit a Gauloise. Over the main bridge again. Through the street Tom had taken last evening, and then Bernard turned

right in the Getreidegasse. Tom had a glimpse of his sharp, rather
handsome profile, his firm mouth – and of a hollow that made a shadow
in his olive cheek. His desert boots had collapsed. Bernard was going
into the Mozart Museum. Admission twelve Schillings. Tom pulled his
raincoat collar up and went in.

One paid admission in a room at the top of the first flight of steps.
Here were glass cases full of manuscripts and opera programmes.
Tom looked into the main front room for Bernard, and not seeing him,
assumed he had gone up to the next floor, which as Tom recalled had
been the living quarters of the Mozart family. Tom climbed the second
flight.

Bernard was leaning over the keyboard of Mozart's clavichord, a keyboard protected by a panel of glass from anyone who might wish to press
a key. How many times had Bernard looked at it, Tom wondered?

There were only five or six people drifting about in the museum, or
at least on this floor, so Tom had to be careful. In fact, at one point he
stepped back behind a door jamb, so Bernard would not see him if he
looked his way. Actually, Tom realized, he wanted to watch Bernard to
try to see what state of mind he was in. Or – Tom tried to be honest
with himself – was he merely curious and amused, because for a short
time he could observe someone whom he knew slightly, someone in a
crisis, who was not aware of him? Bernard drifted into a front room on
the same floor.

Eventually, Tom followed Bernard up the next and last stairs. More
glass cases. (In the clavichord room had been the spot, a labelled corner,
where Mozart's cradle had rested, but no cradle. A pity they hadn't put
at least a replica there.) The stairs had slender iron banisters. Windows
were set at angles in some corners, and Tom, awed as always by Mozart,
wondered on what view the Mozart family had looked out? Surely not
the cornice of another building just four feet away. The miniature stage
models – *Idomeneo* ad infinitum, *Così fan tutte* – were dull and rather
clumsily done, but Bernard drifted through them, staring.

Bernard turned his head unexpectedly towards Tom – and Tom stood
still in a doorway. They stared at each other. Then Tom fell back a step
and moved to the right, which put him behind a doorway and in another
room, a front room. Tom began to breathe again. It had been a funny
instant, because Bernard's face –

Tom did not dare pause to think any more, and made for the stairway
down at once. He was not comfortable, and even then not much, until
he was in the busy Getreidegasse, in the open air. Tom took the little

short street towards the river. Was Bernard going to try to follow him? Tom ducked his head and walked faster.

Bernard's expression had been one of disbelief, and after a split-second fear, as if Bernard had seen a ghost.

Tom realized that that was exactly what Bernard had thought he had seen: a ghost. A ghost of Tom Ripley, the man he had killed.

Tom turned suddenly and started back towards the Mozarthaus, because it had occurred to him that Bernard might want to leave the town, and Tom did not want this to happen without his knowing where Bernard was going. Should he hail Bernard now, if he saw him on a pavement? Tom waited a few minutes across the street from the Mozart museum, and when Bernard did not appear, Tom started walking towards Bernard's pension. Tom did not see Bernard along the way, and then as Tom drew nearer the pension, he saw Bernard walking rather quickly on the other side, the pension side, of the Linzergasse. Bernard went into his hotel-pension. For nearly half an hour, Tom waited, then decided Bernard was not going out for a time. Or perhaps Tom was willing to risk Bernard's leaving, Tom himself didn't know. He much wanted a coffee. He went into a hotel which had a coffee bar. He also made a decision, and when he left the bar, he went straight back to Bernard's pension with an idea of asking the desk to tell Herr Tufts that Tom Ripley was downstairs and would like to speak with him.

But Tom could not get past the modest, drab entrance. He had one foot on the doorstep, then he drifted back onto the pavement, feeling for an instant dizzy. It's indecision, he told himself. Nothing else. But Tom went back to his hotel on the other side of the river. He walked into the comfortable lobby of the Goldener Hirsch, where the grey-and-green uniformed porter at once handed him his key. Tom took the self-operating lift to the third floor and entered his room. He removed the awful raincoat and emptied its pockets – cigarettes, matches, Austrian coins mingled with French. He separated the coins, and tossed the French into a top pocket of his suitcase. Then he took off his clothes and fell into bed. He had not realized how tired he was.

When he awakened, it was after 2 p.m. and the sun was shining brightly. Tom went for a walk. He did not look for Bernard, but rambled around the town like any tourist, or rather not like a tourist, because he had no objective. What was Bernard doing here? How long was he going to stay? Tom felt now wide awake, but he did not know what he should do. Approach Bernard and try telling him that Cynthia wanted to see him? Should he talk to Bernard and try to persuade him – of what?

Between four and five in the afternoon, Tom suffered a depression. he had had coffee and a Steinhäger somewhere. He was far up (as the river flowed, up the river) beyond Hohensalzburg but still on the quay on the old side of town. He was thinking of the changes in Jeff, Ed and now Bernard since the Derwatt fraud. And Cynthia had been made un-happy, the course of her life had been changed because of Derwatt Ltd – and this seemed to Tom more important than the lives of the three men involved. Cynthia by now would have married Bernard and might have had a couple of children, though since Bernard would have been equally involved, it was impossible for Tom to say why he thought the alteration of Cynthia's life of more importance than that of Bernard's. Only Jeff and Ed were pink-cheeked and affluent, their lives outwardly changed for the better. Bernard looked exhausted. At thirty-three or thirty-four.

Tom had intended to dine in the restaurant of his hotel, which was considered the best restaurant of Salzburg also, but he found himself not in the mood for such fine food and surroundings, so he wandered up the Getreidegasse, past the Bürgerspitalplatz (Tom saw by a streetmarker) and through the Gstättentor, a narrow old gateway wide enough for a single lane of traffic, one of the original gates of the town at the foot of the Mönchsberg which loomed darkly beside it. The street beyond was almost equally narrow and rather dark. There'd be a small restaurant somewhere, Tom thought. He saw two places with almost identical menus outside: twenty-six Schillings for soup-of-the-day, Wienerschnitzel with potatoes, salad, dessert. Tom went into the second, which had a little lantern-shaped sign out in front, the Café Eigler or some such.

Two Negro waitresses in red uniforms were sitting with male customers at one table. There was a juke box playing, and the light was dim. Was it a whorehouse, a pick-up joint, or just a cheap restaurant? Tom had taken only a step into the place, when he saw Bernard in a booth by himself, bending over his bowl of soup. Tom hesitated.

Bernard lifted his eyes to him.

Tom looked like himself now, in a tweed jacket, with his muffler round his neck against the chill – the muffler that Heloise had washed the blood from in the Paris hotel. Tom was on the brink of going closer, of extending his hand, smiling, when Bernard half stood up with a look of terror on his face.

The two plump coloured waitresses looked from Bernard to Tom. Tom saw a waitress get up with what seemed like the slowness of Africa, with an obvious intention of going to Bernard to ask, eventually, if something was the matter, because Bernard looked as if he had swallowed something that was going to kill him.

Bernard waved his hand negatively, rapidly – against the waitress or him, Tom wondered?

Tom turned and went through the inside door (the place had a storm door), then walked out onto the pavement. He pushed his hands into his pockets and ducked his head, much like Bernard, as he walked back through the Gstättentor, towards the more lighted part of town. Had he done wrong, Tom asked himself. Should he have simply – advanced? But Tom had felt that Bernard would let out a scream.

Tom went past his hotel and on to the next corner, where he turned right. The Tomaselli was a few yards on. If Bernard was following him – Tom was sure Bernard was going to leave the restaurant – if Bernard wanted to join him here, very well. But Tom knew it was something different. Bernard thought he was seeing a vision, really. So Tom sat at a conspicuous middle table, ordered a sandwich and a carafe of white wine, and read a couple of newspapers.

Bernard did not come in.

The big wood-framed doorway had an arched brass curtain rod which supported a green curtain, and every time the curtain moved, Tom glanced up, but the person entering was never Bernard.

If Bernard did come in and walk towards him, it would be because Bernard wanted to make sure he was real. That was logical. (The trouble was, Bernard was not doing anything logical, probably.) Tom would say, 'Sit down and have some wine with me. I'm not a ghost, you see. I spoke with Cynthia. She'd like to see you again.' *Pull Bernard out of it.*

But Tom doubted that he could.

TWENTY-THREE

By the next day, Tuesday, Tom made another decision: to speak to Bernard by hook or by crook, even if he had to tackle him. He would try also to make Bernard go back to London. Bernard must have some friends there, apart from Jeff and Ed whom he would probably shun. Didn't

Bernard's mother still live there? Tom wasn't sure. But he felt he had to do something, because Bernard's air of misery was pitiable. Each glimpse of Bernard sent a weird pain through Tom: it was as if he were seeing someone already in the throes of death, yet walking about.

So at 11 a.m., Tom went to the Blaue Something, and spoke to a dark-haired woman of about fifty at the downstairs desk. 'Excuse me, there is a man called Bernard Tufts – ein Englischer – staying here?' Tom asked in German.

The woman's eyes went wider. 'Yes, but he has just checked out. About an hour ago.'

'Did he say where he was going?'

Bernard had not. Tom thanked her, and he felt her eyes following him as he left the hotel, staring at him as if he were just as odd as Bernard, simply because he knew Bernard.

Tom took a taxi to the railway station. There were probably few planes out of Salzburg airport, which was small. And trains were cheaper than planes. Tom did not see Bernard at the railway station. He looked on platforms and in the buffet. He then walked back towards the river and the centre of town, watching for Bernard, for a man in a limp beige rain-coat carrying a duffelbag. Around 2 p.m. Tom took a taxi to the airport, in case Bernard was flying to Frankfurt. No luck there, either.

It was just after 3 p.m. when Tom saw him. Bernard was on a bridge over the river, one of the smaller bridges that had a handrail and one-way traffic. Bernard leaned on his forearms, gazing down. His duffelbag was at his feet. Tom had not started across the bridge. He had seen Bernard from quite a distance. Was he thinking about jumping in? Bernard's hair lifted and fell over his forehead with the wind. He was going to kill himself, Tom realized. Maybe not this instant. Maybe he would walk around and come back in an hour, in two hours. Maybe this evening. Two women, walking past Bernard, glanced at him with a brief curiosity. When the women had gone by, Tom walked towards Bernard, neither fast nor slowly. Below, the river foamed quickly over the rocks that bordered its banks. Tom had never seen a boat on the river, that he could recall. The Salzach was perhaps rather shallow. Tom, at a distance of four yards, was ready to say Bernard's name, when Bernard turned his head to the left and saw him.

Bernard straightened up suddenly, and Tom had the feeling that his staring expression did not change at the sight of him, but Bernard picked up his duffelbag.

'Bernard!' Tom said, just as a noisy motorcycle pulling a trailer passed by them, and Tom was afraid Bernard hadn't heard him. '*Bernard!*'

Bernard ran off.

'*Bernard!*' Tom collided with a woman, and would have knocked her down, except that she struck the handrail instead. 'Oh! – I'm *terribly* sorry!' Tom said. He repeated it in German, picking up a parcel the woman had dropped.

She replied something to him, something about a 'football player'.

Tom trotted on. Bernard was in sight. Tom frowned, embarrassed and angry. He felt a sudden hatred for Bernard. It made him tense for a moment, then the emotion passed away. Bernard was walking briskly, not looking behind him. There was a madness in the way Bernard walked, with nervous but regular strides that Tom felt he could keep up for hours until he simply dropped. Or would Bernard ever simply drop? It was curious, Tom thought, that he felt Bernard was as much a kind of ghost as Bernard apparently thought he was.

Bernard began to zigzag meaninglessly in the streets, but he stayed rather close to the river. They walked for half an hour, and now they had left the town proper behind them. The streets were thin now, with an occasional florist's shop, woods, gardens, a residence, a tiny *Konditorei* with a now empty terrace giving a view of the river. Bernard at last went into one of these.

Tom slowed his steps. He was not tired or out of breath after all his fast walking. He felt odd. Only the pleasant coolness of the wind on his forehead reminded him that he was still among the living.

The little square café had glass walls, and Tom could see that Bernard was seated at a table with a glass of red wine in front of him. The place was empty, save for a skinny and rather elderly waitress in black uniform with a white apron. Tom smiled, relieved, and without thinking or pondering anything, he opened the door and went in. Now Bernard looked at him as if he were a bit surprised, puzzled (Bernard was frowning), but there was not the same terror.

Tom smiled a little and nodded. He didn't know why he nodded. Was it a greeting? Was it an affirmation? If so, an affirmation of what? Tom imagined pulling out a chair, sitting down with Bernard and saying, 'Bernard, I'm not a ghost. There wasn't much earth on top of me and I dug my way out. Funny, isn't it? I was just in London and I saw Cynthia and she said ...' And he imagined lifting a glass of wine also, and he would slap Bernard on the sleeve of his raincoat and Bernard would know that Tom was real. But it was not happening. Bernard's expression changed to one of weariness and, Tom thought, hostility. Tom felt again a slight pique of anger. Tom stood up straighter, and opened the door behind him and stepped smoothly and gracefully out, though he did it backwards.

That had been rather deliberate on his part, Tom realized.

The waitress in the black uniform had not glanced at Tom, because presumably she had not seen him. She had been doing something at the counter on Tom's right.

Tom crossed the road, walking away from the café where Bernard was, and farther away from Salzburg. The café was on the land side, not the river side of the street, so Tom was now quite near the river and its embankment. There was a telephone booth full of glass panels near the kerb, and Tom took refuge behind this. He lit a French cigarette.

Bernard came out of the café, and Tom walked slowly around the booth, keeping it between him and Bernard. Bernard was looking for him, but his glances seemed merely nervous, as if he did not really expect to see Tom. At any rate, Bernard did not see him, and kept on walking rather quickly in a direction away from the town of Salzburg and on the land side of the street. Tom eventually followed him.

The mountains rose up ahead, cut by the narrowing Salzach, mountains covered with dark-green trees, mainly pine. It was still a pavement that they walked on, but Tom could see where it finished ahead, and the road became a two-lane country road. Was Bernard going to walk straight up some mountain with his crazy energy? Bernard glanced behind him once or twice, so Tom stayed out of sight – at least from a glance – and Tom could tell from Bernard's behaviour that he had not seen him.

They must be eight kilometres from Salzburg, Tom thought, and paused to wipe his forehead, to loosen his tie under his muffler. Bernard moved out of sight around a curve in the road, and Tom walked on. Tom ran in fact, thinking as he had thought in Salzburg that Bernard might walk right or left and disappear somewhere that Tom could not find him.

Tom saw him. Bernard looked behind him in that instant, and Tom stopped and held both his arms out sideways – to be better seen. But Bernard turned away as quickly as he had turned away several times before, and Tom was left with a feeling of doubt: had Bernard seen him or not? Did it even matter? Tom walked on. Bernard had again disappeared around a curve, and again Tom trotted. When Tom came to the next straight section of road, Bernard was not in sight, so Tom stopped and listened, in case Bernard had gone into the woods. All Tom heard was the twittering of a few birds, and from afar the bells of a church.

Then on his left, Tom heard a faint crackling of branches, which soon stopped. Tom walked a few feet into the woods, and listened.

'Bernard!' Tom yelled, his voice hoarse. Surely Bernard heard that.

There seemed to be complete silence. Was Bernard hesitating?

Then there was a remote thud. Or had Tom imagined it?

Tom walked farther into the woods. Some twenty yards in, there was a slope down towards the river, and beyond this a cliff of light grey rock, which went down thirty or forty feet, it seemed, and perhaps more. At the top of this cliff was Bernard's duffelbag, and Tom knew at once what had happened. Tom went closer, listening, but even the birds seemed silent just now. At the edge of the cliff, Tom looked down. It was not sheer, and Bernard would have had to walk or start falling down a slope of rocks before he jumped or simply toppled over.

'Bernard?'

Tom moved to the left, where it was safer to look down. By clinging to a small tree, and with another tree in sight in case he slipped and had to catch hold of something, Tom looked down and saw a grey, elongated form on the stones below, one arm flung out. It was something like a four-storey drop, and onto rocks. Bernard was not moving. Tom made his way back to safer ground.

He picked up the duffelbag, a pitiably light weight.

It was a few moments before Tom could think of anything at all. He was still holding the duffelbag.

Was anyone going to find Bernard? From the river, could anyone see him? But who was ever on the river? It was not likely that a hiker would see him or come across him, not soon, anyway. Tom could not face going closer to Bernard now, looking at him. Tom knew he was dead.

It had been a curious murder.

Tom walked back along the downward sloping road towards Salzburg, and he encountered no one. Somewhere, down near the town, Tom saw a bus and hailed it. He had not much idea where he was, but the bus seemed to be going in the Salzburg direction.

The driver asked Tom if he were going to a certain place, a name which Tom did not know.

'Nearer Salzburg,' Tom said.

The driver took a few Schillings from him.

Tom got off as soon as he recognized something. Then he walked.

Finally, he was trudging across Residenzplatz, then into the Getreidegasse, carrying Bernard's duffelbag.

He entered the Goldener Hirsch, breathed suddenly the pleasant scent of furniture wax, the aroma of comfort and tranquillity.

'Good evening, sir,' said the porter, and handed Tom his key.

TWENTY-FOUR

Tom awakened from a dream of frustration in which some eight people (only one of whom was recognizable, Jeff Constant) in some house, mocked him and chuckled, because nothing went right for him, he was late for something, he had difficulty settling a bill he owed, he was in shorts when he should have been in trousers, he had forgotten an important engagement. The depression caused by the dream lingered for minutes after he had sat up. Tom put out his hand and touched the thick, polished wood of his night-table.

Then he ordered a Kaffee Komplett.

The first sips of coffee helped. He had been vacillating between doing something about Bernard – what? – and ringing Jeff and Ed to tell them what had happened. Jeff might be more articulate, but Tom doubted if either he or Ed could come up with an idea about the next move he should make. Tom felt anxious, with the kind of anxiety that got him nowhere. The reason he had to speak with Jeff and Ed was simply that he felt scared and alone.

Rather than wait in a noisy, crowded post office, Tom lifted his telephone and gave Jeff's number in London. The next half hour or so while he waited for the call was a curious but not unpleasant limbo. Tom began to realize that he had willed or wished Bernard's suicide, while at the same time, since he had known Bernard was going to kill himself, Tom could hardly accuse himself of forcing suicide upon Bernard. On the contrary, Tom had showed himself pretty clearly alive – several times – unless Bernard had preferred to see a ghost. Also Bernard's suicide had not much and maybe nothing to do with Tom's belief that he had killed him. Hadn't Bernard hanged himself as a dummy already in Tom's cellar, days before Bernard attacked him in the woods?

Tom also realized that he wanted Bernard's corpse, and that this had been in the back of his mind. If he used the corpse as Derwatt's, this would leave the question of what happened to Bernard Tufts. Settle that problem later, Tom thought.

The telephone rang and Tom leapt for it. Jeff spoke.

'This is Tom. In Salzburg. Can you hear me?'

The connection was excellent.

'Bernard – Bernard's dead. Down a cliff. He jumped.'

'You don't mean it. He's killed himself?'

'Yes. I saw him. What's happening in London?'

'They're – The police are looking for Derwatt. They don't know where he is in London or – or elsewhere,' Jeff said, stuttering.

'We've got to make an end of Derwatt,' Tom said, 'and this is a good chance to. Don't mention Bernard's death to the police.'

Jeff didn't understand.

The next exchanges were awkward, because Tom could not tell Jeff what he intended to do. Tom conveyed that he would somehow get Bernard's remains out of Austria and possibly into France.

'You mean – Where is he? He's still lying there?'

'Nobody's seen him. I'll simply have to do it,' Tom said with laborious and painful patience, trying to reply to Jeff's blunt or half-formed questions, 'as if he incinerated himself or wanted to be incinerated. There's no other way, is there?' Not if he tried once more to help Derwatt Ltd.

'No.' Helpful as usual, Jeff.

'I will soon notify the French police, and Webster if he's still there,' Tom said more firmly.

'Oh, Webster's back. They're looking for Derwatt *here* and one man – a plain-clothes man yesterday suggested that Derwatt could have been impersonated by someone.'

'Are they onto *me* about it?' Tom asked anxiously, but with a rush of defiance.

'No, they're not, Tom. I don't think so. But somebody – I'm not sure if it was Webster – said they were wondering where you were in Paris,' Jeff added, 'I think they've checked the Paris hotels.'

'Just now,' Tom said, 'you don't know where *I* am, naturally, and you must say that Derwatt seemed depressed. You have no idea where he might have gone.'

Seconds later, they had hung up. If the police investigated at some later date Tom's doings in Salzburg, and found this call on his bill, Tom would say he had rung because of Derwatt. He would have to create a story that he followed Derwatt to Salzburg, for some reason. Bernard would have to figure in the story, too. If Derwatt for instance –

Derwatt, depressed and disturbed by Murchison's disappearance and possible death, might have rung Tom Ripley at Belle Ombre. Derwatt could also have known, through Jeff and Ed, that Bernard had visited Belle Ombre. Derwatt might have proposed that they meet in Salzburg, where Derwatt wanted to go. (Or Tom might attribute to Bernard that suggestion of Salzburg.) Tom would say that he saw Derwatt at least two or three times in Salzburg, probably with Bernard. Derwatt was depressed. Why, particularly? Well, Derwatt had not told Tom everything. Derwatt had spoken little about Mexico, but had asked about Murchison, and had said that his trip to London had been a mistake. In Salzburg, Derwatt had insisted on going to out-of-the-way places to drink coffee, to have a bowl of gulyassuppe, or a bottle of Grinzing. True to his character, Derwatt had not told Tom where he was stopping in Salzburg, had always left Tom and walked off alone when they had said good-bye. Tom had assumed he was staying somewhere under another name.

Tom would say that he had not wished to tell even Heloise that he was going to Salzburg in order to meet Derwatt.

The story, so far as it went, began to fall into place.

Tom opened his window onto Sigmundsplatz, which was now filled with pushcarts displaying huge white radishes, bright oranges and apples. People stood dipping long sausages into mustard on paper plates.

Perhaps now he could face Bernard's duffelbag. Tom knelt on the floor and opened the zipper. A soiled shirt was on top. Below were shorts and a singlet. Tom tossed them onto the floor. Then he turned the key in his door – though unlike the staff of many hotels, the maids did not come plunging in without knocking here. Tom continued. A *Salzburger Nachrichten* two days old, a London *Times* of the same age. Toothbrush, razor, a much-used hairbrush, a pair of beige chino pants rolled up, and at the bottom the worn brown notebook that Bernard had produced to read from at Belle Ombre. Below this was a drawing pad with a spiral binding, on its cover the Derwatt signature that was the trademark of the art supply company. Tom opened it. Baroque churches and towers of Salzburg, some rather leaning, embellished with extra curlicues. Birds resembling bats flew above some of them. Shadows had been achieved here and there by a wetted thumb moved across the paper. One sketch had been heavily crossed out. In a corner of the duffelbag was a bottle of India ink, the top of its cork broken off, but still the cork was holding, and a bundle of drawing-pens and a couple of brushes held together by a rubber band. Tom dared to open the brown notebook to see if there were any late entries. Nothing since October 5th of this year, but Tom could not read it now. He detested reading other people's letters or personal papers. But he recognized the folded notepaper of Belle Ombre, two sheets. This was what Bernard had written the first evening at Tom's house, and at a glance Tom saw that it was an account of Bernard's forging, beginning six years ago. Tom did not want to read it, and tore the pages into small bits which he dropped into the wastebasket. Tom put the things back into the duffelbag, zipped it, and set it into his closet.

How to buy gasoline, petrol, to burn the corpse?

He could say his car had run out. It couldn't all be done today, certainly, because the only plane was at 2.40 p.m. going towards Paris. He had a return ticket. He could, of course, take a train, but would the luggage inspection be more severe? Tom didn't want a customs inspector to open a suitcase and find a parcel of ashes.

Would a corpse burn enough, in the open, to become ashes? Didn't it require a sort of oven? To augment the heat?

Tom left his hotel shortly before noon. Across the river, he bought a smallish pigskin suitcase at a shop in the Schwarzstrasse, and bought also several newspapers and put them into the suitcase. It was a cool, gusty day, though there was sunlight. Tom caught a bus going up the river on the old side of the town, in the direction of Mariaplain and Bergheim, two towns on the way which he had looked up. Tom got off in what he thought was the right area, and began to look for a petrol station. It took him twenty minutes to find one. He left the new suitcase in the woods before approaching the station.

The attendant was courteous and offered to drive him to his car, but Tom said it was not far, and could he purchase the container also, because he didn't want to come back? Tom bought ten litres. He did not look back as he walked up the road. He picked up his suitcase. He was, at least, on the right road, but it was a long walk, and he twice investigated areas in the woods which were not the right ones.

At last he found the spot. He saw the grey rocks ahead. Tom left the suitcase and descended with the petrol in a roundabout way. Blood had run in wild little veins to right and left below Bernard. Tom looked around. He needed a cave, a recess, something overhanging to increase the heat. It would take a lot of wood. He recalled pictures of Indian corpses on high burning ghats. That took a lot of wood, apparently. Tom found a suitable place below the cliff, a sort of cavity among the rocks. The easiest thing would be to roll the body down.

First Tom removed the one ring that Bernard wore, a gold ring with what looked like a worn-out crest on it. He started to hurl it into the woods, but reflected that there was always a chance it would be found at some time, so he pocketed it with an idea of dropping it into the Salzach from a bridge. Next the pockets. Nothing but a few Austrian coins in the raincoat, cigarettes in a jacket pocket which Tom left, billfold in a trousers pocket, and Tom took the contents out and crumpled them, money and papers, and put them in his own pocket to start the fire with, or to toss on the fire later. Then he lifted the sticky body and rolled it. It tumbled down the rocks. Tom climbed down, and pulled the body towards the recess he had found.

Then, glad to turn away from the thing, he began gathering wood energetically. He made at least six trips to the pale little vault he had discovered. He avoided looking at Bernard's face and head, all of which was of a general darkness now. At last he gathered handfuls of dried leaves and twigs, such as he could find, and stuck the papers and money from Bernard's billfold among them. Then he dragged the body onto the heap of wood, holding his breath as he pushed the legs, shoved one arm with his foot, into place. The body was stiff, with one arm extended. Tom got the gasoline, and poured half of it over the raincoat, soaking it. He decided to gather more wood to put on top, before he lit the whole thing.

Tom struck one match and from a distance tossed it.

The flames sprang up at once, yellow and white. Tom – with eyes half shut – found a spot away from the smoke. There was a lot of crackling. He did not look.

Nothing alive was in sight, not even a flying bird.

Tom gathered more wood. There couldn't be too much, he thought. The smoke was pale but abundant.

A car went by on the road, a truck, judging from the grinding sound of its motor. It was out of sight to Tom because of the trees. Its sound faded, and Tom hoped it had not stopped to investigate. But for three or four minutes nothing happened, and Tom assumed the driver had gone on. Without looking at the remains of Bernard, Tom poked branches nearer the flames. He was using a long stick. He felt he was doing things clumsily, that the fire was not hot enough – nowhere near the intense heat needed to cremate a body properly. The only thing he could do, therefore, was make the fire burn as long as possible. It was now 2.17 p.m. Quite a heat came from the fire, because of the overhang, and Tom had to toss branches finally. He did this steadily for several minutes. When the flames died down a little, he could approach the fire, pick up the half burnt branches, and throw them back again. There was still half the can of gasoline left.

With some method in mind, Tom gathered still more wood, from a greater distance, for a final effort. When he had a heap of wood, he tossed the gasoline tin onto the body – which still had a discouragingly bodylike shape. The raincoat and trousers were burnt, but not the shoes, and the flesh, what he could see of it, was black, but not burnt, evidently only smoked. The gasoline tin made a drumlike boom, not an explosion. Tom was constantly listening for footfalls, or twigs crackling, in the woods. It was possible that someone might come because of the smoke. Finally, Tom withdrew a few yards, took off his raincoat and held it over his arm as he sat down on the ground, his back to the burning. Let a good twenty minutes pass, he thought. The bones were not going to burn, not going to collapse, he knew. It would mean another grave. He'd have to get a shovel somewhere. Buy one? To steal one would be wiser.

When Tom faced the pyre again, it was black, ringed by red embers. Tom poked these back. The body remained a body. As a cremation, it had failed, Tom knew. He debated whether to finish the job today or to come back tomorrow, and decided to finish today, if there remained enough light for him to see what he was doing. What he needed was something to dig with. He poked with the same long stick at the body, and found it jelly-like. Tom put the suitcase flat on the ground, in a little clump of trees.

Then he almost ran up the slope towards the road. The smell of the smoke was awful, and in fact he had not been breathing much for several minutes. He could give the search for the shovel an hour, he thought, if it would take an hour. He liked to have *some* plan, because he felt quite lost and inexpert just now. He walked down the road, free of suitcase, empty-handed. After several minutes, he arrived at the stretch of thinly scattered houses, not far from the café where Bernard had had his glass of red wine. There were a few neat gardens, there were glass-enclosed greenhouses, but there was no shovel leaning conveniently against a brick wall.

'Grüss' Got!' said one man, digging in his garden with the kind of narrow, sharp spade Tom could have used.

Tom returned his greeting casually.

Then Tom saw a bus-stop, one he hadn't noticed yesterday, and a young girl, or woman, was walking towards it, towards Tom. A bus must be due. Tom wanted to take it when it came, to forget about the corpse, the suitcase. Tom walked past the girl without glancing at her, hoping she would not remember him. Then Tom saw a metal wheelbarrow full of leaves beside the kerb, and across the wheelbarrow lay a shovel. He couldn't believe it. A small gift of God – except that the shovel was blunt. Tom slowed his steps, and glanced into the woods, thinking that the work-man to whom these things belonged might have disappeared for a moment.

The bus came. The girl got on it, and the bus went on.

Tom took the shovel, and walked back as casually as he had come, holding the shovel as nonchalantly as he might have held an umbrella, except that he had to carry the shovel horizontally.

Back at the spot, Tom dropped the shovel and went in search of more wood. The time was getting on, and while it was still light enough to see quite well, Tom ventured farther into the woods for fuel. He would have to demolish the skull, he realized, above all get rid of the teeth, and he did not want to come back tomorrow. Tom stoked the fire once more, then took up the shovel and began to dig in an area of damp leaves. It was not so easy as with a fork. On the other hand, the remains of Bernard would not be of interest to any wandering animal, so the grave did not have to be deep. When he grew tired, he turned back to the fire, and without pausing brought the shovel down on the skull. It wasn't going to work, he saw. But another couple of strokes removed the jawbone, and Tom raked it out with the shovel. He pushed more wood near the skull.

Then he went to the suitcase and deployed the newspapers over its interior. He would have to take something from the corpse. He recoiled at the idea of a hand or foot. Some of the flesh from the corpse, perhaps. Flesh was flesh, this was human and could not be mistaken for the flesh of a cow, for instance, Tom supposed. For a few moments, he suffered nausea and crouched, leaning against a tree. Then he went directly to the fire with his shovel, and raked out some of the flesh at Bernard's waist. The stuff was dark and a little damp. Tom carried it in the shovel to the suitcase and dropped it in. He left the suitcase open. Then he lay down on the ground, exhausted.

Perhaps an hour passed. Tom did not sleep. He was aware of the dusk closing in around him, and realized that he had no torch. He got to his feet. Another try with the shovel at the head brought no results. Nor would his foot if he stamped on it, Tom knew. It would have to be a rock. Tom found a rock, and rolled it towards the fire. Then he lifted it with a new-found, and perhaps brief energy, and let it drop on the skull. The rock lay there. The skull was crushed under it. Tom pushed the rock off with his shovel, stepping back quickly to avoid the heat of the rosy red fire. Tom poked, and brought forth with his shovel a strange mess of bones and what should have been the upper teeth.

This activity brought a relief, and Tom now began tidying the fire. Optimistically, he felt that the elongated form bore no resemblance even to a human being. He returned to his digging. It was a narrow trench, and soon it was nearly three feet deep. Tom worked with his shovel, and rolled the smoking form towards the grave he had dug. Now and again he smacked out little flames on the ground with his shovel. He checked, before burying the skeleton, to see if he had got the upper teeth, and he had. He buried the remains, and covered it over with earth. Some wreaths of smoke rose up through the leaves that he scattered on at the last. He tore some newspaper from those of the suitcase, and wrapped the bits of bones that contained the upper teeth, picked up the lower jaw also and put it in.

He pushed the fire together and made as sure as he could that embers were not going to pop out and start a fire amid the trees. He dragged leaves back from the fire, so that this would not happen. But he could not afford to spend more time here, because of the growing dark. Tom folded the newspapers in the suitcase around the small parcel, and walked back up the slope, with suitcase and shovel.

When he reached the bus-stop, the wheelbarrow was not where it had been. Tom left the shovel on the kerb, however.

At the next bus-stop, quite a way on, Tom waited. A woman joined him in the wait. Tom did not glance at her.

As the bus rolled and bumped springily, letting passengers off and on with a wheeze of its door, Tom tried to think, and he thought in erratic jumps, as usual. How would it be for all of them – Bernard, Derwatt and himself – to have met here in Salzburg, to have spoken together several times? Derwatt had spoken of suicide. He had said he wanted to be cremated, not in a crematory, but in the open. He had asked Bernard and Tom to do it. Tom had tried to persuade both men out of their depression, but Bernard had been depressed because Cynthia (Jeff and Ed could vouch for that), and Derwatt –

Tom got off the bus, not caring where he was, because he wanted to think while walking.

'Take your bag, sir?' It was the bellhop at the Goldener Hirsch.

'Oh, it's very light,' Tom said. 'Thank you.' He went up to his room.

Tom washed his hands and face, then took off his clothes and bathed. He was imagining conversations with Bernard and Derwatt in various

Salzburg Bier- and Weinstübl. It would have been the first time Bernard
had seen Derwatt since Derwatt had gone off to Greece five or more years
ago, because Bernard had avoided seeing him on Derwatt's return to
London, and Bernard had not been in London during Derwatt's second
brief visit. Bernard had already been in Salzburg. Bernard had spoken
to Tom in Belle Ombre about Salzburg (true), and when Derwatt had
rung Heloise in Belle Ombre, she had told Derwatt that Tom had gone
to Salzburg to see Bernard, or to try to find him, therefore Derwatt had
gone, too. Under what name had Derwatt come? Well, that would have
to remain a mystery. Who knew what name Derwatt was using in Mexico,
for example? It remained for Tom to tell Heloise (but only when and if
someone asked her) that Derwatt had telephoned Belle Ombre.

Maybe that wasn't all perfect and ironed out as yet, but it was a
beginning.

For the second time, he faced Bernard's duffelbag, and now he looked
for recent notes by Bernard. The October 5th note said, 'I sometimes feel
I am already dead. There is curiously enough of me to realize that my
identity, my self has disintegrated and somehow vanished. I never was
Derwatt. But now am I really Bernard Tufts?'

Tom couldn't let that last pair of sentences stand, so he tore out the
whole page.

Some of the drawings had notes on them. A few about colours, the
greens of Salzburg buildings. 'Mozart's noisy public shrine – not a single
portrait of him that one feels is any good.' Then, 'I gaze often at the
river. It's a fast river and that's nice. That's perhaps the best way to
go, off a bridge one night hopefully when no one is around to shout
"Save him!"'

That was what Tom needed, and he closed the drawing-pad quickly
and dropped it back into the duffel.

Were there any entries about him? Tom looked again through the pad
for his name or initials. Then he opened the brown notebook. Most of
this was the copied excerpts from Derwatt's journals, and the last few
entries at the end, made by Bernard, were all dated, all during the time
Bernard had been in London. Nothing about Tom Ripley.

Tom went down to the restaurant in the hotel. It was late, but he
could still order something. After a few bites of food, he began to feel
better. The cool, light white wine was inspiring. He could afford to leave
on tomorrow afternoon's plane. If his telephone call to Jeff yesterday was
questioned, Tom would say he had rung Jeff on his own initiative to tell
him that Derwatt was in Salzburg and that Tom was worried about him.

Tom would also have to say he had asked Jeff not to tell anyone where he was – least of all 'the public'. And Bernard? Tom might have mentioned to Jeff that Bernard was also in Salzburg, because why not? The police were not looking for Bernard Tufts. Bernard's disappearance, surely a suicide and probably in the River Salzach, must have taken place the night of the day Tom and Bernard cremated Derwatt's body. Best to say Bernard had helped him with that.

He was going to be censured for aiding and abetting a suicide, Tom foresaw. What did they do to people who did that? Derwatt had insisted on taking a massive dose of sleeping pills, Tom would say. The three of them had spent the morning in the woods, walking. Derwatt had taken a few pills before they joined one another. It had been impossible for them to prevent his taking the rest and – Tom would have to confess it – he had not wished to interfere with a desire so strong on Derwatt's part. Nor had Bernard.

Tom returned to his room, opened his window, then opened the pigskin suitcase. He removed the smaller newspaper-wrapped bundle, and added more newspaper. It was still hardly bigger than a grapefruit. Then he closed the suitcase lest a maid come in (though the bed had already been turned down), left his window slightly open, and went downstairs with his little parcel. He took the bridge to the right, the bridge with the handrail, where he had seen Bernard leaning yesterday. Tom leaned on the rail in the same fashion. And when there were no passers-by, Tom opened his hands and let the thing drop. It dropped lightly, and was lost to sight soon in the darkness. Tom had brought Bernard's ring, and he dropped this in the same manner.

The next morning, Tom made his flight reservation, and then went out to buy some things, mostly for Heloise. He bought a green waistcoat for her and a Wolljanker of clear blue like the colour of the Gauloise packet, a white ruffled blouse, and for himself a darker green waistcoat and a couple of hunting knives.

This time, his little plane was called the *Ludwig van Beethoven*.

Orly by 8 p.m. Tom presented his own passport. A glance at him and his photograph, and no stamping was done. He took a taxi to Villeperce. He had been afraid Heloise would have visitors, and he was right, he saw from the slumping dark red Citroën in front of the house. The Grais' car.

They were finishing dinner. There was a comfortable little fire going.

'Why didn't you telephone?' Heloise complained, but she was happy to see him.

'Don't let me interrupt you,' Tom said.

'But we are finished!' said Agnès Grais.

It was true. They were about to have coffee in the living-room.

'Have you had dinner, M. Tome?' Mme Annette asked.

Tom said he had, but he would like some coffee. Tom, in quite a normal way, he thought, told the Grais he had been in Paris to see a friend who was in some personal difficulties. The Grais were not inclined to pry. Tom asked why Antoine, the busy architect, was home in Villeperce on a Thursday evening?

'Self-indulgence,' said Antoine. 'The weather is good, I convince myself I am making notes for a new building, and what is more important, I am designing a fireplace for our guest-room.' He laughed.

Only Heloise, Tom thought, noticed that he was not quite as usual. 'How was Noëlle's party Tuesday?' Tom asked.

'Lots of fun!' said Agnès. 'We missed you.'

'What about the mysterious Mur-*chee*-son?' asked Antoine. 'What is happening?'

'Well – they still can't find him. Mrs Murchison came here to see me – as Heloise might have told you.'

'No, she didn't,' said Agnès.

'I couldn't help her very much,' Tom said. 'Her husband's painting, one by Derwatt, was stolen at Orly also.' No harm in telling that, Tom thought, because it was true and it had been in the papers.

After his coffee, Tom excused himself, saying he wanted to open his suitcase, and he would be back in a moment. To his annoyance, Mme Annette had carried his suitcases up, and his casual request to leave them downstairs had gone unheeded. Upstairs, Tom was relieved to see that Mme Annette had not opened either of the suitcases, probably because she had enough to do downstairs. Tom set the new pigskin suitcase into a closet, and opened the lid of the other suitcase, which was full of his new purchases. Then he went downstairs.

The Grais were early risers, and left before eleven.

'Did Webster ring again?' Tom asked Heloise.

'No.' She said softly in English, 'Is it all right if Mme Annette knows you were in Salzburg?'

Tom smiled, a smile of relief because of Heloise's efficiency. 'Yes. In fact now you must say I was there.' Tom wanted to explain, but he couldn't tell Heloise about Bernard's remains tonight, or maybe any night. The ashes of Derwatt–Bernard. 'I'll explain later. But now I must ring London.' Tom took the telephone and put in a call to Jeff's studio.

'What happened in Salzburg? Did you see the *fou*?' Heloise demanded, with more concern for Tom than annoyance with Bernard.

Tom glanced towards the kitchen, but Mme Annette had said good night and closed the door. 'The *fou* is dead. A suicide.'

'*Vraiment*! You are not joking, Tome?'

But Heloise knew he wasn't joking. 'The important thing – to tell anybody – is that I went to Salzburg.' Tom knelt on the floor beside her chair, put his head in her lap for a second, then stood up and kissed her on both cheeks. 'Darling, I've got to say Derwatt is dead, too, also in Salzburg. And – in case you are asked, Derwatt rang Belle Ombre from London, and asked if he could see me. So you told him, "Tom went to Salzburg." All right? It's easy to remember, because it is the truth.'

Heloise looked at him askance, a little mischievously. 'What is true, what is not true?'

Her tone sounded oddly philosophic. It was indeed a question for philosophers, and why should he and Heloise bother about it? 'Come upstairs and I'll prove I was in Salzburg.' He pulled Heloise up from her chair.

They went up to Tom's room and looked at the things in his suitcase. Heloise tried on the green waistcoat. She embraced the blue jacket. She tried it on, and it fitted.

'And you've bought a new suitcase!' she said, seeing the brown pigskin in his closet.

'That's quite ordinary,' Tom said in French, as the telephone rang. He waved her away from the suitcase. Tom was told that Jeff's telephone did not answer, and Tom asked the operator to keep trying. It was nearing midnight.

Tom took a shower, while Heloise talked to him. 'Bernard is *dead*?' she asked.

Tom was rinsing soap off, delighted to be home, to feel a tub he was acquainted with under his feet. He put on silk pyjamas. He did not know where to begin explaining. The telephone rang. 'If you listen,' Tom said, 'you will understand.'

'Hello?' Jeff's voice said.

Tom stood up straight and tense, and his voice was serious. 'Hello. Tom here. I'm ringing to say that Derwatt is dead ... He died in Salzburg ...'

Jeff stammered, as if his telephone were being tapped, and Tom continued like an ordinary honest citizen:

'I haven't yet told the police anywhere. The death – it was in circumstances I don't care to describe over the telephone.'

'Are you – c-coming to London?'

'I am not, no. But would you speak to Webster and tell him I rang you, that I went to Salzburg to find Bernard ... Well, never mind Bernard just now, except for one important thing. Can you get into his studio and destroy every sign of Derwatt?'

Jeff understood. He and Ed knew the superintendent. They could get the keys. They could say that Bernard needed something. And this would account, Tom hoped, for sketches, the unfinished canvases possibly, that they might have to carry out.

'Do a thorough job,' Tom said. 'To continue, Derwatt is supposed to have rung my wife a few days ago. My wife told him I'd gone to Salzburg.'

'Yes, but why did –'

Why did Derwatt want to go to Salzburg, Tom supposed Jeff was going to ask. 'I think the important thing is that I'm ready to see Webster here. In fact I want to see him. I have news.'

Tom hung up and turned to Heloise. He smiled, hardly daring to smile. And yet, wasn't he going to succeed?

'What do you mean,' Heloise asked in English, 'Derwatt died in Salzburg, when he died three years ago in Greece, you told me?'

'He's got to be proven to be dead. You know, darling, I did all this to preserve the – the honour of Philip Derwatt.'

'How can one kill a man already dead?'

'Can you leave that to me? I have –' Tom looked at his wristwatch on his night-table. 'I have thirty minutes' work to do tonight and after that I would love to join in –'

'Work?'

'Little things to do.' Goodness, if a woman couldn't understand little things to do, who could? 'Little duties.'

'Can't they wait until morning?'

'The Inspector Webster *might* arrive tomorrow. Even in the morning. And by the time you get undressed, almost, I shall be with you.' He pulled her up. She got up willingly, so he knew she was in a good mood. 'Any news from Papa?'

Heloise burst into French saying something like, 'Oh, the hell with Papa on an evening like this! ... Two men dead in Salzburg! You must mean one, chéri. or do you mean any at all?'

Tom laughed, delighted with Heloise's irreverent attitude, because it resembled his own. Her propriety was a veneer only, Tom knew, or surely she'd never have married him.

When Heloise went across the hall, Tom went to his suitcase and took out Bernard's brown notebook and the drawing-pad, and put them neatly on his writing-table. He had disposed of Bernard's chino pants and his shirt in a rubbish bin in a Salzburg street, and of the duffelbag itself in another rubbish bin. Tom's story was going to be that Bernard had asked him to keep his duffelbag while he went off to look for another hotel. Bernard had never returned, and Tom had kept only what was of value. Then from his stud-box, Tom took his Mexican ring that he had worn in London the first time he had impersonated Derwatt. He went downstairs with it, silent and barefoot. Tom put the ring in the centre of what was left of the embers. It might melt to a glob, he supposed, because Mexican silver was pure and soft. Something would remain, and he would add this to Derwatt's – rather Bernard's ashes. He must get up early tomorrow, before Mme Annette cleaned the ashes out of the fireplace.

Heloise was in bed, smoking a cigarette. He did not like to smoke her blond cigarettes, but he liked the smell of the smoke when she smoked them. Tom held Heloise more tightly, when they had turned the light out. A pity he hadn't tossed Robert Mackay's passport into the fire tonight. Was there ever a moment's peace?

TWENTY-FIVE

Tom extricated himself from the sleeping Heloise, withdrawing an arm from under her neck, daring to turn her over and kiss one breast before he eased himself from the bed. She hadn't wakened much, and would probably think he was off to the loo. Tom went on bare feet to his room and got the Mackay passport from a pocket of his jacket.

He went downstairs. A quarter to seven by the clock near the telephone. The fire looked like white ashes, but was no doubt still warm. Tom took a twig and scraped for the silver ring, prepared at the same time to conceal the green passport in his hand – he had bent the passport in half – in case Mme Annette came in. Tom found the ring, blackened and somewhat out of shape, but not the collapsed thing he had expected. He put the ring on the hearth to cool, stirred up the embers, and tore apart the passport. He used a match to hasten the burning of the passport, and watched until it was done. Then he went upstairs with the ring, and put it with the indescribable black and red stuff in the pigskin suitcase from Salzburg.

The telephone rang, and Tom caught it at once.

'Oh, Inspector Webster, hello! ... That's quite all right, I was up.'

'If I understand Mr Constant – Derwatt is *dead*?'

Tom hesitated an instant, and Webster added that Mr Constant had rung his office late last night to leave a message. 'He killed himself in Salzburg,' Tom said. 'I was just in Salzburg.'

'I'd like to see you, Mr Ripley, and the reason I ring so early is because I find I can take a nine o'clock plane. Can I come to see you this morning round eleven?'

Tom agreed readily.

Tom then went back to Heloise's bedroom. They would be awakened – in case Tom slept – in another hour by Mme Annette with her tray of tea for Heloise and coffee for him. Mme Annette was used to finding them both in one or the other's bedroom. Tom did not sleep, but some repose, such as he had with Heloise, was just as restorative.

Mme Annette arrived around 8.30 a.m., and Tom signalled that he would take his coffee but Heloise would prefer to sleep longer. Tom sipped his coffee and thought what he must do, how he must behave. Honest above all, Tom thought, and he went over the story in his mind. Derwatt ringing because he was distressed about Murchison's disappearance (over distressed, oddly, just the sort of illogical thing that would ring true, an unexpected reaction that would sound real), and could he come to see Tom? And Heloise telling him that Tom had gone to Salzburg to look for Bernard Tufts. Yes, best if Heloise mentioned Bernard to Webster. To Derwatt, Bernard Tufts was an old friend whose name he would have responded to at once. In Salzburg, he and Derwatt had been more concerned over Bernard than Murchison.

When Heloise stirred, Tom got out of bed and went downstairs to ask Mme Annette to make fresh tea. It was about 9.30 a.m.

Tom went out to look at the former grave of Murchison. Some rain had fallen since he had last seen it. He left the few branches over it as they were, because they looked natural, not as if someone had tried to conceal the spot, and Tom had no reason anyway to conceal the policemen's digging.

Around ten, Mme Annette went out to do the shopping.

Tom told Heloise that Inspector Webster was due and that he would like her to be present. 'You can say quite frankly I went to Salzburg to try to find Bernard.'

'Is M. Webster going to accuse you of anything?'

'How could he?' Tom replied, smiling.

Webster arrived at a quarter to eleven. He came in with his black attaché case, looking as efficient as a doctor.

'My wife – whom you've met,' Tom said. He took Webster's coat and asked him to sit down.

The Inspector sat on the sofa. First he went through the times of things, making notes. Tom had heard from Derwatt when? November the third, Sunday, Tom thought.

'My wife spoke to him when he rang,' Tom said. 'I was in Salzburg.'

'You spoke to Derwatt?' Webster asked Heloise.

'Oh, yes. He would like to speak with Tome, but I told him Tome was in Salzburg – to look for Bernard.'

'Um-m. At what hotel did you stop?' Webster asked Tom. He had his usual smile, and from his jolly expression, there might have been no death involved.

'The Goldener Hirsch,' Tom said. 'I went first to Paris, looking for Bernard Tufts on a hunch, then I went to Salzburg because Bernard had mentioned Salzburg. He hadn't said he was going there, but he said he'd like to see it again. It's a small town and it's not difficult to find someone you're looking for. Anyway, I found Bernard on the second day.'

'Whom did you see first, Bernard or Derwatt?'

'Oh, Bernard, because I was looking for him. I didn't know Derwatt was in Salzburg.'

'And – go on,' said Webster.

Tom sat forward on his chair. 'Well – I suppose I spoke to Bernard alone once or twice. With Derwatt the same. Then we were a few times together. They were old friends. I thought it was Bernard who was the more depressed. His friend Cynthia in London doesn't want to see him again. Didn't Derwatt –' Tom hesitated. 'Derwatt seemed more concerned with Bernard than himself. I have by the way a couple of notebooks of Bernard's that I think I ought to show you.' Tom stood up, but Webster said:

'I'll just get a few facts down first. Bernard killed himself how?'

'He disappeared. This was just after Derwatt's death. From what he wrote in his notebook, I think he might have drowned himself in the river in Salzburg. But I wasn't sure enough to report that to the police there. I wanted to speak with you first.'

Webster looked a bit puzzled, or benumbed, which didn't surprise Tom. 'I'm most interested in seeing Bernard's notebooks, but Derwatt – what happened there?'

Tom glanced at Heloise. 'Well, on Tuesday, we all had an appointment to meet around ten in the morning. Derwatt had taken sedatives, he said. He'd talked before of killing himself and said he wanted to be cremated – by us, Bernard and me. I at least hadn't taken it too seriously until he turned up groggy Tuesday and sort of – making jokes. He took more pills as we walked. We were in the woods, where Derwatt wanted to go.' Tom said to Heloise, 'If you don't want to listen, dear, you should go upstairs. I have to tell it as it happened.'

'I will listen.' Heloise put her face in her hands for a moment, then took her hands down and stood up. 'I shall ask Mme Annette for some tea. All right, Tome?'

'A good idea,' Tom said. He continued to Webster, 'Derwatt jumped off a cliff onto rocks. You could say he killed himself in three ways, by the pills, by jumping over – and by being burnt, but he was certainly dead when we burnt him. He died from the jump. Bernard and I returned – the next day. We burnt what we could. We buried the rest.'

Heloise came back.

Webster said, writing, 'The next day. November the sixth, Wednesday.' Where had Bernard been staying? Tom was able to say Der Blaue Something in the Linzergasse. But after Wednesday, Tom was not sure. Where and when had they bought the petrol? Tom was vague about the place, but it was Wednesday noon. Where had Derwatt been staying? Tom said he had never tried to find out.

'Bernard and I had promised to meet around nine-thirty Thursday morning in the Alter Markt. Wednesday night, Bernard gave me his duffelbag and asked me to keep it while he found another hotel that night. I asked him to say at my hotel, but he didn't want to. Then – he didn't keep our date Thursday. I waited an hour or so. I never saw him again. He had left no message at my hotel. I felt Bernard didn't want to keep that date, that he'd destroyed himself probably – probably by drowning himself in the river. I came home.'

Webster lit a cigarette, more slowly than usual. 'You were to keep his duffelbag overnight on Wednesday?'

'Not necessarily. Bernard knew where I was, and I rather expected him to pick the bag up later that night. I did say, "If I don't see you tonight, we'll meet tomorrow morning."'

'You asked at hotels for him yesterday morning?'

'No. I didn't. I think I'd lost all hope. I was upset and discouraged.'

Mme Annette served the tea, and exchanged a *'Bonjour'* with Inspector Webster.

Tom said, 'Bernard hung a dummy downstairs in our cellar a few days ago. It was meant to be himself. My wife found it and it gave her quite a scare. Bernard's trousers and jacket hanging from a belt from the ceiling with a note attached.' Tom glanced at her. 'Heloise, sorry.'

Heloise bit her lip and shrugged. Her reaction was indisputably genuine. What Tom had said had happened had happened, and she did not enjoy recalling it.

'Have you got the note he wrote?' Webster said.

'Yes. It must be still in the pocket of my dressing-gown. Shall I get it?'

'In a moment.' Webster almost smiled again, but not quite. 'May I ask why you went to Salzburg exactly?'

'I was worried about Bernard. He'd mentioned wanting to see Salzburg. I felt Bernard might be going to kill himself. And I wondered – why should he have looked me up after all? He knew I had two Derwatt paintings, true, but he didn't know me. Yet he talked very freely on his first visit here. I thought perhaps I could help. Then as it turned out, both Derwatt and Bernard killed themselves, Derwatt first. One doesn't want to meddle somehow – with a man like Derwatt, anyway. One feels one is doing the wrong thing. I don't really mean *that*, but I mean, to tell somebody not to kill himself when one knows it won't be accepted by the other person who's determined to kill himself. That's what I mean. It's wrong and it's hopeless, and why should someone be reproached for *not* saying something, when he knows it's not good to say it?' Tom paused.

Webster was listening attentively.

'Bernard went off – probably to Paris – after hanging himself in effigy here. Then he came back. That's when Heloise met him.'

Webster wanted the date Bernard Tufts had returned to Belle Ombre. Tom did the best he could. October twenty-fifth, he thought.

'I tried to help Bernard by telling him his girl-friend Cynthia might see him again. Which I don't think was true, not from what I could gather from Bernard. I was simply trying to pull him out of his depression. I think Derwatt tried even harder. I'm sure they saw each other alone a few times in Salzburg. Derwatt was fond of Bernard.' Tom said to Heloise. 'Are you understanding this, darling?'

Heloise nodded.

It was probably true that she understood all of it.

'Why was Derwatt so depressed?'

Tom thought for a moment. 'He was depressed about the whole world. Life. I don't know if there was something personal – in Mexico – contributing to it. He mentioned a Mexican girl who had married and gone away. I don't know how important this was. He seemed disturbed because he'd come back to London. He said it was a mistake.'

Webster stopped taking notes at last. 'Shall we go upstairs?'

Tom took the Inspector into his room, and went to the closet for his suitcase.

'I don't want my wife to see this,' Tom said, and opened the suitcase. He and Webster stooped beside it.

The small remains were wrapped in Austrian and German newspapers that Tom had bought. Tom noticed that Webster looked at the dates of the newspapers before he lifted the bundle out and set it on the rug. He put more newspaper under the bundle, but Tom knew it was not damp. Webster opened it.

'Um-m. Dear me. What did Derwatt want you to do with this?'

Tom hesitated, frowning. 'Nothing.' Tom went to the window, and opened it a little. 'I don't know why I took it. I was upset. So was Bernard. If Bernard said we should take some back to England, I don't remember. But I took that. We'd expected ashes. It wasn't.'

Webster was poking in the stuff with the end of his ballpoint pen. He came upon the ring and fished it out with the pen. 'A silver ring.'

'I took that on purpose.' Tom knew the two snakes on the ring were still visible.

'I'll take this back to London,' Webster said, standing up. 'If you have a box, perhaps –'

'Yes, certainly,' Tom said, starting for the door.

'You spoke of Bernard Tufts's notebooks.'

'Yes.' Tom turned back, and pointed to the notebook and the drawing-pad on the corner of his writing-table. 'They're here. And the note he wrote –' Tom went to his bathroom, where his dressing-gown hung on a hook. The note was still in the pocket. *I hang myself in effigy* ... Tom handed it to Webster, and went downstairs.

Mme Annette saved boxes, and there was always a variety of sizes. 'What is it for?' she asked, trying to help him.

'This will do very well,' Tom said. The boxes were on top of Mme Annette's clothes cupboard, and Tom pulled one down. It held a few remnants of knitting wool, neatly coiled, which he handed to Mme Annette with a smile. 'Thank you, my treasure.'

Webster was downstairs, talking in English on the telephone. Heloise had perhaps gone up to her room. Tom took the box upstairs and put the little bundle into it, and wadded some newspaper to fill out the box. He got string from his workroom and tied it. It was a shoe box. Tom took the box downstairs.

Webster was still on the telephone.

Tom went to the bar and poured a neat whisky for himself, and decided to wait to see if Webster wanted a Dubonnet.

'... the Buckmaster Gallery people? Can you wait till I'm there?'

Tom changed his mind and went to the kitchen for ice to make Webster's Dubonnet. He got the ice and, seeing Mme Annette, asked her to finish making the drink and not to forget the lemon peel.

Webster was saying, 'I'll ring you again in about an hour, so don't go to lunch ... No, not a word to anyone just now ... I don't know yet.'

Tom felt uneasy. He saw Heloise on the lawn, and went out to speak to her, though he would have preferred to stay in the living-room. 'I think we should offer the Inspector lunch or sandwiches, something like that. All right, darling?'

'You gave him the ashes?'

Tom blinked. 'A small thing. In a box,' he said awkwardly. 'It is wrapped. Don't think about it.' Tom led her by the hand back towards the house. 'It's appropriate that Bernard should give his remains to be thought of as Derwatt.'

Maybe she understood. She understood what had happened, but Tom did not expect her to understand Bernard's adoration of Derwatt. Tom asked Mme Annette if she would make some sandwiches of tinned lobster and things like that. Heloise went to help her, and Tom rejoined the Inspector.

'Just for formality's sake, Mr Ripley, can I have a look at your passport?' Webster asked.

'Certainly.' Tom went upstairs and came down with his passport at once.

Webster had his Dubonnet now. He looked slowly through the passport, seemingly as interested in months-old dates as in the recent ones. 'Austria. Yes. Hm-m.'

Tom recalled, with a sense of safety, that he had not been to London as himself, Tom Ripley, when Derwatt had shown himself for the second time. Tom sat down tiredly on one of the straight chairs. He was supposed to be rather weary and depressed because of the events of yesterday.

'What became of Derwatt's things?'

'Things?'

'His suitcase, for instance.'

Tom said, 'I never knew where he was staying. Neither did Bernard, because I asked him – after we'd – after Derwatt was dead.'

'You think he just abandoned his things in a hotel?'

'No.' Tom shook his head. 'Not Derwatt. Bernard said he thought Derwatt had probably destroyed every trace of himself, left his hotel and – Well, how does one get rid of a suitcase? Drop the contents in various rubbish bins or – maybe drop the whole thing into the river. That's quite easy in Salzburg. Especially if Derwatt had done it the night before, in the dark.'

Webster mused. 'Did it occur to you that Bernard might have gone back to the place in the woods and thrown himself over the same cliff?'

'Yes,' Tom said, because in some odd way this idea had crossed his mind. 'But I couldn't bring myself to go back there yesterday morning. Maybe I should have. Maybe I should have looked longer in the streets for Bernard. But I felt he was dead – somehow, somewhere, and that I'd never find him.'

'But from what I understand, Bernard Tufts could still be alive.'

'That's perfectly true.'

'Had he enough money?'

'I doubt that. I offered to lend him some – three days ago – but he refused it.'

'What did Derwatt say to you about Murchison's disappearance?'

Tom thought for a moment. 'It depressed him. As to what he said – He said something about the burden of being famous. He disliked being famous. He felt it had caused a man's death – Murchison's.'

'Was Derwatt friendly towards you?'

'Yes. At least, I never noticed any unfriendliness. My talks alone with Derwatt were brief. There were only one or two of them, I think.'

'Did he know about your association with Richard Greenleaf?'

A tremble that Tom hoped was invisible went through his body. Tom shrugged. 'He never mentioned it, if he did.'

'Nor Bernard? He didn't mention it either?'

'No,' Tom said.

'You see, it is odd, you must agree, that three men disappear or die around you – Murchison, Derwatt and Bernard Tufts. So did Richard Greenleaf disappear – his body was never found, I think. And what was his friend's name? Fred? Freddie something?'

'Miles, I think,' Tom said. 'But I can't say Murchison was very near me. I hardly knew Murchison. Or Freddie Miles for that matter.' At least Webster was not yet thinking of the possibility that he had impersonated Derwatt, Tom thought.

Heloise and Mme Annette came in, Mme Annette pushing the cart that held a plate of sandwiches and a wine bottle in an ice bucket.

'Ah, some refreshment!' Tom said. 'I didn't ask if you had a lunch engagement, Inspector, but this little –'

'I have with the Melun police,' Webster said with a quick smile. 'I must ring them shortly. And by the way I'll reimburse you for all these telephone calls.'

Tom waved a hand in protest. 'Thank you, madame,' he said to Mme Annette.

Heloise offered Inspector Webster a plate and napkin, then presented the sandwiches. 'Lobster and crab. The lobsters are these,' she said, indicating.

'How could I resist?' said the Inspector, accepting one of each. But Webster was still on the subject. 'I must alert the Salzburg police – via London because I can't speak German – to look for Bernard Tufts. And perhaps tomorrow we can arrange to meet in Salzburg. Are you free tomorrow, Mr Ripley?'

'Yes – I could be, of course.'

'You've got to lead us to that spot in the woods. We must dig up the – you know. Derwatt was a British subject. Or was he, in fact?' Webster smiled with his mouth full. 'But surely he wouldn't have become a Mexican citizen.'

'That's something I never asked him,' Tom said.

'It will be interesting to find his village in Mexico,' Webster remarked, 'this remote and nameless village. What town is it near, do you know?'

Tom smiled. 'Derwatt never dropped a clue.'

'I wonder if his house will be abandoned – or if he had a caretaker or a lawyer with the authority to wind things up there, once it's known he's dead.' Webster paused.

Tom was silent. Was Webster casting about, hoping for Tom to drop a piece of information? As Derwatt, in London, Tom had told Webster that Derwatt had a Mexican passport and lived under another name.

Webster said. 'Do you suppose Derwatt entered England and travelled about with a false name? A British passport possibly but with a false name?'

Tom replied calmly, 'I always supposed that.'

'So he probably lived in Mexico under a false name also.'

'Probably. I hadn't thought of that.'

'And shipped his canvases from Mexico under the same false name.'

Tom paused, as if he were not very interested. 'The Buckmaster Gallery ought to know.'

Heloise presented the sandwiches again, but the Inspector declined.

'I feel sure they wouldn't tell,' Webster said. 'And maybe they don't even know the name, if Derwatt sent his paintings under the name Derwatt, for instance. But he must have entered England under the false name, because we have no record of his comings and goings. May I ring the Melun police now?'

'But of course,' Tom said. 'Would you like to use my phone upstairs?'

Webster said the downstairs telephone was quite all right. He consulted his notebook, and proceeded to speak with the operator in his adequate French. He asked for the *commissaire*.

Tom poured white wine into the two glasses on the tray. Heloise had her wine.

Webster was asking the Melun *commissaire* if they had any news about Thomas Murchison. Tom gathered not. Webster said that Mrs Murchison was in London at the Connaught Hotel for the next few days, anxious for any information, if the Melun police would pass it on to Webster's office. Webster also inquired about the missing painting 'L'Horloge'. Nothing.

When he had hung up, Tom wanted to ask what was happening in the search for Murchison, but Tom did not want it to appear that he had listened to Webster's words over the phone.

Webster insisted on leaving a fifty-franc note for his telephone calls. No, he thanked Tom, he did not care for another Dubonnet, but he sampled the wine.

Tom could see Webster speculating, as he stood there, as to how much Tom Ripley was concealing, *where* was he guilty, how was he guilty, and where and how did Tom Ripley stand to gain anything? But it was obvious, Tom thought, that no person would have murdered two people – or even three, Murchison, Derwatt and Bernard Tufts, to protect the value of the two Derwatt paintings which hung on Tom's walls. And if Webster should go as far as to investigate the Derwatt Art Supply Company, through whose bank Tom received a monthly income, that income was sent without name to a numbered account in Switzerland.

However, there was still Austria tomorrow, and Tom would have to accompany the police.

'Can I ask you to ring for a taxi for me, Mr Ripley? You know the number better than I.'

Tom went to the telephone and ran a Villeperce taxi service. They would arrive at once, they said.

'You'll hear from me later this evening,' Webster said to Tom, 'about Salzburg tomorrow. Is it a difficult place to get to?'

Tom explained the change of planes at Frankfurt, and said he had been told a bus from Munich to Salzburg, if one landed at Munich, was quicker than waiting at Frankfurt for the plane to Austria. But this would have to be co-ordinated by telephone, once Webster found the time of the plane from London to Munich. He would be travelling with a colleague.

Then Inspector Webster thanked Heloise, and Heloise and Tom accompanied him to the door as the taxi arrived. Webster saw the shoe box on the hall table before Tom could fetch it, and picked it up.

'I have Bernard's note and his two notebooks in my case,' Webster said to Tom.

Tom and Heloise were on their front doorsteps as Webster's taxi drove away, with Webster smiling his rabbit smile through the window. Then they walked back into the house.

A peaceful silence reigned. Not of peace, Tom knew, but at least it was silence. 'This evening – today – can we just do nothing? Watch television tonight?' This afternoon Tom wanted to garden. That always straightened him out.

So he gardened. And in the evening they lay in pyjamas on Heloise's bed and watched television and sipped tea. The telephone rang just before 10 p.m. and Tom answered it in his room. He had been braced for Webster, and had a pen in hand ready to take down the schedule for tomorrow, but it was Chris Greenleaf in Paris. He had returned from the Rhineland and wondered if he could visit, with his friend Gerald?

Tom, when he had finished talking with Chris, came back to Heloise's room and said, 'That was Dickie Greenleaf's cousin Chris. He wants to come to see us Monday and bring his friend Gerald Hayman. I told him yes. I hope it's all right, darling. They'll just stay overnight, probably. It'll be a nice change – a little tourism, nice lunches. Yes? Peaceful.'

'You are back from Salzburg when?'

'Oh, I should be back Sunday. I don't see why that business should take more than one day – tomorrow and part of Sunday. All they want is for me to show them the spot in the woods. And Bernard's hotel.'

'Um-m. Très bien,' Heloise murmured, propped against her pillows. 'They arrive Monday.'

'They'll ring again. I'll make it Monday evening.' Tom got back into bed. Heloise was curious about Chris, Tom knew. Boys like Chris and his friend would amuse her, for a while. Tom was pleased with the arrangement. He stared at the old French film unreeling before them on the television screen. Louis Jouvet, dressed like a Vatican Swiss guard, was threatening someone with a halberd. Tom decided he must be solemn and direct tomorrow in Salzburg. The Austrian police would have a car, of course, and he would lead them directly to the place in the woods, while it was still light, and tomorrow evening directly to Der Blaue Something in the Linzergasse. The dark-haired woman behind the desk would remember Bernard Tufts, and that Tom had once asked for him there. Tom felt secure. As he was beginning to follow the soporific dialogue on the screen, the telephone rang.

'That's no doubt Webster,' Tom said, and got out of bed again.

Tom's hand stopped in the act of reaching for the telephone – only for a second, but in that second he anticipated defeat and seemed to suffer it. Exposure. Shame. Carry it off as before, he thought. The show wasn't over as yet. Courage! He picked up the telephone.

RIPLEY'S GAME

ONE

'There's no such thing as a perfect murder,' Tom said to Reeves. 'That's just a parlour game, trying to dream one up. Of course you could say there are a lot of unsolved murders. That's different.' Tom was bored. He walked up and down in front of his big fireplace, where a small but cosy fire crackled. Tom felt he had spoken in a stuffy, pontificating way. But the point was, he couldn't help Reeves, and he'd already told him that.

'Yes, sure,' said Reeves. He was sitting in one of the yellow silk armchairs, his lean figure hunched forward, hands clasped between his knees. He had a bony face, short, light-brown hair, cold grey eyes – not a pleasant face but a face that might have been rather handsome if not for a scar that travelled five inches from his right temple across his cheek almost to his mouth. Slightly pinker than the rest of his face, the scar looked like a bad job of stitching, or as if perhaps it had never been stitched. Tom had never asked about the scar, but Reeves had volunteered once, 'A girl did it with her compact. Can you imagine?' (No, Tom couldn't.) Reeves had given Tom a quick, sad smile, one of the few smiles Tom could recall from Reeves. And on another occasion, 'I was thrown from a horse – dragged by the stirrup for a few yards.' Reeves had said that to someone else, but Tom had been present. Tom suspected a dull knife in a very nasty fight somewhere.

Now Reeves wanted Tom to provide someone, suggest someone to do one or perhaps two 'simple murders' and perhaps one theft, also safe and simple. Reeves had come from Hamburg to Villeperce to talk to Tom, and he was going to stay the night and go to Paris tomorrow to talk to someone else about it, then return to his home in Hamburg, presumably to do some more thinking if he failed. Reeves was primarily a fence, but lately was dabbling in the illegal gambling world of Hamburg, which he was now undertaking to protect. Protect from what? Italian sharks who wanted to come in. One Italian in Hamburg was a Mafia button man, sent out as a feeler, Reeves thought, and the other might be from a different family. By eliminating one or both of these intruders, Reeves hoped to discourage further Mafia attempts, and also to draw the attention of the Hamburg police to a Mafia threat, and let the police handle the rest, which was to say, throw the Mafia out. 'These Hamburg boys are a decent batch,' Reeves had declared fervently. 'Maybe what they're doing is illegal, running a couple of private casinos, but as clubs they're not illegal, and they're not taking outrageous profits. It's not like Las Vegas, *all* Mafia-corrupted, and right under the noses of the American cops!'

Tom took the poker and pushed the fire together, put another neatly cut third-of-a-log on. It was nearly 6 p.m. Soon be time for a drink. And why not now? 'Would you –'

Mme Annette, the Ripleys' housekeeper, came in from the kitchen hall just then. 'Excuse me, messieurs. Would you like your drinks now, M. Tome, since the gentleman has not wanted any tea?'

'Yes, thank you, Mme Annette. Just what I was thinking. And ask Mme Heloise to join us, would you?' Tom wanted Heloise to lighten the atmosphere a little. He had said to Heloise, before he went to Orly at 3 p.m. to fetch Reeves, that Reeves wanted to talk to him about something, so Heloise had pottered about in the garden or stayed upstairs all afternoon.

'You wouldn't,' Reeves said with a last-minute urgency and hope, 'consider taking it on yourself? You're not connected, you see, and that's what we want. Safety. And after all, the money, ninety-six thousand bucks, isn't bad.'

Tom shook his head. 'I'm connected with *you* – in a way.' Dammit, he'd done little jobs for Reeves Minot, like posting on small, stolen items, or recovering from toothpaste tubes, where Reeves had planted them, tiny objects like microfilm rolls from the unsuspecting toothpaste carriers. 'How much of this cloak and dagger stuff do you think I can get away with? I've got my reputation to protect, you know.' Tom felt like smiling at that, but at the same time his heart had quickened with genuine feeling, and he stood taller, conscious of the fine house in which he lived, of his secure existence now, six whole months after the Derwatt episode, a near-catastrophe from which he had escaped with no worse than a bit of suspicion upon him. Thin ice, yes, but the ice hadn't broken through. Tom had accompanied the English Inspector Webster and a couple of forensic men to the Salzburg woods where he had cremated the body of the man presumed to be the painter Derwatt. Why had he crushed the skull, the police had asked. Tom could still wince when he thought of it, because he had done it to try to scatter and hide the upper teeth. The lower jaw had easily come away, and Tom had buried it at a distance. But the upper teeth – Some of them had been gathered by one of the forensic men, but there had been no record of Derwatt's teeth with any dentist in London, Derwatt having been living (it was believed) in Mexico for the preceding six years. 'It seemed part of the cremation, part of the idea of reducing him to ashes,' Tom had replied. The cremated body had been Bernard's. Yes, Tom could still shudder, as much at the danger of that moment as at the horror of his act, dropping a big stone on the charred skull. But at least he hadn't killed Bernard. Bernard Tufts had been a suicide.

Tom said, 'Surely among all the people you know, you can find somebody who can do it.'

'Yes, and that would be a connection – more than you. Oh, the people
I know are sort of known,' Reeves said with a sad defeat in his voice. 'You
know a lot of respectable people, Tom, people really in the clear, people
above reproach.'

Tom laughed. 'How're you going to *get* such people? Sometimes I think
you're out of your mind, Reeves.'

'No! You know what I mean. Someone who'd do it for the money, just
the money. They don't have to be experts. We'd prepare the way. It'd be
like – public assassinations. Someone who if he was questioned would look
– absolutely incapable of doing such a thing.'

Mme Annette came in with the bar cart. The silver ice bucket shone.
The cart squeaked slightly. Tom had been meaning to oil it for weeks. Tom
might have gone on bantering with Reeves because Mme Annette, bless
her soul, didn't understand English, but Tom was tired of the subject, and
delighted by Mme Annette's interruption. Mme Annette was in her sixties,
from a Normandy family, fine of feature and sturdy of body, a gem of a
servant. Tom could not imagine Belle Ombre functioning without her.

Then Heloise came in from the garden, and Reeves got to his feet.
Heloise was wearing bell-bottom pink-and-red-striped dungarees with
LEVI printed vertically down all the stripes. Her blonde hair swung long
and loose. Tom saw the firelight glow in it and thought, 'What purity compared to what we've been talking about!' The light in her hair was gold,
however, which made Tom think of money. Well, he didn't really need
any more money, even if the Derwatt picture sales, of which he got a
percentage, would soon come to an end because there would be no more
pictures. Tom still got a percentage from the Derwatt art supplies company, and that would continue. Then there was the modest but slowly
increasing income from the Greenleaf securities which he had inherited
by means of a will forged by Tom himself. Not to mention Heloise's
generous allowance from her father. No use being greedy. Tom detested
murder unless it was absolutely necessary.

'Did you have a good talk?' Heloise asked in English, and fell back
gracefully on to the yellow sofa.

'Yes, thank you,' said Reeves.

The rest of the conversation was in French, because Heloise was not
comfortable in English. Reeves did not know much French but he got
along, and they were not talking about anything important: the garden,
the mild winter that seemed really to have passed, because here it was

early March and the daffodils were opening. Tom poured champagne for
Heloise from one of the little bottles on the cart.

'How ees eet in Hambourg?' Heloise ventured again in English, and Tom
saw amusement in her eyes as Reeves struggled to get out a conventional
response in French.

It was not too cold in Hamburg either, and Reeves added that he had
a garden also, as his *petite maison* found itself on the Alster which was
water, that was to say a sort of bay where many people had homes with
gardens and water, meaning they could have small boats if they wished.

Tom knew that Heloise disliked Reeves Minot, mistrusted him, that
Reeves was the kind of person Heloise wanted Tom to avoid. Tom reflected
with satisfaction that he could honestly say to Heloise tonight that he had
declined to cooperate in the scheme that Reeves had proposed. Heloise was
always worried about what her father would say. Her father, Jacques
Plisson, was a millionaire pharmaceutical manufacturer, a Gaullist, the
essence of French respectability. And he had never cared for Tom. 'My
father will not stand for much more!' Heloise often warned Tom, but Tom
knew she was more interested in his own safety than in hanging on to
the allowance her father gave her, an allowance he frequently threatened
to cut off, according to Heloise. She had lunch with her parents at their
home in Chantilly once a week, usually Friday. If her father ever severed
her allowance, they could not quite make it at Belle Ombre, Tom knew.

The dinner menu was *médaillons de bœuf*, preceded by cold artichokes
with Mme Annette's own sauce. Heloise had changed into a simple dress
of pale blue. She sensed already, Tom thought, that Reeves had not got
what he had come for. Before they all retired, Tom made sure that Reeves
had everything he needed, and at what hour he would like tea or coffee
brought to his room. Coffee at 8 a.m., Reeves said. Reeves had the guest
room in the left centre of the house, which gave Reeves the bathroom that
was usually Heloise's, but from which Mme Annette had already removed
Heloise's toothbrush to Tom's bathroom, off his own room.

'I am glad he is going tomorrow. Why is he so tense?' Heloise asked,
while brushing her teeth.

'He's always tense.' Tom turned off the shower, stepped out and quickly
enveloped himself in a big yellow towel. 'That's why he's thin – maybe.'
They were speaking in English, because Heloise was not shy about speaking English with him.

'How did you meet him?'

Tom couldn't remember. When? Maybe five or six years ago. In Rome?
Who was Reeves a friend of? Tom was too tired to think hard, and it didn't

matter. He had five or six such acquaintances, and would have been hard pressed to say where he had met each and every one.

'What did he want from you?'

Tom put his arm around Heloise's waist, pressing the loose nightdress close to her body. He kissed her cool cheek. 'Something impossible. I said no. You can see that. He is disappointed.'

That night there was an owl, a lonely owl calling somewhere in the pines of the communal forest behind Belle Ombre. Tom lay with his left arm under Heloise's neck, thinking. She fell asleep, and her breathing became slow and soft. Tom sighed, and went on thinking. But he was not thinking in a logical, constructive way. His second coffee was keeping him awake. He was remembering a party he had been to a month ago in Fontainebleau, an informal birthday for a Mme – who? It was her husband's name that Tom was interested in, an English name that might come to him in a few seconds. The man, the host, had been in his early thirties, and they had a small son. The house was a straight-up-and-down three-storey, on a residential street in Fontainebleau, a patch of garden behind it. The man was a picture framer, that was why Tom had been dragged along by Pierre Gauthier, who had an art supply shop in the Rue Grande, where Tom bought his paints and brushes. Gauthier had said, 'Oh, come along with me, M. Reeply. Bring your wife! He wants a lot of people. He's a little depressed ... And anyway, since he makes frames, you might give him some business.'

Tom blinked in the darkness, and moved his head back a little so his eyelashes would not touch Heloise's shoulder. He recalled a tall blond Englishman with a certain resentment and dislike, because in the kitchen, that gloomy kitchen with worn-out linoleum, smoke-stained tin ceiling with a nineteenth-century bas-relief pattern, this man had made an unpleasant remark to Tom. The man – Trewbridge, Tewksbury? – had said in an almost sneering way, 'Oh yes, I've heard of you.' Tom had said, 'I'm Tom Ripley. I live in Villeperce,' and Tom had been about to ask him how long he'd been in Fontainebleau, thinking that perhaps an Englishman with a French wife might like to make acquaintance with an American with a French wife living not far away, but Tom's venture had been met with rudeness. Trevanny? Wasn't that his name? Blond, straight hair, rather Dutch-looking, but then the English often looked Dutch and vice versa.

What Tom was thinking of now, however, was what Gauthier had said later the same evening. 'He's depressed. He doesn't mean to be unfriendly. He's got some kind of blood disease – leukaemia, I think. Pretty serious.

Also as you can see from the house, he's not doing too well.' Gauthier had a glass eye of a curious yellow-green colour, obviously an attempt to match the real eye, but rather a failure. Gauthier's false eye suggested the eye of a dead cat. One avoided looking at it, yet one's eyes were hypnotically drawn to it, so Gauthier's gloomy words, combined with his glass eye, had made a strong impression of Death upon Tom, and Tom had not forgotten.

Oh, yes, I've heard of you. Did that mean that Trevanny or whatever his name was thought he was responsible for Bernard Tufts's death, and before that Dickie Greenleaf's? Or was the Englishman merely embittered against everyone because of his ailment? Dyspeptic, like a man with a constant stomach ache? Now Tom recalled Trevanny's wife, not a pretty but a rather interesting-looking woman with chestnut hair, friendly and outgoing, making an effort at that party in the small living-room and the kitchen where no one had sat down on the few chairs available.

What Tom was thinking was: would this man take on such a job as Reeves was proposing? An interesting approach to Trevanny had occurred to Tom. It was an approach that might work with any man, if one prepared the ground, but in this case the ground was already prepared. Trevanny was seriously worried about his health. Tom's idea was nothing more than a practical joke, he thought, a nasty one, but the man had been nasty to him. The joke might not last more than a day or so, until Trevanny could consult his doctor.

Tom was amused by his thoughts, and eased himself gently from Heloise, so that if he shook with repressed laughter for an instant, he wouldn't awaken her. Suppose Trevanny was vulnerable, and carried out Reeves' plan like a soldier, like a dream? Was it worth a try? Yes, because Tom had nothing to lose. Neither had Trevanny. Trevanny might gain. Reeves might gain – according to Reeves, but let Reeves figure that out, because what Reeves wanted seemed as vague to Tom as Reeves' microfilm activities, which presumably had to do with international spying. Were governments aware of the insane antics of some of their spies? Or those whimsical, half-demented men flitting from Bucharest to Moscow and Washington with guns and microfilm – men who might with the same enthusiasm have put their energies to international warfare in stamp-collecting, or in acquiring secrets of miniature electric trains?

TWO

So it was that some ten days later, on 22 March, Jonathan Trevanny, who lived in the Rue St Merry, Fontainebleau, received a curious letter from his good friend Alan McNear. Alan, a Paris representative of an English electronics firm, had written the letter just before leaving for New York on a business assignment, and oddly the day after he had visited the Trevannys in Fontainebleau. Jonathan had expected – or rather not expected – a sort of thank-you letter from Alan for the send-off party Jonathan and Simone had given him, and Alan did write a few words of appreciation, but the paragraph that puzzled Jonathan went:

Jon, I was shocked at the news in regard to the old blood ailment, and am even now hoping it isn't so. I was told that you knew, but weren't telling any of your friends. Very noble of you, but what are friends for? You needn't think we'll avoid you or that we'll think you'll become so melancholy that we won't want to see you. Your friends (and I'm one) are here – always. But I can't write anything I want to say, really. I'll do better when I see you next, in a couple of months when I wangle myself a vacation, so forgive these inadequate words.

What was Alan talking about? Had his doctor, Dr Perrier, said something to his *friends*, something he wouldn't tell him? Something about not living much longer? Dr Perrier hadn't been to the party for Alan, but could Dr Perrier have said something to someone else?

Had Dr Perrier spoken to Simone? And was Simone keeping it from him, too?

As Jonathan thought of these possibilities, he was standing in his garden at 8.30 a.m., chilly under his sweater, his fingers smudged with earth. He'd best speak with Dr Perrier today. No use with Simone. She might put up an act. *But, darling, what're you talking about?* Jonathan wasn't sure he'd be able to tell if she was putting up an act or not.

And Dr Perrier – could he trust him? Dr Perrier was always bouncing with optimism, which was fine if you had something minor – you felt fifty per cent better, even cured. But Jonathan knew he hadn't anything minor. He had myeloid leukaemia, characterized by an excess of yellow matter in the bone marrow. In the past five years, he'd had at least four blood transfusions per year. Every time he felt weak, he was supposed to get to his doctor, or to the Fontainebleau hospital for a transfusion. Dr Perrier had said (and so had a specialist in Paris) that there would come a time when the decline might be swift, when transfusions wouldn't do the trick any longer. Jonathan had read enough about his ailment to know that himself. No doctor as yet had come up with a cure for myeloid leukaemia. On the average, it killed after six to twelve years, or six to eight even. Jonathan was entering his sixth year with it.

Jonathan set his fork back in the little brick structure, formerly an outside toilet, that served as a tool shed, then walked to his back steps. He paused with one foot on the first step and drew the fresh morning air into his lungs, thinking, 'How many weeks will I have to enjoy such mornings?' He remembered thinking the same thing last spring, however. Buck up, he told himself, he'd known for six years that he might not live to see thirty-five. Jonathan mounted the eight iron steps with a firm tread, already thinking that it was 8.52 a.m., and that he was due in his shop at 9 a.m. or a few minutes after.

Simone had gone off with Georges to the Ecole Maternelle, and the house was empty. Jonathan washed his hands at the sink and made use of the vegetable brush, which Simone would not have approved of, but he left the brush clean. The only other sink was in the bathroom on the top floor. There was no telephone in the house. He'd ring Dr Perrier from his shop the first thing.

Jonathan walked to the Rue de la Paroisse and turned left, then went on to the Rue des Sablons which crossed it. In his shop, Jonathan dialled Dr Perrier's number, which he knew by heart.

The nurse said the doctor was booked up today, which Jonathan had expected.

'But this is urgent. It's something that won't take long. Just a question really – but I must see him.'

'You are feeling weak, M. Trevanny?'

'Yes, I am,' Jonathan said at once.

He got an appointment for twelve noon. The hour had a certain doom about it.

Jonathan was a picture framer. He cut mats and glass, made frames, chose frames from his stock for clients who were undecided, and once in a blue moon, in buying old frames at auctions and from junk dealers, he got a picture that was of some interest with the frame, a picture which he could clean and put in his window and sell. But it wasn't a lucrative business. He scraped along. Seven years ago he'd had a partner, another Englishman, from Manchester, and they had started an antique shop in Fontainebleau, dealing mainly in junk which they refurbished and sold. This hadn't paid enough for two, and Roy had pushed off and got a job as a garage mechanic somewhere near Paris. Shortly after that, a Paris doctor had said the same thing that a London doctor had told Jonathan: 'You're inclined to anaemia. You'd better have frequent check-ups, and it's best if you don't do any heavy work.' So from handling armoires and sofas, Jonathan had turned to the lighter work of handling picture frames and glass. Before Jonathan had married Simone, he had told her that he might not live more than another six years, because just at the time he met Simone, he'd had it confirmed by two doctors that his periodic weakness was caused by myeloid leukaemia.

Now, Jonathan thought as he calmly, very calmly began his day, Simone might remarry if he died. Simone worked five afternoons a week from 2.30 p.m. until 6.30 p.m. at a shoe shop in the Avenue Franklin Roosevelt, which was within walking distance of their house, and this was only in the past year when Georges had been old enough to be put into the French equivalent of kindergarten. He and Simone needed the two hundred francs per week that Simone earned, but Jonathan was irked by the thought that Brezard, her boss, was a bit of a lecher, liked to pinch his employees' behinds, and doubtless try his luck in the back room where the stock was. Simone was a married woman, as Brezard well knew, so there was a limit as to how far he could go, Jonathan supposed, but that never stopped his type from trying. Simone was not at all a flirt – she had a curious shyness, in fact, that suggested that she thought herself not attractive to men. It was a quality that endeared her to Jonathan. In Jonathan's opinion, Simone was supercharged with sex appeal, though of the kind that might not be apparent to the average man, and it annoyed Jonathan especially that the cruising swine Brezard must have become aware of Simone's very different kind of attractiveness, and that he wanted some of it for himself. Not that Simone talked much about Brezard. Only once had she mentioned that he tried it on with his women employees who were two besides Simone. For an instant that morning, as Jonathan presented a framed watercolour to a client, he imagined Simone, after a discreet interval, succumbing to the odious Brezard, who after all was a bachelor and financially better off than Jonathan. Absurd, Jonathan thought. Simone hated his type.

'Oh, it's lovely! Excellent!' said the young woman in a bright red coat, holding the watercolour at arm's length.

Jonathan's long, serious face slowly smiled, as if a small and private sun had come out of clouds and begun to shine within him. She was so genuinely pleased! Jonathan didn't know her, in fact she was picking up the picture that an older woman, perhaps her mother, had brought in. The price should have been twenty francs more than he had first estimated, because the frame was not the same as the older woman had chosen (Jonathan had not had enough in stock), but Jonathan didn't mention this and accepted the eighty francs agreed upon.

Then Jonathan pushed a broom over his wooden floor, and feather-dusted the three or four pictures in his small front window. His shop was positively shabby, Jonathan thought that morning. No colour anywhere, frames of all sizes leaning against unpainted walls, samples of frame wood hanging from the ceiling, a counter with an order book, ruler, pencils. At the back of the shop stood a long wooden table where Jonathan worked with his mitre boxes, saws and glass cutters. Also on the big table were his carefully protected sheets of mat board, a great roll of brown paper, rolls of string, wire, pots of glue, boxes of variously sized nails, and above the table on the wall were racks of knives and hammers. In principle, Jonathan liked the nineteenth-century atmosphere, the lack of commer-cial frou-frou. He wanted his shop to look as if a good craftsman ran it, and in that he had succeeded, he thought. He never overcharged, did his work on time, or if he was going to be late, he notified his clients by postcard or a telephone call. People appreciated that, Jonathan had found.

At 11.35 a.m., having framed two small pictures and fixed their owners' names to them, Jonathan washed his hands and face at the cold water tap in his sink, combed his hair, stood up straight and tried to brace himself for the worst. Dr Perrier's office was not far away in the Rue Grande. Jonathan turned his door card to OUVERT at 14.30, locked his front door, and set out.

Jonathan had to wait in Dr Perrier's front room with its sickly, dusty rose laurel plant. The plant never flowered, it didn't die, and never grew, never changed. Jonathan identified himself with the plant. Again and again his eyes were drawn to it, though he tried to think of other things. There were copies of *Paris Match* on the oval table, out of date and much thumbed, but Jonathan found them more depressing than the laurel plant. Dr Perrier also worked at the big Hôpital de Fontainebleau, Jonathan reminded himself, otherwise it would have seemed an absurdity to entrust one's life, to believe an opinion of whether one lived or died, to a doctor who worked in such a wretched little place as this looked.

The nurse came out and beckoned.

'Well, well, how's the interesting patient, my most interesting patient?' said Dr Perrier, rubbing his hands, then extending one to Jonathan.

Jonathan shook his head. 'I feel quite all right, thank you. But what is this about – I mean the tests of two months ago. I understand they are not so favourable?'

Dr Perrier looked blank, and Jonathan watched him intently. Then Dr Perrier smiled, showing yellowish teeth under his carelessly trimmed moustache.

'What do you mean unfavourable? You saw the results.'

'But – you know I'm not an expert in understanding them – perhaps.'

'But I explained them to you – Now what is the matter? You're feeling tired again?'

'In fact no.' Since Jonathan knew the doctor wanted to get away for lunch, he said hastily, 'To tell the truth, a friend of mine has learned somewhere that – I'm due for a crisis. Maybe I haven't long to live. Naturally, I thought this information must have come from you.'

Dr Perrier shook his head, then laughed, hopped about like a bird and came to rest with his skinny arms lightly outspread on the top of a glass-enclosed bookcase. 'My dear sir – first of all, if it were true, I would not have said it to anybody. That is not ethical. Second, it is not true, as far as I know from the last test. Do you want another test today? Late this afternoon at the hospital, maybe I –'

'Not necessarily. What I really wanted to know is – is it true? You wouldn't just not tell me?' Jonathan said with a laugh. 'Just to make me feel better?'

'What nonsense! Do you think I'm that kind of a doctor?'

Yes, Jonathan thought, looking Dr Perrier straight in the eye. And God bless him, maybe, in some cases, but Jonathan thought he deserved the facts, because he was the kind of man who could face the facts. Jonathan bit his underlip. He could go to the lab in Paris, he thought, insist on seeing the specialist Moussu again. Also he might get something out of Simone today at lunch-time.

Dr Perrier was patting his arm. 'Your friend – and I won't ask who he is! – is either mistaken or not a very nice friend, I think. Now then, you should tell me when and if you become tired, *that* is what counts . . .'

Twenty minutes later, Jonathan was climbing the front steps of his house, carrying an apple tart and a long loaf of bread. He let himself in with his key, and walked down the hall to the kitchen. He smelled frying potatoes, a mouth-watering smell always signifying lunch, not dinner, and Simone's potatoes would be in long slender pieces, not short chunks like the chips in England. Why had he thought of English chips?

Simone was at the stove, wearing an apron over her dress, wielding a long fork. 'Hello, Jon. You're a little late.'

Jonathan put an arm around her and kissed her cheek, then held up the paper box, swung it towards Georges who was sitting at the table,

blond head bent, cutting out parts for a mobile from an empty box of
cornflakes.

'Ah, a cake! What kind?' Georges asked.

'Apple.' Jonathan set the box on the table.

They had a small steak each, the delicious fried potatoes, a green salad.

'Brezard is starting inventory,' Simone said. 'The summer stock comes
in next week, so he wants to have a sale Friday and Saturday. I might be
a little late tonight.'

She had warmed the apple tart on the asbestos plate. Jonathan waited
impatiently for Georges to go in the living-room where a lot of his toys
were, or out to the garden. When Georges left finally Jonathan said:

'I had a funny letter today from Alan.'

'Alan? Funny how?'

'He wrote it just before he went to New York. It seems he's heard –'
Should he show her Alan's letter? She could read English well enough.
Jonathan decided to go on. 'He's heard somewhere that I'm worse, due
for a bad crisis – or something. Do you know anything about it?' Jonathan
watched her eyes.

Simone looked genuinely surprised. 'Why no, Jon. How would I hear –
except from you?'

'I spoke with Dr Perrier just now. That's why I was a bit late. Perrier
says he doesn't know of any change in the situation, but you know
Perrier!' Jonathan smiled, still watching Simone anxiously. 'Well, here's
the letter,' he said, pulling it from his back pocket. He translated the
paragraph.

'Mon dieu! – Well, where did he hear it from?'

'Yes, that's the question. I'll write him and ask. Don't you think?'
Jonathan smiled again, a more genuine smile. He was sure Simone didn't
know anything about it.

Jonathan carried a second cup of coffee into the small square living-
room where Georges was now sprawled on the floor with his cut-outs.
Jonathan sat down at the writing desk, which always made him feel like
a giant. It was a rather dainty French écritoire, a present from Simone's
family. Jonathan was careful not to put too much weight on the writing
shelf. He addressed an air-letter to Alan McNear at the Hotel New Yorker,
began the letter breezily enough, and wrote a second paragraph:

I don't know quite what you mean in your letter about the news (about me)
which shocked you. I feel all right, but this morning spoke with my doctor here to
see if he was giving me the whole story. He disclaims any knowledge of a worse
condition. So dear Alan, what does interest me is where did you hear it? Could you

possibly drop me a line soon? It sounds like a misunderstanding, I'd he delighted to forget it, but I hope you can understand my curiosity as to where you heard it.

He dropped the letter in a yellow box *en route* to his shop. It would probably be a week before he heard from Alan.

That afternoon, Jonathan's hand was as steady as ever as he pulled his razor knife down the edge of his steel ruler. He thought of his letter, making its progress to Orly airport, maybe by this evening, maybe by tomorrow morning. He thought of his age, thirty-four, and of how pitifully little he would have done if he were to die in another couple of months. He'd produced a son, and that was something, but hardly an achievement worthy of special praise. He would not leave Simone very secure. If anything, he had lowered her standard of living slightly. Her father was only a coal merchant, but somehow over the years her family had gathered a few conveniences of life around them, a car for instance, decent furniture. They vacationed in June or July down south in a villa which they rented, and last year they had paid a month's rent so that Jonathan and Simone could go there with Georges. Jonathan had not done as well as his brother Philip, two years older than himself, though Philip had looked physically weaker, had been a dull, plodding type all his life. Now Philip was a professor of anthropology at Bristol University, not brilliant, Jonathan was sure, but a good solid man with a solid career, a wife and two children. Jonathan's mother, a widow now, had a happy existence with her brother and sister-in-law in Oxfordshire, taking care of the big garden there and doing all the shopping and cooking. Jonathan felt himself the failure of his family, both physically and as to his work. He had first wanted to be an actor. At eighteen he'd gone to a drama school for two years. He'd not a bad face for an actor, he thought, not too handsome with a big nose and wide mouth, yet good-looking enough to play romantic roles, and at the same time heavy enough to play heavier roles in time. What pipe dreams! He'd hardly got two walk-on parts in the three years he'd hung around London and Manchester theatres – always supporting himself, of course, by odd jobs, including one as a veterinary's assistant. 'You take up a lot of space and you're not even sure of yourself,' a director once said to him. And then, working for an antique dealer in another of his odd jobs, Jonathan had thought he might like the antique business. He had learned all he could from his boss, Andrew Mott. Then the grand move to France with his chum Roy Johnson, who had also had enthusiasm, if not much knowledge, for starting an antique shop via the junk trade. Jonathan remembered his dreams of glory and adventure in a new country, France, dreams of freedom, of success. And instead of success, instead of a series of educational mistresses, instead of making friends with the bohemians, or with some stratum of French society which Jonathan had imagined existed but perhaps didn't – instead of all this Jonathan had continued to limp along, no better off really than when he'd been trying to get jobs as an actor and had supported himself any old way.

The only successful thing in his whole life was his marriage to Simone, Jonathan thought. The news of his disease had come in the same month he had met Simone Foussadier. He'd begun to feel strangely weak and had romantically thought that it might be due to falling in love. But a little extra rest hadn't shaken the weakness, he had fainted once in a street of Nemours, so he had gone to a doctor – Dr Perrier in Fontainebleau, who had suspected a blood condition and sent him to a Dr Moussu in Paris. The specialist Moussu, after two days of tests, had confirmed myeloid leukaemia, and said that he might have from six to eight, with luck twelve years to live. There would be an enlargement of the spleen, which in fact Jonathan already had without having noticed it. Thus Jonathan's proposal to Simone had been a declaration of love and death in the same awkward speech. It would have been enough to put most young women off, or to have made them say they needed time to think about it. Simone had said yes, she loved him too. 'It is the love that is important, not the time,' Simone had said. None of the calculations that Jonathan had associated with the French, and with Latins in general. Simone said she had already spoken to her family. And this after they had known each other only two weeks. Jonathan felt himself suddenly in a world more secure than any he had ever known. Love, in a real and not a merely romantic sense, love that he had no control over, had miraculously rescued him. In a way, he felt that it had rescued him from death, but he realized that he meant that love had taken the terror out of death. And here was death six years· later, as Dr Moussu in Paris had predicted. perhaps. Jonathan didn't know what to believe.

He must make another visit to Moussu in Paris, he thought. Three years ago, Jonathan had had a complete change of blood under Dr Moussu's supervision in a Paris hospital. The treatment was called Vincainestine, the idea or the hope being that the excess of white with accompanying yellow components would not return to the blood. But the yellow excess had reappeared in about eight months.

Before he made an appointment with Dr Moussu, however, Jonathan preferred to wait for a letter from Alan McNear. Alan would write at once, Jonathan felt sure. One could count on Alan.

Jonathan, before he left his shop, cast one desperate glance around its Dickensian interior. It wasn't really dusty, it was just that the walls needed repainting. He wondered if he should make an effort to spruce the place up, start soaking his customers as so many picture framers did, sell lacquered brass items with big mark-ups? Jonathan winced. He wasn't the type.

That day was Wednesday. On Friday, while bending over a stubborn screw-eye that had been in an oak frame for perhaps a hundred and fifty years and had no intention of yielding to his pliers, Jonathan had suddenly to drop the pliers and look for a seat. The seat was a wooden box against a wall. He got up almost at once and wet his face at the sink, bending as low as he could. In five minutes or so, the faintness passed, and by lunch-time he had forgotten about it. Such moments came every two or three months, and Jonathan was glad if they didn't catch him on the street.

On Tuesday, six days after he had posted his letter to Alan, he received a letter from the Hotel New Yorker.

Sat. March 25

Dear Jon,

Believe me, I'm glad you spoke with your doctor and that the news is good! The person who told me you were in a serious way was a little balding fellow with moustache and a glassy eye, early forties maybe. He seemed really concerned, and perhaps you shouldn't hold it too much against him, as he may have heard it from someone else.

I'm enjoying this town and wish you and Simone were here, esp. as I'm on an expense account ...

The man Alan meant was Pierre Gauthier, who had an art supply shop in the Rue Grande. He was not a friend of Jonathan's, just an acquaintance. Gauthier often sent people to Jonathan to have their pictures framed. Gauthier had been at the house the night of Alan's send-off party, Jonathan remembered distinctly, and must have spoken to Alan then. It was out of the question that Gauthier had spoken maliciously. Jonathan was only a little surprised that Gauthier even knew he had a blood ailment, though the word did get around, Jonathan realized. Jonathan thought the thing to do was speak to Gauthier and ask him where he'd heard the story.

It was 8.50 a.m. Jonathan had waited for the post, as he had yesterday morning also. His impulse was to go straight to Gauthier's, but he felt this would show unseemly anxiety, and that he'd better get his bearings by going to his shop and opening as usual.

Because of three or four customers, Jonathan hadn't a break till 10.25

a.m. He left his clock card in the glass of his door indicating that he would be open again at 11 a.m.

When Jonathan entered the art supply shop, Gauthier was busy with two women customers. Jonathan pretended to browse among racks of paint brushes until Gauthier was free. Then he said:

'M. Gauthier! How goes it?' Jonathan extended a hand.

Gauthier clasped Jonathan's hand in both his own and smiled. 'And you, my friend?'

'Well enough, thank you ... *Ecoutez*. I don't want to take your time – but there is something I would like to ask you.'

'Yes? What's that?'

Jonathan beckoned Gauthier farther away from the door which might open at any minute. There was not much standing room in the little shop. 'I heard from a friend – my friend Alan, you remember? The Englishman. At the party at my house a few weeks ago.'

'Yes! Your friend the Englishman. Alain.' Gauthier remembered and looked attentive.

Jonathan tried to avoid even glancing at Gauthier's false eye, but to concentrate on the other eye. 'Well, it seems you told Alan that you'd heard I was very ill, maybe not going to live much longer.'

Gauthier's soft face grew solemn. He nodded. 'Yes, m'sieur, I did hear that. I hope it's not true. I remember Alain, because you introduced him to me as your best friend. So I assumed he knew. Perhaps I should have said nothing. I am sorry, it was perhaps tactless. I thought you were – in the English style – putting on a brave face.'

'It's nothing serious, M. Gauthier, because as far as I know, it's not true! I've just spoken with my doctor. But –'

'*Ah, bon!* Ah well, that's different! I'm delighted to hear that, M. Trevanny! Ha! Ha!' Pierre Gauthier gave a clap of laughter as if a ghost had been laid, and he found not only Jonathan but himself back among the living.

'But I'd like to know where you heard this. Who told you I was ill?'

'Ah – yes!' Gauthier pressed a finger to his lips, thinking. 'Who? A man. Yes – of *course*!' He had it, but he paused.

Jonathan waited.

'But I remember he said he wasn't sure. He'd heard it, he said. An incurable blood disease, he said.'

Jonathan felt warm with anxiety again, as he had felt several times in the past week. He wet his lips. 'But who? How did he hear it? Didn't he say?'

Gauthier again hesitated. 'Since it isn't true – shouldn't we best forget it?'

'Someone you know very well?'

'No! Not at all well, I assure you.'

'A customer.'

'Yes. Yes, he is. A nice man, a gentleman. But since he *said* he wasn't sure – Really, *m'sieur*, you shouldn't bear a resentment, although I can understand how you could resent such a remark.'

'Which leads to the interesting question how did the gentleman come to hear I was very ill,' Jonathan went on, laughing now.

'Yes. Exactly. Well, the point is, it isn't true. Isn't that the main thing?'

Jonathan saw in Gauthier a French politeness, and unwillingness to alienate a customer, and – which was to be expected – an aversion to the subject of death. 'You're right. That's the main thing,' Jonathan shook hands with Gauthier, both of them smiling now, and bade him adieu.

That very day at lunch, Simone asked Jonathan if he had heard from Alan. Jonathan said yes.

'It was Gauthier who said something to Alan.'

'Gauthier? The art shop man?'

'Yes.' Jonathan was lighting a cigarette over his coffee. Georges had gone out into the garden. 'I went to see Gauthier this morning and I asked him where he'd heard it. He said from a customer. A man. Funny, isn't it? Gauthier wouldn't tell me who, and I can't really blame him. It's some mistake, of course. Gauthier realizes that.'

'But it's a shocking thing,' said Simone.

Jonathan smiled, knowing Simone wasn't really shocked, since she knew Dr Perrier had given him rather good news. 'As we say in English, one must not make a mountain out of a molehill.'

In the following week, Jonathan bumped into Dr Perrier in the Rue Grande, the doctor in a hurry to enter the Société Générale before it shut at twelve sharp. But he paused to ask how Jonathan was.

'Quite well, thank you,' said Jonathan, whose mind was on buying a plunger for the toilet from a shop a hundred yards away which also shut at noon.

'M. Trevanny –' Dr Perrier paused with one hand on the big knob of the bank's door. He moved away from the door, closer to Jonathan. 'In regard to what we were talking about the other day – no doctor can be *sure*, you know. In a situation like yours. I didn't want you to think I'd given you a guarantee of perfect health, immunity for years. You know yourself –'

'Oh, I didn't assume that!' Jonathan interrupted.

'Then you understand,' said Dr Perrier, smiling, and dashed at once into his bank.

Jonathan trotted on in quest of the plunger. It was the kitchen sink stopped up, not the toilet, he remembered, and Simone had lent a neighbour their plunger months ago and – Jonathan was thinking of what Dr Perrier had said. *Did* he know something, suspect something from the last test, something not sufficiently definite to warrant telling him about?

At the door of the droguerie, Jonathan encountered a smiling, dark-haired girl who was just locking up, removing the outside door handle.

'I am sorry. It is five minutes past twelve,' she said.

THREE

Tom, during the last week in March, was engaged in painting a full-length portrait of Heloise horizontal on the yellow satin sofa. And Heloise seldom agreed to pose. But the sofa stayed still, and Tom had it satisfactorily on his canvas. He had also made seven or eight sketches of Heloise with her head propped upon her left hand, her right hand resting on a big art book. He kept the two best sketches and threw the others away.

Reeves Minot had written him one letter, asking Tom if he had come up with a helpful idea – as to a person, Reeves meant. The letter had arrived a couple of days after Tom had spoken with Gauthier, from whom Tom usually bought his paints. Tom had replied to Reeves: 'Am trying to think, but meanwhile you should go ahead with your own ideas, if you have any.' The 'am trying to think' was merely polite, even false, like a lot of phrases that served to oil the machinery of social intercourse, as Emily Post might say. Reeves hardly kept Belle Ombre oiled financially, in fact Reeves' payments to Tom for occasional services as go-between and fence would hardly cover the dry-cleaning bills, but it never hurt to maintain friendly relations. Reeves had procured a false passport for Tom and had got it to Paris fast when Tom had needed it to help defend the Derwatt industry. Tom might one day need Reeves again.

But the business with Jonathan Trevanny was merely a game for Tom.

He was not doing it for Reeves' gambling interests. Tom happened to dislike gambling, and had no respect for people who chose to earn their living, or even part of their living from it. It was pimping, of a sort. Tom had started the Trevanny game out of curiosity, and because Trevanny had once sneered at him – and because Tom wanted to see if his own wild shot would find its mark, and make Jonathan Trevanny, who Tom sensed was priggish and self-righteous, uneasy for a time. Then Reeves could offer his bait, hammering the point of course that Trevanny was soon to die anyway. Tom doubted that Trevanny would bite, but it would be a period of discomfort for Trevanny, certainly. Unfortunately Tom couldn't guess how soon the rumour would get to Jonathan Trevanny's ears. Gauthier was gossipy enough, but it just might happen, even if Gauthier told two or three people, that no one would have the courage to broach the subject to Trevanny himself.

So Tom, although busy as usual with his painting, his spring planting, his German and French studies (Schiller and Molière now), plus supervising a crew of three masons who were constructing a greenhouse along the right side of Belle Ombre's back lawn, still counted the passing days and imagined what might have happened after that afternoon in the middle of March, when he had said to Gauthier that he'd heard that Trevanny wasn't long for this world. Not too likely that Gauthier would speak to Trevanny directly, unless they were closer than Tom thought. Gauthier would more likely tell someone else about it. Tom counted on the fact (he was sure it was a fact) that the possibility of anyone's imminent death was a fascinating subject to everyone.

Tom went to Fontainebleau, some twelve miles from Villeperce, every two weeks or so. Fontainebleau was better than Moret for shopping, for having suede coats cleaned, for buying radio batteries and the rarer things that Mme Annette wished for her cuisine. Jonathan Trevanny had a telephone in his shop, Tom had noted in the directory, but apparently not in his house in the Rue St Merry. Tom had been trying to look up the house number, but he thought he would recognize the house when he saw it. Around the end of March, Tom became curious to see Trevanny again, from a distance, of course, and so on a trip to Fontainebleau one Friday morning, a market day, for the purpose of buying two round terracotta flower tubs, Tom, after putting these items in the back of the Renault station wagon, walked through the Rue des Sablons where Trevanny's shop was. It was nearly noon.

Trevanny's shop looked in need of paint and a bit depressing, as if it belonged to an old man, Tom thought. Tom had never patronized

Trevanny, because there was a good framer in Moret, closer to Tom. The little shop with 'Encadrement' in fading red letters on the wood over the door stood in a row of shops – a launderette, a cobbler's, a modest travel agency – with its door on the left side and to the right a square window with assorted frames and two or three paintings with handwritten price tags on them. Tom crossed the street casually, glanced into the shop and saw Trevanny's tall, Nordic-looking figure behind the counter some twenty feet away. Trevanny was showing a man a length of frame, slapping it into his palm, talking. Then Trevanny glanced at the window, saw Tom for an instant, but continued talking to the customer with no change in his expression.

Tom strolled on. Trevanny hadn't recognized him, Tom felt. Tom turned right, into the Rue de France, the next most important street after the Rue Grande, and continued till he came to the Rue St Merry where he turned right. Or had Trevanny's house been to the left? No, right.

Yes, there it was, surely, the narrow, cramped-looking grey house with slender black handrails going up the front steps. The tiny areas on either side of the steps were cemented, and no flower pots relieved the barrenness. But there was a garden behind, Tom recalled. The windows, though sparkling clean, showed rather limp curtains. Yes, this was where he'd come on the invitation of Gauthier that evening in February. There was a narrow passage on the left side of the house which must lead to the garden beyond. A green plastic garbage bin stood in front of the padlocked iron gate to the garden, and Tom imagined that the Trevannys usually got to the garden via the back door off the kitchen, which Tom remembered.

Tom was on the other side of the street, walking slowly, but careful not to appear to be loitering, because he could not be sure that the wife, or someone, was not even now looking out one of the windows.

Was there anything else he needed to buy? Zinc white. He was nearly out of it. And that purchase would take him to Gauthier the art supply man. Tom quickened his step, congratulating himself because his need of zinc white was a real need, so he'd be entering Gauthier's on a real errand, while at the same time he might be able to satisfy his curiosity.

Gauthier was alone in the shop.

'Bonjour, M. Gauthier!' said Tom.

'Bonjour, M. Reepley!' Gauthier replied, smiling. 'And how are you?'

'Very well, thank you, and you? – I find I need some zinc white.'

'Zinc white.' Gauthier pulled a flat drawer from his cabinet against a wall. 'Here they are. And you like the Rembrandt, as I recall.'

Tom did. Derwatt zinc white and other Derwatt-made colours were available, too, their tubes emblazoned with the bold, downward slanting signature of Derwatt in black on the label, but somehow Tom did not want to paint at home with the name Derwatt catching his eye every time he reached for a tube of anything. Tom paid, and as Gauthier was handing him his change and the little bag with the zinc white in it, Gauthier said:

'Ah, M. Reepley, you recall M. Trevanny, the framer of the Rue St Merry?'

'Yes, of course,' said Tom who had been wondering how to bring Trevanny up.

'Well, the rumour that you heard, that he is going to die soon, is not true at all.' Gauthier smiled.

'No? Well, very good! I'm glad to hear that.'

'Yes. M. Trevanny went to see his doctor even. I think he was a bit upset. Who wouldn't be, eh? Ha-ha! – But you said somebody told *you*, M. Reepley?'

'Yes. A man who was at the party – in February. Mme Trevanny's birthday party. So I assumed it was a fact and everybody knew it, you see.'

Gauthier looked thoughtful.

'You spoke to M. Trevanny?'

'No – no. But I did speak to his best friend one evening, another evening at the Trevannys' house, this month. Evidently he spoke to M. Trevanny. How these things get around!'

'His best friend?' Tom asked with an air of innocence.

'An Englishman. Alain something. He was going to America next day. But – do you recall who told *you*, M. Reepley?'

Tom shook his head slowly. 'Can't recall his name and not even how he looked. There were so many people that night.'

'Because –' Gauthier bent closer and whispered, as if there were someone else present. 'M. Trevanny asked *me*, you see, who had told me, and of course I didn't say it was *you*. These things can be misinterpreted. I didn't want to get *you* into trouble. Ha!' Gauthier's shiny glass eye did not laugh but looked out from his head with a bold stare, as if there were a different brain from Gauthier's behind that eye, a computer kind of brain that at once could know everything, if someone just set the programming.

'I thank you for that, because it is not nice to make remarks which are not true about people's health, eh?' Tom was grinning now, ready to take his leave, but he added, 'M. Trevanny does have a blood condition, however, didn't you say?'

'That is true. I think it's leukaemia. But that is something he lives with. He once told me he'd had it for years.'

Tom nodded. 'At any rate, I'm glad he's not in danger. *A bientôt*, M. Gauthier. Many thanks.'

Tom walked in the direction of his car. Trevanny's shock, though it may have lasted just a few hours until he consulted his doctor, must at least have put a little crack in his self-confidence. A few people had believed, and maybe Trevanny himself had believed, that he was not going to live more than a few weeks. That was because such a possibility wasn't out of the question for a man with Trevanny's ailment. A pity Trevanny was now reassured, but that little crack might be all that Reeves needed. The game could now enter its second stage. Trevanny would probably say no to Reeves. End of game, in that case. On the other hand Reeves would approach him as if of course he was a doomed man. It would be amusing if Trevanny weakened. That day after lunch with Heloise and her Paris friend Noëlle, who was going to stay overnight, Tom left the ladies and wrote a letter to Reeves on his typewriter.

March 28, 19—

Dear Reeves,

I have an idea for you, in case you have not yet found what you are looking for. His name is Jonathan Trevanny, early thirties, English, a picture-framer, married to Frenchwoman with small son. [Here Tom gave Trevanny's home and shop addresses and shop telephone number.] He looks as if he could use some money, and although he may not be the *type* you want, he looks the picture of decency and innocence, and what is more important for you, he has only a few more months or weeks to live, I have found out. He's got leukaemia, and has just heard the bad news. He might be willing to take on a dangerous job to earn some money now.

I don't know Trevanny personally, and need I emphasize that I don't wish to make his acquaintance, nor do I wish you to mention my name. My suggestion is, if you want to sound him out come to F'bleau, put yourself up at a charming hostelry called the Hôtel de L'Aigle Noir for a couple of days, contact Trevanny by ringing his shop, make an appointment and talk it over. And do I have to tell you to give another name besides your own?

Tom felt a sudden optimism about the project. The vision of Reeves with his disarming air of uncertainty and anxiety – almost suggestive of probity – laying such an idea before Trevanny who looked as upright as a saint, made Tom laugh. Did he dare occupy another table in the Hôtel de L'Aigle Noir's dining-room or bar when Reeves made his date with Trevanny? No, that would be too much. This reminded Tom of another point, and he added to his letter:

If you come to F'bleau, please don't telephone or write a note to me under any circumstances. Destroy my letter here, please.

                                                            Yours ever,
                                                            Tom

FOUR

The telephone rang in Jonathan's shop on Friday afternoon 31 March. He was just then gluing brown paper to the back of a large picture, and he had to find suitable weights – an old sandstone saying LONDON, the glue pot itself, a wooden mallet – before he could lift the telephone.

'Hello?'

'*Bonjour, m'sieur*. M. Trevanny? ... You speak English, I think. My name is Stephen Wister, W-i-s-t-e-r. I'm in Fontainebleau for a couple of days, and I wonder if you could find a few minutes to talk with me about something – something that I think would interest you.'

The man had an American accent. 'I don't buy pictures,' Jonathan said. 'I'm a framer.'

'I didn't want to see you about anything connected with your work. It's something I can't explain over the phone. I'm staying at the Aigle Noir.'

'Oh?'

'I was wondering if you have a few minutes this evening after you close your shop. Around seven? Six-thirty? We could have a drink or a coffee.'

'But – I'd like to know why you want to see me.' A woman had come into the shop – Mme Tissot, Tissaud? – to pick up a picture. Jonathan smiled apologetically to her.

'I'll have to explain when I see you,' said the soft, earnest voice. 'It'll take only ten minutes. Have you any time at seven today, for instance?'

Jonathan shifted. 'Six-thirty would be all right.'

'I'll meet you in the lobby. I'm wearing a grey plaid suit. But I'll speak to the porter. It won't be difficult.'

Jonathan usually closed around 6.30 p.m. At 6.15 p.m., he stood at his cold-water sink, scrubbing his hands. It was a mild day and Jonathan had worn a polo-neck sweater with an old beige corduroy jacket, not elegant enough for l'Aigle Noir, and the addition of his second-best mac would have made things worse. Why should he care? The man wanted to sell him something. It couldn't be anything else.

The hotel was only a five-minute walk from the shop. It had a small front court enclosed by high iron gates, and a few steps led up to its front door. Jonathan saw a slender, tense-looking man with crew-cut hair move towards him with a faint uncertainty, and Jonathan said:

'Mr Wister?'

'Yes.' Reeves gave a twitch of a smile and extended his hand. 'Shall we have a drink in the bar here, or do you prefer somewhere else?'

The bar here was pleasant and quiet. Jonathan shrugged. 'As you like.' He noticed an awful scar the length of Wister's cheek.

They went to the wide door of the hotel's bar, which was empty except for one man and woman at a small table. Wister turned away as if put off by the quietude, and said:

'Let's try somewhere else.'

They walked out of the hotel and turned right. Jonathan knew the next bar, the Café du Sport or some such, roistering at this hour with boys at the pinball machines and workmen at the counter, and on the threshold of the bar-café Wister stopped as if he had come unexpectedly upon a battlefield in action.

'Would you mind,' Wister said, turning away, 'coming up to my room? It's quiet and we can have something sent up.'

They went back to the hotel, climbed one flight of stairs, and entered an attractive room in Spanish décor – black ironwork, a raspberry-coloured bedspread, a pale green carpet. A suitcase on the rack was the only sign of the room's occupancy. Wister had entered without a key.

'What'll you have?' Wister went to the telephone. 'Scotch?'

'Fine.'

The man ordered in clumsy French. He asked for the bottle to be brought up, and for plenty of ice, please.

Then there was a silence. Why was the man uneasy, Jonathan wondered. Jonathan stood by the window where he had been looking out. Evidently Wister didn't want to talk until the drinks arrived. Jonathan heard a discreet tap at the door.

A white-jacketed waiter came in with a tray and a friendly smile. Stephen Wister poured generous drinks.

'Are you interested in making some money?'

Jonathan smiled, settled in a comfortable armchair now, with the huge iced scotch in his hand. 'Who isn't?'

'I have a dangerous job in mind – well, an important job – for which I'm prepared to pay quite well.'

Jonathan thought of drugs: the man probably wanted something delivered, or held. 'What business are you in?' Jonathan inquired politely.

'Several. Just now one you might call – gambling. Do you gamble?'

'No.' Jonathan smiled.

'I don't either. That's not the point.' The man got up from the side of the bed and walked slowly about the room. 'I live in Hamburg.'

'Oh?'

'Gambling isn't legal in city limits, but it goes on in private clubs. However, that's not the point, whether it's legal or not. I need one person eliminated, possible two, and possibly a theft – to be done. Now that's putting my cards on the table.' He looked at Jonathan with a serious, hopeful expression.

Killed, the man meant. Jonathan was startled, then he smiled and shook his head. 'I wonder where you got my name!'

Stephen Wister didn't smile. 'Never mind that.' He continued walking up and down with his drink in his hand, and his grey eyes glanced at Jonathan and away again. 'I wonder if you're interested in ninety-six thousand dollars? That's forty thousand pounds, and about four hundred and eighty thousand francs – new francs. Just for shooting one man, maybe two, we'll have to see how it goes. It'll be an arrangement that's safe and foolproof for you.'

Jonathan shook his head again. 'I don't know where you heard that I'm a – a gunman. You've got me confused with someone else.'

'No. Not at all.'

Jonathan's smile faded under the man's intense stare. 'It's a mistake ... Do you mind telling me how you came to ring me?'

'Well, you're –' Wister looked more pained than ever. 'You're not going to live more than a few weeks. You know that. You've got a wife and a small son – haven't you? Wouldn't you like to leave them a little something when you're gone?'

Jonathan felt the blood drain from his face. How did Wister know so much? Then he realized it was all connected, that whoever told Gauthier he was going to die soon knew this man, was connected with him somehow. Jonathan was not going to mention Gauthier. Gauthier was an honest man, and Wister was a crook. Suddenly Jonathan's scotch did not taste so good. 'There was a crazy rumour – recently –'

Now Wister shook his head. 'It is not a crazy rumour. It may be that your doctor hasn't told you the truth.'

'And you know more than my doctor? My doctor doesn't lie to me. It's true I have a blood disease, but – I'm in no worse a state now –' Jonathan broke off. 'The essential thing is, I'm afraid I can't help you, Mr Wister.'

As Wister bit on his underlip, the long scar moved in a distasteful way, like a live worm.

Jonathan looked away from him. Was Dr Perrier lying after all? Jonathan thought he should ring up the Paris laboratory tomorrow morning and ask some questions, or simply go to Paris and demand another explanation.

'Mr Trevanny, I'm sorry to say it's you who aren't informed, evidently. At least you've heard what you call the rumour, so I'm not the bearer of bad tidings. It's a matter for your own free choice, but under the circumstances, a considerable sum like this, I would think, sounds rather pleasant. You could stop working and enjoy your – Well, for instance, you could take a cruise around the world with your family and still leave your wife ...'

Jonathan felt slightly faint, and stood up and took a deep breath. The sensation passed, but he preferred to be on his feet. Wister was talking, but Jonathan barely listened.

'... my idea. There're a few men in Hamburg who would contribute towards the ninety-six thousand dollars. The man or men we want out of the way are Mafia men.'

Jonathan had only half recovered. 'Thanks, I am not a killer. You may as well get off the subject.'

Wister went on. 'But exactly what we want is someone not connected with any of us, or with Hamburg. Although the first man, only a button man, must be shot in Hamburg. The reason is, we want the police to think that two Mafia gangs are fighting each other in Hamburg. In fact, we want the police to step in on our side.' He continued to walk up and down, looking at the floor mostly. 'The first man ought to be shot in a crowd, a U-Bahn crowd. That's our subway, underground you'd call it. The gun would be dropped at once, the – the assassin blends into the crowd and vanishes. An Italian gun, with no fingerprints on it. No clues.' He brought his hands down like a conductor finishing.

Jonathan moved back to the chair, in need of it for a few seconds. 'Sorry. No.' He would walk to the door, as soon as he got his strength back.

'I'm here all tomorrow, and probably till late Sunday afternoon. I wish you'd think about it. Another scotch? Might do you good.'

'No, thanks.' Jonathan hauled himself up. 'I'll be pushing off.'

Wister nodded, looking disappointed.

'And thanks for the drink.'

'Don't mention it.' Wister opened the door for Jonathan.

Jonathan went out. He had expected Wister to press a card with his name and address into his hand. Jonathan was glad he hadn't.

The street lights had come on in the Rue de France. 7.22 p.m. Had Simone asked him to buy anything? Bread, perhaps. Jonathan went into a boulangerie and bought a long stick. The familiar chore was comforting.

The supper consisted of a vegetable soup, a couple of slices of leftover *fromage de tête*, a salad of tomatoes and onions. Simone talked about a wallpaper sale at a shop near where she worked. For a hundred francs, they could paper the bedroom, and she had seen a beautiful mauve and green pattern, very light and art nouveau.

'With only one window that bedroom's very dark, you know, Jon.'

'Sounds fine,' Jonathan said. 'Especially if it's a sale.'

'It *is* a sale. Not one of these silly sales where they reduce something five per cent – like my stingy boss.' She wiped breadcrust in her salad oil and popped it into her mouth. 'You're worried about something? Something happened today?'

Jonathan smiled suddenly. He wasn't worried about anything. He was glad Simone hadn't noticed he was a little late, and that he'd had a big drink. 'No, darling. Nothing happened. The end of the week, maybe. Almost the end.'

'You feel tired?'

It was like a question from a doctor, routine now. 'No ... I've got to telephone a customer tonight between eight and nine.' It was 8.37 p.m. 'I may as well do it now, my dear. Maybe I'll have some coffee later.'

'Can I go with you?' Georges asked, dropping his fork, sitting back ready to leap out of his chair.

'Not tonight, *mon petit vieux*. I'm in a hurry. And you just want to play the pinball machines, I know you.'

'Hollywood Chewing Gum!' Georges shouted, pronouncing it in the French manner: '*Ollyvoo Schvang Gom!*'

Jonathan winced as he lifted his jacket from the hall hook. Hollywood Chewing Gum, whose green and white wrappers littered the gutters and occasionally Jonathan's garden, had mysterious attractions for infants of the French nation. '*Oui, m'sieur,*' Jonathan said, and went out the door.

Dr Perrier had a home number in the directory, and Jonathan hoped he was in tonight. A certain *tabac*, which had a telephone, was closer than Jonathan's shop. A panic was taking hold of Jonathan, and he began to trot towards the slanted lighted red cylinder that marked the *tabac* two streets away. He would insist on the truth. Jonathan nodded a greeting to the young man behind the bar, whom he knew slightly, and pointed to the telephone and also to the shelf where the directories lay. '*Fontaine-bleau!*' Jonathan shouted. The place was noisy, with a juke box going besides. Jonathan searched out the number and dialled.

Dr Perrier answered, and recognized Jonathan's voice.

'I would like very much to have another test. Even tonight. Now – if you could take a sample.'

'Tonight?'

'I could come to see you at once. In five minutes.'

'Are you – You are weak?'

'Well – I thought if the test went to Paris tomorrow –' Jonathan knew that Dr Perrier was in the habit of sending various samples to Paris on Saturday morning. 'If you could take a sample either tonight or early tomorrow morning –'

'I am not in my office tomorrow morning. I have visits to make. If you are so upset, M. Trevanny, come to my house now.'

Jonathan paid for his call, and remembered just before he went out the door to buy two packages of Hollywood Chewing Gum, which he dropped into his jacket pocket. Perrier lived way over on the Boulevard Maginot, which would take nearly ten minutes. Jonathan trotted and walked. He had never been to the doctor's home.

It was a big, gloomy building, and the concièrge was an old, slow, skinny woman watching television in a little glass-enclosed room full of plastic plants. While Jonathan waited for the lift to descend into the rickety cage, the concièrge crept into the hall and asked curiously:

'Your wife is having a baby, m'sieur?'

'No. No,' Jonathan said, smiling, and recalled that Dr Perrier was a general practitioner.

He rode up.

'Now what is the matter?' Dr Perrier asked, beckoning him through the dining-room. 'Come into this room.'

The house was dimly lighted. The television set was on somewhere. The room they went into was like a little office, with medical books on the shelves, and a desk on which the doctor's black bag now sat.

'*Mon dieu*, one would think you are on the brink of collapse and you've just been running, obviously, and your cheeks are pink. Don't tell me you've heard another rumour that you're on the edge of the grave!'

Jonathan made an effort to sound calm. 'It's just that I want to be sure. I don't feel so splendid, to tell the truth. I know it's been only two months since the last test but – since the next is due the end of April, what's the harm –' He broke off, shrugging. 'Since it's easy to take some marrow, and since it can go off tomorrow early –' Jonathan was aware that his French was clumsy at that moment, aware of the word *moelle*, marrow, which had become revolting, especially when Jonathan thought of his as being abnormally yellow. He sensed Dr Perrier's attitude that he must humour his patient.

'Yes, I can take the sample. The result will probably be the same as last time. You can never have complete assurance from the medical men, M. Trevanny ...' The doctor continued to talk, while Jonathan removed his sweater, obeyed Dr Perrier's gesture and lay down on an old leather sofa. The doctor jabbed the anaesthetizing needle in. 'But I can appreciate your anxiety,' Dr Perrier said seconds later, pressing and tapping on the tube that was going into Jonathan's sternum.

Jonathan disliked the crunching sound of it, but found the slight pain quite bearable. This time, perhaps, he'd learn something. Jonathan could not refrain from saying, before he left, 'I must know the truth, Dr Perrier. You don't think, really, that the laboratory might not be giving us a proper summing up? I'm ready to believe their *figures* are correct –'

'This summing up or prediction is what you can't get, my dear young man!'

Jonathan then walked home. He had thought of telling Simone that he'd gone to see Perrier, that he again felt anxious, but Jonathan couldn't: he'd put Simone through enough. What could she say, if he told her? She would only become a little more anxious herself, like him,

Georges was already in bed upstairs, and Simone was reading to him. Astérix again. Georges, propped against his pillows, and Simone on a low stool under the lamplight, were like a tableau vivant of domesticity, and the year might have been 1880, Jonathan thought, except for Simone's slacks. Georges' hair was as yellow as cornsilk under the light.

'*Le schvang gom?*' Georges asked, grinning.

Jonathan smiled and produced one packet. The other could wait for another occasion.

'You were a long time,' said Simone.

'I had a beer at the café,' Jonathan said.

The next afternoon between 4.30 and 5 p.m., as Dr Perrier had told him to do, Jonathan telephoned the Ebberle-Valent Laboratoires in Neuilly. He gave his name and spelt it and said he was a patient of Dr Perrier's in Fontainebleau. Then he waited to be connected with the right department, while the telephone gave a *blup* every minute for the pay units. Jonathan had pen and paper ready. Could he spell his name again, please? Then a woman's voice began to read the report, and Jonathan jotted figures down quickly. Hyperleucocytose 190,000. Wasn't that bigger than before?

'We shall of course send a written report to your doctor which he should receive by Tuesday.'

'This report is less favourable than the last, is it not?'

'I have not the previous report here, *m'sieur.*'

'Is there a doctor there? Could I speak with a doctor, perhaps?'

'*I am a doctor, m'sieur.*'

'Oh. Then this report – whether you have the old one or not there, is not a good one, is it?'

Like a textbook, she said, 'This is a potentially dangerous condition involving lowered resistance ...'

Jonathan had telephoned from his shop. He had turned his sign to FERME and drawn his door curtain, though he had been visible through the window, and now as he went to remove the sign, he realized he hadn't locked his door. Since no one else was due to call for a picture that afternoon, Jonathan thought he could afford to close. It was 4.55 p.m.

He walked to Dr Perrier's office, prepared to wait more than an hour if he had to. Saturday was a busy day, because most people didn't work and were free to see the doctor. There were three people ahead of Jonathan, but the nurse spoke to him and asked if he would be long, Jonathan said no, and the nurse squeezed him in with an apology to the next patient. Had Dr Perrier spoken to his nurse about him, Jonathan wondered?

Dr Perrier raised his black eyebrows at Jonathan's scribbled notes, and said, 'But this is incomplete.'

'I know, but it tells something, doesn't it? It's slightly worse – isn't it?'

'One would think you want to get worse!' Dr Perrier said with his customary cheer, which now Jonathan mistrusted. 'Frankly, yes, it is worse, but only a little worse. It is not crucial.'

'In percentage – ten per cent worse, would you say?'

'M. Trevanny – you are not an automobile! Now it is not reasonable for me to make a remark until I get the full report on Tuesday.'

Jonathan walked homeward rather slowly, walked through the Rue des Sablons just in case he saw someone who wanted to go into his shop. There wasn't anyone. Only the launderette was doing a brisk business, and people with bundles of laundry were bumping into each other at the door. It was nearly 6 p.m. Simone would be quitting the shoe shop sometime after 7 p.m., later than usual, because her boss Brezard wanted to take in every franc possible before closing for Sunday and Monday. And

Wister was still at l'Aigle Noir. Was he waiting only for him, waiting for him to change his mind and say yes? Wouldn't it be funny if Dr Perrier was in conspiracy with Stephen Wister, if between them they might have fixed the Ebberle-Valent Laboratories to give him a bad report? And if Gauthier were in on it, too, the little messenger of bad tidings? Like a nightmare in which the strangest elements join forces against – against the dreamer. But Jonathan knew he was not dreaming. He knew that Dr Perrier was not in the pay of Stephen Wister. Nor was Ebberle-Valent. And it was not a dream that his condition was worse, that death was a little closer, or sooner, than he had thought. True of everyone, however, who lived one more day, Jonathan reminded himself. Jonathan thought of death, and the process of ageing, as a decline, literally a downward path. Most people had a chance to take it slowly, starting at fifty-five or whenever they slowed up, descending until seventy or whatever year was their number. Jonathan realized that his death was going to be like falling over a cliff. When he tried to 'prepare' himself, his mind wavered and dodged. His attitude, or his spirit, was still thirty-four years old and wanted to live.

The Trevannys' narrow house, blue-grey in the dusk, showed no lights. It was a rather sombre house, and that fact had amused Jonathan and Simone when they had bought it five years ago. 'The Sherlock Holmes house', Jonathan had used to call it, when they were debating his house versus another in Fontainebleau. 'I still prefer the Sherlock Holmes house,' Jonathan remembered saying once. The house had an 1890 air, suggestive of gas lights and polished banisters, though none of the wood anywhere in the house had been polished when they had moved in. The house had looked as if it could be made into something with turn-of-the-century charm, however. The rooms were smallish but interestingly arranged, the garden a rectangular patch full of wildly overgrown rose bushes, but at least the rose bushes had been there, and all the garden had needed was a clearing out. And the scalloped glass portico over the back steps, its little glass-enclosed porch, had made Jonathan think of Vuillard, and Bonnard. But now it struck Jonathan that five years of their occupancy hadn't really defeated the gloom. New wallpaper would brighten the bedroom, yes, but that was only one room. The house wasn't yet paid for: they had three more years to go on the mortgage. An apartment, such as they'd had in Fontainebleau in the first year of their marriage, would have been cheaper, but Simone was used to a house with a bit of garden – she'd had a garden all her life in Nemours – and as an Englishman, Jonathan liked a bit of garden too. Jonathan never regretted that the house took such a hunk of their income.

What Jonathan was thinking, as he climbed the front steps, was not so much of the remaining mortgage, but the fact that he was probably going to die in this house. More than likely, he would never know another, more cheerful house with Simone. He was thinking that the Sherlock Holmes house had been standing for decades before he had been born, and that it would stand for decades after his death. It had been his fate to choose this house, he felt. One day they would carry him out feet first, maybe still alive but dying, and he would never enter the house again.

To Jonathan's surprise, Simone was in the kitchen, playing some kind of card game with Georges at the table. She looked up, smiling, then Jonathan saw her remember: he was to have rung the Paris laboratory this afternoon. But she couldn't mention that in front of Georges.

'The old creep closed early today,' Simone said. 'No business.'

'Good!' Jonathan said brightly. 'What goes on in this gambling den?'

'I'm winning!' Georges said in French.

Simone got up and followed Jonathan into the hall as he hung his raincoat. She looked at him inquiringly.

'Nothing to worry about,' Jonathan said, but she beckoned him farther down the hall to the living-room. 'It seems to be a trifle worse, but I don't feel worse, so what the hell? I'm sick of it. Let's have a Cinzano.'

'You were worried because of that story, weren't you, Jon?'

'Yes. That's true.'

'I wish I knew who started that.' Her eyes narrowed bitterly. 'It's a nasty story. Gauthier never told you who said it?'

'No. As Gauthier said, it was some mistake somewhere, some kind of exaggeration.' Jonathan was repeating what he had said to Simone before. But he knew it was no mistake, that it was a story quite calculated.

FIVE

Jonathan stood at the first-floor bedroom window, watching Simone hang the wash on the garden line. There were pillow-cases, Georges' sleep suits, a dozen pairs of Georges' and Jonathan's socks, two white nightdresses, bras, Jonathan's beige work trousers – everything except sheets, which

Simone sent to the laundry, because well-ironed sheets were important to her. Simone wore tweed slacks and a thin red sweater that clung to her body. Her back looked strong and supple as she bent over the big oval basket, pegging out dishcloths now. It was a fine, sunny day with a hint of summer in the breeze.

Jonathan had wriggled out of going to Nemours to have lunch with Simone's parents, the Foussadiers. He and Simone went every other Sunday as a rule. Unless Simone's brother Gérard fetched them, they took the bus to Nemours. Then at the Foussadiers' home, they had a big lunch with Gérard and his wife and two children, who also lived in Nemours. Simone's parents always made a fuss over Georges, always had a present for him. Around 3 p.m., Simone's father Jean-Noël would turn on the TV. Jonathan was frequently bored, but he went with Simone because it was the correct thing to do, and because he respected the closeness of French families.

'Do you feel all right?' Simone had asked, when Jonathan had begged out.

'Yes, darling. It's just that I'm not in the mood today, and I'd also like to get that patch ready for the tomatoes. So why don't you go with Georges?'

So Simone and Georges went on the bus at noon. Simone had put the remains of a *bœuf bourguignon* into a small red casserole on the stove, so all Jonathan had to do was heat it when he felt hungry.

Jonathan had wanted to be alone. He was thinking about the mysterious Stephen Wister and his proposal. Not that Jonathan meant to telephone Wister today at l'Aigle Noir, though Jonathan was very much aware that Wister was still there, not three hundred yards away. He had no intention of getting in touch with Wister, though the idea was curiously exciting and disturbing, a bolt from the blue, a shaft of colour in his uneventful existence, and Jonathan wanted to observe it, to enjoy it in a sense. Jonathan also had the feeling (it had been proven quite often) that Simone could read his thoughts, or at least knew when something was preoccupying him. If he appeared absent-minded that Sunday, he didn't want Simone to notice it and ask him what was the matter. So Jonathan gardened with a will, and day-dreamed. He thought of forty thousand pounds, a sum which meant the mortgage paid off at once, a couple of hire-purchase items paid off, the interior of his house painted where it needed to be painted, a television set, a nest-egg put aside for Georges' university, a few new clothes for Simone and himself – ah, mental ease! Simply freedom from anxiety! He thought of one, maybe two Mafia figures – burly, dark-haired thugs exploding in death, arms flailing, their bodies falling. What Jonathan was incapable of imagining, as his spade sank into the earth of his garden, was himself pulling a trigger, having aimed a gun at a man's back, perhaps. More interesting, more mysterious, more dangerous, was how Wister had got hold of his name. There was a plot against him in Fontainebleau, and it had somehow got to Hamburg. Impossible that Wister had him mixed up with someone else, because even Wister had spoken of his illness, of his wife and small son. Someone, Jonathan thought, who he considered a friend or at least a friendly acquaintance, was not friendly at all towards him.

Wister would probably leave Fontainebleau around 5 p.m. today, Jonathan thought. By 3 p.m., Jonathan had eaten his lunch, tidied up papers and old receipts in the catch-all drawer of the round table in the centre of the living-room. Then – he was happily aware that he was not tired at all – he tackled with broom and dustpan the exterior of the pipes and the floor around their *mazout* furnace.

At little after 5 p.m., as Jonathan was scrubbing soot from his hands at the kitchen sink, Simone arrived with Georges and her brother Gérard and his wife Yvonne, and they all had a drink in the kitchen. Georges had been presented by his grandparents with a round box of Easter goodies including an egg wrapped in gold foil, a chocolate rabbit, coloured gumdrops, all under yellow cellophane and as yet unopened, because Simone forbade him to open it, in view of the other sweets he had eaten in Nemours. Georges went with the Foussadier children into the garden.

'Don't step on the soft part, Georges!' Jonathan shouted. He had raked the turned ground smooth, but left the pebbles for Georges to pick up. Georges would probably get his two chums to help him fill the red wagon. Jonathan gave him fifty centimes for a wagonful of pebbles – not ever full, but full enough to cover the bottom.

It was starting to rain. Jonathan had taken the laundry in a few minutes ago.

'The garden looks marvellous!' Simone said. 'Look, Gérard!' She beckoned her brother on to the little back porch.

By now, Jonathan thought, Wister was probably on a train from Fontainebleau to Paris, or maybe he'd take a taxi from Fontainebleau to Orly, considering the money he seemed to have. Maybe he was already in the air, *en route* to Hamburg. Simone's presence, the voices of Gérard and Yvonne, seemed to erase Wister from the Hôtel de l'Aigle Noir, at any rate, seemed to turn Wister almost into a quirk of Jonathan's imagination. Jonathan felt also a mild triumph in the fact that he had not telephoned

Wister, as if by not telephoning him he had successfully resisted some kind of temptation.

Gérard Foussadier, an electrician, was a neat, serious man a little older than Simone, with fairer hair than hers, and a carefully clipped brown moustache. His hobby was naval history, and he made model nineteenth-century and eighteenth-century frigates in which he installed miniature electric lights that he could put completely or partially on by a switch in his living-room. Gérard himself laughed at the anachronism of electric lights in his frigates, but the effect was beautiful when all the other lights in the house were turned out, and eight or ten ships seemed to be sailing on a dark sea around the living-room.

'Simone said you were a little worried – as to your health, Jon,' Gérard said earnestly. 'I am sorry.'

'Not particularly. Just another check-up,' Jonathan said. 'The report's about the same.' Jonathan was used to these clichés, which were like saying, 'Very well, thank you,' when someone asked you how you felt. What Jonathan said seemed to satisfy Gérard, so evidently Simone had not said much.

Yvonne and Simone were talking about linoleum. The kitchen linoleum was wearing out in front of the stove and the sink. It hadn't been new when they bought the house.

'You're really feeling all right, darling?' Simone asked Jonathan, when the Foussadiers had left.

'Better than all right. I even attacked the boiler-room. The soot.' Jonathan smiled.

'You are mad. Tonight you'll have a decent dinner at least. Mama insisted that I bring home three *paupiettes* from lunch and they're delicious!'

Then close to 11 p.m., as they were about to go to bed, Jonathan felt a sudden depression, as if his legs, his whole body had sunk into something viscous – as if he were walking hip-deep in mud. Was he simply tired? But it seemed more mental than physical. He was glad when the light was turned out, when he could relax with his arms around Simone, her arms around him, as they always lay when they fell asleep. He thought of Stephen Wister (or was that his real name?) maybe flying eastward now, his thin figure stretched out in an aeroplane seat. Jonathan imagined Wister's face with the pinkish scar, puzzled, tense, but Wister would no longer be thinking of Jonathan Trevanny. He'd be thinking of someone else. He must have two or three more prospects, Jonathan thought.

The morning was chill and foggy. Just after 8 a.m., Simone went off with

Georges to the Ecole Maternelle, and Jonathan stood in the kitchen, warming his fingers on a second bowl of *café au lait*. The heating system wasn't adequate. They'd got rather uncomfortably through another winter, and even now in spring the house was chilly in the mornings. The furnace had been in the house when they bought it, adequate for the five radiators downstairs, but not for the other five upstairs which they had installed hopefully. They'd been warned, Jonathan remembered, but a bigger furnace would have cost three thousand new francs, and they hadn't had the money.

Three letters had fallen through the slot in the front door. One was an electricity bill. Jonathan turned a square white envelope over and saw Hôtel de l'Aigle Noir on its back. He opened the envelope. A business card fell out and dropped. Jonathan picked it up and read 'Stephen Wister chez', which had been written above:

Reeves Minot
159 Agnesstrasse
Winterhude (Alster)
Hamburg 56
629–6757

There was a letter also.

                                                                1 Apr. 19—
Dear Mr Trevanny,

   I was sorry not to hear from you this morning or so far this afternoon. But in case you change your mind, I enclose a card with my address in Hamburg. If you have second thoughts about my proposition, please telephone me collect at any hour. Or come to talk to me in Hamburg. Your round-trip transportation can be wired to you at once when I hear from you.

   In fact, wouldn't it be a good idea to see a Hamburg specialist about your blood condition and get another opinion? This might make you feel more comfortable.

   I am returning to Hamburg Sunday night,

                                                    Yours sincerely,
                                                    Stephen Wister

Jonathan was surprised, amused, annoyed all at once. *More comfortable.* That was a bit funny, since Wister was sure he was going to die soon. If a Hamburg specialist said, '*Ach, ja,* you have just one or two more months.' would that make him feel more comfortable? Jonathan pushed the letter and the card into a back pocket of his trousers. A return trip to Hamburg gratis. Wister was thinking of every enticement. Interesting that he'd sent the letter Sunday afternoon, so he would receive it early Monday, though

Jonathan might have rung him at any time Sunday. But there was no collection from post boxes in town on Sunday.

It was 8.52 a.m. Jonathan thought of what he had to do. He needed more mat paper from a firm in Melun. There were at least two clients he should write a postcard to, because their pictures had been ready for more than a week. Jonathan usually went to his shop on Mondays, and spent his time doing odds and ends, though the shop was not open, as it was against French law to be open six days a week.

Jonathan got to his shop at 9.15 a.m., drew the green shade of his door, and locked the door again, leaving the FERME sign in it. He pottered about, thinking still about Hamburg. The opinion of a German specialist might be a good thing. Two years ago Jonathan had consulted a specialist in London. His report had been the same as the French, which had satisfied Jonathan that the diagnoses were true. Mightn't the Germans be a little more thorough or up to date? Suppose he accepted Wister's offer of a round trip? (Jonathan was copying an address on to a postcard.) But then he'd be beholden to Wister. Jonathan realized he was toying with the idea of killing someone for Wister – not for Wister, but for the money. A Mafia member. They were all criminals themselves, weren't they? Of course, Jonathan reminded himself, he could always pay Wister back, if he accepted his round-trip fare. The point was, Jonathan couldn't pull the money out of the bank funds just now, there wasn't enough. If he really wanted to make sure of his condition, Germany (or Switzerland for that matter) could tell him. They still had the best doctors in the world, hadn't they? Jonathan was now putting the card of the paper supplier of Melun beside his telephone to remind him to ring tomorrow, because the paper place wasn't open today either. And who knew, mightn't Stephen Wister's proposal be feasible? For an instant, Jonathan saw himself blown to bits by the crossfire of German police officers: they'd caught him just after he fired on the Italian. But even if he were dead, Simone and Georges would get the forty thousand quid. Jonathan came back to reality. He wasn't going to kill anybody, no. But Hamburg, going to Hamburg seemed a lark, a break, even if he learned some awful news there. He'd learn *facts*, anyway. And if Wister paid now, Jonathan could pay him back in a matter of three months, if he scrimped, didn't buy any clothes, not even a beer in a café. Jonathan rather dreaded telling Simone, though she'd agree, of course, since it had to do with seeing another doctor, presumably an excellent doctor. The scrimping would come out of Jonathan's own pocket.

Around 11 a.m., Jonathan put in a call to Wister's number in Hamburg, direct, not collect. Three or four minutes later, his telephone rang, and Jonathan had a clear connection, much better than Paris usually sounded.

'... Yes, this is Wister,' Wister said in his light, tense voice.

'I had your letter this morning,' Jonathan began. 'The idea of going to Hamburg –'

'Yes, why not?' said Wister casually.

'But I mean the idea of seeing a specialist –'

'I'll cable you the money right away. You can pick it up at the Fontaine-bleau post office. It should be there in a couple of hours.'

'That's – that's kind of you. Once I'm there, I can –'

'Can you come today? This evening? There's room here for you to stay.'

'I don't know about today.' And yet, why not?

'Call me again when you've got your ticket. Tell me what time you're coming in. I'll be in all day.'

Jonathan's heart was beating a little fast when he hung up.

At home during lunch-time, Jonathan went upstairs to the bedroom to see if his suitcase was handy. It was, on top of the wardrobe where it had been since their last holiday, nearly a year ago, in Arles.

He said to Simone, 'Darling, something important. I've decided to go to Hamburg and see a specialist.'

'Oh, yes? Perrier suggested it?'

'Well – in fact, no. My idea. I wouldn't mind having a German doctor's opinion. I know it's an expense.'

'Oh, Jon! Expense! Did you have any news this morning? But the laboratory report comes tomorrow, doesn't it?'

'Yes. What they say is always the same, darling. I want a fresh opinion.'

'When do you want to go?'

'Soon. This week.'

Just before 5 p.m. Jonathan called at the Fontainebleau post office. The money had arrived. Jonathan presented his *carte d'identité* and received six hundred francs. He went from the post office to the Syndicat d'Initia-tives in the Place Franklin Roosevelt, just a couple of streets away, and bought a round-trip ticket to Hamburg on a plane that left Orly airport at 9.25 p.m. that evening. He would have to hurry, he realized, and he liked that, because it precluded thinking, hesitating. He went to his shop and telephoned Hamburg, this time collect.

Wister again answered. 'Oh, that's fine. At eleven fifty-five, right. Take the airport bus to the city terminus, would you? I'll meet you there.'

Then Jonathan made one telephone call to a client who had an impor-tant picture to pick up, to say that he would be closed Tuesday and

Wednesday for 'reasons of family', a common excuse. He'd have to leave a sign to that effect in his door for a couple of days. Not a very important matter, Jonathan thought, since shopkeepers in town frequently closed for a few days for one reason or another. Jonathan had once seen a sign saying 'closed due to hangover'.

Jonathan shut up shop and went home to pack. It would be a two-day stay at most, he thought, unless the Hamburg hospital or whatever insisted that he stay longer for tests. He had checked the trains to Paris, and there was one around 7 p.m. that would do nicely. He had to get to Paris, then to Les Invalides for a bus to Orly. When Simone came home with Georges, Jonathan had his suitcase downstairs.

'Tonight?' Simone said.

'The sooner the better, darling. I had an impulse. I'll be back Wednesday, maybe even tomorrow night.'

'But – where can I reach you? You arranged for a hotel?'

'No. I'll have to telegraph you, darling. Don't worry.'

'You've got everything arranged with the doctor? Who is the doctor?'

'I don't know yet. I've only heard of the hospital.' Jonathan dropped his passport, trying to stick it into the inside pocket of his jacket.

'I never saw you like this,' said Simone.

Jonathan smiled at her. 'At least – obviously I'm not collapsing!'

Simone wanted to go with him to the Fontainebleau-Avon station, and take the bus back, but Jonathan begged her not to.

'I'll telegraph right away,' Jonathan said.

'Where is Hamburg?' Georges demanded for the second time.

'Allemagne! Germany!' Jonathan said.

Jonathan found a taxi in the Rue de France, luckily. The train was pulling into the Fontainebleau-Avon station as he arrived, and he barely had time to buy his ticket and hop on. Then it was a taxi from the Gare de Lyon to Les Invalides. Jonathan had some money left over from the six hundred francs. For a while, he was not going to worry about money.

On the plane, he half slept, with a magazine in his lap. He was imagining being another person. The rush of the plane seemed to be rushing this new person away from the man left behind in the dark grey house in the Rue St Merry. He imagined another Jonathan helping Simone with the dishes at this moment, chatting about boring things such as the price of linoleum for the kitchen floor.

The plane touched down. The air was sharp and much colder. There was a long lighted motorway, then the city's streets, massive buildings looming up into the night sky, street lights of different colours and shape from those of France.

And there was Wister smiling, walking towards him with his hand extended. 'Welcome, Mr Trevanny! Had a good trip? ... My car is just outside. Hope you didn't mind coming to the terminus. My driver – not my driver but one I use sometimes – he was tied up till just a few minutes ago.'

They were walking out to the kerb. Wister droned on in his American accent. Except for his scar, nothing about Wister suggested violence. He was, Jonathan decided, too calm, which from a psychiatric point of view might be ominous. Or was he merely nursing an ulcer? Wister stopped beside a well-polished black Mercedes-Benz. An older man, wearing no cap, took care of Jonathan's medium-sized suitcase, and held the door for him and Wister.

'This is Karl,' Wister said.

'Evening,' Jonathan said.

Karl smiled, and murmured something in German.

It was quite a long drive. Wister pointed out the Rathaus, 'the oldest in all Europe, and the bombs didn't get it,' and a great church or cathedral whose name Jonathan didn't get. He and Wister were sitting together in the back. They entered a part of the town with a more countrylike atmosphere, went over still another bridge, and on to a darker road.

'Here we are,' Wister said. 'My place.'

The car had turned into a climbing driveway and stopped beside a large house with a few lighted windows and a lighted, well-kept entrance.

'It's an old house with four flats, and I have one,' Wister explained. 'Lots of such houses in Hamburg. Converted. Here I have a nice view of the Alster. It's the Aussen Alster, the big one. You'll see more tomorrow.'

They rode up in a modern lift, Karl taking Jonathan's suitcase. Karl pressed a bell, and a middle-aged woman in a black dress and white apron opened the door, smiling.

'This is Gaby,' said Wister to Jonathan. 'My part-time housekeeper. She works for another family in the house and sleeps with them, but I told her we might want some food tonight. Gaby, Herr Trevanny aus Frankreich.'

The woman greeted Jonathan pleasantly, and took his coat. She had a round, pudding-like face, and looked the soul of goodwill.

'Wash in here, if you like,' said Wister, gesturing to a bathroom whose light was already on. 'I'll get you a scotch. Are you hungry?'

When Jonathan came out of the bathroom, the lights – four lamps – were on in the big square living-room. Wister was sitting on a green sofa, smoking a cigar. Two scotches stood on the coffee-table in front of Wister. Gaby came in at once with a tray of sandwiches and a round, pale yellow cheese.

'Ah, thank you, Gaby.' Wister said to Jonathan. 'Late for Gaby, but when I told her I had a guest coming, she insisted on staying on to serve the sandwiches.' Wister, though making a cheerful remark, still didn't smile. In fact his straight eyebrows drew together anxiously as Gaby arranged the plates and the silverware. When she departed, he said, 'You're feeling all right? Now the main thing is – the visit to the specialist – I have a good man in mind, Dr Heinrich Wentzel, a haematologist at the Eppendorfer Krankenhaus, which is the main hospital here. World famous. I've made an appointment for you for tomorrow at two, if that's agreeable.'

'Certainly. Thank you,' Jonathan said.

'That gives you a chance to catch up on your sleep. Your wife didn't mind too much, I hope, your taking off on such short notice? ... After all it's only intelligent to consult more than one doctor about a serious ailment ...'

Jonathan was only half listening. He felt dazed, and he was also a bit distracted by the décor, by the fact it was all supposed to be *German*, and that it was the first time he'd been in Germany. The furnishings were quite conventional and more modern than antique, though there was a handsome Biedermeier desk against the wall opposite Jonathan. There were low bookshelves along all the walls, long green curtains at the windows, and the lamps in corners spread the light pleasantly. A purple wooden box lay open on the glass coffee-table, presenting a variety of cigars and cigarettes in compartments. The white fireplace had brass accessories, but there was no fire now. A rather interesting painting which looked like a Derwatt hung over the fireplace. And where was Reeves Minot? Wister was Minot, Jonathan supposed. Was Wister going to announce this or assume that Jonathan realized it? It occurred to Jonathan that he and Simone ought to paint or paper their whole house white. He should discourage the idea of the art nouveau wallpaper in the bedroom. If they wanted to achieve more light, white was the logical –

'... You might've given some thought to the other proposition,' Wister was saying in his soft voice. 'The idea I was talking about in Fontaine-bleau.'

'I'm afraid I haven't changed my mind about that,' Jonathan said. 'And so this leads to – obviously I owe you six hundred francs.' Jonathan forced a smile. Already he felt the scotch, and as soon as he realized this, he nervously drank a little more from his glass. 'I can repay you within three months. The specialist is the essential thing for me now. First things first.'

'Of course,' said Wister. 'And you mustn't think about any repayment. That's absurd.'

Jonathan didn't want to argue, but he felt vaguely ashamed. More than anything, Jonathan felt odd, as if he were dreaming, or somehow not himself. It's only the foreignness of everything, he thought.

'This Italian we want eliminated,' Wister said, folding his hands behind his head and looking up at the ceiling, 'has a routine job. Ha! That's funny! He only pretends it's a job with regular hours. He's hanging around the clubs off the Reeperbahn, pretending he has a taste for gambling, and he's pretending he has a job as an oenologist, and I'm sure he has a chum at the – whatever they call the wine factory here. He goes to the wine factory every afternoon, but he spends his evenings in one or another of the private clubs, playing the tables a little and seeing who he can meet. Mornings he sleeps, because he's up all night. Now the point is,' Wister said, sitting up, 'he takes the U-bahn every afternoon to get home, home being a rented flat. He's got a six-months lease and a real six-month job with the wine place to make it look legitimate. Have a sandwich!' Wister extended the plate, as if he had just realized the sandwiches were there.

Jonathan took a tongue sandwich. There were also cole slaw and dill pickle.

'The important point is he gets off the U-bahn at the Steinstrasse station every day around six-fifteen by himself, looking like any other business-man coming back from the office. That's the time we want to get him.' Wister spread his bony hands palm downwards. 'The assassin fires once if you can get the middle of his back, twice for sure maybe, drops the gun and – Bob's your uncle as the English say, isn't that right?'

The phrase was indeed familiar, out of the long ago past. 'If it's so easy, why do you need me?' Jonathan managed a polite smile. 'I'm an amateur to say the least. I'd botch it.'

Wister might not have heard. 'The crowd in the U-bahn *may* be rounded up. Some of them. Who can tell? Thirty, forty people maybe, if the cops get there fast enough. It's a huge station, the station for the main railway terminus. They might look people over. But suppose they look you over?' Wister shrugged. 'You'll have dropped the gun. You'll have used a thin stocking over your hand, and you'll drop the stocking a few seconds after you fire. No powder marks on you, no fingerprints on the gun. You have no connection with the man who's dead. Oh, it really won't come to all that. But one look at your French identity card, the fact of your appointment with Dr Wentzel, you're in the clear. My point is, *our* point, we don't want anyone connected with us or the clubs . . .'

Jonathan listened and made no comment. On the day of the shooting, he was thinking, he would have to be in a hotel, he could hardly be a house-guest of Wister, in case a policeman asked him where he was staying. And what about Karl and the housekeeper? Did they know anything about this? Were they trustworthy? *It's all a lot of nonsense*, Jonathan thought, and wanted to smile, but he wasn't smiling.

'You're tired,' Wister informed him. 'Want to see your room? Gaby already took your suitcase in.'

Fifteen minutes later, Jonathan was in pyjamas after a hot shower. His room had a window at the front of the house, like the living-room which had two windows on the front, and Jonathan looked out on a surface of water where there were lights along the near shore, and some red and green lights of tied-up boats. It looked dark, peaceful and spacious. A searchlight's beam swept protectively across the sky. His bed was a three-quarter width, neatly turned down. There was a glass of what looked like water on his bed-table and a package of Gitane *maïs*, his brand, and an ashtray and matches. Jonathan took a sip from the glass and found that it was indeed water.

SIX

Jonathan sat on the edge of his bed, sipping coffee which Gaby had just brought. It was coffee the way he liked it, strong with a dash of thick cream. Jonathan had awakened at 7 a.m., then gone back to sleep until Wister had knocked on the door at 10.30 a.m.

'Don't apologize, I'm glad you slept,' said Wister. 'Gaby is ready to bring you some coffee. Or do you prefer tea?'

Wister had also added that he had made a reservation for Jonathan at the Hotel – Victoria was its name in English, anyway, where they would go before lunch. Jonathan thanked him. No further conversation about the hotel. But that was the beginning, Jonathan thought, as he had thought last night. If he were to carry out Wister's plan, he mustn't be

a house-guest here. Jonathan, however, felt glad he was going to be out
from under Wister's roof in a couple of hours.

A friend or acquaintance of Wister's named Rudolf something arrived
at noon. Rudolf was young and slender with straight black hair, nervous
and polite. Wister said he was a medical student. Evidently he did not
speak English. He reminded Jonathan of photographs of Franz Kafka. They
all got into the car, driven by Karl, and set off for Jonathan's hotel.
Everything looked so new compared to France, Jonathan thought, and
then recalled that Hamburg had been flattened by bombs. The car stopped
in a commercial-looking street. It was the Hotel Victoria.

'They all speak English,' Wister said. 'We'll wait for you.'

Jonathan went in. A bellhop had taken his suitcase at the door. He
registered, looking at his English passport to get the number right. He
asked for his suitcase to be sent up to his room, as Wister had told him
to do. The hotel was of middle category, Jonathan saw.

Then they drove to a restaurant for lunch, where Karl did not join them.
They had a bottle of wine at their table before the meal, and Rudolf became
more merry. Rudolf spoke in German and Wister translated a few of his
pleasantries. Jonathan was thinking of the hour 2 p.m., when he was due
at the hospital.

'Reeves –' said Rudolf to Wister.

Jonathan thought Rudolf had said it once before, and this time there was
no mistake. Wister – Reeves Minot – took it calmly. And so did Jonathan.

'Anaemic,' said Rudolf to Jonathan.

'Worse.' Jonathan smiled.

'Schlimmer,' said Reeves Minot, and continued to Rudolf in German,
which seemed to Jonathan as clumsy as his French, but was probably
equally adequate.

The food was excellent, the portions enormous. Reeves had brought his
cigars. But before they could finish the cigars, they had to leave for the
hospital.

The hospital was a vast assembly of buildings set among trees and
pathways lined with flowers. Karl had again driven them. The wing of the
hospital where Jonathan had to go looked like a laboratory of the future
– rooms on either side of a corridor as in a hotel, except that these rooms
held chromium chairs or beds and were illuminated by fluorescent or
variously coloured lamps. There was a smell not of disinfectant but as of
some unearthly gas, somewhat resembling the smell Jonathan had known
under the X-ray machine which five years ago had done him no good with
the leukaemia. It was the kind of place where laymen surrendered utterly

to the omniscient specialists, Jonathan thought, and at once he felt weak enough to faint. Jonathan was walking at that moment down a seemingly endless corridor of sound-proofed floor surface with Rudolf, who was to interpret if Jonathan needed it. Reeves had remained in the car with Karl, but Jonathan was not sure if they were going to wait, or of how long the examination would take.

Dr Wentzel, a heavy man with grey hair and walrus moustaches, knew a little English, but he did not try to construct long sentences. 'How long?' Six years. Jonathan was weighed, asked if he had had any weight loss recently, stripped to the waist, his spleen palpated. All the while, the doctor murmured in German to a nurse who was taking notes. His blood pressure was taken, his eyelids looked at, urine and blood samples taken, finally the sternum marrow sample taken with a punch-like instrument that operated faster and with less discomfort than Dr Perrier's. Jonathan was told he could have the results tomorrow morning. The examination had taken only about forty-five minutes.

Jonathan and Rudolf walked out. The car was several yards away among some other cars in a parking area.

'How was it? ... When will you know?' Reeves asked. 'Would you like to come back to my place or go to your hotel?'

'I think to my hotel, thanks.' Jonathan sank with relief into a corner seat of the car.

Rudolf seemed to be singing Wentzel's praises to Reeves. They arrived at the hotel.

'We'll pick you up for dinner,' said Reeves cheerfully. 'At seven.'

Jonathan got his key and went to his room. He took off his jacket and fell on to the bed face down. After two or three minutes, he pushed himself up and went to the writing desk. There was notepaper in a drawer. He sat down and wrote:

April 4, 19—

My dear Simone,

I have just had an examination and will know the results tomorrow morning. Very efficient hospital, doctor looking like Emp. Franz Josef, said to be the best haematologist in the world! Whatever the result tomorrow I shall feel more at ease knowing it. With luck I may be home tomorrow before you get this, unless Dr Wentzel wants to do some other tests.

Will telegraph now, just to say I am all right. I miss you, I think of you and Cailloux.

A bientôt with all my love,

Jon

Jonathan hung up his best suit, which was a dark blue, left the rest of his things in his suitcase, and went downstairs to post his letter. He had changed a ten-pound traveller's cheque, from an ancient book of three or four, last evening at the airport. He wrote a short telegram to Simone saying he was all right and that a letter was arriving. Then he went out, took note of the street's name and of the look of the neighbourhood – a huge beer advertisement struck him most forcibly – then went out for a walk.

The pavements bustled with shoppers and pedestrians, with dachs-hunds on leads, with hawkers of fruit and newspapers at the corners. Jonathan gazed into a window full of beautiful sweaters. There was also a handsome blue silk dressing-gown set off against a background of creamy white sheep pelts. He started to figure out its price in francs and gave it up, not being really interested. He crossed a busy avenue where there were both tramways and buses, came to a canal with a footbridge, and decided not to cross it. A coffee, perhaps. Jonathan approached a pleasant-looking coffee bar which had pastry in the window, a counter as well as small tables inside, and then could not bring himself to go in. He realized that he was terrified of what the report tomorrow morning would say. He had suddenly a hollow feeling with which he was familiar, a feeling of thinness as if he had become tissue paper, a coolness on his forehead as if his life itself were evaporating.

What Jonathan knew also, or at least suspected, was that tomorrow morning he would receive a phoney report. Jonathan mistrusted Rudolf's presence. A medical student. Rudolf had been no help, because he hadn't been needed. The doctor's nurse had spoken English. Mightn't Rudolf write up a phoney report tonight? Substitute it somehow? Jonathan even imagined Rudolf pinching hospital stationery that afternoon. Or maybe he was losing his mind, Jonathan warned himself.

He turned back in the direction of his hotel, taking the shortest way possible. He reached the Victoria, claimed his key, and let himself into his room. Then he took his shoes off, went into the bathroom and wet a towel, and lay down with the towel across his forehead and his eyes. He did not feel sleepy, just somehow odd. Reeves Minot was odd. To advance a total stranger six hundred francs, to make the insane proposal that he had – promising more than forty thousand pounds. It couldn't be true. Reeves Minot would never deliver. Reeves Minot seemed to live in a world of fantasy. Maybe he wasn't even a crook, but merely a bit cracked, a type that lived on delusions of importance and power.

The telephone awakened Jonathan. A man's voice said in English:

'A chentleman waits on you below, sir.'

Jonathan looked at his watch and saw that it was a minute or two past 7 p.m. 'Would you tell him I'll be down in two minutes?'

Jonathan washed his face, put on a polo-neck sweater, then a jacket. He also took his topcoat.

Karl was alone with the car. 'You had a nice afternoon, sir?' he asked in English.

In the course of the small talk, Jonathan found that Karl had quite a vocabulary in English. How many other strangers had Karl ferried around for Reeves Minot, Jonathan wondered? What business did Karl think Reeves was in? Maybe it simply didn't matter to Karl. What business was Reeves supposed to be in?

Karl stopped the car in the sloping driveway again, and this time Jonathan took the lift alone to the second floor.

Reeves Minot, in grey flannels and a sweater, greeted Jonathan at the door. 'Come in! Did you take it easy this afternoon?'

They had scotches. A table was set for two, and Jonathan assumed that they were going to be alone this evening.

'I would like you to see a picture of this man I have in mind,' Reeves said, hauling his thin form from the sofa, going to his Biedermeier desk. He took something from a drawer. He had two photographs, one a front view, the other a profile in a group of several people bending over a table.

The table was a roulette-table. Jonathan looked at the front-view picture, which was as clear as a passport photograph. The man looked about forty, with the square, fleshy face of lots of Italians, creases already curving from the flanges of his nose down to the level of his thick lips. His dark eyes looked wary, almost startled, yet in the faint smile there was an air also of 'So what've I done, eh?' Salvatore Bianca, Reeves said his name was.

'This picture,' Reeves said, pointing to the group picture, 'was taken in Hamburg about a week ago. He doesn't even gamble, just watches. This is a rare moment when he's looking at the wheel ... Bianca's probably killed half a dozen men himself or he wouldn't even be a button man. But he's not important as a Mafioso. He's expendable. Just to start the ball rolling, you see ...' Reeves went on, while Jonathan finished his drink, and Reeves made him another. 'Bianca wears a hat all the time – outdoors that is – a homburg. A tweed overcoat usually ...'

Reeves had a gramophone, and Jonathan would have enjoyed some music, but felt it would have been rude to ask, though he could imagine Reeves flying to the gramophone to play precisely what he wanted.

Jonathan interrupted finally, 'An ordinary-looking man, homburg pulled down and coat collar turned up – and one's supposed to spot him in a crowd after seeing these two pictures?'

'A friend of mine is going to ride the same underground from the Rathaus stop, where Bianca gets on, to the Messberg, which is the next stop and the only stop before the Steinstrasse. Look!'

This had set Reeves off again, and he showed Jonathan a street map of Hamburg which folded like an accordion and showed the U-bahn routes in blue dots.

'You'll get on the U-bahn with Fritz at the Rathaus. Fritz is coming over after dinner.'

I'm sorry to disappoint you, Jonathan wanted to say. He felt a twinge of guilt for having led Reeves on to this extent. Or had he led him on? No. Reeves had taken a crazy gamble. Reeves was probably used to such things, and he might not be the first person Reeves had approached. Jonathan was tempted to ask if he were the first person, but Reeves' voice droned on.

'There is definitely the possibility of a second shooting. I don't want to mislead you ...'

Jonathan was glad of the bad side of it. Reeves had been presenting it all in a rosy light, the Bob's-your-uncle shooting followed by pockets full of money and a better life in France or wherever, a cruise around the world, the best of everything for Georges (Reeves had asked his son's name), a more secure life for Simone. *How would I ever explain all the lolly to her?* Jonathan wondered.

'This is *Aalsuppe*,' Reeves said, as he picked up his spoon. 'Specialty of Hamburg and Gaby loves to make it.'

The eel soup was very good. There was an excellent cool Moselle.

'Hamburg has a famous zoo, you know. Hagenbeck's Tierpark in Settlingen. A nice drive from here. We might go tomorrow morning. That is' – Reeves looked suddenly more troubled – 'if something doesn't turn up for me. I'm half-way expecting something. I should know by tonight or early tomorrow.'

One would have thought the zoo was an important matter. Jonathan said, 'Tomorrow morning I get the results from the hospital. I'm supposed to be there at eleven.' Jonathan felt a despair, as if 11 a.m. might be the hour of his death.

'Yes of course. Well, the zoo maybe in the afternoon. The animals are in a natural – natural habitat ...'

Sauerbraten. Red cabbage.

The doorbell rang. Reeves did not get up, and in a moment Gaby came in and announced that Herr Fritz had arrived.

Fritz had a cap in his hand, and wore a rather shabby overcoat. He was about fifty.

'This is Paul,' said Reeves to Fritz, indicating Jonathan. 'An Englishman. Fritz.'

'Good evening,' Jonathan said.

Fritz gave a friendly wave to Jonathan. Fritz was a tough one, Jonathan thought, but he had an amiable smile.

'Sit down, Fritz,' said Reeves. 'Glass of wine? Scotch?' Reeves spoke in German. 'Paul is our man,' he added in English to Fritz. He handed Fritz a tall, stemmed glass of white wine.

Fritz nodded.

Jonathan was amused. The oversized wine glasses looked like something out of Wagnerian opera. Reeves was sitting sideways in his chair now.

'Fritz is a taxi-driver,' Reeves said. 'Taken Herr Bianca home many an evening, eh, Fritz?'

Fritz murmured something, smiling.

'Not many an evening, twice,' Reeves said. 'Sure, we don't –' Reeves hestitated, as if not knowing in what language to speak, then continued to Jonathan, 'Bianca probably doesn't know Fritz by sight. It doesn't matter too much if he does, because Fritz gets off at Messberg. The point is, you and Fritz will meet outside the Rathaus U-bahn station tomorrow, and then Fritz will indicate our – our Bianca.'

Fritz nodded, apparently understanding everything.

Tomorrow now. Jonathan listened in silence.

'Now you both get on at the Rathaus stop, that'll be around six-fifteen. Best to be there just before six, because Bianca for some reason might be early, though he's pretty regular at six-fifteen. Karl will drive you, Paul, so there's nothing to worry about. You don't go anywhere near each other, you and Fritz, but it may be that Fritz has to get on the train, the same train as Bianca and you, in order to point him out definitely. In any case, Fritz gets off at Messberg, the next stop.' Then Reeves said something in German to Fritz and extended a hand.

Fritz produced from an inside pocket a small black gun and gave it to Reeves. Reeves looked at the door, as if anxious lest Gaby came in, but he didn't seem very anxious, and the gun was hardly bigger than his palm. After fumbling a little, Reeves got the gun open and peered at its cylinders.

'It's loaded. Has a safety. Here. You know a little about guns, Paul?'

Jonathan had a smattering. Reeves showed him, with assistance from Fritz. The safety, that was the important thing. Be sure how to get it off. This was the Italian gun.

Fritz had to leave. He said good-bye, nodding to Jonathan. *'Bis morgen! Um sechs!'*

Reeves walked with him to the door. Then Reeves came back from the hall with a brownish-red tweed topcoat, not a new coat. 'This is very loose,' he said. 'Try it on.'

Jonathan didn't want to try it on, but he got up and put the coat on. The sleeves were longish. Jonathan put his hands into the pockets, and found, as Reeves was now informing him, that the right-hand pocket was cut through. He was to carry the gun in his jacket pocket, and reach for it through the pocket of the coat, fire the gun preferably once and drop the gun.

'You'll see the crowd,' Reeves said, 'a couple of hundred people. You step back afterwards, like everybody else, recoiling from an explosion.' Reeves illustrated, his body leaning backwards, walking backwards.

They drank Steinhäger with their coffee. Reeves asked him about his home life, Simone, Georges. Did Georges speak English or only French?

'He's learning some English,' Jonathan said. 'I'm at a disadvantage, since I'm not with him a lot.'

SEVEN

Reeves telephoned Jonathan at his hotel the next morning just after 9 a.m. Karl would pick him up at 10.40 a.m. to drive him to the hospital. Rudolf would come along too. Jonathan had been sure of that.

'Good luck,' said Reeves. 'I'll see you later.'

Jonathan was downstairs in the lobby, reading a London *Times*, when Rudolf walked in a few minutes early. Rudolf was smiling a shy, mouselike smile, looking more like Kafka than ever.

'Morning, Herr Trevanny!' he said.

Rudolf and Jonathan got into the back of the big car.

'Luck with report!' said Rudolf pleasantly.

'I intend to speak with the doctor too,' said Jonathan just as pleasantly.

He was sure Rudolf understood this, but Rudolf looked a little confused and said, '*Wir werden versuchen—*'

Jonathan went with Rudolf into the hospital, though Rudolf had said he could fetch the report and also find out if the doctor was free. Karl had helpfully translated, so that Jonathan understood perfectly. Karl, in fact, seemed neutral, Jonathan thought, and probably was. The atmosphere to Jonathan was strange, however, as if everyone were acting, acting badly, even himself. Rudolf spoke with a nurse at a desk in the front hall, and asked for the report of Herr Trevanny.

The nurse looked at once in a box of sealed envelopes of various sizes, and produced one of business-letter size with Jonathan's name on it.

'And Dr Wentzel? Is it possible to see him?' Jonathan asked the nurse.

'Dr Wentzel?' She consulted a ledger with isinglass slots, pushed a button and lifted a telephone. Then she spoke in German for a minute, put the telephone down and said to Jonathan in English, 'Dr Wentzel is busy all day today, his nurse says. Would you care to make an appointment for tomorrow morning at ten-thirty?'

'Yes, I would,' Jonathan said.

'Very good, I will make it. But his nurse says you will find a – a lot of information in the report.'

Then Jonathan and Rudolf walked back to the car. Rudolf was disappointed, Jonathan thought, or was he imagining? Anyway, Jonathan had the thick envelope in his hand, the genuine report.

In the car, Jonathan said, 'Excuse me,' to Rudolf, and opened the envelope. It was three typewritten pages, and Jonathan saw at a glance that many of the words were the same as the French and English terms he was familiar with. The last page, however, was two long paragraphs in German. There was the same long word for the yellow components. Jonathan's pulse faltered at 210,000 leucocytes, which was higher than the last French report, and higher than it had ever been. Jonathan did not struggle with the last page. As he refolded the sheets, Rudolf said something in a polite tone, extending his hand, and Jonathan handed him the report, hating it, and yet what else could he do, and what did it matter?

Rudolf told Karl to drive on.

Jonathan looked out the window. He had no intention of asking Rudolf to explain anything. Jonathan preferred to work it out with a dictionary, or to ask Reeves. Jonathan's ear began to ring, and he leaned back and made an effort to breathe deeply. Rudolf glanced at him and at once lowered a window.

Karl said over his shoulder, '*Meine Herrn*, Herr Minot expects you both to come to lunch. Then perhaps to the zoo.'

Rudolf gave a laugh and replied in German.

Jonathan thought of asking to be driven back to his hotel. But to do what? Stew over the report, not understanding all of it? Rudolf wanted to be let out somewhere. Karl dropped him beside a canal, and Rudolf extended his hand to Jonathan, shook Jonathan's hand firmly. Then Karl drove on to Reeves Minot's house. Sunlight twinkled on the Alster's water. Little boats bobbed gaily at anchor, and two or three boats were sailing about, simple and clean as brand-new toys.

Gaby opened the door for Jonathan. Reeves was on the telephone, but he soon finished.

'Hello, Jonathan! What's the news?'

'Not too good,' said Jonathan, blinking. The sunlight in the white room was dazzling.

'And the report? Can I see it? Can you understand all of it?'

'No – not all of it.' Jonathan handed the envelope to Reeves.

'You saw the doctor too?'

'He was busy.'

'Sit down, Jonathan. Maybe you could use a drink.' Reeves went to the bottles on one of his bookshelves.

Jonathan sat on the sofa and put his head back. He felt blank and discouraged, but at least not faint at the moment.

'A worse report than you've been getting from the French?' Reeves returned with a scotch and water.

'That's about it,' Jonathan said.

Reeves looked at the back page, the prose. 'You've got to watch out about minor wounds. That's interesting.'

And nothing new, Jonathan thought. He bled easily. Jonathan waited for Reeves' comment, in fact for Reeves' translation.

'Rudolf translated this for you?'

'No. But then I didn't ask him to.'

'"... cannot tell if this represents a worsened condition, not having seen a former – diagnosis ... sufficiently dangerous in view of the length of time – *et cetera*". I'll go through it word for word, if you like,' said Reeves. 'One or two words I'll need the dictionary for, these compound words, but I've got the essentials.'

'Then just tell me the essentials.'

'I must say they might've written this out for you in English,' Reeves said, then scanned the page again. '"... a considerable granulation of cells as well as – of the yellow – matter. As you have had X-ray treatment, this is not to be advised again at the moment, as the leukaemia cells become resistant to it ..."'

Reeves went on for a few moments. There was no prediction of remaining time, Jonathan noticed, no hint of a deadline.

'Since you couldn't see Wentzel today, would you like me to try to make an appointment for you tomorrow?' Reeves sounded genuinely concerned.

'Thanks, but I made an appointment for tomorrow morning. Ten-thirty.'

'Good. And you said his nurse speaks English, so you don't need Rudolf. Why don't you stretch out for a few minutes?' Reeves pulled a pillow to the corner of the sofa.

Jonathan lay back with one foot on the floor, the other foot dangling over the sofa's edge. He felt weak and drowsy, as if he could sleep for several hours. Reeves strolled towards the sunny window, talking about the zoo. He spoke of a rare animal – the name went out of Jonathan's mind as soon as he heard it – that had recently been sent from South America. A pair of them. Reeves said they must see these animals. Jonathan was thinking of Georges tugging his wagon of pebbles. *Cailloux*. Jonathan knew he would not live to see Georges much older, never by any means see him grow tall, hear his voice break. Jonathan sat up abruptly, clenched his teeth, and tried to will his strength back.

Gaby came in with a large tray.

'I asked Gaby to make a cold lunch, so we can eat whenever you feel up to it,' Reeves said.

They had cold salmon with mayonnaise. Jonathan could not eat much, but the brown bread and butter and the wine tasted good. Reeves was talking about Salvatore Bianca, of the Mafia's connection with prostitution, of their custom of employing prostitutes in their gambling establishments, and of taking 90 per cent of the girls' earnings from them. 'Extortion,' Reeves said. 'Money's their objective – terror's their method. See Las Vegas! For example, the Hamburg boys want *no* prostitutes,' Reeves said with an air of righteousness. 'Girls are there, a few, helping at the bar, for instance. Maybe they're available, but not on the premises, no indeed.' Jonathan was hardly listening, certainly not thinking about what Reeves was saying. He poked at his food, felt the blood rose to his cheeks, and held a quiet debate with himself. He would try the shooting. And it was not because he thought he was going to die in a few days or weeks, it was simply because the money was useful, because he wanted to give it to

Simone and Georges. Forty thousand pounds, or ninety-six thousand dollars or – Jonathan supposed – only half of that, if there wasn't another shooting to do, or if he got caught on the first shooting.

'But you will, I think, won't you?' Reeves asked, wiping his lips on a crisp white napkin. He meant fire the gun this evening.

'If something happens to me,' Jonathan said, 'can you see that my wife gets the money?'

'But –' Reeves scar twitched as he smiled. 'What can happen? Yes, I'll see that your wife gets the money.'

'But if something does happen – if there's only one shooting –'

Reeves pressed his lips together as if he didn't like replying. 'Then it's half the money. But there'll likely be two, to be honest. Full payment after the second. But that's splendid!' He smiled, and it was the first time Jonathan had seen a real smile from him. 'You'll see how easy it is tonight. And later we'll celebrate – if you're in the mood.' He clapped his hands over his head, Jonathan thought as a gesture of jubilation, but it was a signal to Gaby.

Gaby arrived and took away the plates.

Twenty thousand pounds, Jonathan was thinking. Not so impressive, but better than a dead man with funeral expenses.

Coffee. Then the zoo. The animals Reeves had wanted him to see were two small bearlike creatures the colour of butterscotch. There was a small crowd in front of them, and Jonathan never got a good view. He was also not interested. Jonathan had a good view of some lions walking in apparent freedom. Reeves was concerned that Jonathan did not become tired. It was nearly 4 p.m.

Back at Reeves' house, Reeves insisted on giving Jonathan a tiny white pill which he called a 'mild sedative'.

'But I don't need a sedative,' Jonathan said. He felt quite calm, in fact, quite well.

'It's best. Please take my word for it.'

Jonathan swallowed the pill. Reeves told him to lie down in the guest-room for a few minutes. He did not fall asleep, and Reeves came in at 5 p.m. to say it would soon be time for Karl to drive him to his hotel. The topcoat was at Jonathan's hotel. Reeves gave him a cup of tea with sugar, which tasted all right, and Jonathan assumed there was nothing in it but tea. Reeves gave him the gun, and showed him the safety-catch again. Jonathan put the gun in his trousers pocket.

'See you tonight!' Reeves said cheerily.

Karl drove him to his hotel, and said he would wait. Jonathan supposed he had five or ten minutes. He brushed his teeth – with soap, because he'd left the toothpaste at home for Simone and Georges and hadn't bought any as yet – then lit a Gitane and stood looking out the window until he realized he wasn't seeing anything, wasn't even thinking of anything, and then he went to the closet and got the largish coat. The coat had been worn, but not much. Whose had it been? Appropriate, Jonathan thought, because he could pretend to be acting, in someone else's clothes, pretend the gun was a blank gun in a play. But Jonathan knew he knew exactly what he was doing. Towards the Mafioso he was going to kill (he hoped) he felt no mercy. And Jonathan realized he felt no pity for himself, either. Death was death. For different reasons, Bianca's life and his own life had lost value. The only interesting detail was that Jonathan stood to be paid for his action of killing Bianca. Jonathan put the gun in his jacket pocket and the nylon stocking in the same pocket with it. He found he could draw the stocking on to his hand with the fingers of the same hand. Nervously, he wiped the gun of fingerprints real and imaginary with the stocking-covered fingers. He would have to hold the coat aside slightly when he fired, otherwise there'd be a bullet-hole in the coat. He had no hat. Curious that Reeves hadn't thought of a hat. It was too late now to worry about it.

Jonathan went out of his room door and pulled it firmly shut.

Karl was standing on the pavement by his car. He held the door for Jonathan. Jonathan wondered how much Karl knew, and if he knew everything? Jonathan was leaning forward in the back seat, to ask Karl to go to the Rathaus U-bahn station, when Karl said over his shoulder:

'You are to meet Fritz at the Rathaus station. That is correct, sir?'

'Yes,' said Jonathan, relieved. He sat back in a corner and lightly fingered the little gun. He pushed the safety on and off, remembering that forward was off.

'Herr Minot suggested here, sir. The entrance is across the street.' Karl opened the door but did not get out, because the street was crowded with cars and people. 'Herr Minot said I am to find you at your hotel at seven-thirty, sir,' said Karl.

'Thank you.' Jonathan felt lost for an instant, hearing the thud of the car door closing. He looked around for Fritz. Jonathan was at a huge intersection marked Gr. Johannesstrasse and Rathausstrasse. As in London, Piccadilly for instance, there seemed to be at least four entrances to the U-bahn here because of so many streets intersecting. Jonathan looked around for the short figure of Fritz with his cap on his head. A group of men, like a football team in topcoats, dashed down the U-bahn steps, revealing Fritz standing calmly by the metal post of the stairs, and Jonathan's heart gave a leap as if he had met a lover at a secret rendezvous. Fritz gestured towards the steps, and went down himself.

Jonathan kept an eye on Fritz's cap, though there were now fifteen or more people between them. Fritz moved to one side of the throng. Evidently Bianca had not come on the scene yet, and they were to await him. There was a hubbub of German around Jonathan, a burst of laughter, a shouted 'Wiedersehen, Max!'

Fritz stood against a wall some twelve feet away, and Jonathan drifted in his direction but kept a safe distance away from him, and before Jonathan reached the wall, Fritz nodded and moved diagonally away from the wall, towards a ticket gate. Jonathan bought a ticket. Fritz shuffled on in the crowd. Tickets were punched. Jonathan knew Fritz had sighted Bianca, but Jonathan didn't see him.

A train was standing. When Fritz made a dash for a certain carriage, Jonathan dashed too. In the carriage, which was not particularly crowded, Fritz remained standing, holding to a chromium, vertical bar. He pulled a newspaper from his pocket. Fritz nodded forward, not looking at Jonathan.

Then Jonathan saw the Italian, closer to Jonathan than to Fritz – a dark, square-faced man in a smart grey topcoat with brown leather buttons, a grey homburg, staring rather angrily straight ahead of him as if lost in thought. Jonathan looked again at Fritz who was only pretending to read his newspaper, and when Jonathan's eyes met his, Fritz nodded and smiled slightly in confirmation.

At the next stop, Messberg, Fritz got off. Jonathan looked again at the Italian, briefly, although Jonathan's glance seemed in no danger of distracting the Italian from the rigid stare into space. Suppose Bianca didn't get off at the next stop, but rode on and on to a remote stop where there'd be almost no people getting off?

But Bianca moved to the door as the train slowed. Steinstrasse. Jonathan had to make an effort, without bumping anyone, to stay just behind Bianca. There was a flight of steps up. The crowd, perhaps eighty to a hundred people, flowed together more tightly in front of the stairway, and began to creep upward. Bianca's grey topcoat was just in front of Jonathan, and they were still a couple of yards from the stairs. Jonathan could see grey hairs among the black at the back of the man's neck, and a jagged dent in his flesh like a carbuncle scar.

Jonathan had the gun in his right hand, out of his jacket pocket. He removed the safety. Jonathan pushed his coat aside and aimed at the centre of the man's topcoat.

The gun made a raucous '*Ka-boom!*'

Jonathan dropped the gun. He had stopped, and now he recoiled, backwards and to the left, as a collective '*Oh-h-a – Ah-h-h!*' rose from the crowd. Jonathan was perhaps one of the few people who did not utter an exclamation.

Bianca had sagged and fallen.

An uneven circle of space surrounded Bianca.

'...*Pistole* ...'

'... *erschossen* ... !'

The gun lay on the cement, someone started to pick it up, and was stopped by at least three people from touching it. Many people, not enough interested or in a hurry, were going up the stairs. Jonathan was moving a little to the left to circle the group around Bianca. He reached the stairs. A man was shouting for the '*Polizei!*' Jonathan walked briskly, but no faster than several other people who were making their way to pavement level.

Jonathan arrived on the street, and simply walked on, straight ahead, not caring where he walked. He walked at a moderate pace and as if he knew where he was going, though he didn't. He saw a huge railway station on his right. Reeves had mentioned that. There were no footsteps behind him, no sound of pursuit. With the fingers of his right hand, he wriggled the piece of stocking off. But he did not want to drop it so close to the underground station.

'Taxi!' Jonathan had seen a free one, making for the railway station. It stopped, and he got in. Jonathan gave the name of the street where his hotel was.

Jonathan sank back, but he found himself glancing to right and left out the windows of the cab, as if expecting to see a policeman gesticulating, pointing to the cab, demanding that the driver stop. Absurd! He was absolutely in the clear.

Yet the same sensation came to him as he entered the Victoria – as if the law must have got his address somehow and would be in the lobby to meet him. But no. Jonathan walked quietly into his own room and closed the door. He felt in his pocket, the jacket pocket, for the bit of stocking. It was gone, had fallen somewhere.

7.20 p.m. Jonathan took off the topcoat, dropped it in an upholstered chair, and went for his cigarettes which he had forgotten to take with him. He inhaled the comforting smoke of Gitane. He put the cigarette on the edge of the basin in the bathroom, washed his hands and face, then stripped to the waist and washed with a face towel and hot water.

As he was pulling on a sweater, the telephone rang.

'Herr Karl waits on you below, sir.'

Jonathan went down. He carried the topcoat over his arm. He wanted to give it back to Reeves, wanted to see the last of it.

'*Good* evening, sir!' said Karl, beaming, as if he had heard the news and deemed it good.

In the car, Jonathan lit another cigarette. It was Wednesday evening. He'd said to Simone that he might be home tonight, but she probably wouldn't have his letter till tomorrow. He thought of two books due back Saturday at the Bibliothèque pour Tous by the church in Fontainebleau.

Jonathan was again in Reeves' comfortable apartment. He handed the topcoat to Reeves, rather than to Gaby. Jonathan felt awkward.

'*How* are you, Jonathan?' Reeves asked, tense and concerned. 'How did it go?'

Gaby went away. Jonathan and Reeves were in the living-room.

'All right,' Jonathan said. 'I think.'

Reeves smiled a little – even the little making his face look radiant. '*Very* good. Fine! I hadn't heard, you know? – May I offer you champagne, Jonathan? Or scotch? Sit down!'

'A scotch.'

Reeves bent over the bottles. He asked in a soft voice, 'How many – how many shots, Jonathan?'

'One.' And what if he wasn't dead, Jonathan thought suddenly. Wasn't that quite possible? Jonathan took the scotch from Reeves.

Reeves had a stemmed glass of champagne, and he raised the glass to Jonathan and drank. 'No difficulties? – Fritz did well?'

Jonathan nodded, and glanced at the door where Gaby would appear if she came back. 'Let's hope he's dead. It just occurs to me – he might not be.'

'Oh, this'll do all right if he's *not* dead. You saw him fall?'

'Oh, yes.' Jonathan gave a sigh, and realized he had been hardly breathing for several minutes.

'The news may have reached Milan already,' Reeves said cheerfully. 'An Italian bullet. Not that the Mafia always use Italian guns, but it was a nice little touch, I thought. He was of the Di Stefano family. There are a couple of the Genotti family here in Hamburg now too, and we hope these two families will start shooting at each other.'

Reeves had said that before. Jonathan sat down on the sofa. Reeves walked about in a glow of satisfaction.

'If it suits you, we'll have a quiet evening here,' Reeves said. 'If anyone telephones, Gaby's going to say I'm out.'

'Does Karl or Gaby – How much do they know?'

'Gaby – nothing. Karl, it doesn't matter if he does. Karl simply isn't interested. He works for other people besides me, and he's well paid. It's in his interest *not* to know anything, if you follow me.'

Jonathan understood. But Reeves' information did not make Jonathan feel any more comfortable. 'By the way – I'd like to go back to France tomorrow.' This meant two things, that Reeves could pay him or make the arrangement to pay him tonight, and that any other assignment ought to be discussed tonight. Jonathan intended to say no to any other assignment, whatever the financial arrangement, but he thought he should be entitled to half the forty thousand pounds for what he had done.

'Why not, if you like,' said Reeves. 'Don't forget you have the appointment tomorrow morning.'

But Jonathan didn't want to see Dr Wentzel again. He wet his lips. His report was bad, and his condition was worse. And there was another element: Dr Wentzel with his walrus moustaches represented 'authority' somehow, and Jonathan felt that he would be putting himself in a dangerous position by confronting Wentzel again. He knew he wasn't thinking logically, but that was the way he felt. 'I don't really see any reason to see him again – since I'm not staying any longer in Hamburg. I'll cancel the appointment early tomorrow. He's got my Fontainebleau address for the bill.'

'You can't send francs out of France,' Reeves said with a smile. 'Send me the bill when you get it. Don't worry about that.'

Jonathan let it go. He certainly didn't want Reeves' name on a cheque to Wentzel, however. He told himself to come to the point, which was his own payment from Reeves. Instead, Jonathan sat back on the sofa and asked rather pleasantly, 'What do you do here – as to work, I mean?'

'Work –' Reeves hesitated, but looked not at all disturbed by the question. 'Various things. I scout for New York art dealers, for example. All those books over there –' He indicated the bottom row of books in a bookshelf. 'They're art books, mainly German art, with names and addresses of individuals who own things. There's a demand in New York for German painters. Then, of course, I scout among the young painters here, and recommend them to galleries and buyers in the States. Texas buys a lot. You'd be surprised.'

Jonathan was surprised. Reeves Minot – if what he said was true – must judge paintings with the coldness of a Geiger counter. Was Reeves possibly a *good* judge? Jonathan had realized that the painting over the fireplace, a pinkish scene of a bed with an old person lying in it – male or female? – apparently dying, really *was* a Derwatt. It must be extremely valuable, Jonathan thought, and evidently Reeves owned it.

'Recent acquisition,' Reeves said, seeing Jonathan looking at his painting. 'A gift – from a grateful friend, you might say.' He had an air of wanting to say more, but of thinking he shouldn't.

During the dinner, Jonathan wanted to bring up the money again, and couldn't, and Reeves started talking about something else. Ice-skating on the Alster in winter, and iceboats that went like the wind and occasionally collided. Then nearly an hour later, when they were sitting on the sofa over coffee, Reeves said:

'This evening I can't give you more than five thousand francs, which is absurd. No more than pocket money.' Reeves went to his desk and opened a drawer. 'But at least it's in francs.' He came back with the francs in his hand. 'I could give you an equal amount in marks tonight too.'

Jonathan didn't want marks, didn't want to have to change them in France. The francs, he saw, were in hundred-franc notes in pinned together batches of ten, the way French banks issued them. Reeves laid the five stacks on the coffee-table, but Jonathan did not touch them.

'You see I can't get any more until the rest contribute. Four or five people,' Reeves said. 'But there's no doubt at all that I can get the marks.'

Jonathan was thinking, somewhat vaguely because he was anything but a bargainer himself, that Reeves was in a weak position asking other people for money after the deed was done. Shouldn't his friends have put up the money first, in trust somehow, or at least more money? 'I don't want it in marks, thanks,' said Jonathan.

'No, of course. I understand. That's another thing, your money ought to be in Switzerland in a secret account, don't you think? You don't want it showing on your account in France, or you don't want to keep it in a sock like the French, do you?'

'Hardly. When can you get the half?' Jonathan asked, as if he was sure it was coming.

'Within a week. Don't forget there might be a second job – in order to make the first job count for something. We'll have to see.'

Jonathan was irked and tried to conceal it. 'When will you know that?'

'Also within a week. Maybe even in four days. I'll be in touch.'

'But – to be frank – I think more money than this is only fair, don't you? Now, I mean.' Jonathan felt his face grow warm.

'I do. That's why I apologized for this paltry sum. I tell you what. I shall do the very best I can, and the next you will hear from me – via me – is the pleasant news of a Swiss bank account and a statement of the sum you have in it.'

That sounded better. 'When?' Jonathan asked.

'Within a week. My word of honour.'

'That is – a half?' Jonathan said.

'I'm not sure I can get a half before. You know I explained to you, Jonathan, this was a double-barrelled deal. The boys who are paying this kind of money want a certain kind of result.' Reeves looked at him.

Jonathan could see Reeves was asking, silently, was he going to do the second shooting or was he not? And if he wasn't, say so now. 'I understand,' Jonathan said. A little more, a third of the money even, wouldn't be bad, Jonathan was thinking. Something like fourteen thousand pounds. For the work he had done, that was a comfortable little sum. Jonathan decided to sit tight and stop arguing tonight.

He flew back to Paris the next day on a midday plane. Reeves had said he would cancel Dr Wentzel, and Jonathan had left it to him to do. Reeves had also said he would telephone him Saturday, day after tomorrow, in his shop. Reeves had accompanied Jonathan to the airport, and had shown him the morning paper with a picture of Bianca on the U-bahn platform. Reeves had an air of quiet triumph: there was not a clue except the Italian gun, and a Mafia killer was suspected. Bianca was labelled a Mafia soldier or button man. Jonathan had seen the front pages of the newspapers on the stands that morning when he went out to buy cigarettes, but he had had no desire to buy a newspaper. Now in the plane, he was handed a newspaper by the smiling stewardess. Jonathan left the paper folded on his lap, and closed his eyes.

It was nearly 7 p.m. when Jonathan got home, via train and taxi, and he let himself into the house with his key.

'Jon!' Simone came down the hall to greet him.

He put his arms around her. 'Hello, darling!'

'I was expecting you!' she said, laughing. 'Somehow. Just now. What's the news? Take off your coat. I had your letter this morning that you might be home last night. Are you out of your mind?'

Jonathan flung his overcoat on the hook, and picked up Georges who had just crashed against his legs. 'And how's my little pest? How's Cailloux?' He kissed Georges' cheek. Jonathan had brought Georges a truck which dumped things and this was in the plastic bag with the whisky, but Jonathan thought the truck could wait, and he pulled out the drink.

'Ah, *quel luxe*!' Simone said. 'Shall we open it now?'

'I insist!' said Jonathan.

They went into the kitchen. Simone liked ice with scotch and Jonathan was indifferent.

'Tell me what the doctors said.' Simone took the ice tray to the sink.

'Well – they say about the same as the doctors here. But they want to try out some drugs on me. They're going to let me know.' Jonathan had, on the plane, decided to say this to Simone. It would leave the way open for another trip to Germany. And what was the real *use* of telling her things were a trifle worse, or looked worse? What could she do about it but worry a little more? Jonathan's optimism had risen on the plane: if he'd come well through the first episode, he might make it through the second.

'You mean you'll have to go back?' she asked.

'That's possible.' Jonathan watched her pour the two scotches, generous ones. 'But they're willing to pay me for it. They're going to let me know.'

'Really?' said Simone, surprised.

'Is that scotch? What do *I* get?' Georges said in English, with such clarity that Jonathan burst out laughing.

'Want some? Take a sip,' Jonathan said, holding out his glass.

Simone restrained his hand. 'There's orange juice, Georgie!' She poured orange juice for him. 'They're trying a certain cure, you mean?'

Jonathan frowned, but he still felt master of the situation. 'Darling, there's no cure. They're – they're going to try a lot of new pills. That's about all I know. Cheers!' Jonathan felt a bit euphoric. He had the five thousand francs in his inside jacket pocket. He was safe, for the moment, safe in the bosom of his family. If all went well, the five thousand was merely pocket money, as Reeves Minot had said.

Simone leaned on the back of one of the straight chairs. 'They'll *pay* for your going back? That means there's some danger attached?'

'No. I think – there's some inconvenience attached. Going back to Germany. I only mean they'll pay my transportation.' Jonathan hadn't worked it out: he could say that Dr Perrier would give the injections, administer the pills. But for the moment he thought he was saying the right thing.

'You mean – they consider you a special case?'

'Yes. In a way. Of course I'm not,' he said, smiling. He wasn't, and Simone knew he wasn't. 'They just *might* want to try some tests. I don't know yet, darling.'

'Anyway you look awfully happy about it. I'm glad, darling.'

'Let's go out to dinner tonight. The restaurant on the corner here. We can take Georges,' he protested over her voice. 'Come on, we can afford it.'

EIGHT

Jonathan put four thousand of the francs into an envelope in a certain drawer among eight such drawers in a wooden cabinet at the back of his shop. This drawer was the next from the bottom drawer, and held nothing but ends of wire and string and some tags with reinforced holes – junk that only a frugal person or an eccentric would save, Jonathan thought. It was a drawer, like the one below it (Jonathan had no idea what that contained) which Jonathan never opened ordinarily, therefore neither would Simone open it, he thought, on the rare occasions when she helped out in the shop. Jonathan's real cash drawer was the top one on the right under his wooden counter. The remaining thousand francs Jonathan put into the joint account at the Société Générale on Friday morning. It could be two or three weeks before Simone noticed the extra thousand, and she might not comment, even if she saw it in their cheque book. And if she did, Jonathan could say that a few customers had suddenly paid up. Jonathan usually signed cheques to pay their bills, and the bankbook lived in the drawer of the *écritoire* in the living-room, unless one or the other of them had to take it out of the house to pay for something, which happened only about once a month.

And by Friday afternoon, Jonathan had found a way to use a little of the thousand. He bought a mustard-coloured tweed suit for Simone from a shop in the rue de France for 395 francs. He'd seen the suit days ago, before Hamburg, and thought of Simone – the rounded collar, the dark yellow tweed flecked with brown, the four brown buttons set in a square on the jacket had seemed created just for Simone. The price had been shocking to his eyes, more than a bit out of line, he'd thought. Now it seemed almost a bargain, and Jonathan gazed with pleasure at the new material being folded with care between snowy sheets of tissue paper. And Simone's appreciation gave Jonathan pleasure all over again. Jonathan thought it was the first new thing she'd had, the first pretty clothes, in a couple of years, because the dresses from the market or the Prisunic didn't count.

'But it must've been terribly expensive, Jon!'

'No – not really. The Hamburg doctors gave me an advance – in case I have to go back. Quite generous. Don't think about that.'

Simone smiled. She didn't want to think about money, Jonathan saw. Not just now. 'I'll count this as one of my birthday presents.'

Jonathan smiled too. Her birthday had been almost two months ago.

On Saturday morning Jonathan's telephone rang. It had rung a few times that morning, but this was the irregular ring of a long distance call.

'This is Reeves ... How is everything?'

'All right, thanks.' Jonathan was suddenly tense and alert. There was a customer in his shop, a man staring at lengths of sample frame wood on Jonathan's wall. But Jonathan was speaking in English.

Reeves said, 'I'm coming to Paris tomorrow and I'd like to see you. I have something for you – you know.' Reeves sounded as calm as usual.

Simone wanted Jonathan to go to her parents' home in Nemours tomorrow. 'Can we make it in the evening or – around six p.m., say? I've got a long lunch.'

'Oh, sure, I understand. French Sunday lunches! Sure, around six. I'll be at the Hotel Cayré. That's on Raspail.'

Jonathan had heard of the hotel. He said he would try to be there by 6 or 7 p.m. 'There're fewer trains on Sunday.'

Reeves said not to worry. 'See you tomorrow.'

Reeves was bringing some money, evidently. Jonathan gave his attention to the man who wanted a frame.

Simone looked marvellous on Sunday in the new suit. Jonathan asked her, before they left for the Foussadiers, not to say that he was being paid anything by the German doctors.

'I'm not a fool!' Simone declared with such quick duplicity Jonathan was amused, and felt that Simone really was more with him than with her parents. Often Jonathan felt the opposite.

'Even today,' Simone said at the Foussadiers, 'Jon has to go to Paris to talk to a colleague of the Germans.'

It was a particularly cheerful Sunday lunch. Jonathan and Simone had brought a bottle of Johnny Walker.

Jonathan got the 4.49 p.m. train from Fontainebleau, because there had been no train convenient from St Pierre-Nemours, and arrived in Paris around 5.30 p.m. He took the Métro. There was a Métro stop right beside the hotel.

Reeves had left a message for Jonathan to be sent up to his room. Reeves was in shirt-sleeves, and had apparently been lying on the bed reading newspapers. 'Hello, Jonathan! How is life? ... Sit down – somewhere. I have something to show you.' He went to his suitcase. 'This – as a starter.' Reeves held up a square white envelope, and took a typewritten page from it and handed it to Jonathan.

The letter was in English, addressed to the Swiss Bank Corporation, and it was signed by Ernst Hildesheim. The letter requested a bank account to be opened in the name of Jonathan Trevanny, and gave Jonathan's shop address in Fontainebleau, and said that a cheque for eighty thousand marks was enclosed. The letter was a carbon, but it was signed.

'Who's Hildesheim?' Jonathan asked, meanwhile thinking that the German mark was worth about one and six-tenths French franc, so that eighty thousand marks would convert to something over a hundred and twenty thousand French francs.

'A businessman of Hamburg – for whom I've done a few favours. Hildesheim's not under any kind of surveillance and this won't appear on his company books, so nothing for him to worry about. He sent a personal cheque. The point is, Jonathan, this money has been deposited in your name, posted yesterday from Hamburg, so you'll be getting your private number next week. That's a hundred and twenty-eight thousand French francs.' Reeves didn't smile, but he had an air of satisfaction. He reached for a box on the writing-table. 'Dutch cigar? They're very good.'

Because the cigars were something different, Jonathan took one, smiling. 'Thanks.' He puffed it alight from the match that Reeves held. 'Thanks also for the money.' It was not quite a third, Jonathan realized. It wasn't a half. But Jonathan couldn't say this.

'Nice start, yes. The casino boys in Hamburg are quite pleased. The other Mafia who're cruising around, a couple of the Genotti family, claim they don't know anything about Salvatore Bianca's death, but of course they would say that. What we want to do now is knock off a Genotti as if in retaliation for Bianca. And we want to get a big shot, a *capo* – a chief just under the boss, you know? There's one named Vito Marcangelo who travels nearly every week-end from Munich to Paris. He has a girl-friend in Paris. He's the chief of the dope business in Munich – at least for his family there. Munich by the way is even more active than Marseille now, as far as dope goes ...'

Jonathan listened uneasily, waiting for an opening in which he could say that he didn't care to take on another job. Jonathan's thoughts had changed in the last forty-eight hours. And it was curious, too, how Reeves' very presence stripped Jonathan of a sense of daring – maybe made the deed more real. Then there was the fact that he had, apparently, a hundred and twenty-eight thousand francs in Switzerland already. Jonathan had sat down on the edge of an armchair.

'... on a moving train, a day train, the Mozart Express.'

Jonathan shook his head. 'Sorry, Reeves. I really don't think I'm up to it.' Reeves could block the cheque in marks, Jonathan thought suddenly. Reeves could simply cable Hildesheim. Well, so be it.

Reeves looked crestfallen. 'Oh. Well – so am I sorry. Really. We'll just have to find another man – if you don't do it. And – I'm afraid he'll get the better part of the money too.' Reeves shook his head, puffed his cigar and stared out the window for a moment. Then he bent and gripped Jonathan's shoulder firmly. 'Jon, the first part went so well.'

Jonathan sat back, and Reeves released him. Jonathan squirmed, like someone forced to make an apology. 'Yes, but – to shoot somebody on a train?' Jonathan could see himself nabbed at once, unable to escape anywhere.

'Not a shooting, no. We couldn't have the noise. I was thinking of a garrotte.'

Jonathan could hardly believe his ears.

Reeves said calmly. 'It's a Mafia method. A slender cord, silent. A noose! And you pull it tight. That's all.'

Jonathan thought of his fingers touching a warm neck. It was revolting. 'Absolutely out of the question. I couldn't.'

Reeves took a breath, going into another gear, shifting. 'This man is well guarded, two bodyguards as a rule. But on a train – people get bored sitting and walk in the aisle a bit, or they go to the bog once or twice, or the dining-car, maybe alone. It might not work, Jonathan, you might not – find the occasion, but you could try. Then there's pushing, just pushing him out the door. Those doors can open when the train's moving, you know. But he'd yell – and it might not kill him either.'

Ludicrous, Jonathan thought. But he didn't feel like laughing. Reeves dreamed on silently, looking up at the ceiling. Jonathan was thinking that if he were caught as a murderer or in an attempt at murder, Simone wouldn't touch any of the money from it. She'd be appalled, ashamed. 'I simply cannot help you,' Jonathan said. He stood up.

'But – you could at least *ride* the train. If the right moment doesn't present itself, we'll just have to think of something else, another *capo* maybe, another method. But we'd love to get this guy! He's going to move from dope to the Hamburg casinos – organizing – that's the rumour, anyway.' Reeves said on another note, 'Would you try a gun, Jon?'

Jonathan shook his head. 'I haven't the nerve, for God's sake. On a train? No.'

'Look at this garrotte!' Reeves pulled his left hand quickly from his trousers pocket.

He held what looked like a thin, whitish string. The end slipped through a loop, and was prevented from going all the way through by a small lump at the end of the cord. Reeves tossed it round the bedpost and pulled, jerking the cord to one side.

'You see? Nylon. Strong as wire almost. No one can even grunt more than once –' Reeves broke off.

Jonathan was disgusted. One would have to touch the victim with the other hand – somehow. And wouldn't it take about three minutes?

Reeves seemed to give it up. He strolled to a window and turned. 'Think about it. You can ring me up or I'll ring you in a couple of days. Marcangelo usually leaves Munich noonish Fridays. It would be ideal if it could be done next week-end.'

Jonathan drifted towards the door. He put his cigar out in an ashtray on the bed-table.

Reeves was looking at him shrewdly, yet he might have been gazing far behind him, thinking already of someone else for the job. His long scar looked, as it did in certain lights, thicker than it was. The scar had probably given him an inferiority complex with women, Jonathan thought. Yet how long had he had it? Maybe just two years, one couldn't tell.

'Like a drink downstairs?'

'No, thanks,' Jonathan said.

'Oh, I have a book to show you!' Reeves went to his suitcase again, and pulled a book with a bright red jacket from a back corner. 'Take a look. Keep it. It's a wonderful piece of journalism. Documentary. You'll see the kind of people we're dealing with. But they're flesh and blood like everyone else. Vulnerable, I mean.'

The book was called *The Grim Reapers: The Anatomy of Organized Crime in America.*

'I'll telephone you Wednesday,' Reeves said. 'You'd come to Munich Thursday, spend the night, I'd be there at some hotel also, then you'd return Friday night to Paris by train.'

Jonathan's hand was on the door-knob, and now he turned it. 'Sorry, Reeves, but I'm afraid it's no go. Bye-bye.'

Jonathan walked out of the hotel and directly across the street to the Métro. On the platform, awaiting a train, he read the blurb on the book-jacket. On the back of the jacket were police photographs, front and profile, of six or eight unpleasant-looking men with downturned mouths, faces loose and grim at once, all with dark, staring eyes. It was curious, the similarity of their expressions, whether the faces were plump or lean. There was a section of five or six pages of photographs in the book. The chapters were titled by American cities – Detroit, New York, New Orleans, Chicago, and at the back of the book, besides an index, was a section of Mafia families like family trees, except that these people were all con-temporaries: bosses, sub-bosses, lieutenants, button men, the latter numbering fifty or sixty in the case of the Genovese family of which Jonathan had heard. The names were real, and in many cases addresses were given in New York and New Jersey. Jonathan browsed in the book on the train to Fontainebleau. There was 'Icepick Willie' Alderman, of whom Reeves had spoken in Hamburg, who killed his victims by bending over their shoulder as if to speak to them and sticking an icepick through their eardrum. 'Icepick Willie' was photographed, grinning, among the Las Vegas gambling fraternity of half a dozen men with Italian names and a cardinal, a bishop, and a monsignor (their names also were given) after the clergy had 'received a pledge of $7,500 to be spread over five years'. Jonathan closed the book in brief depression, then opened it again after a few minutes of staring out the window. The book held facts, after all, and the facts were fascinating.

Jonathan rode the bus from the Fontainebleau–Avon station to the *place* near the château, and walked up the Rue de France to his shop. He had his shop key with him, and he went in to leave the Mafia book in the seldom-used drawer with the hidden francs before he walked to his house in the Rue St Merry.

NINE

Tom Ripley had noticed the sign FERMETURE PROVISOIRE POUR RAISONS DE FAMILLE in the window of Jonathan Trevanny's shop on a certain Tuesday in April, and had thought that Trevanny might have gone to Hamburg. Tom was very curious indeed to know if Trevanny had gone to Hamburg, but not curious enough to telephone Reeves to ask. Then on a Thursday morning around 10 a.m. Reeves had rung from Hamburg and said in a voice tense with repressed jubilation:

'Well, Tom, it's done! It's all – Everything's fine. Tom, I thank you!'

Tom for the nonce had been wordless. Trevanny had really come through? Heloise had been in the living-room where he was, so there had been little Tom could say except, 'Good. Glad to hear it.'

'No need of the phoney doctor's report. Everything went fine! Last night.'

'So – and – he's coming back home now?'

'Yes. Due tonight.'

Tom had made that conversation short. He had thought of Reeves' substituting a report of Trevanny's condition that would be worse than the truth, and Tom had suggested it in jest, although Reeves was the type to have tried it – a dirty, humourless trick, Tom thought. And it hadn't even been necessary. Tom smiled with amazement. Tom could tell from Reeves' joy that his intended victim was actually *dead*. Killed by Trevanny. Tom was indeed surprised. Poor Reeves had so wanted a word of praise from Tom for his organization of the coup, but Tom hadn't been able to say anything: Heloise knew quite a bit of English, and Tom didn't want to take any chances. Tom thought suddenly of looking at Mme Annette's *Le Parisien Libéré* which she bought every morning, but Mme Annette was not yet back from her shopping.

'Who was that?' Heloise asked. She was looking over magazines on the coffee-table, weeding out old ones to be thrown away.

'Reeves,' Tom said. 'Nothing of importance.'

Reeves bored Heloise. He had no talent for small talk, and he looked as if he did not enjoy life.

Tom heard Mme Annette's steps crunching briskly on the gravel in front of the house, and he went into the kitchen to meet her. She came in through the side door, and smiled at him.

'You would like some more coffee, M. Tome?' she asked, setting her basket on the wooden table. An artichoke toppled from the peak.

'No, thank you, Mme Annette, I came to have a look at your *Parisien*, if I may. The horses –'

Tom found the item on the second page. There was no photograph. An Italian named Salvatore Bianca, forty-eight, had been shot dead in an underground station in Hamburg. The assassin was unknown. A gun found on the scene was of Italian manufacture. The victim was known to be of the Di Stefano family of Mafiosi of Milan. The account was hardly three inches long. But it might be an interesting beginning, Tom thought. It might lead to much greater things. Jonathan Trevanny, the innocent-looking, positively square Trevanny, had succumbed to the temptation of money (what else?), and committed a successful murder! Tom had once succumbed himself, in the case of Dickie Greenleaf. Could it be that Trevanny was one of *us*? But us to Tom was only Tom Ripley. Tom smiled.

Last Sunday, Reeves had rung Tom from Orly in a dejected state, saying that Trevanny was so far declining the job, and could Tom come up with anybody else? Tom had said no. Reeves said he had written Trevanny a letter which would arrive Monday morning, inviting Trevanny to Hamburg for a medical examination. That was when Tom had said, 'If he comes, you could perhaps see that the report is slightly worse.'

Tom might have gone to Fontainebleau on Friday or Saturday to satisfy his curiosity and catch a glimpse of Trevanny in his shop, perhaps bring a drawing to be framed (unless Trevanny was taking the rest of the week off to recuperate), and in fact Tom had intended to go to Fontainebleau Friday for stretchers from Gauthier's shop, but Heloise's parents had been due for the week-end – they had stayed Friday and Saturday nights – and on Friday the household had been in a tizzy preparing for them. Mme Annette was worried, unnecessarily, about her menu, the quality of the fresh *moules* for Friday night, and after Mme Annette had prepared the guest-room to perfection, Heloise had made her change the bedlinen and the bathroom towels, because they all bore Tom's monogram TPR and not the Plissot family's. The Plissots had given the Ripleys two dozen magnificent heavy linen sheets from the family stock as a wedding present, and Heloise thought it only courteous and also diplomatic to use them when the Plissots visited. Mme Annette had suffered a slight slip of memory about this, for which she certainly wasn't reprimanded by either Heloise or Tom. Tom knew the change of bedlinen was also due to the fact that Heloise did not want her parents to be reminded by his monogram that she was married to him when they got into bed. The Plissots were critical and stuffy – a fact made somehow worse by the fact that Arlène Plissot, a slender, still attractive woman of fifty, made a real effort to be informal, tolerant of the young and all that. It just wasn't in her. The weekend had been a real ordeal, in Tom's opinion, and good heavens, if Belle Ombre wasn't a well-run household, then what was? The silver tea-service (another wedding gift of the Plissots) was kept polished to perfection by Mme Annette. Even the birdhouse in the garden was swept of droppings daily as if it were a miniature guesthouse on the property. Everything of wood in the house gleamed and smelled pleasantly of lavender-scented wax that Tom brought over from England. Yet Arlène had said, while stretched out on the bear-skin before the fireplace in a mauve trouser suit, warming her naked feet, 'Wax is not enough for such floors, Heloise. From time to time they need a treatment with linseed oil and white spirit – *warm*, you know, so it soaks better into the wood.'

When the Plissots left on Sunday afternoon after tea, Heloise had snatched her middy top off and flung it at a french window which had given an awful crack because of a heavy pin on the middy, but the glass had not broken.

'Champagne!' Heloise cried, and Tom dashed down to the cellar to fetch it.

They'd had champagne, though the tea things were not cleared away (Mme Annette was for once putting her feet up), and then the telephone had rung.

It was Reeves Minot's voice, sounding downcast. 'I'm at Orly. Just leaving for Hamburg. I saw our mutual friend in Paris today and he says no to the next – the next, you know. There's got to be one more, I know that. I explained that to him.'

'You've paid him something?' Tom watched Heloise waltzing with her champagne glass in hand. She was humming the grand waltz from *Der Rosenkavalier*.

'Yes, about a third, and I think that's not bad. I've put it in Switzerland for him.'

Tom thought he recalled a promised sum of nearly five hundred thousand francs. A third was not munificent, but it was reasonable, Tom supposed. 'You mean another shooting,' Tom said.

Heloise was singing and twirling. 'La-da-da – la-dee-dee ...'

'No.' Reeves' voice cracked. He said softly, 'It's got to be a garrotte. On a train. I think that's the hitch.'

Tom was shocked. Of course Trevanny wouldn't do it. 'Must it be on a train?'

'I've got a plan ...'

Reeves always had a plan. Tom listened politely. Reeves' idea sounded dangerous and uncertain. Tom interrupted. 'Maybe our friend has had enough at this stage.'

'No, I think he's interested. But he won't agree – to come to Munich, and we need the job done by next week-end.'

'You've been reading *The Godfather* again, Reeves. Make some arrangement with a gun.'

'A gun makes noise,' Reeves said without a flicker of humour. 'I'm wondering – either I come up with someone else, Tom, or – Jonathan's got to be persuaded.'

Impossible to persuade him, Tom thought, and Tom said rather impatiently, 'There's no better persuasion than money. If that doesn't work, I can't help you.' Tom was unpleasantly reminded of the visit of the Plissots. Would he and Heloise have bent over backwards, strained themselves for nearly three days, if they didn't need the twenty-five thousand francs a year that Jacques Plissot gave Heloise as an allowance?

'I'm afraid if he's paid any more,' Reeves said, 'he really will quit. I've told you, maybe, I can't get it – the rest of the dough – until he does the second job.'

Tom was thinking that Reeves didn't understand Trevanny's type at all. If Trevanny was paid in full, he'd either do the job or return half the money.

'If you think of something in regard to *him*,' Reeves said with apparent difficulty, 'or if you know of anyone else who could do it, telephone me, will you? In the next day or so?'

Tom was glad when they'd hung up. He shook his head quickly, and blinked his eyes. Reeves Minot's ideas often gave Tom the feeling of being befogged by some heavy dream that hadn't even the reality of most dreams.

Heloise hurdled the back of the yellow sofa, one hand gently touching the sofa back, the other holding her glass of champagne, and she landed silently, seated. Elegantly, she lifted her glass to him. '*Grace à toi ce week-end était très réussi, mon trésor!*'

'Thank you, my darling!'

Yes, life was sweet again, they were alone again, they could dine tonight barefoot if they chose. Freedom!

Tom was thinking of Trevanny. Tom didn't really care about Reeves, who always scraped through, or pulled out in the nick of time from a situation that became too dangerous. But Trevanny – there was a bit of a mystery. Tom cast about for a way of making better acquaintance with Trevanny. The situation was difficult, because he knew that Trevanny didn't like him. But there was nothing simpler than taking a picture to Trevanny to frame.

On Tuesday, Tom drove to Fontainebleau and went first to Gauthier's art supply shop to buy stretchers. Gauthier might volunteer some news about Trevanny, something about his Hamburg trip, Tom thought, since ostensibly Trevanny had gone to consult a doctor. Tom made his purchases at Gauthier's, but Gauthier did not mention Trevanny. Just as he was leaving, Tom said:

'And how is our friend – M. Trevanny?'

'*Ah, oui*. He went to Hamburg last week to see a specialist.' Gauthier's glass eye glared at Tom, while the live eye glistened and looked a bit sad. 'I understand the news was not good. A little worse, perhaps, than what his doctor here tells him. But he is courageous. You know these English, they never show their real feelings.'

'I'm sorry to hear he's worse,' Tom said.

'Yes, well – so he told me. But he carries on.'

Tom put his stretchers in his car, and took a portfolio from the back seat. He had brought a watercolour for Trevanny to frame. His conversation with Trevanny might not go well today, Tom thought, but the fact that he would have to pick up his picture at some future date would ensure that he had a second chance to see Trevanny. Tom walked to the Rue des Sablons, and went into the little shop. Trevanny was discussing a frame with a woman, holding a strip of wood against the top of an etching. He glanced at Tom, and Tom was sure Trevanny recognized him.

'It may look heavy now, but with a white mat –' Trevanny was saying. Trevanny's accent was quite good.

Tom looked for some change in Trevanny – a sign of anxiety, perhaps – but so far he saw none. At last it was Tom's turn. '*Bonjour*. Good morning. Tom Ripley,' Tom said, smiling. 'I was at your house in – in February, wasn't it? Your wife's birthday.'

'Oh, yes.'

Tom could see in Trevanny's face that his attitude hadn't changed since that night in February when he had said, 'Oh, yes, I've heard of you.' Tom opened his portfolio. 'I have a watercolour. Done by my wife. I thought perhaps a narrow dark-brown frame, a mat – say, two and a half inches at the widest, at the bottom.'

Trevanny gave his attention to the watercolour which lay on the notched, sleek-worn counter between them.

The picture was mainly green and purple, Heloise's free interpretation of a corner of Belle Ombre backgrounded by the pine wood in winter. It was not bad, Tom thought, because Heloise had known when to stop. She had no idea Tom had saved it, and to see it framed was going to be a pleasant surprise for her, Tom hoped.

'Something like this, perhaps,' Trevanny said, pulling down a length of wood from a shelf where a confusion of pieces stuck out. He laid it above the picture at a distance that the mat would take up.

'I think that's nice, yes.'

'Mat off-white or white? Such as this?'

Tom made his decision. Trevanny printed Tom's name and address carefully on a pad. Tom gave his telephone number too.

What to say now? Trevanny's coolness was almost palpable. Tom knew Trevanny would decline, but felt he had nothing to lose, so he said, 'Perhaps you and your wife would come to my house for a drink some time. Villeperce isn't far. Bring your little boy, too.'

'Thanks. I have no car,' Trevanny said with a polite smile. 'We don't go out very much, I'm afraid.'

'A car's no problem. I could fetch you. And of course count on having some dinner with us too.' The words tumbled out of Tom. Now Trevanny shoved his hands into the pockets of his coat sweater, and shifted on his feet as if his will were shifting. Tom sensed that Trevanny was curious about him.

'My wife's shy,' said Trevanny, smiling for the first time. 'She doesn't speak much English.'

'Neither does my wife, really. She's French too, you know. However – if my house is too far away, what's the matter with a *pastis* now? Aren't you about to close?'

Trevanny was. It was a little after noon.

They walked to a bar-restaurant at the corner of Rue de France and Rue St Merry. Trevanny had stopped at a bakery to buy bread. He ordered a draught beer, and Tom had the same. Tom put a ten-franc note on the counter.

'How did you happen to come to France?' Tom asked.

Trevanny told Tom about starting an antique shop in France with an English chum. 'And you?' asked Trevanny.

'Oh, my wife likes it here. And so do I. I can't think of a more pleasant life really. I can travel if I wish. I have lots of free time – leisure you'd call it. Gardening and painting. I paint like a Sunday painter, but I enjoy it. Whenever I feel like it, I go to London for a couple of weeks.' That was cards on the table, in a way, naïve, harmless. Except that Trevanny might wonder where the money came from. Tom thought it probable that

Trevanny had heard the Dickie Greenleaf story, forgotten most of it as most people did, except that certain things stayed in the memory, like Dickie Greenleaf's 'mysterious disappearance', though later Dickie's suicide had been accepted as fact. Possibly Trevanny knew that Tom got some income from what Dickie Greenleaf had left in his will (a will that Tom had forged), because this had been in the papers. Then there'd been the Derwatt affair last year, not so much 'Derwatt' in the French papers as the strange disappearance of Thomas Murchison, the American who had been a guest at Tom's home.

'Sounds a pleasant life,' Trevanny remarked dryly, and wiped foam from his upper lip.

Trevanny wanted to ask him something, Tom felt. What? Tom was wondering whether, for all his English cool, Trevanny could suffer a fit of conscience and either tell his wife or go to the police and confess? Tom thought he was right in assuming Trevanny hadn't and wouldn't tell his wife what he had done. Just five days ago Trevanny had pulled a trigger and killed a man. Of course Reeves would have given Trevanny pep-talks, morale-building lectures on the viciousness of the Mafia and the positive good Trevanny or anybody would do by eliminating one of them. Then Tom thought of the garrotte. No, he could not see Trevanny using a garrotte. How did Trevanny feel about the killing he had done? Or had he had time to feel anything yet? Maybe not. Trevanny lit a Gitane. He had large hands. He was the type who could wear old clothes, unpressed trousers, and still have the air of a gentleman. And he had rugged good looks that he himself seemed quite unaware of.

'Do you happen to know,' said Trevanny, looking at Tom with his calm blue eyes, 'an American called Reeves Minot?'

'No,' Tom said. 'Lives here in Fontainebleau?'

'No. But he travels a lot, I think.'

'No.' Tom drank his beer.

'I'd better push off. My wife's expecting me.'

They went out. They had to go in different directions.

'Thanks for the beer,' Trevanny said.

'A pleasure!'

Tom walked to his car which was in the parking area in front of the Hôtel de l'Aigle Noir, and drove off for Villeperce. He was thinking about Trevanny, thinking that he was a rather disappointed man, disappointed in his present situation. Surely Trevanny had had aspirations in his youth. Tom remembered Trevanny's wife, an attractive woman who looked steady and devoted, the kind of woman who would never push her husband to better his situation, never nag at him to earn more money. In her way, Trevanny's wife was probably as upright and decent as Trevanny himself. Yet Trevanny had succumbed to Reeves' proposal. That meant that Trevanny was a man who could be pushed or pulled in any direction, if one did it intelligently.

Mme Annette greeted Tom with the message that Heloise would be a little late, because she had found an English *commode de bateau* in an antique shop in Chilly-en-Bière, had signed a cheque for it, but had to accompany the antique man to the bank. 'She will be home with the commode at any minute!' said Mme Annette, her blue eyes sparkling. 'She asks you to wait lunch for her, M. Tome.'

'But of course!' said Tom just as cheerily. The bank account was going to be slightly overdrawn, he thought, which was why Heloise had to go to the bank and talk to someone – and how would she manage that during the lunch period when the bank was closed? And Mme Annette was joyous because still another piece of furniture was entering the house which she could get to work on with her indefatigable waxing. Heloise had been looking for a nautical, brassbound chest of drawers for Tom for months. It was a whim of hers to see a *commode de bateau* in his room.

Tom decided to seize the moment and try Reeves, and he ran up to his room. It was 1.22 p.m. Belle Ombre had had two new dial telephones for about three months, and one no longer had to get a long-distance number through the operator.

Reeves' housekeeper answered, and Tom used his German and asked if Herr Minot was in. He was.

'Reeves, hello! Tom. I can't talk long. I just wanted to say I've seen our friend. Had a drink with him ... In a bar in Fontainebleau. I think –' Tom was standing up, tense, staring through the window at the trees across the road, at the empty blue sky. He was not sure what he wanted to say, except that he wanted to tell Reeves to keep trying. 'I don't know but I think it might work with him. It's only a hunch. But try again with him.'

'Yes?' said Reeves, hanging on his words as if he were an oracle that never failed.

'When do you expect to see him?'

'Well, I'm hoping he'll come Thursday to Munich. Day after tomorrow. I'm trying to persuade him to consult another doctor there. Then – on Friday the train leaves around two-ten from Munich to Paris, you know.'

Tom had once taken the Mozart Express, boarding it at Salzburg. 'I would say, give him a choice of a gun and – the other thing, but advise him not to use the gun.'

'I did *try* that!' Reeves said. 'But you think – he might still come around, eh?'

Tom heard a car, two cars, roll on to the gravel in front of the house. It was no doubt Heloise with the antique dealer. 'I've got to sign off, Reeves. Right now.'

Later that day, alone in his room, Tom examined more closely the handsome commode which had been installed between his two front windows. The chest was of oak, low and solid, with shining brass corners and countersunk brass drawer pulls. The polished wood looked alive, as if animated by the hands of the maker, or maybe by the hands of the captain or captains or officers who had used it. A couple of shiny, darkish dents in the wood were like the odd scars that every living thing acquired in the course of life. An oval plaque of silver was set into the top, and on it was engraved in scrolly letters Capt. Archibald L. Partridge, Plymouth, 1734, and in much smaller letters the name of the carpenter, which Tom thought a nice touch of pride.

TEN

On Wednesday, as Reeves had promised, he telephoned Jonathan at his shop. Jonathan was unusually busy and had to ask Reeves to ring back just after noon.

Reeves did ring back, and after his usual courtesies, asked if Jonathan would be able to come to Munich the following day.

'There are doctors in Munich too, you know, very good ones. I have one in mind, Dr Max Schroeder. I've found out he could see you early Friday, around eight in the morning. All I have to do is confirm it. If you –'

'All right,' said Jonathan, who had anticipated that the conversation would go exactly like this. 'Very good, Reeves. I'll see about my ticket –'

'One way, Jonathan. Well, that's up to you.'

Jonathan knew. 'When I find out the plane time, I'll ring you back.'

'I know the times. There's a plane leaving Orly at one-fifteen p.m. direct to Munich, if you can make it.'

'All right. I'll aim for that.'

'If I don't hear from you, I'll assume you're on it. I'll meet you at the town terminus as before.'

Absent-mindedly, Jonathan went to his sink, smoothed his hair with both hands, then reached for his mac. It was raining a little and rather chilly. Jonathan had made his decision yesterday. He would go through the same movements again, visit a doctor in Munich this time, and he would board the train. The dubious part to Jonathan was his own nerve. Just how far would he be able to go? He walked out of his shop and locked the door with his key.

Jonathan bumped into a dustbin on the pavement, and realized that he was trudging along instead of walking. He raised his head a little. He'd demand to have a gun as well as the noose, and if he balked at using the noose because of a failure of nerve (which Jonathan fully expected), and he used the gun, then that was that. Jonathan would make an arrangement with Reeves: if he used the gun, if it was obvious that he was going to be caught, then he would use the next bullet or two for himself. That way he could never possibly betray Reeves and the other people Reeves was connected with. For this, Reeves would pay the rest of the money to Simone. Jonathan realized that his corpse couldn't be taken for that of an Italian, but he supposed it was possible that the Di Stefano family could have hired a non-Italian killer.

Jonathan said to Simone, 'I had a telephone call from the Hamburg doctor this morning. He wants me to go to Munich tomorrow.'

'Oh? So soon?'

Jonathan remembered he had told Simone it might be a fortnight before the doctors wanted to see him again. He had said Dr Wentzel had given him some pills whose result he would want to check. There had in fact been a conversation about pills with Dr Wentzel – there was nothing really to do with leukaemia except try to slow it up with pills – but Dr Wentzel had not given him any. Jonathan was sure Dr Wentzel would have given him pills if he had seen him a second time. 'There's another doctor in Munich – someone called Schroeder – Dr Wentzel wants me to see.'

'Where is Munich?' asked Georges.

'In Germany,' Jonathan said.

'How long will you be gone?' Simone asked.

'Probably – till Saturday morning,' Jonathan said, thinking that the train might come in so late Friday night, there wouldn't be a train out of Paris to Fontainebleau.

'And what about the shop? Would you like me to be there tomorrow morning? And Friday morning? What time must you leave tomorrow?'

'There's a plane at one-fifteen. Yes, darling, it would be a help if you could look in tomorrow morning and Friday morning – even for an hour. There'll be a couple of people calling for pictures.' Jonathan stabbed his knife gently into a piece of Camembert which he had taken and didn't want.

'You're worried, Jon?'

'Not really. No, on the contrary, any news I get ought to be slightly better news.' Polite cheerfulness, Jonathan thought, and it was really rubbish. The doctors couldn't do anything against time. He glanced at his son who looked a bit puzzled, but not puzzled enough to ask another question, and Jonathan realized that Georges had been overhearing such conversations since he could understand speech. Georges had been told, 'Your father has a germ. Like a cold. It makes him tired sometimes. But you cannot catch it. Nobody can catch it, so it is not going to hurt you.'

'Will you sleep at the hospital?' Simone asked.

Jonathan didn't understand what she meant at first. 'No. Dr Wentzel – his secretary said they'd booked a hotel for me.'

Jonathan left the house the next morning just after 9 a.m., in order to catch the 9.42 a.m. to Paris, because the next train later would have made him too late for Orly. He had bought his ticket, one-way, the preceding afternoon, and he had also put another thousand francs into the account at the Société Générale, and five hundred in his wallet, which left two thousand five hundred in the drawer in his shop. He had also removed *The Grim Reapers* from the drawer and stuck it into his suitcase to give back to Reeves.

Just before 5 p.m., Jonathan got off the bus which had brought him to the Munich city terminus. It was a sunny day, the temperature pleasant. There were a few sturdy, middle-aged men in leather shorts and green jackets, and a hurdy-gurdy played on the pavement. He saw Reeves trotting towards him.

'I'm a little late, sorry!' Reeves said. 'How are you, Jonathan?'

'Quite well, thank you,' Jonathan said, smiling.

'I've got you a hotel room. We'll get a taxi now. I'm in a different hotel, but I'll come up with you and we'll talk.'

They got into a taxi. Reeves talked about Munich. He talked as if he really knew the city and liked it, not as if he were talking out of nervousness. Reeves had a map, and pointed out 'the English Garden', which their taxi was not going to pass, and the section bordering the river Isar, where Reeves told him his appointment was tomorrow morning at 8 a.m. Both their hotels were in the central area, Reeves said. The taxi stopped at a hotel, and a boy in dark red uniform opened the taxi door.

Jonathan registered. The lobby had lots of modern stained-glass panels depicting German knights and troubadours. Jonathan was pleasantly aware that he felt unusually well and therefore cheerful. Was it a prelude to some awful news tomorrow, some awful catastrophe? It struck Jonathan as insane to feel cheerful, and he cautioned himself, as he might if he were on the verge of taking a drink too many.

Reeves came with him up to his room. The bellhop was just leaving, having deposited Jonathan's suitcase. Jonathan stuck his topcoat on a hook in the hall, as he might have done at home.

'Tomorrow morning – even this afternoon we might get you a new topcoat,' Reeves said, looking with a somewhat pained expression at Jonathan's.

'Oh?' Jonathan had to admit his coat was pretty shabby. He smiled a little, unresentful. At least he'd brought his good suit, his rather new black shoes. He hung up the blue suit.

'After all, you'll be in first class on the train,' Reeves said. He walked to the door and slid the button which made it impossible for anyone outside to enter. 'I've got the gun. Another Italian gun, a little different. I couldn't get a silencer but I thought – to tell you the truth – a silencer wouldn't make all that much difference.'

Jonathan understood. He looked at the small gun that Reeves had pulled from some pocket, and felt for an instant empty, stupid. To fire this gun at all meant that he'd have to shoot himself immediately afterwards. That was the only meaning the gun had for him.

'And this, of course,' said Reeves, pulling the garrotte from his pocket. In the brighter light of Munich, the cord had a pallid, fleshlike colour. 'Try it on the – the back of that chair,' Reeves said.

Jonathan took the cord and dropped its loop over a projection at the back corner of a chair. He pulled it indifferently until it was tight. He was not even disgusted now, he merely felt blank. Would the average person, he wondered, finding the cord in his pocket or anywhere, know at once what it was? Probably not, Jonathan thought.

'You must jerk it, of course,' said Reeves, solemnly, 'and keep it tight.'

Jonathan felt suddenly annoyed, started to say something ill-tempered and checked himself. He took the cord off the chair, and was about to drop it on the bed, when Reeves said:

'Keep that in your pocket. Or the pocket of whatever suit you're going to wear tomorrow.'

Jonathan started to put it in the pocket of the trousers he was wearing, then went and stuck it in a pocket of the trousers of his blue suit.

'And these two pictures I'd like to show you.' Reeves took an envelope from his inside jacket pocket. The unsealed white envelope held two photographs, one glossy and the size of a postcard, the other a neatly clipped newspaper picture folded twice. 'Vito Marcangelo.'

Jonathan looked at the glossy photograph, which was cracked in a couple of places. It showed a man with a round head and face, heavy curvaceous lips, with wavy black hair. A streak of grey at either temple gave an impression of steam spewing from his head.

'He's about five six,' Reeves said. 'His hair is still grey there, he doesn't touch it up. And here he is partying.'

The newspaper photograph was of three men and a couple of women standing behind a dinner-table. An inked arrow pointed to a short, laughing man with a grey blaze at his temple. The caption was in German.

Reeves took the pictures back. 'Let's go down for the topcoat. Something'll be open. By the way the safety on that gun works as on the other gun. It's loaded with six bullets. I'll put it in here, all right?' Reeves took the gun from the foot of the bed, and put it in a corner of Jonathan's suitcase. 'Briennerstrasse's very good for shopping,' Reeves said as they rode down in the lift.

They walked. Jonathan had left his topcoat in his hotel room.

Jonathan chose a dark green tweed. Who was paying for it? That didn't seem to matter much. Jonathan also thought that he might have only about twenty-four hours to wear it. Reeves insisted on paying for the coat, though Jonathan said he could pay Reeves back when he changed some francs into marks.

'No, no, my pleasure,' said Reeves, jerking his head a little, which was sometimes his equivalent of a smile.

Jonathan wore the coat out of the shop. Reeves pointed out things to him as they walked – Odeonsplatz, the beginning of Ludwigstrasse which Reeves said went on to Schwabing, the district where Thomas Mann had had his house. They walked to the Englischer Garten, then took a taxi to a beerhall. Jonathan would have preferred tea. He realized that Reeves was trying to make him relax. Jonathan felt relaxed enough, and was not even worried about what Dr Max Schroeder would say tomorrow morning. Rather, whatever Dr Schoeder would say simply wouldn't matter.

They dined in a noisy restaurant in Schwabing, and Reeves informed him that practically everyone in the place was 'an artist or a writer'. Jonathan was amused by Reeves. Jonathan felt a bit swimmy in the head from all the beer, and now they were drinking Gumpoldsdinger.

Before midnight, Jonathan stood in his hotel room in his pyjamas. He had just had a shower. The telephone would ring at 7.15 tomorrow morning, followed at once by a continental breakfast. Jonathan sat down at the writing-table, took some notepaper from the drawer and addressed an envelope to Simone. Then he remembered he'd be home the day after tomorrow, even perhaps tomorrow night late. He crumpled the envelope and tossed it into the waste-basket. Tonight during dinner he had said to Reeves, 'Do you know a man called Tom Ripley?' Reeves had looked blank and said, 'No. Why?' Jonathan got into bed and pressed a button which, conveniently, extinguished all the lights, including the one in the bath-room. Had he taken his pills tonight? Yes. Just before his shower. He'd put the pill bottle in his jacket pocket, so he could show them to Dr Schroeder tomorrow, in case the doctor was interested.

Reeves had asked, 'Did the Swiss bank write you yet?' They hadn't, but a letter from them might well have come this morning to his shop, Jonathan thought. Would Simone open it? The chances were fifty-fifty, Jonathan thought, depending on how busy she was in the shop. The Swiss letter would confirm a deposit of eighty thousand marks, and there'd probably be cards for him to sign as samples of his signature. The envelope, Jonathan then supposed, would have no return address on it, or nothing identifiable as a bank. Since he was returning Saturday, Simone might leave any letters unopened. Fifty-fifty, he thought again, and slid gently into sleep.

In the hospital the next morning the atmosphere seemed strictly routine and curiously informal. Reeves was present the whole time, and Jonathan could tell, though the conversation was all in German, that Reeves did not tell Dr Schroeder about a previous examination in Hamburg. The Hamburg report was now in the charge of Dr Perrier in Fontainebleau, who must by now have sent it to the Ebberle-Valent Laboratoire, as he had promised to do.

Again a nurse spoke perfect English. Dr Max Schroeder was about fifty, with black hair modishly down to his shirt collar.

'He says more or less,' Reeves told Jonathan, 'that it is a classic case with – not so cheerful predictions for the future.'

No, there was nothing new for Jonathan. Not even the message that the results of the examination would be ready for Jonathan tomorrow morning.

It was nearly 11 a.m. when Jonathan and Reeves walked out of the hospital. They walked along an embankment of the Isar, where there were children in prams, stone apartment buildings, a pharmacy, a grocery shop, all the appurtenances of living of which Jonathan felt not in the least a part that morning. He had to remember even to breathe. Today was going to be a day of failure, he thought. He wanted to plunge into the river and possibly drown, or become a fish. Reeves' presence and his sporadic talking irked him. He managed not to hear Reeves finally. Jonathan felt that he was not going to kill anyone today, not by the string in his pocket, not by the gun either.

'Shouldn't I think about getting my suitcase,' Jonathan interrupted, 'if the train's at two something?'

They found a taxi.

Almost beside the hotel there was a shop window of twinkling objects, glowing with gold and silver lights like a German Christmas tree. Jonathan drifted towards the window. It was mostly tourist trinkets, he saw with disappointment, but then he noticed a gyroscope poised at a slant against its square box.

'I want to buy something for my son,' Jonathan said, and went into the shop. He pointed and said, '*Bitte*', and acquired the gyroscope without noticing the price. He had changed two hundred francs at the hotel that morning.

Jonathan had already packed, so all he had to do was close his suitcase. He took it down himself. Reeves stuck a hundred-mark note into Jonathan's hand, and asked him to pay the hotel bill, because it might look odd if Reeves paid it. Money had ceased to matter to Jonathan.

They were early at the station. In the buffet, Jonathan didn't want anything to eat, only coffee.

So Reeves ordered coffee. 'You'll have to make the opportunity yourself, I realize, Jon. It may not work out, I know, but this man we *want* . . . Stay near the restaurant car. Smoke a cigarette, stand at the end of the carriage next to the restaurant car, for instance . . .'

Jonathan had a second coffee. Reeves bought a *Daily Telegruph* and a paperback for Jonathan to take with him.

Then the train pulled in, daintily clicking on the rails, sleek grey and blue – the Mozart Express. Reeves was looking for Marcangelo, who was supposed to board now with at least two bodyguards. There were perhaps sixty people getting on all along the platform, and as many getting off. Reeves grabbed Jonathan's arm and pointed. Jonathan was standing with suitcase in hand by the carriage he was supposed to enter, according to his ticket. Jonathan saw – or did he? – the group of three men that Reeves was talking about, three shortish men in hats climbing the steps two carriages away from Jonathan's and more towards the front of the train.

'It's him. I saw the grey in his hair even,' Reeves said. 'Now where's the restaurant car?' He stepped back to see better, trotted towards the front of the train, and came back. 'It's the one in front of Marcangelo's.'

The train's departure was being announced in French now.

'You've got the gun in your pocket?' Reeves asked.

Jonathan nodded. Reeves had reminded him, when he went up to his hotel room for his suitcase, to put it in his pocket. 'See that my wife gets the money, whatever happens to me.'

'That's a promise.' Reeves patted his arm.

The whistle blew for a second time, and doors banged. Jonathan got on the train and didn't look back at Reeves who he knew would be following him with his eyes. Jonathan found his seat. There were only two other people in the compartment, which was for eight passengers. The upholstery was dark red plush. Jonathan put his suitcase on an overhead rack, then his new coat, folded inside out. A young man entered the compartment, and hung out of the window, talking to someone in German. Jonathan's other companions were a middle-aged man sunk in what looked like office papers, and a neat little woman wearing a small hat and reading a novel. Jonathan's seat was next to the businessman, who had the window seat facing the way the train was moving. Jonathan opened his *Telegraph*.

It was 2.11 p.m.

Jonathan watched the outskirts of Munich glide past, office buildings, onion towers. Opposite Jonathan were three framed photographs – a château somewhere, a lake with a couple of swans, some snow-topped alps. The train purred over smooth rails and rocked gently. Jonathan half closed his eyes. By locking his fingers and putting his elbows on the armrests, he could almost doze. There was time, time to make up his mind, change his mind, change back again. Marcangelo was going to Paris like him, and the train didn't arrive until 11.7 p.m. tonight. A stop came at Strassburg around 6.30 p.m., he remembered Reeves saying. A few minutes later, Jonathan came awake and realized there was a thin but regular traffic of people in the aisle beyond the glass-doored compartment. A man came partway into the compartment with a trolley of sandwiches, bottles of beer and wine. The young man bought a beer. A stocky man stood smoking a pipe in the aisle, and from time to time pushed himself against the window to let others pass him.

No harm in strolling past Marcangelo's compartment, as if *en route* to the restaurant car, Jonathan thought, just to size up the situation a bit, but it took Jonathan several minutes to muster his initiative, during which time he smoked a Gitane. He put the ashes into the metal receptacle fixed under the window, careful not to drop any on the knees of the man reading office papers.

At last Jonathan got up and walked forward. The door at the end of the carriage was sticky to open. There was another pair of doors before he reached Marcangelo's carriage. Jonathan walked slowly, bracing himself against the gentle but irregular swaying of the train, glancing into each compartment. Marcangelo's was instantly recognizable, because Marcangelo was facing Jonathan in a centre seat, asleep with hands folded across his abdomen, jowls sunk into his collar, the grey streak at the temple flowing back and up. Jonathan had a quick impression of two other Italian types leaning towards each other, talking and gesticulating. There was no one else in the compartment Jonathan thought. He went on to the end of the carriage and on to the platform, where he lit another cigarette and stood looking out the window. This end of the carriage had a W.C., which now showed a red tag in its circular lock, indicating that it was occupied. Another man, bald and slender, stood by the opposite window, perhaps waiting for the W.C. The idea of trying to kill anyone here was absurd, because there were bound to be witnesses. Or even if only killer and victim were on the platform, wouldn't someone very likely appear in a matter of seconds? The train was not at all noisy, and if a man cried out, even with the garrotte already around his neck, wouldn't the people in the first compartment hear him?

A man and a woman came out of the restaurant car, and went into the carriage aisle, not closing the doors, though a white-jacketed waiter at once did this.

Jonathan walked back in the direction of his own carriage, and glanced once more into Marcangelo's compartment, but very briefly. Marcangelo was smoking a cigarette, leaning forward fatly, talking.

If it was done, it ought to be done before Strassburg, Jonathan thought. He imagined quite a lot of people getting on at Strassburg to go to Paris. But maybe in this he was wrong. In about half an hour, he thought, he ought to put on his topcoat and go and stand on the platform at the end of Marcangelo's carriage and wait. And suppose Marcangelo used the loo at the *other* end of his carriage? There were loos at both ends. And suppose he didn't go to the loo at all? That was possible, even though it wasn't likely. And suppose the Italians simply didn't choose to patronize the restaurant car? No, they would logically go to the restaurant car, but they'd go all together, too. If he couldn't do anything, Reeves would simply have to make another plan, a better one, Jonathan thought. But Marcangelo, or someone comparable, would have to be killed, by him, if he was to collect any more money.

Just before 4 p.m., Jonathan forced himself to get up, to haul down his topcoat carefully. In the aisle, he put on the topcoat with its heavy right-hand pocket, and went with his paperback to stand on the platform at the end of Marcangelo's carriage.

ELEVEN

When Jonathan passed the Italians' compartment, not glancing in this time, he had seen out of the corner of his eye a confusion of figures, men pulling down a suitcase, or perhaps struggling playfully. He had heard laughter.

A minute later, Jonathan stood leaning against a metal-framed map of Central Europe, facing the half-glass door of the corridor. Through the glass, Jonathan saw a man approaching, bumping the door open. This man looked like one of Marcangelo's bodyguards, dark-haired, in his thirties, with the sour expression and the sturdy build that ensured he would one day look like a disgruntled toad. Jonathan recalled the photographs on the jacket of *The Grim Reapers*. The man went straight to the W.C. door and entered. Jonathan continued to look at his open paperback. After a very short time, the man reappeared and went back into the corridor.

Jonathan found that he had been holding his breath. Suppose it had been Marcangelo, wouldn't it have been a perfect opportunity, with no one passing from the carriage or the restaurant car? Jonathan realized he would've stood just where he was, pretending to read, if it *had* been Marcangelo. Jonathan's right hand, in his pocket, pushed the safety on and off the little gun. After all, what was the risk? What was the loss? Merely his own life.

Marcangelo might come lumbering forward at any minute, push the door open, and then – It could be like before, in the German underground. Couldn't it? Then a bullet for himself. But Jonathan imagined firing at Marcangelo, then tossing the gun at once out the door by the W.C., or out the door's window which looked as if it opened, then walking casually into the restaurant car, sitting down and ordering something.

It was quite impossible.

I'll order something now, Jonathan thought, and went into the restaurant car, where there were plenty of free tables. On one side, the tables were for four people, on the other side for two. Jonathan took one of the smaller tables. A waiter came, Jonathan ordered a beer, then quickly changed it to wine.

'*Weisswein, bitte,*' Jonathan said.

A cold quarter-bottle of Riesling appeared. The *cluckety-cluck* of the train sounded more muffled and luxurious here. The window was bigger, yet more private somehow, making the forest – the Black Forest? – look spectacularly rich and verdant. There were endless tall pines, as if Germany had so many it did not need to cut any down for any purpose. Not a scrap of débris or paper was to be seen, nor was any human figure to be seen caring for it, which was equally surprising to Jonathan. When did the Germans do their tidying? Jonathan tried to summon courage from the wine. Somewhere along the line he had lost his momentum, and it was just a matter of getting it back. He drank off the last of the wine as if it were an obligatory toast, paid his bill, and pulled on his coat, which he had laid on the chair opposite. He would stand on the platform until Marcangelo appeared, and whether Marcangelo was alone or with two bodyguards, he would shoot.

Jonathan tugged at the carriage door, sliding it open. He was back in the prison of the platform, leaning against the map again, looking at the stupid paperback ... *David had wondered, did Elaine suspect? Desperate now, David went over the events of* ... Jonathan's eyes moved over the print like an illiterate's. He remembered something he'd thought of before, days ago. Simone would refuse the money, if she knew how he had got it, and of course she'd know how he had got it, if he shot himself on the train. He wondered if Simone could be persuaded by Reeves, by somebody, convinced – that what he had done wasn't exactly like murder. Jonathan almost laughed. It was quite hopeless. And what was he doing standing here? He could walk straight ahead now, back to his seat.

A figure was approaching, and Jonathan looked up. Then he blinked. The man coming towards him was Tom Ripley.

Ripley pushed open the half-glass door, smiling a little. 'Jonathan,' he said softly. 'Give me the thing, would you? The garrotte.' He stood side-ways to Jonathan, looking out the window.

Jonathan felt suddenly blank with shock. Whose side was Tom Ripley on? Marcangelo's? Then Jonathan started at the sight of three men approaching in the corridor.

Tom moved a bit closer to Jonathan to get out of their way.

The men were talking in German, and they went on into the restaurant car.

Tom said over his shoulder to Jonathan, 'The string. We'll give it a try, all right?'

Jonathan understood, or partly understood. Ripley was a friend of Reeves. He knew Reeves' plan. Jonathan was wadding the garrotte up in his left-hand trousers pocket. He pulled his hand out and gave the garrotte into Tom's willing hand, Jonathan looked away from Tom, and was aware of a sense of relief.

Tom pushed the garrotte into the right-hand pocket of his jacket. 'Stay there, because I might need you.' Tom went over to the W.C., saw it was empty, and went in.

Tom locked the toilet door. The garrotte wasn't even through its loop. Tom adjusted it for action, and put it carefully into the right-hand pocket of his jacket. He smiled a little. Jonathan had gone pale as a sheet! Tom had rung up Reeves the day before yesterday, and Reeves had told him Jonathan was coming but would probably hold out for a gun. Jonathan must have a gun now, Tom thought, but Tom considered a gun impossible in such conditions.

Stepping on the water pedal. Tom wet his hands, shook them, and passed his palms over his face. He was feeling a bit nervous himself. His first Mafia effort!

Tom had felt that Jonathan might botch this job, and having got Trevanny into this, Tom thought it behoved him to try to help him out. So Tom had flown to Salzburg yesterday, in order to board the train today. Tom had asked Reeves what Marcangelo looked like, but rather casually, and Tom didn't think Reeves suspected that he was going to be on the train. On the contrary, Tom had told Reeves that he thought his scheme was hare-brained, and had told Reeves that he might let Jonathan off with half the money and find someone else for the second job, if he wanted to make a success of it. But not Reeves. Reeves was like a small boy playing a game he had invented himself, a rather obsessive game with severe rules – for other people. Tom wanted to help Trevanny, and what a great cause it was! Killing a big shot Mafioso! Maybe even two Mafiosi!

Tom hated the Mafia, hated their loan-sharking, their blackmail, their bloody church, their cowardliness in forever delegating their dirty work to underlings, so that the law couldn't get its hands on the bigger bastards among them, never get them behind bars except on charges of income tax evasion or some other triviality. The Mafiosi made Tom feel almost virtuous by comparison. At this thought, Tom laughed out loud, a laugh which rang in the tiny metal-and-tile room in which he stood. (He was aware too that he just might be keeping Marcangelo himself waiting outside the door.) Yes, there were people more dishonest, more corrupt, decidedly more ruthless than himself, and these were the Mafiosi – that charming, squabbling batch of families which the Italian–American League claimed did not exist, claimed were a figment of fiction-writers' imagination. Why, the church itself with its bishops making blood liquefy at the festival of San Gennaro, and little girls seeing visions of the Virgin Mary, all *this* was more real than the Mafia! Yes, indeed! Tom rinsed his mouth and spat and ran water into the basin and let it drain. Then he went out.

There was no one but Jonathan Trevanny on the platform, Jonathan now smoking a cigarette, but he at once dropped the cigarette like a soldier who wanted to appear more efficient under the eyes of a superior officer. Tom gave him a reassuring smile, and faced the side window by Jonathan.

'Did they go by, by any chance?' Tom had not wanted to peer through the two doors into the restaurant car.

'No.'

'We may have to wait till after Strassburg, but I hope not.'

A woman was emerging from the restaurant car, having trouble with the doors, and Tom sprang to open the second for her.

'*Danke schön,*' she said.

'*Bitte,*' Tom replied.

Tom drifted to the other side of the platform and pulled a *Herald-Tribune* from a pocket of his jacket. It was now 5.11 p.m. They were to arrive at Strassburg at 6.33 p.m. Tom supposed the Italians had had a big lunch, and were not going to go into the restaurant car.

A man went into the lavatory.

Jonathan was looking down at his book, but Tom's glance made Jonathan look at him, and Tom smiled once more. When the man came out, Tom moved over towards Jonathan. There were two men standing in the aisle of the carriage, several yards away, one smoking a cigar, both looking out the window and paying no attention to him and Jonathan.

'I'll try to get him *in* the loo,' Tom said. 'Then we'll have to heave him out the door.' Tom jerked his head to indicate the door on the lavatory side. 'If I'm in the loo with him, knock twice on the door when the coast is clear. Then we'll give him the old heave-ho as fast as poss.' Very casually Tom lit a Gauloise, then slowly and deliberately yawned.

Jonathan's panic, which had reached a peak when Tom had been in the W.C., was subsiding a little. Tom wanted to go through with it. Just why he did was beyond Jonathan's power to imagine just now. Jonathan also had a feeling that Tom might intend to botch the thing, and leave Jonathan holding the bag. And yet, why? More likely Tom Ripley wanted a cut of the money, maybe all the rest of it. At that moment, Jonathan simply didn't care. It didn't matter. Now Tom himself looked a bit worried, Jonathan thought. He was leaning against the wall opposite the W.C. door, newspaper in hand, but he wasn't reading.

Then Jonathan saw two men approaching. The second man was Marcangelo. The first man was not one of the Italians. Jonathan glanced at Tom – who at once looked at him – and Jonathan nodded once.

The first man looked around on the platform, saw the W.C. and made for it. Marcangelo passed in front of Jonathan, saw that the W.C. was occupied, and turned back and returned to the carriage aisle. Jonathan saw Tom grin and make a sweeping gesture with his right arm, as if to say, 'Dammit, the fish got away!'

Marcangelo was in plain view of Jonathan, waiting just a few feet away in the aisle, looking out the window. It occurred to Jonathan that Marcangelo's guards, who were in the middle of the carriage, wouldn't know that Marcangelo had had to wait, so that this extra time would arouse their anxiety sooner if Marcangelo didn't come back. Jonathan nodded slightly at Tom, which he hoped Tom would understand to mean that Marcangelo was waiting near by.

The man in the loo came out and returned to the carriage.

Now Marcangelo approached, and Jonathan gave a glance at Tom but Tom was sunk in his newspaper.

Tom was aware that the dumpy figure entering the platform was Marcangelo again, but he did not look up from his newspaper. Just in front of Tom, Marcangelo opened the door of the W.C., and Tom sprang forward like a person who was determined to get into the toilet first, but at the same time he flipped the garrotte over the head of Marcangelo whose cry Tom hoped he stifled as he dragged him, with a jerk of the garrotte like a boxer's right cross, into the little room and closed the door. Tom yanked the garrotte viciously – one of Marcangelo's own weapons in his prime, Tom supposed – and Tom saw the nylon disappear in the flesh of the neck. Tom gave it another whirl behind the man's head and pulled still tighter. With his left hand Tom flicked the lever that locked the door. Marcangelo's gurgle stopped, his tongue began to protrude from the awful wet mouth, his eyes closed in misery, then opened in horror, and began to have the blank, what's-happening-to-me stare of the dying. Lower false teeth clattered to the tiles. Tom was nearly cutting his own thumb and the side of his forefinger because of the force he was exerting on the string, but he felt it a pain worth enduring. Marcangelo had slumped to the floor, but the garrotte, or rather Tom, was holding him in more or less a seated position. Marcangelo was now unconscious, Tom thought, and it was impossible for him to be breathing at all. Tom picked up the teeth, and dropped them into the toilet, and managed to step on the pedal which dumped the pan. He wiped his fingers with disgust on Marcangelo's padded shoulder.

Jonathan had seen the flick of the latch that changed the colour from green to red. The silence was alarming to Jonathan. How long would it last? What was happening? How much time had passed? Jonathan kept glancing through the glass half of the door into the carriage.

A man came from the restaurant car, started for the toilet, and seeing that it was occupied, went on into the carriage.

Jonathan was thinking that Marcangelo's friends would appear at any moment, if Marcangelo was in the least long in getting back to his compartment. Now the coast was clear, and was it time to knock? There *must* have been time for Marcangelo to die. Jonathan went and rapped twice on the door.

Tom stepped calmly out, closed the door and surveyed the situation, and a woman in a reddish tweed suit entered the platform just then – a smallish, middle-aged woman who was plainly headed for the toilet. The indicator was now showing green.

'Sorry,' Tom said to her. 'Someone – a friend of mine is being sick in there, I'm afraid.'

'*Bitte?*'

'*Mein Freund ist da drinnen ziemlich krank,*' Tom said with an apologetic smile. '*Entschuldigen Sie, gnädige Frau. Er kommt sofort heraus.*'

She nodded and smiled, and went back into the carriage.

'Okay, give me a hand!' Tom whispered to Jonathan, and started for the W.C.

'Another one's coming,' Jonathan said. 'One of the Italians.'

'Oh, Christ.' The Italian might simply wait on the platform, Tom thought, if he went into the loo and locked the door.

The Italian, a sallow chap of about thirty, gave Jonathan and Tom a look, saw that the lavatory said *libre*, then went into the restaurant car, no doubt to see if Marcangelo was there.

Tom said to Jonathan, 'Can you bash him with the gun after I hit him?'

Jonathan nodded. The gun was small, but Jonathan's adrenalin was at last stirring.

'As if your life depended on it,' Tom added. 'Maybe it does.'

The bodyguard came back from the restaurant car, moving more quickly. Tom was on the Italian's left, and pulled him by the shirtfront suddenly, out of view of the restaurant car's doors, and hit him in the jaw. Tom followed this with a left fist in the man's abdomen, and Jonathan cracked the Italian on the back of the head with the gun butt.

'The door!' Tom said, jerking his head, trying to catch the Italian who was falling forward.

The man was not unconscious, his arms flailed weakly, but Jonathan already had the side door open, and Tom's instinct was to get him out without spending a second on another blow. The noise of the train wheels came with a sudden roar. They pushed, kicked and poured the bodyguard out, and Tom lost his balance and would have toppled out, if not for Jonathan catching him by his jacket tails. *Bang* went the door shut again.

Jonathan pushed his fingers through his tousled hair.

Tom motioned for Jonathan to go to the other side of the platform, where he could see down the aisle. Jonathan went, and Tom could see him making an effort to collect himself and look like the ordinary passenger again.

Tom raised his eyebrows in a question, and Jonathan nodded, and Tom nipped into the W.C. and swung the latch, trusting that Jonathan would have the wit to knock again when it was safe. Marcangelo lay crumpled on the floor, head next to the basin pedestal, his face pale now with a touch of blue in it. Tom looked away from him, heard the rustle of doors outside – the restaurant car doors – and then a welcome two knocks. This time Tom opened the door just a crack.

'Looks all right,' Jonathan said.

Tom kicked the door open past Marcangelo's shoes which the door bumped, and signalled for Jonathan to open the side door of the train. But in fact they worked together, Jonathan having to help Tom with some of Marcangelo's weight before the side door was in a fully open position. The door tended to close because of the direction of the train. They tumbled Marcangelo through it head-first, heels over head, and Tom, giving him a final kick, didn't touch him at all, because his body had already fallen clear on to a cinder bank so close to Tom that he could see individual ashes and blades of grass. Now Tom held Jonathan's right arm while Jonathan reached for the door's lever and caught it.

Tom pulled the toilet door shut, breathless, trying to assume a calm air. 'Go back to your seat and get off at Strassburg,' he said. 'They'll be looking at everyone on this train.' He gave Jonathan a nervous pat on the arm. 'Good luck, my friend.' Tom watched Jonathan open the door that went into the carriage aisle.

Then Tom started to enter the restaurant car, but a party of four was coming out, and Tom had to step aside while they waddled, talked and laughed through the two doors. Tom at last entered and took the first vacant table. He sat down in a chair facing the door he had just come through. He was expecting the second bodyguard at any moment. He drew the menu towards him and casually studied it. Cole slaw. Tongue salad. Gulaschsuppe ... The menu was in French, English and German.

Jonathan, walking down the aisle of Marcangelo's carriage, came face to face with the second Italian bodyguard who rudely bumped into him in getting past. Jonathan was glad he felt a bit dazed, otherwise he might have reacted with alarm at the physical contact. The train gave one whistle followed by two shorter ones. Did that mean something? Jonathan got back to his seat and sat down without removing his overcoat, careful not to glance at any of the four people in the compartment. His watch said 5.31 p.m. It seemed more than an hour since he had looked at his watch and it had been a couple of minutes past 5 p.m. Jonathan squirmed, closed his eyes, cleared his throat, imagining the bodyguard and Marcangelo, having rolled under the train wheels, being chewed into various bits. Or maybe they hadn't rolled under. Was the bodyguard even dead? Maybe he'd be rescued and would describe him and Tom Ripley with accuracy. Why had Tom Ripley helped him? Or should he call it help? What did Ripley want out of it? He was now under Ripley's thumb, he realized. Ripley probably wanted only money, however. Or was he due for worse? Some kind of blackmail? Blackmail had a lot of forms.

Should he try to get a plane from Strassburg to Paris tonight, or stay at a hotel in Strassburg? Which was safer? And safer from what, the Mafia or the police? Wouldn't some passenger, looking out the window, have seen one body, maybe two, falling beside the train? Or had the two bodies fallen too close to the train to be seen? If anybody had seen anything, the train wouldn't have stopped, but word could be radioed, Jonathan supposed. Jonathan was on the alert for a train guard in the aisle, for any sign of agitation, but he didn't see any.

At that moment, having ordered Gulaschsuppe and a bottle of Carlsbad, Tom was looking at his newspaper which he had propped against a mustard pot, and nibbling a crisp roll. And he was amused by the anxious Italian who had waited patiently outside the occupied loo, until to the Italian's surprise a woman had emerged. Now the bodyguard was for the second time peering down the dining-car through the two glass doors. And here he came, still trying to keep his cool, looking for his *capo* or his thug chum or both, walking the whole length of the car as if he might find Marcangelo sprawled under one of the tables or chatting with the chef at the other end of the car.

Tom had not lifted his eyes as the Italian came through, but Tom had felt his glance. Now Tom risked a look over his shoulder, such as a man who was expecting his food might give, and saw the bodyguard – a blondish, crinkly-haired type in a chalk-stripe suit, broad purple tie – talking with a waiter at the back of the car. The busy waiter was shaking his head and pushing past him with his tray. The bodyguard bustled down the aisle between the tables again and went out.

Tom's paprika-red soup arrived with the beer. Tom was hungry, as he had had only a small breakfast in his Salzburg hotel – not the Goldener Hirsch this time, because the staff knew him there. Tom had flown to Salzburg instead of Munich, not wanting to encounter Reeves and Jonathan Trevanny at the railway station. He'd had time in Salzburg to buy a green leather jacket with green felt trim for Heloise, which he intended to hide away until her birthday in October. He had told Heloise he was going to Paris for one night, maybe two, to see some art exhibits, and since Tom did this now and then, staying at the Inter-Continental or the Ritz or the Pont Royal, Heloise had not been surprised. Tom in fact varied his hotels, so that if he told Heloise he was in Paris when he wasn't, she wouldn't be alarmed at not finding him at, say, the Inter-Continental, if she telephoned. He had also bought his ticket at Orly, instead of at the travel agencies at Fontainebleau or Moret where he was known, and he had used his false passport provided by Reeves last year: Robert Fiedler Mackay, American, engineer, born in Salt Lake City, no wife. It had occurred to Tom that the Mafia could get the passenger list of the train with a bit of effort. Was he on the Mafia's list of interesting people? Tom hesitated to attribute such an honour to himself, but some of Marcangelo's family might have noticed his name in the newspapers. Not recruitable material, not promising as extortion victim either, but still a man on the borderline of the law.

But this Mafia bodyguard, or button man, hadn't given Tom as long a look as he'd given a husky young man in a leather jacket across the aisle from Tom. Perhaps all was well.

Jonathan Trevanny would need some reassuring. Trevanny no doubt thought he wanted money, that he was intending to blackmail him somehow. Tom had to laugh a little (but he was still looking at his newspaper and might have been reading Art Buchwald) at the memory of Trevanny's face when Tom had walked on to the platform, and at that funny moment when Trevanny had realized that he meant to help him. Tom had done some thinking in Villeperce, and decided to lend a hand with the nasty garrotting, so that Jonathan could at least collect the money that had been promised. Tom was vaguely ashamed of himself, in fact, for having got Jonathan into it, and so coming to Jonathan's aid relieved a bit of Tom's guilt. Yes, if all went well, Trevanny would be a lucky and much happier man, Tom was thinking, and Tom believed in positive thinking. Don't hope, *think* the best, and things would work out for the best, Tom felt. He would have to see Trevanny again to explain a few things, and above all Trevanny should take full credit for the Marc-angelo murder in order to collect the rest of the money from Reeves. He and Trevanny mustn't be seen to be chummy, that was a vital point. They mustn't *be* chummy, at all. (Tom wondered now what was happening to Trevanny, if the second bodyguard was cruising the whole train?) The dear old Mafia would try to track the killer down, the killers maybe. The Mafia often took years, but they never gave up. Even if the man they wanted fled to South America, the Mafia might get him, Tom knew. But it seemed to Tom that Reeves Minot was in more danger than either himself or Trevanny at the moment.

He'd try to ring Trevanny tomorrow morning in his shop. Or tomorrow afternoon, in case Trevanny didn't make it to Paris tonight. Tom lit a Gauloise and glanced at the woman in the reddish tweed suit, whom he and Trevanny had seen on the platform, who was now dreamily eating a dainty salad of lettuce and cucumber. Tom felt euphoric.

When Jonathan got off at Strassburg, he imagined that there were more police than usual in evidence, six perhaps instead of the usual two or three. One police officer seemed to be examining a man's papers. Or had the man simply asked a direction, and the cop was consulting a guidebook? Jonathan walked straight out of the station with his suitcase. He had decided to stay the night in Strassburg which, for no real reason, seemed a safer place than Paris tonight. The remaining bodyguard was probably going on to Paris to join his friends – unless by some chance the bodyguard was at this moment tailing him, ready to plug him in the back. Jonathan felt a light sweat breaking out, and he was suddenly aware of being tired. He let his suitcase down on a kerb at a street intersection, and gazed around at unfamiliar buildings. The scene was busy with pedestrians and cars. It was 6.40 p.m., no doubt the Strassburg rush hour. Jonathan thought of registering under another name. If he wrote a false name plus a false card or identity number, no one would ask to see his real card. Then he realized that a false name would make him even more uneasy. Jonathan was becoming aware of what he had done. He suffered a brief nausea. Then he picked up his suitcase and trudged on. The gun weighed heavily in his overcoat pocket. He was afraid to drop it down a street drain, or into a rubbish bin. Jonathan saw himself getting all the way to Paris and into his own house with the little gun still in his pocket.

TWELVE

Tom, having left the green Renault station-wagon near the Porte d'Italie in Paris, got home to Belle Ombre a little before 1 a.m. Saturday. There was no light visible at the front of the house, but when Tom climbed the stairs with his suitcase, he was delighted to see that there was a light in Heloise's room in the back left corner. He went in to see her.

'Back finally! How was Paris? What did you do?' Heloise was in green pyjamas with a pink satin eiderdown pulled up to her waist.

'Ah, I chose a bad film tonight.' Tom saw that the book she was reading was one he had bought, on the French socialist movement. That would not improve relations with her father, Tom thought. Often Heloise came out with very leftist remarks, principles which she had no idea of practising. But Tom felt he was slowly pushing her to the left. Push with one hand, take with the other, Tom thought.

'Did you see Noëlle?' Heloise asked.

'No. Why?'

'She was having a dinner-party – tonight, I think. She needed one more man. Of course she invited us both, but I told her you were probably at the Ritz and to telephone you.'

'I was at the Crillon this time,' Tom said, pleasantly aware of the scent of Heloise's cologne mingled with Nivea. And he was unpleasantly aware of his own filth after the train ride. 'Is everything all right here?'

'Very all right,' said Heloise in a manner that sounded seductive, though Tom knew she didn't mean it that way. She meant she had had a happy and ordinary day and she was happy herself.

'I feel like a shower. See you in ten minutes.' Tom went to his own room, where he had a real shower in the tub, not the telephone-shower of Heloise's bathroom.

A few minutes later – Heloise's Austrian jacket having been tucked away in a bottom drawer under sweaters – Tom was dozing in bed beside Heloise, too tired to look at *L'Express* any longer. He was wondering if *L'Express* might have a picture of one of the two Mafiosi, or both, beside the railway track in next week's edition? Was that bodyguard dead? Tom devoutly hoped he had fallen under the rails somehow, because Tom was afraid he hadn't been dead when they tossed him out. Tom recalled Jonathan pulling him back when he'd been about to fall out, and with his eyes closed Tom winced at the memory. Trevanny had saved his life, or at least saved him from an awful fall, and possibly from having a foot cut off by the train wheels.

Tom slept well, and got up around 8.30 p.m., before Heloise was awake. He had coffee downstairs in the living-room, and in spite of his curiosity didn't switch on the radio for the 9 a.m. news. He took a stroll around the garden, gazed with some pride at the strawberry patch which he had recently snipped and weeded, and stared at three burlap sacks of dahlia roots that had been kept over the winter and were due for planting. Tom was thinking of trying Trevanny by telephone this afternoon. The sooner he saw Trevanny, the better for Trevanny's peace of mind. Tom wondered if Jonathan had also noticed the blondish bodyguard who had been in such a tizzy? Tom had passed him in an aisle when he had been making his way from the restaurant car back to his carriage, three carriages back, the bodyguard looking ready to explode with frustration, and Tom had had a great desire to say in his best gutter Italian, 'You'll get the sack if this kind of work keeps up, eh?'

Mme Annette returned before 11 a.m. from her morning shopping and, hearing her close the side door into the kitchen, Tom went in to have a look at *Le Parisien Libéré*.

'The horses,' Tom said with a smile, picking up the newspaper.

'Ah *oui*! You have a bet, M. Tome?'

Mme Annette knew he didn't bet. 'No, I want to see how a friend made out.'

Tom found what he was looking for at the bottom of page one, a short item about three inches long. Italian garrotted. Another gravely wounded. The garrotted man was identified as Vito Marcangelo, fifty-two, of Milan. Tom was more interested in the gravely wounded Filippo Turoli, thirty-one, who had also been pushed from the train and suffered multiple concussions, broken ribs and a damaged arm that might require amputation in a hospital of Strassburg. Turoli was said to be in a coma and in critical condition. The report went on to say that a passenger had seen one body on the train embankment and alerted a train official, but not before kilometres had been covered by the luxurious Mozart Express, which had been going *à pleine vitesse* towards Strassburg. Then two bodies had been discovered by the rescue team. It was estimated that four minutes had elapsed between the fall of each body, and police were actively pursuing their inquiries.

Obviously there would be more on the subject, with photographs probably, in later editions, Tom thought. That was a nice Gallic touch of detection, the four minutes, like a problem in arithmetic for children also, Tom thought. If a train is going at one hundred kilometres per hour, and one Mafioso is tossed out, and a second mafioso is found tossed out six and two-thirds of a kilometre distant from the first Mafioso, how much time has elapsed between the tossing out of each Mafioso? Answer: four minutes. There was no mention of the second bodyguard who was evidently keeping his mouth shut and lodging no complaints about the service on the Mozart Express.

But the bodyguard Turoli wasn't dead. And Tom realized that Turoli had perhaps had a look at him before Tom hit him in the jaw, had some idea of him. He might be able to describe him or identify him, if he ever saw Tom again. But Turoli had probably not taken in Jonathan at all, since Jonathan had hit him from behind.

Around 3.30 p.m., when Heloise had gone off to vist Agnès Grais on the other side of Villeperce, Tom looked up Trevanny's shop number in Fontainebleau, and found that he had it correct in his memory.

Trevanny answered.

'Hello. This is Tom Ripley. Um-m – about my picture. Are you alone just now?'

'Yes.'

'I'd like to see you. I think it's important. Can you meet me, say – after you close today? Around seven? I can –'

'Yes.' Trevanny sounded as tense as a cat.

'Suppose I hold my car around the Salamandre bar? You know the bar I mean on the Rue Grande?'

'Yes, I know it.'

'Then we'll drive somewhere and have a talk. Quarter to seven?'

'Right,' said Trevanny as if through his teeth.

Trevanny was going to be pleasantly surprised, Tom thought as he hung up.

A little later that afternoon, when Tom was in his atelier, Heloise telephoned.

'Hello, Tom! I am not coming home, because Agnès and I are going to cook something wonderful and we want you to come. Antoine is here, you know. It's Saturday! So come around seven-thirty, all right?'

'How is eight, darling? I'm working a little.'

'*Tu travailles?*'

Tom smiled. 'I'm sketching. I'll be there at eight.'

Antoine Grais was an architect with a wife and two small children. Tom looked forward to a pleasant, relaxing evening with his neighbours. He drove off for Fontainebleau early so that he could buy a plant – he chose a camellia – as a present for the Grais, and give this as an excuse for being a little late, in case he was.

In Fontainebleau Tom also bought a *France-Soir* for the latest news about Turoli. There was nothing about any change in his condition, but the paper did say that the two Italians were believed to be members of the Genotti family of Mafia, and might have been victims of a rival gang. That at least would please Reeves, Tom thought, as that was Reeves' objective. Tom found a vacant spot at the kerb a few yards from the Salamandre. He looked through his back window and saw Trevanny walking towards him, in his rather slow stride, then Trevanny caught sight of Tom's car. Trevanny was wearing a mac of impressive decrepitude.

'Hello!' Tom said, opening the door. 'Get in and we'll go to Avon – or somewhere.'

Trevanny got in, barely mumbling a hello.

Avon was a twin town with Fontainebleau, though smaller. Tom drove down the slope towards the Fontainebleau-Avon railway station and bore to the right on the curve that led into Avon.

'Everything all right?' Tom asked pleasantly.

'Yes,' Trevanny said.

'You've seen the papers, I suppose.'

'Yes.'

'That bodyguard isn't dead.'

'I know.' Jonathan had imagined, since 8 a.m. that morning when he had seen the papers in Strassburg, that Turoli was going to come out of his coma at any moment and give a description of him and of Tom Ripley, the two men on the platform.

'You got back to Paris last night?'

'No I – I stayed in Strassburg and got a plane this morning.'

'No trouble in Strassburg? No sign of that second bodyguard?'

'No,' Jonathan said.

Tom was driving slowly, looking for a quiet spot. He slid up to a kerb in a little street of two-storey houses, stopped, and switched off his lights. 'I think,' Tom said, pulling out his cigarettes, 'considering the papers haven't reported clues – not the right ones anyway – we did a rather good job. That comatose bodyguard is the only rub.' Tom offered Jonathan a cigarette, but Jonathan took his own. 'Have you heard from Reeves?' Tom asked.

'Yes. This afternoon. Before you rang.' Reeves had rung this morning and Simone had answered. *Someone in Hamburg. An American,* Simone had said. That was also making Jonathan nervous, simply the fact that Simone had spoken with Reeves, although Reeves hadn't given his name.

'I hope he's not being sticky about the money,' Tom said. 'I prodded him, you know. He ought to come up with all of it right away.'

And how much would you like, Jonathan wanted to ask, but decided to let Ripley get to it himself.

Tom smiled and slumped behind the wheel. 'You're probably thinking that I want some of the – forty thousand quid isn't it? But I don't.'

'Oh. Frankly I was thinking you wanted some. Yes.'

'That's why I wanted to see you today. One of the reasons. The other reason is to ask if you're worried –' Jonathan's tension was making Tom feel awkward, almost tongue-tied. He gave a laugh. 'Of course you're worried! But there're worries and worries. I might be able to help – that is if you talk to me.'

What *did* he want, Jonathan wondered. He surely wanted something. 'I don't quite understand, I suppose, why you were on the train.'

'Because it was a pleasure! A pleasure for me to eliminate, or help to eliminate such people as those two yesterday. Simple as that! Also a pleasure for me to help you put a little money in your pocket. However, I meant worried about what we did – in any way. It's hard for me to put into words. Maybe because I'm not at all worried. Not yet anyway.'

Jonathan felt off balance. Tom Ripley was being evasive – somehow – or joking. Jonathan still felt a hostility towards Ripley, a wariness of him. And now it was too late. Yesterday on the train, seeing Ripley about to take over the job, Jonathan might have said, 'All right, it's all yours,' and walked off, back to his seat. That would not have erased the Hamburg affair which Ripley knew about, but – Yesterday the money hadn't been the motivation. Jonathan had simply been in a panic, even before Ripley had arrived. Now Jonathan felt he couldn't find the right weapon for his defence. 'I gather it was you,' Jonathan said, 'who put out the story that I was on my last legs. You gave my name to Reeves.'

'Yes,' Tom said a little contritely but firmly. 'But it was a choice, wasn't it? You could've said no to Reeves' idea.' Tom waited, but Jonathan didn't answer. 'However, the situation is considerably better now, I trust. Isn't it? I hope you're not anywhere near dying, and you've got quite a bit of dough – lolly, you'd call it.'

Jonathan saw Tom's face light up with his innocent-looking American smile. No one, seeing Tom Ripley's face now, would imagine that he could kill anyone, garrotte someone, and yet he'd done just that about twenty-four hours ago. 'You have a habit of playing practical jokes?' Jonathan asked with a smile.

'No. No, certainly not. This might be the first time.'

'And you want – nothing at all.'

'I can't think of anything I want from you. Not even friendship, because that'd be dangerous.'

Jonathan squirmed. He made himself stop drumming his fingers on a matchbox.

Tom could imagine what he was thinking, that he was under Tom Ripley's thumb, in a way, whether Ripley wanted anything or not. Tom said, 'You're no more in my grip than I am in yours. I did the garrotting, didn't I? You could as well say something against me as I against you. Think of it that way.'

'True,' Jonathan said.

'If there's one thing I'd like to do it's protect you.'

Now Jonathan laughed and Ripley didn't.

'Of course it may not be necessary. Let's hope not. The trouble is always other people. Ha!' Tom stared through the windshield for an instant. 'For instance, your wife. What've you told her about the money coming in?'

That was a problem, real, tangible and unsolved. 'I said I was being paid something by the German doctors. That they're making tests – using me.'

'Not bad,' Tom said musingly, 'but maybe we can think of something better. Because obviously you can't account for the whole sum like that, and you both may as well enjoy it. How about somebody dying in your family? In England? A recluse cousin, for instance.'

Jonathan smiled and glanced at Tom. 'I've thought of that, but frankly there isn't anybody.'

Tom could see that Jonathan wasn't in the habit of inventing. Tom could have invented something for Heloise, for example, if he'd suddenly come into a great deal of money. He would create an eccentric recluse tucked away in Santa Fe or Sausalito all these years, a third cousin of his mother's, something like that, and embroider the personage with details remembered from a brief meeting in Boston when Tom had been a small boy, orphaned as Tom really had been. Little had he known that this cousin had a heart of gold. 'Still it ought to be easy with your family so far away in England. We'll think about it,' Tom added, when he saw that Jonathan was about to say something in the negative. Tom looked at his watch. 'I'm afraid I'm due for dinner, and I suppose you are too. Ah, one more thing, the gun. A small matter, but did you get rid of it?'

The gun was in the pocket of the raincoat Jonathan was wearing. 'I've got it now. I'd very much like to get rid of it.'

Tom extended his hand. 'Let's have it. One thing out of the way.' Trevanny handed it to him, and Tom stuck it into the glove compartment. 'Never used, so it's not too dangerous, but I'll get rid of it because it's Italian.' Tom paused for thought. There must be something else, and now was the time to think of it, because he did not intend to see Jonathan again. Then it came to him. 'By the way, I will assume that you tell Reeves you did this job alone. Reeves doesn't know I was on the train. It's much better that way.'

Jonathan had rather assumed the opposite, and took a moment to digest this. 'I thought you were a rather good friend of Reeves.'

'Oh, we're friendly. Not too. We keep a distance.' In a way Tom was thinking out loud, and also trying to say the right thing in order not to scare Trevanny, in order to make Trevanny feel more sure of himself. It was difficult. 'No one knows I was on that train but you. I bought my ticket under another name. In fact I was using a false passport. I realized you were having trouble with the garrotte idea. I spoke with Reeves on the telephone.' Tom started his motor and put on the lights. 'Reeves is a bit cracked.'

'How so?'

A motorcycle with a strong headlight came roaring round the corner and passed them, drowning out the car's hum for a moment.

'He plays games,' Tom said. 'He's mainly a fence, as you may know, receives goods, passes them on. It's as silly as spy games, but at least Reeves hasn't been caught yet – caught and released and all that. I understand he's doing quite well in Hamburg, but I haven't seen his place there. He shouldn't be dabbling in *this* sort of thing. Not his dish.'

Jonathan had been imagining Tom Ripley a frequent visitor at Reeves Minot's place in Hamburg. He remembered Fritz turning up with a small package at Reeves' that night. Jewellery? Dope? Jonathan watched the familiar viaduct, then the dark green trees near the railway station come into view, their tops bright under the street lights. Only Tom Ripley next to him was unfamiliar. Jonathan's fear rose afresh. 'If I may ask – how did you come to pick on me?'

Tom was just then making the difficult turn left at the top of the hill into the Avenue Franklin Roosevelt, and had to pause for oncoming traffic. 'For a petty reason, I'm sorry to say. That night in February at your party – you said something I didn't like.' Now Tom was clear of traffic. 'You said, "Yes, I've heard of you," in a rather nasty way.'

Jonathan remembered. He also remembered he'd been feeling particularly tired and consequently bloody-minded that evening. So for a slight rudeness, Ripley had got him into the mess he was in now. Rather, he'd got himself into it, Jonathan reminded himself.

'You won't have to see me again,' Tom said. 'The job has been a success. I think, if we don't hear anything from that bodyguard.' Should he say 'I'm sorry' to Jonathan? To hell with it, Tom thought. 'And from a moral point of view, I trust you don't reproach yourself. Those men were murderers also. They often murder innocent people. So we took the law into our own hands. The Mafia would be the first to agree that people should take the law into their own hands. That's their cornerstone.' Tom turned right into the Rue de France. 'I won't take you all the way to your door.'

'Any place here. Thanks very much.'

'I'll try to send a friend to pick up my picture.' Tom stopped his car.

Jonathan got out. 'As you like.'

'Do ring me if you're in straits,' Tom said with a smile.

At least Jonathan smiled back, as if he were amused.

Jonathan walked towards the Rue St Merry, and in the next seconds began to feel better – relieved. Much of his relief was due to the fact that Ripley didn't seem to be worried – not by the bodyguard still alive, not by the fact they'd both stood for what seemed an unlikely length of time on that platform in the train. And the money situation – that was as incredible as the rest of it.

Jonathan slowed his steps as he approached the Sherlock Holmes house, though he knew he was later than usual. The signature cards from the Swiss bank had come to his shop yesterday, Simone had not opened the letter, and Jonathan had signed the cards and put them into the post at once that afternoon. He had a four-figure number for his account which he had thought he would remember, but which he had already forgotten. Simone had accepted his second visit to Germany to see a specialist, but there wouldn't be any more visits, and Jonathan would have to account for the money – not all of it but a good deal of extra money, for instance – by stories of injections, pills, and perhaps he'd have to make another trip or two to Germany just to substantiate his story that the doctors were continuing their tests. It was difficult, not at all Jonathan's style. He was hoping that some better explanation might occur to him, but he knew it wouldn't unless he racked his brains to think of one.

'You're late,' Simone said as he came in. She was in the living-room with Georges, picture books spread all over the sofa.

'Customers,' Jonathan said, and flung his mac on a hook. The absence of the gun's weight was a relief. He smiled at his son. 'And how are you, Pebble Boy? What're you up to?' Jonathan spoke in English.

Georges grinned like a little blond pumpkin. One front tooth had vanished while Jonathan had been on the Munich trip. 'I am weeding,' Georges said.

'Reading. You weed in the garden. Unless of course you have a speech defect.'

'Wot's a peach defect?'

Worms, for example. But it could go on for ever. What's worms? A town in Germany. 'Speech defect – like when you st-stutter. *B-b-bégayer* – that's a –'

'Oh Jon, look at this,' Simone said, reaching for a newspaper. 'I didn't notice it at lunch. Look. Two men – no, one man was killed on the train from Germany to Paris yesterday. Murdered and pushed off the train! Do you think that was the train you were on?'

Jonathan looked at the photograph of the dead man on the slope of ground, looked at the account of it as if he had not seen it before ... *garrotted ... an arm of the second victim may require amputation* ... 'Yes – the Mozart Express. I didn't notice anything on the train. But then there were about thirty carriages.' Jonathan had told Simone he had come in too late last night to make the last train to Fontainebleau, and that he had stayed at a small hotel in Paris.

'The Mafia,' Simone said, shaking her head. 'They must've had a compartment with the blinds drawn to do that garrotting. Ugh!' She got up to go to the kitchen.

Jonathan glanced at Georges, who was bent over an Astérix picture book at that instant. Jonathan would not have wanted to explain what garrotting meant.

That evening, though he felt a bit tense, Tom was in the best of spirits at the Grais's. Antoine and Agnès Grais lived in a round stone house with a turret, surrounded by climbing roses. Antoine was in his late thirties, neat and rather severe, master in his own house and tremendously ambitious. He worked in a modest studio in Paris all week, and came to the country at weekends to join his family, and knocked himself out further with gardening. Tom knew that Antoine considered him lazy, because if Tom's garden was equally neat, what miracle was it, since Tom had nothing else to do all day? The spectacular dish that Agnès and Heloise had created was a lobster casserole with a great variety of sea-food in the rice, and a choice of two sauces to go with it.

'I've thought of a wonderful way to start a forest fire,' Tom said musingly when they were having coffee. 'Especially good down in the South of France, where there're so many dry trees in summer. You fix a hand lens in a pine tree, you could do it even in winter, and then when the summer comes the sun shines through it and the magnifying glass starts a little blaze in the pine needles. You place it near the house of somebody you dislike, of course, and – snap, crackle and pop! – the whole thing goes up in blazes! The police or the insurance people wouldn't very likely find the hand lens in all the charred wood and even if they did – Perfect, isn't it?'

Antoine chuckled grudgingly, while the women gave appreciative shrieks of horror.

'If that happens to my property down South, I will know who did it!' said Antoine in his deep baritone.

The Grais owned a small property near Cannes which they let in July and August when rents were highest, and used themselves in the other summer months.

Mainly, however, Tom was thinking of Jonathan Trevanny. A stiff, repressed kind of fellow, but basically decent. He was going to need some more assistance – Tom hoped merely moral assistance.

THIRTEEN

Because of Vincent Turoli's uncertain state, Tom drove to Fontainebleau on Sunday to buy the London papers, the *Observer* and the *Sunday Times*, which he usually bought from the Villeperce *journaux-tabac* on Monday morning. The news kiosk in Fontainebleau was in front of the Hôtel de l'Aigle Noir. Tom glanced around for Trevanny, who probably bought the London Sundays habitually too, but he didn't see him. It was 11 a.m., and perhaps Trevanny already had the papers. Tom got into his car and looked at the *Observer* first. It had nothing about the train incident. Tom wasn't sure the English papers would bother reporting the story, but he looked into the *Sunday Times* and found an item on page three, one short column which Tom fell upon eagerly. The writer had given it a light touch: '. . . It must have been an exceptionally fast Mafia job . . . Vincent Turoli of the Genotti family, one arm missing, one eye damaged, regained conscious-ness early on Saturday, and his condition is improving so rapidly he may soon be flown to a Milan hospital. But if he knows anything, he is not talking.' That was no news to Tom, that he wasn't talking, but plainly he was going to live. That was unfortunate. Tom was thinking that Turoli had probably already given a description of him to his chums. Turoli would have been visited in Strassburg by family members. Important Mafiosi in the hospital were protected day and night by guards, and maybe Turoli would get this treatment too, Tom thought, as soon as the idea of eliminating Turoli crossed his mind. Tom recalled the Mafia-guarded hospitalization of Joe Colombo, head of the Profaci family, in New York. Despite overwhelming evidence to the contrary, Colombo denied that he was a member of the Mafia or that the Mafia existed. Nurses had had to step over the legs of bodyguards sleeping in the halls when Colombo had been in. Best not to think about getting rid of Turoli. He had probably already talked about a man in his thirties, with brown hair, a little over average height, who had socked him in the jaw and the stomach, and there must have been another man behind him too, because he had got a crack on the back of the head. The question was would Turoli be absolutely sure if he spotted him again, and Tom thought there was a good chance of this. Oddly Turoli, if he had seen him, might recall Jonathan a little more clearly, simply because Jonathan didn't look like everyone else, was taller and blonder than most people. Turoli of course would compare notes with the second bodyguard who was alive and well.

'Darling,' Heloise said when Tom walked into the living-room, 'how would you like to go on a cruise on the Nile?'

Tom's thoughts were so far away, he had to think for a moment what the Nile was and where. Heloise was barefoot on the sofa, browsing in travel brochures. Periodically she received a slew of them from an agency in Moret, sent on the agency's initiative, because Heloise was such a good customer. 'I don't know. Egypt –'

'Doesn't this look *séduisant*?' She showed Tom a picture of a little boat called the *Isis* which rather resembled a Mississippi steamboat, sailing past a reedy shore.

'Yes. It does.'

'Or somewhere else. If you don't want to go anywhere, I will see how Noëlle feels,' she said, returning to the brochures.

Spring was stirring in Heloise's blood. Tickling her feet. They had not been anywhere since just after Christmas, when they'd had a rather pleasant time on a yacht, sailing from Marseille to Portofino and back. The owners of the yacht, friends of Noëlle and rather elderly, had had a house in Portofino. Just now Tom didn't want to go anywhere, but he didn't say this to Heloise.

It was a quiet and pleasant Sunday, and Tom made two good preparatory sketches of Mme Annette at her ironing board. She ironed in the kitchen on Sunday afternoons, watching her TV which she wheeled into position against the cupboards. There was nothing more domestic, more French, Tom thought, than Mme Annette's sturdy little figure bent over her iron on a Sunday afternoon. He wanted to capture the spirit of this on canvas – the very pale orange of the kitchen wall in sunlight, and delicate blue-lavender of a certain dress of Mme Annette's that set off so well her fine blue eyes.

Then the telephone rang just after 10 p.m., when Tom and Heloise were lying in front of the fireplace, looking at the Sunday papers. Tom answered.

It was Reeves, sounding extremely upset. The connection was bad.

'Can you hold on? I'll try it from upstairs,' Tom said.

Reeves said he would, and Tom went running up the stairs, saying to Heloise, 'Reeves! A lousy connection!' Not that the telephone was necessarily better upstairs, but Tom wanted to be alone for this.

Reeves said, 'I said my *flat*. In Hamburg. It was *bombed* today.'

'What? My God!'

'I'm ringing you from Amsterdam.'

'Were you hurt?' Tom asked.

'*No!*' Reeves shouted, his voice cracking. 'That's the miracle. I just happened to be out around 5 p.m. So was Gaby because she doesn't work Sundays. These guys, they – must've tossed a bomb through the *window*. Quite a feat. The people below heard a car rush up and rush away after a minute, then two minutes later an *awful* explosion – which knocked all the pictures off their walls, too.'

'Look – how much are they on to?'

'I thought I better get elsewhere for my health. I was out of town in less than an hour.'

'How did they *find out?*' Tom yelled into the telephone.

'I dunno. I really dunno. They might've got something out of Fritz, because Fritz failed to keep a *date* with me today. I sure hope old Fritz is okay. But he doesn't know – you know, our friend's name. I always called him Paul when he was here. An Englishman, I said, so Fritz thinks he lives in England. I honestly think they're doing this on suspicion, Tom. I think our plan has essentially *worked*.'

Good old optimistic Reeves, with his flat bombed, his possessions lost, his plan was a success. 'Listen, Reeves, what about – What are you doing with your stuff in Hamburg? Your papers, for instance?'

'Strongbox at the bank,' Reeves said promptly. 'I can have those sent. Anyway what papers? If you're worried – I just have *one* little address book and that's always on me. I'm sure as hell sorry to lose a lot of records and paintings I've got there, but the police said they'd protect everything they could. Naturally they questioned me – nicely of course, for a few minutes, but I explained I was in a state of shock, damn near true, and I had to go somewhere for a while. They know where I am.'

'Do the police suspect the Mafia?'

'Didn't say so if they did. Tom old boy, I'll ring you again tomorrow maybe. Take my number, will you?'

Half reluctantly, though he realized he might need it for some reason, Tom took down Reeves' hotel name, the Zuyder Zee, and its number.

'Our mutual friend sure did one hell of a good job, even if that second bastard is still alive. For a fellow who's anaemic –' Reeves broke off with a laugh that was almost hysterical.

'You've paid him in full now?'

'Did that yesterday,' said Reeves.

'So you don't need him any more, I suppose.'

'No. We've got the police interested here. I mean in Hamburg. That's what we wanted. I heard more Mafia have *arrived*. So that's –'

Abruptly they were cut off. Tom felt a swift annoyance, a sense of stupidity, as he stood there with the buzzing, dead telephone in his hand. He hung up and stood in his room for a few seconds, wondering if Reeves would ring back, thinking he probably wouldn't, trying to digest the news. From what Tom knew of the Mafia, he thought they might leave it at that, bombing Reeves' flat. They might not be out for Reeves' life. But evidently the Mafia knew that Reeves had had something to do with the killings, so the idea of creating the impression of rival Mafia gang-war had failed. On the other hand, the Hamburg police would make an extra effort to clear the Mafia out of the town, out of private gambling clubs, too. Like everything Reeves did, or dabbled in, this situation was vague, Tom thought. The verdict ought to be: not quite successful.

The only happy fact was that Trevanny had his money. He should be informed of that by Tuesday or Wednesday. Good news from Switzerland!

The next days were quiet. No more telephone calls and no letter from Reeves Minot. Nothing in the newspapers about Vincent Turoli in the hospital at Strassburg or Milan, and Tom also bought the Paris *Herald-Tribune* and the London *Daily Telegraph* in Fontainebleau. Tom planted his dahlias, a three-hour job one afternoon, because he had them in smaller packages within the burlap bags, labelled for colour, and he tried to plan his colour patches as carefully as if he were imagining a canvas. Heloise spent three nights at Chantilly, where her parents had their home, because her mother was undergoing a minor operation for a tumour somewhere, which luckily turned out to be benign. Mme Annette, thinking Tom was lonely, comforted him with American food which she had learned to prepare to please him: spareribs with barbecue sauce, clam chowder and fried chicken. Tom wondered from time to time about his own safety. In the peaceful atmosphere of Villeperce, this sleepy, rather proper little village, and through the tall iron gates of Belle Ombre which appeared to guard the castle-like house but actually didn't – anyone might scale them – a murderer might arrive, Tom thought, one of the Mafia boys who would knock on the door or ring the bell, push past Mme Annette, dash up the stairs and plug Tom. It would take the police from Moret a good fifteen minutes to get here, probably, assuming Mme Annette could telephone them at once. A neighbour hearing a shot or two might assume a hunter was trying his luck with owls, and probably wouldn't attempt to investigate.

During the time that Heloise was in Chantilly, Tom decided to acquire a harpsichord for Belle Ombre – for himself, too, of course and possibly for Heloise. Once, somewhere, he had heard her playing some simple ditty on a piano. Where? When? He suspected she was a victim of childhood lessons, and knowing her parents Tom assumed they had knocked any joy out of her endeavours. Anyway, a harpsichord might cost a goodly sum (it would be cheaper to buy it in London, of course, but not with the 100 per cent tax the French would demand for bringing it in), but a harpsichord certainly came in the category of cultural acquisitions, so Tom did not reproach himself for the desire. A harpsichord was not a swimming pool. Tom telephoned an antique dealer in Paris whom he knew fairly well, and though the man dealt only in furniture, he was able to give Tom the name of a reliable place in Paris where he might buy a harpsichord.

Tom went up to Paris and spent a whole day listening to harpsichord lore from the dealer, looking at instruments, trying them out with timid chords, and making his decision. The gem he chose, of beige wood embellished with gold-leaf here and there, cost more than ten thousand francs, and would be delivered on Wednesday, 26 April, along with the tuner who would at once have to get to work, because the instrument would have been disturbed by the move.

This purchase gave Tom a heady lift, made him feel invincible as he walked back to his Renault, impervious to the eye and maybe even the bullets of the Mafia.

And Belle Ombre had not been bombed. Villeperce's tree-bordered, unpavemented streets looked as quiet as ever. No strange characters loitered. Heloise returned in a good mood on Friday, and there was the surprise for her for Tom to look forward to, the arrival of the large and delicately handled crate containing the harpsichord on Wednesday. It was going to be more fun than Christmas.

Tom did not tell Mme Annette about the harpsichord either. But on Monday he said, 'Mme Annette, I have a request. On Wednesday we have a special guest coming for lunch, maybe for dinner too. Let's have something nice.'

Mme Annette's blue eyes lit up. She liked nothing better than extra effort, extra trouble, if it was in the cooking department. '*Un vrai gourmet?*' she asked hopefully.

'I would think so,' Tom replied. 'Now you reflect. I am not going to tell you what to prepare. Let it be a surprise for Mme Heloise also.'

Mme Annette smiled mischievously. One would have thought she had been given a present too.

FOURTEEN

The gyroscope Jonathan bought for Georges in Munich turned out to be the most appreciated toy Jonathan had ever given his son. Its magic remained, every time Georges pulled it from its square box where Jonathan insisted that he keep it.

'Careful not to drop it!' Jonathan said, lying on his stomach on the living-room floor. 'It's a delicate instrument.'

The gyroscope was forcing Georges to learn some new English words, because in his own absorption, Jonathan didn't bother speaking French. The wonderful wheel spun on the tip of Georges' finger, or leaned sideways from the top of a plastic castle turret – the latter a resurrected object from Georges' toy box, pressed into service instead of the Eiffel Tower shown on the pink page of instructions for the gyroscope.

'A larger gyroscope,' Jonathan said, 'keeps ships from rolling on the sea.' Jonathan did a fairly good job of explaining, and thought if he fixed the gyroscope inside a toy boat in a bath-tub of tossing water, he might be able to illustrate what he meant. 'Big ships have three gyroscopes going at once, for instance.'

'Jon, the sofa.' Simone was standing in the living-room doorway. 'You didn't tell me what you think. Dark green?'

Jonathan rolled over on the floor, propped on his elbows. In his eyes the beautiful gyroscope still spun and kept its miraculous balance. Simone meant for the re-covering of the sofa. 'What I think is that we should buy a new sofa,' Jonathan said, getting up. 'I saw an advertisement today for a black Chesterfield for five thousand francs. I'll bet I can get the same thing for three thousand five hundred, if I look around.'

'Three thousand five hundred *new* francs?'

Jonathan had known she would be shocked. 'Consider it an investment. We can afford it.' Jonathan did know of an antique dealer some five kilometres out of town who dealt in nothing but large, well-restored pieces of furniture. Up to now he hadn't been able to think of buying anything from this shop.

'A Chesterfield would be magnificent – but don't go overboard, Jon. You're on a spree!'

Jonathan had talked today about buying a television set, too. 'I won't go on a spree,' he said calmly. 'I wouldn't be such a fool.'

Simone beckoned him into the hall, as if she wanted to be out of Georges' hearing. Jonathan embraced her. Her hair got mussed against the hanging coats. She whispered in his ear:

'All *right*. But when is your next trip to Germany?'

She didn't like the idea of his trips. He had told her they were trying new pills, that Perrier was giving them to him, that though he might stay in the same condition, there was a chance the condition would improve, and certainly it wouldn't get worse. Because of the money Jonathan said he was being paid, Simone didn't believe that he wasn't taking a risk of some kind. And even so, Jonathan hadn't told her how much money, the sum now in the Swiss Bank Corporation in Zürich. Simone knew only that there was six thousand francs or so in the Société Générale in Fontainebleau, instead of their usual four to six hundred – which sometimes went down to two hundred, if they paid a mortgage instalment.

'I'd love a new sofa. But are you sure it's the best thing to buy now? At such a price? Don't forget the mortgage.'

'Darling, how could I? Bloody mortgage!' He laughed. He wanted to pay off the mortgage at a whack. 'All right, I'll be careful. I promise.'

Jonathan knew he had to think of a better story, or elaborate on the story he'd already told. But for the moment he preferred to relax, to enjoy merely the thought of his new fortune – because spending any of it wasn't easy. And he could still die within a month. The three dozen pills that Dr Schroeder of Munich had given him, pills that Jonathan was now taking at the rate of two a day, were not going to save his life or wreak any great change. A sense of security might be a fantasy of sorts, but wasn't it as real as anything else while it lasted? What else was there? What else was happiness but a mental attitude?

And there was the other unknown, the fact that the bodyguard called Turoli was still alive.

On 29 April, a Sunday evening, Jonathan and Simone went to a concert of Schubert and Mozart played by a string quartet at the Fontainebleau Theatre. Jonathan had bought the most expensive tickets, and had wanted to take Georges, who could behave well if he were sufficiently cautioned beforehand, but Simone had been against it. She was more embarrassed than Jonathan, if Georges was not the model child. 'In another year, yes,' said Simone.

During the interval they went into the big foyer where one could smoke. It was full of familiar faces, among them Pierre Gauthier the art dealer, who to Jonathan's surprise was sporting a wing collar and black tie.

'You are an embellishment of the music this evening, madame!' he said to Simone, with an admiring look at her Chinese-red dress.

Simone acknowledged the compliment gracefully. She did look especially well and happy, Jonathan thought. Gauthier was alone. Jonathan suddenly remembered that his wife had died a few years ago, before Jonathan had really become acquainted with him.

'All of Fontainebleau is here tonight!' said Gauthier, making an effort to speak above the hubbub. His good eye roved over the scores of people in the domed hall, and his bald head shone under the grey-and-black hair he had carefully combed over it. 'Shall we have a coffee afterwards? In the café across the street?' Gauthier asked. 'I shall be pleased to invite you.'

Simone and Jonathan were about to say yes, when Gauthier stiffened a little. Jonathan followed Gauthier's glance and saw Tom Ripley in a group of four or five, only three yards away. Ripley's eyes met Jonathan's and he nodded. Ripley looked as if he might come over to say hello, and at the same time Gauthier sidled to the left, leaving. Simone turned her head to see who both Jonathan and Gauthier had been looking at.

'Tout à l'heure, peut-être!' said Gauthier.

Simone looked at Jonathan and her eyebrows went up a little.

Ripley stood out, not so much because he was rather tall as because he looked un-French with his brown hair touched with gold under the chandeliers' lights. He wore a plum-coloured satin jacket. The striking blonde girl who seemed to be wearing no make-up at all must be his wife.

'So?' Simone said. 'Who is that one?'

Jonathan knew she meant Ripley. Jonathan's heart was beating faster. 'I don't know. I've seen him before but I don't know his name.'

'He was at our house – that man,' Simone said. 'I remember him. Gauthier doesn't like him?'

A bell rang, the signal for people to return to their seats.

'I don't know. Why?'

'Because he seemed to want to get away!' Simone said, as if the fact was obvious.

The pleasure of the music had vanished for Jonathan. Where was Tom Ripley sitting? In one of the boxes? Jonathan did not look up at the boxes. Ripley might have been across the aisle from him, for all Jonathan knew. He realized that it wasn't Ripley's presence that had spoilt the evening, but Simone's reaction. And Simone's reaction had been caused, Jonathan knew also, by his own uneasiness at seeing Ripley. Jonathan deliberately tried to relax in his seat, propped his chin on his fingers, knowing all the while that his efforts were not deceiving Simone. Like a lot of other people, she had heard stories about Tom Ripley (even though at this moment she might not recall his name), and she was perhaps going to connect Tom

Ripley with – with what? At the moment, Jonathan really didn't know. But he dreaded what would come. He reproached himself for having shown his nervousness so plainly, so naïvely. Jonathan realized he was in a mess, a very dangerous situation, and that he had to play it calmly, if he possibly could. He had to be an actor. A little different from his effort to succeed on the stage when he'd been younger. This situation was quite real. Or if one liked, quite phoney. Jonathan had never before tried to be phoney with Simone.

'Let's try to find Gauthier,' Jonathan said when they were moving up the aisle. The applause was still pattering around them, gathering itself into the co-ordinated palm-pounding of a French audience which wanted still another encore.

But somehow they didn't find Gauthier. Jonathan missed Simone's reply. She did not seem interested in finding Gauthier. They had the babysitter – a girl who lived in their street – at home with Georges. It was almost 11 p.m. Jonathan did not look for Tom Ripley and did not see him.

On Sunday, Jonathan and Simone had lunch in Nemours with Simone's parents and her brother Gérard and his wife. As usual, there was television after lunch, which Jonathan and Gérard did not watch.

'That's excellent that the *boches* are subsidizing you for being one of their guinea-pigs!' Gérard said with one of his rare laughs. 'That is, if they don't do you any harm.' He had come out with this in rapid slang, and it was the first thing he had said that really caught Jonathan's attention.

They were both smoking cigars. Jonathan had bought a box at a tabac in Nemours. 'Yes. Lots of pills. Their idea is to attack with eight or ten drugs all at once. Confuse the enemy, you know. It also makes it more difficult for the enemy cells to become immune.' Jonathan rambled on quite well in this vein, half-convinced he was inventing it as he went along, half recollecting it as a proposed method for combating leukaemia that he had read about months ago. 'Of course there's no guarantee. There could be side-effects, which is why they're willing to pay me a bit of money for going through with it.'

'What kind of side-effects?'

'Maybe – a decrease in blood-congealing level.' Jonathan was getting better and better at the meaningless phrases, and his attentive listener inspired him. 'Nausea – not that I've noticed any so far. Then of course they don't know all the side-effects as yet. They're running a risk. So am I.'

'And if it succeeds? If they call it a success?'

'A couple of more years of life,' Jonathan said pleasantly.

On Monday morning, Jonathan and Simone drove with a neighbour, Irène Pliesse – the woman who kept Georges every afternoon after school until Simone could fetch him – to the antique dealer on the outskirts of Fontainebleau where Jonathan thought he might find a sofa. Irène Pliesse was easy-going, large-boned, and had always struck Jonathan as rather masculine, though perhaps she wasn't in the least. She was the mother of two small children and her house in Fontainebleau was more than commonly full of frilly doilies and organdy curtains. At any rate, she was generous with her time and her car, and had often volunteered to drive the Trevannys to Nemours on the Sundays when they went, but Simone with characteristic scrupulousness had never once accepted, because Nemours was a regular family affair. Therefore the pleasure of using Irène Pliesse's services for the sofa-hunting was an unguilty one, and Irène took as much interest in the purchase as if the sofa was to be in her own home.

There was a choice of two Chesterfields, both with old frames and both recently covered in new black leather. Jonathan and Simone preferred the larger one, and Jonathan managed to knock the price down five hundred to three thousand francs. Jonathan knew it was a bargain, because he had seen the same sized sofa advertised, with a picture of it, for five thousand. Now this vast sum, three thousand, nearly one month's earnings of himself and Simone combined, seemed positively trifling. It was amazing, Jonathan thought, how quickly one could adjust to having a little money.

Even Irène, whose house looked opulent compared to the Trevannys', was impressed by the sofa. And Jonathan noticed that Simone didn't at once know what to say to pass it off smoothly.

'Jon had a little windfall from a relative in England. Not much but – we wanted to get something really nice with it.'

Irène nodded.

All was well, Jonathan thought.

The next evening, before dinner, Simone said, 'I dropped in to say hello to Gauthier today.'

Jonathan felt at once on guard, because of Simone's tone of voice. He was drinking a scotch and water and looking at the evening paper. 'Oh, yes?'

'Jon – wasn't it this M. Ripley who told Gauthier that – that you hadn't long to live?' Simone spoke softly, though Georges was upstairs, probably in his room.

Had Gauthier admitted it, when Simone asked him a direct question? Jonathan didn't know how Gauthier would behave, being asked a direct question – and Simone could be gently persistent until she got her answer.

'Gauthier told me,' Jonathan began, 'that – Well, as I told you, he wouldn't say who told him. So I don't know.'

Simone looked at him. She was sitting on the handsome black Chesterfield sofa, which had since yesterday transformed their living-room. It was due to Ripley, Jonathan was thinking, that Simone was sitting where she was. It didn't help Jonathan's state of mind.

'Gauthier told you it was Ripley?' Jonathan asked with an air of surprise.

'Oh, he wouldn't say. But I simply asked him – was it M. Ripley. I described Ripley, the man we saw at the concert. Gauthier knew whom I meant. You seem to know too – his name.' Simone sipped her Cinzano.

Jonathan fancied her hand shook slightly. 'It could be, of course,' Jonathan said with a shrug. 'Don't forget, Gauthier told me whoever told him –' Jonathan gave a laugh. 'All this tale-bearing! Anyway Gauthier says, whoever it was – the man said he could have been mistaken, that things got exaggerated. Darling, it really is best forgotten. It's silly to blame strangers. Silly to make too much out of it.'

'Yes, but –' Simone tilted her head. Her lips twisted somewhat bitterly, in a way Jonathan had seen only once or twice before. 'The curious thing is, it *was* Ripley. I know that. Not that Gauthier said it, no. He didn't. But I could tell ... Jon?'

'Yes, dear.'

'It's because – Ripley is very close to being a crook. Maybe he is a crook. Lots of crooks are not caught, you know. That is the reason I ask. I ask *you*. Are you – All this money, Jon – Are you getting it by any chance, somehow, from this M. Ripley?'

Jonathan made himself look straight at Simone. He felt that he had to protect what he already had, and it wasn't *so* connected with Ripley that it would be a lie if he said it wasn't. 'How could I? For what, darling?'

'Just because he is a crook! Who knows for what? What has he got to do with these German doctors? Are they really doctors you are talking about?' She was beginning to sound hysterical. The colour had risen to her cheeks.

Jonathan frowned. 'Darling, Perrier has my two reports!'

'There is something very dangerous about the tests, Jon, or they wouldn't pay you so much, isn't that true? I have the feeling you're not telling me the whole truth.'

Jonathan laughed a little. 'What could Tom Ripley, that do-nothing – He's an American, anyway. What could he have to do with German doctors?'

'You saw the German doctors because you were afraid you were going to die soon. And it was Ripley – I am pretty sure – who started the story you were going to die soon.'

Georges was bumping his way down the stairs, talking to some toy that he was dragging down. Georges in his dream-world, but he was a presence, just a few yards away, and it rattled Jonathan. He found it incredible that Simone had discovered so much, and his impulse was to deny all of it, at any cost.

Simone was waiting for him to say something.

Jonathan said, 'I don't know who it was told Gauthier.'

Georges was standing at the door. Now his arrival was a relief for Jonathan. It effectively stopped the conversation. Georges was asking a question about a tree outside his window. Jonathan didn't listen, and let Simone answer.

During dinner, Jonathan had the feeling Simone did not quite believe him, that she wanted to believe him, but couldn't. Yet Simone (maybe because of Georges) was almost her usual self. She wasn't sulking or cool. But the atmosphere for Jonathan was uncomfortable. And it was going to continue, he realized, unless he could come up with some more specific reason for extra money from the German hospitals. Jonathan hated the idea of lying, exaggerating the danger for himself in order to account for the money.

It even crossed Jonathan's mind that Simone would speak to Tom Ripley himself. Mightn't she telephone him? Make an appointment to see him? Jonathan dismissed that idea. Simone didn't like Tom Ripley. She would not want to come anywhere near him.

The same week, Tom Ripley came into Jonathan's shop. His picture had been ready for several days. Jonathan had a customer in his shop when Ripley arrived, and Ripley proceeded to look over some ready-made frames that leaned against a wall, obviously content to wait till Jonathan should be free. At last the customer left.

'Morning,' Tom said pleasantly. 'It wasn't so easy after all to get someone to pick up my picture, so I thought I'd come myself.'

'Yes, fine. It's ready,' Jonathan said, and went to the back of his shop to get it. It was wrapped in brown paper, but the paper was not tied, and it was labelled RIPLEY, the label fastened with scotch tape to the paper. Jonathan carried it to his counter. 'Like to see it?'

Tom was pleased with it. He held it at arm's length. 'That's great. Very nice. What do I owe you?'

'Ninety francs.'

Tom pulled his billfold out. 'Is everything all right?'

Jonathan was aware that he took a couple of breaths before he answered. 'Since you ask –' He took the hundred-franc note with a polite nod, pulled out his cash drawer and got the change. 'My wife –' Jonathan looked at the door, and was glad to see that no one was approaching at the moment. 'My wife spoke to Gauthier. He didn't tell her that you started that story about my – demise. But my wife seems to have guessed it. I really don't know how. Intuition.'

Tom had foreseen this happening. He was aware of his reputation, that many people mistrusted him, avoided him. Tom had often thought that his ego could have been shattered long ago – the ego of the average person would have been shattered – except for the fact that people, once they got to know him, once they came to Belle Ombre and spent an evening, liked him and Heloise well enough, and the Ripleys were invited back. 'And what did you say to your wife?'

Jonathan tried to speak quickly, because there might not be much time. 'What I've said from the start, that Gauthier always refused to tell me who started the story. That's true.'

Tom knew. Gauthier had gallantly refused to tell his name. 'Well, keep cool. If we don't see each other – Sorry about the other night at the concert,' Tom added with a smile.

'Yes. But – it's unfortunate. The worst is, she associates you – she's trying to – with the money we've got now. Not that I've told her how much it is.'

Tom had thought of that too. It was irritating. 'I won't bring you any more pictures to frame.'

A man with a large canvas on a stretcher was struggling through the door.

'*Bon, m'sieur!*' Tom said, waving his free hand. '*Merci. Bonsoir.*'

Tom went out. If Trevanny was seriously worried, Tom thought, Trevanny could telephone him. Tom had already said that at least once. It was unfortunate, troublesome for Trevanny, that his wife suspected that he had started the nasty rumour. On the other hand, that wasn't easily connected with money from hospitals in Hamburg and Munich, still less connected with the murder of two Mafiosi.

On Sunday morning, when Simone was hanging laundry on the garden line, and Jonathan and Georges were making a stone border, the doorbell rang.

It was one of their neighbours, a woman of about sixty whose name Jonathan wasn't sure of – Delattre? Delambre? She looked distressed.

'Excuse me, M. Trevanny.'

'Come in,' said Jonathan.

'It is M. Gauthier. Have you heard the news?'

'No.'

'He was hit last night by a car. He is dead.'

'Dead? Here in Fontainebleau?'

'He was coming home around midnight from an evening with a friend, someone in the Rue de la Paroisse. You know M. Gauthier lives in the Rue de la République just off the Avenue Franklin Roosevelt. It was that cross-roads with the little triangle of green where there is a traffic light. Someone saw the people who did it, two boys in a car. They didn't stop. They went through a red light and hit M. Gauthier and *didn't stop!*'

'Good lord! Won't you sit down, Mm –'

Simone had come into the hall. 'Ah *bonjour*, Mme Delattre!' she said.

'Simone, Gauthier is dead,' Jonathan said. 'Run over by a hit-and-run driver.'

'Two boys,' said Mme Delattre. 'They didn't stop!'

Simone gasped. 'When?'

'Last night. He was dead when they got him to the hospital here. Around midnight.'

'Won't you come in and sit down, Mme Delattre?' Simone asked.

'No, no, thank you. I must be off to see a friend. Mme Mockers. I am not sure if she knows yet. We all knew him so well, you know?' She was near tears, and set her shopping basket down for a moment to wipe her eyes.

Simone pressed her hand. 'Thank you for coming to tell us, Mme Delattre. That was kind of you.'

'The funeral is on Monday,' Mme Delattre said. 'At St Louis.' Then she departed.

The news somehow didn't register on Jonathan. 'What's her name?'

'Mme *Delattre*. Her husband's a plumber,' Simone said, as if, of course, Jonathan should know.

Delattre wasn't the plumber they used. Gauthier dead. What would happen to his shop, Jonathan wondered. he found himself staring at Simone. They were standing in the narrow front hall.

'Dead,' Simone said. She put her hand out and gripped Jonathan's wrist, not looking at him. 'We should go to the funeral on Monday, you know.'

'Of course.' A Catholic funeral. It was all in French now, not Latin. He imagined all the neighbours, faces familiar and unfamiliar, in the cool church full of candles.

'Hit-and-run,' Simone said. She walked stiffly down the hall, and looked back over her shoulder at Jonathan. 'It's really shocking.'

Jonathan followed her through the kitchen, out into the garden. It was good to get back into sunlight.

Simone had finished hanging her washing. She straightened some things on the line, then picked up the empty basket. 'Hit-and-run – Do you really think so, Jon?'

'That's what she said.' They were both talking softly. Jonathan still felt a bit dazed, but he knew what Simone was thinking.

She came a step closer, carrying the basket. Then she beckoned him towards the steps that led to the little porch, as if neighbours on the other side of the garden wall might hear them. 'Do you think he could've been killed purposely? By someone hired to kill him?'

'Why?'

'Because perhaps he knew something. That's why. Isn't it possible? Why should an innocent person be struck down like that – accidentally?'

'Because – these things happen sometimes,' Jonathan said.

Simone shook her head. 'You don't think possibly that M. Ripley had something to do with it?'

Jonathan saw an irrational anger in her. 'Absolutely not. I certainly don't think so.' Jonathan could have bet his life that Tom Ripley hadn't had anything to do with it. He started to say that, but it would've sounded a bit strong – and if he wanted to look at it in another way, a rather comical bet.

Simone started to pass him and enter the house, but she stopped close to him. 'It's true Gauthier didn't tell me anything definite, Jon, but he might have known something. I think he did. I have the feeling he was killed on purpose.'

Simone was simply shocked, Jonathan thought, like himself. She was putting into words ideas that she hadn't thought out. He followed her into the kitchen. 'Known something about what?'

Simone was putting the basket away in the corner cupboard. 'That's just it. I don't know.'

FIFTEEN

The funeral service for Pierre Gauthier took place at 10 a.m. Monday in the church of St Louis, the main church of Fontainebleau. The church was filled, and people stood even on the pavement outside where the two black automobiles waited dismally – one a shiny hearse, the other a boxlike bus to carry the family relations and friends who had no car of their own. Gauthier was a widower without children. He perhaps had a brother or sister, maybe therefore some nieces or nephews. Jonathan hoped so. The funeral seemed a lonely thing, despite all the people.

'Do you know he lost his glass eye on the street?' a man next to Jonathan whispered to him in church. 'It fell out when he was hit.'

'Oh?' Jonathan shook his head in sympathy. The man who had spoken to him was a shopkeeper. Jonathan knew his face, but could not connect him with any shop. Jonathan could see clearly Gauthier's glass eye on the black tar road, maybe crushed by a car wheel by now, maybe found in the gutter by some curious children. What did the back of a glass eye look like?

Candles twinkled yellow-like, barely illuminating the church's dreary grey walls. It was an overcast day. The priest intoned in French the formal phrases. Gauthier's coffin stood short and thick in front of the altar. At least, if Gauthier had little family, he had many friends. Several women, a few men, were wiping away tears. And other people were murmuring to each other, as if their own exchanges could give them more comfort than the rote the priest was reciting.

There were some soft bells, like chimes.

Jonathan looked to his right, at the people in the rows of chairs across the aisle, and his eyes were caught by the profile of Tom Ripley. Ripley was looking straight ahead towards the priest who was speaking again, and he seemed to be following the ceremony with concentration. His face stood out among the faces of the French. Or did it? Was it merely because he knew Tom Ripley? Why had Ripley troubled to come? In the next instant Jonathan wondered if Tom Ripley might be putting on an act by coming? If, as Simone suspected, he really had had something to do with Gauthier's death, even arranged it and paid for it?

When the people all stood up to file out of the church, Jonathan tried to avoid Tom Ripley, and he thought the best way to succeed in this was not to try to avoid him, above all not to glance another time in his direction. But on the steps in front of the church, Tom Ripley suddenly dashed up at one side of Jonathan and Simone and greeted them.

'Good morning!' Ripley said in French. He wore a black muffler around his neck, a dark blue raincoat. '*Bonjour*, madame. I'm glad to see you both. You were friends of M. Gauthier, I think.'

They were all walking slowly down the steps, because of the dense crowd, so slowly it was hard to keep one's balance.

'*Oui*,' Jonathan replied. 'He was one of our neighbourhood shopkeepers, you know. A very nice man.'

Tom nodded. 'I haven't seen the papers this morning. A friend in Moret rang me – and told me. Have the police any idea who did it?'

'I haven't heard,' Jonathan said. 'Just "two boys". Did you hear anything else, Simone?'

Simone shook her head which was covered in a dark scarf. 'No. Not a thing.'

Tom nodded. 'I was hoping you might've heard something – living closer than I do.'

Tom Ripley seemed genuinely concerned, Jonathan thought, not just putting on a show for them.

'I must buy a paper. Are you going to the cemetery?' Tom asked.

'No, we're not,' said Jonathan.'

Tom nodded. They had all now reached the pavement level. 'Nor am I. I'll miss old Gauthier. It's too bad. – Very nice to have seen you.' With a quick smile, Ripley went away.

Jonathan and Simone walked on, around the corner of the church into the Rue de la Paroisse, the direction of their house. Neighbours nodded to them, gave them brief smiles, and some said, 'Good morning, Madame, M'sieur,' in a way they wouldn't have done on ordinary mornings. Car motors started up, ready to follow the hearse to the cemetery – which Jonathan recalled was just behind the Fontainebleau Hospital where he had so often gone for transfusions.

'*Bonjour*, M. Trevanny! Et Madame!' It was Dr Perrier, sprightly as ever, and almost as beaming as usual. He pumped Jonathan's hand, at the same time making a small bow to Simone. 'What a dreadful thing, eh? ... No, no, no, no, they haven't found the boys at all. But someone said it was a Paris licence on the car. A black D.S. That's all they know ... And how are you feeling, M. Trevanny?' Dr Perrier's smile was confident.

'About the same,' Jonathan said. 'No complaints.' He was glad that Dr Perrier took off at once, because Jonathan was aware that Simone knew he was supposed to be seeing Dr Perrier rather frequently now for pills and injections, though he hadn't been to Perrier for at least a fortnight, when he had delivered Dr Schroeder's report that had come to him at his shop.

'We must buy a paper,' said Simone.

'Up at the corner,' Jonathan said.

They bought a paper, and Jonathan stood on a pavement still a bit crowded with people dispersing from Gauthier's service, and read about 'the disgraceful and wanton act of young hoodlums' which had taken place late Saturday evening in a street of Fontainebleau. Simone looked over his shoulder. The week-end paper had not had time to print the story, so this was the first account they had seen. Someone had seen a large, dark car with at least two young men in it, but no mention was made of a Paris licence number. The car had gone on in the direction of Paris, but had vanished by the time police tried to give pursuit.

'It *is* shocking,' said Simone. 'It isn't often, you know, that there are hit-and-run drivers in France ...'

Jonathan detected a note of chauvinism.

'That's what makes me suspect –' She shrugged. 'Of course I could be completely wrong. But it is quite in character if this type Ripley makes an appearance at M. Gauthier's funeral service!'

'He –' Jonathan stopped. He had been going to say that Tom Ripley had certainly seemed concerned that morning, and also that he bought his art supplies at Gauthier's shop, but Jonathan realized that he was not supposed to know this. 'What do you mean by "in character"?'

Simone shrugged again, and Jonathan knew she was in a mood in which she might refuse to say another word on the subject. 'I think it is just possible this Ripley found out from M. Gauthier that I spoke with him, asking him who started this story about you. I told you I though it was Ripley, even though M. Gauthier wouldn't say so. And now – this – the *very* mysterious death of M. Gauthier.'

Jonathan was silent. They were nearing the Rue St Merry. 'But that story, darling – it couldn't possibly be worth killing a man for. Be reasonable.'

Simone suddenly remembered they needed something for lunch. She went into a charcuterie, and Jonathan waited on the pavement. For a few seconds Jonathan realized – in a different way, as if he saw it through Simone's eyes – what he had done in killing one man by gunshot, and by helping to kill another. Jonathan had rationalized it by telling himself that the two men had been gunmen themselves, murderers. Simone, of course, wouldn't see it that way. They were human life, after all. Simone was sufficiently upset because Tom Ripley might have hired someone to kill Gauthier – just might have. If she knew that her own husband had pulled a trigger. Or was he influenced at the moment by the funeral service he had just been to? The service had after all been about the sanctity of human life, despite saying that the next world was even better. Jonathan smiled ironically. It was the word *sanctity* –

Simone came out of the charcuterie, awkwardly holding little packages, because she hadn't her shopping net with her. Jonathan took a couple of them. They walked on.

Sanctity. Jonathan had given the Mafia book back to Reeves. If he ever had serious qualms about what he had done, all he needed to do was remember some of the murderers he had read about.

Nevertheless, Jonathan felt apprehensive as he climbed the steps of the house behind Simone. It was because Simone was now so hostile towards Ripley. Simone hadn't cared for Pierre Gauthier all this much, to be so affected by his death. Her attitude was composed of a sixth sense, conventional morality and wifely protectiveness. She believed that Ripley had started the story about his dying soon, and Jonathan foresaw that nothing would shake her, because no other person could easily be substituted as a source of the story, especially now that Gauthier was dead, and couldn't back Jonathan up if he tried to invent another person.

Tom shed his black muffler in his car, and drove southwards towards Moret and home. It was a pity about Simone's hostility, that Simone suspected he had arranged Gauthier's death. Tom lit a cigarette with the lighter from his dashboard. He was in the red Alfa-Romeo, and felt tempted to go fast, but he held his speed back prudently.

Gauthier's death had been an accident, Tom was sure. A nasty, unfortunate thing, but still an accident, unless Gauthier was mixed up in stranger things than Tom knew about.

A big magpie swooped across the road, beautiful against a background of a pale green weeping willow. The sun had begun to come out. Tom thought of stopping in Moret to buy something – there seemed always something that Mme Annette needed or might like – but today he couldn't recall anything that she'd asked for, and he didn't really feel like stopping. It was his usual framer in Moret who had rung him yesterday to tell him about Gauthier. Tom must have mentioned to him at some point that he bought his paints at Gauthier's in Fontainebleau. Tom let his foot down on the accelerator and passed a truck, then two speeding Citroëns, and soon he was at the turn-off to Villeperce.

'Ah, Tome, you had a long-distance telephone call,' Heloise said when he came into the living-room.

'From where?' But Tom knew. It was probably Reeves.

'Germany, I think.' Heloise went back to the harpsichord, which now had a place of honour near the french windows.

Tom recognized a Bach *chaconne* whose treble she was reading. 'They'll ring back?' he asked.

Heloise turned her head and her long blonde hair swung out. 'I don't know, *chéri*. It was only the operator I spoke to, because they wanted person·to-person. There it is!' she said as the telephone rang on her last words.

Tom dashed upstairs to his room.

The operator ascertained that he was M. Ripley, then Reeves' voice said: 'Hello, Tom. Can you talk?' Reeves sounded calmer than the last time.

'Yes. You're in Amsterdam?'

'Yeah, and I have a little news you won't find in the newspaper that I thought you might like to hear. That bodyguard died. You know, the one they took to Milan.'

'Who said he died?'

'Well, I heard it from one of my friends in Hamburg. A usually reliable friend.'

It was the kind of story the Mafia might put out, Tom thought. He would believe it when he saw the corpse. 'Anything else?'

'I thought it might be good news for our mutual friend, that this guy is dead. You know.'

'Sure. I do understand, Reeves. And how are you?'

'Oh, still alive.' Reeves forced the sound of a laugh. 'Also I'm arranging for my things to be sent to Amsterdam. I like it here. I feel much safer than in Hamburg, I can tell you that. Oh, there is one thing. My friend Fritz. He telephoned me, got my number from Gaby. He's now with his cousin in some little town near Hamburg. But he got beaten up, lost a couple of teeth, poor guy. Those swine beat him up for what they could get out of him ...'

That was close to home, Tom thought, and felt a pang of sympathy for this unknown Fritz – Reeves' driver, or package-runner.

'Fritz never knew our friend as anything else but "Paul",' Reeves went on. 'Also Fritz gave them an opposite description, black hair, short and plump, but I'm afraid they might not believe him. Fritz did pretty well, considering he was getting the treatment. He said he stuck to his story – the way our friend looks, and that's all he knows about him. *I'm* the one in a mess, I think.'

That was certainly true, Tom thought, because the Italians knew what Reeves looked like, all right. 'Very interesting news. I don't think we should talk all day, my friend. What're you really worried about?'

Reeves' sigh was audible. 'Getting my things here. But I sent Gaby some money, and she's going to get things shipped. I've written my bank and all that. I'm even growing a beard. And of course I'm using a – another name.'

Tom had supposed Reeves would be using another name, with one of his false passports. 'And what's your name?'

'Andrew Lucas – of Virginia,' Reeves said, with a 'Hah' by way of a laugh. 'By the way, have you seen our mutual friend?'

'No. Why should I? Well, Andy, let me know how things go.' Tom was sure Reeves would ring if he were in trouble, if it was the kind of trouble in which he was still able to ring, because Reeves thought Tom Ripley could pull him out of anything. But mainly for Trevanny's sake, Tom wanted to know if Reeves was in trouble

'I'll do that, Tom. Oh, one more thing! A Di Stefano man was plugged in Hamburg! Saturday night. You might see it in the papers and you might not. But the Genotti family must've got him. That's what we wanted ...'

Reeves at last signed off.

If the Mafia got to Reeves in Amsterdam, Tom was thinking, they'd torture some facts out of him. Tom doubted if Reeves could stand up as well as Fritz apparently had done. Tom wondered which family, the Di Stefanos or the Genottis, had got hold of Fritz? Fritz probably knew only about the first operation, the shooting in Hamburg. That victim had been merely a button man. The Genottis would be far more livid: they had lost a capo, and, it was said now, a button man or bodyguard. Didn't both families know by now that the murders had started with Reeves and the Hamburg casino boys, and not through family warfare? Were they finished with Reeves? Tom felt quite incapable of protecting Reeves, if he should need protection. If it was only one man they were up against, how easy it would be! But the Mafia were beyond count.

Reeves had said at the last that he had been ringing from a post office. That was at least safer than if he had rung from his hotel. Tom was thinking about Reeves' first call. Hadn't that been from the hotel called the Zuyder Zee? Tom thought so.

Harpsichord notes came purely from below stairs, a message from another century. Tom went down the stairs. Heloise would want him to tell her about the funeral service, say something about it, though when he had asked her if she wanted to go with him, she had said that funeral services depressed her.

Jonathan stood in his living-room, gazing out the front window. It was just after 12 noon. He had turned on the portable radio for the noonday news, and now it was playing pop music. Simone was in the garden with Georges, who had stayed in the house alone while he and Simone went to the funeral service. On the radio a man's voice sang 'runnin' on along ... runnin' on along ...' and Jonathan watched a young dog that looked like an Alsatian loping after two small boys on the opposite pavement. Jonathan had a sense of the temporariness of everything, of life of all kinds – not only of the dog and the two boys, but of the houses behind them, a sense that everything would perish, crumble finally, shapes destroyed and even forgotten. Jonathan thought of Gauthier in his coffin being lowered into the ground perhaps at this moment, and then he didn't think about Gauthier again but about himself. He hadn't the energy of the dog that had trotted past. If he'd had any prime, he felt past it. It was too late, and Jonathan felt that he hadn't the energy to enjoy what was left of his life, now that he had a little wherewithal to enjoy it. He ought to close up his shop, sell it or give it away, what did it matter? Yet on second thought he couldn't simply squander the money with Simone, because what would she and Georges have when he died? Forty thousand quid wasn't a fortune. His ears were ringing. Calmly Jonathan took deep, slow breaths. He made an effort to raise the window in front of him, and found he hadn't the strength. He turned to face the centre of the room, his legs heavy and nearly uncontrollable. The ringing in his ears had completely drowned the music.

He came to, sweating and cool, on the living-room floor. Simone was on her knees beside him, lightly passing a damp towel across his forehead, down his face.

'Darling, I just *found* you! How are you? Georges, it is all right. Papa is *all right*!' But Simone sounded frightened.

Jonathan put his head down again on the carpet.

'Some water?'

Jonathan managed to sip from the glass she held. He lay back again. 'I think I might have to lie here all afternoon!' His voice warred with the ringing in his ears.

'Let me straighten this.' Simone pulled at his jacket which was bunched under him.

Something slipped out of a pocket. He saw Simone pick up something, then she looked back at him with concern, and Jonathan kept his eyes open, focusing on the ceiling, because things were worse if he closed his eyes. Minutes passed, minutes of silence. Jonathan was not worried, because he knew he would hang on, that this wasn't death, merely a faint.

Maybe first cousin to death, but death wouldn't come quite like this. Death would probably have a sweeter, more seductive pull, like a wave sweeping out from a shore, sucking hard at the legs of a swimmer who'd already ventured too far, and who mysteriously had lost his will to struggle. Simone went away, urging Georges out with her, then returned with a cup of hot tea.

'This has a lot of sugar. It will do you good. Do you want me to telephone Dr Perrier?'

'Oh no, darling. Thanks.' After some sips of the tea, Jonathan got himself to the sofa and sat down.

'Jon, what's this?' Simone asked, holding up the little blue book that was the Swiss bank's passbook.

'Oh – that –' Jonathan shook his head, trying to make himself more alert.

'It's a bankbook. Isn't it?'

'Well – yes.' The sum was in six figures, more than four hundred thousand francs, which were indicated by an 'f' after them. He also knew that Simone had looked into the little book in all innocence, assuming it was a record of some household purchase, some kind of record they had in common.

'It says francs. French francs? Where did you get it? What *is* it, Jon?'

The sum was in French francs. 'Darling, that's sort of an advance – from the German doctors.'

'But –' Simone looked at a loss. 'It's French *francs* isn't it? This sum!' She laughed a little, nervously.

Jonathan's face was suddenly warm. 'I told you where I got it, Simone. Naturally – I know it's a biggish sum. I didn't want to tell you at once. I –'

Simone laid the little blue book carefully on top of his wallet on the low table in front of the sofa. Then she pulled the chair from in front of the writing-table and sat down on it, sideways, holding to its back with one hand. 'Jon –'

Georges suddenly appeared in the hall doorway, and Simone got up with determination and turned him by the shoulders. 'Chou-chou, papa and I are talking. Now leave us alone for a minute.' She came back and said quietly, 'Jon, I don't believe you.'

Jonathan heard a trembling in her voice. It wasn't only the sum of money, startling though it was, but also his secrecy lately – the trips to Germany. 'Well – you've got to believe me,' Jonathan said. Some strength had returned. He stood up. 'It's an advance. They don't think I'm going to be able to use it. I won't have time. But you can.'

Simone did not respond to his laugh. 'It's in your name – Jon, whatever you are doing, you are not telling me the truth.' And she waited, just
those few seconds when he might have told her the truth, but he didn't
speak.

Simone left the room.

And lunch was a sort of duty. They barely talked. Jonathan could see
that Georges was puzzled. Jonathan could foresee the days ahead – Simone
perhaps not questioning him again, just coolly waiting for him to tell the
truth, or to explain – somehow. Long silences in the house, no more love-
making, no more affection or laughter. He had to come up with something
else, something better. Even if he said he ran the risk of dying under the
German doctors' treatment, was it logical that they'd paid him this much?
Not really. Jonathan realized that his life wasn't worth as much as the lives
of two Mafiosi.

SIXTEEN

Friday morning was lovely with light rain alternating with sunlight every
half-hour or so, just the thing for the garden, Tom thought. Heloise had
driven up to Paris, because there was a dress sale at a certain boutique
in the Faubourg St-Honoré, and Tom felt sure she would come back also
with a scarf or something more important from Hermès as well. Tom sat
at the harpsichord, playing the base of a Goldberg variation, trying to get
the fingering in his head and in his hand. He had bought a few music books
in Paris the same day he had acquired the harpsichord. Tom knew how
the variation should sound, because he had Landowska's recording. As
he was going over it for the third or fourth time and feeling that he had
made progress, the telephone jangled.

'Hello?' said Tom.

''Ello – ah – to whom am I speaking, please?' a man's voice asked in
French.

Tom, more slowly than usual, felt an unease. 'You wished to speak to
whom?' he asked with equal politeness.

'M. Anquetin?'

'No, this is not his house,' said Tom, and put the telephone back in its cradle.

The man's accent had been perfect – hadn't it? But then the Italians would get a Frenchman to make the call, or an Italian whose French accent was perfect. Or was he over anxious? Frowning, Tom turned to face the harpsichord and the windows, and shoved his hands into his back pockets. Had the Genotti family found Reeves in his hotel, and were they checking all the telephone numbers Reeves had called? If so, this caller wouldn't be satisfied with his answer. An ordinary person would have said, 'You are mistaken, this is so-and-so's residence.' Sunlight came through the windows slowly, like something liquid pouring between the red curtains on to the rug. The sunlight was like an arpeggio that Tom could almost hear – this time Chopin, perhaps. Tom realized that he was afraid to ring Reeves in Amsterdam and ask what was happening. The call hadn't sounded like a long-distance call, but it wasn't always possible to tell. It could have come from Paris. Or Amsterdam. Or Milan. Tom had an unlisted number. The operator wouldn't give his name or address, but from the exchange – 424 – it would be easy for the man who had the number to find the district, if he cared to. It was part of the Fontainebleau area. Tom knew it wouldn't be impossible for the Mafia to find out that Tom Ripley lived in this area, in Villeperce even, because the Derwatt affair had been in the newspapers, Tom's photograph also, just six months ago. Much depended, of course, on the second bodyguard, alive and uninjured, who had walked the train in search of his capo and his colleague. This one might remember Tom's face from the restaurant car.

Tom was again on the Goldberg variation base when the telephone rang a second time. Ten minutes had passed, he thought, since the first call. This time he was going to say it was the house of Robert Wilson. There was no concealing his American accent.

'*Oui*,' Tom said in a bored tone.

'Hello –'

'Yes. Hello,' Tom said, recognizing Jonathan Trevanny's voice.

'I'd like to see you,' Jonathan said, 'if you've got some time.'

'Yes, of course. Today?'

'If you could, yes. I can't – I don't want to make it around the lunch hour, if you don't mind. Later today?

'Sevenish?'

'Even six-thirty. Can you come to Fontainebleau?'

Tom agreed to meet Jonathan at the Salamandre Bar. Tom could guess what it was about: Jonathan couldn't explain the money properly to his wife. Jonathan sounded worried, but not desperate.

At 6 p.m., Tom took the Renault, because Heloise was not back with the Alfa. Heloise had telephoned to say she was going to have cocktails with Noëlle, and might also have dinner with her. And she had bought a beautiful suitcase at Hermès, because it had been on sale. Heloise thought that the more she bought at sales, the more she was being economical, and positively virtuous.

Tom found Jonathan already in the Salamandre, standing at the counter drinking dark beer – probably good old Whitbread's ale, Tom thought. The place was unusually busy and noisy this evening, and Tom supposed it would be all right to talk at the counter. Tom nodded and smiled in greeting, and ordered the same dark beer for himself.

Jonathan told him what had happened. Simone had seen the Swiss bankbook. Jonathan had told her it was an advance from the German doctors, and that he was running a risk in taking their drugs, and that this was a kind of payment for his life.

'But she doesn't really believe me.' Jonathan smiled. 'She's even suggested I impersonated somebody in Germany to get an inheritance for a gang of crooks – something like that – and that this is my cut. Or that I've borne false witness for something.' Jonathan gave a laugh. He actually had to shout to be heard, but he was sure no one was listening in the vicinity, or could understand if they did. Three barmen were working frantically behind the counter, pouring Pernods and red wine and drawing glasses of lager from the tap.

'I can understand,' Tom said, glancing at the noisy fray around him. He was still concerned about the telephone call he had got that morning, which hadn't been repeated in the afternoon. He had even looked around Belle Ombre and Villeperce, as he drove out at 6 p.m., for any strange figures on the streets. It was odd how one finally knew everybody in the village, by their figures, even at a distance, so that a newcomer at once caught the eye. Tom had even been afraid, a little, when he started the motor of the Renault. Fixing dynamite to the ignition was a favourite Mafia prank. 'We'll have to think!' Tom shouted, earnestly.

Jonathan nodded and quaffed his beer. 'Funny she's suggested nearly everything I might've done short of murder!'

Tom put his foot on the rail and tried to think in all the din. He looked at a pocket of Jonathan's old corduroy jacket where a rip had been neatly mended, no doubt by Simone. Tom said in sudden desperation, 'I wonder what's the matter with telling her the truth? After all, these Mafiosi, these *morpions* –'

Jonathan shook his head. 'I've thought of that. Simone – she's a Catholic. *That* –' Being regularly on the pill was a kind of concession for Simone to have made. Jonathan saw the Catholic retreat as a slow one: they didn't want to be seen to be routed, even if they gave in here and there. Georges was being raised as a Catholic, inevitable in this country, but Jonathan tried to make Georges see that it wasn't the only religion in the world, tried to make him understand that he would be free to make his own choice when he grew a little older, and his efforts had so far not been opposed by Simone. 'It's so different for her,' Jonathan shouted, now getting used to the noise and almost liking its protective wall. 'It'd be really a shock – something she couldn't forgive, you know. Human life and all that.'

'Human! Ha-ha!'

'The thing is,' Jonathan said, serious again, 'it's almost like my whole marriage. I mean, as if my marriage itself was at stake.' He looked at Tom, who was trying to follow him. 'What a hell of a place to talk about something serious!' Jonathan began again with determination. 'Things are not the same between us, to put it mildly. And I don't see how they're going to get any better. I was simply hoping you might have an idea – as to what I should do or say. On the other hand, I don't know why you *should*. It's my problem.'

Tom was thinking they might find a quieter place, or sit in his car. But would he be able to think any better in a quieter place? 'I will try to get an idea!' Tom yelled. Why did everyone – even Jonathan – suppose that he could come up with an idea for them? Tom often thought he had a hard enough time trying to steer a course for himself. His own welfare often required ideas, those inspirations that came sometimes while he was under the shower, or gardening, those gifts of the gods that were presented only after his own anxious pondering. A single person hadn't the mental equipment to take on the problems of another and maintain the same degree of excellence, Tom thought. Then Tom reflected that his own welfare was tied up with Jonathan's after all, and if Jonathan cracked up – but Tom couldn't imagine Jonathan saying to anyone that Tom had been on the train with him, helping him. There shouldn't be any need to say that, and Jonathan as a matter of principle wouldn't. *How does one suddenly acquire about ninety-two thousand dollars?* That was the problem. It was the question Simone was asking Jonathan.

'If we could only make a double-barrelled thing out of it,' Tom said finally.

'What do you mean?'

'Something added to the sum the doctors might have paid you – How about a *bet*? One doctor has bet another in Germany, and they've both deposited the money with you, a sort of trust fund – I mean it's in *trust* with you. That could account for – let's say fifty thousand dollars of it, more than half. Or are you thinking in francs? Um-m – more than two hundred and fifty thousand francs, perhaps.'

Jonathan smiled. The idea was amusing, but rather wild. 'Another beer?'

'Sure,' said Tom, and lit a Gauloise. 'Look. You might say to Simone that – that because the bet seemed so frivolous, or ruthless or whatever, you hadn't wanted to tell her, but there's a bet on your life. One doctor has bet that you'll live – a full life span, for instance. That would leave you and Simone with a little more than two hundred thousand francs of your own – which by the way I hope you've already begun to enjoy!'

Tock! Tock! A hectic barman set down Tom's fresh glass and bottle. Jonathan was already on his second.

'We've bought a sofa – much needed,' Jonathan said. 'We could treat ourselves to a telly too. Your idea *is* better than nothing. Thank you.'

A stocky man of about sixty greeted Jonathan with a brief handshake and walked on towards the back of the bar with no glance at Tom. Tom stared at two blonde girls who were being chatted up by a trio of boys in bell-bottom trousers standing by their table. A roly-poly old dog with skinny legs looked miserably up at Tom as he waited on his leash for his master to finish his *petit rouge*.

'Heard from Reeves lately?' Tom asked.

'Lately – not in about a month, I think.'

Then Jonathan didn't know about Reeves' flat being bombed, and Tom saw no reason to tell him. It would only shake his morale.

'Have you? Is he all right?'

Tom said casually, 'I really don't know,' as if Reeves was not in the habit of writing or telephoning. Tom felt suddenly ill-at-ease, as if eyes were on him. 'Let's take off, shall we?' He beckoned to the barman to take his two ten-franc notes, though Jonathan had pulled out his money also. 'My car's outside to the right.'

On the pavement, Jonathan began awkwardly, 'You feel you're all right yourself? Nothing to worry about?'

Now they were beside his car. 'I'm the worrying type. You'd never think so, would you? I try to think of the worst before it happens. Not quite the same as being pessimistic.' Tom smiled. 'You going home? I'll drop you off.'

Jonathan got into the car.

When Tom got in and closed the door, he at once had a sense of privacy, as if they were in a room in his own house. And how long would his house be safe? Tom had an unpleasant vision of the ubiquitous Mafia, like black cockroaches darting everywhere, coming from everywhere. If he fled his house, getting Heloise and Mme Annette out before him or with him, the Mafia might simply set fire to Belle Ombre. Tom thought of the harpsichord burning, or going up in pieces from a bomb. Tom admitted that he had a love of house and home usually found only in women.

'I'm in more danger than you, if that bodyguard, the second one, can identify my face. I've had a few pictures in the newspapers, that's the trouble,' Tom said.

Jonathan knew. 'I apologize for asking to see you today. I'm afraid I'm awfully worried about my wife. It's because – how we get along is the most important thing in my life. It's the first time I've ever tried to deceive her about anything, you see. And I've rather failed – so it's shattering to me. But – you were a help. Thanks.'

'Yes. It's all right this time,' Tom said pleasantly. He meant their seeing each other this evening. 'But it occurs to me –' Tom opened the glove compartment, and took out the Italian gun. 'I think you ought to have this handy. In your shop, for instance.'

'Really? – To tell you the truth, I'm afraid I'd be hopeless in a shoot-out.'

'It's better than nothing. If someone comes into your shop who looks odd – Haven't you got a drawer just behind your counter?'

A tingle went up Jonathan's spine, because he'd had a dream a few nights ago of exactly that: a Mafia gunman coming into his shop and shooting him point-blank in the face. 'But why do you think I'll need it? There's some reason, isn't there?'

Suddenly Tom thought, why not tell Jonathan? It might inspire him to more caution. At the same time Tom knew that caution wasn't of much help. It also occurred to Tom that Jonathan would be safer if he took his wife and child away on a trip for a while. 'Yes, I had a telephone call today that bothered me. A man who sounded French, but that doesn't mean anything. He asked for some French name. It may not mean anything and yet I can't be sure. Because as soon as I open my mouth, I sound like an American, and he may have been verifying –' Tom trailed off. 'To fill you in further, Reeves' place in Hamburg was bombed – I suppose it was around the middle of April.'

'His flat. Good God! Was he injured?'

'No one was in the place at the time. But Reeves went to Amsterdam in a hurry. He's still there as far as I know, under another name.'

Jonathan thought of Reeves' flat being looked over for names and addresses, of his and maybe Tom Ripley's also being found. 'Then how much does the enemy know?'

'Oh, Reeves says he has all his important papers under control. They got hold of Fritz – I suppose you know Fritz – and beat him up a bit, but according to Reeves, Fritz was heroic. He gave them an opposite description of you – you being the man Reeves hired, or somebody hired.' Tom sighed. 'I'm assuming they suspect Reeves and a few casino club men – only.' He glanced at Jonathan's wide eyes. Jonathan didn't look so much frightened as jolted.

'Good Christ!' Jonathan whispered. 'Do you suppose they got hold of my address – or our addresses?'

'No,' Tom said, smiling, 'or they'd have been here already, I can tell you that.' Tom wanted to get home. He turned on the ignition and manoeuvred himself into the traffic of the Rue Grande.

'Then – assuming the man who phoned you was one of them, how did he get your number?'

'Now we enter the realm of guesswork,' Tom said, getting his car into the clear at last. He was still smiling. Yes, it was dangerous, and this time he wasn't getting a penny out of it, not even protecting his own money, which was what he had done at least in the Derwatt near-fiasco. 'Maybe because Reeves was stupid enough to ring me from Amsterdam. I'm toying with the possibility that the Mafia boys might've traced him to Amsterdam, because for one thing he's having his housekeeper send his possessions there. Pretty stupid move, so soon,' Tom said as if in parentheses. 'I'm wondering, you see, if – even if Reeves got out of his Amsterdam hotel, the Mafia boys didn't check on the phone calls he made. In which case my number might be there. By the way, he didn't ring you, I trust, when he was in Amsterdam. You're sure?'

'The last call I had was from Hamburg, I know.' Jonathan remembered Reeves' cheerful voice, telling him his money, all of it, would be deposited at once in the Swiss bank. Jonathan was worried about the bulge of the gun in his pocket. 'Sorry, but I'd better go to my shop first to get rid of this gun. Drop me anywhere here.'

Tom pulled up to a kerb. 'Take it easy. If you're seriously – alarmed about anything, go ahead and ring me. I mean that.'

Jonathan gave an awkward smile, because he felt scared. 'Or if I can be of help – do the same.'

Tom drove on.

Jonathan walked towards his shop, one hand in his pocket supporting the weight of the gun. He put the gun into his cash drawer which slid under the heavy counter. Tom was right, the gun was better than nothing, and Jonathan knew he had another advantage: he didn't care much about his own life. It wouldn't be like Tom Ripley getting shot or whatever, losing his life while in the best of health, and for literally nothing, it seemed to Jonathan.

If a man walked into his shop with intent to shoot him, and if he was lucky enough to be able to shoot the man first, it would be the end of the game, anyway. Jonathan didn't need Tom Ripley to tell him that. The gunshot would bring people, the police, the dead man would be identified, and the question would be asked, 'Why should a Mafia man want to shoot at Jonathan Trevanny?' The train journey would be the next thing exposed, because the police would ask his movements in the last weeks, would want to see his passport. He'd be finished.

Jonathan locked his shop door and walked on towards the Rue St Merry. He was thinking of Reeves' flat bombed, all those books, the records, the paintings. He was thinking of Fritz who had guided him to the button man called Salvatore Bianca, of Fritz beaten up and not betraying him.

It was nearly 7.30 p.m., and Simone was in the kitchen. *'Bonsoir!'* Jonathan said, smiling.

'Bonsoir,' Simone said. She turned the oven down, then straightened and removed her apron. 'And what were you doing with M. Ripley this evening?'

Jonathan's face tingled a little. Where had she seen them? When he'd got out of Tom's car? 'He came to talk about some framing,' Jonathan said. 'So we had a beer. It was near closing time.'

'Oh?' She looked at Jonathan, not moving. 'I see.'

Jonathan hung his jacket in the hall. Georges was coming down the stairs to greet him, saying something about his hovercraft. Georges was assembling a model Jonathan had bought for him, and it was a little too complicated for him. Jonathan swung him up over his shoulder. 'We'll have a look at it after dinner, all right?'

The atmosphere did not improve. They had a delicious purée of vegetable soup, made in a six-hundred-franc mixer that Jonathan had just bought: it made fruit juices and pulverized almost everything, including some chicken bones. Jonathan tried without success to talk about other things. Simone could soon bring any subject to a halt. It wasn't impossible, Jonathan was thinking, that Tom Ripley should want him to frame some pictures. After all, Tom had said he painted. Jonathan said:

'Ripley is interested in framing several things. I might have to go to his house to look at them.'

'Oh?' in the same tone. Then she said something pleasant to Georges.

Jonathan disliked Simone when she was like this, and hated himself for disliking her. He had been going to plunge into the explanation – the bet explanation – of the sum of money in the Swiss bank. That evening, he simply couldn't.

SEVENTEEN

After dropping Jonathan, Tom had an impulse to stop at a bar-café and ring his house. He wanted to know if all was well, and if Heloise was home. To his great relief Heloise answered.

'*Oui, chéri*, I just got home. Where are you? No, I had only a drink with Noëlle.'

'Heloise, my pet, let's do something nice tonight. Maybe the Grais or the Berthelins are free ... I know it's late to ask anyone for dinner, but for after dinner. Maybe the Cleggs ... Yes, I feel like seeing some people.' Tom said he would be home in fifteen minutes.

Tom drove fast, but carefully. He felt curiously shaky about tonight. He was wondering about any telephone calls that Mme Annette might have got since he left the house.

Heloise, or Mme Annette, had put the front light on at Belle Ombre, though the dusk had not yet fallen. A big Citroën cruised slowly past, just before Tom turned into his gates, and Tom looked at it: dark blue, lumbering on the slightly uneven road, with a licence plate ending in 75, meaning a Paris car. There had been two people in it at least. Was it casing Belle Ombre? He was probably over anxious.

'Hello, Tome! *Les* Clegg can come for a quick drink, and *les* Grais can come for dinner, because Antoine didn't go to Paris today. Does that please you?' Heloise kissed his cheek. 'Where were you? Look at the suitcase! – I admit it's not very big –'

Tom looked at the dark purple suitcase with a red canvas band around it. The clasps and the lock appeared to be brass. The purple leather looked like kid, and perhaps was. 'Yes. It really *is* pretty.' It really was, like their harpsichord, or like his *commode de bateau* upstairs.

'And look – inside.' Heloise opened it. 'Really str-rong,' she said in English.

Tom stooped and kissed her hair. 'Darling, it's lovely. We can celebrate the suitcase – and the harpsichord. The Cleggs and the Grais haven't seen the harpsichord, have they? No ... How is Noëlle?'

'Tome, something is making you nervous,' Heloise said in a soft voice, in case Mme Annette might hear.

'No,' said Tom. 'I just feel like seeing some people. I had a very quiet day. Ah, Mme Annette, *bonsoir*! People tonight. Two for dinner. Can you manage?'

Mme Annette had just arrived with the bar cart. '*Mais oui*, M. Tome. It will have to be *à la fortune du pot*, but I shall try a ragoût – my Normandy style, if you remember ...'

Tom didn't listen to her ingredients – there was beef, veal and kidney, because she'd had time to pop out to the butcher's this evening, and it was not going to be pot-luck at all, Tom was sure. But Tom had to wait until she finished. Then he said, 'By the way, Mme Annette, were there any telephone calls since six when I left?'

'No, M. Tome.' With expertise Mme Annette extracted the cork of a small bottle of champagne.

'None at all? Not even a wrong number?'

'*Non*, M. Tome.' Mme Annette poured champagne carefully into a wide glass for Heloise.

Heloise was watching him. But Tom decided to persist, rather than go into the kitchen to speak with Mme Annette. Or should he not go into the kitchen? Yes. That was quite easy. when Mme Annette went back to the kitchen, Tom said to Heloise, 'I think I'll get a beer.' Mme Annette had left him to make his own drink, as Tom often preferred to do.

In the kitchen, Mme Annette had her dinner in full swing, vegetables washed and ready, and something already boiling on the stove. 'Madame,' Tom said, 'it's very important – today. Are you quite sure nobody telephoned at all? Even somebody – even by error?'

This seemed to jog her memory, to Tom's alarm. '*Ah, oui*, the telephone rang around six-thirty. A man asked for – some other name I can't recall, M. Tome. Then he hung up. An error, M. Tome.'

'What did you say to him?'

'I said it was not the residence of the person he wanted.'

'You told him it was the Ripley residence?'

'Oh no, M. Tome. I simply said it was not the right number. I thought that was the correct thing to do.'

Tom beamed at her. It had been the correct thing to do. Tom had reproached himself for going off at 6 p.m. today without asking Mme Annette not to give his name under any circumstances, and she'd handled everything properly on her own initiative. 'Excellent. That's always the correct thing to do,' Tom said with admiration. 'That's why I have an unlisted number, in order to have a little privacy, *n'est-ce pas?*'

'*Bien sûr,*' said Mme Annette, as if it were the most natural thing in the world.

Tom went back to the living-room, forgetting all about beer. He poured a scotch for himself. He was not much reassured, however. If it had been a Mafioso looking for him, he might be doubly suspicious because two people at this house had refrained from giving the name of the proprietor. Tom wondered if some checking was going on in Milan or Amsterdam or perhaps Hamburg? Didn't Tom Ripley live in Villeperce? Couldn't this 424 number be a Villeperce number? Yes, indeed. Fontainebleau numbers began with 422, but 424 was an area southward, including Villeperce.

'What is worrying you, Tome?' Heloise asked.

'Nothing, darling. – What's happening with your cruise plans? Have you seen anything you like?'

'Ah, yes! Something which is not *casse-pied* swank, just nice and simple. A cruise from Venice around the Mediterranean, including Turkey. Fifteen days – and one doesn't have to dress for dinner. How does that sound, Tome? Every three weeks during May and June, for instance, the boat leaves.'

'I'm not much in the mood at the moment. Ask Noëlle if she'd go with you. It would do you good.'

Tom went upstairs to his room. He opened the bottom drawer of his bigger chest of drawers. On top was Heloise's green jacket from Salzburg. At the back on the bottom of the drawer lay a Luger which Tom had acquired just three months ago from Reeves, oddly enough, not directly from Reeves but from a man whom Tom had had to meet in Paris in order to get something the man was delivering, something that Tom had had to hold for a month before posting it. As a favour, as a kind of payment really. Tom had requested a Luger, and it had been given him – a 7.65 mm with two little boxes of ammunition. Tom verified that the gun was loaded, then he went to his closet and looked at his French-made hunting rifle. It was loaded also, with the safety on it. It was the Luger he would need in case of trouble, Tom supposed, tonight or tomorrow or tomorrow night. Tom looked out the two windows of his room, which gave in two directions. He was looking for cruising cars with dimmed lights, but he didn't see any. It was already dark.

A car approached with a determined air from the left: this was the dear, harmless Cleggs, and they turned in smartly through the gates of Belle Ombre. Tom went down to welcome them.

The Cleggs – Howard, fiftyish, an Englishman, and his English wife Rosemary – stayed for two drinks, and the Grais joined them. Clegg, a retired lawyer, retired because of a heart condition, nevertheless was more animated than anyone else. His grey, neatly cut hair, seasoned tweed jacket and grey flannels, lent the air of country stability that Tom needed. Clegg, standing with his back to the curtained front window, scotch in hand, telling a funny story – What could happen tonight to shatter this rural conviviality? Tom had left his room light on, and he had turned on the bedside lamp in Heloise's room also. The two cars were parked carelessly on the gravel. Tom wanted his house to present the picture of a party in progress, a party bigger than it was. Not that this would really stop the Mafia boys, if they chose to toss a bomb, Tom knew, and therefore he was putting his friends in danger, perhaps. But Tom had the feeling the Mafia would prefer a quiet assassination for him: get him alone and then attack, maybe without a gun, just a sudden beating up that would be fatal. The Mafia could do it on the streets of Villeperce, and be away before the townspeople knew what had happened.

Rosemary Clegg, slim and beautiful in a middle-aged way, was promising Heloise some kind of plant that she and Howard had just brought back from England.

'Are you intending to set any fires this summer?' Antoine Grais asked.

'Not really my dish,' Tom said, smiling. 'Come out and take a look at the greenhouse-to-be.'

Tom and Antoine walked out the french windows and down the steps on to the lawn, Tom with a flashlight. The foundation had been laid with cement, the pieces for the steel frame were stacked alongside, doing the lawn no good, and the workmen hadn't been around for a week. Tom had been warned by one of the villagers about this crew: they had so much work this summer, they hopped from one job to the next, trying to please everybody, or at least keep a lot of people on the hook.

'That's coming along, I think,' said Antoine finally.

Tom had consulted Antoine as to the best type of greenhouse, paid him for his services, and Antoine had also been able to get the materials for him at a professional discount, or anyway more cheaply than the mason would have got them. Tom found himself glancing towards the lane through the woods behind Antoine, where there were no lights at all, certainly no car lights now.

But by 11 p.m., after dinner when the four of them were drinking coffee and Bénédictine, Tom made up his mind to get both Heloise and Mme Annette out of the house by tomorrow. Heloise would be the easier. He'd persuade her to stay with Noëlle for a few days – Noëlle and her husband had a very large flat in Neuilly – or to stay with her parents. Mme Annette had a sister in Lyon, and fortunately the sister had a telephone, so something might be arranged quickly. And the explanation? Tom shrank from the idea of putting on an act of crotchetiness, such as, 'I must be alone for a few days', and if he admitted that there was danger, Heloise and Mme Annette would be alarmed. They'd want to alert the police.

Tom approached Heloise that evening, as they were getting ready for bed. 'My dear,' he said in English, 'I have a feeling something awful is going to happen, and I don't want you here. It's a matter of your safety. Also I would like Mme Annette to leave tomorrow for a few days – so I hope, darling, you can help me persuade her to visit her sister.'

Heloise, propped up on pale blue pillows, frowned a little and set down the yoghurt she was eating. '*What* is happening that is awful? – Tome, you must tell me.'

'No.' Tom shook his head, then he laughed. 'And maybe I'm only anxious. Maybe it's for nothing. But there's no harm in playing it safe, is there?'

'I don't want a lot of words, Tome. What has happened? Something with Reeves! It is that, isn't it?'

'In a way.' It was a lot better than saying it was the Mafia.

'Where is he?'

'Oh, he's in Amsterdam, I think.'

'Doesn't he live in Germany?'

'Yes, but he's doing some work in Amsterdam.'

'But who else is involved? Why are you worried? – What have you done, Tome?'

'Why, nothing, darling!' It was Tom's usual answer under the circumstances. He wasn't even ashamed of it.

'Then you're trying to protect Reeves?'

'He's done me a few favours. But I want to protect you now – and us, and Belle Ombre. Not Reeves. So you must let me try, darling.'

'Belle Ombre?'

Tom smiled and said calmly, 'I don't want any disturbance at Belle Ombre. I don't want anything broken, not a pane of glass. You must trust me, I'm trying to avoid anything violent – or dangerous!'

Heloise blinked her eyes and said in a slightly piqued tone, 'All right, Tome.'

He knew that Heloise would ask no more questions, not unless there was an accusation by the police, or a Mafia corpse to account for to her. A few minutes later, they were both smiling, and Tom slept in her bed that night. How much worse it must be for Jonathan Trevanny, Tom thought – not that Simone appeared difficult, prying or neurotic in the least, but Jonathan was not in the habit of doing anything out of the ordinary, not even of telling white lies. It must be, as Jonathan had said, shattering if his wife had begun to mistrust him. And because of the money, it was natural that Simone would think of crime, of something shameful that Jonathan couldn't admit.

In the morning, Heloise and Tom spoke to Mme Annette together. Heloise had had her tea upstairs, and Tom was drinking a second coffee in the living-room.

'M. Tome says he wants to be alone and think and paint for a few days,' said Heloise.

They had decided this was best after all. 'And a little vacation wouldn't do you any harm, Mme Annette. A little one before the big one in August,' Tom added, though Mme Annette, sturdy and lively as always, looked in the best of form.

'But if you wish, Madame et M'sieur, of course. That is the big thing, is it not?' She was smiling, her blue eyes not exactly twinkling now, but she was agreeable.

Mme Annette at once agreed to ring her sister Marie-Odile in Lyon.

The post came at 9.30 a.m. In it was a square, white envelope with a Swiss stamp, the address printed – Reeves' printing, Tom suspected – and no return address. Tom wanted to open it in the living-room, but Heloise was talking with Mme Annette about driving her to Paris for the train to Lyon, so Tom went up to his room. The letter said:

May 11

Dear Tom,

I am in Ascona. Had to leave Amsterdam because of a near thing in my hotel, but have managed to put my belongings in store in Amsterdam. God, I wish they would lay off! I am here in this pretty town, known as Ralph Platt, staying at an inn up the hill called Die Drei Baeren – cosy? At least it is very out of the way and family pension style. Wishing the very best to you and Heloise,

As ever,
R.

Tom crushed the letter in his hand, then shredded it into his waste-basket. It was exactly as bad as Tom had thought: the Mafia had caught up with him at Amsterdam, and had doubtless got Tom's telephone number by checking all the numbers Reeves had called. Tom wondered what the near thing at the hotel had been? He swore to himself, not for the first time, that he'd never have anything to do with Reeves Minot in future. In this case, all he'd provided was an idea for Reeves. That should have been harmless, and it was harmless. Tom realized his mistake had been to try to help Jonathan Trevanny. And of course Reeves didn't know that, or Reeves wouldn't have been stupid enough to ring him at Belle Ombre.

He wanted Jonathan Trevanny to come to Belle Ombre by this evening, even this afternoon, though he knew Jonathan worked on Saturday. If anything happened, the situation could be more easily handled by two people, at front and back of the house, for instance, because one person couldn't be everywhere. And who else had he to call on but Jonathan? Jonathan wasn't a promising fighter, and yet in a crisis he might come through, just as he had on the train. He'd done all right there, and had also, Tom remembered, yanked him back to safety when he'd been surely going to fall out of the train door. He wanted Jonathan to stay the night, and he'd have to fetch him, too, because there was no bus, and Tom didn't want him to take a taxi, in view of what might happen tonight, didn't want any taxi-driver to recall that he'd driven a man from Fontainebleau to Villeperce, a rather unusual distance.

'You will telephone me tonight, Tome?' Heloise asked. She was packing a big suitcase in her room. She was going first to her family.

'Yes, my love. Around seven-thirty?' He knew Heloise's parents dined promptly at 8 p.m. 'I'll ring and say "All is well", probably.'

'Is it only tonight you are worried about?'

It wasn't, but Tom didn't want to say so. 'I think so.'

When Heloise and Mme Annette were ready to leave around 11 a.m.,

Tom managed to enter the garage first, before he even helped them with their luggage, though Mme Annette had the old French school idea that she should carry the luggage of both in instalments, simply because she was a servant. Tom looked under the hood of the Alfa. The motor presented the familiar picture of metal and wires. He started the motor. No explosion. Tom had gone out and padlocked the garage doors last evening before dinner, but Tom believed anything when it came to the Mafia. They'd pick a padlock and snap it shut again.

'We will be in touch, Mme Annette,' Tom said, kissing her cheek. 'Enjoy yourself!'

'Bye-bye, Tome! Ring me tonight! And take care!' Heloise shouted.

Tom grinned as he waved good-bye. He could tell that Heloise wasn't very worried. That was all to the good.

Tom then went into his house to telephone Jonathan.

EIGHTEEN

The morning had been a rough one for Jonathan. Simone had said, in a pleasant enough tone, because she was then helping Georges tug himself into a turtle-neck sweater:

'I don't see how this ambience can go on for ever, Jon. Do you?'

Simone and Georges had to leave for Georges' school in a couple of minutes. It was almost 8.15 a.m.

'No, I don't. And about that Swiss sum –' Jonathan determined to plunge on, now. He spoke quickly, hoping Georges wouldn't grasp all of it. 'They've made a bet, if you must know. I'm holding the take for both of them. So that –'

'Who?' Simone looked as puzzled and angry as ever.

'The doctors,' Jonathan said. 'They're trying a new treatment – one is – and somebody's betting against him. Another doctor. I thought you'd think it rather macabre, so I wasn't going to tell you about it. But that means there's really only about two hundred thousand, less now, belonging to us. They're paying me that, the Hamburg people, for trying out their pills.'

Jonathan could see that she tried, and couldn't believe him. 'It's absurd!' she said. 'All that money, Jon! For a *bet*?'

Georges looked up at her.

Jonathan glanced at his son and wet his lips.

'Do you know what I think, and I don't care if Georges hears me! I think you are holding – concealing dishonest money for this dishonest type Tom Ripley. And of course he's paying you a little, letting you have a little of it for doing him the favour!'

Jonathan realized he was trembling, and set his bowl of *café au lait* down on the kitchen table. Both he and Simone were standing. 'Couldn't Ripley conceal his own money himself in Switzerland?' Jonathan's instinct was to go to her and grasp her by the shoulders, tell her that she had to believe him. But he knew quite well she'd push him back. So he simply stood up straighter and said, 'I can't help it if you don't believe me. That's the way it is.' Jonathan had had a transfusion last Monday afternoon, the day he had fainted. Simone had gone to the hospital with him, and then he had gone by himself afterwards to Dr Perrier, whom he'd had to ring earlier to make the appointment for the transfusion for him. Dr Perrier had wanted to see him as a matter of routine. But Jonathan had told Simone that Dr Perrier had given him more of the medicaments sent by the Hamburg doctor. The Hamburg doctor, Wentzel, hadn't sent pills, but the pills he recommended were available in France, and Jonathan had a supply at home now. It was the Hamburg doctor Jonathan had decided should be betting 'for' and the Munich doctor who should be betting 'against', but he hadn't got that far with Simone as yet.

'But I *don't* believe you,' Simone said, her voice gentle and also sinister. 'Come along, Georges, we've got to go.'

Jonathan blinked, and watched Simone and Georges go up the hall towards the front door. Georges picked up his satchel of books, and perhaps startled by the heated conversation, forgot to say good-bye to Jonathan, and Jonathan was silent too.

Since it was Saturday, Jonathan's shop was busy. The telephone rang several times. Around 11 a.m., the voice on the other end of the telephone was Tom Ripley's.

'I'd like to see you today. It's rather important,' Tom said. 'Are you able to talk now?'

'Not really.' There was a man at the counter in front of Jonathan, waiting to pay for his picture which lay wrapped between them.

'I'm sorry to bother you on a Saturday. But I'm wondering how soon you could get to my house – and stay the evening?'

Jonathan was jolted for a second. Close the shop. Inform Simone. Inform her what? 'Of course I can. Yes.'

'How soon? I'll pick you up. Say at twelve noon? Or is that too soon?'

'No. I'll make it.'

'Pick you up at your shop. Or on the street there. One other thing – bring the gun.' Tom hung up.

Jonathan attended to the people in his shop, and while there was still someone in his shop, he stuck the FERME sign in his door. He wondered what had happened to Tom Ripley since yesterday? Simone was home that morning, but she was more often out than in on Saturday mornings, because she did marketing and chores like going to the dry cleaners. Jonathan decided to write Simone a note and push it through the letter slot in the front door. Jonathan had the note written by 11.40 a.m., and went off with it, up the Rue de la Paroisse, the quickest way, where there was a fifty-fifty chance of encountering Simone, but he didn't. He stuck the note through the slot marked LETTRES, and walked back quickly the way he had come. He had written:

My dear,

Won't be home for lunch or dinner and have closed the shop. Chance of a big job some distance away and am being taken there by car.

J.

It was inexplicit, not at all like him. And yet, how could things get any worse than they'd been that morning?

Jonathan went into his shop again, grabbed his old mac, and stuck the Italian gun into its pocket. When he went out on the pavement again, Tom's green Renault was approaching. Tom opened the door, barely stopping, and Jonathan got in.

'Morning!' Tom said. 'How are things?'

'At home?' Jonathan was, despite himself, glancing about for Simone who might be anywhere on the streets here. 'Not very good, I'm afraid.'

Tom could imagine. 'But you're feeling all right?'

'Yes, thanks.'

Tom made the right turn by the Prisunic into the Rue Grande. 'I had another telephone call,' Tom said, 'rather my housekeeper did. Same as before, a wrong number, and she didn't tell him whose house it was, but it's made me nervous. By the way I've sent my housekeeper and also my wife away. I have a hunch something might happen. So I called on you to hold the fort with me. I have no one else to ask. I'm afraid to ask the police to keep a watch. If they were to find a couple of the Mafia around my house, there'd be unpleasant inquiries as to why they were there, of course.'

Jonathan knew that.

'We're not at my house yet,' Tom went on, passing the Monument now and entering the road that led towards Villeperce, 'so there's time for you to change your mind. I'll drive you back gladly and you needn't apologize if you don't want to join me. There may be danger and there may not. But it's easier for two people to be on the look-out there than for one.'

'Yes.' Jonathan felt curiously paralysed.

'It's just that I don't want to leave my house.' Tom was driving rather fast. 'I don't want it to go up in smoke or be blown up like Reeves' place. Reeves by the way is now in Ascona. They tracked him to Amsterdam and he had to run.'

'Oh?' Jonathan experienced a few seconds of panic, of nausea. He felt that everything was collapsing. 'You've – Have you seen anything odd around your house?'

'Not really.' Tom's voice was cool. His cigarette stuck up at a jaunty angle.

Jonathan was thinking, he *could* pull out. Now. Just say to Tom he didn't feel up to it, that he might well faint if it came to the crunch. He could go home and be safe. Jonathan took a deep breath and lowered the window a bit more. He'd be a bastard if he did that, a coward and a shit. He might at least try. He owed it to Tom Ripley. And why should he be so concerned about his own safety? Why suddenly now? Jonathan smiled a little, feeling better. 'I told Simone about the bet on my life. It didn't go down too well.'

'What did she say?'

'The same thing. She doesn't believe me. What's worse, she saw me with you yesterday – somewhere. Now she's thinking I'm holding some money for you – in my name. Dishonest money, you know.'

'Yes.' Tom saw the situation. But it didn't seem important compared to what might happen to Belle Ombre, to himself and maybe Jonathan too. 'I'm no hero, you know,' Tom said out of the blue. 'If the Mafia got me and tried to beat some facts out of me, I doubt if I'd be as brave as Fritz.'

Jonathan was silent. He sensed that Tom was feeling as queasy as he himself had a few seconds ago.

It was a particularly fine day, the air liquid with summer, the sunlight brilliant. It was a shame to have to work on such a day, to have to be indoors as Simone would be this afternoon. She didn't have to work any more, of course. Jonathan had wanted to say that to her for the past couple of weeks.

They were entering Villeperce now, a quiet village of the kind that would have perhaps only one butcher's and one bakery.

'That's Belle Ombre,' Tom said, nodding towards a domed tower that showed above some poplars.

They had driven perhaps half a kilometre from the village. The houses on the road were far apart and large. Belle Ombre looked like a small château, its lines classic and sturdy, but softened by four rounded corner towers which came all the way down to the grass. There were iron gates, and Tom had to get out and open them with a huge key he had taken from the glove compartment. Then they rolled on to the gravel in front of the garage.

'What a beautiful place!' Jonathan said.

Tom nodded and smiled. 'A wedding present from my wife's parents, mainly. And every time I arrive lately, I'm delighted to see that it's still standing. Please come in!'

Tom had a key for the front door, too.

'Not used to locking up,' Tom said. 'Usually my housekeeper's here.'

Jonathan walked into a wide foyer paved with white marble, then into a square living-room – two rugs, a big fireplace, a comfortable-looking yellow satin sofa. And a harpsichord stood beside french windows. The furniture was all good, Jonathan saw, and it was well cared for.

'Take off your mac,' Tom said. For a moment, he felt relieved – Belle Ombre was quiet, and he hadn't seen anything out of the ordinary in the village. He went to the hall table and took his Luger from the drawer. Jonathan watched him, and Tom smiled. 'Yes, I'm going to carry this thing all day, hence these old trousers. Big pockets. I can see why some people prefer shoulder-holsters.' Tom pushed the gun into a pocket of his trousers. 'Do the same with yours, if you don't mind.'

Jonathan did.

Tom was thinking of his rifle upstairs. He was sorry to get down to business so quickly, but he thought it might be for the best. 'Come up. I want to show you something.'

They climbed the stairway, and Tom took Jonathan into his room. Jonathan at once noticed the *commode de bateau* and went over for a closer look.

'A recent present from my wife – Look –' Tom was holding his rifle. 'There's this. For long range. Fairly accurate, but not like an army rifle, of course. I want you to look out this front window.'

Jonathan did. There was a nineteenth-century three-storey house across the road, set well back and more than half-obscured by trees. Trees bordered the road on either side in a haphazard way. Jonathan was imagining a car pausing on the road outside the house gates, and that was what Tom was talking about: the rifle would be more accurate than a pistol.

'Of course it depends on what they do,' Tom said. If they intend to throw an incendiary bomb, for instance. Then the rifle will be the thing to use. Of course there are back windows too. And side windows. Come this way.'

Tom led Jonathan into Heloise's room, which had a window giving on the back lawn. Here were denser trees beyond the lawn, and poplars bordering the lawn on the right.

'There's a lane going through those woods. You can faintly see it on the left. And in my atelier –' Tom went into the hall and opened a door on the left. This room had windows on the back lawn and in the direction in which the village of Villeperce lay, but only cypresses and poplars and the tiles of a small house were visible. 'We might keep a look-out on both sides of the house, not that we have to stay glued to the windows but – The other important point is, I want the enemy to think I'm alone here. If you –'

The telephone was ringing. Tom thought for a moment that he wouldn't answer it, then that he might learn something if he did. He took it in his room.

'Oui?'

'M. Ripley?' said a Frenchwoman's voice. '*Ici*, Mme Trevanny. Is my husband there by any chance?'

She sounded very tense.

'Your husband? *Mais non*, madame!' Tom said with astonishment in his voice.

'*Merci, m'sieur. Excusez-moi.*' She hung up.

Tom sighed. Jonathan was indeed having troubles.

Jonathan was standing in the doorway. 'My wife.'

'Yes,' Tom said. 'I'm sorry. I said you weren't here. You can send a *pneu*, if you like. Or telephone. Maybe she's in your shop.'

'No, no, I doubt that.' But she could be, because she had a key. It was only a quarter past 1 p.m. How else could Simone have obtained his number, Tom thought, if not from Jonathan's notation in his shop? 'Or if you like, I'll drive you back now to Fontainebleau. It's really up to you, Jonathan.'

'No,' Jonathan said. 'Thanks.' Renunciation, Jonathan thought. Simone had known Tom was lying.

'I apologize for lying just now. You can always blame me. I doubt if I can sink any lower in your wife's mind anyway.' Tom at that moment didn't give a damn, didn't have the time or the inclination to sympathize with Simone. Jonathan wasn't saying anything. 'Let's go down and see what the kitchen has to offer.'

Tom drew the curtains in his room almost closed, but open enough so that one could see out without stirring the curtains. He did the same in Heloise's room, and also downstairs in the living-room. Mme Annette's quarters he decided to let alone. They had windows on the lane side and the back lawn.

There was plenty of Mme Annette's delicious ragoût of last evening. The window over the kitchen sink had no curtains, and Tom made Jonathan sit out of view at the kitchen table, with a scotch and water.

'What a shame we can't potter in the garden this afternoon,' Tom said, washing lettuce at the sink. He had a compulsion to glance out the window at every passing car. Only two cars had passed in the last ten minutes.

Jonathan had noticed that both garage doors were wide open. Tom's car was parked on the gravel in front of the house. It was so quiet, any footstep would be heard on the gravel, Jonathan thought.

'And I can't turn on any music, because I might drown out some other noise. What a bore,' Tom said.

Though neither ate much, they spent a long time at the table in the dining area off the living-room. Tom made coffee. Since there was nothing substantial for dinner that evening, Tom telephoned the Villeperce butcher and asked for a good steak for two.

'Oh, Mme Annette is taking a short holiday,' Tom said in response to the butcher's question. The Ripleys were such good customers, Tom had no hesitation in asking the butcher to pick up some lettuce and a nice vegetable of some kind at the grocery next door.

The very audible crunching of tyres on gravel half an hour later announced the arrival of the butcher's van. Tom had jumped to his feet. He paid the genial butcher's boy, who was wearing a blood-spattered apron, and tipped him. Jonathan was now looking at some books on furniture, and seemed quite content, so Tom went upstairs to pass some time by tidying his atelier, a room which Mme Annette never touched.

A telephone call just before 5 p.m. came like a scream in the silence, a muffled scream to Tom, because he had dared to go out in the garden and was messing about with the secateurs. Tom ran into the house, though he knew Jonathan wouldn't touch the telephone. Jonathan was still lounging on the sofa, surrounded by books.

The call was from Heloise. She was very happy because she had rung Noëlle, and a friend of Noëlle's Jules Grifaud, an interior decorator, had bought a chalet in Switzerland, and was inviting Noëlle and her to drive there with him and keep him company for a week or so while he arranged his things in the house.

'The country around is so beautiful,' Heloise said. 'And we can also help him ...'

It sounded deadly to Tom, but if Heloise was enthusiastic, that was what mattered. He had known she wouldn't go on that Adriatic cruise, like an ordinary tourist.

'Are you all right, darling? ... What are you doing?'

'Oh – a little gardening ... Yes, everything is *very* tranquil.'

NINETEEN

Around 7.30 p.m., when Tom was standing at the front window of his living-room, he saw the dark-blue Citroën – the same one he'd seen that morning, he thought – cruise past the house, this time at a faster speed, but still not as fast as the usual car which intended to get somewhere. Was it the same? In the dusk, colours were deceiving – the difference between blue and green. But the car had been a convertible with a dirty white upper trim, like the one this morning. Tom looked at the gates of Belle Ombre, which he had left ajar, but which the butcher's boy had closed. Tom decided to leave them closed, but not locked. They creaked a little.

'What's up?' Jonathan asked. He was drinking coffee. He hadn't wanted tea. Tom's unease was making him uneasy, and as far as he had been able to find out, Tom had no real reason to be so anxious.

'I think I saw the same car as I saw this morning. A dark-blue Citroën. The one this morning had a Paris plate. I know most of the cars around here, and only two or three people have cars with Paris plates.'

'Could you see the licence now?' It looked dark to Jonathan, and he had a lamp on beside him.

'No – I'm going to get the rifle.' Tom went upstairs as if borne on wings, and returned at once with the rifle. He had left no lights on upstairs. He said to Jonathan, 'I definitely don't want to use a gun if I can avoid it, because of the noise. It's not the hunting season, and a gunshot might bring the neighbours – or *someone* might investigate. Jonathan –'

Jonathan was on his feet. 'Yes?'

'You might have to wield this rifle like a club.' Tom illustrated, so that the weightiest part of it, the butt, could be used to best effect. 'You can see how it works, in case you have to shoot with it. Safety's on now.' Tom showed him.

But they're not here, Jonathan was thinking. And at the same time he was feeling odd and unreal, as he had felt in Hamburg and in Munich, when he had known that his targets were real, and that they would materialize.

Tom was calculating how much time it would take the Citroën to cruise or drive around the circular road that led back to the village. They could of course turn at some convenient place on the road and come straight back. 'If anyone comes to the door,' Tom said, 'I have the feeling I'm going to be plugged when I open the door. That would be the simplest for them, you see. Then the fellow with the gun jumps into the waiting car and off they go.'

Tom was a bit overwrought, Jonathan thought, but he listened carefully. 'Another possibility is a bomb through that window,' Tom said, gesturing towards the front window. 'Same as Reeves had. So if you're – um – agreeable – Sorry, but I'm not used to discussing my plans. I usually play it by ear. But if you're willing, would you hide yourself in the shrubbery to the right of the door here – it's thicker on the right – and clout anyone who walks up and rings the doorbell? They may not ring the doorbell, but I'll be watching with the Luger for signs of bomb throwing. Clout him fast if he's at the door, because he'll be fast. He'll have a gun in his pocket, and all he wants is a clear view of me.' Tom went to the fireplace, where he had meant to light a fire and forgot, and took one of the third-of-a-log pieces from the wood basket. This he put on the floor to the right of the front door. It was not as heavy as the amethyst vase on the wooden chest by the door, but much easier to handle.

'How about,' Jonathan said, 'if I open the door? If they know what you look like, as you say, they'll see I'm not you and –'

'No.' Tom was surprised by Jonathan's courageous offer. 'First, they might not wait to see, just fire. And if they did look at you, and you said I don't live here, or I'm not in, they'd only push in and see or –' Tom gave it up with a laugh, imagining the Mafia blasting Jonathan in the stomach and pushing him into the house at the same time. 'I think you should take up the post by the door now, if you're willing. I don't know how long you'll have to stay there, but I can always bring you refreshments.'

'Sure.' Jonathan took the rifle from Tom and went out. The road in front of the house was quiet. Jonathan stood in the shadow of the house, and practised a swing with the rifle, high up so as to catch a man standing on the steps in the head.

'Good,' Tom said. 'Would you care for a scotch now by any chance? You can leave the glass in the bushes. Doesn't matter if it breaks.'

Jonathan smiled. 'No, thanks.' He crept into the shrubbery – cypress-like bushes four feet high, and laurel also. It was very dark where Jonathan was, and he felt absolutely concealed. Tom had closed the door.

Jonathan sat on the ground, his knees under his chin, and the rifle alongside near his right hand. He wondered if this could last for an hour? Longer? Or was it even a game Tom was playing. Jonathan couldn't believe it was entirely a game. Tom wasn't out of his head, and he believed something might happen tonight, and that small possibility made it wise to take precautions. Then as a car approached, Jonathan felt a start of real fear, an impulse to run straight into the house. The car went by at a fast clip. Jonathan hadn't even a glimpse of it through the bushes and the house gates. He leaned a shoulder against a slender trunk of something and began to feel sleepy. Five minutes later, he lay at full length on his back, but still quite awake, beginning to feel the chill of the earth penetrating his shoulder-blades. If the telephone rang again, it might well be Simone. He wondered if she would, in some frenzy of temper, come to Tom's house in a taxi? Or would she ring her brother Gérard in Nemours and ask him to bring her in his car? A bit more likely. Jonathan stopped thinking about that possibility, because it was so awful. Ludicrous. Unthinkable. How would he explain lying outside the house in the shrubbery, even if he concealed the rifle?

Jonathan heard the house door opening. He had been dozing.

'Take this blanket,' Tom whispered. The road was empty, and Tom stepped out with a steamer rug and handed it to Jonathan. 'Put it under you. That ground must be awful.' Tom's own whispering made him realize that the Mafia boys might sneak up on foot. He hadn't thought of that before. He went back into the house without another word to Jonathan.

Tom went up the stairs, and in the dark surveyed the situation from the windows, front and back. All looked calm. A streetlight glowed brightly, but without extending its light very far, on the road about a hundred yards to the left in the direction of the village. None of its light fell in front of Belle Ombre, as Tom knew well. It was extremely silent, but that was normal. Even the footsteps of a man walking on the road might have been heard through the closed windows, Tom thought. He wished he could put on some music. He was about to turn from the window, when he heard the faint *crunch-crunch-crunch* of someone walking on the dirt-road, and then he saw a not very strong flashlight beam, moving from the right towards Belle Ombre. Tom felt sure this wasn't a person who would turn in at Belle Ombre, and the figure didn't, but went on and was lost to view before it reached the streetlight. Male or female, Tom couldn't tell.

Jonathan was perhaps hungry. That couldn't be helped. Tom was hungry, too. But of course it could he helped. Tom went down the stairs, still in the dark, his fingertips on the banister, and into the kitchen – the living-room and kitchen were lighted – and made some caviare canapés. The caviare was left over from last night, in its jar in the fridge, so the job was quick. Tom was bringing the plate for Jonathan, when he heard the purr of a car. The car went past Belle Ombre from left to right, and stopped. Then there was the feeble click of a car door, the sound of a car door when it hadn't quite closed. Tom set the plate down on the wooden chest by the door, and pulled out his gun.

Steps crunched firmly, at a polite-sounding pace, on the road, then the gravel. This wasn't a bomb-thrower, Tom thought. The doorbell rang. Tom waited a few seconds, then said in French. 'Who is it?'

'I would like to ask a direction, please,' the man's voice said with a perfect French accent.

Jonathan had been crouching with the rifle since the approach of footsteps, and now he leapt out of the bushes just as he heard Tom slide the bolt of the door. The man was two steps up from Jonathan, but Jonathan was almost as tall nevertheless, and he swung his rifle butt with all his power at the man's head – which had turned just slightly towards Jonathan, because the man must have heard him. Jonathan's blow caught him behind the left ear, just under the hat-brim. The man swayed, bumped the left side of the doorway, and dropped.

Tom opened the door and dragged him by the feet into the house, Jonathan helping, lifting the man's shoulders. Then Jonathan recovered the rifle and came in the door, which Tom closed softly. Tom picked up the piece of firewood and walloped the man's blondish head with it. The man's hat had fallen off and lay upside down on the marble floor. Tom extended his hand for the rifle, and Jonathan handed it to him. Tom came down with the steel butt of it on the man's temple.

Jonathan couldn't believe his eyes. Blood flowed on to the white marble. This was the husky bodyguard with crinkly blond hair who had been so upset on the train.

'Got the bastard!' Tom whispered with satisfaction. 'This is that body-guard. Look at the gun!'

A gun had fallen half out of the man's right side jacket pocket.

'Farther into the living-room,' Tom said, and they hauled and pushed the man across the floor. 'Mind the rug with that blood!' Tom kicked the rug out of the way. 'Next guy's due in a minute, no doubt. Bound to be two, maybe three.'

Tom took a handkerchief – lavender, monogrammed – from the man's breast pocket and tidied a splotch of blood on the floor near the door. He kicked the man's hat and sent it flying over the body, and it fell near the hall door to the kitchen. Then Tom bolted the front door, holding his left hand over the bolt so it would not make a noise. 'Next one might not be so easy,' he whispered.

There were footsteps on gravel. The bell rang – nervously twice.

Tom laughed without making a sound, and pulled his Luger. He motioned for Jonathan to take his gun also. Tom was suddenly convulsed, and doubled over to repress his mirth, then straightened and grinned at Jonathan, and wiped the tears from his eyes.

Jonathan didn't smile.

The bell rang again, a long steady peal.

Jonathan saw Tom's face change in a split-second. Tom frowned, grimaced, as if he didn't know what he should do.

'Don't use the gun,' Tom whispered, 'unless you have to.' His left hand was extended towards the door.

Tom was going to open the door and fire, Jonathan supposed, or cover the man.

Then steps crunched again. The man outside was walking towards the window behind Jonathan, a window now quite covered by the curtains. Jonathan edged away from the window.

'Angy? – *Angy!*' the man's voice whispered.

'Ask him at the door what he wants,' Tom whispered. 'Talk in English – as if you were the butler. Let him in. I'll have him covered. – Can you do it?'

Jonathan didn't care to think whether he could or not. Now there was a knocking, then another ring of the bell. 'Who is it, please?' Jonathan called to the door.

'*Je – je voudrais demander mon chemin; s'il vous plaît.*' The accent was not so good.

Tom smirked.

'Whom did you wish to speak to, sir?' Jonathan asked.

'*Une direction! – S'il vous plaît!*' the voice yelled. Desperation had entered in.

Tom and Jonathan exchanged a glance, and Tom gestured for Jonathan to open the door. Tom was immediately to the left of the door to anyone standing outside, but out of sight if the door were opened.

Jonathan slid the bolt, turned the knob of the automatic lock, and opened the door partway, fully expecting a bullet in his abdomen, but he stood tall and stiffly with his right hand in his jacket pocket on the gun.

The somewhat shorter Italian, wearing a hat like the other man, also had his hand in his pocket and was plainly surprised to see a tall man in ordinary clothes in front of him.

'Sir?' Jonathan noticed that the man's left jacket sleeve was empty.

As the man took a step inside the house, Tom poked him in the side with his Luger.

'Give me your gun!' Tom said in Italian.

Jonathan's gun was also pointed at him now. The man heaved his jacket pocket up as if to fire, and Tom pushed him in the face with his left hand. The man didn't fire. The Italian looked paralysed at finding himself suddenly so close to Tom Ripley.

'Reeply!' the Italian said, in a tone of mingled terror, surprise, and maybe triumph.

'Oh, never mind that and give us the gun!' Tom said in English, poking the man again in the ribs and knocking the door shut with his foot.

The Italian got the idea, at least. He dropped the gun on the floor, when Tom indicated that was what he wanted. Then the Italian saw his chum on the floor yards away, and started, wide-eyed.

'Bolt the door,' Tom said to Jonathan. Then Tom said in Italian, 'Any more of you?'

The Italian shook his head vigorously, which meant nothing, Tom thought. Tom saw that his arm was in a sling under his jacket. So much for the newspaper reports.

'Cover him while I do this,' Tom said, beginning to frisk the Italian. 'Off with your jacket!' Tom took the man's hat off and threw it in Angy's direction.

The Italian let his jacket slide off and drop. His shoulder-holster was empty. There were no weapons in his pockets.

'Angy –' said the Italian.

'Angy *è morto*,' Tom said. 'So will you be, if you don't do what we say. You want to die? What's your name? – What's your *name*?'

'Lippo. Filippo.'

'Lippo. Keep your hands up and don't move. Your hand. Go stand over there.' He motioned for Lippo to go stand by the dead man. Lippo lifted his good right arm. 'Cover him, Jon, I want to have a look at their car.'

With his Luger ready, Tom went out and turned right on the road, approaching the car cautiously. He could hear the motor. The car was at the side of the road with parking lights on. Tom stopped and closed his eyes for a few seconds, then opened them wide, trying to see if there was any movement at the sides of the car or behind the back window. He advanced slowly and steadily, expecting possibly a shot from the car Silence. Could they have sent only two men? Tom hadn't brought a torch in his nervousness. With his gun pointed at someone who might be crouched in the front seat, Tom opened the left-side door. The interior light came on. The car was empty. Tom closed the door enough to shut the light off, stooped, and listened. He didn't hear anything. Tom trotted back and opened the gates of Belle Ombre, then went back to the car and backed it on to the gravel. A car passed just then on the road, coming from the village direction. Tom turned off the ignition and the parking lights. He knocked and announced himself to Jonathan.

'It seems this is all of them,' Tom said.

Jonathan was standing where Tom had seen him last, pointing his gun at Lippo, who now had his good arm down and hanging a little out from his side.

Tom smiled at Jonathan, then at Lippo. 'All alone now, Lippo? Because if you're lying, it's *finito* for you, you get me?'

Mafia pride seemed to be returning to Lippo, and he merely narrowed his eyes at Tom.

'*Risponde*, you ...!'

'*Sì!*' said Lippo, angry and scared.

'Getting tired, Jonathan? Sit down.' Tom pulled up a yellow upholstered chair for him. 'You can sit down, too, if you want to,' Tom said to Lippo. 'Sit next to your pal.' Tom spoke in Italian. His slang was returning.

But Lippo remained standing. He was a bit over thirty, Tom supposed, about five feet ten, with round but strong shoulders and a paunch already starting, hopelessly dumb, not capo material. He had straight black hair, a pale olive face that was now faintly green.

'Remember me from the train? A little bit?' Tom asked, smiling. He glanced at the blond hulk on the floor. 'If you behave well, Lippo, you won't end up like Angy. All right?' Tom put his hands on his hips, and smiled at Jonathan. 'Suppose we have a gin and tonic for fortification? You're all right, Jonathan?' Jonathan's colour had returned, Tom saw.

Jonathan nodded with a tense smile. 'Yep.'

Tom went into the kitchen. While he was pulling out the ice tray, the telephone rang. 'Never mind the phone, Jonathan!'

'Right!' Jonathan had a feeling it was Simone again. It was now 9.45 p.m.

Tom was wondering how to force Lippo to get his chums off his trail. The telephone rang eight times and stopped. Tom had unconsciously counted the rings. He went into the living-room with a tray of two glasses, ice, and an open tonic bottle. The gin was on the bar cart near the dining-table.

Tom handed Jonathan his drink and said, 'Cheers!' He turned to Lippo. 'Where's your headquarters, Lippo? Milano?'

Lippo chose to maintain an insolent silence. What a bore. Lippo would have to be beaten up a little. Tom glanced with distaste at the splotch of drying blood under Angy's head, set his glass down on the wooden chest by the door, and went back to the kitchen. He wet a sturdy floor-cloth – called a *torchon* by Mme Annette – and mopped up the blood from Mme Annette's waxed parquet. Tom pushed aside Angy's head with his foot, and stuck the cloth under it. No more blood was coming, Tom thought. With sudden inspiration, Tom searched Angy's pockets more thoroughly, trousers, jacket. He found cigarettes, a lighter, small change. A wallet in the breast pocket, which he left. There was a wadded handkerchief in a hip pocket, and when Tom pulled it out a garrotte came with it. 'Look!' Tom said to Jonathan. 'Just what I was wanting! Ah, these Mafia rosaries!' Tom held it up and laughed with pleasure. 'For you, Lippo, if you're not a good boy,' Tom said in Italian. 'After all, we don't want to make any noise with guns, do we?'

Jonathan looked at the floor for a few seconds as Tom strolled towards Lippo. Tom was whirling the garrotte around one finger.

'You are of the distinguished Genotti family, *non è vero*, Lippo?'

Lippo hesitated, but very briefly, as if it only flitted across his mind to deny it. '*Si*,' he said firmly, with a trace of *vergogna*.

Tom was amused. Strength in number, in togetherness, the families had. Alone like this one, they turned yellow, or green. Tom was sorry about Lippo's arm, but he wasn't torturing him yet, and Tom knew the tortures the Mafia put its victims to if they didn't come across with money or services – yanked toenails and teeth, cigarette burns. 'How many men have you killed, Lippo?'

'*Nessuno!*' cried Lippo.

'No one,' Tom said to Jonathan. 'Ha, ha.' Tom went to rinse his hands in the little loo opposite the front door. Then he finished his drink, picked up the piece of log beside the front door, and approached Lippos with it. 'Lippo, you're going to telephone your boss tonight. Maybe your new capo, eh? Where is he tonight? Milano? Monaco di Bavaria?' Tom gave Lippo a swat over the head with the wood, just to show he meant business, but the blow was fairly hard, because Tom was nervous.

'Stop it!' yelled Lippo, staggering up from a near collapse, one hand pitifully on top of his head. 'Me a guy with one arm?' he shrieked, talking like himself now, the gutter Italian of Naples, Tom thought, though it could have been of Milan, because Tom was not an expert.

'*Sissi!* And two against one even!' Tom replied. 'We don't play fair, eh? Is that your complaint?' Tom called him something unspeakable, and turned on his heel to get a cigarette. 'Why don't you pray to the Virgin Mary?' Tom said over his shoulder. 'Another thing,' he said to Lippo in English, 'no more shouting or you'll get this over your head in no time flat!' He came down with the piece of firewood in the air – *whish!* – to show what he meant. 'This is what killed Angy.'

Lippo blinked, his mouth slightly open. He was breathing shallowly and audibly.

Jonathan had finished his drink. He was holding the gun pointed at Lippo, holding it in two hands, because the gun had become heavy. He was not at all sure he could hit Lippo if he had to fire it, and anyway Tom was frequently between him and Lippo. Now Tom was shaking the Italian by his belt. Jonathan couldn't understand all of what Tom was saying, some of it being in clipped Italian, the rest in French and in English. Tom was mostly muttering, but his voice finally rose in anger, and he shoved the Italian back and turned round. The Italian had hardly said anything.

Tom went to the radio, pressed a couple of buttons, and a 'cello concerto came on. Tom made the volume medium. Then he made sure the front curtains were completely closed. 'Isn't this dreary,' Tom said apologetically to Jonathan. 'Sordid. He won't tell me where his boss is, so I've got to hit him a bit. Naturally he's as afraid of his boss as he is of me.' Tom gave Jonathan a quick smile, and went and changed the music. He found some pop. Then he picked up the wood with determination.

Lippo brushed the first blow aside, but Tom bashed him in the temple with a backhand stroke. Lippo had yelped, and now he cried, '*No! Lasciame!*'

'Your boss's number!' Tom yelled.

Crack! That was a swat at Lippo's middle, which caught the hand Lippo had put there to protect himself. Glass particles fell on the floor. Lippo wore his watch on his right wrist, the watch must have been shattered, and Lippo held his hand in pain against his abdomen, while he looked at the glass on the floor. He gasped for breath.

Tom waited. The log was poised.

'Milano!' Lippo said.

'All right, you're going to –'

Jonathan missed the rest.

Tom was pointing to the telephone. Then Tom went to the table near the front windows where the telephone was and got a pencil and paper. He was asking the Italian the number in Milan.

Lippo gave a number and Tom wrote it down.

Then Tom made a longer speech, after which he turned to Jonathan and said, 'I've told this guy he's going to be garrotted if he doesn't ring his boss and tell him what I want him to say.' Tom adjusted the garrotte for action, and as he turned to face Lippo, the sound of a car came from the road, the sound of a car stopping at the gates.

Jonathan stood up, thinking it was either Italian reinforcements or Simone in Gérard's car. Jonathan didn't know which would be the worse fate, both seeming a death of sorts at that moment.

Tom didn't want to part the curtains to look out. The motor purred on. Lippo's face showed no change, no sign of relief that Tom could see.

Then the car moved on, towards the right. Tom looked between the curtains. The car was going on, very much on, and all was well, unless the car had let out a few men to hide in the bushes and fire through the windows. Tom listened for several seconds. It might have been the Grais, Tom thought, might have been the Grais who had telephoned a few minutes ago, and maybe they'd seen the strange car on the gravel inside the gates, and decided to go on, thinking the Ripleys had visitors.

'Now, Lippo,' Tom said calmly, 'you're going to telephone your boss, and I'm going to listen with this little gadget.' Tom picked up the round earpiece that was clipped to the back of his telephone, which the French employed for the second ear to augment the sound. 'And if anything doesn't sound *perfect* to me,' Tom continued in French now, which he could see the Italian understood, 'I won't hesitate to pull this suddenly tight, you see?' Tom illustrated with the noose around his wrist, then he walked towards Lippo and flipped the garrotte over Lippo's head.

Lippo jerked back a little in surprise, then Tom led him forward like a dog on a leash towards the telephone. He pushed Lippo down in the chair there, so Tom was in a position to apply strength on the garrotte.

'Now I'll get the number for you, collect, I'm afraid. You will say you are in France, and you and Angy think you are being followed. You will say you have seen Tom Ripley, and Angy says he is not the man you were looking for. Right? Understand? Any funny words, code words and – this –' Tom tightened the garrotte, but not so tight that it disappeared into Lippo's neck.

'Sissi!' said Lippo, staring in terror from Tom to the telephone.

Tom dialled the operator, and asked for the long-distance operator, for Milan, Italy. When the operator asked for his number, as French operators always did, Tom gave it.

'From whom?' asked the operator.

'Lippo. Just Lippo,' Tom replied. Then he gave the number. The operator said she would ring Tom back. He said to Lippo, 'If this turns out to be a corner grocery or one of your girl friends, I'll choke you just the same! Capish?'

Lippo squirmed, looking as if he were desperate to try something by way of escape, but as if he didn't know what, as yet.

The telephone rang.

Tom motioned for Lippo to pick the telephone up. Tom took the earpiece and listened. The operator was saying that the call would be accepted.

'Pronto?' a male voice said at the other end.

Lippo held the telephone with his right hand to his left ear. 'Pronto. Lippo here. Luigi!'

'Sì,' said the other voice.

'Listen, I –' Lippo's shirt was sticking to his back with sweat. 'We saw –'

Tom jerked the garrotte a little to make Lippos get on with it.

'You are in France, no? With Angy?' the other voice said with some impatience. 'Allora – what's the matter?'

'Nothing. I – We saw this fellow. Angy says he is not the man ... No ...'

'And you think you are being followed,' Tom whispered, because the connection was not good, and he hadn't any fear that the man in Milan could hear him.

'And we think – maybe we're being followed.'

'Followed by who?' asked Milan sharply.

'I dunno. So what the — should we do?' Lippos asked, in fluent argot with a word Tom didn't understand. Lippo sounded genuinely scared now.

Tom's ribs tensed with laughter, and he glanced at Jonathan who was still dutifully covering Lippo with his gun. Tom could understand not quite all of what Lippo was saying, but Lippo didn't seem to be pulling any tricks.

'Return?' said Lippo.

'*Sì!*' said Luigi. 'Abandon the car! Take a taxi to the nearest airport! Where are you now?'

'Tell him you've got to hang up,' Tom whispered, gesturing.

'Got to sign off. *Rivederch*, Luigi,' said Lippo and hung up. He looked up at Tom with eyes like a miserable dog's.

Lippo was finished and he knew it, Tom thought. For once Tom was proud of his reputation. Tom had no intention of sparing Lippo's life. Lippo's family wouldn't have spared anyone's life under the circumstances.

'Stand up, Lippo,' Tom said, smiling. 'Let's see what else you've got in your pockets.'

When Tom started to search them, Lippo's good arm twitched back as if to strike him, but Tom didn't bother ducking. Just nerves, Tom thought. Tom felt coins in one pocket, a crumpled bit of paper which on inspection turned out to be a decrepit strip of Italian tram ticket, then in the hip pocket a garrotte, this one a sportif red-and-white striped cord that reminded Tom of a barber's pole, fine as cat-gut, and Tom thought it was.

'Look at this! Still another!' Tom said to Jonathan, holding up the garrotte as if it were a pretty pebble he had found on a beach.

Jonathan barely glanced at the dangling string. The first garrotte was still around Lippo's neck. Jonathan did not look at the dead man who was hardly two yards from him, one shoe turned inward in an unnatural way on the polished floor, but Jonathan kept seeing the prone figure in the margin of his vision.

'My goodness,' Tom said, looking at his watch. He hadn't realized it was so late, after 10 p.m. It had to be done now, he and Jonathan had to drive hours' distance away and get back before sun-up, if possible. They had to dispose of the corpses some distance from Villeperce. South, of course, in the direction of Italy. South-east, perhaps. It didn't really matter, but Tom preferred south-east. Tom took a deep breath, preparatory to action, but the presence of Jonathan inhibited him. However, Jonathan had seen corpses' removal before, and there was no time to lose. Tom picked up the wood from the floor.

Lippo dodged, flung himself on the floor, or tripped and fell, but Tom came down on his head, and again a second time, with the wood. At the same time, Tom had not put his full strength into it – the thought of getting more blood on Mme Annette's floors being in the back of his mind.

'He's only unconscious,' Tom said to Jonathan. 'He's got to be finished, and if you don't want to see it – go in the kitchen, perhaps.'

Jonathan had stood up. He definitely didn't want to see it.

'Can you drive?' Tom asked. 'My car, I mean. The Renault.'

'Yes,' Jonathan said. He had a licence from the early days in France with Roy, his chum from England, but the licence was at home.

'We've got to drive tonight. Go in the kitchen.' Tom motioned Jonathan away. Then Tom bent to his task of pulling the garrotte tight, not a pleasant task – the trite phrase crossed his mind – but what about people who hadn't the merciful anaesthetic, unconsciousness? Tom held the cord tight, the cord had disappeared in flesh, and Tom fortified himself with the thought of Vito Marcangelo succumbing on the Mozart Express by the same means: Tom had brought that job off, and this was his second.

He heard a car, tentative on the road, then rolling up, stopping, with a pull of the handbrake.

Tom kept his grip exactly the same on the garrotte. How many seconds had passed? Forty-five? Not more than a minute, unfortunately.

'What's *that*?' Jonathan whispered, coming in from the kitchen.

The motor of the car was still running.

Tom shook his head.

They both heard light footsteps trotting on the gravel, then a knock at the door. Jonathan felt suddenly weak, as if his knees would give way.

'I think it's Simone,' Jonathan said.

Tom desperately hoped that Lippo was dead. Lippo's face looked merely dark pink. Damn him!

The knock came again. 'M. Ripley? *Jon!*'

'Ask her who's with her,' Tom said. 'If she's with somebody, we can't open the door. Tell her we're busy.'

'Who are you with, Simone?' Jonathan asked through the closed door.

'No one! I've told the taxi to wait. What is happening, Jon?'

Jonathan saw that Tom had heard what she said.

'Tell her to get rid of the taxi,' Tom said.

'Pay off the taxi, Simone,' Jonathan called.

'He is paid!'

'Tell him to leave.'

Simone went away towards the road to do this. They heard the taxi drive off. Simone came back, up the steps and this time she didn't knock, only waited.

Tom straightened up from Lippo, leaving the garrotte on him. Tom was wondering if Jonathan could go out and explain to her that she couldn't come into the house? That they had other people? That they would send for another taxi for her? Tom was thinking of the taxi-driver's impressions. Best to have dismissed this one, rather than *not* show signs of letting Simone into a house that plainly had lights and at least one person in it.

'Jon!' she called. 'Will you open the door? I would like to speak with you.'

Tom said softly, 'Can you wait with her outside while I ring for another taxi? Tell her we're talking business with a couple of other people.'

Jonathan nodded, hesitated an instant, then slid back the bolt. He opened the door not widely, intending to slip out himself, but Simone thrust the door against him suddenly. She was in the foyer.

'Jon! I am sorry to –' Breathless, she glanced around as if looking for Tom Ripley, master of the house, then she saw him, and at the same time saw the two men on the floor. She gave a short cry. Her handbag slipped from her fingers and dropped with a soft thud on the marble. '*Mon dieu!* What is happening here?'

Jonathan gripped one of her hands tightly. 'Don't look at them. These –' Simone stood rigid.

Tom walked towards her. 'Good evening, madame. Don't be frightened. These men were invading the house. They are unconscious. We had a bit of trouble! Jonathan, take Simone into the kitchen.'

Simone didn't walk. She was swaying, and leaned against Jonathan for a moment, then lifted her head and looked at Tom with hysterical eyes. 'They look dead! Murderers! *C'est épouvantable!* Jonathan! I cannot believe that it is you – *here!*'

Tom was going to the bar-cart. 'Can Simone take some brandy, do you think?' he called to Jonathan.

'Yes. We'll go in the kitchen, Simone.' He was prepared to walk between her and the corpses, but she wouldn't move.

Tom, finding the brandy more difficult than the whisky to open, poured whisky into one of the glasses on the cart. He took it to Simone, neat. 'Madame, I realize this is dreadful. These men are of the Mafia – Italians. They came to the house to attack us – me, anyway.' Tom was much relieved to see that she was sipping the whisky, barely grimacing, as if it were medicine that was good for her. 'Jonathan helped me, for which I'm very grateful. Without him –' Tom stopped. Anger was rising again in Simone.

'Without him? What is he doing here?'

Tom stood straighter. He went into the kitchen himself, thinking it was the only way to draw her from the living-room. She and Jonathan followed him. 'That I can't explain tonight, Madame Trevanny. Not now. We've got to leave now – with these men. Would you –' Tom was thinking, had they time, had he time to take her back to Fontainebleau in the Renault, then return to remove the corpses with Jonathan's assistance? No. Tom absolutely didn't want to waste that much time which would mean a good forty minutes. 'Madame, shall I ring for a taxi to take you back to Fontainebleau?'

'I will not leave my husband. I want to know what my husband is doing here – with such filth as you!'

Her fury was directed entirely against him. Tom wished it could all come out now and for ever, in a great burst. He could never deal with angry women – not that he had had to deal with many. To Tom it was a circular chaos, a ring of little fires, and if he successfully extinguished one, the woman's mind leapt to the next. Tom said to Jonathan, 'If Simone could only take a taxi back to Fontainebleau –'

'I know, I know. Simone, it really is best if you go back to our house.'

'Will you come with me?' she asked.

'I – I can't,' Jonathan said, desperate.

'Then you don't want to. You are on his side.'

'If you'll let me talk with you later, darling –'

Jonathan went on in that vein, while Tom thought, perhaps Jonathan wasn't willing, or had changed his mind. Jonathan was getting nowhere with Simone. Tom interrupted:

'Jonathan.' Tom beckoned to him. 'You must excuse us a moment, madame.' Tom spoke with Jonathan in the living-room, in a whisper. 'We've got six hours' work ahead – or I have. I've got to take these two away and dispose of them – and I'd prefer to be back by dawn or before. Are you really willing to help?'

Jonathan felt lost in the sense that he might be lost in the middle of a battle. But the situation seemed already lost in regard to Simone. He could never explain. Going back to Fontainebleau with her would gain him nothing. He had lost Simone, and what else was there to lose? These thoughts flashed in Jonathan's mind like a single image. 'I am willing, yes.'

'Good. Thanks.' Tom gave a tense smile. 'Surely Simone doesn't want to stay here. She could of course stay in my wife's room. Maybe I can find a sedative. But for Christ's sake, she can't come *with* us.'

'No.' Simone was his responsibility. Jonathan felt powerless either to persuade or command. 'I have *never* been able to tell her –'

'There's some danger,' Tom interrupted, then stopped. There was no time to lose in talking, and he went back into the living-room, felt compelled to glance at Lippo whose face was now bluish, or so Tom thought. At any rate, his clumsy body had that abandoned look of the dead – not even dreamlike or sleeplike, but simply an empty look as if consciousness had departed for ever. Simone was coming in from the kitchen, which Tom had been heading for, and he saw that her glass was empty. He went to the bar cart and brought the bottle. He poured more into the glass in her hand, though Simone indicated that she didn't want any more. 'You don't have to drink it, madame,' Tom said. 'Since we must leave, I must tell you there is some danger if you stay in this house. I simply don't know if more of these won't turn up.'

'Then I will go with you. I will go with my husband!'

'That you *cannot*, madame.' Tom was firm.

'What are you going to do?'

'I'm not sure, but we have to get rid of these – this carrion!' Tom gestured. '*Charogne!*' he repeated.

'Simone, you have got to take a taxi back to Fontainebleau,' Jonathan said.

'*Non!*'

Jonathan grabbed her wrist, and with his other hand took the glass, so it wouldn't spill. 'You must do as I say. It's your life, it's my life. We cannot stay and argue!'

Tom leapt up the stairs. He found, after nearly a minute's searching, Heloise's little bottle of quarter-grain pheno-barbitols, which she so seldom took that they were at the back of everything in her medicine cabinet. He went down with two in his fingers, and dropped them casually into Simone's glass – which he had taken from Jonathan – as he topped the glass up with a splash of soda.

Simone drank this. She was sitting on the yellow sofa now. She seemed calmer, though it was too soon for the pills to have taken effect. And Jonathan was on the telephone now, Tom presumed phoning for a taxi. The slender Seine-et-Marne directory was open on the telephone-table. Tom felt a little dazed, the way Simone looked. But Simone looked also stunned with shock.

'Just Belle Ombre, Villeperce,' said Tom when Jonathan glanced at him.

TWENTY

While Jonathan and Simone waited for the taxi, both standing in terrible silence near the front door, Tom went out to the garden via the french windows, and from the toolhouse got the jerry can of spare petrol. To Tom's regret it was not full, but it felt three-quarters full. Tom had his torch with him. When he came round the front corner of the house, he heard a car approaching slowly, the taxi, he hoped. Tom, instead of putting the jerry can in the Renault, set it in the laurels, out of sight. He knocked on the front door and was admitted by Jonathan.

'I think the taxi's here,' Tom said.

Tom said good night to Simone, and let Jonathan escort her to the taxi which was waiting beyond the gates. The taxi drove off, and Jonathan came back.

Tom was refastening the french windows. 'Good Christ,' Tom said, not knowing what else to say, and being immensely relieved to find himself alone with Jonathan again. 'I hope Simone isn't too livid. But I can hardly blame her.'

Jonathan shrugged in a dazed way. He tried to speak and couldn't.

Tom realized his state and said, like a captain giving orders to a shaken crew, 'Jonathan, she'll come round.' And she wouldn't ring the police either, because if she did, her husband would be implicated. Tom's fortitude, his sense of purpose was returning. He patted Jonathan's arm as he walked past him. 'Back in a minute.

Tom got the jerry can from the bushes and put it in the back of his Renault. Then he opened the Italians' Citroën, the interior light came on, and he saw that the fuel gauge registered slightly over half full. That might do; he wanted to drive for more than two hours. The Renault, he knew, had only slightly more than half a tankful, and the bodies were going to be in there. He and Jonathan hadn't had any dinner. That wasn't wise. Tom went back into the house and said:

'We ought to eat something before this trip.'

Jonathan followed Tom into the kitchen, glad to escape for a few moments from the corpses in the living-room. He washed his hands and face in the kitchen sink. Tom smiled at him. Food, that was the answer – for the moment. He got the steak from the fridge and stuck it under the glowing bars. Then he found a plate, a couple of steak knives and two forks. They sat down finally, eating from the same plate, dipping morsels of steak into a saucer of salt and another of HP. It was excellent steak. Tom had even found a half-full bottle of claret on the kitchen counter. There'd been many a time when he'd dined worse.

'That will do you good,' Tom said, and tossed his knife and fork on to the plate.

The clock in the living-room gave a ping, and Tom knew it was 11.30 p.m.

'Coffee?' asked Tom. 'There's Nescafé.'

'No, thanks.' Neither Jonathan nor Tom had spoken while they had bolted the steak. Now Jonathan said, 'How are we going to do it?'

'Burn them somewhere. In their car,' Tom said. 'It isn't necessary to burn them, but it's rather Mafia-like.'

Jonathan watched Tom rinsing a thermos at the sink, careless now of the fact he stood before an open window. Tom was running the hot water. He tipped some of the jar of Nescafé into the thermos and filled it with steaming water.

'Like sugar?' Tom asked. 'I think we'll need it.'

Then Jonathan was helping Tom carry out the blond man, who was now stiffening. Tom was saying something, making a joke. Then Tom said he had changed his mind: both bodies were going into the Citroën.

'... even though the Renault,' Tom said between gasps, 'is bigger.'

It was dark in front of the house now, the distant street lamp not even shedding a glow this far. They tumbled the second body on to the first on the back seat of the Citroën convertible, and Tom smiled because Lippo's face seemed to be buried in Angy's neck, but he refrained from comment. He found a couple of newspapers on the floor of the car and spread them over the dead men, tucking them in as best he could. Tom made sure that Jonathan knew how the Renault worked, showed him the turn signals, the headlights and the bright lights.

'Okay, start it. I'll close the house.' Tom went into the house, left one light on in the living-room, came out and closed the front door and double-locked it.

Tom had explained to Jonathan that their first objective was Sens, then Troyes. From Troyes they would go farther eastwards. Tom had a map in his car. They would rendezvous first at Sens at the railway station. Tom put the thermos in Jonathan's car.

'You're feeling all right?' Tom asked. 'Don't hesitate to stop and drink some coffee if you feel like it.' Tom waved him a cheerful good-bye. 'Go ahead out first. I want to close the gates. I'll pass you.'

So Jonathan drove out first, Tom closed his gates and padlocked them, then soon passed Jonathan on the way to Sens, which was only thirty minutes away. Jonathan seemed to be doing all right in the Renault. Tom spoke briefly to him at Sens. At Troyes, they were again to go to the railway station. Tom didn't know the town, and on the road it was dangerous for one car to try to follow another, but the way to 'La Gare' was pretty well marked in every town.

It was about 1 a.m. when Tom got to Troyes. He hadn't seen Jonathan behind him for more than half an hour. He went into the station café for a coffee, a second coffee, and kept a look-out through the glass door for the Renault which might pull into the parking area in front of the station. Finally Tom paid and went out, and as he walked towards his own car, his Renault came down the slope into the parking area. Tom gave a wave, and Jonathan saw him.

'You're all right?' Tom asked. Jonathan looked all right to Tom. 'If you want some coffee here, or to use the loo, best go in alone.'

Jonathan didn't want either. Tom persuaded him to drink some coffee out of the thermos. No one was giving them a glance, Tom saw. A train had just come in and ten or fifteen people were heading for their parked cars or to the cars of people who had come to meet them.

'From here we take the National Nineteen,' Tom said. 'We'll aim for Bar – Bar-sur-Aube – and meet again at the railway station. All right?'

Tom started off. The highway became clearer, with very little traffic except two or three elephantine trucks, their rectangular rears outlined in white or red lights, moving forms which might have been blind, Tom felt, blind at least to the two corpses in the back of the Citroën under newspaper, such a tiny cargo compared to theirs. Tom was not going fast now, not more than ninety kilometres or around fifty-five miles per hour. At the Bar railway station he and Jonathan leaned out of their windows to speak with one another.

'Petrol's getting low,' Tom said. 'I want to go beyond Chaumont, so I'm going to pull in at the next petrol station, okay? And you do the same.'

'Right,' said Jonathan.

It was now 2.15 a.m. 'Keep on the old N nineteen. See you at the railway station in Chaumont.'

Tom pulled in at a Total station as he was leaving Bar. He was paying the man, when Jonathan drove in behind him. Tom lit a cigarette and didn't glance at Jonathan. Tom was walking about, stretching his legs. Then he pulled his car a little aside and went to the toilet. It was only forty-two kilometres to Chaumont.

And there Tom arrived at 2.55 a.m. Not even a taxi stood at the railway station, only a few parked and empty cars. There were no more trains tonight. The station bar-café was closed. When Jonathan arrived, Tom approached the Renault on foot, and said:

'Follow me. I'm going to look for a quiet spot.'

Jonathan was tired, but his fatigue had switched into another gear: he could have gone on driving for hours more, he felt. The Renault handled tightly and quickly, with the minimum of effort on his part. Jonathan was totally unfamiliar with the country here. That didn't matter. And now it was easy, he merely kept the red tail-lights of the Citroën in view. Tom was going more slowly, and twice paused tentatively at side roads, then went on. The night was black, the stars not visible, at least not with the glow of the dashboard before him. A couple of cars passed, going in the opposite direction, and one lorry overtook Jonathan. Then Jonathan saw Tom's right indicator pulse, and Tom's car disappeared to the right. Jonathan followed, and barely saw the black gorge that was the road, or lane, when he came to it. It was a dirt road that led at once into forest. The road was narrow, not wide enough for two cars to pass, the kind of road often found in the French countryside, used by farmers or men gathering wood. Bushes scraped delicately at the front fenders, and there were potholes.

Tom's car stopped. They had gone perhaps two hundred yards from the main road in a great curve. Tom had cut his lights, but the interior of the car lit when he opened the door. Tom left the door open, and walked towards Jonathan, waving his arms cheerfully. Jonathan was at that instant cutting his own motor and his lights. The image of Tom's figure in the baggy trousers, green suede jacket, stayed in Jonathan's eyes for a moment as if Tom had been composed of light. Jonathan blinked.

Then Tom was beside Jonathan's window. 'It'll be over in a couple of minutes. Back your car about fifteen feet. You know how to reverse?'

Jonathan started the car. The car had backing lights. When he stopped, Tom opened the second door of the Renault and pulled out the jerry can. Tom had his torch.

Tom poured petrol on to the newspapers over the two corpses, then on their clothing. Tom splashed some on the roof, then the upholstery – unfortunately plastic, not cloth – of the front seat also. Tom looked up, straight up where the branches of the trees almost closed together above the road – young leaves, not yet in their fullness of summer. A few would get singed, but it was for a worthy cause. Tom shook the last drops from the jerry can on to the floor of the car where there was rubbish, the remains of a sandwich, an old road map.

Jonathan was walking slowly towards him.

'Here we go,' Tom said softly, and struck a match. He had left the front door of the car open. He flung the match into the back of the car, where the newspapers flared up yellow at once.

Tom stepped back, and grabbed Jonathan's hand as his foot slipped in a depression at the side of the road. 'In the car!' Tom whispered, and trotted towards the Renault. He got into the driver's seat, smiling. The Citroën was taking nicely. The roof had started to burn in one central, thin yellow flame, like a candle.

Jonathan got in on the other side.

Tom started his motor. He was breathing a little hard, but it soon became laughter. 'I think that's all *right*. Don't you? I think that's just great!'

The Renault's lights burst forward, diminishing the growing holocaust in front of them for an instant. Tom backed, fairly fast, his body twisted so he could see through the back window.

Jonathan stared at the burning car, which completely disappeared as they backed along the curve in the road.

Then Tom straightened out. They were on the main road.

'Can you see it from here?' Tom asked, shooting the car forward.

Jonathan saw a light like that of a glowworm through the trees, then it vanished. Or had he imagined it? 'Not a thing now. No.' For an instant, Jonathan felt frightened by this fact – as if they had failed somehow, as if the fire had died out. But he knew it hadn't. The woods had simply swallowed the fire up, hidden it utterly. And yet, someone would find it. When? How much of it?

Tom laughed. 'It's burning. They'll burn! We're in the clear!'

Jonathan saw Tom glance at his speedometer, which was climbing to a hundred and thirty. Then Tom eased back to a hundred.

Tom was whistling a Neapolitan tune. He felt well, not tired at all, not even in need of a cigarette. Life afforded few pleasures tantamount to disposing of Mafiosi. And yet –

'And yet – ' Tom said cheerfully.

'And yet?'

'Disposing of two does so little. Like stepping on two cockroaches when the whole house is full of them. I believe, however, in making the effort, and above all it's nice to let the Mafia know now and then that people can diminish them. Unfortunately in this case they're going to think another family got Lippo and Angy. At least I hope they'll think that.'

Jonathan was now feeling sleepy. He fought against it, forcing himself to sit up, pressing his nails into his palm. My God, he thought, it was going to be hours before they got home – back to Tom's or to his own house.

Tom seemed fresh as a daisy, singing now in Italian a tune he'd been whistling before.

> '... *papa ne meno*
> *Como faremo fare l'amor ...*'

Tom was chatting on, about his wife now, who was going to stay with some friends in a chalet in Switzerland. Then Jonathan awakened a little as Tom said:

'Put your head back, Jonathan. No need to stay awake. You're feeling all right, I hope?'

Jonathan didn't know how he was feeling. He felt a bit weak, but he often felt weak. Jonathan was afraid to think about what had just happened, about what was happening, flesh and bone being burnt, smouldering on hours from now. Sadness came over Jonathan suddenly, like an eclipse. He wished he could erase the last few hours, cut them out of his memory. Yet he had been there, he had acted, he had helped. Jonathan put his head back and fell half asleep. Tom was talking cheerfully, casually, as if he were having a conversation with someone who now and then replied to him. Jonathan had in fact never known Tom in such good spirits. Jonathan was wondering what he was going to say to Simone? Merely to be aware of that problem exhausted him.

'Masses sung in English, you know,' Tom was saying, 'I find simply embarrassing. Somehow one gives the English-speaking people credit for believing what they're saying, so a mass in English ... you feel either the choir has lost its mind or they're a pack of liars. Don't you agree? Sir John Stainer ...'

Jonathan woke up when the car stopped. Tom had pulled on to the edge of the road. Smiling, Tom was sipping coffee from the thermos cup. He offered some to Jonathan. Jonathan drank a little. They then drove on.

Dawn came over a village that Jonathan had never seen before. The light had awakened Jonathan.

'We're only twenty minutes from home!' Tom said brightly.

Jonathan murmured something, and half shut his eyes again. Now Tom was talking about the harpsichord, his harpsichord.

'The thing about Bach is that he's instantly civilizing. Just a phrase ...'

TWENTY-ONE

Jonathan opened his eyes, thinking he had heard harpsichord music. Yes. It wasn't a dream. He hadn't really been asleep. The music came from downstairs. It faltered, recommenced. A sarabande, perhaps. Jonathan lifted his arm wearily and looked at his wristwatch: 8.38 a.m. What was Simone doing now? What was she *thinking*?

Exhaustion sucked at Jonathan's will. He sank deeper into the pillow, retreating. He'd taken a warm shower, put on pyjamas at Tom's insistence. Tom had given him a new toothbrush and said, 'Get a couple of hours' sleep, anyway. It's terribly early.' That had been around 7 a.m. He had to get up. He had to do something about Simone, had to speak to her. But Jonathan lay limp, listening to the single notes of the harpsichord.

Now Tom was fingering the bass of something, and it sounded correct, the deepest notes a harpsichord could pluck. As Tom had said, *instantly civilizing.* Jonathan forced himself up, out of the pale blue sheets and the darker blue woollen blanket. He staggered, and with an effort stood straight as he walked towards the door. Jonathan went down the stairs barefoot.

Tom was reading the notes from a music book propped in front of him. Now the treble entered, and sunlight came through the slightly parted curtains at the french windows on to Tom's left shoulder, picking out the gold pattern in his black dressing-gown.

'Tom?'

Tom turned at once and got up. 'Yes?'

Jonathan felt worse, seeing Tom's alarmed face. The next thing Jonathan knew, he was on the yellow sofa, and Tom was wiping his face with a wet cloth, a dishtowel.

'Tea? Or a brandy? ... Have you got any pills you take?'

Jonathan felt awful, he knew the feeling, and the only thing that helped was a transfusion. It hadn't been so long since he'd had one. The trouble now was that he felt worse than he usually did. Was it only from losing a night's sleep?

'What?' Tom said.

'I'm afraid I'd better get to the hospital.'

'We'll go,' said Tom. He went away and came back with a stemmed glass. 'This is brandy and water, if you feel like it. Stay there. I'll just be a minute.'

Jonathan closed his eyes. He had the wet towel over his forehead, down one cheek, and felt chilly and too tired to move. It seemed only a minute until Tom was back, dressed. Tom had brought Jonathan's clothing.

'Matter of fact, if you put on your shoes and my topcoat, you won't have to dress,' Tom said.

Jonathan followed this advice. They were in the Renault again, heading for Fontainebleau, and Jonathan's clothes were folded neatly between them. Tom was asking him if he knew exactly where they should go when they got to the hospital, if he could get a transfusion right away.

'I've got to speak with Simone,' Jonathan said.

'We'll do that – or you will. Don't worry about that now.'

'Could you bring her?' Jonathan asked.

'Yes,' said Tom firmly. He hadn't been worried about Jonathan until that instant. Simone would hate the sight of him, but she would come to see her husband, either with Tom or on her own. 'You still have no phone at your house?'

'No.'

Tom spoke to a receptionist in the hospital. She greeted Jonathan as if she knew him. Tom held Jonathan's arm. When Tom had seen Jonathan into the charge of the proper doctor, Tom said, 'I'll have Simone come, Jonathan. Don't worry.' To the receptionist, who was in nurse's uniform, Tom said, 'Do you think a transfusion will do it?'

She nodded pleasantly, and Tom left it at that, not knowing whether she knew what she was talking about or not. He wished he'd asked the doctor. Tom got into his car and drove to the Rue St Merry. He was able to park a few yards from the house, and he got out and walked towards the stone steps with the black handrails. He'd had no sleep, was in slight need of a shave, but at least he had a message that might be of interest to Mme Trevanny. He rang the bell.

There was no answer. Tom rang again, and looked on the pavement for Simone. It was Sunday. No market in Fontainebleau, but she might well be out buying something at 9.50 a.m., or might be at church with Georges.

Tom went down the steps slowly, and as he reached the pavement, he saw Simone walking towards him, Georges beside her. Simone had a shopping basket over her forearm.

'*Bonjour*, madame,' Tom said politely, in the face of her bristling hostility. He continued, 'I only wanted to bring you news of your husband. – *Bonjour*, Georges.'

'I want nothing from you,' Simone said, 'except to know where my husband is.'

Georges stared at Tom alertly and neutrally. He had eyes and brows like his father. 'He is all right, I think, Madame, but he is –' Tom hated saying it on the street. 'He is in the hospital for the moment. A transfusion, I think.'

Simone looked both exasperated and furious – as if Tom were to blame for it.

'May I please speak with you inside your house, madame. It is so much easier.'

After an instant's hesitation, Simone agreed to this, out of curiosity, Tom felt. She unlocked the door with a key which she produced from her coat pocket. It wasn't a new coat, Tom noticed. 'What has happened to him?' she asked when they were in the little hall.

Tom took a breath and spoke calmly. 'We had to drive nearly all night. I think he is merely tired. But – of course I thought you would want to know. I've just brought him to the hospital now. He's able to walk. I do think he's not in danger.'

'Papa! I want to see papa!' Georges said rather petulantly, as if he had asked for papa last evening too.

Simone had set her basket down. '*What* have you done to my husband? He is not the same man I knew – since he met *you*, m'sieur! If you see him again, I – I will –'

It seemed only the presence of her son that kept her from saying that she would kill him, Tom thought.

She said with bitter control of herself, '*Why* is he in your power?'

'He is not in my power and never was. And I think now the job is finished,' Tom said. 'It's quite impossible to explain now.'

'What job?' Simone asked. And before Tom could open his mouth, she continued, 'M'sieur, you are a crook, and you corrupt other people! What sort of blackmail have you subjected him to? And why?'

Blackmail – thé French word *chantage* was so off the beam, Tom stammered as he began to reply. 'Madame, no one is taking money from Jonathan. Or anything from him. Quite the contrary. And he has done nothing to give people power over him.' Tom spoke with genuine conviction, and he certainly had to, because Simone looked the picture of wifely virtue, probity, her fine eyes flashing, and her brows concentrated against him, powerful as the Winged Victory of Samothrace. 'We have spent the night cleaning things up.' Tom felt shabby saying that. His more eloquent French had suddenly deserted him. His words were no match for the virtuous helpmeet who stood before him.

'Cleaning what up?' She stooped to pick up her basket. 'M'sieur, I will be grateful if you leave this house. I thank you for informing me where my husband is.'

Tom nodded. 'I would also be happy to take you and Georges to the hospital, if you like. My car is just outside.'

'*Merci*, non.' She was standing midway in the hall, looking back, waiting for him to leave. 'Come, Georges.'

Tom let himself out. He got into his car, thought of going to the hospital to ask how Jonathan was, because it would be at least ten minutes before Simone could get there either by taxi or on foot. But Tom decided to telephone from his house. He drove home. And once home, he decided not to telephone. By now Simone might be there. Hadn't Jonathan said the transfusion took several hours? Tom hoped it wasn't a crisis, that it wasn't the beginning of the end.

He turned on France Musique for company, opened his curtains wider to the sunlight, and tidied the kitchen. He poured a glass of milk, went upstairs and got into pyjamas again and went to bed. He could shave when he woke up.

Tom hoped that Jonathan could straighten things out with Simone. But it was the same old problem: how did the Mafia get tied up, how could they possibly be tied up with two German doctors?

This unsolvable problem began to make Tom sleepy. And Reeves. What was happening to Reeves in Ascona? Madcap Reeves. Tom still had a lurking affection for him. Reeves was now and then maladroit, but his crazy heart was in the right place.

Simone sat beside the flat bed, more wheels than bed, on which Jonathan lay taking in blood through a tube in his arm. Jonathan as usual avoided looking at the jar of blood. Simone was grim. She had spoken with the nurse out of Jonathan's hearing. Jonathan thought his condition now wasn't serious (assuming Simone had heard anything), or Simone would have been more concerned about him, kinder. Jonathan was propped on a pillow, and there was a white blanket pulled up to his waist for warmth.

'And you're wearing that man's pyjamas,' Simone said.

'Darling, I had to wear something – to sleep in. It must've been six in the morning when we got back –' Jonathan broke off, feeling hopeless and tired. Simone had told him that Tom had called at the house to tell her where he was. Simone's reaction had been anger. Jonathan had never seen her so grim. She detested Tom as if he were Landru or Svengali. 'Where's Georges?' Jonathan asked.

'I telephoned Gérard. He and Yvonne are coming to the house at ten-thirty. Georges will let them in.'

They would wait for Simone, Jonathan thought, then they would all go to Nemours for Sunday lunch. 'They want me to stay here till at least three, I know,' Jonathan said. 'The tests, you know.' He knew she knew, probably another marrow sample would be taken, which required only ten or fifteen minutes, but there were always other tests, urine, the spleen-feeling. Jonathan still did not feel well, and he didn't know what to expect. Simone's hardness further upset him.

'I cannot understand. I cannot,' she said. 'Jon, why do you *see* this monster?'

Tom was not really such a monster. But how to explain? Jonathan tried again. 'Do you realize that last night – those men were killers? They had guns, they had garrottes. *Tu comprends, garrottes* – They came to Tom's house.'

'And why were you there?'

Gone was the excuse of paintings that Tom wanted framed. One didn't help Tom kill people, help him get rid of corpses, because one was going to frame a few pictures. And what was the favour Tom Ripley had done him to make him cooperate so? Jonathan closed his eyes, gathering strength, trying to think.

'Madame –' That was the nurse's voice.

Jonathan heard the nurse telling Simone that she should not tire her husband. 'I promise you that I will explain, Simone.'

Simone had stood up. 'I think you cannot explain. I think you are afraid to. This man has trapped you – and why? For money. He pays you. But why? You want me to think that you are a criminal too? Like that monster?'

The nurse had gone away and couldn't hear. Jonathan looked at Simone through half-closed eyes, desperate, wordless, defeated, for the moment. Couldn't he make her see, some time, that it was not so black and white as she thought? But Jonathan felt a chill of fear, a premonition of failure, like death.

And Simone was leaving, as if on a final word – *her* word, *her* attitude. At the doorway she blew him a kiss, but perfunctorily, like a person in church genuflecting barely, without thinking, as he passed some object. She was gone. The day ahead stretched like a bad dream to come. The hospital might decide to keep him overnight. Jonathan closed his eyes and moved his head from side to side.

They were almost finished with the tests by 1 p.m.

'You have been under a strain, haven't you, m'sieur?' asked a young doctor. 'Any unusual exertions?' Unexpectedly, he laughed, 'Moving house? Or too much gardening?'

Jonathan smiled politely. He was feeling a little better. Suddenly Jonathan laughed too, but not at what the doctor had said. Suppose it had been the beginning of the end, this morning's collapse? Jonathan was pleased with himself because he had pulled through it without losing his nerve. Maybe he could do that one day with the real thing. They let him walk down a corridor for the final test, the spleen palpation.

'M. Trevanny? There is a telephone call for you,' a nurse said. 'Since you are so near –' She motioned towards a desk and a telephone, which was off the hook.

Jonathan felt sure it was Tom. 'Hello?'

'Jonathan, hello. Tom. How is everything? ... Can't be too bad if you're on your feet now ... That's fine.' Tom sounded really pleased.

'Simone was here. Thank you,' Jonathan said. 'But she's –' Even though they were talking in English, Jonathan couldn't get the words out.

'You had a tough time, I can understand.' Platitudes. Tom at his end heard the anxiety in Jonathan's voice. 'I did my best this morning, but do you want me to – to try to talk with her again?'

Jonathan moistened his lips. 'I don't know. It's not of course that she –' He'd been going to say 'threatened anything', such as taking Georges and leaving him. 'I don't know if you *can* do anything. She's so –'

Tom understood. 'Suppose I try? I will. Courage, Jonathan! You're going home today?'

'I'm not sure. I think so. By the way, Simone is with her family in Nemours for lunch today.'

Tom said he wouldn't try to see her till about 5 p.m. If Jonathan was home then, that would be fine.

It was a bit awkward for Tom, Simone's not having a telephone. On the other hand, if there'd been a telephone, she would probably have given him a firm 'No' if he asked if he might come to see her. Tom bought flowers, yellow forced dahlias, from a vendor near the château in Fontainebleau, as he had nothing presentable as yet from his own garden. Tom rang the Trevanny doorbell at 5.20 p.m.

There were steps, them Simone's voice, '*Qui est-ce?*'

'Tom Ripley.'

A delay.

Then Simone opened the door with a stony face.

'Good afternoon – *bonjour, encore,*' Tom said. 'Could I speak with you for a few minutes, madame? Has Jonathan returned?'

'He will be home at seven. He is having another transfusion,' Simone replied.

'Oh?' Tom boldly took a step into the house, not knowing if Simone would flare up or not. 'I brought these for your house, madame.' He presented the flowers with a smile. 'And Georges. *Bonjour*, Georges.' Tom extended his hand, and the child took it, smiling up at him. Tom had thought of bringing sweets for Georges, but he hadn't wanted to overdo it.

'What is it you want?' Simone asked. She had given Tom a cool '*Merci*' in regard to the flowers.

'I definitely must explain. I must explain last night. That is why I am here, madame.'

'You mean – you can explain?'

Tom returned her cynical smile with a fresh and open one. 'As much as anyone can explain the Mafia. Of course! Yes! Come to think of it, I could have bought them off – I suppose. What else do they want except money? However, in this case I'm not so sure, because they had a special grudge against me.'

Simone was interested. But this fact did not diminish her antipathy to Tom. She had taken a step back from him.

'Can't we go into your living-room – perhaps?'

Simone led the way. Georges followed them, gazing fixedly at Tom. Simone motioned Tom to the sofa. Tom sat down on the Chesterfield, gently slapped its black leather and started to pay Simone a compliment on it and didn't.

'Yes, a special grudge,' Tom resumed. 'I – You see, I happened – just happened to be on the same train as your husband when he was returning from a visit to Munich recently. You remember.'

'Yes.'

'Munich!' said Georges, his face lighting up as if in anticipation of a story.

Tom smiled back at him. 'Munich – *Alors*, on this train – for reasons of my own – I will not hesitate to tell you, madame, that sometimes I take the law into my own hands just as much as the Mafia do. The difference is, I don't blackmail honest people, I don't need protection money from people who wouldn't need protection if not for my threats.' It was so abstract, Tom was sure Georges was not following it, despite Georges' intense gaze at Tom.

'What're you getting at?' Simone asked.

'At the fact that I killed one of those beasts on the train, and nearly killed the other – pushed him out – and Jonathan was there and saw me. You see –' Tom was only briefly daunted by the shock in Simone's face, by her fearful glance at Georges who was following the story avidly, and perhaps thought that 'beasts' were indeed animals, or maybe that Tom was making it up as he went along. 'You see, I had time to explain the situation to Jonathan. We were on the platform – on the moving train. Jonathan kept a look-out for me, that's all he did. But I'm grateful. He helped. And I hope you see, Madame Trevanny, that it was for a good cause. Look at the way the French police are fighting the Mafia down in Marseille, the drug merchants. Look at the way *everyone* is fighting the Mafia! Trying to. But one must expect dangerous retaliations from them, you know that. So that's what happened last night. I –' Did he dare say he had asked for Jonathan's help? Yes. 'It was entirely my fault that Jonathan was at my house, because I asked him if he would be willing to help me again.'

Simone looked puzzled, and highly suspicious. 'For money, of course.'

Tom had expected this, and remained calm. 'No. No, madame.' It was a matter of honour, Tom started to say, but that didn't completely make sense, even to him. Friendship, but Simone wouldn't like that. 'It was kindness on Jonathan's part. Kindness and courage. You shouldn't reproach him.'

Simone shook her head slowly, disbelieving. 'My husband is not a police agent, m'sieur. Why don't you tell me the truth?'

'But I am,' Tom said simply, opening his hands.

Simone sat tensely in the armchair, her fingers working together now. 'Very recently,' she said, 'my husband has received quite a bit of money. Are you saying that that has nothing to do with you?'

Tom leaned back on the sofa and crossed his feet at the ankles. He was wearing his oldest, nearly worn-out desert boots. 'Ah, yes. He told me a little about that,' Tom said with a smile. 'The German doctors are making a bet together, and they've entrusted the take to Jonathan. Isn't that right? I thought he'd told you.'

Simone merely listened, waiting for more.

'In addition, Jonathan told me they'd given him a bonus – or prize money. After all they are using him to experiment on.'

'He also told me there was no – no real danger in the drugs, so why should he be paid?' She shook her head and laughed briefly. 'No, m'sieur.'

Tom was silent. His face showed disappointment, and he meant it to. 'There are stranger things, madame. I'm simply telling you what Jonathan told me. I have no reason to think it isn't true.'

That was the end of it. Simone stirred restlessly in her chair, then stood up. She had a lovely face, clear, handsome eyes and brows, an intelligent mouth that could be soft or stern. Just now it was stern. She gave him a polite smile. 'And what do you know about the death of M. Gauthier? Anything? I understand you often bought things at his shop.'

Tom had stood up, and he faced this, at least, with a clear conscience. 'I know that he was run over, madame, by a hit-and-run driver.'

'That is all you know?' Simone's voice was a little higher pitched, and it trembled.

'I know that it was an accident.' Tom wished that he hadn't to speak in French. He felt he was being blunt. 'That accident makes no sense. If you think I – that I had anything to do with it, madame – then perhaps you will tell me for what purpose. Really, madame –' Tom glanced at Georges, who was now reaching for a toy on the floor. Gauthier's death was like something in a Greek tragedy. But no, Greek tragedies had reasons for everything.

Her mouth twitched a little, bitterly. 'I trust you won't have need of Jonathan again?'

'I won't call on him if I do,' Tom said pleasantly. 'How is –'

'I would think,' she interrupted, 'the people to call are the police. Don't you agree? Or perhaps you are already in the secret police? Of America, perhaps?'

Her sarcasm had very deep roots, Tom realized. He was never going to succeed with Simone. Tom smiled a little, though he felt slightly wounded. He'd endured worse words in his life, but in this case it was a pity because he had so wanted to convince Simone. 'No, that I am not. I get into scrapes now and then, as I think you know.'

'Yes. I know.'

'Scrapes, what is scrapes?' Georges piped up, his blond head turning from Tom to his mother. He was on his feet, very near them.

Tom had used the word *pétrins* – which he'd had to grope for.

'Sh-h, Georges,' said his mother.

'But in this case, you must admit to take on the Mafia is not a bad thing.' Whose side are you on, Tom wanted to ask, but that would be rubbing it in.

'M. Ripley, you are an extremely sinister personage. That is all I know. I would be most grateful if you left both me and my husband alone.'

Tom's flowers lay on the hall table, waterless.

'How is Jonathan now?' Tom asked in the hall. 'I hope he's better.' Tom was even afraid to say he hoped Jonathan would be home tonight, lest Simone think he intended to use him again.

'I think he is all right – better. Good-bye, M. Ripley.'

'Good-bye and thank you,' Tom said. '*Au revoir*, Georges.' Tom patted the boy's head, and Georges smiled.

Tom went out to his car. Gauthier! A familiar face, a neighbourhood face, now gone. It piqued Tom that Simone thought he had had something to do with it, had arranged it, even though Jonathan had told him days ago that Simone thought this. My God, the taint! Well, yes, he had the taint, all right. Worse, he had killed people. True. Dickie Greenleaf. *That* was the taint, the real crime. Hot-headedness of youth. Nonsense! It had been greed, jealousy, resentment of Dickie. And of course Dickie's death – rather his murder – had caused Tom to the kill the American slob called Freddie Miles. Long past, all that. But he had done it, yes. The law half-suspected it. But they couldn't prove it. The story had crept through the public, the public mind, like ink creeping through a blotter. Tom was ashamed. A youthful, dreadful mistake. A fatal mistake, one might think, it was just that he had had amazing luck afterwards. He'd survived it, physically speaking. And surely his – murder since then, Murchison for instance, had most certainly been done to protect others as much as himself.

Simone was shocked – what woman wouldn't have been – at seeing two corpses on the floor when she walked into Belle Ombre last night. But hadn't he been protecting her husband as well as himself? If the Mafia had caught him and tortured him, wouldn't he have come out with the name and address of Jonathan Trevanny?

This made Tom think of Reeves Minot. How was he faring? Tom thought he ought to ring him. Tom found himself staring with a frown at the handle of his car door. His door was not even locked, and his keys, in Tom's usual style, were hanging in the dashboard.

TWENTY-TWO

The evidence of the marrow test, which a doctor took in mid-afternoon Sunday, was not good, and they wanted to keep Jonathan overnight and give him the treatment called Vincainestine, which was a complete change of blood, and which Jonathan had had before.

Simone came to see him just after 7 p.m. They had told Jonathan that she had telephoned earlier. But whoever had spoken to her had not told her that he had to stay overnight, and Simone was surprised.

'So – tomorrow,' she said, and seemed not to find any more words.

Jonathan lay with his head a little raised by pillows. Tom's pyjamas had been changed for a loose garment, and he had a tube in both arms. Jonathan felt a terrible distance between Simone and himself. Or was he imagining it? 'Tomorrow morning, I suppose. Don't trouble to come here, my dear, I'll get a taxi – How was the afternoon? How's your family?'

Simone ignored the question. 'Your friend M. Ripley paid a visit to me this afternoon.'

'Oh, yes?'

'He is so – absolutely full of lies, it is hard to know even what smallest part to believe. Maybe none of it.' Simone glanced behind her, but there was no one. Jonathan's was one of many beds in the ward, not all of them occupied, but the ones on either side of Jonathan were occupied, and one man had a visitor.

They couldn't easily talk.

'Georges will be disappointed that you don't come back tonight,' Simone said.

Then she left.

Jonathan went home the next morning, Monday, around 10 a.m. Simone was at home, ironing some of Georges' clothing.

'Are you feeling all right? ... Did they give you breakfast? ... Would you like some coffee? Or tea?'

Jonathan felt much better – one always did just after a Vincainestine, until his disease got to work and ruined the blood again, he thought. He wanted only a bath. He had a bath, then put on different clothes, old beige corduroy trousers, two sweaters because the morning was cool, or perhaps he was feeling the chill more than usually. Simone was ironing in a short-sleeved woollen dress. The morning newspaper, the *Figaro*, lay folded on the kitchen table with its front page outermost, as usual, but it was obvious from the looseness of the paper that Simone had looked at it.

Jonathan picked up the paper, and since Simone did not look up from her ironing, he walked into the living-room. He found a two-column item in a bottom corner of the second page.

TWO CORPSES INCINERATED IN CAR

The dateline was 14 May, Chaumont. A farmer named René Gault, fifty-five, had found the still-smoking Citroën early on Sunday morning, and had at once alerted the police. The still unburnt papers in the wallets of the dead men identified them as Angelo Lippari, thirty-three, contractor, and Filippo Turoli, thirty-one, salesman, both of Milan. Lippari had died of skull fractures, Turoli of unknown causes, though he was believed to have been unconscious or dead when the car was set alight. There were no clues at the moment, and police were making investigations.

The garrotte had been completely burnt, Jonathan supposed, and evidently Lippo so badly burnt that the signs of garrotting had been destroyed.

Simone came into the doorway with folded clothing in her hands. 'So? I saw it too. The two Italians.'

'Yes.'

'And you helped M. Ripley to do that. That is what you called "cleaning up".'

Jonathan said nothing. He gave a sigh, sat down on the luxuriously squeaking Chesterfield sofa, but he sat up rather straight, lest Simone think he was retreating on grounds of weakness. 'Something had to be done with them.'

'And you simply had to help,' she said. 'Jon – now that Georges is not here – I think we should talk about this.' She put the clothes on top of the waist-high bookcase by the door, and sat down on the edge of the arm-chair. 'You are not telling me the truth, and neither is M. Ripley. I am wondering what else you are going to be obliged to do for him.' On the last words, her voice rose with hysteria.

'Nothing.' Jonathan did feel sure of that. And if Tom asked him to do anything else, he could quite simply refuse. At that moment, it seemed quite simple to Jonathan. He had to hold on to Simone at any cost. She was worth more than Tom Ripley, more than anything Tom could offer him.

'It is beyond my understanding. You knew what you were doing – last night. You helped to kill those men, didn't you?' Her voice dropped, and it trembled.

'It was a matter of protecting – what had gone before.'

'Ah, yes, M. Ripley explained. By accident you were on the same train as he was, coming from Munich, is that right? And you – assisted him in – in *killing* two people?'

'Mafia,' Jonathan said. What *had* Tom told her?

'You – an ordinary passenger, assist a murderer? You expect me to believe that, Jon?'

Jonathan was silent, trying to think, miserable. The answer was no. *You don't seem to realize they were Mafia,* Jonathan wanted to repeat. *They were attacking Tom Ripley.* Another lie, at least in regard to the train. Jonathan pressed his lips together, and sat back on the generous sofa. 'I don't expect you to believe it. I have only two things to say, this is the end of it, and the men we killed were criminals and murderers themselves. You must admit that.'

'Are you a secret police agent in your spare time? *Why* are you being paid for this, Jon? You – a killer!' She stood up with her hands clenched. 'You are a stranger to me. I have never known you before now.'

'Oh, Simone,' Jonathan said, standing up too.

'I cannot like you and I cannot love you.'

Jonathan blinked. She had said that in English.

She continued in French: 'You are leaving out something, I know. And I don't even want to know what it is. Do you understand? It is some horrible connection with M. Ripley, that odious personage – and I wonder what,' she added with the bitter sarcasm again. 'Plainly it is something too disgusting for you to tell me, I shouldn't wonder. You've no doubt covered up some other crime for him, and for this you're being paid, for this you're in his power. Very well, I don't want –'

'I am not in his power! You'll see!'

'I've seen enough!' She went out, taking the clothes with her, and climbed the stairs.

When it came time for lunch, Simone said she wasn't hungry. Jonathan made himself a boiled egg. Then he went to his shop, and kept the FERME sign in the door, because he was not officially open on Mondays. Nothing had changed since Saturday noon. He could see that Simone hadn't been in. Jonathan suddenly thought of the Italian gun, usually in a drawer, now at Tom Ripley's. Jonathan cut one frame, cut the glass for it, but lost heart when it came to driving the nails in. What was he to do about Simone? What if he told her the whole story, just as it had been? Jonathan knew, however, that he was up against a Catholic attitude about taking human life. Not to mention that Simone would consider the original proposition to him '*Fantastic! Disgusting!*' Curious that the Mafia was a hundred per cent Catholic, and they didn't mind about human life. But he, Simone's husband, was different. He shouldn't take human life. And if he told her it was a 'mistake' on his part, that he regretted it – Hopeless. First of all, he didn't particularly believe it had been a mistake, so why tell another lie?

Jonathan went with more determination back to his worktable, and got the glue and nails in the picture frame, and sealed it neatly with brown paper on the back. He clipped the owner's name to the picture wire. Then he looked over his orders to be filled, and tackled one more picture, which like the other needed no mat. He went on working until 6 p.m. Then he bought bread and wine, and some ham slices from a charcuterie, enough for dinner for the three of them in case Simone hadn't done any shopping.

Simone said, 'I am in terror that the police will knock on the door at any moment, wanting to see you.'

Jonathan, setting the table, said nothing for a few seconds. 'They will not. Why should they?'

'There is no such thing as no clues. They will find M. Ripley, and he will tell them about you.'

Jonathan was sure she hadn't eaten all day. He found some left-over potatoes – mashed potatoes – in the fridge, and went about preparing the dinner himself. Georges came down from his room.

'What did they do to you in the hospital, papa?'

'I have completely new blood,' Jonathan replied with a smile, flexing his arms. 'Think of that. All new blood – oh, at least eight litres of it.'

'How much is that?' Georges spread his arms also.

'Eight times this bottle,' said Jonathan. 'That's what took all night.'

Though Jonathan made an effort, he couldn't lift the gloom, the silence of Simone. She poked at her food and said nothing. Georges couldn't understand. Jonathan's efforts, failing, embarrassed him, and over coffee he too was silent, not able even to chat with Georges.

Jonathan wondered if she had spoken with her brother Gérard. He steered Georges into the living-room to watch the television, the new set which had arrived a few days ago. The programmes – there were only two channels – weren't interesting for kids at this hour, but Jonathan hoped he would stay with one of them for a while.

'Did you talk to Gérard by any chance?' Jonathan asked, not able to repress the question.

'Of course not. Do you think I could possibly tell him – this?' She was smoking a cigarette, a rare thing for her. She glanced at the doorway to the hall, to be sure Georges was not coming back. 'Jon – I think we should make some arrangement to separate.'

On the television, a French politician was speaking about *syndicats*, trade unions.

Jonathan sat down again in his chair. 'Darling, I do know – It's a shock to you. Will you let a few days pass? I know, somehow, I can make you understand. Really.' Jonathan spoke with utmost conviction, and yet he realized he was not convinced himself, not at all. It was like an instinctive clinging to life, Jonathan thought, his clinging to Simone.

'Yes, of course you think that. But I know myself. I am not an emotional young girl, you know.' Her eyes looked straight at him, hardly angry now, only determined, and distant. 'I am not interested in all your money now, not any of it. I can make my own way – with Georges.'

'Oh, Georges – my God, Simone, I'll support Georges!' Jonathan could hardly believe they were saying these words. He got up, drew Simone up from her chair a little roughly, and some coffee spilled out of her cup into the saucer. Jonathan embraced her, would have kissed her, but she squirmed away.

'Non!' She put her cigarette out, and started clearing the table. 'I am sorry to say also that I don't want to sleep in the same bed with you.'

'Oh, yes, I assumed that.' And you'll go to church tomorrow and say a prayer for my soul, Jonathan thought. 'Simone, you must let a little time go by. Don't say things now that you don't mean.'

'I will not change. Ask M. Ripley. I think he knows.'

Georges came back. Television was forgotten, and he looked at them both with puzzlement.

Jonathan touched Georges' head with his fingertips as he went into the hall. Jonathan had thought to go up to the bedroom – but it wasn't their bedroom any more, and anyway what would he do up there? The television droned on. Jonathan turned in a circle in the hall, then took his raincoat and a muffler, and went out. He walked to the Rue de France and turned left and at the end of the street went into the bar-café on the corner. He wanted to telephone Tom Ripley. He remembered Tom's number.

'Hello?' Tom said.

'Jonathan.'

'How are you? ... I telephoned the hospital, I heard you stayed the night. You're out now?'

'Oh, yes, this morning. I –' Jonathan gasped.

'What's the matter?'

'Could I see you for a few minutes? If you think it's safe. I'm – I suppose I could get a taxi. Surely.'

'Where are you?'

'The corner bar – the new one near the Aigle Noir.'

'I could pick you up. No?' Tom suspected Jonathan had had a bad scene with Simone.

'I'll walk towards the Monument. I want to walk a little. I'll see you there.'

Jonathan felt at once better. It was spurious, no doubt, it was postponing the situation with Simone, but for the moment that didn't matter. He felt like a tortured man momentarily relieved of the torture, and he was grateful for a few moments of the relief. Jonathan lit a cigarette and walked slowly, because it would take Tom nearly fifteen minutes. Jonathan went into the Bar des Sports, just beyond the Hôtel de l'Aigle Noir, and ordered a beer. He tried not to think at all. Then one thought rose to the surface on its own: Simone *would* come round. As soon as he thought consciously about this, he feared that she wouldn't. He was alone now. Jonathan knew he was alone, that even Georges was more than half cut off from him now, because surely Simone was going to keep Georges, but Jonathan was aware that he didn't yet realize it fully. That would take days. Feelings were slower than thoughts. Sometimes.

Tom's dark Renault in a thin stream of other cars came out of the darkness of the woods into the light around the Obelisque, the Monument. It was a little past 8 p.m. Jonathan was on the corner, on the left side of the road, and Tom's right. Tom would have to make the complete circle to regain his road homeward – if they went to Tom's. Jonathan preferred Tom's house to a bar. Tom stopped and unlatched the door.

'Evening!' Tom said.

'Evening,' Jonathan replied, pulling the door shut, and at once Tom moved off. 'Can we go to your place? I don't feel like a crowded bar.'

'Sure.'

'I've had a bad evening. And day, I'm afraid.'

'So I thought. Simone?'

'It seems she's finished. Who can blame her?' Jonathan felt awkward, started to take a cigarette, and found even that purposeless, so he didn't.

'I tried my best,' Tom said. He was concentrating on driving as fast as possible without bringing down a motor-cycle cop, some of whom lurked in the woods at the edge of the road here.

'Oh, it's the money – it's the corpses, good Christ! As for the money, I said I was holding the stake for the Germans, you know.' It was suddenly ludicrous to Jonathan, the money, the bet also. The money was so concrete in a way, so tangible, so useful, and yet not nearly so tangible or meaningful as the two dead men that Simone had seen. Tom was driving quite fast. Jonathan felt unconcerned whether they hit a tree or bounced off the road. 'To put it simply,' Jonathan went on; 'it's the dead men. The fact that I helped – or did it. I don't think she's going to change.' What profiteth it a man – Jonathan could have laughed. He hadn't gained the whole world, nor had he lost his soul. Anyway, Jonathan didn't believe in a soul.

Self-respect was more like it. He hadn't lost his self-respect, only Simone. Simone was morale, however, and wasn't morale self-respect?

Tom did not think Simone was going to change towards Jonathan either, but he said nothing. Maybe he could talk at home, and yet what else could he say? Words of comfort, words of hope, of reconciliation, when he didn't really believe there'd be one? And yet who knew about women? Sometimes they appeared to have stronger moral attitudes than men, and at other times – especially as to political skulduggery and the political swine they could sometimes marry – it seemed to Tom that women were more flexible, more capable of double-think than men. Unfortunately, Simone presented a picture of inflexible rectitude. Hadn't Jonathan said she was a church-goer too? But Tom's thoughts were equally on Reeves Minot now. Reeves was nervous, for no very strong reason that Tom could see. Suddenly Tom was at the turn-off at Villeperce, guiding the car slowly through the familiar, quiet streets.

And there was Belle Ombre behind the tall poplars, a light glowing above the doorway – all intact.

Tom had just made coffee, and Jonathan said he would join him in a cup. Tom heated the coffee a bit, and brought it with the brandy bottle to the coffee-table.

'Speaking of problems,' Tom said, 'Reeves wants to come to France. I phoned him today from Sens. He's in Ascona staying at a hotel called The Three Bears.'

'I remember,' Jonathan said.

'He imagines he's being spied on – by people in the street. I tried to tell him – our enemies don't waste time with that sort of thing. He should know. I tried to discourage him from coming even to Paris. Certainly not to my place, here. I wouldn't call Belle Ombre the safest spot in the world, would you? Naturally, I couldn't even hint at Saturday night, which might've reassured Reeves. I mean, we at least got rid of the two people who saw us on the train. I'm not sure how long the peace and quiet will last.' Tom hitched forward, elbows on his knees, and glanced at the silent windows. 'Reeves doesn't know anything about Saturday night, or didn't say anything, anyway. Might not even connect it, if he reads the papers. I suppose you saw the papers today?'

'Yes,' Jonathan said.

'No clues. Nothing on the radio tonight either, but the TV boys gave it a spot. No clues.' Tom smiled, and reached for one of his small cigars. He extended the box to Jonathan, but Jonathan shook his head. 'What's equally good news, not a question from the townsfolk here. I bought bread

and went to the butcher's today – on foot, taking my time – just to see.
And around seven-thirty p.m. Howard Clegg arrived, one of my neighbours, bringing me a big plastic sack of horse manure from one of his farmer
friends where he buys a rabbit now and then.' Tom puffed on his cigar
and relaxed with a laugh. 'It was Howard who stopped his car outside
Saturday night, remember? He thought we had guests, Heloise and I, and
that it mightn't be the time to deliver horse manure.' Tom rambled on,
trying to fill in the time, while Jonathan, he hoped, lost a little of his
tension. 'I told him Heloise was away for a few days, and I said I'd been
entertaining some friends from Paris, hence the Paris car outside. I think
that went down very well.'

The clock on the mantel struck nine, with pure little pings.

'However, back to Reeves,' Tom said. 'I thought of writing him, saying
I had some grounds for thinking the situation had improved, but two
things stopped me. Reeves might leave Ascona at any hour now, and
second, things haven't improved for him, if the wogs still want to get him.
He's using the name Ralph Platt now, but they know his real name and
what he looks like. There's nothing for Reeves but Brazil, if the Mafia still
wants to get him. And even Brazil –' Tom smiled, but not happily now.

'But isn't he rather used to it?' Jonathan asked.

'Like this? No. Very few people, I suppose, get used to the Mafia and live
to talk about it. They may live, but not very comfortably.'

But Reeves had brought it on himself, Jonathan was thinking. And
Reeves had drawn him into it. No, he'd walked into it of his own free will,
let himself be persuaded – for money. And it was Tom Ripley who had –
at least tried to help him collect that money, even if it had been Tom's idea
from the start, this deadly game. Jonathan's mind spun back to those
minutes on the train between Munich and Strassburg.

'I *am* sorry about Simone,' Tom said. Jonathan's long, cramped figure,
hunched over his coffee cup, seemed to illustrate failure, like a statue.
'What does she want to do?'

'Oh –' Jonathan shrugged. 'She talks about a separation. Taking
Georges, of course. She has a brother, Gérard, in Nemours. I don't know
what she'll say to him – or to her family there. She's absolutely shocked,
you see. And ashamed.'

'I do understand.' So is Heloise ashamed, Tom thought, but Heloise was
more capable of double-think. Heloise knew he dabbled in murder, crime
– yet was it crime? At least recently, with the Derwatt thing, and now the
accursed Mafia? Tom brushed the moral question aside for the moment,
and at the same time found himself flicking a bit of ash off his knee. What

was Jonathan going to do with himself? Without Simone, he'd have no morale at all. Tom wondered if he should try talking to Simone again? But his memory of yesterday's interview discouraged him. Tom didn't fancy trying again with Simone.

'I am finished,' Jonathan said.

Tom started to speak, and Jonathan interrupted:

'You know I'm finished with Simone – or she is with me. Then there's the old business of how long will I live anyway? Why drag it on? So Tom –' Jonathan stood up. 'If I can be of service, even suicidal, I'm at your disposal.'

Tom smiled. 'Brandy?'

'Yes, a little. Thanks.'

Tom poured it. 'I've spent the last few minutes trying to explain why I think – I *think* we're over the hump. That is with the wogs. Of course we're not out of the woods if they catch Reeves – and torture him. He might talk about both of us.'

Jonathan had thought of that. It simply didn't matter much to him, but of course it mattered to Tom. Tom wanted to stay alive. 'Can I be of any service? As a decoy, perhaps? A sacrifice?' Jonathan laughed.

'I don't want any decoys,' Tom said.

'Didn't you say once the Mafia might want a certain amount of blood, as revenge?'

Tom had certainly thought it, but he wasn't sure if he had said it. 'If we do nothing – they may get Reeves and finish him,' Tom said. 'This is called letting nature take its course. I didn't put this idea – assassinating Mafiosi – into Reeves' head, and neither did you.'

Tom's cool attitude took the wind out of Jonathan's sails a little. He sat down. 'And what about Fritz? Any news? I remember Fritz well.' Jonathan smiled, as if recollecting halcyon days, Fritz arriving at Reeves' flat in Hamburg, cap in hand, with a friendly smile and the efficient little pistol.

Tom had to think for a moment who Fritz was: the factotum, the taxi-driver-messenger in Hamburg. 'No. Let's hope Fritz has returned to his folks in the country, as Reeves said. I hope he's staying there. Maybe they're finished with Fritz.' Tom stood up. 'Jonathan, you've got to go home tonight and face the music.'

'I know.' Tom had, however, made him feel better. Tom was realistic, even about Simone. 'Funny, the problem isn't the Mafia any more, it's Simone – for me.'

Tom knew. 'I'll go with you, if you like. Try to talk with her again.'

Jonathan shrugged again. He was on his feet now, restless. He glanced at the painting that Tom had said was called *Man in Chair*, by Derwatt, over the fireplace. He was reminded of Reeves' flat, with another Derwatt over the fireplace, maybe destroyed now. 'I think I'll be sleeping on the Chesterfield tonight – whatever happens,' Jonathan said.

Tom thought of turning on the news. It wasn't the right time to get anything, though, not even to get Italy. 'What do you think? Simone can always forbid me the door. Unless you think it'll make it worse for you if I'm with you.'

'Things could not be worse. All right. I'd like you to come, yes. But what'll we say?'

Tom pushed his hands into the pockets of his old grey flannels. In his right pocket was the small Italian gun which Jonathan had carried on the train. Tom had slept with it under his pillow since Saturday night. Yes, what to say? Tom usually relied on inspiration of the moment, but hadn't he already shot his bolt with Simone? What other brilliant facet of the problem could he come up with, to dazzle her eyes, her brain, and make her see things their way? 'The only thing to do,' Tom said thoughtfully, 'is try and convince her of the safety of everything – now. I admit that's hard to do. That's hurdling the corpses all right. But much of her trouble is anxiety, you know.'

'Well – are things safe?' Jonathan asked. 'We can't be sure, can we? It's Reeves, I suppose.'

TWENTY-THREE

They were in Fontainebleau at 10 p.m. Jonathan led the way up the front steps, knocked, then put his key into the lock. But the door was bolted inside.

'Who is it?' Simone called.

'Jon.'

She slid the bolt. 'Oh, Jon – I was worried!'

That sounded hopeful, Tom thought.

In the next second, Simone saw Tom, and her expression changed.

'Yes – Tom's with me. Can't we come in?'

She looked on the brink of saying no, then she stepped back a little stiffly. Jonathan and Tom went in.

'Good evening, madame,' Tom said.

In the living-room the television was on, some sewing – what looked like a repair on a coat lining – lay on the black leather sofa, and Georges was playing with a toy truck on the floor. The picture of domestic calm, Tom thought. He said hello to Georges.

'Do sit down, Tom,' said Jonathan.

But Tom didn't, because Simone showed no sign of sitting.

'And what is the reason for this visit?' she asked Tom.

'Madame, I –' Tom stammered on, 'I've come to take all the blame on myself, and to try to persuade you to – to be a little kinder to your husband.'

'You are telling me that my husband –' She was suddenly aware of Georges, and with an air of nervous exasperation took him by the hand. 'Georges, you must go upstairs. Do you hear me? Please, darling.'

Georges went to the doorway, looked back, then entered the hall and mounted the stairs, reluctantly.

'Dépêche-toi!' Simone yelled at him, then closed the living-room door. 'You are telling me,' she resumed, 'that my husband knows nothing about these – events, until he just walked in on them. That this sordid money comes from a bet between doctors!'

Tom took a breath. 'The blame is mine. Perhaps – Jon made a mistake in helping me. But can't that be forgiven? He is your husband –'

'He has become a criminal. Perhaps this is your charming influence, but it is a fact. Is it not?'

Jonathan sat down in the armchair.

Tom decided to take one end of the sofa – until Simone ordered him out of the house. Bravely, Tom started again. 'Jon came to see me tonight to discuss this, madame. He is most upset. Marriage – is a sacred thing, you know that well. His life, his courage would be quite destroyed if he lost your affections. You surely realize that. And you should think also of your son, who needs his father.'

Simone was a little affected by Tom's words, but she replied, 'Yes, a father. A real father to respect. I agree!'

Tom heard footsteps on the stone steps, and looked quickly at Jonathan.

'Expecting someone?' Jonathan asked Simone. She had probably telephoned Gérard, he thought.

She shook her head. 'No.'

Tom and Jonathan jumped up.

'Bolt the door again,' Tom whispered in English to Jonathan. 'Ask who it is.'

A neighbour, Jonathan thought as he went to the door. He slid the bolt quietly shut. *'Qui est-ce, s'il vous plaît?'*

'M. Trevanny?'

Jonathan didn't recognize the man's voice, and looked over his shoulder at Tom in the hall.

There'd be more than one, Tom thought.

'Now what?' asked Simone.

Tom put his finger to his lips. Then, not caring what Simone's reaction might be, Tom went down the hall towards the kitchen, which had a light on. Simone was following him. Tom looked around for something heavy. He still had one garrotte in his hip pocket, and of course it wouldn't be necessary if the caller was a neighbour.

'What're you doing?' Simone asked.

Tom was opening a narrow yellow door in a corner of the kitchen. It was a broom closet, and here he saw what he might need, a hammer, and besides that a chisel, plus several innocuous mops and brooms. 'I might be more useful here,' Tom said, picking up the hammer. He was expecting a shot through the door, the sound of the front door being assaulted by shoulders from outside, perhaps. Then he heard the faint click of the bolt being slid – open. Was Jonathan mad?

Simone at once started off boldly into the hall, and Tom heard her gasp. There was a scuffling sound in the hall, then the door slammed shut.

'Mme Trevanny?' said a man's voice.

Simone's cry was shut off before it became a real cry. The sounds came up the hall now towards the kitchen.

Simone appeared, sliding on the heels of her shoes, manhandled by a thick fellow in a dark suit, who had his hand over her mouth. Tom, to the left of the man as he entered the kitchen, stepped out and hit him with the hammer just below his hat-brim in the back of the neck. The man was by no means unconscious, but he released Simone, and straightened up a little, so that Tom had an opportunity to bash him on the nose, and this Tom followed – the man's hat having fallen off – by a blow on the forehead, straightforward and true, as if he had been an ox in a slaughter-house. The man's legs sank under him.

Simone got to her feet, and Tom drew her towards the broom closet corner, which was concealed from the hall. As far as Tom knew, there

was only one other man in the house, and the silence made Tom think
of the garrotte. With his hammer, Tom went up the hall towards the
front door. Quiet as he tried to be, he was still heard by the Italian in
the living-room, who had Jonathan on the floor. It was indeed the old
garrotte again. Tom sprang at him with the hammer raised. The Italian
– in a grey suit, grey hat – released the garrotte and was pulling his
gun from a shoulder-holster when Tom hit him the cheek-bone. More
accurate than a tennis racket, the hammer! The man, who had not quite
stood up, lurched forward, and Tom removed his hat quickly with his
left hand and with his right came down again with the hammer.

Crack! Little Leviathan's dark eyes closed, his pink lips relaxed, and
he thudded to the floor.

Tom knelt beside Jonathan. The nylon cord was already well into
Jonathan's flesh. Tom turned Jonathan's head this way and that, trying
to get at the cord to loosen it. Jonathan's teeth were bared, and he was
trying with his own fingers, but feebly.

Simone was suddenly beside them, holding something that looked like
a letter-opener. She pried with the point of it into the side of Jonathan's
neck. The string loosened.

Tom lost his balance on his heels, sat down on the floor, and sprang
up again. He yanked the curtains of the front window shut. There had
been a gap of six inches between them. Tom thought that a minute and
a half had passed since the Italians had come in. He picked up the hammer
from the floor, went to the front door and bolted it again. There was no
sound from outside, except for the normal-sounding steps of someone
walking past on the pavement, and the hum of a passing car.

'Jon,' said Simone.

Jonathan coughed and rubbed his neck. He was trying to sit up.

The porcine man in grey lay motionless, with his head propped by
accident against a leg of the armchair. Tom tightened his grip on the
hammer, and started to give the man one more blow, but hesitated,
because there was already some blood on the carpet. But Tom thought
the man was still alive.

'Pig,' Tom murmured, and pulled the man up a little by his shirt front
and flamboyant tie, and smashed the hammer head into his left temple.

Georges stood wide-eyed in the doorway.

Simone had brought Jonathan a glass of water. She was kneeling beside
him. 'Go *away*, Georges!' she said. 'Papa is all right! Go in the – Go upstairs, Georges!'

But Georges didn't. He stood there, fascinated by a scene that was perhaps unsurpassed on the television. By the same token, he wasn't taking it too seriously. His eyes were wide, absorbing it all, but he was not terrified.

Jonathan got to the sofa, helped by Tom and Simone. He was sitting up, and Simone had a wet towel for his face. 'I'm really all right,' Jonathan mumbled.

Tom was still listening for footsteps, front or back. Of all times, Tom thought, when he'd meant to create a peaceable impression on Simone! 'Madame, is the garden passageway locked?'

'Yes,' said Simone.

And Tom remembered ornamental spikes along the top of the iron door. He said in English to Jonathan, 'There's probably at least one more of them in a car outside.' Tom supposed Simone understood this, but he couldn't tell from her face. She was looking at Jonathan, who seemed to be quite out of danger, and then she went to Georges who was still in the doorway.

'Georges! Will you –!' She shooed him upstairs again, carried him halfway up the stairway, and spanked his bottom once. 'Go into your room and close the door!'

Simone was being splendid, Tom thought. It would be a matter of seconds until another man, just as at Belle Ombre, came to the door, Tom supposed. Tom tried to imagine what the man in the car would be thinking: from the absence of noise, of screams, of gunshots, the waiting man or men probably supposed that everything had gone as planned. They must be expecting their two chums to come out the door at any moment, mission accomplished, the Trevannys garrotted or beaten to death. Reeves must have talked, Tom thought, must have told them Jonathan's name and address. Tom had a wild idea of Jonathan and himself putting on the Italians' hats, making a dash out the door to the Italians' car (if any), and taking them by surprise with – the one small gun. But he couldn't ask Jonathan to do that.

'Jonathan, I'd better go out before it's too late,' Tom said.

'Too late – how?' Jonathan had wiped his face with the wet towel, and some blond hair stood on end above his forehead.

'Before they come to the door. They'll be suspicious if their chums don't come out.' If the Italians saw the situation here, they'd blast the three of them with guns and make a getaway in their car, Tom was thinking. Tom went to the window and stooped, looking out just above the sill level. He listened for a car motor idling somewhere, looked for a car stationed with parking lights on. Parking was permitted on the opposite side of the street today. Tom saw it – maybe it – to the left, some twelve yards away diagonally. The big car's parking lights were on, but Tom could not be sure the motor was, because of the hum of other noises on the street.

Jonathan was up, walking towards Tom.

'I think I see them,' Tom said.

'What should we do?'

Tom was thinking of what he would do alone, stay in the house and try to shoot anyone who broke in the door. 'There's Simone and Georges to consider. We don't want a fight in here. I think we should rush them – outside. Otherwise they'll rush us here, and it'll be guns if they break in – I can do it, Jon.'

Jonathan felt a sudden rage, a desire to guard his house and home. 'All right – we'll go together!'

'What are you going to do, Jon?' Simone asked.

'We think there might be more of them – coming,' Jonathan said in French.

Tom went to the kitchen. He got the hat from the linoleum floor near the dead man, stuck it on his head and found it fell over his ears. Then he suddenly realized that these Italians, both of them, had guns in their shoulder-holsters. Tom took this man's gun from the holster. He went back into the living-room. 'These guns!' he said, reaching for the gun of the man on the floor. The drawn gun was hidden under his jacket. Tom took the man's hat, found that it fitted him better, and handed Jonathan the hat from the kitchen. 'Try this. If we can look like them till we cross the street, it's a slight advantage. Don't come with me, Jon. It's just as good if one person goes out. I just want them to move off!'

'Then I'll go,' Jonathan said. He knew what he had to do: scare them off, and perhaps shoot one first if he could, before he was shot himself.

Tom handed a gun to Simone, the small Italian gun. 'It might be useful, madame.' But she looked shy of taking the gun, and Tom laid the gun on the sofa. The safety was off.

Jonathan pushed the safety off the gun in his hand. 'Could you see how many are in the car?'

'Couldn't see a thing inside.' On his last words, Tom heard someone walking up the front steps, cautiously, with an effort to be silent. Tom jerked his head at Jonathan. 'Bolt the door after us, madame,' he whispered to Simone.

Tom and Jonathan, both wearing hats now, walked up the hall, and Tom slid the bolt and opened the door in the face of the man standing

there. At the same time, Tom bumped him and caught him by the arm,
turning him back down the stairs again. Jonathan had grabbed his other
arm. At a glance, in the near darkness, Tom and Jonathan might have
been taken for his two chums, but Tom knew the illusion wouldn't last
more than a second or two.

'To the left!' Tom said to Jonathan. The man they held was struggling,
but not yelling, and his efforts nearly lifted Tom off his feet.

Jonathan had seen the car with its parking lights on, and now he saw
the lights come full on, and heard the motor revving. The car backed
a little.

'Dump him!' Tom said, and he and Jonathan, like a pair that had re-
hearsed it, hurled the Italian forward, and his head hit the side of the
slowly moving car. Tom was aware of the clatter of the Italian's drawn
gun on the street. The car had stopped, and the door in front of Tom
was opening: the Mafia boys wanted their chum back, apparently. Tom
pulled his gun from his trousers pocket, aimed at the driver, and fired.
The driver, with the aid of a man in the back, was trying to get the
dazed Italian into the front seat. Tom was afraid to fire again, because
a couple of people were running towards them from the Rue de France.
And a window opened in one of the houses. Tom saw, or thought he
saw, the other back door of the car being opened, someone being pushed
out on to the pavement.

One shot came from the back of the car, then a second, just as Jonathan
stumbled or walked right in front of Tom. The car was moving off.

Tom saw Jonathan slump forward, and before Tom could catch him,
Jonathan fell on the place where the car had been. Damn it, Tom thought, if
he'd hit the driver, it must have been only in the arm. The car was gone.

A young man, then a man and woman came trotting up.

'What's happening?'

'He's shot?'

'Police!' The last was the cry of a young woman.

'Jon!' Tom thought Jonathan had merely tripped, but Jonathan wasn't
getting up, and was barely stirring. With the assistance of one of the
young men, Tom got Jonathan to the kerb, but he was quite limp.

Jonathan had been shot in the chest, he thought, but he was mainly
aware of numbness. There had been a jolt. He was going to faint soon,
and maybe it was more serious than fainting. People dashed around him,
shouting.

Only now did Tom recognize the figure on the sidewalk – Reeves! Reeves
was crumpled, apparently trying to recover his breath.

'... ambulance!' a Frenchwoman's voice was saying. 'We must call an ambulance!'

'I have a car!' a man cried.

Tom glanced at Jonathan's house windows, and saw the black silhouette of Simone's head as she peered through the curtains. He shouldn't leave here there, Tom thought. He had to get Jonathan to the hospital, and his car would be quicker than any ambulance. 'Reeves! – Hold the fort, I'll be back in one minute – *Oui, madame*,' Tom said to a woman (now there were five or six people around them), I'll take him to the hospital in my car at once!' Tom ran across the street and banged on the house door. 'Simone, it's Tom!'

When Simone opened the door, Tom said:

'Jonathan has been hurt. We must go to the hospital at once. Just take a coat and come. And Georges too!'

Georges was in the hall. Simone didn't waste time with a coat, but she did grope in a coat pocket, in the hall, for her keys, then hurried back towards Tom. 'Hurt? Was he shot?'

'I'm afraid so. My car is to the left. The green one.' His car was twenty feet behind where the Italians' car had been. Simone wanted to go to Jonathan, but Tom assured her that the most useful thing she could do was open the doors of his car, which was unlocked. There were more people, but no policeman as yet, and one officious little man asked Tom who in hell he thought he was, taking charge of everything?

'Stuff yourself!' Tom said in English. He was struggling with Reeves to lift Jonathan in the gentlest way possible. It would have been wiser to have brought the car closer, but having got Jonathan off the ground, they continued, and a couple of people assisted, so after a few steps it was not difficult. They braced Jonathan in a corner of the back seat.

Tom got into his car, dry in the mouth. 'This is Mme Trevanny,' Tom said to Reeves. 'Reeves Minot.'

'How do you do?' said Reeves with his American accent.

Simone got into the back, where Jonathan was. Reeves took Georges in beside him, and Tom pulled out, heading for the Fontainebleau hospital.

'Papa has fainted?' Georges asked.

'*Oui*, Georges.' Simone had begun to weep.

Jonathan heard their voices, but couldn't speak. He couldn't move, not even a finger. He had a grey vision of a sea running out – somewhere on an English coast – sinking, collapsing. He was already far away from Simone whose breast he leaned against – or so he thought. But Tom was alive. Tom was driving the car, Jonathan thought, like God himself. Somewhere there had been a bullet, which somehow no longer mattered. This was death now, which he had tried to face before and yet had not faced, tried to prepare and yet hadn't been able to. There was no preparation possible, it was merely a surrender, after all. And what he had done, misdone, accomplished, striven for – all seemed absurdity.

Tom passed an ambulance just coming up, wailing. He drove carefully. It was only four or five minutes' drive. The silence among all of them in the car became eerie to Tom. It was as if he and Reeves, Simone, Georges, Jonathan if he was conscious of anything, had been frozen in one second that went on and on.

'This man is *dead*!' said an intern in an astonished voice.

'But –' Tom didn't believe it. He couldn't get another word out.

Only Simone gave a cry.

They were standing on the concrete at one entrance to the hospital. Jonathan had been put on a stretcher, and two helpers held the stretcher poised, as if they didn't know what to do next.

'Simone, do you want –' But Tom didn't even know what he had been going to say. And Simone was now running towards Jonathan who was being borne inside, and Georges followed her. Tom ran after Simone, thinking to get her keys from her, to remove the two corpses from her house, or do *something* with them, then he stopped abruptly and his shoes slid on the concrete. The police would be at the Trevanny house before he was. The police were probably already breaking in, because the people in the street would have told them that the disturbance started from the grey house, that after the shots one person (Tom) had run back to the house, and he and a woman and small boy had come out and got into a car.

Simone was now disappearing round a corner, following the stretcher of Jonathan. It was as if Tom saw her already in a funeral procession. Tom turned and walked back to Reeves.

'We take off,' Tom said, 'while we can.' He wanted to take off before someone asked questions or made a note of his licence number.

He and Reeves got into Tom's car. Tom drove off, towards the Monument and home.

'Jonathan's *dead* – do you think?' Reeves asked.

'Yes. Well – you heard the intern.'

Reeves slumped and rubbed his eyes.

It wasn't sinking in, Tom thought, not to either of them. Tom was apprehensive lest a car from the hospital be trailing him, even a police car.

One didn't deposit a dead man and drive off with no questions asked. What was Simone going to say? They'd excuse her for not saying anything this evening, perhaps, but tomorrow? 'And you, my friend,' Tom said, his throat hoarse. 'No bones broken, no teeth knocked out?' He'd talked, Tom remembered, and maybe at once.

'Only cigarette burns,' Reeves said in a humble voice, as if burns were nothing compared to a bullet. Reeves had an inch-long beard, reddish.

'I suppose you know what's at the Trevannys' house – two dead men.'

'Oh. Good. – Yes, of course I know. They're missing. They never came back.'

'I'd have gone by the house to do something, try to, but the police must be there now.' A siren behind Tom made him grip the wheel in sudden panic, but it turned out to be a white ambulance with a blue light on its roof, which passed Tom at the Monument, and whisked away in a quick right turn towards Paris. Tom wished it might have been Jonathan, being taken to a Paris hospital where they were better able to deal with him. Tom thought that Jonathan had deliberately stepped between him and a man's gun in the car. Was he wrong? No one overtook them, or sirened them to a stop, in the drive to Villeperce. Reeves had fallen asleep against the door, but he woke up when the car stopped.

'This is home sweet home,' Tom said.

They got out in the garage, and Tom locked the garage, then opened his house door with a key. All was serene. It was rather unbelievable.

'Do you want to flop on the sofa while I make some tea?' Tom asked. 'Tea is what we need.'

They had tea and whisky, more tea than whisky. Reeves, with his usual apologetic manner, asked Tom if he had any anti-burn ointment, and Tom produced something from the downstairs loo medicine cabinet, and Reeves retired there to dress his wounds, which he said were all on his stomach. Tom lit a cigar, not so much because he craved a cigar as because a cigar gave him a sense of stability, perhaps illusory, but it was the illusion, the attitude towards problems that counted. One simply had to have a confident attitude.

When Reeves came into the living-room, he took note of the harpsichord.

'Yes,' Tom said. 'A new acquisition. I'm going to see about taking lessons in Fontainebleau – or somewhere. Maybe Heloise will take lessons too. We can't go on twiddling on the thing like a pair of monkeys.' Tom felt curiously angry, not against Reeves, not against anything specific. 'Tell me what happened in Ascona.'

Reeves sipped his tea and whisky again, silent for a few seconds like a man who had to drag himself back inch by inch from another world. 'I'm thinking about Jonathan. Dead. – I didn't want that, you know.'

Tom recrossed his legs. He was thinking about Jonathan too. 'About Ascona. What did happen there?'

'Oh. Well, I told you I thought they'd spotted me. Then a couple of nights ago – yes – one of these fellows approached me on the street. Young fellow, summer sports clothes, looked like an Italian tourist. He said in English "Get your suitcase packed and check out. We'll be waiting." Natch. I – I knew what the alternative was – I mean if I'd decided to pack my suitcase and run. This was around seven p.m. Sunday. Yesterday?'

'Yesterday was Sunday, yes.'

Reeves stared at the coffee-table, but he sat upright, one hand delicately against his midriff, where perhaps the burns were. 'By the way, I never took my suitcase. It's still in the lobby of the hotel in Ascona. They just beckoned me out the door and said "Leave it".'

'You can telephone the hotel,' Tom said, 'from Fontainebleau, for instance.'

'Yes. So – they kept asking me questions. They wanted to know the master-mind of it all. I told them there wasn't any. Couldn't have been *me*, a master-mind!' Reeves laughed weakly. 'I wasn't going to say *you*, Tom. Anyway it wasn't you who wanted to keep the Mafia out of Hamburg. So then – the cigarette burns started. They asked me who'd been on the train. I'm afraid I didn't do as well as Fritz. Good old Fritz –'

'He's not dead, is he?' asked Tom.

'No. Not that I know of. Anyway to make this disgraceful story short, I told them Jonathan's name – where he lived. I said it – because they were holding me down in the car in some woods somewhere, giving me the cigarette burns. I remember thinking that if I screamed like mad for help, no one would have heard me. Then they started holding my nose, pretending they were going to suffocate me.' Reeves squirmed on the sofa.

Tom could sympathize. 'They didn't mention my name?'

'No.'

Tom wondered if he could dare to believe that his coup with Jonathan had come off. Perhaps the Genotti family really thought that Tom Ripley had been a wrong trail. 'These were the Genotti family, I presume.'

'Logically, yes.'

'You don't know?'

'They don't mention the family, Tom, for goodness' sake!'

That was true. 'No mention of Angy – or Lippo? Or a capo called Luigi?'

Reeves thought. 'Luigi – maybe I heard the name. I'm afraid I was scared stiff, Tom –'

Tom sighed. 'Angy and Lippo are the two Jonathan and I did in Saturday night,' Tom said in a soft voice as if someone might overhear them. 'Two of the Genotti family. They came to the house here, and we – They were incinerated in their own car, miles from here. Jonathan was here and he was marvellous. You should see the paper!' Tom added, smiling. 'We made Lippo phone his boss Luigi and tell him that I wasn't the man he wanted. That's why I'm asking you about the Genottis. I'm very interested to know whether it was a success or not.'

Reeves was still trying to remember. 'They didn't mention your name, I know. Killed two of them here. In the house! That's something, Tom!' Reeves sank back on the sofa with a gentle smile, looking as if it were the first time he'd relaxed in days. Perhaps it was.

'However, they know my name,' Tom said. 'I'm not sure whether the two in the car recognized me tonight. That's – in the stars.' He was surprised at the phrase coming from his lips. He meant it was fifty-fifty, something like that. 'I mean,' Tom continued on a firmer note, 'I don't know whether their appetites are satisfied by getting Jonathan tonight or not.'

Tom stood up, turning away from Reeves. Jonathan dead. And Jonathan hadn't even needed to go out with Tom to the car. Hadn't Jonathan deliberately stepped in front of him, between him and the pistol pointing from the car? But Tom wasn't quite sure he'd seen a pistol pointing. It had all happened so quickly. Jonathan had never reconciled Simone, never had a word of forgiveness from her – nothing but those few minutes of attention she had given him after he'd been nearly garrotted.

'Reeves, shouldn't you think about turning in? Unless you'd like to eat something first. Are you hungry?'

'I think I'm too bushed to eat, thanks. I'd really like to turn in. Thanks, Tom. I wasn't sure you could put me up.'

Tom laughed. 'Neither was I.' Tom showed Reeves up to the guest-room, apologized for the fact Jonathan had slept for a few hours in the bed, and offered to change the sheets, but Reeves assured him that it didn't matter.

'That bed looks like bliss,' Reeves said, weaving with exhaustion as he started to undress.

Tom was thinking, if the Mafia boys tried another attack tonight, he had the bigger Italian gun, plus his rifle, the Luger also, with a tired Reeves instead of Jonathan. But he didn't think the Mafia would come tonight. They would probably prefer to get a great distance from Fontaine-bleau. Tom hoped he had wounded the driver, at least, and badly.

The next morning, Tom let Reeves sleep on. Tom sat in his living-room with his coffee, with the radio tuned to a French popular programme which gave the news every hour. Unfortunately it was just after 9 a.m. He wondered what Simone was saying to the police, and what she had said last night? She wouldn't, Tom thought, mention him, because that would expose Jonathan's part in the Mafia killings. Or was he right? Couldn't she say that Tom Ripley had coerced her husband – But how? By what kind of pressure? No, it was more likely that Simone would say, more or less, 'I can't imagine why the Mafia (or the Italians) came to our house.' 'But who was the other man with your husband? The wit-nesses say there was another man – with an American accent.' Tom hoped none of the bystanders would remark on his accent, but probably they would. 'I don't know,' Simone might say. 'Somebody my husband knew. I have forgotten his name ...'

Things were a bit uncertain, at the moment.

Reeves came down before 10 a.m. Tom made more coffee, and scrambled some eggs for him.

'I must take off for your sake,' Reeves said. 'Can you drive me to – I was thinking of Orly. Also I want to telephone about my suitcase, but not from your house. Could you take me to Fontainebleau?'

'I can take you to Fontainebleau and Orly. Where are you headed?'

'Zürich, I was thinking. Then I could swoop back to Ascona and get my suitcase. But if I telephone the hotel, they might send the suitcase to Zürich care of American Express. I'll just say I forgot it!' Reeves laughed a boyish, carefree laugh – or rather, forced it out of himself.

Then there was the money situation. Tom had about thirteen hundred francs in cash in the house. He said he could easily let Reeves have some for the plane ticket and to change into Swiss francs once he got to Zürich. Reeves had traveller's cheques in his suitcase.

'And your passport?' Tom asked.

'Here.' Reeves patted his breast pocket. 'Both of them. Ralph Platt with the beard and me without. Had the picture taken by a chum in Hamburg, me wearing a phoney beard. Can you imagine the Italians didn't take the passports off me? That's luck, eh?'

It certainly was. Reeves was unkillable, Tom thought, like a slender lizard flitting over stone. Reeves had been kidnapped, cigarette-burnt.

intimidated God knew how, dumped, and here he was eating scrambled eggs, both eyes intact, not even his nose broken.

'I'm going back to my own passport. So I'll shave off my beard this morning, take a bath too, if I may. I just came down in a hurry, because I thought I'd slept pretty late.'

Tom telephoned while Reeves was bathing, and found out about planes to Zürich. There were three that day, the first taking off at 1.20 p.m., and the girl at Orly said there would very likely be a single seat available.

TWENTY-FOUR

Tom was at Orly with Reeves a few minutes past noon. He parked his car. Reeves telephoned the hotel Three Bears in Ascona about his suitcase, and the hotel agreed to send it to Zürich. Reeves was not much concerned, not as concerned as Tom would have been if he'd left behind an unlocked suitcase with an interesting address book in it. Reeves would probably recover his suitcase with all its contents undisturbed tomorrow in Zürich. Tom had insisted on Reeves' taking one of his small suitcases with an extra shirt, a sweater, pyjamas, socks and underwear, and Tom's own toothbrush and toothpaste, which Tom thought essential for a suitcase to look normal. Somehow Tom hadn't wanted to give Reeves the new toothbrush that Jonathan had used only once. Tom also gave Reeves a raincoat.

Reeves looked paler without the beard. 'Tom, don't wait to see me off, I'll manage. Thanks infinitely. You saved my life.'

That wasn't quite true, unless the Italians had been going to plug Reeves on the pavement, which Tom doubted. 'If I *don't* hear from you,' Tom said with a smile, 'I'll assume you're all right.'

'Okay, Tom!' A wave of the hand, and he vanished through the glass doors.

Tom got his car and drove homeward, feeling wretched and increasingly sad. He didn't care to try to shake if off by seeing people this evening, not the Grais again, not the Cleggs either. Not even a film in Paris. He'd ring Heloise around 7 p.m., and see if she'd departed on the Swiss jaunt. If she had, her parents would know her telephone number in the Swiss chalet, or some way of reaching her. Heloise always thought of things like that, leaving a telephone number or an address where she could be found.

Then of course he might have a visit from the police, which would put an end to his efforts to shake off his depression. What could he say to the police, that he had been home all last evening? Tom laughed, and the laugh was a relief. He ought to find out first, of course, what Simone had already said, if he could.

But the police did not come, and Tom made no effort to speak with Simone. Tom suffered his usual apprehension that the police were spending this time in amassing evidence and testimony before they dumped it on him. Tom bought some things for his dinner, practised some finger exercises on the harpsichord, and wrote a friendly note to Mme Annette in care of her sister in Lyon:

My dear Mme Annette,

Belle Ombre misses you painfully. But I hope you are relaxing and enjoying these beautiful days of early summer. Everything is all right here. I will telephone one of these evenings and see how you are. All the best wishes.

Affectionately,

Tom

The Paris radio reported a 'shoot-up' in a Fontainebleau street, three men killed, no names given. The Tuesday paper (Tom bought *France-Soir* in Villeperce) had a five-inch-long item: Jonathan Trevanny of Fontaine-bleau shot dead, and two Italians also shot in Trevanny's house. Tom's eyes glided over their names as though he didn't want to remember them, though he knew they might linger a long time in his memory: Alfiori and Ponti. The Italians had invaded the house for no reason that Mme Simone Trevanny knew, she had told the police. They had rung the doorbell, then burst in. A friend whom Mme Trevanny did not name had aided her husband, and later driven them both, with their small son, to the hospital in Fontainebleau where her husband had been found dead on arrival.

Aided, Tom thought with amusement, in view of the two Mafiosi with their skulls bashed in in the Trevanny house. Pretty handy with a hammer, that friend of the Trevannys, and maybe Trevanny himself, con-sidering they had been up against a total of four men with guns. Tom began to relax, to laugh even – and if there was a little hysteria in the laugh, who could blame him? He knew that more details were going to come out in the newspapers, and if not the newspapers then via the police themselves – direct to Simone, direct to him, maybe. But Mme Simone was going to try to protect her husband's honour and her nest-egg in Switzerland, Tom believed, otherwise she would have told them a bit more already. She could have mentioned Tom Ripley, and her suspicion of him. The newspapers could have said that Mme Trevanny promised to make a more detailed statement later. But evidently she hadn't.

The funeral of Jonathan Trevanny was to be held Wednesday afternoon, 17 May, at 3 p.m. in the church of St Louis. On Wednesday, Tom wanted to go, but he felt it would have been exactly the wrong thing to do, from Simone's point of view, and after all funerals were for the living, not the dead. Tom spent that time in silence, working in his garden. (He must prod those blasted workmen about the greenhouse.) Tom became more and more convinced that Jonathan had on purpose shielded him from that bullet by stepping in front of him.

Surely the police were going to question Simone in the days to come, demand to know the name of the friend who had aided her husband. Hadn't the Italians, maybe identified by now as the Mafia, been in pursuit of the friend, perhaps, not Jonathan Trevanny? The police would give Simone a few days to recover from her grief, and then they would question her again. Tom could imagine Simone's will strengthened even more in the direction in which she had started: the friend didn't want his name given, he was not a close friend, he had acted in self-defence, as had her husband, and she wanted to forget the whole nightmare.

About a month later, in June, when Heloise was long back from Switzerland, and Tom's speculations on the Trevanny affair had come true – there had been no further statements from Mme Trevanny in the newspapers – Tom saw Simone approaching him on the same pavement in the Rue de France in Fontainebleau. Tom was carrying a heavy urn-like thing for the garden, which he had just bought. Tom was surprised to see Simone, because he had heard that she had already removed herself and her son to Toulouse where she had bought a house. Tom had heard this news via the young and thrusting owner of the new and expensive delicatessen shop into which Gauthier's art supply shop had been converted. So with his arms nearly giving out from the load which he had almost entrusted to the clerk at the florist's, the unpleasant memory of céleri rémoulade and herrings-in-cream in his mind instead of the as yet odourless tubes of paint, virgin brushes and canvases that he was used to seeing in Gauthier's premises, plus the belief that Simone was already hundreds of miles away – Tom had the feeling he was seeing a ghost, having a vision. Tom was in shirtsleeves, beginning to crumple, and if not for Simone, he might have set the urn down to rest for a moment. His car was at the next corner. Simone saw him and at once began to glare like a focusing enemy. She paused briefly beside him, and as Tom almost came to a stop also, thinking at least to say 'Bonjour, madame,' she spat at him. She missed his face, missed him entirely, and plunged on towards the Rue St Merry.

That, perhaps, corresponded to the Mafia revenge. Tom hoped that would be all that there was to it – either from the Mafia or Mme Simone. In fact, the spit was a kind of guarantee, unpleasant to be sure, whether it hit or not. But if Simone hadn't decided to hang on to the money in Switzerland, she wouldn't have bothered spitting and he himself would be in prison. Simone was just a trifle ashamed of herself, Tom thought. In that, she joined much of the rest of the world. Tom felt, in fact, that her conscience would be more at rest than that of her husband, if he were still alive.

THE BOY WHO
FOLLOWED RIPLEY

To Monique Buffett

ONE

Tom crept forward as silently as possible on his parquet floor, crossed the threshold of his bathroom, and paused and listened.

Zz-zzz---zz-zzz---zz-zzz.

The industrious little beasts were at it again, though Tom could still smell the Rentokil he had painstakingly injected into their exit holes, or whatever they were, that afternoon. The sawing went on and on, as if his efforts had been for nothing. He glanced at a folded pink hand towel below one of the wooden shelves and saw – already – a minuscule heap of fine, tan sawdust.

'Shut *up*!' Tom said, and slammed the cabinet with the side of his fist.

They did shut up. Silence. Tom imagined the little bugheads with saws in their hands pausing, looking at each other with apprehension, but maybe nodding also as if to say, 'We've had this before. It's the "master" again, but he'll be gone in a minute.' Tom had had it before too: if he walked into his bathroom with a normal tread, not even thinking of carpenter ants, he could sometimes detect their diligent buzz before they detected him, yet one more step of his, or the turning on of a tap would shut them up for a few minutes.

Heloise thought he took it too seriously.'It will be years before they make the cabinet *fall*.'

But Tom disliked the fact that he had been defeated by the ants, that they caused him to blow their dust off clean folded pyjamas when he took a pair off a shelf, that his purchase and application of a French product called Xylophene (fancy name for kerosene), and his consulting two encyclopaedias at the house had been futile. *Camponotus* gnaws galleries in wood and constructs its nest. See *Campodea.* Wingless, blind, but serpentine, fleeing light, lives under rocks. Tom couldn't imagine his pests serpentine, and they were not living under rocks. He had made a special trip to Fontainebleau for good old Rentokil yesterday. Yes, yesterday he'd launched his Blitzkrieg, second attack today, and he was still defeated. Difficult of course to fire Rentokil upwards, as one had to do, because the holes were on the underside of the shelves.

The zz-zz-zz resumed, just as the music of *Swan Lake* from the gramophone below stairs swung gracefully into another gear too, an elegant waltz as if to mock him, as the insects were doing.

All right, give it up, Tom told himself, *for today anyway.* But he had wanted today and yesterday to be constructive: he had cleaned out his desk, thrown papers away, swept the greenhouse, written business letters, one an important one to Jeff Constant at Jeff's private address in London. Tom had been putting that letter off, but today he had written a letter which he asked Jeff to destroy at once: Tom advised absolutely no more pretended discoveries of Derwatt canvases or sketches, and Tom had asked rhetorically weren't the profits from the still flourishing art materials company and the art school in Perugia sufficient? The Buck-master Gallery, specifically Jeff Constant, a professional photographer but now a part owner of the Buckmaster Gallery along with Edmund Banbury, journalist, had been toying with the idea of selling more of Bernard Tufts' failures, or not-so-good imitations of Derwatt's work. They had succeeded up to now in this, but Tom wanted it stopped for safety reasons.

Tom decided to take a walk, have a coffee at Georges's and change his thoughts. It was only half past 9 p.m. Heloise was in the living room, talking away with her friend Noëlle in French. Noëlle, a married woman who lived in Paris, was staying the night, but without her husband.

'*Succès, chéri?*' Heloise asked brightly, sitting up on the yellow sofa.

Tom had to laugh, a little wryly. '*Non!*' He went on in French. 'I admit defeat. I am vanquished by carpenter ants!'

'A-a-aaaaah,' Noëlle groaned sympathetically, then laughter bubbled out of her.

She was no doubt thinking about something else, dying to get back to her conversation with Heloise. Tom knew they were planning an Adventure Cruise in late September or early October together, maybe to the Antarctic, and they wanted Tom to come too. Noëlle's husband had already firmly declined: business reasons.

'I'm going to take a little walk. Back in half an hour or so. Need any cigarettes?' he asked both of them.

'*Ah, oui!*' said Heloise. She meant a pack of Marlboros.

'I stopped!' said Noëlle.

For at least the third time that Tom could remember. Tom nodded, and went out the front door.

Mme Annette had not closed the front gates as yet. He would do it on his return, Tom thought. He turned left and walked towards the centre of Villeperce. It was coolish, for mid-August. Roses bloomed in profusion in his neighbours' front gardens, visible behind wire fences. Daylight Saving Time made it lighter than normal, but Tom suddenly wished he had brought a torch for the walk home. There were no proper sidewalks on this road. Tom breathed deeply. Think of Scarlatti tomorrow, of the harpsichord instead of carpenter ants. Think of taking Heloise to America in late October, maybe. It would be her second trip. She had loved New York, and found San Francisco beautiful. And the blue Pacific.

Yellowish lights had come on in some of the small houses in the village. There was Georges's slanting red *tabac* talisman above the door, with a glow of light below it.

'Marie,' Tom said with a nod as he walked in, greeting the proprietress who was just then slamming a beer down on the counter for a customer. This was a working-class bar, nearer to Tom's house than the other bar in the village, and often more amusing.

'*Monsieur Tome! Ça va?*' Marie tossed her curly black hair with a trace of coquetry, and her big mouth, bright with lipstick, gave Tom a reckless smile. She was fifty-five if she was a day. '*Dis donc!*' she yelled, plunging back into conversation with two male customers who were hunched over pastis at the counter. 'That asshole – that *asshole!*' she shouted as if to gain an ear by this word which was bandied about many times a day in the establishment. With no attention from the roaring men who were now talking simultaneously she continued, 'That *asshole* spreads himself like a whore who takes on too much work! He deserves what he got!'

Was she talking about Giscard, Tom wondered, or a local mason? '*Café,*' Tom put in, when he got a split second of Marie's attention, 'and a packet of Marlboros!' He knew Georges and Marie were pro-Chirac, the so-called Fascist.

'Eh, Marie!' Georges boomed in baritone from Tom's left, trying to quieten his wife down. Georges, a tub of a man with fat hands, was polishing stemmed glasses, putting them back daintily on the shelf to the right of the cash register. Behind Tom a noisy table football game was in progress: four adolescent boys whirled rods, and little lead men in lead shorts kicked a marble-sized ball as they spun backwards and forwards. Tom suddenly noticed, on his extreme left round the curve of the bar, a teen-aged boy whom he had seen on the road near his house a few days ago. The boy had brown hair and wore a workman's jacket of the usual French blue, blue jeans too, as Tom recalled. When Tom had first seen him – Tom had been opening his gates one afternoon for an expected visitor – the boy had moved from his position under a big chestnut tree across the road and walked off, away from Villeperce. Had he been casing Belle Ombre, watching the family's habits? Another minor worry, Tom thought, like the carpenter ants. Think about something else. Tom stirred his coffee, sipped it, glanced at the boy again and found the boy looking at him. The boy at once lowered his eyes and picked up his beer glass.

"*Coutez, Monsieur Tome!*' Marie was leaning over the counter towards Tom, and she jerked a thumb towards the boy. '*Américain,*' she whispered loudly over the awful racket of the juke box which had just started up. 'Says he's over here to work this summer. Ha-ha-haah!' She laughed hoarsely, as if it were hilarious for an American to work, or maybe because she believed there wasn't any work to be had in France, hence the unemployment. 'Want to meet him?'

'*Merci, non.* He works where?' Tom asked.

Marie shrugged, and picked up a cry for beer. 'Oh, you know where to stick *that*!' Marie yelled merrily at another customer as she pulled the beer tap.

Tom was thinking about Heloise and the possible American tour. They ought to go up to New England this time. Boston. The fish market there, Independence Hall, Milk Street and Bread Street. It was Tom's native territory, even though he would hardly know it now, he supposed. Aunt Dottie, of the grudging $11.79 presents in the form of cheques in the old days, had died, leaving him $10,000, but not her stuffy little house there, which Tom would have liked. Tom could at least show Heloise the house in which he had grown up, show it from the outside. Tom supposed that Aunt Dottie's sister's kids had inherited the house, since Aunt Dottie had no children of her own. Tom put seven francs down on the bar top for his coffee and cigarettes, glanced at the boy in the blue jacket again and saw him paying too. Tom put out his cigarette, called "*Soir!*' to no one in particular and went out.

Now it was dark. Tom crossed the main road under the not very bright light of a street lamp, and entered the darker road on which his house sat a couple of hundred yards away. Tom's road was almost straight, two-lane and paved, and Tom knew it well, but was glad of the approach of a car whose lights enabled him to see the left side of the road on which he was walking. As soon as the car had passed, Tom became aware of quick but soft steps behind him, and turned.

A figure had a flashlight. Tom saw blue jeans and tennis shoes. The boy from the bar.

'Mr Ripley!'

Tom tensed. 'Yes?'

'Good evening.' The boy stopped, fiddled with the flashlight. 'B-Billy

Rollins, my name is. Since I've got a flashlight – maybe I can walk you home?'

Tom vaguely saw a squarish face, dark eyes. He was shorter than Tom. His tone was polite. Was this going to be a mugging, or was he over-anxious tonight? Tom had only a couple of ten-franc notes on him, but he didn't fancy a scuffle tonight either. 'I'm all right, thanks. I live very near by.'

'I know. Well – I'm going the same way.'

Tom cast an apprehensive glance at the darkness ahead, then walked on. 'American?' he asked.

'Yes, sir.' The boy was pointing his flashlight at a careful angle ahead, convenient for both of them, but his eyes were more on Tom than on the road.

Tom kept his distance from the boy, and his hands hung free for action. 'You're on vacation?'

'In a way. Working a bit too. Gardener.'

'Oh? Where?'

'In Moret. Private house.'

Tom wished another car would approach, so he might get a better look at the boy's expression, because Tom sensed a tension that might be dangerous. 'Where in Moret?'

'Chez Madame Jeanne Boutin, seventy-eight Rue de Paris,' the boy replied promptly. 'She has a fairly big garden. Fruit trees. But mainly I do weeding – mowing.'

Tom clenched his fists nervously. 'You sleep in Moret?'

'Yes. Madame Boutin has a little house in the garden. There's a bed and a sink there. Cold water, but it's all right in summer.'

Now Tom was genuinely surprised. 'Unusual for an American to choose the country instead of Paris. Where're you from?'

'New York.'

'And how old are you?'

'Going on nineteen.'

Tom would have thought younger. 'You've got working papers?' Tom saw the boy smile for the first time. 'No. Informal arrangement. Fifty francs a day, which is cheap, I know, so Madame Boutin lets me sleep there. She even invited me for lunch once. Of course I can buy bread and cheese and eat in the little house. Or in a café.'

The boy wasn't from the gutter, Tom could tell from the way he spoke, and from the way he pronounced Mme Boutin, he knew some French. 'How long has this been going on?' Tom asked in French.

'*Cinq, six jours,*' the boy replied. His eyes were still on Tom.

Tom was glad to see the big elm which slanted towards the road, which meant his house was some fifty paces farther. 'What brought you to this part of France?'

'Oh – maybe the forest of Fontainebleau. I like to walk in the woods. And it's near Paris. I stayed in Paris a week – looking around.'

Tom was walking more slowly. Why was the boy interested in him enough to know his house? 'Let's cross.'

The beige gravel of Belle Ombre's front court showed below the door light just a few yards away now. 'How is it you knew where my house is?' Tom asked, and sensed the boy's embarrassment in the duck of his head, the twist of the torch's light. 'I saw you on the road here – two or three days ago, wasn't it?'

'Yes,' Billy replied in a deeper voice. 'I'd seen your name in the newspapers – in the States. I thought I'd like to see where you lived, since I was near Villeperce.'

In the newspapers when, Tom wondered, and why? Tom knew he had a dossier, however. 'You left a bike in the village here?'

'No,' said the boy.

'How're you getting back to Moret tonight?'

'Oh, I hitchhike. Or I walk.'

Seven kilometres. Why did anyone who slept in Moret come seven kilometres to Villeperce after 9 p.m. with no transportation? Tom saw a faint glow of light to the left of the trees: Mme Annette was still up, but in her own room. Tom's hand was on one of his iron gates, which were not quite closed. 'You're welcome to come in for a beer, if you like.'

The boy's dark brows frowned a little, he bit his underlip and looked up dismally at Belle Ombre's two front turrets, as if whether to come in were a big decision. 'I –'

His hesitation puzzled Tom still more. 'My car's right there. I can drive you to Moret.' Indecision. Did the boy really work and sleep in Moret?

'All right. Thank you. I'll come in a minute,' the boy said.

They walked through the gates, and Tom closed them but did not lock them. The big key was in the lock on the inside. At night it was hidden at the foot of a rhododendron near the gate.

'My wife has a friend visiting tonight,' Tom said, 'but we can have a beer in the kitchen.'

The front door was unlocked. One light was on in the living room, but Heloise and Noëlle had evidently gone upstairs. Often Noëlle sat up late talking to Heloise either in the guestroom or in Heloise's room.

'Beer? Coffee?'

'What a nice place!' the boy said, looking around from where he stood. 'Can you play the harpsichord?'

Tom smiled. 'Taking lessons – twice a week. Let's go in the kitchen.'

They went into the hall on the left. Tom put a light on in the kitchen, opened the fridge and took out a six-pack of Heineken.

'Hungry?' Tom asked, seeing the remains of their roast beef on a platter under aluminium foil.

'No, sir. Thank you.'

Back in the living room, the boy looked at the painting 'Man in Chair' over the fireplace, then at the slightly smaller but genuine Derwatt called 'The Red Chairs' on the wall near the french windows. The boy's glances had taken only seconds, but Tom had remarked them. Why the Derwatts and not the bigger Soutine, of striking reds and blues, which hung above the harpsichord?

Tom gestured towards his sofa.

'I can't sit there – in these levis. They're too dirty.'

The sofa was covered in yellow satin. There were a couple of un-upholstered straight chairs, but Tom said, 'Let's go up to my room.'

They climbed the curving stairway, Tom carrying the beer pack and the opener. Noëlle's room was open, a light on there, and Heloise's door slightly open, and from Heloise's room Tom heard voices, laughter. Tom went left towards his room, and put on the light.

'Take my chair. Wooden,' Tom said, turning his desk chair, which had arms, towards the centre of the room. He opened two bottles.

The boy's eyes lingered on the square Wellington chest, its surface and brass corners and countersunken drawer pulls now as always polished to perfection by Mme Annette. The boy nodded with approval. He had a handsome face, a bit serious looking, a strong and beardless jaw. 'It's a nice life you have, isn't it?'

The tone might have been mocking or wistful. Had the boy looked up his dossier and labelled him a crook? 'Why not?' Tom handed him a beer bottle. 'Forgot glasses, sorry.'

'Would you mind if I washed my hands first?' the boy asked with earnest politeness.

'Certainly not. Right there.' Tom put on his bathroom light.

The boy bent at the basin, scrubbing away for nearly a minute. He had not shut the door. He returned smiling. He had smooth lips, strong teeth, straight dark brown hair. 'That's better. Hot water!' He smiled at his own hands, then picked up his beer. 'What's that smell in there, turpentine? Do you paint?'

Tom laughed a little. 'I do sometimes, but today I was attacking carpenter ants in the shelves there.' Tom did *not* want to talk about carpenter ants. When the boy had sat down – Tom was seated on another wooden chair – Tom asked, 'How long do you intend to stay in France?'

The boy appeared to think. 'Maybe another month or so.'

'Then you go back to college? Are you in college?'

'Not yet. I'm not sure I want to go to college. I'll have to decide.' He shoved his fingers through his hair, pushing it towards the left side of his head. Some of his hair wanted to stand straight up on top. He seemed embarrassed by Tom's inspection, and took a gulp of beer.

Now Tom noticed a small spot, a mole, on the boy's right cheek. Tom said casually, 'You're welcome to take a hot shower. No trouble at all.'

'Oh, no, thanks very much. Maybe I look grubby. But really I *can* wash in cold water. I do. Anybody can.' The full young lips attempted a smile. The boy set his beer bottle on the floor, and caught sight of something in the waste-basket by his chair. He looked more closely. '*Auberge Réserve des Quatre Pattes,*' Billy read from a discarded envelope. 'Now that's funny! You've been there?'

'No. They send me mimeographed letters now and then, asking for donations. Why?'

'Because just this week I was walking in the woods somewhere – east of Moret on a dirt road, and I met a man and woman who asked me if I knew where this Auberge Réserve was, because it was supposed to be near Veneux les Sablons. These people said they'd been looking for it for a couple of hours. Said they'd sent money to it a couple of times and they wanted to see the place.'

'They say in their bulletins they don't welcome visitors, because they make the animals nervous. They try to find homes by post – then they write success stories about how happy the dog or cat is in his new home.' Tom smiled, recalling the sentimentality of some of the stories.

'You've sent them money?'

'Oh – thirty francs a couple of times.'

'Where did you send it?'

'They have a Paris address. Post box. I think.'

Billy smiled now. 'Wouldn't it be funny if the place didn't *exist?*'

This possibility amused Tom too. 'Yes. Just a charity racket. Why didn't that occur to me?' Tom opened two more beers.

'May I look at this?' asked Billy, meaning the envelope in the waste-basket.

'Why not?'

The boy fished out also the mimeographed pages that had come in the envelope. He glanced over them, and read out loud, '. . . "adorable little creature who deserves the paradi–sical home that providence has found her." That's a kitten. "And now to our doorstep has strayed an extremely thin brown and white terrier – fox – who is in need of penicillin and other protective injections . . ."' The boy looked up at Tom. 'I just wonder where their doorstep is? What if it's a *fraud?*' He pronounced fraud as if he relished the word. 'If that place exists, I'm not too lazy to find it. I feel curious.'

Tom watched him with interest. Billy – Rollins, was it? – had suddenly come alive.

'*Poste Restante* Box two hundred eighty-seven, eighteenth arrondisse-ment,' the boy read. 'I wonder which post office in the eighteenth? Can I keep this, since you seem to be throwing it away?'

The boy's zeal impressed Tom. And what had given him, at such an early age, an enthusiasm for exposing frauds? 'Of course, keep it.' Tom reseated himself. 'You've been the victim of fraud yourself, perhaps?'

Billy laughed quickly, then looked as if he were reflecting on the past to see if he had been. 'No, not really. Not out and out fraud.'

Some kind of deception, perhaps, Tom thought, but decided not to pry further. 'And wouldn't it be amusing,' Tom said, 'to send these people a letter signed with a phony name saying we're wise to you, making money on non-existent animals, so prepare yourself for a visit from the police at your – post box.'

'We shouldn't warn them, we should find out where they're based and crash in. Just suppose it's a couple of tough guys living in a fancy Paris apartment! We'd have to trail them – from the post box.'

Just then Tom heard a knock at his door and got up.

Heloise stood in the hall, in pyjamas and a pink seersucker robe. 'Oh, you have someone with you, Tome! I thought the voices were your radio!'

'An American I just met in the village. Billy –' Tom turned, drawing Heloise by the hand. 'My wife, Heloise.'

'Billy Rollins, *Enchanté, madame.*' Billy, on his feet, made a small bow.

Tom continued in French. 'Billy is working in Moret as a gardener. He is from New York. A good gardener, Billy?' Tom smiled.

'My – intentions are good,' Billy replied. He ducked his head, and again set his beer bottle carefully on the floor beside Tom's desk.

'I hope you have a pleasant sojourn in France,' Heloise said lightly, but her quick eyes had looked the boy over. 'I just came to say good night, Tome, and tomorrow morning – Noëlle and I go to the antique shop at Le Pavé du Roi, then to Fontainebleau for lunch at l'Aigle Noir. Want to join us for lunch?'

'I don't think so, thank you, dear. Enjoy yourselves. I'll see you both tomorrow morning before you leave, won't I? Good night, sleep well.' He kissed Heloise on the cheek. 'I'll drive Billy home, so don't be alarmed if you hear me come in later. I'll lock the house when I go out.'

Billy said he could catch a ride easily, he was sure, but Tom insisted on driving him. Tom wanted to see if the Moret house in the Rue de Paris existed.

In the car with Billy, Tom said, 'Your family's in New York? What does your father do, if that's not an impertinent question?'

'He's – in electronics. They make measuring equipment. For measuring all kinds of things electronically. He's one of the managers.'

Tom sensed that Billy was lying. 'You're on good terms with your family?'

'Oh, sure. They –'

'They write to you?'

'Oh, sure. They know where I am.'

'And after France, where're you going? Home?'

A pause. 'I might go to Italy. Not sure.'

'Is this the right road? We turn here?'

'No, the other way,' the boy said just in time. 'But it's the right road, all right.'

Then the boy indicated where Tom should stop, at a medium-sized, modest-looking house with windows all dark now, front garden bordered with a low white wall along the pavement, closed carriage gates to one side.

'My key,' Billy said, fishing a rather long key from his inside jacket pocket. 'I have to be quiet. I thank you very much, Mr Ripley.' He opened the car door.

'Tell me what you find out about the animal home.'

The boy smiled. 'Yes, sir.'

Tom watched him walk to the dark gates, shine the torch on the lock, then turn the key. Billy passed through, waved at Tom, then closed the gates. As Tom backed to turn the car, he saw the number 78 plainly visible on its blue official metal plaque beside the main door. Odd, Tom thought. Why should a boy want a boring job like this, even for a short time, unless he was hiding from something? But Billy didn't look like a delinquent. The most likely thing, Tom thought, was that Billy had had a quarrel with his parents or suffered a disappointment with a girl, and had hopped on an aeroplane to try to forget it. Tom had the feeling the boy had plenty of money, and was in no need of garden work at fifty francs a day.

TWO

Three days later, on a Friday, Tom and Heloise sat at the table in the alcove off the living room, breakfasting and looking over letters and newspapers that had arrived at 9.30. It was Tom's second coffee, Mme Annette having brought the first to him, along with Heloise's tea, at eight or so. A storm was blowing up, or brewing, creating an atmosphere of tension that had awakened Tom at eight, before Mme Annette's arrival. It was now ominously dark, not a breeze stirred outside, and there were distant rumbles of thunder.

'A postcard from the Cleggs!' Heloise exclaimed, discovering it under letters and a magazine. 'Norway! They're on their cruise. Remember, Tome? Look! Isn't that beautiful?'

Tom looked up from his *International Herald Tribune*, and took the postcard Heloise extended. It showed a white ship cruising up a fjord between very green mountains, with a few cottages nestling in a crease of the shore in the foreground. 'Looks deep,' Tom said, for some reason suddenly thinking of drowning. He was afraid of deep water, hated swimming or trying to, and often thought that somehow his end might be watery.

'Read the postcard,' Heloise said.

It was in English, signed by both Howard and Rosemary Clegg, their English neighbours who had a house about five kilometres away. '"Divinely restful cruise. We play Sibelius on the cassette to keep in the mood. Love from Rosemary. Wish you both were here in the midnight sunshine with us –"' Tom paused as thunder cracked and rumbled like a determined dog. 'We're going to get it today,' Tom said. 'I hope the dahlias stand up.' He had staked them all, however.

Heloise reached for the card which Tom handed back. 'You're so nervous, Tome. We have had storms before. I am glad it comes now and not tonight at six. I have to go to Papa's, you know.'

Tom knew. Chantilly. Heloise had a standing date with her parents for dinner on Friday nights, and usually she kept it. Sometimes Tom went and sometimes he didn't. He preferred not to go, because her parents were stuffy and they bored him, not to mention that they had never cared much for him. Tom found it interesting that Heloise always said she had to go to 'Papa's' instead of to her 'parents''. Papa held the purse strings. Mama was considerably more generous by nature, but in case of a real crisis – if Tom stepped out of line in some way as had nearly happened in the Derwatt mess with Bernard and the American Murchison – Tom doubted if Mama would have much clout if Papa wanted to cut off Heloise's allowance. The proper running and upkeep of Belle Ombre depended on Heloise's allowance. Tom lit a cigarette, braced himself for the next shaft of lightning with a mixture of pleasure and anxiety, and thought of Jacques Plisson, Heloise's father, a plump, pompous man with the strings of destiny in his hands (purse strings) which he held like a twentieth-century charioteer. A pity money had such power, yet of course it had.

'*Monsieur Tome, encore du café?*' Mme Annette stood suddenly at Tom's elbow with the silver pot that Tom noticed trembled ever so slightly.

'I'm all right, Madame Annette, but leave the pot, I may want some later.'

'I'm going to check the windows,' Mme Annette said, setting the pot on a mat in the centre of the table. 'Such a darkness! This will be a storm!' Her blue eyes under the Norman lids met Tom's for an instant, then she bustled away towards the staircase. She had checked the windows once, Tom thought, maybe even closed some shutters, but to check them again pleased her. It pleased Tom too. He got up restlessly, went near the window where there was a bit more light, and looked at the *People* column on the back page of the *Trib. Frank Sinatra* was making another final appearance, this time in a forthcoming film. Sixteen-year-old *Frank Pierson*, favourite son of the later super-food tycoon *John Pierson*, had taken off from the family home in Maine, and the family was anxious after nearly three weeks with no word from him. Frank had been extremely upset by his father's death in July.

Tom remembered a write-up of John Pierson's death. Even the *Sunday Times* of London had given it a few inches. John Pierson had been a wheelchair case, something like George Wallace of Alabama, and for the same reason, someone had attempted to assassinate him. He had been enormously wealthy, not quite as wealthy as Howard Hughes, but still with a fortune that went into hundreds of millions gained by his food products, gourmet, health and diet foods. Tom had remembered the obituaries especially because it had not been determined whether he had committed suicide by pushing himself off a cliff on his estate or whether it had been an accident. John Pierson had been fond of watching the sunsets from a cliff, and had refused to have a handrail put up, because it would have spoiled the view.

Ka-a-*rack*!

Tom flinched from the french windows, and looked wide-eyed outside to see if his greenhouse's glass windows were still intact. Now the wind came, rattling something down the tiles of the roof, Tom hoped nothing more than a twig.

Heloise was reading a magazine, indifferent to the elements.

'Must get dressed,' Tom said. 'You haven't a lunch date, have you?'

'*Non, chéri.* I am not going out till five. You are always nervous about the wrong things. This house is very solid!'

Tom managed to nod, but it seemed natural to be nervous with lightning striking all over the place. He took the *Trib* from the table and went upstairs, and showered and shaved, day-dreaming. When was old Plisson going to die, die a natural death? Not that Tom and Heloise needed money, more money, not at all. But he was such a pain in the neck, classic, like the awful mother-in-law. Jacques Plisson was of course plumping for Chirac too. Dressed now, Tom opened the side window in his bedroom and got a gust of rain-filled wind in his face, which he breathed in because it was refreshing and exciting, but he closed the window at once. What a good smell, rain over dry land! Tom went to Heloise's bedroom, and saw that the windows were closed. They hissed with the rain now. Mme Annette was just tucking the bedcover properly over the pillows on the double bed where he and Heloise had slept.

'All secure, Monsieur Tome,' she said, patting a pillow, finished, straightening herself up. Her rather short, sturdy figure seemed charged with energy like that of a much younger person. She was in her late sixties, but she had many more years ahead of her, Tom thought, and the thought was comforting.

'I'm going to take a quick look at the garden,' Tom said, and turned and left the room.

He ran down the stairs, out the front door and around to the back lawn. His dahlia stakes and their strings were still holding. The Crimson Sunbursts nodded their heads crazily, but they weren't going to be blown over, neither were the frizzy orange dahlias, Tom's favourites.

Lightning broke out in the slate-coloured sky to the south-west, and Tom stood waiting for the thunder as the rain wet his face. It came with an arrogant, rending sound, hollow.

What if the boy he met the other night were Frank Pierson? Sixteen years old. That was certainly more like it than the nineteen the boy had told him. Maine, not New York. When old Pierson died, hadn't there been a picture of the whole family in the *IHT*? There had been a picture of the father, anyway, whose face Tom realized he couldn't at all remember. Or had that been in the *Sunday Times*? But the boy of three days ago he remembered better than he usually remembered people. The boy's face was rather brooding and serious, and he didn't smile easily. A firm mouth, and level dark eyebrows. And the mole on his right cheek, not large enough to show up in the average photograph, perhaps, but a mark. The boy had been not only polite, but cautious.

'Tome! – come *in*!' That was Heloise, shouting from the french windows.

Tom ran towards her.

'Do you want to be hit by the lightning?'

Tom wiped his desert boots on the doormat. 'I'm not wet! I was thinking of something else!'

'Of what? Dry your hair.' She handed him a blue towel from the downstairs loo.

'Roger's coming this afternoon at three,' Tom said, wiping his face. 'Scarlatti for me. I must practise this morning and after lunch too.'

Heloise smiled. In the rainlight, her blue-grey eyes showed lavender spoke-like radiations from their pupils, which Tom adored. Had she chosen a lavender-coloured skirt especially for today, Tom wondered? Probably not, and it was merely a piece of aesthetic luck.

'I was just sitting down to practise myself,' Heloise replied primly in English, 'when I saw you standing on the lawn like an idiot.' She went to the harpsichord and sat down, sat up straight and shook her hands – like a professional, Tom thought.

He went to the kitchen. Mme Annette was clearing out the cabinet above the sideboard to the right of the sink. She had a dust-rag in her hand, and was wiping one spice jar after another from her perch of a three-legged wooden stool. It was too early for lunch preparations, and she had probably postponed her shopping in the village to this afternoon, because of the rainstorm.

'Just want to have a look at the old newspapers,' Tom said, stooping near the threshold of the next hall, which led to Mme Annette's quarters on the right. The old newspapers were kept in a basket with a handle, the type of basket used for firewood.

'Something in particular, Monsieur Tome? May I help you?'

'Thank you. I'll know in a minute. American newspapers I need. I think I can do it.' Tom spoke absently as he riffled through July *IHTs*. Obituary page or the news, that was the question, but he had a recollection of the Pierson items being in an upper left column of a right-hand page, with a photograph. There were only ten or so *IHTs* to look at, the others having been discarded. Tom went up to his room. Here he found more *IHTs*, but none had the write-up of John Pierson.

Heloise's Bach Invention sounded quite good from Tom's room. Was he jealous? Tom wanted to laugh. Was his own Scarlatti not going to be as good (in the ears of Roger Lepetit, of course) as Heloise's Bach this afternoon? Now Tom did laugh, put his hands on his hips, and looked at the little heap of newspapers on the floor with disappointment. *Who's Who*, he thought, and crossed the hall to the other front, turreted room which was their library. Tom pulled the *Who's Who* down, and found no entry for John Pierson. He tried *Who's Who in America*, an older volume than the English, but still found nothing on John Pierson. Both his *Who's Whos* were about five years old. And John Pierson might have been the type to refuse permission for an entry.

Heloise's third performance of the Invention concluded with a delicately ringing Schlussakkord.

Was the boy called Billy going to look him up again? Tom thought he would.

Tom practised his Scarlatti after lunch. He could now practise with concentration for thirty minutes or more without taking a break in the garden, which was progress from the original fifteen-minute session of months ago. Roger Lepetit (anything but petit, a tall plump young man, a French Schubert, Tom thought, spectacles and curly hair) said that gardening was ruinous for a pianist's or harpsichordist's hands, but Tom preferred to compromise: he didn't want to give up gardening, but he could perhaps leave the wrenching of milk-wort or whatever to their part-time gardener Henri. After all, he was not aiming to become a concert harpsichordist. All life was a compromise.

By 5.15, Roger Lepetit was saying, 'This is *legato* here. You must make an *effort* with the harpsichord to achieve a *legato* –'

The telephone rang.

Tom had been trying to achieve the correct tension, the correct degree of relaxation to do the simple piece properly. He now took a deep breath and got up, excusing himself. Heloise was upstairs, dressing to go off to her parents', having had her lesson. Tom picked up the downstairs telephone.

Heloise had already answered upstairs, and was talking in French. Tom recognized the voice of Billy, and interrupted.

'Mr Ripley,' Billy said. 'I've been to Paris. You know – about the Auberge thing. Interesting – it was.' The boy sounded shy.

'You found out something?'

'A little and – since it might amuse you, I thought – if you have a few minutes around seven tonight –'

'Tonight is fine,' said Tom.

They hung up abruptly, before Tom had time to ask how the boy would get here. Well, he had gotten here before. Tom flexed his shoulders and went back to the harpsichord. He sat up straight. He fancied his next rendition of the Scarlatti piccola sonata was better.

Roger Lepetit pronounced it fluent. High praise.

The rainstorm had exhausted itself by noon, and in late afternoon the garden shone bright and clean in unusually dustless sunlight. Heloise departed, saying she would be home by midnight or before. It was a drive of an hour and a half to Chantilly. She and her mother always talked after dinner, while her father retired no later than 10.30.

'The American boy you met is coming tonight at seven,' Tom said. 'Billy Rollins.'

'Oh. Of the other night, yes.'

'I'll offer him something to eat. He might be here when you get back.'

It was of no importance, and Heloise did not reply. 'Bye-bye, Tome!' she said, picking up her bouquet of long-stemmed shasta daisies with a single red peony, almost their last. Providently she wore a raincoat over her skirt and blouse.

Tom was listening to the seven o'clock news, when the outside gate bell rang. Tom had told Mme Annette he was expecting a caller at seven, and Tom intercepted her in the living room and said he would let his friend in himself.

Billy Rollins was walking across the gravelled stretch between the gates, which had been open, and the front door. Now he wore grey flannel trousers, a shirt and jacket. He carried something flat in a plastic bag under his arm.

'Evening, Mr Ripley,' he said, smiling.

'Evening. Come in. How did you get here – so punctually?'

'Taxi. Blowing it today,' said the boy, wiping his shoes on the doormat. 'This is for you.'

Tom opened the plastic bag and pulled out a record of Schubert's Lieder sung by Fischer-Dieskau, a new recording of which Tom had recently heard. 'Thank you very much. Just what I wanted, as they say. But I mean it, Billy.'

The boy's clothes looked immaculate, in contrast to the other evening. Mme Annette entered to ask what they wished. Tom introduced them.

'Sit down, Billy. A beer or something else?'

Billy sat down on the sofa. Mme Annette went to fetch beer to be added to the bar cart's offerings.

'My wife went to visit her parents,' Tom said. 'It's a usual Friday evening date with her.'

Tonight Mme Annette was attempting Tom's gin and tonic, with a slice of lemon. The more work Mme Annette had, the happier she was, and Tom had no complaint about the drinks she made for him.

'You had a harpsichord lesson today?' Billy had noticed the music books on the open harpsichord.

Tom said yes, Scarlatti, and for his wife a Bach Invention. 'Much more fun than playing bridge in the afternoon.' Tom was grateful that Billy did not suggest that he play something. 'Now your Paris trip – our four-footed friends.'

'Yes,' said Billy, tilting his head back as if he were thinking carefully before beginning. 'I spent Wednesday morning making sure the Auberge really didn't exist. I asked in a café, also at a garage which said they'd had a couple of people asking too – and I even asked the police in Veneux. They said they'd never heard of it, and they couldn't find it on a detailed map. Then I asked at a big hotel there, and *they'd* never heard of it.'

Tom knew, the Hotel Grand Veneux, probably, a name which had always made Tom think of 'the big venery', suggesting a huge lech of some kind. Tom winced at his own thoughts. 'You were pretty busy Wednesday morning, it seems.'

'Yes, and of course I worked Wednesday afternoon, because I do put in five or six hours a day for Madame Boutin.' He took a gulp of beer from his glass. 'Then Thursday, yesterday, I went to Paris, to the eighteenth arrondissement starting with Les Abbesses metro stop. Then Place Pigalle. I went to their post offices and asked about box two hundred and eighty-seven. That was not information for the public, they said. I asked the name of the person who was collecting, you see.' Billy smiled a little. 'I was in my work clothes, and I said I wanted to give ten francs to an animal fund, and wasn't that box number an animal fund. You'd have thought *I* was a crook, the way they looked at me!'

'But do you think you asked at the right post office?'

'I couldn't tell, because all the post offices in the eighteenth – or four of them – refused to say if they *had* a box two eighty-seven. So I did the next best thing – the logical thing, I thought,' Billy said, looking at Tom as if he expected him to guess what he had done.

Tom couldn't, at the moment. 'What?'

'I bought some paper and a stamp, went to the next café and wrote a letter to the Auberge saying, "Dear Auberge et cetera, your mimeographed establishment does not exist. I am one of the many duped – *trompés*, you know –"'

Tom nodded appreciatively.

'"– and I have allied myself with other well-meaning friends of your charitable – *fraud*. Therefore be prepared for an invasion by the legal authorities."' Billy sat forward, and there seemed to be a struggle going on in his face, or mind, between amusement and righteous indignation. His cheeks had pinkened, he smiled and frowned at the same time. 'I said their *post box* would be watched.'

'Excellent,' said Tom. 'I hope they're squirming.'

'I did hang around one promising post office, hoping. I said to a girl behind the window, how often do they come to collect? She wouldn't tell me. That's typically French, of course. Not that she was trying to protect anybody necessarily.'

Tom knew. 'How is it you know so much about the French? And you speak a pretty good French too, don't you?'

'Oh – we had it in school, of course. Then – a couple of years ago I – my family spent a summer in France. Down south.'

Tom had the feeling the boy had been brought several times to France, maybe starting at the early age of five. No one learned decent French in an ordinary American high school. Tom opened another Heineken at the bar cart and brought it to the coffee table. He had decided to plunge in. 'Did you read about the death of the American John Pierson – about a month ago?'

Surprise showed in the boy s eyes for an instant, then he seemed to be trying to remember. 'I think I heard something – somewhere.'

Tom waited, then said, 'One of the two boys in the family disappeared. The one called Frank. The family's worried.'

'Oh? I didn't know.'

Had the boy's face gone paler? 'It just occurred to me – he might be you,' Tom said.

'Me?' The boy sat forward, beer glass in hand, and his eyes left Tom and fixed on the fireplace. 'I wouldn't be working as a gardener, I think, if –'

Tom let some fifteen seconds pass. Nothing more came from the boy. 'Shall we try your record? How did you know I liked Fischer-Dieskau? From the harpsichord?' Tom laughed. He switched on the hi-fi controls, which were on a shelf to the left of the fireplace.

The piano began, then Fischer-Dieskau's light baritone came in, singing in German. Tom felt instantly more alive, happier, then he smiled, thinking of an awful deep baritone he had happened to catch on his transistor only last evening, a groaning Englishman singing in English and making Tom think of a dying water buffalo, maybe lying in mud with its feet in the air, though the words had been about a dainty Cornish maiden he had loved and lost years ago, a good many years ago, judging from the maturity of the voice. Tom suddenly laughed out loud, and realized that he was unusually tense.

'What's funny?' asked the boy.

'I was thinking of a title I made up for a Lied. "My soul has not been the same since Thursday afternoon, when on opening a book of Goethe's poems, I discovered an old laundry list." It goes better in German. *"Seit Donnerstag Nachmittag ist meine Seele nicht dieselbe, denn ich fand beim Durchblättern eines Bandes von Goethegedichten eine alte Wäscheliste."'*

The boy was laughing too – with the same kind of tension? He shook his head. 'I don't understand many German words. But it's funny. Souls! Ha!'

The lovely music continued, and Tom lit a Gauloise and walked slowly about the living room, wondering how he should proceed. Really force it and ask to see the boy's passport, ask to see something – such as a letter addressed to him – by way of settling the matter?

At the end of a song, the boy said, 'I don't think I want to listen to the whole side, if you don't mind.'

'Of course not.' Tom switched the machine off. He put the record back into its sleeve.

'You were asking me – about the man called Pierson.'

'Yes.'

'What if I were to say –' The boy's voice sank low, as if someone else in the room or maybe Mme Annette in the kitchen might be listening. '– I'm his son who ran away?'

'Oh,' Tom said calmly, 'I would say that's your business. If you wanted to come to Europe – incognito – it's been done before.'

The boy's face looked relieved, a corner of his mouth twitched. But he kept silent, rolling his half-full glass between his palms.

'Except that the family is worried, it seems,' Tom said.

Mmé Annette came in. 'Excuse me, Monsieur Tome, will there be –'

'Yes, I think so,' said Tom, because Mme Annette had been about to ask if there would be two for dinner. 'You can stay for a bite, can't you, Billy?'

'Yes, I'd like to. Thank you.'

Mme Annette smiled at the boy, more with her eyes than her lips. She liked guests, liked making them happy. 'About fifteen minutes, Monsieur Tome?'

When Mme Annette left the living room, the boy squirmed to the edge of the sofa and asked, 'Can we take a look at your garden before it gets dark?'

Tom stood up. They went out through the french windows, down the few steps to grass level. The sun was sinking in the left corner of the horizon, glowing orange and pink through the pine trees. Tom sensed that the boy wanted to get farther away from Mme Annette's ears, but for the moment he was taken by the scenery.

'Now this has some quality – as a layout. Nice – but not too formal.'

'I can't take credit for the design. It was here. I just try to maintain it.'

The boy bent to look at some London Pride (not blooming now), and he knew it by name, to Tom's surprise. Then he turned his attention to the greenhouse.

Here were multi-coloured leaves, blossoms, plants ready to be given away to friends, all in proper dampness and rich soil. The boy inhaled as if he loved it. Was this really the son of John Pierson, raised in luxury to take over the business reins – unless that was the older son's duty? Why didn't he talk now, in the privacy of the greenhouse? But the boy kept peering at pots, and touched one plant gently with a fingertip.

'Let's go back,' Tom said, a bit impatient.

'Yes, sir.' The boy straightened as if he had done something wrong, and followed Tom out.

What kind of school demanded 'Yes, sir' these days? A military school?

They had dinner in the alcove off the living room. The main dish was chicken with dumplings, the dumplings laid on after the boy's telephone call this afternoon, at Tom's request. Tom had taught Mme Annette how to make dumplings in the American style. The boy ate well and seemed to enjoy the Montrachet also. He asked polite questions about Heloise, where did her parents live, and what were they like? Tom restrained himself from giving his real opinion of the Plissons, especially the father.

'Does your – does Madame Annette speak English?'

Tom smiled. 'She doesn't even say "Good morning." Doesn't like English, I think. Why?'

The boy moistened his lips and leaned forward. More than a metre of table still separated them. 'What if I were to tell that that I am the – person you were speaking of – Frank?'

'Yes, you asked that before,' Tom said, realizing that Frank was feeling what he had drunk. All to the good! 'You're here – just to get away from home for a while?'

'Yes,' Frank said in an earnest way. 'You won't give me away, will you? I hope not.' He was almost whispering, trying to look at Tom steadily, but his eyes swam a little.

'Certainly not. You can trust me. You probably had your own reasons –'

'Yes. I would like to be somebody else,' the boy interrupted, 'for maybe –' He stopped. 'I was sorry to run off the way I did, but – but –'

Tom listened, sensing that Frank was coming out with only part of the truth, and might not come out with much more tonight. Tom felt grateful for the power of vino and its veritas. There was a limit to how much one could lie with it, at least someone as young as Frank Pierson. 'Tell me about your family. Isn't there a John Junior?'

'Yes, Johnny.' Frank twirled the stem of his wine glass. He was now staring at the middle of the table. 'I took his passport. I stole it from his room. He's eighteen, nearly nineteen. I can forge his signature – or at least well enough to get by. I don't mean I ever tried it before – not at all till now.' Frank paused, and swayed his head as if confused by many thoughts at the same time.

'Then what did you do after you ran away?'

'I took a plane to London, stayed there for – I think five days. Then I went to France, Paris.'

'I see. And you had enough money? You weren't forging Travellers Cheques?'

'Oh, no, I took some cash, two or three thousand. That was easy – from the house. I can open the safe, of course.'

At this moment, Mme Annette came in to remove some dishes and to serve the strawberry – fraises des bois – shortcake with whipped cream.

'And Johnny,' Tom said to start the ball rolling again, when Mme Annette was gone.

'Johnny's at Harvard. On vacation now, of course.'

'And where's the house?'

Frank's eyes swam again, as if he were thinking, which house? 'Maine. Kennebunkport. That house?'

'The funeral was in Maine, was it? I seem to remember. You left from the Maine house?' Now Tom was surprised at the boy's apparent shock at the question.

'Kennebunkport, yes. We're usually there at this time of the year. The funeral was there – the cremation.'

Do you think your father killed himself, Tom wanted to ask, but he thought the question was vulgar, would be only to satisfy his curiosity, so he did not put it. 'And how is your mother?' Tom asked instead, as if he knew Frank's mother and was inquiring about her health.

'Oh, she's – she's rather pretty – even though she's forty something. Blonde.'

'You get along well with her?'

'Yes, sure. She's more cheerful than – than my father was. She likes social life. And politics.'

'Politics? What kind?'

'Republican.' Here Frank smiled and looked at Tom.

'Your father's second wife, I think.' Tom thought he remembered that from the obituary.

'Yes.'

'And you told your mother where you are?'

'Well, no. I left a note saying I was going to New Orleans, because they know I like New Orleans. I've stayed before at the Hotel Monteleone – by myself. I had to walk to the bus stop from the house, otherwise Eugene – he's the driver – would've driven me to the railroad station and somehow – they might've know I wasn't going to New Orleans. I just wanted to get away on my own feet, so I did, and I got to Bangor, then New York and caught a plane over. May I?' Frank reached for a cigarette from a silver cup. 'No doubt my family rang up the Monteleone, and found out I wasn't there, so this accounts for – I know, I read it in the *Trib* which I buy sometimes.'

'How long after the funeral did you leave?'

Frank struggled for the exact answer. 'A week – maybe eight days after.'

'Now why don't you send your mother a cable and say you're okay and in France and want to stay a while longer? It's a bore to have to hide, isn't it?' But maybe the game amused Frank, Tom thought also.

'At the moment, I happen not to want – any contact with them. I'd like to be on my own. Free.' He said it with determination.

Tom nodded. 'At least now I know why your hair stands up. You used to part it on the left.'

'I did.'

Mme Annette was bringing a tray of coffee to the living room. Frank and Tom got up, Tom glancing at his watch. It was not even ten as yet. Why had Frank Pierson decided that Tom Ripley would be sympathetic? Because Ripley had a shaky reputation, according to the newspaper files which the boy perhaps had seen? Had Frank done something wrong too? Killed his father, maybe, pushed him over the cliff?

'Ah-hem,' Tom said for no reason, swinging a foot as he walked towards the coffee table. Disturbing thought, that. And was it the first time, even, that it had crossed his mind? Tom wasn't sure. Anyway, he would let the boy come out with that one, if and when he wished to. '*Coffee,*' Tom said firmly.

'Maybe you want me to take off?' asked Frank, having seen Tom glance at his watch.

'No, no, I was thinking about Heloise. She said she'd be back before midnight, but it's a long time till midnight. Sit down.' Tom fetched the brandy bottle from the bar cart. The more Frank talked tonight, the better, and Tom would see him home. 'Cognac.' Tom poured, and poured the same amount for himself, though he disliked cognac.

Frank looked at his own wristwatch. 'I'll leave before your wife gets back.'

Heloise, Tom supposed, was one more person who might discover Frank's identity. 'Unfortunately, they're going to widen the search, Frank. Don't they know already that you're in France?'

'I don't know.'

'Sit down. They must know. The search might even get to a small town like Moret, once they've finished with Paris.'

'Not if I wear old clothes and have a job – and another name.'

Kidnapping, Tom thought. That might come next, certainly was a possibility. Tom didn't want to remind Frank of the Getty boy's kidnapping, that fine-tooth-comb search that had still been futile. The kidnappers had snipped off an ear lobe to prove that they had the boy, and the three million dollars ransom had been paid. Frank Pierson was hot property also. If crooks recognized him (and they would be trying more than the general public), it would be more profitable to kidnap him than to turn the attention of the police to him. 'Why,' Tom asked, 'did you take your brother's passport? Haven't you got a passport?'

'Yes. A new one.' Frank had sat down, in the same corner of the sofa as before. 'I don't know. Maybe because he's older and I felt safer. We look a little bit alike. Only he's blonder.' Frank winced as if with shame.

'You get along with Johnny? You like him?'

'Oh, pretty well. Sure.' Frank looked at Tom.

That was a genuine answer, Tom felt. 'Got along all right with your father?'

Frank looked towards the fireplace. 'It's hard to talk about since –'

Tom let him struggle.

'First he wanted Johnny to take an interest in Pierson – the company, I mean, then he wanted me to. Johnny can't make it into Harvard Business School, or he doesn't want to. Johnny's interested in *photography*.' Frank said it as if it were something bizarre, and gave Tom a glance. 'So Dad then started on me. This was – oh, more than a *year* ago. I kept saying I wasn't sure, because it's a very big – business, you know, and why should I want to – dedicate my *life* to it.' There was a flash of wrath in Frank's brown eyes.

Tom waited.

'So – maybe no, we didn't get along so well – if I'm honest.' Frank picked up his coffee cup. He had not tasted the brandy, and maybe didn't need it, because he was talking quite well.

The seconds passed, nothing more came from Frank, and out of mercy, because Tom could see there was more pain to come, Tom said, 'I noticed you looking at the Derwatt.' He nodded towards 'Man in Chair' over the fireplace. 'Do you like it? It's my favourite.'

'It's one I don't know. I know that one – from a catalogue,' Frank said with a glance over his left shoulder.

He meant 'The Red Chairs', a genuine Derwatt, and Tom knew at once which catalogue the boy had probably looked at, a recent one from the Buckmaster Gallery. The gallery now made an effort to keep the forgeries out of its catalogues.

'Were some really forged?' Frank asked.

'I don't know,' Tom said, with his best effort at sincerity. 'Never was proven. No. I seem to remember Derwatt came to London to verify – certain ones.'

'Yes, I thought maybe you were there, because you know the people at that gallery, don't you?' Now Frank perked up a bit. 'My father has a Derwatt, you know.'

Tom was glad to veer slightly. 'What one?'

'It's called "The Rainbow". Do you know it? Beige colours below, and a rainbow mostly red above. All fuzzy and jagged. You can't tell what city it is, Mexico or New York.'

Tom knew. A Bernard Tufts forgery. 'I know,' Tom said, as if with fond memory of a genuine. 'Your father liked Derwatt?'

'Who doesn't? There's something warm about his stuff – human, I mean, which you don't find in modern painting all the time. I mean – if someone wants warmth. Francis Bacon is tough and real, but so is *this*, even if it's just a couple of little girls.' The boy looked over his left shoulder at the two little girls in the red chairs, flaming red fire behind them, a picture that could certainly be called warm because of its subject matter, but Tom knew Frank meant a warmth of attitude on Derwatt's part, which showed in his repeated outlines of bodies and faces.

Tom felt a curiously personal affront, because apparently the boy did not prefer 'Man in Chair', which showed an equal warmth on the part of the painter, though neither the man nor the chair was on fire. It was a phony, though. That was why Tom preferred it. At least Frank had not yet asked if it might be a phony, a question which if he put it would be based on something he had heard or read, Tom thought. 'You evidently enjoy paintings.'

Frank squirmed a very little. 'I like Rembrandt a lot. Maybe you think that's funny. My father has one. He keeps it away in a *safe* somewhere. But I've seen it several times. Not very big.' Frank cleared his throat and sat up. 'But for pleasure –'

That was what painting was all about, Tom thought, regardless of Picasso saying that paintings were to make war.

'I like Vuillard and Bonnard. *They're* cosy. This modern stuff, abstracts – maybe one day I'll understand it.'

'So at least you had something in common with your father, you both liked paintings. He took you to art exhibits?'

'Well, I went. I mean, I liked them, yes. Since I was about twelve, I remember. But my father was in a wheelchair since I was about five. Someone shot at him, you know?'

Tom nodded, realizing suddenly that John Pierson's condition would have made it a strange life for Frank's mother for the past eleven years.

'All business, charming business,' Frank said cynically. 'My father knew who was behind it, some other food company. Hired killer. But my father never tried to persecute – *prosecute*, because he knew he would only get more of the same. You know? That's the way things are in the States.'

Tom could imagine. 'Try your cognac.' The boy picked it up, sipped and winced. 'Where's your mother now?'

'Maine, I suppose. Or maybe the New York apartment, I don't know.'

Tom wanted to press the matter again, to see if Frank would say something new. 'Call her up, Frank. You must know both numbers. The phone's right there.' It was on a table near the front door. 'I'll go upstairs so I won't hear anything you're saying.' Tom stood up.

'I don't want them to know where I *am*.' Frank looked with steadier eyes at Tom. 'I would call up a girl if I could, but I can't even let *her* know where I am.'

'What girl?'

'Teresa.'

'She lives in New York?'

'Yes.'

'Why *don't* you ring her up? Isn't she worried? You don't have to tell her where you are. I'll still go upstairs –'

But Frank was shaking his head, slowly. 'She might be able to tell it comes from France. I can't risk that.'

Had he perhaps run away from the girl? 'Did you tell Teresa you were going away?'

'I told her I was thinking of taking a short trip.'

'Did you have a quarrel with her?'

'Oh, no. No.' A quiet, happy amusement spread over Frank's face, a look of dreaming that Tom had not seen before. Then the boy looked at his wristwatch and stood up. 'I'm sorry.'

It was only eleven or so, but Tom knew Frank did not want Heloise to see him again. 'Have you got a picture of Teresa?'

'Oh, yes!' Again happiness shone in his face as he reached into the inside pocket of his jacket for his billfold. 'This one. My favourite. Even though it's only a polaroid.' He handed Tom a small square snapshot in a transparent envelope which just fitted it.

Tom saw a brown-haired girl with lively eyes, a mischievous smile with closed lips, eyes slightly narrowed. The hair was straight and shining, shortish, the face more full of fun than mischief, really, as if she had been snapped while dancing. 'She has charm,' Tom said.

Frank nodded, happy and wordless. 'You don't mind driving me back? These shoes are comfortable but –'

Tom laughed. 'Nothing easier.' Frank wore Gucci shoes, black moccasin-style of crinkly leather, well-shined now. His brown and tan tweed jacket, a Harris tweed, had an interesting diamond pattern that Tom might have chosen for himself. 'I'll see if madame is still awake and tell her I'm leaving and coming back. She sometimes gets disturbed by car sounds, but she *is* expecting Heloise. Use the downstairs loo, if you want.' Tom gestured towards a narrow door in the front hall.

The boy went off to use it, and Tom walked through the kitchen to Mme Annette's door. Her light was off, he saw from a look at the crack under the door. Tom scribbled a note on the desk where the telephone was: 'Driving a friend home. Back by midnight probably. T.' Tom left it on the third step of the stairs where Heloise would be sure to see it.

THREE

Tom wanted to see Frank's 'little house' tonight, and on the road he put the request casually. 'Can I see where you're living? Or would that bother Madame Boutin?'

'Oh, she goes to bed around ten! Sure, you can see it.'

They were just then entering Moret. Tom knew the route now, made the left turn into the Rue de Paris and slowed for number 78 on the left. There was a car parked near the Boutin house facing Tom. Since the street was empty of traffic, Tom pulled over to the left to park, his headlights lit the front of the parked car, and Tom noticed that the licence plate ended in 75, which indicated a car registered in Paris.

At the same time, the car's headlights came on at their brightest into Tom's windshield, and the Paris car backed quickly. Tom thought he saw two men in the front seats.

'What's that?' Frank asked, sounding a bit alarmed.

'Just what I was wondering.' Tom watched the car back into the nearest turn on the left, then pull out and roll away at a good speed. 'Paris car.' Tom had stopped, but his lights were still on. 'I'm going to park around the corner.'

Tom did so, in the still darker and smaller road in which the Paris car had made its turn. Tom put out his lights, and locked three doors with the buttons after Frank had got out. 'Maybe nothing to worry about,' Tom said, but he felt a little worried, imagined that there might be one man, or two, lurking in Mme Boutin's garden now. 'A torch,' Tom said, getting his from the glove compartment. He locked the driver's door, and they walked towards the Boutin house.

Frank took the long key from his inside jacket pocket, and opened the gates of the driveway or carriage entrance into the garden.

Tom tensed himself for a possible fistfight just inside the gates – which were only about nine feet high, not difficult to climb even with their spikes at the top. The front gate would have been even easier.

'Lock them again,' Tom whispered as they both went through.

Frank did. Now Frank had the torch, and Tom followed him as he walked between grapevines and some trees that might have been apple towards a small house on the right. Mme Boutin's house on the left was quite dark. Tom heard no sound at all, not even that of a neighbour's television. French villages could be deadly silent by midnight.

'Watch out,' Frank whispered, indicating with the torch a cluster of three buckets that Tom should avoid. Frank pulled a smaller key out, opened the door of the little house, switched on the light, and handed Tom his torch back. 'Simple, but it's home!' Frank said gaily, closing the door behind him and Tom.

It was one not very big room with a single bed, a wooden table painted white, on which lay a couple of paperback books, a French newspaper, ballpoint pens, a mug of half-finished coffee. A workman's blue shirt hung over a straight chair. At one end of the room was a sink and a small wood-burning stove, a waste-basket, a towel rack. A brown leather suitcase, not new, rested on a high shelf, and below the shelf a rod about a yard long served for clothes-hanging, and Tom saw a couple of pairs of trousers, jeans and a raincoat.

'Bed's more comfortable than this chair to sit on,' said Frank. 'I can offer you Nescafé – made with cold water.'

Tom smiled. 'You don't have to offer me anything. I think your place is quite – adequate.' The walls looked freshly whitewashed, maybe by

Frank. 'And that's pretty,' Tom said, noticing a watercolour on a piece of white cardboard (the cardboard that came at the bottom of writing paper tablets) propped against the wall on Frank's bed table. The bedside table was a wooden crate on which stood also a red rose with some wild flowers in a glass. The watercolour was of the gates they had just passed through, partly opened in the picture. It was direct, bold, and not at all worked over.

'Yes, that. I found some kid's watercolours in the drawer of the table here.' Now the boy looked more sleepy than drunk.

'I shall be pushing off,' Tom said, reaching for the door-knob. 'Phone me again when you feel like it.' Tom had the door half open, when he saw a light come on in Mme Boutin's house about twenty yards away straight ahead.

Frank saw it too. 'Now what?' Frank said with irritation. 'We didn't make any noise.'

Tom wanted to flee, but suddenly in the absolute silence he heard her footsteps on what sounded like gravel and pretty near. 'I'm going to hide in the bushes,' Tom whispered, and he moved even as he spoke, out and to the left, where he knew there was darkness either against the garden wall or under a tree.

The old lady was watching her footing with the aid of a feeble pencil-like flashlight. 'C'est Billy?'

'Mais oui, madame!' Frank said.

Tom was crouched, with one hand on the ground, about six yards from Frank's little house. Mme Boutin was saying that two men had arrived around ten o'clock, asking to see him.

'To see me? Who were they?' Frank said.

'They didn't say their names. They wanted to see my gardener, they said. Strangers to me! Bizarre to look for a gardener at ten o'clock, I thought!' Mme Boutin sounded vexed and suspicious.

'It's not my fault,' said Frank. 'What did they look like?'

'Oh, I saw only one. Maybe thirty years old. He asked when you would be back. I didn't know!'

'I am sorry they disturbed you, madame. I am not looking for other work, I assure you.'

'I trust not! I don't like such people ringing my doorbell at night.' Now, her small, rather stooped figure was taking its leave. 'I keep my two gates locked. But I came all the way to the front gate to speak to them.'

'We should – forget it, Madame Boutin. I am sorry.'

'Good night, Billy, and sleep well.'

'And you too, madame!'

Tom waited, watching her progress back to the house. He heard Frank close his house door, then finally the turning of a lock in Mme Boutin's house, the faint creak of a second key, then the firm clunk of a bolt that she slid home. Or was that even final? There were no more noises of closures, but still Tom waited. A light on the floor above the ground floor glowed dimly through clouded glass. Then that went out. Frank was evidently waiting for him to make the first move, which Tom thought intelligent of the boy. Tom crept from the bushes, approached the door of the little house, and tapped with his fingertips.

Frank opened the door partway, and Tom slipped in.

'I heard that,' Tom whispered. 'I think you'd better leave tonight. Now.'

'*Do* you?' Frank looked startled. 'I know you're right. I know, I know.'

'Now – let's get going and pack up. You'll stay at my house tonight and worry about tomorrow tomorrow. This is your only suitcase?' Tom took it from the high shelf, and opened it on the bed.

They worked smoothly, Tom handing Frank things, trousers, shirts, sneakers, boots, toothpaste and toothbrush. Frank worked with his head down, and Tom felt he was on the brink of tears.

'Nothing to worry about if we evade those creeps tonight,' Tom said softly, 'and tomorrow we'll leave the nice old lady a note – maybe saying you phoned your family tonight and you have to get back to the States right away. Something like that. But we can't waste time with it now.'

Frank pressed his raincoat down, and closed the suitcase.

Tom took his torch from the table. 'Wait a sec., I want to see if they've come back.'

Tom walked as noiselessly as possible over the mowed grass towards the gates. He was able to see only some three yards around him without the torch, and he didn't want to put the torch on. No car was in front of the Boutin house, anyway. Could they be waiting near his car around the corner? Nasty thought. The gates were now locked, so Tom couldn't go round the corner and see. He went back for Frank, and found him with suitcase in hand, ready to go. Frank left the key in the lock of the little house, its door locked, and they went on to the gates.

'Stay here for a minute,' Tom said when Frank had unlocked the gates. 'I want to look round the corner.'

Frank lowered his suitcase, and nervously started to come with Tom, but Tom pushed him back, made sure the gate looked closed, and walked towards the corner. He felt rather safe, because the two men certainly weren't after him.

His own car was the only one that Tom could see. That was reassuring. People in this neighbourhood had garages, and no cars were parked at the kerbs. Tom only hoped that the two men had not taken notice of his licence plates, because if they had, they might trace his name and address via the police on some made-up grounds of misdemeanour or affront. Tom walked back for Frank, who was still behind the gates. The boy came out when Tom beckoned.

'I don't know what to do with this key,' Frank said.

'Drop it behind the gate,' Tom whispered. Frank had locked the gate again. 'We'll tell her in the note tomorrow.'

They walked, Frank carrying his suitcase and Tom a small carry-all, round the corner, and got into the car, which seemed a haven to Tom as soon as they had closed its doors. Tom concentrated on getting out of the town, and by a different route. As far as he could see, he was not being followed. In the main part of town, across the old bridge with its four towers, very few street lights were on, one bar was closing, only two or three cars moved, paying no attention to him. Tom took the big N 5, and made a right turn towards the tiny town of Obelique on a road that would take them finally to Villeperce.

'Don't be worried,' Tom said. 'I know where I'm going and I don't think anyone's following us.'

Frank seemed sunk in his own thoughts.

The little world of Mme Boutin was shattered, Tom thought, and the boy didn't know where he was now. 'I'll have to tell Heloise you're staying the night,' Tom said. 'But you'll still be Billy Rollins to her. I'll tell her you want to do some gardening for us, and –' Tom looked into his car mirror again, but nothing was behind them. 'I'll say you're looking for a part-time job. Don't worry.' Tom glanced at Frank. The boy was staring through the windshield and biting his underlip.

They were home. Tom saw the gentle glow of Belle Ombre's front court light, which Heloise had left on for him, and he drove through the open gates into the garage at the right of the house. Tom saw that Heloise had parked the red Mercedes Benz in the right-hand garage space. Tom got out, asked Frank to wait a moment, then he got the big key from under the rhododendrons and locked the front gates.

By then Frank was standing with suitcase and carry-all beside the car. One living room light was on. Tom put on another light which lit the stairs, turned off the living room light, then went out and beckoned for Frank to follow him. They turned left at the top of the stairs, and Tom put on the light in the guest room. Heloise's door was closed.

'Make yourself comfortable,' Tom said to Frank. 'Closet's here –' He opened a cream-coloured door. 'Drawers there – and use my bathroom tonight, because the one here is Heloise's. I won't be asleep for another hour probably.'

'Thank you.' Frank had put his suitcase on the short oak bench at the foot of one of the twin beds.

Tom went into his room, put on the light, and also the light in the bathroom. Then he couldn't resist going to his front window, whose curtains had been drawn by Mme Annette, and peering out to see if any car was cruising past or parked. He saw nothing but darkness, except for the area of light under a street lamp to the left. Of course a lightless car could be parked out there, but Tom preferred to think none was.

Frank knocked on the partly open door, and came in in pyjamas, toothbrush in hand, barefoot. Tom gestured towards the bathroom.

'All yours,' Tom said, 'and take your time.' Tom smiled, watching the tired boy – shadows under his eyes now – walk into the bathroom and close the door. Tom got into pyjamas. He would be interested to see what the *IHT* might have to say in the next days about the disappearance of Frank Pierson. Surely the search would be hotting up. Tom went down the hall to Heloise's room, looked through the keyhole through which he could always see some light, if any light was on, though the key remained in the lock inside. No light.

Tom went back to his own room, and was in bed browsing in a French grammar when Frank came out of the bathroom, smiling, with dampish hair.

'A hot shower! Wow!'

'Go and get some sleep. Sleep as late as you like.'

Then Tom went to wash. He was thinking about the car in front of Mme Boutin's. Whoever the two men had been, they had not wanted to risk a noisy fight, or even a meeting with Frank and another person. Still it boded no good. On the other hand, it might be petty curiosity: someone in Moret might have mentioned seeing a new boy, an American, who might be Frank Pierson, and the same person might have a Paris friend. The men hadn't asked for Frank, it seemed, just for Mme Boutin's 'gardener'. Tom thought he would deliver Frank's note to Mme Boutin tomorrow without the boy, and as quickly as possible.

FOUR

A solitary bird – not a lark – awakened Tom with a six-note song. What bird was it? Its voice sounded questioning, almost timid, yet curious too, and full of vigour. This bird or one of its family often woke Tom in summer. Now with barely opened eyes he looked at his grey walls, darker grey shadows – which looked like a wash drawing. Tom liked it, the lump of brass-cornered chest, the darker lump of desk. He sighed, and snuggled deeper into his pillow for a final snooze.

Frank!

Tom suddenly remembered the boy was in the house, and came full awake. 7.35 now by his watch. Tell Heloise that Frank was here – rather, Billy Rollins. Tom put on slippers and dressing gown, and went downstairs. It would be comforting to speak with Mme Annette first, and he was ahead of her as to time for his coffee at eight. Guests never bothered Mme Annette, and she never asked how long they were staying, except in regard to the next several meals.

The kettle had just begun to hum as Tom walked into the kitchen. '*Bonjour, madame!*' he called cheerily.

'*Monsieur Tome! Vous avez bien dormi?*'

'Excellently, thank you. We have a guest this morning, the young American you met last night – Billy Rollins. He is in the guest room and may be here for a few days. He likes to do gardening.'

'Oh, yes? A *nice* young man!' Mme Annette said with an air of approval. 'And what time would he like his breakfast? – Your coffee, Monsieur Tome.'

Tom's coffee had dripped, the kettle was for Heloise's tea. He watched Mme Annette pour black coffee into a white cup. 'Don't trouble yourself. I told him to sleep as late as he wished. He may come down. I can see about that.' Heloise's tray was ready, and Mme Annette picked it up. 'I'll go up with you,' said Tom, and followed her with his cup of coffee.

Tom waited until Mme Annette had knocked and entered Heloise's room with the tray of tea, grapefruit and toast, then went to the open door.

Heloise was awakening. 'Ah, Tome, come in! I was so tired last night –'

'But at least you weren't late. I was home by midnight, I think. Listen, my dear, I asked the American boy to stay the night. He's going to do some gardening for us. He's in the guest room. Billy Rollins. You met him.'

'Oh,' said Heloise, and spooned some grapefruit into her mouth. She was not much surprised, but she asked, 'Hasn't he a place to live? He has no money?'

Tom answered carefully. They were talking in English. 'I'm sure he has some money, enough to put himself up somewhere, but he said last night he was not too happy with the place where he's staying, so I said come to our house for the night, and we fetched his things. He's a well brought up boy.' Tom added, 'Eighteen, likes gardening and seems to know quite a bit. If he wants to work for us for a while – there're cheap lodgings at the Jacobs'.' The Jacobs were a couple in Villeperce who ran a bar-restaurant, with a three-room 'hotel' on the floor above.

Munching into toast now, Heloise was more alert and said, 'You are so impulsive, Tome. An American boy in our house – just like that! And suppose he is a thief? You ask him to stay the night – and how do you know he is there now?'

Tom lowered his head for a moment. 'You are right. But this boy isn't one of the – hitchhiker types. You've –' At that moment, Tom heard a gentle buzz like that of his own travel clock's alarm. Heloise seemed not to have heard it, as she was not so near the hall. 'I think he's set his alarm. See you in a while.'

Tom went out, still carrying his coffee, closed Heloise's door, and rapped on Frank's door.

'Yes? Come in.'

Tom found Frank sitting up on one elbow. On his night table was a travel clock much like Tom's own. 'Morning.'

'Good morning, sir.' Frank pushed his hair back, and swung his legs over the edge of the bed.

Tom was amused. 'Want to sleep some more?'

'No, I thought eight was a good time to get up.'

'Coffee?'

'Yes, thank you. I can come down.'

Tom said he preferred to bring him coffee, and went down to the kitchen. Mme Annette had already prepared a tray of orange juice, toast and the usual, and Tom started to pick it up, but Mme Annette told him she had not poured the coffee as yet.

She poured coffee into the pre-heated silver pot on the tray. 'Do you really want to take it up, Monsieur Tome? If the young man wishes an egg –'

'I think this will be perfect, Madame Annette.' Tom went up.

Frank tried the coffee and said, 'Um-m!'

Tom replenished his own cup from the new pot, and sat down on a chair. He had put the tray on the writing table. 'You must write that note to Madame Boutin this morning. The sooner the better, and I'll deliver it.'

'Right.' Frank was savouring his coffee, waking up. The hair on top of his head now stood straight up, as if in a wind.

'And where the gate key is. Just behind the gates.'

The boy nodded.

Tom let him bite into some toast and marmalade. 'Do you remember the date you left home?'

'July twenty-seventh.'

It was now Saturday the nineteenth of August. 'You were in London a few days and then – where did you stay in Paris?'

'Hôtel d'Angleterre, Rue Jacob.'

Tom knew the hotel, but he had never stayed there. It was in the Saint-Germain-des-Prés area. 'Can I see the passport you've got now? Your brother's?'

Frank went at once to his suitcase, got the passport from the suitcase's top pocket, and handed it to Tom.

Tom opened it and turned it sideways to see a picture of a more blond young man, hair parted on the right, with thinner face, yet with some resemblance to Frank in eyes, brows and mouth. How had he made it, however, Tom wondered. Luck, so far. This boy would be almost nineteen, five feet eleven, therefore a bit taller than Frank was at present. In French hotels it was no longer necessary to present a passport or card of identity. But the immigration bureaux of England and France must have been informed by now that Frank Pierson was missing, might have been sent a photograph of Frank. And wouldn't his brother have missed his passport by now?

'You may as well give up, you know,' Tom said, trying a new tack. 'How are you going to go on in Europe like this? They'll stop you at any border. Maybe especially the French border.'

The boy looked stunned, also affronted.

'I don't understand why you want to hide.'

The boy's eyes shifted, but not with dishonesty. Frank seemed to be asking himself what he wanted to do. 'I'd like to be *quiet* – just for a few more days.'

Tom noticed a tremble in the boy's hand as he started to put the napkin back on the tray, then absently half folded it and dropped it. 'Your mother must know by now that you took Johnny's passport, that yours is at home. They could easily trace you to France. It's going to be more unpleasant to be picked up by the police here than if you simply tell them now.' Tom set his cup on Frank's tray. 'I'll leave you so you can write that note to Madame Boutin. I told Heloise you're here. Got some paper you can write on?'

'Yes, sir.'

Tom had been about to offer him some typewriter paper and a cheap envelope, because the notepaper in the guest room drawer had Belle Ombre's address on it. Tom went into his room, shaved with his battery razor, and put on old green corduroy trousers that he often wore when gardening. It was a lovely day, coolish and sunny. He did some watering in his greenhouse, thought about what he and Frank might do that morning, and put out the secateurs and fork. He was interested in the morning post, due in a few minutes. When Tom heard the familiar creak of the post van's handbrake, he walked towards his front gates.

He wanted to see if the *IHT* had an item anywhere in it about Frank Pierson, and he looked for this first, even though he saw a letter from Jeff Constant of London. Oddly, Jeff, a free-lance photographer, was a better correspondent than Edmund Banbury who hardly did anything else but manage the Buckmaster Gallery and spend most of his time there. Nothing in the news pages or in the *People* column about Frank Pierson. Tom suddenly thought of *France-Dimanche*, the old gossip rag of the weekend. Today was Saturday, and there would be a fresh edition. *France-Dimanche* was almost exclusively concerned with people's sexual activities, but money came next in their interest. He opened Jeff's letter in the living room.

Jeff didn't mention Derwatt's name, Tom saw from a glance at the typewritten page. Jeff said he agreed with Tom that a stop should be put, and had so informed the right people, after discussing it with Ed. Tom knew he meant by the right people a young painter in London called Steuerman, who had been attempting Derwatt forgeries for them – maybe five by now – but whose work could not hold a candle to that of the dedicated Bernard Tufts. Though Derwatt was presumed deceased by now, in his little Mexican village whose name he had never disclosed, Jeff and Ed had been keen for years now on 'finding' old efforts of Derwatt's, and trying to market them. Jeff went on: 'This will cut our intake considerably, but as you know, we've always listened to your advice, Tom . . .' He ended by asking Tom to tear up his letter. Tom felt a bit relieved, and began to tear up Jeff's letter, slowly, into little bits.

Frank came down with an envelope in his hand. He wore blue jeans. 'It's done. Could you take a look? I think it's all right.'

He made Tom think of a schoolboy handing a paper to a teacher. Tom noticed two small mistakes in the French, which he thought normal. Frank had written that he had telephoned home, and had to return at once because of an illness in the family. He thanked Mme Boutin for her kindness, and said that the gate key was just inside the garden gates where he had dropped it.

'Quite okay, I think,' Tom said. 'I'll run over with it now. You can look at the paper or go out in the garden. I'll be back in half an hour.'

'The paper,' said Frank softly, with a wince that showed his teeth.

'Nothing in that. I looked.' Tom indicated the *IHT* on the sofa.

'I'll go out in the garden.'

'But not in front of the house, all right?'

Frank understood.

Tom went out and took the Mercedes, whose keys he had picked up from the hall table. The car was low on gasoline, and he would buy some on the way back. Tom drove as fast as the speed limit permitted. A pity the letter was in Frank's handwriting, but it would have been odd if he had written on a typewriter. Not unless the police knocked on Mme Boutin's door would anyone be interested in Frank's handwriting, Tom hoped.

In Moret, Tom parked a hundred yards from the Boutin house, and went on foot. Unfortunately a woman was standing outside the front door gate, talking with Mme Boutin, Tom supposed, though he couldn't see the latter. They might be talking about Billy's disappearance. Tom turned and walked the other way, slowly, for a couple of minutes. When he looked again, the woman who had been standing on the pavement was now walking towards him. Tom walked in the direction of the Boutin house, and did not glance at the woman as he passed her. Tom dropped the envelope into the slit marked LETTRES in the closed front gate, circled the block and arrived back at his car. Then he headed for the centre of town, towards the bridge over the Loing river, where he knew there was a newspaper shop.

Tom stopped and bought a *France-Dimanche*. It had red headlines as usual, but these were about Prince Charles's girl friend, and the second headline about the catastrophic marriage of a Greek heiress. Tom crossed the bridge and bought gas, and opened the paper while the tank was filling. A full-face picture of Frank – left-side hair part, right cheek showing the little mole – made Tom start. It was a square, two-column item. AMERICAN MILLIONAIRE'S SON HIDES IN FRANCE, said the caption, and below the photograph: Frank Pierson. Have you seen him?

The item read:

Hardly a week after the death of multi-millionaire John J. Pierson, American food magnate, his younger son Frank, only 16, quit his luxurious home in Maine, USA, having taken his older brother John's passport. The sophisticated Frank is known for his independence, and was also extremely troubled by his father's death, said his beautiful mother Lily. The young Frank left a note saying he was going to New Orleans, Louisiana, for a few days. But the family and police found no evidence that he ever went there. The search has since led to London and now to France, according to authorities.

The fabulously wealthy family is desperate, and the older brother John may come to Europe with a private detective in an attempt to find Frank. 'I can spot him better, because I know him,' said John Pierson, Jr.

John Pierson, Sr, a wheelchair invalid since an attempt on his life eleven years ago, died on July 22 last, when he fell from a cliff on his Maine estate. Was he a suicide or was it an accident? The American authorities attributed his death to 'accidental causes'.

But – what is the mystery behind the boy's flight from home?

Tom paid the station attendant, and gave him a tip. He should tell Frank at once, show him the newspaper, Tom thought. It would surely jog the boy into making a move of some kind. Then he should get rid of the newspaper in case Heloise or Mme Annette (more likely) looked at it.

It was 10.30 when Tom rolled through the gates of Belle Ombre, and into the shade of the garage. He folded the newspaper, stuck it under his arm, and walked around the house to the left, past Mme Annette's door, which had prim pots of blossoming red geraniums, one on either side – a touch of pride, Tom thought, as she had bought them herself. He saw Frank at the far end of the garden, stooped and apparently pulling weeds. From the house, through the slightly opened french windows, he heard Heloise virtuously practising Bach. After one half hour, Tom knew, she would either put on a record of someone playing the same thing, or something to change her mood entirely, such as rock music.

'Bil-ly,' Tom called gently, trying to fix in his mind that he must call him Billy and not Frank.

The boy stood up from the grass and smiled. 'You delivered it? Did you see her?' he asked, just as gently, as if someone in the woods beyond might hear.

Tom was also wary of the woods behind the garden – after ten yards of scrubby underbrush the trees became thicker. Tom had once been buried there, for maybe a quarter of an hour. One couldn't see through the waist-high nettles, the wild and thorny blackberry vines three or four yards long, that produced no fruit, not to mention the tall limes just beyond, so thick that their trunks could conceal a man who wished to hide behind one. Tom jerked his head, and the boy came closer to him. They moved towards the friendly structure of the greenhouse. 'Something about you in the gossip rag,' Tom said, opening the newspaper. He had turned his back on the house, whence Heloise's playing was still audible. 'I thought you should see it.'

Frank took the paper, and Tom saw his shock in the sudden twitch of his hands. 'Damn,' he said softly. He read it with his jaw clenched.

'Do you think your brother might come over?'

'I think it's – yes. But to say my family's "desperate" – that's absurd.'

Tom said lightly, 'What if Johnny were to turn up here today and say, "Well, here you are!"'

'Why should he turn up here?' asked Frank.

'Did you ever talk about me, mention me to your family? Or to Johnny?'

'No.'

Tom was whispering now. 'What about the Derwatt painting? Weren't there conversations about that? Do you remember? A year or so ago?'

'I remember. My father mentioned it, because of what was in the newspapers. It wasn't particularly about *you*, not at all.'

'But when you – you said you read about me – in the newspapers.'

'In the Public Library in New York. That was just a few weeks ago.'

He meant the newspaper archives. 'You didn't mention me then to your family or to anybody?'

'Oh, *no*.' Frank looked at Tom, then his eyes fixed on something behind Tom, and his anxious frown came back.

Tom turned around, and what should he see but the Old Bear Henri ambling towards them, looking big and tall as something out of a kid's fairy tale. 'Our part-time gardener. Don't run and don't worry. Mess your hair up a little. And let it grow – for future use. Don't talk, just say "Bonjour." He'll quit at noon.'

By this time the French giant was almost within hearing, and Henri's own booming voice, deep and loud, called out, *''Jour, Monsieur Reeply!'*

''Jour,' Tom replied. *'François,'* Tom said, gesturing towards Frank. 'Cleaning out some weeds.'

'Bonjour,' Frank said. He had mussed his hair by scratching the top of his head, and now he assumed a slouch, and went off to where he had been pulling horsetail weeds and convolvulus at the back edge of the lawn.

Tom was pleased by Frank's performance. In his scruffy blue jacket, he might have been a local boy who had asked to do a couple of hours' work at the Ripley house, and God knew Henri couldn't be depended on, so Henri could hardly complain about competition. Henri could not tell the difference between Tuesday and Thursday, it seemed. Any day he set for himself was never the day he appeared. Henri didn't show surprise now at the sight of the boy, but kept his absent-minded smile, visible in encircling brown moustache and untrimmed beard. He wore baggy blue work trousers, a checked lumberjack shirt and a pale blue-and-white striped cotton cap with a bill, like an American railwayman's cap. Henri had blue eyes. He gave the impression of being slightly fuzzy with drink always, but was never very drunk as far as Tom could see, and Tom thought perhaps that drink had done its damage at some period in the past. Henri was about forty. Tom paid him fifteen francs an hour, whatever he did, even if they just stood around and discussed potting soil or the methods of storing dahlia tubers over the winter.

Now Tom suggested that they make another attack on the hundred-metre-long back edge of the garden, where Frank was still working, but Frank was far on their left near the little road which went into the woods there. Tom handed Henri the secateurs, and himself took the fork and rake, a strong metal rake.

'Build a low stone wall here, and you won't have this trouble,' Henri murmured cheerfully, taking the spade. He had made the remark many times before, and Tom did not mean to compound its boredom by repeating that he and his wife preferred the garden to appear to blend into the woods. Henri would have then told Tom that the woods were blending into the garden.

They both worked, and when Tom looked over his shoulder some fifteen minutes later, Frank was not in sight. Good, Tom thought. If Henri asked what had happened to the boy, Tom would say that he had probably drifted off, not really wanting to work. But Henri said nothing; all the better. Tom went into the kitchen via the service door. Mme Annette was washing something at the sink.

'Madame Annette, a small request.'

'Oui, Monsieur Tome!'

'The young man with us – he has just had an unhappy experience with his girl friend from America. He was with a few young Americans in France. So he wants to stay quiet and with us for a few days, I think. It is best if you don't tell anyone in the village that Billy is staying with us. He doesn't want his friends to look him up here, you see?'

'Ah-h.' Mme Annette understood. Affairs of the heart were personal, dramatic, wounding, and the boy was so young, her face seemed to say.

'You haven't mentioned Billy to anyone, have you?' Mme Annette often visited Georges's bar-café for a cup of tea, sitting down at a little table, Tom knew. So did other housekeepers.

'Certainly not, monsieur.'

'Good.' Tom went out to the garden again.

It was nearly noon when Henri showed signs of slowing his already slow work, and remarked that it was warm. It was not warm, but Tom didn't mind stopping his raking. They went into the greenhouse, where Tom kept a reserve of six or more bottles of Heineken lager in a square cement recess in the floor which was for drainage. Tom hauled up two bottles and opened them with a rusty bottle-opener.

The next few minutes passed vaguely for Tom, because he was thinking about Frank, wondering where he was. Henri kept up his murmuring about the meagre crop of raspberries this summer, as he stalked about with his little beer bottle, bending to look at this and that plant on Tom's shelves. Henri wore old laced boots that came high above his ankles, thick mushy soles on them, the picture of comfort though not of chic. He had the biggest feet Tom could remember having seen on any man. Did Henri's feet really fill those boots? But judging from his hands, they might.

'Non, trente,' Henri said. 'Don't you remember the last time? You were short fifteen.'

Tom didn't, but gave Henri thirty francs anyway rather than argue.

Then Henri pushed off, promising to return next Tuesday or Thursday. It was all the same to Tom. Henri was on 'permanent retirement' or 'repos', due to an injury on some job years ago. He had an easy, anxiety-free life, and in many ways was to be envied, Tom thought, as he watched his great figure stalk off and pass the beige turreted corner of Belle Ombre. Tom rinsed his hands at the greenhouse sink.

A few minutes later, Tom entered his house by the front door. A Brahms quartet was playing on the stereo in the living room, and perhaps Heloise was there. Tom went upstairs, looking for Frank. Frank's room door was closed, and Tom knocked on it.

'Come in?' said Frank's voice in the questioning tone Tom had heard before.

Tom went in and saw that Frank had packed his suitcase, removed sheets and blanket from his bed and folded them neatly. He had also changed out of his work clothes. And he also saw that Frank was near breaking, or near tears, though the boy held himself straight. 'Well,' Tom said softly, and closed the door. 'What's up? – Worried about Henri?' Tom knew it wasn't Henri, but he had to lead the boy to talk. The newspaper still poked from a back pocket of Tom's trousers.

'If it isn't Henri, it'll be somebody else,' Frank said in a shaky but rather deep voice.

'Now what's wrong – up to now?' Johnny was coming, with a private detective, and the game might soon be up, Tom thought. But what game? 'Why don't you want to go back home?'

'I killed my father,' Frank said in a whisper. 'Yes, I pushed him over that –' The boy gave up, his mouth seemed to crumple like that of an old man, and he lowered his head.

A murderer, Tom thought. And why? Tom had never seen such a gentle murderer. 'Does Johnny know?'

Frank shook his head. 'No. Nobody saw me.' His brown eyes glistened with tears, but there were not enough tears to fall.

Tom understood, or was beginning to. The boy's conscience had driven him away. Or somebody's words. 'Did anybody *say* anything? Your mother?'

'Not my mother. Susie – the housekeeper. But she didn't see me. She couldn't have. She was in the house. Anyway, she's shortsighted and the cliff isn't even visible from the house.'

'She said something to you or somebody else?'

'Both. The police – didn't believe her. She's old. A little cracked.' Frank moved his head like someone under torture, and sought his suitcase on the floor. 'I've told you – okay. You're the only person in the world I'd tell, and I don't care what you say. I mean, to the police or anyone. But I'd better take off.'

'Come on now, take off to where?'

'I don't know.'

Tom knew. He couldn't get out of France even with his brother's passport. He had nowhere to hide except in fields. 'You're not going to be able to go anywhere outside of France and not far inside it. Look, Frank, we'll talk about this after lunch. We have all the –'

'Lunch?' Frank's tone sounded as if he were affronted by the word.

Tom advanced towards him. 'I'm giving you orders now. It's lunch-time. You can't just disappear now, it'd look strange. Now you pull yourself together, eat a good lunch, and we'll talk afterward.' Tom reached out to shake the boy's hand, but Frank edged back.

'I'll go while I can!'

Tom grabbed the boy's shoulder with his left hand, his throat with his right. 'You will not. You will *not!*' Tom gave his throat a shake, then released him.

The boy's eyes were wide and thoroughly shocked. That was what Tom wanted. 'Come on with me. Downstairs.' Tom gestured, and the boy preceded him towards the door. Tom went into his own room for a minute to get rid of the *France-Dimanche*. For good measure, he stuck it in a back corner of his closet among shoes. He did not want Mme Annette to find it even in the waste-basket.

FIVE

Downstairs, Heloise was arranging orange and white gladioli – Tom knew she disliked them and that Mme Annette must have cut them – in a tall vase on the coffee table. She looked up and smiled at Tom and Frank. To relax himself, Tom deliberately shrugged as if he were adjusting a jacket on his shoulders: he meant to be calm and cool.

'Nice morning?' Tom asked Heloise in English.

'Yes. I see that Henri decided to appear.'

'Doing the minimum as usual. Billy's better.' Tom motioned for Frank to follow him into the kitchen, whence Tom could smell – he thought – broiling lamb chops. 'Madame Annette – *excusez-nous*. I would like a small apéritif before lunch.'

She was indeed inspecting lamb chops in the over-the-stove grill. 'But Monsieur Tome, you should have told me! *Bonjour, monsieur!*' she said to Frank.

Frank replied politely.

Tom went to the bar cart, which was now in the kitchen, and poured a scotch, not too big or too small, into a glass and poked it into Frank's hand. 'Water?'

'A little.'

Tom added some water from the sink tap, and handed the glass back to Frank. 'This will loosen *you* up, not necessarily your tongue,' Tom murmured. Tom made himself a gin and tonic without ice, though Mme

Annette wanted at once to get some out of the refrigerator. 'Let's go back,' Tom said to Frank, nodding towards the living room.

They went back, took their places at the table with their drinks, and Mme Annette almost at once brought the first course of her home-made jellied consommé. Heloise chattered away about her Adventure Cruise for late September. Noëlle had rung her that morning with some more details.

'The Antarctic,' said Heloise with joy. 'We may need – oh – just imagine the kind of clothes! Two pairs of gloves at once!'

Longjohns, Tom was thinking. 'Or do they turn on central heating somewhere at that price?'

'O-oh, Tome!' Heloise said with good humour.

She knew he didn't give a damn about the cost. Jacques Plisson was probably making Heloise a present of the trip, since he knew Tom was not going.

Frank asked how long the cruise would last, and how many people would be on the boat – this from Frank in French – and Tom found himself appreciative of the boy's upbringing, those old customs of writing thank-you letters three days after receiving a present, whether one liked the present or the aunt who had given it, or not. The average American boy aged sixteen would not have been able to keep such cool, Tom thought, under the circumstances. When Mme Annette passed the lamb chop platter for the second helping – four remained on the platter and Heloise had eaten only one – Tom served Frank with a third chop.

Then the telephone rang.

'I'll get it,' Tom said. 'Excuse me.' Odd to have a 'phone call in the sacred French lunch hour, and Tom was not expecting a call. 'Hello,' Tom said.

'Hello, Tom! It's Reeves.'

'Hang on, would you?' Tom laid the telephone down on the table and said to Heloise, 'Long distance. I'll take it upstairs so I don't shout.' Tom ran up the stairs, lifted the telephone in his room, and told Reeves to hang on again. Tom went down and hung up the downstairs telephone. Meanwhile he was thinking that it was a piece of luck that Reeves had rung, because a new passport for Frank might well be in order, and Reeves was just the man for that. 'Back again,' said Tom. 'What's new, my friend?'

'Oh, not too *much*,' Reeves Minot said in his hoarse, naïve-sounding American voice. 'Just a little – uh – well, that's why I'm calling. Can you put a friend up – for one night?'

Tom did not like the idea just now. 'When?'

'Tomorrow night. His name is Eric Lanz. Coming from here. He can make it to Moret, so you won't have to pick him up at the airport, but – best if he doesn't stay at an hotel in Paris overnight.'

Tom squeezed the telephone nervously. The man was carrying something, of course. Reeves was a fence, mainly. 'Sure. Yes, sure,' Tom said, thinking if he demurred, Reeves would not be so forthcoming when Tom put in his own request. 'For one night only?'

'Yes, that's all. Then he's going to Paris. You'll see. Can't explain more.'

'I'm to meet him at Moret? What does he look like?'

'He'll know you. He's in his late thirties, not very tall, black hair. Got the timetable here, Tom, and Eric can make the eight-nineteen tomorrow night. *Arrival* time, that is.'

'Very – good,' said Tom.

'You don't sound very keen. But it's sort of important, Tom, and I'd be –'

'Of course I'll do it, Reeves old boy! While you're here – on the line – I'm going to need an American passport. I'll send a photo to you express Monday and you ought to have it by Wednesday latest. I assume you're in Hamburg?'

'Sure, same place,' said Reeves cosily, as if he were running a teashop, but Reeves's apartment house on the Alster – Reeves's apartment specifically – had been bombed once. 'For yourself?' asked Reeves.

'No, someone younger. Not over twenty-one, Reeves, so not an old well-used passport. Can you do that? – You'll hear from me.'

Tom hung up and went downstairs again. Raspberry ice had been served. 'Sorry,' Tom said. 'Nothing important.' He noticed that Frank looked better, that some colour had returned to his face.

'Who was that?' Heloise asked.

Seldom did she ask him who rang, and Tom knew she mistrusted Reeves Minot, or at least didn't much like him, but Tom said, 'Reeves from Hamburg.'

'He's going to come here?'

'Oh, no, just wanted to say hello,' Tom replied. 'Want coffee, Billy?'

'No, thank you.'

Heloise did not usually take coffee at lunch, and she didn't now. Tom said that Billy wanted to look at his *Jane's Fighting Ships* books, so the three left the table, and Tom and the boy went up to Tom's room.

'Damned annoying phone call,' Tom said. 'Friend of mine in Hamburg wants me to put up a friend of his tomorrow night. Just for the night. I couldn't say no, because he's very helpful – Reeves.'

Frank nodded. 'Would you like me to go to an hotel or something – near here? – Or just *go*?'

Tom shook his head. He was lying on his bed, propped on an elbow. 'I'll give him your room, you'll take mine – and I'll sleep in Heloise's room. So this room will remain closed and – I'll tell our guest we're fumigating the carpenter ants and the door can't be opened.' Tom laughed. 'Don't worry. I'm pretty sure he'll leave Monday morning. I've had overnight guests of Reeves's before.'

Frank had sat down on the wooden chair that Tom used at his desk. 'Is the fellow coming one of your – interesting friends?'

Tom smiled. 'The fellow coming is a stranger.' *Reeves* was one of his interesting friends. Maybe Frank had seen Reeves Minot's name in newspapers too. Tom wasn't going to ask. 'Now,' Tom said quietly, 'your situation.' Tom waited, noting the boy's uneasiness, the frown. Tom felt uneasy also, and deliberately pushed off his shoes and swung his feet up on the bed, pulled a pillow under his head. 'By the way, I thought you did very well at lunch.'

Frank glanced at Tom, but his expression did not change. 'You asked me before,' the boy said softly, 'and I told you. You're the only person who knows.'

'We shall keep it that way. Don't confess to anyone – ever. Now tell me – what time of day did you do it?'

'Around seven, eight.' The boy's voice cracked. 'My father always watched the sunset – nearly every evening in summer. I hadn't –'

Here there was a long pause.

'I absolutely had not planned to do it. I was not even very angry, not angry at all. Later – even the next day, I couldn't believe I'd *done* it – somehow.'

'I believe you,' Tom said.

'I didn't usually walk out with my father for those sunsets. In fact I think he liked to be alone there, but that day he asked me to come with him. He'd just been talking with me about my doing well in school, and how Harvard Business School would come soon and how easy it – well, the usual. He even tried to say a nice word about Teresa, because he knew I – that I like her. But up to then, *no*. He'd been stuffy about Teresa coming to the house – twice only she was there – and saying it was stupid to be in love at sixteen, get married early or something, even though I never said a *word* about getting married, never even asked

Teresa! She'd laugh! Anyway, I suppose I suddenly had it that day. The phonyness, the all-round phonyness, everywhere I looked.'

Tom started to say something, and the boy nervously interrupted.

'The two times Teresa did come to the Maine house, my father was a bit rude to her. Unfriendly, you know? Just because she's pretty, maybe, and my Dad knows she's popular. Knew. You'd have thought she was some girl I picked up off the streets! But Teresa's *very* polite, she knows how to behave! And she didn't like it – natch. She wasn't going to come to the house again, and she more or less told me so.'

'That must've been very tough for you.'

'*Yes.*' Then Frank was silent for several seconds, looking at the floor. He seemed stuck.

Tom supposed that Frank could visit at Teresa's house, or meet her in New York now and then, but Tom didn't want to get side-tracked from the essentials. 'Who was at the house that day? The housekeeper Susie. Your mother?'

'And my brother too. We were playing croquet, then Johnny quit the game. Johnny had a date. He has a girl friend whose family lives – Well, anyway my Dad was on the front porch when Johnny went off in his car, and Dad said good-bye to him. Johnny had a lot of roses from the garden to give his girl, I remember, and I remember thinking if it weren't for my Dad's attitude, Teresa could've been at the house that evening, *somehow*, and we could've gone out somewhere. My Dad won't even let me drive yet, but I can drive. Johnny taught me on the dunes. My father always thought I'd have a wreck and kill myself, but fellows fifteen and younger in Louisiana or Texas, they're driving if they feel like it.'

Tom knew. 'Then what? After Johnny left. You'd been talking with your father –'

'I'd been listening to him – in the library downstairs. I wanted to escape, but he said, "Come out with me, watch the sunset, it'll do you good." I was in a lousy mood and I tried to hide it. I should've said, "No, I'm going up to my room," but I didn't. And then Susie – she's all right but a little in her second childhood, makes me nervous – she was around and made sure my Dad got down the ramp in his wheelchair. There's a ramp from the back terrace down to garden level, made just for my father. But she needn't have bothered, because my Dad can make it by himself. Then she went back in the house, and my father went on up the path – it's wide, flagstones – towards the woods and the cliff. And when we got there, he started talking again.' Frank lowered his head, clenched his right fist and opened it. 'Somehow after four or five minutes of it, I just couldn't stand it any more.'

Tom blinked, unable to look any longer at the boy who was looking at him now. 'The cliff's steep there? Down to the sea?'

'It's pretty steep, but not straight down. But anyway – enough to – to kill someone, certainly. Rocks there.'

'Lots of trees there?' Tom was still wondering who might have seen him. 'Boats?'

'No boats, no. No harbour there, anyway. Trees, sure. Pines. Part of our land, but we let it grow wild up there, and just cut a path to the cliff.'

'You couldn't've been seen from the house even with binoculars?'

'No, I know. Even in winter, if my father was on the cliff – it's not visible from the house.' The boy gave a heavy sigh. 'I thank you for listening to all this. Maybe I should write it out or try to – somehow – to get it off my mind. It's terrible. I don't know how to analyse it. Sometimes I can't believe I did it. It's strange.' Frank looked suddenly at the door, as if the existence of other people had just crossed his mind, but there had been no sound from the direction of the door.

Tom smiled a little. 'Why not write it out? You could show it only to me – if you feel like it. Then we could destroy it.'

'Yes,' Frank said softly. 'I remember – I had the feeling I couldn't look at his shoulders and the back of his head one second longer. I thought – I don't know *what* I thought, but I rushed forward and kicked the brake lever off and hit the forward button and I gave the chair a shove besides. Then it went forward, head over. Then I didn't look. I just heard a clatter.'

Tom had an instant's sickish feeling, imagining it. Fingerprints on the wheelchair, Tom wondered? But they might have been expected, if Frank had accompanied his father to the cliff. 'Did anyone talk about fingerprints on the chair?'

'No.'

Fingerprints would have been looked for at once, Tom thought, if there had been any suspicion of foul play. 'On that button you mentioned?'

'I think I hit it with the side of my fist.'

'The motor must've been still running when they got to him.'

'Yes, I think somebody said it was.'

'Then what did you do – just afterwards?'

'I didn't look down. I started walking back to the house. I felt suddenly very tired. It was strange. Then I started trotting towards the house, sort of to wake up. Nobody was on the lawn but Eugene – our driver, kind of butler too – he was in the big downstairs *dining room*, in fact, by himself, and I said, "My father just went over the cliff." Then Eugene told me to tell my mother and to ask her to call the hospital, and he ran out towards the cliff. My mother was with Tal in the upstairs living room watching TV, and I told her, and then Tal called the hospital.'

'Who's Tal?'

'A New York friend of my mother's. Talmadge Stevens. He's a lawyer, but not one of father's lawyers. Big fellow. He –' The boy stopped again.

Was Tal possibly his mother's lover? 'Did Tal say anything to you? Ask any questions?'

'No,' Frank said. 'Well – I said my father sent the chair over himself. Tal didn't ask anything.'

'So – the ambulance – and then I suppose the police came?'

'Yes. Both. It seemed like an hour before they got him up. Plus the wheelchair. They were using big spotlights. Then of course the journalists, but Mom and Tal got rid of them pretty fast. They're both good at that. Mom was furious at the journalists, but they were just the local journalists that night.'

'And later – the journalists?'

'My Mom had to see a couple of them. I spoke to one at least, had to.'

'And you said what – exactly?'

'I said my father was near the edge. It seemed to me that he really did mean to send himself over.' On the last word, Frank sounded as if he had no breath left. He got up from the chair and walked to the window, which was partly open. Frank turned. 'I lied. I told you.'

'Does your mother suspect you – at all?'

Frank shook his head. 'I'd know if she did, and she doesn't. I'm considered rather – um – *serious* – if you know what I mean. Honest too.' Frank smiled nervously. 'Johnny was more rebellious at my age, they had to have tutors for him, he was so often running away from Groton, going to New York. Then he sobered up – a little. I don't mean he ever drank booze, but pot sometimes, sure. A little cocaine. He's better now. But I mean, I'm considered something like a Boy Scout by comparison. That's why Dad put the pressure on me, you see, to take an interest in his company, the Pierson *empire*!' Frank flung his arms out and laughed.

Tom saw that the boy was tired.

Frank wandered back to the chair, sat down and tipped his head back with his eyes half shut. 'You know what I sometimes think? That my father was so near to being dead anyway. Half dead in his chair and maybe going to die pretty soon. And I wonder if I think that just to excuse myself a little? Awful to think that!' Frank said with a gasp.

'Back to Susie for a minute. She thinks you sent the chair over and she said that to you?'

'Yes,' Frank looked at Tom. 'She even said she saw me from the house, so that's why no one believes her. You can't see the cliff from the house. But Susie was very upset when she said that. Sort of hysterical.'

'Susie also talked to your mother?'

'Oh, sure, I know. My mother didn't believe her. My mother doesn't like Susie really. My father liked her, because she's very reliable – was – and she's been with us so many years, since Johnny and I were babies almost.'

'She was your governess?'

'No, she was more the housekeeper. We always had separate – women as governesses. Mostly English.' Frank smiled. 'Mother's helpers. We only got rid of the last one when I was about twelve.'

'And Eugene? Did he say anything?'

'About me? No. Not a thing.'

'Do you like him?'

Now Frank laughed a little. 'He's all right. He's from London. Has a sense of humour. But whenever Eugene and I used to joke, my Dad would say to me later that I shouldn't joke with the butler or the chauffeur. Eugene was both most of the time.'

'Anyone else in the household? Other servants?'

'Not just now. Part-time people now and then. Vic the gardener, on vacation in July, maybe longer, so we have part-time fellows sometimes. My father always wanted the minimum of servants and secretaries around.'

Tom was thinking that perhaps Lily and Tal were not so unhappy at John Pierson's demise. What went on there? He got up and went to his desk. 'Just in case you do feel like writing it all out,' Tom said, handing the boy some twenty sheets of typewriter paper, 'with a pen or on the typewriter. Anyway, they're both here.' Tom's typewriter sat in the middle of his desk.

'Thank you.' Frank stared at the sheets in his hand, musingly.

'You'd probably like to take a walk – but unfortunately you can't.'

Frank stood up, paper in hand. 'Just what I'd like to do.'

'You could try the back road there,' Tom said. 'It's a one-lane, nobody ever on it but an occasional farmer. You know, beyond where we were working this morning.' The boy knew, and moved towards the door. 'And don't run,' Tom said, because Frank looked charged with nervous energy. 'Come back in half an hour, or I'll be worried. You've got a watch?'

'Oh, yes. Two-thirty-two.'

Tom checked his own, early by one minute. 'If you want the type-writer later, just come in and get it.'

The boy went to his room next door to deposit the paper, then went down the stairs. From a side window, Tom could see Frank crossing the lawn, plunging through a section of the underbrush, jumping, tripping once and falling on his hands, then springing up as lithely as an acrobat. The boy turned to the right and became hidden by trees as he followed the narrow road.

A moment later, Tom found himself switching on his transistor. It was partly because he wanted to catch the French news at 3 p.m., partly because he felt a need to change the atmosphere after Frank's story. Amazing, in fact, that the boy hadn't broken down even more while telling it. Would that come, or wouldn't it? Or had it come in the night, perhaps nights before, when the boy was in London or alone at the house of Mme Boutin, his mind in terror of an imagined judgement from somewhere? Or had the few seconds of tears, today before lunch, been enough? There were boys (and girls) aged ten or so in New York, who had witnessed murder, murdered in gangs their contemporaries or strangers, but Frank was hardly that type. Such guilt as Frank's would show itself in some way, some time. Tom thought that every strong emotion such as love, hatred, or jealousy eventually showed itself in some gesture, and not always in the form of a clear illustration of that emotion, not always what the person himself, or the public, might have expected.

Restless, Tom went downstairs to speak with Mme Annette, who was engaged in the gruesome task of dropping a live lobster into a huge pot of boiling water. She was just lifting it towards the steam, the crustacean's limbs were stirring, and Tom recoiled at the threshold, making a gesture to indicate that he would wait a moment in the living room.

Mme Annette gave him an understanding smile, because she had seen such a reaction in him before.

Had Tom heard a hiss of protest from the lobster? Was Tom even now, with some highly attuned part of his own auditory nerve, hearing a cry of pain and outrage from the kitchen, a final high-pitched shriek as the life went out? Where had the unfortunate creature spent the night, because Mme Annette must have bought it yesterday Friday from the mobile *poissonnerie* van that parked itself in Villeperce? This lobster was a big one, not like some of the little creatures Tom had seen wriggling vainly, tied upside down to the shelf bars in the fridge. When Tom heard the clunk of the vessel's lid, he approached the kitchen again, head a little down.

'Ah, Madame Annette,' he said. 'Nothing important, just –'

'Oh, Monsieur Tome, you are always so worried about the lobsters! Even the mussels, isn't it?' She laughed with real mirth. 'I tell my chums – *mes copines* Geneviève and Marie-Louise –' These were other servants of local gentry, whom Mme Annette encountered while marketing, and who sometimes visited one another on good TV evenings, because they all had TV, and rotated their get-togethers.

Tom admitted his weakness with a nod and a polite smile. 'Liver of yellow,' Tom said in French, the phrase useless, he realized, because he had meant to translate either lily-livered or yellow-bellied. No matter. 'Madame Annette, *another* guest tomorrow, but just for Sunday night till Monday morning. A gentleman. I'll bring him home around eight-thirty for dinner, and he'll have the young man's room, and I'll sleep in the room of my wife. Monsieur Billy will sleep in my room. I'll remind you tomorrow.' But he knew he wouldn't need to remind her.

'Very good, Monsieur Tome. An American also?'

'No, he – European,' Tom said with a shrug. He fancied he could smell the lobster, and he backed from the kitchen. '*Merci, madame!*'

Tom went back to his room, listened to the news at three on a French pop station, and heard nothing about Frank Pierson. When the news was over, Tom realized that a half hour had passed, just, since Frank's departure. Tom looked out of his side window again. The woods at the corner of his garden showed no human figure. Tom waited, lit a cigarette, and went back to the window. Seven past three now.

Absolutely no reason to feel worried. Tom told himself. Ten minutes one way or the other. Whoever used that road? Sleepy-looking farmers leading or driving a horse and wagon, an old fellow driving a tractor now and then, headed for a field across the main road. Still, Tom was worried. Suppose someone had been watching, since Moret, and had trailed Frank to Belle Ombre? Tom had walked alone one night to Georges's and Marie's noisy café to take a coffee and see if any new character had appeared who showed curiosity even in him. Tom hadn't seen any new personage, and more important, the talkative Marie had asked nothing about a boy staying in his house. Tom had been slightly relieved.

At twenty past three, Tom went downstairs again. Where was Heloise? Tom went out by way of the french windows, and walked slowly across the lawn towards the little road. His eyes were on the grass, and he expected the boy to shout a 'Hello!' at any moment. Or did he? Tom picked up a stone from the grass and threw it awkwardly with his left hand towards the woods. He kicked away a wild blackberry vine, and finally stepped on to the road. Now he could see at least thirty yards along the road, even if it was a bit overgrown, because the road was straight. Tom began walking, listening, but he heard only the innocent and absent-minded tweets of sparrows, and from somewhere a turtle dove.

He certainly didn't want to call Frank's name or even 'Billy!' Tom stopped and listened again. Really nothing, no sound of a car motor, not even from behind him on the Belle Ombre road. Tom started trotting, thinking he'd better have a look at the end of the road – and what *was* the end? Tom thought it went on for a kilometre or so, and met another road more important, while all around were farm fields, corn for cattle, cabbages sometimes, mustard. Tom had by now begun to look for broken branches on either side of the lane, which might indicate a struggle, but he knew a wagon could have broken some just as well, and also he did not see anything unusual in the foliage. He walked again. He had by now come to the crossroad, a bigger road though still not paved, that ended what he thought of as the woods. Beyond lay cleared fields, belonging to farmers whose houses he could not see. Tom took a deep breath, and turned back. Had the boy possibly gone back to the house, got back, before Tom went out? Was he even now in his room? Tom leaned forward and again ran.

'Tom?' The voice had come from Tom's right.

Tom skidded in his desert boots and looked into the woods.

Frank came from behind a tree – or so it seemed to Tom, materializing suddenly from green leaves and brown tree trunks in grey trousers and beige sweater almost blending with the verdure in the spotty sunlight. He was alone.

Tom felt relief, like an ache. 'What happened? You're okay?'

'Sure.' The boy lowered his head and began to walk with Tom, back towards Belle Ombre.

Tom understood. The boy had deliberately hidden, to see if Tom cared

about finding him. Frank had wanted to see if he could trust him. Tom
shoved his hands into his pockets and lifted his head. He felt the boy
glance at him, shyly. 'You *were* a bit late, later than you said you'd be.'

The boy said nothing, and rammed his hands in his pockets, exactly
like Tom.

SIX

Around 5 o'clock that same Saturday afternoon, Tom said to Heloise, 'I
don't feel like going to the Grais's tonight, dear. Is that so serious? *You*
can go.' They were invited for dinner and due around eight.

'Oh, Tome, why not? We can ask if they will have Billy. I'm sure they
will say yes.' Heloise looked up from the triangular table that she had
bought that afternoon at an auction, and which she was now waxing.
She knelt on the floor in blue jeans.

'It's not Billy,' Tom said, though it was exactly Billy. 'They always
have a couple of other people –' Tom meant other people to amuse
Heloise. 'What does it matter? I'll phone them and make some excuse, if
you like.'

Heloise brushed back her blond hair. 'Antoine insulted you the last
time. Is that it?'

Tom laughed. 'Did he? If so, I forgot. He *can't* insult me, I'd just
laugh.' Antoine Grais, a hard-working architect of forty, diligent gardener at his country house, had a certain scorn for Tom's leisurely life,
but his slightly insulting remarks bounced right off Tom, and Tom
thought Heloise picked up fewer of them than Tom did. 'Old Puritan,'
Tom added. 'Belongs in America three hundred years ago. I just feel like
staying home. I hear enough about Chirac from the locals.' A right-
winger, Antoine Grais, pretentious enough not to be caught dead with
France-Dimanche, but just the type to sneak a look at someone else's in a
bar-café. The last thing Tom wanted was Antoine to recognize Billy as
Frank Pierson. Antoine and his wife Agnès, a little less strait-laced but
not much, would never keep it quiet. 'Want me to ring them, darling?'
Tom asked.

'No, I shall just – arrive,' said Heloise, going on with her waxing.

'Say I've got one of my awful friends coming. Someone socially unacceptable,' Tom said. He knew Antoine thought his social list suspect also. Who was it Antoine had once met by accident? Yes, the genius Bernard Tufts, who had often looked scruffy, and was sometimes too daydreamy to be polite.

'I think Billy is quite nice,' said Heloise, 'and I know you are not worried about Billy, you just don't like *les Grais*.'

Tom was bored with this, and so nervous, because of Billy in the house, that he had to repress another remark about the Grais – that they *were* arch-bores. 'They have a right to live – I suppose.' Tom decided suddenly not to mention the man called Eric Lanz turning up tomorrow evening, though he had meant to tell Heloise now.

'But how do you really like the table? It's for my room, in that corner, the side where you sleep. Then my table there would look better between the *twin* beds in the guest room,' Heloise said, admiring the shine now on the table top.

'I do like it – really,' Tom said. 'How much did you say?'

'Only four hundred francs. *Chêne* – and it's a Louis Quinze copy – a hundred years old itself. I bargained. Hard.'

'You did well,' said Tom, meaning it, because the table was handsome and looked sturdy enough to sit on, though no one ever would, and Heloise adored to think she had got a bargain, when often she hadn't. His mind was on other things.

Tom went back to his room, where he had set himself the boring task of spending one hour, by the clock, on his monthly income and expenses for his accountant. Rather, Heloise's father's accountant. This man, one Pierre Solway, kept Tom's and Heloise's accounts separate from the august Jacques Plisson accounts, of course, but Tom was glad enough to be relieved of the accountant's fee (paid by Jacques Plisson), and also to know that the accounts met Plisson's approval, because the old gentleman certainly found time to look them over. Heloise's income or allowance from her father was given her in cash, so was not liable for income tax on the Ripley bill. Tom's Derwatt company income – maybe ten thousand francs a month or close to two thousand dollars if the dollar was strong enough – came also under the table in the form of Swiss franc cheques, this money being filtered almost entirely through Perugia where the Derwatt Art Academy was, though some came back from the Buckmaster Gallery sales too. Tom's ten per cent of Derwatt profits derived also from Derwatt-labelled art supplies, from easels to erasers, but it was easier to smuggle money from northern Italy into Switzerland than to get it from London to Villeperce. Then there was the income from about eighteen hundred dollars a month from the original Dickie Greenleaf's bequest to Tom, which had risen to three or four hundred years ago. On this, curiously enough, Tom did pay full USA income tax, considerable because it was capital gains. Ironic and a bit fitting, Tom thought, because he had forged Dickie's will after Dickie's death, writing it on Dickie's own Hermes in Venice, and signing it with Dickie's forged signature.

But when you came down to it, Tom thought, as he thought every month, what was Belle Ombre apparently living on? Peanuts. After a fifteen-minute swat at listing expenditures, Tom's mind started to swim with ennui, and he stood up and smoked a cigarette.

Yes, well, why should he complain, he thought as he stared out of his window. Tom declared some of the Derwatt company income, but not all of it, to the French, origin being labelled stocks in Derwatt Ltd. Tom now had his own stocks and a few US Treasury Bonds, on which he had to declare the interest. His French Déclaration was for French-source income only (a bit for Heloise, not him), while the Americans wanted to know his global income. Tom was a French resident, though he still kept his American passport. Tom had to make a separate worksheet for Pierre Solway in English, as Solway dealt also with the Ripleys' USA taxes. Mind-boggling. Papers were the curse of the French populace, and even the humblest citizen had to fill out a score of forms to acquire state health insurance. Fond as Tom was of mathematics or plain arithmetic, it bored him to copy postal expenses from last month's record, and he stared down at the efficient-looking pale green graph paper, income above, output below, and cursed it filthily. One more swat, and he'd have filled out the hour and have it done. This was for July, should have been done at the end of that month, and now it was late August.

Tom was thinking of Frank, who was writing his account of his father's last day. Now and again, Tom faintly heard his typewriter clicking. The boy had taken it into his room. Once Tom heard an 'Oof!' from Frank. Was he going through agony? There were such long silences from the typewriter, that Tom wondered if the boy were writing some of it in longhand.

Seizing his little batch of receipts – telephone, electricity, water bill, car repair – Tom sat down for a final onslaught, determined to finish. He did, and finally the worksheet and the receipts, but not the cancelled cheques, because the French bank kept those, went into a manilla envelope to be kept in a bigger envelope with the other monthly reports for Pierre Solway. Tom stuck the big envelope into a lower left drawer of his desk, and stood up with a sense of joy and virtue.

He stretched. And just at that moment one of Heloise's rock 'n' roll records started playing below stairs. Just what he needed! This was a Lou Reed. Tom went into the bathroom and washed his face in cold water. What time was it? 6.55 already! Tom decided to tell Heloise about Eric now.

Frank just then came out of his room. 'I heard the music,' he said to Tom in the hall. 'Radio? No, it's the record, isn't it?'

'Heloise's,' Tom said. 'Come down.'

The boy had changed from sweater to a shirt now, and the tails hung out of his trousers. He glided down the stairs with a happy smile, like one in a trance, Tom thought. The music had really struck a chord.

Heloise had it up loud, and was dancing by herself, with shoulder shrugging movements, but she stopped shyly as Tom and the boy came down the steps, and she turned the music lower.

'Don't turn it down for me! It's nice,' said Frank.

Tom could see that they were going to get on well in the music and dance department. 'Finished the bloody accounts!' Tom announced loudly. 'All dressed? You look nice!' Heloise wore a pale blue dress with a black patent leather belt, and high-heeled shoes.

'I telephoned Agnès. She said come early so we could talk,' Heloise said.

Frank looked at Heloise with a new admiration. 'You like this record?'

'Oh, yes!'

'I play it at home.'

'Go ahead and dance,' Tom said cheerfully, but he saw that Frank, at least, was a bit constrained at the moment. What a life for the boy, Tom thought, writing about murder minutes ago, and now plunged into rock. 'Progress this afternoon?' Tom asked softly.

'Seven and a half pages. Some in my writing. I was switching.'

Heloise, standing near the gramophone, had not heard the boy's words.

'Heloise,' Tom said, 'I'm picking up a friend of Reeves's tomorrow night. The friend stays the night only. Billy can take my room, so I'll be with you.'

Heloise turned her pretty, made-up face towards Tom. 'Who is coming?'

'Reeves said his name was Eric. I'll pick him up at Moret. We have no date for tomorrow evening, have we?'

She shook her head. 'I think I will go now.' She went to the telephone table, where she had left her handbag, and got a transparent raincoat from the front closet, as the weather looked uncertain.

Tom walked out with her to the Mercedes Benz. 'By the way, darling, don't mention to the Grais that anyone is staying with us. Don't say anything about an American boy. Say I'm expecting a phone call tonight. That's simple.'

Her face lit with a sudden idea. 'Are you maybe *hiding* Billy? To render Reeves a service?' She was talking through the open car window.

'No, dear. Reeves has never heard of Billy! Billy's just an American kid doing some gardening for us. But you know what a bourgeois snob Antoine is. "Putting up a gardener in your guest room!" Have a nice evening.' Tom bent and kissed her cheek. 'Promise?' Tom added.

He meant promise to say nothing about Billy, and he could see from her calm, amused smile and her nod that she did promise. She knew Tom did favours now and then for Reeves, some of which she had an inkling of, others of which she hadn't. Somehow his favours meant money earned, or acquired, anyway, and that was useful. Tom had opened the big gates for her, and he waved as she drove through and turned right.

By a quarter past nine that evening, Tom was lying on his bed with his shoes off, reading Frank's manuscript, or account. It went:

Saturday 22nd July had started like an ordinary day for me. Nothing unusual. The sun was shining and it was what everybody called a great day, meaning the weather. The day is doubly strange to me now, because I had no idea in the morning how it was going to end. I had no plans about anything. I remember Eugene asked me around three that afternoon if I wanted to play some tennis, since there were no visitors (guests) and he had some time. I said no, don't know why I said no. I tried to phone Teresa then, and her mother said she was out (Bar Harbor) and for the evening too and wouldn't be home till maybe after midnight. I felt very jealous, wondering whom she was with, even a lot of people or just one, it would have been the same feeling. I decided I would go to New York the next day no matter what, even if I couldn't use our apartment which was closed for the summer with drapes over the furniture and all. I would telephone Teresa and persuade her to come to New York, and we could either take a hotel room for several days or she could stay with me in the New York apartment. I wanted to make a *move*, and N Y seemed great to suggest to her, to look forward to. I might have been in New York already except for the fact that my father wanted me to have 'talks' with a guy called Bumpstead or something that sounded like that, who was going to be in Hyannisport for a couple of weeks vacationing. This Bumpstead is a businessman of some kind about 30, my Dad said. My Dad thought 30 would be young enough to convert me, I'm sure. To his way of life, business. This Bumpstead was due the next day. He didn't come because of what happened.

(Here Frank had switched to a ballpoint pen.)

But I was trying to think of bigger things, of my whole life, if I could. I was trying to sum my life up, as Maugham says in a paperback I have called *The Summing Up*, but I am not sure I could or that I got very far with it. I had been reading some Somerset Maugham short stories (very good), and they seemed to understand everything, in just a few pages. I tried to think what is my life *for*, as if my life of course had a meaning, which is not necessarily so. I tried to think what I wanted from life, and all I could think of was Teresa, because I am so happy when I am with her, and she seems happy too, and I thought with the two of us together, we'd arrive at something called a meaning, or happiness, or going forward. I know I want to be happy and I think everyone should be happy and not confined by anything or anyone. By this I mean comfortable physically, and as to how they live. But

(Frank had crossed out the but and switched to the typewriter again.)

I remember after lunch my mother's friend Tal with us, my father as usual made some remark about having the grandfather clock in the downstairs hall repaired. It hasn't run for about a year, and Dad was always talking about getting it repaired, but he didn't trust any of the local places to do it and didn't want to send it to NY. It is an old clock from his family. I was bored at lunch. My mother and Tal managed to laugh a lot but they have their own jokes about people they know in NY.

After lunch I heard my father screaming on the telephone to Tokyo in the library. I switched off and waited in the hall. My father said he had something he wanted to say to me. Finally, this was to come and see him in the library around 6 p.m. I thought he could have told me that at lunch. I then went to my room, feeling angry. The others started playing croquet on the side lawn.

I detested my father, that I will admit, and I have heard that a lot of people detest their fathers. This does not mean that a person has to kill his father. I think I am unable as yet to realize what I did, and for this reason can walk around like a more or less ordinary human being, although I should not, and inside I feel different, uptight, and maybe I will never get over it. This is why after I did it I decided to look up T.R. who for some reason I felt very interested in. This was partly because of the Derwatt picture mystery. My family has a Derwatt, my father was interested a couple of years ago when some Derwatt paintings were suspected of being fakes or forgeries. I was around 14. Several names mentioned in the newspapers, mainly English names in London. Derwatt lived in Mexico, and I was reading a lot of spy stuff then, and I got interested and went to the big library in NY and looked up the records of all those names in the newspaper files, the way detectives have to do in their work. T.R.'s entries seemed the most interesting. American living in Europe, had lived in Italy, something about a friend of his bequeathing him his income when he died – so he must have liked T.R. – and also something about a missing American called Murchison, in connection with the Derwatt mystery, the American disappearing after visiting T.R.'s house. I thought T.R. might also have killed someone, just maybe, but that anyway he did not look tough or like a stuffed shirt even, because there were two pictures of him in the newspaper items I saw. He was rather good looking and did not look cruel. And whether he killed anybody seemed rather unproven.

(Frank here picked up the pen again.)

I thought that day, not for the first time, why should I join the old system, which had already killed the rats who joined it? Or had killed and would kill a lot of them with suicide, breakdowns, maybe simple insanity? Johnny had already absolutely refused, and he was older than I and therefore must know what he is doing, I thought. Why shouldn't I follow Johnny instead of my father?

This is a confession, and I confess now to only one person T.R. that I killed my father. I sent his chair over that cliff. Sometimes I cannot believe that I did it and yet I know that I did it. I have read about cowards who do not want to face up to what they have done. I do not want to be like that. Sometimes I have a cruel thought: my father had lived long enough. He was cruel and cold to Johnny and me – most of the time. He could switch. Okay. But he tried to break us or change us. He had his life, with two wives, girls in the past, money galore, luxury. He was not able to walk for the last eleven years, because a 'business enemy' tried to shoot him dead. How bad *is* what I did?

I am writing these lines to T.R. only, because he is the only person in the world I would tell these facts to. I know he does not detest me, because at this moment I am under his roof and he is giving me hospitality.

I want to be free and feel free. I just want to be free and be myself, whatever that is. I think T.R. is free in spirit, in his attitudes. He also seems kind and polite to people. I think I should stop here. Maybe it's enough.

Music is good, any kind of music, classic or whatever it is. Not to be in any kind of prison, that is good. Not to manipulate other people, that is good.

                                                                Frank Pierson

The signature was straight and clear, and underlined with what looked like an attempt at a dash. Tom suspected that the underlining was not usual for Frank.

Tom was touched, but he had hoped for a description of the very instant when Frank had sent his father over the cliff's edge. Was that hoping for too much? Had the boy blotted it out of his memory, or was he incapable of putting the instant of violence into words – which would require an analysis as well as a description of physical action? Probably, Tom thought, a healthy drive towards self-preservation was preventing Frank from going back in thought to that very moment. And Tom had to admit to himself that he would not care to analyse or relive the seven or eight murders he had committed, the worst undoubtedly having been the first, that of Dickie Greenleaf, beating that young man to death with the blade or the butt of an oar. There was always a curious secret, as well as a horror, about taking the life of another being. Maybe people didn't want to face it, because they simply couldn't understand it. It was so easy to kill someone, Tom supposed, if one were a hired killer, to dispose of some gang member or political enemy whom one didn't know. But Tom had known Dickie very well and Frank had known his father. Hence the blackout, perhaps, or so Tom suspected. Anyway, Tom did not intend to pump the boy further.

But Tom knew the boy would be anxious to hear what Tom thought of his account, would probably want a word of praise for his honesty at least, and Tom felt the boy had really tried to be honest.

Frank was now in the living room. Tom had switched on the television for him after their dinner, but evidently Frank had been bored (very likely on a Saturday night), because he had put on the Lou Reed record again, though not so loudly as Heloise had played it. Tom went down, having left the boy's pages in his room.

The boy lay on the yellow sofa, his feet carefully over the edge so as not to soil the yellow satin, his hands behind his head, eyes closed. He had not even heard Tom come down the stairs. Or was he asleep?

'Billy?' Tom said, again trying to fix 'Billy' in his mind for as long as he would need it, and how long would that be?

Frank sat up at once. 'Yes, sir.'

'I think what you wrote is very good – interesting as far as it goes.'

'Do you? – What do you mean as far as it goes?'

'I was hoping –' Tom glanced towards the kitchen, but the light there was already off, Tom saw through the half-open door. Tom had decided to stop, however. Why force his own thoughts into the mind of a sixteen-year-old? 'Still, the moment when you rushed forward towards the edge of the cliff –'

The boy shook his head quickly. 'Amazing I didn't go over myself. I often think of that.'

Tom could imagine, but it wasn't what he meant. He meant the realization that he had stopped the life of someone else. If the boy had so far escaped that mystery, or its puzzlement, then perhaps so much the better, because what could be accomplished by pondering it, even finally understanding it? Was it even possible?

Frank was waiting for a further word from Tom, but Tom had none.

'Did you ever kill a person?' the boy asked.

Tom moved nearer the sofa, a movement to relax himself, also to be farther from Mme Annette's quarters. 'Yes, I did.'

'Even more than one?'

'To be honest, yes.' The boy must have combed quite well through his dossier in the newspaper files of the New York Public Library, and used a bit of imagination too. Suspicion, rumours, nothing more, Tom knew, never an outright charge against him. Bernard Tufts' death over a mountainside near Salzburg oddly enough had been Tom's closest call in the direction of being accused, and Bernard – God rest his troubled soul – had been a suicide.

'I don't think what I did has sunk into me yet,' Frank said in a voice barely audible. Now his left elbow rested on the sofa arm, a more relaxed attitude than that of a few minutes before, but he was far from relaxed. 'Does it ever sink in?'

Tom shrugged. 'Maybe we can't face it.' The we had a special meaning for Tom then. He wasn't talking to a hired killer, and he had met a few.

'I hope you don't mind that I put this music on again. I used to play it with Teresa. She has it. We both have the record. So –'

The boy couldn't go on, but Tom understood, and he was glad to see that Frank's face looked more inclined to self-confidence, even inclined to a smile, rather than to the tears of a breakdown. *What about buzzing Teresa now,* Tom wanted to say, *and if you boomed the music up and told her you're okay and coming home?* But Tom had said this to Frank before and got nowhere. Tom pulled up one of the upholstered chairs. 'You know – Frank, if no one suspects you, you have no reason to hide. Maybe now that you've written it out, you can go back home – soon. Don't you think?'

Frank's eyes met Tom's. 'I just need to be *with* you for a few days. I'll work, you know? I don't want to be a drag in the house. But maybe you think I'm some kind of danger to you?'

'No.' He was, slightly, but Tom couldn't have said how, exactly, except that the name Pierson was dangerous, because kidnappers would be interested. 'I'm getting a new passport for you – by next week. Different name.'

Frank smiled as if Tom had given him a surprise, a present. 'You are? How?'

Tom again glanced unnecessarily towards the kitchen. 'Let's go to Paris Monday for a new photograph. The passport will be done in – Hamburg.' Tom was not used to betraying his Hamburg connection, Reeves Minot. 'I ordered it today. That phone call at lunch. You'll have a different American name.'

'Great!' said Frank.

The record moved into another song, a different, simpler rhythm. Tom watched the dream in the boy's face. Was he thinking of the new identity he would have, or of the pretty girl called Teresa? 'Is Teresa in love with you too?' Tom asked.

Frank lifted his lip at one side, and it was not quite a smile. 'She doesn't *say* so. She did say so once, weeks ago now. But there're a couple of other fellows – not that she likes them, but they're always hanging around. I know, because I told you, I think, her family has a house near Bar Harbor – also an apartment in New York. So I know. It's better not to make speeches about how *I* feel – to her or to anybody. But *she* knows.'

'She's your only girl friend?'

'Oh, yes.' Frank smiled. 'I can't imagine liking two girls at once. A little bit, maybe. But not really.'

Tom left him to listen to the music.

Tom was upstairs in his room, in pyjamas, reading Christopher Isherwood's *Christopher and his Kind*, when he heard a car turning in at Belle Ombre. Heloise. Tom glanced at his watch: five to midnight. Frank was still downstairs, playing records, in a trance of his own, Tom supposed, and he hoped a happy one. Tom heard the car give a *br-room* before the engine cut, and he realized that it was not Heloise. He leapt off the bed, grabbed his dressing gown and put it on as he went down the stairs. Tom opened the front door slightly and saw Antoine Grais's cream-coloured Citroën on the gravelled area in front of the steps. Heloise was getting out on the passenger side. Tom closed the door and turned the key.

Frank was on his feet in the living room, looking worried.

'Go upstairs,' Tom said. 'It's Heloise. She's come home with a visitor. Just go up and close your door.'

The boy ran.

Tom was walking towards the door as Heloise tried the handle. Tom unlocked the door and Heloise entered, followed by Antoine who was smiling genially. Tom saw Antoine's eyes lift in the direction of the staircase. Had he heard something? 'How *are* you, Antoine?' Tom asked.

'Tome, the strangest thing!' Heloise said in French. 'The car wouldn't start just now, just wouldn't! So Antoine kindly brought me home. Come in, Antoine! Antoine thinks it's only –'

Antoine's baritone voice interrupted: 'I think a bad connection of the battery. I looked. It needs a big wrench, a cleaning with a file. Simple. But I haven't got a big wrench. Ha-ha! And how are you, Tome?'

'Very well, thank you.' They were by now in the living room where music still played. 'May I offer you something, Antoine?' Tom asked. 'Sit down.'

'Ah, no more the harpsichord music,' said Antoine, referring to the gramophone, and he seemed to be sniffing the air as if in hopes of picking up a scent of perfume. He had black and grey hair, and a stocky figure which swivelled now, on its toes.

'What's the matter with rock?' Tom asked. 'My tastes are catholic, I hope.' As Tom watched Antoine's eyes drift over the living room, looking for a clue as to what kind of person might have run up the stairs, possibly, Tom was reminded of the boring argument he and Antoine had got into over the pale blue rubber-tube-like structure called the Centre Pompidou, or Beaubourg. Tom detested it, Antoine defended it, saying it was 'too new' for Tom's uneducated eye (that was the implication) to appreciate.

'You have a friend? I am sorry to disturb you,' Antoine said. 'Male or female?' This was meant to be funny, but had a nasty curiosity in it.

Tom could have hit him with pleasure, but only smiled, tight-lipped, and said, 'Guess.'

Heloise was in the kitchen during this, and appeared very soon with a small coffee for Antoine. 'Here you are, Antoine dear. *Force* for the drive home.'

The abstemious Antoine drank only a bit of wine at dinner.

'Sit down, Antoine,' said Heloise.

'No, my dear, this is fine,' said Antoine, sipping. 'We saw the light in your room, you know, and the living room light on, so – I invited myself in.'

Tom nodded politely, like a toy ducking bird. Was Antoine thinking that a girl or boy had fled at once to Tom's bedroom, and that Heloise connived at it? Tom folded his arms, and just then the record came to its end.

'Tome will take me to Moret tomorrow, Antoine,' Heloise said. 'We'll tell the garage mechanic and bring him to your house for the car. Marcel. Do you know him?'

'Very good, Heloise.' Antoine set his coffee cup down, efficient as always, even at drinking hot coffee fast. 'Now I must be off. Good night, Tome.'

Antoine and Heloise exchanged French kisses at the door, smacks on the cheeks, one, two. Tom hated it. Not French kisses in the American sense, certainly, nothing sexy about them, just damned silly. Had Antoine been able to see Frank's legs dashing up the stairs? Tom didn't think so. 'So Antoine thinks I might have a girl friend!' Tom said with a chuckle after Heloise had closed the door.

'Of course he does not! But why are you hiding Billy?'

'I'm not hiding him, he's hiding himself. He's even a little shy with Henri, of all people. Anyway darling, I'll take care of the Mercedes – Tuesday.' It had to be Tuesday because tomorrow was Sunday, and Monday their usual garage was closed, as were most French garages, since they stayed open Saturday.

Heloise slipped out of her high-heeled shoes. Now she was barefoot.

'Nice evening? Any other people?' Tom put a record back in its sleeve.

'A couple from Fontainebleau, another architect – younger than Antoine.'

Tom hardly listened. He was thinking of Frank's pages on his desk in the place where the typewriter usually sat. Heloise was now going up the stairs. She used his bathroom most of the time, now that the boy had the guest room. But Tom continued putting away records – only one more to go. Heloise was not inclined to pause and look at pages of any kind on his desk. Tom turned out the living room lights, locked the front door, and went upstairs. Heloise was in her own room undressing, Tom supposed. He took the boy's pages, put a paperclip on them, and stuck them in his top right drawer, then on second thought into a folder marked 'Personal'. The boy would have to get rid of those pages, regardless of their literary merit, Tom thought. Burn them. Tomorrow. With the boy's consent, of course.

SEVEN

On the following day, Sunday, Tom took Frank for an outing in the Fontainebleau woods, west of Fountainebleau where Frank had not been before, and to a section Tom knew where there were few or no hikers or tourists. Heloise had not wanted to come, and said she preferred to lie in the sun and read a novel that Agnès Grais had lent her. Heloise tanned amazingly well for a blonde. She never overdid her sunbathing, but sometimes her skin became a bit darker than her hair. Perhaps she had conveniently mixed genes, as her mother was blonde, and her father evidently brunette, because his hair, what was left of it, was a fringe of dark brown with an inner circle of grey, suggesting saintliness to Tom, though nothing was further from the truth.

Near noon, Tom and Frank were driving towards Larchant, a quiet village several kilometres west of Villeperce. The cathedral at Larchant had been half destroyed by fire a couple of times since the tenth century. The little private houses, all close together in cobble-stoned lanes, looked like illustrations from children's books, cottages almost too small for man and wife to live in, which made Tom think it might be interesting to live alone again. But when had he ever lived alone? With bloody Aunt Dottie – dotty about everything except money – from childhood, until he left her Boston establishment in his teens, then crummy apartments in Manhattan for brief periods, unless he shacked up with more affluent friends who had a spare bedroom or a living-room sofa. And then Mongibello and Dickie Greenleaf when he had been twenty-six. And why should all that go through his head as he stood looking up at the cream-and-dust-coloured interior of the Larchant cathedral?

The cathedral was empty but for them. Larchant attracted so few tourists, Tom was not afraid of Frank's being spotted. Tom would have been afraid of the château at Fontainebleau, for instance, with its international clientèle, and probably Frank had already seen it. Tom didn't ask.

At an unattended counter by the door, Frank acquired some postcards of the cathedral, and dutifully dropped the correct sum into the slot in a wooden box, then seeing that his palm was still full of francs and centimes, Frank tipped his hand and dropped the lot in.

'Your family go to church?' Tom asked as they walked down a steep cobbled slope towards the car.

'Na-a-ah,' Frank said. 'My father always called the church a cultural lag and my mother's plain bored with it. She won't be pressured.'

'Is your mother in love with Tal?'

Frank gave Tom a glance and laughed. 'In love? My mother plays it cool. Maybe she *is*. But she'd never act silly, never show it. She was an actress, you know. I think she can act even in real life, I mean.'

'Do you like Tal?'

Frank shrugged. 'I suppose he's all right. I've seen worse. He's an outdoor type, very strong physically, considering he's a lawyer. I leave them alone, you know?'

Tom was still curious whether Frank's mother might marry Talmadge Stevens, but why should he be? Frank was more important, and Frank didn't care about his family's money, from what Tom could see, if his mother and Tal should for some reason, maybe even suspicion of patricide, decide to cut the boy off.

'Those pages you wrote,' Tom said, 'they ought to be destroyed, you know. Dangerous to keep, don't you think?'

The boy, watching his footing, seemed to hesitate. 'Yes,' he said firmly.

'If anyone found them, you couldn't say it's a short story, with all those names in it.' Of course the boy could, Tom thought, but it would be a bit mad. 'Or are you toying with the idea of confessing?' Tom asked, in a tone that implied that this would be total madness, out of the question.

'Oh, no. *No*.'

The strength of that negative pleased Tom. 'Okay then. With your permission I'll get rid of the pages this afternoon. Maybe you want to read them once more?' Tom was opening the car door.

The boy shook his head. 'I don't think so. I read it over once.'

After lunch at Belle Ombre Tom went out to the garden (because Heloise was practising on the harpsichord in the living room where the fireplace was) with the pages folded twice in his hand. Frank was wielding the spade near the greenhouse, wearing his blue jeans, which Mme Annette had washed in her machine for him and also ironed. Tom burned the pages in a back corner of the garden, near where the woods began.

Shortly before eight that evening, Tom drove to Moret to fetch Reeves's friend Eric Lanz from the railway station. Frank wanted to come with him for the ride, and to walk back, and insisted that he could get back to Belle Ombre on foot. Tom had reluctantly agreed. Tom had said to Heloise before leaving, 'Billy's having dinner in his room tonight. He doesn't want to meet a stranger, and I don't want this friend of Reeves to meet him either.' Heloise had said, 'Oh? Why?' and Tom had replied, 'Because he might try to engage Billy for some little job. I don't want the boy to get into trouble, even if he's paid well for it. You know Reeves and his chums.' Indeed Heloise did, and Tom often had to say to her, 'Reeves *is* useful – sometimes,' which could and had meant that Reeves could do services that were sometimes much needed, such as providing new passports, acting as go-between, a safe house in Hamburg. Sometimes Heloise half understood what was going on, and the half that she did not know, she didn't want to know. All to the good. Her nosy father couldn't pump much out of her that way either.

At a clearing at the edge of the road, Tom pulled over and stopped the car. 'Now let's compromise, Billy. You're three or four kilometres from Belle Ombre, a nice walk. I don't want to take you all the way to Moret.'

'Right.' The boy started to open the car door.

'And this. Just a sec.' Tom pulled a flat box from his trousers pocket. It was pancake make-up that he had taken from Heloise's room. 'I don't want that mole showing.' He put a little of the paste on the boy's cheek and rubbed it smooth.

Frank grinned. 'Makes me feel silly.'

'Keep this. I don't think Heloise'll miss it, she's got so much other stuff. I'm going back one kilometre.' Tom turned the car around. There was almost no traffic.

The boy said nothing.

'I want you to be home before I get back. I can't have you coming in the front door.' Tom stopped the car only one kilometre from Belle Ombre. 'Have a nice walk. Madame Annette's put your supper in my room – or she will. I told her you wanted to go to bed early. Stay in my room. All right, Billy?'

'Yes, sir.' Now the boy smiled, and with a wave of his hand, walked away towards Belle Ombre.

Tom again turned the car and headed for Moret. He arrived just as the train from Paris was disgorging its passengers. Tom felt a bit awkward, because Eric Lanz knew what he looked like, and he didn't know Eric from Adam. Tom walked slowly towards the exit gate, where a scruffy little ticket-taker in a peaked cap bent over every passenger's ticket to see if it was valid for today, though Tom thought three-quarters of French passengers, being students, elderly, civil servants, war-damaged, travelled at half-fare anyway. No wonder the French railway was always crying bankruptcy. Tom lit a Gauloise and looked up at the sky.

'Miss-ter –'

Tom looked from the blue sky into the smiling face of a rather short, rosy-lipped man with a black moustache, who wore a horrible checked jacket and a necktie of gaudy stripes. He had also round, black-rimmed spectacles. Tom waited, saying nothing. The man looked not at all German, but one never knew.

'Tom?'

'Tom, yes.'

'Eric Lanz,' he said with a short bow. 'How do you do? And thank you for meeting me.' Eric was carrying two cases of brown plastic, both so small, they could be considered hand luggage on an aeroplane. 'And greetings from Reeves!' Now his smile was broader as they walked towards Tom's car, whose position Tom had indicated with a gesture. Eric Lanz spoke with a German accent, though a slight one.

'Did you have a good trip?' Tom asked.

'Yes! And I always enjoy France!' Eric Lanz said, as if he were setting foot on a Côte d'Azur beach, or maybe walking into a splendid museum of French culture somewhere.

Tom felt in a thoroughly sour mood for some reason, but what did it matter? He would be polite, offer Eric dinner and bed and breakfast, and what else could Eric want? Eric declined to put his cases even in the back of the front seats of the Renault station wagon, but kept them at his own feet. Tom zoomed off towards home.

'Ah-h,' said Eric, ripping off his moustache. 'That's better. And these Groucho Marx things.'

Off came his spectacles, Tom saw with a glance to his right.

'That Reeves! Too – much, as the English say. Two passports for something like *diss*?' Eric Lanz proceeded to effect the change in his passports from inside jacket pocket to something at the bottom and apparently in a bottom compartment of a shaving kit which he took from one of the awful plastic carry-alls.

Now in his pocket he had a passport looking more like himself, Tom supposed. What was his real name? Was his hair really black? What else did he do besides odd jobs for Reeves? Safe-cracking? Jewellery thieving on the Côte d'Azur? Tom preferred not to ask. 'You live in Hamburg?' Tom asked in German, by way of being polite and also practising his German.

'*Nein!* West Berlin. Much more fun,' said Eric, in English.

Maybe more remunerative too, Tom thought, if this chap was a runner for dope or illegal immigrants. What was the fellow carrying now? Only his shoes looked of quality, Tom noticed. 'You have an appointment with someone tomorrow?' Tom asked, again in German.

'Yes, in Paris. I shall be out of your ha-ar, as they say, by eight o'clock tomorrow morning, if that is agreeable to you. I am sorry, but it could not be arranged by Reeves that the – man I am supposed to see would meet me at the airport. Because he is not here yet. Could not be.'

They arrived at Villeperce. Since Eric Lanz seemed quite outgoing, Tom ventured to ask:

'You're bringing him something? What – if I may be so rude?'

'Jewellery!' said Eric Lanz, almost giggling. 'Ver-ry pretty. Pearls – which I know nobody these days cares about, but these are real ones. Also a necklace of *Smaragd*! Emeralds!'

Well, well, Tom thought, and said nothing.

'You like emeralds?'

'Frankly no.' Tom particularly disliked emeralds, perhaps because Heloise, being blue-eyed, disliked green. Tom also thought he would not or did not care for women who would like emeralds or who wore green.

'I was thinking of showing them to you. I am very pleased that I have got here,' Lanz said with an air of relief, as Tom drove through the open gates of Belle Ombre. 'Now I can see your wonderful house which I have heard about from Reeves.'

'Would you mind waiting here for a moment?'

'You have guests?' Eric Lanz looked on the alert.

'No-o.' Tom pulled his handbrake. He had seen a light in the window of his own room, and he supposed Frank was there. 'Back in a sec.' Tom leapt up the front steps and entered the living room.

Heloise lay face down on the yellow sofa, reading a book, with her bare feet over the sofa's arm. 'By yourself?' she asked with surprise.

'No, no, Eric's outside. Billy's back?'

Heloise turned and sat up. 'He is upstairs.'

Tom went back to bring Eric Lanz in. He introduced the German to Heloise, then offered to show him to his room. Mme Annette came into the living room then, and Tom said, 'Monsieur Lanz, Madame Annette. Don't trouble, madame, I shall show our guest his room.'

Upstairs, in the room which had just been Frank's and where there was no sign of Frank now, Tom asked, 'Was that all right? I introduced you to my wife as Eric Lanz?'

'Ha-ha, my real name! Of course it's all right here.' Eric set his plastic bags on the floor near the bed.

'Good,' said Tom. 'There's the bath. Come down soon and have a drink with us.'

Had there been any need, Tom was thinking by ten that evening, for Eric Lanz to spend the night at his house? Lanz was taking the 9.11 a.m. train tomorrow from Moret to Paris, and he could get a taxi to Moret, he assured Tom, if Tom preferred. Tom was driving all the way to Paris tomorrow with Frank, but he wasn't going to tell Eric that.

Over coffee, Eric Lanz talked about Berlin, and Tom only half listened. Such fun! Lots of places open all night. All kinds of people, *individuals*, free-wheeling, anything went. Not many tourists, just the mainly stuffy foreigners who came invited to attend one kind of conference or another. Excellent beer. Lanz was drinking a brand called Mützig, available at the Moret supermarket, and declared it better than Heineken. 'But for me it's Pilsener-Urquell – *vom Fass!*' Eric Lanz seemed to admire Heloise and to be trying to put his best foot forward for her. Tom hoped Eric would not become inspired to haul out his gems tonight to show her. That would be funny! Showing a pretty women his jewellery, then snatching it away again, because it wasn't his to bestow.

Now Eric was talking about possible industrial strikes in Germany which he said would be, if they came, the first since before Hitler. There was a certain fussiness about Eric, a neatness. He got up for a second time to admire the beige and black keyboard of the harpsichord. Heloise, bored to the point of nearly yawning, excused herself before coffee.

'I wish you a pleasant night's sleep, Monsieur Lanz,' said Heloise with a smile, and went upstairs.

Eric Lanz was still gazing at her, as if he would have liked to make his night's sleep more pleasant by sharing her bed. He was on his feet, almost falling forward, and he made a second little bow. '*Madame!*'

'How is Reeves doing?' Tom asked casually. 'Still in that flat!' Tom chuckled. Reeves and Gaby, the part-time house-maid, had not been in when the flat was bombed.

'Yes, and with the same maid! Gaby! She is a darling. Fearless! Well, she likes Reeves. He gives a little excitement to her life, you know?'

Tom shifted. 'Could I see the jewels that you mentioned?' Tom thought he might as well improve his education.

'Why not?' Eric Lanz was on his feet again, giving what Tom hoped was a final glance at his empty coffee cup, his empty Drambuie glass.

They went up the stairs, into the guest room. The light showed under the door of Tom's room. He had told the boy to lock the door from the inside, and Tom thought Frank would have done this, because it was a bit dramatic. Now Eric had opened one of the pudgy plastic cases and he groped at its very bottom – maybe into a false bottom – and produced a purple velvet-like cloth which he spread on the bed. Within this cloth were the jewels.

The diamond and emerald necklace left Tom cold. He would not even have bought the thing, if he could have afforded it, not only not for Heloise, but not for anyone. There were also three or four rings, one a diamond of goodly size, another a separate emerald.

'And these two – sapphire,' said Eric Lanz, relishing the word. 'I won't tell you where these came from. But they are valuable indeed.'

Had Elizabeth Taylor been robbed lately, Tom wondered. Amazing, Tom thought, that people put value in such essentially ugly objects – garish even – as this diamond and emerald necklace. Tom would have preferred to own a Dürer etching or a Rembrandt. Perhaps his taste was improving. Would he have been impressed by these jewels at the age of twenty-six, when he had been with Dickie Greenleaf in Mongibello? Maybe, but strictly by the monetary value of the objects. And that was bad enough. But now he wasn't even impressed by that. He had improved. Tom sighed, and said, 'Very pretty. And no one took a look in your cases at Charles de Gaulle?'

Eric laughed gently. 'No one bothers with me. With my crazy moustache, my boring? – yes, boring clothes, cheap and with no taste, nobody pays any attention. They say passing customs is a technique, an attitude. I have the right one, not too casual, but not at all anxious. That's why Reeves likes me. To take things around for him, I mean.'

'Where are these going to end up?'

Eric was now refolding the purple cloth with the finery inside. 'I do not know. That is not my worry. I have a date tomorrow in Paris.'

'Where?'

Now Eric smiled. 'Very public place. Saint-Germain area. But I don't think I should tell you exactly where or exactly the time,' he said teasingly, and laughed.

Tom smiled also, not caring. It was almost as silly as the Italian Count Bertolozzi affair. The Count had been an overnight guest at Belle Ombre carrying, unbeknownst to the Count, microfilm in his toothpaste tube. Tom had had to steal the toothpaste tube, he recalled, on Reeves's request, from the bathroom which Eric Lanz had now. 'Have you a clock, or shall I ask Madame Annette to awaken you, Eric?'

'Oh, I have a *Wecker* – a waker-clock, thank you. I should say we take off a little after eight? I should like to avoid taking a taxi, but if the hour is too early for you –'

'No problem,' Tom interrupted pleasantly. 'I'm very flexible as to hours. Sleep well, Eric.' Tom went out, aware that Eric thought he had not sufficiently admired his jewels.

Tom realized that he had forgotten his pyjamas, and he disliked sleeping nude. Nudity could come later in the night, if one wanted it, was Tom's feeling. With some hesitation, he rapped gently on the door of his room with his fingertips. A light was still visible under the door. 'Tom,' he whispered at the crack of the door, hearing the boy's light and probably barefoot tread.

Frank opened the door, smiling broadly.

Tom put a finger to his lips, went in, relocked the door, and whispered, 'Pyjamas, sorry.' He got them from his bathroom, and also his house slippers.

'He's in there? What kind of fellow?' Frank asked, indicating the next room.

'Never mind that. He'll be gone tomorrow morning just after eight. You stay in this room till I get back from Moret. All right, Frank?' Tom noticed that the mole on the boy's right cheek was again visible, because Frank had washed or had a bath.

'Yes, sir,' Frank said.

'Good night.' Tom hesitated, then gave the boy a pat on his arm. 'Glad you're home safe.'

Frank smiled. 'G'night, sir.'

'Lock the door,' Tom whispered, before he opened the door and went out. Tom paused long enough to hear the slide of the lock. Under the German's door a light showed, and Tom faintly heard running water in the bathroom, a melodious humming, and Tom recognized 'Frag Nicht Warum Ich Weine' – a sweet, sentimental little waltz! Tom bent over with silent laughter.

Tom paused in front of Heloise's door, wondering suddenly if and when Johnny Pierson might turn up in France with a private detective to look for his brother. That was a nuisance, a little problem. When he and the boy went to the American Embassy area tomorrow – the neighbourhood was convenient for passport photos – couldn't Johnny be making inquiries at the Embassy about his brother? Why worry, since it hadn't happened yet, Tom told himself. And what if it did? Why should he guard Frank so zealously, just because Frank wanted to hide himself? Was he becoming as cloak-and-dagger as Reeves Minot? Tom tapped on Heloise's door.

'Come in,' said Heloise.

*

The next morning, Tom drove Eric Lanz, still moustacheless, to Moret for the 9.11 train. Eric was in good spirits, talking about the farmland they were driving through, the inferior corn for cattle which people could be eating if it were better corn, the all-round subsidized inefficiency of the French farmer.

'Still – it is nice to be in France. I shall visit a couple of art exhibits today, since my rendezvous will be finished at – um – early.'

Tom didn't care what time the rendezvous was, but he had thought to visit Beaubourg with Frank, as there was a major exhibit on now called 'Paris-Berlin', and it would be a hell of a coincidence if Eric were there when he and the boy were, because Eric just might be aware of the disappearance of Frank Pierson. Funny, Tom thought, that so far no newspaper had suggested that Frank might have been kidnapped, though of course kidnappers usually announced their ransom demands pretty quickly. Evidently the family believed that Frank had run away on his own and was still on his own. It would be a splendid time for crooks to demand ransom money, claiming that they had the boy when they hadn't. Why not? Tom smiled at the idea.

'What is funny? I should think it is not very funny for you as an American,' said Eric, trying to be light, but at his most Germanic. He had been talking about the falling dollar, and the inadequate policies of President Carter, as compared with the sagacious housekeeping of Helmut Schmidt's government.

'Sorry,' Tom said, 'I was thinking of Schmidt's or somebody's remark – "The financial affairs of America are now in the hands of rank amateurs".'

'*Correct!*'

They were at the Moret station now, and Eric had no time to continue. Hand-shaking and many thanks.

'Have a good day!' Tom called.

'Same to you!' Eric Lanz smiled and was off, with his two plastic carry-alls firmly in his hands.

Tom drove back to Villeperce, spotted the postman's yellow van in mid-village making its usual rounds, and knew that the post would be on time today at 9.30. But it reminded Tom of a little chore that would be easier to do here than in crowded Paris. He stopped outside the post office, and went in. That morning, with his first coffee, he had gone downstairs and written a note to Reeves. '. . . The boy is 16, 17, but *not* younger, 5 ft. 10 in., brown straight hair, born anywhere in the USA. Send the thing to me soon as pos express. Tell me what I'll owe you.

Thanks in advance, in haste. E.L. here. All okay, it seems. Tom.' In the Villeperce post office, Tom paid the extra nine francs for the red EXPRESS label, which the girl behind the grille pasted on the envelope for him. She started to take his letter, remarked that it wasn't sealed, and Tom told her that he had something else to put in it. Tom took the envelope home with him.

Frank was in the living room, dressed, finishing his breakfast.

Heloise was evidently still upstairs.

'Good morning. How are you?' Tom asked. 'Sleep well?'

Frank had stood up, with his air of respect for Tom which made Tom a bit uneasy. The boy's face was sometimes radiant, almost as if he were looking at the girl Teresa with whom he was in love. 'Yes, sir. You took your friend to Moret, Madame Annette told me.'

'He's gone, yes. We'll take off in maybe twenty minutes. Okay?' Tom looked at the boy's tan polo-neck sweater, and supposed it would be all right for a passport photo. In the photograph in *France-Dimanche*, maybe his passport photograph, Frank wore a shirt and tie. All the better if Frank looked less formal. Tom went closer to the boy and said, 'Keep the right-hand part in your hair, but loosen it as much as you can top and sides for the photograph today. I'll remind you again. Got a comb to take with you?'

Frank nodded. 'Yes, sir.'

'And that pancake?' The boy had covered the mole, Tom saw, but he had to keep it covered all day.

'Got it, yes.' The boy touched his right back pocket.

Tom went upstairs and saw that Mme Annette was changing the sheets in the room that had been Eric Lanz's, and thriftily replacing them with the same ones Frank had been sleeping on before. It reminded Tom of yesterday, when the boy had insisted that Mme Annette not change Tom's sheets. Frank had seemed to prefer to sleep on them, and Mme Annette had appeared to think this quite sensible.

'You and the young man will be back tonight, Monsieur Tome?'

'Yes, in time for dinner, I should think.' Tom heard the postman's van and his handbrake. From the closet in his room, Tom got an old blue blazer, which had always been a bit small for him. Tom didn't want the passport photograph to include Frank's interesting diamond-patterned tweed jacket, in case Frank elected to wear it today.

The row of shoes on the floor of his closet caught Tom's eye. All shined to perfection! All lined up like soldiers! He had never seen such a gleam on the Gucci loafers, such a deep glow in the cordovans. Even his patent leather evening slippers, with their silly grosgrain bows, had new highlights. Frank's work, Tom knew. Mme Annette occasionally gave them a brush-up, but nothing like this. Tom was impressed. Frank Pierson, heir to millions, polishing his shoes! Tom closed his closet door and went down with the blazer.

The post looked uninteresting, two or three bank envelopes which Tom did not bother opening, a letter to Heloise whose envelope was addressed in her friend Noëlle's handwriting. Tom ripped the brown paper off the *International Herald-Tribune*. Frank was still in the living room, and Tom said, 'Brought this for you to wear instead of that tweed. Old one of mine.'

Frank put the jacket on carefully, and with obvious pleasure. The sleeves were a bit long, but the boy flexed his arms gently and said, 'Just marvellous! Thank you.'

'In fact, you can keep it.'

Frank's smile widened. '*Thank* you – really. Excuse me, I'll be down in a minute.' He ran upstairs.

Tom glanced over the *Trib*, and found a small item at the bottom of page two. Pierson Family Sends Detective, said the modest headline. There was no photograph. Tom read:

Mrs Lily Pierson, widow of the late John J. Pierson, food manufacturing magnate, has sent a private detective to Europe to look for her missing son Frank, 16, who left their Maine home in late July and has been traced to London and Paris. Accompanying the detective is her older son John, 19, whose passport the younger brother took when he left his home. It is believed the search will begin in the Paris area. No kidnapping is suspected.

Tom felt an unease akin to embarrassment on reading this, yet what would happen if they ran smack into Frank's brother and the detective today? The family simply wanted to find the boy. Tom was not going to mention the item to Frank, and he would leave the *IHT* at home. Heloise gave the paper barely a glance, usually, but just might miss it if he took it with him and got rid of it. However, what were the French papers going to say about the private detective and the older brother? And would they oblige with a reprint of Frank's photograph?

Frank was ready. Tom went up to say good-bye to Heloise.

'You could have taken me,' Heloise said.

The second sour note of the morning. It was unlike Heloise. She always had things to do. 'I wish you'd said it last night.' She was wearing pink and blue striped jeans, a sleeveless pink blouse. It didn't matter what someone as pretty as Heloise wore in Paris in August, but Tom didn't want Heloise to know that Frank was getting a passport photograph made. 'We're going to Beaubourg, and you've already seen the show with Noëlle.'

'What's the matter with this Billy?' she asked with a puzzled twitch of her blond eyebrows.

'The matter?'

'He looks troubled about something. And he seems to adore you. Is he a *tapette?*'

That meant a homosexual. 'Not that I can see. Do you think so?'

'How long does he want to stay with us? He's been here nearly a week, no?'

'I do know that he wants to go to a travel agency today. In Paris. He was talking about Rome. He'll be taking off this week.' Tom smiled. 'Bye-bye darling. Back around seven.'

When he left the house, Tom picked up the *IHT*, folded it and jammed it into a back pocket.

EIGHT

Tom took the Renault, though he would have preferred the Mercedes. He reproached himself for not having asked Heloise if she needed a car today, because the Mercedes was still at the Grais'. Heloise would have said something, if she needed a car, Tom thought. Frank looked happy with his head back, and the wind blowing through the open window. Tom put on a cassette, Mendelssohn for a change.

'I always leave my car here. Parking's a bore in mid-town.' Tom had stopped at a garage near the Porte d'Orléans. 'Back around – eighteen hours,' Tom said in French to an attendant whom he knew by sight. Tom had passed through the gate which mechanically presented him with a ticket and his hour of arrival stamped on it. Then he and Frank got a taxi. 'Avenue Gabriel, if you please,' Tom said to the driver. He did not want to get out right at the Embassy, and had forgotten the name of the street at a right angle to Avenue Gabriel in which the photography place was. When they were in the neighbourhood, Tom intended to ask the driver to let them out.

'This is the life, riding with you in a taxi in Paris!' Frank said, still in his dream of – what? Freedom? The boy insisted on paying the taxi. He took his wallet from the inside jacket pocket of Tom's old blazer.

Tom wondered what else was in the wallet, in case the boy was searched. Tom asked the driver to stop just off Avenue Gabriel in the street he wanted. 'There's the photo place,' Tom said, indicating a small shingle hanging from a doorway twenty yards away. 'Called Marguerite or something. I don't want to go in with you. That mole looks all right now, but don't touch it. Muss your hair. Maybe put on a – slight smile. *Don't* look serious.' Tom said this because the boy did look serious most of the time. 'They'll ask you to sign your name. Sign Charles Johnson, for instance. They won't ask for identity, I know, because I've recently been through this with them. All right?'

'Okay. Yes, sir.'

'I'll be here,' Tom said, pointing to a bar-café across the street. 'Come out and join me, because they'll tell you you have an hour to wait for the photos, but really it's about forty-five minutes.'

Then Tom walked to Avenue Gabriel and went left towards Concorde, where he knew there was a news-stand. He bought *Le Monde*, *Figaro*, and *Ici Paris*, a gaudy scandal sheet, with blue, green, red and yellow on the front page. Tom saw at a quick glance as he walked back towards the bar-café, that *Ici Paris* had given a whole page to Christina Onassis's surprising marriage to a Russian prole, and another page to Princess Margaret's probably imaginary new escort, an Italian banker slightly younger than she. All sex, as usual, who was doing it to whom, who might start doing it, and who had knocked it off with whom. When Tom had sat down and ordered a coffee, he took a look at every page of *Ici Paris*, and found nothing about Frank. No sex angle there, of course. On the penultimate page were a lot of advertisements, how to meet your true partner – 'Life is short, so realize your dream now' – and ads with illustrations of various inflatable rubber dolls, ranging in price from fifty-nine francs to three hundred and ninety, the dolls said to be shippable in plain wrapper and to be capable of everything. How did one blow them up, Tom wondered. It would take all the breath out of a man to do it, and what would a man's housekeeper or his friends say, if they saw a bicycle pump and no bicycle in his apartment? Funnier, Tom thought, if a man just took the doll along to his garage with his car, and asked the attendant to blow her up for him. And if the man's housekeeper found the doll in bed and thought it was a corpse? Or opened a closet door and a doll fell out on her? A man could buy more than one doll, certainly, one his wife and two or three others his mistresses, and could lead quite a busy fantasy life that way.

His coffee had arrived, and Tom lit a Gauloise. He found nothing in *Le Monde*, nothing in *Figaro*. What if the French police had put a man *in* the photography place, a man who might be on the watch for Frank Pierson along with other wanted people? Wanted people often had to change their passports as well as their identification papers.

Frank came back, smiling. 'They said an hour. Just like you told me.'

'Just *as* you told me,' said Tom. The mole was still covered, Tom saw, the boy's hair still standing up a little on top. 'You signed another name?'

'In the book there, yes. Charles Johnson.'

'Well, we can take a walk – for forty-five minutes,' Tom said. 'Unless you'd like a coffee here.'

Frank had not yet sat down at the little table, and suddenly his body went rigid as he stared at something across the street. Tom looked also, but cars were just then passing. The boy sat down, averted his face, and rubbed a hand across his forehead nervously. 'I just saw –'

Tom stood up now, looked on the pavement, the pavement across the street, and at that instant one of two men's figures turned to look back, and Tom recognized Johnny Pierson. Tom sat down again. 'Well, well,' Tom said, and glanced at the waiters behind the bar, who seemed to be paying no attention to them, so Tom at once got up and went to the doorway to look again. The detective (Tom assumed he was the detective) wore a grey summer suit and was bareheaded, with wavy reddish hair, a stocky build. Johnny was taller and blonder than Frank, wearing a waist-length, nearly white jacket. Tom wanted to see if they went into the passport photograph shop – which was not so labelled, it was just a place that sold cameras and took photographs for passports – and to Tom's relief, they walked past it. But they had probably made inquiries at the United States Embassy which was just around the corner. 'Well –' Tom said again, sitting down. 'They didn't find out anything at the Embassy, that's for sure. Nothing that *we* don't know, anyway.'

The boy said nothing. His face was noticeably paler.

Tom took a five-franc piece from his pocket, ample for one cup of coffee, and motioned to the boy.

They went out and turned left, towards Concorde and the Rue de Rivoli. Tom looked at his watch, and saw that the photographs should be ready by a quarter past twelve. 'Take it easy.' Tom was not walking fast. 'I'll go back to that shop on my own first, and see if they're possibly waiting there. But they just walked past it.'

'They did?'

Tom smiled. 'They did.' Of course they could turn and go back, into the shop, if they had inquired of the Embassy where people usually had photographs made. They might ask if a boy fitting Frank's description had come in recently, and so forth. But Tom was tired of fretting over things he couldn't do anything about. They gazed into windows in the Rue de Rivoli – silk scarves, miniature gondolas, swanky looking shirts with French cuffs, postcards on racks out in front. Tom would have enjoyed looking into W. H. Smith's bookshop, but he steered Frank away, saying that the place was always full of Americans and English. Tom would have liked to think the cloak-and-dagger game amused the boy, but Frank's face looked stricken since he had seen his brother. Then it was time to walk back to the photography shop. Tom told Frank to walk slowly along the pavement, and to turn and go back to the arcades of the Rue de Rivoli in case he saw his brother and the detective again, and Tom would find him.

Tom walked to the shop and went in. An American-looking couple sat waiting on straight chairs and the same skinny, tall young man whom Tom remembered from a couple of months ago, the photographer himself, was offering the name-signing book to a new customer, an American girl. Then the young man disappeared with the girl behind a curtain, where Tom knew the studio was. Tom had pretended to be looking at cameras in a glass case, and now he went out. He told Frank that the coast was clear.

'I'll be on the street here,' Tom said. 'You've paid for the pictures, haven't you?' Tom knew the procedure, and the boy had paid thirty-five francs in advance. 'Just take it easy, and I'll be here.' Tom gave him an encouraging smile. 'Slowly,' Tom said, as the boy went off.

Frank obediently slowed his pace, and did not look back.

Tom walked not fast, but as if he might have a destination, to the end of the street. He was keeping an eye out for the return of Johnny and the detective, but he did not see them. When Tom reached the Avenue Gabriel end of the block, and turned, Frank was walking towards him from the shop. Frank crossed the street, pulled a small white envelope from his jacket pocket and handed it to Tom.

The pictures did look different from the one Tom had seen in *France-Dimanche*, hair more mussed on top, the vague smile that Tom had suggested, the mole not visible, but still the eyes and brows were much the same. Under careful inspection, the two photographs would of course be seen to be of the same boy.

'As good as can be expected,' Tom said. 'Now let's get a taxi.'

Frank had hoped for higher praise, Tom could see. They got a taxi by good luck before Concorde. Tom put one of the photographs into the envelope he had prepared for Reeves Minot. Tom sealed the envelope and felt relieved. He had asked the driver to go to Beaubourg, near which place there was bound to be a snack bar and a post box. Tom found both these things within yards of the bulbous exterior of the Centre Pompidou.

'Amazing, isn't it,' Tom said, referring to the blue monstrosity of the museum's exterior. 'I find it ugly – outside, anyway.'

It looked like many long blue balloons inflated to near bursting point and wrapped around each other. There was definitely something like plumbing about it, but one hesitated to guess whether the ten-foot diameter balloons might contain water or air. Tom again thought of the inflated dolls for sexual purposes, and imagined one bursting under a man, which surely must happen occasionally. What a letdown! Tom bit his lip to stop his laughter. They had a mediocre steak with potato chips in a bar-café-tabac, outside which Tom had dropped his express letter into a yellow box. The collection time was at 16.00 hours.

At the 'Paris-Berlin' show, Frank seemed most impressed by Emil Nolde's 'Dance Before the Golden Calf', a violently prancing trio or quartet of vulgar ladies, one quite naked. 'Golden calf. That's money, isn't it?' said Frank, looking dazed and glassy-eyed with what he had seen already.

'Money, yes,' said Tom. It was not an exhibit to give one quietude, and Tom felt tense also because he thought he ought to look around now and then for Johnny Pierson and the detective. It was strange to try to take in artist's statements on German society of the 1920s, anti-Kaiser posters from World War I, Kirchner, portraits by Otto Dix – plus his brilliant 'Three Prostitutes on the Street' – and at the same time to be worried about the possible appearance of a pair of Americans who would put a sudden end to his pleasure. To hell with the Americans, Tom thought, and said to Frank, 'You keep an eye out for – you know, your brother. I'd like to enjoy this.' Tom spoke a bit severely, but the pictures that surrounded him were like music pouring into his ears in silence, or into his eyes anyway. Tom took a deep breath. Ah, the Beckmanns!

'Does your brother,' Tom asked, 'like art exhibits?'

'Not as much as I do,' was the reply, 'but he does like them.'

That was not very cheering. Now Frank was riveted by what looked like a charcoal drawing of a room's interior with a window at the back on the left, and a masculine figure standing in the foreground in an attitude of strain and confinement. The perspective of the walls and floor suggested confinement. Not a brilliant drawing, perhaps, but the conviction and intensity in the artist's mind was plain. It was prison-like, whatever kind of room it was. Tom knew why Frank was fixated.

Tom had to put his hand on the boy's shoulder to tear him away.

'Sorry.' Frank shook his head a little, and looked at the two doors of the room in which they stood. 'My Dad used to take us to exhibits. He always liked Impressionists. Mainly French. Snowstorms in Paris streets. We have a Renoir at home – of that. Snowstorm, I mean.'

'So that's one thing nice about your father, he liked paintings. And he could also afford to buy them.'

'Well – at least. I mean, *paintings* – a few hundred thousand dollars –' Frank said it as if it were nothing. 'I notice you're always trying to say something nice about my father,' he added a bit resentfully.

Was he? The exhibition was bringing out some emotion in Frank. '*De mortuis,*' Tom said, shrugging.

'He could buy Renoirs? Certainly.' Frank flexed his arms as if he were getting ready to hit somebody, but he looked rather emptily straight ahead of him. 'His market was the whole world, everybody. Well, everybody who could afford it. A lot of his stuff was luxury goods. "More than half of America is too fat," he used to say.'

They were walking slowly back through a room where they had already been. One of the three or four miniature cinema shows was going on to their left, six or eight people sat on chairs looking at it, others stood. On the screen Russian tanks were attacking Hitler's army.

'I told you,' Frank continued, 'besides the ordinary and gourmet stuff, there's the same stuff with a low calorie count. It reminds me of what they say about gambling or prostitution – they make money out of other people's vices. You fatten them up, then make them thin, and start over again.'

Tom smiled at the boy's intensity. What bitterness! Was he trying to justify himself in having killed his father? It was like a little steam being let out of a kettle, when the lid rises and falls again. How was Frank ever going to achieve the big justification, which would take away all his guilt? He might never find a total justification, but he had to find an attitude. Every mistake in life, Tom thought, had to be met by an attitude, either the right attitude or the wrong one, a constructive or self-destructive attitude. What was tragedy for one man was not for another, if he could assume the right attitude towards it. Frank felt guilt, which was why he had looked up Tom Ripley, and curiously Tom had never felt such guilt, never let it seriously trouble him. In this, Tom realized that he was odd. Most people would have experienced insomnia, bad dreams, especially after committing a murder such as that of Dickie Greenleaf, but Tom had not.

Frank clenched his hands suddenly – but he hadn't seen anything. The gesture was due to his own thoughts.

Tom took his arm. 'Had enough? Let's go out this way.' Tom steered him towards what he thought was an exit room, back through still another room, where Tom had a feeling of walking past one soldier after another – the pictures – as if they were an army of variously attired fighters, somehow armed to the teeth, even though some were in evening clothes. Tom felt in a curious way conquered, and he didn't like that. What caused it? Something besides the pictures, he was sure. He would have to send the boy away. The situation was getting a bit warm, emotional, worse.

Suddenly Tom laughed.

'What?' asked Frank, alert as ever to Tom, and he glanced around to see what might be funny.

'Never mind,' Tom said. 'I'm always thinking of crazy things.' Tom had been thinking, if the detective and Johnny saw Tom Ripley with Frank, they might at first think Tom had kidnapped him, since Tom had such a bad reputation. That could still arise, Tom thought, if the detective even thought to discover his residence and learned that a boy had been staying at the Ripleys' house. On the other hand, who in Villeperce knew that, besides Mme Annette, and also Tom had not presented any ransom demand.

They took a taxi to the garage, and were back at Belle Ombre at a little after six. Heloise was upstairs, washing her hair, which would take another twenty minutes, Tom knew, with the dryer. All to the good, because he wanted to try once again with Frank. The boy had sat down in the living room and was looking at a French magazine.

'Why don't you ring up Teresa and tell her you're okay?' Tom asked in a cheerful voice. 'You won't have to tell her *where* you are. She must know you're in France anyway.'

At the name Teresa, the boy sat up a little. 'I think you'd like to – you'd like me to get lost. I can understand that.' Frank stood up.

'If you want to stay in Europe, you can. That's your affair. But it'll make you happier if you speak to Teresa and tell her you're all right. Won't it? Don't you think she's worried?'

'Maybe. I hope so.'

'It's around noon in New York. She's in New York? You dial nineteen, one, then two one two. I can go upstairs so I won't hear a word.' Tom waved a hand towards the telephone, and walked towards the stairs. The boy was going to do it, Tom could tell. Tom went up to his room and closed the door.

Less than three minutes later, the boy knocked on Tom's door. He came in at Tom's word, and said, 'She's out playing tennis.' He announced this as if it were dreadful news.

Frank couldn't imagine Teresa so unconcerned about him that she would be out playing tennis, Tom supposed, and a further agony must be that she was playing tennis with a boy she liked more than she liked Frank. 'You spoke to her mother?'

'No, the maid – Louise. I know her. She told me to call back in an hour. Louise said she was out with a few boys.' Frank put the last phrase in miserable-sounding quotes.

'You said you were all right?'

'No,' the boy said after an instant's reflection. 'Why should I? I suppose I sounded all right.'

'I'm afraid you can't call back from here,' Tom said. 'If the – if Louise mentions it, the family may want to get the call traced if you ring back. Anyway it's too likely for me to risk it. Post office in Fontainebleau is closed now, otherwise I'd drive you. I don't think you can reach Teresa tonight, Billy.' Tom had hoped that the boy could reach Teresa tonight, and that she might have said something like, 'Oh, Frank, you're okay! I miss you! When are you coming home?'

'I understand,' the boy said.

'Billy,' Tom said firmly, 'you must make up your mind what you want to do. You're not suspected. You're not going to be accused. Susie doesn't seem to count for much or anything, because she didn't see anything. Just what are you afraid of? You have to come to terms with that.'

Frank shifted and shoved his hands in his back pockets. 'Of myself, I think. I already said that.'

Tom knew. 'If I weren't here, what would you do?'

The boy shrugged. 'Maybe kill myself. Maybe be sleeping in Piccadilly. You know the way they hang around the fountain there, the statue. I'd send Johnny's passport back to him, and then I don't know what I'd do

– till somebody checked on me. Then I'd be sent home –' Another shrug. 'And then I don't know. Maybe I wouldn't ever *confess* –' He emphasized the word, but spoke in a whisper. 'But maybe I'd kill myself in a couple of weeks. Then there's Teresa. I admit I'm hung up – and if something goes wrong there – if something's already gone wrong – She can't *write* me, you know. So it's hell.'

Tom didn't want to remark that Frank would probably be in love with seventeen more girls before he found the one he might finally marry.

Wednesday just after noon, Tom was pleasantly surprised by a telephone call from Reeves. The object in question would be ready by late that night, and would be in Paris by tomorrow noonish. If Tom was in a hurry and wanted to pick it up himself, he could go to a certain Paris apartment, otherwise it could be sent from Paris to Tom by registered post. Tom preferred to pick it up. Reeves gave him an address, a name, third floor.

Tom asked for the telephone number there in case of need, and Reeves gave him this too. 'Very fast work, Reeves, I thank you.' It would have been quite all right, Tom thought, to have sent it registered from Hamburg, but the aeroplane delivery did save one day.

'And for this little job,' said Reeves in his creaky, old man's voice, though he was not yet forty, 'two thousand, if you don't mind, Tom. Dollars. Cheap at the price, because this wasn't easy, sort of a new one, you know. And I should think your friend can afford it, eh?' Reeves's tone was amused and friendly.

Tom understood. Reeves had recognized Frank Pierson. 'Can't talk any more here,' said Tom. 'I'll get it to you via the usual, Reeves.' Tom meant via a request to his Swiss bank. 'Are you going to be home in the next days?' Tom had no plans, but wanted to know this. Reeves could be wonderfully helpful.

'Yes, why? Thinking of coming?'

'No-o,' said Tom cautiously, ever fearful that his line might be being tapped.

'You're staying put.'

Tom supposed that Reeves knew he was sheltering Frank Pierson, if not under his own roof, then somewhere.

'What's all the trouble? Impossible to say, huh?'

'Impossible, yes, just now. I do thank you, Reeves.'

They hung up. Tom walked to the french windows and saw Frank in his levis and darker blue workshirt plying the spade at the edge of a long bed of roses. He worked slowly and steadily, like a peasant who knew what he was doing, not like an amateur who would have knocked himself out in fifteen minutes of a fast attack on something. Strange, Tom thought. Maybe the work was some kind of penance in the boy's mind? Frank had been spending his time yesterday and today reading, listening to music, and doing chores such as car-washing and sweeping out Belle Ombre's cellar, which had involved shifting rather heavy racks of wine and putting them back in place. Frank had thought the tasks up himself.

Should they go to Venice, Tom wondered. A change of scene might shape the boy up, make him come to a decision, and Tom might be able to put him on a plane from Venice to New York, and return home himself. Or Hamburg? Same thing. But Tom didn't want to involve Reeves in the sheltering of Frank Pierson, and Tom in fact didn't care to involve himself much longer. Maybe with the new passport, Frank would find his courage and take off on his own, finish his personal adventure in his own style.

Thursday noon, Tom rang the Paris number in the Rue du Cirque, and a woman answered. They spoke in French.

'This is Tom here.'

'*Ah, oui.* I think everything is in order. You are coming this afternoon?' She didn't sound like a maid, but like the woman of the house.

'Yes, if that is convenient. Around three-thirty?'

That would be all right.

Tom told Heloise that he was going to make a quick trip to Paris to talk with their bank manager, and would be back between 5 and 6 p.m. Tom was not in trouble with an overdraft, but one of the managers of Morgan Guarantee Trust did sometimes give him stock market advice, very general and minor, Tom considered, as Tom preferred to let his stocks ride rather than waste time in the dangerous game of playing the market. Anyway, Tom's excuse was good enough, because Heloise's mind was on her mother that afternoon. Her mother, a youthful fifty-odd and not inclined to illness, had had to go to hospital for an examination which might result in an operation for a tumour. Tom remarked that doctors always prepared people for the worst.

'She looks in the pink of health. Give her my good wishes when you speak with her,' Tom said.

'Billy is going with you?'

'No, he's staying. He's got some little jobs he wants to do – for us.'

In the Rue du Cirque, Tom was able to find a parking meter free, then he went to the house, an old well-kept edifice with the usual street door button to press, and then the door opened on a hall or foyer with a concierge's door and window, which Tom didn't bother with. He took the lift to the third floor, and rang the bell on the left marked Schuyler.

A tall woman with a lot of red hair opened the door slightly.

'Tom.'

'Ah, come in! This way, please.' She led him towards a living room which was across a hall. 'You have met before, I think.'

In the living room stood Eric Lanz, smiling, hands on hips. There was a coffee tray on a low table in front of a sofa. Eric was standing. 'Hello, Tom. Yes, me again. How are you?'

'Quite well, thanks. And you?' Tom was also smiling with surprise.

The red-headed woman had left them. There was a low drone of sewing machines from another room of the flat. What went on here, Tom wondered. Maybe another fence depot, as was Reeves's Hamburg apartment? With a couturière cover?

'And here we are,' said Eric Lanz, opening a beige cardboard portfolio, which had strings to close it. He produced a white envelope from among other thicker envelopes.

Tom took the envelope, and glanced over his shoulder before he opened it. No one else had come into the room. The envelope was not sealed, and Tom wondered if Eric had already looked at the passport? Perhaps. Tom did not want to look at it in Eric's presence, but at the same time wanted to know if Hamburg had done a good job.

'I think you will be pleased,' Eric said.

Frank's photograph had the official stamp which raised the surface, plus PHOTOGRAPH ATTACHED DEPARTMENT OF STATE PASSPORT AGENCY NEW YORK partly on and below it. BENJAMIN GUTHRIE ANDREWS was the name, born in New York, and height and weight and date of birth corresponded well enough to Frank's, though the date made him seventeen now. No matter. The job looked good to Tom, who had some experience, and maybe only a magnifying glass could detect that the raised stamp on the photograph might be a bit off from the stamp on the page – or was it? Tom couldn't tell. Inside of front page, full address was apparently that of parents in New York. The passport was some five months old, with a Heathrow entry stamp, then France, then Italy where the unfortunate bearer must have been relieved of it. No current French entry, but unless a passport control officer's suspicions were aroused by Frank's appearance, no one was going to peer at entry and exit stamps, Tom knew. 'Very good,' Tom said finally.

'Nothing to do but sign it across the photograph.'

'Do you happen to know if the name has been changed, or is the real Benjamin Andrews going to be looking for his passport?' Tom hadn't detected any sign of erasure in the typewritten name inside the front cover, and any previous signature fragment had been neatly obliterated from beside the photograph.

'It has been changed, the last name, Reeves told me. Coffee? This is finished, but I can ask the maid to make some.' Eric Lanz looked slimmer, even of better social class since Tom had seen him three days ago, as if he were a miracle man who could effect a transformation just by thinking about it. Now he wore the trousers of a dark blue summer suit, a good white silk shirt, and the shoes which Tom recognized. 'Sit down, Tom.'

'Thanks, I said I'd be home soon. You travel a lot, it seems.'

Eric laughed – rosy lips, white teeth. 'Reeves always has work for me. Berlin too. I am selling hi-fi gadgets this time,' he said in a lower tone and glanced at the door behind Tom. '*Supposed* to be. Ha-ha! When are you coming to Berlin?'

'No idea. No plans.' Tom had put the passport back into its envelope, and he gestured with it before sticking it into his inside jacket pocket. 'I've arranged to settle for this with Reeves.'

'I know.' Now Eric pulled a billfold from his blue jacket which lay on the sofa. He extracted a card and handed it to Tom. 'If you are ever in Berlin, it would be a pleasure to see you, Tom.'

Tom glanced at the card. Niebuhrstrasse. Tom didn't know where that was, but it was in Berlin, with a telephone number. 'Thanks. You've known Reeves a long time?'

'Oh – two, three years, *ja*.' His rosy, neat mouth smiled again. 'Luck to you, Tom – and to your friend!' He moved to the door with Tom to see him out. '*Wiedersehen!*' said Eric, softly but clearly.

Tom went down to his car and drove homeward. Berlin, Tom was thinking. Not for the presence of Eric Lanz at all, if he ever was at home, but because Berlin was off the beaten tourist track. Who wanted to visit Berlin, except perhaps scholars of the World Wars, or as Eric had said businessmen invited to conferences. If Frank wanted to hide out a few days longer, Berlin might be an idea for him. Venice – more attractive and beautiful, but also a place where Johnny and the detective might spend a couple of days, looking. What Tom didn't want was that pair to knock on his own door in Villeperce.

NINE

'Benjamin. Ben. I like that name,' Frank said, beaming now as he sat on the edge of his bed, gazing at his new passport.

'I hope it gives you courage,' Tom said.

'I know this cost something. You can tell me how much, and if I can't – do it just now, I can do it later.'

'Two thousand dollars ... Now you're free. Keep letting your hair grow. You've got to sign that passport across the photograph, you know.' Tom made him try the entire name on a sheet of typewriter paper. The boy had rather quick and angular handwriting. Tom told him to round the capital B of Benjamin, and made him write the whole name out three or four more times.

At last the boy signed with one of Tom's black ballpoint pens. 'How is this?'

Tom nodded. 'All right. Remember when you sign anything else – take it easy so you'll round everything.'

It was after dinner. Heloise had wanted to watch something on television, and Tom had asked the boy to come upstairs with him.

The boy looked at Tom and his eyelids blinked quickly. 'Will you come with me, if I go somewhere? To another town, I mean? City?' He wet his lips. 'I know it's been a pain having me – hiding me. If you'd come with me to another country, you could just leave me.' Now he looked with sudden dismalness towards the window, and back at Tom. 'It'd be so awful, somehow, leaving from here, *your* house. But I could, I suppose.' He stood up straighter, as if to illustrate that he could stand on his own feet.

'Where're you thinking of going?'

'Venice. Rome, maybe. They're big enough to get lost in.'

Tom smiled, thinking Italy was a hotbed of kidnappers. 'Yugoslavia? Doesn't appeal to you?'

'Do you like Yugoslavia?'

'Yes,' Tom said, but not in a tone that implied he would like to go there now. 'Go to Yugoslavia. But I wouldn't advise Venice or Rome – if you want to stay free for a while. Berlin is another possibility. Off the tourist track.'

'Berlin. I've never been there. Would you go to Berlin with me? Just for a few days?'

The idea was not unattractive, because Tom found Berlin interesting. 'If you promise to go home after Berlin,' Tom said quietly and firmly.

Frank's face was smiling again, as broadly as when he had received the new passport. 'All right, I promise.'

'Okay, we'll go to Berlin.'

'Do you know Berlin?'

'I've been there – twice, I think.' Tom suddenly felt picked up. Berlin would be all right for three or four days, fun in fact, and he would hold the boy to his promise to take off for home from there. Maybe it wouldn't be necessary to remind the boy of that promise.

'When shall we go?' Frank asked.

'The sooner the better. Maybe tomorrow. I'll see about plane tickets in Fontainebleau tomorrow morning.'

'I've still got some money.' Then the boy's expression changed. 'Not much, I suppose, only about five hundred dollars' worth of francs.'

'Never mind about money. We'll settle up later. I'll say good night. I want to go down and speak with Heloise. Of course you can come downstairs again if you want to.'

'Thanks, I think I'll write to Teresa.' Frank looked happy.

'All right, but we'll post it from Düsseldorf tomorrow, not from here.'

'Düsseldorf?'

'Planes to Berlin have to touch down somewhere inside Germany first, and I always aim for Düsseldorf instead of Frankfurt, because you don't change planes at Düsseldorf, just get out for a few minutes – passports. One other thing, most important, don't tell Teresa you're going to Berlin.'

'All right.'

'Because she might tell your mother, and I assume you want to be let alone in Berlin. The Düsseldorf postmark will let her know you're in Germany, but tell her you're – going to Vienna. How about that?'

'Yes – *sir*.' Frank sounded like a newly promoted soldier, delighted to take orders.

Tom went downstairs. Heloise was lying on the sofa, watching a news programme. 'Look,' she said. '*How* can they go on killing each other?'

A rhetorical question. Tom looked blankly at the television screen, which showed an apartment building blowing up, darts of red and yellow flame, an iron beam tumbling in the air. He supposed it was Lebanon. A few days ago it had been Heathrow, the aftermath of an attack on the Israeli airlines. Tomorrow the world, Tom thought. He was thinking that Heloise would have news of her mother tomorrow morning maybe by about ten, and Tom hoped the hospital tests would not mean surgery. Tom intended to go to Fontainebleau before ten, get the tickets, and tell Heloise that it was a most urgent job for Reeves Minot, which he had learned about by telephone during the night, something like that. There was no telephone in Heloise's room, and with her door closed, she could not hear the telephone in his room or in the living room downstairs. Awful news continued on the television set, and Tom postponed any kind of speech to Heloise.

Before he went to bed that night, Tom knocked on Frank's door and handed him some booklets on Berlin and a map. 'Might interest you. Tells you about the political situation and so forth.'

By breakfast time, Tom had altered his plans somewhat. He would use a Moret travel agency for the ticket – his own – and telephone the airport in regard to Frank's ticket. He told Heloise that Reeves had rung in the small hours and wanted him to come to Hamburg at once to lend both his presence and his advice on an art deal.

'I spoke with Billy this morning. He wants to come with me to Hamburg,' Tom said, 'and he'll be going back to America from there.' Tom had told her that Billy had not made up his mind Monday in Paris where he wanted to go.

Heloise was visibly pleased that the boy would be going off with Tom, as Tom had thought she would be. 'And you'll be coming back – when?'

'Oh – I'd say in three days. Maybe Sunday, Monday.' Tom was dressed and having a second coffee and toast in the living room. 'I'll take off in a few minutes to see about the tickets. And I hope the news is good, darling, by ten.'

Heloise was supposed to ring a doctor at a Paris hospital at ten in regard to her mother. 'Merci, chéri.'

'I have a feeling there's nothing wrong with your mother.' Tom meant that, because her mother looked very fit. Just then Tom saw that Henri the gardener had arrived – today being neither Tuesday nor Thursday but Friday – and was lazily filling big metal pitchers with rainwater from the tank by the greenhouse. 'Henri's here. That's nice!'

'I know. Tome, there's nothing dangerous about Hamburg, is there?'

'No, dear. Reeves knows that I know about a Buckmaster sale that's a little like this one in Hamburg. A nice launching place for Billy too. I'll show him a bit of the city. I never do anything dangerous.' Tom smiled, thinking of the shoot-outs, which he considered he had never been in, but he also recalled an evening at Belle Ombre, when a Mafia corpse or two had been lying on the marble floor right here in the living room, oozing blood which Tom had had to wipe up with Mme Annette's sturdy grey floor rags. Heloise hadn't seen that. Not a shoot-out, anyway. The Mafiosi had had guns, but Tom had bashed one over the head with a piece of firewood. Tom did not like to remember that.

Tom telephoned Roissy from his room, and learned that there were seats available on an Air France flight taking off at 3.45 p.m. that afternoon. He reserved a place for Benjamin Andrews, the ticket to be picked up at the airport. He then drove to Moret and bought his round-trip ticket in his own name. When he came back, he informed Frank. They would leave the house around one o'clock for Roissy.

Tom was glad that Heloise did not ask for Reeves' telephone number in Hamburg. On some other occasion, Tom had certainly given it to her, but maybe she had mislaid it. If she found it and rang Reeves, it would be awkward, so Tom thought he should telephone Reeves once he got to Berlin, but somehow Tom didn't want to do it now. Frank was packing. And Tom was casting an eye over his house as if it were a ship he would soon abandon, although the house was in good hands with Mme Annette. Only three or four days? That was nothing. Tom had thought of taking the Renault and leaving it at the Roissy garage, but Heloise wanted to drive them or at least accompany them in the Mercedes, which was now running well. So Tom drove the Mercedes to Roissy-Charles de Gaulle airport, and thought how friendly and convenient Orly airport had been a year or so ago, between Villeperce and Paris, until they opened the north-of-Paris Roissy and routed everything from there, even flights to London.

'Heloise – I thank you for putting me up so many days,' Frank said in French.

'A pleasure, Billy! And you have been a help to us – in the garden and in the house. I wish you luck!' She extended her hand through the car's open window, and rather to Tom's surprise she kissed Frank on both cheeks as he bent towards her.

Frank grinned, embarrassed.

Heloise drove off, and Tom and Frank went into the terminus with their luggage. Heloise's affectionate goodbye reminded Tom that she had never asked him what he was paying the boy for his work. Nothing. Tom was sure the boy would not have accepted anything. Tom had given the boy five thousand francs this morning, the maximum one was allowed to take out of France, and Tom had the same amount himself, though he had not as yet ever been searched by the French on departure. If they should run out in Berlin, which was unlikely, Tom could wire for money from a bank in Zurich. Now he told Frank to go and buy his ticket at the Air France counter.

'Benjamin Andrews, flight seven-eight-nine,' Tom reminded him, 'and on the plane we won't sit together. Don't look at me. See you in Düsseldorf maybe, otherwise Berlin.' He started for the luggage check-in, then found himself lingering to see if Frank was going to get his ticket without difficulty. One or two people were ahead of Frank, then the boy was at the counter, and Tom saw from the girl's scribbling and the money exchange that all was well.

Tom checked in his suitcase, then proceeded to one of the upward sloping escalators which eased him towards gate number six. These gates, called simply gates in England or anywhere else, were here absurdly labelled 'Satellites', as if they were somehow detached from and whirling around the airport proper. Tom lit a cigarette in the last hall where one could smoke, and looked over his fellow passengers, nearly all men, one concealed behind a copy of the *Frankfurter Allgemeine* already. Tom was among the first to board. He did not look back to see if Frank had even come into the lounge. Tom settled himself in his smoking-section seat, half closed his eyes and glanced at the passengers bumping up the aisle with attaché cases, but he did not see Frank.

At Düsseldorf, the passengers were told they could leave their hand luggage on board, but everyone had to get off. Here they were herded like sheep towards an unseen destination, but Tom had been here once before, and knew they were destined for nothing worse than a passport checking and stamping.

Then came a small waiting area to which they were also herded, and Tom saw Frank negotiating for a stamp for his letter to Teresa. Tom had forgotten to give the boy some of the German paper money and coins which Tom had in his pocket, left over from earlier trips, but the German woman was smiling now, apparently accepting Frank's French money, and the letter changed hands. Tom boarded the plane for Berlin.

Tom had said to Frank, 'You'll love the Berlin-Tegel airport.' Tom liked it, because it looked like an airport of human size: no frills, no escalators, triple levels or eye-dazzling chromium, just a mostly yellowish-painted reception hall with a round bar-café counter in the centre, and a single W C in evidence without a kilometre's walk to it. Near the circular refreshment counter Tom lingered with his suitcase, and gave Frank a nod when he saw him approaching, but Frank was evidently so dutifully obeying orders that he did not look at Tom, and Tom had to intercept him.

'Fancy seeing you here!' said Tom.

'Good afternoon, sir,' said Frank, smiling.

The forty or so passengers who had debarked at Berlin seemed to have dwindled to less than a dozen now, which was another treat to the eye.

'I'll see about an hotel room,' Tom said. 'Wait here with the luggage.' Tom went to a telephone booth a few yards away, looked up the number of the Hotel Franke in his business address book, and dialled it. Tom had once visited an acquaintance at this middle-category hotel, and had noted its address for possible future use. Yes, they had two rooms to offer, said the Hotel Franke, and Tom booked them under his name, and said he would be arriving in about half an hour. The few persons left in the homey-looking terminus appeared so innocuous to Tom that he risked a taxi together with the boy.

Their destination was the Albrecht-Achillesstrasse off the Kurfürsten-damm. They rode at first through what seemed kilometres of flat plains, past warehouses, fields and barns, then the city began to show itself in a few very new-looking buildings, beige and cream near-skyscrapers, a bit of chrome on aerial-like spires. They were approaching from the north. Tom slowly and rather uncomfortably became aware of the pocket-like, island-like entity called West Berlin, surrounded by Soviet-controlled territory. Well, they were within the Wall, and protected at least for the nonce by French, American and British soldiers. The one jagged, not new edifice made Tom's heart leap, rather to his own surprise.

'That's the Gedächtniskirche!' Tom said to Frank with almost proprietary pride. 'Very important landmark. Bombed, as you see, but they let it stand the way it was.'

Frank was looking out the open window, rapt, almost as if it were Venice, Tom thought, and in its way Berlin was just as unique.

The broken, reddish-brown tower of the Gedächtniskirche passed by them on their left, then Tom said, 'All this was flattened around here – what you're looking at. That's why everything looks so new now.'

'*Ja*, and *kaputt* it was!' said the middle-aged driver in German. 'You are tourists? Just here for pleasure?'

'Yes,' said Tom, pleased that the driver wanted to chat. 'How's the weather?'

'Yesterday rain – today like this.'

It was overcast, but not raining. They sped along the Kurfürsten-damm, and halted for a red light at Lehninplatz.

'Look how new all these shops are,' Tom said to Frank. 'I'm really not mad about the Ku'damm.' He remembered his first trip to Berlin, alone, when he had walked up and down the long straight Kurfürstendamm, vainly trying to sense an atmosphere which one couldn't get from pretty shop windows, chrome and glass pavement booths that displayed porcelain and wristwatches and handbags. Kreuzberg, the slummy old section of Berlin, now so full of Turkish workers, had more personality.

The driver made a left turn into Albrecht-Achillesstrasse, past a corner pizzeria which Tom remembered, then past a supermarket, now closed, on the right. The Hotel Franke stood on the left around a little curve in the street. Tom paid the driver with some of his left-over marks, of which he had nearly six hundred.

They filled out little white cards that the receptionist gave them, and both consulted their passports for the correct numbers. Their rooms were on the same floor, but not adjacent. Tom had not wanted to go to the more elegant Hotel Palace near the Gedächtniskirche, because he had stayed there once before, and thought that for some reason they might remember him, and notice that he was with a teen-aged boy not related to him. Just what anybody would make of that, even also at the Hotel Franke, Tom didn't care, but he thought a modest hotel like the Franke less apt to recognize Frank Pierson.

Tom hung up a pair of trousers, pulled the bedcover back and tossed his pyjamas on to the white, button-sheeted, feather-filled top item, which served both as blanket and sheet, a German institution that Tom knew of yore. From his window he had a thoroughly dull view of a greyish court, of another six-storey cement building set at an angle, and a couple of distant tree tops. Tom felt inexplicably happy suddenly, felt a sense of freedom, maybe illusory. He stuck his passport case with his French francs in it at the bottom of his suitcase, closed the suitcase lid, and went out and locked his door. He had told Frank he would pick him up in five minutes. Tom knocked on Frank's door.

'Tom? Come in.'

'Ben!' said Tom, smiling. 'How are things?'

'Look at this crazy *bed*!'

They both suddenly laughed out loud. Frank had also pulled the bedcover back and laid his pyjamas on the buttoned feather blanket.

'Let's go out and take a walk. Where're those two passports?' Tom made sure that the boy's new passport was out of sight, found Johnny's passport in the suitcase and put it in an envelope from the writing table drawer. This he stuck at the bottom of the boy's suitcase. 'You don't want to whip out the wrong one.' Tom wished they had burned

Johnny's passport at Belle Ombre, since Johnny must have had to acquire a new one anyway.

They went out and could have taken the stairs, but Frank wanted to see the elevator again. He looked as happy as Tom felt. Why, Tom wondered.

'Press E. That's the *Erdgeschoss.*'

They left their keys, went out and turned right towards the Kurfürstendamm. Frank stared at everything, even at a dachshund being aired. Tom proposed a beer at the corner pizzeria. Here they bought chits and queued up at a counter for beer only, then carried their big mugs to the only partly free table where two girls were eating pizzas. With a nod, they gave permission for Tom and the boy to sit down.

'Tomorrow we'll go to Charlottenburg,' Tom said. 'Museums there and a beautiful park too. Then there's the Tiergarten.' And there was tonight. Lots of places to go to in Berlin at night. Tom looked at the boy's cheek and saw that the mole was covered. 'Keep up the good work,' Tom said, pointing to his own cheek.

By midnight or a little after, they were at Romy Haag's, and Frank was a bit drunk on three or four more beers. Frank had won a toy bear at a throwing-game stall outside a beerhall, and Tom was now carrying the little brown bear, the symbol of Berlin. Tom had been to Romy Haag's on his last visit to Berlin. It was a bar-disco, slightly touristy, and with a late show of transvestites.

'Why don't you dance?' Tom said to Frank. 'Ask one of these to dance.' Tom meant the two girls seated on stools at the bar with their drinks in front of them, but with their eyes on the dance floor over which a grey sphere kept turning. Spotted lights, shadows and white, played slowly over the walls. The rotating grey object, no bigger than a beachball and quite ugly *per se*, looked like a relic of the Thirties, evocative of pre-Hitler Berlin, and strangely fascinating to the eye.

Frank squirmed as if he hadn't the courage to approach the girls. He and Tom were standing at the bar.

'Not prostitutes,' Tom added over the noise of the music.

Frank went off to the toilet near the door. When the boy came back, he walked past Tom and went on to the dance floor where Tom for a few minutes lost sight of him, and then saw him dancing with a blonde girl under the revolving sphere, along with a dozen other couples and maybe a few singles. Tom smiled. Frank was jumping up and down, having fun. The music was non-stop, but Frank came back after a couple of minutes, triumphant.

'I thought you'd think I was a coward if I didn't ask a girl to dance!' Frank said.

'Nice girl?'

'Oh, very! Pretty! Except that she was chewing gum. I said *"Guten Abend"* and I even said *"Ich liebe dich"* but I only know that from songs. I think she thought I was pissed. She laughed, anyway!'

He certainly was pissed, and Tom steadied him by one arm so he could slide a leg over a stool. 'Don't drink the rest of that beer, if you don't want it.'

A roll of drums heralded the floorshow. Three sturdy men pranced out in floor-length, ruffled dresses of pink, yellow and white, in broad-brimmed flowered hats, and with huge plastic breasts entirely exposed and sporting red nipples. Enthusiastic applause! They sang something from *Madame Butterly*, and then came several skits of which Tom understood barely half, but which the spectators seemed to appreciate.

'They *are* funny to look at!' Frank roared into Tom's ear.

The muscular trio wound up with *'Das ist die Berliner Luft'*, flouncing their skirts and kicking high, as posies from the audience showered upon them.

Frank clapped and shouted 'Bravo! – *Bravo!*' and nearly fell off his stool.

A few minutes later, Tom was walking arm in arm with the boy – mainly to keep Frank upright – along a darkish pavement, which however at half past two in the morning still had several pedestrians.

'What's *that*?' Frank asked, seeing a pair in strange costume approaching.

They seemed to be a man and a woman, the man in harlequin tights and a hat with pointed brim fore and aft, while the woman resembled a walking playing card, and on closer inspection Tom saw that she was the ace of clubs. 'Probably just come from a party,' Tom said, 'or going to one.' Tom had noticed before in Berlin that people liked to change their clothing from one extreme to another, even disguise themselves. 'It's a who-am-I game,' Tom said. 'The whole city's like this.' Tom could have gone on. The city of Berlin was bizarre enough, artificial enough – at least in its political status – and so maybe its citizens attempted to outdo it sometimes in their dress and behaviour. It was also a way for Berliners to say, *'We exist!'* But Tom was in no mood to get his thoughts together. He said only, 'To think it's surrounded by these boring *Russians* with no sense of humour at all!'

'Hey, Tom, can we take a look at East Berlin? I'd love to see that!'

Tom clutched the little Berlin bear, and tried to think of any peril there for Frank, and couldn't. 'Sure. They're more interested in taking a few DM off their visitors than in knowing who the visitors are. There's a taxi! Let's get it!'

TEN

Tom telephoned Frank from his room the next morning at nine. How was Ben feeling?

'All right, thank you. I woke up just two minutes ago.'

'I'll order breakfast for us in my room, so come over. Four fourteen, And lock your door when you go out.'

Tom had checked around three a.m., when they had returned to the hotel, to see if his passports were still in his suitcase, and they had been.

Over breakfast, Tom suggested Charlottenburg, followed by East Berlin, and then the West Berlin zoo, if they had energy left. He gave the boy an item from the London *Sunday Times* by Frank Giles, which Tom had cut out and carefully kept, because it told a lot about Berlin in a few words. 'Is Berlin Split Forever?' was its title. Frank read it as he ate toast and marmalade, and Tom said it didn't matter if he got butter on the cutting, because he had had it so long.

'Only fifty miles from the Polish border!' said Frank in a tone of wonder. 'And – ninety-three thousand Soviet troops within twenty miles of – the suburbs of Berlin.' Then Frank looked at Tom and said, 'Why're they so worried about Berlin? All this Wall stuff.'

Tom was enjoying his coffee and did not want to embark upon a lecture. Maybe the reality would sink into Frank today. 'The Wall goes all the way up and down Germany, not just Berlin. The Berlin Wall is talked about the most because it surrounds West Berlin, but the Wall goes down to Poland and Romania too. You'll see it – today. And maybe tomorrow we'll take a taxi out to the Glienicker-Brücke where they exchange prisoners sometimes, West and East. I mean spies, really. They even divide the river there, you can see a wire above the surface dividing the river down the middle.' At least some of it was sinking in,

Tom thought, because the boy perused the article thoroughly. It explained the triple military occupation or control of Berlin by English, French and American troops, which helped to explain (but not really to Tom, who always felt that something was just out of his grasp in regard to Berlin) why the German airline Lufthansa could not land at Berlin-Tegel airport. Berlin was artificial, something special, not even a part of West Germany, and perhaps it didn't even wish to be, since Berliners had always taken a pride in being Berliners.

'I'll get dressed and knock on your door in about ten minutes,' Tom said, standing up. 'Bring your passport, Ben. That's for the Wall.' The boy was dressed, but Tom was still in pyjamas.

They caught an old-fashioned streetcar from the Kurfürstendamm to Charlottenburg, and spent more than an hour in the museums of archaeology and paintings. Frank lingered over the models of activities of long ago in the Berlin area, copper-mining by men in animal pelt garments three thousand years before Christ. As at Beaubourg, Tom found himself watching out for anyone who might show an interest in Frank, but Tom saw only parents with chattering and curious children peering into cases. Berlin, so far, presented a mild and harmless scene.

Then another streetcar back to the Charlottenburg S-Bahn stop for the ride to the Friedrichstrasse stop and the Wall. Tom had his map. They were above ground all the way, though this was now an underground or subway type of train, and Frank stared out of the window at the passing apartment houses, mostly rather old and drab, which meant that they had not been bombed. Then the Wall, grey and ten feet high as promised, topped with barbed wire, sprayed with covering paint in spots by East German soldiers, Tom remembered, before President Carter's visit a couple of months ago, so that West German television could not send the anti-Soviet slogans painted on the Wall into the homes of East Berliners and of many East Germans who could get West German television programmes on their sets. Tom and Frank waited in a room with some fifty other tourists and West Berliners, many laden with shopping bags, baskets of fruit, tinned hams, and what looked like boxes from clothing stores. These were mostly elderly people, probably visiting for the umptieth time their siblings and cousins cut off by the Wall since 1961. Tom and Frank's seven-digit numbers were finally called out by a girl behind a grilled window, which meant that they could file through to another room with a long table manned by East German soldiers in grey-green uniforms. A girl returned their passports, and a few yards on they had to buy from a soldier six DM fifty pfennigs' worth of East German money, which came to more in East German marks. Tom had an aversion to touching it, and stuck it in an empty back pocket.

Now they were 'free'. Tom smiled at the thought as they began walking along the Friedrichstrasse which continued here, beyond the Wall. Tom pointed out the still uncleaned palaces of the Prussian royal family. Why the hell didn't they clean them, Tom wondered, or plant some hedge boxes around them, if they wanted to make a good impression on the rest of the world?

Frank looked all around him, speechless for several minutes.

'Unter den Linden,' Tom said, not in a merry tone. A sense of self-preservation made him try, however, for something cheering, so he took Frank by the arm and swung him into a street on the right. 'Let's go this way.'

They were back on a street – yes, Friedrichstrasse again now – where long stand-up counters projected from snack cafés halfway across the pavement, patrons stood spooning soup, eating sandwiches, drinking beer. Some of them looked like construction workers in plaster-dusty overalls, some were women and girls who might have been office workers.

'I might buy a ballpoint pen,' said Frank. 'It'd be fun to buy *something* here.'

They approached a stationer's shop which had an empty news-stand in front, only to be greeted by a sign on the front door saying: CLOSED BECAUSE I FEEL LIKE CLOSING. Tom laughed, translating it for Frank.

'Bound to be another shop along here,' said Tom as they walked on.

There was another, but it was also closed, and another handwritten sign said: CLOSED BECAUSE OF HANGOVER. Frank thought this hilarious.

'Maybe they do have a sense of humour, but otherwise it's just like what I read about it, sort of – drab, maybe.'

Tom also felt a creeping depression that he remembered from his first trip to East Berlin. The people's clothes looked limp. This was Tom's second visit, and he would not have come if the boy hadn't wanted to see it. 'Let's have some lunch, cheer ourselves up,' Tom said, gesturing towards a restaurant.

This was a big, modest, efficient-looking restaurant and some of the long tables bore white tablecloths. If they hadn't enough money on them, Tom thought, the cashier would be delighted to take DM. They sat down, and Frank studied the clientèle thoughtfully – a man in a dark suit with spectacles, eating by himself, and two plumpish girls chattering away over their coffee at a nearby table – as if he watched animals of a new species in a zoo. Tom was amused. These were 'Russians' to Frank, he supposed, tinged with Communism.

'They're not all Communists, really,' Tom said. 'They're Germans.'

'I know. But it's just the idea that they can't go and live in West Germany if they want to – can they?'

'That is correct,' Tom said, 'they can't.'

Their food was arriving, and Tom waited until the blonde waitress, who had a friendly smile, had departed. 'But the Russians say they built the Wall to keep the capitalists *out*. That's their pitch, anyway.'

They went up to the top of the Alexanderplatz tower, pride of East Berlin, to take coffee and admire the view. Then both were seized by a desire to leave.

West Berlin, surrounded as it was, felt like the wide open spaces once they had quit the district of the Wall and were rattling along on the elevated train towards the Tiergarten. They had changed a few more ten-DM notes, and Frank was now poring over his East Berlin coins.

'I might keep these as souvenirs – or send a couple to Teresa for fun.'

'Not from here, please,' Tom said. 'Keep them till you get back home.'

It was refreshing to see the lions strolling in apparent freedom in the Tiergarten, tigers lounging by their swimming pool, yawning in the faces of the public, though there was a moat between them and the visitors. The trumpeter swan, just as Tom and Frank walked by, lifted his long neck and trumpeted. They made their way slowly towards the aquarium. Here Frank fell in love with the Druckfisch.

'Unbelievable!' Frank's lips parted in astonishment, and he looked suddenly like a child of twelve. 'Those eyelashes! Just like *make-up*!'

Tom laughed and stared at the little fish of brilliant blue, hardly six inches long, cruising at what could be called moderate speed, apparently in quest of nothing, except that its little round mouth kept opening and closing as if it were asking something. The lids of its oversized eyes were outlined in black, and above and below were what looked like long black lashes, gracefully curved, as if a cartoonist had drawn them on its blue scales with a grease pencil. It was one of the wonders of nature, Tom thought. He had seen the fish before. It astounded him again, and it pleased Tom that the Druckfisch evoked more admiration from Frank than the celebrated Picassofisch. The Picassofisch, equally smallish, bore a black zigzag on its yellow body, suggesting a Picasso brushstroke of his Cubist period, and a blue band across its head with several raised antennae – odd enough, surely, but somehow no match for the Druck-fisch's eyelashes. Tom turned his eyes away from their watery world, and felt like a clumsy lump as he walked on, breathing air.

The crocodiles in their heated and glass-enclosed quarters with a pedestrian bridge through, had a few slightly bleeding wounds on them, no doubt inflicted by their fellows. But just now they were all dozing, with fearful grins.

'Had enough?' Tom asked. 'I wouldn't mind going to the Bahnhof.'

They left the aquarium and walked a few streets to the railway station where Tom got some more German money with his French francs. Frank changed some also.

'You know, Ben,' Tom said as he pocketed his marks, 'one more day here, and you have to think about – home, maybe?' Tom had cast an eye about the Bahnhof interior, meeting place for hustlers, fences, gays, pimps, drug addicts and God knew what. He walked as he spoke, wanting to get out of the place, in case one of the loitering people, for some reason, might be interested in him and the boy.

'I might go to Rome,' Frank said as they walked towards the Ku'damm.

'Don't go to Rome. Save it for another time. You've been to Rome, didn't you say?'

'Only twice when I was a little kid.'

'Go home first. Get things straightened out. Also with Teresa. You could still go to Rome this summer. It's only the twenty-sixth of August.'

Some thirty minutes later, when Tom was relaxing in his room with the *Morgenpost* and *Der Abend*, Frank rang him from his room.

'I reserved a ticket to New York for Monday,' Frank said. 'Take-off eleven-forty-five Air France, then I switch to Lufthansa in Düsseldorf.'

'Very good – Ben.' Tom felt relief.

'You might have to lend me a little money. I can buy the ticket, but it'll leave me maybe a little short.'

'No problem,' Tom said patiently. Five thousand francs was over a thousand dollars, and why should the boy need more if he was going straight home? Was he so in the habit of carrying big sums, he felt uncomfortable without a lot? Or had money, from him, become a symbol of love to Frank?

That evening they went to a cinema, walked out before the end, and since it was after eleven and they had had no dinner, Tom steered them towards the Rheinische Winzerstuben which was just a few steps away. Half-drawn glasses of beer, at least eight, stood lined up beside the beer taps, awaiting customers. The Germans took several minutes to draw a beer properly, a fact which Tom appreciated. Tom and Frank chose their food from a counter offering homemade soups, ham, roast beef and lamb, cabbage, fried or boiled potatoes, and half a dozen kinds of bread.

'It's true what you said about Teresa,' Frank said when they had found a table. 'I should get things clearer with her.' Frank gulped, though he had not yet eaten a bite. 'Maybe she likes me, maybe she doesn't. And I realize I'm not *old* enough. Five more years of school if I finish college. Good Christ!'

Frank seemed furious with the school system suddenly, but Tom knew his problem was uncertainty about the girl.

'She's different from other girls,' the boy went on. 'I can't describe it – in words. She's not silly. She's very sure of herself – that's what scares me sometimes, because I don't look as self-confident as she does. Maybe I'm *not*. Maybe one day you'll meet her. I hope so.'

'I hope so too. Eat your meal while it's hot.' Tom felt that he never would meet Teresa, but illusion, hope such as the boy was trying to hang on to now – what else kept people going? Ego, morale, energy, and what people so vaguely called the future – wasn't it for most people based on another person? So very few people could make it alone. And himself? Tom tried for a few seconds to imagine himself in Belle Ombre without Heloise. No one to talk to in the house except Mme Annette, no one to switch on the gramophone and fill the house suddenly with rock music or sometimes Ralph Kirkpatrick on the harpsichord. Even though Tom kept from Heloise so much of his life, his illegal and potentially dangerous activities which could put an end to Belle Ombre if discovered, she had become a part of his existence, almost of his flesh, as they said in the marriage vows. They didn't often make love, didn't always when Tom shared her bed, which was hardly half the time, but when they did, Heloise was warm and passionate. The infrequency of their making love didn't seem to bother her at all. Curious, since she was only twenty-seven, or was it twenty-eight? But convenient too, for him. He couldn't have borne a woman who made demands several times a week: that really would have turned him off, maybe at once and permanently.

Tom summoned his courage and asked in a tone both light and polite, 'May I ask if you've been to bed with Teresa?'

Frank glanced up from his plate with a quick and shaky smile. 'Once. I – Well, of course it was wonderful. Maybe too wonderful.'

Tom waited.

'You're the only person I would tell this to,' Frank continued in a lower voice. 'I didn't do very well. I think I was too excited. She was excited too, but nothing happened – really. It was at her family's apartment in New York. Everybody was out, we had all the doors locked. And she laughed.' Frank looked at Tom as if he had made a statement of fact, not one that hurt him, even, just a fact.

'Laughed at you?' Tom asked, trying to assume an attitude of only mild interest. He lit a Roth-Haendle, the German equivalent of a Gauloise.

'*At me*, I dunno. Maybe. I felt awful. Embarrassed. I was ready to make love to her and then I couldn't finish. You know?'

Tom could imagine. 'Laughed *with* you, maybe.'

'I *tried* to laugh. Don't ever tell anybody, will you?'

'No. Who would I tell, anyway?'

'Other guys at school, they're always boasting. I think half the time they're lying. I know they are. Pete – one year older – I like him a lot, but I know he doesn't always tell the truth. About girls, I mean. Sure, it's easy, I think, if you *don't* like a girl so much. You know? Maybe. Then you just think about yourself and being tough and making it and everything's fine. But – I've been in love with Teresa for *months*. Seven months now. Since the night I met her.'

Tom was trying to compose a question: had Teresa other boy friends with whom she might be going to bed? Tom didn't get the question out before a loud introductory chord rang out over the beerhall's clatter and chatter.

Something was happening on the far wall opposite them. Tom had seen the show once before. Lights had come on there, and the rumbustious overture to *Der Freischütz* boomed out from a rather rusty gramophone somewhere. From the wall, a flat tableau of spooky houses made of cut-out silhouettes projected a few inches – an owl perched in a tree, the moon shone, lightning flashed, and a real rain of water drops slanted down from the right. There was also thunder, which sounded like big pieces of tin being shaken backstage. A few people got up from their tables for a better view.

'That's *mad*!' Frank said, grinning. 'Let's go look!'

'You go,' said Tom, and the boy went. Tom wanted to stay seated to assess Frank from a distance, to see if anyone paid attention to him.

Frank, in Tom's blue blazer and his own brown corduroy trousers – a bit short, the trousers, and the boy must have grown since he bought them – watched the tableau-almost-vivant with his hands on his hips. No one that Tom could see paid the boy any attention.

The music ended with crashes of cymbals, the lights went off, the raindrops trickled out, and people returned to their seats.

'What a great idea!' Frank said, ambling back, looking relaxed. 'The rain falls in a little gutter in front, you know? – Can I get you another beer?' Frank was eager to be of service.

It was nearly one when Tom asked a taxi driver to take them to a bar called the Glad Hand. Tom didn't know what street it was on. He had heard of it from someone, maybe even Reeves.

'Maybe you mean the Glad Ass,' said the driver in German, smiling, though the name of the bar remained in English.

'Whatever you say,' said Tom. He knew the Berliners changed the names of their bars when they spoke about them among themselves.

This bar had no sign at all outside it, just a lighted list of beverage and snack prices behind glass on the outside wall by the door, but booming disco was audible from within. Tom pushed the brown door open, and a tall, ghostlike figure pushed Tom back in a playful way.

'No, no, you can't come in *here*!' said the figure, then grabbed Tom by his sweater and pulled him in.

'You're looking *charming*!' Tom shouted at the figure that had pulled him in – over six feet tall in a sloppy muslin gown that swept the floor, his face a mask of pink and white paste.

Tom made sure that Frank was in tow as he forged towards the bar, which looked impossible to get to because of the crowd – entirely men and boys, all yelling at each other. There seemed to be two big rooms for dancing, maybe even three. Frank was much stared at and greeted as he endeavoured to follow Tom. *'What the hell?'* Tom said to him, with a cheerful shrug, meaning he didn't think he would ever make it to the bar to order beer or anything else. There were tables against the walls, but these were taken and more than taken with fellows standing and talking to the ones seated.

'Hoppla!' roared another figure in drag into Tom's ears, and Tom realized, almost with a twinge of shame, that it was perhaps because he looked straight. A miracle they didn't throw him out, and maybe he had Frank to thank for being in. This led to a happier thought: Tom himself was an object of envy for having a nice looking boy of sixteen in his company. Tom could in fact see that now, and it made him smile.

A leather figure was asking Frank to dance.

'Go ahead!' Tom shouted to Frank.

Frank looked for an instant bewildered, scared, then seemed to collect himself, and he went off with the leather chap.

'. . . my cousin in *Dallas!*' an American voice was shouting to someone on Tom's left, and Tom moved away from that.

'Dallas-Fort *Vort!*' said his German companion.

'Naw, that's the fuckin' *airport!* I mean Dallas! *Friday* the bar's called. Gay bar! Boys and girls!'

Tom turned his back to them, somehow got a hand on the bar edge, and managed to order two beers. The three barmen or barmaids wore beaten up blue jeans but also wigs, rouge, ruffled blouses and very gay lipsticky smiles. No one looked drunk, but everyone seemed wildly happy. Tom clung with one hand to the bar, and stood on tiptoe to look for Frank. He saw the boy dancing with even more abandon than with the girl in Romy Haag's. Another fellow seemed to be joining them, though Tom couldn't be certain. Now an Adonis-like statue, bigger than life and painted gold, descended from the ceiling and rotated horizontally over the dance floor, while from above coloured balloons floated down, twisting, rising, stirred by the activity below. One of the balloons said MOTHERFUCKER in Gothic black letters, others sported drawings and words Tom couldn't make out from where he was.

Frank was coming back, pressing his way through to Tom. 'Look! Lost a button, sorry. Couldn't find it on the floor and I got knocked down trying to look for it.' He meant the middle button on the blazer.

'No importance! Your beer!' Tom said, handing the boy a tall, tapering glass.

Frank drank through the foam. 'They're having such a good time –' he yelled, 'and *no girls!*'

'Why'd you come *back?*'

'The other two got in an argument – a little bit! The first guy – he said something I didn't understand.'

'Never mind,' said Tom, quite able to imagine. 'You should've asked him to say it in *English!*'

'He did and I *still* didn't understand!'

Frank was being eyed by a couple of men behind Tom. Frank was trying to tell Tom it was a very special night, somebody's birthday, hence the balloons. The loudness of the music almost prevented talking. Talking of course was unnecessary, as customers could see one another's wares, and either walk out together or exchange addresses. Frank said he didn't feel like dancing again, so they left after their one beer.

*

Sunday morning Tom awakened just after ten, and rang down to ask if breakfast was still available. It was. Then he rang the boy's room. No answer. Was Frank taking a morning walk? Tom shrugged. Had he made himself shrug? Had it been involuntary? What if the boy ran into trouble on the street, got spoken to by some alert policeman? 'May I ask your name? May I see your passport or identification?' Was there an umbilical cord between him and Frank? No. Or if so, cut it, Tom thought. It was going to be cut tomorrow, anyway, when the boy took the plane for New York. Tom hurled a wadded cigarette package at the waste-bucket, missed, and had to go and pick it up.

Tom heard a gentle tapping on his door, with fingertips, the way he himself knocked.

'Frank.'

Tom opened the door.

Frank had a transparent green plastic bag of fruit. 'Went for a walk. They said you'd ordered breakfast, so I knew you were up. I asked them in German. How about that?'

Just before noon, they were standing at a Schnell-Imbiss wagon in Kreuzberg, both with tinned beers, Frank with a *Bulette* or bunless hamburger, cold but cooked meat that one could hold in one's fingers and dip into mustard. A Turk standing with beer and a frankfurter next to them wore the last word in casual summer gear: no top at all, hairy abdomen bulging over short green shorts not only worn out but eaten nearly to pieces perhaps by a dog. His dirty feet were in sandals. Frank looked this chap up and down with an unfazed eye, and said:

'I think Berlin is quite big. Not cramped at all.'

That gave Tom an idea for the afternoon's activities: Grunewald, the big forest. But first perhaps the Glienicker-Brücke.

'I'll never forget this day – my last day with you,' Frank said. 'And I don't know when I'll see you again.'

The words of a lover, Tom thought, and would Frank's family – his mother in particular – be overjoyed if Tom looked up Frank on his next trip to America in October of this year? Tom doubted that. Did his mother know anything about the suspicion of forgery in regard to Derwatt paintings? Very likely, since Frank's father had talked about it, maybe at the dinner table. Would his name ring a sour bell with Frank's mother? Tom did not want to ask.

They had a late lunch at an outdoor table on a height overlooking the Pflauen-Insel in the Wannsee, a blue lake below. Pebbles and earth underfoot now, leaves shading them, a portly and friendly waiter.

Sauerbraten with potato dumplings, red cabbage, and beers. They were in the southwest area of West Berlin.

'Gosh, it's marvellous, isn't it? Germany,' Frank said.

'Really? Nicer than France?'

'The people seem friendlier here.'

Tom felt the same way about Germany, but Berlin seemed a funny place to say it in. That morning they had driven past a long section of the Wall, unguarded by visible soldiers, but of the same ten-foot height as at Friedrichstrasse, and the attack dogs on sliding leashes behind the Wall had barked at the mere sound of their taxi. The driver had been delighted to make the tour, and had talked a blue streak. Beyond the Wall, out of sight and behind the dogs even, lay a strip of minefield 'Fifty metres wide!' their driver had said in German, and beyond that a nine-foot-deep anti-vehicle trench, and yet beyond that a strip of land ploughed so as to reveal footprints. 'Such trouble they take!' Frank had said. And Tom, inspired, had replied, 'They call themselves revolutionaries but they happen to be the most backward just now. They say every country needs a revolution, but why some groups still ally themselves with *Moscow* –' He had tried to say it in German to the driver. 'Oh, Moscow just has the military now, to show force here and there. Ideas, no,' the driver had said, resigned, or with an air of resignation. At the Glienicker-Brücke, Tom had translated for Frank the statement written in German on a big placard:

Those who gave this bridge the name Bridge of Unity built the Wall also, laid barbed wire, created deathstrips, and so hinder unity.

Tom translated it thus, but the boy wanted it in the German original, and Tom copied it out for him. The driver, Hermann, had been so friendly, Tom had asked him if he would like some lunch, and then he could take them on somewhere else. Hermann had agreed to the lunch, but politely suggested that he eat by himself at another table.

'Grunewald,' Tom said to Hermann after he had settled their bills. 'Can you do that? Then you can get rid of us, because we want to walk around a little.'

'Absolutely! Okay!' said Hermann, hauling himself up from his chair, looking as if he had taken on a couple of kilos with his lunch. It was a warmish day, and he wore a short-sleeved white shirt.

Now it was nearly a four-mile drive generally northward. Tom had his map of Berlin on his lap to show Frank where they were. They crossed the Wannsee bridge and turned north, went through a lot of wooded areas that held clusters of small houses. At last Grunewald where, Tom had told Frank, the troops of Fance, England and America often did their tank exercises and fired guns for practice. War Games.

'Can you let us off at the Trümmerberg, Hermann?' Tom asked.

'Trümmerberg, ja, neben dem Teufelsberg,' he replied.

Hermann did this, his taxi climbed a slope, then the Trümmerberg, a mountain made from the rubble of war ruins, covered with earth, rose still higher. Tom gave Hermann his tariff and an extra twenty DM.

'Danke schön und schönen Tag!'

A small boy stood a little way up the mountain, manoeuvring a toy aeroplane by electronic control. There was a curving groove down the side of the Trümmerberg for skiing and toboganning.

'They ski here in winter,' Tom said to Frank. 'Fun, isn't it?' Tom didn't know really what was fun about it just now – with no snow – but he felt euphoric. It was fantastic to see vast woods on one side and the city of Berlin, low and remote in the distance, on the other. Unpaved lanes led into Grunewald, a wild-looking forest, something like twelve miles square, Tom judged from his map, and that this forest could lie within the city limits of Berlin struck Tom as amazing, or as a kind of blessing, since the whole of West Berlin was hemmed in, including, of course, Grunewald itself.

'Let's go this way,' Tom said.

They took one of the lanes into the woods, and after a couple of minutes the trees closed over them, shutting out much of the sunlight. A boy and girl picnicked a few yards away on a blanket spread on pine needles. Frank looked at them dreamily, maybe with envy. Tom picked up a small pine cone, blew on it, and stuck it into his trousers pocket.

'Aren't the birches great! I love birches!' Frank said.

Speckled birches stood everywhere, of all sizes, among pine trees and the occasional oak.

'Somewhere – there's the sector for the military. Barbed wire fences around it, red warning signs, I remember.' But Tom was feeling vague, not like talking, about anything. He sensed a sadness in the boy.

Around this time tomorrow Frank would be flying westward towards New York. And what would he be going back to? A girl he was not quite sure of, and a mother who had once asked him if he had killed his father – and had seemed to believe him when he had said no. And would anything in America have changed? New evidence come up against Frank? Maybe. Tom couldn't guess how, but he supposed there was a possibility of new evidence. Had Frank really killed his father, or was it a fantasy of Frank's? It was not the first time Tom had wondered about that. Was it because the sunlit woods were so beautiful, the day so pleasant, that he didn't want to believe the boy had killed anyone? Tom noticed a big fallen tree on their left. Tom motioned towards it, and the boy followed him.

Tom leaned against the tree which he now saw had been felled, lit a cigarette and glanced at his watch: thirteen minutes to four. Tom felt like turning back towards the Trümmerberg, where he knew there were a few cars and a chance of a taxi. It would be easy to get lost if they wandered farther. 'Cigarette?' Tom asked. Last evening the boy had smoked one.

'No thanks. Excuse me a minute. Got to pee.'

Tom pushed himself from the tree as the boy walked past him. 'I'll be around here.' He gestured towards the lane they had just come from. Tom was thinking that he could go back to Paris tomorrow afternoon, unless he decided to look up Eric Lanz, and perhaps spend the evening with him. That might be amusing, to see what kind of apartment Eric had here in Berlin, what kind of life he led. It would also give him time to buy Heloise a present, something nice from the Ku'damm, a handbag, for instance. Tom glanced to his right, thinking he had heard something, maybe voices. He looked for the boy. 'Ben?' he called. Tom went back a few paces. 'Hey, Ben, are you lost? This way!' Tom walked back to the tree they had been leaning against. 'Ben!' Did he hear a crackling of underbrush far ahead in the woods, or was it the wind?

Frank was playing a trick again, Tom supposed, as he had on the little road near Belle Ombre. Waiting for Tom to find him. Tom didn't fancy walking through the scruff, the bushes that would tear his trouser cuffs. He knew the boy was within hearing, so he yelled, 'Okay, Ben! Stop the kidding! Let's go!'

Silence.

Tom swallowed, with sudden difficulty. What was he worried about? Tom wasn't quite sure.

Suddenly Tom broke into a run for the area ahead of him and slightly on his left, where he thought he had heard some rustling of branches. 'Ben!'

No answer, and Tom plunged on – paused only once to look back into empty, dense forest – then ran again. 'Ben?'

Abruptly he came to a dirt road and took it, going still left. The road soon bent to the right. Should he keep going or turn back? Tom was curious enough to keep going, trotting now, at the same time deciding that if he didn't see the boy in another thirty yards, he would turn back and try the woods again. Was the boy running away again? That would be too stupid, Tom thought, for Frank to do, and where would he get without his passport which was at the hotel? Or had Frank been nabbed?

Ahead of him, on a lower level than the road and in a small clearing, Tom suddenly had that answer before him: a dark blue car faced Tom with both its front doors open. The driver at that moment started the engine with a zoom, and banged his door shut. Another man ran from behind the car, started to jump into the passenger's seat, but saw Tom and stopped with one hand on the door, while the other hand reached for something inside his jacket.

They had Frank, Tom was sure. Tom advanced. 'What the hell are you –'

Tom found himself looking at a black pistol pointed straight at him, perhaps five yards away. The man held the gun with both hands. Then the man slipped into the car, closed the door, and the car backed. B-RW-778 the registration plate read. The driver was blondish, the man who had jumped in was a heavy fellow with straight black hair and a moustache. And they had seen him clearly, Tom realized.

The car moved away, not even going very fast now. Tom could have sprinted after it, but for what? To get a bullet in his stomach? What would a little thing like the death of Tom Ripley matter compared to a boy worth a few million dollars? Was Frank in the trunk in back, gagged? Or hit over the head and unconscious? Hadn't there been one more man, a third, in the back seat? Tom thought so.

This went through his head before the car, an Audi, rolled quite out of sight around the next curve in the woods.

Tom had a ballpoint pen, but finding no paper, pulled out his pack of Roth-Haendle cigarettes, took off the cellophane and wrote on the pink package the car's licence number while it was still in his head. They might abandon the car or change its plates, knowing he had had a glimpse, Tom thought. Or the car might have been stolen for this job.

There was also the uncomfortable possibility that they had recognized him as Tom Ripley. Maybe they had been following him and Frank since yesterday or so. Would it be useful for them to eliminate him? Fifty-fifty, Tom thought. He really couldn't think clearly at the moment, and his hand had shaken when he wrote the licence number. Of course he had heard voices in the woods! The kidnappers might have approached Frank with some harmless sounding question.

Best for him not to stay one more day in Berlin. Tom plunged into the unpleasantly thick woods again, taking a short cut to the path, because he was afraid the kidnappers might decide to come back along the road and have a shot at him.

ELEVEN

Tom made his way back along the lane he had walked with Frank to the Trümmerberg, where he had an irritating wait of nearly twenty minutes for a taxi, and then one came only by accident, as most visitors to Grunewald came in their own cars. Tom asked the driver to go to the Hotel Franke, Albrecht-Achillesstrasse.

Wouldn't it be great, as Frank often said, if the boy were back in his hotel room, having played another trick, and if the people Tom had seen with the car and the gun had been up to some different mischief? But such wasn't the case. Frank's key hung on its hook at the hotel desk, as did Tom's.

Tom took his key and went to his room, locked his door nervously on the inside, sat on his bed and reached for the telephone directory. The police department's numbers should be in the front, he thought, and so they were. He dialled the 'emergency' number, and put the cigarette packet with the car number before him.

'I think I have seen a kidnapping,' Tom said. Then he answered the man's questions. When? Where?

'Your name, please?'

'I do not wish to give my name. I took the licence number of the car.' Tom proceeded to give it, and the colour of the car, dark blue, an Audi.

'Who was the victim? Do you know the victim?'

'No,' Tom said. 'A boy – he looked sixteen, seventeen. One of the men had a gun. May I telephone you again in a couple of hours to ask what you have found out?' Tom was going to phone, whatever the man said.

The man said 'yes', and with a brusque thank you hung up.

Tom had said the kidnapping took place about 4 p.m. in Grunewald not far from the Trümmerberg. It was now nearly half past five. He should get in touch with Frank's mother, he thought, warn her that she might be presented with a ransom demand, though what good it would do to warn her, he didn't know. Now that the Pierson detective had a real job to do, he was in Paris, and Tom didn't know how to reach him. Mrs Lily Pierson, however, would know.

Tom went down to the hotel desk, and asked for the key to Herr Andrews's room. 'My friend is out and he needs something.'

The key was handed to Tom without question.

Tom went up and entered Frank's room. The bed was made, the room tidy. Tom glanced at the writing table for an address book, then thought of Johnny's passport in Frank's suitcase. Johnny's address in the United States was a Park Avenue address in New York. His mother would probably be in Kennebunkport now, but the New York address was better than nothing, and Tom took note of it, and replaced the passport in the suitcase. Then in the pocket of the suitcase lid he found a little brown address book and opened it eagerly. Under Pierson there was only a Florida address and telephone number, the entry headed Pierson Sunfish. Tough luck. Most people, Tom supposed, didn't write down their own addresses, because they knew them by heart, but with as many houses as the Piersons must have, Tom had had hopes.

Tom thought it best after all to go down to the desk for what he wanted – post offices being closed today, Sunday. But first he went back to his own room, dropped Frank's key on his bed, took his sweater off and wet a towel. He washed his face and his body down to his trouser tops, put his sweater back on, and tried to assume an air of calm. He realized that he was thoroughly shattered by the boy's – rape, in the sense that he had been snatched away. Tom had never felt thus shaken by something that he himself had done, because in such cases in the past, he had been in control of things. Now he was anything but in control. He went out of his room and locked it, and took the stairs down.

At the hotel desk, he printed on some note-paper: John Pierson, Kennebunkport, Maine (Bangor). Tom thought Bangor was the closest big town, and might be able to provide the Kennebunkport number. 'Could you ask information in Bangor, Maine, to give me the Pierson telephone number?' Tom asked the man behind the desk, who looked at what Tom had written and said, 'Yes, right away,' and went at once to a girl on Tom's right who sat at a switchboard.

The man came back to Tom and said, 'Maybe two, three minutes. Do you wish to speak to a certain person?'

'No. First I'd like just to get the number, please.' Tom lingered in the lobby, wondering if the girl would succeed, if the American operator was going to say the number was unlisted and could not be given out?

'Herr Ripley, we have the number,' said the desk man, who had a paper in his hand.

Tom smiled. He copied it on another piece of paper. 'Can you ring this? And I'll take it in my room. Please don't give my name. Just Berlin calling.'

'Very good, sir.'

Back in his room, Tom had hardly a minute's wait before his telephone rang.

'This is Kennebunkport, May-yun,' said a female voice. 'Am I speaking to Berlin, Germany?'

The Hotel Franke operator confirmed this.

'Go ahead, please,' said Maine.

'Good morning, Pierson residence,' said an Englishman's voice.

'Hello,' said Tom. 'May I speak with Mrs Pierson, please?'

'May I ask who's speaking?'

'This is in regard to her son Frank.' The formality at the other end gave Tom the cool that he needed.

'One moment, please.'

It was more than a moment that Tom had to wait, but at least it seemed that Frank's mother was home. Tom heard a woman's voice, a man's also, as Lily Pierson perhaps approached the telephone accompanied by the butler whose name was Eugene, as Tom recalled.

'Hel-*lo-o*,' came the high-pitched voice.

'Hello, Mrs Pierson, can you tell me at what hotel your son Johnny and your private detective are staying? In Paris?'

'Why are you asking that? You're an American?'

'Yes,' Tom said.

'May I ask your name?' She sounded cautious and frightened.

'That's of no importance. It's more important that –'

'Do you know where Frank *is*? He's with *you*?'

'No, he is not with me. I would simply like to know how to reach your private detective in Paris. I'd like to know what hotel they're in.'

'But I don't know why you want to know that.' Her voice was becoming shriller. 'Are you holding my son somewhere?'

'No, indeed, Mrs Pierson. I can find out where your detective is, I think, by telephoning the French police. So can't you tell me now and save me the trouble? It's no secret, is it, where they're staying in Paris?'

Slight hesitation. 'They're at the Hôtel Lutetia. But I'd like to know *why* you want to know.'

Tom had what he wanted. What he did not want was the police of Berlin to be alerted by Mrs Pierson or by her detective. 'Because I may have seen him in Paris,' Tom said, 'but I'm not sure. Thank you, Mrs Pierson.'

'Seen him in Paris?'

Tom wanted to hang up. 'In the American Drugstore, Saint-Germain-des-Prés. I've just come from Paris. Goodbye, Mrs Pierson.' Tom put the telephone down.

He began to pack. The Hotel Franke seemed suddenly a very unsafe place. The duet or trio who had Frank might well have followed him and Frank to the hotel at some time since Friday evening, and might think nothing of firing a shot at him as he left the hotel, or even of coming up to his room to do it. Tom picked up the telephone and told the desk that he would be leaving in a few minutes, and could they make up his bill and also the bill for Herr Andrews? Then Tom closed his suitcase, and went to Frank's room with its key. He had thought a moment ago of ringing Eric Lanz. Eric might be willing to put him up, but if Eric couldn't, then any hotel in Berlin was safer than this one. Tom packed Frank's things, shoes from the floor, toothpaste and toothbrush from the bathroom, the Berlin bear, closed the suitcase and went out with it, leaving the key in the lock. He took the suitcase to his own room, found Eric's card in his jacket pocket still, and dialled the number.

A German voice, deeper than Eric's, answered, and asked who was calling.

'Tom Ripley. I'm in Berlin.'

'Ach, Tom Ripley! Einen Moment, bitte! Eric ist im Bad!'

Tom smiled. Eric home and having a bath! After a few seconds, Eric came on.

'Hello, Tom! Welcome to Berlin! When can we see each other?'

'Now – if possible,' Tom said as calmly as he could. 'Are you busy?'

'No-o. Where are you?'

Tom told him. 'I'm about to check out of the hotel.'

'We can fetch you! Have you got some time?' Eric asked gaily. 'Peter! Albrecht-Achillesstrasse, easy for us . . .' His voice faded away in German, then came back. 'Tom! We shall see you in less than ten minutes!'

Tom put the telephone down, much comforted.

The desk man had not sounded surprised at Tom's request for the bills, but might think it odd that he was leaving with the boy's suitcase. Tom was prepared to say that Herr Andrews was waiting at the air terminus. Tom paid the two bills, plus the extra for his telephone calls, and no questions were asked. Fine. He might have been one of Frank's kidnappers, Tom thought, or in cahoots with them, simply taking away Frank's belongings.

'Have a good trip!' said the desk man, smiling.

'Thank you!' Then Tom saw Eric walking into the lobby.

'Hello, Tom!' said Eric, beaming. His dark hair looked still damp from his bath. 'You are finished?' he asked with a glance at the desk. 'I'll take one suitcase, shall I? – By yourself?'

There was a bellhop, but he was lingering near another man who had three suitcases.

'Yes, just now. My friend's waiting at the Flughafen,' Tom said in case the desk man or anyone else might be able to hear them.

Eric had Frank's suitcase. 'Come! Peter's car is just here to the right. Mine's at the garage till tomorrow. Temporarily kaputt. Ha!'

A pale green Opel sat at the kerb not far away, and Eric introduced Tom to Peter Schubler, or so the name sounded, a tall slender man of about thirty, with a lantern jaw and black hair cut quite short as if from a fresh haircut. The luggage went easily on the back seat and floor. Eric insisted that Tom sit in front with Peter.

'Where is your friend? Really at the airport?' Eric leaned forward with interest as Peter started the car.

Eric didn't know who his friend was, though he might suspect he was Frank Pierson, recipient of the passport Eric had brought for Tom to Paris. 'No,' Tom said. 'Tell you later. Can we possibly go to your house now, Eric, or is it awkward for you?' Tom spoke in English, not knowing if Peter understood.

'But of course! Yes, we go *home*, Peter! Peter was going home anyway. We thought you might have a little time free.'

Tom was looking on either side of the street, as he had on coming out of the hotel, at the people on the pavement, even at cars parked at the kerbs, but by the time they arrived at the Kurfürstendamm, Tom was feeling easier.

'You're with the boy?' Eric asked in English. 'Where is he?'

'Taking a walk. I can reach him later,' Tom said casually, and suddenly felt sick and awful. He lowered his window all the way.

'My house is your home, as the Spanish say,' said Eric, pulling out a key-ring inside the front door of an old but refurbished apartment house. They were in Niebuhrstrasse, parallel with the Ku'damm.

The three of them rode up with the suitcases in a roomy elevator, and Eric opened another door. More words of welcome from Eric, and with Peter's help Tom set the suitcases in a corner of the living room. It was a bachelor's flat with no frills, substantial old furniture, and only a highly polished silver coffee-pot flashed a bit of glitter from a sideboard. There were several nineteenth-century German landscapes and woodland paintings on the walls, which Tom recognized as valuable, but such paintings bored Tom to a degree.

'Excuse us a minute, Peter. Take a beer, if you like,' said Eric.

The taciturn Peter nodded, picked up a newspaper, and prepared to sit on a large black sofa under a lamp.

Eric beckoned Tom into an adjacent bedroom and closed the door. 'Now what's the matter?'

They did not sit down. Tom told his story quickly, including his telephone conversation with Lily Pierson. 'It occurred to me that the kidnappers might like to get rid of me. It's possible that they recognized me in Grunewald. Or they can get it out of the boy. So I'd be more than grateful, Eric, if you can put me up tonight.'

'Tonight? Two nights! More! What a happening, *mein Gott*! And now – the ransom request, I suppose? To the mother?'

'I suppose.' Tom drew on a cigarette, and shrugged.

'I doubt if they will try to get the boy *out* of West Berlin, you know. Too difficult. Every car searched thoroughly at the East borders.'

Tom could imagine. 'I'd like to make two phone calls tonight, one to the police to ask if they found out anything about that Audi in Grunewald, and one to the hotel to ask if Frank possibly turned up. It occurred to me that the kidnappers might get cold feet and let the boy go. But I –'

'But?'

'I shall not give your phone number or address to anybody. That's not necessary.'

'Thank you, not to the police anyway. Important.'

'I could even ring from outside, if you prefer.'

'My telephone!' Eric waved a hand. 'Your calls are innocent compared to what goes on here! Often in code, I will admit! Go ahead, Tom, and ask Peter to do it for you!' Eric sounded sure of himself. 'For the moment, Peter is my chauffeur, secretary, bodyguard – all! Come out and have a drink!' He pulled Tom's arm.

'You trust Peter.'

Eric whispered. 'Peter escaped from East Berlin. The second attempt he made it. I should say, they threw him out. The first attempt, they threw him in prison, where he made himself such a nuisance, they couldn't stand him. Peter – he looks *mild und leise*, but he has – um – guts.'

They went into the living room where Eric poured whiskies, and Peter went at once to the kitchen to fetch ice. It was almost eight now.

'I shall ask Peter to ring the Hotel Franke and ask if there has been a message from – What was his name?'

'Benjamin Andrews.'

'Ah, yes.' Eric looked Tom up and down. 'You are nervous, Tom. Sit down.'

Peter pressed ice from a black rubber tray into a silver bucket. Tom soon had a scotch in his hand. Eric turned to Peter and related the story in rapid German.

'*Wa-as?*' Peter said, astounded, and he gave Tom a respectful look, as if he suddenly realized that Tom had been through a bit of hell that day.

'. . . the emergency department,' Eric was saying to Peter in German. 'And the number of the car, you said. You didn't tell them your name, I suppose.'

'Certainly not.' Tom copied out the number from the Roth-Haendle packet more legibly on some paper by Eric's telephone, and added 'dark blue Audi'.

'Maybe early to get news on the car,' said Eric. 'Maybe they will abandon it, if it is stolen. That gets us nothing, unless the police will take fingerprints.'

'Ring the hotel first, Peter,' Tom said. He got the number from his hotel bill. 'The less they hear my voice there, the better, somehow. Can you ask if there is a message from Herr Andrews?'

'Andrews,' Peter repeated, and dialled the number.

'Or any message for Herr Ripley.'

Peter nodded, and put those questions to the Hotel Franke. After a few seconds, Peter said, 'Okay. Thank you.' To Tom he said, 'No messages.'

'Thank you, Peter. Now could you try the police about the car?' Tom looked in Eric's telephone directory, and made sure the emergency number was the same one he had dialled, and pointed it out to Peter. 'This one.'

Peter dialled, spoke to someone for a couple of minutes, with long pauses, and finally hung up. 'They have not found such a car,' Peter said.

'We can try again later – both places,' Eric said.

Peter went into the kitchen, and Tom heard a rattle of plates, the fridge door closing. Peter seemed quite familiar with the house.

'Frank Pierson,' said Eric with his neat little smile, oblivious of Peter who was coming in with a tray. 'Didn't his father die not so long ago? *Yes.* I read that.'

'Yes,' Tom said.

'Suicide, wasn't it?'

'So it seems.'

Peter was setting the table. He had brought out a cold roast beef, tomatoes, and a bowl of sliced fresh pineapple which gave out an aroma of kirsch. They pulled up chairs and sat down at a long table.

'You spoke with the mother. Are you supposed to speak with the detective in Paris?' Eric poked red meat into his mouth, and followed it with a sip of red wine.

Eric's casualness annoyed Tom slightly. This was merely a little crooked situation, and Eric was willing to help Tom a bit, because Tom was a friend of Reeves Minot. Eric had never even met Frank. 'I don't have to speak with Paris, no,' Tom said, meaning that he didn't have to appoint himself as go-between. 'As I said, the mother doesn't know my name.'

Peter was listening carefully, maybe understanding everything.

'But I hope that detective doesn't put the Berlin police on to this – after Mrs Pierson gets a ransom demand. Police don't always help in a case like this.'

'No, not if you want the boy back alive,' Eric said.

Tom was wondering if the American detective was going to come to Berlin? The boy would very likely be released in Berlin, since it was so difficult to get him out to anywhere else. And where would the kidnappers want the money deposited? That was anybody's guess, Tom thought.

'What are you worried about now?' asked Eric.

'Not worried,' Tom said, smiling. 'I was thinking that Mrs Pierson might tell her detective to beware of an American in Berlin who is either playing tricks or is in cahoots with the kidnappers. I told her –'

'Cahoots?'

'Working with them. I told her I thought I'd seen Frank in Paris, you know. Unfortunately she knows I rang from Berlin, because the Hotel Franke operator said it.'

'Tom, you worry too much. But maybe that is why you are successful.' Successful? Was he?

Peter said something to Eric in German so fast that Tom missed it.

Eric laughed, and when he had swallowed his food, he said to Tom, 'Peter hates kidnappers. He says they pretend to be leftists, all that political *Scheiss*, when all they want is money, just like any other crooks.'

'I think I would like to ring the Hôtel Lutetia tonight to see if they have any news,' Tom said. 'The kidnappers may have 'phoned Mrs Pierson. I can hardly imagine them sending her a telegram or an express letter.'

'No,' said Eric, pouring more wine for everybody.

'By now the Paris detective might know where the money's to be delivered and where the boy's to be released and all that.'

'Is he going to tell *you* all that?' Eric asked, reseating himself.

Tom smiled again. 'Maybe not. But I'll still pick up something, I imagine. By the way, Eric, I'll be responsible for my telephone bill.' Tom was envisaging more calls.

'What an idea! Very English, friends and guests paying telephone bills. Not in my house – which is *your* house. What time is it? Would it help if I telephoned the Lutetia instead of you, Tom?' Eric looked at his wristwatch and spoke before Tom could answer. 'Just about ten now, same time in Paris. Let us give the detective time to finish the Fr-rench dinner – at the Piersons' expense. Ha-ha!'

Eric switched on his television, while Peter made the coffee. There was a news programme after a few minutes. Eric had to answer his telephone twice, and the second time spoke in rather awful Italian. Then Eric and Peter listened to a political figure who spoke for several minutes, and they chuckled throughout and made comments to each other. Tom was not interested enough to try to follow what the man on the screen was saying.

Around eleven, Eric proposed ringing the Hôtel Lutetia. Tom had refrained from mentioning it, lest Eric call him nervous again.

'I think I have the number right here.' Eric consulted a black leather address book. '*Ja*, here we are –' He began to dial.

Tom was standing by. 'Ask for Johnny Pierson, would you, Eric? Because I don't know the detective's name.'

'Don't they know your name by now?' Eric asked. 'Wouldn't the boy have said –' Eric pointed to the little round receiver at the back of his telephone.

Tom picked it up and put it to his ear.

'Hello. May I speak to John Pierson, if you please?' Eric said in French, and gave a satisfied nod to Tom as the operator promised to connect him.

'Hello?' said a young American voice, much like Frank's.

'Hello. I am ringing to ask if you have news of your brother.'

'Who are you?' asked Johnny, and there were sounds of his being spoken to by another male voice.

'Hello?' said a deeper voice.

'I am calling to ask for news about Frank. Is he all right? Have you had news?'

'May I ask your name? Where are you calling from?'

Tom nodded at Eric's questioning glance.

'Berlin,' said Eric. 'What is the message for Mrs Pierson?' Eric asked with almost bored matter-of-factness.

'Why should I tell *you*, if you don't identify yourself,' replied the detective.

Peter was leaning against the sideboard, listening.

Tom motioned for Eric to pass the telephone to him, and Tom handed Eric the little receiver. 'Hello, this is Tom Ripley.'

'Oh! – Yes. Was it you who spoke with Mrs Pierson?'

'Yes, it was. I would like to know if the boy is all right, and what the arrangements are.'

'We don't know if the boy is all right,' the detective replied frigidly.

'They've asked for a ransom?'

'Y-yes-s.' It came out as if the detective had reflected that he had nothing to lose by disclosing this.

'Money to be delivered in Berlin?'

'I don't know why you're interested, Mr Ripley.'

'Because I'm a friend of Frank's.'

The detective refrained from comment.

'Frank can tell you that – when you speak with him,' Tom said.

'We haven't spoken with him.'

'But they'll let him speak to prove they've got him – won't they? Anyway, Mr – May I ask your name?'

'Yes-s. Thurlow. Ralph. How did you know that the boy was kidnapped?'

Tom couldn't answer or didn't want to. 'Have you informed the Berlin police?'

'No, they don't want us to do that.'

'Any idea where they are in Berlin?' Tom asked.

'No.' Thurlow sounded discouraged.

Not easy to have a call traced without police cooperation, Tom supposed. 'What kind of proof are they going to give you?'

'They said he'd speak to us – maybe later tonight. Said he'd had some sleeping pills. Can you give me your telephone number there?'

'Sorry, I can't. But I can reach you. Night, Mr Thurlow.' Tom put the telephone down as Thurlow was saying something else.

Eric looked at Tom brightly, as if the conversation had been a success, and put back the receiver.

'Yes, well, I've learned something,' Tom said. 'The boy *has* been kidnapped and I wasn't – mistaken.'

'What's the next step?' asked Eric.

Tom poured still more coffee for himself from the silver pot. 'I want to stay in Berlin till something happens. Till I know Frank is safe.'

TWELVE

Peter left then, promising Eric to visit the garage tomorrow morning and see that Eric's car was delivered in front of his apartment house. 'Tom Ripley – good success!' Peter said to Tom, and his handshake was firm.

'Isn't he wonderful?' Eric said after he had closed his apartment door. 'I helped Peter get out of the East, and he has never forgotten it. He is an accountant by profession. He could get a job here. He had one for a while. But just now he does so much work for me, he doesn't need a job. He is very good also with my income tax forms.' Eric chuckled.

Tom was listening, but thinking also that he would ring Paris again tonight, maybe at two or three in the morning, to find out if Thurlow had spoken with Frank. Sleeping pills, of course. That was to be expected.

Eric produced a cigar box, but Tom declined. 'You were right not to give my telephone number to that detective. He might give it to the kidnappers! Lots of detectives are boobs – wanting to get all the information they can, and to hell with anybody else. *Boobs!* – I love American slang.'

Tom refrained from saying that boobs had another meaning too. 'Must send you a book of it. – Zurich, Basel, which,' Tom mused, enjoying being able to muse out loud in the presence of Eric, because usually he had to keep his thoughts to himself.

'You think that's where the money will change hands?'

'Don't you think it's likely? Unless the kidnappers want it in marks in Berlin for their anti-establishment activities or something. But Switzerland's always safer – I'd think.'

'How much do you think they'll ask?' Eric drew gently on his cigar.

'One, two million dollars? Thurlow might know the sum already. Maybe he's leaving for Switzerland tomorrow.'

'Why are you so interested in this kidnapping event – if I may ask you, Tom?'

'Oh. Well – I'm interested in the boy's safety.' Tom walked around the room with his hands in his pockets. 'He's an odd boy, considering his family's so wealthy. He has a fear of money or a hatred of it. Do you know he shined every pair of shoes I possess? These, for instance.' Tom lifted his right foot. The shine still remained on the loafer, despite the plunge through Grunewald. Tom thought of Frank's murder of his father. Tom was sympathetic because of *that*. But to Eric Tom added only, 'He's in love with a girl in New York. She hasn't been able to write to him while he's been in Europe, because he couldn't give her an address. He wanted to be incognito for a while. So he's on tenterhooks – uncertain, I mean, whether the girl still cares for him. He's only sixteen. You know how it is.' But had Eric ever been in love? It was hard for Tom to imagine. There was something strongly selfish and self-preserving about Eric.

Eric was nodding thoughtfully. 'He was in your house when I was. I knew there was somebody there. I thought – maybe a girl – or a –'

Tom laughed. 'A girl I was hiding from my wife?'

'Why did he run away from home?'

'Oh – boys do. Maybe upset about his father's death. Maybe his girl friend too. He wanted to hide for a few days – to be quiet. He worked in the garden at my house.'

'Did he do something illegal in America?' Eric sounded almost prudish.

'Not that I know of. But for a while he didn't want to be Frank Pierson, so I got him another passport.'

'And you brought him to Berlin.'

Tom took a deep breath. 'I thought I could persuade him to go home from here, which I did. He has a plane ticket reserved for tomorrow, back to New York.'

'Tomorrow,' Eric repeated, without any emotion.

Why should Eric have any emotion, Tom thought. Tom looked at the buttons of Eric's silk shirt, which were strained by the bulge of his abdomen. The buttons looked the way Tom felt. 'I'd like to ring Thurlow again tonight. Maybe quite late. Two or three in the morning. I hope it won't disturb you, Eric?'

'Certainly not, Tom. The telephone is here at your disposal.'

'Maybe I should ask you where I'm to sleep. Here, maybe?' Tom meant the big horsehair sofa.

'Ach, I'm glad you said that! You do look tired, Tom. On this sofa, yes, but it is a *bed* sofa. Watch!' Eric removed a pink pillow from the sofa. 'It looks like an antique, maybe, but it is the latest thing. One button –' Eric pressed something, and out zoomed the seat, the back fell flat, and it was the size of a double bed. 'Look!'

'Marvellous,' said Tom.

Eric fetched blankets and sheets from somewhere, and Tom helped him. A blanket first to fill in the indentations caused by the sofa's buttons, then the sheets. 'Yes, time you turned in. Turn in, turn out, over, on, off, turn against and turn up. Really I think sometimes that English is just as – movable as German,' said Eric, plumping pillows now.

Tom, taking off his sweater, realized that he was going to sleep like a top tonight, but he didn't want to get into an etymological discussion about sleeping like a top, in case Eric was interested in the phrase, so Tom said nothing, and dragged his pyjamas from the bottom of his suitcase. He was thinking that the kidnappers might have forced Frank to reveal his name. Would Mrs Pierson trust him to deliver the ransom money? Tom realized that he dearly wanted a swat of some kind at the kidnappers. Maybe that was foolhardy, quite mad, because just now he felt vaguely angry and much too tired to be logical.

'The bathroom is yours, Tom,' said Eric. 'I shall say good night, so I don't disturb you any more. Do you want me to set my *Wecker* for you at two, maybe, so you can telephone?'

'I think I'll make it – wake up,' Tom replied. 'Thank you – very much, Eric.'

'Oh, while I think of it, one little question. Do you say "waken somebody, wake somebody or – awaken somebody"?'

Tom shook his head. 'I don't think the English know.'

Then Tom took a shower and went to bed, trying to fix in his mind the hour of three a.m., so he would wake up, exactly one hour and twenty minutes from now. Was it worth it to risk getting kidnapped himself, or worse shot dead, to deliver the ransom money, when anyone else could do it? The kidnappers might appoint their own man. Who? Might the kidnappers insist that Tom Ripley deliver it? Quite possible. If the kidnappers managed to seize him, they could get some more money, and Tom tried to imagine Heloise getting his ransom money together – how much, a quarter of a million? – and asking her father – Good Lord, no! Here Tom had to laugh into his pillow. Would Jacques Plisson cough up money for son-in-law Tom Ripley? Not bloody likely! A quarter of a million would certainly take all the investments he and Heloise had, and maybe even Belle Ombre would have to be sold. Unthinkable!

And maybe none of what he was thinking about would come to pass.

Tom awakened from an anxiety dream in which he had been trying to drive a car up an impossibly steep road, more vertical than any hill of San Francisco, and the car had been about to topple over backward before it reached the top. His forehead and chest were sleek with perspiration. But it was one minute to three, just right.

He dialled the Lutetia number from Eric's address book, where Eric had written also the dial code for Paris. Tom asked for Monsieur Ralph Thurlow.

'Hello. Yes – Mr Ripley. Thurlow here.'

'What's the news? Have you spoken with the boy?'

'Yes, we spoke with him about an hour ago. Says he's not hurt. Sounded very sleepy.' And Thurlow sounded tired.

'And the arrangements?'

'They haven't set the place. They –'

Tom waited. He supposed Thurlow was hesitant about mentioning money, and maybe Thurlow had had a tough day at the Hôtel Lutetia. 'But they told you what they wanted?'

'Yes, that will be coming from Zurich tomorrow – I mean today. Mrs Pierson is having it telexed to three Berlin banks. They want three banks. And Mrs Pierson thinks it's safer too.'

Maybe the sum was so big, Mrs Pierson wanted to draw as little attention to it as possible, Tom thought. 'You're coming to Berlin?'

'I haven't arranged that as yet.'

'Who's picking it up at the banks?'

'I don't know. They want to know if the money's in Berlin – first. And they're going to tell me later where it's to be delivered.'

'To be delivered in Berlin, you think?'

'I would think. I don't know.'

'The police are not in on this – listening to your phone?'

'No, indeed,' said Thurlow. 'That's the way we want it.'

'What's the sum?'

'Two million. USA. In German marks.'

'Do you expect a bank messenger to handle it all?' The idea made Tom smile.

'They – they sound as if they're arguing among themselves,' Thurlow's American voice droned on. 'About place and time. One man talks to me – German accent.'

'Shall I call you again around nine this morning? Won't the money be here by then?'

'I should think so.'

'Mr Thurlow, I'm willing to pick up the money and take it to wherever they want it. Might be faster, in view of –' Tom stopped. 'Don't mention my name to them, please.'

'The boy told them your name, said you were his friend, and said that to his mother too.'

'Very well, but if they ask about me, say you haven't heard a word from me, and since I live in France, I may have gone home. Please say the same thing to Mrs Pierson, as I assume they're 'phoning her.'

'They're mainly 'phoning *me*. They just let the boy talk with her once.'

'You might ask Mrs Pierson to tell her Swiss bank or the Berlin banks that I'm to pick the money up – if Mrs Pierson is agreeable to that.'

'I'll see about that,' said Thurlow.

'I'll ring you in a few hours. And I'm delighted that the boy's okay – or that he's not suffering anything worse than sleepiness at the moment.'

'That's right, let's *hope*!'

Then Tom hung up and went back to bed. Eric's quiet bustling in the kitchen awakened him, the clink of a kettle, the buzz of an electric coffee-grinder, comforting sounds. It was twelve minutes to nine, Monday 28th August. Tom went into the kitchen to tell Eric the results of his three a.m. telephone call.

'Two million dollars!' said Eric. 'Just what you have guessed, is it not?'

That seemed to be more interesting to Eric than the fact that Frank was alive and well enough to talk to his mother. Tom let it go, and drank his coffee.

Tom dressed, then managed to put his bed into the form of a sofa again, and he folded his sheets neatly, thinking he might need them tonight. When the living room looked tidy again, Tom glanced at his watch, thinking of Thurlow, and then out of curiosity went to the long Schiller section of Eric's bookcase, and pulled out *Die Räuber*. It really was an individual, leather-bound book. Tom has suspected that the row of Schiller's complete works was a façade concealing a safe or a secret compartment perhaps in the books themselves.

Tom picked up the telephone, dialled the Lutetia number, and asked for Monsieur Ralph Thurlow.

Thurlow answered. 'Yes, Mr Ripley, hello. I have the banks' names now, three of them.' Thurlow sounded considerably more awake and cheerful.

'The money's arrived here?'

'Yes, and Mrs Pierson is willing for you to pick it up today – as soon as you can, in fact. She's told Zurich that this is a transfer with her approval and Zurich has done the same with the Berlin banks. The banks seem to have odd hours there for opening, but that doesn't matter. You should 'phone each bank and tell them when you'll arrive and they'll – uh –'

'I understand.' Tom knew, some banks didn't open until half past three, others closed at one. 'So – the banks –'

Thurlow interrupted. 'The people who – are 'phoning me, they'll 'phone me later to make sure the money's been collected, and then they'll set a place where it's to be left.'

'I see. You didn't mention my name to them?'

'Certainly not. I just said it will be picked up, it will be delivered.'

'Good. Now the banks, if you will.' Tom had a ballpoint pen and proceeded to write. The first was the A D C A Bank at Europa-Center, which was to have a million and a half D M. The second the Berliner Disconto Bank with the same sum. The third the Berliner Commerz Bank with 'not quite' a million D M. 'Thank you,' Tom said as he finished writing. 'I'll try to collect this in the next couple of hours and ring you back around noon – with luck.'

'I'll be here.'

'By the way, did our friends say they were with any group?'

'Group?'

'Or gang? Sometimes they give themselves names and are pleased to tell them. You know, like the Red Saviours.'

Ralph Thurlow chuckled nervously. 'No, they didn't.'

'Do you think they're 'phoning from a private apartment?'

'No, mainly not. Maybe when the boy spoke with his mother. *She* seemed to think so. But this morning they were dropping coins somewhere. They 'phoned around eight to ask if the money got to Berlin. We've been at this all night.'

When Tom hung up, he heard the click of Eric's typewriter in Eric's bedroom, and Tom didn't want to interrupt him. He lit a cigarette, and thought he should ring Heloise, since he had promised to be home today or tomorrow, but now he did not want to take the time. And where might he be at this time tomorrow?

Tom imagined Frank confined in a room somewhere in Berlin, maybe not tied with ropes, but under surveillance day and night. Frank was the kind of boy who would make a dash to escape, who might even jump out of a window if the ground were not too far away, and the kidnappers might have realized that. Tom also knew that the anti-establishment people, the groups who kidnapped, had friends among the public who would give them shelter. Reeves had spoken with Tom about this not long ago on the telephone. The situation was complex, because the revolutionaries, the gangs, claimed to be part of the political left wing movement, although they were rejected by its majority. These gangs seemed directionless to Tom, except for their obvious efforts to create an atmosphere of disturbance, provoking the authorities to crack down and show their presumably true, that was to say fascist, colours. The kidnapping and murder of Hanns-Martin Schleyer, who had been decried by some as an old Nazi representative of management and factory owners, had unfortunately inspired a witchhunt by the authorities against intellectuals, artists and liberals. And right-wingers, seizing the moment, insisted that the police were still not cracking down hard enough. Nothing in Germany was black or white and simple, Tom thought. Were Frank's captors 'terrorists' or even political in any way? Were they going to drag out negotiations, publicize them? Tom hoped not, because he simply couldn't afford any more publicity.

Eric came into the living room, and Tom told him about the banks.

'What sums!' Eric looked for a moment stunned, then blinked his eyes. 'Peter and I could help you this morning, Tom. Those banks are mostly on the Ku'damm. We could go in my car or Pete's car. Peter keeps a gun in his car, but I do not. Certainly not allowed here.'

'I thought your car was on the blink.'

'On the blink?'

'Kaputt,' Tom said.

'Oh, just till this morning. Peter said he would try to get it here by ten, I remember. Nine-thirty-five now. For safety, you know, Tom, we should all go together this morning, don't you think so?' Eric looked at his most cautious, about to approach the telephone.

Tom nodded. 'We collect the money and bring it here – with your permission, Eric.'

'Ye-es – of course.' Eric glanced at his walls as if he might find them stripped in a few hours. 'I'll give Peter a call.'

Peter's line did not answer.

'He is maybe seeing about my car,' Eric said. 'If he buzzes me from downstairs – soon – I shall ask him if he can come with us this morning. And where does the money go later, Tom?'

Tom smiled. 'I hope to find that out by noon. By the way, Eric, I think I'll need a suitcase for this morning's haul, don't you think so? Could I borrow one from you, perhaps, instead of emptying mine or Frank's?'

Eric was at once obliging, went to his bedroom, and came back with a medium-sized brown pigskin suitcase, not new or expensive looking, and perhaps just the right size, though Tom had no idea of the bulk of nearly four thousand banknotes of a thousand DM each.

'Thank you, Eric. If Peter can't come with us, we can do this by taxi, I should think. First I've got to ring those banks. Now.'

'I shall ring them for you, Tom. The ADCA Bank, didn't you say?'

Tom put his list by Eric's telephone, and consulted the directory for the number of the ADCA Bank. While Eric dialled the ADCA Bank, Tom wrote down the numbers of the other two banks. Eric did it calmly and smoothly: he asked for the Herr Direktor, and said he was telephoning in regard to collecting some money being held in the name of Thomas Ripley. This took several minutes, during which time Tom pocketed his passport for identification, and listened. Eric was not able to speak with each manager personally, but all three banks confirmed that money was being held. Eric said that Herr Ripley would arrive in the next hour.

During the last telephone call, Eric's doorbell rang, and Eric motioned for Tom to press the release button in the kitchen. Tom pressed the speaker button and asked, 'Who is it?'

'Peter here. The car of Eric is downstairs.'

'Just a minute, Peter,' Tom said. 'Here's Eric.'

Eric took over the speaker, and Tom left the kitchen.

Tom heard Eric asking if Peter had some time this morning for a 'very important couple of errands'. Then Eric came into the living room and said, 'Peter has time, and he says also my car is downstairs. Isn't he marvellous?'

Tom nodded, and pocketed his list of banks. 'Yes.'

Eric put on a jacket. 'Let us go.'

Tom picked up the empty suitcase, Eric double-locked his door, and they went down Eric's stairs.

Peter was sitting in his car at the kerb, and Eric's Mercedes was parked not far from Eric's doorway. Eric got into Peter's passenger seat, and motioned for Tom to get into the back seat.

'I have to explain this behind closed doors,' Eric said to Peter. Then he said in German that Tom had to call at three banks now to collect some money for the kidnappers' ransom, and would Peter drive them, or should they all go in his, Eric's, car?

Peter glanced at Tom with a smile. 'My car, all right.'

'You have your gun, Peter?' Eric asked, laughing a little. 'I hope we shall not need it!'

'Right here, ja,' said Peter, pointing to his glove box, and he smiled as if it would be an absurdity to use it under these circumstances, when Tom's collecting of the money had been authorized.

They decided at once on the ADCA Bank at Europa-Center first, since the other two banks were on the Ku'damm and on the way back to Eric's apartment house. They were able to park quite near the ADCA Bank, because there was a curved parking area in front of the Hotel Palace meant for patrons of the hotel and for taxis coming and going. This bank was open. Tom went alone to the bank doors, and he did not take the suitcase with him.

Tom gave his name to the receptionist, and said in English that the manager was expecting him. The girl spoke into a telephone, then indicated a door at the rear on Tom's left. It was opened by a blue-eyed man in his fifties, with grey hair, straight posture, and a pleasant smile. A man carrying a few briefcases, who had been in the room, departed almost at once, giving Tom no special look, which made Tom feel easier.

'Mr Ripley? Good morning,' the man said in English. 'Would you like to sit down?'

'Good morning, sir.' Tom did not at once take the leather armchair that was offered, but took his passport from his pocket. 'May I? My passport.'

Standing behind his desk, the Herr Direktor or manager put on his spectacles and looked at the passport carefully, compared the photograph with Tom's face, then sat down and made a note on a pad. 'Thank you.' He handed the passport back to Tom, and pressed a button on his desk. 'Fred? Alles in Ordnung. Ja, bitte.' The man folded his hands and looked at Tom with still smiling but slightly puzzled eyes. Then the same man Tom had seen before came in, bearing two large tan envelopes. The door closed behind him automatically with a deep click, and Tom felt it was extremely locked.

'Would you care to count the money?' asked the Herr Direktor.

'I'm sure I should take a look,' Tom said politely, as if accepting a canapé at a party, but he had no desire to count all that. He opened the two manilla envelopes, which had been closed with rubber bands, and saw that they contained bundles of DM held by brown paper strips. Tom saw what looked like at least twenty little bundles in one envelope, and both envelopes seemed of equal weight. The notes were all of one thousand DM each.

'One million five hundred thousand DM,' said the Herr Direktor. 'One hundred such notes in each band.'

Tom was riffling through the end of one bundle, which looked to be a hundred. Tom nodded, wondering if the bank had noted serial numbers, but he did not want to ask. Let the kidnappers worry. The kidnappers must have said nothing about denomination either, or Thurlow surely would have told him. 'I shall believe you.'

The two Germans smiled, and the man who had brought the envelope left the room.

'And the receipt,' said the Herr Direktor.

Tom signed a receipt for one million five hundred thousand DM, and the manager initialled it, kept the carbon, and handed Tom the top paper. Tom was on his feet, and extended his hand. 'Thank you.'

'Have a nice stay in Berlin,' the Herr Direktor said, as he shook Tom's hand.

'Thank you.' The man's words had sounded as if he thought Tom might be intending to have a spree on the money he was taking away. Tom tucked the thick envelopes under his arm.

The manager looked amused. Was he thinking of a joke he would tell at lunch, or was he going to tell a story about an American picking up nearly a million dollars in marks and walking out with it under his arm? 'Would you like an escort to where you are going?'

'No, thanks,' said Tom.

Tom walked through the bank without looking at anyone. Eric sat in Peter's car, and Peter stood smoking a cigarette with one hand in his trousers pocket, his face turned up to the sunlight.

'*Alles gut gegangen?*' asked Peter, seeing the envelope.

'Fine,' Tom said. In the back seat, he opened the suitcase, stuck the envelopes in, and zipped it closed. Tom noticed that Eric was glancing about at people on the pavement as they moved off. Tom did not. Tom deliberately yawned, leaned back, and watched Peter make a left turn that brought them into the Kurfürstendamm.

The next two banks were rather near to each other on the broad avenue which was neatly bordered by its young trees. All chromium and sparkling glass shop fronts again. The edifices Tom wanted were also brand-new and had their names in broad letters above their windows which were perhaps bulletproof. Peter had stopped in front of one bank at a corner, where there was no parking meter free, but Eric said he would be outside somewhere on the pavement to tell Tom where the car was, when Tom came out.

This transaction went as the first: the receptionist, a manager, Tom's passport for identification, and then the money and the receipt for the same sum as that of the ADCA Bank. This time the money was in a single larger envelope. Again Tom was asked if he wished to count it, and Tom declined. Would he like a bank guard to accompany him to his destination?

'No, thank you,' Tom said.

'Shall I seal the envelope – for safety?'

Tom glanced into the big envelope, and saw bundles of DM with paper wrappers around their middles, similar to the bundles he already had. Tom handed over the envelope, and the manager sealed it with some broad tan tape which he pulled from a gadget on his desk.

Now Eric was on the pavement, looking as if he expected a friend to come from right or left, anywhere but from the bank door. Eric gestured towards the right. Peter was double-parked. Eric and Tom got in, Tom in the back again, and he deposited this envelope in the suitcase.

Tom collected some six hundred thousand DM from the third bank, and walked out with a green envelope, and again found Eric on the pavement. Peter was around a corner to the right.

Bang! The closing of the car door was a pleasure. Tom sank back, the green envelope on his lap. Peter was driving towards Eric's apartment, Tom knew from his next turn. Peter and Eric exchanged pleasantries, which Tom did not try to follow. Something about bank robbers. Laughter. Tom stuck the final envelope into the suitcase.

In Eric's apartment the good humour continued, Peter and Eric chuckling over the suitcase which Peter had insisted on carrying, because he was the chauffeur. Peter set the suitcase against the wall by the sideboard, on the opposite side of the room from the apartment door.

'No, no, in my closet where it always is!' said Eric. 'It looks just like a couple of others there.'

Peter did as he was told.

A quarter to noon. Tom was thinking of ringing Thurlow. Eric put on a record of Victoria de los Angeles, which he said he always played when he felt euphoric. Eric looked in a good humour, but more nervous than euphoric, Tom thought.

'Maybe I'll meet Frank tonight,' Eric said to Tom. 'I hope so! He can stay here, have my bed. I'll sleep on the floor. Frank will be my guest of honour!'

Tom only smiled. 'I'll have to ask you to turn the music down a little while I try Thurlow again.'

'With pleasure, Tom!' Eric did so.

Peter had come in with a tray of cold beers, and Tom took one, put it by the telephone, and dialled.

Thurlow's line was engaged, and Tom told the hotel operator he would wait. It was a short wait before Thurlow came on.

'Everything is in order here,' Tom said, trying to sound calm.

'You've got it?' asked Thurlow.

'Yes. And you've got the place?'

'Yes, I have. It's in the northern part of Berlin, they said. Lub – I can spell it for you. L – u – two dots – b – a – r – s. Got that? And the streets –'

Tom was writing, and motioned for Eric to pick up the little receiver at the back of the telephone, which Eric did quickly.

Thurlow gave a street-name, then spelt it: Zabel-Krüger-Damm, which he said crossed a street called Alt-Lübars. 'The first street runs east and west, Alt-Lübars goes north when it intersects there. *You* keep going north on Alt-Lübars on to a little dirt road so it sounds like – which hasn't got any name. About a hundred metres or yards on, you'll see a shed on the left side of the road. Got that so far?'

'Yes, thanks.' Tom had, and Eric gave him a reassuring nod, as if to say the streets were not so difficult to find as Tom might think.

Thurlow continued, 'You're to leave the – the sum in a box or a sack at four o'clock in the morning. That is tonight, you understand.'

'Yes,' said Tom.

'Set it behind the shed and leave. One messenger, they said.'

'And what about the boy?'

'They'll call me once they get the money. Can you 'phone me after four in the morning to tell me if all went well?'

'Yes, of course, sure.'

'And very good luck to you, Tom.'

Tom put the telephone down.

'Lübars!' Eric put his little receiver back. He turned to Peter. 'Lübars, Peter, at four o'clock in the morning! That is an old farm district, Tom, north. Up by the Wall. Not many people living there. The Wall borders Lübars on the north. Have you got a map, Peter?'

'*Ja-a.* I was there once, I think, maybe twice – driving around.' Peter spoke in German. 'I can take Tom tonight. One must have a car there.'

Tom was grateful. He trusted Peter's driving and Peter's nerve, and Peter had a gun in his car.

Peter and Eric produced some lunch, a bottle of wine.

'I have a date this afternoon in Kreuzberg,' Eric said to Tom. 'Come with me. Change your thoughts, as the French say. Takes just about an hour, maybe less. Then I have to meet Max later tonight. Come with me too!'

'Max?' Tom asked.

'Max and Rollo. Friends of mine.' Eric was eating.

Peter's rather pale face smiled at Tom, and he lifted his eyebrows slightly. Peter looked calm and sure of himself.

Tom could not eat much, and barely listened to Eric's and Peter's jocular conversation about an anti-dog-dropping campaign now being waged in Berlin in imitation of New York's campaign, which involved little scoops and paper bags being carried by dog owners. The Berlin sanitation department intended now to build *Hundetoiletten*, dog W Cs big enough for German shepherds to enter, which Peter remarked might inspire the dogs to start using their owners' houses, if they couldn't tell the difference.

THIRTEEN

Eric and Tom drove off in Eric's car for the Kreuzberg area of Berlin, which Eric said was less than fifteen minutes away. Peter had departed, promising to come to Eric's apartment around one a.m. Tom had said to Peter that he would be grateful if they could get an early start for the Lübars rendezvous. Even Peter admitted that the driving plus the finding of the place might take an hour.

Eric stopped in a dismal-looking street of reddish-brown, old four- or five-storey apartment houses near a corner bar with an open front door. A couple of kids – the word urchins sprang to Tom's mind – rushed up and begged pfennigs from them, and Eric fished in his pocket, saying if he didn't give them some coins, they might do something to his car, though the boy looked only about eight years old, and the girl perhaps ten, with lipstick messily applied to her lips and rouge on her cheeks. She wore a pavement-length gown which looked as if it had been fashioned from a brownish-red and pinned-together window curtain to create something like a dress. Tom erased his first idea, that the girl was playing with her mother's make-up and wardrobe: there was something more sinister going on here. The little boy had a thick mop of black hair which had been hacked in places by way of a haircut, and his dark eyes were glazed or maybe simply elusive. His projecting underlip seemed to indicate a fixed contempt for all the world around him. The boy had pocketed the money that Eric had given the girl.

'Boy's a Turk,' said Eric, locking his car, keeping his voice low. Eric gestured towards a doorway they were supposed to enter. 'They can't read, you know? Puzzles everyone. They speak Turkish and German fluently, but can't read *anything*!'

'And the girl? She looks German.' The little girl was blonde. The strange juvenile pair were watching them still, standing by Eric's car.

'Oh, German, yes. Child prostitute. He's her pimp – or he is trying to be.'

A buzz released the door and they went in. They climbed three flights of badly lit stairs. The hall windows were dirty, and let in almost no light. Eric knocked on a dark brown door, its paint scarred as if from kicks and blows. When clumping footsteps approached, Eric said, 'Eric' at the door crack.

The door was unlocked, a tall, broad man beckoned them in, talking in mumbled German in a deep voice. Another Turk, Tom saw, with a swarthiness of face that not even dark-haired Germans ever achieved. Tom walked into a terrible smell of what he thought was stewing lamb mingled with cabbage. Worse, they were promptly ushered into the kitchen whence the smell originated. A couple of small children played on the linoleum floor, and an old woman with a tiny-looking head and fuzzy, thin grey hair stood at the stove, stirring a pot nervously. The grandmother, Tom supposed, and maybe German, as she didn't look Turkish, but he couldn't really tell. Eric and the burly man sat down at a round table to which Tom was urged also, and Tom sat down reluctantly, yet he meant to enjoy the conversation if he could. Just what was Eric doing here? Eric's slangy German, and the Turk's hash of it made it difficult indeed for Tom to understand anything. They were talking numbers. 'Fifteen . . . twenty-three' and prices, 'Four hundred marks . . .' Fifteen what? Then Tom remembered that Eric had said the Turk did some work as go-between for the Berlin lawyers who issued papers to Pakistanis and East Indians, permitting them to remain in West Berlin.

'I don't like this nasty little work,' Eric had said, 'but if I don't cooperate to some extent, as go-between of papers myself, Haki won't do jobs for me that are more important than his smelly immigrants.' Yes, that was it. Some of the immigrants, illiterate even in their own language, and unskilled, simply took the underground from East Berlin to West Berlin, and were met by Haki who steered them to the right lawyers. Then they could go on relief, at West Berlin expense, while their claims to be 'political refugees' were investigated, a process that might take years.

Haki was either a full-time crook or on unemployment too – maybe both – otherwise what was he doing home at this hour? He looked no more than thirty-five, and strong as an ox. His trousers, which he had long ago outgrown as to belly, were now held together at the waist by a piece of string that bridged the gap. A few fly buttons showed, unfastened.

An awful white-lightning-type of home-made vodka (Tom was told) was brought forth by Haki, or would Tom prefer beer? Tom did prefer beer, after sampling the vodka. The beer arrived in a big half-empty bottle, flat and tepid. Haki went off to fetch something from another room.

'Haki is a construction worker,' Eric explained to Tom, 'but on leave because of some injury – at work. Not to mention that he enjoys the – *Arbeitslosenunterstützung* – the –'

Tom nodded. Unemployment benefits. Haki was lumbering back with a dirty shoebox. His tread made the floor shake. He opened the shoebox, and produced a brown-paper-wrapped parcel the size of a man's fist. Eric shook the parcel and it rattled. Like pearls? Drug pellets? Eric pulled out his wallet and gave Haki a hundred-mark note.

'Only a tip,' said Eric to Tom. 'Are you bored? We'll leave in a minute.'

'*Inna minnit!*' repeated the grubby little girl on the floor, staring.

It gave Tom a small jolt. How much of all this were the kids understanding? The old woman, stirring the pot like a *Macbeth* witch, or maybe an inmate of an insane asylum, also stared at Tom. She appeared to tremble slightly, as if she might have a disease of the nerves.

'Where's the wife?' Tom murmured to Eric. 'The mother of these kids?'

'Oh, she's working. German – from East Berlin. Sad type but she works. Well –' Eric spoke softly, and gestured with his smooth fingers as if to say he could not speak further just now.

Tom was delighted when Eric got to his feet. They had been there half an hour, and it seemed to Tom much longer. Goodbyes, and suddenly Tom and Eric were on the pavement, where the sunlight fell cleanly on their faces. The little parcel bulged Eric's jacket pocket. Eric looked around before he opened his car door. They drove off. Tom was curious about what was in the package, but thought it might be rude to ask.

'It is funny – about his wife, as you called her. East Berlin prostitute, and she was smuggled over in something like a jeep by American soldiers! And here her life was a little *better* – as a prostitute, but she is a drug addict too. She manages to hold some kind of a job, maybe cleaning public toilets, I don't know. Do you know – American soldiers cannot afford West Berlin prostitutes now, because the dollar has sunk so low, so they have to go to East Berlin for them? The Communists are furious, because they are not supposed to have any prostitutes – officially.'

Tom smiled, mildly amused, and tried to shift himself into another gear in order to get through the hours ahead. What kind of people were the kidnappers? Young amateurs? Reasonably clever professionals? A girl with them? So useful to make an innocent impression on the public sometimes, a girl. And maybe all they wanted was money, as Eric had said, and they had no intention of harming Frank or anyone else physically.

Back at Eric's flat, Tom dialled Belle Ombre. It had the same dial code as Paris. The telephone rang six, seven times, and Tom imagined Heloise perhaps in Paris, having had an impulse to go to an afternoon film with Noëlle, and Mme Annette sitting over a tea or a cold soda pop in Marie's and Georges's café, exchanging the latest gossip with another *femme de ménage* of Villeperce. Then on the ninth ring Mme Annette said:

"Allo?"

'Madame Annette, *c'est Tome ici!* How is everything at home?'

'*Très bien, Monsieur Tome!* When are you returning home?'

Tom smiled, relieved. 'Wednesday, probably, not sure. Don't worry. Is Madame Heloise there?'

She was, but Mme Annette had to summon her from upstairs.

'*Tome!*' Heloise came to the telephone so quickly, Tom knew she had picked it up in his room. 'Where are you? Hamburg?'

'N-no, moving about a little. Did I wake you up from a nap?'

'I was soaking my finger in something Madame Annette made for me, so I thought I would let her answer.'

'Soaking your finger?'

'A vasistas in the greenhouse fell on it yesterday when I was watering. It is swollen, but Madame Annette does not think the nail will fall off.'

Tom gave a sympathetic sigh. She meant one of the windows that propped up in the greenhouse. 'Let *Henri* take care of the greenhouse!'

'Ah, Henri! – the boy is still with you?'

'Yes,' Tom said, wondering if someone had rung Belle Ombre and asked about Frank. 'Flying home tomorrow maybe. Heloise,' Tom said quickly before she could put a word in, 'if anybody telephones and asks

where I am, say I've gone out for a walk in Villeperce. That I'm home –
just gone out. Any long distance caller – tell him that.'

'*Why* is this?'

'Because I very soon will be home taking a walk, Wednesday, I think.
I'm moving around here – in Germany – so nobody can reach me just
now anyway.'

That went down reasonably well.

'I kiss you,' were Tom's last words.

Tom felt very much better. Sometimes, he admitted to himself, he felt
liked a married man, solid, loved, or whatever one was supposed to feel.
Even though he had just lied, a little bit, to his wife. It wasn't a lie for
the usual reasons anyway.

Around eleven that evening, Tom was in a gayer place than Kreuzberg, a men's bar considerably more chic than the one he had gone to
with Frank. This one had a glass-enclosed stairway going up to the
toilets, and patrons stood on the stairs making contacts, or trying to,
with other patrons below.

'Amusing, eh?' said Eric, who was waiting for someone. They stood at
the bar, there being no tables free. The place was of course a disco as
well. 'Easier to –' Here Eric was jostled by someone behind him.

Tom supposed Eric had been going to say it was easier to pass things
in a place like this than even on a street corner, because all the
customers, except those who were dancing, were either engrossed in
shouted conversation or staring with their minds on pick-ups and not
contraband goods. Tom had to admire one boy in drag, with a long
black stole – or what was it – of feather partly around his neck and
partly hanging, one end of which he wafted gently as he strolled about.
Few women went to such trouble to look their best.

Eric's contact arrived, a tallish young man in black leather, hands
jammed into the pockets of a short leather jacket. 'This is *Max*!' Eric
yelled to Tom.

Eric didn't say Tom's name. Just as well, Tom thought. The package,
which Eric had wrapped in gift paper with a blue ribbon, changed hands
and went into Max's leather jacket front, which he zipped up again. Max's
hair was cut very short, and his nails were painted in shocking pink.

'No time to take this away,' Max said to Tom in English with a
German accent. 'Busy all day. You like it?' He grinned mockingly,
meaning did Tom like his nails.

'Drink, Max? Dornkaat?' Eric shouted at him over the throbbing
music. 'Or a *vodka?*'

Max's expression suddenly changed. He had seen something in a far corner. 'Thanks, I think I must fuck off.' He nodded in the direction Tom had seen him look, and dropped his eyes with embarrassment. 'Guy over there I don't want to see just now. Painful. I am sorry, Eric. G'night.' He gave Tom a nod, turned and went out the door.

'*Guter Junge!*' Eric shouted at Tom, nodding towards the door where Max had disappeared. '*Good boy*! Gay but just as reliable as Peter! Max's friend is called *Rollo*! You may meet him!' Eric put a hand on Tom's forearm, and pressed him to have one more drink – anything – maybe a beer? Best if they didn't leave right away, Eric conveyed.

Tom consented to a beer and paid the barman in advance. 'I love this crazy fantasy here!' Tom said to Eric. He meant the occasional figure in drag, the make-up, the mock flirtations, and the laughter and good humour everywhere. It gave Tom a lift, *A Midsummer Night's Dream* overture always gave him a lift before he went into battle. Fantasy! Courage was all imaginary, anyway, a matter of mental state. A sense of reality did not help when one was faced with a gun barrel or a knife. Tom was now noticing, not for the first time, Eric's furtive or at least anxiously observant glances over his shoulder. Eric wasn't looking for an old or a new acquaintance among the men and boys. Or was he? No, Tom thought. Eric was a businessman, taking care of his apparently widely scattered business. Looking over his shoulder had become a habit with Eric.

'Ever have any trouble with the police here, Eric?' Tom asked, close to Eric's ear. 'I mean this kind of bar?'

But still Eric hadn't heard him, thanks to a crash of cymbals in the music just now, a quivering climax of some kind that went on for several seconds before the deep heartbeat set in again, seeming to hit the walls as if they were drumheads. On the dance floor, male figures hopped up and down and twirled as if in a trance. Tom gave it up, shook his head and picked up his fresh beer. He wasn't going to yell the word 'police' at the top of his lungs.

FOURTEEN

Berlin, the city's lights, dwindled behind them, and Peter and Tom drove on through semi-rural, rather boring little communities, where nearly all the café lights were off now. Their direction was north. Eric had decided to stay at home, which was just as well, because Tom couldn't imagine what good he could have done by coming, and if the kidnappers saw a third man in Peter's car, they might suspect a police officer.

'Now – this is the beginning of Lübars,' Peter said after some forty minutes of driving. 'Now I go to the correct street and we shall have a look.' He sat up straight, as if he had an important job to do. He had drawn a little sketch, which he had shown Tom in Eric's flat, and which now lay above his dashboard. 'I think I have taken an unright road. *Verdammt!* But it does not matter, as we have plenty of time. It is only thirty-five minutes past three.' Peter took a small torch from the shelf over his dashboard, and focused it on his sketch. 'I know what I did. I must turn.'

As Peter turned, his headlights illuminated a dark field of cabbages or lettuce in rows, buttoning the earth down with their neat green dots. Tom readjusted the thick suitcase between his feet and knees. The night was pleasantly cool, and there seemed to be no moon.

'Sure – this is the Zebel-Krüger-Damm again and I should go left up here. They go to bed so early here – get up early too! – Alt-Lübars, yes.' Peter made a careful left turn. 'Up here to the right should be the village green,' Peter said softly in German, 'according to my little map at home. Church and so on. And do you see those lights ahead?' His voice took on a rise of tension that Tom had not heard before. 'That is the Wall.'

Tom saw a fuzzy, whitish-yellow glow ahead, low and long, a bit lower than the road level, the searchlights on the other side of the Wall. The road sloped a little downward. Tom looked around for other cars, another car, but all was black except for a couple of perhaps obligatory street lights in the direction of what Peter had called the village green. Now Peter's car barely crept. The kidnappers, as far as Tom could see, had not arrived as yet.

'This little road is not for cars, which is why I am going so slowly. Now we should soon see the – *Lagerhalle* on the left. There, maybe?'

The shed. Tom saw it, a low structure, longer than it was high, and it appeared to be open on the side facing the road. Tom could vaguely see a few structures that might be horse paddocks in a field to the right. Peter stopped by the shed.

'Go ahead. Put the suitcase behind the shed. Then we'll back out,' said Peter in German. 'I cannot turn here.' Peter had dimmed his lights.

Tom was ready to get out. 'You go ahead and back. I'll stay. I'll make it back to Berlin, don't worry.'

'What do you mean, "stay"?'

'Stay. I have a sudden inspiration.'

'Do you want to *meet* that gang?' Peter's hands twisted on the steering wheel. '*Fight* them? Don't be crazy, Tom!'

Tom said in English, 'I know you have a gun. Can I borrow it?'

'Sure, sure, but I can wait for you too – if –' Peter looked puzzled, pushed the knob of his glove compartment, and took a black gun from under a cloth. 'It is loaded. Six shots. Safety here.'

Tom took the gun. It was smallish and did not weigh much, but looked lethal enough. 'Thank you.' Tom put it in the right side pocket of his jacket, then peered at his watch. Three-forty-three. He saw Peter glance nervously at the clock in the dashboard, which was one minute fast.

'Look, Tom. You see that little hill of land over there?' Peter pointed behind them and to the right, towards the village green. 'Where the church is. I shall wait for you there. With my lights out.' Peter said it like a command, as if he had compromised enough by letting Tom take his gun.

'Don't wait. There's even a bus running all night on this Krüger-Damm, you told me.' Tom opened the door and took the suitcase out.

'I just mentioned the bus. I didn't mean for you to *take* it!' Peter whispered. 'Don't shoot at them! They will only shoot back and kill you!'

Tom closed Peter's door as softly as he could, and headed for the shed.

'This!' Peter whispered through his window. He was handing Tom his small torch.

'Thanks, my friend!' The torch was certainly a help, because the ground was rough. Tom felt he had left Peter bereft – of gun and torch. Tom clicked off the little torch when he was behind the back corner of the shed, and lifted his arm to Peter in a sign of farewell, whether Peter could see him or not. Peter backed, slowly and straight, on the dirt road that Peter surely could not see well if at all with his parking lights. Tom saw Peter's car reach Alt-Lübars, then turn slowly to Tom's left, headed for the village green. Peter was going to wait.

Now there was a faint, but very faint sign of dawn coming, though Lübars' sparse street lights remained on. Peter's car was not in sight. Tom heard distant dog barks, and realized with a slight chill that they were the barks of the East German attack dogs beyond the Wall. The dogs did not sound excited. A breeze blew from the Wall's direction, and perhaps he had heard merely a bit of dog conversation as the animals slid along their wires. Tom turned his eyes from the eerie glow of the Wall's searchlights, and concentrated on listening.

He listened for the sound of a car motor. Surely the collector of the money wouldn't come via the field behind him?

Tom had set the suitcase against the wooden back of the shed, and he shoved it gently even closer with his foot. He took Peter's gun from his jacket pocket, pushed the safety off, and stuck it back in his pocket. Silence. It was so silent, Tom felt he could have heard the breathing of any person who might be in the shed, on the other side of the boards. Tom felt the wooden planks with his fingertips. There were a few chinks in the rough wood.

He had to pee, and it reminded him of Frank in Grunewald, but he went ahead and relieved himself anyway, while he could. And what did he want? Why was he staying here? To get a look at the kidnappers again? In this darkness? To scare them off and save the money? Certainly not. To save Frank? His staying was not necessarily a help in that direction, maybe just the opposite. Tom realized that he hated the kidnappers, and that he would relish a blow back at them. He also knew this was illogical, since he would probably be outnumbered. Yet here he was, vulnerable, an easy target for a bullet, and it would be an easy getaway for the kidnappers too, most likely.

Tom straightened up at the sound of a car's motor from the Alt-Lübars direction. Or was it Peter departing? The car purred forward, however, Tom could see its dim parking lights. Very slowly the car entered the unpaved road on which the shed stood, and lumbered on, swaying with the lane's irregularities. The car stopped about ten yards to Tom's right. The car looked to be dark red, but Tom was not sure. Tom was now pressed against the back of the shed, and peering around the back corner, because the car's lights did not reach the shed.

The left side back door of the car opened, and one figure got out. The car's lights went off, and the man who had got out switched on a torch. He looked sturdy and not tall, and he walked on with assurance, but slowed when he left the road and stepped on to the field. Then he paused, and waved a hand at his chums in the car, as if to say that all looked well so far.

How many were in the car, Tom wondered? One? Two? Maybe there were two others, since the man had got out of a back seat.

The man approached the shed slowly, torch in his left hand, and his right hand moved to his trouser pocket and pulled out what might have been a gun. He came on to Tom's right, towards the back of the shed.

Tom picked up the suitcase and gripped its handle, and as the man rounded the corner, Tom swung the suitcase and caught him on the left side of his head with it. The impact made not a loud thud but a solid one, and there was a second bump as the man's head hit the back of the shed. Tom brought the suitcase down once more, aiming at the left side of the man's head as he was falling. The paleness of the shirt-collar above what might have been a black sweater guided Tom as he brought the butt of Peter's gun down on the man's left temple. Now the man was not stirring, nor had he cried out. The torch beamed to Tom's left on the ground. Tom gripped Peter's gun in a firing position, and pointed it upward.

'Got the swine!' Tom yelled hysterically, or maybe, 'Gott, das Schwein!' and at the same time he fired two shots into the air.

Tom yelled again, shouted another phrase of nonsense, maybe a curse, and kicked the shed's back. He realized that his voice had gone shrill, that he was yelling at nothing.

Behind the Wall the dogs yelped, excited by the shots.

The click of a car's door closing startled Tom as if he had been shot himself. He looked around the shed's corner just in time to see a man in the driver's seat draw his leg in. The interior light had been on for a moment. This door then closed, and without parking lights, the car moved backwards to Tom's right, and the parking lights came on. The car backed to the left in Alt-Lübars, then went off at faster speed towards the bigger avenue.

The kidnappers were abandoning their chum. They could of course afford to abandon him and even the money just now, because they still had Frank Pierson. They had probably thought it a police trick, with no money on the scene. Tom breathed through his mouth, as if he had been in a fight. He pushed the safety on to Peter's gun, stuck it in his right trouser pocket, picked up the fallen torch and shone it for a couple of seconds on the man on the ground. His left temple looked all blood, was perhaps crushed, and to Tom he looked indeed like the Grunewald Italian type, though now his moustache was gone. Search his pockets? With the torch still on, Tom felt quickly in the one back pocket of the man's black trousers, found nothing, then with difficulty reached into the left front pocket, which yielded a box of matches, a couple of coins and a key which looked like a house key. Tom pocketed the key quickly and almost absently, and avoided looking at the red splotch of the man's temple and face, which was making him feel faint, or so he thought. The right front pocket felt flat and empty. Tom took the man's gun from the ground near his hand, stuck it into a corner of the suitcase, and zipped the suitcase shut again. He rubbed the torch against his trousers, cut if off, and dropped it on the ground.

Then Tom made his way to the road without putting on Peter's small torch – tripping once badly – and walked towards Alt-Lübars, backed by the yelps of attack dogs. Tom didn't as yet see anyone who had ventured out of his house to investigate the shots, so he dared to put on the little torch for a second or two at a time, so he could see his footing. Once at Alt-Lübars, he didn't need the torch as the road was smoother. Tom did not look to the left, where Peter might still be, because he did not want to run into an inhabitant of the village who might just be coming out his door.

Behind him somewhere, a window opened, a voice cried something. Tom did not look back.

What had the voice said? 'Who is there?' or 'Who is that?'

The dogs' barks had faded out, and Tom wet his lips as he rounded the corner to the right into Zebel-Krüger-Damm. The suitcase suddenly seemed weightless. Here cars were parked, a couple of cars even zoomed past. Dawn was definitely rising, and as if to confirm him half the street lights went out. In the distance, not more than a hundred yards away, Tom saw what he thought was a bus-stop sign. Peter had mentioned a number 20 bus going to Tegel. That was the airport area, in the direction of Berlin at any rate. Tom dared to lift the suitcase and to glance at its corners for the red or pink of blood. He could hardly be sure in the dim light, and what was earth or mud might have looked the same as blood, but he saw nothing to be concerned about. He made himself walk at a moderate pace, as if he had somewhere to go, but was not in a hurry. There were only two other people on the pavement now, both men, one elderly and a bit stooped. They seemed to pay him no attention.

How often did the buses run? Tom paused by the bus-stop, and looked back. A car appeared, full lights on, and passed Tom.

'*Äpfel, Äpfel!*' That was from a small boy who came running and fell against the elderly man, who nearly embraced him.

Tom watched. Where had the little boy come from? Why was he crying 'Apples!' when he had none in his hands? The elderly man took the boy's hand, and they walked on, away from Berlin.

Here came the yellowish lights of what looked like a bus. Tom saw 20 TEGEL on its lighted front. When Tom paid for his ticket, he noticed that a couple of knuckles of his left hand were dark red with blood. How had that happened? Tom took a seat in the nearly empty bus, suitcase between his feet, stuck his left hand in his jacket pocket, and avoided looking at the other passengers. Tom gazed out the window on his left, at the encouragingly increasing houses, cars, people. It was now light enough to see the colours of cars. What had happened to Peter? Tom hoped he had fled at the sound of the gunshots.

How soon would the body be found? In an hour, by some curious dog, the dog maybe in the company of a farmer? The body would not be visible from the road. Tom felt reasonably sure it was a body, not an unconscious man. Tom sighed, almost gasped, shook his head, and stared at the brown pigskin suitcase between his knees which contained two million dollars in paper. He leaned back and relaxed. Tegel must be the terminal stop, he thought, and he could almost afford to sleep. But he didn't sleep, only rested his head against the window.

The bus arrived at Tegel, which seemed a U-Bahn station rather than the air terminus. Tom was interested in a taxi, and after a few seconds, he found the taxi rank. He asked a driver if he could to go Niebuhrstrasse. Tom did not give the number, and told the driver he would know the house once he got to the street. Tom settled back and lit a cigarette. His knuckles were scraped, nothing serious there, and it was his own blood at least. Wouldn't the kidnappers try again, ring up Paris and make another date? Or would they be so scared or rattled now, they would turn Frank loose? The last idea seemed amateurish to Tom, but how professional were these kidnappers?

Tom got out somewhere in Niebuhrstrasse, paid and tipped the driver, and walked in the direction of Eric's apartment house. He had the two keys on a ring which Eric had given him, and he opened the front door with one, and took the lift. At Eric's door Tom knocked, and gave the bell one short push. It was now nearly half past six.

Tom heard footsteps, then Eric's voice asked in German:

'Who is there?'

'Tom.'

'A-ah!' A chain rattled, a couple of bolts slid.

'Back again!' Tom whispered cheerfully, and set the suitcase down in Eric's hall, near where it became the living room.

'Tom, why did you make Peter *leave?* Peter is so worried, he telephoned twice! – And you brought the suitcase back!' Eric smiled and shook his head, as if at a silly economy.

Tom took off his jacket. The August sunlight was starting to blaze beyond Eric's window.

'Two shots, Peter told me. Now what happened? – Sit down, Tom! Would you like a coffee? Or a drink?'

'A drink first, I think. Could you manage a gin and tonic?'

Eric could and while he was making it, Tom went to the bathroom and washed his hands with warm water and soap.

'How did you get back? Peter said you took his gun.'

'I still have his gun.' Now Tom was standing with a Gauloise in one hand and his drink in the other. 'I took a bus and a taxi. The money's still there.' Tom nodded towards the suitcase. 'That's why I brought your suitcase back.'

'Still there?' Eric's pink lips parted. 'Who fired the shots?'

'I did. But only in the air.' Tom's voice had gone hoarse. He sat down. 'I hit one with your suitcase. The Italian type, I think. I think he's dead.'

Eric nodded. 'Peter saw him.'

'Did he?'

'Yes. I must put on something, Tom, I feel silly.' Eric, in pyjamas, hurried into his bedroom, and came back tying the belt of his black silk dressing gown. 'Peter waited, he said, maybe ten minutes, and then he went back to look, thinking you might be dead or wounded. He saw a man lying behind the shed.'

'True,' Tom said.

'So you just – Why didn't you go back to Peter who was waiting at the church?'

Waiting at the church! Tom laughed, and stretched his legs out in front of him. 'I don't know. Maybe I was scared. I didn't think. I didn't even look towards the church.' Tom sipped more of his glass, and said, 'Coffee, yes, please, Eric, and then a little sleep.'

On his last words, the telephone rang.

'That certainly is Peter again.' Eric went to his telephone. 'Just come back!' Eric said. 'No, he is all right, not hurt. He took a bus and a taxi!' Then Eric laughed at something Peter was saying. 'I shall tell Tom, yes. Very funny. Yes, at least we are all safe. Here! Can you believe it?' Eric put the telephone against his chest, still smiling broadly. 'Peter cannot believe the money is back *here*! Peter wants to talk to you.'

Tom got up. 'Hello, Peter . . . Yes, I am okay. My infinite thanks to you, Peter, you did well.' Tom said that in German. 'No, I did not shoot the man.'

'I could not see well in the dark – with no light,' Peter said. 'I only saw he was not you. So I went away.'

He was brave to go back, Tom thought. 'I've still got your gun and your torch.'

Peter chuckled. 'Let us both get some sleep.'

Eric made coffee for Tom – Tom knew it was not going to disturb his sleep in the least – and then together they opened the horsehair sofa and spread the sheets and blanket.

Tom carried the brown suitcase to the window, and looked at it for signs of blood. He saw none, but he took, with Eric's permission, a floor rag from the kitchen, moistened it at the sink, and went over the exterior of the suitcase with it, then rinsed the rag out and hung it on a rod to dry.

'You know,' Eric said to Tom, 'a man approached Peter as he was walking away from that little road, and said, "Did you hear the shots?" and Peter said yes, that was why he had walked on to the road. Then the man asked what Peter was doing there, since Peter was a stranger and Peter said, "Oh, I am only with my girl friend by the church!"'

Tom was not in a mood to laugh. He washed in a perfunctory way in the bathroom, and pulled on his pyjamas. He was thinking that if the kidnappers released Frank, they would not necessarily inform Thurlow. Frank might know and probably did know that his brother and Thurlow were at the Hôtel Lutetia in Paris, and Frank might make his way there on his own, if he were freed. Or – the kidnappers might simply kill the boy with an overdose and leave his body in some Berlin apartment which they would abandon.

'What are you thinking about, Tom? Let us both go back to bed for a little while. A long while. Sleep as late as you like! My housekeeper does not come tomorrow. And I have locked and chained the door.'

'I'm thinking I have to ring Thurlow in Paris, because I said I would.'

Eric nodded. 'Yes – what *is* going to happen now? Go ahead and do it, Tom.'

Tom went in his pyjamas and loafers to the telephone, and dialled.

'How many were there?' Eric asked. 'Could you see?'

'Not really. In the car? Three maybe.' Two now, Tom thought. He turned off the lamp by Eric's telephone. There was light enough from the window.

'Hello!' Thurlow said. 'What happened there?'

Thurlow had heard from them, Tom could tell. 'Can't say on the telephone. Are they willing to make another date?'

'Ye-es, I'm pretty sure, but they're sounding scared – nervous, I mean, and a little threatening. They said if there were any police –'

'No police. There won't be any police. Tell them we're willing to make another date, would you?' Tom suddenly had an idea as to a meeting place. 'I think they still want the money. Make them prove the boy's still alive, would you? Then I'll call you back later today when I've had a little sleep.'

'Where *is* the money now?'

'Safe with me.' Tom put the telephone down.

Eric stood with Tom's empty coffee cup, listening.

Tom lit a final cigarette. 'Asking about the money,' he said to Eric, smiling. 'I'm betting they still want the money. Much nicer than killing the boy and having a corpse on their hands.'

'*Ja*, sure it is. I took the suitcase back into my bedroom. Did you notice?'

Tom hadn't.

'Good night, Tom. Sleep long!'

Tom glanced at the chain on the door, then said, 'Good night, Eric.'

FIFTEEN

'Eric, I'd like to borrow some drag – for tonight probably. Do you think your friend Max would be kind enough to lend me some?'

'Drag?' Eric gave a mystified smile. 'Drag for what? A party?'

Now Tom laughed. They were breakfasting, or Tom was, at a quarter past one in the afternoon. Tom sat in pyjamas and dressing gown on Eric's smaller sofa. 'Not a party, but I have an idea. Might work, and anyway it would be fun. I thought I'd try to make a date with the kidnappers at the Hump tonight. And maybe Max can even come with me.' Der Hump was the name of the gay bar with the glass stairway.

'You will deliver the money at the Hump in *drag*?'

'No, no money. Just drag. Can you reach Max now?'

Eric stood up. 'Max may be working. Rollo is more likely. He sleeps till noon usually. They live together. I shall try – yes.' Eric dialled a number which he had not needed to look up. After a few seconds, he said, 'Hello, Rollo! How are you? . . . is Max there? . . . So. Listen,' he went on in German, 'my friend Tom would like – Well, Max has met him. Tom is staying with me. Tom would like some drag for tonight . . . *Ja!* A long dress –' Eric glanced at Tom and nodded. '*Ja*, a wig certainly, make-up – shoes.' Eric looked at Tom's loafers and said, 'Max's maybe, yours are *too* big, ha-ha! . . . At the Hump maybe! . . . Ha-ha! Oh, I am sure you can come if you want to.'

'Some kind of *handbag*,' Tom whispered.

'Oh, and a handbag,' said Eric. 'I don't know. Fun, I suppose.' Eric chuckled. 'You think so? Good, I'll tell Tom. *Wiedersehen*, Rollo.' Eric hung up and said, 'Rollo thinks Max can arrive tonight around ten – here, I mean. Max is working in a beauty parlour till nine, and Rollo goes out at six to do a window-dressing job until ten, but he says he will leave a note for Max to find.'

'Thank you, Eric.' Tom felt cheered, even though nothing was as yet arranged.

'Again I have a date at three this afternoon,' Eric said. 'Not Kreuzberg. Want to come?'

This time Tom didn't. 'No, thanks, Eric. I think I might take a little walk – buy a present for Heloise, maybe. And I must ring Paris again. I shall owe you a thousand dollars for your 'phone bill.'

'Ha-ha! – To leave money for 'phone bills! No. We are all friends, Tom.' Eric went off to his bedroom.

His words lingered in Tom's ears as he lit a Roth-Haendle. They were friends, and so was Reeves a friend of theirs. They used one another's telephones, houses, lives sometimes, and somehow it all evened out. Tom could, however, send Eric an American slang dictionary, at least.

Once more, Tom dialled the Lutetia.

'Hel-lo, I am glad to hear from you,' said Thurlow, sounding as if he were chewing something. 'Yes,' he said in answer to Tom's question, 'they 'phoned around noon today, this time with what sounded like fire engines in the background. Anyway they would like another definite place and time and they've set it up. It's a restaurant – I'll give you the address – and you're simply to leave a *package* to be picked –'

'I have a place to suggest,' Tom interrupted. 'A bar called the Hump. That's H-u-m-p, just the way it sounds. In – Just a minute.' Tom put his hand over the telephone and called, 'Eric! – Sorry to bother you. What is the street of Der Hump?'

'Winterfeldstrasse!' said Eric promptly.

'Winterfeldstrasse,' Tom said to Thurlow. 'Oh, never mind the number, let them find it ... Oh, yes, just an ordinary bar, but a pretty big one. I'm sure the taxi drivers will know it ... Around midnight. Between eleven and midnight, let's say. They are to ask for Joey, and Joey will have what they want.'

'That will be *you*?' Thurlow asked in an interested tone.

'Well – not sure. But Joey will be there. I assume you've heard that the boy is still all right?'

'Only their word. We didn't speak with him. With fire engines in the background, they must've been calling from the street.'

'Thank you, Mr Thurlow. I expect success tonight,' Tom said in a firm tone, firmer than he felt. Tom plunged on. 'Once they've got the money, I trust they'll acknowledge it and tell you where the boy's to be released. Can you ask them to do that? I suppose they'll ring you again before tonight to confirm a date?'

'I *hope* so. They gave me orders to tell *you*. About that restaurant, I mean – So you'll call me back when, Mr Ripley?'

'I can't say an exact time just now. But I'll call back, yes.' Tom hung up, vaguely dissatisfied, wishing he could be sure the people who had Frank would ring Thurlow again today.

Eric walked in from the hall with a purposeful air, licking an envelope. 'Success? What is the news there?'

Eric's lack of anxiety gave Tom a bit of cool. They were both going to quit the apartment in a few minutes and leave two million dollars in it, unguarded. 'I made a date for between eleven and twelve tonight at the Hump. The kidnappers are supposed to ask for Joey.'

'And you are not taking the money?'

'No.'

'And then what?'

'I shall plan things as I go along. Has Max got a car?'

'No – they haven't.' Eric adjusted his dark blue jacket on his shoulders, and looked at Tom, smiling. 'I shall see you to a taxi in your drag tonight.'

'Want to come?'

'Not sure,' Eric wagged his head. 'Tom, make yourself at home. But double-lock the door if you go out – please.'

'Definitely. I shall.'

'Would you like to see where the suitcase is – in my closet?'

Tom smiled. 'No.'

'Bye-bye, dear Tom. Back by six, I think I am.'

A few minutes later, Tom also went out, double-locking the door as Eric had requested.

Niebuhrstrasse looked peaceful and ordinary to Tom, no figure anywhere that appeared to be loitering or paying attention to him. Tom walked left into Leibnizstrasse, and left again when he reached the Kurfürstendamm. Here were the shops, the book-and-record stores, the four-wheeled snack wagons on the pavements, life, people – a small boy running with a big cardboard box, a girl trying to scrape chewing gum from the heel of her boot without having to touch it. Tom smiled. He bought a *Morgenpost*, and took a brief look at it, not expecting and not finding anything that had to do with a kidnapping.

Tom stopped in front of a shop window full of good attaché cases, handbags and wallets. He went in and bought a dark-blue suede handbag with a shoulder strap. Heloise would like it, he thought. Two hundred and thirty-five DM. And maybe he had bought it as a guarantee that he would get back home and be able to present it to her. That was a bit illogical. He bought a couple of packets of Roth-Haendle at a Schnell-Imbiss wagon. Convenient, Tom thought, that they sold cigarettes and matches as well as food and beer. Did he want a beer? No. He strolled back towards Eric's.

Tom held Eric's front door open for a woman coming out with an empty shopping trolley. She thanked him, but barely glanced at him.

He did not like going into Eric's silent apartment, wondered for an instant if someone might be hiding in Eric's bedroom. Absurd. But he went into the bedroom – which was quiet and neat with the bed made – and looked into the closet. The brown suitcase stood at the back, behind a larger suitcase, and in front of the larger suitcase was a row of shoes. Tom lifted the brown suitcase, and felt its familiar weight.

In the living room, Tom found himself staring at one of Eric's woodland paintings – hating it – of an antlered stag with terrified and bloodshot eyes under dark-blue storm clouds. Were dogs pursuing the stag? If so, Tom didn't see any. He looked in vain for a rifle barrel poking from anywhere in the picture. Maybe the stag had hated the painter.

The telephone rang, and Tom jumped almost off his feet. It had sounded unusually loud. Could the kidnappers have got Eric's number? Of course not. Should he answer it? Put on a different voice? Tom picked up the telephone and spoke in his usual voice.

'Hello?'

'Hello, Tom. This is Peter,' Peter said calmly.

Tom smiled. 'Hello, Peter. Eric's not here, back around six, he said.'

'Not important. You are okay? Slept?'

'Yes, thank you – Are you free tonight, Peter? Say from ten-thirty or eleven for a little bit?'

'Ja-a. I have only to see a cousin for dinner. What is happening tonight?'

'I am visiting Der Hump, maybe with Max. Again I am requesting your taxi service, but tonight should be safer. Well,' Tom added hastily, 'I *hope* it will be safer, but that would be my problem, not yours.'

Peter said he could come to Eric's between ten-thirty and eleven.

Max laid out his drag offerings in Eric's living room like a salesman displaying something which would probably interest the customer, though this was the only outfit Max had brought. 'This is my best one,' Max said in German, clumping around the living room in his boots and black leather gear, spreading the long gown to best advantage against himself.

Tom was relieved to see that it had long sleeves. The gown was pink and white and transparent, with a triple row of ruffles at the hem. 'Terrific,' said Tom. '*Very* pretty,' he added.

'And this, of course.' From his red canvas carry-all, Max pulled a white slip or petticoat that looked as long as the dress. 'Put the dress on first, it will inspire me for the make-up,' Max said with a smile.

Tom lost no time, took off his dressing gown under which he wore shorts, pulled on the slip and followed it with the dress. This caused a problem with the tights which looked like a wraith of beige and which Max said he had to sit down to put on properly, but finally Max said, 'What the hell?' if the shoes felt all right without the tights, because the dress came nearly to the floor. Max was as tall as Tom. The gown had no belt but fell loose.

Then Tom sat down before a rectangular looking-glass that Eric had fetched from his bedroom. Max had spread his paraphernalia on Eric's sideboard, and now he got to work on Tom's face. Eric watched all this with folded arms and silent amusement. Max slapped heavy white cream on Tom's eyebrows and spread it, humming as he worked.

'Never mind this,' said Max. 'I'll get the eyebrows back. Just what you need.'

'Music!' said Eric. 'We need *Carmen*!'

'No, we *don't* need *Carmen*!' Tom said, hating the idea of *Carmen*, mainly because it wasn't funny enough, or he wasn't in the mood for

Bizet. The transformation in Tom's lips amazed him. His upperlip had become thinner, the underlip fuller. He would hardly have recognized himself!

'Now the wig,' Max murmured in German, shaking out the auburn, rather frightening thing that had been lying on a corner of Eric's sideboard. It had dangling curls that Max proceeded to comb out delicately.

'Sing something,' Tom said. 'Do you know that song about the slick little girl?'

'Ach! – The things you do to your *face* – *Make*-up!' Max was off, singing, doing a fine imitation of Lou Reed. 'Rouge and colouring, incense and ice . . .' Max swayed with his work.

It reminded Tom of Frank, of Heloise, of Belle Ombre.

'Open *your* ice!' Max sang to him, concentrating on Tom's eyes now. Max paused for a look at Tom, then a look into the mirror.

'Are you free tonight, Max?' Tom asked in German.

Max laughed, adjusting the wig, viewing his product. 'Are you serious?' Max had a broad, generous mouth, now spread in a smile, and Tom thought that Max blushed. 'I keep my hair very short, so these wigs fit better, but really it is silly to be so fussy. I think this looks nice.'

'Yes.' Tom gazed into the mirror as if at another person, but without much interest at the moment. '*Ernsthaft*, Max. Have you got an hour to spend with me at the bar? At the Hump tonight? Around midnight or even earlier? Bring Rollo. Be my guests. Just for an hour or so, eh?'

'Am I left out?' Eric asked in German.

'Oh, up to you, Eric.'

Now Max was helping Tom into the high-heeled patent leather pumps, which were rather full of cracks.

'Second-hand from a thrift shop in Kreuzberg,' Max said, 'but they don't torture my feet like a lot of these high heels. Look! They fit!'

Tom sat down again before the mirror, and felt in a fantasy world as Max created a beauty spot on his left cheek with one masterly black dot.

The doorbell rang, and Eric went into his kitchen.

'You really want Rollo and me to join you at the Hump tonight?' Max asked.

'You can't expect me to sit there or stand there all by myself like a wall-flower, can you, Max? I'll need you both. Eric isn't the right type.' Tom was practising a lighter voice.

'All this just for fun?' Max asked, touching Tom's auburn curls again.

'Just for fun. I think I'll stand up an imaginary date. He won't know me when he walks in, anyway.'

Max laughed.

'Tom!' Eric said, walking back into the living room.

Don't call me Tom, Tom felt like saying.

Eric stared, speechless for a moment, into the mirror which reflected Tom's transformed face. 'P-Peter's downstairs, says he cannot park so easily, so maybe you can come down?'

'Oh, indeed,' said Tom. Coolly, Tom picked up his handbag, a largish thing of red leather and black patent leather which criss-crossed in a basket pattern. Coolly too, he reached in a pocket of his jacket that hung in Eric's front closet, and took the key that he had found on the Italian type, and from the back right corner of the closet floor picked up the gun that belonged to Peter. Eric and Max were chatting, looking at Tom's attire, and neither of them noticed his putting the gun into his handbag. Tom had his back to them. 'Ready, Max? Who's escorting me down?'

Max did. Max had been a bit late in getting to Eric's, and he said Rollo might already be at the Hump, but Max wanted to dash home first to 'partly' change his clothes, because he had been working all day in the shirt he was wearing.

Peter's cigarette nearly fell from his mouth. He was sitting in his car.

'Tom,' Tom said. 'Hello, Peter.'

Peter and Max apparently knew each other. Max told Tom that he lived so near, it was better for him to run home on foot, since the Hump was in the other direction. He would see Tom in a few minutes. Peter and Tom drove off towards Winterfeldstrasse.

'Now what is all this? For fun?' Peter asked, a bit tense.

Had Tom detected a slight coolness in Peter? 'Not entirely.' Tom realized that he could have rung Thurlow back, and hadn't, to find out if the kidnappers would keep the date tonight. 'While we have a minute – you went back to that *shed*, Peter.'

Peter shrugged or squirmed. 'I went on foot, yes, not wanting to make noise with the car motor. Very dark without a light.'

'I can imagine.'

'I thought maybe you were dead there – wounded maybe, which would have been worse. Then I saw the man there on the ground – not you. So I went away. You did not shoot him?'

'I hit him with the suitcase.' Tom swallowed. He did not feel like saying that he had also bashed his temple with Peter's gun butt. 'I think the kidnappers thought I was more numerous than I was. I fired your gun twice in the air and yelled. But I think the fellow on the ground there was dead.'

Peter chuckled, perhaps nervously, but it made Tom feel better. 'I didn't stay long enough to find out. Didn't see the papers tonight – and I wasn't watching the news tonight either.'

Tom said nothing. For a moment, he was in the clear, Tom thought, and he had to think about the present. Did he dare ask Peter to wait again, outside the Hump? Peter could be extremely useful tonight.

'And they drove away,' Peter said. 'I saw their car going away, and then I waited for you – more than five minutes, I think.'

'That was when I walked back to that avenue – the Krüger-Damm and caught the bus. I didn't even look towards the church. My fault, Peter.'

Peter turned a corner. 'All that money in Eric's house now! – And what will they do to the boy if they don't get it?'

'Oh, I think they would rather have the money than the boy.' They had now entered the street where the bar was, and Tom was watching for the pink neon sign which said *Der Hump* in script with a horizontal underlining on the side of a building, but he didn't yet see it. Tom had to enlighten Peter about the possible events of tonight, and Tom with difficulty tried to get started. His drag, at that moment, made him feel silly and vulnerable, and he lifted nervously the black and red handbag on his lap: it was heavyish because of Peter's gun. 'I've got your gun with me. Four bullets left.'

'Now? You have the gun?' Peter asked in German, and glanced at Tom's handbag.

'Yes. I made a date with the kidnappers tonight – and maybe just one of them will turn up, I don't know – at the Hump – between eleven and midnight. So, Peter, if you're willing to wait for me – It's eleven now and a little after. I'm going to ignore them inside, and then I hope to be able to follow them. I think they may come in a car, but I'm not sure of that. If they haven't a car, I'll do what I can on foot by way of following them.'

'O-oo-oh,' said Peter dubiously.

Was Peter thinking of his high-heeled shoes, Tom wondered? 'If they don't show up at all, at least it's fun tonight and nobody gets hurt.' Tom had just seen the pink *Der Hump* sign, not nearly as large as he had remembered it. Now Peter was trying to park. 'There's a place!' Tom said, having spotted a gap in a line of cars parked on the right side of the street.

Peter was taking it.

'Are you willing to wait nearly an hour? Maybe more?'

'Sure, sure,' Peter said, parking.

Tom explained: if the kidnappers kept this date, they were going to ask for 'Joey', ask the barman or a waiter, and when Joey did not appear after a while, they would leave, and then Tom wanted to follow them. 'I doubt if they'll wait till closing time at dawn. They'll know it's a trick by midnight or a little after. But if you have to pee, you had better go somewhere now.'

Peter's long jaw dropped slightly and he laughed. 'No, I am okay. You are alone there? By yourself?'

'Do I look so delicate? Max is coming. Probably Rollo too. Bye-bye, Peter. See you here later. If it gets to be quarter past twelve, I'll come out and speak with you.'

Tom looked at Der Hump's door. One masculine figure came out, two others slipped in, and the beat of the disco music came louder through the opened door. BOOM-PAH . . . BOOM-PAH . . . BOOM-PAH . . . like a heartbeat, not fast, not too slow, either, but strong. A little phony too, Tom thought, artificial, electronic not exactly human. Tom knew what Peter was thinking.

'You think this is intelligent to do?' Peter asked in German.

'I want to find out where the boy is.' Tom took up his handbag. 'If you don't want to wait, Peter, I don't blame you. I can try to get a taxi in time to follow them.'

'I'll wait.' Peter smiled, tense. 'If you have trouble – I'm here.'

Tom got out and crossed the street. The evening breeze made him feel naked, and he glanced down to make sure he wasn't, that his skirt hadn't blown up. His ankle turned as he stepped on to the kerb, and he warned himself to take it easy. Tom touched his wig nervously, and with slightly parted lips pulled open the door of Der Hump. The disco pulse engulfed him, created echoing vibrations in his eardrums. Tom moved – under the gaze of at least ten customers, many of whom smiled at him – towards the bar. The air smelled of pot.

Again there was no room at the bar, but it was amazing how four or five men stepped aside so Tom could finally touch the round, shiny chromium rim of the bar.

'And who are you?' asked a young man in levis so worn out, they revealed the absence of any underwear.

'Mabel,' Tom said, and fluttered his eyelashes. Coolly he opened his handbag, in order to get at the loose marks and change at the bottom for a drink. Tom suddenly realized he had not thought of nail polish, and neither had Max. The hell with it. It seemed masculine to dump coins on the counter in the English manner, so Tom didn't.

Men and boys on the dance floor twisted and pumped to the din of pounding rock, as if the floor were exploding or undulating beneath them. Figures hovered, gazed, drifted up the glass-enclosed stairway which led to the loos, and as Tom watched, one figure fell down the stairs, was righted by two other men, and walked on down apparently undamaged. There were at least ten other figures in long-dress drag, Tom noticed, but now Tom was looking around for Max. With infinite slowness, Tom extracted a cigarette from his handbag and lit it, in no hurry to catch the eye of a barman and order a drink, for the nonce. It was now a quarter past eleven, and Tom looked around – especially at the bar where it would be logical for someone to ask a barman about a Joey – but so far Tom did not see anyone who could by any stretch of the imagination be called straight, and he assumed the kidnappers were.

And here came Max in a Western white shirt with pearl buttons, black leather trousers and boots still, from the back part of the establishment where most of the dancing was going on. He was followed by a tall figure in a long dress that seemed made of beige tissue paper, and with crew-cut hair that had slender yellow ribbons somehow tied in it above both ears.

'*Good* evening,' Max said, smiling. 'Rollo.' He gestured to the tissue paper figure.

'Mabel,' said Tom, smiling merrily.

Rollo's thin red lips turned up at the corners. Otherwise his face was a floury white. His blue-grey eyes seemed to glitter like cut diamonds. 'You wait a friend?' asked Rollo. He was carrying a long black cigarette holder without a cigarette.

Was Rollo kidding or not? '*Ja-a*,' said Tom, letting his eyes roll again over what he could see of the fellows against the walls in the tables department. Tom could hardly imagine one of the kidnappers or even two of them dancing, but perhaps anything was possible.

'What to *drink?*' Rollo asked Tom.

'I shall do it. Beer, Tom?' Max asked.

Beer seemed unladylike, but Tom at once thought this absurd, was about to say yes, when he noticed an espresso machine behind the bar. '*Kaffee, bitte!*' Tom took some of the loose coins from the bottom of his handbag and put them on the counter. He had not brought his wallet.

Max and Rollo wanted Dornkaats.

Tom manoeuvred himself so that he could face the door, lean against the bar, and chat with Max and Rollo who were now facing him.

Chatting was a bit difficult in the noise. Every few seconds, a male figure or two came in the door, and fewer seemed to depart.

'Who are you standing up?' Max shouted into Tom's ear. 'Do you *see* him?'

'Not yet!' Just then Tom noticed a young man with dark hair in the very corner or end of the bar which curved to Tom's right and stopped against the wall. This one could be straight. He looked in his late twenties, wore a tan canvas-like jacket, and he held a cigarette in his left hand which rested on the bar. He was drinking beer, and he kept looking around, slowly and alertly, glancing at the door too. But many other people were also looking at the door, so Tom didn't know what to think. Sooner or later the man Tom wanted would ask the barman – possibly for a second time, if he had already done it once – if he knew or saw or had a message from someone called Joey.

'*Dance?*' said Rollo, bending politely towards Tom, because Rollo was even taller.

'Why not?' He and Rollo forged their way to the dance floor.

Within seconds, Tom had to remove his high-heeled shoes, which Rollo gallantly took and began to clap together over his head like castanets. Whirling skirts, everybody laughing, but not at them, and in fact no one paid any attention to him and Rollo. *DEW-IT . . . DEW-IT . . . DEW-IT . . .* Or the words might have been *CHEW IT* or *PEE WIT* or *BLEW IT*, it didn't matter. The floor felt good under Tom's bare feet. Now and then he put his hand on the top of his head to straighten his wig, and once Rollo did it for him. Rollo had had the good sense to wear flat sandals, Tom noticed. Tom felt exhilarated and stronger, as if he were having a workout in a gym. No wonder Berliners liked disguises! One could feel free, and in a sense like *oneself* in a disguise.

'Shall we go back to the bar?' Tom knew it was 11.40 at least, and he wanted to have another look.

Tom didn't put his shoes back on till he got to the bar, where his unfinished coffee still stood. Max had been guarding his handbag. Tom resumed his place from which he could watch the door. The man Tom had noticed was no longer at the end of the bar, and Tom glanced around, looking for a tan jacket among the men milling around the tables, or those standing and staring at the dance floor or the stairway. Then Tom saw him just a couple of yards behind him at the bar, nearly concealed by the customers between, trying to catch the attention of a barman. Max started to yell something at Tom, and Tom silenced him with a wave of a finger, and watched the man through his nearly closed false eyelashes.

The barman leaned forward – he wore a curly blond wig – and shook his head.

The tan-jacketed man was still speaking, and Tom stood on tiptoe to try to see his lips. Was he saying 'Joey'? It looked like it, and now came a nod of the barman's head, a nod that might mean, 'I'll tell you if he turns up.' Then the man in the tan jacket slowly made his way through standing groups and solitary figures towards the wall opposite the bar. Here he spoke with a blondish man in a bright blue open-necked shirt who was leaning against the wall. The blue shirt said nothing in reply to whatever the other man had said to him.

'What were you saying?' Tom asked Max.

'*That* your friend?' Max asked, grinning, nodding towards the tan jacket.

Tom shrugged. He pushed his pinkish ruffled sleeve back, and saw that it was eleven minutes to midnight. Tom finished his coffee. He leaned towards Max and said, 'I *may* have to leave in a minute. Not sure. So I'd better say good night and *thank* you, Max – in case I have to run – like Cinderella!'

'You want a taxi?' Max asked, puzzled, polite.

Tom shook his head. 'Another Dornkaat?' Tom signalled for two by pointing at Max's glass, holding up two fingers, then put out two ten-mark notes over Max's protest. At the same time, Tom was watching the tan-jacketed man make his way back to the bar, aiming for the same place by the wall, which was now occupied by a man and a boy, deep in conversation. Then the tan jacket seemed to give up the bar idea, and moved nearer the door. Tom saw him lift an arm to get the eye of the barman who happened to be near the end of the bar just then. The barman shook his head at once, and then Tom knew that the man in the tan jacket was the one looking for Joey. Or Tom felt sure enough of it. The man looked at his wristwatch, then at the door. Three teen-aged boys came in, all in levis, all eyes, all swinging empty hands. The man in the tan jacket looked in the direction of the blue shirt, and gave a movement of his head in the direction of the door. The tan jacket went out.

'Good night, Max,' Tom said, picking up his handbag. 'Lovely to meet you, Rollo!'

Rollo gave a bow.

Tom saw the blue shirt moving towards the door, and let him go out

first. Then in an unhurried manner, Tom made his way to the door and
out. Tom saw both men on the pavement to his right, the tan jacket
waiting as the blue shirt walked towards him. Tom went left, towards
Peter's car, which was headed in the wrong direction, Tom realized.
Some more fellows were entering the Hump, and one whistled at Tom,
and the others chuckled.

Peter had his head back, but snapped to attention when Tom tapped
his half-closed window.

'Me *again*!' said Tom, and went round the car and got in. 'You'll have
to turn. I just saw them. On this street. Two men.'

Peter was already turning. The street was darkish, full of parked cars,
but there was no traffic just now.

'Go slow, they're on foot,' Tom said. 'Pretend you're looking for a
parking place.'

Tom saw them walking, not looking behind them, and apparently
engaged in conversation. Then they stopped at a parked car, and at a
gesture from Tom, Peter slowed still more. A car was behind Peter's but
had room to pass, and it did. 'I'd like to follow them without being
noticed,' Tom said. 'Give it a try, Peter. If they suspect we're following
them, they'll give us a bum steer or zoom off somewhere – one or the
other.' Tom tried to put bum steer into German, but Peter seemed to
understand well enough.

Some fifteen yards in front of them, the car pulled out, and turned
smartly left into the next cross-street. Peter followed, and they saw the
car turn right into a busier street. Two cars then got between them, but
Tom kept the men's car in view, and at its next left turn saw in the
headlights of another car that the car's colour was maroon.

'The car's dark red. That's the car!'

'You know it?'

'It's the car that was in Lübars.'

They followed, for what seemed to Tom five minutes but was perhaps
half that, through two more turns, Tom navigating all the way, until
Tom saw the car slow at a parking place on the left side of a street full
of four- or six-storey dwellings, whose windows looked mostly unlighted
now.

'Can you stop here and back a bit,' Tom said quickly.

Tom wanted to try to see which house they went into. And then, if
possible, see if a light came on on a certain floor. These were again the
dreary middle-class or lower middle-class apartment buildings which
had escaped the bombs of World War II. Thanks to the tan jacket, Tom

was able to make out a fuzzy shadow, lighter than the background, which mounted some steps at one of the front doors. He saw the light jacket disappear into the house.

'Go ahead about three metres – please, Peter.'

As Peter inched ahead, Tom saw a third floor light grow brighter, and a second floor light grow dim to non-existence. A minuterie system? Hall lights? A third floor light to the left then came on more strongly. A second floor light on the right remained bright and unchanged. Tom groped in the bottom of his handbag, where coins and paper money lay disorganized, and found the key he had taken from the pocket of the Italian type.

'Right, Peter, you can drop me here,' Tom said.

'You want me to wait?' Peter whispered. 'What are you going to do?'

'Not sure.' Peter's car now stood on the right side of the street close to a row of parked cars, not annoying anyone. Peter might have been able to stay here fifteen minutes, but Tom did not know how long he would be, and he did not want to endanger Peter's life, in case a couple of them stormed out of the house shooting at him, and Peter tried to pick him up. Tom knew he sometimes imagined the worst, the absurdest. Did the key he had work the front door, the apartment door, or neither? Tom envisaged himself pressing half a dozen buttons downstairs until some innocent soul, not the kidnappers, let him into the building. 'I'll just try to scare them,' Tom said, tapping his fingertips on the door handle.

'You don't want me to telephone the police? Now or in five minutes?'

'No.' Tom was going to get the boy or not, accomplish something or not, before the police could get here, and if the police arrived in time or too late, Tom's name would be dragged in by them, and that he did not want. 'The police don't know anything about this, and I want it that way.' Tom opened the car door. 'Don't wait, and slam the car door when you're farther away.' He half closed the door after himself, so that it made only a faint click.

A woman in a light coloured dress passed Tom on the pavement, gave Tom a rather startled glance and walked on.

Peter's car slid onwards into darkness, into safety, and Tom heard its door slam. Tom concentrated on getting up the few front steps in his high heels, holding his long skirt a few inches above step level, so he wouldn't trip.

Inside the first front door, there was a panel of at least ten buttons, most marked with unclear names and not all with apartment numbers indicated. Discouraging, Tom thought, as he might have dared ring 2A or 2B, if he had seen it. That had been a second floor light by European counting, third floor by American. Tom tried the Yale-lock-type of key which he had in his hand. It worked in the lock. Tom felt a shock of surprise. Perhaps each of the gang carried such a house key, and there was always someone in the apartment to open the apartment door? Which apartment now? Tom pressed the minute-light button, and saw an uninviting brown stairway of unpolished wood, and two closed doors, one on either side of where he stood.

He dropped the key into his handbag, and felt for the gun. He pushed the safety to an off position, left the gun in the handbag, and began climbing the stairs, again holding up his skirt in front. As Tom approached the next floor, a door closed, a man appeared in the hall, and another minute-light came on when the man pressed a wall button. Tom was confronted by a thick, middle-aged man in trousers and sports shirt, who wished to descend the stairs, and who stepped aside less out of politeness than as if alarmed by the sight of Tom.

Tom supposed the man might think he was a prostitute making a call, or some such, rather than a man in drag, and kept on climbing and turned to go to the next floor.

'Do you live here?' asked the old gent in German.

'*Jawohl*,' Tom replied softly, but with conviction.

'Strange goings on here,' the man murmured to himself, and went on down the stairs.

Tom climbed another flight. The stairs creaked a little. He saw lights under the two doors, left and right. There seemed to be two other flats at the rear, doors anyway. The apartment Tom was interested in would be on the left, but Tom listened briefly at the door on the right, heard what he thought was a television voice, then went to the left hand door. He heard a very low hum of voices, at least two voices. Tom pulled Peter's gun out. He had pressed the minute-light on this floor, and it had perhaps thirty seconds of light left. The door appeared to have a single lock, but it looked strong enough. What the hell to do next? Tom was not sure, but he knew his best ploy was to surprise them, get them off balance.

Tom pointed his gun at the lock, just as the light went out. Then Tom knocked loudly on the door with the knuckles of his left hand, causing his handbag to slide down to his left elbow.

There was a sudden silence behind the door. Then after a few seconds, a man's voice asked in German, 'Who is it?'

'*Polizei!*' Tom yelled in a firm, no-nonsense voice. '*O-pen!*' he added in German.

Tom heard a scurrying, a scrape of chair legs, which however sounded not yet panicky. He again heard low voices. '*Polizei, öffnet!*' he said, and banged on the door with the side of his fist. '*Ihr seid umringt!*'

Were they even now getting out via some window? Tom took the precaution of stepping to the right of the door, in case they fired through the door, but his left hand rested on the door lock, just under the knob, so he knew where it was.

The minute-light went out.

Then Tom stepped in front of the door and set the muzzle of the gun at the crack between metal and wood and fired. The gun bounced back in his hand, but he kept his grip on it, and at the same time he gave the door a push with his shoulder. The door did not yield completely: it appeared to have a chain. Tom wasn't sure. Tom yelled again, '*Open!*' in a voice that might terrorize even the people on the same floor behind their closed doors, and Tom hoped they stayed there, but now one door opened slightly behind him, Tom saw from a glance over his shoulder. Tom didn't care about the door behind him. He heard someone opening the door in front of him. They might be giving up, Tom thought.

The young blond man in the blue shirt had opened the door, the light from behind him fell on Tom. The man started with surprise, and reached for his back pocket. Tom had his gun pointed at the blue shirt front. Tom took a step into the room.

'Surrounded!' Tom repeated in German. 'Get out over the *roof!* You are not going to get out the door *below!* – Where is the boy? Is he here?'

The man in the tan jacket – open-mouthed in the middle of the room – made an impatient gesture, and said something to a third man, a sturdy type with brown hair, shirt-sleeves rolled up. The blue shirt had kicked the shattered door shut – it would not shut and hung partly open – and then had run into a room on Tom's left, where the front window would be. There was a big oval table in the room where Tom stood. Someone had turned out a ceiling light, which left one standing lamp's light on.

All was confusion for a few seconds, and Tom even thought of fleeing while he could. *They* might flee and plug him on the way. Had he made a mistake in not having Peter get the police, complete with sirens below? Tom yelled suddenly in English:

'Get out while you *can!*'

The blue shirt, after quick words with the man in shirt-sleeves, handed his gun to the tan jacket, and went into a room on Tom's right. Tom at once heard a thud from there, as if a suitcase had fallen.

Tom was afraid to look for the boy, as long as he had his own gun focused on the man in the tan jacket – for what Tom's gun was worth, because the tan jacket also had a gun in his hand. Tom heard a voice behind him ask in German:

'What's going on *here*?'

Tom glanced behind him. That had come from a curious neighbour in the hall – so it seemed – a man in house slippers and with wide-eyed fear in his face, ready to duck back into his apartment.

'Get away from here!' yelled the man in the tan jacket.

The shirt-sleeved man, who had been in the front room, hurried into the room where Tom was, and Tom was aware of the neighbour fading away behind him.

'Okay, *schnell*!' said the shirt-sleeved man, grabbing a jacket that had been over a chair by the oval table. He put the jacket on, and his free hand for an instant pointed upward. He ran across the room towards the door on Tom's right, and collided with the man in the blue shirt who was coming through the door with a suitcase.

Had they really seen something on the street, Tom wondered, cops already, due to the shot he had fired? Not likely! Past him now ran the man in the blue shirt with the suitcase, and then the man in the tan jacket. They were taking the stairs to the roof, Tom saw, and either the roof door was open by prearrangement, or they had the key. Tom knew there were no fire escapes in such houses, only central courts for fire engines, and roof exits. The man in the ordinary jacket now dashed past Tom, carrying what looked like a brown briefcase. He went up the stairs, slipping, recovering. He had run into Tom in his dash and nearly knocked him down. Tom now closed the door as well as he could. A big splinter of old wood made closing impossible.

Tom went into the room on the right. He still held Peter's gun pointed forward, as if at an enemy.

This room was a kitchen. On the floor lay Frank with a towel tied to cover his mouth, hands behind his back, ankles tied, on a blanket. But the boy moved, rubbed his face against the blanket as if in an effort to get the towel off.

'He-ey, *Frank*!' Tom knelt by the boy and pushed the tied dish towel down over Frank's chin to his neck.

The boy drooled, bleary with drugs or sleeping pills, Tom supposed, unable to focus his eyes.

'F'God's sake!' Tom murmured, and looked around for a knife. He found one in a drawer of the kitchen table, but it felt so dull to his thumb, he seized a bread knife from the drainboard. There were a couple of empty Coca-Cola tins on the drainboard. 'Have you loose in a minute, Frank,' Tom said, and began sawing away at the rope around Frank's wrists. The rope was strong and half an inch in diameter, but the knot looked much too tight to try to untie. During this sawing, Tom listened for another entry at the apartment door.

The boy spat, or tried to, on to the blanket. Tom slapped him nervously on the cheek.

'Wake up! It's *Tom*! We're leaving in a minute!' Tom wished there were time for him to make some instant coffee, even with cool water from the sink, but Tom did not dare take the time even to look for instant coffee. He attacked the ankle ropes now, sawed half the wrong loop first, and cursed. Finally he got the rope off, and hauled the boy up. 'Can you walk, Frank?' Tom had lost one high-heeled pump, and he kicked off the other. Better to be barefoot under the circumstances.

'T-to-um?' said the boy, looking one hundred per cent drunk.

'Here we go, boy!' Tom swung one of Frank's arms around his neck, and they started in the direction of the apartment door, Tom hoping that some movement might wake the boy up a little. As they struggled towards the door, Tom looked around in the carpetless living room for anything the men might have left, a notebook, a scrap of paper, but he saw nothing like that. Evidently they had been neat and efficient, with all their gear gathered in one place. Tom saw only what looked like a dirty shirt that had been dropped in a corner. He saw that he had still, somehow, the handbag on his left arm, and remembered sticking the gun back into it, and shoving the handbag on his arm, before lifting Frank. In the hall, three neighbours confronted him, two men and one woman, astounded, scared.

'*Alles geht gut!*' Tom said, realizing that he sounded mad and shrill, and the three did fall back slightly as Tom made for the stairs.

'Is that a woman?' one of the men asked.

We have telephoned the *police*!' the woman said menacingly.

'All is in order!' Tom replied. It sounded so good in German.

'*Drugged* the boy is!' said one of the men. 'Who *are* these animals?'

But Tom and Frank continued down the stairs, Tom supporting nearly all of the boy's weight, and suddenly they were out the front door – having passed only two slightly opened apartment doors with curious eyes peering out. Tom nearly fell going down the stone front steps, as there was no wall to lean against.

'*Sacred holy spirits!*' This came from one of a pair of young men walking on the pavement, and they laughed loudly. 'May we help you, *gnädige Frau?*' This was exaggerated politeness.

'Yes, thank you, we need a taxi,' Tom replied in German.

'That we can easily see! Ha-ha! A taxi, *meine Dame!* At once!'

'Never did a lady need a taxi *more!*' the other contributed.

With the aid of these two, Tom and Frank got to the next corner without much difficulty, the two young men guffawing at Tom's bare feet, and asking such questions as, 'What have you two been *doing?*' But the two stood by, and one of the young men went out into the street and energetically tried to hail a taxi. Tom glanced up at a street signpost and saw that the street he had just walked through, where the kidnappers' apartment was, was called Binger Strasse. Tom now heard police sirens. But a taxi had been found! It slid up. Tom got into the taxi first and pulled the boy after him, much helped by the cheerful young men.

'Happy trip!' one yelled, closing the door.

'*Niebuhrstrasse, bitte,*' Tom said to the driver, who gave Tom a look somewhat longer than necessary, then put his meter on and started off.

Tom opened a window. 'Breathe,' he said to Frank, and squeezed his hand to try to waken him further, not giving a damn what the driver thought. Tom snatched off his wig.

'Good party?' asked the driver, looking straight ahead.

'*Oo-oh, ja,*' Tom groaned, as if it had been a hell of a good party.

Niebuhrstrasse, thank God! Tom began groping for money. Out came a ten-mark note at once, ample as the fare was only seven. The driver wanted to give him change, but Tom told him he could keep it. Now Frank seemed slightly more awake, though still weak-kneed. Tom held his arm firmly and pressed Eric's bell. This time he had not Eric's key with him, but Tom thought surely Eric would be in, because of the money in his apartment, and then the blessed buzzer sounded, and Tom pushed the door open.

Peter came, lanky and swift, down the stairs. 'Tom!' he whispered. Then 'Oh oh – *Oh!*' at the sight of the boy.

Frank was now trying to hold his head up, and it wobbled as if his neck were broken. Tom felt like laughing – from nerves and hysteria – and bit his underlip as he and Peter got the boy into the elevator.

Eric had his door open slightly, and opened it wider when he saw them. '*Mein Gott!*' said Eric.

Tom still had the wig in his hand. He dropped this and the handbag on Eric's floor, and he and Peter got Frank seated on the horsehair sofa. Peter went off for a wet towel, Eric to fetch a cup of coffee.

'I don't know *what* they've been giving him,' Tom said. 'And I've lost Max's shoes –'

Peter smiled nervously, and stared at the boy as Tom wiped his face. Eric was ready with the coffee.

'Cool but good for you – coffee,' Eric said to Frank in a gentle voice. 'My name is Eric. Friend of Tom's. Don't be afraid.' Eric said over his shoulder to Peter, '*Mein Gott*, is he *out*!'

But Tom could see that the boy was looking better, sipping a bit of coffee, though still in no condition to hold the cup for himself.

'Hunger?' Peter asked the boy.

'No, no, he might choke,' said Eric. 'This coffee has sugar in it. Good for him.'

Frank smiled at all of them, like a drunken child, and smiled especially at Tom. Tom, dry in the mouth, had taken a cold Pilsener Urquell from Eric's fridge.

'What happened, Tom?' Eric asked. 'You went *in* their *house*? Peter said so.'

'I shot the lock off. But nobody was hurt. They scared – got scared.' Tom felt suddenly exhausted. 'Dying for a wash,' he murmured, and went off to the bathroom. He showered under hot water, then cool. His dressing gown hung luckily on the back of the bathroom door. Tom folded his gown and slip neatly to return to Max.

When Tom, went back to the living room, Frank was eating a bit of something Peter was holding for him: buttered bread.

'Ulrich – is one,' said Frank. 'And Bobo ...' Something else he said was unintelligible.

'I asked him their names!' Peter said to Tom.

'Tomorrow–' said Eric. 'He'll remember tomorrow.'

Tom went to see if the chain was on Eric's door, and it was.

Peter was smiling at Tom, looking happy. 'It's marvellous! – Where did they go to? They ran out?'

'I think they took to the roofs,' Tom said.

'Three of them.' Peter spoke in a tone of awe. 'Maybe your drag scared them.'

Tom smiled, too tired to talk. Or he might have been able to talk about anything else but what he had just been through. Tom laughed suddenly. 'You should've been at the Hump tonight, Eric!'

'I must go,' said Peter, hovering, not really wanting to go.

'Oh, your gun, Peter, and the torch, while I think of it!' Tom got the gun from the handbag, the torch from the closet. 'Many, many thanks! Three shots fired, three shots left.'

Peter pocketed his gun, smiling. 'Good night, sleep well,' he said in a soft voice, and went out.

Eric said good night to him, and replaced the chain on the door. 'Now let's get this bed open, don't you think so, Tom?'

'Yes. Come on, Frank old boy.' Tom smiled at the sight of Frank sitting with an elbow on an arm of the sofa, viewing them with a silly smile and half-open eyes, like a sleepy spectator in a theatre. Tom hauled the boy up and sat him in an armchair.

Then he and Eric got the sofa undone, the sheets on.

'Frank can sleep with me,' Tom said. 'Neither of us is going to know *where* we are.' Tom started undressing Frank, who gave him some cooperation but not much. Then Tom fetched a big glass of water. He meant to encourage Frank to drink all he could.

'Tom, should you not telephone Paris?' Eric asked. 'To say the boy is all right? Just suppose that gang tries something else with Paris!'

Eric was right, but the thought of ringing Paris bored him. 'I'll do it.' He got Frank on to his back in bed, and pulled the sheet up to his neck, and also drew a light blanket over him. Then he dialled the Hôtel Lutetia, whose number he had to make an effort to recall, but he got it right.

Eric lingered.

And Thurlow answered sleepily.

'Hello, this is Tom. Everything is all right here . . . Yes, that's what I mean . . . Quite all right, but sleepy. Tranquillizers . . . I don't care to go into details tonight . . . No, I'll explain that later. It's untouched. . . . *Yes* . . . Not before noon, Mr Thurlow, we are very tired here.' Tom hung up as Thurlow was saying something else. 'Asking also about the money,' Tom said to Eric, and laughed.

Eric laughed too. 'The suitcase is in my bedroom closet! – Good night, Tom.'

SIXTEEN

For the second time in Eric's apartment, Tom awakened to the cosy hum of the coffee-grinder. This morning he was happier. Frank lay face down, asleep and breathing. Tom had yielded to an impulse to check if he was breathing by looking at his ribs. Tom put on his dressing gown and went in to see Eric.

'Now tell me more about last night,' Eric said. 'One shot –'

'Yes, Eric. Only one. At the door lock.'

Eric was putting various kinds of bread, rolls, and jams on a tray – extra festive in Frank's honour, perhaps. 'We'll let the boy sleep, of course. Isn't he a nice-looking boy!'

Tom smiled. 'You think so? Yes. Rather handsome and unaware of it. That's always attractive.'

They sat on Eric's smaller sofa in the living room, which had a coffee table in front of it. Tom narrated the evening's events, even to Max and Rollo standing by him in the Hump, and said that the two who had been looking for Joey finally left, disappointed.

'They sound amateurish – to let you follow them,' Eric said.

'Evidently. They looked young, in their twenties.'

'And the neighbours there in Binger Strasse. Did they recognize the boy, do you think?'

'Doubt it.' He and Eric were keeping their voices low, though Frank showed no sign of waking. 'What can the neighbours do now? They should be more familiar with the kidnappers' faces, since they were going in and out of the house. One of them said she'd called the police. I think she did. Anyway the police'll surely look the apartment over, get a lot of fingerprints if they take the trouble. But do the neighbours know what was going *on*? – The police will find Max's pumps there. That'll throw them off!' Tom was feeling much better with Eric's strong coffee. 'I'd like to get the boy out of Berlin as soon as possible – and get myself out too. I'd like to take off for Paris this afternoon, but I don't think the boy's up to it.'

Eric looked at the bed, then back at Tom. 'I shall miss you,' he said, sighing. 'Berlin can be dull. Maybe you don't think so.'

'Really? – There is one chore today, Eric, returning the money to the banks here. Can't we get messengers for that? Maybe one messenger can do it all? I certainly don't want to do it.'

'I'm sure, yes. We shall telephone.' Eric suddenly bubbled with laughter and looked rather Chinese in his shiny black dressing gown. 'I am thinking of all that money here, and that *boob* in Paris is there doing nothing!'

'No, he is collecting his fee,' said Tom.

'Imagine,' Eric went on, 'the boob in drag! I bet he could not have done it! I wish I had been at the Hump last night. I would have taken polaroids of you with Max and Rollo!'

'Please return Max's drag with my thanks. Oh – and I must get that Italian's gun out of that suitcase. No need for the bank messenger to see that. May I?' Tom motioned towards Eric's bedroom.

'Of course! Back of my closet. You will find it.'

Tom got the suitcase from the depths of Eric's closet, carried it into the living room, and unzipped its top. The longish muzzle of the gun pointed right at him, because its handle had fallen between a manilla envelope and the side of the suitcase.

'Something missing?' Eric said.

'No, no.' Tom took the gun out carefully, and made sure the safety was on. 'I'll make someone a present of this. I doubt if I could fly out of Berlin with it. Would you like it, Eric?'

'Ach, the guns of yesterday! Most welcome, Tom. Not easy to get here, guns, even flick-knives beyond a certain length. Very strict regulations here.'

'House present,' Tom said, handing the gun to Eric.

'I do thank you, Tom.' Eric disappeared with it into his bedroom.

Now Frank stirred, and lay on his back. 'Is-no-*no*.' He said it in a reasoning tone of voice.

Tom watched the boy's frown tighten.

'To g'up, you said, I dunno so – *stop*!' The boy arched his back.

Tom shook his shoulder. 'Hello, it's Tom. You're okay, Frank.'

Frank opened his eyes, frowned again, and pushed himself nearly to a sitting position. 'Wow!' He shook his head, and smiled fuzzily. 'Tom.'

'Coffee.' Tom poured a cup for him.

Frank looked all around him, at walls and ceiling. 'I – How did we get here?'

Tom didn't answer. He brought the coffee and held it while the boy had a sip.

'Is this an hotel room?'

'No, Eric Lanz's house. Remember the man you had to hide from at my house? A week or so ago?'

'Yes . . . Sure.'

'His apartment. Have some more coffee. Got a headache?'

'No . . . Is this Berlin?'

'Yes. Apartment house. Third floor . . . I think we ought to leave Berlin today if you feel up to it. Maybe this afternoon. Back to Paris.' Tom brought a plate of bread and butter and jam. 'What were they giving you there? Sleeping pills? Injections?'

'Pills. They put them in cokes – made me drink it. In the car they gave me a needle – in my thigh.' Frank spoke slowly.

In Grunewald. That sounded a little more professional. The boy was able to take a bite of toast and chew it, Tom was glad to see. 'They feed you anything?'

Frank tried to shrug. 'I threw up a couple of times. And they – w-would not let me go to the john often enough. Think I wet my trousers – awful! My clothes –' The boy looked around, frowning, as if these unmentionable items might be in sight. '*That* I –'

'No importance, Frank, really.' Eric was coming back, and Tom said, 'Eric, meet Frank. He's a bit more awake now.'

Frank was covered to the waist by the sheet, but he pulled the sheet higher. His eyelids still sagged. 'Good morning, sir.'

'I am delighted to meet you,' said Eric. 'You are feeling better?'

'Yes, thank you.' Frank was now looking at the horsehair edge of his bed, which the sheet did not cover, in apparent wonderment. 'Your house – Tom told me. Thank you.'

Tom went into Eric's bedroom, where Frank's brown suitcase was, and took Frank's pyjamas from it. He brought them in to Frank and tossed them on the bed. 'So you can walk around,' Tom said. 'Your suitcase is here, Frank,'so nothing's lost. I'd love to take him for a walk in the fresh air, but I don't think it's advisable,' Tom said to Eric. 'The next thing really is to ring up one of those banks. The ADCA Bank or the Disconto. The Disconto sounds bigger, doesn't it?'

'Banks?' asked Frank, pulling pyjama pants on under the sheet. 'Ransom money?' But his voice was still sleepy, and he sounded un-concerned.

'Your money,' said Tom. 'What do you think you're worth, Frank? Guess.' Tom was trying to wake the boy up by talking to him. Now he looked in his wallet for the three receipts he had, which would also have the telephone numbers of the banks.

'Ransom money – Who has it?' Frank asked.

'I have it. It's going back to your family. Tell you about that later, not now.'

'I know there was a date,' Frank said, drawing on his pyjama jacket. 'One was talking in English on the 'phone. Then they went out – once – all except one.' Frank's speech was still slow, but he sounded sure of his statements.

Eric reached for a black cigarette from a silver bowl on his coffee table.

'You know –' Frank's eyes began to swim again. 'I was always in the kitchen there – but I think that's right.'

Tom poured more coffee for Frank. 'Drink that.'

Eric was now on the telephone, asking to speak with the Herr Direktor. Tom heard him give his own address in regard to money collected yesterday by Thomas Ripley. Eric also mentioned the two other banks. Tom felt relieved. Eric was handling it well.

'A messenger will come before noon,' Eric said to Tom. 'They have got the Swiss account number and they can telex it back.'

'Excellent. I thank you, Eric.' Tom watched Frank crawl out of bed.

Frank looked at the open suitcase on the floor with the fat manilla envelopes inside. 'Is that it?'

'Yes.' Tom took some clothes and started for the bathroom to dress. Glancing behind him, he saw Frank edging around the suitcase as if it were a poisonous snake. Under the shower, Tom remembered that he had promised to ring Thurlow around noon. Maybe Frank would also like to talk with his brother.

When Tom came back to the living room, he told Frank that he had to ring Paris, and that he had rung last night and the detective Thurlow knew he was safe. Frank showed little interest in Paris. 'Wouldn't you like to talk with Johnny?'

'Well, Johnny – yes.' Frank was still barefoot and walking around, which Tom thought was good for him.

Tom dialled the Lutetia number. He got Thurlow, and said, 'Yes, the boy's right here. Would you like to speak with him?'

Frank frowned and shook his head, but Tom pressed the telephone on him.

'Give him some proof,' Tom said, smiling. Tom whispered, 'Do *not* mention Eric's name.'

'Hello? ... Yes, I'm fine ... Yes, sure, Berlin ... *Tom*,' Frank said. 'Tom got me last night ... I don't know, really ... Yes, it's *here*.'

Eric pointed to the little receiver for Tom's use, but Tom didn't want to listen in.

'I'm sure not,' Frank said. 'Why should Tom want any of it, it's going –'

Longish listening now on Frank's part. 'How do you expect me to talk about something like that over the 'phone?' Frank said with some irritation. 'I don't know, I just don't know ... Okay, fine.' Then Frank's expression softened, and he said, 'Hi, Johnny ... Sure, I'm okay, I just said so ... Oh, I dunno, I just woke up. But quit worrying. I haven't got even a broken bone or anything!' Now a long speech from Johnny, and Frank squirmed. 'Okay, okay, but – What do you mean?' Now the boy frowned. 'Not in a hurry!' he said mockingly. 'What you really mean – you really mean she's not coming and doesn't – doesn't care.'

Tom could hear Johnny's easy chuckle as he spoke from Paris.

'Well, at least she *telephoned*.' Frank's face looked paler. 'All right, all right, I see.' he said impatiently.

From where he stood, Tom heard Thurlow's voice come on, and then Tom picked up the little receiver.

'... when you're coming *here*. Something holding you there? – You there, Frank?'

'Why should I go to Paris?' Frank asked.

'Because your mother wants you home. We want you – safe.'

'I *am* safe.'

'Is – Tom Ripley trying to persuade you to stay on there?'

'Nobody is persuading me,' said Frank, shaping every word.

'I'd like to speak with Mr Ripley, if he's there, Frank.'

Frank grimly handed the telephone to Tom. 'That f—' He didn't get the second word out. Suddenly Frank had become an ordinary American boy, furious.

'Tom Ripley,' said Tom. He watched Frank walk into the hall, maybe in quest of the bathroom, which he found on the right.

'Mr Ripley, as you can understand, we want the boy safe and back in America, that's why I'm here. Can you tell us – I'm most grateful for what you've done, but I have to tell his mother a few facts, namely when the boy will be coming home. Or should I come to Berlin and get him?'

'No-o, I'll consult with Frank. He's just been held under unpleasant conditions for the last couple of days, you know. He's been given a lot of tranquillizers.'

'But he sounds pretty much all right.'

'He's not hurt.'

'And as for the German marks, Frank said –'

'Those will be returned to the bank or the banks today, Mr Thurlow.' Tom laughed a little. 'Fine subject in case your 'phone is being tapped.'

'Why should it be tapped?'

'Oh, because of your profession,' Tom said, as if his profession might be anything bizarre, even call-girl.

'Mrs Pierson was glad to hear that the marks are safe. But I can't just stay here in Paris while you or Frank or both of you make up your minds when Frank comes home. You can probably understand that, Mr Ripley.'

'Well – there are worse cities than Paris,' Tom said in a pleasant tone. 'Could I perhaps speak with Johnny?'

'Yes. Johnny?'

Johnny came on. 'We're very glad about Frank! Can't tell you!' Johnny sounded open and friendly, with an accent like Frank's but a deeper voice. 'Have the police got the gang or whoever it was?'

'No, no police involved.' Tom heard Thurlow trying to shush Johnny on the subject of police, or so it seemed.

'You mean, you got Frank all by yourself?'

'No – with a little help from my friends.'

'My mother's *so* happy! She was – uh –'

Dubious about him, Tom knew. 'Johnny, you said something to Frank about somebody 'phoning? From America?'

'Teresa. She was going to come over, but now she's not. I'm sure she's not, now that Frank's okay, but – I know she's sort of tied up with someone else, so I know she won't. She didn't say it to me, but I happen to know the fellow, I introduced them and – he told me before I left America.'

Now Tom understood. 'You told Frank that?'

'I thought the sooner he knew it the better. I know he's pretty hung up. I didn't tell him who the fellow was. I just said I know Teresa's got another interest.'

In that Tom saw a world of difference between Johnny and Frank. Easy come, easy go with Johnny, evidently. 'I see.' Tom didn't even feel like saying, what a pity you had to spill it just now. 'Well, Johnny, I'll sign off.' Tom heard faintly Thurlow asking to be put on again, or Tom thought so. 'Bye-bye,' Tom said, and hung up. '*Asses – both* of them!' Tom shouted.

But no one heard him. Frank was flat out asleep again on the bed, and Eric was somewhere else in the apartment.

The bank messenger might arrive at any minute.

When Eric came into the living room, Tom said, 'How about lunch at Kempinski? Are you free for lunch, Eric?' Tom had a desire to see Frank eat a steak or a big portion of Wiener Schnitzl and get some colour back in his face.

'I am, yes.' Eric was dressed now.

The doorbell rang. The bank messenger.

Eric pressed his release button in the kitchen.

Tom shook Frank's shoulder. 'Frank, old boy – up! Take my dressing gown.' Tom snatched it from his suitcase. 'Go into Eric's bedroom, because we have to see someone here for a couple of minutes.'

Frank did as Tom told him. Tom spread the blanket over the sheets, so the bed would look a bit neater.

The bank messenger, a short, bulky man in a business suit, was accompanied by a taller guard of some kind in uniform. The messenger presented his credentials, and said he had a car waiting downstairs with a driver, but he was in no hurry. He carried two big briefcases. Tom didn't feel like looking at the credentials, so Eric examined them. Tom did watch the first few seconds of the counting. One envelope had been sealed and still was. The paper-banded bundles of DM had not been touched in the other envelopes, but it would have been possible to slip a thousand-mark note from any or several of the bundles. Eric watched.

'Can I leave this to you, Eric?' Tom asked.

'*Aber sicherlich*, Tom! But you must sign something, you know?' Eric and the messenger were standing at the sideboard, envelopes separated, money stacks separated.

'Back in a couple of minutes.' Tom went off to speak with Frank.

Frank was in Eric's bedroom, barefoot, holding a damp towel against his forehead. 'I felt faint for a minute just now. Funny –'

'We're going out to lunch soon. We'll have a good lunch and cheer up, all right, Frank? – Want a cool shower?'

'Sure.'

Tom went into the bathroom and adjusted the shower for him. 'Don't slip,' Tom said.

'What're they doing in there?'

'Counting dough. I'll bring you some clothes.' Tom went back into the living room, found a pair of blue cotton trousers in Frank's suitcase, a polo neck sweater, and he took a pair of his own shorts, not finding any of Frank's. Tom knocked on the bathroom door which was not quite closed.

The boy was drying himself with a big towel.

'How do you feel about Paris? Want to go back today? Tonight?'

'No.'

Tom noticed that the boy's eyes were shiny with tears under a very determined and grown-up frown. 'I know what Johnny said to you – about Teresa.'

'Well, that's not *everything*,' Frank said, hurled the towel at the side of the tub, and at once picked it up and hung it properly on a rod. He took the shorts Tom was holding out to him and turned his back as he put them on. 'I don't want to go back just yet, I just don't!' Frank's eyes flashed with anger as he looked back at Tom.

Tom knew: it would be two defeats, the loss of Teresa, and being recaptured. Maybe after lunch, Tom thought, Frank would calm down, see things differently. However, Tom knew that Teresa *was* everything.

'Tom!' Eric called.

Tom had to sign. Tom did look over the receipt. The three banks were listed, the sums due each. The bank messenger was now on Eric's telephone, and Tom heard him say a couple of times that things were *in Ordnung*. Tom signed. The name Pierson still did not appear, only the Swiss Bank Corporation number. Much handshaking upon leaving, and Eric accompanied the two men to the elevator.

Frank came into the living room, dressed but for shoes, and Eric returned, beaming with relief, wiping his forehead with a pocket handkerchief.

'My apartment deserves – a Gedenktafel! How do you call it?'

'A plaque?' said Tom. 'As I was saying, lunch at Kempinski. Do we have to make a reservation?'

'It would be wiser. I shall do it. Three.' Eric went to his telephone.

'Unless we can reach Max and Rollo. It'd be nice to invite them. Or are they – working?'

'Oh!' Eric chuckled. 'Rollo's hardly awake by now. He likes to stay up very late, till seven or eight in the morning. Then Max is free-lance – a hairdresser when certain places need him. I never can reach them except sometimes around six in the evening.'

He would send them a present from France, Tom thought, maybe a couple of interesting wigs, when he got their address from Eric. Eric was now making the reservation for a quarter to one.

They went in Eric's car. Tom had applied a flesh-coloured salve – for cuts and abrasions, the tube said – from Eric's medicine cabinet to Frank's famous cheek mole. Somewhere Frank had lost Heloise's pancake from his back pocket, which did not surprise Tom.

'I want you to eat, my friend,' Tom said to Frank at the table, starting to read the huge à la carte menu. 'I know you like smoked salmon.'

'Ah, I shall have my favourite!' said Eric. 'There is a liver dish here, Tom – out of this world!'

The restaurant had high ceilings, gilt and green scrolls on its white walls, elegant tablecloths, and uniformed waiters who put on a grand air. A grill – another part of the restaurant – served people who were not quite properly attired, Tom had noticed while they were waiting to be shown to their table. This had meant a pair of men in blue jeans, though with neat enough sweaters and jackets, who had been told in German, somehow politely, that the grill was *that* way.

Frank did eat, aided by a couple of Tom's jokes, dredged up, because he didn't feel like telling jokes. He knew Frank was under a black cloud of Teresa, and he wondered if Frank suspected or knew definitely who Teresa's new interest was? Tom could not possibly ask. Tom knew only that Frank had begun that painful process known as turning loose, turning loose emotionally of a moral support, of a mad ideal, of what had been to him embodied, and still was, in the only girl in the world.

'Chocolate cake, Frank?' Tom suggested, and refilled Frank's glass of white wine. It was their second bottle.

'That is good here and so is the Strudel,' Eric said. 'Tom, a meal to remember!' Eric wiped his lips carefully. 'A morning to remember too, no? Ha-ha?'

They were in one of the little alcoves against the restaurant wall, nothing so primitive as a booth, rather a romantic curve giving semi-privacy, yet enabling them to see what they wished of the other patrons. Tom had seen no one paying attention to them. And Tom suddenly realized, pleasantly, that Frank would be leaving Berlin under his false passport as Benjamin Andrews. The passport was in Frank's suitcase at Eric's.

'When shall I next see you, Tom?' Eric asked.

Tom lit a Roth-Haendle. 'Next time you have a little thing for Belle Ombre? And I don't mean a house present.'

Eric chuckled, pink with food and wine now. 'That reminds me, I have a three o'clock date. Excuse me for this rudeness.' He looked at his wristwatch. 'Only a quarter past two. I am fine.'

'We can take a taxi back. Leave you free.'

'No, no, it is on the way, my house. Easy.' Eric poked with his tongue at something in a tooth, and looked speculatively at Frank.

Frank had eaten nearly all of his chocolate cake, and was pensively turning the stem of his wine glass.

Eric lifted his eyebrows at Tom. Tom said nothing. Tom got the bill and paid. They walked the one street to Eric's car in bright sunlight. Tom smiled and patted Frank impulsively on the back. But what could he say? He wanted to say, 'Isn't this better than the floor of a kitchen?' But Tom couldn't. Eric was the type to come out with it, but Eric didn't. Tom would have liked a longer walk, but he did not feel a hundred per cent safe, or unnoticed, walking with Frank Pierson, so they both got into Eric's car. Tom had Eric's housekeys, and Eric dropped them off at a corner.

Tom approached Eric's house carefully, on the watch for loiterers, but saw none. The downstairs hall was empty. The boy was silent.

In the apartment, Tom took off his jacket and opened the window for fresh air. 'About Paris,' Tom began.

Frank suddenly plunged his face into his hands. He was seated on the small sofa by the coffee table, elbows on his spread knees.

'Never mind,' Tom said, embarrassed for the boy. 'Get it out.' Tom knew it wouldn't last long.

After a few seconds, the boy snatched his hands down, stood up and said, 'Sorry.' He stuffed his hands in his pockets.

Tom strolled into the bathroom, and brushed his teeth for a good two minutes. Then he went back into the living room with a calm air. 'You don't want to go to Paris, I know. What about Hamburg?'

'Anywhere!' Frank's eyes had the intensity of madness or hysteria.

Tom looked down on the floor and blinked. 'You don't just say "anywhere" like a madman, Frank. I know – I understand about Teresa. It's a –' what was the right word? '– a letdown.'

Frank stood stiff as a statue, as if defying Tom to say more. *Still you'll have to face your family at some point,* Tom thought of saying. But wouldn't that be unsympathetic, just now? Wouldn't it be a good idea to see Reeves? Have a change of atmosphere? Tom needed it, anyway. 'I find Berlin a bit claustrophobic. I feel like seeing Reeves in Hamburg. Didn't I mention him in France? Friend of mine.' Tom made an effort to sound cheerful.

The boy looked more alert, polite again. 'Yes, I think you did. You said he was a friend of Eric's.'

'True. I'm –' Tom hesitated, looking at the boy who, with hands still in pockets, stared back at him. Tom could easily put the boy on a plane to Paris – insist – and say goodbye to him. But Tom had the feeling the boy would lose himself again, in Paris, as soon as he got off the plane. He wouldn't go to the Hôtel Lutetia. 'I'll try Reeves,' Tom said, and moved towards the telephone. Just then it rang. Tom decided to answer it.

'Hello, Tom, this is Max.'

'Max! How are you? I have your wig and your drag here – safe!'

'I wanted to telephone this morning and I was – stuck, *ja*? Not home was I. Then by Eric an hour ago nobody was home. So last night? The boy?'

'He's here. He's okay.'

'You got him? You are not hurt, nobody is hurt?'

'Nobody,' Tom blinked away a sudden vision of the Italian type with the smashed head on the ground in Lübars.

'Rollo thought last night you looked wonderful. I was almost jealous. Ha! – Is Eric there? I have a message.'

'Not here because he has a three o'clock date. Can I take a message?'

Max said no, he would call back.

Tom then consulted the telephone book for the Hamburg code, and dialled Reeves' number.

''Allo?' said a female voice.

This was Reeves' *Putzfrau* and part-time housekeeper, Tom supposed, a figure more portly than Mme Annette, but equally dedicated. 'Hello – Gaby?'

'*Ja-a?*'

'This is Tom Ripley. How are you, Gaby? – Is Herr Minot there?'

'*Nein, aber er* – I *hear* something,' she went on in German. 'One minute.' A pause, then Gaby came back and said, 'He comes in just now!'

'Hello, *Tom!*' said Reeves, breathless.

'I'm in Berlin.'

'*Berlin!* Can you come and see me? What're you doing in Berlin?' Reeves' voice sounded gravelly and naïve, as usual.

'Can't say now, but I was thinking of coming to see you – even tonight, if that's all right with you.'

'Of course, Tom. You've always got priority and I'm not even busy tonight.'

'I have a friend with me, an American. Could you possibly put us up for one night?' Tom knew Reeves had a guest room.

'Even two nights. When're you arriving? Got your plane tickets?'

'No, but I'll try for this evening. Seven, eight or nine. If you're in I won't ring you again, just turn up. I'll ring you if I can't make it. Okay?'

'Okay and I'm *very* pleased!'

Tom turned to Frank, smiling. 'That's settled. Reeves is glad to have us.'

Frank was sitting on the smaller sofa, smoking a cigarette, unusual for him. The boy stood up, and he seemed suddenly as tall as Tom. Had he grown in the last few days? That was possible. 'I'm sorry I was in the dumps today. I'll pull out.'

'Oh, sure you'll pull out.' The boy was trying to be polite. Maybe that was why he looked taller.

'I'm glad about Hamburg. I don't want to see that detective in Paris. Good *Christ*!' Frank whispered the last, but with venom. 'Why don't they both go home now?'

'Because they want to be sure you're coming home,' Tom said patiently.

Tom then telephoned Air France. He made two reservations for a take-off at 7.20 p.m. for Hamburg. Tom gave their names, Ripley and Andrews.

Eric arrived while Tom was on the telephone, and Tom told him their plans. 'Ah, Reeves! A nice idea!' Eric glanced at Frank, who was folding something away in his suitcase, and motioned for Tom to come into his bedroom.

'Max rang up,' Tom said as he followed Eric. 'Said he'd ring you back.'

'Thank you, Tom. Now this.' Eric closed his bedroom door, pulled a newspaper from under his arm, and showed the front page to Tom. 'I thought you should see this,' Eric said with one of his twitching smiles, more full of nerves than amusement. 'No clues, it seems – now.'

The front page of *Der Abend* had a two-column photograph of the Lübars shed with the Italian type just as Tom had seen him last, prone, head turned slightly to the left, and the left temple a darkened mass of blood, some of which had run down the face. Tom read quickly the five-line comment below. An as yet unidentified man wearing clothing made in Italy, underwear made in Germany, had been found dead early Wednesday in Lübars, his temple crushed by blows of a blunt instrument. Police were trying to identify him, and were making inquiries among residents of the region to find out if they had heard any disturbances.

'You understand it all?' asked Eric.

'Yes.' Tom had fired two shots into the air. Surely a resident was going to remark hearing two shots, even if the man had not been killed by a bullet. Some neighbour might describe a stranger with a suitcase. 'I don't like to look at this.' Tom folded the newspaper and put it on a writing table. He glanced at his watch.

'I can drive you to Tegel. Plenty of time,' said Eric. 'The boy really doesn't want to go home, does he?'

'No, and he had some bad news today about a girl he likes in America. The brother told him that she has a new boy friend. So there's that. If he were twenty, it might be easier for him.' Or would it? Frank's murder of his father was keeping him from going back home too.

SEVENTEEN

As the plane began its descent to Hamburg, Frank woke from a doze and caught between his knees a newspaper that had nearly slipped to the floor. Frank looked out of the window on his side, but they were still too high for anything but clouds to be visible.

Tom finished a cigarette covertly. The stewardesses bustled up and down the aisle, collecting last glasses and trays. Tom saw Frank lift the German newspaper from his lap and look at the picture of the dead man in Lübars. To Frank it would be just another newspaper photograph. Tom had not told Frank that his date with the kidnappers had been in Lübars, he had simply said that he stood the kidnappers up. 'Then you followed them?' Frank had asked. Tom had said no, he had got on their trail via the gay bar and the message passed to the kidnappers by Thurlow to ask for Joey there. Frank had been amused, full of awe at Tom's daring – maybe his courage too, Tom liked to think – in crashing in on the kidnappers single-handed. Tom had found nothing in this newspaper about any of the three kidnappers having been caught in the vicinity of Binger Strasse or anywhere else. Of course no one but Tom knew them as kidnappers. They might have criminal records and no fixed addresses, but that was about it.

Their passports were rather quickly glanced at and handed back, then they got their luggage and took a taxi.

Tom pointed out landmarks to Frank, what he could see in the gathering darkness, a church spire that he remembered, the first of the many filled-in canals or 'fleets' which had little bridges over them, then the Alsters. They got out in the upward sloping driveway leading to

Reeves' white apartment house, a large, formerly private house which had been partitioned to make several apartments. It was Tom's second or third visit to Reeves. Tom pressed a button downstairs, and Reeves at once let him in after Tom said his name into the speaker. Tom and Frank went up in the elevator, and Reeves was waiting outside his apartment door.

'Tom!' Reeves kept his voice low, because of at least one other apartment on the same floor. 'Come in, both of you!'

'This is – Ben,' said Tom, introducing Frank. 'Reeves Minot.'

Reeves said 'How do you do' to Frank, and closed his door behind them. As ever, Reeves' flat struck Tom as spacious and immaculately clean. Its white walls bore Impressionist and more recent paintings, nearly all in frames. Rows of low bookcases, containing mostly art books, bordered the walls. There were a couple of tall rubber plants and philodendrons. The two big windows on the Aussenalster's water had their yellow curtains drawn now. A table was set for three. Tom saw that the pinkish Derwatt (genuine) of a woman apparently dying in bed still hung over the fireplace.

'Changed the frame of that, didn't you?' asked Tom.

Reeves laughed. 'How observant you are, Tom! Frame got damaged somehow. Fell in that bombing, I think, and cracked. I prefer this beige frame. The other frame was too white. Look now, put your suitcases in here,' Reeves said, showing Tom the guest room. 'I hope they didn't give you anything to eat on the plane, because I have something for us. But now we must have a glass of cold wine or something and talk!'

Tom and Frank set their suitcases in the guest room which had a three-quarter bed with its side against the front wall. Jonathan Trevanny had slept here, Tom remembered.

'What did you say your friend's name was?' Reeves asked softly, but he did not bother to be out of the boy's hearing as he and Tom went back into the living room.

Tom knew from Reeves' smile that Reeves knew who the boy was. Tom nodded. 'Talk to you later. It was not –' Tom felt awkward, but why did he have to hide anything from Reeves? Frank was in a far corner of the living room now, looking at a painting. 'It was not in the papers, but the boy was just kidnapped in Berlin.'

'Ree-eally?' Reeves paused with the corkscrew in one hand, a wine bottle in the other. He had an unpleasant pink scar down his right cheek almost to the corner of his mouth. Now with his mouth open in surprise, the scar looked even longer.

'Last Sunday night,' Tom said. 'In Grunewald. You know, the big woods there.'

'Yes, I do. Kidnapped how?'

'I was with him, but we were separated for a couple of minutes and – Sit down, Frank. You're among friends.'

'Yes, sit down.' Reeves said in his hoarse-sounding voice, and drew the cork.

Frank's eyes caught Tom's, the boy nodded his head as if to indicate that Tom could tell the truth if he wished. 'Frank was released just last night. The men holding him gave him sedatives and I think he's still a bit drowsy,' Tom said.

'No, I hardly notice it now,' Frank said politely and firmly. He got up from the sofa he had just sat down on, and went to look more closely at the Derwatt over the fireplace. Frank shoved his hands in his back pockets and glanced at Tom with a quick smile. 'Good, yes, Tom?'

'Isn't it?' said Tom with satisfaction. He loved the dusty pinkness of it, suggesting an old lady's bedcover, or maybe her nightdress. The background was murky brown and dark grey. Was she dying or simply tired and bored with life? But the title was 'Dying Woman'.

'Woman or a man here?' Frank asked.

Tom had just been thinking that Edmund Banbury or Jeff Constant at the Buckmaster Gallery had probably given the picture its title – often Derwatt hadn't bothered with titles – and one could not really tell if the figure was male or female.

'"Dying Woman", it's called,' Reeves said to Frank. 'You like Derwatt?' he asked in a tone of pleased surprise.

'Frank says his father has one at home – in the States. One or two, Frank?' Tom asked.

'One. "The Rainbow".'

'Ah-hah,' said Reeves, as if he could see it before his eyes.

Frank drifted away towards a David Hockney.

'You delivered a ransom?' Reeves asked Tom.

Tom shook his head. 'No, had it and didn't deliver it.'

'How much?' Reeves smiled as he poured wine.

'Two million American.'

'Well, well. And now what?' Reeves nodded towards the boy who had his back to them.

'Oh, he's going back home. I thought if we could, Reeves, we'd stay tomorrow night also with you, and leave Friday for Paris. I don't want the boy to be recognized in an hotel, and another day's rest would do him good.'

'Certainly, Tom. No problem.' Reeves frowned. 'I don't quite understand. The police are still looking for him?'

Tom shrugged nervously. 'They were *before* the kidnapping, and I'm
assuming the detective in Paris has notified at least the French police
that the boy's been found.' Tom explained that there had been no police
anywhere informed of the kidnapping.

'You're supposed to take him where?'

'To the detective in Paris. He's employed by the family. Frank's
brother Johnny is there with the detective too. Thank you, Reeves.' Tom
took his glass.

Reeves carried another glass to Frank. Then Reeves went into his
kitchen, and Tom followed him. From his refrigerator, Reeves produced
a platter of sliced ham, cole slaw, and a variety of sliced sausages and
pickles. Reeves said it was Gaby's production. Gaby lived in the building
with some other people who employed her, and she had insisted on
coming in at seven this evening after her late shopping to 'arrange'
what she had bought for Reeves' guests. 'I'm lucky, she likes me,'
Reeves said. 'Finds my place more interesting than where she sleeps – in
spite of that damned bomb here. Well, she happened to be out at the
time it hit.'

The three sat down at the table, and talked of other things than
Frank, but it was still of Berlin. How was Eric Lanz? Who were his
friends? Had he a girl friend? A laugh from Reeves along with the
question. Had Reeves a girl friend, Tom wondered. Were Reeves and
Eric so lukewarm, girls and women just didn't matter? It was nice to
have a wife, Tom thought, as the wine began to warm him. Heloise had
once said to him that she liked him, or had she said she loved him,
because he let her be herself, and gave her room to breathe. Tom had
been gratified by her remark, though he had never thought about
giving Heloise *Lebensraum.*

Reeves was watching Frank. And Frank was looking extremely
sleepy.

They got Frank to bed by a little after eleven. Frank took the guest
room bed.

Then with another bottle of Piesporter Goldtröpfchen, Reeves and
Tom installed themselves on the living room sofa, and Tom narrated the
events of the last days, even the first days, when Frank Pierson,
working as a part-time gardener, had looked him up in Villeperce.
Reeves laughed at the drag bit in Berlin, and wanted every detail. Then
something dawned on Reeves, and he said:

'That Berlin picture then – in the papers today. They said Lübars, I remember.' Reeves leapt up to look for his newspaper, and found it on a book-shelf.

'That's it,' Tom said. 'I saw it in Berlin.' Tom felt sickish for a moment, and set his wine glass down. 'The Italian type that I mentioned.' Tom had told Reeves that he had only knocked the man out.

'No one saw you? You're sure? Getting away?'

'No. Shall we wait for tomorrow's news?'

'The boy knows?'

'I didn't tell him. Don't mention Lübars to him. Reeves, old pal, could I trouble you for some coffee?'

Tom went with Reeves into the kitchen, not wanting to sit by himself. It was not pleasant, the realization that he had killed a man, even though the Italian type was not the first. He saw Reeves glance at him. There was one thing he had not told Reeves, and was not going to tell him, which was that Frank had killed his father. Tom took a little comfort from the fact that though Reeves had read about Pierson Senior's death, and the question of suicide or accident, which had not been answered, Reeves had not thought to ask Tom if someone could have murdered Pierson Senior by pushing him over the cliff.

'What was it made the boy run away?' Reeves asked. 'Upset by his father's death? – Or maybe the girl? Her name's Teresa, you said?'

'No, I think the Teresa situation was all right when he left. He was writing to her from my house. It's only yesterday that he heard she has a new boy friend.'

Reeves chuckled in an avuncular way. 'The world is full of girls, even pretty ones. Certainly Hamburg is! Shall we try to distract him – take him to a club? You know?'

Tom said as lightly as he could, 'He's only sixteen. It's hit him pretty hard. The brother's a bit thick-skinned, or he wouldn't have blurted it out as he did – now.'

'You expect to meet the brother? And the detective?' Reeves laughed as if at the word detective, as he might laugh at anybody whose job it was presumably to try to track down crime in the world.

'I rather hope not,' Tom said, 'but I may have to put the boy right in their charge, because he's not keen to go home.' Tom was standing in the kitchen with his coffee. 'I'm getting sleepy, even though your coffee tastes great. I'm going to have another cup.'

'Won't bother your sleep?' Reeves asked hoarsely, but with the concern of a mother or a nurse.

'Not in my state. Tomorrow I'll take Frank around Hamburg. One of those boat rides around the Alster, you know? I'll try to cheer him up. Can you meet us for lunch, Reeves?'

'Thanks, Tom, but I have a date tomorrow. I can give you a key. I'll do it now.'

Tom walked out of the kitchen with his cup. 'How's business been?' Tom meant the fence business, and a little bit of legitimate talent-scouting among German painters, and some art-dealing, the latter activities being Reeves' front, at least.

'Oh –' Reeves put a ring of keys into Tom's hand, then cast an eye around his living room walls. 'That Hockney's – on loan, I might say. Really it's stolen. It's from Munich. I put it on the wall because I like it. After all, I'm very careful about the people I let *in* here. The Hockney's being collected very soon.'

Tom smiled. It struck him that Reeves led a delightful life in a most pleasant city. Something was always happening. Reeves never worried, he always bungled through even the very awkward moments, once for instance when he had been beaten up and tossed unconscious out of a moving car. Reeves hadn't suffered even a broken nose on that occasion, which had been in France, Tom remembered.

When Tom crept into bed that night, Frank didn't stir. The boy was face down with his arms around his pillow. Tom felt safe, safer than in Berlin. Reeves' flat had been bombed, maybe burgled, but it felt as snug as a little castle. He might ask Reeves what kind of protection he had, besides perhaps a burglar alarm. Did he have to pay off anybody? Had Reeves ever asked the police for extra protection, because of the valuable pictures he sometimes dealt with? Not very likely, Tom thought. But maybe it would be rude to inquire into Reeves' safety measures.

A gentle knock awakened Tom, and he opened his eyes and realized where he was. *'Herein!'*

Gaby came in, heavy and shy, talking in German, carrying a tray of coffee and rolls. 'Herr Tom . . . we were so glad to see you again after such a long time! How long has it been? . . .' She spoke softly because of Frank, still asleep. Gaby was in her fifties, with black straight hair done in a bun behind her head. Her cheeks were rather blotchily pink.

'I am so glad to be here, Gaby. And how have you been? – You can put it here, that is fine.' Tom meant on his lap. The tray had legs.

'Herr Reeves has gone out, but he says you have the keys.' She looked, smiling, at the sleeping boy. 'There is still more coffee in the kitchen.' Gaby spoke stolidly, giving the facts, and only her dark eyes

showed liveliness and a childlike curiosity. 'I am here another hour –
not quite – in case you want something.'

'Thank you, Gaby.' Tom wakened himself further with coffee and a
cigarette, then went off to take a shower and shave.

When he came back into the guest room, he saw Frank standing with
one bare foot on the sill of the window which he had opened. Tom had
the feeling the boy was about to jump. 'Frank?' The boy hadn't heard
him come in.

'Great view, isn't it?' said Frank, both feet on the floor now.

Had the boy shuddered, or had Tom imagined it? Tom moved to the
window and looked out at excursion boats ploughing towards the left
on the Alster's blue water, at a half dozen little sailboats scooting about,
at people strolling on the quay beside the water. Bright pennants flew
everywhere, and the sun shone. It was like a Dufy, only German, Tom
thought. 'You weren't thinking of jumping out just now, were you?'
Tom asked as if he were joking. 'Only a few storeys here. Not very
satisfying.'

'Jumping?' Frank shook his head quickly, and took a step back from
Tom, as if he were shy about standing so close to him. 'Certainly not . . .
Okay if I wash?'

'Go ahead. Reeves is out but Gaby's here, the housekeeper. Just say
"Guten Morgen" to her. She's very friendly.' Tom watched the boy take
his trousers and go across the hall. He thought perhaps he had been
wrong to be anxious. Frank had a purposeful air this morning, as if the
pills had worn off.

By mid-morning, they were at St Pauli. They had taken a look at the
sex-shop windows in the Reeperbahn, at the garish fronts of the non-
stop blue-film cinemas, at shop windows with astounding underwear
for all sexes. Rock music poured from somewhere, and even at this hour
there were customers browsing and buying. Tom found himself blinking,
maybe with amazement, maybe at the glaring colours that seemed
circus-like in the clear sunlight. Tom realized that he had a prudish side,
maybe due to his childhood in Boston, Massachusetts. Frank looked
cool, but then he would make an effort to look cool, confronted by
dildoes and vibrators with price tags.

'Place must be hopping at night,' Frank remarked.

'Doing all right now,' Tom said, seeing two girls approaching them
with intent. 'Let's hop a streetcar – or taxi. Let's go to the zoo, that's
always fun.'

Frank laughed. 'The zoo again!'

'Well, I like zoos. Wait till you see this zoo.' Tom saw a taxi.

The two girls, one of whom looked in her teens and rather attractively unmade-up, seemed to think the taxi might be for all four of them, but Tom waved them away with a polite smile and shook his head.

Tom bought a newspaper at the kiosk in front of the Tierpark entrance, and took a minute to glance at it. He went through it a second time, looking now for a small item that might have to do with the kidnappers in Berlin, or Frank Pierson. His second search was not thorough, but he didn't see anything. This was *Die Welt*.

'No news,' Tom said to Frank, 'is good news. Let's go.'

Tom bought tickets which came in orange-coloured perforated strips. These enabled them to ride the toylike trains that travelled all over the Carl Hagenbeck Tierpark. Frank looked enchanted, and Tom was pleased. The little train had perhaps fifteen carriages; one stepped aboard from the ground without opening a side door, and the train had no roof. They rolled along almost noiselessly past adventure playgrounds where kids hung from rubber tyres that slid along cables from a height, or crawled in and out of two-storey plastic constructions with holes, tunnels and slopes. They passed lions and elephants with, apparently, no barrier between them and the human race. In the bird section, they detrained, bought beer and peanuts at a stand, then got aboard another passing train.

Then a taxi to a big restaurant on the harbour which Tom remembered from a previous trip. Its walls were glass, and one could look down at the port where tankers, white cruise liners and barges lay moored, being loaded and unloaded, while water poured from their automatic pumps. Seagulls cruised, and occasionally dived.

'We go to Paris tomorrow,' Tom said after they had begun their meal. 'How about that?'

Frank at once looked on guard, but Tom could see him collecting himself. It was either Paris tomorrow, Tom thought, or the boy would blow up in another day and insist on striking out somewhere from Hamburg on his own. 'I don't like to tell people what they should do. But you've got to face your family at some point, haven't you?' Tom glanced to right and left, but he was speaking softly, the wall of glass was just to his left, and the nearest table was more than a yard away behind Frank. 'You can't hop one plane after another for months to come, can you? – Eat your *Bauernfrühstück*.'

The boy fell to again, more slowly. He had been amused by 'Farmer's Breakfast' on the menu and ordered it: fish, home-fried potatoes, bacon, onions, all mixed on a king-sized platter. 'You'll be coming to Paris too tomorrow?'

'Sure, since I'm going home.'

After lunch, they walked, crossed a Venice-like inlet of water bordered by beautiful old peak-roofed houses. Then on the pavement of a commercial street, Frank said, 'I want to change some money. Can I go in here for a minute?'

He meant a bank. 'Okay.' Tom went into the bank with him and waited while the boy stood in a short queue and made a transaction at the window marked 'Foreign Exchange'. Frank hadn't his Benjamin Andrews passport with him, as far as Tom knew, but he wouldn't need it if he was changing French francs into marks. Tom did not try to see. Tom had put some other kind of cream on Frank's mole that morning. Why was he always thinking about that damned mole? What if anybody *did* recognize Frank now? Frank came back smiling, pushing marks into his billfold.

They walked on to the museum of Völkerkunde und Vorgeschichte, where Tom had been once before. Here were table models of fire bomb implosions that had flattened much of the Hamburg dock area in World War II: nine-inch high warehouses on fire, sculpted yellow and blue flames. Frank pored over a model of ship-raising, the little ship three inches long resting on sand and under what appeared to be metres of sea. As usual, after an hour of this, including oil paintings of Hamburg Bürgermeisters signing this and commemorating that, all in dress of the Benjamin Franklin period, Tom was rubbing his eyes and longing for a cigarette.

Minutes later, in an avenue of shops and pushcarts of flowers and fruit, Frank said, 'Will you wait for me? Five minutes?'

'Where're you going?'

'I'll be back. By this tree.' Frank pointed to a plane tree near the kerb beside them.

'But I'd like to know where you're going,' Tom said.

'Trust me.'

'All right.' Tom turned away, walked slowly several paces on, doubting the boy, and at the same time reminding himself that he couldn't play nursemaid to Frank Pierson forever. Yes, if the boy disappeared – and how much money had he cashed at the bank, how much had he left in French or American? – Tom would take Frank's suitcase to Paris and deliver it to the Lutetia. Had Frank possibly taken his passport with him this morning? Tom turned back and walked towards the plane tree, which he recognized from others only because of an elderly gentleman sitting on a chair and reading a newspaper under it. The boy was not there, and more than five minutes had passed.

Then Frank reappeared through a trickle of pedestrians, smiling, carrying a big red-and-white plastic bag. 'Thanks,' Frank said.

Tom was relieved. 'Bought something?'

'Yep. Show you later.'

Next, then Jungfernstieg. Tom remembered the name of the street or promenade, because Reeves had once told him it was where the pretty girls of Hamburg strolled in the old days. The sight-seeing boats set off for round-the-Alsters cruises from a quay at right angles to the Jungfernstieg, and Tom and Frank boarded one.

'My last day of freedom!' Frank said on the boat. The wind blew his brown hair back and whipped his trousers against his legs.

Neither wanted to sit down, but they were not in anyone's way, hanging on to a corner of the superstructure. A jolly man in a white cap spoke through a meagaphone, explaining the sights they were passing, the big hotels on sloping green lawns overlooking the water, where he assured everyone the tariff was 'among the highest in the world'. Tom was amused. The boy's eyes had focused on some distant point, maybe on a seagull, maybe on Teresa, Tom didn't know.

When they got back to Reeves' at just after six, Reeves was not home, but he had left a message in the middle of the neatly made bed in the guest room: 'Back at seven or before. R.' Tom was glad Reeves was still out, because he wanted to speak with Frank alone.

'You remember what I told you at Belle Ombre – in regard to your father,' Tom said.

Frank looked puzzled for an instant, then said, 'I think I remember everything you ever said to me.'

They were in the living room, Tom standing near the window, the boy sitting on the sofa.

'I said, never tell anyone what you did. Don't confess. Don't entertain for a minute the idea of confessing.'

Frank looked from Tom to the floor.

'Well – are you thinking about telling someone? Your brother?' Tom threw it out in the hope of eliciting something.

'No, I'm not.'

The boy's voice was firm and deep enough, but Tom was not sure he could believe him. He wished he could take the boy by the shoulders and shake some sense into him. Did he dare? No. And what was he afraid of, Tom wondered, failure to shake any sense into the boy? 'This you ought to know. Where is it?' Tom went to the little heap of newspapers at one end of the sofa and found yesterday's. He opened it to the front page on which was the picture of the dead man in Lübars. 'I saw you looking at this yesterday on the plane. This – this man I killed in Lübars, north Berlin.'

'*You?*' Frank's voice rose an octave with astonishment.

'You never asked me where the meeting place was for the ransom. Never mind. I hit him over the head. As you can see.'

Frank blinked and looked at Tom. 'Why didn't you tell me before? Sure, I recognize this fellow now. He was the Italian in the apartment there!'

Tom lit a cigarette. 'I tell you this because –' Because, why? Tom had to pause to collect his words. There was no comparison, really, between pushing one's father off a cliff, and bashing the skull of a kidnapper who was walking towards you with a loaded gun. But both involved the taking of life. 'The fact that I killed this man – It's not going to change my life. Granted he was probably a criminal himself. Granted he wasn't the first man I ever killed. I don't think I have to tell you that.'

Frank was looking at him with wonder. 'Did you ever kill a woman?'

Tom laughed. That was just what he had needed, a laugh. Tom was aware of relief also, because Frank had not asked him about Dickie Greenleaf, the one murder Tom felt a bit of guilt about. 'Never – a woman. Never had to,' Tom added, and thought at once of the joke about the Englishman who told a friend he had had to bury his wife, simply because she was dead. 'Situation never arose. A woman. Surely not on your mind, Frank . . . Who?'

Now Frank smiled. 'Oh, no one! Gosh!'

'Good. The only reason I bring this up –' Tom was again at a loss, but plunged on. 'It – I mean the –' He gestured towards the newspaper. 'The act shouldn't be devastating – to the rest of your life. There's no reason to collapse.' Did the boy, could he, know the meaning of collapse at his age? To collapse from a sense of total failure? But many adolescents did collapse, even committed suicide, because they had met a problem they couldn't cope with, sometimes just schoolwork.

Frank was brushing the knuckles of his right fist against the sharp corner of Reeves' coffee table. Was the top made of glass? It was black and white, but not marble. Frank's gesture made Tom nervous.

'Do you understand what I mean? You either let some event ruin your life or not. The decision is yours. You're lucky, Frank, in your case the decision *is* yours, because no one is accusing you.'

'I know.'

And Tom knew that part – how much? – of the boy's mind was on the apparently lost love, Teresa. That was a sickness Tom felt unable to deal with, quite another subject than murder. Tom said nervously, 'Don't hit your knuckles against that table, will you, because it won't solve anything. You'll only get to Paris with bleeding knuckles. *Don't be silly!*'

The boy had made a downward swipe at the table, but not quite hit it. Tom tried to relax, and looked away.

'I wouldn't be that stupid, don't worry, don't worry.' Frank stood up and pushed his hands into his pockets, walked to a window, then turned to Tom. 'The plane tickets for tomorrow. Shall I do it? I can make the reservations in English, can't I?'

'I'm sure. Go ahead.'

'Lufthansa,' said Frank, picking up the telephone directory. 'What time, around ten tomorrow morning?'

'Even earlier.' Tom felt much relieved. Frank seemed to be standing on his feet at last, or if he wasn't quite, he was trying.

Reeves came in as Frank was fixing the time for tomorrow. 9.15 take-off. Frank gave the names, Ripley and Andrews.

'Did you have a nice day?' Reeves asked.

'Very fine, thanks,' Tom said.

'Hello, Frank. Got to wash my hands,' Reeves said in his croaky voice, at the same time displaying his palms which were visibly grey. 'Handling pictures today. Not a dirty –'

'A real day's work, Reeves?' said Tom. 'I admire your hands!'

Reeves cleared his hoarse throat in vain, and began again. 'I was about to say not a dirty day's work but a day's *dirty* work. Did you make yourself a drink, Tom?' Reeves went off to his bathroom.

'Would you like to go out for dinner, Reeves?' Tom asked, following him. 'It's our last night.'

'I really don't, if you don't mind. Always something here, you know. Gaby sees to that. I think she made a casserole or something.'

Reeves never liked restaurants, Tom remembered. Reeves probably kept a low profile on the Hamburg scene.

'Tom.' Frank beckoned Tom into the guest room, and pulled a box out of the red and white plastic bag. 'For you.'

'For me? – Thank you, Frank.'

'You haven't opened it yet.'

Tom untied some blue and red ribbon, then opened the white box which had a lot of white tissue paper inside. He found something reddish, shiny, golden, pulled it out and it became a dressing gown with a belt of the same dark-red silk, with black tassels. The red material was flecked with gold in the form of arrowheads. 'Really pretty,' said Tom. 'Very handsome.' Tom took his jacket off. 'Shall I try it on?' he asked, trying it on. It fitted perfectly, or would with pyjamas underneath instead of his sweater and trousers. Tom glanced at the sleeve length and said, 'Perfect.'

Frank ducked his head, and swung away from Tom.

Tom took the dressing gown off carefully and laid it across the bed. It made a fine and impressive rustle. The colour was maroon, the same as the kidnappers' car in Berlin, a colour Tom didn't like, but if he made himself think of it as Dubonnet, maybe he could forget that car.

EIGHTEEN

On the plane going to Paris, Tom noticed that Frank's hair had grown so long, it was falling partly over his cheek where the mole was. Frank had not had a haircut since the middle of August, which was the time Tom had advised Frank to let it grow. Between noon and one o'clock, he would be delivering Frank to Thurlow and Johnny Pierson at the Lutetia. Tom had reminded Frank, last evening at Reeves', that he ought to see about getting a genuine passport, unless Thurlow had had the wit to bring his passport or ask his mother to send it from Maine.

'You see this?' Frank asked, showing Tom a page in a glossy little magazine donated by the airline. 'That's where we were.'

Tom read a small item about Romy Haag and its transvestite show. 'I bet they haven't got the Hump there! That magazine's for tourists.' Tom laughed, and stretched his legs as far as the seat in front of him permitted. Airplanes were getting increasingly uncomfortable. He could travel first class, though probably with a sense of guilt about spending so much extra when the inter-European rates were already inflated, and moreover Tom would have felt embarrassed at being seen in first class. Why? He always had a desire to step on the toes of people in the roomy first class when he boarded an airplane and had to pass through their more luxurious quarters, where champagne corks started to pop before take-off.

This time, not looking forward to the encounter at the Lutetia, Tom proposed the train from the airport to the Gare du Nord, and a taxi from there. At the Gare du Nord they queued for a taxi, the queue kept in order by no less than three policemen in white spats and with guns on their hips, and then they rode towards the Hôtel Lutetia. Frank, tense and silent, stared out the window. Was he planning his stance, Tom wondered, and what would it be? A don't-touch-me attitude towards Thurlow? An awkward explanation to brother Johnny? A defiance even? Was Frank going to insist on staying in Europe?

'I think you'll like my brother all right,' Frank said nervously.

Tom nodded. He wanted Frank to get home safely, resume his life which was bound to mean school again, face what he had to face, and learn to live with it. Kids of sixteen, at least from Frank's kind of family, could not leave home and expect to cope, as a boy from the slums might, or a boy from such a wretched home that the street might be better. They slid up in front of the Lutetia.

'I have francs,' Frank said.

Tom let him pay. A doorman carried their two suitcases in, but once inside the rather pretentious lobby, Tom said to the doorman, 'I'm not staying in the hotel, so could you check mine for half an hour or so?'

Frank wanted his checked too, and a bellhop returned and gave them two tickets, which Tom pocketed. Frank came back from the desk, and reported that Thurlow and his brother were out, but due back in less than an hour.

Amazing to find them out, Tom thought, and looked at his watch. It was 12.07. 'Maybe they're out for lunch? I'm going to the next bar-café and ring home. Want to come?'

'Sure!' said Frank, and led the way to the door. On the pavement, he hung his head as he walked.

'Stand up straight,' Tom said.

Frank did so at once.

'Order me a coffee, Frank?' Tom said as they went into a *bar-tabac*. Tom went down some winding stairs to the *toilettes-téléphones*. He put two francs into the telephone slot, not wanting to be cut off for being a few seconds late with his money, and dialled Belle Ombre. Mme Annette answered.

'Ah-h!' She sounded as if she were fainting at the sound of his voice.

'I'm in Paris. All goes well?'

'*Ah, oui!* But Madame is not here at the moment. She went out to lunch with a friend.'

A female friend, Tom noticed. 'Tell her I'll be home this afternoon, maybe around – oh, by four, I hope. By six-thirty anyway,' he added, remembering the gap between trains from a little past 2 p.m. until 5 p.m. something at Gare de Lyon.

'You do not wish Madame Heloise to fetch you in Paris?'

Tom didn't. He went back to Frank and his coffee.

Frank, with a hardly touched Coca-Cola in front of him at the bar, spat out chewing gum into an empty and crushed cigarette packet that he took from a big ashtray. 'Sorry. I hate chewing gum. Don't know why I bought it. Or this.' He pushed the Coca-Cola away.

Tom watched the boy drift towards the juke box near the door. The box was now playing something, an American song sung in French.

Frank came back. 'Is everything all right at home?'

'I think so, thanks.' Tom pulled some coins from his pocket.

'This is paid for.'

They went out. Again the boy's head sank, and Tom said nothing.

Ralph Thurlow, at any rate, was in. Tom had let Frank ask at the desk. They rode up in a decorated lift that suggested to Tom a bad performance of Wagner. Was Thurlow going to be cool, self-important? That at least would be amusing.

Frank knocked on the door of 620, and the door opened at once. Thurlow beckoned the boy in enthusiastically and without a word, then saw Tom. Thurlow's smile remained. Frank made a gracious gesture, ushering Tom in. No one said a word until the door was closed. Thurlow wore a shirt with sleeves rolled up and no tie. He was a chunky man in his late thirties, perhaps, with rippling short-cut reddish hair and a rather tough face.

'My friend Tom Ripley,' Frank said.

'How d'you do, Mr Ripley? – Please sit down,' said Thurlow.

There was plenty of space, and chairs and sofas, but Tom did not at once sit down. A door to the right was closed, a door to the left by the windows open, and Thurlow went to it and called to Johnny, saying to Frank and Tom that he thought Johnny was taking a shower. There were newspapers and a briefcase on a table, and more newspapers on the floor, a transistor radio, a tape recorder. This was not a bedroom but a sitting room between two bedrooms, Tom supposed.

Johnny came in, tall and smiling, in a fresh pink shirt he had not yet stuffed into his trousers. He had straight brown hair lighter than Frank's, and his face was more narrow than Frank's. 'Franky!' He swung his brother's right hand and almost embraced him. 'How *are* yuh?'

Or so it sounded to Tom. How are yuh. Tom felt that he had entered America, just by stepping into room 620. Tom was introduced to Johnny and they shook hands. Johnny looked like a straightforward, happy and easy-going boy, even younger than nineteen, which Tom knew he was.

Then down to business, which Tom let Thurlow stumble on with. Thurlow first assured Tom, with thanks from Mrs Pierson, that the marks had been reported in Zurich by the bank there.

'Every last one, except the bank charges,' said Thurlow. 'Mr Ripley, we don't know the details, but . . .'

You never will, Tom thought, and barely listened to what followed from Thurlow. Reluctantly, Tom sat down on a beige upholstered sofa, and lit a Gauloise. Johnny and Frank were talking fast and quietly by the window. Frank looked angry and tense. Had Johnny said the name Teresa? Tom thought so. He saw Johnny shrug.

'You said there were no police,' said Thurlow. 'You went to their apartment – How did you do it?' Now Thurlow fairly laughed, maybe in what he thought was a tough guy to tough guy manner. 'It's fantastic!'

Tom felt one hundred per cent turned off in regard to Mr Thurlow. 'Professional secret,' said Tom. How long could he endure this? Tom stood up. 'Got to be pushing on, Mr Thurlow.'

'Pushing on?' Thurlow had not yet sat down. 'Mr Ripley, besides meeting you – thanking you – We don't even know your exact address!'

In order to send him a fee, Tom wondered? 'I am in the book. Villeperce, seventy-seven, Seine et Marne. Frank?'

'Yes, sir!'

Suddenly the boy's anxious expression looked like the one Tom remembered from mid-August at Belle Ombre. 'May we go in here for a minute?' Tom asked, indicating what he supposed was Johnny's room, whose door was still open.

They could, Johnny said, so Tom and Frank went in, and Tom closed the door.

'Don't tell them all the details of that night – in Berlin,' Tom said. 'Above all, don't tell them about the dead man – will you?' Tom glanced around, but saw no tape-recorder in this room. There was a *Playboy* on the floor by the bed, and a few big bottles of orange soda pop on a tray.

'Of course I *won't*' said Frank.

The boy's eyes seemed older than his brother's. 'You can say – all right – that I failed to keep the date with the money. That's how I still had the money. All right?'

'All right.'

'And that I followed one of the kidnappers after I made a second date, so I knew where you were being held. But don't mention that crazy *Hump!*' Now Tom burst out laughing, and bent over.

They both laughed, with nearly hysterical mirth.

'I gotcha,' Frank whispered.

Tom caught the boy suddenly by the front of his jacket, then released him, embarrassed by his gesture. 'Never anything about that dead man! You promise?'

Frank nodded. 'I know, I know what you mean.'

Tom started to walk back to the other room, then turned. 'I mean,' he whispered, 'so far and no farther – with everything. If you mention Hamburg, don't give Reeves' name. Say you forgot it.'

The boy was silent, but he looked steadily at Tom, then nodded. They went into the other room.

Now Thurlow sat on a beige chair. 'Mr Ripley – please sit down again, if you've got just a couple of minutes.'

Tom did so to be polite, and Frank at once joined him on the beige sofa. Johnny was still standing by the window.

'I must apologise for my brusqueness several times on the telephone,' Thurlow said. 'I couldn't know, you know –' Thurlow paused.

'I'd like to ask you,' Tom said, 'what the situation is now in regard to Frank's being missing or looked for. You told the police here – what?'

'Well – I first told Mrs Pierson that the boy was safe in Berlin – with you. Then with her agreement I informed the police here. Of course I didn't need her agreement to do it.'

Tom bit his underlip. 'I hope you and Mrs Pierson didn't mention my name to the police anywhere. That wouldn't've been necessary at all.'

'Not here, I know,' Thurlow assured Tom. 'Mrs Pierson – I – yes, I told her your name, of course, but I certainly asked her not to mention your name to the police in the States. There were no police in the States. This was a private detective situation. I told her to say to any journalists – whom she hates, by the way – that the boy had been found taking a holiday in Germany. Didn't even say *where* in Germany, because that could've led to another kidnapping!' Ralph Thurlow chuckled, leaning back in his chair, and adjusting his brass-buckled belt with a thumb.

He was smiling as if another kidnapping might have landed him in some other comfortable spot, such as Palma de Majorca, Tom thought.

'I wish you'd tell me what happened in Berlin,' Thurlow said. 'At least a description of the kidnappers. It might –'

'You're not intending to *look* for them,' Tom said in a tone of surprise, and smiled. 'Hopeless.' Tom stood up.

So did Thurlow, looking unsatisfied. 'I've recorded my telephone conversations with them. Well, maybe Frank can tell me a little more. What made you go to Berlin, Mr Ripley?'

'Oh – Frank and I wanted a change of scene from Villeperce,' Tom said, feeling like a travelogue or brochure, 'and I thought Berlin was off the tourist trail. Frank wanted to be incognito for a while ... By the way, have you got Frank's passport here?' Tom asked before Thurlow might ask why he had sheltered the boy.

'Yep, my mother sent it by registered post,' Johnny said.

Tom said to Frank, 'You'd better get rid of the Andrews one, you know? I can take it if you go downstairs with me.' Tom was thinking of returning it to Hamburg, where it could certainly be made use of again.

'*What* passport?' asked Thurlow.

Tom edged towards the door.

Thurlow seemed to give up the passport matter, and walked towards Tom. 'Maybe I'm not a typical detective. Maybe there aren't any such animals. We're all different, not all of us capable of a physical fight, if it came to it.'

But wasn't he the usual, Tom thought, glancing at Thurlow's well-fed body, at his heavy hands with a school ring on one little finger. Tom thought of asking him if he had ever been on the police force, but really Tom didn't care.

'You've had some experience with the underworld before, haven't you, Mr Ripley?' Thurlow asked this in a genial way.

'Haven't we all,' Tom said, 'anyone who's ever bought an oriental rug. Well, Frank, with your passport, you seem all set.'

'I'm not going to stay here tonight,' Frank said, getting up.

Thurlow looked at the boy. 'What do you mean, Frank? – Where's your suitcase? You have no suitcase?'

'Downstairs with Tom's,' Frank replied. 'I want to go home with Tom now. And tonight. We're not leaving for the States today, are we? I'm not.' Frank looked determined.

Tom gave a twitch of a smile and waited. He had expected something like this.

'I thought we'd leave tomorrow,' With equal determination and a little puzzlement, Thurlow folded his arms. 'Do you want to 'phone your mother now, Frank? She's expecting a call from you.'

Frank shook his head quickly. 'Just tell her I'm okay if she calls up.'

Thurlow said, 'I wish you'd stay here, Frank. It's just one night here, and I want you in sight.'

'Come on, Franky,' Johnny said. 'Stay with *us*! Natch!'

Frank gave his brother a look, as if he objected to being called Franky, made a kicking movement with his right foot, though there was nothing to kick. He walked nearer to Tom. 'I want to leave.'

'Now look,' said Thurlow. 'One night –'

'*Can* I go to Belle Ombre with you?' Frank asked Tom. 'I can, can't I?'

In the next seconds, everyone but Tom talked at the same time. Tom wrote his telephone number on a pad by the telephone, and added his name below.

'If we just tell my mother, it's all *right*,' Johnny was saying to Thurlow. 'I *know* Frank.'

Did he, Tom wondered. Evidently Johnny trusted his brother usually.

'– cause a delay,' Thurlow was saying with irritation. 'Use your influence, Johnny.'

'I haven't any!' said Johnny.

'I'm leaving.' Frank stood as tall as Tom or anyone else could have wished. 'Tom wrote his 'phone number. I just saw it. Good-bye, Mr Thurlow. See you soon, Johnny.'

'Tomorrow morning, yes?' asked Johnny, following Tom and Frank out of the room. 'Mr Ripley –'

'You can call me Tom,' They were now in the hall, walking towards the lifts.

'Not much of a meeting,' Johnny said with a serious air to Tom. 'This has been a crazy time. I know you've taken care of my brother, really saved him.'

'Well –' Tom could see freckles on Johnny's nose, eyes that were shaped like Frank's, yet looked so much happier.

'Ralph's rather abrupt – the way he speaks,' Johnny went on.

Now Thurlow was joining them. 'We want to leave tomorrow, Mr Ripley. Can I 'phone you tomorrow morning around nine? I'll have our reservations by then.'

Tom nodded calmly. Frank had pushed the elevator button. 'Yes, Mr Thurlow.'

Johnny extended his hand. 'Thank you, Mr R – Tom. My mother kept thinking –'

Thurlow made a gesture as if he preferred that Johnny keep silent.

Johnny went on. 'She didn't know what to think about you, I know.'

'Oh, can it!' said Frank, squirming with embarrassment.

The lift doors slid open like a pair of arms saying, 'Welcome!' and Tom was delighted to step in. Frank followed at once, Tom pressed the button, and down they went.

'Whew!' said Frank, hitting himself in the forehead with his palm.

Tom laughed, and leaned against the Wagnerian interior. Two floors down, a man and a woman got on, the woman with a perfume that made Tom cringe, though perhaps it was expensive. Her yellow-and-blue-striped dress certainly looked expensive, and her black patent leather pumps reminded Tom of the one, or maybe two, that he had left in the kidnappers' flat in Berlin. A surprising find for the neighbours or the police, Tom supposed. In the lobby, Tom reclaimed their suitcases, but felt that he didn't breathe until he was standing on the pavement, waiting for the doorman to get a taxi. One came almost at once, letting off two women, and Tom and Frank took it, bound for the Gare de Lyon. They could make the 14.18 with a few minutes to spare, which was nice, as it avoided the awful wait for the next train at 5 p.m. or so. Frank was gazing out of the window with eyes at once intense and dreaming, his body stiff as a statue. In fact, Tom thought of a statue of an angel, one of the dazed but supportive figures at the sides of the church doors. At the station, Tom bought first class tickets, and a copy of *Le Monde* from the news-stand by the trains.

Once the train started moving, Frank pulled out a paperback that he had bought at a bookshop in Hamburg, Tom remembered. *The Country Diary of an Edwardian Lady*, of all things. Tom glanced at *Le Monde*, read a column about *gauchistes* which seemed to have nothing new in it, put *Le Monde* on the seat beside Frank and stuck his feet up on it. Frank did not look at him. Was Frank pretending his absorption?

'Is there any reason why . . .' Frank said.

Tom leaned forward, not having heard the rest in the train's roar. 'Reason why what?'

Frank asked earnestly, 'Is there any simple reason why Communism doesn't *work*?'

Tom thought the train was just then roaring towards its next stop, hadn't begun to put on the brakes, which would be even louder. Across the aisle, a small child had begun to wail, and his father smacked him gently. 'What made you think of that? That book?'

'No, no. *Berlin*,' said Frank, frowning.

Tom took a deep breath, hating talking over the train's noise. 'It does work. Socialism works. It's individual initiative that's lacking – they say. The Russian form just now doesn't allow enough initiative – so everyone becomes discouraged.' Tom glanced around, glad to see that no one was listening to his unprepared lecture. 'There's a difference –'

'A year ago I thought I was a Communist. You know, Moscow even. Depends on what you read. If you read the *right* things . . .'

What did Frank mean by the right things? 'If you read –'

'Why do the Russians need the *Wall*?' Frank asked with frowning brows.

'Well, that's it. If it comes to freedom of choice – Even now people can ask for citizenship in Communist countries and probably get it. But if you're in a Communist country, try and get *out*!'

'That's what's so – uh – unfair!'

Tom shook his head. The train roared on, as if they had passed Melun even, but that was impossible. He was glad the boy was asking naïve questions. How else could a boy learn anything? Tom leaned forward again. 'You saw the Wall. The barriers are on *their* side, yet they claim they built it to keep capitalists out. But it could've been marvellous, sure. Russia became more and more a police state. They seem to think they need all that control over people.' How to finish, Tom wondered. Jesus Christ was an early Communist. 'But of course the idea is *great*!' Tom yelled. Was this the way to instruct the young? By screaming platitudes?

Melun. The boy returned to his book, and minutes later pointed out a sentence to Tom. 'We've got these in our garden in Maine. My father ordered them from England.'

Tom read a sentence about an English wild flower he had never heard of: yellow, sometimes purple, blooming in early spring. Tom nodded. He was worried, thinking of a lot of things, therefore of nothing, he realized, nothing that was profitable or conclusive, anyway.

At Moret, they got off, and Tom engaged one of the two waiting taxis. Then he began to feel better. This was home, familiar houses, familiar trees even, the towered bridge over the Loing. He remembered the first time he had brought the boy back to Mme Boutin's here, remembered his suspicion of the boy's story, his wondering why the boy had looked him up. The taxi rolled through the open gates of Belle Ombre on to the gravel, and stopped near the front steps. Tom smiled at the sight of the red Mercedes in the garage, and since the door of the second garage was closed, Tom supposed the Renault was there too, and Heloise was home. Tom paid the driver.

'*Bonjour, Monsieur Tome!*' Mme Annette called from the front steps. 'And Monsieur Billy! Welcome!'

She seemed not much surprised by Billy, Tom saw. 'And how goes everything?' He gave Mme Annette a peck on the cheek.

'All very well, but Madame Heloise was so worried – for a day or so. Come in.'

Heloise walked towards him in the living room, and then she was in his arms. 'Finally, Tome!'

'Was I gone so long? And Billy's here.'

'Hello, Heloise. I am intruding on you again,' the boy said in French. 'But just for the night – if I may.'

'*Not* intruding. Hello.' She blinked her eyes and extended a hand.

In that blink of her eyes, Tom realized that she knew who the boy was. 'Lots to talk about,' Tom said cheerfully, 'but I want to get our suitcases up first. S-so –' He motioned to Frank, not knowing for the moment what to call him, and they both went upstairs with their luggage.

Mme Annette was in process of baking something, Tom judged from the aroma of orange and vanilla, otherwise she would have seized upon the suitcases and have been relieved of them by Tom, because he still disliked seeing women carrying men's suitcases.

'Christ, is it good to get home!' Tom said in the upstairs hall. 'Take the spare room, Frank, unless –' A peak into the room assured Tom that no one else was using the guest room at the moment. 'But use my john. I'd like to speak with you, so come in in a minute.' Tom went to his room, and took some things out of his suitcase to hang up or to be washed.

The boy came in with a troubled face, and Tom knew that he had noticed Heloise's manner.

'Well, Heloise knows,' Tom said, 'but what's there to worry about?'

'As long as she doesn't think I'm a hundred-per-cent phony.'

'I wouldn't worry about that either. I wonder if that delicious-smelling cake or whatever is for tea or dinner?'

'And what about Madame Annette?' Frank asked.

Tom laughed. 'She seems to want to call you Billy. But she probably knew who you were before Heloise did. Madame Annette reads gossip sheets. It'll be out in the open tomorrow anyway, when you show your passport. What's the matter? Are you ashamed of *yourself*? – Let's go down. Throw your stuff to be washed here on the floor. I'll tell Madame Annette, and everything will be ready by tomorrow morning.'

Frank went back to his room, and Tom down to the living room. The day was lovely, and the french windows stood open on the garden.

'I knew, of course, from the photographs. I saw two,' Heloise said. 'Madame Annette showed me the first. Why did he run away?'

Mme Annette just then came in with a tea tray.

'He wanted to get away from home for a while. He took his older brother's passport when he left America. But he's going back home tomorrow, back to the States.'

'Oh?' said Heloise, surprised. 'Is he?'

'I just met his brother Johnny – and the detective his family hired. They're at the Hôtel Lutetia in Paris. I've been in touch with them from Berlin.'

'Berlin? I thought you were in Hamburg – mostly.'

The boy was coming down the stairs.

Heloise poured tea. Mme Annette had gone back to the kitchen.

'Eric lives in Berlin, you know.' Tom went on. 'Eric Lanz who was here last week. Sit down, Frank.'

'What were you doing in Berlin?' Heloise asked, as if it were a military outpost, or a place anyone on vacation would never dream of visiting.

'Oh – just looking around.'

'You will be happy to get home, Frank?' Heloise asked as she served him orange cake.

The boy was going through a bad moment, and Tom pretended not to notice. Tom got up from the sofa and went to look at the letters stacked where Mme Annette often put them, by the telephone. There were only six or eight, and a couple looked like bills. One was from Jeff Constant, and Tom was curious about that, but he did not open it.

'Did you speak with your mother when you were in Berlin?' Heloise was asking Frank.

'No,' said Frank, swallowing cake as if it were dry as dust.

'How was Berlin?' Heloise looked at Tom now.

'Nothing in the world like it. As they say of Venice,' Tom said. 'Everyone can do his own thing. Isn't that right, Frank?'

Frank rubbed a knuckle into his left eye, and writhed.

Tom gave up. 'Hey – Frank. Go up and take a nap. I insist.' He said to Heloise, 'Reeves kept us up late last night in Hamburg. I'll call you at dinner time, Frank.'

Frank got up and bowed slightly to Heloise, evidently with his throat too tight for him to get a word out.

'Something the matter?' Heloise whispered. '*Hambourg* – last night?'

The boy had by now gone up the stairs.

'Well – never mind Hamburg. Frank was kidnapped last Sunday in Berlin. I couldn't get to him till early Tuesday morning. They gave him –'

'Kidnapped?'

'I know it wasn't in the papers. The kidnappers gave him a lot of sedatives, and I know he's still feeling the effect.'

Heloise was wide-eyed, blinking again but in a different manner, her eyes so wide that Tom could see the little dark blue lines that radiated from the pupils and crossed the blue irises. 'No, I didn't hear a thing about a kidnapping. His family paid a ransom?'

'No. Well, yes, but it wasn't paid. I'll tell you some time when we're alone. You suddenly remind me of the Druckfisch in the Berlin aquarium. Most amazing little fish! I bought some postcards of it, I'll show you! *Eyelashes* – as if someone had drawn them around its eyes. Long black ones!'

'*I* haven't got long black eyelashes! – Tom, this kidnapping. You could not get to him, what do you mean?'

'Some other time, the details. We're not hurt, you can see that.'

'And his mother, she knows about this?'

'She had to, because the money had to be put up. I only – began telling you this to explain why the boy seems a bit strange tonight. He's –'

'He's very strange. Why should he run away from home in the first place? Do you know?'

'No. Not really.' Tom knew he never would tell Heloise what the boy had told him. There was a limit to what Heloise should know, and Tom knew it as if it were a mark on a scale.

NINETEEN

Tom read Jeff Constant's letter, and was reassured because Jeff promised firmly to see that the half-finished or downright unsuccessful sketches done by the successor to Bernard Tufts in imitation of Derwatt were 'torn-up'. These efforts, by some hack, seemed inexhaustible. Tom had checked his greenhouse, plucked a ripe tomato that must have escaped Mme Annette's attention, had taken a shower and put on clean blue jeans. He had also helped Heloise polish a clothes tree she had just bought somewhere. From the top of the clothes tree curved wooden hooks sprang out, tipped with brass, reminding Tom of western American cowhorns. To Tom's surprise the thing really had come from America, Heloise told him, and this must have added to its price, which Tom did not ask. Heloise liked it because it was comical in their house, being *style rustique* of the American variety.

Around eight, Tom called Frank down for dinner, and opened two beers for them. Frank had not been asleep, but Tom hoped he had had a nap. Tom caught up on Heloise's family news: her mother was quite all right now, no operation necessary, but the doctor had put her on a régime of no salt and no fats, the time-honoured French prescription, Tom thought, when the doctor didn't know what else to say or do. Heloise said she had rung up her family that afternoon to say she would not have her usual date with them tonight, because Tom had just come back.

They had coffee in the living room.

'I'll play the record you like,' said Heloise to Frank, and she started the Lou Reed *Transformer*. 'Make-up' was the first song on the second side.

> Your face when sleeping is sublime,
> And then you open up your eyes . . .
> Then comes pancake Factor Number One,
> Eyeliner, rose lips, oh, it's such fun!
> You're a slick little girl . . .

Frank ducked his head over his coffee.

Tom looked for a box of cigars on the telephone table, and it wasn't there. Maybe that box was finished. And the new ones he had bought were up in his room. Tom didn't want one badly enough to go up. Tom was sorry Heloise had put the record on, because he knew it reminded the boy of Teresa. Frank seemed to be suffering inwardly, and Tom wondered if he wanted to be 'excused', or did he prefer their company in spite of the music? Maybe the second song was easier on him.

> Sa – tel – lite . . .
> Gone way up to Mars . . .
> I've been told that you've been bold
> With Harry, Mark and John . . .

Things like that drive me out of my mind . . .
I watched it for a little while . . .
I love to watch things on TV . . .

The easy American voice went on, the words light and simple, yet – if one chose to take them that way – the words could be about an individual's crisis. Tom made a sign to Heloise, meaning, 'Please turn it off', and Tom got up from an armchair. 'I like it but – How about a bit of the classics? Maybe the Albeniz? I'd like that.' They had a new recording of *Iberia* played on the piano by Michel Block, whose perform-ance topped all contemporaries in this work, according to the most respected reviewers. Heloise put it on. This was better! This was musical poetry by comparison, unfettered by human words with a message. Frank's eyes met Tom's for an instant, and Tom saw a flicker of gratitude.

'I shall be going upstairs,' said Heloise. 'Good night, Frank. I shall see you tomorrow morning, I hope.'

Frank stood up. 'Yes. Good night, Heloise.'

She went up the stairs.

Tom sensed that Heloise's early departure was a hint for him to come upstairs early too. She wanted to ask him some more questions, of course.

The telephone rang, and Tom turned the music down and answered. It was Ralph Thurlow in Paris, wanting to know if Tom and the boy had got to Tom's house, and Tom assured him that they had.

'I have reservations for a twelve forty-five take-off from Roissy tomor-row,' Thurlow said. 'Can you see that Frank makes that? Is he there? I'd like to speak with him.'

Tom looked at Frank who made a vigorously negative gesture. 'He's upstairs and I think he's gone to bed, but I can see that he gets to Paris, certainly. What airline?'

'TWA, flight number five six two. I think it would be simplest if Frank came to the Lutetia between ten and ten-thirty tomorrow morning, and we'll take a taxi from here.'

'Okay, that can be done.'

'I didn't mention it this afternoon, Mr Ripley, but I'm sure you've had some expenses. Just inform me and I'll see that the matter is taken care of. Write me care of Mrs Pierson. Frank can give you her address.'

'Thank you.'

'Will I see you tomorrow morning too? I'd rather you – uh – brought Frank here,' said Thurlow.

'All right, Mr Thurlow.' Tom was smiling when he hung up. He said to Frank, 'Thurlow has tickets reserved for tomorrow noonish. You're supposed to be at their hotel around ten. That's easy. Lots of trains in the morning. Or I could drive you up.'

'Oh, no,' said Frank politely.

'But you'll be there?'

'I'll be there.'

Tom felt a relief that he tried to hide.

'I was thinking of asking you to come with me – but that would be the bottom, I suppose.' Frank's hands were clenched in the pockets of his trousers, and his jaw seemed to shake.

Come with him where, Tom wondered. 'Sit down, Frank.'

The boy didn't care to sit down. 'I've got to face everything, I know that.'

'What do you mean by everything?'

'Tell them what I did – about my father,' Frank replied, as if it were a sentence of death for himself.

'I told you not to,' Tom said softly, though he knew that Heloise was upstairs in her room or in her bathroom at the back of the house. 'You don't have to, and you know that, so why do you bring it up again?'

'If I had Teresa, I wouldn't, I swear. But I haven't even got her.'

Here was the impasse again, Tom thought. Teresa.

'Maybe I'll kill myself. What else? I'm not saying this to you as a threat, some stupid threat.' He looked Tom in the eyes. 'I'm just being reasonable. I thought my life out upstairs this afternoon.'

At sixteen. Tom nodded, then said what he didn't believe. 'Teresa may not be lost. Maybe for a couple of weeks she's interested in someone else, or thinks she is. Girls like to play, you know. But surely she knows you're serious.'

Frank smiled a little. 'Where does that get me? This other fellow is *older.*'

'Now look, Frank –' Would it do any good to keep the boy another day at Belle Ombre and try to talk some sense into him? Tom at once doubted the success of that. 'The one thing you don't have to do – is tell anyone.'

'I think I have to decide that for myself,' Frank said with surprising coolness.

Tom wondered if he should go to America with Frank, see him over the first day or so with his mother, make sure the boy was not going to blurt anything out? 'Suppose I go with you tomorrow?'

'To Paris?'

'I meant to the States.' Tom had expected a relaxation of the boy's tension, a visible lift of some kind, but Frank merely shrugged.

'Yes, but after all what good –'

'Frank, you're not going to collapse. Have you any objection to my coming with you?'

'No. You're really the only friend I have.'

Tom shook his head. 'I'm not your only friend, just the only person you've talked to. All right, I'll come with you, and I want to tell Heloise now. Come upstairs and get some sleep. Will you?'

The boy came upstairs with Tom, and Tom said, 'Good night, see you tomorrow,' then went to Heloise's door and knocked. She was in bed, propped against pillows and on one elbow, reading a paperback. Tom noticed that it was their well-worn copy of Auden's *Selected Poems*. She liked Auden's poems because they were 'clear', she said. A funny time to be reading poetry, Tom thought, but maybe it wasn't. He watched her eyes swim back to the present, to him and to Frank.

'I'm going to the States with Frank tomorrow,' Tom said, 'probably just for two or three days.'

'Why? – Tom, you haven't told me very much. Hardly anything.' She tossed the paperback aside, but not angrily.

Tom suddenly realized there was something he could tell Heloise. 'He's in love with a girl in America, and the girl's recently found somebody else, so the boy's very depressed about that.'

'Is that a reason why you have to go to America with him? – What really happened in Berlin? You are still protecting him from – a gang?'

'No! A kidnapping happened in Berlin. When Frank and I were taking a walk in some woods there. Frank and I were separated for a minute or two – and they snatched him. I made a date with the kidnappers –' Tom paused. 'Anyway I was able to get Frank from their apartment. He was very sleepy from sedatives – still is, a little.'

Heloise looked incredulous. 'All this in Berlin – the city?'

'Yes, West Berlin. It's bigger than you may think.' Tom had sat down at the foot of Heloise's bed, but now he stood up. 'And you're not to worry about tomorrow, because I'll be back very soon and – when is it exactly that you go on this Adventure Cruise? Not till late September, isn't it?' Today was September first.

'The twenty-eighth. Tom, what is really worrying you? You think they are going to try to kidnap this boy again? The same people?'

Tom laughed. 'No, certainly not! They were like a bunch of juveniles in Berlin! Just four of them. And I'm sure they're scared now, lying low.'

'You are not telling me everything.' Heloise was not angry, not taunting, but something between the two.

'Maybe not, but I will tell you later.'

'That's what you said about –' Heloise stopped and looked down at her hands.

Murchison? His disappearance, still not accounted for? The American whom Tom had killed in the cellar of Belle Ombre by hitting him with a wine bottle. A bottle of good Margaux, Tom remembered. No, he had never told Heloise about dragging Murchison's corpse out, or told the truth about the big dark-red splotch that still refused to come out of the cement floor of their cellar, and which was not entirely due to wine. Tom had scrubbed at that spot. 'Anyway –' Tom edged towards the door.

Heloise lifted her eyes to him.

Tom knelt by the bed, put his arms around her as much as he could, and pressed his face against the sheet that covered her.

She brushed her fingers in his hair. 'What kind of danger is this? Can't you tell me that?'

Tom realized that he didn't know. 'No danger at all.' He stood up. 'Good night, darling.'

When Tom went into the hall, he saw that the boy's room light was still on. Tom was walking past, when the guest room door opened slightly. Frank beckoned to him. Tom went in, and the boy closed the door. Frank was in pyjamas, his bed was turned down, but he had not been in it.

'I think I was a coward downstairs,' Frank said. 'I think it's the *way* I said things. With the wrong words. And nearly shedding tears, good Christ!'

'So what? Never mind.'

The boy walked across the carpet, looking down at his bare feet. 'I feel like losing myself. It's not so much killing myself as losing myself. That's because of Teresa – I think. If I could just vaporize like steam – you know?'

'You mean lose your identity? Lose what?'

'Everything. Once with Teresa I thought I'd lost my billfold.' Frank smiled suddenly. 'We were having lunch at a restaurant in New York, and I wanted to pay the check and couldn't find my billfold. I had the feeling I'd pulled it out a couple of minutes ahead of time, and maybe it had dropped on the floor. I looked under the table – we were on a sort of bench – and I couldn't find it, then I thought, maybe I'd left it at home! I'm always in a daze, I think, when I'm with Teresa. That's how it is – I want to faint. When I first see her – every time – I feel I can hardly breathe.'

Tom closed his eyes for a second in sympathy. 'You mustn't ever look nervous with a girl, Frank, even if you feel nervous.'

'Yes, sir. Anyway, that day, Teresa said, "I'm sure you haven't lost it, look again," and by this time even the waiter was helping me, and Teresa said she could pay the bill, and when she started to, she found I'd stuck my billfold in *her* handbag, because I'd had it out ahead of time and I was nervous. That's the way things always went with Teresa. I'd think things were awful – then things were rather lucky.'

Tom understood. So could Freud have understood. Was this girl really lucky for Frank? Tom doubted that.

'I could tell you another story like that, but I don't want to bore you.'

What was he getting at? Or did he just want to talk about Teresa?

'I really want to lose everything, Tom. Even my life, yes. It's hard for me to say in words. Maybe I could explain it to Teresa or at least say something, but now she doesn't even care. She's bored with me.'

Tom pulled his cigarettes out and lit one. The boy was in a dream world and needed a jolt of reality. 'While I'm thinking of it, Frank, your Andrews passport. May I?' Tom gestured towards a straight chair where Frank had hung his jacket.

'Go ahead, it's there,' the boy said.

Tom got it from the inside pocket. 'This goes back to Reeves.' Tom cleared his throat and continued. 'Shall I tell you that I once murdered a man in this house? Awful, isn't it? Under this roof. I could tell you the reason. That picture downstairs over the fireplace, "Man in Chair" –' Tom suddenly realized that he couldn't tell Frank that it was a forgery, and that a lot of Derwatts were forgeries now. When might Frank tell it to someone else months or years from now?

'Yes, I like it,' Frank said. 'The man was stealing it?'

'No!' Tom put his head back and laughed. 'I don't want to say any more. We are alike in a way, don't you think, Frank?' Did he see the least relief in the boy's eyes or not? 'Good night, Frank. I'll wake you around eight.'

In his room, Tom found that Mme Annette had unpacked his suitcase, so he would have to start over again with shaving kit and so on. Heloise's present, the blue handbag, was on his desk now, still in its white plastic bag. It was in a box, and Tom decided to smuggle the box to her room some time tomorrow morning, so that she would find it after he had gone. Five past eleven now. Tom went downstairs to ring Thurlow, even though there was a telephone in his room.

Johnny answered, and said that Thurlow was taking a shower.

'Your brother wants me to come with him tomorrow, so I will,' Tom said. 'I mean to America.'

'Oh. Really? Well!' Johnny sounded pleased. 'Here's Ralph. It's Tom Ripley,' Johnny said, and passed the telephone to Thurlow.

Tom explained again. 'Can you get a place for me on the same 'plane, do you think, or shall I try tonight?'

'No, I'll handle it. I'm sure I can do it,' Thurlow said. 'This is Frank's idea?'

'His wishes, yes.'

'Okay, Tom. I'll see you tomorrow around ten then.'

Tom took another warm shower, and looked forward to sleeping. Just that morning he had been in Hamburg, and what was dear old Reeves doing at this moment? Making another deal with someone over cool white wine in his apartment? Tom decided to leave all his packing until the morning.

In bed and with the light out, Tom found himself pondering the generation gap, or trying to. Didn't it turn up in every generation? And didn't generations overlap, so that one could never point out a definite twenty-five year period of change? Tom tried to imagine what it was like for Frank to have been born when the Beatles were getting started in London (after Hamburg), then making their American tour, and changing the face of pop songs, to have been about seven when a man landed on the moon, when the United Nations as a peace-keeping organization was beginning to be laughed at and to be used. And before that, the League of Nations, hadn't it been? Ancient history, the League of Nations, which had failed to stop Franco and Hitler. Every generation seemed to have to turn loose of something, and then try desperately to find something new to hang on to. Now for the young it was gurus sometimes, or Hare Krishna, or the cult called the Moonies, and pop music all the time – social protesters sang to their souls sometimes. Falling in love, however, was out of date, Tom had heard or read somewhere, but he had not heard it from Frank. Frank was perhaps exceptional in even admitting that he was in love. 'Play it cool, no strong emotions' was the tenet of youth. A lot of young people didn't believe in marriage, just in living together and having children sometimes.

Now where was he? Frank had said he wanted to lose himself. Did he mean turning loose of the Pierson family responsibilities? Suicide? Changing his name? What did Frank want to hang on to? Tom's sleepiness put an end to his efforts. Beyond his window an owl was calling 'Chou-*ette*! chou-*ette*!' In early September, Belle Ombre was sliding into autumn and winter.

TWENTY

Heloise drove Tom and Frank to the Moret railway station, and had offered to drive them to Paris. But she was going to Chantilly tonight to see her parents, so Tom persuaded her not to make the Paris drive besides. She sent them both off with well wishes and an extra kiss for Frank, Tom noticed.

Tom could not buy a *France-Dimanche*, the gossip sheet, at the Moret station, but it was the first thing he did when they arrived at the Gare de Lyon. It was only a little after nine, and Tom paused in the station to give the paper a look. He found Frank Pierson on page two, with the familiar old passport picture in one column instead of spread over two or more. MISSING AMERICAN HEIR WAS ON HOLIDAY IN GERMANY said the headline. Tom looked through the column, worried about finding his own name, but it was not there. Had Ralph Thurlow finally done a commendable piece of work? Tom felt relieved.

'Nothing alarming,' Tom said to Frank. 'Want to see it?'

'No, I don't, thanks.' Frank lifted his head with what looked like a deliberate effort. He was again in a head-hanging mood.

They joined the taxi queue and rode to the Lutetia. Thurlow was in the lobby at the desk, paying his bill, in the act of writing a cheque.

'Good morning, Tom – Hello, Frank! Johnny's upstairs making sure the luggage gets down.'

Tom and Frank waited. Johnny emerged from an elevator, carrying a couple of airline bags. He smiled at his brother. 'You see the *Trib* this morning?'

They had left Tom's house too early to see the *Trib*, and Tom hadn't thought of buying it. Johnny informed his brother that the *Trib* said he had been found in Germany, taking a vacation. And where was Frank supposed to be now, Tom wondered, though he did not put the question.

Frank said, 'I know,' and looked uncomfortable.

They needed two taxis. Frank wanted to ride with Tom, but Tom suggested that he go with his brother. Tom wanted a few minutes with Ralph Thurlow, for what they might be worth.

'You've known the Piersons for quite a while?' Tom began in a pleasant tone to Thurlow.

'Yes. I knew John for six or seven years. I was a partner of Jack Diamond. Private detective. Jack went back to San Francisco, where I'm from, but I stayed on in New York.'

'I'm glad the papers didn't make much of Frank's reappearance. Is that due to your efforts?' Tom asked, eager to pay Thurlow a compliment, if he could.

'I hope so.' Thurlow showed satisfaction. 'I did my best to cool it. I'm hoping there're no journalists at the airport – Frank hates all that, I know.'

Thurlow smelled of some presumably masculine scent, and Tom inched back into the corner of his seat. 'What kind of man was John Pierson?'

'Oh –' Thurlow slowly lit a cigarette. 'A genius, I'm sure. Maybe I can't figure people like that out. He lived for his work – or money, which was like a score to him. Maybe it gave him emotional security, even more than his family. But he certainly *knew* his business. Self-made man, too, no rich father to get him started. John started out by buying a grocery store in Connecticut that was going broke, and then he went on from there, always in the food product line.'

Another source of emotional security, Tom had always heard. Food. Tom waited.

'His first marriage. He married a well-to-do Connecticut girl. I think she bored him. Fortunately no children. Then she met another man, maybe with a little more time to give her. So they got a divorce. Quietly.' Thurlow glanced at Tom. 'I didn't know John in those days, but I heard about all this. John was always a hard worker, wanted the best for himself *and* his family.' Thurlow spoke with some respect.

'Was he a happy man?'

Thurlow looked out the window and wagged his head. 'Who can be happy trying to manage so much money? It's like an empire. A nice wife, Lily, nice sons, nice houses everywhere – but maybe incidental to

a man like that. I don't know. He certainly was a lot happier than
Howard Hughes.' Thurlow laughed. 'That man lost his mind!'

'Why do you think John Pierson killed himself?'

'I'm not sure he *did*.' Now Thurlow looked at Tom. 'What do you
mean? Frank said that?' Thurlow's tone was easy.

Was Thurlow sounding him out? Trying to sound Frank out? Tom
also wagged his head with deliberate slowness, even though the taxi
was making a heavy swerve just then to pass a truck on the *périphérique*
as they sped on northward. 'No Frank said nothing. Or he said what
the papers said, that it could've been an accident or a suicide. What's
your opinion?'

Thurlow seemed to ponder, but his thinnish lips had a smile, a safe
smile. Tom saw at a glance. 'I do think suicide rather than an accident.
I don't *know*,' Thurlow assured Tom, 'it's only my guess. He was
already in his sixties. How could a man be happy in a wheelchair – for a
decade – half-paralysed? John always tried to be cheerful – but maybe he'd
had enough? I don't know. But I know he'd been to that cliff hundreds
of times. There wasn't any kind of wind to blow him over that day.'

Tom was pleased. Thurlow didn't seem to suspect Frank. 'And Lily?
What's she like?'

'She's another world. She was an actress when John met her. Why're
you asking?'

'Because I suppose I'll meet her,' Tom said, smiling. 'Has she a
favourite between the two boys?'

Thurlow smiled, relieved at an easy question. 'You must think I know
the family pretty well. I don't know them that well.'

There Tom let the matter rest. They had exited at Porte de la Chapelle
from the *périphérique* and entered the boring stretch of fifteen kilometres
towards the horror called Charles de Gaulle airport, nearly as offensive
to Tom's eye as Beaubourg, but at least inside Beaubourg there were
beautiful things to look at.

'How do you spend your time, Mr Ripley?' Thurlow asked. 'Someone
told me you haven't a usual job. You know, an office –'

That was an easy question for Tom, because he had answered it many
a time. There was gardenihng, he was studying the harpsichord, Tom
said, he liked reading French and German, and he was always trying to
improve himself in those languages. He could feel Thurlow regarding
him as if he were a man from Mars, possibly also regarding him with
distaste. Tom didn't mind at all. He had weathered worse than Thurlow.
He knew Thurlow thought he was a borderline crook, with the luck to

have married a well-to-do Frenchwoman. A gigolo, perhaps, a sponger, loafer and parasite. Tom kept a bland expression on his face, since he might need Thurlow's help in the days ahead, even Thurlow's allegiance. Had Thurlow ever fought as hard for anything, Tom wondered, as he had to protect the Derwatt name – the Derwatt forgeries, really, but of course the earlier half of the paintings were *not* forgeries. Had Thurlow slain one or two Mafiosi, as had Tom? Or was it more correct now to call them 'organized criminals', those sadistic pimps and blackmailers?

'And Susie?' Tom began again pleasantly. 'I suppose you've met her?'

'Susie? Oh, Susie the housekeeper. Sure. She's been there for ages. Geting on in years, but they don't want to – retire her.'

At the airport, they could not find any luggage carts, so they hauled everything by hand to the check-in at TWA. Suddenly two or three photographers crouched with cameras on both sides of the queue. Tom lowered his head, and saw Frank cover his face calmly with one hand. Thurlow shook his head sympathetically at Tom. One journalist addressed Frank in French-accented English:

'You enjoy your holiday in Germany, Monsieur Pierson? – Have you something to say about France? – Why – why did you try to hide?'

His camera hung big and black in front of him from a cord around his neck, and Tom had an impulse to seize it and break it over his head, but the man swung it up and snapped Frank, just as Frank turned his back on him.

After the check-in, Thurlow sprang to the fore in a manner that Tom admired, shouldering aside the press – four or five by now – like a football linesman as they made directly for Satellite Number Five escalator and the passport control that would give them a barrier.

'I am going to sit next to my friend,' Frank said firmly to the stewardess when they were all aboard the plane. Frank meant Tom.

Tom let Frank handle it, and one man was willing to change his seat, so Tom and Frank were side by side in a row that held six. Tom had the aisle seat. It was not Concorde, and Tom did not relish the thought of the next seven hours. A bit strange Thurlow had not bought first class, Tom thought.

'What did you and Thurlow talk about?' Frank asked.

'Nothing important. He was asking how I spent my time.' Tom chuckled. 'And you and Johnny?'

'Also nothing important,' Frank replied rather curtly, but Tom knew the boy by now and didn't mind.

Tom hoped that Frank and Johnny had not talked about Teresa, because Johnny seemed to have no sympathy for the department of lost loves. Tom had brought three books to read, which he had in a plaid carry-all. There were the inevitable, indefatigable small children – all of three of them American – who started running up and down the aisle, though Tom had thought he and Frank might escape their racket, being seated at least eighteen rows away from the kids' presumable base. Tom tried reading, snoozing, thinking – though it was not always good to try to think. Inspiration, good or productive ideas seldom came that way. Tom woke up from a semi-doze with the word 'Showmanship!' strongly in his ears or in his brain, and sat up, blinked at the technicolour Western now in progress on the screen in the middle of the plane, silent to him, because he had declined earphones. Showmanship how? What was he supposed to do at the Piersons'?

Tom picked up a book again. When one of the odious four-year-olds ran for the umteenth time up the aisle towards him, babbling nonsense, Tom stretched back and put a foot out slightly into the aisle. The little monster fell on its belly with, seconds afterwards, a wail like that of a wronged banshee. Tom feigned sleep. A bored stewardess came from somewhere to set the little thing upright. Tom saw a satisfied smirk from a man seated across the aisle from him. Tom was not alone. The child was steered back to its place forward, no doubt to recover *pour mieux sauter*, as the French said, in which case Tom thought he might leave the pleasure of tripping it to another passenger.

When they got to New York, it was early afternoon. Tom craned to look out the window, thrilled as always by the Manhattan skyscrapers made hazy as an Impressionst painting now by fluffy white and yellow clouds. Beautiful and admirable! Nowhere in the world did so many buildings stretch so high in such a tiny area! Then they were down with a dull thud, moving like cogs again, passports, luggage, frisking. And then the rosy-cheeked man whom Frank identified to Tom as Eugene, the chauffeur. Eugene, rather short and balding, looked happy to see Frank.

'Frank! How *are* you?' Eugene seemed friendly and at the same time polite and correct. He had an English accent, and wore ordinary clothes with shirt and tie. 'And Mr Thurlow. Greetings! – And Johnny!'

'Hello, Eugene,' Thurlow said. 'And this is Tom Ripley.'

Tom and Eugene exchanged a 'How do you do?' then Eugene continued, 'Mrs Pierson had to go to Kennebunkport early this morning. Susie wasn't feeling well. Mrs Pierson said either to come to the apartment and stay the night, or we can take a 'copter from the Heliport.'

They were all standing in bright sunshine, luggage on the pavement, hand luggage still in hand, at least Tom's was.

'Who's at the apartment?' Johnny asked.

'No one just now, sir. Flora's on vacation,' said Eugene. 'We've rather closed the apartment, in fact. Mrs Pierson said she *might* come down midweek, if Susie –'

'Let's go to the apartment,' Thurlow interrupted. 'It's on the way, anyway. All right with you, Johnny? I'd like to 'phone the office. I might have to drop in there today.'

'Sure, it's okay. I also want to look at my mail,' said Johnny. 'What's the matter with Susie, Eugene?'

'Not quite sure, sir. Sounded as if she might've had a slight heart attack. I know they sent for the doctor. This was at noon today. Your mother telephoned. I drove down yesterday with her and we stayed the night at the apartment. She wanted to meet you in New York.' Eugene smiled. 'I'll just go get the car. Back in two minutes.'

Tom wondered if it was Susie's first heart attack. Flora, Tom supposed, was one of the servants. Eugene returned, driving a large black Daimler-Benz, and they all got in. There was even room for their luggage. Frank sat in the front with Eugene.

'Everything's okay, Eugene?' Johnny asked. 'My mother?'

'Oh, yes, sir, I think so. She's been worried about Frank – of course.' Eugene drove stiffly and efficiently, reminding Tom of a Rolls-Royce brochure he had once read, informing drivers that they should never rest an elbow on the windowsill, because it looked sloppy.

Johnny lit a cigarette and pushed something in the beige leather upholstery which caused an ashtray to appear. Frank was silent.

Third Avenue now. Lexington. Manhattan looked like a honeycomb compared to Paris, little cells everywhere, buzzing with activity, human insects crawling in and out, carrying things, loading, walking, bumping into one another. In front of an apartment house with an awning that extended to the kerb, the car came to a quiet stop, and a smiling doorman in a grey uniform opened the door of the car, after a touch of his fingers to his cap.

'*Good* afternoon, Mr Pierson,' the doorman said.

Johnny greeted him by name. Glass doors, and then they rode up in an elevator, while the suitcases went up in another elevator.

'Anybody got the key?' asked Thurlow.

'I have,' Johnny said with an air of pride, and pulled a key ring from his pocket.

Eugene was putting the car away somewhere.

The apartment was marked 12A. They went into a spacious foyer. Some of the chairs in the big living room bore protective covers, the ones nearest the windows, though the windows now had their venetian blinds down and closed, so that one needed electric light to see properly. Johnny took care of both – smiling as if he were happy to be home, if this were home – slid the blind cords so that more light came in, then turned on a standing lamp. Tom saw Frank lingering in the hall, looking through a stack of some dozen letters. The boy's face remained tense, a bit frowning. Nothing from Teresa, Tom thought. But the boy's step into the living room was almost a saunter. He looked at Tom and said:

'Well, well, Tom – this is it. Or part of it. Our home.'

Tom gave a polite smile, because Frank wanted that. Tom strolled towards a mediocre oil above the fireplace – did the fireplace work? – of a woman Tom supposed was Frank's mother: blonde, pretty, made-up, posed with hands not in lap but stretched out, as were the arms, along the back of a pale green sofa. She wore a black sleeveless dress with an orange-red flower in her belt. The mouth was gently smiling, but so worked over by the painter, Tom did not look for reality or character in it. What had John Pierson had to pay for this mess? Thurlow was on the telephone in the foyer, speaking perhaps to his office. Tom was not interested in what he might have to say. Now Tom saw Johnny in the hall looking at the letters, pocketing two, opening a third. Johnny looked cheerful.

In the living room two large brown leather sofas – Tom could just see the bottom part of the side of one under the white sheet – made a right angle, and there was a grand piano with a music score propped up. Tom moved closer to see what the music was, but two photographs atop the piano distracted him. One was of a dark-haired man holding a baby of perhaps two, the baby laughing and blond: Johnny, Tom supposed, and the man was John Pierson, looking hardly forty, smiling with friendly dark eyes in which Tom thought he saw a resemblance to Frank's. The second picture of John looked equally attractive, John in white shirt with no tie, wearing no glasses, in the act of taking a pipe from his smiling mouth as a wraithe of smoke drifted up. It was difficult to imagine John the elder a tyrant or even a tough businessman from these pictures. The sheet music on the piano had *Sweet Lorraine* written in scrolly letters on its cover. Did Lily play? Tom had always liked *Sweet Lorraine*.

Eugene arrived, and Thurlow came in just then from another room,

carrying what looked like a scotch and soda. Eugene at once asked Tom
if he would like some refreshment, tea or a drink, and Tom declined.
Then Thurlow and Eugene discussed the next move. Thurlow was for
taking a helicopter, and Eugene said of course that could be done, and
were they all going? Tom looked at Frank, and would not have been
surprised if Frank had said he preferred to stay in New York and with
Tom, but Frank said:

'All right, yes. We'll all go.'

Then Eugene made a telephone call.

Frank beckoned Tom into a hall. 'Would you like to see my room?' The
boy opened the second door on the right in the hall. Again venetian blinds
had been drawn, but Frank pulled a cord so that they admitted light.

Tom saw a long trestle-based table, books neatly set in a row at the
back against the wall, stacked spiral-backed school notebooks, and two
pictures of the girl he recognized as Teresa. In one picture she was by
herself with a tiara, a lei of flowers, white dress, pink lips smiling a
mischievous smile, eyes bright. The belle of the ball that night, Tom
supposed. The other picture, also in colour, was smaller: Frank and
Teresa standing in what looked like Washington Square, Frank holding
her hand, Teresa in bell-bottomed beige jeans and blue denim shirt,
with a little sack of something – peanuts maybe – in one hand. Frank
looked handsome and happy, like a boy who was sure of his girl.

'My favourite picture,' said Frank. 'Makes me look older. That was
just – maybe two weeks before I went to Europe.'

Meaning about a week before he killed his father. Tom again had the
disturbing, very strange doubt: *had* Frank killed his father? Or was it
fantasy? Adolescents did have fantasies and hung on to them. And
might Frank? Frank had an intensity of a kind that Johnny showed not
at all. It was going to take ages for Frank to recover from Teresa, for
instance, and by ages Tom thought of perhaps two years. On the other
hand, to fantasize about killing his father, and to have told Tom about
it, would have been a way of calling attention to himself, and Frank
was not the type to do that.

'What're you thinking about?' Frank asked. 'Teresa?'

'Are you telling me the truth about your father?' Tom asked softly.

Frank's mouth became suddenly firm in a way that Tom knew well.
'Why would I ever lie to you?' Then he shrugged as if ashamed of being
so serious. 'Let's go out.'

He just might lie, Tom thought, because he believed more in fantasy
than in reality. 'Your brother doesn't suspect at all?'

'My brother – he asked me and I said I didn't – push –' Frank broke off. 'Johnny believed me. I think he wouldn't even want to believe the truth if I told him.'

Tom nodded, and also nodded towards the door of the room. Before he went out, Tom glanced at the hi-fi and the handsome three-tiered case of records near the door. Then Tom went back and pulled the venetian blinds' cord the way it had been. The rug was dark purple, as was the cover of the bed. Tom found the colour pleasing.

They all went down and got two taxis, and headed for the Midtown Heliport on West Thirtieth Street. Tom had heard of the Heliport, but never been here. The Piersons had their own helicopter, with room for a dozen people, it seemed, though Tom didn't count the seats. There was leg room, a bar, an electronic kitchen.

'I don't know these people,' Frank said to Tom, referring to the pilot and the steward who was taking drink and food orders. 'They're employed by the Heliport.'

Tom ordered a beer and a cheese sandwich on rye. It was now just after five, and the trip was going to take about three hours, someone had said. Thurlow sat beside Eugene in seats nearer the pilot. Tom looked out of his window and watched New York drop below them.

Chop-chop-chop, as the comic strips said. Mountains of buildings sank below, as if being sucked downward, reminding Tom of a film being turned in reverse. Frank sat across the aisle from Tom. There was no one behind them. Now the steward and the pilot up front were telling jokes, or so it seemed from their laughter. On their left, an orange sun hung above the horizon.

Frank sank himself in another book, one he had taken from his room. Tom tried to snooze. It seemed the best thing to do, in view of the fact they all might be up late tonight. For Tom, Frank and Thurlow, also Johnny, it was about two in the morning. Thurlow was already asleep, Tom saw.

A different pitch of the motor's buzz awakened Tom. They were descending.

'We're landing on the back lawn,' Frank said to Tom.

It was almost dark. Now Tom saw a big white house, impressive yet somehow friendly with its yellowish lights glowing under two porch roofs on two sides. And maybe mother would be standing on one porch, Tom thought, as if welcoming a son who came trudging home with a handkerchief of possessions on a stick over his shoulder. Tom realized that he was curious about the Pierson establishment here, not their only house, of course, but an important one. The sea lay on their right, and Tom could see a couple of lights out there, of buoys or of small craft. And there, suddenly, *was* Lily Pierson – mama – on the porch, waving! She appeared to be wearing black slacks and blouse, in the semi-darkness Tom couldn't tell, but her fair hair showed in the porch's light. Beside her stood a thicker figure, a woman wearing mostly white.

The helicopter touched ground. They descended steps that had been flipped out.

'*Franky!* Welcome *home!*' called his mother.

The woman beside her was a black, smiling also, coming forward to help with the luggage which Eugene and the steward were taking from a side hatch.

'Hello, Mom,' said Frank. He put his arm nervously or a bit tensely around his mother's shoulder, and did not quite kiss her cheek.

Tom watched from a distance, as he was still on the lawn. The boy was shy, but he did not dislike his mother, Tom thought.

'This is Evangelina,' Lily Pierson was saying to Frank, indicating the black woman walking towards them with somebody's suitcase now. 'My son Frank – and Johnny,' she said to Evangelina. 'And how are you, Ralph?'

'Very fine, thank you. This is –'

Frank interrupted Thurlow. 'Mom, this is Tom Ripley.'

'I'm so happy to meet you, Mr Ripley!' Lily Pierson's made-up eyes gave Tom a searching inspection, though her smile looked friendly enough.

They were ushered into the house, assured by Lily that they could leave their jackets and raincoats in the hall or anywhere. And had they had anything to eat, or were they exhausted? Evangelina had prepared a cold supper, if anyone wished to partake. Lily's voice did not sound nervous, only hospitable. Her accent combined New York and California, Tom thought.

Then they all sat down in the large living room. Eugene disappeared in the same direction as Evangelina, perhaps to the kitchen where the helicopter crew probably was. And there was the painting, the Derwatt that Frank had mentioned on his second visit to Belle Ombre. This was 'The Rainbow', a Bernard Tufts forgery. Tom had never seen the painting, simply remembered its title from a Buckmaster Gallery report to him on sales maybe four years ago. Tom recalled also Frank's description of it: beige below, being the tops of a city's buildings, and a mostly dark-reddish rainbow above with a little pale green in it. *All fuzzy and jagged*, Frank had said. *You can't tell what city it is, Mexico or New York.* And so it was, and well pulled off by Bernard, with dash and assurance in that rainbow, and Tom took his eyes away with reluctance, not wanting to be asked by Mrs Pierson if he was especially fond of Derwatts. Thurlow and Lily Pierson were talking now, Thurlow telling the Paris events (telephone calls), and about Frank and Mr Ripley spending a couple of nights in Hamburg after Berlin, which of course Lily Pierson must already have known. It was strange, Tom thought, to be sitting on a sofa much bigger than his own, in front of a fireplace also bigger than his own, over which hung a phony Derwatt, just as 'Man in Chair' at his own house was phony.

'Mr Ripley, I've heard through Ralph about your fantastic *help* to us,' said Lily, blinking her eyelids. She sat on an oversized green hassock between Tom and the fireplace.

To Tom fantastic was an adolescent's word. He realized that he used the word fantastic in his thoughts, but not in his speech. 'A little realistic help, maybe,' Tom said modestly. Frank had left the living room, and so had Johnny.

'I do want to thank you. I can't put it into words because – I know for one thing you risked your life. That's what Ralph said.' She had the clear diction of an actress.

Had Ralph Thurlow been so kind?

'Ralph says you didn't even use the *police* in Berlin.'

'I thought it best to do without the police, if I could,' said Tom. 'Sometimes kidnappers panic. As I said to Thurlow, I think the kidnappers were amateurs in Berlin. Rather young and not well organized.'

Lily Pierson was observing him closely. She looked hardly forty, but was probably a bit more, slender and fit, with the blue eyes that Tom had seen in the oil painting in New York, suggesting that her blonde hair was real. 'And Frank was not hurt at all,' she said, as if she marvelled at the fact.

'No,' said Tom.

Lily sighed, glanced at Ralph Thurlow, then back at Tom. 'How did you and Frank meet?'

Frank came back into the living room just then. The corners of his mouth looked tighter. Tom supposed that he had looked for a letter or a message here from Teresa, and again found none. The boy had changed his clothes, and now wore blue jeans, sneakers, and a yellowish viyella shirt. He had heard the last question, and said to his mother, 'I looked Tom up in the town where he lives. I had a part-time job in a town nearby – gardening.'

'Really? Well – you always wanted to be that – do that.' His mother looked a bit stunned, and blinked her eyes again. 'And where are these towns?'

'Moret,' Frank said. 'That's where I was working. Tom lives about five miles away. His town is called Villeperce.'

'Villeperce,' his mother repeated.

Her accent made Tom smile, and he stared at 'The Rainbow', loving it.

'Not far south of Paris,' said Frank, standing straight, and speaking with what Tom thought was unusual preciseness. 'I knew Tom's name, because Dad mentioned Tom Ripley a couple of times – in connection with our Derwatt painting. Remember, Mom?'

'No, I frankly don't,' said Lily.

'Tom knows the people at the gallery in London. Isn't that true, Tom?'

'Yes, I do,' said Tom calmly. Frank was in a way boasting about him as an important friend and – maybe, Tom thought – deliberately creating an opening for either his mother or Thurlow to bring up the matter of the authenticity of some pictures signed Derwatt. Was Frank going to defend Derwatt and all the Derwatts, even the possible phonies? They didn't get that far.

Evangelina slowly and surely brought platters and wine to a long table in a room behind Tom, and she was aided by Eugene. While this was going on, Lily proposed showing Tom his room.

'I'm so pleased you can stay at least a night with us,' said Lily, leading Tom up some stairs.

Tom was taken into a large square room with two windows, which Lily said looked on to the sea, though the sea was not visible now, only blackness. The furniture was white and gold, and there was a bathroom adjoining, also in white and gold, and even the towels were yellow, and some of the fixtures including a small chest of drawers were adorned with gold scrolls in imitation of the room's furniture which was Louis Quinze *véritable*.

'How is Frank really?' asked Lily with a frown that put three anxious lines across her forehead.

Tom took his time. 'I think he's in love with a girl called Teresa. Do you know anything about Teresa?'

'Oh – *Teresa* –' The room door was ajar, and Lily glanced at it. 'Well, she's the third or fourth girl that *I've* heard of. Not that Frank talks to me at all about his girl friends – or even much else – but *Johnny* finds out somehow. What do you mean about Teresa? Frank's been talking a lot about her?'

'Oh, no, not a lot. But it seems he's in love with her now. She's been to the house here, hasn't she? You've met her?'

'Yes, sure. *Very* nice girl. But she's only sixteen. So is Frank.' Lily Pierson looked at Tom as if to say, of what importance can this be?

'Johnny told me in Paris that Teresa has another interest. An older man, shall we say. I think that upset Frank.'

'Oh, probably. Teresa's so pretty, she's awfully *popular*. A girl of sixteen – she'll prefer somebody of twenty or even older.' Lily smiled, as if the subject were finished.

Tom had been hoping to draw from Lily some remark on Frank's character.

'Frank'll get over *Teresa*,' Lily added cheerfully, but in a soft voice, as if Frank might be in the hall and able to listen.

'One more question, Mrs Pierson, while I have the chance. I think Frank ran away from home because he was upset about his father's death. Isn't that the main reason? More than because of Teresa, I mean, because at that time from what Frank told me, Teresa hadn't cooled off.'

Lily seemed to be choosing her words before she spoke. 'Frank was upset about John's death, more than Johnny was, I know. Johnny's sometimes in the clouds with his photography and *his* girls.'

Tom looked at Lily's twisted face, and wondered if he dared ask her if she thought her husband had killed himself? 'Your husband's death was called an accident, I read in the newspapers. His wheelchair went over that cliff.'

Lily gave a shrug, like a twitch. 'I really don't *know*.'

The room door was still ajar, and Tom thought of closing it, of suggesting that Lily sit down, but would that interrupt the flow of truth, if she knew it? 'But you think it was an accident rather than a suicide?'

'I don't *know*. The ground slopes up a little there, and John never sat at the very edge. That would've been stupid. And his chair had a brake, of course. Frank said he just zoomed over suddenly – and why should he have put the power on unless he wanted to?' Again the troubled frown, and she glanced at Tom. 'Frank came running towards the house –' She did not go on.

'Frank told me your husband was disappointed because neither of the boys wanted to – They didn't take much interest in his work. The Pierson business, I mean.'

'Oh, *that*, true. I think the boys are terrified of the *business*. They consider it too complicated or they just don't like it.' Lily glanced towards the windows as if the *business* might have been a big black storm coming up outside. 'It was a disappointment to John, certainly. You know how a father wants *one* of his sons anyway to take over. But there're other people in John's family – he always called his office people his family too – who *can* take over. Nicholas Burgess, for instance, John's right-hand man and only forty now. It's hard for me to believe a disappointment in the boys could've made John want to kill himself, but I think he could've done it because he really felt – ashamed of being in a chair. Tired of it, I know that. And then at sunset – He always got emotional about sunsets. Not emotional, but *affected.* Happy and sad, like the end of something. Not even the sun there, but dusk falling over the water in front of him.'

So Frank had come running towards the house. Lily had spoken as if she had seen him. 'Frank often went out with his father? On the cliff?'

'No.' Lily smiled. 'Bored Frank. He said John wanted him to go with him that afternoon. John often *did* ask Frank. John was always counting on Frank more than on Johnny – between you and me.' She laughed a little, mischievously. 'John said, "There's something more solid in Frank, if I can just bring it out. Shows in his face." He meant compared to Johnny, who's more of a – I don't know – a dreamer type.'

'I was reminded of George Wallace's case, when I read about your husband. John perhaps had periods of depression.'

'Oh-h, not really,' said Lily with a smile now. 'He could be serious and grim about his work, pull a long face one day if something went wrong, but that's not the same as being depressed. Pierson, Incorporated, business, whatever he called it, was like a big chess game to John. That's what a lot of people said. You win a little one day and lose a little the next, and the game is never *over* – not even now that John's gone. No, I think John was an optimist by nature. He could always smile – nearly always. Even in the years when he was in his chair. We always called it his *chair*, not a wheelchair. But it was sad for the boys, so far as having a father went, because that's all the boys have known of him for such a long time in their lives – a businessman in a chair, talking about markets and money and people – everything invisible somehow. Not able to go out for walks or teach the boys judo or whatever fathers usually do.'

Tom smiled. 'Judo?'

'John used to do judo in this very room! It wasn't always a guest room, this room.'

They were moving towards the door. Tom glanced at the high ceiling, the wide floor that would have provided space for mats and somersaults.

Downstairs the others were in the living room buffeting themselves, as Tom always thought when he encountered the word buffet, but in this case there was plenty of room and no elbowing crowd. Frank was drinking a Coca-Cola from the bottle. Thurlow stood by the table with Johnny, holding a scotch highball and a plate of food.

'Let's go out,' Tom said to Frank.

Frank set his bottle down at once. 'Out where?'

'Out on the lawn.' Lily had joined Johnny and Thurlow, Tom saw. 'Did you ask about Susie? How is she?'

'Oh, conked out asleep,' said Frank. 'I asked Evangelina. What a name! She belongs to some nutty soul group. Been here just a week, she says.'

'Susie's here?'

'Yes, she has a room in the back wing upstairs. We can go out this way.'

Frank was opening a large french window in what must be their main dining room, Tom thought. There was a long table with chairs around it, and smaller tables with chairs near the walls, sideboards and some bookcases also. There were platters and a cake on the table now. Frank had put on an outside light, so they could see their way across a terrace and down four or five steps to the lawn. To the left of the steps sloped the ramp that Frank had told him about. After that, it was dark, but Frank said he knew the way. A stone path was palely visible, extending across the lawn, then curving to the right. As Tom's eyes became more adjusted to the darkness, he could see tall trees, pine or poplar, ahead.

'This is where your father used to walk?' Tom asked.

'Yes, well – not walk. He had his chair.' Frank slowed and stuck his hands into his pockets. 'No moon tonight.'

The boy had stopped and was ready to go back to the house, Tom saw. Tom took a couple of deep breaths and looked back at the two-storey white house with its yellowish lights. The house had a peaked roof, the porches' roofs projected to the left and right. Tom didn't like the house. It looked newish, and of no definable style. It was not like an American southern house or a New England colonial house. John Pierson had probably had it built to order, but at any rate Tom didn't care for the architect. 'I wanted to see the cliff,' Tom said. Didn't Frank know that?

'All right, it's this way,' Frank said, and they walked on along the flagstone path into deeper darkness.

The flagstones were still visible, and Frank walked as if he were sure of every inch of it. The poplars closed in, then parted, and they were on the cliff, and Tom could see its edge, defined by light coloured stones or pebbles.

'The sea's out there,' said Frank, gesturing. He hung back from the edge.

'I assumed that.' Tom could hear waves below, gentle, not pounding and not rhythmic, but rather lapping. And far out in the blackness, Tom saw a boat prow's white light, and imagined he saw a pinkish port light. Something like a bat whizzed by overhead, but Frank seemed not to have noticed it. *So here is where it happened*, Tom thought, then he saw Frank walking past him, hands in the back pockets of his jeans, to the edge of the cliff, and he saw the boy look down. Tom had an instant's fear for Frank, because it was so dark, and the boy seemed so near the edge, even though the edge did slope up a little, Tom could now see. Frank turned back suddenly and said:

'You were talking with Mom tonight?'

'Oh, yes, a bit. I asked her about Teresa. I know Teresa's been here. I suppose she didn't write to you?' Tom thought it better to ask him outright than not to say anything about a letter.

'No,' Frank said.

Tom went closer to him, until they were only four or five feet apart. The boy stood straight. 'I'm sorry,' Tom said. He was thinking that the girl had troubled to telephone Thurlow in Paris, once, days ago, and now that Frank was found, and safe, she was simply dropping out, with no explanation.

'Is that all you talked about? Teresa?' Frank asked in a light tone that might have implied that that was not very much to talk about.

'No, I asked her if she thought your father's death was a suicide or an accident.'

'And what did she say?'

'That she didn't know. You know, Frank –' Now Tom spoke softly. 'She doesn't suspect you *at* all – and you'd better let this thing blow over. Just that. Maybe it has. It's done. Your mother said, "Suicide or accident, it's done." Something like that. So you must pick yourself up, Frank, and get rid of – I wish you wouldn't stand so near the edge.' The boy was facing the sea, raising and lowering himself on his toes, whether aggressively or absent-mindedly, Tom couldn't tell.

Then Frank turned and walked towards Tom, and passed Tom on the left. The boy turned again and said, 'But you know I did send that chair over. I know you were talking to my Mom about what she might think or believe, but I *told* you. I mean, I said to my mother my father did it himself, and she believed me, but that's not true.'

'All right, all right,' Tom said gently.

'When I sent my father's chair over, I even thought I was with Teresa – that she – liked me, I mean.'

'All right, I understand,' Tom said.

'I thought, I'll get my father out of my life, out of our lives, for me and Teresa. I felt my father was spoiling – life. It's funny that Teresa gave me courage then. And now she's gone. Now there's nothing but silence – nothing!' His voice cracked.

Odd, Tom thought, that some girls meant sadness and death. Some girls looked like sunlight, creativity, joy, but they really meant death, and not even because the girls were enticing their victims, in fact one might blame the boys for being deceived by – nothing at all, simply imagination. Tom laughed suddenly. 'Frank, you *have* to realize that there are other girls in the world! You must see it by now that Teresa – She's turned loose of you. So you must turn loose of her.'

'I have. I did that in Berlin, I think. The real crisis was there, when I heard what Johnny said.' Frank gave a shrug, but was not looking at Tom. 'Sure, I looked for a letter from her, I admit that.'

'So you go on from here. Things look rotten now, but there are a lot of weeks and years ahead for you. Come on!' Tom slapped the boy on the shoulder. 'We'll go back to the house in a minute. Wait.'

Tom wanted to see the edge, and moved forward towards the lighter coloured rocks. He could feel pebbles and a bit of grass under his shoes. He could feel also the emptiness below, now black, but giving out something like a sound of hollow space. And there, unable to be seen now, were the jagged rocks that Frank's father had fallen on to. Tom turned at the sound of the boy's steps towards him, and at once moved away from the edge. Tom had had a sudden feeling that the boy might rush him and push him over. Was that insane on his part, Tom wondered. The boy adored him. Tom knew that. But love was strange too.

'Ready to go back?' Frank asked.

'Sure,' Tom felt the coolness of sweat on his forehead. He knew he was more tired than he thought, and that he had lost track of time because of the airplane trip.

TWENTY-ONE

Tom fell asleep almost before he got into bed. Some time later, he awakened with a violent twitch of his entire body. A bad dream? If so, he didn't remember a dream. How long had he been asleep? An hour?

'*No!*' That had been a whisper or a soft voice outside his room in the hall.

Tom got out of bed. The voices outside went on, a cooing, pigeon-like female voice mingling with Frank's. Tom knew Frank's room was next to his on the right. Only a few words came through, said by the woman: '. . . *so impatient* . . . I *know* . . . what, *what* will you do . . . not matter to *me!*'

That had to be Susie, and she sounded angry. Tom could detect her German accent. And in fact he could have put his ear to the door and heard more, but Tom had an aversion to eavesdropping. He turned his back to the door, groped forward towards his bed, and found his night table on which lay cigarettes and matches. Tom struck a match, put on his reading lamp, lit a cigarette and sat down on his bed. That was better.

Had Susie knocked on Frank's door? More likely than that Frank had knocked on hers! Tom laughed, and lay back on his bed. He heard a door close gently nearby, and that would be Frank's door. Tom stood up, put his cigarette out, and stepped into his loafers which were serving again as house-slippers as they had in Berlin. He went into the hall, and saw a light under Frank's closed door. Tom rapped with his fingertips.

'Tom,' he said, when he heard a soft, quick tread coming towards the door.

Frank opened the door, hollow-eyed with fatigue, but smiling. 'Come *in*!' he whispered.

Tom did. 'That was Susie?'

Frank nodded. 'Got a fag for me? Mine are downstairs.'

Tom had his in the pocket of his pyjamas. 'Well, what's she on about?' He lit the boy's cigarette.

Frank said, 'Fwoop!' and blew out smoke, nearly laughing. 'She still says she saw me on the cliff.'

Tom shook his head. 'She's going to have another heart attack. Want me to talk with her tomorrow? – I'm curious to meet her.' He looked behind him at the closed door, because Frank had looked at it. 'Does she wander around at night? I thought she was ill.'

'Strength of an ox, maybe.' Frank was weaving with tiredness, and fell back on his bed with his bare feet in the air for an instant.

Tom glanced around the room, saw an antique brown table on which stood a radio, a typewriter, books, a tablet of writing paper. On the floor near half-open closet doors he saw ski boots and a pair of riding boots. Pop singer posters were tacked to a vast green pin-up board above the brown table, the Ramones slouching in blue jeans, and below all this were cartoons, a couple of photographs, maybe of Teresa, but since Tom did not want to bring that subject up, he did not look closely. 'Damn her ass,' Tom said, meaning Susie, 'she *didn't* see you. You don't expect another visit from her tonight, do you?'

'Old witch,' Frank said, with his eyes half closed.

Tom waved a hand, and went out and back into his room. He noticed that his own room door had a key in the lock on the inside. Tom did not lock it.

The next morning, after the breakfast ritual, Tom asked Mrs Pierson's permission to cut a few flowers from the garden to bring to Susie. Lily Pierson said of course he could. As Tom had supposed, Frank knew more about the garden than his mother, and assured Tom that his mother wouldn't care what they cut. They amassed a bouquet of white roses. Tom preferred to make his visit to Susie without preparation, as it were, but Tom asked Evangelina – appropriate name – to herald his advent. The black maid did so, then asked him to wait, please, for two minutes in the hall.

'Susie likes to comb her hay,' said Evangelina with a happy smile.

After a couple of minutes, Tom was summoned by a guttural or sleepy 'Come in,' and he knocked first, then entered.

Susie was propped against pillows in a whitish room now made whiter by sunlight. Susie's hair looked yellowish and greyish also, her face round and seamed, eyes tired and wise. She reminded Tom of some German postage stamps of famous women whom, usually, Tom had never heard of. Her left arm, in a long white nightdress sleeve, lay outside the covers.

'Good morning. Tom Ripley,' Tom said. Friend of Frank's, he thought of saying, but stopped himself. Maybe she had heard of him already, via Lily. 'How are you feeling this morning?'

'Reasonably well, thank you.'

A television set was facing her bed, reminding Tom of some hospital rooms he had visited, but the rest of the room was personal enough, with old family pictures, crocheted doilies, a bookcase full of knick-knacks, souvenirs, even an old top-hatted minstrel doll that might have been a relic of Johnny's childhood. 'I'm glad to hear that. Mrs Pierson told me that you had a heart attack. I'm sure that's frightening.'

'Yes, when it is the first,' she replied in a grumbling voice. She was keeping a sharp, pale blue eye on Tom.

'I was just – Frank was with me for several days in Europe. Maybe Mrs Pierson told you.' Tom got no response to this, and looked for a vase to put the flowers in, and didn't see one. 'I brought these to brighten your room a little.' Tom advanced with a smile, with his bouquet.

'Thank you very much,' said Susie, taking the bouquet with one hand – Frank had put a napkin around it – and pressing a bell at her bedside with the other.

In no time, there was a knock, Evangelina entered, and was handed the bouquet and requested by Susie to find a vase, please.

Tom was not offered a chair, but he took a straight chair anyway. 'I suppose you know –' Tom wished he had ascertained Susie's last name. '– that Frank was very upset by his father's death. Frank looked me up in France, where I live. That's how I met him.'

She looked at him, still sharply, and said, 'Frank is not a good boy.'

Tom stifled a sigh, and tried to look pleasant and polite. 'He seems quite a nice boy to me – stayed in my house several days.'

'*Why* did he run away?'

'I think he was upset. Well, all he did –' Did Susie know about Frank taking his brother's passport? 'Lots of young people run away. And then come back.'

'I think Frank killed his father,' said Susie tremulously, wagging the forefinger of the hand that lay outside the covers. 'And that is a terrible thing.'

Tom inhaled slowly. 'Why do you think that?'

'You are not surprised? Has he confessed it to you?'

'He certainly has not. No. I'm asking you why you think he did.' Tom frowned with seriousness, and he was affecting some surprise too.

'Because I saw him – almost.'

Tom paused. 'You mean on the cliff there.'

'*Yes.*'

'You saw him – You were out on the lawn?'

'No, I was upstairs. But I saw Frank go out with his father. He *never* went out with his father. They had just finished a game of croquet. Mrs Pierson –'

'Mr Pierson played croquet?'

'Yes, sure! He could move his chair just where he wanted it. Mrs Pierson always wanted him to play a little – to take his mind off – you know, business worries.'

'Frank was playing that day too?'

'Yes, and Johnny too. I remember Johnny had a date – went off. But they all played.'

Tom crossed his legs, wanted a cigarette and thought it best not to light one. 'You told Mrs Pierson,' Tom began with an earnest frown, 'that you thought Frank pushed his father over?'

'Yes,' said Susie firmly.

'Mrs Pierson doesn't seem to think that.'

'Did you ask her?'

'Yes,' said Tom with equal firmness. 'She thinks it was either an accident or a suicide.'

Susie sniffed, and looked towards her TV, as if she wished it were on.

'Did you say the same thing to the police – about Frank?'

'Yes.'

'And what did they say?'

'Ah, they said I couldn't have seen it, because I was upstairs. But there are some things a human being *knows*. You know, Mr –'

'Ripley. Tom. I am sorry I don't know your last name.'

'Schuhmacher,' she replied, just as Evangelina entered with the roses in a pink vase. 'Thank you, Evangelina.'

Evangelina set the vase on the night table between Tom and Susie, and left the room.

'Unless you did see Frank do it – which must be impossible if the police said so – you should not say it. It has troubled Frank very much.'

'Frank was with his father.' Again the plump but slightly wrinkled hand lifted and fell on the bedcover. 'If it was an accident, even a suicide, Frank could have stopped him, no?'

Tom at first thought Susie was right, then he thought of the speed the chair controls must have been capable of. But he didn't want to go into this with Susie. 'Couldn't Mr Pierson have sent his chair over by himself, before Frank knew what was happening? That's what *I* thought.'

She shook her head. 'Frank came back running, they said. I didn't see him till I went downstairs. Everyone was talking then. Frank said his father drove his chair over, I know.' The pale blue eyes were fixed on Tom.

'That's what Frank told me too.' The moment of lying must have been like a second crime for Frank. If the boy had only come back calmly, let half an hour pass, as if he had left his father on the cliff! That, Tom realized, was what he would have done – nervous though he might have been, he would have done a little bit of *planning*. 'What you think or believe – can certainly never be proven,' Tom said.

'Frank denies it, I know.'

'Do you want the boy to have a breakdown because of your – accusation?' At least Susie seemed to pause at this, and Tom pushed his advantage, if he had any, and he wanted to imagine that he had for the moment. 'Unless there's a witness or some real evidence, an act such as you describe can never be proven – or even believed in this case.' And when was the old lady going to die, Tom wondered, and let Frank off the hook? Susie Schuhmacher looked capable of another few years, and Frank could hardly separate himself from her, because she was installed in the Kennebunkport house, where the family evidently stayed quite often, and she probably went to their New York apartment also, when the family was there.

'Why should I care what Frank makes of his life? He –'

'You don't like Frank?' Tom asked, as if amazed.

'He is – not friendly. He is rebellious – unhappy. You never know what he is thinking. He gets ideas and hangs on to them. Attitudes.'

Tom frowned. 'But would you call him dishonest?'

'No,' Susie replied, 'he is too polite. It goes beyond dishonesty, what I mean. More important even –' She seemed to be getting tired. 'But what should I care what he does with his life? He has everything. He does not appreciate what he has, never did. He gave his mother worries, running off the way he did. He doesn't even care about that. He is not a good boy.'

It was not a time, Tom thought, to launch into Frank's fear or dislike of his father's business empire or even to ask what she might know of the influence of Teresa. Now Tom heard a telephone ringing remotely from somewhere. 'But Mr Pierson liked Frank very much, I think.'

'Maybe too much. Did the boy deserve it? Look!'

Tom uncrossed his legs and squirmed. 'I think I've taken enough of your time, Mrs Schuhmacher –'

'That's all right.'

'I'll be leaving tomorrow, maybe even this afternoon, so I'll say good-bye now and give you my good wishes for your health. In fact, I think you look very well,' he added, meaning it. He had stood up.

'You live in France.'

'Yes.'

'I think I remember Mr Pierson mentioning your name. You know the art people in London.'

'Yes, indeed,' Tom replied.

She lifted her left hand again, and let it fall, and looked towards the window.

'Bye-bye, Susie.' Tom made a bow, but Susie didn't see it. Tom left the room.

In the hall, Tom ran into Johnny, lanky and smiling.

'I was just coming to rescue you! Would you like to see my dark room?'

'Sure,' Tom said.

Johnny turned and led Tom to a room on the left side of the hall. Johnny switched on red lights, which gave the effect of a black cavern with pink air in it, something like a stage set. The walls looked black, even the lump of a sofa black, and in a far corner Tom barely detected the paleness of what looked like a long sink. Johnny switched off the red and put on ordinary light. A couple of cameras stood on tripods. The black sheets now seemed minimal. It was not a big room. Tom was not knowledgeable about cameras. He didn't know what to say when Johnny pointed to a camera that he had just acquired, except, 'Really impressive.'

'I could show you some of my work. Nearly all of it's in portfolios here, except one downstairs in the dining room which I call "White Sunday", but it's not snow. But – I think just now Mom wants to talk with you.'

'Now? Does she?'

'Yes, because Ralph's leaving, and Mom said she wanted to see you after he left. How was Susie?' There was amusement, or anticipation of it, in the boy's smile.

'Pleasant enough. Looking pretty strong, I thought. Of course I don't know how she usually looks.'

'She's a bit cracked. Don't pay too much attention to anything she says.' Johnny stood straight, still smiling a little, but his words sounded like a warning.

Johnny was protecting his brother, Tom felt. Johnny knew what Susie was saying, and Frank had told Tom that Johnny didn't believe it. Tom went downstairs with Johnny, and found Mrs Pierson and Ralph Thurlow with his raincoat over his arm. Thurlow must have slept late today, because Tom had not seen him until now.

'Tom –' Ralph Thurlow extended a hand. 'If you ever need a job – along the same lines –' He fished for something in his billfold, and extended a card. 'Ring my office, would you? My home address is there too.'

Tom smiled. 'I'll remember.'

'I really mean, let's have an evening in New York some time. I'm off to New York now. Bye-bye, Tom.'

'Bon voyage,' Tom said.

Tom had thought that Thurlow was going to depart in the black car in the driveway, but Mrs Pierson and Thurlow went out on to the porch and walked to the left. Tom saw that a helicopter had landed or been rolled out on to the cement circle on the back lawn. The property was so vast, Tom supposed that the Piersons might have their own hangar somewhere at the end of the cement runway which disappeared among the trees. This helicopter looked smaller than the one they had taken from New York, but perhaps he was simply getting used to the scale on which the Piersons lived. Tom looked at the black Daimler-Benz whose exhaust pipe gave out faintly visible fumes, and saw that Frank was at the wheel alone. The car moved forward two yards or so, then reversed, smoothly.

'What're you doing?' Tom asked.

Frank smiled. He was in shirt sleeves – the same yellowish viyella shirt – and sat very straight as if he were a chauffeur in livery. 'Nothing.'

'You've got a driving licence?'

'Not yet, but I know how to drive. Do you like this car? I like it. Conservative.'

It was similar to the car Eugene had driven in New York, but the upholstery of this one had brown leather instead of beige.

'Don't take off anywhere without a licence,' Tom said. The boy looked in a mood to take off, though he was working the gears very slowly and meticulously. 'See you later. I'm supposed to speak with your mother.'

'Oh?' Frank switched off the ignition and looked at Tom through the open window. 'And what did you think of Susie?'

'She was – the same as always, I suppose.' Susie was giving the same old story, Tom meant. Frank looked both amused and thoughtful, and at that moment he looked very handsome, perhaps a few years older than he was. It crossed Tom's mind that Frank might have had a telephone call from Teresa that morning, but Tom was afraid to ask. Tom went back to the house.

Lily Pierson, wearing pale blue slacks this morning, was giving Evangelina instructions about lunch. Part of Tom's mind was on his own departure. Should he try to get to New York this evening? Stay a night in New York? He should give Heloise a ring today.

Lily turned to him, smiling. 'Sit down, Tom. Oh no, let's go in here – more cheerful.' She led him towards a sunny room off the living room.

It was a library, full of economics books in bright new jackets, Tom saw at a glance, with a big square desk on which sat a pipe rack with five or six pipes in it. The dark green leather swivel chair behind the desk looked both old and unused, and it occurred to Tom that John Pierson might not have found it worth the trouble to move himself from the wheelchair to the leather chair, when he was in this room.

'And what did you think of Susie?' Lily asked in the same tone as her sons, smiling with her lips pressed together, as were her hands. She looked eager to be amused.

Tom nodded with an air of thought. 'Just what Frank told me. A bit stubborn – perhaps.'

'And she still thinks Frank pushed his father over the cliff?' Lily asked in a tone that implied that the idea was absurd.

'So she thinks, yes,' Tom said.

'No one believes her. There's nothing to believe. She didn't *see* anything. I really can't keep on worrying about Susie. She could make anyone as eccentric as *she* is. I wanted to say to you, Tom, that I realize you've had a lot of expenses due to Frank, and so without any more words about it, would you please accept this cheque from me, from the family.' She had pulled a folded cheque from the pocket of her blouse.

Tom looked at it. Twenty thousand dollars. 'My expenses were nothing like this. Anyway, it was a pleasure to meet your son.' Tom laughed.

'It would give *me* pleasure.'

'My expenses weren't half this.' But in an instant, in the way she brushed her hair back from her forehead unnecessarily, Tom knew that it would please her if he accepted the cheque. 'All right, then.' Tom put the cheque into his trousers pocket, and kept his hand there. 'With my thanks also.'

'Ralph told me about Berlin. You risked your life.'

Tom was not interested in that now. 'Did Frank possibly get a telephone call from Teresa this morning, do you know?'

'I don't think so. Why?'

'I thought he looked more cheerful just now. But I don't know.' Tom really didn't know. He knew only that Frank was in a different mood, one that he had not seen before.

'You can never tell about Frank,' said Lily. 'From the way he acts, I mean.'

Meaning that Frank could act the opposite from the way he felt? Lily was so relieved to have Frank back home, that factors like Teresa just didn't count for much, Tom supposed.

'My friend Tal Stevens is coming this afternoon, and I'd like you to meet him,' Lily said as they walked out of the library. 'One of John's best lawyers, though he never was employed by the company, he was just a freelance counsel.'

This was the friend Lily liked, according to Frank. Lily was saying that Tal had work this afternoon, so probably couldn't arrive until six. 'And I have to see about taking off,' Tom said. 'I thought of staying a day or so in New York.'

'But you're not leaving *today*, I hope. 'Phone your wife in France and tell her. That's the thing to do! – Frank says you have such a pretty house there. He was telling me about your greenhouse and – the two Derwatts you have in your living room and also about your harpsichord.'

'Was he?' His and Heloise's French harpsichord amid helicopters, Maine lobsters, and an American black named Evangelina! It struck a surrealist note to Tom. 'With your permission,' Tom said, 'I will make a 'phone call or two.'

'Make yourself at home here, Tom!'

From his room Tom telephoned the Hotel Chelsea in Manhattan, and asked if they had a single room for that night. A friendly voice said they could probably manage it with a little bit of Irish luck. That was good enough. Tom thought he should take his leave after lunch. Some neighbours called the Hunters were coming at four, Lily had said, because they were very fond of Frank and wanted to see him. Tom supposed that the Pierson household could get him some kind of transportation to Bangor, whence he could take a plane to New York.

Maine lobster was exactly what they had for lunch, as if Tom had received a premonition. Before lunch, he and Frank had driven to the town of Kennebunkport with Eugene at the wheel of a station wagon, and picked up the commanded lobsters. The town had sent a wave of nostalgia over Tom that had almost brought tears to his eyes: white house fronts and store fronts, a freshness in the sea air, sunlight, and American sparrows in trees still heavy with summer foliage – all of which had made Tom think he had made a mistake in leaving America. But this he had put out of his head at once, since it was a depressing and baffling feeling, and he had reminded himself that he was going to bring Heloise to America in late October, or whenever she got back and recovered from her Adventure Cruise, which as Tom recollected was to the Antarctic.

Though Frank had looked surprised and disappointed when Tom said he was leaving that afternoon, the boy appeared cheerful at lunch. Was Frank pretending good humour, Tom wondered? Frank had put on a handsome pale blue linen jacket, though he still wore his blue jeans. 'The same wine we drank at Tom's,' he said to his mother, lifting his stemmed glass with a flourish. 'Sancerre. I asked Eugene to find it. In fact I went to the cellar with him to get it.'

'It is *delicious*,' said Lily, smiling at Tom, as if it were Tom's wine and not hers.

'Heloise is very pretty, Mom,' Frank said, and dipped a fork with lobster into his melted butter.

'You think so? I'll tell her,' said Tom.

Frank placed a hand over his stomach and pretended to belch, a silent performance that was also half a bow, for Tom's benefit.

Johnny devoted himself to his food, and said only something to his mother about a girl called Christine possibly coming at seven, and he didn't know whether they would go somewhere for dinner or stay in.

'Girls, girls, girls,' Frank said contemptuously.

'Shuddup, you little twit,' murmured Johnny. 'Are you jealous maybe?'

'Now stop it, both of you,' said Lily.

It sounded like a usual family lunch.

By three, Tom had made his arrangements, reserved a place on an early evening flight from Bangor to Kennedy Airport, and Eugene would drive him to Bangor. Tom packed his suitcase but did not close it. He went into the hall and tapped on Frank's slightly open door. There was no answer. Tom pushed the door wider and went in. The room was empty and tidy, the bed probably having been made by Evangelina. On Frank's desk sat the Berlin bear, some twelve inches high, its beady brown eyes ringed with yellow, its mouth jolly though closed. Tom remembered Frank's amusement at the hand-written sign: 3 WÜRFE I MARK. Frank had thought *Würfe* a funny word for throws, because it sounded like something to eat, or maybe a dog's bark. How had the little bear survived a kidnapping, a murder, a couple of airplane trips, and come out looking as fluffy and cheerful as ever? Tom had wanted to ask Frank to join him for another walk to the cliff. Tom had the feeling that if he could get the boy used to the cliff, though used wasn't quite the right word for it, Frank's guilt might be diminished.

'I think Frank went off with Johnny to get his bicycle tyres pumped up,' Lily said to Tom downstairs.

'I thought he might come for a little walk, since I've got about an hour,' Tom said.

'They should be back any minute, and I'm sure Frank *would*. He thinks you hung the *moon*, Tom.'

Tom hadn't heard this complimentary term since he had been a teenager in Boston. He went out on to the lawn, on to the flagstone path. He wanted to see the cliff by daylight. Somehow the path seemed longer, then suddenly he was beyond the trees, with the beautiful view of blue water before him, perhaps not as blue as the Pacific, but still very blue and clean now. Sea gulls let themselves be borne on the wind, and three or four little boats, one a sailboat, moved slowly on the wide surface. And then the cliff. It was a sudden ugliness to Tom. He walked closer to its edge, looking down at the grass that merged with stones then rock, and finally with his feet eight or ten inches from the drop. Below, just as he had imagined, boulder-sized beige and white rocks lay tumbled as if by some landfall or rockfall in the not too distant past. Down where the water began, he could see little white waves lapping against the smaller rocks. He looked, stupidly, for some sign of the John Pierson catastrophe, such as a piece of chrome from the chair. He saw nothing man made down there. John Pierson, if he had merely toppled his chair over at not much speed, would have hit jagged rocks thirty feet below, and would possibly have tumbled another couple of yards downward. Not even any bloodstains on the rocks now, Tom saw, and shuddered. He backed from the edge and turned.

He glanced towards the house which was hardly visible through the trees, just its dark grey roof ridge showing, and then he saw Frank on the path coming towards him, still in his blue jacket. Was the boy looking for him? Without thinking, Tom stepped to his right into a cluster of trees and behind some bushes. Would the boy look around? Call his name, if Frank thought he might have walked here? Tom realized that he was curious – maybe just to see the expression on the boy's face as he approached the cliff. Now Frank was so close, Tom could see his straight brown hair bobbing a little with his steps.

Frank's eyes looked to left and right, at the trees, but Tom was well hidden.

And also, Tom thought, probably his mother hadn't told Frank that he had gone to the cliff, because Tom hadn't said that. At any rate, Frank did not call Tom's name, and did not look round again. Frank had his thumbs hooked in the front pocket of his levis, and he strode slowly towards the cliff's edge, a little arrogantly, swinging his feet. Now the boy's whole figure was silhouetted against the beautiful blue sky, just perhaps twenty feet from Tom. The boy looked down. But mostly he looked at the sea, and he seemed, to Tom, to take a deep breath and to relax. Then he stepped backward, as Tom had done, looking down at his sneakered feet. He kicked his right foot backward, scattering a few pebbles, and took his thumbs from his pockets. He bent forward and at once ran.

'Hey!' Tom shouted, and drove forward himself. Somehow he tripped, or perhaps had merely launched himself horizontally, but his hands had been extended, and he had Frank by one ankle.

Frank was flat down, gasping, and his right arm hung over the cliff's edge.

'God's *sake*!' Tom said, and gave Frank's ankle a nervous tug towards him. Tom got to his feet, and hauled Frank up by one arm.

The breath was knocked out of the boy, and his eyes looked glazed and unfocused.

'What the hell were you doing?' Tom realized that his voice had gone hoarse suddenly. 'Wake up!' Tom steadied Frank, felt in a state of shock himself, and pulled the boy by his arm towards the woods, the path. A bird cried just then, an odd squeak, as if the bird also was shocked. Tom stood up straighter and said, 'All right, Frank. You almost did it. Same as doing it, isn't it? – Quick reflex from hearing my voice? You flopped down like a football player!' Or had he? Had Tom stopped him by catching one ankle? Tom slapped the boy nervously on the back. 'You've done it once now, okay. All right?'

'Yep,' said Frank.

'You mean it,' Tom said, as if asking him. 'Don't just say "Yep" to me. You proved what you wanted to prove. Okay?'

'Yes, sir.'

They were walking back towards the house. The wobbliness slowly left Tom's legs, and he deliberately breathed deeply. 'I won't mention this. Let's not mention this to anybody. All right, Frank?' He glanced at the boy who seemed as tall as himself suddenly.

Frank was looking straight ahead, not at the house but beyond. 'Right, Tom, sure.'

TWENTY-TWO

When Tom and Frank got back to the house, the Hunters had arrived.
Tom would not have known this, if Frank had not pointed out a green
car in the driveway. Tom would have thought it one of the Piersons'
cars.

'I'm sure they're up in the ocean *view* room,' Frank said, as if putting
ocean view in quotes. 'Mom always serves tea up there.' He looked at
Tom's suitcase, which someone had taken down and set near the front
door.

'Let's have a drink of something. I could use one,' Tom said, and
went to the sideboard or bar table which was nearly three yards long.
'Any Drambuie, I wonder?'

'Drambuie? I'm sure there is.'

Tom watched him bend over the double row of bottles, index finger
extended to the left, then the right, and he found it and hauled it up,
smiling.

'I remember this from your house.' Frank poured some into two
brandy glasses.

Frank's hand was steady, Tom saw, but his face looked still pale as
he lifted his glass. Tom joined him, and touched the boy's glass. 'This
will do you good.'

They drank. Tom noticed that the bottom button of his jacket front
was hanging by a couple of threads, so he pulled it off and pocketed it,
and brushed some dust away. The boy's jacket had a rent about an inch
long on the right breast.

Frank swung on one heel of his sneaker, made a complete turn, and
asked, 'What time do you have to leave?'

'Around five.' Tom saw by his wristwatch that it was a quarter past
four. 'I don't feel like saying good-bye to Susie,' Tom said.

'Oh, let it go!'

'But your mom –'

They went upstairs. Some colour had returned to Frank's cheeks, and
his step was springy. Frank rapped on a white, half-open door, and he
and Tom went in. This was a large room with wall-to-wall carpeting
and three broad windows which took up the whole opposite wall and
gave a view on the sea. Lily Pierson sat near a round low table, and a
middle-aged couple who Tom supposed were the Hunters sat in armchairs. Johnny was standing up with a handful of photographs.

'Where have you *been?*' asked Lily. 'Come in, both of you. Betsy, this is Tom Ripley – who I've been *talking* so much about. Wally – finally *Frank* is back.'

'Frank!' said the Hunters almost simultaneously, as the boy strolled forward, bowed a little, and shook Wally's hand. 'Are you boring these people with your junk again?' Frank asked his brother.

'Finally I've met you,' said Wally Hunter, shaking Tom's hand and looking into Tom's eyes as if he, Tom, might be a miracle-worker – or someone who might not really have existed – but Tom's hand hurt.

The Hunters, he in a tan cotton suit and his wife in a mauve cotton dress, looked the picture of Maine summer chic.

'Tea, Frank?' asked his mother.

'Yes, please.' Frank had not yet sat down.

Tom declined tea. 'I should be taking off, Lily.' She had asked him to call her Lily. 'Eugene said he could drive me to Bangor.'

Both Johnny and his mother spoke at once. Of course Eugene would drive him to Bangor. 'Or I can,' Johnny said. They informed Tom that there were at least ten minutes to spare before he had to leave. Tom did not want to talk about events in Europe, and Lily managed to steer Wally Hunter off, promising to tell him about France and Berlin at some other time. Betsy Hunter kept rather cool grey eyes on Tom, but Tom felt indifferent to what she might be thinking about him. Tom also felt indifferent to the arrival of Talmadge Stevens, earlier than expected. The Hunters seemed to know him and like him, judging from their greetings.

Lily introduced him to Tom. He was a bit taller than Tom, looked in his mid-forties, and was the rugged type who perhaps jogged. Tom at once sensed that Lily and Tal had an affair going. And so what? Where was Frank? He had slipped out of the room. Tom slipped out too. Tom thought he had heard music – maybe one of Frank's records – a minute ago.

Frank's room was across the hall and more towards the back of the house. His door was closed. Tom knocked and got no answer. He opened the door a little. 'Frank?'

Frank was not in the room. The gramophone cover was off, with a record on it, but the machine was not turning. Tom saw that it was the Lou Reed *Transformer*, the second side which Heloise had put on at Belle Ombre. Tom glanced at his watch: nearly five, and he and Eugene were supposed to leave at five. Probably Eugene was downstairs at the back of the house where the servants' quarters seemed to be.

Tom went downstairs to the empty living room, and just then heard a clap of laughter from upstairs in the ocean view room. Tom made his way across another central living room with windows on the garden, found the hall again and continued towards the back of the house, where he thought the kitchen was. The kitchen doors stood open, and the walls glowed with copper-bottomed pans and skillets. Eugene stood drinking a cup of something, rosy-cheeked, talking with Evangelina, and jumped to attention at the sight of Tom. Tom had somehow expected to see Frank here.

'Excuse me,' Tom said. 'Have you–'

'I'm watching the time, sir, for five o'clock. I have seven to. May I help you with your luggage?' Eugene had set his cup and saucer down.

'Thanks, no, it's down. Where's Frank? Do you know?'

'I think he's upstairs, sir, having tea,' Eugene said.

No, he's not, Tom started to say, and didn't. Tom felt suddenly alarmed. 'Thanks,' he said to Eugene, and hurried through the house to the nearest exit, which was what Tom thought of as the front door, on to a porch, then around to the right to the lawn. Maybe Frank was upstairs, again, in the room where people were having tea, but Tom wanted to go to the cliff first. He imagined seeing the boy standing at the edge again, contemplating – what? Tom ran all the way. Frank was not there. Tom slowed, gasping, not from lack of breath but from relief. As he walked closer to the edge, he became again afraid. He kept going.

There below was the blue jacket, the darker blue of the levis, the dark head of hair with an outline of red – flower-like, unreal, yet real against nearly white rocks. Tom opened his mouth, as if he were about to yell something, but he did not. He did not even breathe for several seconds, until he realized that he was shaking, and in danger of falling over the edge himself. The boy was dead, and there was no use of anything, of trying anything by way of saving him.

Tell his mother, Tom thought, as he started back towards the house. Good Christ, all the people up there!

When Tom entered the house, he encountered Eugene, pink and alert. 'Something the matter, sir? It's just two minutes to five now, so we –'

'I think we have to call the police now – an ambulance or something.'

Eugene looked Tom up and down as if for injuries.

'It's *Frank*! He's on the cliff there,' Tom said.

Eugene suddenly understood. 'He's *fallen*?' He was ready to run out.

'I'm sure he's dead. Can you telephone the hospital or whatever you're supposed to do? I'll tell Mrs Pierson. Hospital first!' Tom said, when Eugene showed a sign of wanting to dash out of the french windows.

Tom braced himself for the upstairs, and went on. He knocked on the tea party door, and entered. They all looked comfortable now, Tal leaning on the end of the sofa near Lily, Johnny still standing, talking to Mrs Hunter. 'Can I speak with you for a minute?' Tom said to Lily.

She got up. 'Something the matter, Tom?' she asked, as if she thought he might only have changed his travel plans, which would not have inconvenienced anyone.

Tom spoke with her in the hall, after he had closed the door. 'Frank just jumped off the cliff there.'

'Wha-at? Oh, *no!*'

'I went to look for him. And I saw him below. Eugene's 'phoning the hospital – but I think he's dead.'

Tal suddenly opened the door, and his expression at once changed. 'What's up?'

Lily Pierson could not speak, so Tom said, 'Frank just jumped off the cliff.'

'That *cliff?*' Tal was about to run down the hall, but Tom made a gesture, as if to say *it's done.*

'What's the trouble?' Johnny came through the door, and behind him the two Hunters.

Tom heard Eugene pounding up the stairs, and went down the hall to meet him.

'Ambulance *and* the police should be here in a few minutes, sir,' Eugene said quickly, and went past Tom.

Tom looked farther up the hall, and saw a white figure – no, pale blue, paler than Frank's jacket – Susie. Eugene, who had passed the others, said a word to Susie. Susie nodded, and gave even a faint smile, Tom thought. Johnny just then ran past Tom, on his way to the stairs.

Two ambulances came, one bearing reviving apparatus, from what Tom could see as two white-clad men hurried across the lawn, guided by Eugene. Then came a folding ladder. Had Eugene instructed them, or did they remember the cliff from John Pierson's mishap? Tom hung back near the house. He emphatically did not want to see the boy's smashed face, wanted to leave at once, in fact, though knew that he couldn't. He would have to wait until the boy was up to the lawn level, until he had said a few more words to Lily. Tom went back into the house, glanced at his suitcase which was still by the front door, then he went up the stairs. He had an impulse to go into Frank's room again, for the last time.

In the upstairs hall, he saw Susie Schuhmacher standing at the far end of the hall, her hands spread behind her and touching the wall. She looked at him and nodded, or Tom thought she did. He walked on to Frank's door and a little past it. Susie was nodding. What did she want? Tom looked at her as if fixated, but he also frowned at her.

'You see?' Susie said.

'No,' Tom said firmly. Was she trying to cow him, convince him? Tom felt an animal-like hostility towards her, a sense of self-preservation that would see him through. He continued to walk towards her. He stopped about eight feet from her. 'What are you talking about?'

'Frank – of course. He was a bad boy and at least he *knew* it.' Now she was moving with just a little feebleness towards Tom and to her right, to go back to her room. 'And you are maybe the same,' she added.

Tom retreated one step back, mainly to keep a certain distance from her. He turned and went back to Frank's door, and into the room. He closed the door, feeling angry, but the anger ebbed a little. That terribly neat bed! Where Frank would never sleep again. And the Berlin bear. Tom moved towards it slowly, wanting it. Who would ever know or care, if he took it? Tom picked it up gently by its furry sides. A square of paper on the table caught Tom's eye. It lay to the left of where the bear had sat. Teresa, I love you forever, Frank had written. Tom let his held breath out. Absurd! But of course it was true, because Frank had died in the last half hour. Tom didn't touch the note, though it crossed his mind to take the note away and destroy it, as one might do a service for a dead friend. But Tom went out only with the bear, and closed the door.

Downstairs, he stuck the bear into a corner of his suitcase, turning its nose inward so it would not be mashed. The living room was empty. They were all on the lawn, Tom saw, and one ambulance was departing. Tom did not want to look out again on to the lawn. He wandered around in the living room, and lit a cigarette.

Eugene appeared, and said that he had telephoned the airport at Bangor. There was another plane Tom might get, if he should wish, if they left in fifteen minutes. Eugene was the servant again, though a lot paler in the face.

'That's fine,' Tom said. 'Thank you for seeing about that.' Tom went out on to the lawn to speak with Frank's mother, just at the moment when a stretcher covered in white was being slid into the back of the one remaining ambulance.

Lily sank her face on to Tom's shoulder. There were words, from everybody, but Lily's tight grip on Tom's shoulders had more meaning. Then Tom was in the back seat of one of the big cars, being driven by Eugene towards Bangor.

He arrived at the Hotel Chelsea by midnight. People were singing in the lobby, which had a square fireplace and black-and-white plastic sofas, chained to the floor against theft. The lyric was a limerick, Tom recognized, and amid much laughter the levi-clad boys and a few girls were trying to fit it to guitar music. Yes, there was a room for Mr Ripley, said the tweedy man behind the desk. Tom glanced at the oil paintings on the walls, some donated by clients who couldn't pay their bills, Tom knew. He had a general impression of tomato red. Then he went up in an old-fashioned elevator.

Tom took a shower, put on his least good trousers, and lay on his bed for a few minutes, trying to relax. It was hopeless. The best thing to do was to eat something, though he wasn't hungry, walk around a bit, and then try to sleep. At Kennedy Airport he had made a reservation for tomorrow evening to go to Paris.

So Tom went out and walked up Seventh Avenue, passed the closed and still-open delicatessen shops, snack shops. The pavement dully glistened with discarded metal beer top rings. Taxis lurched drunkenly into potholes and rumbled out and onward, reminding Tom somehow of Citroëns in France, big, lumbering and aggressive. Ahead and on both sides of the avenue rose tall black buildings, some office buildings, some residences, like solid hunks of land up there in the sky. Lots of windows were lighted. New York never slept.

Tom had said to Lily, 'There is no reason for me to stay now.' Tom had meant stay for the funeral, but he had also meant that he couldn't do anything more for Frank. Tom had not told her about the boy's first attempt to kill himself hardly an hour earlier. Lily just might have said, 'Why didn't you keep an eye on him afterward?' Well, Tom had thought, wrongly, that Frank's crisis had passed.

He went into a corner snack shop which had stools at a counter, and ordered a hamburger and a coffee. He did not want to sit down, and standing up was certainly permitted. Two black customers were having an argument over a bet they had made, over the possible crookedness of the bookie they had both used. It sounded fantastically complicated, and

Tom stopped listening. He could ring up a couple of friends in New York tomorrow, he thought, just to say hello. The idea, however, did not attract him. He felt lost and purposeless, awful. He ate half the hamburger, drank half the weak coffee, paid and went out, and walked up to Forty-second Street. Now it was nearly two in the morning.

This was more cheerful, like a crazy circus or a stage-set through which he was permitted to wander. Huge cops in blue short-sleeved shirts swung their wooden nightsticks and joshed with the prostitutes whom they were supposed to round up, Tom had read lately. Had the cops rounded up the same ones so often, that they'd got tired of it? Or were they in process of rounding these up? Teenaged boys with make-up and very wise eyes sized up the older men, some with money already in their hands, who were ready to buy them.

'No,' Tom said softly, ducking his head at the approach of a blonde girl whose thighs bulged horribly under shiny black plastic. Tom read with amazement the blunt and banal film titles on the cinema marquées. Such a lack of talent in the porn department! But this cliéntèle didn't want subtlety or wit. And all the blown-up colour photos of men and women, men and men, women and women, naked and presumably making it, and Frank had not made it with Teresa the one time he had tried! Tom laughed a little, with a bizarre amusement. Suddenly he had had enough, and went trotting through the shuffling blacks, the pasty-faced whites towards the darkish blob of the big Public Library on Fifth Avenue. He didn't go as far as Fifth, but turned southward on Sixth Avenue.

A sailor hurtled out of a bar on Tom's right and collided with Tom. The sailor fell on the ground, and Tom hauled him up, steadied him with one hand and reached for his white cap which had fallen off. The boy looked in his teens and was swaying like a mast in a storm.

'Where're your chums?' Tom asked. 'Haven't you got chums in there?'

'I wanna taxi and I wanna girl,' said the boy, smiling.

He looked healthy, and probably a couple of scotches and six beers had put him into this state. 'Come on.' Tom took his arm and pushed the bar door open, looking for other sailor uniforms. Tom saw two at the bar, but a barman came round towards Tom and said:

'We don't want him in here and we're not serving him!'

'Aren't these his friends?' Tom asked, pointing to the two sailors.

'We do' *want* him!' said one of the two sailors, also a bit drunk. 'He can get the fuck *out*!'

Tom's charge was now leaning against the door jamb, resisting the efforts of the barman to wrestle him out.

Tom went up to the two at the bar, not caring a damn if he got a sock in the jaw for his trouble. Tom said with as tough a New York accent as he could put on, 'Take care of your pal! That's a hell of a way to treat a guy in the same uniform, no?' Tom looked at the second sailor, who was not quite so under the influence, and saw that he had got through to him, because he shoved himself from the bar. Tom walked towards the door and looked back.

The soberer sailor was approaching his drunken pal, reluctantly.

Well, that was something, Tom thought as he went out, though very little. He walked back to the Chelsea. Here people were a bit pissed, or gay, or merry in the lobby, but the scene was sedate compared to Times Square. The Chelsea was famous for its eccentric patrons, but usually they kept themselves within a certain bound.

Tom thought of ringing Heloise, since it would be around nine in the morning there, and didn't. He realized that he was shattered. *Shattered.* And how had he escaped a punch in the ribs from the sailors in that bar? Tom realized that he had been lucky once again. He fell into bed, not caring when he woke up.

Should he telephone Lily tomorrow? Or would it even disturb her, upset her? Was she taking care of such things as deciding what kind of coffin would be appropriate? Would Johnny suddenly grow up and take charge? Would Tal take charge? Would Teresa be told, and would she come to the funeral, the cremation or whatever it would be? Did he have to think about this tonight, Tom asked himself as he tossed in his bed.

Only by 9 p.m. the next evening did Tom regain some kind of composure, a sense of returning to himself. The engines had started on the airplane, and he seemed suddenly to wake up, as if he were home already. He felt happy, or happier, and he was escaping from – what? He had acquired another suitcase, at Mark Cross this time, as Gucci had become so ultra snob. Tom was inclined to boycott it, and the new suitcase was full of things he had bought: a sweater for Heloise, an art book from Doubleday's, a blue and white striped apron for Mme Annette with a red pocket on which was printed OUT TO LUNCH, plus a small gold pin, also for Mme Annette because her birthday was soon, the pin in the shape of a flying goose with little spiked reeds of gold below, a good looking passport case for Eric Lanz. Tom had not forgotten Peter in Berlin. He would look for something special for him in Paris. Tom watched Manhattan's fairyland of lights gently rising and falling with the plane's movement, and he thought of Frank being buried soon in the same body of land. When the American coast was out of sight, Tom closed his eyes and tried to fall asleep. But he kept thinking of Frank, and finding it hard to believe that the boy was dead. It was a fact, and yet that fact was something that Tom could not make real as yet. He had thought sleep would be a help, but he had awakened this morning with the same sense of fantasy about Frank's death – as if he might look now across the plane's aisle and see Frank sitting there, smiling at him, surprising him. Tom had to remember the white sheet over the stretcher. No intern would pull a sheet all the way over someone's head, unless the person beneath was dead.

He would have to write to Lily Pierson, a proper letter in longhand, and Tom knew he could do it, politely and tenderly and all that, but what could Lily ever know about the little garden house in Moret where Frank had slept, or about Berlin, or even about Teresa's power over her son? Tom wondered what had been Frank's last thought as he fell downward on to the rocks? Teresa? A memory of his father falling fatally downward on to the same rocks? Had the boy possibly thought of him? Tom shifted in his seat and opened his eyes. The stewardess had begun to circulate. Tom sighed, not caring what he ordered, beer, a scotch, food or nothing.

What a joke, Tom thought, how useless now were the rather carefully considered lectures he had given Frank on the subject of 'money' or 'money and power'! Use it a little, even enjoy it a little, Tom had said, and stop feeling guilty. Give some to charity, to art projects, to whatever you like and to whomever needs it. Yes, and he had also said, as had Lily, that there were others who could take over the administration of Pierson at least until Frank finished school and even after that. But Frank would have had to poke his nose a little bit further into Pierson, have his name (maybe along with his brother's) at the head of the directors' list, and Frank hadn't wanted even that.

At some point, miles high and in a black sky, Tom went to sleep under a blanket provided by a red-headed stewardess. When he woke up, the sun was rising and blazing – as out of step with time, it seemed, as anything else, and the airplane was over France, according to the announcement which had awakened Tom.

Roissy again, and the Satellites' shiny escalators, one of which Tom rode down with his hand luggage. He could have run into trouble with his new suitcase and its contents, but Tom put on a glassy unconcern, and made it through the Nothing to Declare barrier. He checked the timetable in his wallet, decided on a train, then rang Belle Ombre.

'Tome!' Heloise said. 'You are *where?*'

She couldn't believe that he was at Charles de Gaulle Airport, and he couldn't believe that she was so close. 'I can be in Moret at twelve-thirty easily. I just looked it up.' Tom was suddenly smiling. 'Everything okay?'

Everything was, except that Mme Annette had a sprained knee from a fall or slip on the stairway. But even that did not sound serious, as she was getting about as usual, Heloise said. 'Why didn't you write me – or telephone?'

'I was there such a short time!' Tom replied. 'Just two days! I'll tell you about it when I see you. Twelve thirty-one.'

'*A bientôt, chéri!*' She was going to fetch him.

Tom taxied to the Gare de Lyon with his luggage – which had still not been overweight – and boarded the train for Moret with *Le Monde* and *Le Figaro*. He was nearly finished scanning the papers, before he realized that he had not looked for anything about Frank, and realized also that there would barely have been time for a report of his death in these papers. Was it going to be, again, a possible 'accident'? What was his mother going to say? He thought that Lily was going to say that her son was a suicide. And let history or gossip make what they wished of the two deaths there within the same summer.

Heloise awaited him beside the red Mercedes. The breeze blew her hair about. She saw him and waved, though he couldn't wave back with two suitcases plus a plastic bag of Dutch cigars, newspapers and paperbacks. He kissed Heloise on both cheeks and on her neck.

'How are you?' Heloise asked.

'Ah-h,' said Tom, loading his suitcases into the trunk.

'I thought you might be back again with Frank,' she said, smiling.

It was amazing to Tom how happy she looked. When, he thought as they drove away from the station, should he tell her about Frank? Now Heloise – who had said she wanted to drive – was in the clear of traffic and light signals and heading for Villeperce. 'I may as well tell you now, Frank died the day before yesterday.' Tom glanced at the steering wheel as he spoke, but Heloise's hands only tightened on it for a second.

'What do you mean *died?*' she asked in French.

'He jumped over that same cliff where his father died. I'll explain better at the house, but I somehow didn't want to say it in front of Madame Annette, even in English.'

'What cliff do you mean?' Heloise asked, still in French.

'The cliff on their land in Maine. It overlooks the sea.'

'Ah, yes!' Heloise suddenly remembered, perhaps from the newspaper stories. 'You were there? You *saw* him?'

'I was at the house. I didn't see him, no, because the cliff's some distance away. I'll –' Tom was finding it difficult to speak. 'Really there isn't much to tell. I spent one night at the house. I was intending to leave the next day – which I did. His mother and a couple of her friends were having tea. I went out to look for the boy.'

'And you saw he had jumped?' Heloise said in English now.

'Yes.'

'How awful, Tome! – That is why you look so – absent.'

'Do I? Absent?' They were now approaching Villeperce, and Tom gazed at a house he knew and liked, and then the post office, then the bakery, before Heloise made the turn to the left. She had taken the route quite through the village, maybe by accident, maybe because she was nervous and wanted to go by a slower way. Tom went on, 'Maybe I found him ten minutes after he'd jumped. I don't know. I had to go back and tell the family. It's quite a steep cliff – rocks down there. I will tell you more later maybe, darling.' But what more would there be to tell? Tom glanced at Heloise who was driving through the gates of Belle Ombre now.

'Yes, you *must* tell me,' she said as she got out of the car.

Tom could see that this was a story she expected to hear in full, because Tom had not done anything wrong, and was not going to conceal anything from her.

'I liked Frank, you know?' Heloise said to Tom, and her lavender-blue eyes met his for a second. 'Finally, I mean. I didn't like him at first.'

Tom knew.

'This is a new suitcase?'

Tom smiled. 'And a few new things in it.'

'Oh! – Thank you for the German handbag, Tome!'

'*Bonjour, Monsieur Tome!*' Mme Annette stood on the sunlit doorstep, and Tom could just see a pale elastic band below her skirt hem, under her beige stockings or maybe tights, around one knee.

'How are you, dear Madame Annette?' Tom said, putting an arm half around her, and she replied that she was very well, and gave him a token kiss, but paused hardly at all before crossing the gravel to take the suitcase Heloise was carrying.

Mme Annette insisted upon carrying both suitcases up, one at a time, despite her sprained knee, so Tom let her do it, because it gave her pleasure.

'It's so good to be *home*!' Tom said, looking around at the living room, the table set for lunch, the harpsichord, the phony Derwatt over the fireplace. 'You know, the Piersons have "The Rainbow"? Did I mention that or not? You know, one of the – a very good Derwatt.'

'Rea-ally?' said Heloise, rather mockingly, as if she had or maybe had not heard of this particular Derwatt, or maybe because she suspected it was a fake.

Tom simply couldn't tell. But he laughed with relief, with happiness. Mme Annette was coming down the stairs, carefully now, with one hand on the banister. At least he had dissuaded Mme Annette years ago from polishing the stair steps.

'How can you look so cheerful, when the boy is dead?' Heloise had asked that in English, and Mme Annette, reaching now for the second suitcase, paid no attention.

Heloise was right. Tom didn't know why he could feel so cheerful. 'Maybe it hasn't sunk in as yet. It was so sudden – a shock to everyone at the house. Frank's older brother was there, Johnny. Frank was very unhappy because of a girl. I told you that. Teresa. Plus his father's death –' That was as far as Tom wanted to go. John Pierson Senior's death would always be a suicide or an accident, whenever he spoke to Heloise about it.

'But that is terrible – to kill oneself at sixteen! More and more young people are killing themselves, you know? I am always reading about it in the newspapers. Would you like some? Or anything?' Heloise extended the wine glass full of Perrier which she had just poured for herself, Tom knew.

Tom shook his head. 'I want to wash up.' He went towards the downstairs W C and basin, and en route glanced at the little stack of four letters on the telephone table, yesterday's and today's post. That could wait.

During lunch, Tom told Heloise about the Kennebunkport house of the Piersons, about the odd old servant called Susie Schuhmacher, who had been housekeeper and in a way governess of the boys years ago, and who was now laid low with a heart attack. He succeeded in making the house a mixture of luxury and gloom, which was the truth, Tom thought, or anyway the way he had felt about it. From Heloise's slight frown, Tom knew that she knew he was not telling the whole truth.

'And you went away the same evening – just after the boy died?' she asked.

'Yes. I didn't see what good I could do by staying longer. The funeral – it might have been two days away.' Might be today Tuesday, Tom thought.

'I don't think you could face the funeral.' Heloise said. 'You were very fond of the boy – weren't you? I know.'

'Yes,' said Tom. He could look at Heloise steadily now. It had been strange to try to steer a young life like that, as he had tried – and to have failed. Maybe one day he could admit that to Heloise. But on the other hand, he couldn't, because he was never going to tell her that the boy pushed his father over the cliff, and that was the whole explanation of the boy's suicide, or at least it was more important than Teresa, Tom felt.

'Did you meet Teresa?' Heloise asked. She had already asked for a full description of Lily Pierson, the former actress who had married such wealth and Tom had done his best there, including a description of the attentive Tal Stevens, whom Tom suspected she would marry.

'No, no, I didn't meet Teresa. I think she was in New York.' And Tom doubted that Teresa would even come to Frank's funeral, and did that matter, either? Teresa to Frank had been an idea, intangible almost, and so she would remain, as Frank had written, 'forever'.

Tom went upstairs after lunch to look at his post, and to unpack. Another letter from Jeff Constant of the Buckmaster Gallery, London, and at a glance Tom saw that all was well. The news was that the Derwatt Accademia in Perugia had had a change of managership to two artistically inclined young men from London (Jeff supplied their names), and they had the idea of acquiring a nearby palazzo which could be converted into an hotel for the art students. Did Tom like the idea? Did he possibly know the palazzo to the south-west of the art school? The new London boys were going to send a photo next post. Jeff wrote:

'This means expansion, which sounds all to the good, don't you think, Tom? Unless you have some inside information about Italian internal conditions that might make the purchase inadvisable just now.'

Tom had no inside information. Did Jeff think him a genius? Yes. Tom knew he would agree to the purchase idea. Expansion, yes, as to hotels. The art school made most of its money from the hotel. The real Derwatt would cringe with shame.

He pulled off his sweater, strolled into his blue and white bathroom, and threw the sweater behind him on to a chair. He fancied he heard

the carpenter ants shut up at his step, or had he heard the ants in the
first place? He put his ear to the wooden shelf side. No! He had heard
them, and they hadn't shut up. There was the faintest whir which
augmented even as he listened. At it still, the little zealots! On a folded
pyjama top on one shelf, Tom saw a miniature pyramid of fine reddish-
tan dust which had fallen from excavations above. What were they
building in there? Beds for themselves, egg repositories? Had these little
carpenters put their wits together and constructed maybe a tiny bookcase in there, composed of spit and sawdust, a little monument to their
know-how, their will to live? Tom had to laugh out loud. Was he going
mad himself?

From the corner of his suitcase, Tom took the Berlin bear, fluffed its
fur out gently, and set it at the back of his desk against a couple of
dictionaries. The little bear was made to sit, its legs didn't bend for it to
stand up. Its bright eyes looked at Tom with the same innocent gaiety
as in Berlin, and Tom smiled back at it, thinking of the '3 Würfe 1
Mark' which had won it. 'You will have a good home for the rest of
your life,' Tom said to the bear.

He would take a shower, flop on the bed, and look at the rest of his
letters, he thought. Try to get back to normal in time, twenty to three
now, French time. Frank would be lowered into a grave today, Tom felt
sure, and he didn't care to figure out just when it might be, because for
Frank time had ceased to matter.

FOR THE BEST IN PAPERBACKS, LOOK FOR THE 🐧

In every corner of the world, on every subject under the sun, Penguin represents quality and variety – the very best in publishing today.

For complete information about books available from Penguin – including Puffins, Penguin Classics and Arkana – and how to order them, write to us at the appropriate address below. Please note that for copyright reasons the selection of books varies from country to country.

In the United Kingdom: Please write to *Dept JC, Penguin Books Ltd, FREEPOST, West Drayton, Middlesex, UB7 0BR.*

If you have any difficulty in obtaining a title, please send your order with the correct money, plus ten per cent for postage and packaging, to *PO Box No 11, West Drayton, Middlesex*

In the United States: Please write to *Dept BA, Penguin, 299 Murray Hill Parkway, East Rutherford, New Jersey 07073*

In Canada: Please write to *Penguin Books Canada Ltd, 2801 John Street, Markham, Ontario L3R 1B4*

In Australia: Please write to the *Marketing Department, Penguin Books Australia Ltd, P.O. Box 257, Ringwood, Victoria 3134*

In New Zealand: Please write to the *Marketing Department, Penguin Books (NZ) Ltd, Private Bag, Takapuna, Auckland 9*

In India: Please write to *Penguin Overseas Ltd, 706 Eros Apartments, 56 Nehru Place, New Delhi, 110019*

In the Netherlands: Please write to *Penguin Books Netherlands B.V., Postbus 3507, NL–1001 AH, Amsterdam*

In West Germany: Please write to *Penguin Books Ltd, Friedrichstrasse 10–12, D–6000 Frankfurt/Main 1*

In Spain: Please write to *Alhambra Longman S.A., Fernandez de la Hoz 9, E–28010 Madrid*

In Italy: Please write to *Penguin Italia s.r.l., Via Como 4, I-20096 Pioltello (Milano)*

In France: Please write to *Penguin France S.A., 17 rue Lejeune, F-31000 Toulouse*

In Japan: Please write to *Longman Penguin Japan Co Ltd, Yamaguchi Building, 2–12–9 Kanda Jimbocho, Chiyoda-Ku, Tokyo 101*

BY THE SAME AUTHOR

Ripley Under Water

Tom Ripley's past would not bear too much close scrutiny. But he has carefully covered his tracks as far as murder and forgery are concerned. Or so he thinks . . . 'The Ripley books are marvellous, insanely readable' – H. R. F. Keating in *The Times*

Carol

First published under a pseudonym in 1952, *Carol* is that rarest of stories, a gay love story with a happy ending told with consummate wit and eroticism, and consummate tenderness. 'An original, honest novel, a remarkable imaginative achievement by any standard . . . as compelling as any of Highsmith's thrillers . . . memorable' – *Financial Times*

Edith's Diary

In the neat little Pennsylvania house, with senile, dribbling Uncle George and her sly son Cliffie, Edith watches the stranglehold of everyday life tighten its grip. Slowly, inevitably she retreats into her diary. A sumptuous leather-bound volume where she begins to build a perfect fantasy of a very different life, with Cliffie happily married and two adorable grandchildren.

The Glass Cell

For six long years Philip Carter suffered for a crime he did not commit. Brutalized by prison guards who strung him up by his thumbs, he became addicted to morphine. He suspected his wife of having an affair with his lawyer. It was a cumulative process and when release came, Carter was ready to kill . . .

BY THE SAME AUTHOR

People Who Knock on the Door

Patricia Highsmith pitilessly dissects the prying suburban self-righteousness which leads to frenzies for which ultimately we all must pay. 'She has an uncanny feeling for the rhythms of terror ... a great gift to create excitement out of apprehension' – *The Times Literary Supplement*

Mermaids on the Golf Course

Beware not the trained killer or the psychopath – beware the average man – in these effortlessly chilling stories. For Patricia Highsmith the everyday turns out to be more surprising and more dangerous than most of us would care to imagine.

Little Tales of Misogyny

There are women who destroy their men and women who destroy themselves; girls who notch up their conquests and girls who go too far. From 'Oona, the Jolly Cave Woman' to 'The Fully Licensed Whore, or, The Wife', here are seventeen ironical, bizarre and sophisticated stories.

The Black House

Eleven sinister stories reveal Patricia Highsmith's characters breaking the social laws (often unconsciously) and paying the price. 'Nothing is certain when we have crossed this frontier. It is not the world as we once believed we knew it, but it is frighteningly more real to us than the house next door' – Graham Greene

BY THE SAME AUTHOR

The Cry of the Owl

Robert Forester didn't look like the kind of man to be a prowler. His ex-wife had told the police he was erratic, liable to violence, had even fired a gun at her. Maybe he was a psychopathic murderer . . .

Deep Water

'The most outstanding merit of *Deep Water* is the dexterity with which it develops the psychopath's portrait from the first faint agreeable outline to the full dark horrific colours of schizophrenia. If you read crime stories at all, or perhaps especially if you don't, you should read *Deep Water*' – Julian Symons in the *Sunday Times*

A Suspension of Mercy

Alicia Bartleby had died at least twenty times in Sydney's imagination: he was a thriller writer. So when Alicia decided to take a trip to Brighton incognito, Sydney took the opportunity of doing some first-hand research into the sensations of a suspected wife-murderer.

The Blunderer

Walter Stackhouse's love for his wife is dead: now he wishes *she* was. His wish comes true when Clara's body is found lying at the bottom of a cliff. But there are uncanny similarities between her death and that of a woman called Helen Kimmel, who was, in fact, murdered by her husband . . . 'Ingenious . . . makes a cold clutch at the reader's deeper security' – *Punch*